NEW YORK REVIEW BOOKS
CLASSICS

ANNIVERSARIES

UWE JOHNSON (1934–1984) grew up in the small town of Anklam
in the German state of Mecklenburg-Vorpommern. At the end of World
War II, his father, who had joined the Nazi Party in 1940, disappeared
into a Soviet camp; he was declared dead in 1948. Johnson and his mother
remained in Communist East Germany until his mother left for the
West in 1956, after which Johnson was barred from regular employment.
In 1959, shortly before the publication of his first novel, *Speculations
About Jakob*, in West Germany, he emigrated to West Berlin by streetcar,
leaving the East behind for good. Other novels, *The Third Book About
Achim*, *An Absence*, and *Two Views*, followed in quick succession. A
member of the legendary Gruppe 47, Johnson lived from 1966 until
1968 with his wife and daughter in New York, compiling a high-school
anthology of postwar German literature. On Tuesday, April 18, 1967,
at 5:30 p.m., as he later recounted the story, he saw Gesine Cresspahl,
a character from his earlier works, walking on the south side of Forty-
Second Street from Fifth to Sixth Avenue alongside Bryant Park; he
asked what she was doing in New York and eventually convinced her
to let him write his next novel about a year in her life. *Anniversaries* was
published in four installments—in 1970, 1971, 1973, and 1983—and was
quickly recognized in Germany as one of the great novels of the century.
In 1974, Johnson left Germany for the isolation of Sheerness-on-Sea,
England, where he struggled through health and personal problems to
finish his magnum opus. He died at age forty-nine, shortly after it was
published.

DAMION SEARLS grew up on Riverside Drive in New York City,
three blocks away from Gesine Cresspahl's apartment. He is the author
of three books and has translated more than thirty, including six for
NYRB Classics.

ANNIVERSARIES

From a Year in the Life of Gesine Cresspahl

Volume One

UWE JOHNSON

Translated from the German by
DAMION SEARLS

NEW YORK REVIEW BOOKS

New York

The translation of this work was supported by a grant from Goethe-Institut using funds provided by the German Ministry of Foreign Affairs. It was made possible in part by the New York State Council on the Arts with the support of Governor Andrew Cuomo and the New York State Legislature.

The translator and publisher wish to thank the John Simon Guggenheim Foundation, the Dorothy and Lewis B. Cullman Center for Scholars and Writers at the New York Public Library, and the Uwe Johnson Society's Peter Suhrkamp Stipend for their generous support.

Library of Congress Cataloging-in-Publication Data
Names: Johnson, Uwe, 1934–1984 author. | Searls, Damion translator.
Title: Anniversaries : from a year in the life of Gesine Cresspahl / by Uwe
    Johnson ; translated by Damion Searls.
Other titles: Jahrestage. English
Description: New York : New York Review Books, 2018. | Series: New York
    Review Books classics
Identifiers: LCCN 2018010220 (print) | LCCN 2018012166 (ebook) | ISBN
    9781681372044 (epub) | ISBN 9781681372037 (alk. paper)
Classification: LCC PT2670.O36 (ebook) | LCC PT2670.O36 J313 2018 (print) |
    DDC 833/.914—dc23
LC record available at https://lccn.loc.gov/2018010220

CONTENTS

With thanks to
Peter Suhrkamp
Helen Wolff

PART ONE

August 1967–December 1967

LONG WAVES beat diagonally against the beach, bulge hunchbacked with cords of muscle, raise quivering ridges that tip over at their very greenest. Crests stretched tight, already welted white, wrap round a cavity of air crushed by the clear mass like a secret made and then broken. The crashing swells knock children off their feet, spin them round, drag them flat across the pebbly ground. Past the breakers, the waves pull the swimmer across their backs by her outstretched hands. The wind is fluttery; in low-pressure wind like this, the Baltic Sea used to peter out into a burble. The word for the short waves on the Baltic was: *scrabbly*.

The town is on a narrow spit of the Jersey shore, two hours south of New York by train. They've fenced off the wide sandy beach and sell tickets to out-of-towners for forty dollars a season; retirees in uniforms slump at the entrances and keep an eye out for the badges on the visitors' clothes that grant admission. The Atlantic is free for those who live in the beach houses, which sit sedately on the stone embankment above the hurricane line, with their verandas, two-story galleries, colorful awnings, under complicatedly slanting roofs. The dark-skinned help who live here fill their own church, but Negroes are not supposed to buy houses or rent apartments or lie on the coarse white sand. Jews, too, are not welcome here. She is not sure whether Jews were still allowed to rent houses in the fishing village near Jerichow before 1933; she cannot remember any signs prohibiting it from the years that followed. Here, she has borrowed a bungalow on the bay side for ten days, from friends. The people in the house next door receive the mail and read the postcards that the child writes to "Dear Miss C." from summer camp, but they insist on calling her "Mrs. Cresspahl," and seem to want to see her too as a Catholic of Irish descent.

Guh-ZEE-neh CRESS-påll
Kick er heel n make er fåll

3

The sky has been bright for a long time, blue with white clouds, the horizon line hazy. The light presses her eyelids shut. Much of the sand between the expensive deck chairs and the blankets is unoccupied. Words from nearby conversations penetrate her sleep as though from a past. The sand is still heavy with yesterday's rain and can be pushed and shoved into firm soft pillows. Tiny airplanes pull banners across the sky praising drinks and stores and restaurants. Farther out, over the crowded mass of sport-fishermen's boats, two jet fighters practice getting their bearings. The waves crash with the impact of heavy artillery and spray apart with the same thundering sounds as in the war movies that the village movie house plays at night. A few drops of rain wake her up and again she sees the bluish field of a sloping roof's shingles in the darkening light as a furry thatched roof in a part of Mecklenburg, on another shore.

To the municipal council of Rande, near Jerichow: As a former citizen of Jerichow, and a formerly regular visitor to Rande, may I politely request the following information: How many summer guests of the Jewish faith were recorded in Rande before 1933? Thank you for your assistance.

In the evening the beach is hard from the wetness, drilled with pores, and it presses the fragments of mussel shells more sharply against her soles. The waves surging back out to sea hit her ankles so hard that she often stumbles. When she stands still, the water digs the ground out from under her feet in two streams, washes it away. After rains like this, the Baltic washed a delicate, almost even foam onto the land. There was a game played while running along the Baltic shore, where a child would give a sudden knock to the side of the foot of the child in front, the child who she was, at just the moment when she'd lifted that leg to move it forward, and this would hook her foot behind the heel of the leg her weight was on. The first time she fell she had no idea what had happened. She heads toward the lighthouse whose recurring flash cuts larger and larger segments out of the blue shadows. Every few steps, she tries to let the waves push her off her feet, but she cannot recapture that feeling somewhere between stumbling and hitting the ground.

Can you teach me the trick, Miss C.? It might not be known in this country.

Shooting has resumed on the Israeli-Jordanian front. In New Haven, citizens of African descent are said to be breaking shopwindows, throwing Molotov cocktails.

The next morning, the earliest coast train to New York, a decrepit thing with mortgage plates mounted on the sides under the railroad company's name, has pulled up to the open field by the bay. Jakob wouldn't have let such neglected train cars leave the siding. The streaky windows frame pictures of whitewashed wooden houses in gray light, private docks in the marinas, breakfast terraces half awake under thick leafy shadows, mouths of rivers, last glimpses of the sea past the harbors, views of vacations in years past. Were they vacations? In the summer of 1942, in Gneez, Cresspahl put her on a train to Ribnitz and explained how to get from the station to the harbor. The separation upset her so much that she didn't think to be scared of the trip. To her, the Fischland steamboat ferry in the Ribnitz port had looked like a fat black duck. Setting out on the Saal lagoon, she had kept her eyes on the Ribnitz church tower, and the Körkwitz tower, then memorized the Neuhaus dune, facing backward the whole way to Althagen. She didn't want to get lost on the way back to the railroad, to Jerichow, later. In the summer of 1942, Cresspahl wanted his child out of town. In 1951 he'd sent her away to southeast Mecklenburg, five hours from Jerichow. The Wendisch Burg train station was at a higher elevation than the city and from the end of the blue sand platform you could see the eastern edge of Bottom Lake, dull in the afternoon light. Only when she reached the barrier did she notice that Klaus Niebuhr had been watching her stand there indecisively—he'd been there the whole time, not saying a word, leaning comfortably on the railing, nine years older than the child that she was remembering. He had brought a girl named Babendererde with him. She was one those girls with a carefree smile, and Gesine nodded cautiously when Klaus said her name. She was also afraid he knew why Cresspahl didn't want her in Jerichow for the time being. Those were hardly vacations. The train rolls unhurriedly into small-town squares, commuters in suits step out of the early-morning half-light under the shelters, each one alone with his briefcase, and go to sleep in reclined seats on the train. Now the sun is darting out over the rooftops, hurling fistfuls of light across low-lying fields. The branch line from Gneez to Jerichow ran in large detours around the villages; the stations were toy red-brick buildings with gabled tar roofs and a few people with shopping bags waiting in front. The students taking the train to school lined up on the platforms in such a way that by Gneez they would all be gathered in the third and fourth compartments behind the luggage car. Jakob learned the railroad along this line. Jakob, in his black work smock, looked down from his brakeman's cab at the group of high-school students with such tolerant impassivity that it was as though he didn't want to acknowledge Cresspahl's daughter. At nineteen he might have still categorized people by their social class. From New Jersey's blighted rusty morasses the train tottered over spindly bridges up into the Palisades and down into the tunnel under the Hudson to New York, and she has been standing in the center aisle, in the line of weekenders and day-trippers, for a while now, occasionally moving six inches forward, ready to run for the train door, the escalator, the maze of construction fences in Penn Station, to the West Side subway line, the train to Flushing, up the escalator from the blue dome on the corner of Forty-Second Street at Grand Central Terminal. She is not allowed to get to her desk more than an hour late, and that hour late is permitted only today, after her vacation.

August 21, 1967 Monday

Clearing weather in North Vietnam permitted air attacks north of Hanoi. The navy bombed coastal targets from the air and fired eight-inch guns into the demilitarized zone. Four helicopters were shot down in South Vietnam. The racial disorders in New Haven continued yesterday with fires, shattered store windows, and looting; another 112 people arrested.

Next to the pile of newspapers sits a small, cast-iron bowl. The merchant's hand darts out, curled into a scoop, even before she has had a chance to toss her coin in. He seems hostile—his money has been snatched up one too many times by people walking past on the open street.

I got my neck shot up for this, lady.

Yesterday afternoon, the body of the American who failed to return to his hotel in Prague last Wednesday night was found in the Vltava River.

Mr. Jordan, fifty-nine years old, had worked for the Joint, a Jewish relief organization. He had gone out to buy a newspaper.

The canyon floor of Lexington Avenue is still in shadow. She remembers the taxis jostling on the street in the morning, stopped mid-turn by a traffic light whose red the pedestrians can exploit to cross the eastbound one-way street and during whose green they are permitted to obstruct the waiting cars. She did not hesitate to walk toward its warning words. She has been coming here a long time, elbows tucked in, attentive to the rhythm of the people alongside her. She avoids the blind beggar clinking his out-held cup and grunting angrily. She didn't understand him this time either. She is walking too slow, her gaze wanders, she is still in the process of returning to the city. The wail of sirens—swelling, dwindling, erupting fiercely again behind faraway blocks—has hung in the air between the tall towers of windows ever since she left. Hot backlight blasts down at an angle from the side street. She walks with her eyes on the dazzling concrete, next to a black marble facade whose mirror tints the faces, painted sheet metal, canopies, shirts, shopwindows, and dresses darker. She turns off into a white-lit passage from which the smell of ammonia detaches itself bite by bite from the narrow spring-loaded door and wafts into the air. Only employees know about this entrance.

She is thirty-four years old now. Her daughter is almost ten. She has lived in New York for six years. She has worked in this bank since 1964.

I imagine: The tiny grooves under her eyes were lighter than the tanned skin of her face. Her hair, almost black, cut short on all sides, has gotten lighter. She looked sleepy. She hasn't had a real conversation with anyone for a while. She took off her sunglasses only after she was behind the door's flashing panes of glass. She never wears sunglasses pushed up into her hair.

She took barely any pleasure in the rage of the drivers defeated, day after day, by a traffic light on Lexington Avenue. She came to New York with a car, a Swedish convertible, that spent two years being eaten away by de-icing salt at the base of Ninety-Sixth Street, across from the three garages. She has always taken the subway to work.

I imagine: During her lunch break she rereads that a man was rowing on the Vltava in Prague until he reached the May First Bridge. There he saw a New York Jew who had left his hotel to buy a newspaper, hanging on a water barrier. (She's heard that in Prague English-language newspapers are sold only in hotels.)

Until five years ago, all she knew of Prague were the nighttime streets a taxi takes to get from the main train station to the Střed station.

You American? Hlavní nádraží dříve, this station, earlier, Wilsonovo nádraží. Sta-shun. Woodrow Wilson!

She would have had to say yes because she was carrying an American passport in her pocket. She's forgotten the name on the passport. This was in 1962.

I imagine: In the evening, under a sky already grown cloudy, she comes up out of the Ninety-Sixth Street subway station onto Broadway and sees, in the opening of the bridge under Riverside Drive, a green glade—sees past the fringes of foliage in the park the flat river whose hidden banks guide its flow into an inland lake in an August forest in dry, scorched silence.

She lives on Riverside Drive, in a three-room apartment below the tops of the trees. The light inside is tinged green. To the south, next to thick clouds of leaves, she can see the lights on the bridge, and behind them the lights on the parkway. The fading light makes the streetlights brighter. The sound of the motors blends together and beats against the window in regular, even waves, not unlike the surf at the sea. From Jerichow to the shore was an hour on foot, along the marsh and then between the fields.

August 22, 1967   Tuesday

Two US Navy jets were shot down yesterday over mainland China. The Department of Defense identified 32 men as killed in action in Vietnam. US Marines counted 109 North Vietnamese killed. The gang in the South promises completely honest and impartial elections.

Yesterday in New Haven, shopwindows were broken and fires set once again. The policemen, wearing blue helmets and carrying rifles, fired tear gas. Arrests brought the total to 284, nearly all Negroes and Puerto Ricans.

The newspaper stand on the southwest corner of Broadway and Ninety-

Sixth Street is a green tent built around a core of aluminum boxes. The local magazines are laid out in overlapping rows on the left; the piles of daily newspapers are on the right, at the front; outside, on the right, are the European imports, secured with crusted-over weights. The stand gives advance notice of the day's weather to the people who live around the corner: when it adds on more roof, with bars and cloth, rain is on the way. The old man with the greasy visored cap who works the morning shift feels entitled to his moods. His right hand is deformed but he insists on having clients put their money between his crooked fingers, and every morning he practices digging coins out of the pit of his crippled hand with his fat thumb. This morning he doesn't return her greeting.

He knows this customer: she comes walking up Ninety-Sixth Street at ten past eight every workday, she always has exact change, and she tries to read the *New York Times* headlines while she's slipping the paper out from under its paperweight. She usually goes to work empty-handed; she goes down into the subway station with the paper under her arm, always catching the same train (which he hears through the grating in the middle of Broadway, arriving right after she goes down the stairs). She says Good morning as though she had learned it at a school up north, but she was not born in this country. The vendor also knows this customer's child, from Saturdays, when they walk down the street together with their shopping cart; the child, a ten-year-old girl with a round head like her mother's but sandy-blond foreign braids, says Good morning as though she had learned it at P.S. 75, a block away, and she comes in secret on Sunday mornings to get a paper consisting solely and entirely of comic strips. The customer knows nothing about that, nor the fact that the child rarely has to pay for it. The customer never buys any paper but *The New York Times*.

You won't say Good morning tomorrow, lady. All this fuss.

Gesine Cresspahl buys *The New York Times* at the stand on weekdays; home delivery might not make it before she has to leave. On the platform she folds the pages lengthwise and then again, so that she can keep hold of the paper during the crush through the subway doors and can read the first page of the eight-column wand from top to bottom, squeezed between the elbows and shoulders, swept along underground for fifteen minutes until she is able to proceed on foot. When she travels to Europe, she asks her neighbor to keep his issues, and when she returns she spends whole weekends catching up from the foot-high piles on the New York time she has missed. On her lunch break she clears off her desk and reads around in the pages behind the front page, her elbows planted on the edge of the desk, European-style. Once, on a visit to Chicago, she walked two miles down a snowy, windswept street of boarded-up apartment buildings until she found a New York City edition, not from that date, in a pro-Chinese bookstore, as though only what was printed out of town could be believed. On her way home from work, the three lengthwise folds have been so strongly carved into the paper that the columns submissively fall open, fold down to the right, swivel over to the left, under the fingers of one hand, like the keys of a musical instrument; she uses her other hand to hold the strap in the crowded, swaying subway car. Once, after midnight, she walked cautiously down the hot side streets, keeping her eyes straight ahead, past groups of whispering people and a brawl around a drunk or unconscious woman, to Broadway, filled at that hour with policemen, prostitutes, and drug addicts, and bought the earliest edition of *The New York Times* and opened it under the acetylene lamp on the gable of the kiosk and found the news that was now truer than the sensational headline she had not been able to believe from the afternoon paper (namely that in Berlin Mrs. Enzensberger had tried to finish off the vice president with bombs made of custard powder). She keeps the crumpled, floppy paper under her arm until she has passed through her apartment door and then reads the financial pages again over dinner—this time for work. If spending a day at the beach has made her miss getting the paper, then that evening she keeps her eye on the subway floor and every garbage can she passes, in search of a thrown-out, torn-up, stained *New York Times* from that day, as though it alone were proof of the day having existed. *The New York Times* accompanies her and stays home with her like a person, and when she studies the large gray bundle she gets the feeling of someone's presence, of a conversation with someone, whom she listens to and politely answers, with the concealed skepticism, the repressed grimace, the forgiving smile, and all the other gestures she would nowadays make to an aunt, not a relative but a universal, imagined Auntie: her idea of an aunt.

August 23, 1967 Wednesday

The air force flew 132 missions over North Vietnam yesterday. Under a picture of the wreckage of an airplane in Hanoi, the newspaper writes that the Communists say that the picture shows a US plane that has been shot down. The photo was important enough for the front page, but only on the sixth page, set below news from Jerusalem, do we find the official death tally: forty soldiers, with only the dead from the New York area listed by name, fifteen lines of local news.

Last night, five hundred police patrolled the Negro neighborhoods in New Haven, stopping and searching cars, shining floodlights into windows, arresting one hundred. And if she had been at Foley Square yesterday afternoon instead of walking down West Ninety-Fifth Street toward the park—still wetly blurred, with the river in the middle of the picture—she could have heard a leader of the radical African Americans shout that they were at war with the whites and they better get themselves some guns. She imagines she would have watched the policemen's faces, one of which is visible under the raised black fist in the newspaper with a skeptical expression, almost that of a wise elder, still with an aftertaste of the beatings that had just taken place.

In August 1931, Cresspahl was sitting on a shady lawn in Travemünde with his back to the Baltic, reading a five-day-old English newspaper.

He was in his forties then, big-boned, broad-shouldered, with a firm stomach above his belt. In his gray-green corduroy suit with knickerbockers he looked more rustic than the other spa guests around him; he carried himself carefully, his hands were massive, but the waiter saw when he raised one and soon put a beer down next to it, not without a comment or two. Cresspahl answered with a soft, inattentive grunt. He looked over the top of his crumpled newspaper at a table in the sunny middle of the lawn, where a family from Mecklenburg was sitting, but in an absentminded way, as though he'd had enough of his out-of-date news. He was chubby in the face then, with dry, already tough skin. His long face was narrower at the brow. His hair was still blond, cut short, unruly. He had an observant look, hard to interpret, and his lips were slightly protruding, as in the picture in his passport that I stole from him twenty years later.

He had left England five days before. In Mecklenburg he had married

his sister off to Martin Niebuhr, a foreman for the Department of Waterways. He'd paid for the dinner at the Waren Ratskeller. He'd looked
Niebuhr over for two long days before giving him a thousand marks, as a
loan. He'd paid the fees for the next twenty years for his father's grave in
the Malchow cemetery. He'd set up an annuity for his mother. He'd bought
his way free, had he not? He'd spent one day visiting a cousin in Holstein
and helping him bring in the grain crop. He'd renewed his passport for
five years, as required by the naturalization regulations. He still had twenty-
five pounds in his pocket and did not want to spend much of it before he
was back in Richmond, with his workshop full of expensive equipment,
with a reliable clientele, with his two rooms on Manor Grove in a house
he had made an offer on. He'd revisited during this trip the places where
he had been a child, where he had learned his trade, where he had been
called up into the war, where the Kapp putschists had locked him in a
potato cellar, where now the Nazis and the Communists were beating one
another up. He was not planning to come back to Germany again.

The air was dry and moved swiftly. Warm shadows fluttered. The sea
breeze pushed scraps of the spa concert into the lawn. It was peacetime.
The picture is chamois-colored, yellowing slightly. What did Cresspahl see
in my mother?

In 1931 my mother was twenty-five years old, the second-youngest of
the Papenbrock daughters. In family photos she stands in the back, hands
clasped, head tilted slightly to one side, unsmiling. You could tell by looking at her that she'd never had to work. She was the same medium height
as me and wore her hair, our hair, in a chignon—dark hair, falling loosely,
framing her small, submissive, faintly yellowish face. At that particular
moment she looked worried. She seldom raised her eyes from the tablecloth
and was kneading her fingers as though she were practically helpless. She
alone had noticed that the man watching her, steadily, without a nod, had
followed them from the Priwall ferry to the nearest free table on the lawn.
Old Papenbrock leaned back in his chair with his whole weight and grouched
with the waiter, or else with his wife when the waiter was busy at another
table. My grandmother, the sheep, said as though in church: Yes, Albert.
Of course, Albert. The waiter stood next to Cresspahl and said: Not that
I know of. For the weekend. A lot of people come up from the country.
Good families. Yes, sir.

I was pretty, Gesine.
But he looked like a workman.
That's what we liked, Gesine.

Cresspahl was waiting for the ferry to Priwall when the Papenbrocks
came and stood in the front row; on the ferry he leaned against the barrier,
his back to them. On the other side, he let them walk past him to Albert's
delivery truck and was soon lost among the people strolling beneath leafy
trees through the streets of mansions. That evening, Cresspahl drove in a
rented car back to Mecklenburg, via Priwall, along the Pötenitzer Wiek,
along the coast, to Jerichow. My father, when his boat to England sailed
from Hamburg, took a room at the Lübeck Court in Jerichow.

Gesine Cresspahl is invited out for lunch sometimes, to an Italian
restaurant on Third Avenue. There is a garden in back, between ivy-covered
brick walls. The tables beneath the brightly colored umbrellas are covered
with red-and-white-checked tablecloths, the street noise comes over the
roof muffled, and the conversation is about the Chinese. What are the
Chinese doing?

The Chinese are setting fire to the British diplomatic compound in
Peking and beating up the British envoy. That's what the Chinese are doing.

August 24, 1967 Thursday

Five American warplanes have been shot down in North Vietnam. Seventeen military personnel were killed in combat in South Vietnam, among
them Anthony M. Galeno of the Bronx.

Police in the Bronx have discovered a cache of weapons: submachine
guns, an antitank gun, dynamite, ammunition, hand grenades, rifles,
shotguns, pistols, detonators. The four collectors—private citizens, patriots, members of the John Birch Society—had planned to kill the Communist Herbert Aptheker first, then protect the nation from its other
enemies.

When Gesine Cresspahl came to this city in the spring of 1961, it was
supposed to be for two years. The porter had put the child on his luggage
cart and dashed her exuberantly around the somewhat run-down French

Line terminal; when he doffed his cap and tried to shake hands, the child put both of hers behind her back. Marie was almost four years old. After six days at sea she'd lost heart and no longer expected the new country to have the Rhine, her Düsseldorf kindergarten, her grandmother. Gesine still always thought of Marie as "the child," and the child was of course powerless to stop her. Gesine was worried—this child, squinting darkly, shyly into the grimy light of West Forty-Eighth Street from under a white bonnet, could thwart the move.

She had twenty days to find an apartment, and the child resisted New York on every last one of them. The hotel found her a German-speaking babysitter, an elderly, stiff-necked woman from the Black Forest in a tar-black dress, all ruffles and buttons. She could sing lieder by Uhland in a thin soprano voice, but she had retained more of her local dialect than she did the High German spoken in Freudenstadt twenty-five years ago; the child didn't answer her. The child marched through the city with Gesine, refusing to let go of her hand, pressing against her in buses and subways, watchful to the point of suspicion, and letting herself be tricked into sleep by the monotonous movements of some vehicle only late in the afternoon. She hunched her head between her shoulders when Gesine read to her from the apartment listings in *The New York Times*: she couldn't care less about doorman buildings or air-conditioning; she asked about ocean liners. She looked around with a kind of satisfaction in the apartments Gesine could afford, with their stingily chopped-up, shabbily furnished rooms, three windows looking out on a courtyard black as night and one on the bleak hard opposite facade, expensive only because it was free of Negro neighbors; these windows were nothing compared to the garden ones in Düsseldorf, she didn't have to stand for these. The child did not take in one single English word, letting the shouts and hellos and compliments in hotel lobbies in buses in coffee shops pass over her as though she had gone entirely deaf. She answered only with a delayed furious shake of the head, eyelids lowered. She was so silently bent on going back that people called her well brought up again and again. She started to refuse her food, because the bread, the fruit, the meat tasted different. Gesine let herself resort to bribery and told her she could watch cartoons on TV; the child turned away from the screen, and not defiantly. The child stood at the window and looked down at the street, dark between the high buildings, where everything was different: the packs of taxis in blazing color, the whistling uniformed porters under their baldachins, the American flag on the Harvard Club, the policemen playing with their nightsticks, the white steam coming out of the central system vents, glowing in the strange and foreign night. She asked about airplanes. Gesine was relieved when the child, after days of observation, asked why some of the people here had dark skin, or why old women from the Black Forest were Jews. Most of their conversation was wordless, conducted in looks, in thoughts:

can't you just forget the whole thing, for me?
Give me these two years. Then we'll go back to West Germany for as long as you want.
So you might change your mind

On the twelfth day, for the child's sake, Gesine stopped looking in Manhattan and tried one of the nicer residential parts of Queens. The train clambered out of the tunnel under the East River onto the tall stilts opposite the United Nations, and the child, dispirited and bossy, looked at the jagged, superhumanly high skyline of the other shore and then at the low squalid boxes, the single-story wasteland (as a writer once said) on either side of the tracks. In Flushing, though, they found wide park boulevards between grassy slopes in the shade of old trees, loosely ringed by white wooden houses keeping their distance from one another, rustic-style slate roofs, and Gesine was no longer secretly apologizing to the child. The child said: Shouldn't we look near the water instead?

The broker on the main street was a staid man with a soft voice, over fifty, white. When he took off his glasses, he looked experienced. Age made him seem reliable. He had some furnished apartments in the wooded areas, with steps down to the gardens, swimming pools around the corner. Gesine could afford to live here. The man smiled at the child, now stiff with anger that the move seemed to have really happened. He talked about the area, called it respectable and Jewish, and said: Don't worry, we keep the shwartzes out. Gesine snatched the child from the chair and her bag from the table in one motion and was out on the sidewalk, making sure to slam the glass door with a bang behind her, too.

That evening they sat in a restaurant at Idlewild Airport and watched the planes taxi out onto the runways and start across the ocean against a swarthy sky. She tried to explain to the child that the broker had thought she was Jewish, and thought she was a better person than a Negro. The child wanted to know what *You bastard of a Jew* meant, and realized that miracles do exist. She saw the suitcase with her toys being wheeled out of the hotel, felt herself on the plane already, back home tomorrow. Gesine was ready to give up. You can't live among such people.

The West German government wants to completely eliminate the statute of limitations for any murder and genocide committed during the Nazi regime, maybe.

Light artillery can be ordered by mail, but a license is required for a handgun, and she doesn't want to go to the police.

August 25, 1967 Friday

Rain has been falling in the city since last night, the thudding sound of the cars on the Hudson River parkway muffled to a low whoosh. This morning, the slurping sound of the tires on the dripping-wet pavement under her window wakes her up. The rainy light has hung darkness between the office buildings on Third Avenue. The small stores tucked into the base of the skyscrapers cast meager, small-town light out into the wetness. When she switched on the overhead fluorescent light in her office, its glow hemmed in by the darkness painted a picture of homeyness in her boxy cell, for a moment. The child comes back from summer camp today.

In the evening, the bank building's brow, not far above her floor, is draped in fog. Seen from the street, the executives' windows give a watery twinkle. Sinking ships.

Later that evening, she's waiting for the child at the snack counter of the George Washington Bridge bus station, smoking and chatting lazily with the waitress, newspaper under her arm. The paper is folded along the same crease as when she fished it out from under the canopy of the newspaper stand; she's saved it for the hour she has to wait. She gives herself permission not to start on the front page and instead choose articles from the table of contents.

A federal court has indicted twenty-five persons in connection with the

$407,000 in travel checks that disappeared from J. F. Kennedy Airport last summer. They've tracked down the man who resold the checks for a quarter of their face value, as well as the man who disposed of them at half their value, and also the people who cashed them, but have yet to find whoever actually knocked the package of checks off the luggage truck. The man who presumably squealed the information was found on July 11, shot dead in a ditch outside of Monticello. A little message from the Mafia.

The child had sent her a postcard with her arrival time: on the front is a photo showing her in a rowboat with other children. Marie has one leg trailing in the water and a wide dark bandage around her shin. She looks quiet and fearless amid the others' grimaces. She'd banged her shin against her water-ski binding. She is not one meter forty-seven: she is four foot ten. Her handwriting has the curves and loops of the American model. When she multiplies, she writes the multiplicator under, not next to, the multiplicand. She thinks in Fahrenheit, gallons, miles. Her English is better than Gesine's, better in articulation, intonation, accent. German is for her a foreign language, which she uses with her mother to be polite, in a flat tone, pronouncing her vowels the American way, often hunting for the right word. When she speaks English the way she does naturally, Gesine doesn't always understand her. She wants to be baptized when she turns fifteen, and she has managed to make the nuns in the private school farther uptown on Riverside Drive call her M'ri instead of Mary. She was supposed to be expelled from that school anyway, for refusing to take off her GET OUT OF VIETNAM button in class. She changes out of her blue school uniform with the crest over the heart as soon as she gets home; she likes to wear sneakers and tight pants made of white poplin, whose hems she's cut off with a kitchen knife. She has lost almost none of the friends she's made during her six years here, and she still talks about Edmondo from Spanish Harlem, who even in kindergarten could express his feelings only with his fists and who was institutionalized for life in 1963. She has slept over in many apartments on Riverside Drive and West End Avenue. She is in demand as a babysitter for small children, but she is strict with them, occasionally rough. She knows Manhattan's subway system by heart—she could work at an information booth. What she types in her room she keeps in a portfolio tied with knots that cannot be reproduced. She secretly looks in Gesine's box of photographs, and she used her own pocket money to make a copy of a picture that shows Jakob and Jöche outside the train conductor's school in Güstrow. She has forgotten her Düsseldorf friends. She knows West Berlin from the newspapers. A lot of businesses on Broadway are obliged to pay her tribute—Maxie's with peaches, Schustek's with slices of bologna, the liquor store with chewing gum. When she slips up and says that after all Negroes are just Negroes, she bobs up and down and makes a gesture with her outturned palms as though pushing back against Gesine and says: Okay! Okay!

On page 2 of the paper is a photograph showing an American pilot pointing to a map to show where he'd shot down two North Vietnamese pilots and their planes; he is in profile, his lips pulled back from his teeth in what looks to be a tired, satisfied smile. The official death toll of Americans is on page 12 today, seven lines, with no connection to the news immediately above it. LONG ISLAND MAN AMONG WAR DEAD reads the headline. The following report lists twenty-eight.

Marie says:
– My braids are my property, I'll cut them off when I want to.
– My grandfather was a rich man.
– Mrs. Kellogg shaves.
– I don't mind the sight of blood. I want to be a doctor.
– My mother thinks Negroes have the same rights, and that's where she stops thinking.
– Negroes have different bodies than us too.
– President Johnson is in the Pentagon's pocket.
– James Fenimore Cooper is the greatest.
– My father was a delegate at the European Railway Timetable Conference in Lisbon, representing the German Democratic Republic.
– Düsseldorf-Lohausen is an international hub for air travel.
– My friends in England write to me twelve times a year.
– My mother is in banking.
– My mother is from a small town on the Baltic, but don't rub it in.
– My mother has the best legs on the whole number 5 bus above Seventy-Second Street.
– Fathers have such a starved look.
– Bring our boys home!

– Sister Magdalena is an old bag.

– John Vliet Lindsay is the greatest.

– My mother always flies in the same plane as me so that we'll die to-gether.

– Everything would be better if John Kennedy was still alive.

– My best friends are Pamela, Edmondo, Rebecca, Paul and Michelle, Stephen, Annie, Kathy, Ivan, Martha Johnson, David W., Paul-Erik, Mayor Lindsay, Mary-Anne, Claire and Richard, Mr. Robinson, Esmeralda and Bill, Mr. Maxie Fruitmarket, Mr. Schustek, Timothy Shuldiner, Dmitri Weiszand, Jonas, D. E., and Senator Robert F. Kennedy.

– My mother knows the Swedish ambassador.

– Go ahead and get married, but I don't want a father.

– I speak Spanish better than my mother.

– My mother wanted to go back to Germany after two years, and I said: We're staying.

The New York Times reports as national news the death of an industrialist who in 1895 started as an errand boy working for $1.50 a week and died with assets of $2.5 billion, and the paper devotes more than two hundred lines to his memory.

The child walks past the glass wall of the station restaurant. She hasn't turned her head, she just keeps walking amid the crush of parents and goodbyes. She has gotten skinny; her skin is tanned and dry. She looks older than ten. She is wearing the Vietnam pin on the collar of her windbreaker. Her braids swing a little from side to side when she tries to look back in the glass panes of the exit. She stops and turns around without letting her left shoulder slip out from under Gesine's outstretched hand.

Ich ha-be dich ge-se-hen: she says, stressing every syllable, speaking every word equally slowly. She repeats: *I sawwww you!* and this time gives the verb its own separate, triumphant soprano pitch. She doesn't look like her father.

August 26, 1967 Saturday

Two US Army sergeants have been arrested and charged with delivering classified documents to Mr. Popov of the Soviet embassy and Mr. Kireyev of the United Nations—in shopping centers, in restaurants, just like in the movies. The Soviet gentlemen have now left the country, by air.

US fighter-bomber raids came within 18 miles of the Chinese border, and the United States lost its 660th plane, and the US secretary of defense tells astonished senators that North Vietnam cannot be bombed to the negotiating table.

Consumer prices rose so much that we had to pay 4.6 percent more in July for fruit and vegetables than we did in June, and a member of the American Nazi Party shot and killed his leader in the act of taking his clothes to a coin-operated Laundromat in Arlington, Virginia, and a swirl of soap flakes fluttered down around the dead man.

Would she have stayed in this country if not for the apartment by the river? Probably not. But after giving up the search, she found the tiny ad promising three rooms on Riverside Drive, "all with a view of the Hudson," available for one year at $124 a month. The voice on the telephone seemed surprised at Gesine's questions. Of course the apartment was overrun with applicants, "but we're waiting to find someone we like." Children were permitted. "If you happen to be colored, come anyway, don't worry about that." On her first trip to New York, Gesine had ridden the number 5 bus down Riverside Drive, the inside edge of a wide artificial landscape that starts with a promenade along the river, then continues, as you move inland, with a multilane divided expressway and practically horticultural on-ramp loops, then a spacious, hilly park fifty blocks long, with monuments, playgrounds, sports fields, sunbathing lawns, and bench-lined paths for strolling. Only then comes the actual street bordering the park, curved in numerous places, rising gently over graceful knolls and hills, stretching out slender exit fingers toward apartment buildings behind farther green islands: a rarity in Manhattan, a showpiece of the gardener's art, and a street with views of trees, the water, a landscape. Back then, Gesine had hoped to someday live in one of these towering fortresses of prosperity, richly ornamented in Oriental, Italian, Egyptian, in any case magnificent style, their weather-beaten state making them if anything even more dignified. She'd thought she could never afford it.

Broadway, where it crosses Ninety-Sixth Street, is a marketplace of mostly small buildings with lots of foot traffic to the Irish bar, the drugstore on the southwest corner, the restaurant across the street, at the newsstand.

Now as then, scruffy men stand leaning against the buildings: thieves and fences, drunks, crazies, many of African descent, jobless, sick, some begging. This Broadway is polyglot, with accents from every continent confusingly tackling American English: as you walk along you can hear Spanish from Puerto Rico and Cuba, Caribbean French, Japanese, Chinese, Yiddish, Russian, various vernaculars of the illegal, and again and again German as it was spoken thirty years ago in East Prussia, Berlin, Franconia, Saxony, Hesse. The child heard a high-bosomed matron, wearing an old-fashioned dress with a large flower pattern and ribbons, harangue in German a short downcast man in a black hat creeping alongside her, and she stood there, forgetting all else, and noticed Gesine's tugging hand only after a while. It was a whitish-gray morning, with lots of people on the street moving carefully through air thick with moisture, and the intersection promised a memory of Italy on many mornings to come. Ninety-Seventh Street, sloping down to the west, was gloomier between the decrepit, age-worn hotels, dirty with slimy garbage in the gutter and splotchy bags and dented garbage cans on the sidewalk, and at the end it opened onto a wide, undulating field made up of the swift-flowing roadway of Riverside Drive, grassy slopes, wooded parkland. In the playground, children were jumping and frolicking under sparkling jets of water. In the shade by the park fence, families sat and lay on the cool grass. Behind puffy clouds of leaves hung the blue-gray picture of the mile-wide river and the opposite bank. They stood on the street for a while looking up at the building: yellow bricks, a band with an exotic bull pattern winding around it not far from the ground. To live here seemed so out of reach that Gesine mentally started parceling out her savings into bribes, imagined herself entering into complicated and shady dealings

If only I could send you in ahead
You say: You won't regret it, sir. You say: The advantages of this apartment move me to offer you a token of my gratitude.
You'd never be able to talk like that.

The apartment door opens into a tiny hallway. There is a kitchenette in the wall on the left, with the massive refrigerator at the end. On the right the hallway opens into a large room. Two women Gesine's age, one with a

Danish accent and one with a Swiss, were packing paperbacks into cardboard boxes; they said hello to the child first, serious, polite, as though speaking to a real person. The room has two windows out onto the bright open space above the street, over the park. The apartment continues to the right with a smaller room, behind curtained glass double doors, with another window facing the park. That was the Dane's bedroom. On the other side of the apartment, behind a sturdy door, next to the bathroom, which has a window looking out over the park, is what was the Swiss woman's room, with a window overlooking the park. In winter the cliffs of New Jersey are visible through the bare branches, and the breadth of the river and the hazy air can blur the architectural wasteland on the other side into an illusion of unspoiled countryside, a phantasm of openness and distance. Both women were stewardesses being transferred to Europe. They wanted to be able to leave their furniture behind for one year. They wanted to give up the apartment right away. It would not cost anything besides the rent. They asked Marie if she wanted to stay here, and Marie said an English word: "Yes." The super, a heavyset, somewhat formal black man with a resplendent British accent, gave Gesine exact change, to the penny, for her deposit. The women took them out to lunch and let them help with the packing and then helped them bring their suitcases from the hotel, and the child seemed sad when the women left for the airport that night. After a year they didn't come back, but we visited the Danish one on our vacation. We had an apartment and didn't ask any questions. Over the next seven years, handmade pieces replaced much of the factory-made furniture, first in Marie's room (the Swiss room), then in the middle room too: dark wood, a lime-green bookshelf with glass doors, blue burlap curtains, a fleecy rug on which the child reads the newspaper out loud, lying on her belly, chin in her hands, swinging her legs back and forth. All day long an even, regular, sonic field of rushing rain surrounds the apartment. Here there will be no flooding.

Marie collects pictures from the newspaper, and today she cuts out the one that in the foreground shows the body of the Nazi leader lying on his side, next to his car, and in the background, on the roof of the Laundromat, a policeman standing where the sniper had shot him from. "Rabbi Lelyveld," she reads out loud from the article, "said that Rockwell was a nuisance rather than a menace." Then the child says in English, in a lecturing tone: I can hear what the rabbi's not saying when he says that.

August 27, 1967 Sunday

The East Germans in power say: We are introducing a five-day workweek, forty-three and three-quarters hours, a unique Socialist achievement. The American Nazi Party says: Our leader's body belongs to the party. The wife of the arrested army sergeant says: It can't be true, my husband isn't a spy. *The New York Times* says: In America the forty-hour workweek was introduced in 1938.

And the weather in North Vietnam has cleared up enough to allow bombing to resume, and the Pentagon suggests that the North Vietnamese are tucking away planes of their own in China, and yesterday morning three men raided the Schuyler Arms Hotel on Ninety-Eighth Street, shot and wounded the night clerk, and got away with $68 in cash. It was about three a.m., two blocks from here.

And *The New York Times* devotes more than eight full columns, starting on the front page—184 inches—to Stalin's daughter. This wayward daughter of Attila was sitting, according to the *Times*, among the Goths on Long Island, in a garden chair under a black oak tree, and she said: She is in favor of freedom, as a general principle.

She says: *The New York Times* relays: I believe that when people have freedom to do whatever they want, and to express whatever they like, and even have the freedom to riot—they will.

She means the race riots in Detroit.

She was wearing a simple white dress and beige flats as she sat there, in a small group of friends and journalists, expressing her thoughts in a relaxed and cheerful way. *The New York Times* considers it necessary that we know this.

This hope of salvation says: I like dogs better than cats. I used to have a dog—but no more.

When asked whether she has a bank account, the daughter of the leader of the Socialist camp answers yes. Then she giggles and asks back: Do you?

The New York Times vouchsafes us the information that this voluntary refugee has had to learn how to write checks.

The daughter of the most powerful Socialist statesman says: Although I always felt a personal attachment to my father, I was never an admirer of what was called "Stalinism" as a system.

Then she asked for a glass of water, "with ice, please."

When she spoke of her children, she lowered her voice and looked off into the woods at the edge of the lawn.

She says: The chief evil influence in my father's life was what made him leave his priesthood and become a Marxist.

She says: I think a religious feeling is inborn, just as a person is born a poet.

The New York Times, says *The New York Times,* will print excerpts from Stalin's daughter's book starting on September 10. It says so neither at the beginning nor at the end but in passing, on the edge of a page, near the bottom. *The New York Times* trusts its readers.

In an article on coordinated Vietcong attacks throughout South Vietnam, *The New York Times* reports the losses on our side (killed or wounded) as 268 (later 248) in Cantho, 79 in Hoian, 1 in Hue, 53 or more in Quangda and Dienban, moderate casualties near Pleiku, 13 at Banmethuot, and light casualties near Saigon, and gives the total as 335.

In the early thirties, Jerichow was one of the smallest towns in Mecklenburg-Schwerin: a market town of 2,151 inhabitants, located near the Baltic Sea between Lübeck and Wismar. It was a backwater with low brick buildings lining a cobblestone street, from the two-story town hall with fake classical fluting to a Romanesque church with a tower like a bishop's miter, high and sharply pointed and with small protruding gables on all four sides, like a miter. On the north side of the market square, toward the sea, stood a hotel, the mayor's office, a bank, the credit union, Wollenberg's hardware store, Papenbrock's house and business, and the old town center, with side streets branching off from there: Kattrepel, the Bäk, Short Street, School Street, Station Street. To the south was where the original town had been, around the church and the cemetery, five lanes of half-timber houses, until it burned down in 1732, rebuilt only in the nineteenth century with squat red-brick buildings shoulder to shoulder under skimpy roofs. Now the post office was there, the co-op department store, the brickworks past the churchyard, the brickworks owner's villa. A lot of barns still stood on the outskirts of town, the side streets quickly turned into country lanes, and farmyard gates of old wood stood next to shopwindows on the main street. Townsmen-farmers lived there, on three hundred acres, along with merchants and tradesmen. Cresspahl came in from the south, on the Gneez country road, and drove up the main street past the market square and out the other side of Jerichow, just thinking that this must be the start of town when actually it was where the town ended. There were fields all the way to the sea.

Jerichow was not in fact a town. It had a town charter dating back to 1240, it had a municipal council, it purchased electricity from the Herrenwyk power plant, it had an automatic telephone exchange and a train station, but it belonged to the nobility whose estates surrounded it. This was not because of the fire. The nobility had taken the farms of the peasants who had made the land arable, annexed them to their own land, and made the peasants serfs; the weak princely house of Mecklenburg, up to its ears in debt, had confirmed their right to do so in the Constitutional Inheritance Law of 1755. Of the villages that had made Jerichow strong, only three remained—tiny, impoverished settlements. In this corner of the world, the gentry, in the form of employers, mayors, judges ruled over their day laborers, gained fame as robber barons, gained wealth as industrialists. Jerichow, for its part, had all but reverted to its original state as a village clearing. Its distance from the sea and the larger Baltic harbors were insurmountable obstacles to a shipping trade. Where a Jerichow harbor might have been lay the fishing village of Rande, rich enough even at the turn of the century for a Grand Hotel, an Archduke Hotel, a City of Hamburg Hotel. Jerichow had remained a way station on the road to Rande, a place in which the carriages, now the omnibuses, never dropped off their big-spending summer visitors. Trade did not travel along the narrow country lanes; the large roads bypassed Jerichow far to the south. The nobility liked Jerichow the way it was, as an office, a warehouse district, a trading post, a loading station for their wheat and sugar beets. The nobility had no need of a town. Jerichow got its train line to Gneez, on the Hamburg–Stettin main line, because the nobility needed a means of transportation. Jerichow was too poor to build a sewer system; the nobility did not need one. There were no movie theaters in Jerichow: the nobility did not approve of that particular invention. Jerichow's industry, brickmaking, belonged to the nobility, as did the bank, most of the buildings, the Lübeck Court Hotel. The Lübeck

Court had a septic tank. The nobility bought replacement parts for their machines in Jerichow, made use of the municipal administration, the police, the lawyers, Papenbrock's granaries, but they handled their important business in Lübeck, sent their children to boarding schools in Prussia, held religious services in their own private chapels, and had themselves buried behind their manor houses. At harvest time, when Ratzeburg or Schwerin was too far away, the gentlemen rode to the Lübeck Court of an evening and played cards at their own special table—ponderous, affable, droning men wallowing in their Low German, their Plattdeutsch. They thought Cresspahl, with his beer, was a traveling salesman because of the big-city license plate on his car.

Jerichow called its main street, a narrow cutting from when the forest was being cleared, Town Street.

At breakfast, Cresspahl asked about the weather. He stepped inside the little shops, bought stationery or shirts of a better sort, asked casual questions. He stood for a while on the path behind Heinz Zoll's yard—Zoll did the higher-end woodworking around here—and had a good long look at the lumber stored in the open shed. He started taking his beer in at Peter Wulff's pub. Wulff was his age, less fat in those days, a hands-off tight-lipped bartender who observed Cresspahl's patient waiting the same way Cresspahl did his. Cresspahl wrote a postcard for all to see and gave it to the hotel porter to mail to Richmond. He stopped in to see Jansen, the lawyer. He walked to Rande and had dinner in the City of Hamburg Hotel. He read all the advertisements on the page for the Jerichow area in *The Gneez Daily News*. He did not slow down when he passed by Papenbrock's gate, but his walks did take him past it, and after a while he knew that the young man in charge of unloading the sacks in the yard was Horst Papenbrock, the son and heir, then thirty-one years old. Between its receding chin and its receding brow, Horst's face was as sharply pointed as a fish's. Through the open window, Cresspahl saw old Papenbrock at his desk, sweating above his comfortable, delicate stomach, his polite nods so vigorous that he seemed to be bowing in his seat. Apparently he did not like bargaining with his aristocratic clientele, or not for long, this Papenbrock who was so cheap that he never bought a car and drove his family to Travemünde for coffee in the delivery truck. Cresspahl did not see my mother. Cresspahl did see my grandmother helping out behind the counter in the bakery, a submissive, spry old lady with a rather treacly way of speaking, especially to children. Here he did nod hello through the open door as he walked past.

and I was never a sheep, Gesine.
They threw you down on your side, they tied your hooves together, they pinned your neck to the barn floor with their knees, they stripped off your wool with dull shears, and you never once opened your mouth, Louise née Utecht from Hageböcker Street in Güstrow, you sheep

Cresspahl knew that Horst Papenbrock and the farmer Griem were Nazis who had to go to Gneez for their street fighting because the Social Democrats in Jerichow were their neighbors, their relatives, their city councilmen. He knew that Papenbrock, with his grain business, his bakery, his deliveries to the surrounding countryside, was the richest man in Jerichow and a moneylender. He knew that history had left no trace in Jerichow except a Napoleonic fortification on the coast, five miles away. He knew that Jerichow could not support a second master carpenter.

Jerichow is surrounded by wheat fields. To the south, past the marsh, are the Countess Woods, then meadows bordered with hedges over six feet high. The weather is maritime. The wind comes mostly from the west, especially in midsummer and winter. It's cool here. There are more overcast days per year here than anywhere else in the country. It rains less often here than elsewhere in Mecklenburg, and storms are rare. The apple trees blossom late, in mid-May; the winter rye is ripe on July 25. The frost sets in later and leaves earlier than in the rest of the county, but it barely penetrates the soil, because the air is always in motion from the wind, here.

August 29, 1967 Tuesday
There are still town houses dating from the last century on Third Avenue north of Forty-Second Street: four or five stories high, once-elegant brownstone or expensive brick facades, now grimy, the windows smeared and covered with dust, and only the ground floors occupied, with small businesses, snack shops, bars, whose neon signs and awnings conceal the corpses

of the buildings above them. The businesses have enough walk-in customers, they could hardly get by on the tenants. The street's future is supposed to lie in the glass-and-steel office buildings set back atop block-wide ten-story pedestals, stacked high in identical strata starting from the twentieth story, still sixty-five feet wide on the fiftieth floor. The frosted glass and metal between the ribbon windows can look dark blue, gray, green, or yellow; some buildings have brick columns stuck onto the facade at the bearing struts; another distinguishing feature is the names on the ground-floor marble facing. The buildings are easy to dismantle, their names neither inscribed on nor inlaid in the walls, only stuck on or screwed on, for easy removal.

The building in which Miss Cresspahl earns her salary consists of a block-long twelve-story plinth with a terrace atop it, set back, crowned by a smooth tower. The glass between the shining ribs has blue-gray stripes wrapping around it. Most of the windows show the slats of venetian blinds but a little fluorescent light still shimmers through the cracks. From across the street, with her head tilted all the way back, she should be able to make out which two windows are hers, but she always loses count. At street level, half of the front of the building is laid out as a normal bank, behind plate-glass windows taller than the people inside and out, neither tinted nor curtained nor ribbed with blinds, drawing a passerby's gaze in to the fake-leather seats, low tables, desks on islands of carpet, counters, teller windows under the eye of automatic cameras, and brightly polished giant-frying-pan vault door. This parlor as big as a train station's waiting room is still empty. The other half of the ground floor is a restaurant, shielding its customers from the light of day with lime-green curtains. The building's main entrance with its four swinging doors pulls in so many people from the sidewalk that the rest hurrying past get out of step. Behind a wall of pale marble, the foyer opens onto three elevator lanes to the left, the building's maintenance area branches off in the back, and the right wall is taken up by a long counter selling newspapers, candy, and tobacco products. Every elevator lane is managed by its own supervisor, whose blue-gray uniform bears the company's name in embroidered script above the heart. She manages to nod to him. As she enters an elevator car, its green light indicating an upward course, she sees the building's street number set into the floor, intended to alert the passenger if he has made a mistake. Among the approximately twenty-five occupants today, she sees no one she recognizes. When the steel double doors snap shut before her, it is nine minutes to nine o'clock.

The death toll for today is twenty Americans, fifteen South Vietnamese, and ninety-eight North Vietnamese, the latter estimated. The newspaper gives only two names from the list of the dead, who happened to be from the state of New York, as though the exact total counted for nothing really compared to the hundred and ninety-five million citizens of America. The slain Nazi will be permitted a burial of honor at a national military cemetery, since his only crime was incitement to the murder of Negroes and Jews. A Mrs. Hart is opposed to having his grave next to the graves of those who fell in the war against the Nazis. Four Germans have gone on trial in Westphalia on charges of having drowned prisoners and tortured them to death under ice-cold showers at the Mauthausen concentration camp. At least one million American housewives are alcoholics. And this time Stalin's daughter is in the paper for not wanting $250,000 for a television interview. She'll do it for free. She seems to have substantial future earnings in view.

– How was work today, Gesine?

Mrs. Williams is back in the office, she didn't go to Greece after all, she was afraid of the military. A third memo has requested that employees lock their desks during lunch hour and keep their handbags with them at all times because of more thefts on the tenth floor. The latest rumor is that we've bought Xerox. My boss had to leave for Hawaii this afternoon, his son is being sent there for R&R from South Vietnam.
– And what did the paper say?

Mahalia Jackson was taken to a hospital in West Berlin.

August 30, 1967 Wednesday
Vietcong guerillas broke into a jail in the northern city of Quangngai and freed eight hundred prisoners. The paper gives the names of four men from

the New York–New Jersey area killed in action, but not the total count. The soldiers on guard at the Culpeper National Cemetery in Virginia denied the dead Nazi burial because the party refused to take their swastika off of the hearse; now he is back in the funeral home.

"Dear Gesine,

I waited for you till eight, then Pamela Blumenroth invited me to sleep over. Please don't call.

No mail, except for me.

What you need is in the fridge.

Mrs. Ferwalter is mad at you or at me. She hasn't called for a week.

We have to do something about D. E. He doesn't believe that you were in New Jersey alone.

The phone lines got crossed again. This time he said his name was George and that he wanted to talk to a Luise. He was calling from Rhode Island.

Were you in New Jersey alone?

If there's any news about Mahalia Jackson's condition, bring it for me.

This Griem, from Jerichow, did you know him? Is he still alive?

The truth is I only waited until seven thirty. What kind of office is that, where people have to stay working till eight at night? Is that worth it for us?

With affectionate greetings,

Mary Fenimore Cressp. Cooper"

She uses British slang, "fridge," out of loyalty to London SE.

What are the Chinese doing? In London they are starting a fight with the police, attacking them with baseball bats, iron bars, and axes. The one holding the ax is lanky, with glasses, still a schoolboy.

How did the Chinese find a baseball bat in England?

August 31, 1967 *Thursday*

The Vietcong are continuing their attacks in the South. The Soviets are conducting a secret trial of three writers. The Chinese forced a British chargé d'affaires in Peking to bend his head by pulling down on his hair—in retaliation, they say. Six other cemeteries rejected the body of the Nazi leader; the party has had him cremated and his ashes are under armed guard.

What kind of person does Gesine picture when she thinks of *The New York Times* as an aunt?

An older person. Teachers at the high school in Gneez used to be called "Auntie"—ladies of a certain age, humanistically educated, good-naturedly disapproving of the course of things but only in one-on-one conversations, helplessly. Once they had wanted to change the course of things: by studying at the universities under the Kaiser, by camping out and canoeing with men and without marriage certificates, by earning their own living despite the concerns of their middle-class families whose articles of faith they themselves defended against the changing times once they reached the same age and their hair turned gray and they tromped around in comfortable shoes and slacks whenever possible: It doesn't do to put a revolution in the saddle, it might not have had enough riding lessons. And you have to think of the horse, too. It's true that expressing such an opinion during class would have led to their dismissal. They were called Auntie with a certain indulgence, not unkindly, not unsympathetically. The term was malicious when applied to kindergarten teachers, those champion caregivers. Unathletic boys and overly timid girls were called Auntie, too, as a term of contempt.

That said, *The New York Times* strikes Gesine as like an aunt from a good family that has acquired a certain fortune on the backs of others but not in any brutal way, simply as the age dictates. It has rendered services to every government, and every government is in the history books. This surviving aunt carries on the family tradition. Gesine pictures age, a gaunt figure, a deeply lined face, a bitter twist to the mouth, but elegant dark clothes, an insistence on hairpins, a scratchy voice, smiles only in the corners of the eyes. Never, never losing her temper. In her bearing, in the way she holds her legs, she flirts with her age—a sign of her experience. She has been around, looked life straight in its tight-lipped face; no chance of anyone pulling the wool over her eyes. She has had her affairs but was certainly no adventuress; they were in the best hotels in Europe, as befit her station; that's all in the past now. She so obviously expects respect that she almost invites one to refuse it. She is a little stubborn, almost pushy when she feels excluded by younger people. She likes the young people to have their fun as long as she is the one doling it out. Gesine pictures a living room, a salon, furnished in Empire style, where the aunt holds court.

Everything proceeds in civilized fashion; one listens to one's elders first. Tea is served, whiskey is served. Then tea again. Old lovers come for memory's sake, the younger generation for instruction. The servants are fanatically discreet. Auntie smokes (cigarillos) and drinks, the hard stuff too; she gets jokes, except when forced to pronounce them unacceptable in the interests of the public. She keeps up with the times. She can cook, she can bake. Auntie has remained unmarried, a tacit indication of the requirements one would have had to meet. She gives advice on marital questions; she can imagine what it's like to be married. (Anyway, a music critic's job is to criticize music, not to write symphonies. Not even sonatas.) She is modern. (Gesine has no such aunt in her family.) This is someone you can go steal horses with whenever the law demands horse thefts.

And yet this person is not only pleasant.

Her bearing is useful, educational.

She does not raise her voice, she delivers a lecture.

On fifteen by twenty-three inches, over eight columns, she offers more than twenty stories for you to choose from.

She does not call an accused person guilty, not yet. Of the two murders a day in the city, she mentions only the instructive ones.

She does not use the president's first name, at most a murder victim's.

She describes hearsay as hearsay.

She lets even those she despises have their say.

She talks to sportsmen in the language of sportsmen.

Changes in the weather, too, she points out.

She helps the poor with charitable donations, and investigates poverty using the latest scientific methods.

She decries disproportionate sentencing.

At least she has pity.

She is impartial toward all forms of religion.

She safeguards purity of language—even correcting it in her clients' advertisements.

She offers the reader at most two pages of ads without a news story (except on Sunday).

She never swears or takes the Lord's name in vain.

She occasionally admits to errors.

She can restrain herself and call a murderer a controversial figure, from brigadier general up.

She drank in propriety with her mother's milk. Why shouldn't we trust her?

September 1, 1967   Friday

The American commander in South Vietnam says: The North Vietnamese are lying. Radio Hanoi reports US losses (killed, wounded, missing) as 110,000 for the first six months of this year. He says: 37,038.

As of today, New York State's divorce law of 1787 is no longer valid. Those who marry now have to wait two years before they are free again.

You don't have to marry me: D. E. says: you should just live with me.

D. E. sends flowers, telegrams, theater tickets, books. He takes Marie out to eat, has made friends with Esther, listens to Mr. Robinson's stories about his military service in West Germany. D. E. lives in New Jersey but spends a lot of time in the bars around Ninety-Sixth Street and Broadway, two blocks from Riverside Drive. On the phone he can almost always say: I'm in the neighborhood. D. E. is close to forty, tall, dressed in Italian jackets and Irish tweed, with a long, fleshy, patient face above which he wears his gray hair long and parted, as if trying to conceal his age. D. E. weighs two hundred and twenty-five pounds and moves nimbly on small feet. D. E. drives a large English car, the colors of his suits are carefully chosen, he lacks for little. D. E. works in the arms industry.

D. E. says: I work for the Defense Department.

Gesine first heard D. E.'s name in Wendisch Burg, in 1953. He'd gone to the same school that Klaus Niebuhr and the Babendererde girl had had to withdraw from that spring; he was about to be expelled from his physics program in East Berlin after standing up in a faculty meeting and calling the Babendererde case a violation of the constitution of the German Democratic Republic (on the part of the German Democratic Republic). Not then, but after the June 1953 uprising, he left the country. He will have made his decision using a list of positive and negative factors, the same kind of list that he draws up today when he can't make up his mind between different cars or houses or political opinions. Back then, what stood in one column was Wendisch Burg, Socialism in the East German fashion, and a drawn-out love affair with Eva Mau; on the other side of the balance sheet was: The prospects for my education here are not good. So he hadn't had to make up his mind himself.

Gesine had seen him for the first time in the Marienfelde refugee center in West Berlin: a skinny young man with a slim steep head, blond hair at the time, paying somewhat absentminded attention to her by asking her questions about Jerichow and holding forth on political theories with extensive recourse to physics vocabulary. The only thing they could talk about easily was the Babendererde incident. He made no effort to be assigned to the same city as her. She saw him for only two days before he was flown out to West Germany. He apparently told the immigration board: I chose the lesser evil. So they sent him to Stuttgart; he finished his doctorate in Hanover, moved from West Germany to England, and Defense bought his way to the United States in 1960. He did send postcards, sometimes letters, mainly about the actions and exploits of Eva Mau; from Stuttgart, young Mrs. Niebuhr née Babendererde sent reports of D. E.'s string of quick love affairs in a marveling, almost devoted tone. Even today she talks about D. E. as though about an older relative, as though grateful to him for something. Gesine had been in New York for eleven months before he found her while flipping through the phone book, and he invited her out to their first dinner, a hulking, uncommunicative, rather solemn patron. After meeting Marie, he proposed marriage.

D. E. works in a place called Industrial Park in New Jersey, for a firm involved in the DEW Line. DEW stands for Distant Early Warning, a line of radar stations around the territories of the North Atlantic Treaty Organization, designed to detect Soviet rockets in time for an American counterstrike. He must have given the military greater assurances than that he'd chosen the lesser evil before they let him join them and felt their secrets would be safe with him. He is barely a scientist anymore, he is a technician. He earns $25,000 a year by now, and his duties include inspection trips to England, Italy, France, Denmark, and Norway, and someone from the embassy is waiting for him at passport control. According to D. E., his Soviet opposite number sits locked in a military airport, buying and selling technical literature on the black market. His firm can count

on government contracts for the improved systems of the seventies, and
D. E. can count on the firm's confidence in his abilities. D. E. does his best
to impair these abilities through the regular intake of alcohol.

The house D. E. offers us is situated by a wide stream in a wooded area
of New Jersey. It is an old colonial wooden house, white clapboard and
blue slate roof. He owns almost half of it so far. D. E.'s mother keeps
house—a shy, bony, finicky woman who learned her English from her
maids. D. E. was one of the few people smart enough to get their families
out of East Germany before the open border in Berlin was closed. The place
where they now live consists of a few scattered houses, and D. E.'s mother
has arrived at her image of America from a certain similarity to the landscape around Wendisch Burg, and mostly from TV shows. She is so proud
of her son that she wants to be buried where he found success. Around
Gesine her behavior is careful, almost formal, as though trying to dispel
some kind of fear. She sighs over D. E. when he betakes himself to his study
in the evening with the French red wine that he orders by the case from
an importer, but she says nothing, and every morning she has two new
bottles ready for him. D. E. sits at his metal behemoth of a desk, a heavy,
sorrowful figure in the night, and phones the island of Manhattan. He
says: Dear Miss Mary, quite contrary, come see me, the weekend is so long.
We'll have a cookout in the yard. I'll take you to the shore. He says: If she
doesn't want to, let me come see the two of you.

You just don't want to die alone.
But with me the child would be taken care of.

Unfortunately, D. E. has won the child over. Marie laughs at his funny
faces, especially the wounded-dignity one; she laughs at his demonstrations
of drawling Mecklenburg German, where to amuse her he ends every other
sentence with a squeaking *"Nich?,"* and at his performances of Southern
or New England dialects, and she envies him his English, because D. E. is
like a parrot with languages. Marie believes his stories full of sudden twists
and turns—about the lady who beat a policeman over the head with her
shoe outside St. Patrick's Cathedral, about his cats who can count, about
the vice presidents of his firm waging war against each other on the eighth
floor. Marie designs secret codes ever since he taught her ciphering systems.

Marie admires his behavior in restaurants, and the fact that he can afford restaurants on the fifty-second floor. Marie keeps her door open a crack on nights when D. E. is sitting at the table with his bottles and talking about lasers, about the political history of Mecklenburg, about Tom's Bar. Marie thinks of the two upstairs guest rooms in D. E.'s house as her inalienable personal property. She even gave D. E. this name, because she liked the little hiccup between "Dee" and "Ee." She doesn't hold his drinking against him (he doesn't lie on the steps in front of the emergency exit of the movie theater on Ninety-Seventh Street, dressed in rags, crusted with dirt, unshaven, snoring loudly, hand still on the bottle in its brown paper bag; he's not a Broadway bum, he's a professor). Once, when D. E. said he was coming over, Marie went to the phone and ordered a supply of red wine and Gauloises and paid with the grocery money. But D. E. arrives with bags in both hands, flowers tucked under his arm, chocolate bars clamped between his fingers, and you can already hear his booming teasing voice in the hall saying something to Mr. Robinson, and Mr. Robinson stands in the elevator door to watch D. E. enter the Cresspahl residence with head raised, sniffing the air, shouting in awe and wonder: Smell That Dee-li-cious Meck-len-burg Cooking! And Marie laughs.

September 2, 1967 Saturday

Through the night, till the early-morning hours, cars were inching bumper to bumper along the river into the long weekend, sending short bursts of dull noise into the open windows on Riverside Drive. D. E. could not be dissuaded from a comparison with approaching artillery fire. Now the weekenders have left silence in their wake, and up to 660 of them, it is predicted, will have died in traffic accidents by the evening of Labor Day.

The morning is cool, bright, and dry in the park. This playground, sprinkled with white light, is a part of Gesine's earliest days in New York; here is where Marie brought her in contact with her first neighbors. This morning she is sitting on one of the benches around the edge of the arena and looking down at the half-naked children running in circles in the taut, intersecting jets of water from the three sprinklers. She is waiting for Mrs. Ferwalter, who spends Sabbath mornings here during the summer. If she turns halfway around, she can see between the leaves the window with the blue curtain behind which D. E. is sleeping off his wine, spread out across the whole bed, naked, arms at his sides, breathing shallowly with angrily protruding lips, alone in the apartment.

Mrs. Ferwalter, Rebecca's mother, is a short, fat woman—a stocky individual who likes to wear loose-fitting red dresses. Her cheekbones are wide, her forehead is narrow above almost black eyes and eyebrows, and the curve with which her head tapers to a narrow chin recalls her face as a girl. Now that face is in the firm grip of age and locked in a rigid expression of disgust that she doesn't realize it has. She was born in 1922 and looks like she's sixty. Six years ago, here in this playground, Mrs. Ferwalter heard Gesine speaking German to her child and stood up from the neighboring bench, walked heavily over on her pudgy legs, and sat down next to Gesine. – Maybe with yours can my child play, she said good-naturedly, in an accent that made her German sound almost Russian. She looked like someone who had recently been through a dangerous illness. Her coarse brown hair was cut short, unevenly, as if after a skull operation. She was wearing a sleeveless dress, and when she held the back of the bench for support as she sat down, Gesine saw the number tattooed on the inside of her left forearm. She looked away, at the woman's plump legs, but there she saw varicose veins bulging out.

You stay right there on that bench. You don't know why I had to send Gronberg away. You don't know anything.
If only I'd known how easy it is for the dead to talk. The dead should keep their mouths shut.

– I'm from Germany, Gesine had said, and Mrs. Ferwalter had answered, with a sigh, from the dry heat or perhaps it was a sigh of longing: I could hear. Europe . . .

She had already called Rebecca over, who was five years old then, a well-behaved child with her mother's hair, doll-like with her small suspicious mouth, dark eyebrows, wide starched collar, ironed jacket-and-skirt set, and like a puppet she made a jerky curtsy to Gesine. Marie came warily over, feet swinging in slow wide arcs, sometimes half turning away altogether, but her curiosity was too much for her. The two children held their hands behind their backs and looked scornfully at each other, but Mrs. Ferwalter ordered severely: Go and play nicely! and Rebecca obediently took the strange child over to the swings. Mrs. Ferwalter started to praise Marie: Your child is so quiet. She doesn't race around. Doesn't scream at her mother. She's not American, she's European. It's a good way to raise children, the European way, she had said, in her broken English, her broken German, following both children with her always narrowed, almost squinting eyes, her thin lips pursed in disgust.

Mrs. Ferwalter is from a Ruthenian village in eastern Slovakia, "where the Jews lived a comfortable life." She emphasizes that it was a "good" village. The Christians tolerated those of a different faith, and the fifteen-year-old girl was not harassed even at night by the teenage boys on the Christian side. We can't ask her about her parents. "I wasn't pretty. They said I looked striking." "My hair hung down to my waist." In 1944, she was handed over to the Germans, probably by the Hungarians (we can't ask her about that). The Germans took her to Mauthausen concentration camp. "One of the wardens, she was so nice, she had five children and had to, everything, yes." She means a female SS guard. We can't ask her about that. In a photograph from 1946 she has the face of a smooth-skinned thirty-five-year-old. She tried to stay in Czechoslovakia and in 1947 she married a leatherworker with a small leather-goods shop in Budweis. The Communist putsch made the country where she had grown up unsafe, and in 1958 she arrived in the United States via Turkey, Israel, and Canada. The doctors say that the fat in her shoulders, her neck, her whole body is a manifestation of concentration camp syndrome, whose symptoms also include her anxiety, her insomnia, and a chronic inflammation of the respiratory tract, which she has only one way of dealing with: sucking mucus down into her throat with a harsh, scratching sound. All of these facts are things we didn't ask her about. She has mentioned them casually and in passing over the course of six years, the way friends bring up pieces of their lives.

Mrs. Ferwalter was the first of the European émigrés on Riverside Drive to give Gesine advice about the neighborhood. She recommended a kindergarten for Marie, showed her the stores selling imported food, warned her away from the ones run by "bad Jews," and always pointed out everything "European" on Manhattan's Upper West Side. She is homesick for the taste of the bread in Budweis. Maybe she has clung to Gesine for these six years, with phone calls and walks and conversations in Riverside Park, because this German knows what the bread she misses tastes like.

On Saturday mornings she waits in the park for her husband and son who have gone to synagogue. She herself takes certain liberties with her God, but she makes sure that Rebecca does not break the Sabbath and, for instance, start running around with other children or get too close to the ice-cream man. When she shouts for her daughter, her voice can be heard across the whole playground, a shrill shriek, and Rebecca sulks and trudges around the bench from which Mrs. Ferwalter reigns. When Mrs. Ferwalter thinks no one is watching, though, she leans over to Gesine and says, with a wink in Rebecca's direction and a conspiratorial smile: Look at her strolling around, that child. She's got long legs, that child.

She lets Gesine read to her from the newspaper; she would never spend money on a paper herself. Rebecca's school is expensive, and her husband doesn't make much as the manager of a little shoe store on Broadway. She arranges her legs this way and that, crosses and uncrosses her ankles, fidgets on the bench. She cannot sit still. She nods with her fat chin—disgusted, sickened—at the news that the Soviets have expelled two US diplomats because the United States had previously expelled two Soviet diplomats. She nods, as though she knows all about espionage.

The latest news about the Mafia. Apparently all five Mafia families in the New York area have gotten out of the drug-dealing business for good. They now prefer to use their cash reserves to seize power in legitimate undertakings. The prison sentences for some members of the families, up to forty years, were deterrent enough. For another thing, the Corsican and French heroin suppliers were mad that the Mafia refused to pay for a shipment worth $2.8 million ($100 million retail) on the grounds that they did not receive the delivery, the FBI did. Heroin trafficking now seems to run via Cuban and South American middlemen. The French like to pack the stuff in oscilloscopes.

Mrs. Ferwalter has stood up and walked over to the playground entrance, where, between her husband and her son, each formally dressed in black suit and stubby black fur hat, Marie wheels up the grocery cart with the provisions for next week, intent, lips pursed tight with responsibility, and Mrs. Ferwalter leads her into the playground, one arm affectionately around her shoulder, and deposits her in front of Gesine, and cries: She's a sport! Just like a real Czech!

And her mouth is relaxed now, her eyes wide open.

September 3, 1967 Sunday

On a day like this, thirty-six years ago. On a white day like this, cool under a hard blue, in clean, briskly moving air. On the beach promenade in Rande, by the gray-and-green sea, across from the sharp, dark contour of the Holstein coast. Keeping on the sunny side under the flickering leaves. Cresspahl's voice must have been a deep bass then, vowels starting way back in the throat in the Malchow version of Plattdeutsch; my mother's voice small, supple, a high alto. Sometimes a turn of phrase in High German creeps into her speech: "God willing" or "for my mother's sake." She has lagged behind her parents, and Louise Papenbrock keeps turning her head to look back at the stranger who is asking her daughter something, maybe what time it is.

But what'll happen then?
Shouldn't we wait and see?
But they're planning something.
That's what I'm waiting to find out.

Page 1. From *The New York Times* Special Correspondent in Bonn. Ilse Koch, "the Beast of Buchenwald," was found dead in her prison cell yesterday. Her neck hung in a noose made from bedsheets and tied to the door latch. She was sixty.

My name is Cresspahl. I'm forty-three years old. My father was a wheelwright on the Bobzin estate near Malchow am See and is now dead. My mother has an annuity in Malchow. I am a master carpenter.
A cabinetmaker.
I can make wagon wheels too.
I'm twenty-five and supposed to marry someone in Lübeck.

Ilse Koch, a plump woman with vivid green eyes and flaming red hair (according to the description in *The New York Times*), was born in Dresden and in 1937 married a friend of Hitler's, the commander of the Buchenwald concentration camp, in a spectacular nighttime outdoor pagan ceremony. The Kochs then lived in a mansion not far from the camp.

"Would you care to be my wife?"
Yes, I learned my English at boarding school. Rostock accent.

51,572 political enemies, Jews, and forced laborers from all over Europe died in Buchenwald. On morning rides through the camp, Ilse Koch beat prisoners she came across with her riding crop. She ordered others beaten and killed, and forced prisoners to participate in orgies involving sadism and perversity. She ordered the killing of tattooed prisoners and made lampshades, gloves, and book covers from their skin and their bones.

Will we change our names when we become British citizens?
If you want.
I want to keep your name.

During the trial of Ilse Koch in 1947, a Dr. Konrad Morgen—investigator, prosecutor, judge for the SS—was called as a witness. He had investigated the Koch case in 1943, on orders from the SS authorities. According to his findings, she was an incurable moral degenerate, a perverted, nymphomaniacal, hysterical, power-mad she-devil. Her handicrafts disappeared after this investigation. Karl Koch was later shot by the Nazis.

My older brother didn't do too well. He's in South America. My sister is in Krakow, married
  to a lawyer, who embezzles money.
And Horst doesn't have much going for him. So now I'm the favorite, unfortunately, and I'm supposed to move up to the city. You have to say you make four thousand marks a year.
  I can say six.
And that Hitler's an Austrian.

Say that to Horst?
To my father.
If you want me to.

During her detention, Ilse Koch became pregnant, and the Allies sentenced her merely to life imprisonment. Later her sentence was reduced to four years (in the opinion of one witness: because she had helped the Allies gather incriminating evidence for the Nuremberg trials). The West Germans arrested her in 1949 when she was released from Landsberg and sentenced her to life imprisonment in a new trial.

Do you sleep with a pillow? Do you believe in God? Is Richmond far from the sea?

In October 1966, the Bavarian government rejected Ilse Koch's application for a pension. In 1962 she had even appealed to the European Commission of Human Rights.

Do you want children, Heinrich Cresspahl?

September 4, 1967 Monday, Labor Day
We're supposed to believe that? That more than three hundred Czechoslovak intellectuals around the world have appealed to Western writers to join a protest against their own censors? To John Steinbeck, of all people? We don't want to believe it. Steinbeck paid a visit to Vietnam to see the war, and nothing there bothered him. Still, *The New York Times* seems to believe the news. *The New York Times* prints it on the front page.

The Vietcong marked election day in South Vietnam by staging a series of terrorist attacks and shellings against voters in twenty-one provinces. At least twenty-six civilians are dead. The Americans bombed near Hanoi.

The New York Times would like to draw our attention to the weather. It offers as evidence a photograph showing the corner of Eighty-Ninth Street and Riverside Drive: thick lumpy treetops surrounding a monument bathed in light, hardly any pedestrians, cars parked. Nearer, Arcadia, to thee.

The city is completely quiet. The ear misses the sounds of car engines, helicopters, sirens. The light is white, like yesterday. The wind from the Great Lakes has pushed all the dirty clouds from above the city out to the Atlantic, the chimneys have been idle for two days, and the air is brisk, clear, and cool. It is the first weekend this summer that it hasn't rained. From Riverside Drive, seen across the whole width of the Hudson, the brownish boxes and cylinders on the New Jersey side are sharp and unde-niable: modern architecture, the view set aside for Riverside Drive in the 1880s destroyed.

The buildings on this street, hardly any of them under ten stories tall, were built for the new aristocracy of the nineteenth century, for the new money—railroad money, mining money, natural gas money, oil money, speculation money, all the money of the industrial explosion. Riverside Drive was meant to surpass Fifth Avenue as a residential area, with its magnificent entryways, formal lobbies, eight-room suites, servant's quarters, hidden service entrances, liveried employees, and private views of the river, of the forest of wild clouds atop the other shore's cliffs, of nature. There is not a single store or business along all of Riverside Drive, and only two or three hotels, even these residential hotels for long-term guests. The dwell-ing places of Business were meant to be Noble. Figures such as William Randolph Hearst lived here, in fact on three floors that he later converted to a three-story atrium with his own private elevator, then on still more floors, until by 1913 he had bought all twelve. In that era, an address on Riverside Drive meant wealth and credit, power and princely status. It was a street for whites, Anglo-Saxons, Protestants. After the First World War, they were joined by the Jews from Harlem who felt that their formerly exclusive neighborhood no longer befitted their station, as well as by im-migrants from the Lower East Side whose income now made such a pres-tigious address affordable—émigrés who had made it. In the thirties, the Jews from Germany came, first with their household belongings in crates, then without any luggage, then from the German-occupied countries of Europe, and after the war came the survivors of the camps, and finally the citizens of the State of Israel, inveterate Europeans who had not been able to cope with Israel's climate and besiegement. As a result, a Jewish colony had formed on Riverside Drive and West End Avenue just behind it, joined by religion, blood ties, and memories of Europe.

The Belgians called me Madame, *and the Americans say* Darling. *In Europe children bow to grown-ups. My family was in Germany for five hundred years. My father used to come home with long baguettes under his arm. My father—*
   Your father was killed by the Germans, Mrs. Blumenroth.
   My father died young, Mrs. Cresspahl.

Riverside Drive did not overtake Fifth Avenue as a residential address; President Kennedy's widow does not live here. Retirees live here, middle-income people, office workers, students with roommates. Countess Seydlitz lives here. Ellison, the writer, lives here. (The assistant at Schustek the butcher's refuses to move here; he believes in having his own lawn in front of his own house.) Most of the buildings still consider themselves too genteel to rent to dark-skinned citizens: Negroes are permitted to super-intend them, keep them clean, operate the elevators, polish the brass. And old age lurks in these monuments of prosperity, like a neglected disease. Many of the elegant suites have been divided up into stingy little apart-ments; neighbors complain about leaky pipes, rattling plumbing, repeated malfunctions in the elevators, and a sheen of grime against which broom and water are powerless on the marble paneling and antiquated furniture in the lobbies. In some buildings the rents have been frozen by law since the war. Doormen, not only to greet the tenants but also to scare away burglars and child-snatchers, are a rare sight nowadays; often, the manned elevators have been replaced with automatic ones, in which the passengers eye strangers warily. Apartments here are still much sought after and change hands privately. There are high ceilings, old-fashioned floor plans; the walls do a good job muffling sound; the management takes care of the garbage and repairs. The street is considered practically safe. (On the park benches, there is a lot of talk these days about the homosexuals cruising one another at the Soldiers' and Sailors' Monument, which they call the Wedding Cake.) And the street is one of the quiet ones. At most it sees two parades a year. Long grass grows in the cracks between the squares of the sidewalk. For half the year, the sound of cars from the highway along the Hudson is filtered through leaves in the park, and except during rush hour Riverside Drive carries only local traffic, it is empty and noiseless at night until six in the morning, when the first people will drive to work and the hollow whistles of the railroad under the hills of the park will force their way into our shallow sleep, tomorrow. This is where we live.

September 5, 1967 Tuesday

At six thirty yesterday evening, four policemen came upon four or five Negro youths assaulting an old white man in one of the ghettos of Brooklyn. They managed to arrest one youth and shot another in the back of the head. A crowd quickly gathered, hurling bottles and rocks at the police and shouting: Kill 'em! Teenagers looted one liquor store; other shopwindows were smashed. The police lifted their barricades in the area around ten p.m., but shortly after eleven, fifteen Molotov cocktails exploded in the street. By that time, the shot young man had been dead for two hours. Richard Ross, fourteen years old.

The Soviet Union is believed to have provided $500 million in weapons to developing countries since 1955.

Sometimes the elevator in the bank building falls a short way down as it starts up, as though genuflecting. Almost twenty people in the ascending cabin listen to two girls complain, insistently but not angrily, about the store on the corner. They haven't raised the price of their coffee, true, but they're selling it in smaller cups. Gesine meets the amused looks of the people next to her, who start exchanging nods. The little movements of their necks make them look like people just waking up. All the buttons on the panel next to the door are filled with yellow light: the elevator is going to stop on every floor. Yes, it's a local today, she agrees, smiling, not paying attention. In the lit rectangles over the doors, the name of the firm appears twelve times over, the same three words twelve times with the same symbol—five red lines—but without indicating the department, except for the third floor: Reception. On the third floor, visitors are screened and the regular customers' account records are kept. On the fourth floor, the two girls with their bags of coffee get out, and some of the passengers smile once more, as though a probable event had in fact happened. Fourth floor is data entry. Her first job in this country had been in data entry, at a three-foot-wide desk, third from the left in a row of twelve, in front of a calculating machine whose clattering reached her ear strangely detached from the fog of noise in the large room. On the fifth floor are the stockroom and central mail room. She never goes to the fifth floor anymore, now that Mrs. Williams takes care of keeping her supplied with paper, pencils, and typewriter ribbons. At first she'd resisted being waited on like that; then she realized Mrs. Williams liked these short walks away from her desk, spread throughout the day. The sixth floor, called East and West after the coasts, was where she'd started at this bank, at a metal desk in an open office, visible from all four sides, with her typewriter and a department head's extension telephone. On the seventh floor are the cafeteria and conference rooms. This cafeteria still uses the larger coffee cups, and a good number of people get out of the elevator here. On the eighth floor are the technology and human resources departments; on the ninth, the bank's memory; on the tenth, the legal department and library. Coming from the frosted-glass sky of the elevator, within which a loose tube gives off little flickers of darkness as in a rainstorm, is muffled muzak that blends in with the clatter of the doors shearing open and the ding of the journey's signals. On the eleventh floor, Gesine gets out and turns west. The elevator shafts and utility pipes divide the building in half, and on this floor the eastern half is the South America department, the western half is part of Western Europe. She calls it the eleventh floor, even to herself, counting the way the Americans do, not the tenth as it would be called in Germany. The door closes behind her with a heavy smack.

Good morning Gee-sign.
Good morning.

September 6, 1967 Wednesday

Since yesterday morning, 54 Americans marines and 160 North Vietnamese troops have been killed in continued fighting in the Queson Valley, 136 North Vietnamese near Tamky, 3 Americans by Nuibaden Mountain, 16 Vietnamese at Cantho, 5 Americans and 37 Vietnamese near Conthien, 34 Vietnamese in Quangngai Province.

Again last night Negroes pelted policemen and firefighters with stones, bottles, and Molotov cocktails in the Brownsville section of Brooklyn. Garbage fires in trash cans and on the street filled the air with smoke. Mayor Lindsay met with spokesmen from the ghetto at the station house. *The New York Times* mentions that he was wearing a blue suit and blue knit sport shirt.

In the early hours of yesterday morning, a man rushed into the Bluebird Tavern in the Bronx, fired eight rifle shots, and left without saying a word. One dead, two wounded.

In 1920, during the Kapp Putsch, Baron Stephan le Fort, retired cavalry captain, owner of the Boek estate (6,479 acres), shelled the town of Waren on Lake Müritz with a cannon because workers had taken over. The scars in Town Hall are still visible today. When the farmworkers in the area heard about the five dead in Waren, they set out with hunting guns and scythes to search the nearby estates for the rifles, machine guns, and ammunition that the Güstrow armed forces had sent to the owners. The estate holder in Vietsen, Papenbrock, whose household included five men who'd fought in the Baltic—officially as tutors, apprentices, a secretary—sent them out through the back when the gardener came running up to report the enemy's approach. Papenbrock, then fifty-two years old, took up a post on the outside staircase, shoulders thrown back, belly hanging over his belt, in English breeches and boots, and he said: Gentlemen, I give you my word as an officer. There are no weapons here. (If you want to look anyway, please be quiet in the children's room and let the girls sleep.)

My mother, a girl of fourteen, stood on the floorboards in her ankle-length white nightgown winding her hair around her wrist and looking back and forth between Papenbrock, her sister Hilde, and the laborers questioning her in Platt. The expression on Papenbrock's face alternated between threatening and affectionate. Finally, taking a deep breath, and with downcast eyes, she said: Through the door. In the children's room there was a door hidden behind the oak wardrobe that weighed hundreds of pounds with all the linens inside, and through that door were nine infantry rifles and two hundred and ten bullets in ammo belts. My mother was put on bread and water for two weeks. Papenbrock spoke of betrayal by his own flesh and blood. His wife spoke of the Christian's love of truth. Papenbrock's hand flashed out to her cheek and he didn't go to church all that summer. There was talk on the surrounding estates about Papenbrock's honor as an officer. In 1922, Papenbrock gave up the estate.

In Vietsen we girls each had our own chambermaid.

Then there were the maids for the ironing room, the kitchen, the laundry, there were the housekeepers, and the mamsell.

Louise Papenbrock had a private chaplain for a while.

Once, Hilde asked someone to fetch her stockings from the wardrobe, because the four steps down the hall were too far for her, and Papenbrock yelled at her. She had to give the maid half a mark.

When Papenbrock wanted to go somewhere, he would phone the village stationmaster and have him stop the train he wanted in the middle of the field near the estate. The man would say: Yes, sir. For two Christmas chickens.

And when Papenbrock came back, he would pull the emergency brake near the estate, pay the two hundred mark fine, and climb into the carriage that Fritz had driven up the country lane to meet the train.

Fritz came with us to Jerichow. He died there.

When Robert was seventeen, Hilde always had to wake him up two hours before school started, so that Louise Papenbrock wouldn't find the maid in his bed.

Her name was Gerda. She was my age. She married someone in the village when she got pregnant.

And Papenbrock paid for the trousseau.

And yet again Louise Papenbrock could not understand what her husband was doing.

Robert rode a horse to death once in a race against a car.

When Robert wanted to try to ride to Teterow in an hour, I took the horse by the halter and led it to the stable. He stood next to me and kept saying, softly because of the stable boys: Gimme th'horse. It was dark in the stable, it was cloudy that evening, just before a storm, and I didn't see him take his revolver out of his pocket. He said: Gimme th'horse or I'll shoot.

Go ahead.

I ducked, as a joke, and all I lost was a hair.

And the horse reared up. It was ruined for riding.

Don't tell Mama, he said.

Mama never found out anything.

Your uncle Robert would show up drunk at school, run up debts in res-
taurants, shoot at sparrows in the middle of town and hit windows. When
he got a teacher's daughter pregnant, he had to be sent off to Parchim. In
Parchim

he took a room at the Count Moltke Hotel.

And strolled around town with a little silver-handled cane.

He was sitting in the Golden Grapes on Long Street with his roast duck
and red wine and he saw out the window the principal passing by with his
wife and he invited the shocked couple in for roast duck and red wine, and
that was the end of him in Parchim.

After Parchim I don't know.

From Parchim he went to Hamburg.

With three marks in silver, from Parchim to Hamburg?

First Robert got cash for two horses he'd borrowed then he drank the leg
off the devil.

In Vietsen, they said he was learning the import-export business in Rio de
Janeiro.

In Vietsen they used to say: Open the door, the grain Jews are coming.

In Vietsen your great-grandmother was still alive. She was the one who
always killed the geese.

Henrietta was her name. She was from a noble family. She used words
like: perron, dependency. Or: lavoir-basin.

During the search of the house, one of the laborers said to me: Put something
on your feet, kid.

Papenbrock gave up Vietsen because the nobility cut him dead after March
1920.

Papenbrock's lease in Vietsen was not renewed because he hadn't drained
the land as the contract required.

Because everyone was laughing about his children's room.

Because he hadn't drained the land.

We don't know, Gesine.

Why do you want to know, Gesine.

Because of Cresspahl. Why did Cresspahl want anything to do with a
family like that?

September 7, 1967 Thursday

The newspaper vendor on the southwest corner of Broadway and Ninety-Sixth Street prefers his customer to put her ten cents in his hand and not, as one would if his crooked fingers worked like uninjured ones, next to the pile of papers. On the steps leading underground, whose metal treads are more worn down on the left, you have to take short steps. It is expedient to have the subway token between your thumb and index finger five steps before the turnstiles. After you take the tunnel under the local track to the southbound platform, the first door of the last car stops one and a half paces from the stair rail. The train has passed through Harlem; the seats are packed tight with sleeping dark-skinned passengers. *The New York Times* has to be folded in the seconds remaining before the jolt of departure, before the passenger steadies himself against the lurches of the train with the strap hanging above every seat. The administration sees its forecast of a strong economic expansion confirmed; the administration reports convincing indications of rising inflationary tendencies. In the mornings, the passageways and stairs under Times Square are divided with chains and by transit policemen into lanes for the streams of pedestrians moving among the four subway lines; of the three tracks for the shuttle to Grand Central Terminal, the middle one is considered best. At this time of day, physical contact with other passengers is almost impossible to avoid. The autoworkers in Detroit are on strike against Ford. Years ago, in the large main hall of Grand Central Terminal, under the blue and gold starry sky of the barrel-vault ceiling, an express train to Chicago was being announced; never again has she hit that precise moment. Groggy commuters thread their way out from underground, heading east toward Lexington Avenue, not yet up for the battle for taxis. In the meantime, of the seven hundred faces she has seen this morning, almost all have been forgotten. Now the smiling starts.

She has learned to do it. Only rarely is she still startled by the smile that every morning instantaneously shows up on, slips aside from, and crashes down off the face of the girl at the department reception desk. She feels she is too slow for the elaborate, unvarying exchange: the hello, the inquiry into how it's going, the answer, the counterquestion, the counteranswer, the goodbye. She has trouble making it to the end of the script within the four strides of a hallway encounter. She hasn't learned that. Still, she feels that her smile covers her and she ramps it up to the point of downright merriment.

She's our German. Germans are different though.

The department consists of an inner core of frosted-glass cubicles, an open room with groups of desks, and an outer fringe of offices with outside windows. After the metal door that clicks shut behind her, she passes the reception desk, four desks on the left, three inner offices on the right. She walks past Mrs. Agnolo's typewriter feigning distraction and a conversation with the person at the next desk; Mrs. Agnolo has a son in Vietnam. Yesterday 36 Americans and 142 Vietnamese were killed south of Danang. She dreads the morning when the death notice will be brought to the office; the boy still has four months left to serve. Most of the inner offices are already lit up fluorescent white, the chairs in the open room are all occupied, but the girls are still taking out their work, digging around in their handbags, showing each other newspaper ads. In Brownsville, Brooklyn, the Negroes threw bottles and rocks at policemen. Looting, arson—the other side of the East River. In Central Park, a fifteen-year-old girl was raped by two men who stomped her friend so severely that he might die. In two minutes, a net of keyboard noise will hang in the air, suddenly, as though someone had thrown a switch. A removable brown plastic nameplate has been slid into the little rails next to her workspace, imprinted with the name "Miss Cresspahl" in white letters. The cell measures three and a half by three meters, or twelve by ten feet here, with wall-to-wall carpeting, a steel filing cabinet, a desk, the typewriter stand, a dictation machine, telephone, swivel chair, double-decker filing tray, and chair for visitors. The coffee cart comes by at eleven, lunch is at twelve, the secretarial staff can leave at five, the telephone switchboard shuts down at six, the elevators stop working at eight. As Employee Cresspahl, eleventh floor, takes her mail from the in-box on Mrs. Williams's desk, she looks through her open door at the slats of the blinds on the opposite building bordered by frosted blue glass, the mirror in which this day will sink down into darkness, leaving no trace.

September 8, 1967 Friday

The secretary of defense explains the wall he plans to build along the northern border of South Vietnam. He speaks of barbed wire, land mines, and sophisticated electronics; he says absolutely nothing.

In the four days of fighting around Danang, 114 Marine infantry were killed and 283 wounded. The casualties on the other side were put at 376, but for them *The New York Times* does not tally the wounded separately.

Always ready to be of service, the paper describes future curtailments among Ford's suppliers: at stake is some $5 billion a year in parts and materials that won't be able to be produced. Picketers are not harassed. Thirty years ago, at the River Rouge plant in Dearborn, Michigan, there were riots, beatings, and shootings. Thirty years ago, a child of Cresspahl's fell into the water butt behind his house.

You have a mind like a man's, Mrs. Cresspahl!: says James Shuldiner, preoccupied. It is broad daylight in a Scandinavian sandwich shop on Second Avenue, at a tiny side table, elbow to elbow with eavesdroppers, and Mr. Shuldiner has never once asked Mrs. Cresspahl out to dinner, to one of the velvet-dark restaurants in the East Fifties, to a tablecloth, to checks discreetly delivered in leather covers, to intimacies. James Shuldiner is a thin gentleman with moist eyes, brooding, with clumsy movements, stiff, and under his shock of dark hair, still like the high-school student he was eleven years ago, a boy from Union City whom neither gang wanted, beaten up by both, who went straight from his last vacation into the army—Mr. Shuldiner, a careworn tax professional who might well take pride in a masculine mind. He has not put his hand on the lady's, he looks not at her but at his egg salad; he has discovered something new to worry about. Still, he waits.

– Thank you, kind sir: she says.

Mrs. Cresspahl is not particularly proud of her mind. Mr. Shuldiner is amazed at her reference to the Cash and Carry law of 1937, which allowed the United States to supply weapons to nations at war; Mr. Shuldiner does not insist on calling her by her first name, and he talks to her not about his own concerns but those of international politics. She had searched her memory for the year 1937 and once again retrieved nothing but a static, disconnected fragment. This is how her mind's storage system arbitrarily selects things for her, stored up in quantities beyond her control, only sometimes responsive to commands and intentions:

In 1937, Stalin had much of his military staff executed,

in 1937, Hitler had fully worked out his war plans,

we have to buy at least one record by Pete Seeger because the TV networks have put him on the blacklist for an antimilitary song,

(Marie says),

today's issue of *The New York Times* is the 40,039th,

an advertising poster in the Ninety-Sixth Street/Broadway subway station has had handwritten on it since the day before yesterday: Fuck the Jews:

this mind has helped her get through school exams, tests, interrogations, it gets her through her daily work, a man sees it as an ornamental trinket; what mattered most to her was one of its functions—memory, not the storage but the retrieval, the return to the past, the repetition of what was: being inside it once more, setting foot there again. There is no such thing.

If only the mind could contain the past in the same receptacles we use for categorizing present reality! But the brain, in recalling the past, does not use the same many-layered grid of terrestrial time and causality and chronology and logic that it uses for thinking. (The concepts of thinking do not even apply there. And this is what we're supposed to live our life with!) The repository of the mind is not organized to provide copies, in fact it resists retrieving things that have happened. When triggered, even by mere partial congruence, or at random, out of the blue, it spontaneously volunteers facts and figures, foreign words, isolated gestures. Give it an odor that combines tar, rot, and a sea breeze, the sidelong smell from Gustafsson's famous fish salad, and ask it to fill with content the emptiness that was once reality, action, the feeling of being alive—it will refuse to comply. The blockade lets scraps, splinters, shards, and shavings get through, merely so that they can be scattered senselessly across the emptied-out, spaceless image, obliterating all traces of the scene we were in search of, leaving us blind with our eyes open. The piece of the past that is ours, because we were there, remains concealed in a mystery, sealed shut against Ali Baba's magic words, hostile, inapproachable, mute and alluring like a huge gray cat behind a windowpane seen from far below as though with a child's eyes.

It can sit wherever it wants.

Mr. Shuldiner interrupted his analysis of the latest violations of international law when Mrs. Cresspahl picked up her purse, her hand clutching the flabby black fabric like the nape of a cat's neck, put it on her other wrist, and said something out loud in a dialect of German. Unoffended, leaning forward as an attentive listener, he asked her to explain:

That's what my father said once, when a cat sitting under the table scared me. It had laid down on the leather of his clogs to go to sleep. That must have been in 1937, too. The day I fell into the water butt.

And your mother? Your mother just stood there? Mr. Shuldiner said eagerly.

Lisbeth I'll kill you.

My mother was not just standing there. I'm sorry. My mind was elsewhere, Mr. Shuldiner.

James Shuldiner dutifully accompanies Mrs. Cresspahl down Second Avenue, into one store after another, and watches with embarrassment as she tries to buy one apple. The gourmet markets sell apples in packages, or by the pound, not individually. After Mrs. Cresspahl has managed to steal an apple from a supermarket, he tries to say goodbye. He watches her bite into the apple and says: That's a pretty dress, Mrs. Cresspahl. He won't say why he asked her out this time either. He walks uphill up the street, a haggard, somewhat bent man, black and white in his business suit. Maybe he is shaking his head.

Say I saw a cat lying inside the kitchen window, and I climbed up on an upside-down bucket and from there up onto the water butt. Say the lid wasn't there, and my mother was nearby. Say Cresspahl pulled me out, and she was watching. What am I supposed to do about it!

September 9, 1967 Saturday

This morning, justice almost reigns in New York. The air is still. The air cannot move under stationary warm fronts in the upper atmosphere; since yesterday it has not been able to rise into the cold and rid itself of what the city pumps into it from power stations, gasworks, chimneys, cars, jet engines, and steamships: the inversion has set an impenetrable dome over the city. The dirt in the air—soot, boiler ash, hydrocarbon emissions, carbon monoxide, sulfur dioxide, nitrogen oxide—passes without regard of person through window cracks, into eyes, into wrinkles on skin; it scratches throats, dries mucous membranes, weighs on hearts, blackens tea, spices food, creates more work for lung doctors, shoe shiners, car washers, window cleaners, and Mr. Fang Liu in his basement shop near Broadway, who is now taking the Cresspahls' laundry from Marie with swift, enthusiastic gestures. Few in the city can hide behind sealed double-glass windows and high-powered air conditioners, and they, imprisoned in their bare, musty towers on the East Side, miss out on the bright clouds in lurid colors that the moisture in the air paints in as a backdrop to Riverside Park, on the dull-colored tatters of haze draping the Hudson. In all the stores on Broadway where Marie is currently pushing her grocery cart around, the mere word *pollution* is enough to get a conversation going and call forth the New Yorker's pride in the incomparably difficult life of a New Yorker. She can swap sighs and trade smiles of mutual sympathy when she brushes her hair back from her sweaty brow with her forearm. Outside on the muggy street she will feel like her face is hitting a wall of hot water.

For Marie goes shopping on Broadway, some Saturdays. Early in the morning she sneaks barefoot up to Gesine's bed, steals her alarm clock, and tiptoes to the front door, letting it click softly shut against the calibrated counterpressure of her springy fingertips. Although she has a sneaking suspicion that Gesine is deliberately keeping her breath regular, that she is awake and has long since been lying on her back, hands clasped behind her head, listening.

Because six years ago, the four-year-old clung tight to Gesine at the kindergarten's swinging doors, screamed with rage and beat against the doors of the elevator into which her mother had disappeared, often lay on the classroom floor during playtime, sad and unspeaking, deaf to persuasion, her face turned to the door. The teacher admonished Gesine over the phone. Three weeks later, she gave Gesine a list of the most important words that the child had refused to learn, which included *hand* and *foot*, *stand*, *hold*, *look*, and Gesine started buying West German newspapers, for the want ads. The child listened to the English Gesine spoke with politely resistant looks, never taking her eyes off her, and Gesine realized that what English meant for Marie was the outside world, the foreign, what at least at home she should be spared. She did not want to bribe the child to learn, though. She refused to let herself feel pity when she sent Marie up to the ice-cream truck at the park entrance by herself and had to watch her, clutching the quarter behind her back, take half a step back for every step forward, pushed aside by the other thronging children, unnoticed by the ice-cream man until he had already turned to drive on. Marie even refused to reveal the English she did know. When a supermarket cashier showed her a dollar bill and asked if she knew who that stout worthy gentleman in the middle was, and the customers behind her prompted her, loudly or in whispers, Marie just stood there, waiting, silent and sulking, to see if these people would finally give up and start speaking German. (Out on the street, she said, indignantly: George Washington! As if I didn't know that! Who were all those ladies anyway!) For her, it had been a test of her self-confidence. It was only on a trip up the Hudson, when she let two boys rope her into a game of tag on the stairs and down the corridors of the multistory, building-like steamship, that she tipped her hand, running down the aisle between the rows of seats, past Gesine without realizing it, and saying to her, as though to a stranger: *Excuse me!* Later she could be found with the dazzled boys on the steps leading up to the bridge, telling them stories about Düsseldorf and the Rhine in an effervescent mix of shards of German and the sonic curves into which she had translated the sentence melodies of the radio announcers. But the boys were on their way back to their riverless city in Ohio that same night, and Marie was shoved and teased in the playground for the blubber-lipped, droning sounds that she thought Americans used. The children had learned from TV movies how to cage a victim against a wall with stiff outstretched arms, and Gesine waded into the scuffle and pulled her child out because Marie wasn't defending herself.

But Marie, now wheeling the whole week's groceries out the elevator door as soon as the scissor gate clatters open, is talking at the top of her lungs to Mr. Robinson, and again Mr. Robinson holds the door and watches as the child pushes her way into the Cresspahl apartment and repeats her story about the bum who tried to rob her grocery cart on Broadway. *And*

I didn't worry about being a lady! At Schustek's, it was Mr. Schustek himself, not an assistant, who'd served her, and she'd tasted three different kinds of sausage before she bought any. Gesine spends a long time standing in supermarket aisles, she is taken in by new product packaging, she buys on impulse, or out of curiosity, or because she's hungry; the child marches straight through the traps and snares, blind to posters, deaf to announcements over the loudspeakers, looking slowly and steadily up and down the shelves, and she puts not an ounce, not a package in her cart except what's on her list. Today she caught the same cashier to whom she had once refused to give information about George Washington overcharging her by twenty-one cents, and the cashier apologized without argument to the child and the customers in earshot. The child tries to reproduce for Gesine the face that one of these customers in earshot made, who up until then had gone on and on about the shenanigans at the cash register and now was scandalized that a ten-year-old had caught the criminal red-handed: the child contorts her face, all the way up to her hairline, with the matron's sour disgust. Nor did Marie forget today's *New York Times*, a tidy bale, its vending-machine crease unmarred: the consciousness of the day. She puts the paper down next to Gesine's breakfast like a gift.

The secretary of defense will not rule out the possibility that Red China will enter the Vietnam War. However, he says that it would be a most ill-advised decision.

Only on page 48, between Business and Real Estate, does the circumspect organ of the press report that more than five hundred civilians in North Vietnam have been killed by American attacks during the first six months of 1967, by seventy-seven thousand tons of bombs in March alone.

– And the twenty-one cents: the child says, after a prolonged account of everything she'd bought, with the ragged, catarrhal voice that six years in the contaminated New York air has given her: I gave it to the beggars. Sixteen cents to the one with blue hair, five to the one on Ninety-Eighth Street.

September 10, 1967 Sunday
Agriculture needs tax relief! The Treasury simply must accept payments in kind! The collective-bargaining laws need changing! What the government

should do is crack down on price gouging from the middlemen! If only Berlin would at least curb imports!

So ran the lament of Papenbrock Senior. Only such measures might get the Mecklenburg nobility at least through 1931!

The old man did not raise his voice or even try to conceal his asthma in the pauses his cigar forced him to take; he leaned back in his upholstered armchair, limp, with eyes half closed, in the sharply slanting reddish rays of sunlight that made it impossible to see out of his office windows. He was only playing for time with his visitor, a man by the name of Cresspahl who had sent a note on the stationery of the Lübeck Court requesting a private conversation. Besides, this Cresspahl was acting genuinely interested in the cares and troubles of the East Elbian aristocracy.

– The landowner's tax burdens probably should be covered, yes: Cresspahl said earnestly, in the same formal Plattdeutsch as Papenbrock spoke, sitting properly upright on the visitors' sofa, keeping his gaze on Papenbrock's bald head shining in the evening light. No matter how hard he looked, the father of the bride could find nothing undeferential about him.

Papenbrock didn't know what to do with him. He was sturdy, not fat, not to be talked down. He could afford a room in the Lübeck Court for a week and counting. The telegram he had received from England mentioned various jobs, although Frieda Klütz, the Jerichow telegraphist, had been unable to give Papenbrock a precise translation of the business matters in question. Papenbrock's daughter had told him about £3,000 in an account in the Surrey Bank of Richmond, and Papenbrock had stifled his contemptuous snort because he had a certain respect for ready cash. The man hadn't tried to impress his prospective father-in-law with a bank account in Jerichow, having learned his lesson from the German banking collapse in July. He had served in the army, and Papenbrock's comrades-in-arms on the Russian front had made him an NCO. He was from Mecklenburg. But Papenbrock couldn't bring himself to accept him.

– Well if you, as a shrewd businessman, support the aristocracy's policy demands ... : Cresspahl said, encouragingly, leaning his shoulders slightly forward as though eager to hear about Papenbrock's deals in the Mecklenburg-Schwerin ministries.

Papenbrock did not yet want Cresspahl to know who his friends were. This Cresspahl came from an area in the southeast where Papenbrock had once lost a lease on an estate. This Cresspahl might have been sitting behind a desk in the Waren town hall when Papenbrock had had to turn over his weapons to a worker's committee. This Cresspahl had, in the meantime, lived ten years abroad—in the Netherlands, in England, with the winners of the war—and even Capt. (Ret.) Papenbrock would have a hard time making such a son-in-law acceptable to the Steel Helmet paramilitary. This Cresspahl didn't even seem to realize that Papenbrock could have been his superior officer a few short years ago. However much his proper bourgeois frugality in Jerichow's stores might count in his favor, he did sometimes sit in the back room with Peter Wulff, after closing time, talking with people who came from Wismar on bicycles and not even the police knew where they would spend the night.

It was a couple weeks ago, in Itzehoe. The Nazis were having a meeting in Oesauer Berg, and when the Communists came after them, what do you think they had with them? Stanchions, pitchforks, bicycle chains, clubs wrapped in razor wire, two-by-fours with nails, billy clubs. Look it up in The Lübeck Gazette!

The one man killed was a Communist, you know.

I read that only the Nazis were shooting. So where would the Nazis have gotten their gunshot wounds from?

Hey, why don't you tell us about England.

Papenbrock would prefer not to befriend a man who went around not wearing a hat. Who let himself be seen on the patio of the Archduke Hotel in Rande with a Dr. Semig. Arthur Semig, Dr. Vet. Med., might have two diplomas hanging on his wall and might wear his war medals through the streets of town on the Kaiser's birthday, but Papenbrock thought that paying his bills on time, and by return mail, was more than enough. And yet there he was, sitting outside a Christian hotel under a sun umbrella, drinking cognac in front of other guests, rattling on to strangers about the state of the world.

My dear Herr Cresspahl, do you want to know something? Only one offer was placed on a preserve in Schönberg recently, and do you know how high it was? Eight hundred centner. No. My dear Cresspahl, if you want to know the truth I should have been an innkeeper, not a veterinarian. You've seen it yourself, the bars are filled to bursting, it's standing room only in the pubs by afternoon. Do you know what, a liter of milk brings in seven and a half cents. No. When a horse is colicky, the farmers wait and see, by God. The nobility hasn't picked up the phone for an average-size pig in a long time. And who has his whole herd vaccinated against erysipelas nowadays? But when they do call, they arrange a price with me in advance. It used to be I would have hung up on the spot. But in times like these, and as a Jew...

Really?

But my dear Cresspahl, can't you tell? They can see it, you know. Look at me, Cresspahl! Now you can tell, right?

And Papenbrock did not know what to do with this Cresspahl. Who said he was free to meet after dinner, who let Papenbrock smoke his cigar alone, who did not insist on the glass of Rotspon the occasion warranted, who refused to be insulted by anything. He had money, almost as much as the gentleman in Lübeck. He wouldn't go so far as to invite Dr. Semig to the wedding, most likely. And so Papenbrock slid out of his armchair, groped around in the room grown nearly black as night, bent down with all the weight of his sixty-three years, reached under his desk, put the open bottle on the table, poured, and said, unexpectedly switching to High German: "Herr Cresspahl..." He gestured for my speechless father to stand up, and began: Herr Cresspahl, it seems that we are going to be relatives. Tell me the first name they gave you, son.

Lisbeth Papenbrock had my grandfather well trained.

Gesine Cresspahl is spending this Sunday on Staten Island, in Tottenville and later on the Midland Beach boardwalk. The child had insisted on waiting out the rain there. The towers of Brooklyn are visible to the northeast, across the Atlantic bay, smudged gray by the weather but occasionally flashing white under breaks in the clouds. Beyond those coastal palaces, in the two-story slums, they're killing each other.

The outing made her miss *The New York Times*. She catches a glimpse of the remains of today's edition in a garbage can. A large photograph facing up shows, not entirely clearly, a plump dark-haired girl of about fourteen lying in the arms of a man in peasant clothing who is about to give her a kiss. The man has a mustache; the collar of his shirt is not American. He bears a certain resemblance to Stalin in his prime.

– And then? the child asks. Your mother was engaged, the way they do it in Europe?

Then she and Heinrich Cresspahl, master carpenter from Richmond, were engaged. Louise Papenbrock had quietly set the table in the dining room again and was busy polishing the glasses when the men came in from the office. Cloth in hand, she clutched at Cresspahl's, tried to look him in the eye, and said something about the need for God's benevolence, which Cresspahl thought was harmless enough. Papenbrock, blinking, had already turned to go down to the wine cellar. My mother again acted the part of Papenbrock's favorite daughter, circling the table, serving drinks, quiet, calm, satisfied. Louise Papenbrock cried at moments that seemed appropriate. Papenbrock alternated between cognac and Mosel and spoke of the beautiful children that his daughter and Cresspahl would bring into the world,

but any girls better not have those bones of yours, Heinrich Cresspahl, prost!

and of Heinz Zoll, Jerichow's master carpenter whom he would buy out. And my mother sat down next to him and looked pleadingly at Cresspahl, but Cresspahl nodded his head seriously, and she said, a little anxious but not entirely unmischievous: *We're not staying Daddy.* And Papenbrock clutched at his heart, where her hand already was, and grinned, a little embarrassed because he had shown his shock and was on the point of exaggerating it.

– And Horst Papenbrock? the child asks.

Horst Papenbrock wasn't there. My mother had made sure of that. He was spending the evening with his Nazi buddies in Gneez.

September 11, 1967 Monday
In yesterday's edition of *The New York Times*, Stalin's daughter described "The Death of My Father"; in today's, "Life With My Father and Mother." The world's best newspaper supplies photos of its own to enhance the

defector's memoirs—today a picture from 1935, in which Stalin is thumbing his nose at his chief bodyguard's camera.

And we've been loyal to this paper for six years! There was a time when we were at the mercy of a chained dog on an East German military base, trapped in an inner chicken-wire kraal within the outside fencing so that it could never befriend a civilian and thus it had no choice but to become a hypochondriac, introverted, and acutely irritable type that would stand outside its kennel barking like crazy even in the pouring rain, and while it was something besides zeal that made the dog's voice crack, that cracking voice was the voice of *Neues Deutschland*; there was a time when we relied on the democratic virtues of an old maid—the officiousness, the love of bickering, the hypocrisy, the abstract conscience, the self-righteousness of spinsters left untouched for so long that they prefer to deny the existence of carnal intercourse altogether and on principle: the establishment press in the confines of the West German military base. We knew we could never entirely fail to appreciate an honest old Auntie like *The New York Times*. And in 1961 we had the choice between her and the *Herald Tribune*! Between a conservative dark suit of hard work and devotion to duty and, on the other hand, the more appealing layout and snazzier photos of another elderly figure, but one with her white hair wrapped in a silk scarf, bows at her neck, fashionable colors at her hips, and ankle boots bought on Via Condotti. For us it was no choice at all. Also in 1961, not like a blind chicken finding a lost piece of grain but like a watchful magpie stealing silver, *The New York Times* could be counted on to see which way the wind was blowing and where the Wall was going up around West Berlin, and to describe both of these things to us in firsthand quotations, second-order analyses, with glosses, photos, preliminary summaries, the lesser narrative forms, and when all the strands of the rhapsodic subject were tied up and the first level of the dividing wall built, she channeled all her means of description into an epic river and delivered, in the serial form of daily dispatches from the construction site, a story that for her was already history. How could we doubt her? Back then she only cost five cents, too. Not just paper printed on both sides but the justified expectation that this housewife would refuse to sweep any news under the rug, would see dirty laundry as suitable for airing, would feel that every closet could and should be opened and that one needn't fear finding a skeleton—all for five cents!

This trustworthy individual furnished us with reasons to live in New York! For the first time, we could add logical reasons to the other ones meant to justify our presence, and could honestly say that a newspaper here was putting the news from Germany into a proper relationship, namely a subordinate one, with the news from the rest of the world, and in so doing it helped us and taught us to accept reality with the expectations and judgments our parents had tried to inculcate.

It wasn't just a matter of convenience. We got used to her the way one does to a person with a fixed place at the table, not forced to accept crumbs or exiled among the old folks. We thought about her: Don't ever change. She felt that her country's well-being and prosperity was the most important thing in the world, and we could use that to factor out her biases; her country, in its egotism, often couldn't care less about her scruples and criticisms, and we felt reminded of the theory of tragedy of the classical century of German literature. We treated her obligingly and with consideration, strictly in accord with Brecht's recommendations: what matters most to us is always first and foremost her experience. We watched her advise the Greek king to improve his country with a putsch, and observed that it was not the king but his generals who could understand the words of the oracle of Times Square, but cunning is the least we can ascribe to old aunts. And is it not to her that we owe our prompt knowledge of the fact that the Western bloc was making a place at the table for Fascists in Greece too? She stayed true to her principles and immediately expressed revulsion at the torture of politically suspect Greeks. And neither the newspaper's owners nor the monopolies and political parties are responsible for dictating this picture of the present,

they write what the subscribers expect; it's you who're naive, Gesine:

as Countess Seydlitz says. Mrs. Albert Seydlitz means: Gesine, in her mistrust of bourgeois traditions, unintentionally also casts aspersions on fundamentally necessary traditions that have merely been abused. We do not live by bread alone, we need hard facts too, child.

We feel a need for Auntie Times's company; we grant her the honor due to our elders. She sets our table with the latest developments; we pay the higher rate and admire her civilized gestures. We find it almost touching, the pains she takes to keep us aware of the most basic information—when she has news to report from Cobh and first mentions that Cobh is located in southeastern Ireland, near Cork, in County Cork, and was once famous as a port of call for transatlantic steamships. We respect her objectivity and let her call herself "a New York newspaper." A detail fanatic, yes, but a mystifier? No. We anxiously, though not without fondness, observe her efforts to at least admit the existence of changes in popular taste, for instance when she suddenly replaced her typeface with a larger one on July 3, 1966, or without warning one day, namely on February 21, 1967, started printing the date at the top of the page in Italics instead of roman; it looks good on her, and we trust her sense of proportion and propriety.

There is one thing, we fondly dream, that she will never do to us: abandon her severe eight-column front page, not for the most modern and far-fetched tailored creation from Madison Avenue; wipe from her brow the uncial Gothic—the adornment of age, the monument to the past, as practically indispensable as the art nouveau ornaments atop the glass-slippered feet of the buildings of Manhattan—for an Antiqua font, howsoever British. Said buildings cannot stand up to the wrecking balls of unadulterated profit motives; it is she who continues to link the centuries together. Meanwhile, conservatively enough, she is now asking ten cents for her services. We'd gladly pay thirty.

What does she care whether we—how shall we put it—approve of her? That must be why she can invite Stalin's daughter into the house, still at age forty-one an immature child, perceptually defective, who has understood nothing about the twentieth century beyond the personal circumstances of her own life. Like any overdependent child, this incurable daughter wants only to unburden her father of the heartless findings of the history books, make excuses for him with the good qualities he showed in his free time, when he was close to her—not close enough, though, to enlighten her for instance about the idea that politics and revolution were not sent down from the heavens of religion, where, nonetheless, she imagines her dearly departed to be.

But it is not merely with schadenfreude that Auntie Times gathers her family together for daily installments of the insights that twenty-five years of instruction in dialectical and historical materialism have produced in a privileged student thereof. It is not simply mockery when Auntie Times identifies Svetlana Stalina as a writer, or permits her to use her mother's name, especially since wide knowledge of the true state of affairs removes the risk of losing readership. It is not only a trick when the *Times* lets pass the infanta's claim that the destiny of the Soviet Union and of international Communism was, at the decisive moment, decided by a man named Lavrenty P. Beria, although an editorial box does mention that his time in office began only in 1938 (so for one thing the eleven million people killed by the Soviet land reforms of 1928 to 1932 would have to be chalked up to Mr. Trotsky, except that he was abroad just then, or else to His Honor Winston S. Churchill, with whom the father of the hapless girl had at least exchanged a few words on the subject ("the worst thing I ever had to do"), rather than with his poor child). It is not solely an occasion for pride when the *Times* deprives its own country of taxes and has the defector's fee forwarded directly to a Liechtensteinian institution. We may suspect the existence of all these motivations, but we can be sure of other, more positive, tender feelings. Because yesterday's edition prefaced its excerpts from the life of Stalin's daughter with a picture of the author in a serious pose, as though graven on a coin, with a black collar, not quite equal to Auntie Times as a witness of History but still somewhere in her vicinity, someone who was there at rabbit hunts and family parties, one of the children pampered by Joseph Vissarionovich Stalin. The author's historical relevance thus preemptively determined, the *Times* could open the second installment of this chat with a different photograph, in which the author appears with a softer hairdo, a cheerful smile, wearing a white collar. A likable picture. Bigger, too. Here *The New York Times* exudes benevolence, sympathy, protectiveness, a suitable attitude to take toward a younger niece, admittedly from the provinces and from more constrained circumstances but still a relative.

Today we salute Mr. William S. Greenawalt from Brooklyn. He wrote a letter to *The New York Times* a good two weeks ago, in which he asked: If the Sanitation Department can manage to keep its white trucks white, why can't the Transit Authority keep its red subway trains red?

And *The New York Times* has decided that this, too, should find its place among the items worthy of and/or suitable for publication: *fit to print.*

September 12, 1967 Tuesday

If: Svetlana Stalina proclaims to the world in a newspaper: If Lavrenty P. Beria had not had the inexplicable support of my father, he would not have been able to kill Stalin's old fellow fighters and half of his family.

The president of the Supreme Soviet has acknowledged, after twenty-three years, that the nation of the Crimean Tatars was exiled to Central Asia unjustly for collaboration with the German Army. Still, the half-million rehabilitated citizens will not be allowed to return to their homeland.

If...

Mrs. Cresspahl receives a request to keep this afternoon free for a drive to Kennedy Airport; a letter there will need translating. An hour before work ends, Mrs. Cresspahl is picked up by a man in livery, an older, heavy-set, dark-skinned man who, with the solemnity of a footman, introduces himself as Vice President de Rosny's chauffeur, refers to her as the latter's interpreter, and adds: My name is Arthur. There are white streaks in his short curly hair, and as he speaks he holds the cap of his uniform somewhere in the vicinity of his heart. Mrs. Cresspahl tries to shake hands with him but he has already stepped aside. Left hanging, she half-heartedly tells him her own first name, and he answers, gravely, indulgently: That's quite all right, Mrs. Cresspahl.

Mrs. Cresspahl has to walk behind him, as though behind a servant. His uniform, his measured stride, his unseeing expression, all put a stop to the end-of-day chitchat passing between the rows of typewriters in the open office; he does not give her time to say goodbye, he is already holding open the door to the main hall so that she can pass through it like something invisible, at least to him. As they wait for the elevator he insists on taking her briefcase. On the way down, alone with her, he remarks on the weather, his face upturned toward the indicator saying what floor they've reached; he ignores her answers and repeats: Very good, ma'am: until, in the basement, he can bow to her and to de Rosny's car, let go of the handle with which he has gently, firmly closed the car door, and place his cap back on his head. She feels sealed, shipped, and delivered like a package for someone.

The vice president's car, from the outside a fifteen-foot-long black battleship, encases a first-class private cabin, fully upholstered, with four seats, telephone, reading light, writing surface. The cabin is cut off from the outside world by dark tinted glass and a thick pane separating the driver's area, and also, apparently, by perfectly smooth suspension, since the interior betrays no sign of the jolt with which the car comes off the steep ramp onto Forty-Sixth Street, nor the spurts with which it descends Second Avenue into the broad trough that leads to the tiled tubes of the Midtown Tunnel. This is one of Mrs. Cresspahl's favorite routes, now that she has gotten used to the white light and cramped vaulted arches under the East River: It is the path to departure. A path out of the city, for the road steadily widens between the industrial buildings of Brooklyn, the spacious homes set back from the street, and finally the Long Island highways, until, near the cemeteries, the sky stretches nearly unobstructed across the horizon. The gravestones clustered in the fields re-create the rises and valleys of the original landscape, flicker low under dusty evergreens. The graveyards are cities, protected by walls, traversed by gracefully curving roads, densely built up with narrow gravestones like the old single-family houses in Manhattan before opening out again into green parklands where solitary mausoleums evoke the inequalities of earthly social relations. The road runs past LaGuardia Airport near the Sound, alongside piers and jetties and sails catching the wind, until finally the scabby scars of industrial exploitation and land speculation are entirely repressed by a luxurious landscape on both sides of the exits—mowed lawns, landscaped copses, right up to the cement corrals in the ring of passenger terminals where cars have been rounded up and wait in crowded rows, a glinting motionless herd. But this time the trip was ruined for Mrs. Cresspahl. She would have liked the man behind the wheel not to hold his fleshy neck quite so still, to lower the glass divider, to turn around just once and admit to having a last name. But at the International Arrivals hall, Arthur is quicker to the door than she is and says goodbye with a bow, every inch the rich man's chauffeur, doffing his cap once more, looking into her face for only a moment, expressionless, and repeating, in his respectful, throatily rumbling voice: Yes, ma'am. Of course, ma'am.

Don't like this country? Go find another one.

Inside the terminal there is a glassed-in passageway suspended above the baggage claim area, which allows a full view of the conveyor belts in the customs lanes, a quarter view of the array of baggage carrousels, and a one-eighth view of the exits from passport control so that travelers below can be spotted from above. The thick teak railing inside the passageway's glass is crowded with the propped elbows of people meeting passengers, those of an Italian family on Gesine's left and those of an Indian couple on her right, all gazing down in comfort at the crushed, confused, exhausted travelers and the contents of their open suitcases, in which customs officers are probing around with firm, shrewd fingers. Gesine is expecting a white man, around sixty, with a flabby, gray, indistinct face, a man in loose gray clothes, a banking executive who will nonetheless have to open and present his leather bags to customs. She remembers what her boss looks like from the interview three years ago, from nods in the elevator lanes, and most clearly from the passport photo in company brochures. It is only from that passport photo that she now recognizes the man coming into view on the far side from the customs inspection area, his unopened suitcases on a porter's luggage cart alongside him, being escorted through an automatic door by a uniformed official and seen off with a police salute. He is clearly not of French descent after all but one of the Irish. Mrs. Cresspahl meets him at the foot of the stairs, a sprightly gentleman in a very blue linen suit, a lean, stooped man with firm muscles supporting his jowls in pleats, a speaker of long and intricate sentences who seamlessly thanks Mrs. Cresspahl for coming, affably bosses the porter around, ushers Mrs. Cresspahl with old-fashioned chivalry through the automatic doors, tips the porter precisely 11 percent, and walks straight over to Arthur, showing not the least surprise, for Arthur who has been circling the airport ring road for fifty minutes in his black limo has now arrived to the minute, pulling up to the curb next to his boss's canvas suitcases. Arthur! this boss says, and Arthur, cap on his head, white teeth smiling beneath the dark brown furrows of his brow, says: So, Chief.

On the drive back, the divider behind Arthur's seat is down; he drives one-handed, the other arm resting on the back of the seat so he can turn around more easily. De Rosny is sitting on the appropriate diagonal in his line of sight and they're catching each other up on what's new in their lives.

Mr. de Rosny has not flown straight back from Hawaii, no no. He's had a stopover in California, had this suit made in Italy, spent two days enduring Parisian cuisine, and just managed to get a seat on an American airline, he's glad to be back in New York. How about you, Arthur?

Arthur has bought his wife a new washing machine. His second-youngest son has passed his med school exams—not aced them, but passed. Arthur spent the weekend in Connecticut, that backyard of his sure is nice. The wife is worried about the teacher's strike, the younger kids are missing school, although the teachers' demands, especially for smaller classes and higher pay...

– And how did you and she get along? the boss asks, tossing his head toward Mrs. Cresspahl. – She was fine: Arthur says, and Mrs. Cresspahl catches his eye in the rearview mirror for a moment. He doesn't wink at her, just gives a tiny, reassuring widening of the eyelids.

I might have known that the boss would put his arm around your shoulders, hold the door for you, let you choose where to sit. Gesine, or whatever your name is.

All right, Arthur. And, go to hell, Arthur.

September 13, 1967 Wednesday

The New York Times illustrates today's round of Svetlana Stalina's reminiscences with a photo from 1941, showing the girl a bit fat for a fifteen-year-old, in a white blouse with two intertwined S's, standing in front of the grille of an imposing ZIS limousine, the "family car." In 1942, the wayward daughter reports, a great many people in camps were shot...I have no idea why it happened...

And more news from the entertainment industry: On Sunday night, Frank Sinatra talked back to an employer of his and was knocked down, losing two teeth in the process...

Federal Judge Dudley B. Bonsal has ordered the transit authority to allow antiwar ad posters in the subway too: because of the Fourteenth Amendment.

Gesine's ten days on the Atlantic have now been buried under three weeks back in the city, and the codes of employee behavior have once again taken over. Again she sets her clocks and watch five minutes fast, so as not to be late to the office. She denies to herself the existence of these five extra minutes, when she goes to sleep, when she wakes up; only when the subway is late does she consciously draw on this reserve. She generalizes occasional subway lateness into a negative rule so as to completely safeguard her commute against delays, and she either mentally stores up any minutes fewer than five that have accrued from finishing breakfast early or else doesn't trust her watch. She tracks her stockpiled time using the announcements on the radio, while at the same time hiding behind mistrust of the speaker's nonchalance:

Well, folks, if you were trying to get out of the house by half past, you're now seven minutes late!

Aside from that, she tries to minimize her empirically derived thirty-five minutes from apartment to typewriter by transferring quickly and interpreting traffic lights in daredevil fashion, without, however, crediting herself with any time thereby gained. The accumulated surplus sometimes sends her forth from the Upper West Side as early as ten past eight, and often brings her under the insistent clock in Grand Central Terminal

This is the clock that wakes up America!

at eight thirty. Not infrequently, she has reached the public electric clock in the office, its spider-leg second hand slicing away at the dial, by a quarter to nine. With the fifteen minutes gained she could in theory unfold her newspaper, but she thinks it would be petty to start work precisely at nine zero zero and zero seconds, so she reaches into her in-box after all. This hamsterish timekeeping has no effect on the pace of her work, because tasks are given to her as they come in; there are half hours on duty when Mrs. Cresspahl reads encyclopedias, bent diligently over her desk, with the door open . . . Not until ten to five does she start to pay her hoarded minutes back into real time. It's easy to lose one or two of the actual temporal units in the process: she usually isn't standing at her apartment door until five forty. She considers this difference of a twelfth of an hour a real loss, whether or not Marie has been waiting for her.

The management has not introduced punch clocks, and the word *punctual* never comes up in their regular memoranda to the staff. Gesine is no more devoted to this particular company than she was to previous employers. Showing up two minutes late in the morning is not enough to give her a bad conscience. Others may interpret her early arrival as overeagerness, even brown-nosing. And yet she cannot forego this juggling with imaginary time. She has nothing else she can count on. She lets Mrs. Williams tease her about German punctuality; she lets D. E. blather on about traumatic punishments for tardiness in school. All she has is the check that comes through interoffice mail at the middle and end of each month, in a sealed envelope, $8,000 a year before taxes. That check is nothing compared to a union that could go on strike, like the workers against Ford, the railwaymen against the LIRR, the teachers against the city. She can be given two weeks' notice at any time, and she has only five months' salary in a savings account to pay for Marie's school until she finds another job. She refuses to pass up any extra guarantee she can find, not even that of optical presence, of being at her place of work on time.

And as for the intimate overtime in the Waldorf Astoria Towers . . . a hundred feet up above the night, above abandoned Lexington Avenue, a hundred feet al fresco above the drunken gentlemen, lost tourists, taxis regally circling in the stinking canal of the street . . . in the musty air of air conditioners, the air from grandmothers' dresser drawers full of curiosities and treasures . . . overtime for Vice President de Rosny, who was brought to his suite like a beloved visiting prince, provided by the hotel with a bar with fresh ice, a second TV set, an electric typewriter in a kind of wheeled cradle . . . overtime to translate a letter from Prague, written in Polish French, about nightclubs, Super 8 film, a girl named Maria-Sofia, government credit tied to the dollar . . . overtime with cocktails . . . overtime that included being driven home in a black chariot, through the reddish backlight of the West Forties, under the gushing arcs from open fire hydrants, up the West Side Highway, high above the gray steaming Hudson and the mist-shrouded other shore, on past the swept and raked Riverside Park, across the world . . . hours spent after closing time, above and beyond the ordinary requirements . . . ?
It was a night out. It was fun. It was an exception. It was overtime, unpaid.

September 14, 1967 Thursday

In an interview about the battles around Dongson yesterday, Lieut. Col. William Rockety mentions a North Vietnamese who pushed through to the American mortar positions and killed two Marine infantrymen before being killed. "One North Vietnamese": Lieut. Col. Rockety tells *The New York Times*: "was really courageous—or crazy."

The intensification of the Vietnam War has created more than one million jobs in the United States over the past two years, in virtually every branch of industry (except shipbuilding and new construction). This is almost one quarter of the total rise in employment opportunities.

How far from disgust was Cresspahl in August 1931, wasting day after day in Jerichow, a healthy man lazing about in the middle of harvest time, blind, trapped by his mental picture of Papenbrock's youngest daughter, as though she were the one thing he needed in life?

The repetition must have disgusted Cresspahl. Fine, at sixteen a girl's proximity, her breath, her glance, her voice, the feel of her skin could still be the most important thing in his world; at sixteen his prospects and plans and whole future might depend on slow persistent pursuit of a fifteen-year-old girl, no longer seeing her as his guild master's granddaughter but as ineluctable necessity, the key to a still-secret plan for his whole life to come. At sixteen, as a carpenter's apprentice in Malchow, in the early years of the century, sure. But in 1931, in Jerichow near Gneez, at forty-three?

The repetition is unbearable, isn't it—that one's need for another person should again and again force consciousness through the same old grid, that feelings stirred up so long ago should return fresh and new, that one's imagination should once again indefatigably interpret someone's mere exterior as a sign of every conceivable correspondence between her and oneself, that one's image of a person should suddenly and without warning mask the real person's lacks and failings, that one's heart pounding faster and faster at the merest glimpse of her should feel as scary and alive as it did at the sight of someone else, five, twelve, twenty-eight years ago, as though here at last some new incomparable reality, never touched, never felt, was about to be revealed? He must have been half out of his mind.

He stood, a sturdy man with strong arms, drowsy, friendly, next to the weighing house on the market square as one cart after another from the surrounding farms drove up to it, walking down the rows of the hot tired horses, past the crouching and sweating carters, as though the work was something for him to contemplate. Next to the weighing house he was not so near Papenbrock's house that he seemed to be waiting, but near enough to see a window swing open.

He went for a drive, in the veterinarian's carriage, past the grain carts crunching along the summer road, innocent as any other summer visitor, simply someone out enjoying the scenery, enjoying the summer, incessantly casually bringing the conversation around to the local grain trade, and hearing in everything Dr. Semig said about Papenbrock's business sense only one thing: You'll be happy with the girl, Cresspahl. Happy.

He walked, in collar and tie, idle, past the groups of mowers in the scorching grain fields, as though on vacation, far from the pounding noise of the threshing machines, under a hard sky stretched above the paths around Jerichow, from manor house to manor house, from the coastal bluffs to the Countess Woods, around the marsh, along all the streets in town, for no other reason than that Papenbrock's daughter had grown up there: he wanted to know what she'd had to give up.

He sat, on a research trip to the station pub, the Nazis' hangout, and drank the sour beer and waited for three nights until Horst Papenbrock turned up, then let him rail against the Dawes Plan and the Reichstag election last September, and matched Horst's Kniesenack pint for pint and his liquor shot for shot. He carried the staggering, merry, weepy Papenbrock son and heir across the market square around midnight and propped him up against his father's gate and went to Peter Wulff's back room to tell him about it, not very drunk himself, very pleased, entirely satisfied.

He traveled, to Hamburg for a day, and came back, and appeared on the road to Papenbrock's house and office, modest, in an English shirt from Ladage & Oelke, a dark suit, and no hat; he had given the people of Jerichow weeks of amusement with his love affair, while his head was full of the secret existing between him and Lisbeth Papenbrock, for no one's eyes but his and hers.

A Protestant. Protestants.
Must have money if he can spend so much time doing whatever he wants.
With Nazis. Goes boozing with a Nazi.
Well he's not in it for the money.

You don't have the guts. You wouldn't make a fool of yourself in front of two thousand people.

That's what he imagines life has to offer: a religious girl.

Yeah, she didn't pick you, Stoffregen.

She'll never come back. She'll go with him wherever he says. She was already holding hands with him just now when they turned onto Field Road from the market.

They were lying there in the woods. He didn't hear me ride by on my bike, and she had her eyes open.

On Rehberge Hill. Where you can see a bit of the sea, over by the cliff.

One person warned him. Meta Wulff joined Peter and Cresspahl after closing time and started talking about Pastor Methling, about Lisbeth sitting in the second row, right under the pulpit, every single church day. Wulff growled at her to stop, but Meta, a fisherman's daughter from the Dievenow River, gave him a slap below the shoulder blades and rubbed his back and went on talking about the Bible study group that Papenbrock's daughter held for children in the parish hall, far above and beyond her Christian duties. Cresspahl took none of it in except: She's good with children, too.

Under Auntie Times's broad skirt sits Stalin's daughter, explaining her mother's 1932 suicide: "People were a lot more honest and emotional in those days. If they didn't like life the way it was, they shot themselves. Who does that kind of thing now?"

He was half out of his mind.

This summer is over.

During the past week, 2,376 people were killed in action in Vietnam. Yesterday, the Soviets denied that they were mistreating one of their writers at a labor camp. Public school teachers continue their strike. South Korea intends to build a wall of barbed wire and electronics along its northern border. Jan Szymczak from Brooklyn says his wife has left him, after arriving from Poland to live with him only in February; he refuses to pay any debts she incurs, as of today.

This summer is over. This summer, Chomba, having made millions from the revolution, was kidnapped and brought to Algeria, and his former friends are sharpening the guillotine. This summer, the thirty-third military conflict since the end of World War II got under way, and the cubicles upstairs in the bank were overcrowded with announcers reporting from Israel on transistor radios, doors that had been open since the building went up were almost shut if not entirely closed, and Mr. Shuldiner talked all through a lunch about Jewish imperialism; on Broadway, the lanky gentlemen with their full beards, sidelocks, and opaque expressions jumped when neighbors slapped them on the shoulders in congratulation, and found it hard to join the sidewalk debates on realpolitik that followed, and one of them, fleeing into the Eighty-Sixth Street subway station, collided with Mrs. Cresspahl, who had been listening to the discussion from five steps away; – I'm no hero, I'm a theologian: he said. In the victory parade down Riverside Drive, Marie walked at the end of a row next to Rebecca Ferwalter, as though she belonged there, not wearing the blue-and-white outfit but waving a little flag, the Star of David. Kosygin drove north up Third Avenue in a black funeral car, and the onlookers in their modern climate-controlled office towers could not open windows to wave to him. Then he went to see Niagara Falls anyway. Nikita Sergeyevich Khrushchev appeared on TV screens once again, a worn-out old man, jabbering on about deeds he shrugged off. On the wall between our windows hangs the photograph of a California housewife who received a telegram telling her that her son had died in Vietnam and then sat down again for the photographer, pretending to read it. Crime is up 17 percent in six months. With two murders a day in New York, how long will it be before one of them takes the life of Mrs. Cresspahl? Which night will be the one when the window is broken in, when a shadow under the bridge comes to life holding a knife, when an arm around her neck drags her off the street into a basement? Three-Finger Brown, a Mafia leader, died in his bed and the police took photographs of the mourners paying their respects at the graveside. Negroes have risen up in 22 cities, their death toll stands at 86 for now, and meanwhile the New York City police number 32,365 men. We sat on the Hudson River promenade, among people fishing, family outings, tennis games, and looked across the turgid river thick with garbage at the red strangled evening light, and listened to civil war in New Jersey, from which there is free access to Manhattan along railroad tracks and the roads under the river. Late one night a call came from West Berlin, from Anita, the bar owner, and she'd wanted to ask: You still alive, Gesine? If we only knew whether John Kennedy had been killed by a lone wolf or someone acting on orders. The air force is losing mini-mines on the Florida coast and doesn't know how it's happening. Railroads, telephone companies, automobile factories, and schools are undergoing strikes. It's not our problem, we're here as guests, we're not responsible. We're not responsible yet. More Americans than South Vietnamese soldiers are being killed in Vietnam, and General Westmoreland has called up more. The legislature is laughing out loud over a law against the plague of rats in the slums. De Gaulle promises freedom to Quebec. Again and again, the great powers photograph the dark side of the moon. Krupp has died, Ilse Koch has killed herself. One of the inventors of the gas chamber, a fat German man in his mid-fifties, was seen entering the dock in a Stuttgart courtroom. This summer is over, it's now our future past, that's what we can expect from life. But still, underneath Broadway, at the Eighty-Sixth Street subway station, when an express thunders past heading north along the center tracks, we look at the stiff and expressionless people in the juddering train windows and fear someday being no longer among them—a future when it is only through our homesickness that we will live in New York City.

September 16, 1967 Saturday

Saturday is South Ferry day. When Marie announces at noon their departure for the Battery, South Ferry day has begun.

Marie first saw the ferries that run between Staten Island and the southern tip of Manhattan from the tourist deck of the *France*, back when she still had to be lifted up to see over the railing. She stared with hostility at the skyscraper cactus of Manhattan, growing to gigantic proportions instead of shrinking to human ones; she observed with curiosity the ferryboats crisscrossing the New York harbor alongside the ocean liner: multistory buildings, orange with blue trim, moving fast like fire engines. She nodded in a daze when Gesine couldn't tell her what the vessels were, but she recognized them when we saw them a second time, on an outing, even though the ferry doors were like blinders blocking her view of the exterior.

The South Ferry was the first thing in New York she longed for, badly enough that she could reliably wait without whining for her wish to come true: the ride on the Brooklyn express to Chambers Street, the slow crawl on the local line to the screeching loop of the train at the South Ferry station, the emergence from underground into the big waiting room, all without rushing and fussing. When the giant doors rolled back into the walls, though, she started to tug at Gesine's hand, pull her through the gangways and over the bridges onto the ship, as though in all that space for three thousand people there was one single spot that was hers and she didn't want to lose it. Back then, she would draw pictures for her Düsseldorf friends that showed New York as nothing but a harbor for floating orange caves with lots of windows, carrying a kindergarten along with a large number of cars. Back then, she didn't mind when people asked her why she wanted to spend Gesine's days off taking trips on the South Ferry, and she answered: because it's a floating house; because it's a street between islands that crosses itself; because it's a restaurant you can take a trip in without needing to say goodbyes.

It was also at the South Ferry turnstiles that, for the first time in the city, she was allowed to pay for a trip herself. This was where she joined the community of citizens.

Nowadays, she invariably begins her use of the ship on the car deck, supervising the ferry workers as they cast off the cables and raise the scissor gate before pulling their gloves off and sauntering through the car tunnel to the other end of the ship. In the smoking areas, on the main deck and down below, she goes looking for the shoeshine man with whom she has a standing arrangement for her Sunday shoes and a running skeptical conversation about his concession and his life on the ferry. At the snack counter, too, among the tourists on the foredeck, among the family outings and retirees and children between the rows of scuffed brown seats, she finds enough people to observe, so carefully, so politely, that she can just happen to slip away and disappear if spoken to. She disappears down the passageway, lost in her observations, a gangly child wearing a faded windbreaker with her braids and brown dress shoes shined to perfection with her slightly worn white pants. She does not tell her mother what she liked about the Negro girl her age hauling a two-year-old around on her hip, teasing the baby's lunging lurching mouth with an ice-cream cone; she says nothing about the old man with the crossword puzzle who asked her for a French word meaning *lobby* (she told him). Only when she thinks no one is watching does she turn her head to the side and take a few nonchalant steps behind the child playing mother. She avoids policemen, as she has every official in uniform since 1965 when she saw film footage of American soldiers in the Dominican Republic; policemen are the only ones she can respond to with nothing but a lopsided, uncertain smile. She only occasionally, keeping a respectful distance, circles the bench where her mother sits turning the pages of her newspaper, conveying with the nod of a stranger that she doesn't want to bother her. During the forty-five minutes it takes to go to Staten Island and back, she has covered the three hundred feet from stem to stern several times.

A Black Muslim on trial before the state supreme court for shooting three policemen was gagged with a small hand towel when his protests against the court proceedings disrupted the court proceedings. The draft board has unexpectedly declared two of the teachers on strike eligible for the draft. An army private in California faces eleven years of hard labor for refusing to board a troop plane to Vietnam (his war, he says, is being fought in the ghettos of Philadelphia). The head of the Egyptian armed forces in the Israeli war has committed suicide by taking poison. The German chemist Albert Widmann, who helped design and test mobile gas chambers, has been released in Stuttgart. For the first time in six days, *The New York Times* spares us the pleading yowls of Svetlana Dzhugashvili.

Only on the trip back, when the ferry has already gotten as far as South Brooklyn, does Marie take Gesine up to the top deck and identify the ships lying in the gloomy fog outside the Narrows, the fortress on Governors Island, and the barracks the army built next to the classic red-and-white buildings from the last century; she doesn't care that her face is getting scoured by the heavy wet wind driving offshoots of Hurricane Doria against the hanging nets of cables on the three bridges over the darkening East River. She says, earnestly, unblinkingly: Thank you very much for taking me, as though she'd needed supervision on the South Ferry. It has never occurred to her to take the South Ferry by herself, not yet.

Then we went to Rande and took the excursion steamer to Travemünde. She came along, to Hamburg. She wasn't sad.

We were very tired, we were very merry.
We had gone back and forth all night on the ferry.

September 17, 1967 Sunday

Yesterday at noon, on Bayswater Road in London, a man was seen being taken into a car against his will by four men. He was heard shouting for the police. That afternoon, Scotland Yard sent squad cars to Heathrow, where they blocked a runway to prevent an Aeroflot plane's departure. The police, after a tug-of-war with the captain and crew of the surrounded airplane, took a young Soviet physicist who had been studying in Birmingham for eight months off the plane. He did not seem very coherent under questioning by the British officers. A Soviet embassy official in London said that Mr. Tkachenko had wanted to leave England earlier than planned due to a nervous breakdown, and that the embassy doctor had given him an injection. (After which Mr. Tkachenko called for the police.)

Cresspahl, back in London at the start of the thirty-sixth tax week of 1931, began preparing in all seriousness for a life with Papenbrock's youngest daughter. The two assistants he now operated the business with often saw him standing in its courtyard surrounded by backyards, eyes on the brick pavement or the chimney of the Richmond gasworks, one hand on the back of his neck, deep in thought, without ever shaking his head at himself. But since both men had worked for him, usually alongside him, for more than a year, they just pointed the old man out to each other with a smile and a tilt of the head, as he stood there in the heat for minutes at a time like a blind man until at last he heard that the wood planer inside had stopped running. The younger assistant, Perceval, went reconnoitering late one night but all he had to report in the end was that the old man had been busy in the workshop at midnight. At that point, they offered to work overtime. But Cresspahl had no intention of firing either one.

Cresspahl didn't own the business. The business, Pascal and Son, was owned by one Albert A. Gosling, Esq. This Albert A. Gosling was a wiry, anxious little man, part owner of a fabric store in Uxbridge, who had gotten himself named Pascal's legal heir. Reggie Pascal, the Son in the company name, had had no children of his own and had wanted to leave his business to the carpenter's guild of Richmond, but Gosling, a distant relative, contested the will. Being a retailer, he saw the workshop merely as a piece of property he could sell. The lawyers, Burse, Dunaway & Salomon, unhappily following their client's alternately warlike and wimplike instructions, pulled themselves together and explained to him that the firm of Pascal and Son, established a generation ago, with a steady middle-class and aristocratic clientele, was a good investment. When Albert A. Gosling signaled that he had grasped at least the fact that capital yields interest, Burse, Dunaway & Salomon put an ad in the *Richmond and Twickenham Times* for a master carpenter prepared to manage a business on the owner's behalf. Cresspahl noticed the listing when he returned from a trip to Dorking with Mrs. Trowbridge and took her out to dinner at Short's Greyhound Restaurant on George Street in Richmond. Or was it she who noticed the ad? That whole spring of 1928, Albert Gosling would show up in the workshop wearing a new bowler hat and trying to keep a sharp eye on Cresspahl. But since he didn't know a rasp from a clamp, he would talk about his lifelong fondness for Reggie Pascal—on whose bones in North Sheen Cemetery he had in fact laid nothing, not a wreath, not a petal—and request advance partial payments. His suspicious whining upset Cresspahl's workers, and Cresspahl insisted that all payments go via the lawyers. Burse, Dunaway & Salomon en masse begged Gosling to leave the workshop alone; Dunaway, in a fit of temper, at one point shoved the file so far across his desk that it hung over the edge and almost fell to the floor. Gosling invested his income in new tailored suits and adopted a neat little goatee and spent more time standing around with assorted young gentlemen at Paddington station than standing with his wife in the shop in Uxbridge; when he came to Richmond, it was more often than not to while away the hours in respectable drinking establishments bad-mouthing the Germans against whom he said he had risked his life. Cresspahl heard about that not only from the waiters but from Perceval, an apprentice at the time. (Perceval would have liked watching the master let Gosling have it, at least once.) To which Mr. Smith added that during the war Gosling had actually worked in the navy supply base in Dartmouth, counting caps. Salomon, who as Burse's and Dunaway's junior partner had been stuck with the Pascal account, had taken a liking to this stubborn craftsman from "Michelinberg" who had things to talk about besides the economic crisis or the Jews. Salomon would have liked very much to advise him to give up the arrangement, but his duty to his client's mandates, especially in light of Cresspahl's tidy profits, took precedence in the end. Cresspahl had met members of the Jewish faith not only as merchants in the villages around Malchow but also as NCOs on the western front, and he had no trouble learning how to get along with Arthur Salomon, so unabashedly proud of his prep school accent, his conservative black, his brazilwood office furniture, the legal tomes ranged behind his small, alert, embittered head. Cresspahl instructed him to fake an offer to buy Pascal's property, although at a lower price. Then he had him draw up a settlement for Mrs. Elizabeth Trowbridge.

For maybe three weeks, how a rather provincial girl had looked waving from the St. Pauli Piers in Hamburg remained fixed in his mind—the whole trip from Hamburg to Kingston on Hull to King's Cross station (one day and ten hours), plus another twenty days at work, including during his last dinner with Elizabeth Trowbridge. Then Lisbeth Papenbrock sent him a work by the Gneez photographer Horst Stellmann, Portraits Our Specialty: a nondescript girl, her center-parted hair tucked behind her ears, Lisbeth Papenbrock, hands folded over her stomach, in front of Stellmann's peculiarly gathered drapery backdrop. Cautiously amused, she is looking at the large-format camera behind which Stellmann is squirming under his black cloth, and her lips were slightly parted, and Cresspahl instantly forgot all the earlier pictures.

A little awry
delights the Lord's eye.

Where we live, Broadway is old. We're far from its legendary stretch above Times Square, where quick turnover has set sandblasters loose polishing the weather-beaten tower of *The New York Times*, where old buildings are torn down in secret behind scaffolds hung with tarps, where the sturdy doorknobs and locks and banisters of the Astor Hotel are auctioned off to make room for glass and plastic and anodized aluminum, where the street is decked with enormous sheets of light: flickering under movie marquees, in the impure colors of neon gases, as messages dashing around surfaces, under spotlights, under searchlights, and as circling, leaping, bursting illuminated advertising. In our neighborhood, on the Upper West Side, the lights are more modest and closer to the ground.

Our Broadway starts at Seventy-Second Street where it intersects Amsterdam Ave. and clips off the Verdi Square park. A roomy median strip, supplied with benches at the intersections and occasionally shrubbery, divides the street into two wide roadways. Specimens of Renaissance architecture, elephantine in scale, tower on either side; the window-covered boxes under lyrical cornices extending far to the north testify to the feverish confidence in a real estate market that began to go crazy around 1900, when the subway was built under Broadway. These are hotels, cinemas, and apartment buildings from an era when profits were reinvested, when buildings still used art nouveau or Italianate embellishments around their knees and brows to advertise their value. The boom was not enough to let these ornate monsters close ranks—between them crouch the more faintheartedly calculated rental buildings, modest, four-story, making less of an effort to conceal their fire escapes, and now their age unmasks them. Few hotels have been able to keep either their well-to-do clientele or the reputation promised by their facade; they now by and large house long-term guests, poor pensioners, hardly anyone with children. The apartment buildings do not have to advertise their vacancies for long: while their addresses may not be especially prestigious, they are well supplied with subway stations, bus lines in all four directions, and ground floors packed with an unbroken line of businesses—delis, supermarkets, laundromats, barbershops, diners, grocery stores, bars, storefront churches, shoe repair shops, dry cleaners, tax advisers, driving schools, and travel agencies—even if the front windows are sometimes a bit dusty, the fabrics tattered, and the countertops not as gleaming as on the East Side. But nothing new has been built on this street for forty years, and despite the teeming lights at the foot of the facades, Broadway brings to mind postcards from the era of horse-drawn carriages, when residents spoke of "the boulevard."

Old people keep quiet on the traffic islands in the middle of Broadway, step gingerly into the quick stream of walkers crossing them, hover at the edge of a crowd that has formed around a peddler, spend long hours over a single cup of coffee in an Automat cafeteria. Abandoned. They failed to save their possessions in Europe from the Nazis, they received no significant compensation, they cannot prolong their bourgeois past into the burnished apartments of Riverside Drive, they live alone. Abandoned by their children, predeceased by their spouse of many decades, by themselves they live out the last warm days on Broadway, where at least they have movement and traffic and business nearby, until it's time to go back to their furnished rooms, to the old age homes on West End Avenue. These are not elderly gentlemen taking a break during a well-planned stroll, not older ladies savoring an impulse purchase on a bench in the middle of Broadway: these are wards of government welfare, and little more than their clean clothes and erect posture separates them from the ragged man with black skin sweating out some dangerous booze on the thrumming subway grate behind them. They are willing to talk to the person next to them, but grudgingly. The *Novoye Slovo*, from which two people read the state of the world together, is not enough; the fact that their mothers were practically neighbors in Ruthenian villages is not enough for solidarity; and what kind of closeness is supposed to arise from reciprocal stories of marriages or children's careers when the children themselves do not come—not for a visit, and not to meet them in the cheap cafeterias where the water is free and sometimes the cream and sugar too. And it's not even true that their twenty cents and years of loyalty bought them any right to be provided by society with a meeting place, because when their cafeteria's lease runs out the owners move on, looking for customers with less time on their hands and more cash. There are still the benches.

The *New York Times* was there last night when the Automat on Seventy-Second Street, just off Broadway, closed its doors. The *Times* observed for us:

– Should auld acquaintance be forgot… ("frail, uncertain voices").
– I've come here for fifteen years, every evening: Ida Bess.
– Fifteen years? Thirty years I'm eating here: Rose Katz.
– It's too bad, I've never seen such faithful customers: Steve Kelly.

Another photo shows an old woman near Danang, stiff with age, pencil legs, grimacing face, being carried on a soldier's back out of an area of heavy fighting to higher ground. "A member of the armed forces helps her": says *The New York Times.*

September 19, 1967   Tuesday
Your child just had to go to a private kindergarten, Gesine Cresspahl, and you didn't mind that it was in a church a Rockefeller had dedicated to God in memory of his mother, clean and spacious classrooms high above the Hudson and Riverside Park, with teachers paid well enough to be patient with middle-class children—Mrs. Jeuken, Mrs. Davidoff, who made Marie believe in a world where kindness and obedience and the absence of envy pay off. For that you pinched and scraped together one and a half months' salary, and your excuse was that "she should have as easy a time as possible learning the new language." She was also learning to have high expectations, wasn't she?

The British have returned the Soviets' runaway physicist to them. Both sides now agree that he is a sick man, and both powers accuse the other of having acted improperly.

And when your child turned six, Gesine Cresspahl, she still wasn't sent to public school—to one of the shabby, boxy brick buildings reeking of fiscal stinginess, to an overcrowded classroom where the children of the poor sleep off their parents' fights and underpaid teachers have to worry more about self-defense than teaching, to a world where what counts is the slap and the punch, the cut and thrust. Did you not like the broken benches, the stinking toilets, the bleak concrete schoolyards behind thick chicken wire? Or was it that your child shouldn't have to do without school during strikes, like this one, six days long so far and today keeping four-fifths of New York's teachers out of school, over not just wages but new schools, smaller classes, and the right to discipline disruptive children? Did you not want the police to turn up in Marie's school and beat representatives of the colored community from the building with billy clubs? Are there some kinds of knowledge you want to keep from your child?

"When Patrolman Clarke was led from the floor with his head bandaged, some of the women demonstrators shouted: 'I hope you die.'"

So, the only place good enough for your child, Mrs. Cresspahl, was a private school on the northern heights of Riverside Drive, a Catholic one too, a concrete block of the finest cut and costliest workmanship, cited in the annals of modern architecture, an institution with a two-year waiting list and annual tuition running as high as three of your paychecks. The discreet bus carrying the children past the slums to pure knowledge didn't bother you; the school uniform, a blue blazer with a gold crest over the heart, didn't embarrass you. Your child already deserves to be treated as an individual, autonomous person, her abilities recognized and fostered early. But why by people in long brown habits, white cords around their waists and limited intelligence under their coifs? It's true that the child will be accepted at exclusive universities with a diploma from this institution, unlike the graduates of P.S. 75, and she will have friends in families wealthier than her own. Why this sham, when two missed tuition payments are enough to blow it apart?

The East Germans are telling the West Germans (according to the *New York Times* correspondent): Give up your militarism, your neo-Fascism, and your monopoly power, then we'll negotiate with you.

Not only that, Mrs. Cresspahl, but when your child needs to see a doctor she doesn't go to a public clinic, doesn't have to wait in moldy bug-infested corridors next to bleeding, unconscious, or mentally ill people—your child goes to a private practice on Park Avenue, where she is announced like a lady and greeted like a friend for fifteen dollars a visit, blood tests forty. Your child knows her doctor by name, writes him letters, feels comfortable calling him on the phone. Your child's doctor got his excellent grades not at a state university but at one called Harvard, and for your child he makes house calls. Where can you find that—a New York doctor, bringing in well over a hundred thousand a year, making a house call for a slight temperature and ending his visit with an unhurried conversation, relaxed in his chair, not a professional businessman but practically like a friend just dropping by? The best is barely good enough for your child, Mrs. Cresspahl, is that how you see it? Why for your child? Incidentally, you've got some mail, Gesine.

Dear Mr./Mrs./Miss <u>Cresspahl</u>,

I have been called up on short notice for active military service. Kindly settle any outstanding accounts with my attorney. You may be sure that I will inform you when I return ...

Washington, Sept. 18 (AP)—The Defense Department today identified the following men killed in action in Vietnam: 2nd Lieut. William D. Huyler, Jr., of Short Hills, N.J., Sgt. Harald J. Canan of Oceanside, Long Island, and Pvt. Laifelt Grier of Brooklyn, from the Army; Lance Cpl. James P. Braswell of the Bronx and PFC Robert C. Wallace of Plattsburgh, N.Y., from the Marines.

September 20, 1967 Wednesday

Thirty-six years ago yesterday or the day after tomorrow, Papenbrock's youngest daughter received an invitation to join Leslie Danzmann on a trip to Graal. Their beds had been next to each other in the Rostock boarding school; Leslie Danzmann was in fact vacationing in Graal. She was the widow of a naval officer and with his pension could only afford off-season on the Baltic. Leslie Danzmann was always ready to help.

Her friend from Jerichow arrived in Graal after breakfast and wrote postcards late into the afternoon in the dining room of the Strandperle spa hotel. Leslie told her the day trips: Moorhof, Wallenstein's camp, the haunted forest, the Markgrafenheide Forest Lodge. When they were back at the train station in the woods, they suddenly hugged each other: a country girl in a skirt-suit with checks that were too big, and a pale-haired young lady in a tennis dress. Both were unusually effusive, one at the favor a true friend was doing for her, the other because she was not inclined to warn her unmarried friend. Then Leslie Danzmann went to the post office, signed the first card to Papenbrock, and dropped it in the mailbox.

In the light that the crowns of tall trees held at a distance, between lush fields of bracken, Lisbeth Papenbrock traveled back along the route she had just come. She did not look out the window in Rostock, nor in Bützow. From behind her *Berlin Daily*, she saw Dr. Erdamer board the train in Bad Kleinen, but Dr. Erdamer walked right past a lady reading a liberal newspaper. In Gneez the express train stopped next to the train to Jerichow, and even though it was pig market day in Gneez, the platform was empty. After five furtive hours she was in Hamburg. It wasn't at all that she was trying to deceive her parents; she was only trying to keep a secret.

The next morning, she took the streetcar to Fuhlsbüttel, picked up the plane ticket she'd ordered in advance, boarded the airplane to London, landed in Bremen, landed in Amsterdam, landed nine hours later in Croydon, and hired an open car to drive her to Richmond: an exhausted, excited tourist staring with mouth slightly open at the reddish colors of the street made heavier by the afternoon haze, almost startled to find that the New Star and Garter Hotel really existed on Richmond Hill, not only in the Grieben's guidebook. (Eight shillings. Twenty percent unemployment in England.) When the cabdriver drove away, annoyed at the tip, she wished she could've run after him. She didn't want to start off here with a mistake.

It was already dark, a thick ashen night, when she reached the courtyard of Cresspahl's workshop. She took her time, she watched him at work, strong and tough in his collarless shirt; he had neglected his blond stubble for days and was busy with some heavy clamps, cursing under his breath. Sometimes he winked to himself, he was so sure he was alone. Finally, when he stepped outside with a pipe, he couldn't see who it was, then he saw who it was.

They were very moved. All the words he had spoken to her about the house and Salomon and Richmond immediately took on for her the shape of his stairs, his kitchen, his room, the gasworks chimney outside his window. His visit to Jerichow grew inexorably more real. She was already afraid of losing him; she hoped she would die first.

Cresspahl was alarmed. (He didn't mind about the money she had thrown away to take the trip; he was uncomfortable with the frugal budget they had agreed on.) He was alarmed at the sudden impulses that after this one he would have to expect from her in the future. He found it bizarre how blindly she seemed to believe that she had joined him in a single bound, in an instant—while he still chafed under a feeling of strangeness and distance, she no longer felt any distance at all. She seemed to him like the child in an egg-and-spoon race who gets so carried away that he forgets his playmates with their own fragile burdens are also trying to reach the goal, playing dirty tricks if necessary; now he felt an added obligation to make sure she got home safely. Now he was her superior in more than age. She had made herself dependent. That's not what he'd wanted.

She let him work during the day, and by evening he had thought of so much he wanted to tell her that he started talking and talking. They felt so sure of each other that they talked back at each other, and not always joking. Deeply moved, they told each other where and when they might have met sooner: in 1914, at the Whitsuntide market in Malchow; in 1920, in the Waren town hall; in 1923, in Amsterdam; in August 1931, for exactly one minute, at the Schwerin train station. All these deprivations seemed inconceivable. Now they were in the clear.

They took each other out to dinner (the German cash-export limit of a hundred marks had just been lifted), and while Cresspahl wanted to take her to Schmidt's, a German restaurant on Charlotte Street, she wanted to go to an English restaurant. (Leslie Danzmann had given her one of her dresses.) He had her order from the menu. She understood that to mean that he wanted her to practice the language, and he saw the waiter tuck his smile under his mustache. (It wasn't so long ago that he'd gone out to the White Horse in Dorking with Elizabeth T. He had to give up the Black Horse, too.) She wasn't trying to reform him when she bought him a safety razor, but she wanted to seem like she was. She was so deliriously happy on the top level of a double-decker streetcar at rush hour that the people sitting nearby had smiles for her, and for Cresspahl too. One time, with her purse on the table, she had paid a bill and put her hand on his tobacco pouch and stuck it in her handbag, so he wouldn't have to carry it, and so he could ask her for it back later, and so she would have something she could give him.

He had made a table, a light and sturdy oak frame, where they and four children could sit. That sounded good to her. He showed her his designs for beds, and she picked one where they could lie together. That sounded good to him.

She told him all about her walks in Richmond, about what she thought of the various shops. The meandering main street reminded her of Gneez, as did the buildings that each had a different facade, the small shops, the often overcrowded sidewalks. (He looked at her; he didn't notice she talked longest about the Parish Church.) He wanted to return the favor and asked about Jerichow, and she turned Jerichow into a series of disparaging stories:

Molten the baker had a hand-painted sign in his shopwindow: Germans, Eat German Bread! She hadn't thought to laugh about it at home, but in front of a window full of pastries on George Street she couldn't hold back a dark-throated titter.

(She didn't tell him that Pastor Methling had thundered down from the pulpit against the surveying of Jerichow land for a Catholic church. "So come to church on Reformation Day in your top hat!" he'd cried. Since Jerichow's tradesmen were counting on large orders from the commission, Pahl the tailor had to put a new top hat in his window every day. Jerichow's tradesmen would give Pastor Methling his top hats all right, though not for his reasons.)

She made her brother sound ridiculous, to please Cresspahl: Horst Papenbrock, showing up for dinner in his brown shirt and shoulder belt, marching up and down Town Street with Griem, who was wearing the same uniform, just because the government had lifted the ban on the Brownshirts. They were giving notice. Horst Papenbrock, who can't get anywhere in the SA because his father refuses to spring for a truck for propaganda trips around the countryside. Horst Papenbrock, whose voice suddenly turns small, almost flaccid, whenever he begs his father for donations for the SA.

Daddy you can't possibly want your son to go around as a common foot soldier.
Berlin has lifted the ban off your necks. Thats all youre gonna get.

And what does *The New York Times* have to offer us today from the life of Stalin's daughter? "It was May. Flowers were in bloom outside the dacha. 'So you want to get married, do you?' my father said. For a long time he stared at the trees and said nothing. 'Yes, it's spring,' he remarked all of a sudden. 'To hell with you. Do as you like.'" (1944)

She'd made sure that he too would get one of the postcards mailed after her departure, showing the steamship port in Graal (with warm greetings from Leslie Danzmann).

I wanted to sleep with you again before we got married, Heinrich Cresspahl. In a bed, I mean.

September 21, 1967 Thursday

Our building on Riverside Drive has another, basement entrance, where Ninety-Sixth Street runs below the overpass—after the yawning caverns of the three garages, before the blackish arch of the bridge, an unexpected lead-gray door opens into a passage between zigzagging walls. Behind this open door, which today has sucked in soggy brown leaves from the park, all the others are locked: the one to the inside fire-escape stairwell, the one to the elevators, the others hiding the maintenance equipment and garbage incinerators. Today, the low passageway is too narrow for Mrs. Cresspahl, and it is with unusual urgency that she presses the button to summon down Mr. Robinson: not because she is rain-soaked, not because she wouldn't be able to defend herself with shopping bags in both arms, but because, in just such a passageway (according to *The New York Times*) in the basement of a building on West 181st Street

   near Fort Washington Avenue
   right around the corner the whole time—when we transferred from the
subway to the long-distance bus, when we took out-of-town visitors up to the
George Washington Bridge, when we ate chicken made Jewish-style, not far
from that respectable building, bricks bundled in elegant sandstone wrapping,
just a few steps away from that basement, so close the whole time

the superintendent, Mr. Hartnett, found two steamer trunks yesterday: "Property of Anne Solomon," the tags said. Her widower knew nothing about any such trunks and gave Mr. Hartnett permission to open them. One was empty. The other held the bodies of three children, as well preserved as mummies, wrapped in roofing tar paper and evening newspapers from January 1920, March 1922, and October 1923. According to Mr. Solomon, who married his wife, Anne, only in 1933, she had previously been a domestic in White Plains. She must have secretly moved the trunk into the basement after 1935, when they moved to 181st Street, so that she could live above it until her own death in 1954.

   – An American mother: Mr. Robinson says, because he notices Mrs. Cresspahl's glance at the *Daily News* spread out on the stool next to him in the elevator. He stands facing the scissor gate as he takes her upstairs from the basement level. – An American mother: he says, in his thin hard

Spanish voice. First one at fourteen, another at sixteen, another at seventeen, then finally got married at twenty-seven. What should she have told Jacob Solomon?

Mr. Robinson, "Robinson with the aquiline profile," one of the three elevator operators in the building for the past two years, early on started greeting Mrs. Cresspahl with phrases that sounded like *Auff'eedesehn* or *Gudnmong'* and only reluctantly settled for replies in English. Mr. Robinson had spent some years of his youth in Germany. He thinks he understands this foreigner.

– The landscape in Germany is *vunnebah*: he would say. He happily took refuge in repeating this sentence, so as not to have to speak certain others—he was trying to be nice to this German lady. For while this refugee from Cuba had been able to buy his citizenship faster by joining the army voluntarily, and before he left North Carolina was grateful for his training as a low-frequency radio technician, the army had held up a mirror to him in the restricted military zone around Schwarzer Berg near Grafenwöhr, and in this mirror he saw his red, almost Indian skin, and the black hair reaching down to his neck in tight shining curls so stiff that his patting pushing fingers never moved it out of place. Technician Fourth Grade Robinson had to be reprimanded over a brawl with pink-skinned individuals outside the Bayreuth train station before he learned to go drinking with the dark-skinned ones, in the dirtier bars where the rum cost more and the girls showed their contempt more openly and for higher prices. The landscape was that of the Upper Palatine Forest, which he saw at night out the window of the radar truck near Flossenbürg on the border of the Czechoslovak Socialist Republic.

The Flossenbürg concentration camp can best be described as a factory dealing in death. Vicious murders of Jews were the order of the day; lethal injections and shots in the back of the neck were everyday occurrences.

T/4 Robinson had himself transferred to West Berlin for his last year. To West Berlin, as to everywhere it went around the world, the US Army exported the ghettos that it didn't allow in its military bases back home; in West Berlin, too, the bars for second-class Americans were more run-down, more often targets of the police, and more expensive than the pubs for ordinary citizens. And in Berlin the Germans laughed at these foreigners parading down Clayallee on July Fourth in their armored vehicles, hands held flat under their chins, sitting ramrod straight in impractical postures, fiercely staring straight ahead, like dolls in a toy car. In Berlin he met a girl who wanted to improve her English; with his English from the streets of the Bronx, this girl was incomprehensible to Americans who had theirs from a school. T/4 Robinson had thought it was a romance. Berlin couldn't keep him in Germany. The army couldn't keep him.

 – Or maybe it was a girlfriend who planted the steamer trunk with the mummies in Anne Solomon's basement: says Mr. Robinson, low-frequency radio technician, elevator operator, maintenance man, plumber, painter, dealer in used TV sets, custodian of the basement storage room (who pretends not to recognize Mrs. Cresspahl when he runs into her on Broadway while with elegantly dressed Negroes—strong, sturdy men with unusually cheerful demeanors), a person who cannot be questioned, cannot be known. He precedes Mrs. Cresspahl out of the elevator and taps on her doorbell until Marie opens the door, cautiously today, only as far as the chain will go, not entirely relieved when she sees him.

We did what you asked: he promises the child, who is keeping her expectant eyes on him, reminding him: We checked. *Puedes estar segura. En nuestra casa no hay cementerio particular.*

Turning away, he winks at Mrs. Cresspahl. While doing so, he lifts his hand and dabs at the skin around the corner of his left eye, several times, with careful fingers, as he always does when we're sure that he's lying.

September 22, 1967 Friday

 – Mrs. Cresspahl? Mrs. Cresspahl! How nice, Mrs. Cresspahl. I mean: nice to meet you, by phone at least. Brewster. I mean: Mrs. Brewster, the wife. Dr. Brewster's wife. Is your daughter there? Aha, she isn't there. She's on her way, she's coming, but she's not with you, is that right? She's not here either. She was here, I mean: she didn't come straight here. First she went to Dr. Brewster's office on Park Avenue, but the only one there was Miss Gibson, yes, like the drink, she was having the super pack up the equipment. Miss Gibson was in tears a little, it always amazes me, the most unexpected people do like my husband, and a girlfriend of hers has a fiancé who has a brother in Vietnam who sent home a photograph where he had a kind of chain of cut-off ears from the Vietcong slung across his shoulder and I said, Nonsense, first of all we are a civilized country, secondly the Vietcong won't take revenge on our doctors, especially not on my husband, the most unexpected people like him, as I said, but I wasn't there, I was already in the Biltmore, we live in Greenwich, Connecticut, do you know Greenwich, Mrs. Cresspahl?

The secretary of state has let his daughter marry a Negro, who is moreover a lieutenant in the Air Force Reserve who requested to serve in Vietnam.

– You simply must come and pay us a visit in Greenwich, once we're past our troubles of course, along with your daughter, I wish I could hug her, the way she comforted Miss Gibson and helped with the packing up and left all of a sudden, a modest child, Miss Gibson said, Miss Gibson called here, let the call go through, she said, because we've stopped picking up, I'm here with my two daughters, seven and nine, lovely children, you simply must meet them, we just can't understand it, Dr. Brewster, a doctor, so respected, the way he got on board an airplane in Newark, already a real soldier, and two days later he'll be in San Francisco and in Vietnam by October, it's horrible, and these children's refugee camps are apparently so unhygienic, what if he catches something, well that's our contribution, our national duty, I'm sure your daughter must understand that too, there's a patient here who's just walked in, a ten-year-old girl, who wants to see him, Dr. Brewster, one more time, before, Miss Gibson said.

Since 1961, approximately 13,365 American citizens have fallen in combat in Vietnam.

– ... such a polite child, Mrs. Cresspahl, you've done a wonderful job, that must have been her Sunday dress, a real lady, you must tell me her school's address, my daughters out here in the country, you know, it can be so expensive, we're thinking of moving to New York, Dr. Brewster will be in Vietnam for at least two years, in Danang, or Danghoi, someone get me a map, so your daughter looked around when she got to our suite, the

Biltmore always gives me a suite, she was looking for Dr. Brewster, you know, and I tell her we already took him to Newark and that we're moving to New York and I ask would she rather have Coke or a Sprite, it does better in the taste tests supposedly, and your daughter just looks at me, you know, I was sitting on the sofa and your daughter looked at me, so quietly, like she really understood what I was going through, like she could see it in my face, and what can I tell you, Mrs. Cresspahl, she turns around, turns on her heel and disappears, I was still in the doorway, she could have stayed of course, I didn't mean it like that, she was gone, such a tactful child, Mrs. Cresspahl, and so brave, taking the subway this late, I haven't been in the subway for ten years, all those drunks and Negroes and ritual murders, you must come and see us, I'll give you my number, and of course your daughter can write to Dr. Brewster, I'll pass the letters along, and I must congratulate you on such a daughter, Mrs. Cresspahl, I'll call again, Mrs. Cresspahl. Mrs. Cresspahl! I only said: It's better if you don't call me. I'll call you. It was a pleasure. Charming.

Today *The New York Times* has decided to offer for our consideration, at last, the final problem plaguing the spirit of self-presentation virtuoso Svetlana Dzhugashvili: Can what is good ever be forgotten?

September 23, 1967 Saturday

In 1931, ten eggs cost seventy-eight pfennigs, a pound of butter one mark thirty. St. Peter's Church in Jerichow charged two marks for wedding decorations and clean-up afterward, three marks for ringing the bells at the bridal car's approach, one mark for lighting the altar candles, three marks for choir and organ during the ceremony, and it sold admission tickets to anyone not in the bride's or groom's family at twenty-five pfennigs each. Fees payable in advance. Lisbeth Papenbrock had ordered everything on offer except for the guest tickets and the painful singing; after lunch on Reformation Day she really and truly found herself being driven down Town Street to church in one of Swenson's black rental cars; but she did not feel entirely at ease. She'd so often anticipated what she would be feeling now that now the hope crumpled and broke, not only under the stares coming from both sidewalks into the slowly driving car, which seemed polite, barely,

I cant help it, I think Im pretty, said the cat, looking at its reflection in the well.
Then in it fell.
And you pushed it!
Shes wearing silk but no honor. The war just thirteen years ago and shes goin to England.
If youve got it long, show it long.
We'll cut hers short!
Ottje Stoffregen's drunk already.
She should have gotten her myrtle from a flowerpot.

not only under the stubborn silence of a family crisscrossed with conflicts since the night before—Louise with her husband and the bride because the wedding procession wouldn't be on foot; Papenbrock with his elder daughter because she'd brought her bankrupt husband and drunk too; she in turn with Horst because he couldn't keep his mouth shut about the anonymous letters Cresspahl had apparently been getting; Horst with his father because the latter wouldn't let him wear his SA uniform to the ceremony (even though Pastor Methling was prepared to accept a detachment of uniformed Brownshirts as a display of patriotism), and because his Krakow brother-in-law had been helped out of his debts again, and because Lisbeth's dowry was coming out of his inheritance; Lisbeth with Horst because he'd called Cresspahl's family proles; Papenbrock with everybody because they'd tried to make him invite the oldest son from "Rio de Janeiro"—
what really bothered her was Cresspahl's acquiescence. She didn't find such behavior appropriate. He had agreed to have the wedding on Reformation Day, the notices drafted for *The Rostock Gazette* and *The Gneez Daily News* and *The Lübeck Gazette* had come back from Richmond without a single edit, he had let her have her choice of the theme of the sermon ("No man, having put his hand to the plough, and looking back, is fit for the kingdom of God": Luke 9:62), he may have insisted on inviting Dr. Semig but hadn't insisted on the Wulffs, in the end he'd accepted one of Papenbrock's hats so he'd have something to doff at the church door—all in exchange for her

promise that, for the certainty that, at half past seven the number 2 express train from Gneez near Jerichow to Hamburg would rescue them. But if it was a deal he was making, why didn't he add anything for her willingness to move abroad, which was, after all, the greater sacrifice?

I'm doing this for you, Cresspahl. It's for you. Do you even see it?

Here is the first picture: The groom and my mother in front of the churchyard wall, her face reduced to eyes and lips, unrecognizable under the edge of the long veil that drew a line across her forehead and followed the shape of her skull above that line, revealing it in the form of a silly and vulnerable vessel; he (long since hatless) to her right, his left arm behind her back without touching her, a country fellow dressed up in a loose-fitting black suit (from Ladage & Oelke, Alster Arcades, Hamburg), not a local, offering to the camera lazily protruding lips instead of a smile, a stranger with faith in the Stettin–Hamburg express. Next comes Cresspahl's mother, an old woman with twisted shoulders, so attentively is she listening with her overstrained, exhausted body; she has thin gray-black hair and her grimace of joy is somewhat spoiled by the yellowed stumps of her teeth. Our li'l grammy, eighteen months before her death. Placed next to her is Gertrud Niebuhr, her second child, shy and embarrassed at the deference and honor, who will relive the ceremony, in words, fully animated, only when she goes home; and Martin Niebuhr, friendly and stiff in his musty Sunday suit; and Peter Niebuhr, forestry student from Berlin, with glints in his glasses that hide his eyes, holding himself as though he has ended up in an all too distant land. They spoke only a very southern form of Plattdeutsch. Stellmann drags his tripod farther and farther back in front of them, sticks a hand out from his black cloth, three fingers raised as though he is taking a vow, and issues sharp orders, trying to enforce a better-synchronized play of facial expressions. Then there is the semicircle of assembled relatives plus a pastor in back obscured by a black block of sturdy men in black top hats, who'd accidentally stepped in front of the camera but let a little pleasure slip into their solemn stony faces because someone, other than them, had come a cropper this Reformation Day.

I never saw that picture.

The other picture is a photograph mounted on varnished cardboard with Stellmann the photographer's name and address embossed on it: a view of a long table with lamplight and the light of the flashbulb reflected in the centerpieces and platters of meat. When I first saw it, it had barely been touched but the sepia had turned almost dark brown in its paperboard folder, blurring the faces. I recognized Papenbrock from his pear-shaped head, and also by the somewhat servile stiffness with which he leaned toward the lady on his right. This lady, in a suit that looked like a uniform, meant to emphasize her square shoulders, was perhaps Isa, a relative of the von Bothmers. The woman on Papenbrock's left is my mother—so I have been told. By this point she is wearing a blouse, maybe greenish, loosely tied at her neck with a thin white cord; the photo catches her with one hand behind her head, touching her helmetlike hairdo, so that she laughs, delighting in her clumsiness, but also as if laughing does not suit her. This face looks like mine did in 1956. The photograph is ruined because Cresspahl is turning half of his broad back toward the lens, talking to the lawyer from Krakow who drank away Hilde Papenbrock's inheritance and saddled her with one misfortune after another, and he, kicked out of the Mecklenburg bar association, thrusting his dark head forward undaunted, having a good time, or maybe just scheming, with his squinting eyes, his firm cheeks—this is the man Cresspahl's drinking a toast to, with cognac. Next to them, the camera has caught a gentleman in the act of leaving: Semig, with his rabbity head, with the wide flat toothbrush mustache sticking out from his shaved rabbity head, Semig with his curved lips and wrinkled nose, but it's not that he's about to sneeze, not at all, he is trying to look amiable. He left before the end of the coffee. He stopped behind my mother and bent over her shoulder, not for long, for four words (You'll be happy with the girl, Cresspahl). He nodded to the others as he left the room, and for a long time thereafter the von Bothmers as well as the Papenbrocks held up his behavior as amazingly tactful for a Jew, and for a university man. Pastor Methling was sore at Semig because now he couldn't decently stay longer himself. The schnapps bottles appeared on the table as soon as he was out the door, and when my mother and Cresspahl arrived in Hamburg on the number 2 express train at around a quarter to ten and walked down Kirchenallee to the Reichshof Hotel,

– . . . they were married: Marie says. (Saturday is South Ferry day when Marie says it is.)

Che Guevara, the revolutionary, found it necessary to have himself photographed in the Bolivian jungle. True, *The New York Times* now shows him surrounded by comrades-in-arms. But does the whole world have to see him risk his neck and lose?

September 24, 1967 Sunday

"GERMAN-AMERICANS MARCH WITH YODELING, PRETTY FRAU-LEINS

There was yodeling on Fifth Avenue and in Yorkville yesterday afternoon as the German-Americans held their annual Steuben Parade for the 10th time.

There were also beer steins in all sizes, pretty girls of the New York Turn Verein turning cartwheels and elderly members of the German War Veterans Association displaying World War I Iron Crosses.

And there was Governor Rockefeller, shaking every hand in a 10-foot radius on the reviewing stand on Fifth Avenue and 69th Street, slapping the backs of visitors from West Germany, applauding every passing lederhosen group and pinning a blue cornflower, the parade symbol, on the lapel of State Attorney General Louis J. Lefkowitz.

As usual during ethnic and other Fifth Avenue parades, East Side traffic was disrupted for hours. In addition to Fifth Avenue, the transverse roads crossing Central Park were temporarily closed to all vehicles except buses.

One of the about 40 floats in the two-hour parade carried a large portrait of the late Chancellor, Dr. Konrad Adenauer, 'Architect of German-American Cooperation.' The display was sponsored by the New York Staats-Zeitung und Herold, a German-language daily.

. . .

Many German-American associations that took part in yesterday's parade carry on the traditions and costumes of areas that never belonged to Germany, like Transylvania (a part of Rumania) or Gottschee (the

Yugoslav Kocevje), or were severed from Germany after World War II, like
Silesia, now a part of Poland."
© The New York Times

"CLOTHIER FOUND SLAIN IN STORE
Queens Man Shot to Death Near Waterfront Here
The survivor of a German concentration camp who had befriended sailors
of many nations in his waterfront haberdashery here was found shot to
death in his store yesterday.

The victim, Max Hahn, 64 years old, of 63-60 102d Street, Rego Park,
Queens, was found on the floor of the store at 680 12th Avenue near 51st
Street with two bullets in his chest. His feet and hands had been tied by
his assailant who apparently had attempted to rob him, the police said.

. . .

Apparently the gunman killed Mr. Hahn after he had tied him up,
shooting him twice in the chest at close range. Mr. Hahn's pockets had
been turned inside out, but the police said they did not think that the killer
had found any money.

Most of Mr. Hahn's customers were members of crews from the ships
that docked in the Hudson River along the avenue. Mr. Hahn, a native of
Poland, would stand in the doorway of the store or sit outside it and josh
with the seamen as they walked by his store. His wife, Ida, helped out in
the store, which was open six days a week, usually from 8 a.m. to 11 p.m.

Their son had returned about two months ago from Israel where he had
been attending college."
© The New York Times

"Fall arrived briskly and brightly yesterday. The official change-over in
seasons occurred at 1:38 p.m. . . ."
© The New York Times

September 25, 1967 Monday
How come: he wonders, she wonders, we wonder: she is suspended, buckled in, tilted back, in a three-engine jet plane in a holding pattern over

Pennsylvania? But the clumpy clouds in the foreground and the previously level strata to the north recall the Arctic (recall pictures of the Arctic), with the edges pictured somehow sharper, icier. Only the clock knew it was afternoon, the white radiance under the blue sphere merely repeating "light," "light." The airplane is tipped about forty degrees; it seems to be aiming at a sea-dark blue hole in which brownish-yellow flecks of dirt indicate human settlements. Only the wing's surface slanting into the swelling balls of cloud shows the plane's repeated turns. This must have been April 1962, when she was obtaining European passports with American visas, which arrived from Milan after a few weeks by registered mail, as though none of them had ever been to East Germany. That morning, in Minneapolis, in the mirror facing the bed, her whole body had looked yellow, one night closer to death. It is the sun, sinking into the cloud cover, that sets the wing's surface ablaze with color. Gradually the white sculptures of the sky are flattened into a bluish, tufted plain. The captain, grumbling on behalf of his passengers, informs them about the new instructions from ground control in New York. New York—will we ever get there? Then the stewardesses serve the second round of Bloody Marys: cheap vodka swimming on a layer of tomato juice. A woman like her can afford weekend trips like this only with a pass, the kind major shareholders get. She cannot cross the Atlantic with it, can cross the Pacific only as far as Hawaii. In Milan, Vito Genovese was Karsch's neighbor for a while. In Minneapolis, at the top of the Foshay Tower, there were two women and one man who turned to look down at the forests and the necklace of lakes to the north whenever other tourists pushed past behind them. (*Je vous assure que vos papiers d'identité ne serviront pas aux but anti-communistes.*) Where was the child? The child was with Mrs. Ferwalter. No, on an eleventh floor. The child is supposed to buy *The New York Times*. The child, Cresspahl's last two eyes, as survivor. Now the plane is circling below the clouds, above a twilit coastal area, tiny house lights, cars not visible. One of those echoing sonorous voices will say into the telephone: Marie, do you have a father, a grandmother, any relatives at all? You need to be brave now! The plane unexpectedly starts to race, hurtling low over the Atlantic toward Brooklyn, alongside the shrouded Verrazano Bridge, the Empire State Building rearing up solitary in the night and vanishing into nothing under its chignons of light. Coney Island—whirling colored lights. Lines of headlights on the expressways. Blue lights wrapped in fog. A long taxi on the runway, delays at the intersections. Once, a glimpse past the wing of a deep tunnel seething with cars. In the cubby for this flight's passengers, there are no messages in the slot labeled "C." The city bus is stuck in traffic. The gravestones to either side flicker under the city lights. The tunnel—the tiled Hades under the river. In the airport train station, numbers for taxis are handed out. This city won't last much longer. What's so special about First Avenue. This city will last maybe another two hundred years. (The doorman in the lobby of the Foshay Tower stood there as anxiously, as reproachfully, as if he were Foshay himself, who in the end lost everything—stocks, cash, tower.) On Ninety-Sixth Street the rails come out from under Park Avenue: the rich live on stilts. Not far from here, from these dilapidated remains of cars and the slimy garbage on the sidewalk, is where the widow of the murdered President Kennedy moved recently: 1040 Fifth Avenue. Their daughter goes to school around the corner. When Mrs. Kennedy's plans to move there became public, the residents of the building started getting outrageous offers for their apartments, just for the chance to run into Secret Service men in the elevator. (One couple, who were planning to move to the country anyway, made a clean $10,000 profit on the sale of their apartment.) Central Park is pitch black. In the middle of the park there is a stable for police horses, a shooting range for policemen. One round trip to Minneapolis. Maybe the child has kept the tea warm and put the newspaper on the table, with a note: "Don't change the alarm." Because even if windswept Singer Bowl stadium in Queens was full of striking public-school teachers yesterday, Marie has her private school tomorrow. Now we want to read the advice column. "My wife having left my bed and board, I will no longer be responsible for any debts contracted by her."

– Gesine, wake up. Where were you.
– A few years ago.

September 26, 1967   Tuesday
"Despite the forecast of milder days ahead, there was a feeling of autumn in the air. And it wasn't entirely welcome.

'Looks like fall is really here,' said a gas station proprietor in Upper Montclair. 'I don't know how many more winters I can stand.'" ©

Cresspahl never reached old age.

The soft gray-white light always new over the conspicuously green clusters of trees where the marsh used to be. His eyes weren't so good anymore. Time and again the smell on the west wind of leaves still undiminished and fresh. So much painful hope. Now there was a brown patch of scrawny sticks in the hollow, and the smell of mold until the ground freezes.

The town was small, like decades before. He could walk from one end to the other, take its measure, look at the children. The others were dead, of course.

A few days ago a sprinkling of snow had fallen, which would have had to go on much longer to turn things white, if it hadn't melted. Two four-year-olds were standing outside the Jerichow post office, catching the flakes in the bigger one's cap; they showed the people walking past, Cresspahl too: Snow.

Winter. Kern's granddaughter had told him about one winter when the ice had shelved off of the coastal cliffs, leaving high piles of slabs. You could walk on the Baltic. For Elke Kern, that had been a First Time.

The field his wife used to call the garden, behind the rack for drying the milk cans—he wanted to break up the soil there again. After his wife died, the fence rotted and the chickens ate up the garden and buried it. Then he'd torn down the wire.

One can also pay one's respects at the cemetery, if one is inclined to do as much as possible one Last Time. But he didn't know the woman there anymore.

Jakob, him he knew. He walked to Jakob's grave. Had a chat with Jakob. So, Jakob. How's things? Yes Cresspahl. Look at me, lying here on show. Creutz fixed up the grave like a display model, now he keeps bringing customers round to see me, and every time he says: I hope I'm laid out as nice as that someday. And then they buy.

Be seeing you, Jakob.

The cat lies all night where the stove has warmed up the floorboards, stretched out full-length. She's listening.

She's listening to the pocket watch on the table, to the creaking of the chair.

America is too far away for me to imagine.

When Jöche wakes up, he'll send his wife to look in on me. See if I'm still alive.

In Malchow, a master would be laid on the wagon and brought to the grave only by other masters. The clothworkers and cobblers, they had hearses of their own.

In Februarys, not from this century, there were market stalls in Malchow where they sold *Heitwecken*: stuffed cinnamon rolls sprinkled with sugar and cinnamon and shaped like a jester's cap. *Sevenny-four years's long enough.*

Now Jöche's bicycle was leaning on the milk rack. Strips of Jöche's living-room carpets were slung over the frame. Crates of empty beer bottles against the wall of the house. Jöche had left the railroad for the brewery. Where does all the beer he drinks go.

Oh, they got along pretty good. Jöche'd split enough wood for two winters. Jöche'd turned the soil after all.

He wants to seed grass.

September 27, 1967 Wednesday

On Monday, a bus driver in Harlem was attacked for the second time. As on the previous Tuesday, two light-skinned Negroes boarded the bus during rush hour and one grabbed the change money ($28.80) while the other put a knife to the driver's throat. The slashes required seven stitches. The other passengers had fled the bus, if only so that they wouldn't have to testify against the robbers. Now there are plainclothes policemen riding the bus in Harlem.

The East Germans are trying to sell several hours of film footage here, showing captured American airmen in Hanoi. Their idea of an appropriate price is half a million dollars.

And the honeymoon was over, wasn't it, Lisbeth Papenbrock?

And with no one to help her! Mrs. Jones, who had put a veneer of cleanliness on Cresspahl's two rooms and still came by for the laundry, couldn't tell her anything about the butchers and greengrocers of Richmond, she did her shopping at Brixton station. And, Mrs. Jones thought of Cresspahl's new wife as a lady, avoiding unseemly conversations where she might have to express her unvarnished opinions. And, she couldn't understand what Mrs. Jones was saying.

Mrs. Jones said: What a distinctive face! Gushing over her grandchild, who had flat cheeks like hers and the same calculating look in the same long narrow eyes, the same mouth pressed tightly together in a line. Lisbeth Papenbrock heard: What a distinct faith! She had to repeat the sound of this English to herself again and again until a memory from her schooldays vaguely snapped into place. This language was so fast. And even though the melody of the sentences seemed stuck on a single high tone, it actually dived lower and swung higher quite often, changing the meaning. She couldn't blame Mary Hahn for it; Mary Hahn had imposed a Scottish English in the Rostock Girls' School. No matter how slowly and clearly Lisbeth Papenbrock tried to talk, the salespeople still interrupted their weighing and looked at her mouth. Cresspahl, who knew English as well as a Puerto Rican after two years in New York, Cresspahl they understood.

And, she didn't have the words! She could carry on a conversation about John Galsworthy or Sir Thomas Beecham but had to point for a Dutch oven or a colander. Every night she had Cresspahl translate for her the next day's recipe from *Frieda Ihlefelds Hauskochbuch* (*Home Cooking*, 9th ed., Friedrich Bahn Books, Schwerin, Mecklenburg), but Cresspahl wasn't very familiar with cooking terms and didn't own a dictionary. (They had to buy a dictionary too. That wasn't saving money.) And then she still had to come home from grocery shopping and go into the workshop and ask how you say *Semmelmehl*, deeply embarrassed in front of the assistants to whom Cresspahl described what the thing was by explaining how it was made, using hand gestures. "Bread crumbs." And, she had to convert all the weights and measurements into English measure. And, she hadn't been expected to mind her sixpence on her trip to Richmond, in the restaurants, at the hotel, but living in Richmond she was expected to mind her pennies.

And, Cresspahl didn't notice how she felt! Cresspahl came upstairs at mealtimes, a satisfied man, stretched his legs out under the table, and praised the cooking. And, she saw something new in him: he could play deaf. What he didn't want to hear ran right off his alert friendly face like water. He looked at her, the corners of his mouth showing his delight; he looked just the tiniest bit past her eyes; he didn't hear her complaints. That wasn't how he'd been when she was still Lisbeth Papenbrock. She couldn't win a fight that way.

Heinrich, listen, terrible news! Pastor Methling wants to retire, he's only sixty-eight, he must be sick.

He's an employee like any other. With a pension, why should he work any longer than he has to.

Heinrich Cresspahl! Let me tell you! His work is for the Lord, and you're making fun of a sick man.

He's lived a healthy life. And if the Lord rewards him for his work, that sounds like a good deal from his employer to me.

After their first fight about church, she served him his meals but refused to eat with him. She left the house between mealtimes on long walks into the city, to punish him. She was cold in the foreign November. It was depressing how closely the historic buildings resembled her ideas of them. Flocks of birds over the rooftops on Parliament Street—she was less at home here than they were. A soldier in the King's Guard marched back and forth with ponderous steps among the passersby, saber in front of his nose, and he looked like a giant rooster, since his helmet covered most of his face and the red plume on top kept moving. Another thing she could never remember: that the Union Jack consisted of a red St. George Cross edged in white, on a diagonal St. Andrew Cross on blue, with a red diagonal Cross of St. Patrick on it. In the grassy field between Westminster Abbey and St. Margaret's, poppy graveyards had been set out for the military, the paramilitary, the groups of firefighters, and so on: little wooden crosses with red rosettes were for sale, pre-sharpened for sticking in the ground. This was how the poppies had bloomed in Flanders at the end of the war. They weren't there to commemorate the dead from her side. And when she finally went back to Cresspahl, past miles and miles of the same semidetached houses with the same balconies, now curved, now square, and the same painted columns, beneath the white-and-yellow streetlamps, her feet in wet leaves, she was not happy with the fact that her Christian duty required her to forgive him. It was hard for her to do that for him. She felt cheated.

Cresspahl thought: A hug is apology enough. (He had no idea what he was apologizing for.)

September 28, 1967 Thursday

In the morning, in the first shaded breadth of five glass doors, I see reflected the opposite side of the street, lit white: its framed section of shop signs, display windows, and pedestrians acts hurt, like some peaceful creature, when I make a fifth of it shear away on an opened door. In the second surface, of the doors in the lobby, the reflection is formed more blurrily and the mirror almost entirely breaks apart into equal-size segments of doors swinging next to me, comes swinging back into place reflecting the pale marble surfaces in the lobby, and now is an image made of shadows, quiet, moving, edged with darkness suspended from above as though by treetops, and between the sliding replicas of shadowy people the background has receded far away, a whitish sea light seen under green leaves, boats on the water, indelible well-known outlines before me, names full of time, and only when I lose the image at the fluorescent-lit corner of the bank of elevators does my mind give the happy sight and moment and memory a sharp edge of danger and misfortune.

The heavily overcast day with mist on the opposite bank of the river, on the parched colors of leaves by the blurry water, promises a morning in Wendisch Burg, sailing weather for a morning fourteen years ago, and produces a longing for a day that wasn't like that, creates for me a past I didn't live, turns me into a false person divided from herself by tricks of memory.

Conversation in the elevator: You know so-and-so? She got married, and he still had to ship out the very next day.

I wouldn't know.

Vietnam probably.

(Eleven people listening.)

Rain showers in the evening.

September 29, 1967 Friday

Now that's how it should be. That's what we expect. In the first section of the paper, our good old *New York Times* has not one word to say about the bullet hole made in the front window of the Franklin Society Savings & Loan yesterday. First do your homework, then you can play, Grete Selenbinder used to say, the namesake auntie, the aunt with the keys, with the crying. The homework here is air battles over Hanoi; teachers accepting a new contract with the city; the government of the ČSSR having robbed its writers of a journal; the left wing of the League of German Socialist Students in West Berlin being led by one Mr. Rudi Dutschke. "He is sometimes called 'Red Rud' or 'Revolutionary Rudy,' but he is no classic Marxist." That takes care of that.

Now you can play. On the first page of the second section, the *Times* makes herself comfortable, with epic photos and elegant printing covering 102 sq. in., and helps the dull-witted along with a nice play on words: "Two Midtown Bandits Ricochet and Retreat When Bullets Fly." She gets any mere pleasure-seeking quickly under control, though, putting this censure right at the start: The two men bungled their holdup "from inept start to ignominious finish." First mistake: They were conspicuous. Walked into the bank at 441 Lexington Avenue with brown paper bags under their arms, the kind we go shopping with, and narrow-brimmed hats pulled low toward their noses. Second mistake: In their nervousness they hit a guard over the head when he tried to ask them a question. Third: Insufficient familiarity with the terrain: when another guard started shooting, one of the robbers tried to pull open a door you had to push. When they finally solved that puzzle, they dashed out onto Lexington Avenue and vanished (in fact, "into the heavy crowds on Lexington Avenue"—an explanation provided for the benefit of the paper's out-of-town subscribers). Fourth mistake: They left clues. They dropped their hats and the paper bags in which they had planned to carry off their loot.

And now *The New York Times* puts on a show, as a well-earned reward for us after all that analysis: the whole story once again, from the top:

It was about 10 a.m.

At 441, that's on East Forty-Fourth Street.

Quiet in the bank.

Just ten customers.

The guard is in uniform. He is struck down!

The two men turn toward the counter.

One has a pistol.

He points it at the office manager, because the office manager stepped forward.

Some of the tellers scream and throw themselves to the floor behind the counter. From behind the counter, a plainclothes guard shoots at the two thugs.

They can't tell where the shots are coming from.

They panic, they flee.

Of the three shots fired, one made the hole in the front window.

Under the hole, out the window (as seen from within), at least eleven men are standing, all serious, practically glowering, deep in thought.

That's what we mean: the great scientific turn of *The New York Times*, its sober yet gripping contribution to the sociology of bank robbing.

And that is how a lady of the old school comports herself. She may condescend to film a bank robbery, but she doesn't tolerate any fuss.

Crumbs fall from the table on which she treats her subjects so importantly. We, forced to miss out in the office, can taste in these crumbs a hint of salvation—from our distance both from places in Asia and from the nearby building. We imagine her holding up for us the life we have missed, reheated but still fresh, as though it were possible to catch up.

On Lexington Avenue the sidewalks are even narrower than elsewhere, both before and after work hours—more crowded than the other avenues with people praying for a cab, cursing at a bus, setting their heart on the next shuttle to Times Square. We won't cross the street to take a look at the hole in the window, of course; we have a picture of it under our arm. Outside Grand Central, two newspaper vendors have set up their stall half immersed in the surging stream of pedestrians, compressing that stream into half the space, and whoever is pushed off the curb by the buffeting that results from the blockage hears them bark: "*Wall Street.* The latest. *Wall Street.* The latest," and, softer, "Thank you, sir. Thank you, sir." It goes lickety-split, coins and papers almost colliding in the same hand, and anyone with both hands already full gets the paper tucked under his arm for him. In the Graybar Building, in the dimly lit hall leading to Grand Central Terminal, two men stand behind a counter made of crates with exactly the same papers—silent, gloomy, blocked by no customers, but even passersby who have not yet purchased the latest from Wall Street don't stop, as though there is something suspect about any goods so unflamboyantly on offer. We don't buy here and we don't buy there, we wait for *The New York Times.*

To get his gun control bill through Congress, President Johnson has allowed states to permit the mail-order sale of rifles and shotguns. It doesn't have to be revolvers.

September 30, 1967 Saturday, South Ferry day

The reopening of schools after the two-week strike did not go off entirely without incident. As one teacher was walking into her school in Brooklyn, someone in a passing car yelled, "Dirty Jew!" The teacher happens to be of Irish descent. Stock certificates worth a million stolen. Fifteen years in an East German prison for an American photographer. The West German government responds to a letter from the East German government, apparently without having read it.

— Was she homesick in Richmond, your mother, this Lisbeth Papenbrock? the child says.

— She was trapped. She'd used up her own money, her christening gifts, on that plane trip via Graal, and on purchases for her kitchen. She had to have a double boiler like the one her mother in Jerichow had, of course.

— In Jerichow they would have just laughed at her, right? I guess she wanted to make the grade.

— And ultimately the people of Richmond forced this Mrs. Cresspahl to deal with them. She was a customer, and if she can't say what she wants then you just pull out all six drawers of rice and explain the various kinds to her and tell her the dishes that each one's good for and she'll eventually buy one. If you pile enough cooking pots on the shop counter, pots for boiling, steaming, roasting, casseroles, she's bound to recognize one of them as the one she wants and buy it. And, not being shy by nature, she showed signs of her mother's attitudes soon enough, her mother who was perfectly capable of telling a saleslady: You can take that one away right now, don't bother showing me anything so cheap. (That was something Louise Papenbrock did only when Albert was out of earshot, though. Albert didn't like her behavior to give clues to his net worth.)

— What about the people who weren't trying to sell her anything?

— At first, Perceval and Jim were embarrassed about taking their meals with the master and his wife, and to start with all they liked about her

Mecklenburg cooking was the money they didn't have to spend at the fish-and-chips stand. Eventually she learned how to cook mutton. (The butcher could tell quickly whether a customer was a decent cook or not, and his recommendations to this customer were good ones.) Then there was Mrs. Jones, with her squinty-eyed granddaughter—she stayed on out of curiosity. Street kids, a ragged freezing pack of them, could count on a piece of bread from her. When they were hanging around the entrance gate to Kew Gardens, she would pay the admission for one of them to come in with her, preferably a girl. There was one dinner for Salomon. Salomon only stayed an hour, but he did come.

– And the pastor.

– Not the pastor. She couldn't recognize her church services in this new language. She had more or less picked up the differences between High Church, Low Church, and Broad Church from the reference books at the library on the Green; none of these was good honest Protestant. Low Church might have worked for her, but she didn't have the courage to walk through the door. There were civilian chairs inside, as for a traveling congregation. The preacher might call himself a pastor, but in her eyes his splendid purple robe made him a priest. And she was confused by all the different denominations in Richmond: Congregationalists, Baptists, Spiritualists, Christian Scientists, Methodists, and Presbyterians on Little Green. In Jerichow there was only St. Peter's Church. (And, she'd checked: Pastor Methling hadn't retired due to illness.)

– Was she as strapped for money as we are?

– She had a hard time asking Cresspahl for more than the household allowance they'd agreed on. It hurt her pride. But she had a bit more to spend than us, and also the newly accrued dignity of a young housewife managing her husband's money for the first time. And she didn't want that house behind the gasworks, the house with a workshop, she wanted a new house designed solely to be lived in, something with bay windows or a balcony, with a garden in back ("for the children"). For lifetime possession of that you needed to put eight hundred pounds on the broker's desk. Cresspahl had left it to her to save up at least half of that. He could have made the down payment for such a house on the spot, from savings; he didn't tell her that. He wanted to give her some time, the way you give a child time.

– What did she write in her letters home?

– She bragged. What she described about Richmond was the park, the nice shops on George Street, equestrians in the park, parades of East Surreys in their red tunics, ice-skating on the rink by Richmond Bridge. She left out the rotting husks of buildings in her own neighborhood, where the working classes were shut away. If she was doing well in a foreign country, it should at least be a foreign country Jerichow could envy. Here in Richmond there were products from the colonies—coffee, tea, cocoa, hot chocolate powder—at incomparably lower prices. And, she wrote: Not a single one of the Communists' twenty-six candidates had gone through in the October election, and twenty-one of them didn't get even an eighth of the vote in their district, so they forfeited their deposit. (She did not write that Cresspahl considered Prime Minister MacDonald a traitor to the Labour Party for having agreed to reduce unemployment benefits.) She'd had dinner out once, at the Original Maids of Honour restaurant, for three shillings a head; she wrote about restaurants as though they went every week.

– Did she show him the letters before she sent them?

– She gave him the letters to read, and he understood what he read to mean that she was happy. He looked at her affectionately, from the side, a little from below, a touch uneasy, but so that she wouldn't see him looking.

– Was Cresspahl still getting anonymous letters from Jerichow?

– She got one anonymous letter, postmarked West Central 1. It was typed, and expressed regret at her refusal to partake of social interactions abroad. On the other hand, it said, she and a certain Mrs. Trowbridge would have a lot in common.

– She didn't show Cresspahl that one.

– No, she kept that one to herself. She hadn't breathed a word to him either about Herbert Wehmke, midshipman. She wasn't planning to keep it from him forever, but for a little while longer.

– Want to make a bet? the child says: I bet it's going to slam. Wanna bet?

Because some captains steer into the ferry slip too late, so that the heavy ship bangs into the wall of wooden pilings as it pulls in, hard the first time, then with a more muffled sound. Then there's the creaking of the thick logs in the frothy water.

October 1, 1967 Sunday; heat turned on
Now our morning dreams are interrupted again by the sounds of the hot water Mr. Robinson is sending up from the basement through floor after floor in exposed pipes. The water recoils from the cold air and pounds on every side under the unequal pressure, which means that while we sleep an old man appears, towering up by the head of the bed, with an iron throat, a jagged pipe in his gullet, breathing razor blades, eating glass and scrap metal. Little pebbles are bouncing up and down too, banging back and forth. The unexpectedly constricted breath of the water delivers quick frightened blows to the metal. The regular rhythm disintegrates into feeble, dwindling heartbeats. The fellow shows no sign of dying and shoves a barbed-wire broom down his throat, with scratching, tickling, scraping noises that sound practically pleasant. To finish the cleaning up, he sends in little men with sharp hammers, who tap the pipe with deliberate blows at unexpected intervals, alternating between the sharp end and the blunt end of the hammer. Then they're all coughed up in several scraping heaves and thud back down with a chirp, like their bones are breaking. The fellow slowly washes them down, but not in one gulp, they go down separately, hopping around like fleas. A heap of broken glass clanks down, the pieces clinking into one another without, however, hitting bottom in the shattering crash it has led us to expect. The shards are clumped together in balls of glass that someone is gargling. Now he gives a little cough. Feeling unobserved, he hacks copiously and repeatedly. Finally, he has a full-on coughing fit, his shoulders shaking convulsively. Finally, our sleep has been worn so threadbare that the images tear apart as they unspool. It is not a dream, it's the morning warming-up of the pipes. The heat's been turned on for the winter.

Dear Superintendent, Once again I cannot believe this noise.
Quite right, Mrs. Cresspahl.
Not in New York!
In New York the people living in slums have to bang on the pipes with hammers for hours before the super turns on the heat.
Is it true that our seventy-year-old building is falling apart? The whole thing?
Absolutely, Mrs. Cresspahl. The whole thing is falling apart. It's the mort-

gages, they're eating their way through the whole building, top to bottom. Good morning, by the way, Mrs. Cresspahl.

Later, when the heating has toned its excitement down to helpless hissing in the radiator valves, the other sounds of Sunday start to emerge. Here is the crinkling with which the fallen leaves yield to the shoes of people walking by. Here is the alarm clock in one of the apartments upstairs, announcing that church service will start in an hour. Here is the flabby mishmash from the classical music station. Here is the whispering wind in the park, bringing children's bored conversations in through the window. Here is the quiet clicking produced by the park attendant hanging with all his weight on the chains of the children's swings, one after the other, to forestall any accidents for one more day.

We mean the quiet park attendant, six and a half feet tall, skinny, taciturn, who greets the children as though they were his employers. We don't mean his assistant from last summer, the Puerto Rican, strolling among the mothers wearing his green Parks Department shirt and pants like a military uniform, gloves tucked into his belt like a canteen, hollering with the children, parading around in a strut until everyone's noticed him. We mean the black man who's been working hard, you can see it on his overalls; his gloves are usually on his hands, as he sweeps up the leaves and garbage, from under and behind the benches too, into a pile, as he would in his own lawn, while the other man, proud too of the glints of gray in his hair, talked to the ladies. The other man could read and write, he didn't have to keep working here. The black man stayed. He says hello to the adults who go to the playground, from long acquaintance but not familiarly, with a casual, as it were forgiving smile. We don't know even his first name.

Among the other early Sunday sounds are the creaking of the elevator cable as Esmeralda takes the boy from the West End newspaper distributor up to the fourteenth floor. He then comes jumping down the booming metal stairs behind the elevator shaft, three at a time, distributing *The New York Times* on floor after floor, five American pounds of paper landing in front of the numbered doors with a whopping slap, including the door to #204. Mrs. Cresspahl does not want to miss the Sunday paper again; as of yesterday, she is one of the clients of this ragged black boy who is about to let the heavy front door of the building bang shut behind him, his load lightened for the few strides separating him from his heavily loaded cart.

Governor Romney has spent nineteen days touring the nation's urban slums. He finds the cities on the brink of open rebellion. The New York psychologist Dr. Clark has described the ghetto Negro of today as cynical, bitter, hostile, and frustrated because the jobs situation, the housing situation, and the school situation in the country's slums show no progress.

The Soviets will put one of their writers on trial for having protested against writers being put on trial.

In the battle around Conthien, American marines have a new expression for death by artillery fire: they say he's "blown away."

Chairmen and shop stewards of seven unions representing employees of *The New York Times* have asked city, state, and federal officials for increased police protection. They do not feel safe from bodily harm while walking on the streets outside the Times building, which for the occasion reports its own address: 229 West 41st Street.

And the usual murders.

The park outside our windows is now entirely lit by the October sun that pushes every color one step closer toward the unbelievable: the yellow sprinkling of leaves on the grass, the elephant skin of the bare plane trees, the bright maze of branches in the thornbushes on the upper promenade, the cold Hudson, the hazy forest mist on the other side of the river, the steely sky. Sundayness has fallen on a Sunday. It is an almost innocent picture, in which children and people strolling along live as if harmlessly. It's an illusion, and it feels like home.

October 2, 1967 Monday

DEJ BŮH ŠTĚSTÍ

is painted in colored Gothic letters on the fluorescent-white glass surfaces cutting the foreground of the U Svatého Václava restaurant in half. The restaurant is tucked away in the East Seventies, in the middle of a Hungarian and German neighborhood. The way there runs from the Lexington Avenue subway, across Third and Second Avenues, past dilapidated buildings, over badly cracked sidewalks, by shop owners standing guard over their wares, under the watchful eyes of neighbors chatting on the stoops, between garbage and scar-encrusted cats, next to dismantled cars and the abandoned wastelands of schoolyards, to a little apartment building whose ground floor shows no sign of a restaurant. The blue door with its thinly outlined white and red rectangles denotes the Republic of Czechoslovakia, and the customers inside, at tables far apart from one another, speak Czech: familiarly, unobtrusively, as though the age of the bourgeoisie in Prague's Lesser Side, the Malá Strana, lived on. The regulars are elderly, formally dressed, dignified, couples silenced by long marriage as well as the solitary gentleman moving his lips above his raised glass as though speaking with the dead, the only ones who still recognize his doughy, old man's face. Younger and more casually dressed are the ČSSR's representatives to the UN, the administrators as well as the new power's spies, who here, unashamed by the presence of newly disempowered compatriots or refugees, eat away at the same homesickness for Bohemian, Czech, European cooking. Maybe they all know what "*Dej Bůh štěstí*" means; we don't, and Dmitri Weiszand won't venture a translation.

Dmitri Weiszand, Mrs. & Miss Cresspahl's host this evening, is embarrassed. He should know what it means. For he—this gentleman with the Slavic bones in his face, the thick Eastern European accent, the warm demeanor—is a Pole by birth, from a country adjacent to Czechoslovakia, and to their language too, no? Then again, he is Polish only by birth. When the Soviet Union annexed eastern Poland from the Nazi spoils of war in 1939, as agreed, it got the boy Weiszand into its clutches too, reassigned his citizenship, taught him Russian in the otherwise unchanged school, and another subject as well, just as difficult, called Patriotism. Even then he had to resign himself to the back bench. When the Germans reclaimed their booty two years later, they pocketed the Weiszand schoolboy too, but they had no citizenship at all for him and no school in which to learn Czech or anything else. Later, as an expedient at one point, he was a German for two years, and the Americans, when they let him into the country, put that in his papers as his country of origin. He can say probably ten words in German. And this Mr. Weiszand, with his youthful shock of brown hair, plump face, skin and expression almost unmarred by age, is in his forties, an alumnus of numerous camps in Eastern Europe, where he could have learned French, Romanian, Italian, Dutch, and even Czech, but the teachers weren't on the ball, and when he was finally unloaded in New Jersey he arrived with no brothers or sisters, no parents, and the memory of them was as hard for him to endure as the Russian and Polish languages in which they appeared. – I have a friend who's a Slavic professor: Mr. Weiszand says, embarrassed: He'll find out for us, *dej Bůh štěstí.*

Marie doesn't like going to St. Wenceslas restaurant; it is one of Gesine's whims that she indulges. She cannot reap amusement from the conversations at the neighboring tables. The distance between the tables, the white tablecloths, the napkins folded into bishop's miters all remind her of trips to Europe, and she doesn't like leaving this country. The story of Saint Wenceslas, put to death by his brother Boleslav on September 28, 935—the management's recollections of the good old days in Malá Strana, printed on the back of the menus—it's too long ago for her. The young students working as servers here still speak with the accent of their homeland and are too attentive for her taste. D. E. wouldn't like coming to a place like this either. Plus, she had to wear her red velvet dress with the lace collar. She uncomfortably eats some of her strange roast pork with the foreign bread dumplings, moves her cutlery stiffly back and forth, listens impatiently to the failed exchange of words between Dmitri and Gesine.

– What do you have to say about the German neo-Nazis winning 8.8 percent in the Bremen election? Mr. Weiszand says, fingering the edge of the Cresspahls' *New York Times.* Whatever these eight seats in the Bremen state legislature might mean, Marie knew that her mother would raise her shoulders in an unpleasant way, stare down at her plate, dodge the question. Now Marie remembers why D. E. avoids European restaurants in New York.

I already know it. If I have to live with it, then I'd rather not do it around Jews.

– What do you think of how Stalin's daughter is acting? Gesine says after a while, and Marie realizes that the question slipped out by accident, that she wishes she hadn't asked it, and in fact Mr. Weiszand's friendly expression goes a tiny bit stiff, and he manages no more than: – It's true, I was one of Mr. Stalin's movable assets for a while, but still . . . : and Marie gives in to her boredom and carefully, craning her neck, starts reading *The New York Times*.

"(Reuters) The newspaper *Bild am Sonntag* said today that Stalin's eldest son was shot by the Nazis in 1944 after refusing to make an anti-Soviet speech to Russian workers at an armament's factory in Berlin."

But Gesine's raised eyebrows, her sidelong look, not accusing but only troubled, is more than Marie can bear, and she makes an effort to redeem her behavior. She walks between the tables to the counter by the entrance, surly under the attention of the other guests, and talks to the old man at the register for a while. He is dressed all in black, he keeps his face impassive, his eyes rarely move, and she isn't happy about turning to him. But he answers her as though she were a grown-up, he doesn't invite the onlookers to smile at her expense, and while giving her the information in a quiet, indifferent voice, he offers her the bowl of olives.

– I can tell you what *dej Bůh štěstí* means: Marie says, back at the table. She says it twice, first in English, to restore Mr. Weiszand's faith in her manners, then in German, for Gesine: God bring you good fortune, that's what it means.

October 3, 1967   Tuesday

Emmy Creutz, the cemetery gardener's wife in Jerichow, sends her bill, as she does every October. Dear Frau Cresspahl, To cover your grave sites for the winter will cost six marks each, bouquet included. In addition, the annual fee for perpetual care is due: three graves, twenty marks each.

From Saigon, *The New York Times* reports bombing raids on North Vietnam. In seven raids in just three days, B-52 bombers have produced 110 secondary explosions. In one attack northwest of Conthien, the bombs produced 44 secondary explosions and three large fires, leaving the entire area in flames.

Emmy Creutz encloses photographs of the grave sites with her bill, for Frau Cresspahl to review. Lisbeth Cresspahl's metal cross has still not been scraped and repainted. Rust stains have been allowed to trickle down from the metal letters on the boulder that the town of Jerichow heaved onto Cresspahl's skull. The slab with Jakob's name, which is supposed to be lying on his mound, is still standing in front of it like a price tag. Where would Emmy Creutz be if she left the looks of the cemetery up to her customers.

Erich Rajakovic, head of deportations in the Hague from 1941 to 1943, has been picked up in Istria. He is wanted in the Netherlands for the murder of 100,000 Jews (approx.).

The photographs of the Jerichow graves show conditions in August, a flurry of wilted floral colors, no dark hues. Only over Lisbeth Cresspahl is the ivy growing that we wanted for all of them. But the Creutzes have to consider their bottom line. – The other two are lying in the midday sun: Emmy Creutz wrote: the ivy won't grow there. We're sorry, ivy isn't that much work.

In honor of the Soviet Revolution, *The New York Times* reports on the effects of the purges of comrades that Stalin carried out through Beria and Alexander N. Poskrebyshev. You could count on Poskrebyshev. He didn't even lift a finger against having his wife, a longtime party member, shot.

Emmy Creutz says she has partly applied our overpayment from billing year 1966–67 toward the planting of pansies (so that there's always something in bloom on the grave, Frau Cresspahl). She seems to consider it a garden. For the remaining balance, and as an advance toward the 1968–69 fees, she requests additional payment in kind.

General Poskrebyshev died his own proper death last fall, pampered in the Kremlin hospital. His memory was undimmed. He told a story there about his friend Beria: When asked whether a certain prominent Communist was still "sitting" (the Russian phrase for being in jail is "to sit"), Beria grinned. Nope, he said, he's not sitting anymore. He's lying flat on the floor. When General Poskrebyshev told the story he, too, roared with laughter.

The payment Emmy Creutz would like is: 1 men's sweater (acrylic), turtleneck, burgundy, size 48–50; 1 wash-and-wear dress shirt, size 43; 1 men's windbreaker, size 56, nylon, lined, not too short, whatever color you think best, Frau Cresspahl. Emmy Creutz can only have heard of these items from ads on West German television.

When asked about another victim, General Poskrebyshev screwed up his face and said: "Must have been shot. We didn't start using poison until 1940, or thereabouts."

This costs us Saturday morning in the department stores around Herald Square. Then we have to send the package to Ite Milenius in Lübeck, so that Emmy Creutz is spared customs for goods mailed from the United States. Ite Milenius has to procure official certificates of disinfection, or else the clothes will be seized for the benefit of the German Democratic Republic. Ite Milenius is then supposed to divide the stuff into three smaller packages for Jerichow—addressed to Emmy, Erich, and Jürgen Creutz— since the German Democratic Republic does not permit three articles of clothing in one parcel. For her troubles, Ite Milenius will present us with a Christmas wish list of her own.

In Darmstadt yesterday, eleven members of SS Sonderkommando 4A went on trial for participating in a total of 80,000 murders of Soviet citizens in 1941, 70,000 of them Jewish. In Kiev they drove 33,771 men, women, and children to the edge of the Babi Yar ravine, shot them, and pushed them in, in the space of less than thirty-six hours.

So who is the burgundy-red sweater for? Creutz, seventy-one years old, or Jürgen, the deputy commander of the Schwerin military district, officer in the East German army, and enemy of West German television advertising? Maybe he wants to wear it with his dress uniform.

In July, 72 percent of the American public were still in favor of continuing the war in Vietnam; in August it was still 61 percent. Now it's fifty-eight out of a hundred.

Amalie Creutz, the first wife, hanged herself in her bedroom in October 1945. She did it in broad daylight, around lunchtime, perhaps hoping she'd be found in time by the two workmen she had to cook for. She was pregnant, in her third month, from one or another of the eleven Soviet soldiers who'd raped her in the Countess Woods. Mayor Cresspahl's petition for an abortion was rejected by the Gneez hospital and the health department in Schwerin. (And Cresspahl was thrown in jail by Red Army counterintelligence.) Now Amalie Creutz was afraid of her husband, still in a French prison. She was afraid of public opinion in Jerichow, which would prevent Creutz from believing her. Jakob's mother helped bury her. In 1950, Creutz took to wife one of his employees: Emmy Burbach, from Reichenberg, Silesia, a widow. She was twelve years younger than him, and at first he was glad she took over running the business from him. He used to write on the top of her invoice letters to Cresspahl's daughter: "Dear

Gesine," and underneath: "Yours, Erich Creutz." Now it says: "Sincerely,
Emmy Creutz."

Then we also have Marie Abs's grave in Hanover, West Germany. That
one lives on automatic bank transfers. *If the sun fell out of the sky, we'd all
be sitting in the dark.*

October 4, 1967 Wednesday

Rosh Hashanah, the Jewish New Year's festival, begins today at sundown
and will last until sundown on Friday. On the occasion and for the duration of the holiday, the city has suspended alternate-side-of-the-street
parking. For the Jews, it is the start of the year 5728.

Rajakovic has escaped safely to Austria. The Yugoslav police had warned
him, not arrested him. (In addition, Rajakovic denies the allegation that he
made his money from supplying Communist countries with strategic goods.)

According to an analysis by Gunnar Myrdal, a Swedish expert on social
crises, the United States will have to shovel trillions of dollars and the
efforts of a whole generation at the problem if it wants to fight poverty in
this country realistically and without regard to race. Marie is entirely
unafraid to live in such a country.

Lisbeth Cresspahl was afraid in England. She was frightened by the
unemployed who came marching to London from Wales, northern England,
and Scotland with the National Unemployed Workers' Movement—a
ragged mass of men in whom even she could see malnutrition and miserable living conditions. She was one of the onlookers standing in a thin line
on Charing Cross, a respectable woman in a new coat, fox-fur collar around
her neck, shoes in that year's fashion, staring at the Hunger March a little
stupidly and deeply shocked. She had not yet grasped that the demonstrators merely wanted to draw attention to their situation; she did not trust
their patient, peaceful conduct. Moreover, the NUWM had been supported
by the Communists. One time she'd had to take a message to Perceval and
met his parents, the Ritchetts, Cresspahl's age, a couple in squalid clothes
and smelling foul who almost rudely tried to stop her from setting foot in
the house. She would have been perfectly happy to leave it at feeling sorry
for the young man for having to go home from work to slovenly parents

in such a filthy hovel. For a long time she preferred not to believe that long periods without work and income produce such indifference, which the Ritchetts too were ashamed of, as though of a personal failing. Then she realized that Perceval was supporting his parents with his salary, siblings too, because the Richmond unemployment office had certain picayune doubts about the extent of their poverty. Now she pictured more such crushed households behind the bare windows on the workers' streets and could almost understand the defiance of the unfed, preserving a sheen of respectability, with occasional shaves and bargain-basement clothes, only on the street and in the pub. She didn't dare try to give the Ritchetts charity; they had made her ashamed too.

Pay the boy more, Cresspahl.
Give him something from your kitchen money, Lisbeth, and don't let the competition find out.

When she was still named Papenbrock, she'd felt safe. She was equipped not with a concept of justice but with a feeling for it. This feeling, under the guidance of the Protestant faith, allowed for differences, but nothing too extreme. The poverty in Mecklenburg had been hidden from her—behind a Mecklenburg soul that was centuries behind the times, behind the Papenbrock family's firm belief in their right to a privileged existence, behind regular donations to the church, behind stupid proverbs like the one about virtue being its own reward or no one ever going hungry in the country. She had never felt unsafe there. Here she did, because she'd gathered from Cresspahl's comments that they were more or less barely staying afloat on the edge of the Depression due to the arbitrary fact that the upper and middle classes still wanted to spend money on restoring and replicating their family furniture. He also tried to explain to her what had stuck with him from Labour Party meetings: that the unemployment was caused by England's declining exports in every major branch of industry, and that a mechanism was at work here. He also seemed to think that the British policy was to sacrifice their own workers to concerns about the exchange rate of the pound sterling. She didn't like hearing that. It meant that her situation depended on economic laws and actual people, not on fate. She could have resigned herself to fate. Now she felt trapped. Charity beyond a certain moderately benevolent level would have cut into her housekeeping money, would have compromised her dream of their own house. That meant she was being unjust, and she believed that injustice would bring down divine punishment, whether or not it manifested first as worldly. How were the two of them supposed to live, in the long run, in a country where the churches and squares were adorned and filled with monuments to the dead in the war against the Germans? How much longer would Cresspahl be allowed to work in a country where craftsmen put ads in the paper with the promise ONLY BRITISH MATERIAL USED, ONLY BRITISH LABOUR EMPLOYED? What could they count on here? And, deep down, again and again, she thought: It's not so bad in Germany. Encountering capitalism for the first time, she saw it as something foreign.

This insolence—she got it from you, Lisbeth.
You got it from me, Gesine. And watch out that your child won't feel she has to make excuses for you someday, the way you do for me.

October 5, 1967 Thursday

Phonopost: one (1) piece.

D. E.,

the ads say this audiotape is "low hiss"; maybe what you're hearing in the background is really the heavy rain washing our windows. We've had Indian summer aplenty, and now it's over.

Here's some news that will make you sad: The St. Louis Cardinals beat your Boston Red Sox two to one in Fenway Park, and apparently it wasn't even an exciting game. What do you say to that?

Second, Marie. Marie insists I keep telling her how it might have been when Grandmother married Grandfather. Her questions sharpen my thoughts, her listening seems attentive. She sits at the table with her hands on either side of her face, making a Mecklenburg coat of arms, your ox head. But what she wants to know is not the past, not even her past. For her it's an introduction to possibilities she feels immune from. In another sense: stories. (I haven't asked her.) That's how we spend some of our evenings.

A lot of the time, my stories feel like a skeleton. I can't drape him in flesh, but at least I've gone looking for a coat for him: at the Institute for the Promotion of British Culture. This is located on Madison Avenue and Eighty-Third Street, not far from the splendid funeral home where people in New York's Social Register are bade farewell. The institute's windows are sealed, for the tony neighbors' sakes, and the facade has been given a face-lift, and the walls inside are covered with eighteenth-century paintings and red paneling. They must have flown in the shabby armchairs from a London club, or else had someone artificially distress them into their current aristocratic condition. The staff acts like this mansion is open to plebes only because of the owner's impecuniousness, and female plebes are hustled up to the archive by the back stairs.

They have on microfilm in this institute the *Richmond and Twickenham Times* from the first number (1873) up to today. The newspaper calls itself a "Journal of Local News, Society, Art, and Literature" and is a distant relation of the old *Times* of London, in its title font and the personal announcements as lead stories, but it's a small-town relation, with sensationalistic, rather common ads on the front page, at least in volume 59 (1932).

There are ads for "Kellogg's Corn Flakes," the same item Marie demands for breakfast today. It's amazing how brand-name products outlive us! After every war they're reborn, stronger than ever—Junker & Ruh, Siemens, Linde, Du Pont, General Motors. You'd say this was one of my disconnected thoughts. It wasn't meant as a thought at all, though. Just a feeling. An emotional reaction, you'd call it.

Right on the front page, in the middle, in bold, in almost every issue of the *Richmond and Twickenham Times*, is an advertisement for Gosling & Sons, Richmond's Department Store, and now you'll think I named Pascal's heir after them. But that was his name, I can't change it: Albert Gosling, patriot and informer.

This isn't how we spend every evening. On Monday, D. W. invited us out to dinner with the Czechs, and I admit it, you're right, he keeps confusing the person with his or her nation-state of origin. For him, I am Germany—the old one and the current two. For him I sometimes have no face at all on my head, just the national colors; to him I am responsible for the West German railroad and the West German Nazis. But it's not because I lack a sense of hygiene that I share his table. You and your fastidiousness. I'm interested in finding out what else he wants from me.

Did the article on the shrapnel bombs appear in the Danish papers too? In *The New York Times*, it says that two little (tiny) children were brought into a press conference in Hanoi, survivors of a raid from September 27, one with such extensive wounds on the face that he was unable to speak. Marie can't stop thinking about it. "D. E. has to do something about this," she says.

You won't be able to reach us this weekend—we'll be in Vermont. Your mother sounds relaxed on the phone. Mr. Robinson asked after you. So, warm regards,

Any unintended person who finds this audiotape is kindly requested to return it, postage paid, to Gesine Cresspahl, 243 Riverside Drive, Apt. 204, New York, NY, 10025; 212-749-2857.

That goes for you too, D. E. But first you should tell it what's going on with you.

And, since you want to hear it, I'll say it, in Platt: *When theres no one else around, youre the best.*

Oh, something you'd be interested in just came on the *New York Times* radio: In Game 2 of the World Series, your Boston Red Sox, thanks to Yastrzemski, beat the St. Louis Cardinals five to nothing. I guess you'll know what that means.

October 6, 1967 Friday

In Miami yesterday, five masked gunmen entered the du Ponts' house (thirty-three rooms, golf course, tennis courts, swimming pool) and left after a leisurely two and a half hours with items valued at $1.5 million. Polite the whole time. When the tied-up du Ponts got chilly, a blanket was draped over them; when a spot on Mr. du Pont's leg itched, one of the men scratched it. The du Ponts describe them not unfriendlily.

Back home, in the Manhattan banking district, $1.7 million in negotiable securities has disappeared. Back home, a well-dressed man (dark fedora, sunglasses, automatic pistol) walked into a Western Union branch in Brownsville, Brooklyn, yesterday morning and asked the manager to write out a $12,500 money order. His confederate had to come back from the bank (2590 Atlantic Avenue) to have the document officially endorsed.

When the bank called Western Union to check, Western Union, with the bore of the automatic on his temple, told the bank it was all right to cash the order. Then the bank tellers had to pool their money for the friendly client, awaiting his money with a smile and his beautiful teeth. It wouldn't have gone so smoothly if it weren't Jewish New Year, with the streets so deserted. This time *The New York Times* finds not a thing to criticize about the bank robbers' technique. *The New York Times* is amused. "Thieves had a busy day today," she says.

– So she couldn't have had anything to complain about in Richmond: the child says about her grandmother, "your mother."

– There's no comparison with Richmond in 1932. The crimes there were burglaries, drunken rowdiness, crossing the yellow line on the highway, traffic violations in general.

– And Richmond's attractions!: the child says, pleading on its behalf.

– Yes, the hardworking city of Richmond, cradled lovingly in a bend in the southern Thames, also strangled between it and the barrier of Richmond Hill so that it couldn't sprawl in land speculation and housing developments, and instead had to go up stone by carefully placed stone in the center; town houses and mansions arranged in terraces around Richmond Hill; a market town, city of gardeners, place of death of Elizabeth the Great, namesake of cities all over the world: Richmond, Kentucky; Richmond, Indiana; Richmond, Virginia...

– I've done my homework: the child says, in English, not unconciliatorily.

– She tried, our Lisbeth Cresspahl did. There was Richmond Bridge, captured on canvas thousands of times, by J. M. W. Turner even—an object of history and culture, late eighteenth century, a hundred yards long between the town and the princely edifices of East Twickenham, idyllically surrounded by pleasure boats and excursion ships. Lisbeth Cresspahl saw in it five white stone arches topped with a humpbacked paved surface; she was polite enough to commit the sight to memory, but it did not move her. Of course she walked to Richmond Hill Park almost regularly (always via Queen's Road, not over Hill Rise, because of the former brewery where war wounded manufactured poppies for all of England); she often stood next to Thatched Cottage (which for her had a Plattdeutsch name: Reetdachhus) and took in the obligatory view down to the Thames, across steeply sloping meadows, between elegantly, pleasantly arranged groups of trees, down to the bushy riverbank, the island groves, the water, bluish in the evening shadows; her letters also listed what you could see in the distance on clear days: Windsor Castle, the Berkshire Downs, St. Ann's Hill, Hog's Back behind clouds of chestnut blossoms over Bushy Park with its tame does and deer—but all this did not console her. The landscape had been laid out sumptuously, wastefully, it was intimidating in the age of its culture, forbidding in its magnificence, thoroughly foreign. And she went there alone, not for the view but to be alone. She didn't like thinking that it might be only with an effort of will that she could put down roots there.

– No one had kept anything secret from her.

– Cresspahl had prepared her. He'd called himself a kind of master tradesman and that's really what was he was, not a fair target for the criticisms she wanted to level. He hadn't described the area around the gasworks as a respectable neighborhood, and she'd gotten used to the gasometer, its pink painted dirty brown halfway up and peeling off above that in big rusty triangles; still, she was stung by the haughtiness with which the *Richmond and Twickenham Times* could take for granted that "few people in this poor part of town are likely to object" to the horrid view. She couldn't expect the good citizens of Richmond to welcome her into their neighborly interactions, but she didn't like how truly alone she was now, below the middle class, barely above the lower, and a foreigner too. Cresspahl had suggested she meet people through church, and she'd screamed at him, furious at herself for being unable to come to grips with the liturgy and ritual here. And now she thought it was horrible of him to veer away from the subject the moment the word *church* came up in conversation, calmly, not put out in the least, as though this was just an area reserved for her which he wasn't allowed to set foot in. To end the fight, she'd bought a King James Bible at Hiscoke, a used bookstore on Hill Street; Cresspahl had picked up the leather-bound volume and silently put it down again and not given any sign of understanding that she was trying. Sometimes she felt like attacking him: You have everything you wanted! and she shrank back in fear of her own answer: That I wanted. She didn't like the fact that such aggression even occurred to her. She put off going to the Aliens' Registration Bureau, often for days; she didn't like watching the official flip through their passports like things that were not going to be valid much longer. She hadn't reached that point yet. And Cresspahl didn't notice a thing! He took her to the Royal Horse Show one bright sunny June day, proud and happy to have Lisbeth Papenbrock on his arm, and that was how they looked in the photograph she had to send back to Germany—a confident pair, a happy couple, not how she felt. One time, she saw Cresspahl through an open door standing at a bar, glass in hand, talking comfortably with the man next to him, so carefree that it was like he didn't need her, so distant that it was like she would never catch up to him. She couldn't even reproach him for spending too much money at the pub. She couldn't complain that he kept putting off getting her pregnant—a Papenbrock daughter had no language for that—and that after promising him children ("Four, Heinrich"), she wanted to get started. (She was afraid of the labor pains.) There were lots of little grievances that she couldn't put into fair and reasonable words, and she felt so adrift that she even wrote some of them down in a little schoolbook so she could look over them later, maybe understand them. One August morning (the 12th, a Friday), in a storm with dangerous flashes of lightning and tropical rain, she was so plagued by the thought of dying and terrified at the thought that Cresspahl might find the hidden notebook afterward that she secretly threw it in the workshop brazier with the wood shavings. She was always making new resolutions but still kept getting into fights with Cresspahl, she didn't know how to back down, turned wordlessly away, and stayed mired for days in silence, concealed from the workmen with strained chattiness, but when she was alone with Cresspahl and the cat she couldn't even talk innocuously to the cat. Cresspahl could do it too; after several failed attempts to talk to her, he could live alongside her without a word, without a glance. What kept them together during these fights were the customary mealtimes, the moments of waking up, and only an awkward, mercurial time for reconciliation, without a word beforehand, in the North German way.

– That's the North German way? the child says. – I didn't inherit that: Marie says, convinced, relieved.

To date, 13,643 American war dead in Vietnam. Can it be that this is still not a high enough proportion of the two hundred million citizens of the United States of America?

October 7, 1967 Saturday

It was Marie who picked out the car in the rental-company garage, the car in which the Cresspahls leave Manhattan this morning: a sedan disguised as a sports car and named after the tough horses of Spanish descent on the American plains. It had to paw the ground for a long time in the traffic jams and construction zones on the Cross Bronx Expressway before, on the interchange above Saint Raymond's Cemetery, it reached the finger of the Bruckner Expressway and could gallop north to the New England Thruway. It was Marie who decided that the Cresspahls should drive slowly up West End Avenue, at practically parade pace, so that her friends might see her too for once as a child with a car. Ultimately, it's because of Marie that we're taking this weekend trip to Vermont at all. But she doesn't know that. She had to force all her wishes through a show of resistance from Gesine.

Whenever I was nice to you you didn't notice, Gesine.
You liked me thinking you were strict, Cresspahl. That made things easier for you.

And Marie smugly looks out at the New York Central Railroad yards alongside Route 95, at the New Rochelle, Larchmont, and Mamaroneck stations where other people go for the weekend. She refuses to react to the people looking out the windows of the Greyhound buses cruising like battleships past the Cresspahls' low yellow car. But she's acting a bit too businesslike when she reads the map, passes Gesine the coins to drop in the payment maw for the toll, scrunches her nose at the two young men in the Oldsmobile passing the Cresspahl car twice, for fun: she's exaggerating, playing. Playing car trip.

– So, if this Lisbeth Cresspahl, your mother: she says. She is staring straight ahead, at the four lanes, frowning, brooding.
– Your grandmother: Gesine says. But the child refuses to react to that.
– If she burned her book of complaints about Cresspahl? How do you know about it?
– She started a new one. It's back home in the safe-deposit box.
– In New York? At Hanover Trust?
– In Düsseldorf.

– Can't you make something like that for me?: the child says, talking fast, afraid to hear a no: Not complaints about me. What you're thinking now, things I won't understand until later. Complaints are okay too.

– On paper, with the date and the weather?

– On tape. Like the phonopost.

– For when I'm dead?

– Yes. For when you're dead.

It's not the same country up here. The Harlem River below the Washington Bridge was lined with dirt, debris, scrap metal, and industry; the northern stretches of New York City, too, were wastelands of garbage between dilapidated shacks beneath the elegant elevated highways; finally, there started to be old lawns in front of surviving old houses, in village-like clusters, a not yet bulldozed past, until they too vanished behind the simulated landscape on both sides of the expressway: soft blankets of grass on the hills the road was cut into, intact groves of trees at the horizon, useless and lovely under the gray overcast sky. Only near the cities does this arcadian picture fall apart—on the sooty empty factory streets of Bridgeport, approaching New Haven, along the black, swampy, stinking shoreline when the view of the Atlantic is taken from us. But afterward the land was once more used for no purpose except to adorn the highway, which gradually widened in long slow rises and declines, pointed to parklands of meadows and towering forests, was interrupted at almost decent intervals by gas stations and the pavilions of the Howard Johnson's. Under one rest stop's village-church spire, Marie orders a second breakfast at around ten o'clock, for her mother too, who has brought with her *The New York Times*.

It's in Canada that Soviet nuclear physicist Boris Dotsenko wants to stay, not at the University of Kiev, which authorized his vacation. There they don't like purely theoretical research: he says: And here it's more democratic: he says.

Earl H. Duncan of Bolivar, Missouri, has sent back President Johnson's letter of sympathy for the death of his son in Vietnam, as a criticism of his conduct of the war. He calls Johnson responsible "for the unnecessary loss of lives of young American men, not to mention the thousands of crippled and maimed." James R. Duncan, his son was called.

Now it's Marie reading out loud from *The New York Times*, just before the Connecticut-Massachusetts border, in bumper-to-bumper traffic moving only a few feet at a time. The taillights in front of the Cresspahls' car force their way into the inside lane, blinking nervously, and the Cresspahls can just make out the circling colored lights of police cars and ambulances up ahead in the mist, near the center divider. It is suddenly surprisingly quiet, above the scaled-down, slowed-down sounds of engines.

"He," Marie reads, at first with the speed of a newscaster, then slower and slower as the meaning of the words sinks in, "lay on his back on the sidewalk, eyes closed, legs sprawled, hair matted, face scarred. The only signs of life were the trickle of blood from the gash in the forehead, and his lips, which every five or six seconds puffed out as he exhaled."

– It's a good description: she adds: I've seen people like that, on the Bowery. In rags, no socks in their shoes. They're the ones who come up to cars stopped at lights when they need money for booze, they wipe the windshields with greasy cloths and don't let them go for less than ten cents. Or more. Now you're going to ask me what I was doing on the Bowery, of all the streets in New York.
– You were lost, right?
– You do realize you got a cutting board for your birthday? They were cheapest at a store on the Bowery.
– Thanks for the tip, Mary Cooper.

It is Marie who, after Springfield, Mass., finds their route on back roads through Polish tobacco-farmer country, an area of low houses built far apart, past Emily Dickinson's birthplace, then up above the Connecticut River, the wide waterway they repeatedly glimpse drowsing between the tall firs of the riverbanks. In the southeast corner of Vermont, between Massachusetts and New Hampshire, on the outskirts of an almost entirely wooden village, surrounded by a wet orchard, she finds our host's white shingle house, advanced in years and sitting peacefully next to a crimson-red barn that earlier generations once painted with the blood of slaughtered animals. Marie refuses to believe that.

Then the door of the added-on kitchen bursts open and a pack of little children, happy and dirty, rush at Marie. She stands in the middle of the group a bit stiffly, conscious of her dignity, her age, her status as a visitor from New York City. Is that what she wanted from this trip?

October 8, 1967 Sunday
– Where did you meet these Fleurys: the child says, not right away when we drive off but sixty miles later, after a thoughtful silence, and not accusingly. Last year Marie had still talked about "Annie," if not so familiarly of "Frederick."

We met Annie Fleury five years ago, when her name was still Annie Killainen and she was explaining to tourists the artworks and symbols in the United Nations buildings—barely twenty years old, a lively, strapping girl with appleblossom coloring, standing in our doorway one day and looking very disappointed. For the Cresspahls do not have their name above the doorbell, and she was trying to visit the previous occupants of #204. She too is from the Baltic, from the Gulf of Bothnia, a farmer's child who went to Helsinki and then Geneva with stipends. She could laugh so brightly—at her stories, her forgetfulness, her two left hands—that we kept her. Once we hurt her feelings by calling the Protestant church a limited liability corporation, but she was distressed for our sake, not her own, and she came over again, and brought Scandinavian toys for the child, and stayed overnight, a friend who insisted on making herself useful. Back then she still pantomimed all the American-style formalities required to make plans, and she had in her purse a photograph of the young man waiting for her in Kaskinen, a wholesaler's son more than happy to get a multilingual secretary as a wife. She accepted not the TV journalist, not the St. Louis soap dealer, but F. F. Fleury, a Romance-language specialist from Boston who earned his living by typewriter. He promised her the right kind of life, a life in the country, and we didn't like his way of speaking French because he, like Pauly Möllendorff in Gneez, did violence to his voice when articulating foreign words, as though contorting not just his mouth but himself, and the invitation to their wedding reached us so late that we couldn't make it even by plane.

When we visit them in their Vermont farmhouse, which he actually was able to put a down payment on with his translations, he doesn't show his face for hours, he lets the afternoon wear on in his attic room while we help Annie put the house in order for Sunday. For not only is the house as venerable as a museum piece, it is also falling apart from age in various places, and because Mr. Fleury does not here show signs of the energy he displayed in abundance in college football, our friend can't keep up with the housework, with three children,

– F. F. Fleury Jr., the boxer: Marie says;
– Annina S., the apple girl: Marie says;
– Francis R., knock-knees: Marie says;

and because she also has to discuss "choice passages" of Mr. Fleury's daily labors at night, and also has to type up a clean copy of these and all the other passages during the day. She seemed happy enough while straightening up and baking, and even though we were alone, with all the children out in the dripping-wet woods, she didn't complain, it's just that she hardly seemed to perceive F. F. Fleury at all when he showed his face in the kitchen and she wordlessly handed him a drink, making him a new one unasked every time, five before dinner, many more throughout the meal and afterward, until he finally found his way out of his stubborn, violent silence into the argument that Annie let pass over her, without defending herself, sitting slightly hunched, with strangely squared shoulders, hands between her knees, almost happy, as though what she'd expected was finally happening.

– You know them as well as I do, Marie.
– No I don't. I was sitting on the stairs in the dark. I heard you all. And I saw Annie.

toi avec ton âme européenne, ou même russe, peut-être. Rien qu'à vous entendre parler, vous autres! Mais la salle de bain? un champ de bataille où chaque jour de nouveau c'est le désordre qui gagne, les saletés des enfants partout où on met les pieds
ne dis pas cela Frédéric
tu ne te sers de ton âme touranienne que pour m'éloigner des enfants. Avec toi, en finnois, ils parlent de toutes choses, avec moi, en anglais, de très peu
ne dis pas cela, Frédéric

ton sacré goût pour la souffrance, ton accablement de ménage mal caché,
tout cela est abstrait, tout cela se plaît dans le reproche
  ne dis pas cela, Frédéric
et ça ne signifie pas comprendre mon travail. Mon travail n'a rien à faire
avec vos traductions simultanées ridicules, il s'agit d'une reconstruction d'art!
dont, apparemment, je ne comprends rien
  ne dis pas cela, Frédéric
vos façons, vos expériences, vos attitudes d'Européens! et tout ça seulement
à cause du petit peu de guerre que vous avez vu. Ce ne sont pas les Américains
morts au Viet-nam qui vous font de la peine, ce sont les Vietnamiens! Retraite
du Viet-nam, paix inconditionelle: c'est une exigence si absolue, si dogmatique,
d'une morale si enfantine et d'une imagination si peu technique!
  tu nous excuseras, Gesine
il n'y a rien à excuser. C'était pour ça que tu l'as fait venir, cette Européenne,
encore une, qu'elle puisse raconter comment le Gros Gorille Américain traite
sa femme. Restez, ne partez pas, Mrs. Cresspahl! Maintenant je vais vous dire
enfin pourquoi vous m'emmerdez. Vous venez dans notre pays, avec des arrière-
pensées. Là où nous tous partageons notre responsabilité, vous vous figez dans
une conscience morale absolue, et vous l'exprimez par votre satané orgueil pour
lequel même mon meilleur français n'est pas assez bon. Je me permets de vous
faire remarquer que, pendant deux ans, j'ai vécu à Paris, j'ai des amis à Paris

In Vietnam the marines will start handing out Purple Hearts only for serious injuries, since three decorations are enough for a transfer out of the war zone and the drain on manpower has gotten too severe.

The main medical problems among the Vietnamese civilian population are tuberculosis, cholera, typhoid, plague, malaria, polio, and intestinal parasites.

Dotsenko, the nuclear physicist so enamored of democracy in Canada, must first get a divorce from his Soviet wife.

And for the holiday *The New York Times* brings us a long article, delicious with specifics, about the Mafia families on Long Island—how they're trying to invest their money in legitimate lines of business and how they're jockeying to succeed Three-Finger Brown, as well as the latest news about Carlo Gambino, Johnny Dio, Joe Bananas, Eddie Toy, Vicious Vivian, and, last but not least, Sonny Franzese, on trial because "The Hawk" Rupolo was fished out of Jamaica Bay on August 24, 1964, with a slashed body, one eye shot out, hands tied, and concrete blocks on his feet. We need to send this article to Milan, to Vito Genovese's former neighbor, Karsch.

The New York Times came to meet us in Vermont, thick piles in a small-town general store where a disgruntled old woman suddenly snapped wide awake with curiosity because our car had the blue-and-yellow license plates of New York and we were there so early, having secretly in the cold morning slipped away from the house of our friends.

The Cresspahls exchange compliments. – You're a good driver: the child says. She says it only because now, in a gray early afternoon, we have made it back to Manhattan's West Hundreds, to the scruffy Puerto Rican kids playing on the dirty street, the crumbling front steps. She says it because we're coming home.

October 9, 1967 Monday

Yesterday morning, when Fred Wright, a handyman, got back to the basement on Avenue B where he sleeps, he found two bodies next to the furnace: that of eighteen-year-old Linda Rae Fitzpatrick and that of twenty-one-year-old James H. Hutchinson, both of them nude and lying on their stomachs, beaten to death, heads bashed in. The girl, from a wealthy Connecticut family, had been having a go at life with the hippies and unemployed in Manhattan's East Village for only a few weeks; the boy was known as a cheap source of LSD, marijuana, and barbiturates. People called him "Groovy," someone who knew the ropes, knew his way around.

Another picture shows a little girl surrounded by dense foliage. Black hair, black dress, a bit preoccupied with her serious task, she is marching a downed US pilot somewhere at the point of a cute little gun. His head is hanging forward as if the tendons in his neck have been torn.

Showers likely today.

Without closing her eyes, Lisbeth Cresspahl could see before them her mother writing the letters Lisbeth received from Jerichow that November 1932. The old woman sitting at the kitchen table where she could stare at the granary wall while she thought, the wall still often painted with yellow and the shadows of swaying branches by the low sun. Long pauses while searching her mind for the week's stories, head raised to the cool courtyard light, gaze fixed and unseeing. On Sunday, Papenbrock would add frivolous underlining and exclamation marks to all the Bible quotations and invocations to God she had put in. The fights between them had long since withered into teasing, and lately Lisbeth Cresspahl was starting to think that she and Cresspahl weren't far from the same arrangement.

Every Monday afternoon, whether the sea wind was sweeping wide shirttails of rain through the city streets or not, Louise Papenbrock would walk to the post office with her letter for England, look everyone on the sidewalk straight in the eye, stand in line with the letter there in her hand for all to see, and every time she would ask Knever, the senior postal clerk, to weigh it again and adjust the postage, so the letter scale in Papenbrock's office became something else they talked about in Jerichow. Her goal was to make sure people knew that she'd married off two daughters—one of them, admittedly, under police observation in Krakow at the moment, but the other prosperous, respected, and even abroad.

The more vaguely she described the news from Krakow, the easier it was to imagine what it might be. Just what you'd suspect from Hilde Papenbrock. She refused to take sides against her husband, Dr. Paepcke, former lawyer and notary, even when he used what his father-in-law had said was absolutely and irrevocably the last loan to lease a brickworks rather than pay back his earlier misappropriations. She let herself be talked into thinking there'd be enough of a profit to take care of their debts, and let him make it up to her for her worries with trips to Berlin, visits to one country estate after another, parties in the Krasemann am See spa hotel. Rumor had it she worshipped the ground her Alexander walked on; the fact was, she didn't want to rob him of any fun. As a child, when she'd done something wrong, her eyelids would flutter, escaping her conscious control for a few seconds. Now, on a calm wet night, the brickworks had burned down. The Paepckes could prove that they were at the city cinema, but when they drove up to their house around midnight the police were there already, and they refused to come in for a drink, and they were inclined to accuse the gentleman of being there, and of arson, given that their insurance policy had just been increased. Hilde Paepcke was asked whether she knew anything about any Hindenburg lights. Whereupon she'd denied it a bit too quickly and categorically.

It's not my family, Cresspahl.
It's our family now, Lisbeth.
Eventually you'll have to bail them out too.
I will not bail out total stupidity. They put a Hindenburg light on a brick
floor. Any child could see how that fire started.

The news about Horst Papenbrock was that the threatened encroachment on his inheritance had made him downright agreeable. Plus he was crestfallen at the Nazis' poor showing in the Reichstag election of November 6: as he saw it, his group's destiny was one smooth swift rise. He even seemed conciliatory to the sister who'd given up Germany for England, and in one letter he enclosed a photograph of a girl: a buxom brunette, her youth making her almost attractive if only she wouldn't keep her face so stiff. Elisabeth Lieplow, from Kröpelin. The picture showed her in a sleeveless white jersey, on its breast the emblem of the Bund Deutscher Mädel, the girls' Hitler Youth. With swastika. He asked for the picture back, but asked Lisbeth to make sure old Papenbrock didn't see it, not yet.

And Lisbeth Cresspahl, at the end of a long and detailed letter about the business situation and Richmond Park and cooking recipes, added a short P.S. – In March: she wrote. – Early March. Cresspahl hopes it's a girl. If I have my way, it'll be a boy, named Heinrich.

You mean Henry.
Yes, Cresspahl, I mean Henry.

That year, Adolf Hitler finally managed, with the help of an amenable senior official in Brunswick, to become an official citizen of the German Reich.

October 10, 1967   Tuesday

– Mrs. Cresspahl is not at her desk at the moment.
  – The police have two suspects.
  – Oh you mean the Linda Fitzpatrick thing.
  – Apparently they were having an LSD party in that basement.

– I wish the suspect wasn't a Negro.

– Well, you know, down on Avenue B.

– She had everything, the *Times* says.

– Daughter of a spice importer in Greenwich, thirty-room house worth $155,000, swimming pool, horses, private school. If that's not enough.

– Mrs. Cresspahl is not at her desk at the moment. May I take a message?

– Yes. Where she is.

– You used to live there too, didn't you? East Eleventh. Wasn't that near Avenue B?

– No, First Ave. It was getting more and more Hispanic. If you came home late there'd be Puerto Rican kids on the stairs, like they'd been waiting for you all day. Friendly kids. Only after they'd cleaned out my apartment for the third time did I move to the Upper East Side.

– My goodness, you know that Earl H. Duncan from Bolivar, Missouri? Turns out he didn't send the sympathy letter back to Johnson because he's against the war. He thinks the war isn't being fought hard enough, he thinks that's why his son was killed.

– That was in the paper?

– Yes, but where?

– We'll have to ask Gesine, she always reads the paper.

– But only *The New York Times*.

– So where is she.

– Mrs. Cresspahl is not at her desk at the moment. This is Amanda speaking. May I take a message?

– She was called up to the Greece office, room 2402.

– I don't know her at all. Is she the Danish translator or the German one?

– The German. Thirtyish. Nice body.

– Oh that one. She sometimes does special assignments for the vice president.

– You should invite us the next time she has a party.

– She doesn't have parties.

– Who's she married to?

– Beats me.

– You remember that picture of this Che Guevara guy, Ernesto or Anselmo or something? In the field, in the *Times* recently?

– Yeah. They've caught him.

– Who's they?

– The Bolivian army.

– Dead?

– Yup, dead.

– It's crazy.

– What, that they shot him?

– No. That he let himself be photographed. I bet that's not in Mao's little book.

– What does the *Times* say about it?

– Just go into Cresspahl's office. She usually has it.

– Mrs. Cresspahl is not at her desk at the moment. This is Amanda speaking.

– This is Cresspahl.

– Oh, it was nothing. Someone sent a sympathy letter back to President Johnson and Naomi said you'd know more details.

– Sorry, I don't know.

– So where was she?

– Didn't say.

– Wait a second. Amanda, where was she?

– Mrs. Cresspahl, I'll connect you.

– Oh shit.

– Yes?

– Sorry Gesine. You were gone half an hour, and naturally we were curious, sorry. Forget it. I'm sorry.

– I was in the vice president's office.

– Of course, Gesine.

– What do you mean, "of course"?

– Mrs. Williams said something about that.

– About the raise? I only just heard about it.

– No. What do you mean raise?

– You know. A salary increase.

– Sorry. Aha. Aha! Congratulations!

– Thank you very much. There'll be bourbon in my office at five. Bring ice.

– It was just a raise.

– That took half an hour?

– De Rosny is like that. I hear.

– And now she's throwing a party after all.

– You should come. She's fun, believe me. You'll like her.

– We're not really supposed to have office parties.

– Scaredy-cat. Where did you go to school?

– It was just half an hour. Don't be all jealous.

– I bet I still make more than she does. Wanna bet?

– Of course you do. Men.

– We don't hold it against her. Really we don't.

– I don't have a Danish girl in my collection yet.

– There you go.

October 11, 1967   Wednesday

How it rained last night! The windowpanes were crackling all afternoon yesterday, and at the end of the workday water was pouring down thick and heavy onto Third Avenue, onto the newspapers and handbags the pedestrians were holding over their heads. Our way to the subway entrance on Forty-Second Street was blocked by a big black lake in the gutter and an interminable red light, thanks to the rain and the police, respectively. Around ten o'clock, the park suddenly fell silent—not another drop to be heard. But between the scarred trunks of the plane trees the streetlamp light was caught in blurry haloes: the air was not clear.

This morning, *The New York Times* brings us the photo the dead rebel Ernesto Che Guevara. His eyes are open, making him look awake. But his features are sickly and his head is supported by a hand, which shows: Now we can do this to him. He can no longer defend himself.

The secretary of defense has stated that the bombing of North Vietnam has not affected that country's ability to wage war.

"So why don't we stop all the bombings up North and just continue to lose American lives in the South?" asked a senator (D-Missouri).

The letters Cresspahl received from Jerichow, that November 1932, were from the people in Peter Wulff's back room: sarcastic comments about their beer and his marital bliss; stories that emerged sentence by sentence from the passing mention of people's first names; and newspapers clippings. The letter writers wrote not about themselves but about the Communists from Gneez and Gadebusch paying nightly visits and having meetings to try to get back into their good graces. And yet these Social Democrats, now out of office, could not forget last August when the Communists had voted with the Nazis against the Prussian government. Back then, they'd talked about the "fat-cat economy" of the Socialists in power, and now here they were proposing a coalition against the Nazis. Not the Social Democrats' idea of dignity, you know.

They're going down hard, Cresspahl. We should get involved with that?

What brought about this political struggle in Jerichow were cigarettes made by a company in Dresden: Drummers. The manufacturer had made a deal with the Nazis to include a picture of a National Socialist politician in every pack. Böhnhase, the tobacconist on Town Street across from Papenbrock's warehouse, had put nice big piles of them next to the lighters. So the Communists asked the Social Democrats to support their own brand, from Berlin, but in vain. Someone came up with the idea of asking Böhnhase in person. Böhnhase refused to carry Collectives, he didn't understand the name, but he did put in a trial order for another Communist brand, Reds, and since Böhnhase was DNVP, the German National People's Party, he wasn't about to let the Social Democrats tell him what to do. The Reds became popular with farmers and farmworkers—the name sounded like something to do with potatoes and beets.

Nor was it the Social Democrats who had freed the monument for the First World War dead from the pretentious memorial wreath Hitler's SA had placed on it. There was talk about that in the Lübeck Court. – I am not aware of these snot-nosed SA brats having shed any of their blood in the war!: an estate holder named Kleineschulte is said to have shouted, arguably drunk and in any case late at night but still to great applause. This in the presence of a young von Plessen. Kleineschulte went on to stick the remains of the wreath on his dung heap. Horst Papenbrock couldn't understand it, this Kleineschulte, owner of some two hundred acres on the Baltic, had earlier contributed money to the Nazi Party. He had recently started squinting one eye at young Papenbrock whenever he rode past in his carriage, which made him look even drowsier and more spiteful than usual, and that was when he was sober.

On the road to Rande, a young shoemaker, a registered member of the Hitler Youth, was beaten so badly it took him three hours to crawl back to the hospital in Jerichow. The country gendarme was on vacation; the city police were busy. The aristocracy didn't object. – You bed em you wed em, Kleineschulte apparently said, and this time not in a back room of the Lübeck Court but at a city council meeting, on the record. The young man, still lying in the hospital with a broken arm, didn't feel comfortable with the hue and cry about his martyrdom from the local Jerichow branch of the NSDAP, and one night, after seeing his picture in the Gneez paper for the second time, he tied two sheets together, climbed down to the street, and skipped town. If you believed Frieda Klütz, he was now in Hamburg, because a telegram had been sent to his parents from there, admittedly unsigned. Frieda Klütz was prepared to say what was in the telegram too, to anyone who would listen, but Peter Wulff knew already and left the old maid hanging, ready to burst with her untold secret. Erich Schulz was the young man's name, one of the Schulzes from Outer Jerichow, the little hamlet east of the Rande country road.

– We have them here too: Cresspahl wrote. – Here they call themselves Fascists. Their headquarters is in Chelsea, with guards at the door and troop transport trucks in the yard. Playing Freikorps. But I don't think they're allowed to kill anyone yet. Do you know someone named Elisabeth Lieplow, from Kröpelin? Drop me a line, stay in touch.

The New York Times has asked around in Manhattan's East Village on our behalf. What do the people who live there have to say about hippies?

– The love thing is dead. The flower thing is dead. (A tall young man with wire-rimmed glasses.)
– The hippies really bug us, because we know they can come down here and play their games for a while and then split. And we can't, man. (A young Negro.)
– They're saying drop out of society. That's not where it's at for our young men—they want in! (A young Negro former gang leader, who now works with local youths.)

– Groovy Hutchinson would have been dead in four years anyway. He was on *meth*, and you know what they say, "speed kills." But he didn't care. He was beautiful. (A girl called Ghost.)

October 12, 1967 Thursday, Columbus Day

The tellers' windows are closed for the holiday, but people are working on every floor of the bank above the lobby. The restaurant in the basement was so crowded at lunchtime that a line of people stood waiting, staring down at seated eaters' necks, while the waitresses whipped away empty plates so greedily that reading the paper was out of the question. We couldn't get our regular waitress either—the brisk, distracted, attentive one who complains so delightfully and says, as though to a comrade in suffering: Oh, Gesine . . .

The New York Times has received a report from La Paz that the guerilla Ernesto Che Guevara probably lived another twenty-four hours after his capture before being killed. Seven bullets, one fatal wound in each lung and a third straight through the heart.

The Soviet Union has replaced 80 percent of the planes, tanks, and artillery that the Arabs lost during the Six-Day War in June, according to the Israelis, who are seeking permits from the Western powers to buy more weapons.

And the mail today is delivered as usual too. The phonopost from Greece is already unpacked and ready to go in the tape player Marie has set up. She is sitting at the other end of the table, waiting to hear it, eager, bright-eyed. She's already listened to it twice.

To phone number SIX-AUKS in New York. To the authorized personnel of apartment 204. Dear colleagues and friends, patriots and traitors, dear six razorbill auks, murrelet auks, Icelandic great auks, puffins, and dovekies. Greetings.

You have you're a bit you've labeled the tape can't I change it do I have to erase one of your words with every word of mine why. Why Gesine are you only lending me your voice not giving it why if you trusted my promises I could have recorded over it anyway oh yes. No.

Dear Mary, Mary, not contrary, I did it the way you guys told me to.

When I got there everybody was there already and I went to your hotel in Copenhagen and had a room up so high where the rooms never stop flying out over the crooked red roofs it smelled like America in the halls not Hilton more like Sheraton Boston. The Danes were all mad that a West German a Defense Department engineer had called Jutland the ideal unsinkable aircraft carrier of the Bundesrepublik they should just sink themselves all right so much for state secrets. With my Danish I don't know something is rotten in it.

Raced a gate agent at Kastrup on the scooters they have there they do Marie airport scooters. Two East German planes standing there in the rain little tear-stained dogs seriously. On the contrary Communism is good for you get some today ask for it by name.

Not Germany. Already knew how to sink it in case of emergency totally perfect nothing but Swiss on the plane a big family on their way home with my French I don't know something is gamy in it. In the West German news magazine they actually without batting an eye printed our daft old Auntie Hallelujah what she calls memoirs no it's true phone-tapping scandal can West Berlin be saved now they've got enough of that. Lake Constance at the Überlingen end like rotting soup then Switzerland blue and white and green colors so pure you could run experiments on them.

Zürich stopover the snack bar was besieged by a group of traveling musicians from New Orleans if you ask me Birmingham two girls delicate as little birds dressed exactly like your great-grandmother as a child Henriette von Heintz did I get that right they wanted Sprite don't have any the men wanted hamburgers don't have any I translated what they wanted into close approximations the waitress asked And what would the Negro gentleman like and I gasped. The shit follows you everywhere I had just been feeling almost homesick.

Dear Mary I have obtained a passel of caran d'ache that's the word the Russians used when they invented the pencil. Karandasch. *Svetlana A. Stalina s karandaschom.*

You can have your Karsch. No answer to my first telegram a big article di Karsch in the paper an analysis of the German firm Quandt one of the bosses just died in a plane crash here near Turin Karsch is leading the Italian business world through the icons of the West German financial pages if you ask me after my second telegram he told me to meet him at a café at

La Scala after waiting two hours I left and that's why I'm landing in Milan now. Milano.

In a letter from a reader in the West German news magazine thirty-seven labels for Düsseldorf including newspaper city city of academic publishing film city the writing desk of the Ruhr city of postmarks city of lakes city of US peace dollars city of rest and relaxation pearl of the world's airports is that where you two lived. Düsseldorf city of local newspapers.

Public outrage in Italy because the Coca-Cola Company is keeping its flavor a secret that breaks the local laws Coke requests a new law and in West Germany they already have one only two people know the recipe for Coke chief chemists in Atlanta they are never allowed to fly on the same plane otherwise not even Coke would know what it's made of anymore the Italian chemists are helpless they would really have liked one of the two special canisters of concentrate that are flown in from Atlanta. No state secrets other than that.

What you can now hear is the unmistakable unique sound of a DC-9 engine starting its descent to the Albanian coast now it's turning around after all I shouldn't say this I'm not saying it obviously I can live without you two but I don't want to many thanks for your nasty remarks about my beloved Boston Red Sox the day will come descending now into Athens.

Dear censor this communiqué is in clear not encrypted Missingsch my Greek I don't know needs brushing up there's nothing more to it everything's on it so kindly be careful when you rewind I demand compensation for any and every erased comma Missingsch is an impure alloy of Plattdeutsch pronunciation and High German linguistic development remember that Marie yours D. E.

I won't say it. End of message.

October 13, 1967 Friday; Yom Kippur, the Jewish Day of Atonement
For a while now Manhattan's buses have been driving ridiculous slogans around on their long temples, on either side of the route number; at night we saw them glowing fluorescent white beneath our windows, urging everyone to SAY HELLO TO A STRANGER, a half-bald Latin American type holding out an inviting hand; DECRY COMPLACENCY, unlike the groggy

overindulger shown here; BE KIND, BE GENTLE, as a lamb, say. We have not yet been able to put these suggestions into practice, we have merely taken note of them. Now they're real, since *The New York Times*, the paper of record, is reporting on them. The Transit Authority received a shipment of new buses before they could sell the advertising space on them. That's what really happened. All these exhortations to good deeds mean nothing more than THIS SPACE AVAILABLE.

The secretary of state, the Honorable Dean Rusk, firmly believes that backing out of our treaty obligations to South Vietnam would subject the country to mortal danger. Incidentally, he is not the least little bit intimidated by antiwar intellectuals; he says Einstein was a genius in mathematical physics, an amateur in music, and a baby in politics.

The Soviet Union has increased its annual military spending by 15 percent, to 16,700,000,000 rubles.

Was it possible in early 1933 to see what was coming?

Cresspahl sent Peter Wulff, Jerichow/Meckl., a clipping from the *News Chronicle*, from the first week in January: Germany, it said, would have a good year, if current indications were not deceiving. The economic recovery anticipated for 1933 would put an end to the Red menace in Germany. This was the kind of thing they sent each other, as hints, as requests for information, as banter. Neither believed in recovery. What Peter Wulff believed from *The Gneez Daily News* were the official announcements and the local news, at least half of it.

– If there is one it won't be in Mecklenburg: he wrote back.

– The government in Schwerin is freezing payments until the end of the month, except for interest payments and their own wages. Now a lawyer from Rostock has opened bankruptcy proceedings against the state, good for him. Stay where you are, man, which is not to say I approve of English beer in the slightest. Warm regards, Wulff.

– How did they get to be friends?

– Maybe it was because they were the same age. Both middle class, for a few years both had been members of the Social Democrats. The main thing was they could be together, sit together, without talking. That only looked like closeness. And they both liked pulling the other's leg, and could take it as well as dish it out. Cresspahl had watched in silent amusement as Meta Wulff kindly, approvingly rubbed her husband's back, while Peter tilted his head, a bit martyred before Cresspahl's eyes. Cresspahl had had to let Meta Wulff talk about May–December marriages, and Peter Wulff had looked at him, apparently neutral but clearly enjoying his defenseless condition.

– Is that North German too?
– It's Mecklenburgish, and that's something you did inherit.
– Well, if it's practical then I don't mind.
– And they'd both seen service on the western front.

The western front came up in the clippings from the *Daily Express* that Cresspahl mailed to Wulff's pub and general store along with a sheet of paper on which Lisbeth Cresspahl had translated the marked passages. In Germany, the war veteran August Jäger had just been sentenced for "desertion and treason." In April 1915, he had been taken prisoner by a French patrol near Langemarck and had revealed details about a planned German gas attack: the date, and how many gas cylinders there were, and where they were stored. On April 14, the English liaison officer for the two French divisions went to English Second Army headquarters and reported that there were sixty gas cylinders just behind the German lines, in bombproof concrete bunkers, one every twenty to forty meters all along the Twenty-Sixth Division front from Langemarck to the hill. General Plumer did nothing but send a squadron of reconnaissance planes over the German positions, who were taken in by the camouflage on the gas bunkers. He believed so firmly that this was deliberate misinformation that he didn't even notify the War Office. On April 22, the gas came and killed British and French men by the thousands. Now the *Daily Express* was calling for a trial of the Allied military officers responsible, to match the one against August Jäger in Germany. Giant headlines.

Cresspahl had no need to add any comment here. They both remembered it. Cresspahl had seen a whole schoolyard full of bluish-black corpses. They were of the same mind, or close enough.

Generals on trial, when's that ever happened.
This Jäger, maybe he had something against gas.
The Students of Langemarck. Stupid jackasses.

Singing the Germany Hymn under heavy fire.
They were in a hole.
They sang out of fear, normal shit-your-pants fear.
The heroes of Langemarck huh.
I'll tell you what you can do with your Langemarck.

At the Jerichow celebration of the anniversary of the founding of the German Reich, Mayor Erdamer had to stop in the middle of his speech and then, with a big harrumph, address a rumor that was going around the city and the estates, about which words failed him, and which, also in the name of the Stahlhelm, the Steel Helmet Brigade, he had decided to put a definite stop to, and also in the name of the heroic Students of Langemarck. He had gotten himself all worked up, he was aghast at ruining this simple story, and every so often he gazed almost pleadingly at his audience, like a little boy begging the bigger boys for mercy. *Don't, please.* Then, a bit uncertain, rubbing his stiff tuft of white hair with one hand, he released them to the fun part of the evening, a comic play followed by dancing late into the night.

Wulff had found out a little about Elisabeth Lieplow from Kröpelin. She was a troop leader in the BDM and had made a bad impression in the village of Beckhorst adjoining the Beckhorst estate, not because she'd had her troop parade around in the currently banned uniform but because she'd sent them out on a Sunday morning, to the field at the edge of the village, and had them undress for gymnastics half an hour before church started. All the churchgoers had to file past a pack of scantily clad girls jerking their bodies this way and that, doing splits and back bends. Wulff made no mention of Horst Papenbrock because he knew Lisbeth would read the letter.

If we'd had breakfast at the 52nd St. Café between Sixth Ave. and Broadway yesterday, we too would have seen six men and a woman, all Negroes around thirty years old, walk in brandishing a sawed-off shotgun and knives and take $3,150 from the cash registers and customers' pockets, then spray their victims with a gas from black aerosol cans that made them unable to fight, to run, to see. The effects were not unlike those of the police substance known as Mace. Mace comes in black cans but is sold only to the police and the military. *The New York Times* seems to be suggesting a question.

Today is Yom Kippur. Since sundown, the Jews have been sitting and kneeling in their synagogues and temples, busy praying, fasting, and accounting for their actions. "Kol Nidre" is how the prayer for forgiveness begins. For a long time now, Marie has wanted to attend such a service with her friend Rebecca, but Rebecca wouldn't take her even if Mrs. Ferwalter didn't say she couldn't. We've never been invited for a meal with the Ferwalters. We're friends with them, but to them we will always be goyim.

October 14, 1967 Saturday

Today there's a picture on the front page of *The New York Times* showing in the foreground the well-known anti-Fascist Willy Brandt as the foreign minister of West Germany, and behind and above him, blurrier, the leader of the so-called Christian Democrats, who, during the reign of the Fascists, had been blind, deaf, and paralyzed. Also on the first page, *The New York Times* addresses the class from the valuable upper-right column, reminding us: "Germany was divided after a series of decisions by the Allies at London and Yalta in World War II." This is how history is absorbed from a distance of 3,800 miles; this is how she tries to make us feel comfortable here in America.

True, our Upper West Side of Manhattan is only an imagined homeland. We have adapted to it—permanently, indissolubly; we cannot hope for reciprocation. Yet an hour's stroll through the neighborhood is enough to inoculate us for years against the prospect of leaving. The bus driver who pulls over and opens the door for us in the rain today lets us wave him onward, and raises three fingers in greeting as the doors clap shut; despite being stopped almost immediately by a light turning red, he looks back at us without anger, friendly, like a neighbor. We'd miss him. The utility pole at the corner of Riverside and Ninety-Seventh, we wouldn't want to do without that. Every time we see it we count its burdens, we greet it like a friend. Not only does it hold the thick end of a whip with which it cracks the light over our heads (as a poet once said), it also supports the signs for both streets, two clusters of traffic lights, the one-way sign, and on top a little yellow light, which indicates the fire alarm fixed to its trunk as one last encumbrance. For us, Ninety-Seventh Street is packed with the past, crowded with presence. In the building on the north corner, behind a window on the second (not first) floor, is Caroline with her sewing machine—where we go to do our sewing. On the south side, there are deep trenches cut between the sidewalk and the buildings, and the Puerto Rican children on the basement stairs aren't there to play, they are on their way down to their apartments. They live down there. Across the street is where an old Jewish woman once stopped us, years ago, to complain about the neighborhood going downhill: it used to be so nice, so Jewish. She was a mess, like she'd gone a long time without a mirror. Four or five paces on the uneven sidewalk opposite—that is now her place. – They've destroyed everything: she complained, a tiny creature swaying on stiff legs. Maybe she thought these apartment buildings at the western end of Ninety-Seventh Street had been built as respectable addresses, for solid middle-class families like, perhaps, her own, who wanted bay windows and stone ornaments on yellow brick facades, among other things, to show the rent they were able to pay. The open trash cans next to the stately portals disgust her, the blaring of record players from the upper floors too—a greeting we've come to expect every time. We already know these songs about a Caribbean sky, from the transistor radio Esmeralda rides up and down the elevator in our building with; the music doesn't ruin a thing as far as we're concerned. It's true that the kids on the front stoops near West End Avenue let us pass through their field of vision as though we were invisible; Marie, too, gives them only surreptitious looks, trying to read from their lips the Spanish she can't quite grasp from hearing it. But these strapping young men lounging in the doorways have never shown anger or envy toward us. Yet we, in Jerichow, in our childhood fights, our childhood fears, could always count on our parents coming to save us.

And you want to live in one of these hotels when you're on your last legs?
Just look at this child, Cresspahl. Now she's promised me a house on Staten Island for my old age.
These hotels, if they promise twenty-four-hour telephone staffing they must be expecting you to call for help.
Don't brag, Cresspahl. Just because you've already gone through with your death. I won't need your help for that.

For years now, the sign hanging outside the Hartcourt Arms has said NO VACANCY, and another of these accommodations has just been given a brand spanking new coat of pink paint—that's business. Then, past the vomit-stained steps of the Riviera Theatre, our Broadway begins. Broadway is our neighborhood's main street, its market square. We hardly need leave it to buy anything we want, whether we're in the mood for Japanese beer, Kamchatka king crabs, Irish honey, Düsseldorf mustard, or Dresden stollen. There are Chinese restaurants where Chinese people eat too, Israeli diners, bodegas, an establishment called the Maharaja, Italian ice-cream parlors and pizzerias; newspapers for the Eastern European émigrés hang alongside the West German tabloids and news magazine. Here, at the shoe repair, the florist, the little delis, at Schustek's, people ask after our health, our holidays, the child's school, and we too resort to this consumerist social lubricant, marveling at Schustek's deft cleaver blows between the pig ribs, complaining about the weather. We are customers in good standing at Schustek's; we could get food for weeks on a tab. Mr. Schustek still has a little of his Westphalian German, and his two Puerto Rican assistants speak and understand enough Yiddish for the store's clientele. He doesn't observe the Sabbath; Mrs. Ferwalter does not shop here. On these sidewalks, we can tell locals from outsiders—the former give us a blank withdrawn look that only just betrays having seen us. We speak to the man working the afternoon shift at the newsstand only when spoken to. That's because last winter, bundled up tight and stamping his feet against the cold, he compared the weather to January in Berlin, and we said: We've been to Berlin too. At which point he pulled out a flask and observed us in silence as he drank, not squinting but imperturbable, until we finally moved off. We had called his time in Berlin a bit too precisely to mind. About the old gentleman nodding to us through the cafeteria window, all we know is that he regularly shouts "Hey, darling!" to us. He is carefully dressed in his old-fashioned clothes, and we can see between his lapels that he has pulled his waistband almost up to his nipples. With a totally empty stare he gazes out over his raised cup and sees something different. Cresspahl used to sit like that after the war—there but far far away, in a time that existed only in his mind. Now the beggar with the blue-black hair is walking toward us up Ninety-Sixth Street and we duck into Good Eats, where we are greeted as neighbors, regular visitors but not regular enough. The children of East Germany born the year I was born call that "perpetuating the capitalist system." Are we supposed to say: Charlie, you just want our money? Charlie would say: You want one of my triple-decker sandwiches, the way only I can make it, and you can get it in exchange for your money, Gesine. Right? Right. And your girl wants toast with maple syrup, the usual. Yeah, it's been almost a year and a half since the building across the street burned down. A ruin on a corner like this! Not that I mind that the cafeteria there is out of commission. It'll probably stay that way too. Takes a long time to start rebuilding because of the insurance companies, they don't want to get involved, our neighborhood's too unsafe for them.

October 15, 1967 Sunday

ALL THE NEWS, promise the words on *The New York Times* factory on the West Side as you drive past it heading north on the highway along the river. Only slowly does the qualification slide into view through the windshield: THAT'S FIT TO PRINT. It's hard to translate, even into English, what exactly the news has to be for the *Times* to print it: appropriate, proper, worthy, serviceable—who knows. The newspaper has long shirked the task of specifying its motto any further, but today it does give a hint, in a headline over an article about another paper, the Communist *Worker*, which comes out only twice a week and has no more than 14,218 paying readers. "All the News That Fits the Line"—the party line, that is. This is how the *Times* takes a dig at the competition, its own self-confidence perfectly intact despite the vaguer promise at the top of the page.

In a Newark tavern on Lafayette Street, the owner and two brothers, all in their thirties, were found dead this morning, shot at close range. Apparently they had been having a drink with their killers. It might have had something to do with dividing the spoils from a wildcat strike by longshoremen in Port Newark.

A sixty-five-year-old man, his throat cut from ear to ear, was found lying in a badly prepared fire in an apartment house in Forest Hills, Queens. His hands were tied behind his back with wire.

West German students have publicly burned newspapers to express their political opinion.

Heinrich Schneider, fifty-three years old, accused of burning eight hundred Polish Jews to death in a Bialystok synagogue in 1941, hanged himself in his prison cell in Wuppertal the night before last.

Marie's homework assignment is: "I look out the window…" She has been sitting by the window half the morning, at the typewriter on which she is drafting her essay. When she stops and thinks, her hands slip down onto her knees, she hunches her back, and she stares so fixedly out at Riverside Park, head to one side, that she doesn't notice a gaze on her, doesn't hear a footstep. Maybe she's taking a stab at the playground, which by now is clearly visible through the bare plane trees. The playground across from our building, surrounded without and watched over within by tall old trees, is a large enclosure on several levels, starting with a big flat area at the north end, full of slides, seesaws, sandboxes, and fenced-in groups of swings and bordered by mostly broken green benches. This zone opens out into a circular space surrounded by high walls, and in it a concentric area ringed by a metal fence; at a break in the wall on the southern edge, steps lead up to a terrace of benches, picnic tables, and an attendant's hut that looks like a little castle, followed by more steps up to the highest level, some fifteen feet above the playground. She might be describing: how the tables will soon be moved indoors. She might be describing: how the buxom babysitter with the rosy farmgirl cheeks has not been seen here for weeks and is now wiping children's noses and applying Band-Aids with her deft, stubby fingers, with the same lilting Irish voice, somewhere else. Marie might be describing: how the colors are tiered under the clear sky, with the blue of the steep New Jersey cliffs between the softer color of the vegetation and the sharper gray of the river, all sprinkled with sand-colored tree boughs and thin patches of leaves on the upper promenade, and, along the lower edge of the view, the poisonous car paint next to the solemn gloom of a park fence deep in shadow. She might be describing: Rebecca Ferwalter, whose muffled scream, in which a certain name can only be surmised, can now be heard from outside below the window. But Marie makes plans with her friend for later that afternoon and goes on tapping away at the typewriter undisturbed for a long time, before pulling the last page out and leaving the draft for Gesine next to the newspaper, not urgently, almost distractedly, as though her mind were still enlarging on what she has seen.

"I look out the window, the big front window of the Good Eats diner on Ninety-Sixth Street and Broadway, facing south. The time is an evening in late May last year. The building across the street is on fire. It is a two-story building with a cafeteria, a drugstore, and offices. The smoke was not billowing, it was coming out the empty windows all white, like fog or breath. There was a crowd of people watching on the sidewalks, mostly colored people, but well-behaved. They made sure they weren't blocking each other's view. I could see over the shoulders of the ones outside the window. The murmur got louder when the jets of water revealed flames on the second floor. The fire hid in the floor until it showed itself again with billows of smoke. Streams of water as thick as an arm shot up from the engine far below, and also stabbed down into the building from a cherry-picker platform and from telescoping ladders. A lot of vehicles were stopped in the intersection: red fire trucks, ambulances (private and city), green-and-white police cars. In the middle of the south lanes of Broadway, two men, not in uniform, stood by themselves. They acted like they owned the fire. The people on the stools next to me craned the necks holding up their chewing heads. They didn't always manage to lean on their elbows. Sometimes one of them tottered when a policeman pushing his way to the phones in the back bumped into him. On the other side of the window, the water was washing the front of the building and knocking the wooden shutters off. The four big billboards still stood high above the roof, lit by floodlights. This was the first time I had ever seen them. The street looked dry even though none of the hydrants sealed tight around the hose couplings. A block away from the intersection it looked like steam was coming up from the asphalt. Policemen were standing there with flashlights, waving aside cars that had no idea what was happening. All the side streets were packed with nervous headlights. My mother said, This is what it's like in a war."

– I did not say that.
– You did too.
– Did not. What I said, the morning after, when there were yellow police planks boarding up the building and the firemen were looking through the charred wood and soggy rubble, when the air was dry again: I said it smelled like war.
– We're not allowed to write about smells.
– Can you say "it looks a little like"?

Marie snorts unhappily through her nose as she changes the ending. Tomorrow Sister Magdalena will ask her if she was thinking about Vietnam. And then it will become a topic at the next parents' meeting. You are not raising your child properly, Mrs. Cresspahl.

October 16, 1967   Monday

It's not only Linda Fitzpatrick's parents who can't believe that their daughter let herself be lured to her death in an East Village basement with LSD, *The New York Times* can't let go of it either. On the front page, along with the 701st plane shot down over Vietnam, next to the vice president's fear of the Chinese Communist Peril, the newspaper prints a private photo showing the dead girl at the tiller of a massive sailboat and goes on to compare (over more than a whole page) the family's description of her with the statements of her East Village companions. The hippies say that the girl thought she was a witch. In Indianapolis she had met two warlocks, or male witches, in their late twenties. One had taken her mind apart and scattered it all over the floor and then put it back together again. She herself stated that ever since then she'd felt that the warlock owned her. The warlock, "Pepsi" by name, stated that she was a real meth monster—a speed freak. A good kid otherwise, he said.

Cresspahl suspected nothing, not in the least.

He had thought Lisbeth Papenbrock was settled in, had gotten used to Richmond, to England. When she heard the phone ring she no longer looked around for him but just picked it up, almost without thinking, and slogged her way through the whole conversation in the foreign language with practically no misunderstandings. English had crept into her German sentences. – *Oewe dat's'n full-time job*, she'd said without realizing it until Cresspahl looked up unexpectedly. – *Or nich?* she added, head to one side, embarrassed and teasing, so that he wouldn't put her mistake into words. In moments like this he believed they were thinking alike. In the Royalty Cinema, as Buster Keaton in *Speak Easily* blossomed from professor of Greek mythology to manager of a musical-comedy troupe, he had secretly watched her; he trusted her quiet, knowing laughter. She had let herself be talked into coming to the Christmas party at the Station Hotel for

Richmond's Anglo-German Circle, had suffered bravely through the singing of German Christmas carols, from "Silent Night" to the address to the
Christmas tree, before insisting they leave at the appearance of the new
member, Father Christmas with his large sack, so that the circle's president,
Mrs. Allen, had had to mail them the present for Mrs. Cresspahl later (a
celluloid baby rattle). He had taken that to mean: she no longer needed
German things.

He had counted on her growing interest in the town. When she expressed
her approval of Ham's incorporation into Richmond, when she mentioned
the mayor's name, Reid, as though she had known it for years, it sounded
like Richmond was her place now—she was participating in at least its
outward life. She'd told him about the work being done on Richmond
Bridge: a pier on the Middlesex side had had to be reinforced; about what
that diver was doing down on the bottom of the Thames, secured with air
lines, lifelines, and signal ropes; about the crowd of children on the river
path, passing critical judgment on the sinking of each bag of concrete and
transposing their dream careers underwater.

December 1932 had been unusually warm, with plenty of sunshine, and
she'd come back from every one of her walks with something from the city,
not with homesickness for Jerichow. She had left the bakery with her coat
open, for a moment her protruding belly could be seen by passersby, and
an old woman, a beggar it seemed, had said to her: God bless you, dearie.
The sixpence the insulted old woman refused went into her savings. When
Wright Brothers, the department store on George Street, announced a sale
in its upstairs windows—the massive corner building was going to be
renovated, adding electric lifts and a new tearoom—Mrs. Cresspahl dialed
RIchmond–3601 and had them put aside, before the crowds turned up,
the baby things she had her eye on, at the sale price of course. She had also
engaged with Richmond in the manner befitting a Papenbrock daughter:
reading up on the history of the town until she could point out to Cresspahl
the actual window in the ruins of the old Tudor palace from which, on
March 24, 1603, the ring had been thrown to the waiting knight, which
meant that Elizabeth, Queen of England and Ireland, had finally died from
her cold, leaving the way free for James VI of Scotland. Lisbeth Cresspahl
even knew this James well enough to call him a libertine.

All the arrangements had been made: hospital, doctor, a woman to help around the house starting on February 10, 1933—not Mrs. Jones, who had wanted to give up two other jobs for this one, but a certified baby nurse who also knew her way around the kitchen. Cresspahl had heard about the ridiculousness of first-time fathers, so he watched to see if his wife laughed when he refused to let her carry anything heavy, or monitored her meals to make sure she was following the doctor's orders. She did not laugh. Sometimes she seemed not to hear him, only the child beneath her folded hands. But since the autumn there had been no more painful silences. He often found himself thinking: It will all be fine.

Once, in January, he ran into her on a side street off of George Street. The sidewalk and street were almost empty. She could have seen him approaching. She was walking slowly, stepping carefully, one hand on her hip, not looking ahead but only up at the buildings. As though looking for something above their pretentious ornaments and domes. She held her face almost motionless. Her skin looked cold, red from the wind. Her gaze was strangely clear, revealing no thoughts. She walked right past him even though he'd stopped. Given a choice between her and the child, he would have decided against the child.

Then, in late January, she asked him to call Moxon, Salt & Co. on Regent Street. This was the agent for the North German Lloyd's. She wanted a steamboat ticket to Hamburg. Cresspahl was so little on his guard that he was about to answer right away. Then he saw that she had prepared for the argument as though for a difficult job, and that she would sit there like that for as long as it took, a little bent forward, her forearms on her knees, supporting her belly, submissive and absolutely unyielding. He cautiously said: You can't have both, a child at home with you and me in Jerichow. And she said, not unfriendly: How is the child any of your business, Cresspahl.

– And that's why I was born in Jerichow.

– Would you significantly prefer it to have been born in Richmond? the child says, Marie says. That's how her German sounds now. She is sitting with her dinner before her, fists propped under her chin, avidly curious.

– That's what I'm saying. To have been born in England, and grown up there, and never left.

– I don't get it. Oh. Right. Right, sorry.

October 17, 1967   Tuesday

GIRLS SAY YES
TO MEN WHO SAY NO
(on a sign at a demonstration against the draft in San Francisco). The
marines have bombed their own positions in Vietnam for the second time
in three days.

The New York Times has been informed in Prague that Miss Zdena
Hendrych, the daughter of the second-in-command in the Communist
Party, stole a Central Committee document from her father's desk out of
love for the writer Jan Beneš. Now the document is with an émigré organization in Paris, Beneš is in prison for five years, and Papa Hendrych is
furious at writers. Even though Vaculik, Liehm, Klima, Kundera, and
Prochazka haven't smuggled the truth across the border, just put pieces of
the truth on public display inside the country.

*Tovarishch Stalin skazal, chto my dolzhny byt' inzhenery chelovecheskikh
dush!*
Comrade Stalin has said that we are to be the engineers of human souls!

– Come on over! Sam says. – Step right up! Hello sweetie! Two teas
with, one coffee without! Who're you talkin to! Let's go! Three Danishes,
right! Here's yours, Gee-sign!
Sam mans the to-go counter in the back of the building cafeteria. The
crowd of people waiting in front of him is thickest in the morning, right
before work starts, with customers off the street as well as from inside the
bank, so he talks almost uninterruptedly and seems almost impatient when
his voice stops. You can't tell Sam's age by looking. Sometimes a familiar
turn of phrase makes him seem close in age to the young typists, whose
lives he knows as well as their names; sometimes his sagging features, wiped
out from work, put him closer to fifty. He is squat, stocky, fat in a very solid
way. When he's talking to a customer, something about his look hooks
into them; in his few idle moments, the eyes under his five-and-dime glasses
look heavy, sad. He moves quickly, making his thin, pajama-like jacket hang
crooked, and a little yellow something on a chain swings back and forth as
if motorized above the neckline of his undershirt. His voice changes volume
like someone's flipped a switch: after saying hello in a casual, conversational

tone he will produce a guttural bark to pass an order to the kitchen behind him, and then, precisely articulated, call out the orders ready for pickup. But he's more than an announcer—he takes money, makes change, grabs filled bags from the service hatch, and writes down new orders coming in over his three phones on the wall, and to these he has to staple the accompanying cash slips, marking them with a quick handwritten swirl that always starts with the same cramped arc, its meaning revealed only by the various executions of the long tail. To write he has to hunch over and rest on his elbows; to take orders he has to stand up straight and tap his fingers in the air to encourage his customer to talk faster; to reach the kitchen hatch he has to turn his hips; when one of his three phones chirps, he has to reach over to the wall while balancing a bag full of coffee cups on his other, open hand. Sometimes he runs out of hands. He never complains; only when he presses the back of his hand against his receding hair is anything like suffering visible.

The first few times, he seemed overwhelmed; by now, he strikes us as being happy at his job, if only because he can do it so well. He talks no differently to the bank employees than he does to the deliverymen, mostly black or shabby white men, who carry the call-in orders upstairs to the bank offices and to the surrounding buildings, except for the encouraging word he occasionally gives the deliverymen along with the order. Something like: Attaboy—almost as if talking to a child. Still, the embattled bag-bearers often acknowledge his good intentions with a martyred smile. Nor does he draw his customers into conversation indiscriminately—his interlocutor needs to be in the mood. Never once has he honored with a single word the gentleman who comes down the long hall toward him five mornings a week, in a leather jacket instead of a suit, even though the bag for this customer is ready on the counter the moment he reaches it, with exact change always in his hand, and the two men briefly glance into each other's eyes and part in silence, so we will never know what's in the man's bag, a full breakfast or a Diet Coke, because his order is never called out. Others he calls Jennifer dear, wishing them an extra good morning, complimenting their haircuts, noticing a new sweater at first glance, and the advice he most often gives is that classic American line: *Take it easy.* He can come up out of his writing crouch and say, with an almost nurturing look: So, something to eat today too?, and it's not a sales pitch, and he never extorts the purchaser's loyalty with even two words inviting them to come again. That's why we do come again, and accept his help getting through the start of the day. – We're very grateful to you, Sam.

The lady who sits at the register some days—elegant, petite, playing with her necklace with hands that show absolutely no trace of work—calls him by another name, though: Jerome, or Jeremy. Maybe he's trying to make it easier and more efficient to deal with him, as Sam.

In the early afternoon, when the herd of tables crouch empty and abandoned by the street window and even the swivel stools at the three horseshoe counters are only sparsely occupied, Sam has nothing but phone orders to deal with, coffee for the hungover and ice for the early drinkers, and he chats on the side with the eaters perched at his counter. Today he's talking about the murdered Linda Fitzpatrick's predilection for methamphetamine hydrochloride, speed, the drug that gives an incredibly racing heightened awareness before felling its victim, broken and shattered. He can't understand it. – If I couldn't stay awake without that, fuggedaboutit: he says.

– And giving the address! A paper like the *Times*! Describing right where you can get the stuff! he says. He is writing something down, he's busy, he can still shake his head, angry and demoralized. – Practically leading the kids there by the hand! he says.

Sometimes, for a few minutes at a time, the telephone and cash register leave him in peace, but he doesn't sit down, he stands stooped over the low counter counting money. Bundle after bundle of green bills appears in his hands, and the way the money glides between his fingers makes it look like he's washing his hands with it.

– Looks good today: Mrs. Cresspahl says. – Oh, Gesine: Sam says, joyless, exhausted, and now she sees something stiff and jerky about his movements, something hidden in the morning and lunchtime rush. She notices, too, for the first time, the deep-cleft wrinkles in the fat of his brow, the color of sick skin under his sweat. – This place: he says:

(and he doesn't just work here. He is not being exploited here. The whole shop is his baby—he pays the rent, he's the one who fitted it out, he pays the wages for three cooks, nine waitresses, two women working the register. He's the boss)

– This place, you know how I'm going to leave this place? If I ever do leave it. In a box, that's how. In a box!

In one of those rounded metal sheaths that the police use to carry off bodies, after two men in little black bowler hats pull their guns out of brown paper bags and shoot Sam for the pile of cash?

No. He must keep a revolver next to the register. He's not going to let them get even a single day's takings.

So there'll be time to fetch a coffin, not the final one but a plain reusable city coffin, after Sam slumps to the floor outside the kitchen, a little surprised, but not angry, at the pain suddenly rising from his heart through his left arm into his brain and snuffing it out. Hopefully he won't lose his glasses in the fall, so that we'll be spared the face concealed behind them. That's the way it'll be.

– Pract'ly there already: Sam says indulgently. Maybe he was beaten a lot as a child.

– Now don't look all scared, Gee-sign!

October 18, 1967 Wednesday

Today at sundown the Jews start their Feast of Booths, Sukkoth. For the Orthodox, it lasts nine days; Reform Jews celebrate only eight. The Bible mandates the festival in the third book of Moses, Leviticus 23:43: "that your generations may know that I made the children of Israel to dwell in booths, when I brought them out of the land of Egypt: I the LORD your God."

Dear Anita Redcross. Dearest.

I've copied this out for you from *The New York Times*, because the young man you're getting out of East Germany needs to know such things if he not only is Jewish but looks so Jewish that you won't want to use any passport without an indication of Jewish faith.

I've had them as neighbors for six years now and I still can't tell by looking. Maybe some people have the gift. I don't. Are East German border officials specially trained in it?

I've found someone who looks like the boy in your photo. Yes, he's twenty, not nineteen. He was raised speaking French, just like you wanted, a Belgian national. He's visiting his grandparents two blocks from our corner, and since we know old Mr. and Mrs. Faure from around Broadway and Riverside Drive, they vouched for me. Actually, they trust me because of Marie. They take the child as a guarantee. Unfortunately, they think we're undertaking this transport to the West out of love for the Jews, and they're touched. The young man who gives me his passport is doing so for reasons he considers political.

You don't have much time, because Henri R. Faure's visa is valid only until November 18, so I have to reattach the Immigration Office form on top of it before then, so that he can prove not only that he hasn't left the country but that the passport has been in his pocket the whole time.

You'll give your "Henri R. Faure" the usual history, I'm sure; here for reference is a CV of the real one. Plus a book about Manhattan's Upper West Side, *The Airtight Cage* by Joseph P. Lyford, so that your ward can tell the checkpoint guards something about his visit to his grandparents in New York, if he has to.

It was just by chance that I could find someone so quickly, and I wouldn't risk Grandma Faure's trust in any other cause. So let it be this one. Your nineteen-year-old couldn't take any more of the GDR's anti-Israeli propaganda after the Six-Day War and started talking, and had to leave his technical college, and now the security services have their eye on him. Someone like that needs to get out, even if he's in for a shock. Just please let it not be some love affair.

I wouldn't lift a finger for that cause anymore. Admit it, Anita! The Wall went up through the middle of Berlin and sympathy turned us into real fools. When one of your needy creatures appeared on your doorstep with some story about their love for a person in the country they were now cut off from, you usually said yes right away so you wouldn't have to hear any more lovey-dovey confidences. We should have listened a little more closely. Some of those people's pride was just hurt—how could the GDR infringe on their rights by depriving them of the object of their affections? Some men wanted to bring a lover or fiancée over just to show her how potent he was, in this regard too. Do you remember that poet from Munich who cried his eyes out in your lap? Two months after getting the girl he'd ordered, he tossed her aside. Remember Dietbert B., the photographer, the man of the world? To hear the two of them talk, you'd think their separation was killing them, that they couldn't live apart, not for anything, but in fact there wasn't enough to keep them together anywhere. Because absolute, unconditional love was only possible in the capitalist free market. What bullshit!

What I'm trying to say is: If you can't get out of this line of business, I hope you're not working Henriettaplatz-style for free anymore. It's not that I want you to turn into a hard-nosed professional, but you should at least earn the butter on your bread with these transports out of the Land of Egypt.

Part II

No. We're not homesick for Germany. Marie definitely isn't. She's already embarrassed when it comes out that she was born in Düsseldorf, not New York. And the house in Düsseldorf, the first place of my own, my first real home—they tore it down. I would love to be sitting under your gray skylight again, as it rattles from the roar of the jet planes on the flight path approaching the airport, but not so I could be in West Berlin again, only so that I could see your faces and hear what you're up to.

Around the corner from us, on West End Avenue, is the Hotel Marseilles, a crenellated tower from the Middle Ages known as the turn of the century, with air conditioners sticking out the windows like rows of false teeth. The establishment offers a Bar & Restaurant & TV in Every Room & Swimming Pool. Taking a walk with Marie last Saturday, the words slipped out of me: Anita the Red could stay there. It was another few steps before I realized what I'd said, and that it's actually possible. So we hereby invite you to New York to celebrate your PhD, some expenses paid. I'd love to tell you about a strange thing that happened to me in Minneapolis, among other things. And we would initiate you into reading *The New York Times*, the most experienced person in the world, the first to cross the Atlantic, the first to fly over the South Pole, the Firm You Can Trust.

Sincerely yours, G. C.

P.S. You are not allowed to put H. R. Faure's passport photo into someone else's documents.

Mr. Mark T. Markshaw, who is putting this in your hand, has been brought up in such a way as to be incapable of opening other people's mail. At this point, he knows only that he is doing me a favor. If he feels like sightseeing in East Berlin, and you try to question him about the latest passport-control ceremonies at the border, he would know somewhat more. You shouldn't ask that of him.

The New York Times is in a fight with another paper. For the fiftieth anniversary of the Bolshevik Revolution it had made the statement, wrapped up with a bow, that the exploitation of man was not over, only transferred to the world's largest employer, the Soviet state. *Pravda* writes back: That cannot be true because there is no evidence with which to prove it.

Three gangsters paid a visit to a liquor-store owner in Brooklyn yesterday. Instead of handing over his cash, the owner starts shooting. One of the bandits grabs the owner's four-year-old son, and one of the father's bullets hits the child in the abdomen.

What did Cresspahl care about the headlines in bold with which British papers reported the naming of one Herr Hitler as the German chancellor of the Reich! The British papers weren't too worked up about it either—after all, who but the leader of the largest party should fill that position, duly overseen by the assembled Right. Markets calm, the mark slightly higher against the pound.

But Cresspahl's wife had sailed away, across the Channel, in the middle of a cold snap from Russia, thirty-one weeks pregnant. England may have been colder than it had been for seven years, but Dassow Lake near Lübeck was frozen over. The fisherman walked out to work and chopped holes in the outlying bays. – I'm cold: she'd said. Then she had sailed into the cold.

The night before her departure, Cresspahl had gone to the meeting of the Richmond Anglo-German Circle, alone. At home he would have had to try to talk her into staying; she would have expected it too. The guest speaker for the evening, Mr. von Dewall, an editor at the *Frankfurter Zeitung*, described it as the Germans' desire not to be looked upon as a minor power. He anticipated a limited rearmament; he pointed to the example of unarmed China at the mercy of Japan. Dr. Jackson asked Wolf von Dewall for his impressions of England. The representative of the *Frankfurter Zeitung* spoke of the development of an entirely new type of person in Germany. The people there even had new faces, he said. Von Dewall admired the English. Slow to take action, pondering a long time first, in the end they invariably took a step in the right direction. Back home, Cresspahl couldn't say anything about the talk; the German hunger for weapons, the stability of England would have looked like still more arguments against going to Jerichow. He did not want to describe Mr. von Dewall to her—she would have taken his anger as directed at her. He sat on the edge of her bed for a while in the darkness. Then he turned on the light, almost without a sound he thought, but her eyes were open, she was smiling like a child who knows the surprise prepared for her and is playacting so as not to spoil the fun, her own or the other person's.

On January 31, 1933, the *Daily Express* reported from Berlin that a certain General Schleicher was attempting to found a military dictatorship with a military coup. The Potsdam garrison, prepared to march on the German capital, had not. The Social Democratic Party had decided to bring a vote of no confidence against the Harzburger Front coalition cabinet. On the inevitable other hand, the Communist Party had requested a vote of no confidence against the Hitler–von Papen government. Nothing new about that. To Cresspahl's amazement, though, everyone seemed to find it normal for a young woman to go home for the birth of her first child. Now that it was about him, he found it not normal. He overheard his assistants talking about Mrs. Cresspahl. Perceval listed the housework he'd had to do for previous masters' wives. Mrs. Cresspahl had had him knead gingerbread dough for a whole hour, but later she'd left a bowl of the finished cookies for him in the workshop. – I was flabbergasted: Perceval said. – But the boss's face: he said. A real lousy sulky spiteful penny-pinching mug he has these days. I don't get it. I'd be happy to have a kid from her! and Mr. Smith said, in a friendly way: Shut your trap, T. P. Mr. Smith, cadaverous from drinking, still had plenty of gritty strength left in his long arms, and he knew he could shut the younger man up with a look from between his bushy brows and the metal frame of his glasses. Mr. Smith's devotion to drink had never made Cresspahl happy before, but that night he sent out for some beer. And not because Mr. Smith was relieving him of the burden of educating Perceval.

In Richmond there were sixty public houses with liquor licenses and Cresspahl was out almost every night, as though he wanted to get to know them all. He drank slowly, almost methodically, until he felt tired enough to fall asleep, but the moment he left the pub, carefully stepping between the freezing kids waiting there for their parents, he forgot the conversations he'd had inside. He had laughed along with the others at the tirades presented to the magistrate by Miss Newton, an elderly social worker, protesting against moving closing time half an hour later, ten thirty instead of ten. He had been asked about the number-one topic of conversation in the city: the incomprehensible closing of the Richmond Gasworks and laying off of all the workers. And they still wouldn't tear down this rusty pink monster of a gasholder! He had to know something about it, had a business right next door didn he, carpentry or something. Only recently started drinking.

What Cresspahl could see before his eyes on his walk home through bare Petersham Road, in the whistling wind from the Channel storms, was Lisbeth's face behind the window of the train leaving Victoria station. He had been so unhelpful while searching for a last possible thing to say that she had taken care of everything with the luggage porter and the ticket collector before he'd even opened his mouth. She'd shown him that she would have all the help she needed on her journey, and that she knew how to get it. That aside, he had realized that what she was doing here she was doing alone, without him, against him. She had pulled herself up into the train car with both arms. She had stood behind the pane of glass, arms hanging, as though she couldn't open the window. She had not looked at anyone or anything but him. Her face was different. She looked younger, too young for her new experiences. She had a girl's face again, a bit uncertain around the eyes, a bit stubborn. In his memory, in the darkness of his deserted unheated room, that face had been still until it swayed with the jerk of the departing train and slid obliquely away.

He sent her a postcard in mid-February, the Richmond Bridge, and under the pier he drew in for her the foundations of elm and oak wood that had lasted in the water for 156 years. He wrote about the progress on the jobs she knew about, and sent greetings from Dr. Salomon and Mrs. Allen. Then he ran out of room on the card. Because, however much he could barely live without her, it wouldn't do for him to write it out for her, would it?

After she'd been gone three weeks, he was more or less convinced that he had agreed to her leaving for Jerichow. If he hadn't exactly urged her to, then at least he hadn't opposed it. Now he was entirely at ease, and in his memory she was, too.

October 20, 1967 Friday

The US losses in Vietnam last week bring the total numbers to 13,907 dead and 88,502 wounded since January 1, 1961.

Students at Brooklyn College, objecting to the presence of two navy recruiters, were roughly treated by the police. One of the pictures in *The New York Times* shows an officer, mouth wide open, venting his feelings on a smaller person, apparently a girl, with a billy club. The photo would be perfect for a wanted poster.

An antiwar protest is scheduled to take place this weekend in Washington, D.C. Paratroop units from the army's Eighty-Second Airborne Division have been flown in to protect the Pentagon.

Cresspahl, on his way from London to Jerichow, wanted to stop over in Lübeck. He kept telling himself he should hurry to Jerichow, and kept not wanting to listen. From the top of the ungainly staircase in the station hall, he could look down at the Stettin express, connection in Gneez to Jerichow. He knew he was supposed to be hurrying. He had a dull and unpleasant feeling of future guilt. Still that was preferable to the prospect of Papenbrock's house, of Louise Papenbrock and the fake piety with which she would lead him to the door of the room which by that point, he imagined, contained a new baby. He wasn't ready for that room yet. In any case, no one there was expecting him. He'd heard that babies in their first few days of life couldn't really see anyway. By the time he stored his overnight bag in the station, procrastination had apparently triumphed. Practically a little vacation.

At customs in Hamburg they'd been almost manically festive. They'd greeted him by name, congratulated him on his return home to Germany. If he hadn't been dressed up, as though for a funeral, they might have nudged him in the ribs. And yet it was an ordinary weekday, March 2, 1933, a Thursday. He thought he'd take a look around the Free Hanseatic City of Lübeck, see if they were acting all crazy there too.

Men in uniform stood partly blocking the station exits: two at each exit, one in policeman's green and one in SA brown, asking everyone to take out their wallets. But the city employee, supposed to pass the travelers along to his partner, kept drifting away from him, seemingly embarrassed, making the inspection of papers in the midst of the gathering crowd look unserious, even indecent. Still, Cresspahl assumed an obliging manner (this was his first move in dealing with officials, all his life), as if happy to wait for the Brownshirt to finger his documents the way he was the papers of two young men, who in their flat tweed caps looked less like workmen than apprentice hairdressers. But the policeman in his shako made it clear to Cresspahl, with an angry swing of his chin, that people paying a visit to Lübeck in a black suit and polished shoes did not need to be checked; out on the sidewalk, Cresspahl caught another disgusted, almost imploring look from him. He seemed sickened by this Hitler fellow's private army. Cresspahl almost gave him a nod.

Erwin Plath lived in the North St. Lorenz neighborhood, on a side street off Schwartauer Allee, near the slaughterhouse on the border, and for a moment before he knocked Cresspahl stood amazed outside the stately, freshly painted gabled house. Plath's wife sprang out at him as though she'd been leaning against the door. – My husband's not home! she screamed, – my husband's not home! she said again, and Cresspahl moved a step back on the sidewalk so she could see him better. That didn't help. Her husband wasn't home!, she cried, as if she wanted the neighbors to hear. Cresspahl slowly opened his top two coat buttons, at a loss, and also because his collar felt tight, and suddenly she whispered something, from which he gathered that Erwin would be at the Hindenburg House that afternoon, "to follow." – My husband's not home! she announced, very loud, and Cresspahl did not even try to answer. Back on Schwartauer Allee, he permitted himself a shake of the head. Years ago, in Hamburg, Erwin had told him about his wife, stubborn but easygoing enough, not about a scared little girl dabbling in drama.

On the railroad bridge, he did not turn right but went straight, toward Ebert Square, crossed over the moat on the Puppenbrücke, past the statues, listened to what the monuments had to tell him, answered back,

all right, Bismarck, say something already

circled the Holsten Gate sunk in its bowl of earth, and disappeared into the city center. Nothing much to see there. He inspected the fully stocked furniture stores, and no one had to explain to him that high unemployment was still weighing down the businesses that sold on installment, that the sawmills were therefore hesitant to buy, and that no one was eager for someone like him here. The department stores had just had their Linens Week sales. Houses at bargain prices filled one real estate broker's window. He was urged repeatedly not to miss the orchard- and pig-count on March 3. He was officially informed that the year 1933–34 was that of the Beetle. He stood with his hands behind his back looking at placards and shop-windows and newspaper pages on display, a sturdy man in holiday clothes, walking lazily down Broad Street, up King Street, bareheaded, his short curly hair in the softly wafting air, a little curious, even then not surprised.

Then he saw something, but time started racing so fast that by the next day he no longer believed everything that had happened. At Hindenburg House, a funeral procession came marching toward him, with muffled drums, navy flags, swastika flags, and, bringing up the rear, far behind the blue and brown uniforms, he really and truly did see Erwin shuffling along, a bit stooped, as though they weren't in fact the same age, and with a vacant stare as if he literally were helping carry someone to his grave. But what was a registered Social Democrat doing with a dead lieutenant captain and a cortege of Storm Troopers? Erwin pretended he didn't see Cresspahl, while Cresspahl joined in, adopting the appropriate dazed expression, and they trotted along to the Old Cemetery side by side in silence, every inch the mourners. Only when the procession turned onto Mittelallee did Erwin slip off down a side path, handkerchief raised to wipe something invisible off his face so that no one would particularly notice him. Cresspahl later found him in the farthest corner of the graveyard, behind a mausoleum wall, anxious, looking over his shoulder, whispering, not cheerful, not the jokester that Cresspahl had known for some twenty years. Erwin was waiting for someone. Not Cresspahl. Basically he was waiting for the police but hoping someone else would find him first.

So it was Cresspahl who rode back from the cemetery on the rear plat-form of the number 2 streetcar down Israelsdorf Allee across Klingenberg Square to Kronsforder Allee with Erwin's envelopes. The address was on a street of town houses with elegantly plastered half-timbered beams or pretty Jugendstil brickwork. Behind the quiet curtains there was nothing more shocking than Marlene Dietrich in pants, nothing more urgent to do than see the talkie *No Answer from F. P. 1* again, nothing more advisable than to hoist the black, white, and red flag up the pole, in heartfelt readi-ness to be agreeable to the state, so that any possible mistake might at least be counterbalanced by the sincerity of the effort. In one of these houses, in a room dark with velvet and mahogany, Cresspahl handed off the two passports, with visas to go abroad, that Erwin had given him. The people around the polished family table seemed to him to be playing school, but impatient, rushed, as if they knew there more urgent things to consider. Namely, the question of whether the Communists had started the Reichstag fire, or Hitler's Storm Troopers had. Also, whether the Social Democrats could now ally themselves with the German Communist Party again and keep their dignity intact. For the Communist representatives from Mecklenburg—Warncke, Schröder, Quandt, Schuldt—were on the run; there was reason to fear that Ernst Thälmann might come knocking at the door next. Thälmann was reported to be on his way to Denmark. And yet the Communists had made a pact with the Nazis against the Social Democrats. Could those who had coined the slur "Social Fascists" ever be forgiven? Leading the discussion was a weak little runt of a man, his rectangular mustache held perfectly still beneath his nose, his shining bald skull tilted to the side as if he were asleep, but when he woke up he railed like a furious, merciless schoolteacher. Cresspahl didn't stay to hear the end of the argument; he and two other men returned to the city, separately, on different streetcars, this time on line 1 via Ratzeburger Allee. On the way to the stop, the other two ranted something at him about *The Lübeck Gazette*. If you believed what it said there, Reichstag Representative Julius Leber had, one February morning, intervened in a fight on Grosse Burgstrasse between Brüggmann the Nazi and Rath the worker with the incitement: Stab 'im! Cresspahl's travel companions were especially bitter that the bourgeois paper had failed to show proper respect toward a Reichstag representative (who was also the editor of the Social Democratic competitor, *The Lübeck Herald*). But after the publisher, Charles Coleman, had voluntarily thrown any Israelite cultural news out of the paper, allowed SA ads with swastikas, and promulgated biographies of Mussolini and Hitler, what else could they expect? And now it had gone so far as to print not only the police report on the burial of party comrade Brüggmann but also the NSDAP District Committee's depiction of it. The ranting sounded timid, like disappointed hopes; Cresspahl seemed bored.

At Klingenberg he didn't meet up with either of his companions and didn't entirely mind, to be honest, since they hadn't let him get a word in edgewise about his own distance from the SPD since 1922. After a while, he headed out to Beckergrube, the street where Erwin had said he'd wait for him, and sat in vain for a long time at a window looking out over the backyard in the parlor of an old woman who treated him like some teenage gang member just looking for trouble. Clearly she was used to such visits. She spoke only Plattdeutsch. She made him eat a plaice fried in very little butter. Then she pleaded with him not to leave, in a downright gentle voice as though she hadn't just been acting quarrelsome. She reminded him of his mother, and that made him laugh. Back outside, he noticed some drunks standing around strangely joyless and halfhearted. On Johannisstrasse, a crowd pushed him right up next to a fight that was just starting, three men casually shoving one another. After every shove they would walk another half a step farther, shoulders thrown back like swaggering children, until one of them blocked a punch to his upper arm with one hand and socked the attacker on the chin with the other. They were still arguing about the parade two weeks ago of the Reichsbanner, the Socialist veteran's group, which the SA had blocked off the street to stop, claiming that shots had been fired, and also that someone had shouted an insult to Reich Chancellor Hitler; the two men left dead, though, were later identified as Reichsbanner members. (And last night, a Nazi parade had allegedly been shot at from the rooftops.) The policeman outside the Reichsbank faced strictly northward, and nothing he heard made him turn his head; clearly he was busy enforcing the renewed prohibition against tearing off twigs and pussy willows, either intentionally or accidentally. Toward evening, Cresspahl was walking down Schüsselbuden, and when he saw the consulate's plaque at number 17 for His Great British Majesty George V, he had the feeling of two different realities and wished he were in only one. He was on his way to the station, by the Salt Depots, when Erwin caught up with him, now standing tall, like a man with great self-respect out for a stroll. He talked loudly about the Sunday excursion he had planned, on the Wakenitz by motorboat to Ratzeburg. But he couldn't stop looking over his shoulder, and he was still waiting. Someone had come by his house around midday, asking for him. Cresspahl didn't want to go back to his house with him, but at the station he found that there were no more trains to Gneez that night, never mind Jerichow, and when he knocked on Erwin's door again he was arrested, just like that, the police sprang out from the dark hall and drove him to the station in the car that he had noticed right off as too fancy for a street like that. The police were prepared to bring him food in his cell in exchange for his money, the British inserts in his passports were good for that at least, but they didn't know what else to do with this slow, dense piece of work who said he'd only wanted to make a little stopover in Lübeck, till the next train, and who sat on his stool so stiff and huddled up so tight that it was almost like he was afraid to get dirt from the walls on his black coat. Back then the Lübeck police still prided themselves on their cleanliness and they took this as some kind of insult. So they questioned him only the next morning, and still he refused to save himself by using his father-in-law's social standing in Lübeck. He felt sure that the only thing that could help him was acting dumb. He insisted on seeing his friend Erwin Plath—he had stopped in Lübeck just to see him, and now time was running out, and he wanted to have done that at least. They finally brought Erwin in and put him in the other corner of the office. Erwin looked a little battered about the shoulders but now he was openly in high spirits, and sly, *swinplietsch* as they say in Mecklenburgish, as though at last the wait was over and what was happening wasn't as bad as what he'd expected. The commissioner, in a scintillating mood after a good night's sleep, launched into a lengthy interrogation, starting off craftily by asking how the two gentlemen knew each other, they were such good friends. At which, striking a military pose, Cresspahl gave a thunderous shout that yanked the stunned interrogator right up out of his swivel chair: Twenty-Fourth Holstein Artillery Regiment, Güstrow, Second Battalion! After the first syllable Erwin joined in, shouting in unison until the proper moment when Cresspahl left him room to add something: Fifth Battalion! Erwin said.

When they were sitting over breakfast in Gerda Plath's kitchen, Erwin had started waiting again. – Who could that have been yesterday, around midday, that you sent me word of at the Hindenburg House: he brooded out loud, kneading the back of his neck. – It was someone who knew the signal, the two coat buttons: he said, looking past Cresspahl, who obviously couldn't know. And Gerda involuntarily glanced at Cresspahl, who up until then had been acting clearly reserved around her, and they both realized at the same time that someone really had failed to turn up yesterday, someone who knew the signal as a signal. – *'E's sittin right ere*: she said, pointing an elbow at Cresspahl. They both watched Erwin's face as delight defended itself against the other realization. Then he said, haltingly, in Plattdeutsch: *What we need is a drink.*

That morning, Friday, the third of March, 1933, Gesine Cresspahl was born in Jerichow.

October 21, 1967 Saturday

A Western correspondent witnessed three air raids, seven bombing waves, numerous isolated flights over the area by the Americans, and another eight alerts in the vicinity of Haiphong (Vietnam) on Tuesday; the day was described to him as normal. Tens of thousands of Chinese are working to restore rail and road communication with their own country. *The New York Times* gave detailed plans and possible alternate routes for the demonstration taking place in Washington today; protestors intended to occupy the Pentagon, for instance; further demonstrations in support are expected in London, Paris, Rome, Stockholm, Bonn, and Copenhagen. In Mississippi, seven whites were found guilty in the murder of three young civil rights workers in 1964, among the seven was Cecil R. Price, the chief deputy sheriff who held the victims in Meridian County jail until the Ku Klux Klan could finish making its preparations, then released them, recaptured them on the highway, and handed them over to the lynch mob, which included Price himself (the bodies were found in the earthen dam of a small pond, buried with the aid of a bulldozer). Five of the convicted men are free and can read their life stories on page 18 of *The New York Times*.

Saturday, South Ferry day.

– So Cresspahl, your father, my grandfather: Marie says: didn't get to Jerichow to see you until the afternoon of March 3, 1933.

– Not quite afternoon, but at the same time the leader of the Communist Party of Germany, Ernst Thälmann, let himself get caught and arrested in a small room on Lützow Street in Berlin. Without a ticket to Denmark on him.

– And Cresspahl wasn't drunk.

– Not visibly. He'd helped Erwin Plath in Lübeck get through not only the morning but also a liter bottle of Doppel-Kümmel aquavit and half a case of beer, and Gerda Plath wouldn't let him go until he'd done justice to her coffee. She wanted to send this Frau Cresspahl a sober husband. The man who arrived in Jerichow, walking upright and rather slowly down

Station Street and under Papenbrock's first sixteen windows, was as wide awake and alert a drunk as you can imagine.

– So he must have been in a good mood: Marie says.

– A blind man seeing everything, retaining nothing. A deaf man who heard a cat run by without understanding what the sound meant. Jerichow seemed very loud. There was music on Market Square. There were more people on the square than he thought lived in the whole town. Papenbrock's door onto the square was locked.

– No one had told him anything.

– He seemed to remember reading *The Gneez Daily News* on the train. He didn't think he'd seen any birth notice for Cresspahl. He walked back to Station Street and found Papenbrock's gate in the high brick wall and a door to the house. In the warm hall, behind all the brown doors, it was quiet. The silence closed in around him and made his ears hum like when you're underwater.

– D. E. says that happens to him?

– He didn't find his wife upstairs, off the hallway where Papenbrock had put the rooms for his children. He padded back down to the front door and left his bag outside, in the middle of the path. The bag was meant to say on his behalf: It was a long trip. Delays sometimes happen on trips.

– Families like that take afternoon naps: Marie says.

– Lisbeth was sleeping nestled in her hair in the room above Papenbrock's office, which only a week ago had been a sitting room. She slept propped up on several other pillows, mouth open, breathing laboriously in the overheated air, installed among the stately formal furniture as though on her deathbed.

– Now the baby.

– The baby lay in a rustic cradle against the wall between the two windows looking out on the market. The baby was wedged in, packed tight in eiderdown. The baby was asleep on her right ear, between two loosely clenched fists. You could see her breathing but not smell her breath. Her chin still stuck out, the forehead receding sharply below the few dark hairs. She was a healthy baby girl with fully formed fingernails, reddish and blue skin, only a few tiny crow's-feet around her eyes.

– You can't know that about yourself: Marie says, as a statement of fact, not an objection.

– I know it about you.

– I'm not like you.

– In July 1957 you were.

– I wish you'd tell the story how it would have been told to you: Marie says.

– I was told that no one even noticed Cresspahl. Suddenly the house woke up and sent one ambassador after another in to see the two sleepers. Mama Laabs, the county midwife, came. Louise Papenbrock came, with hot-water bottles for the baby. The servants came, the cook, the maids, the coachman, the workmen, to offer their congratulations. Edith brought her two children with her and proved to them that the stork had brought the new baby, because look, at the foot of the cradle he had also left some Lübeck marzipan in two gold paper wrappers. Edith of all people. Albert Papenbrock came in, the grandfather, in stocking feet, bringing the best tray with tea the way Lisbeth had learned to make it in Richmond. They didn't have much use for this guy by the north window. Louise Papenbrock nodded at him, contented, imperious, her revenge postponed. To the people who came up from the stable and the granary he seemed appropriately dazed. Edith's children curtsied and looked him in the eye until he coughed up a sixpence. Albert was the only one to put his arm around his shoulders and say something to him with a chuckle, maybe he was trying to laugh, and then he dragged him almost affectionately into the next room and sat him down in front of a bottle of Rotspon and drank a glass with him, keeping the same puckered-up look on his face, like a child needing consolation. But before that, Dr. Berling came too and clapped Cresspahl on the shoulder.

Well, old Swede. Guess you didn't try that hard. It's not a boy.

When can she travel?

When can she go to England?

Go home.

It's up to the mother. Ask her in three weeks.

Not any sooner?

Come on, old Swede. Why do you want to go back to England now anyway?
Now that Germany's finally on the rise again.

That's not how it looks from over there.

– And now the story of the cup tub: Marie says. – The one they gave you baths in because you were so small.

– That was Louise Utecht who was so small. That was in 1871, on Hageböcker Street in Güstrow. That's not my story.

– All right, something about their marriage.

– Cresspahl, when he was walking past the head of his wife's bed to the side room, caught a look from her—dazed, like out of a dream. He wanted to wait until she was alone anyway. At first the red wine only made him sleepy. For a while he couldn't get the picture out of his head of Horst Papenbrock in the uniform of a Hitler Storm Trooper, toasting him, counting something off for him on fingers bent one after the other, like a math teacher giddily proving a theorem. Then he managed to forget him and think about Meta Wulff instead. He could trust Meta Wulff completely, and he told her about his night in the Lübeck jail. He had definitely already seen Dr. Semig, but an exclamation had slipped out when he saw him that he wished he could get back, if only he could find it in some far-flung corner of his memory. Then, after the second bottle, he had drunk himself sober. The afternoon music on Market Square: that had been the SA's 162nd Regiment band from Lübeck. What Horst Papenbrock had been counting off on his fingers: the arrests of Communist functionaries—twenty-seven in Rostock, ten each in Schwerin and Wismar and Güstrow, fifty-eight in the country district of Mecklenburg. The racket under the windows was from one of the loudspeakers the Johs. Schmidt Musikhaus had set up on Town Street and the market square, carrying Hitler's speech from Hamburg. The flickering light between the gables of the buildings came from the torches shining on the uniforms of the SA and the Steel Helmet Brigade as they marched to the Rifle Club, and the gentle breeze came from the door that Papenbrock had now reopened because he felt that this crowd was in no way a threat to his own property. The fire and sparks in the smoke on the other side of town came from the torches thrown into a pyre, and the song drifting in from the low-hanging night was coming out of Papenbrock's mouth as well while he groped his way up the stairs, humming contentedly,

Myself I have surrendered
With all my heart and hand

To you oh land of life and love
My precious Fatherland.

and while Cresspahl bolted his door shut, he suddenly found himself thinking in his version of English: Aw-right. *We* won't surrender. No heart and hand, no body and soul. Precious or not, you want something from us and we're not gonna give it to you.

The baby was a girl, so he owed Lisbeth something in return. But even if the child didn't recognize him, it had seen him.

– Your mother, Lisbeth: Marie says. – Tell me something from her point of view.

– I can't.

– You can't think what she was thinking?

– Not what she was thinking, not how she was thinking. I don't understand her anymore.

That was today, late this afternoon, when the ferry was already halfway back to Whitehall Terminal. A Japanese gentleman had asked Marie for help, pressing his camera into her hand with extraordinarily fulsome apologies, and she had positioned him and his family in front of Manhattan's skyscrapers with expert instructions and hand gestures before flexing her knees to absorb the swayings of the ship's deck and pressing proof of the visitors' trip around the world into their camera. As she disembarked over the gangway and up the stairs and down the ramp alongside the ferry building, she answered the tourists' friendly looks three times, not with a smile but with a slight bow suggested from her shoulders and recognition in her eyes. – *Welcome a Stranger*: I said in English, and even though she obviously recognized the quote from the Transit Authority's buses, she replied, almost in earnest, almost excited: – That's right, Gesine. Welcome a stranger.

October 22, 1967 Sunday

Start, Gesine.
    No you start.

Why didn't you go to the demonstration in Washington yesterday.

Because I don't believe in it. The president's policy in Vietnam won't be changed by the protests of a minority.

You wanted to save the bus fare.

Not even the president decides the president's policies.

Dos Passos.

No. Baran and Sweezy. Monopoly Capital.

There were fifty thousand protestors.

And there are two hundred million Americans. President Johnson was holding a luncheon.

The New York Times *devoted a quarter of the front page to what happened in Washington and abroad, and almost two more pages inside.*

It's The New York Times'*s job to report what happens, isn't it.*

Reports in The New York Times *might change what the nation thinks.*

We don't even know what the paper means with those photographs. That front-page picture of three US marshals beating someone already on the ground with their white nightsticks, is it supposed to elicit outrage from its subscribers? The picture next to it, of the young men shouting, is that one in there because of the unbourgeois beard, the disguising sunglasses, the twisted mouth?

Publicizing the antiwar movement in the media—isn't that an opportunity for the opposition?

A possible opportunity.

So you're saying that as far as you're concerned an opportunity doesn't count unless it's already a certainty.

Something like that.

Were you scared of the white nightsticks, Gesine? Admit it, you're glad you weren't one of the people the soldiers beat back down the Pentagon steps with their rifle butts. That's not your blood on the steps.

I can't raise the child if I'm crippled.

The child, the child. Your patented excuse.

My patented excuse.

You're scared of jail.

What good would I be to anybody in jail? Yes, I'd be scared to go jail, any jail, in any country.

Norman Mailer got arrested at the Pentagon yesterday.

For "technical violation" of a police line. How much you want to bet he's long since back home in Brooklyn Heights?

He declared his opposition to US policy in Vietnam.

And did what writers do, and next he'll be selling us his story about it.

The Vietcong flag in the march, that's what bothered you.

What do I care about the Vietcong? All I want is foreign troops out of Vietnam.

Our troops.

Foreign troops.

All the pot smoke from your fellow demonstrators would have made you doubt the cause.

The cause is clearer when you're high?

One little aesthetic flaw in the act and you won't do it?

It's not just the act that would come back to haunt me but the flaw too.

And you don't like not being in control of what the act means.

I don't want a rejection of North American expansion into Asia to be twisted around into approval of Soviet expansion.

You're jabbering like a goddamn intellectual.

And you're jabbering like people who aren't exactly around anymore.

The fact is, you took the easy way out. You didn't want to be there as someone over thirty. You didn't want to stand out among all those students, children, young people.

Who should I have gone with? The flower children? The New York High School for Music and the Arts?

You didn't want to be recognized as a foreigner.

It's true, I did feel I'd have had to go in disguise.

You wouldn't have been on your own, for once.

That beautiful camaraderie around the campfires in front of the Pentagon, I don't feel that way anymore. Surrounded by soldiers with bayonets fixed and expertly braced against their hips—I don't fall for the line about heroism in the face of danger. The smell of smoke and tear gas in the air wouldn't make me think of the suffering that's scientifically proven to precede inevitable victory. Group sing-alongs of "Down by the Riverside." The prospect of remembering that would have made me squirm even while I was there.

Well, as long as you're not embarrassed, now or later.

As long as I don't do anything I'm ashamed to remember.

Even them burning police barricades in their campfires would have been too much for you.

The point wasn't to destroy public property. That's not going to win taxpayers over to peace marches.

You're a taxpayer. Your taxes go to the war too.

I should be paying taxes for British arms sales to Africa instead? For the West German arms industry? For the costs of the Soviet occupations?

Yesterday, when you got off the ferry, you didn't understand the little demonstration in Battery Park. You didn't get why so many drivers, including those of city buses and police cars, had their headlights on in broad daylight.

They drove around like that in mourning for John F. Kennedy too.

Yesterday they did it in solidarity, to support the nation's war in Vietnam.

I admit it, I was glad not to know. "Mistakes happen sometimes."

"That's what she said"

". . . and then she had her fifth kid."

And just reading in the newspaper about yesterday's demonstrations all over the world, that's enough for you? You can live like that, without being there, joining in, getting involved, taking action?

That's what I have left: I can learn how things work. At least live with my eyes open.

Gesine, why didn't you go to the demonstration in Washington yesterday?

I'm not saying.

You can tell us.

I can't. Not even in a mental conversation.

There's only one thing left it could be.

If I don't think it through, it doesn't exist.

Yesterday Mrs. Ernest Hemingway complained to *The Times* of London about their publishing letters her deceased husband wrote between 1950 and 1956 to one Adriana Ivancich, a young woman who says she was the basis for the character of Renata in Hemingway's novel *Across the River and into the Trees.*

The New York Times was unable to reach this basis, now Countess Rex, by telephone in Milan yesterday afternoon.

October 23, 1967 Monday
You don't want to open your mouth today, Gesine? Not a peep? Keeping your trap shut?

That's normal for New York, apparently. One man described going for twenty-one days without a word—a record. That's typical for alienated life in New York, apparently.

Why don't you want to say anything, Gesine.

I don't feel like talking.

Work conversations don't count. Marie doesn't count, even though she walked out the door without a word after unexpectedly giving Gesine a big hug, briefly but firmly, so that the feeling of her body from knees to shoulders lingered for a few breaths. (Don't ask me anything, Marie.)

Seeing Jason goes off without a word, without a grimace. Where the metal staircase around the elevator shaft opens to the building staff's room, there stood Jason in the doorframe, massive, black, gloomy, melancholy, blocking the noise from the radios and TVs for a moment, then withdrawing into the darkness behind his eyes. (Lovely morning today, Jason.)

The mechanics in the middle garage are awake enough, they call out, greet Mrs. Cresspahl as their sister, one of them whistles. (I'll wear my skirts as short as I want.)

On the corner of Ninety-Sixth and West End Avenue, the police car has driven up and dropped off the guard who watches over the children's walk to Emily Dickinson School every schoolday. As he strides into the center of the intersection, he firmly pulls on his white gloves and eyes the pedestrians on the sidewalk, who, annoyed, embarrassed, have to obey the traffic light this time. (Yes, officer.)

Behind the window of his Good Eats Diner, Charlie stands stock-still, holds his high forehead and gray shock of hair toward Broadway without seeing it, and ignores his hands spatuling up a hamburger. In a corner of the diner's window, a printed card with grease spots recommends Charlie's cooking to clients of a West German travel agency. (What do the Jews in the office upstairs think about that, Charlie?)

The old man at the newsstand has his hands in the pouch of his apron and his eye on the customer exchanging coins for a paper, so intently that it's as if he's looking for something to come out of her mouth. (Today I'm the one who's forgotten how to say good morning.) That wasn't an easy one. She almost went back, to make it up to him with a comment about the weather. (Has *Der Spiegel* come in yet?)

On the stinking stairs down to the subway, a woman steps out of the wall like someone in a dream, dressed respectably, middle-class, of no interest to the male passengers, and she says: Dearie, sweetie, can you spare a dime? (I have a great Brecht poem you might like, you poor crazy housewife.)

The A express train is packed solid today, getting more and more crowded by the minute to the mindlessly flowing monologue of a dark-skinned man talking at the ceiling in a husky, abrasive voice, head thrown back like someone drowning: Theyre tryin tuh corrup the nigguh! Theyre thinkin an schemin an plannin to corrup the nigguh wit sex! (You don't say.)

In the Grand Central Terminal concourse a dignified old lady in a lace blouse and tailored black suit is digging around in the pay phone coin returns for forgotten change, and senses she's being watched, and asks us, in the lilting tones of an expensive college, where she might find the train from Montreal. (Call information, madam.)

At Sam's, we have to count on him having our regular order memorized, and in fact the rush at his counter when our bag is ready prevents him from handing it over with the usual exchange of pleasantries; maybe his nod, the gloomy glance from above his bellowing mouth, wasn't meant for us. (Hi, Sam. Tea with lemon. Thanks, Sam. Don't work too hard, Sam. Back atcha, Sam.)

And so we make it to the first row of elevators in silence, make it up to the eleventh floor, past the girls in the typing pool, to our desk, and then have two hours of silence in front of the humming, clacking machine, until Amanda parks herself on the second chair with a steaming cup of coffee and a lit cigarette, equipped for a long visit, and ask us how it's going. She insists on an answer. Game over. – You can see for yourself, I'm radiant: Mrs. Cresspahl says.

Meanwhile the demonstration in Washington is one for the history books, you can find an analysis of the news in *The New York Times*. If you believe the *Times*, everyone lost. The administration is sad, due to its damaged reputation abroad. The demonstrators are sad, because they didn't win enough people over to their side against the president. The vilification directed at his person ("LBJ the Butcher") might reverse his declining fortunes in the polls. The signs and lines from the theatrical performances are too indecent for publication ("too obscene to print"). Most of the people arrested apparently acted like upstanding bourgeois citizens caught in a misdemeanor while out drinking on a Saturday night; Norman Mailer, though and of course, was visibly and dramatically himself. The various groups involved were united on neither the goal nor the tactics of the protest. Advantage of idealism had been taken. The radicals had wanted a battle and they'd gotten one. That's how it was, according to the *Times*.

The Soviets claim not to know that Yevgeny Y. Runge, the secret agent who defected, ever served in the Soviet army or Soviet security forces. Claim not to know.

On the way home we tried again not to talk. But Mrs. O'Brady at the cigarette stand would only sell us cigarettes in exchange for some chitchat about how dangerous cigarettes are, Mr. Stample (James F. "Shorty" Stample) was not in the mood to drink alone at Grand Central, and when we got rid of him a young man stopped us in the middle of Lexington Avenue and asked us how to get to Times Square, not to any other address in all of New York. (I've never run across that scam. You must have seen the words Times Square somewhere, buddy.) But there really was confusion in his youthful face with its fuzzy rust-red beard, his accent was plausibly British, close enough to be a New Zealander, he really did look like someone set down suddenly and without warning in a foreign country, so we brought him along under Grand Central Terminal to the warren of tunnels under Times Square, talking the whole time, enjoying the other English, the one from another country, from childhood. And Marie was leaning on the railing at the Ninety-Sixth Street subway exit, a determined, somewhat worried child, who allowed us another few steps without talking before the day needed to be cleared up.

– Are you still sad, Gesine?
– No.
– Do you remember what was bothering you?
– No.
– It's these darn Mondays, Gesine. Sometimes I can't take it either, Gesine.

October 24, 1967 Tuesday

Not only has Albert "Kid Blast" Gallo had to cede control of the Brooklyn Mafia to Joseph Colombo, he's been arrested, around seven a.m. yesterday, something about a little racketeering and extortion in a racetrack ticket-cashing scheme.

Leo Held, thirty-nine years old, of Loganton, Pennsylvania, father of four, baldish, six feet tall, two hundred pounds, "a quiet peaceful man devoted to his family," "a respected citizen," former school board member, avid hunter and good shot, with no police record, never treated for mental illness, an employee for twenty-one years at the Hammermill Paper Company plant in Lock Haven, walked into his workplace yesterday with a .38 caliber revolver and a .44 caliber Magnum and shot five of his apparently deliberately chosen colleagues dead and wounded four others. At around eight fifteen he shot and killed the woman at the switchboard of the Lock Haven airport, a neighbor. Back home, 17 kilometers away, he fired at a sleeping couple next door, killing the husband, and took the man's ammunition, then had a shootout with twelve policemen until they finally shot the guns from his hands. He will probably live.

Yesterday afternoon, when Robert Smith, of 470 Sheffield Avenue, Brooklyn, was having a fight with his wife, Clarice, their six-year-old son, Randy, went to the closet, got his father's rifle, .22 caliber, loaded it, aimed, and shot his father in the chest. His father will never start trouble with his mother again.

In Jerichow in 1933, Cresspahl felt that people were trying to keep him from starting trouble. In the morning, standing downstairs in the hall, he'd let his mind wander and before he knew it Louise Papenbrock was hugging him. At breakfast, old Papenbrock waited until he knew his wife was busy with the child ("with the children"), then sent Edith to the Lübeck Court for two pitchers of Kniesenack beer and poured himself and Cresspahl generous glasses of Richtenberg kümmel aquavit to go with them; he was happy for the chance to bend the rules a little and also relieved that this son-in-law of his knew how to drink. He hadn't seen that yet. Papenbrock and Cresspahl walked down Town Street, and back up Town Street, so that people would see them; they stopped into some shops and accepted congratulations from Molten the baker, and Pahl the tailor, and Böhnhase,

and over shots at the counter or in the back room they agreed, as circumstances dictated, that either shop owners or tradesmen were the backbone
of the middle class, and that the Nazis clearly appreciated that about shop
owners or tradesmen. Even Stoffregen didn't run off when Papenbrock
buttonholed him and fished for congratulations. Cresspahl didn't understand why this Stoffregen kept looking so grief-stricken and depressed. At
one point, he realized that Heinz Zoll had ducked into the post office at
their approach. By the time they reached the mayor's office, Papenbrock
was quite red in the face and not uninclined to furious little outbursts
about his wife, Louise, but Louise remembered the time in Vietsen and
not once did she send a message to the Lübeck Court, where by now there
were eight gentlemen drinking to the new baby's health. Papenbrock was
also congratulated on his son, who, due to the "change of government,"
was moving up in the world, but Dr. Erdamer didn't join in those congratulations and Papenbrock did his best to wave them aside, with a long
hand now grown quite fat. Horst had commandeered a police detachment
in Gneez and was now on the hunt for a Communist thing being called a
cabal, with the district group leader's full authority and list of names.
Papenbrock's feelings vacillated between pride and fear—he was proud
that his boy had finally learned how to give orders in forceful, almost
military fashion, and worried that in the end he himself would be held
responsible for his offspring's actions, not least his moves against Dr.
Erdamer, who was not only a Social Democrat but also on Horst's "hit
list." He wanted to keep Cresspahl out of it for now, if only for a few more
days, and Cresspahl suspected nothing, not in the least.

Starting trouble would have suited him just fine. It wasn't just the ridiculous antics of all the women in Papenbrock's house, using the birth to
upstage the men ("My husband's in the hospital. We have a new baby"); it
was that he'd wanted everything different: a private room in a clinic,
medical supervision, trained nurses, visits only by family members, a semblance of proper hygiene. Now his wife was lying in state in the sitting
room, forced to put up with formal visits from families they were on good
terms with, and the baby was picked up and shown to the visitors' children
and put down and picked up again, affectionately pawed by dirty snotty
fingers, and it was probably getting a headache from the bouquets of flowers in the dry heated air, just like him, like Cresspahl. Nor did he manage

to talk freely with Lisbeth (except the first night, which he spent on the floor next to her bed, hands clasped behind his head, speaking softly, until she forgot her sudden fear and could fall asleep). She didn't commit to a departure date but didn't oppose him either. When he looked at the baby, blindly helplessly sipping drops of sugar water from his chapped finger, he felt a powerful sense of urgency.

On Sunday afternoon, while the loudspeakers of the Johs. Schmidt Musik- and Radiohaus blasted the windowpanes with classical music records interspersed with the latest vote counts from the Reichstag election, the child was given a name. She had been announced in *The Gneez Daily News* as simply "a healthy baby girl." Lisbeth Cresspahl had expected a boy and had decided on the boy's name, Henry, not the girl's, and Cresspahl hadn't expected what he wanted to take precedence for once over what she wanted. She asked him for suggestions. She was sitting half upright, propped against three pillows, and she looked at him, alert, receptive, almost cheerful. Her eyes seemed darker than usual; she hadn't regained her color; even the loose hair around her face was not as light as usual. He offered suggestions slowly, not entirely convinced himself; she considered them carefully, parting her lips, chewing the air. It looked like she was testing the seasoning. No, not Elisabeth. – Which Lisbeth is supposed to come when you call one of us? Both, Cresspahl? She knew perfectly well that he only considered the middle name Luise out of politeness to Papenbrock's wife, not because he wanted it. She brought up his sister's name. Cresspahl hesitantly said it should be a name that was hers alone. – Gesine?: he said innocently, and wished he could swallow his words. – All right: Lisbeth said, acquiescent, kind, so that he would be forced to take it as a gift. He was sitting on the edge of her bed, at the foot. Not once had she looked over at the cradle. She lightly kicked his hip under the blanket and said: Gesine Henriette.

Is that you, Gesine?
It's me, Gesine.
In 1904? In Malchow?
I was fifteen. He was sixteen. I was Redebrecht's granddaughter.
What did you look like, Gesine.
I had braids. I was blond. He always wanted me to unpin my braids. The

first time, I went upstairs to the window in the middle of the night, my hair down. Nothing had been planned, nothing said. There he was.

Are you dead too, Gesine?

Not necessarily, Gesine. I'd only be seventy-nine. The old lady standing in your way at the Wendisch Burg station in 1952, I could have been her. The old lady with the cane on the bench outside the old age home in Hamburg, maybe that was me. At least you can think so, Gesine.

I can, Gesine.

Peter Harper, a superintendent, lives at 2015 Monterey Avenue in the South Bronx. He has built himself a garbage shelter over the back door leading to the building's courtyard—a reinforced metal roof. Now he's happy. Now the garbage that the residents throw down into the yard from the upper floors can't hit him anymore. (*The New York Times* is either not au courant enough or too diplomatic, for she leaves out the name for the trash hurtling down, gentle scraps of paper or hard juice bottles: airmail.)

October 25, 1967 Wednesday

The Soviets have decided to get mad after all about the defection of their secret agent, Runge, to the West: they admit that he exists, and they call him an unscrupulous criminal. They also make public the name of an American agent who defected to their side, from New Delhi. It's John Smith.

– Gesine, I'm having a problem with someone.
– Someone I know?
– No. A girl in my class.
– Does she sit next to you?
– They seated her next to me.
– A girl from another school?
– From Harlem.
– Is that the problem?
– The problem is she's colored.
– Watch your language, Marie.
– Okay, okay!

– The right term is "Negro." A black girl.
– Yes, Gesine. I know, all right.

Several children from the Polish, Bulgarian, and Czechoslovakian embassies have been threatened and beaten by American students at Lincoln Middle School in Washington (DC). One boy had to be taken to the hospital. The State Department says: This is very bad for our image abroad.

– She's the only black girl.
– Doesn't she have a name?
– Francine is the only black girl in our class, and out of all twenty-one of us Sister Magdalena had to pick me.
– You're embarrassed.
– No. The thing is, it's pointless. She's an exception.
– An exception among Negroes?
– An exception to life in America. She's an alibi-Negro.
– Miss Cresspahl, explain this concept.
– An alibi-Negro is someone who can go to our school for free.
– So the institution doesn't lose its government funding.
– To trick the law.
– Do you want every black student to have a place at your school, for justice's sake?
– Well until then I have to do all the work with the alibi-Negro for all twenty-one of us and it's not fair.

The playwright LeRoi Jones, on trial in New Jersey over two revolvers found in his car during the July riots, denounced the white judge and white prospective jurors as his oppressors. He was put in handcuffs.

– That's too much to ask of you, Marie?
– It's a lot. Francine is behind in math, she writes English badly, she doesn't know where Montreal is.
– She's also never been taken to Montreal for the weekend, like a certain other girl I know.
– Francine can't even learn. She doesn't remember things and then gets them all mixed up.

– Maybe she doesn't have anywhere at home to study, or peace and quiet, or time.

– That's not my fault.

– Welcome a Stranger.

– That's what I've been doing since Labor Day. I've been checking her notebooks for seven weeks, going over the tests with her during break, listening to her recite the lessons, explaining the homework to her again over the phone. It's not that. When I say all the work I mean something else.

When the Reverend Stephen McKittrick of St. Paul's Lutheran Church heard on his car radio the news about the father of four running amok, he ran into his house and got his over-and-under shotgun, a birthday present from his wife, which he had actually been hoping to use during turkey season.

– So what do you mean by work?

– The work is being nice.

– Is she nice?

– She was paralyzed with fear the first couple weeks. She never looked up. Even now she needs courage, or a nudge in the ribs, to raise her hand. But she feels comfortable around me.

– She thanked you.

– I told her not to.

– So she is nice.

– And I have to be nice back! Otherwise my help doesn't work. Her feelings are hurt. And

– You don't like her.

– Right. I don't. I think she's ugly.

– What Negroes don't you think are ugly?

– Jason. Esther. Shakespeare.

– Because they look like the ones on TV.

– I don't watch TV behind your back.

– Sorry.

– Now she says to my face that she likes me. Next thing she'll want to hug me in the morning and when school gets out. Now she wants me completely.

– She's been taken in by the alibi.
– But I don't want to pay for it anymore.
– Pay for it?
– With Marilyn. With Marcia. With Deborah. They think I'm helping
Francine not only because it's the right thing to do. They think what
Francine thinks: that I'm doing it because I like her. I want out.

Seven years ago, it cost only $5,790 for a family of four in New York to
live a life without luxuries. The US Bureau of Labor Statistics has added
home ownership to this standard of living. As a result of the change, as
well as increased prices and higher taxes, the cost for the same family
in 1966 was $10,195, a 71 percent increase. Maybe we won't make it here
after all.

– Why are you only now telling me about all this?
– I was waiting for a good time.
– Good in what way?
– A good time to talk to you, Gesine. Say one word about the condition
of the Negroes and you can count on a very prickly reaction from Mrs.
Cresspahl.
– You don't want to tell Francine.
– No. I can't.
– Then let her go on thinking what she thinks and keep the real reason
why you're helping her to yourself.
– What about my real friends?
– You can let them know how you feel by asking them to help with
Francine.
– That's not lying?
– Not exactly lying.
– Good. I'm off the hook. Thank you.
– It doesn't bother you that all this is on tape now?
– No. By the way, I want to invite Francine over. For my Halloween
party.
– Now you're trying to trick the tape.
– And you never trick anyone, Gesine. Not even tapes.
– Maybe I'm better at it.

– Sorry. I didn't mean you. I meant: When I recognize a thought even before I've completely said it, does that mean it's actually something I've thought before? Did I mean it, when I maybe thought it? Am I remembering the thought, or remembering wanting to think it? Tell me, Gesine.

That night, no sooner did we get home than an army of thunderbolts and rain showers moved in from the west, battering our windows, striking the city fast and furious, from five until shortly past midnight. The cold weather's here now.

October 26, 1967 Thursday

The Soviets still can't grasp, except as a ruse or a stupid joke on the part of their competition, that their secret agent Runge has crossed over to the other side. The East Germans even claim him as one of their own (criminal and fugitive) citizens. As a countermove, the competition in London is showing around Runge's passports, identity cards, and documents—genuine photocopies.

Dr. Gallup has put a question to the nation once again. Forty-six out of a hundred have confided to him that they regret US involvement in Vietnam. In 1965, it was just half that many.

This Stalina woman has distributed a little of her more than $2.5 million among the needy whom she finds simpatico. Seven-eighths of her booty she's keeping for herself.

The man who ran amok in Pennsylvania died yesterday morning. His incoherent mumbling revealed no further information (six executed, six wounded).

Cresspahl did not have an easy time registering the birth of his child. City Hall was under armed guard.

Horst Papenbrock's own seizure of power hadn't started on Market Square. The Monday after the Reichstag election, when he came back from Gneez having sniffed around for Communists and not caught any, his day felt incomplete, and the Jerichow school flagpole caught his eye. He thought it seemed a bit . . . naked. Later that same afternoon, the SA mustered on Market Square, some of them not much interested in simply standing there

stiff and straight and silent, and they marched off to the right onto School
Street, no songs, a bit wobbly, like a tank with a drunk driver, between the
low buildings and the dogs, and they hoisted the flag of the National Socialist movement over the schoolyard and left a pair of sentries on guard
in the form of the two men who still had both a semblance of their wits
and a relatively complete uniform about and on them, respectively. The
mayor sent the police only at nightfall. The police consisted of Ete Helms,
also not much older than twenty and with the fast-approaching moment
of going off duty very much on his mind, so he didn't object to being dispatched on an errand; only when standing on Papenbrock's threshold and
asking for the young gentleman did he button the jacket of his uniform.
Horst had kept the bottle of Koem next to his plate of ham all through
dinner and he played the superior officer to the younger man for a few
minutes, until he heard that Dr. Erdamer had said: Stupid nonsense! (to
himself, while shutting the door). Five minutes later, Horst was defending
the sentries with pistol drawn, while Ete Helms was left to stand by the
schoolyard fence until almost midnight, now alert, his hands on his belt,
envying the Nazis' supply of hot coffee, impressed by their dashing hourly
changing of the guard, not entirely comfortable amid spectators who hadn't
enjoyed so much nighttime entertainment in years, not least the game of
stepping forward again after every time he'd ordered them to step back.
Around midnight, Dr. Erdamer had the good sense to yield to Geesche
Helms's requests and send her husband home to bed, so that the SA, having lost its audience, also lost interest in saluting and goose-stepping around,
and they cleared the schoolyard, but still it had been a victory for Horst
Papenbrock.

For the next morning, when the children arrived for school, the honor
guard was back in the schoolyard, though not accompanied by the police.
Horst had delegated command to Walter Griem, while he himself had the
Nazi flag hoisted on the roof of Town Hall and posted two uniformed
men to the left and right on the landing at the top of the front steps. Dr.
Erdamer had a good view of them from his window above the stairs, and
also of the fact that members of the Steel Helmets had forced their way
into this sentry duty by that point. On his desk was *The Lübeck Gazette*
from Monday. The newspaper stated on the top of the page that it was for
sale every morning except Mondays. It had appeared on this Monday, in

honor of the Reichstag election and because of the nature of the election's results. In the Mecklenburg district, the Social Democrats had lost one seat, keeping 120. The Communists were down from 100 seats to 81. The Mecklenburg soul had not, however, been satisfied with 195 Nazis in the Reichstag; they provided that party with an additional 93. In his hand was that day's *Lübeck Gazette*. He had read the headline so many times that the bold Gothic type no longer turned into the meaning of the words when he read it, it turned into other meanings. "Lübeck No Longer Red!" the paper exulted. But there hadn't been any Communists in the senate of the Free Hanseatic City of Lübeck—what the headline meant were the Social Democrats. What it meant was him. During eight and a half years of administrative service he had always rejected the label "Red" in his mind, those were the Communists, who wanted to destroy the republic, not serve it. That was what he had tried to do, in the small towns of Mecklenburg, and it wasn't the citizenry or his party that had driven him to move on from one to another but better offers. He had cleaned up both the Jerichow town hall and the road to the sea, the fire station at the gasworks, the employment office, and the weedy vacant lots in the northwest part of town, which he'd started to develop into a residential neighborhood. Neither his law degree from the University of Leipzig nor his party card nor his successful career was what gained him respect; in Jerichow, as elsewhere, he was on good terms with both the nobility and the citizenry, in agreement with them, not only observing the proper formalities of behavior but also evincing the decency these formalities were purported to contain. Now he no longer understood the local nobility. He understood them, he could grasp the economic interests of these people intending to wait out the political turmoil in the safety of their estates, but he was ashamed of them—sitting there calmly, not having their people kick the squads of Nazi thugs out of the laborers' settlements, not proclaiming either directly or through the church that they were against the National Socialist plebs. He was ashamed of the church. It bothered him that Papenbrock didn't give his son a good smack. He used to agree with Papenbrock, not only over wine but also about the decisions he wanted to see emerge from the city council meetings. Papenbrock had been too genteel to put himself up for office, but he had liked having his finger in every pie that Town Hall had in the oven. Now he was letting his brat put a red flag with a swastika on the town hall and set an armed guard to watch over it, a guard who aimed his gun at Ete Helms the moment Helms showed his face at the edge of the dormer window, and that gun wasn't loaded with birdshot either.

Erdamer's colleagues in the senate of the Free Hanseatic City of Lübeck had shown him the way: the ones from the Social Democratic Party had stepped down, even though the Reichstag election had nothing at all to do with the makeup of the local government. It was unconstitutional. It was against the law. And he'd spent his whole life in small towns. He no longer had a chance at a ministerial position in Schwerin. In Jerichow, his daughter was losing a friend, this Lisbeth Papenbrock with her Cresspahl in England. He was losing control over, and responsibility for, the knife fights in the villages, the nightly exchanges of gunfire between Reichsbanner members and the SA auxiliary police. He was losing the weekly wrangles with the Nazis in the city council over Semig the Jew. He was losing the people who had waited until eleven o'clock on Sunday night by Johs. Schmidt's loudspeakers for the election results, enjoying the warm air, practically drunk on each new vote count. They were acting like not only the police but the tax office was about to be abolished. He had been unable to reach anyone on the phone in the Schwerin party office, or even in Gneez. That afternoon, when he called the city council meeting to order, he had not yet decided. Then the Jerichow Social Democrats resigned: Upahl, Stoffregen, Piep, Piepenbrink. Even Stoffregen. Kleineschulte with his Hugenberg Party stayed; Kleineschulte said he'd come see him that night to explain himself. It was not prearranged that he would throw Kleineschulte out. Erdamer was now forty-three years old. When he stood up, his shoulders fell quite naturally into the bearing of an officer. He held his chin so high that he couldn't see anyone who was sitting down. He felt the brief, then lowered glances at his gaunt head, close-cropped all around, at his eyes almost blind with strain, at the contemptuous twitching of the corner of his mouth, and he was sure they were watching not without concern as he walked out the door.

From the top of the town hall steps, he saw Cresspahl approaching across the market square, Papenbrock's son-in-law, clearly wanting to register his child, the child to whose health he had just drunk on Saturday. He decided not to tell him that the registrar was taking minutes at the council meeting and thus unavailable, and then, as he started walking away, a rather haughty upright man in riding boots under a long coat, no further decision was guiding his footsteps. He passed between the two sentries without seeing them (otherwise he could have greeted them by first name), he was through them before they managed to turn Horst Papenbrock's now truly uncertain command into a lopsided present-arms maneuver, he was past Cresspahl without having acknowledged him, and Cresspahl stood there, stopped in three different tracks at once—saying good day, expressing indignation at Horst, and taking a first half step to follow Erdamer—stopped in the middle of Market Square, in full view of the bystanders, baffled, openmouthed, with an expression on his face both deaf and listening, like a trapped rabbit waiting for the blow not a breath away from its neck.

Shut up, Gesine. Shut yer mouth.

October 27, 1967 Friday
is the day on which *The New York Times* reports the following: People tend to forget things associated with unpleasant experiences.

This has been proven to *The New York Times* by means of an experiment two Princeton researchers conducted on sixteen undergraduates. The subjects were volunteers who did not know the objective of the study. First, they were taught a language of ten three-letter nonsense syllables and English-word equivalents for each, for example MEMORY (mental images, recall, retention, etc.) for DAX. Then they were given a second list with ten other English words subliminally associated with the words of the first list. The vocabulary of the second list, like the contents of the first list, was projected on a screen, only this time some of the words were presented simultaneously with an electric shock to the volunteer's hand. The shock created a bridge across the associations to the corresponding made-up word from the first list and incinerated the nexus, while the pain-free correspondences remained in the students' minds. That's the proof. QED. If you don't believe it, that'll be ten cents. *The New York Times* costs ten cents. There it sits next to us, on the visitor's chair, so eager it's on the edge of its seat, hat askew, and it talks and talks and keeps us from our work.

Giving the customers what they want, Gesine.

The latest news of Science.

It's relevant for your problems too, Gesine. You're interested in how forgetting works.

How remembering works.

All these years we've just lived our lives and taken it for granted.

And now at last two men show up in Princeton and lay it all out for us.

That they've proven it.

They say they've proven it.

They have proven it, Gesine.

What was it that they decided they had to prove?

Common knowledge.

"I remember things I don't care about"?

No. "Painful things get forgotten."

Why is this superstition worth an experiment?

So that we can make use of it, should the need arise.

Which forgetting do they mean, then? Vienna-style, London-style, Chicago-style?

Simple obliteration, Gesine. The annihilation of what had been known.

Make use of it for political purposes?

No ethical person would . . .

But Science would, definitely.

For the time being, Science has only observed a learning process.

In no more than sixteen people.

Who are volunteers, so above suspicion.

So not even chosen for their ability to remember, or to forget.

Who are unsuspecting, so they constitute convincing evidence.

So they also have no motivation to remember or forget.

Yes they do. A couple of dollars.

People to whom the learning process itself offers only modest pleasure or profit.

At least they're all the same age.

A Granny Prüss would've not only remembered the electric shock but dug around in her mind for the reason behind it. Granny Prüss holds a grudge.

A learning process culminates in one of two genuine alternatives.

With a shock you forget, with bodily comfort you retain. What a crap choice.

But reasonable.

As reasonable as the cow who gets shock after shock from an electrified fence. The cow just can't learn.

With your cows, the shock is what they're supposed to learn, Gesine.

And with people, forgetting is supposed to be transferrable, or what?

It's indirect, don't you understand?

With just ten word pairs.

Still.

All with a breaking point in the same place, prepared in advance.

The breaking is real, Gesine. It's still real.

An arbitrary grouping of thirty letters into clusters of three, that's what The New York Times *calls "a language."*

As does Science, Gesine. The Times *is strictly following Science.*

A language of unrelated words?

I'm sure that Science has its well-considered reasons.

Learning a language involves using what you've learned.

In that case, forgetting would be too hard.

That's what makes it worth anything.

The experiment was not about semantics, Gesine.

And they gave it no time to mature in the memory.

The existence of a forgetting has been proven.

But no one had any desire to retain this useless vocabulary in the first place.

Everyone was given the same democratic choice between retaining something and forgetting it.

A blind reaction.

An automatic reaction.

The alternatives weren't evenly balanced; they tipped the scale with pain on one side.

And the burdened alternative was destroyed.

And there you have it.

What we have, Gesine, is a functional model of the finest behavioristic provenance.

Bioveristic?

Don't be rude, Gesine. The New York Times *pronounces her words loud and clear.*

Science knows best.

Right you are, Gesine. Where would we be without Science. Where would the USA be without its scientists.
Who prove an experiment with an experiment.
And prove that pain is linked to memory, whether positively or negatively. Somehow.
It's "unambiguous," Gesine. The gentlemen say so themselves.
And Auntie Times protects herself with quotation marks.
Quotation marks prove that the words someone has said are being reliably repeated.
But words were just incinerated, weren't they?
Just words, Gesine. No one was hurt.
What if another newspaper spelled the word "words" with the letters t, h, i, n, g, s?
That would be inexcusable, misleading the reader, a sin against the spirit of journalism, unforgivable for all eternity.
And why does The New York Times *do this?*
All the better to catch you with, my dears.
My, what big teeth you have.

October 28, 1967 Saturday
John Sidney McCain III, for example, was shot down over Hanoi. He'd survived the fire on the USS *Forrestal* aircraft carrier in July. After seeing (his words): "what the bombs and napalm did to the people on our ship, I'm not so sure that I want to drop any more of that stuff on North Vietnam." But he did it anyway, and now Radio Hanoi has reported his capture.

The Soviets have an asset in Great Britain, a married couple of spies, Helen and Peter Kroger, sentenced to prison until 1981. The British have someone of their own, Gerald Brooke, allegedly in a Soviet labor camp until 1970. The Soviets want to trade. The British say no deal.

Yesterday afternoon in a student dorm in Brooklyn, the same dorm where on Thursday night one co-ed had already been raped and another one robbed, a man pushed a student into her apartment and put a wire around her neck ... She fought him off.

DAX, friend of MEMORY, has been murdered by GRANNY. The old

lady used an electric shock, conducted through MEMORY into DAX. MEMORY is said to be doing well; all that's left of DAX is a charred black spot.

The news is from yesterday, and still not forgotten. This procedure aimed to reveal the theoretical underpinning of a real process. We were supposed to be able to transplant it into reality. Something gets lost in the repotting, the circumstances are changed, but still, the plant ought to be recognizable. So, Comrade Writer, give me ten words.

PLISCH
PLUM
SCHMULCHEN
SCHIEVELBEINER
ROOSEVELT
CHURCHILL
BOLSHEVIK
WORLDWIDE-JEWISH-CONSPIRACY
SUBHUMAN
BRAINIAC

These are words Gesine Cresspahl knew at age seven. They are not pathogen-free, not synthetic substances. Now artificial units, like DAX for MEMORY or CEF for STEM (root, shaft, stalk), offer the imagination a not entirely cold shoulder: some combinations are neutral, some ominous, some appealing. The words from PLISCH to BRAINIAC are like DAX and CEF in one important way: their unreality. Like the three-letter words for the Princeton students, these words for a seven-year-old child in small-town Mecklenburg circa 1940 were not real, not actual, they were fictive things. One might have meant dog, or puppy, but the dogs in Jerichow were different. One might have meant whiskey, or cigar, but there was no whiskey, and cigars were rationed, that is to say, tangible enough to take on an entirely different reality through their absence. These words came from children's books, or newspapers, or matters that grown-ups let slip. They were playthings.

The Princeton experiment wouldn't have chosen words from only one semantic cluster, would it? No, and the child in Jerichow, when she learned PLUM and CHURCHILL, had no idea of the connection between those words either. The connection was just an impression, vaguely felt, in any case not without danger. The picture book was locked away at night. Talk about THE JEW turned shamefaced somehow, with a kind of premonition. But there weren't any in Jerichow. I didn't know it about Dr. Semig. It was impossible to incorporate the words into the day-to-day life of the town. They were not words at all, only sonic receptacles for content not belonging to them, slippery mixtures creeping around within the walls of the letters as vague blobs—spreading out, balling up, soft, wiggly, ungraspable. These words were so unreal that they should have gone around only in quotation marks: instead of DAX, "SCHMULCHEN."

So: "PLISCH," "PLUM," "SCHMULCHEN"... —those ten are the first group. And, just as unreal letter clusters were chosen for the Princeton students (instead of RAILROAD or GARTER BELT, the forgetting of which would have meant an irreplaceable loss), it wouldn't much matter if anything happened to "BOLSHEVIK."

The second group, linked to the nonsense syllables by correspondences imposed by reason not animated from within, is: PLISCH, PLUM, SCHMUL-CHEN, SCHIEVELBEINER, ROOSEVELT...

Just as any interaction between CEF and STEM can only be forced, so too "PLISCH" has nothing to say to PLISCH, and "CHURCHILL" has never heard of CHURCHILL, and "SCHIEVELBEINER" did not even know enough about SCHIEVELBEINER to spread nasty rumors about him. Because Schievelbeiner the Jew in the children's book, dancing in terror between the yapping dogs Plisch and Plum to the merry laughter of the German child and man looking on, is not Schievelbeiner the actual person, who bears his name as a name and not out of Austrian spite. That actual person is perfectly capable of defending himself against a couple of misbehaving mutts. The "whiskey-guzzling Churchill with the cigar in his maw and a machine gun in his hand" was one thing—invented, imagined, unreal, "Judaized." The other one was a living English person, male, first name Winston, middle initial S., with a last name invoking a place of Christian worship that was sick, but only in the idle mental games of a schoolgirl learning her first foreign language. Likewise, the "SUBHUMAN" lived on, faceless and without prospects, alongside the imaginable and real human being who found himself in a subordinated position. The same words not in quotes in the second group are the content, the new material to be learned—irreconcilable with the first group, lacking any spontaneous, mutual understanding; battling for sole rule, bent on the other's destruction, forced into having any relationship with the other at all. This, too, we learned, and like experimental subjects we didn't know why.

We can also confirm the existence of a functioning method of administering a shock that produces a guaranteed effect.

The means of administering the shock: a photograph the British took in the Bergen-Belsen concentration camp and printed in the newspaper they authorized in Lübeck after the war.

The effect has not ceased to this day. It affected me as an individual: I am the child of a father who knew about the systematic murder of the Jews. It affected my group: I may have been twelve years old at the time, but I belong to a national group that massacred an excessive number of members of another group (to a child even the spectacle of a single victim would have been excessive). The shock can be proven to have been effective, the evidence being a range of hamstrung reactions. Miss Cresspahl, student in Halle in 1952, could endure a Professor Ertzenberger's lectures only as long as she could block out of her mind the fact that he was one of the surviving Jews. (By that point, Jews dependably appeared in the German language only in the plural, not in the singular with a definite article.) She lost all trust in the East German republic solely because it seemed prepared to perpetuate Stalin's crackdown on the January 1953 "doctors' plot," thereby breaking an anti-Fascist more-or-less promise. Cresspahl the tourist subjected those around her to her miserable French in every foreign country, even where the Germans weren't proven perpetrators of kidnappings or murdering hostages. Cresspahl the immigrant warily, abruptly turned and walked out of a diner near Union Square in New York when she recognized the owners' language as Yiddish. The shock's effectiveness is proven.

At Princeton, the pain introduced along with the projection of the word GRANNY crept into the word MEMORY through secret tunnels and leaped from there across to its other identity, DAX, burning the bridge behind it. DAX alias memory was forgotten.

Maybe the word SLENDER appeared unaccompanied by an electric shock, so STEM could live on for a while with its companion, CEF. In the Mecklenburg experiment, though, every one of the corresponding trigger words came with shocks:

RACE-
BAITING
SAMUEL
DEFAMATION
US PRESIDENT
BRITISH PRIME MINISTER
TAKEOVER OF POWER
GENOCIDE
VICTIM
TALKING HORSE

and they didn't extinguish "PLISCH," and not "PLUM" either. While washing my hands, while driving a car, from out of nowhere, the rhymes from the children's book by the great German anti-Semite Wilhelm Busch come flooding back into consciousness, complete with his drawings and the enchantment of a child circa 1940:

There goes Schmulchen Schivelbeiner.
Surely ours is so much finer.
There he goes with crooked nose,
We like ours much more than those.
*   Oh, woe is me!*

When Roosevelt comes to mind, the justification keeps popping up that he wasn't in fact the head of the Worldwide Jewish Conspiracy; our mourning for Churchill's death grew out of a desire to contradict Fascist propaganda; the Nazi use of the word "BOLSHEVIK" ultimately served to immunize us against postwar bourgeois warnings about the export of Socialism from the Soviet Union. "WORLDWIDE JEWISH CONSPIRACY" and "SUBHUMAN" have survived, but only as symptoms letting us diagnose anyone who speaks those words as a Fascist. And the talking horse, the "BRAINIAC," lives on as an inverted prejudice, a double-edged compliment for intellectuals whether Jewish or Muslim. Nothing has been forgotten. It has taken root. It doesn't pop up during conversations with Jewish people, it doesn't dare emerge from memory at the sight of Jewish newspapers on Broadway, but it's there, extant, retained. These words were, just like CEF and DAX, the weakest links in the chain, sensitive to pressure, fragile, perishable, the way a child can learn them and not see them, not use them, not grasp them, not have them.

Maybe we're wrong? Maybe the reason the Fascist garbage is lodged so firmly in memory is that the schools in the Soviet occupation zone in Germany spent so much time publicizing the . . . the things the Germans as National Socialists had done to the Jews?

No. The schools explained these . . . things to us as predictable symptoms of the decline of capitalism in its most highly developed phase, imperialism. Yet these same lessons gave us ways to understand that what had produced the attempted "Final Solution to the Jewish Problem" was not realpolitik or some economic mechanism but the German variety of madness. (And the schools soon started using the same categories they'd initially labeled as reprehensible: a "Churchill" who was "following the City's orders," a "Roosevelt" who'd been a "pawn in the hands of the business interests.") If the schools had had their way, we would have forgotten "Plisch" and "Plum" altogether. And it was the experimental subject's own efforts, it turns out, that produced the strongest electric shock: when she learned that there'd once been a city in Pommern named Schivelbein; when she discovered that a prophet and judge of Israel lay hidden behind "Schmulchen." The shock was enough to create: the wish to forget, the having of nightmares, the blind futile struggle of the sleeper to defend herself against something that would never entirely disappear upon any awakening.

– Saturday! Marie says. – *Tag der South Ferry!* she says: South Ferry day.

October 29, 1967 Sunday, end of Daylight Saving Time
On Fifty-Third Street near Fifth Avenue yesterday, at around noon, actors handed a woman on the street a red plastic water gun, pushed her into a circle, and told her to shoot a young boy who they said was a member of the Vietcong. The woman, a twenty-year-old German visiting the city, aimed her weapon straight at the boy and pulled the trigger. The boy fell back and lay sprawled on the pavement. When the actors who were mingled with the onlookers disappeared, and for some time afterward, Miss Gritli Kux still didn't know what had happened.

The Protestant church in Jerichow, to which Cresspahl paid a visit to

register the birth of his child, was still Pastor Methling's church; he had
been in Jerichow so long, making himself seen, felt, heard.

Seen, as a man almost six and a half feet tall, some two hundred and
twenty-five pounds, in a cassock wide enough around his belly but too
short at the ankles so that clayey boots often showed under his black gown
as he strode down Town Street, head held high on his way to house visits,
head lowered behind Swenson's hearse, and just as his flock wanted to take
him down a peg in the former case, they didn't believe his show of humility in the latter. Because he was a shouter. In the fall of 1927, when he was
brought in by Provost Swantenius, they had expected a battle-weary shepherd of souls, relegated to a small town to serve out his time on his way to
a pension, barely diligent enough to handle the holiday decorations. But
the new pastor had no truck with mildness. On the contrary. Nor with
the custom of requesting church services for ceremonial occasions solely
to ensure that the wedding or birth lacked for nothing ("everything done
properly"). He went to people's houses uninvited, no one even had to be
sick, and took a seat so assertively that only someone like Peter Wulff dared
refuse him hospitality. And he brought the church into holidays his predecessor had observed in private: the anniversary of the founding of the
German Reich, the Kaiser's birthday, the commemoration of the Battle of
Tannenberg. He started a parish paper, *A Ramble Around St. Peter's*, and
didn't let it be bought by the issue: only full subscriptions, to those who
donated. It only took a few straight Sundays of preaching (or, Ottje Stoffregen's word, "raging") about "hardness of heart," with special reference
to Jerichow, and Maass on Market Square got his money to print the paper,
and additional work too, posters. Though boys as young as ten were put to
work in Jerichow, the pastor started an Iron Ring group and kept the
children in it with badges and exercises in full regalia; he may have not let
them join political groups but the populist young brotherhood did have
to wear uniforms to their meetings, and their motto was "Grab on—Hold
tight," which definitely didn't mean that a German should let go of anything
that was his, whether things or thoughts. Pastor Methling, chin politely
raised, showed his hard-boiled egg of a head with a tiny little face attached
to the front in family photos and in *The Gneez Daily News*, for he was
especially proud of its pronounced features, regarding them as authentically

Mecklenburgish and Low German. No less so was the language he spoke before the city council, whose deliberations now suddenly had to take the "interests of the church" into account—the councilmen had barely realized such things existed before. The nobility, who had summoned the new pastor to come introduce himself when he first arrived in Jerichow, then couldn't get rid of him, and when he greeted, say, Baroness von Plessen on the street, it was not to claim equality—as when, for instance, old Papenbrock did it—but instead an act of unmistakable condescension, bringing his hand to the brim of his hat very slowly and tipping it back with an excessively solemn turn of the wrist, and if Louise Papenbrock might have taken Methling's superior knowledge of the Bible as sufficient excuse for such behavior, Estate Holder Kleineschulte must have understood it rather differently, for he ceased to brandish his hat before Pastor Methling, preferring instead his whip.

He made himself felt. He started by asking the congregation not to hang their hats and caps on the ends of the pews during services; he proceeded by demanding that women who had just given birth give thanks for their recovery by going to church; he prevailed by requiring, through an order of the parish council, Gothic lettering (not Roman) on gravestones, so that a German could be a real German, even when moldering. If the mother of an illegitimate child didn't come voluntarily, he might go to the manager of the estate, find out enough about the girl's case to mortify her completely, then have her summoned to a meeting that inevitably ended in tears. Methfessel the butcher had wanted to pay for his son's christening with only the fee, not the recitation of the promise to raise this new addition to the human race in a Christian spirit and urge him to Christian deeds; the pastor refused, and Methfessel caved, and he was hardly the only one to do so. They put up with Methling's jovial behavior because it brought him, if not exactly into the nobility, at least to a somewhat comparable elevation. Then again, his familiarities, his rigidities, his windbaggery at patriotic proclamations also invited retaliation. Picking a fight with him might cost money but could be fun. No one had ever been able to catch him out with a girl. That he liked a drink or two was something he was only too ready to admit himself, there was no point filing a complaint with the Gneez superintendent's office about that. But even that dirt on his boots, meant as an ostentatious sign of Jerichow's rural circumstances, was good for a shake of the head or a bit of a laugh—for someone well past sixty to let himself go like that! And they'd put one over on him once, on Reformation Day in 1931, when the guildsmen did not, as he'd wanted, come to church in top hats to protest the construction of a Catholic church but rather welcomed the income that would come from the contracts. It was felt around town that only Papenbrock could stand up to Mething; when he'd let his younger daughter work for Mething, he must have gotten something in return, even if what that might have been remained unclear for the time being.

And Pastor Mething made himself heard. Alas, he had something troubling him. Was it a competitor? Even an enemy, perhaps? He sometimes called it a godless element, and the Communist Party might come to his listeners' minds. In the spring of 1932, they discovered their mistake. Mething preached about choosing children's names and warned against those of Jewish-Greek derivation, although the Plattdeutsch accent in his booming bass voice had faded a bit in his seventeen years of service on the border of Brandenburg. Mething, a paying member of every local historical association in Mecklenburg, preached from the pulpit about the clamor among the people for racially pure marriages, and pronounced that clamor justified. Below the pulpit sat Mething's wife: short, slight, noticeably older than him, so intimidated her gaze was almost dumbstruck, her shiny black hair done up in a bun, childless, surrounded on the street by crowds of children, and not of Mething's race. Race, in Mething's view, was an earthly barrier that would be overcome in heaven; he wanted to respect the Jews and love them and convert them to the true faith—but not be ruled by them (that wouldn't be Christian). He accused the Jews of greed for money; the congregation reflected on how Mething preferred to be paid in cash for performing his church duties. Dr. Semig had given discounts often enough. Mething spoke of the Jewish indifference to the ideal of the nation, but he had been home in the fatherland preaching while Semig was fighting in the trenches. He didn't mean Semig, no, not Semig, he didn't mean Tannebaum the clothier on Short Street either—although he'd allow them to buy graves in his cemetery only with a 100 percent surcharge—he meant national character, Teutonic heritage, racial honor. Now Semig no longer showed his face on the street, no longer went to the City of Hamburg Hotel. Now Semig stayed home, next to a telephone that never rang, in front of a calendar that even in December had still had appointments in it but now was almost empty.

Wilhelm Methling was still in Jerichow, even though he'd come into a nice house in Gneez after he retired. From Gneez he continued to edit his rambles around the spire of St. Peter's Church, with the help of Stoffregen the teacher. Stoffregen wrote little local-history essays about places around Jerichow; he published funny things children had said that people sent in, and family news, and photos of the windmills still standing in the area; meanwhile Methling sat in Gneez and wrote about trees—trees in folk songs, in legend, on the country road if necessary, and from every last one he managed a transition to family trees, bloodlines, Staemmler's draft laws against racial mixing, marriage prohibitions, genealogical research (q.v. Jesus's family tree in the book of Luke)—and now he wanted money for a job he used to perform for the honor of it. And it was Methling, at a town meeting in Gneez, who worded the congratulatory telegram to the new chancellor of the Reich, and in *The Gneez Daily News* there was a photo of him reading it: an old man full of childlike joy at seeing the goal of his life not bypassed by history but in power; a big shining Mecklenburg egg of a head, somewhat flat on the top and slightly squeezed and wrinkly at the sides.

Here was where Cresspahl wanted to register the birth of his child.

Standing outside the pastor's house, he saw the nameplate for the new pastor, Brüshaver, and remembered. The front door was locked. Cresspahl went around the side of the house, across the muddy entrance to Creutz's garden, but the gate to the pastor's yard was locked, and no one was moving behind the windows' red reflections.

Here, at the northern end of our neighborhood, stands the Church of St. John the Divine, the largest Gothic cathedral in the world, three blocks wide, from 111th St. to 113th St. on Amsterdam Avenue, begun in 1892, no further construction since 1941, unfinished, without the planned central dome and the two west towers. We've always called it the Cathedral of St. John the Unfinished. Now it shall remain so: as long as Horace W. B. Donegan is the bishop of New York; until the suffering of the disadvantaged citizens in the surrounding slums has been ameliorated. Those are two different dates.

– I don't understand: Marie says. – How can I have gained an hour just by changing the clocks?

– Because you had an hour less sleep on April 30. Daylight saving time got you out of bed too early.

– But if I don't remember it, is it still real?

October 30, 1967 Monday

Once again Mr. George Gallup has turned to the nation. This time with the question: What would you say to handing the war over by stages to the South Vietnamese? Out of every hundred respondents, nine had no idea and twenty were opposed. It sounded like a good idea to the other seventy-one.

Yesterday, in East Berlin, the East German and Soviet armies paraded tanks, heavy artillery, ground-to-ground rockets, antitank rockets, and antiaircraft rockets. The television commentary from an East German military expert described the tanks as "capable of operating in areas contaminated by nuclear explosions."

The first noise was the slapping of the elevator cables. As though the chains were beating against the walls of the shaft.

Above Riverside Park, a brightly colored bird gave off a swishing swinging sound. Then it lifted its tail and hung in the wind over the Hudson and cried *arr-arr*. It was not an ABC TV copter, sir, it was your escaped electric razor, whose motor has had just about enough of its casing.

Then you can talk to me all you want about recessed roller friction: the subway trains lumber, the compressed-air opening of the doors is a human exhalation, even if only the waiting passengers make them that. Inside, as the train stops, all the overhead handholds jolt lightly back against their springs; the passengers start moving their hands and elbows, pulling newspapers, handbags, shopping bags close; everyone turns to face the car doors, hoping that today, as on every other day, the doors will obey their valves and roll aside, half into one wall, half into the other.

The car horns are tuned to a single note, but one modulated as the sound ricochets down brick and concrete channels, sideways, under bridges, upwards. The police sirens are almost an element of the air, adjustable from a polite whimper to the howl of berserkers. They are followed by the cars with beds for the dead.

Desperate shrieking of rails under Park Avenue in the Forties. The approach to Grand Central is the neck of the bottle that the police often use to describe traffic. Who wants to keep seeing all those trains under their feet? Are they anything more than a monument?

In the elevator, the buttons, soft receptacles for pressure, yield with a secret click when touched, as though in response to a good deed, and express their thanks with a yellow glow.

When the thermostats mandate a pause in the blowing of the air conditioners, everybody dies a little, because something they're used to is gone and they can't quite put their finger on what it was. Yet for a little while the ribs of the machine spew out absolutely no more cold air. As though someone would never breathe again.

The coins dance happily in the head of the coin counter that keeps bus drivers from one kind of dishonesty. And the nickels that the driver releases as change from a quarter sound fatter since the fare hike; now I can hear the silver in the dimes I used to get back.

The hospitable clatter of cheap silverware on the dining counters, the slapping down of the bill with what is almost a blow of the fist, and the plate placed with nearly sisterly attentiveness: There you go, darling.

And again the machines contentedly gulping subway token after subway token on behalf of the Transit Authority, down throats grinding with pleasure that the riders set chewing inside the three-armed turnstiles up to five times per minute, maybe six times a minute, that would be some sixteen hundred an hour in the four lanes, that's too many, and yet there are more than that. And again the heavy rumbling noise, audible through all the sways and jolts and braking processes, which betrays the excessive weight of the payload and reflects it in the base of the skull as a feeling of almost dangerous pressure.

In the bar the man behind the counter puts down your glass with an uneven sound, and the other half of the base of the glass follows quick as an afterthought. Hesitantly perhaps he scoops up the coins placed on the counter and lets the prepared selection of three coins skip between two fingers against the countertop before ringing them up, after three inaudible steps to the register, by pressing on three keys, which snap into place and echo for some customers with the violence of thunderclaps, and like fate itself is the rough blow of the side of the hand slapping shut the drawer that has sprung out from the base. Sir.

"Off so soon, Mrs. Cresspahl?"

"Oh, here you are, Gesine."

Late at night, the half-raised window. A defenseless ear to which cars driving by at liberal speeds patiently and yet again explain the Doppler effect, or into which sudden noises blast with no subtleties at all, buses starting up, creating the sonic world anew and carrying off the merely remembered one. Highway traffic noise, filtered through branches as thin as hairs, tests wind strengths of four to six, transmits groundswells and receding breakers, suspends pauses of wind, hurls waves like water—and now the comparison with the Baltic shuts the traffic out of this perception, replacing it with nothing.

In Queens not long ago, four blocks blew up with a noise one would expect from a gas main explosion, and the loved ones the residents the citizens of Queens told the paper: It was like something from outer space, like a cataclysm, somehow inhuman.

This is the sound I now hear from the apartment next door, from the ABC TV evening news, from Vietnam. Like something from outer space, it is cataclysmic like flak shrapnel just before the sudden, dull, earthshaking impact of the bombs, it is human. Sir.

October 31, 1967 Tuesday

In Cologne, former SS officers Carl Schulze and Anton Streitwieser were sentenced to prison and hard labor on charges of accessory to murder in their concentration camps, in nine and three cases, respectively. It is estimated that 120,000 people died in Mauthausen and its subcamps.

The picture of the Vietnamese woman with outstretched hands in the smoke and rubble of her village, pleading with US soldiers that her home be spared, is on page 3.

In Sing Sing, computer programming is to be added to the curriculum.

March 1933 in Jerichow was also, all else aside, a season. The sea wind may have still blown into town, but wisps of rested earth, of coming flowers, fluttered in with it. There were gulls in the air, frisky fliers. Fat pigeons warming themselves in the lee of the chimneys, slipping off in leisurely glides, shitting on the long red flag flying over Town Hall. The sparrows let everyone know they were all taken care of. The light warmed the bricks, dyed the plaster of the town hall yellow, brought the grayed wood of the yard gates to life. Anyone looking could easily get the impression that nothing was amiss. It'll all work out. *Take care a isself.* Now we just need to get the child into the files so she'll have her papers for Richmond. Then we'll pack her in a basket, I'll pick up one handle and you'll take the other, and we'll carry her home.

Avenarius Kollmorgen, licensed attorney, a little short but very stocky, strolled across Market Square with his elbows out, making his face with its parted lips and twinkling eyes even wider, and he doffed his hat to Cresspahl and squeaked in his pinched voice: All's well, Herr Cresspahl? All's well? and he paddled on and didn't turn around and wasn't expecting an answer. All's well, Cresspahl?

In the registrar's office, Fritz Schenk had risen to his feet when handing over the birth certificate and given Cresspahl a handshake to congratulate him on the splendid times in which he had brought a child into the world— Fritz Schenk, the rabbit researcher whose mother hadn't told him where children come from. Clicked his heels, and stuffily looked Cresspahl straight in the eye, and said: Life really is different now. This job is fun again! And in fact the birth rate rose in 1933, for girls it would do so every year until 1942, for boys it declined as early as 1941, and Fritz Schenk was looking forward to having more opportunities to apply his large S, convoluted with curlicues, which devoured the rest of his name in one flourish: Schenk, Records Clerk. Cresspahl returned the handshake in silence. He could think of nothing to say. He didn't think to remember the incident, he thought he had no further reason to. All he had left to take care of now were the church and the certificate from Brüshaver.

If you asked Papenbrock, this Brüshaver was pathetic. He offered the town none of the entertainment you could count on from Pastor Methling. He never dropped by uninvited. He didn't leave the house in his cassock, he walked down Town Street in a suit that was not even black, a man of forty already walking with a stoop, with narrow shoulders, a little square mustache, such a faraway look in his eyes that his prompt reply to a greeting was a bit startling. It was always disappointing to see him take his gown out of his bag in the front hall and put it on, as though getting dressed to do repairs or some other such work, not perform an ineffable act. Well, they said dying with him was nice. But people like Käthe Klupsch—with ancestral seats in the front pew, under the pulpit—missed Methling's loud zeal, said Brüshaver was like a doctor, and not only at sickbeds. And Brüshaver spoke, he didn't preach. He didn't raise his voice, didn't fling out his arms. He acted like church was his job. He thundered no threats when someone had failed to fulfill their religious obligation—he brought up the oversight casually. He issued no proclamations, neither about hats on the pew ends nor about recuperated new mothers. Methling had put on a real show, having beggars stand ten feet from his door and throwing them used clothes and berating them for reeking of alcohol in a hail of abuse, not without sniffing; Brüshaver quietly invited them into the house and they could take what they wanted from the Winter Relief and put it on then and there and come back out onto the street looking like respectable citizens. And Brüshaver stayed home. He didn't turn up at the Lübeck Court. Not only was he missing at Steel Helmet and Tannenberg Society meetings, he was not even a member. What infuriated Papenbrock most was the way Brüshaver had read the Protestant Church's proclamation for the March elections. ("For fourteen years, the forces of centrism, Social Democracy, and Communism, with their *international* connections... Now, in the struggle against these powers, the renewal of Germany must begin *from within* ...") – Like how you'd read a bank statement! Papenbrock had groused. It wasn't grand enough for him, it almost spoiled his mood as he went to go vote.

Brüshaver wasn't home. Cresspahl was received by his wife, who to him seemed like a girl, not only because she was barely thirty but also because of her relaxed, offhand movements, because her blond braids were wound so loosely around her head, because she seemed too young and too bright amid the dark books and furniture of the pastor's office. And she didn't quite manage to treat Cresspahl as a helpless young father. She tried, but not even the dignity of her proxy duties sufficed. When she wrote down the names and dates, she held herself like a schoolgirl. She leaned her face so close to the book, pressed her index finger down so hard without realizing it. – And when? she said, her pencil poised above Brüshaver's appointment book. Then he realized she'd been watching him closely the whole time, appraisingly but without real curiosity. What he'd thought was friendliness was an illusion caused by her youth. She, too, wanted to make him pay for the Papenbrock family. But by then he'd been looking at her steadily and obligingly for too long, he couldn't very well be unfriendly to her now.

– Wednesday morning we have the Voss funeral. Voss, in Rande, whom the Nazis beat to death. Later would be fine, let's say Wednesday at eleven: she said. Now she wasn't looking at him, she paged through her calendar, darted her pencil around the columns for the days, and without looking up took down Lisbeth's request for a church christening (no charge) on Sunday, March 12. She said goodbye to him in the hall, took her apron back off its hook, let him see himself out.

A home christening the very first available morning, Cresspahl.
It costs two marks, it's not the end of the world.
The child would've been ready to travel.
Lisbeth didn't have Berling's permission yet.
And she wanted to be completely sure. She wanted to extend your time in Germany with a later date at the church.
A home christening just wasn't enough for her.
She put one over on you, Cresspahl.
I didn't want to think that, Gesine. And you'll learn soon enough.

November 1, 1967 Wednesday
The authorities of the Soviet Union want to show us what "Socialist humanism" is and plan to release various people from their prisons and labor camps, such as war invalids, decorated veterans, pregnant women, and women with underage children, although not, for instance, two recalcitrant writers.

The authorities of mainland China have issued their 444th "serious warning" against the USA, this time for border violations at sea.

The authorities of the USA are celebrating the longest economic boom in human history, tied with the previous record (eighty months) and still going, and *The New York Times* has given its employees a raise.

Last night a group of Negroes celebrated All Saints' Eve in Montefiore Cemetery in Queens, knocking down gravestones and throwing small stones and eggs at passing cars. By the time the police drove up, first with one radio car and then with forty, the youths bombarding the representatives of law and order with bottles and rocks numbered three hundred, all of them "colored," as a rule of language would have it.

On Broadway in our neighborhood, too, bands of children were running wild—in witch's robes, in witch's hats, faces painted and blackened, but beneath the paint and the blackening their skin was pink and so even a policeman was fair game. He strolled down the sidewalk deep in thought, letting his holster bob against his hip and his nightstick twirl around his wrist, suspecting nothing, when five costumed children surrounded him, hopping and screaming, and offered him the options of paying a tribute or paying the price, until he started feeling around for coins in his back pocket, embarrassed, restrained from defending himself by the watchful eyes of the adult passersby, who not only monitored whether he acted as a Friend and Helper but also wanted to see with their own eyes a policeman publicly coughing up real genuine money. One of the children, keeping to the edge of the holdup, gesticulating and chanting in a not entirely carefree way, a girl about Marie's height, was wearing a long yellow cloak with black tiger stripes much like the one that Marie had made over the weekend. Her face was blackened, and a black hood hid her hair, and even from a distance she couldn't be Marie. Marie had wanted to throw her own party for Halloween, All Hallows, All Saints' Eve, a party at her house, and her friend Francine was going to be allowed to come.

The howling mass had already blown through Maxie's store, and the man that the customers and employees called Max stood stunned amid his neatly laid out fruits and vegetables, for lying on the floor in the sawdust were trampled pears and grapes, flung down by disappointed children who wanted money. At the exit, near the hanging scales, a rearguard was still busy looting an older lady. She was audaciously dressed in bright colors, each piece of clothing a little off in one way or another, and her whitish strands of hair had a bluish shimmer, and she looked outlandish, not all there. She talked strangely. She had clearly collected change for this day, and she chattered on and on about the wonderful opportunity and permission the day afforded her to give these dear innocent young creatures a little joy, and Max's staff watched disapprovingly as she dug coin after coin from the depths of her faded handbag, not only nickels, quarters too, rattling blissfully on, blind to the fact that the young creatures in question looked demanding and extortionate more than anything else. No sooner had she left, head trembling, muttering to herself, than the staff turned on the boys and shooed them out onto the street, and even though they hadn't thought this customer was crazy before—she always paid for her vegetables—they now made gestures behind her back, saying that she was nuts, tapping on their foreheads just like the Germans do. Max said nothing about Marie. For six years now, Max has greeted the child with *Hey, Blondie!* and given her peaches or apples, Marie has gone through hundredweights of fruit in his store, and if he had recognized her among the Halloween marauders he would have mentioned it. – And the grapes that aren't good enough for this generation, they come from California, by air! he'd said. – Maine or Long Island potatoes today, Mrs. Cresspahl?

The plundered policeman was now outside Sloane's supermarket, his back to the wall, standing very straight, unapproachable. His twirling of his nightstick no longer looked quite so playful, more like practice, and however vacant and even-tempered his gaze might be now, no child would ever dare go up to him.

On the east side of West End Avenue, a troop of witch children was marching up the hill, plastic pumpkins on sticks in their hands, arms around one another's shoulders, walking in an almost exactly synchronized rhythm. They looked tiny next to the dark red and gray elephantine buildings, and so innocent, singing in their immature voices:

> *One little, two little, three little witches*
> *Fly over haystacks, fly over ditches,*
> *Fly to the moon without any hitches:*
> *Hi-ho Halloween's here,*

until they swept under the awning outside Marcia's front door, marched past a startled doorman into the lobby with the quick, shrill, badgering battle cry *Trick or treat! Trick or treat!*, and this time Marie was unmistakable, red boots, yellow cloak, black hood, a child who would rather give up her own party and go to someone else's than invite a child of a different skin color into her apartment.

And the child who came back home in blackest darkness had stood in the hall for fifteen minutes before she could bring herself to use her key. When she'd made up her mind, she'd rolled her Halloween costume into an unrecognizable bundle under her arm and walked past the table without a word, without a glance at dinner, straight to her room, and pulled the double door shut behind her, very softly, and wasn't heard from again until morning. Tonight is the second night that she offers the excuse of not being hungry, immediately shuts the doors behind her, and in general is acting uncommunicative but not stubborn (behavior she used to believe she hadn't inherited), but also like a child, with unguarded amazement, as though simply not understanding something.

It wasn't like that.
Tell it to Francine.
It wasn't like that. Marcia invited us before I could invite anyone.
And you're not allowed to bring colored children over to Marcia's.
It wasn't my party.
You promised Francine.
I promised it to you, she doesn't know anything about it.
I do.
Anyway, it wasn't a promise. It was a possible plan.
And so why wasn't it possible after all?
Can't you see I'm ashamed?
And is that a nice feeling?
For two days now you've thought I was lying.
So what happened?
I don't know why I did it.
Do you want me to try to tell you?
No. If you did, I'd think it was the truth.
What do you know so far.
Not the truth anyway.

The truth—as it said for all to read on the roof and side of a truck on Third Avenue—is:

The truth is that NU-Skin Wash is the best way to care for your skin.

That's the truth, and the advice about how to save your skin is free of charge.

November 2, 1967 Thursday

Let it be known to one and all that I, Elinor S. Donati, love my husband dearly, and as such hope to remain Mrs. William R. Donati forever and ever.

Are we supposed to send our congratulations? To: Mrs. William R. Donati, whoever that is, c/o The New York Times, Public Notices Department.

On March 11, 1933, Albert Papenbrock, grain merchant and bakery owner, Jerichow, Mecklenburg-Schwerin, gave a present to his granddaughter Gesine H. Cresspahl. He signed over to her a property on the edge of town, with land, barn, and outbuildings, to be administered for her until her majority by her father, Heinrich Cresspahl, master carpenter, Richmond, Greater London.

Lisbeth. Lisbeth. Lisbeth.
Think of the child, Cresspahl.
Lisbeth. Lisbeth.
We owe it to the child, Cresspahl.
Lisbeth.
What if something happened to us, Cresspahl.
This is why you came back to Germany, Lisbeth.
You knew I was going, Cresspahl.
It's not why I came.
You're here now.
And I didn't want to come.
It was your duty and obligation to come.
What if I hadn't?
Then you'd have had it your way.
I'm not staying in Germany.
But now we own a piece of it.
I don't need one.
But I do, Cresspahl.

You wrote in the birth notice: Jerichow and Richmond.

Because it was true.

Because you were bragging, Lisbeth.

No harm done.

They arrested me in Lübeck.

A misunderstanding.

I didn't see it that way.

We've had Nazis in the Mecklenburg government since last summer.

Silly asses.

See?

Gun-toting idiots.

See? What difference does it make to us, Cresspahl?

You're related to one.

All the better.

A house from your father, connections from your brother.

Another man would be happy about it.

Well I'm not another man.

Oh, Cresspahl, your pride.

Financially it's crazy.

Papenbrock bought out Zoll. Zoll's going to Gneez to join the party.

Him too. You too?

You have Fascists in London too, Cresspahl.

Not in the government.

Not yet.

Never.

You want to gamble when your own child's at stake?

We wouldn't be foreigners much longer, Lisbeth.

Long enough.

Lisbeth, the child would be a British citizen.

Not right away.

Is this why she had to be born in Jerichow?

Yes.

Yes?

It wasn't right for me there, Cresspahl.

You wanted a house in Richmond.

And now I want one here.

You got by just fine in Richmond.
Even the colors were too much for me.
The colors. Lisbeth.
Yes. The red. The blue. On the ships, the mailboxes, the uniforms. Such
cold colors.
The colors that that painter used, Con . . .
John Constable. Now he was a painter. Those were landscapes.
You liked them.
As art, not to live in.
Whose idea was this?
Papenbrock's.
Lisbeth.
I asked him.
When?
When the child was born.
Lisbeth. Lisbeth.
Ach, Cresspahl. When I got here from England.
Lisbeth. Lisbeth. Lisbeth.
You're talking as if we still had a choice.
We?
Yes, I mean we, Cresspahl. We.

Papenbrock informed his son-in-law of the bestowal in his daughter's
presence. He relied on the fact that no one starts shouting with a convalesc-
ing new mother in bed in the room. He'd also wanted to monitor the
couple's initial discussion. In fact, Cresspahl's first comment was that they'd
have to think it over. Him then leaving the room with a downright casual
glance at Lisbeth Cresspahl was not what Papenbrock had expected. He
was still sure he'd get his way, but had lost all hope of enjoying the process.

November 3, 1967   Friday
The chancellor of West Germany, formerly a member and public official
of the Nazis, has named as his government's new spokesman a former
member and public official of the Nazis.

They just never learn. They look at the hand with which they're slapping survivors in the face and they don't understand it: said the writer Uwe Johnson. For that he got a slap in the face.

It turns out that the writer Uwe Johnson had failed to understand something too. Nine months ago now, on the evening of January 16, he took his seat behind the long table covered in green cloth that the Jewish American Congress had set up in the ballroom of the Roosevelt Hotel. Appearing next to the leonine head of Rabbi Joachim Prinz (formerly of Berlin-Dahlem), he waited to tell the Jews of New York something about the election gains of the West German Nazi Party.

> *Where were you sitting, Gesine?*
> *Somewhere I could see you, Comrade Writer.*
> *In the back?*
> *Yes, way in the back, right next to a door.*

Such speakers from Germany have to be introduced the way they deserve. This one was introduced by a functionary of the Jewish American Congress, with the story of a friend who'd recently decided to fly Lufthansa, the German airline, from Philadelphia to Düsseldorf, and had reserved a kosher meal as well as his seat. Once he was buckled into the Germans' airplane, they had no kosher meal for him but they did do, from the English Channel on, what during the First World War was called loop the loops. – So I said to my friend, Why did you have to tell them you were Jewish?

The roomful of Jews laughed, not maliciously, almost charmed. The wave of delight bypassed a few islands of individual audience members, who were quietly, attentively watching the German on the podium polish the bowl of his pipe in the cup of his hand. Another wave of laughter swept through the ballroom when the microphone stopped working and Rabbi Joachim Prinz (formerly of Berlin-Dahlem) comically raised his arms and frantically thundered: They're everywhere! (The Germans, the Nazis.) Even here!

The German who actually was there acted as if he understood not only English but the mood that had been prepared for him in the audience. He looked up at the cheerful, carefree speaker introducing him to the Jews. He was curious. From the room, the expression on his upturned face looked humorless and severe. Yet the jokes had been meant to be laughed at. Invited to the podium, the writer Uwe Johnson did not, say, leave the event at once (with thanks for the introduction) but instead began his talk in all serious- ness, admittedly not with the late Middle Ages but still with the year 1945 and the subsequent development of two German states. He failed, however, to pull off the New England cadences he seemed to be trying to adopt for the occasion, and lapsed back into the wrong vowels, the wrong stresses, the not even British accent his school had let him get away with.

Gesine Cresspahl seems to be embarrassed for a fellow German.
I take it back. Some of it. For your vanity's sake, Writer.
For the sake of one of my teachers, okay?
Fine.

– Ladies and gentlemen: Johnson said. The front half of the room showered him with shouts, not yet collective, of: Louder! – I would like to thank the JAC for the invitation to speak here tonight about: Johnson said. Now the back half of the room was calibrated to the rhythm of the front half, and lagged only slightly in the cry: Louder!! – Let me begin with, and even mention, the East German Republic, also known as the DDR: Johnson said, and this time he entered into the next surge of shrieks from the auditorium, took advantage of the superbly functioning sound system, and sent the full force of his voice bursting from all the loudspeak- ers, unbearably loud: YOU WILL NOT MAKE ME SHOUT!, ladies and gentlemen. After he shouted that, the audience adopted a dozing posi- tion and let him believe that anyone could hear him, or understand him.

I'm sorry, Gesine.
Absolutely not. That was the most reasonable thing you managed to do all night.
They wanted to see if I would defend myself?
Are you always so dense?

At no point did they applaud him, including when he could no longer fail to mention the appointment of a Nazi to the position of chancellor of West Germany. – It wasn't meant as a slap in the face of surviving victims, though the world felt it was. It simply lacked any understanding of the fact that every German government this century will be judged by its distance from the Nazi establishment. The chancellor had not been elected because of his connection with the Nazis, it's just that this side of things had been forgotten. Johnson would have done better not to say anything about forgetting. In any case, his sentences were too long, too German, and even though he sometimes, for short stretches, managed to catch the American melody, he seemed helpless. You couldn't have confidence that he even understood, much less could explain, the country he had made himself responsible for explaining; he had not yet grasped that the time and place had deprived him of a tour guide's blameless neutrality, turning every analytical word in his mouth defensive. He may have realized something during the next speech, by Charles G. Moerdler (formerly of Leipzig, Saxony), before whose lips the technology now really did break down and who was not once urged by the audience to speak louder, who moreover was not merely one of them but also the housing and real estate consultant for the city of New York, making sure that his name, sticking in the mind of signatories to his resolution, would look familiar when seen on future ballots. Johnson sat slumped behind the green table, firmly covering his manuscript with his two hands, his bald head reflecting the spotlights, his eyes scanning the room from between his brows and the rims of his glasses. Strangely, he was wearing a black leather jacket with his dress shirt, the kind of jacket only Negroes wear usually, some Negroes, the Negro with the woolly beard and flashing eyes glancing up from his drowsy face, who we saw Wednesday night in the West Side subway, for instance, but the man in the subway certainly looked more comfortable, in his tight shiny leather, with one hand in his pocket, holding something angular.

Who's telling this story, Gesine?
We both are. You know that, Johnson.

Then the writer got a little taste of reality. The hotel staff set up two microphones on stands in the ballroom's center aisle, and behind them ten and eleven people were waiting their turn to respond to Johnson's declarations, deliberations, disclosures. And they said: My mother. Theresienstadt. My whole family. Treblinka. My children. Birkenau. My life. Auschwitz.

My sister. Bergen-Belsen. Ninety-seven years old. Mauthausen. Two, four, and five years old. Majdanek.

– *He* didn't do it: the rabbi said.
– He's one of them: they said.
– No one's asking you to forgive him: the rabbi said.
– We don't forgive him: they said.
– You should talk with him: the rabbi said.
– You talk with us, Rabbi: they said.
– He's our guest: the rabbi said.
– Outside he's an enemy: they said.
– Be reasonable, my brothers: the rabbi said.
– He's not doing anything against the new Nazis: they said.
– How can he, in his line of work: the rabbi said.
– He shouldn't do it professionally, he should do it as a human being: they said.
– You heard what he said: the rabbi said.
– He should still be ashamed of himself: they said.
– Do you have anything else to say, Mr. Johnson?: the rabbi said.
– Everything has been said already: Johnson said.
– Thank you, Mr. Johnson: the rabbi said.

The writer Johnson appeared once more, in the lobby of the Roosevelt, in the crowd, in conversation with Rabbi Joachim Prinz (formerly of Berlin-Dahlem) and the gentleman who'd introduced Johnson among the Jews. They'd have been happy to grab a drink with their guest, a bite to eat. Their guest put his coat on quickly, as if afraid they might snatch it from him. We were standing just a few steps away and could see from how he was holding his head that he was in the process of telling a genuine, true-blue, colorfast, airtight lie. Then he disappeared around the corner of Madison Avenue onto Forty-Fifth Street, in a hurry, toward Grand Central, toward the subway, toward his lie. He is not going to try to explain his individuality as an individual to the Jews again. In future he will keep his head down for as long as a government speaks in his name. He has absolutely nothing further to say about the new West German press secretary. He's not going to do that again.

Yes, if only I'd asked your advice first, Mrs. Cresspahl.
We weren't talking to each other yet, Mr. Johnson.

The chancellor of West Germany, a member of the Nazi Party, a hench-man to Jew-killers, remembered an old friend from the same department. True, the latter joined the party only in 1938. Still, he too never left it. He is exactly the right person to speak as press secretary for the West German government. The West German government wants friendship with the American people, with the 5,936,000 Jews in North America, two million in this city alone, the city where we live.

November 4, 1967 Saturday, South Ferry day
The secretary of defense has heard that the Soviets will shortly be able to put into orbit around the earth a bomb carrying a payload of up to the equivalent of three million tons of TNT, which could be called down upon any point under its path, with only about three minutes' warning before it hit its target: an excellent city-buster.

– Like a fist slamming into the port: Marie says. She looks into the spitting rain over the water in an appraising way, as if calculating the height of the splash that would blow the ferry with her on it and the steamer on the blurry horizon and the tugboats and the cargo ship with train cars of freight and the zippy Coast Guard greyhounds into the sky.
– And Staten Island too, and Long Island, and Manhattan, and large parts of New Jersey, New York, and Connecticut.
– Are you trying to scare me?
– No.
– Then don't tell me the truth too soon: she says. She hangs from her elbows on the railing of the outer walkway and holds her face to be washed by the wind. Her face is smeared shut with the feel of the weather, covered as though with another skin. If her eyes were shut she'd look blind now. Only the short pale hairs sneaking out of her hood at the sides of her forehead invite recognition. But she's waiting. She is absolutely certain that Borough Hall in Richmond will appear from behind the curtain of mist,

as indestructible in reality as it is in memory. – I don't want to live anywhere but New York: she says.

Cresspahl didn't want to even imagine a life in Jerichow. That would be a life with the Papenbrocks.

He'd gotten mixed up with the Papenbrocks two years earlier, secretly sure he would never have to feel for them, deal with them. What he'd noticed about Lisbeth were the ways she seemed different from her family. Now he was being forced to get to know them after all.

– Is there really no one in the world I'm related to? Marie says.
– No one but me.
– Right, you. But I can choose everyone else.

He'd expected a hostile reception from Horst Papenbrock. Now Horst was behaving almost reasonably at the few meals he ate at home, the few meals his official obligations left him time for. He asked Cresspahl to call him by his first name but answered with Cresspahl's last: something of the behavior proper to a younger man. He didn't try to make his SA activities the topic of conversation, didn't try to enter the conversation at all, even when the granary he was in charge of was discussed. He sat quietly with his plate in front of him, left hand relaxed in his lap, right hand spooning up soup, slurping carefully, looking absolutely fixedly down as though the liquid there were a mirror, or writing. He didn't look tired, more like he was making plans. When Edith announced that some of his followers were out in the hall, he underwent a kind of transformation as he stood up, throwing back his shoulders, raising his chin, striding to the door as though onto a stage, the hand with his napkin slightly swaying at his side so that the cloth caressed his brown boots. He came back after an exchange of words that reached the eaters' ears through the door, sounding strangely sharp and staccato; his doll-like face was filled with delight, out to the tip of the sharp triangle of his nose and suffusing all within; he had a half smile of anticipation and now held the napkin in his fist and struck the side of his boot with it, firmly yet inattentively. Clearly he was not used to showing pleasure. The workers from Papenbrock's yard and granary had never treated him as their boss; they had adopted the old man's nickname for him, "sonny boy," calling him Papenbrock's Sonny Boy. Now they looked away when his military style of giving orders made them want to laugh. He was still in no hurry to impose discipline in the granary. In the pub, Cresspahl had heard tell that young Papenbrock had been driving the car from which Voss had been thrown onto the street in Rande, not bludgeoned to death, incidentally, but whipped to death. The person saying this hadn't known who Cresspahl was, and when a nudge to the ribs had told him that one of Papenbrock's relatives was at the next table, he looked him straight in the eye, as though a fight would be just fine with him. Cresspahl was not unwilling, but this particular cause was not to his taste. Horst denied it about Voss in Rande. Horst said he didn't want anything to do with garbage like that. "Garbage like that" was explained to Cresspahl as meaning, for Horst, settling old scores, old feuds, old insults, as opposed to National Socialism, which Horst spoke of, not insistently but when the occasion called for it, in a shy, halting way, as if it were something sacred. Certainly there were plenty of girls in and around Jerichow who had been happy to do it with someone else, not Horst. Cresspahl wanted no responsibility for him whether in uniform or not, so he parried even Horst's respectful inquiries into his wartime service, fobbed him off like a puppy with preoccupied silence, a nonchalance just barely acceptable. Why bother with a good relationship he had no intention of needing.

Things went all right with the old man. It wasn't exactly fun when Papenbrock tried to rope him into a game where shots had to be gulped down at regular intervals behind Louise's back. It wasn't great when the old man talked about, if not precisely the Cresspahls' return to Germany, then the people in Jerichow, in Gneez, in Schwerin who had always been amenable to Papenbrock's suggestions (that was Papenbrock's idea of tact. He was not trying to influence Cresspahl, he was trying to help). It rubbed Cresspahl the wrong way how the old man watched his son, his youngest hatchling, bleakly but still gleeful, the strict yet permissive father still undecided whether Horst's associations with the new power were good or bad for business, but at bottom ready to accept either eventuality without hesitation. At first, all Horst wanted from his father was a truck, but before Papenbrock would loan his company name to the SA he wanted to hear, again and again, why the national renewal needed it. What he wanted most out of Horst was to hear about the planks in the Nazi program that threatened the department stores and large landowners, and under his amused gaze, in Horst's embarrassed recital, the Nazis' future started to seem unreal, or at least not dangerous. What was not all right was Papenbrock wanting to hear, in detail, how Cresspahl had built up such a large balance at the Surrey Bank of Richmond, and whether Lisbeth's numbers from 1931 were anywhere near accurate. That was not acceptable at all. It was amusing to watch Papenbrock putting his devious ways to work against his own family, for instance when he pontificated vaguely about cobblers' daughters without admitting he'd ever heard of Horst's Miss Lieplow, prompting a disgruntled but still-obedient look from Horst, like that of someone who has suddenly run into an obstacle. Papenbrock had always enjoyed creating problems for his prodigal son; his enjoyment with this one was less obvious. His daughters, on the other hand, he let twist him around their little fingers, "take the butter off his bread," every time. He wanted to smooth the way for his daughters to like him. That was all right. Things with Papenbrock went all right.

Things went better than all right with Hilde. Hilde Paepcke had left Krakow, left her husband to his fights with a fire insurance company that had no intention of forgetting those Hindenburg lights; Hilde wanted to see Lisbeth's baby, she wanted to be the child's godmother, she wanted to go back home. Hilde was pregnant. She wanted children before Alexander completely and totally broke through the floor under their bourgeois feet; she wanted to "save something from the bankruptcy." Or so she told Cresspahl, when promenading with him in Rande, arm in arm, in a sudden closeness, never discussed. When Cresspahl finally realized that she wasn't letting her breasts and hips brush against him by accident, they came to an understanding with a shameless, delighted, sidelong look, and Hilde said, cockily, jauntily, without a hint of regret: *Well now innt that too bad.* – The things you miss out on in life: Cresspahl said. He, on his own, invited Hilde and Alexander to come visit them in Richmond.

He still felt no regret at having resisted bringing Louise Papenbrock to England, even though then Lisbeth would have stayed at home and the child would have been born where it was going to live. Louise Papenbrock in his house—it wouldn't have come off without bickering. At least in

Jerichow he had no right to contradict her. For however naively Papenbrock might think he ran his household, it was Louise, with the old man on a long leash and the children on a short one. The bottle of kümmel that Papenbrock drank his way through in great secrecy—Louise replaced the empty with a new one. Louise decided how much the Papenbrock household donated to the church, and she let the new pastor, Brüshaver, feel how she disapproved of his lack of zeal at the pulpit. The meals served at the table were what she thought proper, and she said grace for as long as she wanted to. She'd had a bed made for Cresspahl in Lisbeth's old room, on the third floor in the back, far away from Lisbeth and the child, without ever asking what he might prefer. And she had completely reorganized the household arrangements for the birth, all her provisions putting a fence up around Lisbeth that Cresspahl had to climb over, not needing Louise's permission but only when instructed. He couldn't even complain, since Louise Papenbrock had brought four children into the world with her hot-water bottles and overheated stoves; on the contrary, he had to be grateful.

He was hardly ever alone with Lisbeth, and never without the likelihood of being disturbed.

The day before the christening was to take place, Gertrud Niebuhr phoned Jerichow. Cresspahl answered the phone, and she took him, with perfect stubbornness, for the person she was expecting to reach: Papenbrock. – Hey, Papenbrock! she said, excited at the long-distance conversation, and it turned out that she, the scatterbrained sister, had lost Cresspahl's Richmond address. She wanted to write to him. She wanted to write to him that it was going "not so good" with their mother. No, nothing serious. – Heinrich, that can't be you on the phone! You're still in Inglant!

The day of the christening, Cresspahl took the train via Blankenberg and Sternberg and Goldberg to Malchow, away from Jerichow, with a sense of relief that would weigh on his conscience for some time.

He had not yet looked at the house for his child, Gesine.

Today is a great day for *The New York Times*. She has calculated her revenue for October and reports: A record of 8,256,618 lines of paid advertising! A record of 963,130 weekday copies sold! A record of 1,588,091 Sunday copies sold! She reports this on a page for which she otherwise could have gotten about $6,000. But she refuses to be miserly or churlish in her rejoicing.

November 5, 1967 Sunday

The North Vietnamese defense minister wrote an article in which he publicly acknowledged China's support in the war. He resisted the urgent request from the Soviets to cut that sentence. Now it's been published in *Krasnaya Zvezda*, so now it's true in the Soviet Union, too.

We walked down Broadway from our house to Seventy-Ninth Street and back up via Riverside Park, the promenade along the river, and the street, and never once saw Marjorie.

Her name's not Marjorie. We don't know her name. We don't know her. She came into our lives last winter, a girl waiting for the number 5 bus on Ninety-Seventh Street. It was a day of biting wind, cold enough to make the wait urgent and pleading. She was not standing huddled and miserable in the cold; she had turned her chilliness into a charming, meticulous pantomime. She seemed to be feeling cold out of camaraderie. We said very little to her, and already she confided in us that: she was glad she hadn't missed out on this weather. She said it as a truth, and since it was her truth it didn't come out too intrusive. She's so confiding.

She knows how to live with such grace. The word *beautiful* still applies to her. She can hide under billowing capes the fact that she has grown for a full sixteen years the way one should, slim but not lanky, with long legs that attract the gazes of female passersby too. It's her face. Her face gives information about her that never disappoints, never has to be taken back. She has pale, transparent skin (one shade below pink), wears her dark brown cloud of hair down over her shoulder blades, has minutely specified eyebrows and heavy dark eyes—those are her resources. We look at her mouth, because it is young; we look at her lips, because of her totally conscious, deliberate smile. It is serious, considered. It means something. It can be understood. It's friendly. What others are granted on special occasions is for her an embarrassment of riches to draw on at will.

She sees us, she beams. She speaks with her dark eyes and we believe her. It's impossible to guess why she'd be happy to see us; we accept her happiness without hesitation. Even when she's walking down Riverside Drive surrounded by her laughing, chatting friends, she has a particular, individual look to give us, separately, us alone, and it says as clearly as if she had whispered the words secretly into our ear: It makes me happy to see you. It's not even embarrassing. There is no doubt. She drapes her truth over us. She can still express only what she is. She has a way of turning toward us, attentive, alert, cheerful, almost deferential with sympathy, in a beautiful movement that comes from the shoulders and neck and is reflected in our feelings like a physical touch. Every time, her look encompasses us as though she recognizes us, and not only her image of us but who we really are. And we believe her. We don't doubt her sincerity. You can exchange kindness with her as though it still mattered. At first we thought she wasn't American.

– She's a general's daughter: Marie says.
– She isn't. Don't say that.
– She is too. Quartermaster general, attorney general . . .

She speaks a precise American English, rich in vocabulary, with almost no slang and only the slight trace of a Midwestern accent. She does not depend on language, she can make herself perfectly clear without this defective means—but it, too, she doesn't use carelessly.

Whenever we see her there's something new about her appearance. She comes up to us with a big wide-brimmed hat—she wants us to appreciate it, to enjoy it. Buttons with demands addressed to the rest of humanity—she wears those too (Bring Our Boys Home! Support the Police: Bribe Your Friends and Helpers!), but on her handbag or the crown of her hat. One day she's wearing her hair tied with four inches of ribbon, then the next time a headband is enough, and the time after that she's embedded fifty grams of hairpins in the interlaced construction. Violet stockings are the only thing to wear on one day, copper-green on another—no other color would have been right. She walks down Broadway in a dress that her grandmother wore in Scarborough by the Great Lake, at the turn of the century (not in Scarborough): a ruffled swirling tale of a dress; she has hit on the height of fashion, and without trying. It's the real dress from the real closet of her genuine grandmother. She says so.

She got on the 5 bus in which we were sitting. She was delighted. We got off the bus at Eighty-Seventh Street, her stop too. She thought that was wonderful. We walked onto Eighty-Seventh Street together. She couldn't be more pleased. We told her our destination. She told us hers. She could not have possibly hoped for more from this day than that we would turn out to have friends on the same street, even. Suddenly she stopped and shouted a name up at the eighteen stories, belting it out, assured of success, pleased at the power in her throat, then she waved to us with her whole long arm, called her friend's name, waved, raised her beaming face to the sky.

In our neighborhood it is only habit that makes us jump when someone taps us from behind on the shoulder. For when it's done with a quick double tap, with light, straight fingers, it's her. Her face isn't scrunched up in a grimace, it is open, relaxed, unfolding in the expectation of pleasure to come. – Hi!: she says, and from her it would be clear to even the most obdurate foreigner that this is a greeting, a welcome. One of the most reasonable, natural, and credible sorts of welcome. She shows you so that you'll learn it too.

Someone out of the *Thousand and One Nights*.

When school has made her tired, two large blots appear on her cheeks, unambiguously red, danger signs.

That winter, she stood on the corner of Broadway and Ninety-Sixth Street where the ice-cold wind from the Hudson can blast unobstructed up the hill, and she sniffed the air, her fragile delicate profile obliviously raised, and she said, mysteriously, mischievously: It's over now. With her face, even the tendons of her neck, she can transmit a feeling clear and entire, express herself beyond words in a language thought to be lost. What she has said is, in its entirety: Ice may go, snow may come, but the new season is in the air and growing stronger. The earth has remembered. Be mindful of this, Mrs. Cresspahl. Consider this smell.

She doesn't know our name. We don't know her name. She wants nothing from us. There is nothing we could want from her. It's unnecessary.

If, Mrs. Cresspahl, the city of New York has ever done you harm or made you suffer, I have been sent to tell you: It shouldn't have happened. It was a mistake. We're sorry, and I will comfort you.

Today she was nowhere to be seen.

November 6, 1967 Monday

The New York Times paid a visit to Rear Admiral Ralph W. Cousins's flagship, the aircraft carrier *Constellation*, whose planes harry the North Vietnamese heartland with their attacks. Cousins is fifty-two years old, clear-eyed, soft-spoken, his black hair beginning to gray. He is a reader of respectable magazines and French mystery novels. After six hours of sleep in his large well-furnished cabin below the flight deck, he is woken at six thirty. Then he gets dressed. Then he drinks a cup of tea. Then he does calisthenics for ten minutes. Then he goes up to the bridge and settles into his white-upholstered revolving chair embroidered with two stars. Now he opens the manila folder containing the top secret messages printed on red paper.

On Saturday evening, Gary Sickler, twenty-six, entered a liquor store in Poughkeepsie. The cuts on his hand were, he said, from an assault by two men and a girl. He led the police to the spot where the assault had occurred, in a fashionable, wooded residential neighborhood, and to a car in which lay the body of Kathleen Taylor, twenty-two, stabbed to death. Sickler, a convicted rapist, had been on parole.

The friendly tobacconist Stephen Zachary Weinstein, from Philadelphia, was being sought for possibly having sedated with drugs, mistreated with blows, and finally strangled an eighteen-year-old student who wanted to buy himself a pipe. The student's body was found in a trunk floating in the Delaware River, and S. Z. Weinstein was found because he'd tried to buy tickets to a play in New York. Many visitors to the city consider the New York theater an attraction not to be missed.

The other picture on the front page of *The New York Times* is eight and a half inches by almost seven inches in size. It shows President Johnson with his wife, daughters, and sons-in-law. The news is the fact that these people had been to church.

Cresspahl found his mother in a village to the southeast of Malchow, in a strange bed. She was not any shorter in death, but when he picked her up, she felt like a sleeping child in his arms.

November 7, 1967 Tuesday

No! No! No! Mrs. Erichson cried. She saw us at her front door and told us No, delight in her face, feigned denial in her voice, as though she didn't see us, as though the telephone couldn't possibly have spoken the truth, as though the Port Authority Bus Terminal must have burned down just that Monday evening, the Hudson engulfed the Lincoln Tunnel on today of all days, Highway 80 collapsed into the swamps of New Jersey, something, anything, so there was never any real chance we would turn up for dinner. – No! she said, more gently this time, simply to relish once more this after-taste of the obvious made piquant with a pinch of doubt, having long since pulled us into the front hall. It was meant to express pleasure. It's a Mecklenburg quirk, this way of welcoming visitors or pieces of news. That's what old people in Mecklenburg do.

Now do make yourself comfortable, Gesine Cresspahl. And you did laugh, you know, against your will but you did.

D. E. has rigged the house. Not only has he made the sagging shingled box as sturdy as a fresh young house with new beams and clamps, he's transformed its lifestyle. The colonial-style furniture in the hall and the living rooms is too well preserved, too expensive for a farmer's house. Behind handmade doors there are unexpected little rooms blazing with light and fitted out with the latest inventions of sanitary science. The old light fixtures never shone so bright before. The discreet grates in the century-old halls may be genuine brass, but central heating sends warm air through them into the antiques showrooms. Every corner of the house is according to plan: the leather cushions might be askew here, a telephone forgotten in the middle of a carpet there, a cat asleep on a typewriter, but the house would still meet the *New York Times* criteria for being an exemplar of tradition and modern technology in interior design. The house has been rethought from top to bottom, divided into a common area and three separate ones: Mrs. Erichson's on the ground floor, next to the household facilities and the living area for all occupants; D. E.'s on the east side of the second floor; and a third domain on the same floor. This last, a row of brown doors running down a hallway of white paint and windows and muslin, is reached by a separate staircase, is separated from the other half of the floor by a door allowed on this side to keep its old bolt and lock. Here there's a room with glass-fronted bookcases and a writing desk, a room for which the Hotel Marseilles on West End Avenue would pocket $35.00 a day and night, a lockable lair for, say, a ten-year-old child who likes being able to get down to the lawn unseen, unquestioned, unhindered, and most of all fast. It's got everything. The child's room has its hammock, its TV set, the towels are piled up extravagantly high in the bathroom, the escritoire in the study contains writing paper all ready, large and small and thick and thin, and arrayed behind the glass doors are the volumes of *Artistic and Historical Monuments of the Grand Duchy of Mecklenburg-Schwerin* along with Professor Wossidlo's collection of local words and Herr Johannes Nichtweiß's opinions on the Mecklenburg peasant clearance, 1st ed., Berlin (East), 1954. This half of the second floor is called the guest wing even though no guests have ever been here other than the Cresspahls. Here is where D. E. puts our suitcases, not inside but in the hall, next to the door.

You could live here, Gesine Cresspahl. At least make yourself comfortable.

The house has its rules, a rhythm that runs like clockwork, but in the kind of clock that merely shows guests the time rather than regulating their lives. In the hour before dinner, D. E. is to be found on one of the stools around the high breakfast counter by the kitchen window, conferring with his mother and his Copenhagen beer; last night Marie sat across from him, chin propped on the palms of both hands for the duration, receiving instruction on the ideas about the boundary layers of the primordial earth that Professor Andrija Mohorovičić fell prey to in 1908, and the American project of drilling holes in the ocean floor in his honor: Moholes. Voices, blending in with the leisurely scraping sound of pans being moved and the clicking open and shut of the refrigerator door, rose up through the wood-work as indistinct noise, more intimate than I was entirely comfortable with. Outside the window, the wind was busy catching handfuls of bare branches; it opened and closed its fist, paused panting to regather its strength. Beneath the sky's darkness, the interior of the house swelled up, spread out, with light and warmth and human life. When Marie walked in with a cat on her shoulder hairily delineated from behind by the lamp's glow, I mistook her for the child I was dreaming about, the child that I was.

Are you sure you don't need any more sleep, Gesine? We can have dinner whenever you want. The guests' wishes are law in this house.

The guests' wishes are read from their eyes in this house. Even during the meal, D. E. didn't talk about himself but used judicious questions, counterquestions, interjected questions to get his mother to tell her own stories. The old woman woke up fully in the night, held her head high. Her large gray bird's eyes held her listeners' gaze, made lowered eyelids feel uncomfortable. She wanted to see her stories mirrored; she didn't want to be exerting herself for nothing. How her father drove to the Güstrow wool market in 1911. Her face is chapped with age. The skin is deeply, sharply incised all over, deeper than the wind of seventy years could carve. How a landowner's daughter was not supposed to marry into the city, not supposed to marry a hairdresser. The dark bags under her eyes make her face even thinner, withered, shrunken. She looks like she's living with her very last strength, but she passed her driving test only last summer, she chops her own firewood. How the Great Depression affected the haircutting trade in Wendisch Burg. How Schusting Brand, the cobbler, came to get his hair cut there out of friendship and wanted to pay only half price out of friend-ship. We'll have to remember him. Things were looking up for the Erich-son Hair Salon after 1933, two girls on the ladies' side and soon three apprentices for the men. Her own hair looks like a snow-white plank bleached under water, gouged by water, then broken off, jagged and splin-tery. She probably no longer washes it with anything but water. Conversa-tions during haircuts. She didn't think much of Herr Hitler. She says that as a favor to me, a favor to D. E. No, by conviction she was a royalist, she would have most liked to see the Mecklenburg princes back in power. So D. E. was a child who had to sweep up cut hair. During the new army's Mecklenburg maneuvers, she saw Mussolini from just ten steps away. Mussolini in Mecklenburg? She went shopping for the Jews when they no longer felt safe on the streets of Wendisch Burg, and yet they were university graduates. If only we could believe that. If only she'd done that. Thank-you letters from Mexico City. Really. How Mr. Erichson senior suddenly started sending unusually friendly letters home from a labor camp near Stalingrad. That we'll believe. In Wendisch Burg there are the fisherman-Babendererdes and the teacher-Babendererdes. They're related to the Dührkops, bookbinders in Neustrelitz, who are related to the Bunges, leatherworkers in Schwerin, who've written just recently: In Schwerin a tourist from West Germany had a balcony fall on her head and now all the buildings in town are going to get their loose stucco knocked off. That we don't believe. Yes, Schwerin is all mottled. But we won't tell her we don't believe it. Good night, Mrs. Erichson.

You've been suffering on a hard chair for three hours, D. E.
She doesn't talk except over meals.
And you risked boring Marie.
She won't take it the wrong way.
You thought I'd appreciate it, D. E.?
Glad to be of service, Gesine.
Okay, well, thanks very much for the stories.

Morning actually does begin with a holiday feeling. In New York it's Election Day, the banks and stock exchange and schools and liquor stores are closed. The sounds from the house do not shatter one's morning sleep. They're so familiar that they transpose themselves into images behind closed eyes. The muffled little clicking is Frau Erichson laying the repolished silverware back in its velvet caddy. The terse double bang is the girl from the village who comes to help out in the mornings; when she has her hands full she pulls doors shut behind her with a sharply angled foot. There's a child, too, singing the Coca-Cola Company song. That child would like to stay here, an hour and a half from New York. Far away, right at the outermost skin of the house, D. E.'s typewriter murmurs. That's where money is being made, money that would be enough for us. Now they're singing in trio in the kitchen, Marie seems to be conducting, and they're asking the powers that be how in the world the Coca-Cola Company does it. It's a day outside of the world. Here we are accepted. At the sound of a single foot being placed outside the door, they will get to work making a second breakfast. On the table will be not only *The Philadelphia Inquirer* but also *The New York Times.* This is how D. E. imagines my life.

November 8, 1967 Wednesday

There are also critics of the American war in Vietnam with the rank of lieutenant general of an airborne division. James M. Gavin does not so much have in mind the inhabitants of Vietnam. He simply considers the war too costly for his own country.

The unemployment rate has increased from 4.1 percent to 4.3 percent, its highest level in two years. That makes 3.8 percent among whites. That makes 8.8 percent among Negroes. But only one in ten American citizens is Negro.

Herr Paul Zapp, sixty-three years old, has been arrested in Bebra, a small Hessian town. He is responsible for the murder of at least 6,400 Jews in the occupied Soviet Union. Until the day before yesterday, an assumed name was all he needed.

Cresspahl came back from Malchow and went to look at the house that had been offered to his child. As he walked down Town Street people stared with curiosity, volunteered greetings, spontaneously, even strangers. Papenbrock had put an announcement of the death of Grete Cresspahl, née Niemann, in *The Gneez Daily News.* He probably was trying to tie his son-in-law to Jerichow, even if he had to start in the minds of the Jerichowers. Cresspahl hadn't known anything about the announcement.

At the south end of Town Street, the pastor's house stands on the right side, red brick, white trim, mossy tiled roof. The garden wall is, on the other side, the cemetery wall. Kids can swing in semicircles on either half of the iron gate. Then the wall takes a sharp right turn to the west, along a sandy path called either Churchyard Road or Brickworks Road because of the long red hops kiln on the other side, whose walls are more boring than the wall that encloses the dead, with its upper stones set diagonally, its glazed green coping. Opposite the middle of the wall surrounding the brickworks, the cemetery wall bulges back with a little door in the center as wide as a man and the large arched gates of the mortuary, so poorly built that it had to be plastered. Standing where you can look through the brickworks gate at the large work yard to the left, you can also see over Creutz's fence to the right. The church owns the land and has leased it to Creutz, since it doesn't yet need it for the dead. Look over your right shoulder: no sign of the dead. Behind the thickly overgrown elder bushes along Creutz's border, the rough dark bricks of the church shimmer through. The gabled tower and spire look tallest from here. Across from the entrance to the brickworks, in a well-tended garden behind a white cast-iron grate next to Creutz's leased land, stands the brickworks owner's villa. The ceremonial flagpole surrounded by flower beds once bore the flag of the fugitive kaiser. There are no buildings past it on the road, which runs between meadows and farmland, rising and falling, before petering out, not even leading to any village. At this point, some ways down toward the sea, the marsh comes into view. There, behind a weeded grassy area to the left, stands a low farmhouse under a black hipped roof. Now I'm home.

Cresspahl didn't go into the house first thing. Some of the windowpanes had been smashed in. That was all he needed to know for the time being.

The farmers who'd developed this land had once been so rich that they'd even put up a brick barn. The barn, placed perpendicularly, was taller than the house, roofed with overlapping tar paper. Its north side was almost entirely doors: a high double door made of wood that the sea wind had eaten away at, with a hinged door for people set into one of the bigger doors. Inside, the compartments of the barn had been swept out. In the end the farmers turned thriftier. They'd left nothing behind but useless junk: a banged-up turnip cutter, broken carriage shafts, sauerkraut vats, and the mudguard of a Sunday carriage, undamaged, paint gleaming. The stalls in the east half stank of rotted straw. There were pig and sheep stalls, crib space for twelve head of cattle and four horses. Ever since they'd been herded off, nothing had lived here but the wind. The building was so chilly that there were no traces of teenage couples or cats. The manure pile must have taken three years to shrivel so dry. There were electric lights in the stalls, but anyone who tried the switch got a surge of current up to his shoulder, making his arm churn. His predecessors were trying to tell him something: Our misfortune is yours now.

Behind the house stood a black tree full of blackbirds.

To the south, the west, the north, there was empty space around the yard. Only the wind spoke. To the north there was a gap between the earth and the sky—a strip of the Baltic.

1. If a person wanted to, he could replace two-thirds of the doors with glass. That would let in enough light for carpentry work.

2. Most of the renovations could be done by Cresspahl himself, if he wanted.

3. If a person wanted to, he could make the inhabitants of the villas put up with the noise of saws during normal working hours.

If a person wanted to.

It's not right to leave New York, not even for a single day. We did and missed the city's first snow. Today the day with its cold sun is acting all innocent.

November 9, 1967 Thursday

Adolf Heinz Beckerle went on trial yesterday in Frankfurt for having, as Hitler's envoy to Bulgaria, assisted in the deportation of 11,343 Jews to death camps. He asserts that, on the contrary, 40,000 Bulgarian Jews owed their lives to him. Fritz Gebhard von Hahn, a former colleague of the West German chancellor, is charged along with him, on account of 20,000 Greek Jews.

It is a short report, appearing far beneath the outermost skirt of *The New York Times*. She expresses her opinion more forcefully today about the mayor's plan to let the business world sponsor a half-hour TV show for him. The old dame tears the Honorable John Vliet Lindsay a new one. – It's about propriety! she cries, and lets fly again. She's not frail yet.

It's Thursday and the wrong-number callers strike again, starting early in the afternoon. The first, still inexperienced in the trade, merely wanted to know whether Marie were "RIverside 9-2857." She answered severely that he had reached 749-2857, and even though the numbers 7 and 4 correspond to the letters R and I on telephone dials, astonishment made the man hang up. – It's like he doesn't know American phones: Marie relays, with gusto. She thinks it's a brand-new trick, and she's discovered it.

At first, we had to use the phone that Mademoiselles Bøtersen and Bertoux had left us along with the apartment. It answered to a number beginning with MOnument, and piped up often. In Germany, phones used to ring implacably, barkingly; here a gentle tinkle trickles out of the device, slowly, gracefully, like a cat stretching after it wakes up. Men asked for Ingrid and wanted to talk to Françoise, and Françoise should bring Ingrid along to Grand Ticino, and hardly anyone could grasp that the girls now lived at the Kastrup and Geneva airports, in post-office boxes, and not a few were keen to know the first name that the new voice on the line had to offer. Then the telephone company operated, extracting the soul from the device's casing and returning it to the warehouse where it would rest in peace for the time being.

That was when RI9-2857 came into our lives, if only to provide a way to reach Dr. Brewster's office or a children's hospital. But the child wanted to play learning how to use a phone, and before long she was the one who took the yoke off the whimpering thing's neck first and asked, American-style: Who's this? not: Who's there? It was on this telephone that Marie learned to tell lies under supervision. Because strangers called and wanted to hear not only that they'd reached the Cresspahl residence but also whether the Cresspahl residence was located on the third or thirteenth floor, numbered 13A or 134, because the phone book hadn't yet relieved criminals of the need to prepare the finer details of their break-ins, and Marie not only described where to find apartment 204 but offered the extra information: I'm alone. Now we had to invent an Uncle Humphrey, a brawler and brute of a man, allegedly sleeping in the guest room, for whom Marie built a matchbox house under the telephone, and these strangers turned out not to want to speak to Uncle Humphrey after all.

Not all the callers were plying the same trade. Some said they were trying to get to sleep by reading the phone book and the name "Cresspahl" had blasted them into alertness and now they desperately yearned to know the national origin of this name and wanted our opinion about the end of the world no less than they wanted a listener for stories of their wartime experiences in Germany. Some couldn't make it through the night alone in a lonely room in a sleeping city and their only means of seeking a connection was by phoning other boroughs of that city (one Mr. Abraxas, from Brooklyn). We were spared the rage of divorced husbands against any and all female sole proprietors of telephone numbers, as well as the sexual fantasies of unknown drunks, because in this country the name "Gesine" failed to provide unambiguous information about the sex of its bearer. The others remained faithful. There were repeat customers, like the Indian engineer who called from New Haven the first time and insisted, come hell or high water, on being connected to a certain Elsa, apparently not only German but with a similar voice, so that he unburdened himself of all his painful disappointment at her behavior onto New York RI9-2857, in the unique German that the Leipzig International Institute in Saxony provided to foreign exchange students in the GDR as a means of making themselves understood. If this Janin Landa called only every month, George Abraxas checked in every two weeks. Then D. E. found us while idly flipping through the Manhattan phone book, and we had ourselves removed and are happy to pay the cost of doing so.

We're left with the ones who roll dice to come up with phone numbers, and those who discover in the course of their meticulous research a gap between 7492856 and 7492858, and those who dial direct from San Francisco to the East Coast just to tell us the time and the weather there, and those who accidentally get lost in the rotary dial and have nothing to say but their apologies. It'll really be a problem when calls are put through automatically under the Atlantic, too, and German millionaires get a new game to play. Then we'll have to rely entirely on Marie, who has recently put her trust in the absurd and repels unwanted calls by saying: This is an unlisted number. This is an unlisted number. It confuses even the most stubborn.

Once, late last September, our phone put through a call like the ones in the fifties in West Berlin. The diaphragm at the other end of the line was set in motion by the vibration not of words but only of breathing. However regular the breaths were, they always sped up at some point and started to sound threatening. Nothing but breathing.

You hear enough voices.
If only the dead would keep their traps shut.

Once, two weeks ago, a woman's voice was reciting something, fast, indifferently, as though reading from an index card: Your name is Gesine Cresspahl, born March 3, 1933, in Jerichow, residing in the United States since April 28, 1961. – Yes: I said, and got only a click in response, and I wished I'd said I was somebody else, anybody.

– This is a nonworking number: Marie is saying now, with the voice of a machine as it might emerge from a worn-down tape player. – This is a nonworking number. Then, unwillingly, unconvinced, she holds the receiver up to me over her shoulder and says: – Some guy named Karsch, doesn't know where we live, doesn't know who I am … How was I supposed to know! You've never told me about him!

– I may need to borrow that child sometime: Karsch says.

– Where are you, Karsch?

– I'd rather not say: Karsch says.

– Do you need something, Karsch?

– It hasn't gotten to that point yet: he says. – See you soon: he says: See you.

He didn't say: Talk to you soon. Him aside, Thursday is the day on which wrong-number callers most often strike.

Early last night, in secret, President Johnson arrived in the city. Five hundred policemen were surrounding the Americana Hotel, posted on the roofs of buildings around the hotel, and another hundred were in the ballroom, where the president told Jewish trade-union leaders: The nation risked a far more terrible war in the future if it did not succeed in this one in a small and distant country in Southeast Asia. Page 1.

On page 17, under the White Plains busing problems and assurance that the mayor of Albany was not driving drunk, *The New York Times* offered the official list of the war dead—eleven and a half lines.

The most important item to her on the front page, though, is the photograph of the West German passport used by Runge, the Soviet spy. Not only does she tell us everything declassified about his life, she also describes the structure of the Soviet intelligence agency, complete with org chart, so now we know who is responsible for the bloody business. Rodin, aka Nikolai B. Korovin. His mailing address is omitted, however.

Lisbeth Cresspahl was not to be spared her mother-in-law's funeral. Her sister, Hilde, spent a whole afternoon telling her about it.

Papenbrock had suddenly had misgivings about none of his family being present for the occasion. So he'd sent at least Hilde to Lake Müritz.

When she arrived the coffin was still open, laid out in the entrance hall of the Schmoog farmhouse. Berta Niemann and Erna Lübbe had been friends since 1873, a bond that continued after Erna married the heir to a farm and Berta married a wheelwright who worked on the village estate. Berta had wanted to visit her friend.

To be polite, old Mrs. Cresspahl wanted to pay another call first, to the nobility for whom her husband had worked for forty-five years and she for forty-one. Since she turned up in city clothes and wasn't recognized, the nobility invited her into the salon of the manor house and entertained her there even after she had given her explanations. She may, in the excitement, have drunk or swallowed something too quickly. She pulled herself together and asked Frau von Haase for permission to lie down for a moment. Frau von Haase took the question as reason for concern that the old woman was going to die on her sofa, and she ordered the horses readied, hitched to the carriage at least. While the carriage was racing wildly through the village street, Mrs. Cresspahl came to slightly and recognized the Schmoog farmhouse. Maybe she was afraid she would die in a hospital, or else she didn't want to forgo the visit she'd actually wanted to pay. She insisted on being unloaded at the Schmoogs'.

She lay in her friend's bed for two days, not agitated, asleep most of the time. She was so tired that she let other people wait on her. When she opened her eyes, Mrs. Schmoog thought she could see in them disappointment at not finding someone else standing at her bedside. When Cresspahl ducked into the little room, the Schmoogs thought she was still alive. So she had been alone when she died.

The Schmoogs' house has a windbreak of two crossed horse's heads on the brow of its thatched roof, and painted there is a year from the early eighteenth century. The roof comes down low over the half-timbered masonry. The front part of the entrance hall led off to stalls for cows and horses. Now the hall had been swept clean with water, making the beaten clay look like uneven stone. The coffin had the place of honor. On the way to either the living room or the kitchen, you had to pay your respects.

Erna Schmoog hadn't managed too well with her friend's hair. Wisps of it lay across the part. She apologized to Cresspahl. Cresspahl reminded her that that's how her hair was when she was alive.

When the mourners gathered from the village, it suddenly became apparent that Mrs. Schmoog was talking to her friend's son in a carefree, almost cheerful way. Mrs. Schmoog was no older than the dead woman. Now she'd been able to show her husband, and the farmhands too, how she wanted her own death observed.

The coffin was about to be closed when the assembled mourners parted, leaving a wide path free for an old man walking stooped down to his bent knees. He had gotten very short with age. He took off his top hat and held it in his hand before he even set foot in the entrance hall. He had not spoken a word to Berta Niemann since she'd married Heinrich Cresspahl senior, never given the Schmoogs the time of day either, first because of their continued friendship with the new Mrs. Cresspahl and second due to a fight from around 1890 over a strip of field. The old man had hardly shown his face in the village since the war. Now he was not embarrassed. He walked slowly over to the coffin. He stood before it for a long time. He tried to keep his back straight. Then it was possible to see from his neck that he had nodded to the dead woman. Then he turned around and shook hands with the dead woman's daughter, then the son, then the other relatives.

Then he walked over to the Schmoogs and shook hands with all of them, including the sons, the daughters-in-law, the grandchildren.

Then everyone crowded around the coffin again so that the pastor wouldn't see anything. Cresspahl put the lid on. Then they helped him loosely screw it on.

It was two hours to Malchow at a walking pace. The village had lent out its hearse. There were not many wreaths propped against the coffin. Still, the Papenbrock family's wreath looked more frugal than the others.

The estate owners had sent a cart with rubber tires and benches. Between that and the third cart, there were enough seats for the elderly and the women. Cresspahl and his sister would doubtless have walked behind the coffin anyway. They let Hilde walk next to them.

In Malchow, the following people carried the coffin into the church: Martin Niebuhr, Peter Niebuhr, Alexander Paepcke. Günter Schmoog, Paul Schmoog, Heinz Mootsaak. They left Cresspahl alone in the church so that he could get his mother settled properly again. When he came out of the church door, the six men went in without him and screwed the coffin shut, this time tightly. Then the service began.

Cresspahl was very friendly to everyone, to Hilde too. At Meininger's, on Long Street, she sat next to him. He carried himself like someone who had brought a task to completion. At one point he stood up and thanked everyone for coming. After that, he watched the eating and drinking around him without impatience. One more bill to be paid. Then he could leave.

Hilde deliberately brought her sister to tears. It'd be better for her if Cresspahl got his way.

She didn't just tell her how it was. She turned what had happened into vague reproaches, as though morality could still frighten her younger sister. By the time Cresspahl got back to Jerichow, Hilde had gotten her sister to the point where he had to console Lisbeth for his own loss. She would have gone to the train station with him then, if he'd asked her then.

November 11, 1967 Saturday, Veterans Day

Karsch may take an *R* for something other than a *7* on an American phone, but he hasn't overlooked that the mail here is not delivered on days when those who took part in past wars are marching. His letter was brought by a man in a chauffeur's uniform. The man didn't wait even a second for a tip, and his face betrayed no hint that he was used to being received in better-maintained buildings. The letter is not from Karsch. It is a written notice from the Italian delegation at the UN, signed by Dr. Pompa, instructing the security guards there to permit the bearer of this document and one child passage through the employee entrance. On the business card that Karsch enclosed, the dot before the name with which Karsch, like General Narses, indicates that his written instructions are not to be followed wasn't there, and if that's the way Karsch wants it, that's what we'll give him.

The 104 bus goes from our house down Broadway and then east on

Forty-Second Street to the UN. Marie prefers the row of seats in the back so that she has windows on both sides, and down to the Seventies she keeps the west sidewalk of Broadway in sight, looking for children, passersby, or policemen she knows. Marie has put on a dress without complaining, almost hurried to the appointment. – Just so I can meet all your friends: she said. She has never been to the part of the UN where visitors aren't allowed.

The government wants to give Thailand a present—about $50 million worth of antiaircraft missiles—if Thailand sends ten thousand soldiers to Vietnam.

Dr. Gallup has once again gone down among the nation and posed questions. This time he learned that out of a hundred people, fifty-nine are in favor of continuing the American war in Vietnam.

Last night, Frank "Frankie the 500" Telleri and the D'Angelo brothers (Thomas and James) gathered for a meal of veal parmigiana and white wine in an upscale restaurant in the Ridgewood section of Queens. In comes a squat guy in a black fedora, black raincoat, glasses, and pulls out some type of machine gun and shoots twenty to twenty-five holes in the three men. The police surmise that the killings were no ordinary incident but a settling of gangland scores.

Marie is disappointed. The UN security guards are Americans, quite possibly from the Bronx and Manhattan; the escalators look like the ones she knows from any of the better subway stations; the restaurant is run by a completely mundane hotel chain; not even the long bar is anything sacred. Mr. Karsch is going to have a hard row to hoe with the child.

Mr. Pompa and Mr. Karsch come walking down the hall like twins, both of them tall and imposing in their casual suits, both with the gait of people afraid to step on small objects, both irrevocably well on in years and perhaps intelligible only to each other now. Except Mr. Pompa's skin sits firm and comfortable on his face, his eyes are commanding, and he still monitors his smile. Karsch is soft in the face. He takes care where he looks, he protects himself, he doesn't want to see everything, God forbid. Now he sees us.

Ti voglio bene.

Ti voglio bene.

It's Karsch, and we can hug him without a second thought, a person changing as he turns in our direction. That doesn't happen—still feeling close to someone after years and years, no question about it, no testing the waters, feeling a totally genuine pleasure at seeing them again. That does happen.

It's Karsch, who keeps his back straight when saying hello to a child, not trying to curry favor, serious, almost formal, so that Marie can't find an opening to take offense. Karsch, the first at the table to notice that the child doesn't speak Italian and switch without a fuss into his undistorted British English that Mr. Pompa, on the other hand, can understand. Karsch, to whom the waiters come like doctors, and he talks to them unabashedly with his fingers, with his hands. Karsch, who talks about the weather and flying conditions for as long as Dr. Pompa is there, who asks about us as soon as the stranger has taken his leave, who tells us about himself without self-pity. He still lives alone in two rooms in Milan. These are not the rooms next door to Vito Genovese anymore; it's not his own house. His son in Hamburg is no longer of an age to collect all the Lufthansa freebies he gets on his flights across the Alps, the boy costs money like a grown-up now. Karsch has come to New York to work on a book.

He looks sick. His hair has turned almost entirely white, with only a few darker strands left. He is wearing it long; it sits on his temples like little clouds. With his hair, and the rumples in his exquisite jacket, and the tie from the store near La Scala half askew, he involuntarily betrays that he has no one in his life to look after him. He isn't sad. His glasses are rimmed in thin flashing steel and the reflections in them mask his eyes. He's not trying to hide, he just doesn't want to show himself much. And when Karsch pours some more red wine, the bottle moves past his glass with neck held high. Karsch no longer drinks.

– What's the book about: Marie says at last, disregarding issues of rudeness and proper behavior to strangers in restaurants. A stranger can't see that she's flustered, that her fingertips are shaking.

– About families, family ties, family visits: Karsch says.

– In Italy?

– In Italy, and in your country: Karsch says.

– Why don't you write about Germany?

– Reading its own books upon publication is not a distinguishing feature of the German people: Karsch says, amused for private reasons, not making fun of Marie. The East Prussian and Hamburg accents have been completely washed away from his German. He talks so evenly that Marie has to look in his eyes to understand that he's not complaining.

– They're not the kind of books you're thinking, Marie: Mrs. Cresspahl says, to distract the child: they're books about real events and real people.

But Marie refuses to be distracted.

– So you want to be read right away, is that it?: she says severely, still in a tone of interrogation. She doesn't let Karsch's lazy nod intimidate her a bit.

– What kinds of families?: she says. Karsch taps the middle of the folded *New York Times*, where there is an article about the stolen credit card scam that the Mafia families—the Gallos in Brooklyn and the Gambinos—have been running until recently.

Have you run into trouble with these people, Karsch?
A little, Gesine.
And now you don't want anyone to know that we know you, so that's why you've brought us here to the depths of the UN?
The food wasn't that bad, Gesine.
Good old considerate Karsch.
I'd rather you tell me why the child is so jealous, Gesine.

For now Marie wants to know who's paying Karsch for these transatlantic trips, whether Karsch really pays his own bills, whether it's true that no government and no university helps him, if he really makes a living the way he lives, if he really does do everything differently than D. E. She's gotten a bit carried away in her agitation, and a stranger can't see how much she'd give for shelter behind impeccable behavior. She manages it only at the goodbyes. It's a promise meant as an apology. – The next time you call us, I'll recognize you: she says.

She looks at Karsch as he innocently ambles away down the corridor, preoccupied and forgetful under his ruffled hair, greeted with waves from colleagues, drawn into conversations by familiar grips on his arm, a man with lots of friends, including famous people, and she says she hates him, and we can believe it. She refuses eye contact. She pulls the collar of her coat up high enough to make the points reach her eyes, as though by accident. – I hate him! she says. – I hate him!

November 12, 1967 Sunday

Time to give you our annual speech about your death. The date doesn't matter.

I understand, you're dead. It's your business.

But it's our business whether we want to keep you. You always want to be in our thoughts. We have enough without you.

You're the one who left. It was obvious five years beforehand, when you took the first steps. You let it happen.

You could have gotten help. You didn't even want to admit you needed help.

Not one single person in all of Jerichow, all of Mecklenburg, all of Germany satisfied your pride. You were too good for them.

You didn't like living like that, and so you went away. Did you think you'd arrive somewhere? (We know, you thought it possible you might arrive some-where, even if a welcome was now ruled out.) So how was it?

You didn't want to hurt everyone. But you hurt him. You hurt me. A child. We don't forgive you, not at all.

Have it your way. We take the trip. We dream the plane, we dream the flight, we travel by night, we fly through the air, we transfer somewhere, we have to keep going through time, all the more impenetrable the more of it there is. Now we're where you were.

There, where you're dead, we don't see you.

Now it's quickly back over England and Ireland and Newfoundland and Canada to New York, ten minutes late. You can follow us here only if we give our permission.

You wouldn't exist if we didn't want you to anymore.

Don't get your useless hopes up.

Don't be impatient. Have we left you in the lurch even once in twenty-nine years?

Behave yourself. No back talk. Not today.

November 13, 1967 Monday

The rumor of Franco's murder that traveled with the snack cart through every floor of the bank this morning did not withstand the light of day. He's still alive.

– Unfortunately: Amanda says. – And we have a list as long as my arm, don't we, Gesine?

Amanda means the list of surviving dictators awaiting assassination. Amanda is Mrs. Williams, and today Mrs. Williams goes home a different way, and Mrs. Cresspahl does too, and they run into each other on the bus that's trudging up Third Avenue like an animal staggering with exhaustion. At five in the afternoon the bus on Third takes twenty minutes to move just ten blocks uptown. The driver has trouble maneuvering the long box away from the stop and back into traffic, has to force it, inch by inch, parallel to the surrounding cars that never jerk forward more than a few steps at a time, and as a result has to watch from afar as the green light comes and goes several times. Once he gets to the intersection, cars turning in from the side streets are stuck in it, and now a new task begins—trying to at least suggest a swerve to the right between the hemmed-in private vehicles and taxis. The stopped bus looms amid the low cars like an elephant good-naturedly performing his dressage routine for now but capable at any moment of breaking out with all the strength currently parked in a bellowing idle. Its green skin just needs to turn gray and wrinkle into hard furrows. The driver, though, has to not only direct the vehicle, steer, step on the gas, step on the gas, brake, signal, but also open the doors, change money, keep an eye on the clattering of the correct fare into the coin counter, monitor the surrounding traffic as well as his passengers' behavior in his rearview mirrors, close the doors, clear the coins from the meter with his free hand and put each denomination into the correct cash-register tube while driving, arrange the exchanged dollar bills by hand, folding them and putting them away, and remain insensitive the whole time to the lumpish clouds of resignation and impatience behind his back. Amanda volunteers the vow that she would never marry a Manhattan bus driver. Amanda's voice is not obtrusively loud, but she doesn't mind being overheard either. She wouldn't even help finance a murder; she would fight tooth and nail not to look at a shot and bleeding dictator; she doesn't mean the actual literal deed, she's just taking a stand on the side of those who share her convictions, a group among which she counts us. The whole long day, since early morning, was not enough to starve out her goodwill; just as she greeted every visitor to our department, every passing vice president, with bursting or muffled joy, from nine o'clock till closing time, a recurring smile still flits across her just twenty-eight-year-old face like an ingrained habit, like a curtain perpetually raised and then bouncing back into place as soon as the stage threatens to become visible. A year and a half ago Mr. Kennicott II, the personnel manager, introduced her to the department as Amanda, so she was on a first-name basis with everyone except for the bosses. Naomi here, Jocelyn there. Then, on the fifth day, she wasn't at the phone when payroll asked for a Mrs. Williams, and neither Naomi nor Jocelyn knew her under that name, only Mrs. Cresspahl, who was still making the faux pas of using last names. Such things don't bother Amanda; she ignores them, assuming unintentional discourtesy. Her friendliness is not indiscriminate. When she hands out the biweekly checks to the girls in her typing pool, she does so with remarks on the ship that's back in the water or the chimney smoking again; she delivers Mrs. Cresspahl's sealed envelope like the mail, though, but puts it next to the in-box, and her expression may be congratulatory but it is not overly familiar. She treats differences in work and in payment discreetly. She takes dictation from Mrs. Cresspahl, gives assignments to her typists; she follows the formalities of request and mutual consultation with everyone except the male heads of the department. She is as eager to hear news of others' private lives as she is to report on her own: in moderation, *fino a un certo punto*. She is from one of the flocks of bungalows near St. Paul and tells stories about Minnesota winters; she flies home for her father's funeral and mentions it three months later, in passing, thereby avoiding the feelings of others. She has married a student who now works as a psychologist for the city police; she had inadvertently recommended a position with the police as a way to avoid being drafted into the Vietnam War. She has a job as a senior secretary solely to furnish her Bleecker Street apartment entirely in Scandinavian style, or for her next summer vacation to southern Europe; she wouldn't admit that she won't consider having children without sufficient savings. She knows Mrs. Cresspahl's real family situation and addresses her around others as a married woman, to shield her; she passes along the lunch invitations from all sorts of different men in an amused way, showing no sign even of curiosity, much less approval; she knows about Marie's missteps in language and thought, not the worst ones, but the most amusing; now and then, the feeling seems like friendship. It's nice to be seen in public with her, even on the M101 bus at rush hour. Bystanders feel refreshed by her tireless, still-girlish voice; approve of her saucy banter; observe with worship or open regret her firm, curvaceous legs, then the abundant shapes in her slim military-style coat, and finally her wide, half-awake face, which comes across as naive to anyone who misses the occasional pursing of the lips, the narrowing of the eyes to a single point. There's room for more people than her in the friendliness she generates. Now she's talking about the purse-snatchings on the South American floor, in her faux-surprised, smart-aleck, flippant tone of voice, hanging at exemplary ease on the strap, absorbing unperturbed the unexpected lurches of the bus, enjoying the indecisive stares of the seated gentlemen. She's a fun person. Is she a friend or isn't she? Ask her for money and she'll check to see how long she can spare it for. Wave her over to your lunch table and she'll look happy, not irritated, at the inconvenience of wasted time before she can leave. Send her on errands and she'll deny that it puts her out in the least. Ask her to lie for you: she'll do it. Why then this certainty that we have only words between us, not understanding? How can anything be missing? The fact is, we do detect the well-meaning superiority of the former student when she discusses the Williamsburg minister who, in his sermon yesterday morning before the president of the United States, asked him for "some logical, straightforward explanation" of the nation's involvement in Vietnam. Amanda finds the request amusing. – Maybe he wanted to take advantage of the president being in the front pew: she says, and her bemused malice applies to both the man of God and the powerful sheep in his parish.

– I don't know much about ministers: Mrs. Cresspahl says, suddenly so intent on creating some distance between them that she didn't even anticipate Amanda's preemptive apology and has to make a greater effort to ward it off than the joke expected of her would have required. Now the conversation is halting.

Meanwhile, since the East Sixties, even though the people on his bus are no longer so crowded together, they are standing almost separated, the driver has given up trying to approach the right-hand curb; even though the downtown traffic is thinning out, he stops only when a ding of the signal asks him to. There are dispatchers stationed every twenty blocks here, who check and note down how closely the schedule is being followed, and the driver has to make up for his delays and get back into the prescribed time. Furthermore, it turns out that Amanda had sized him up correctly in her single passing glance, because the armor of patience and equanimity he'd shown himself steeled with—against private drivers' infelicities, police cars' right of way, and the usual stop-and-go—is starting to crack under his accumulated, compressed rage and may burst by the end of his shift. – All right now, ladies, let's keep it moving: he says, in a tone that invites the remaining passengers to join in his displeasure. Earlier, beneath his cap shoved back on his head to precisely the same extent, he'd looked ready to crack jokes. Mrs. Williams and Mrs. Cresspahl stand on Third Avenue in the East Nineties and neither wants to explain to the other why she was taking a northbound bus to Greenwich Village, an East Side bus to the West Side.

– Getting cold again: Mrs. Williams says. She stamps her feet, she wants to part in a moment of explicit agreement. To the east, the island drops steeply off to the darkly reflective bowl of the East River, at Hell Gate.

– Sorry: Mrs. Cresspahl says. Which can be taken to refer to her hurrying to cross the street while she has a green light, or to something else.

I'm sorry, really, Mrs. Williams.

But there you have it—we don't mentally hear her voice answer.

November 14, 1967 Tuesday

Senator Robert F. Kennedy, not in the administration, does not share the administration's view when it comes to, say, Vietnam. "Despite the killing and despite the destruction, we are in no better position now than we were a year ago, and we will not be in any better position a year from now," he writes, and moreover recommends negotiations with the Vietcong. The administration, though, will hear no talk of missed chances for negotiation.

In Bolivia, Che Guevara, trafficker in revolution, has allowed not only himself to be captured but also his diary.

Four young men were seized yesterday as they loaded what police said was a quarter of a million dollars worth of marijuana into their station wagon on West End Avenue.

– 785 West End Avenue, where's that, Marie?

– Drop the last digit, divide by two, add sixty: it's around the corner from us, Mrs., *madam*, Gesine.

– Did you know that that happened on Ninety-Ninth Street?

– Esmeralda told me, Jason had told her, and Jason saw it. I don't need *The New York Times* for that, unlike a certain lady I know, *madam*, Mrs. Cresspahl.

By the third weekend in March 1933, Cresspahl had wasted his fourteenth day in Mecklenburg, and when he went to pay various calls in Jerichow, people thought he was coming to say his goodbyes. There was no way the man could leave his workshop back in England to take care of itself any longer. That much was clear to them.

Martha Maass saw him walk past the doors of the stationery store and the printer's, and gave up on him as a customer. Why would this Cresspahl need any stationery in Jerichow, what other advertisements did he have to mock up? That night, she and her husband agreed that he'd seemed reasonable enough to them, these being times when they would set to work on announcements smaller than that of the opening of a new woodworking establishment. Still, Maass put the conversation to bed with the somewhat disgruntled remark: People just passin through shouldn let the door hit em on the way out.

Cresspahl walked past Dr. Erdamer's house without glancing over the bushes, even though he heard the doors open and close and thought he heard the daughter calling his name. Then he was sure of it, and he still didn't turn around. It wasn't entirely unfathomable to him why the furloughed mayor might have wanted him to change his mind. The city council meeting had given him not only complete but commendatory recognition of his services in 1931–32, unanimously, maybe because they wanted him to keep managing the town affairs as an unofficial deputy, but definitely because of pressure from old Papenbrock. Papenbrock had also seen to it that the mayor's exit was reformulated as a personal request. Now Erdamer was sending his daughter out hatless and coatless into the street after Papenbrock's son-in-law, who didn't want to take on anything else as a representative of his father-in-law—at least not this.

No one asked Papenbrock questions. He had to explain what he wanted, just to be sure—on the estates, occasionally to the authorities in Schwerin, but not in Jerichow. In Jerichow, the fact that he wanted things a certain way was still enough. And so he was not always understood quite correctly. He'd wanted to avoid an impropriety affecting a civil servant, an educated man, a man of his own standing. As far as Maass, Böhnhase, Pahl, Methfessel, business, trade were concerned, Papenbrock "had put a stop to it." If he demanded decent behavior, then of whom more than Sonny Boy? That fit all the stories of the old man keeping his brat under his thumb even with no one ever there to see it. Not only had Papenbrock refused to bestow a single word or loan on Horst's SA, he was in the new government with the conservative German National People's Party. Papenbrock's voice still carried weight, and maybe the old man had arranged for the quick dismissal of charges against anyone his son turned over to the Gneez courts, whether Sass the customs official, who'd apparently maligned the new Reich chancellor, or the Communist journeyman tailor in whose room they'd found an SA uniform. When the Mecklenburg state legislature decreed that all official buildings should fly the old imperial black-white-and-red flag and the swastika flag from March 13 through March 15, who was it who made sure that the flag of the state of Mecklenburg—merely permitted, not mandated—be run up alongside them, and at the same height too? Papenbrock. Who had ordered three additional blue-yellow-and-red flags from Pahl—the state flag, that is, not merely a banner with the historical Mecklenburg colors of blue, yellow, and red? Papenbrock. True, he hadn't said why, but his actions spoke clearly enough, and they said: that the state of Mecklenburg-Schwerin would outlast this regime, too, the seventh in the space of a year. Then Papenbrock's son-in-law turned up, apparently to say goodbye. Not only was he not a business rival, he had not appeared anywhere in public with his brother-in-law. Well, all right, give the man a drink and wish him bon voyage.

Dr. Semig was out. The door was answered by Dora Semig, born Dora Köster in Schwerin, so like her husband that you felt you were looking at him when you saw her: both were tall, thin, whole body sturdy and strong, with a somewhat stiff, dry-skinned face nonetheless capable of quick, soft, friendly movements. That was the Dora Semig he knew. Today she kept her lips pressed tight together, eyes fixed, and refused to say hello even after she'd recognized Cresspahl. He was standing one stair below her. She held the door firmly. She didn't seem scared, more like hostile. At around two in the morning on March 13 the doorbell had rung at the home of Dr. Spiegel, a Jewish lawyer in Kiel. Mrs. Spiegel, hearing shouts of "Police! Police!" had opened the door. The shouters were not policemen, and they killed Dr. Spiegel with a bullet to the head. Now the Semigs' maid had given notice. Dora Semig had been brought up with maids. Never in her life had she had to answer a door herself. She looked so grumpy that Cresspahl didn't wholly believe her. He moved half a step back to take a look into the courtyard. Semig's carriage wasn't there. Now Cresspahl had made Dora laugh. It started small, against her will. Then her lips parted slightly in the middle. Then the corners of her eyes started to move a little. Then she laughed. She wasn't even offended when Cresspahl said he didn't have time to wait for Dr. Semig.

He went to see a lot of people. Wulff, like the others, was expecting Cresspahl's departure. Plus Cresspahl didn't feel like drinking alone. Wulff put a glass for himself down on the bar a bit abruptly, the same way he did everything that afternoon with a certain satisfied fury, whether sending Elli Wagenführ from table to table with sidelong looks or holding his emptied glass up to Cresspahl with an expression of having had to swallow a bitter pill. Elli Wagenführ, who'd known Peter Wulff for at least six months of evening waitressing and could use her sharp tongue on him when necessary the same way she could rap customers on the knuckles, today had nothing to say to him but drink orders, and when she had to go behind the counter she never budged from the sink. Wulff didn't care whether Cresspahl had something he wanted to discuss, he had a few things to say himself. Warncke, the Communist representative to the state legislature, had gotten himself captured in Neustrelitz. The party branch in Krakow am See had dissolved voluntarily, sending all of its membership records and documents to the Mecklenburg criminal authorities, with the assurance: "We're done with all that!" – We're done with all that!: Peter Wulff remarked to no one in particular and in High German, as though imitating someone speaking High German. – *It stinks like where an owls sat!*: he said in Platt, incensed like a man who may have seen something coming but wasn't so happy, was in fact rather upset, to have been proven right. He reviled Warncke and every other Communist he could think of with thumbnail biographies—this one's grandfather's lapses, that one's childhood bed-wetting. They had disappointed him, so deeply that he felt more hurt than he'd expected. It was as if a separation had existed only in words up until then, and now he was making it real. He was talking like someone who'd prepared to take a trip, one not without danger, but still an entertaining prospect, and now it was finally getting under way, now at last the waiting was over, and he was thinking with grim anticipation of the day to come—but he was talking to no one in particular, not paying much attention to Cresspahl, because he didn't reckon he'd be seeing him in the future, or even after this weekend.

It didn't occur to him that Cresspahl might want something from him. Cresspahl stood there in front of him, unassuming, one hand calmly in his pants pocket and the other resting lightly on the edge of the bar, keeping his head erect and his face impassive. He watched Wulff and gave no response—not with a wrinkle of brow, with his eyes, with the corners of his mouth. Wulff might well think Cresspahl had wrapped up all his affairs. He'd never known him to be especially talkative. He had a hard enough time finding something appropriate to say about the man's dead mother; he didn't want to let himself in for dealing with a departure. He refilled their glasses, raised his to make it clear that this round was on the house, and said: *Well its not for me, sez the wolf.*

– *But a little lamb sure hits the spot, he sez*: Cresspahl said.

He hadn't looked to anyone like a man who maybe didn't exactly need advice, but still would have welcomed some.

November 15, 1967 Wednesday

– I don't like what comes next: Marie says. – Can't you change it?

So what was it the rebel Che Guevara wanted to bring about in Bolivia? A second Vietnam.

The New York Times has dedicated to the roughly three thousand youths protesting against the American war in Vietnam last night around the New York Hilton Hotel not only a thirty-five-square-inch photograph, under a headline of its own, but also her famed column eight. When policemen on motor scooters drove into the line of youths who had linked their hands to block traffic, she heard one of the custodians of law and order say: You want to be treated like animals, we'll treat you like animals.

The Soviet Union lets two of the spies they've turned take the floor. One of them knows that America was trying to stage a military coup in India, and the other says that what he missed about English life were beer and oysters, and an occasional afternoon at the soccer matches. The former's name might actually be Smith.

In Queens, John Franzese, "Sonny" to mafiosi, was on trial for first-degree murder in the 1964 slaying of Ernest "The Hawk" Rupolo. A mistrial had to be declared because several jurors had read about the defendants in the newspaper. Sonny looked relieved, relaxed, and his dear wife, Tina, blew him a kiss from across the courtroom, which, *The New York Times* does not neglect to mention, was wood-paneled.

– Can't you tell it differently? Marie says. – Did every English child really have to be christened in those days?

– But she was a German child, in the country, in Mecklenburg.

– And again Cresspahl did it for this Lisbeth person?

– He did it for his wife, and even arranged for a church ceremony, for Sunday, March 19, 1933. This time he ended up seeing Pastor Brüshaver himself, not Brüshaver's wife. When Cresspahl saw him sitting at his desk he understood why people called him a bureaucrat. Brüshaver wrote down the date, even though it was only two days in the future; he entered the fee he received into a ledger; he acted like a bookkeeper whose firm has been given an order. That's how Cresspahl saw him. Brüshaver was a squat, stout man, not especially strong looking. He had flesh on his bones that wasn't fat or flabby, it sat firmly on him—it was just so visible. His hands were so soft on the desktop. His jowls didn't sag, his chin was no more than round, yet he was swollen with flesh. It moved little, it hadn't worked much. Sad flesh. Cresspahl looked at him not at all like someone who made his living with hands; he'd also noticed that the soil in the garden behind the pastor's house was freshly turned, not too neatly, but deep enough. The two men were roughly the same age; you didn't see the pastor's age in his face, at most you could see it in the eyes, in the even, unwavering, heavy gaze, which suggested not just attention but actual observation. Cresspahl was annoyed that, while they talked, Brüshaver was clearly continuing to think about something else he had no intention of sharing, like a doctor keeping a troubling finding from his patient. Like a doctor! that's what the people of Jerichow said about him. And he had small lips, innocent like a child's. There was also something professional about the way he moved his lips as he wrote out the baptismal reading, as though savoring something, reacquainting himself with his understanding of more than was to be found in the mere words of Psalm 71, verse 6. At least he knew his business and the passage in question. Cresspahl was not inclined to say more than that in his favor.

– Say it in English, if you have to say it: Marie says.

– By thee have I been holden up from the womb: thou art he that took me out of my mother's bowels: my praise *shall* be continually of thee.

– Dam-nation! Marie thunders. But the outrage captured on tape is not real; her laughter unexpectedly follows and lets the modulation of what she's just said reverberate with inner amusement. – My foot! she says.

– Should someone have changed that?

– No. But he changed your name!

– Nobody changed my name, Marie.

– So your name is Gesine Henriette C.?

– No.

– See, Gesine Lisbeth? When you're telling a story you've got to keep track of everything.

– Maybe he just wanted to keep the name Henry free for the next child. For one of the next children.

– Maybe he wanted to do that Lisbeth of yours another favor.

– Maybe he traded it for her permission to let Dr. Semig be godfather at the christening.

– He hadn't picked Semig at his earlier appointment. What happened to Alexander Paepcke?

– Paepcke had something to attend to at the Güstrow courthouse too early the next morning. But there were plenty of people who would have been glad to take his place.

– After what had happened that week, it had to be a Jew?

– A Christian, Marie. A Christian. After this new gambit, Brüshaver had tried to make his client reconsider by giving him another one of his looks, as if he must have been so busy listening to and looking at him that he'd misheard and misseen. Until Cresspahl stated for the record, as though repeating it: Herr Semig is not a Jew, he was baptized like his father, and his grandfather too, and the Kösters wouldn't have turned a blind eye and given away their daughter . . . : all said in the calm, obliging tone that he otherwise used to suggest stepping outside to settle things, and Brüshaver nodded. He didn't nod with his whole head, but he moved his creaseless eyelids in a brief, acquiescent way, and added: People will talk, Mr. Cresspahl. Twaddle, if you ask me, Mr. Cresspahl.

– I don't like it: Marie says.

– That Cresspahl invited a Jerichow veterinarian to a christening?

– If he wanted to pick a fight with Jerichow, he should have stayed in Jerichow. Should have been staying.

– You want me to change that?

– You should tell it differently.

– Well, we'll present it a bit differently.

– Don't forget the child being put on display at Papenbrock's house.

– Now Cresspahl had to disabuse the pastor of the idea that they were in agreement on all points except the one in which the church was, after all, only supposed to assist. When Brüshaver repeated the baptismal reading, just to be sure, Cresspahl misunderstood it as a question, hesitated before answering, and eventually said: Nah. It came out sounding mildly amused, but still like a snub for a foolish presumption. It meant that, first, Lisbeth Papenbrock had to go looking for a Bible passage herself, and second, that Cresspahl didn't expect . . . that the church . . . he wouldn't . . . the church wouldn't . . .

– Third: Marie says: that he wasn't exactly desperate to make friends. That he didn't need friends in Jerichow. Why didn't he leave!

– Pick the child up under his arm and take the train to Hamburg and give her a bite of his steak and a drink of his beer?

– Oh: Marie says: aha. A man with a baby. No can do.

– He no longer had any choice. Now he could keep his child, and his wife, only in Jerichow. Not in Richmond, not in Lisbeth's foreign country.

– What made him so sure?

– She'd told him.

– Weren't men in charge in that land of Mecklenburg?

– Usually, Marie.

– So why didn't he tell her: Take the baby, pull yourself together, and come with me?

– You don't usually approve of using force, Marie.

– He didn't care about not using force. He was scared.

– He was scared of losing her.

– He was chicken! He didn't want to find out what she was capable of!

– I can't change any more than that.

The subway cashiers will no longer accept five-dollar bills, for fear of counterfeits. Some of the money in our purse is probably fake.

November 16, 1967 Thursday

Mr. Josiah Thompson didn't believe the official report about the death of President Kennedy either. After he concluded that there were three perpetrators, not the one officially recognized assassin, FBI agents paid him a visit to warn him that anything he said might be held against him. So he didn't say anything. Then they went away. He still doesn't know what they wanted to ask him about.

The North Vietnamese shelled an airfield and ammunition dump in South Vietnam, setting a whole valley on fire. The American commander in chief in Vietnam finds the situation "very, very encouraging."

The New York Times has to correct herself. The secretary of state did not say that there was no alternative to escalation. He said: Whenever we try to start the process of de-escalation, we face rejection from the other side.

The address Mrs. Ferwalter gave us is on the East Side, on a street in the Nineties near the East River. Where the street starts, the hopes that the small businesses once inspired in their owners are laid out dead behind metal scissor gates: half-demolished shop counters, broken glass, packaging that's now garbage. Almost no children hang out on the street. The abandoned cars from four weeks ago are still sitting there, a little rustier now, a little more thoroughly cannibalized for salvage. The street has so little life left in it that people come from other neighborhoods to throw their bulk trash, from sofas to refrigerators, next to the dumpsters here, whose bellies no longer even stink. The moribund building itself cowers pitifully in a row of four-story fellows. The front steps look unused. The door stands open, wedged back at an angle, revealing that the fear of theft is gone, leaving only indifference. Most of the windows keep the daylight out with dusty blinds. The owner tried, ten years ago maybe, to paint the bricks of the facade a watery blue now that they were no longer sheathed in brownstone; since then the building has received no further assistance. There is not yet deliberate dirt covering the stairwells, just dust and sticky grime, a rotting mix. Behind the doors, it's as quiet as a sickroom, and the faces that appear are lifeless, as though not much cooking goes on there. On the third (fourth) floor, Mr. Kreslil has pinned up his visiting card: yellowed elegant cardstock printed in fancy italics thirty years ago. It doesn't mention that he gives private Czech lessons, and he has crossed out the abbreviation for "Professor" with a neat, unflustered stroke of the pen.

The apartment is guarded by an old woman whose name, as we learned only slowly, is Jitka Kvachkova. The first time, she needed to hear our name and nonthreatening words repeated over and over before she was willing to unhook the door chain. She's short. For all her roundness, she looks harried, fugitive. She has raised the height of her head with hair pulled up in a tight bun, too much for her low steep forehead to bear. Her eyes don't relax once they've recognized the visitor, they keep looking past her for uninvited guests on the stairs, for danger. Her speech is so foreign that at first only her gestures made it clear that the visitor was being asked to wait a moment. She had such trouble believing we'd understood her that her manner seemed severe. There's a rustle at her hips as of many skirts when she marches to the connecting door, hand far outstretched as though determined to lash out in rage. But once she's through the door she speaks in a gentle, utterly submissive voice. The visitor has to wait to be announced, every time. We wait in a room that also functions as a kitchen, and at night as a bedroom; we wait in an armchair whose bottom is half falling out, the armrests still warm from Mrs. Kvachkova's hands. The second time, we tiptoed over to the TV set facing the chair: still warm. By now she's used to us and has continued to learn from TV shows what you say in this country when guests arrive or leave, but what she manages best is a smile that starts at several parts of her face at once, runs together, and eventually forms an overall, completely believable expression. It has also occasionally happened that she's touched our arm and expressed sympathy for our weariness with a sorrowful shake of the head, bringing back thoughts of Jakob's mother, who used to take the groggy Cresspahl child to the train for school in the early-morning darkness. Still, she insists on the ceremony of announcing the visitor. This bare room is hers, she lives there, she works there, but to outsiders it must play the part of Professor Kreslil's anteroom, and she that of the housekeeper, not the woman who lives with him. Perhaps because that's how they did things back in České Budějovice.

The same as at Ottje Stoffregen's, in Jerichow. After the war, Ottje Stoffregen lived in a room upstairs from the pharmacy and kept an evacuee from Pommern in the kitchen, and she had to audibly discuss with him whether or not to admit a visitor, as though he were sitting at his claw-foot desk bent over his work, not over bound volumes of magazines in which he had been permitted to publish before 1938. He would rise to his feet as though surfacing from pressing thoughts, go up to the visitor with outstretched hand, with a pleased but distracted, busy smile and a figure as gaunt as Professor Kreslil's, on which his suits hung similarly loose and askew, the difference being that Stoffregen's English tweed wasn't shabby even after having been worn for ten years while Professor Kreslil's clothes seemed to have been bought in that Czech forest through which the party of the working classes had herded one lone sheep, and the other difference being that Kreslil merely lacks the money for a dentist who could fill out his cheeks with proper dentures while Stoffregen had had his teeth knocked out and bore the gaps like a badge of honor, as though needing to act the part of the witch in the fairy tale, his grin constantly slipping into a familiarity that could not, in fact, be trusted. So it's not the same as at Ottje Stoffregen's. Kreslil, with his bowing and his formal way of speaking, belongs in a black suit at the best table at St. Wenceslas restaurant, and he has never once set foot in it; his coloring is different, too, shocks of white hair bookending healthy pink skin on his bald head while Stoffregen was yellow, and Stoffregen was too good to give lessons, there was nothing to learn from Stoffregen; Kreslil has set up his desk as if for a veritable feast of learning, with abundant pencils and paper and textbooks opened to the right page; his own books are ranked on the bookshelf far behind him, five blue volumes by one Anatol Kreslil, all with the same indecipherable title, and Kreslil sits up straight in a correct, angular way that one used to learn behind schoolroom desks, carefully clears his throat, begins by reviewing the homework from the previous lesson, smiles encouragingly behind his rimless bifocals, and is happy to see what I have learned, in fact it is now possible to tell him that our houses are far from the train station, *naše domy jsou daleko od nádraží,* but we're missing something that would make these Czech words come easily, *tato česká slova . . .*, and there was a time at school when Miss Cresspahl didn't want to learn any more of the language of the occupying power and spent a whole year never getting beyond the story of the little old grandfather and the turnip that just wouldn't be pulled out, and he pulled and he pulled, *tyeshil, tyeshil, a nye vyteshil,* and in Prague a stranger stopped me, a man in a post office uniform, in the middle of the main train station, Wilsonovo nádraží, three steps from the information booth, and he let me direct him there with a *"ptejte se tam"* as though not expecting the usual form *"zeptejte se tam,"* passport please, with that American passport I'd rather have ended up at the police station than the American embassy, but no one came into the compartment during the trip to Berlin East station, all night long, the secret police are not so pedantic when it comes to the function of verbal aspects in Slavic languages, and again and again Kreslil's Czech takes me back to my Russian and then he retreats into a reserved, severe expression and looks disapprovingly at me while I sleep, it's another refresher course in the history of Socialism, I have seen myself sleeping with shoulders slightly hunched and head drooped and face slack, in one of Blach's pictures, sleeping like the dead, Kreslil wakes me up for a single word of German out of a sleep that cost ten dollars and walks me to the door past the outraged Mrs. Kvachkova, I have not spoken Russian, not spoken German, I don't say anything, how could I have fallen asleep here. How can I sleep in these people's home. Wake me up.

November 17, 1967   Friday

It's not him. The old man making his way around the streets of Panama, peddling combs, wine, and secondhand clothes, is not Heinrich Müller. If the head of Hitler's secret police is still alive, then he's still at large.

On page 3, which *The New York Times* usually sets aside for photojournalism from Vietnam, she today shows the 75-foot-long cage in Catanzaro where the Italian justice system is holding 121 members of the Mafia who are on trial. If Karsch can stay in this country now, he must have his people in Calabria.

Avenarius Kollmorgen was looking forward to an enjoyable evening. He spent more than enough nights at home alone; he'd read about the renunciations that come with age, but that wasn't how he felt about it, not with respect to other people, not with respect to pleasures. Not that he needed other people, only their company. At bottom, he wanted to be left alone. He had broken with his parents by studying law, not the arts they'd wanted him to study. He had gotten over his first name, which others had made literarily and philosophically famous as a last name. On top of everything, he didn't even want Richard Wagner as a grandfather. He had also succeeded in creating a self-image as not the "Avi" from Wismar public school, not the "Arius" of Erlangen University, but really and truly the genuine, secret Avenarius Kollmorgen who no longer needed to go around telling anyone about himself. He knew this Avenarius to be a gentle, sensitive creature. Fine, he had made no mark in any art. Yes, he'd left Rostock for a much smaller city by the Baltic, where he wasn't easy to find. Admittedly, he lived alone. Where was the woman to whom he could have explained and explicated himself? The children who ran after him shouting singsong rhymes in the street, the Jerichowers who found his way of talking and way of walking amusing—let them think him a devious sort, arrogant, even crotchety. That wasn't the worst disguise. And if he didn't often set foot in the Lübeck Court, that wasn't because the stairs were a bit too steep for his rather short legs, it was only because he didn't like what they did with their wines. They bought doubtful vintages. Then they stored the bottles in the sunny side of the cellar. Such substances had never been served in the Kollmorgen house. Also, he wasn't so good with crowds. He didn't have much he could talk about, he knew so many secrets that the boundary between them and public knowledge sometimes grew somewhat blurry. No, what he needed were individuals, people he could seat in a particular chair in his own house and who'd play by his rules, unable to prevent Avenarius K. from observing, analyzing, and seeing right through them at his leisure. And, of course, occasional visitors served as a welcome alibi for the neighbors, who saw empty bottles accumulate in the courtyard almost every morning. So it was just fine when Albert Papenbrock came by with his son-in-law, even on a Saturday evening, to discuss the rather unusual gift being deeded to a two-week-old child. Papenbrock was getting on in years himself, too. Possibly, as the night wore on, Papenbrock would reveal certain weaknesses to which a Kollmorgen would not be prey for some time. And he'd been curious about this son-in-law for a long time. In 1931 he'd found his way not to Kollmorgen but to Dr. Jansen. Funny, in a certain sense of the word. Nothing against his colleague Jansen, for that matter. Kollmorgen stood up from his Seneca and marched to the kitchen, his back ramrod straight enough almost to tip him over backward, and he shooed Geesche Helms's sister out of the house. For all her nosiness, she never seemed to find the vintages she was sent to retrieve. Then the short stocky gentleman clambered down to the cellar, sighing happily over the small amount of work that would yield such a generous reward.

When he'd installed his clients in their armchairs—plump stuffed traps they wouldn't have such an easy time getting free of—the two men still seemed to be on the same side. Papenbrock had come for a pleasant evening, not for any long negotiations. No sooner was his cigar lit than he pointed his chin over to the bottles arrayed on one side, and a Kollmorgen doesn't need to be asked twice. The other fellow...—Cresspahl, isn't it?—sat rather straighter, not like a guest, looking a bit drowsy with his pipe, his mind clearly elsewhere. He seemed to be waiting. Yes, Kollmorgen too could hardly stand the suspense. The preliminaries took a certain amount of time, alas unavoidable. First, the weather. Not bad for mid-March. And with that, how business was looking (good) was taken care of too (second). Third, the family. Maybe better not. Politics. Definitely not. Well, down to brass tacks. It won't take long, surely. And, in this hope, Dr. Kollmorgen spread the pages of his draft out on the extensive surface of his bulging thighs, draped his elbows comfortably on the padded armrests of his chair, and began his presentation. He rocked back and forth from sheer anticipation and well-being. To keep his daughter's husband in the country, Papenbrock was giving his granddaughter a property that would be hers not before March 3, 1954. He, Kollmorgen, would not live to see that day, so it was of necessity on this one that he would have to get all the entertainment he was entitled to out of the proceedings.

– And the other children? he said.

He held his round head, flattened in the back and excessively large, very high; raised wild eyebrows up into his forehead; acted as serious as he could. Let the clients do their worst, he could take it. In the event of multiple children, the property could only be divided up by its monetary value, since various different dates of attaining majority would be in play, along with additional legal proceedings, not to mention other official processes. The question was justified; there was nothing the gentlemen could do about it. This . . . —Cresspahl, isn't it?—gave no sign of irritation, he simply nodded quietly, head to one side, the way amateurs in chess acknowledge the opening their opponent has chosen to deploy, as if to say that this one is fine, though another would've been better. It was really too bad that Avenarius was too isolated from the world by this time to befriend anyone even as a chess partner. Then he noticed Papenbrock's hand, frozen in midair holding a full glass then weaving erratically to the point where a drop shot up over the glass's rim. Papenbrock hadn't prepared for this. It was no use trying to get his own back by puffing smoke and suggesting a proviso clause. Well, let Papenbrock think he had rallied. Let him scoff at Kollmorgen's alleged idiosyncrasies. That was just fine.

Since the mother's inheritance is hereby and of her own free will being settled on the child, the property thus deeded would revert upon the death of the child first to the mother and only then to the father, and then to the current owner. The father, as trustee, is not authorized to borrow against the assigned property, nor to encumber it with a mortgage. He is to pay for the property and building maintenance from the usufruct, and is responsible for any and all state and local taxes and fees. The child's ownership is protected against the father top to bottom, back to front. That's how the gentlemen want it, no?

– *Well then theres nothin in it for us*: Cresspahl said, not bitter and no less calm than Papenbrock had been as he'd listened to the terms.

Papenbrock heaved himself upright in two stages, so that he could look his son-in-law straight in the face—not merely surprised but hurt. In an aggrieved tone of voice, he named the sum he had already put into the property, slightly rounded up actually, even though every phase of the purchase had gone through Kollmorgen's office. Avenarius, in his delight, tried to top off Cresspahl's glass. Not enough was missing from it.

– Maintenance!: Cresspahl said. *The way everything theres fallin apart, the wind'll take care a that.*

He made not the slightest protest when Papenbrock, obliged to rein himself in somewhat, brought up a certain account at the Surrey Bank of Richmond; he dismissed it with a nod, and in so doing made it crystal clear to Papenbrock that the account really was as substantial as Lisbeth had said, maybe even more substantial by now. This made him stumble in his calculations, during which time Avenarius reveled in the certainty that Papenbrock had been counting on certain sentimental family feelings. He made a note of this mistake in his head, on the right, just above his fat hairy ear, to savor to the full later. He couldn't afford to miss anything transpiring at the moment. There was no need to pit these two against each other. Observation, innocent undistracted observation—that was his favorite thing.

Papenbrock had been acting like he'd been trying to give his son-in-law an indirect gift, that is to say, via Cresspahl's daughter, so as not to insult him. This Cresspahl, meanwhile, was taking refuge behind his obligation to scrutinize the gift for the advantages it actually gave to his daughter. Avenarius couldn't have planned it any better himself. He leaned back unassumingly, forced his hands together over his belly, without forgoing the rocking on his elbows, and turned his head back and forth from one man to the other so as not to miss a single blow, a single direct hit. He liked how this . . . Cresspahl was landing them. He carried himself not in a defiant or challenging way, as the situation might well have warranted; his manner was slow, thorough, like someone who'd promised to think things over. And now the thinking-over was done. Papenbrock had immediately snatched at the sheet of paper on which Cresspahl had made his calculations, and as a result was torn back and forth between the numbers he was reading and the words he was hearing out of Cresspahl's mouth. That was too bad, Kollmorgen felt, for Papenbrock thus failed to feel the full scope of his defeat. Cresspahl, on the other hand, could recite by heart the fact that the property had no significant market value at the present time. It would nonetheless still be a much more reasonable course to sell it. The money could be placed in a trust account until the child came of age—ideally half in a German account, half in a British one, to cover any divergent economic developments and facilitate the trustee's management of the usufruct. At least that way the gift would incur no further costs. And, speaking of which, the trustee could hardly agree to use his cash on something over which he had no disposal rights. The way things stood now, there was nothing in it at all for them. Not to mention the maintenance, still less to mention the repairs. If Papenbrock seriously wanted to do something for the child, any renovation was up to him. But that was entirely the giver's business. He was perfectly free to have repairs carried out by persons he contracted to do the work, or else to let the child's legal guardian hire contractors, but in either case he would need to be responsible for the full costs, since it was part of his gift. After the deeded property was restored to a normal condition, it still would not meet the demands of the craft that was the trustee's business, and moreover he would still have to establish and build up a business here, and then, Cresspahl said, obligingly, as a good-natured promise: *Then itll be time to talk about my money.*

It was long after midnight that Avenarius Kollmorgen found himself pacing through his three rooms, standing up less than ramrod straight, sometimes hugging himself a little with pleasure. He carried his glass with him, sipping expertly, and as he swallowed he raised a serene and joyous face to the ceiling. He had seen Papenbrock in defeat, observed him closely. Papenbrock had signed over money for his feelings, and a lot more money than he'd wanted to. Papenbrock had thought his son-in-law was at such a disadvantage that he had failed to reckon with his own handicaps. Now Avenarius knew a bit more about Papenbrock. His picture of him had become more complete. He knew all about pictures, there was always some point or another where the picture failed to coincide with the actual person, he knew this from the pictures of himself in circulation, but while people couldn't apply their picture of Avenarius Kollmorgen to him, he knew full well how to exploit his of them. Oh yes indeed. Best of all was recalling the moment when Papenbrock had realized his situation and put the half-drunk glass of wine down and said goodbye to his hopes for an evening chat among like-minded men. Yes, this had been a great and memorable evening for Avenarius K. Even the private army of this Austrian, this . . . Hitler, had refrained for once from rumbling and bellowing in the market square and intruding on the performance taking place here, which had surpassed Avenarius's fondest dreams.

The stocky abbreviated gentleman stopped at one of his windows, stuck his hefty head out through the curtains, and looked out onto the nighttime market square lying before him between the shining white gabled houses like a giant stage. Someday a stage like that should be built for him, Avenarius, so that someday all the audiences from Wismar to Lübeck could see him as the wise and yet deeply sensitive being he really was. They would not understand. But he didn't need their attempts at understanding. They would misjudge him, they could do nothing else. He was content to enjoy his solitude. That way no one disturbed him in the sublime amusement that he and he alone was capable of gleaning from the banal business of others. Still, to give credit where credit was due, he'd had no reason to expect such an evening. He had no right to so much pleasure. And if no right to that, then no right to another bottle of Pommard either; since, however, he had nonetheless been granted the one, he had perforce to go fetch the other. Otherwise the world would be out of joint, and it was he alone who could put it right. All right, down to your cellar, Avenarius.

November 18, 1967 Saturday, South Ferry day,
maybe the last one this year. Because last night, the second snowstorm in a week moved through New York State and New England, and even if it swept past the city with nothing more than rain and isolated flurries, the temperature has been stuck in the low 40s for some time. Gesine still subtracts thirty-two, multiplies by five, then divides by nine to get her 6°C to the same result as Marie, who has long since been able to translate 42°F into a physical sensation: It's cold.

Marie doesn't say so. She runs around the outer walkways during the ferry ride, both ways, and on only the windy side during the trip back to Manhattan, even though Gesine is sitting indoors on the other side. So she can't be seen. So she doesn't have to show herself. So she doesn't have to talk. Yesterday she put the mail next to the phone without sorting it into personal, strangers, and junk, as though she hadn't looked through the envelopes and in particular hadn't noticed the one with her school's official letterhead. She went into her room as if by chance whenever Gesine happened to walk anywhere near the phone, and it's unclear whether she was listening this morning when her mother made an appointment with Sister Magdalena. Two can play at this game. Gesine leaves it to her to bring it up, the same way Marie has left it to Gesine for the past four hours. Now, when the ferry is level with Liberty Island, she comes back inside, rubbing her hands, so cold she's hunched over. She says nothing about school, mentions only the Statue of Liberty, erected in New York Harbor by Frédéric-Auguste Bartholdi and bearing the face of none other than his dear mother.

– She has goose feet: Marie says.

She needs to sit down next to Gesine, a little out of her line of sight while Gesine keeps her eyes looking straight ahead, before she decides.

– Okay, so: she says: I'm sorry.

She pushes her hood back onto her neck but ignores her braid, still stuck in the blue wool fleece. She leans forward, elbows resting on her thighs, and even shakes her head back and forth like a man regretting a piece of foolishness even though in his heart he won't admit responsibility since he can't understand what it is he's done. – I just don't understand how they found out! she says.

Sister Magdalena didn't seem especially upset. She'd set out the tea things in her tiny upstairs room in the new wing of the school, her little wood-paneled cell that, for all the tidiness of bed and desk, still suggested a furnished rented room, a merely temporary place to sleep. Sister Magdalena was wearing the same dark gray dress that she wears to teach classes on other days, the dress Marie suspects she sleeps in, "and on her back, too, without moving." She was very hard to recognize from the little patch of face that her vows permit her to show to the outside world because, in addition, she barely moved it. She kept it firmly in that tolerant expression in which severity and goodness can coexist, and was unaware of prompting thoughts of bald-headed Paris mannequins. Sister Magdalena is thirty or fifty or forty years old: even the age of her voice is hidden in an unchanging tone that blends humility and determination. With her teacup and her hostess manners, she tried to imply an innocuous visit, but she sat stiffly on her chair, knee pressed to knee, shoe to shoe; even her hands resting loosely in each other left no doubt that this visit was a summons. She had concerns about Marie. She presented her complaints as concern for the child, as sympathy, in the pedagogical language that masks findings and the intentions behind them under expressions from life outside of school— detours and interconnections in which any direct question gets wrapped and smothered like a fly caught in a spider's web. She started by saying that children express feelings. Then she described the differences among various feelings. She explained the varying degrees of control that children have over their feelings. Puberty was euphemized as "a change not only in the soul." So, Marie had expressed feelings, was that it? No, that was not it. But she had tried to express feelings. In history class, she'd voiced anger at the way America's conquerors had treated the Indians, and this interfered with the lesson plan and necessitated a discussion that for all its psychological gains jeopardized their adherence to the syllabus. Not only had she made an utterly irrelevant connection to the Vietnam War in an essay she'd written, "I look out the window...", she had also, in conversations during lunch and recess, created difficulties, even confusion, for the other girls with respect to their own feelings about said war. She had raised her voice. So was that what you called me in to discuss? No. The issue was the girl's tendency to take the side of the downtrodden in historical events, to the point of almost moral solidarity. No one would deny that the war in Vietnam was a tragedy, but so were many other historical occurrences, and the school's goal was to convey not the unjust aspects of the topic being taught but the content of the material as such. A child willing to get worked up over established facts might pose a threat to the community in learning and life that the school strives to create. Is that the issue? No, Mrs. Cresspahl. Sister Magdalena had concerns about nothing less than the child's spiritual well-being.

How are we supposed to explain that to Marie? Should we tell her: Marie, you're too biased? Change that, Marie?

Sister Magdalena, mild and inexorable, had continued without a pause in her multistep, terraced deductions. Our interjected questions plagued her like wasp stings, she was not at all equipped to handle interruptions, and when she showed she was suffering, with strains at the corner of her mouth and the mildest creasing of the skin on her brow, she was actually trying to convey a rebuke. She diluted this expression into a wry smile meant to bemoan her human frailties—an only half-hearted pretense of apology. That was how she avoided answering. She seemed to be asking questions herself, although not quite. She spoke of the hardships and deprivations that working parents must suffer, especially in their then passing them along to their children. Especially with single parents, living apart, the refusal to impose authority can have other consequences, worse consequences for children than the desired and to some extent laudable ones. Children calling their parents by their first name, not addressing them as parents, might have a different meaning from family to family. It gave a sense of closeness, an illusory equality more likely to wreak havoc in a child's mind than nurture it. At no point did Sister Magdalena speak concretely. She even mentioned the school psychiatrist merely as a mutual acquaintance who had, of course, performed important services both in his work and in the wider field of human behavior. She was gathering information but refusing to distill it into facts. It was as if impressions were enough. We couldn't possibly explain anything to her. All that mattered was to make the right gestures—being worried about Marie's place in the school, concerned about Sister Magdalena's clearly sleepless nights, willing and eager to improve—in the vague hope of their being more or less plausible. And it wasn't as if we were outright lying. Sister Magdalena is the classroom teacher, and after a summons to see her the next step is being called in to see the administration. The school is overcrowded, in every grade, precisely because of the solid curriculum, and our paying full tuition, having not requested financial aid, won't save us since the other applicants have at their disposal the sacrament of baptism, which Marie cannot produce. The third summons, to the principal's office, is tantamount to the child's expulsion. There is no appeal against the insights of someone who's taught fifth grade for eleven years. The institution recently expelled a child with a congenitally deformed hip because she was ultimately incapable of conforming to the educators' ideas of a desirable child. No outright lying—the lie was elsewhere: in the polite conduct of the conversation, in our expected and unquestioned respect for Sister Magdalena's psychological abilities, everything down to the unwavering friendliness with which we said our goodbyes at the elevator door, Sister Magdalena refusing to walk away until the elevator arrived. On the street, in a worldly guise, we wouldn't recognize her. – It was such a pleasure speaking with you, Mrs. Cresspahl. – Not at all. The pleasure was mine, Sister Magdalena.

I'm sorry, Jakob.
Okay, Gesine. For what now?
That I said "We're not living apart."
Which is true.
That I said "He's dead."
It always helps to do that, doesn't it, Gesine?

I'm sorry Jakob.
Get the child out of there, Gesine.
And take her where, Jakob? To the moon?
Dublin. London. Copenhagen.

Should we order Marie to just kindly respect my authority? Should we scare her—with the bogeyman? with the psychiatrist? with expulsion? Should we tell her: Don't talk in school about what we talk about at home?

The child is so deep in thought that she neglects to watch the ferry arrive in the dock, even though the braking of the boat has long since been making the hull shake and most of the passengers have already headed for the doors and stairways in wedge-shaped crowds. – I don't understand: she says. – I was alone in the classroom when I wrote it on the board, and Sister Magdalena erased it without asking when the next class started.

– What did you write on the blackboard?

It's hard for the child. She doesn't quite squirm but she does hem and haw, holds her head to the side, leaning away.

– "Bugs Bunny for President": she finally admits. – Can I apologize to the old bag in writing, or do I have to do it in person?

The New York Times does not share the view that President Johnson is doing his job worse than that cartoon character who's forever concocting inventions supposedly designed to benefit his fellow creatures but actually designed to hurt and thwart them. *The New York Times* puts three photographs of the president's press conference on the front page, and the article runs to almost two pages: how he stepped out from behind the podium, waved his arms, chopped the air, drew imaginary lines with his fingers, ran the vocal gamut from loudly angry to gently modest, walked up and down in front of the camera like a revival preacher. The real Johnson. About those criticizing his conduct of the war: He did not want to call them unpatriotic. But they were living in glass houses.

November 19, 1967 Sunday

At last it's no longer a trade secret we need to keep: the devaluation of the pound sterling is stated in *The New York Times*.

Edward Ravender, a real estate broker, a Negro among whites, lives in a house with a swimming pool in Oceanside, Long Island. These whites have thrown rocks at his windows, door, and chimney, strewn empty beer cans across his lawn, burned a cross on it. He wanted to stick it out. Last night, they threw a bomb into his dining room. If it had gone off, his three-year-old son and twenty-day-old daughter would not have survived. Now Mr. Ravender is selling his house, worth $50,000, for the first reasonable offer.

Marie wants to know what happens at a church christening. She's disappointed to hear that the baby just has a little warm water brushed onto her forehead and her parents and godparents promise the church to bring up the future person in accord with the church's wishes. In return, the church's authorized representative confirms the child's name. Describing it that way might perhaps convince Marie not to carry out her plan to undergo the ceremony herself in five years. And that was, in fact, the whole procedure after the service in St. Peter's Church in Jerichow on March 19, 1933. Part of the congregation remained in their seats through the sleepy sound of the organ music with which Jule Westphal, the organist, was trying to usher them out of the house of God; some even moved up to vacant front pews set aside for the nobility, under the disapproving eye of the verger who, under Methling's regime, would have been allowed not only to intervene but also to collect the admission fees. Ol' Bastian was not happy with the new pastor. Pathetic, this Brüshaver. Warming up baptismal water, have you ever heard of that! Mollycoddling from the get-go, not to mention the extra work for Pauli Bastian in his declining days. Pauli kept his face stiff as a board while the Cresspahls and Papenbrocks walked up the center aisle with the baby, and the wrinkles that developed on his face, centered on the midpoint of his nose, formed a pattern not suitable for small children. Cresspahl carried the child high on his chest, very tense until he could hand her back to her mother at the altar. The women were all in high spirits. Louise Papenbrock had nodded more gently when she found herself in the front pew next to Dora Semig—born a Köster, after all, from Schwerin. Semig's wife watched everything being done to the child as though everyone were bent on making her laugh and on the point of succeeding. Hilde Paepcke couldn't keep her head still: she looked up at Cresspahl, made signs with her eyes and her lips to Lisbeth, not as an older sister but as a child playing along. Hilde Paepcke was rehearsing the christening ceremony for the child she had in her own belly. Lisbeth, my mother, your grandmother, didn't reveal much, but it was clear from the way she looked at Brüshaver and from her eager and timely joining in the prayers and responses that she was celebrating a very special occasion, and that she had gotten everything she wanted. About Louise Papenbrock it could be said without reservation that she'd lost control of her face, and that possibly the spectacle was letting her retouch her memories of the earlier christenings in her life, at least make them more bearable. Ladies such as Käthe Klupsch, for whom the occasion was proceeding nowhere near tragically and tearfully enough, we will not discuss. Cresspahl's expression showed nothing. He had his work face on. The other godparent, Arthur Semig, Dr. Vet. Med., held his hands loosely clasped over his belly and was unabashedly delighted. He stood next to Lisbeth Cresspahl and looked down at the baby's head turned toward him, at the eyelids twitching in half sleep, the lips opening and closing with relish, the cat's-paws in the corners of her eyes, you call them crow's-feet, and the grown man was so besotted with the baby that he crinkled his nose as oblivious to his surroundings

– as Mr. Fang Liu: Marie says.

– As only Chinese people can act around strangers' children.

Papenbrock sat there like the reigning monarch of the whole affair, but a dissatisfied one, watching something disagreeable taking place under his very nose. He was not seething with rage against Cresspahl, not in the least, though Cresspahl assumed he was. The previous evening, Papenbrock had left Avenarius Kollmorgen and his red wine for the Lübeck Court and Lindemann's Mosel, and stayed past closing time, just to brood silently in Cresspahl's presence. Cresspahl thought he might as well endure the uncomfortable silence if it helped Papenbrock get over his defeat; not in the least did he suspect that the old man was mentally comparing him to Horst Papenbrock, to how Horst spent his time, and was seriously considering changing his will. Here Papenbrock was not entirely paying attention. He was not so absentminded that he failed to notice the moisture in the inner corners of his eyes, but instead of dabbing at it with pleasure, like Louise, he roughly wiped it away as one more annoyance. He didn't hear the child sneeze, they had to tell him that later. He'd started early that morning. He'd waited to see if Horst would come to breakfast in his SA uniform.

The moment he caught sight of the brown boots, he'd started yelling, to Horst's amazement—Horst didn't think anyone was paying attention to him at all. Horst insisted he'd wear the party uniform to church. Papenbrock pushed his plate away, very slowly, with obvious regret. Horst was now in the wrong for forcing his aged father to let his fried eggs get cold. When Papenbrock rose to his feet, he started yelling. Cresspahl had kept his head down, like everyone else at the table, and had almost admired the old man. He roared effortlessly, one imprecation after another occurring to him for people who don't respect the dignity of a religious ceremony, who don't do their work, who don't understand anything except idiotic schoolboy pranks (– Idiotic schoolboy pranks? said Horst, pale, composed, outraged, feeling that the symbols of the new state were under attack. – Yes! Papenbrock roared: Holding hands with shoemaker's daughters!), all in his fast Plattdeutsch laced with obscenities, so that Horst didn't even have the courage to mention in Elisabeth Lieplow's defense that despite being from Kröpelin, the cobbler city, she was certainly not a shoemaker's daughter, she was a tax collector's. When he left the room, the bang of the door echoed behind him. When he came back, dressed in a black Sunday suit, Papenbrock sent him out to feed the horses, and this time Horst showed no rebellion or threat even in his face, and it's harder to stomp off loudly in dress shoes. Now, next to the old man in the pew, admittedly still under observation, he signaled his independence with a bored demeanor, because he thought he had weathered Papenbrock's bad mood. He continued to think that through lunch, although he did notice that while the dish with the roast goose was regularly passed to his place, the white wine was not. In fact, Papenbrock was acting peaceable, almost hedonistic. He gave three speeches: one for Lisbeth, one for Hilde, one for the child sleeping off the hardship of the outing at a safe distance from him. Her second middle name, Albertine, was more than he could have hoped for, he apparently said (according to Mrs. Brüshaver). Then he posed the question: Does one have to forgive one's children for everything? Not even Louise Papenbrock wanted to answer that, but she saw something coming. She hunched forward a little, folded her hands in her lap, to be ready to pray if necessary. Papenbrock, meanwhile, insisted on an answer. Eventually, he even turned to Brüshaver point-blank, and the new pastor, caught by surprise with a half-raised glass in his hand, again acted as though he knew all about this family's internal disputes. He gestured at drinking a toast, nodded slightly, but in such a way that his assent gave Papenbrock the springboard he'd been looking for. Papenbrock reminded his family of Reformation Day 1931, when everyone had accused him of "hard-heartedness" just because he had not wanted to bring his son back from "Rio de Janeiro." Now Brüshaver was looking down into his glass, and Semig would rather have not been in the room. – Lisbeth has a child, Hilde's about to have one: Papenbrock said, not without taking a certain satisfaction in his logical line of argument. – *Youre gonna go get im*: he said, not even looking in Horst's direction. Then he sat down, listening to none of his youngest offspring's objections. On the contrary, he started a conversation with Semig about the effects of the spring rain on clayey soil, about whether Meyer's estate wouldn't have to be re-plowed. He brushed off what was coming from Horst's end of the table like an annoying insect.

Down at that end Horst had a lot to say. He didn't know Brazilian. He was then informed that it's actually called Portuguese and can be learned. His work on the estate and in the warehouse would have to be left undone. That was a bad move. Now he got another talking-to, never mind the presence of guests for the christening. He'd had other people doing his work for three months now, and any single one of them would probably do it better than he would, not with an eye to an inheritance but to a well-earned wage. It wouldn't be easy finding the long-lost eldest. Well then he'd better look hard. It could take a year. If it took two, Papenbrock would survive. It would cost a mint. That's what Papenbrock had money for. Horst couldn't get out of it. His sisters gave him no support, partly to pay him back for numerous insults and partly because they were taken in by Papenbrock's generosity. They were touched, too, and found Horst's attempts to refuse the job disgraceful. Louise cried because tears seemed called for. Cresspahl stared across the table until Semig finally admitted with a glance that he had smiled into his wineglass. Cresspahl was, almost unwillingly, on Papenbrock's side. The old man had no faith in the new government and no desire to let Horst's SA activities get him involved if the regime collapsed. He may even have been trying to protect Horst by sending him halfway around the world. It was amusing to watch Horst, who seemed to think the choice was between staying and going; in fact, he was being offered the choice between the Nazis and his inheritance, and if he decided in favor of bourgeois property then he would probably get only half of it, long-lost Robert Papenbrock getting the other half, and Horst helping him get it, in Portuguese. And Horst didn't dare try to seriously bring up the SA, in which he would miss out on rank and fame while away. It was amusing enough, but sometimes the people around this table seemed alien to Cresspahl. He didn't feel like he belonged there, and in fact his bag was standing packed by the front door and he was once again waiting for the connecting train to the line 2 express to Hamburg. But this time he was traveling alone, and for the last time.

Well youve gotten your way, Lisbeth.
Well youll get yours for the rest of your life, Hinrich.

The business owners along Fifth Avenue have organized a parade on Fifth Avenue to protest against parades on Fifth Avenue. They lose a half a million dollars per parade and want them moved to a street west of Central Park, either West End Avenue or Riverside Drive. We'd have an earful to give them about that.

November 20, 1967 Monday

In a move designed to protect the dollar in the wake of Britain's devaluation of the pound, the Federal Reserve System announced a new discount rate of 4.5 percent, an increase of 0.5 percent. Once again, *The New York Times* does not want any of her readers to neglect the news simply because he or she does not understand it, so she explains, once again: The discount rate is the amount commercial banks pay to borrow money from the Federal Reserve System. She repeats the lesson on her contents page. We've taken courses in political economics at Columbia University for this! The Spanish government, too, has devalued its currency. Work at the bank this week will be even heavier than last week.

Major General William R. Peers, the commander of the Fourth Infantry Division in Vietnam, comments on the fighting near Dakto in the Central Highlands: "There's no use fighting him (the Vietcong) man to man: You make a contact and let him have it with air and artillery."

It started yesterday morning. Marie was talking on the phone in the living room. She said little in response to the person on the other end of the line; it sounded like "Yes" every time. Her obedient tone of voice was incredible. Then she was inaudible, but so was the click of hanging up. When I looked in she was standing with her back to the phone and holding the receiver straight out in front of her. She let out a deep breath when we took it from her. It was emitting the dial tone. She kept her eyes lowered, she kneaded her knuckles, she was trying out what she would say. – It's Karsch: she said.

But then it hadn't actually been Karsch. A stranger had asked for him. He wasn't here. The stranger knew that. He not only knew where Karsch was, he promised that Karsch would be staying there unless $2,000 turned up to replace him. And fast. He had called Marie "Sister," just like she imagines the Mafia doing.

The things children come up with. The stories children tell.

Marie didn't defend her story. She went straight to the green desk the Danish woman had left us, reached into the top drawer, between the passports, and took out the travel money, spreading it out on the table and starting to sort it:

S.fr. 187.00
£ 9/11/-
DM 15.00
Lire 40,000

There was nothing missing from the story in the retelling. The stranger wanted the money in cash, in small bills, by tonight. At one point he'd let her hear Karsch's voice over the phone: it sounded a bit unclear, like a tape recording, so Marie had asked him what he'd ordered eight days ago in the UN restaurant, and he'd told her exactly, down to the Idaho potatoes. – It's really me: he'd said, and further instructions would be coming late this afternoon. The stranger had described himself with the word "we." As though Karsch was sitting tied to a chair, blindfolded, under the watchful eyes of experienced gunmen. The things children are willing to believe.

Marie had answered every objection patiently but with a preoccupied look on her face as she systematically went through the whole apartment.

It seemed like she was trying to make up with her own actions for the time her mother was wasting. She took the housekeeping money from the tea canister in the kitchen cupboard and laid it out next to the foreign money. Then she brought out the box with her own savings. In the end there was about $450 on the table, foreign currency included. And where are you supposed to exchange foreign money on a Sunday in New York!

– Kennedy Airport: Marie said. Her face had gotten very small. She was extremely worried; at least she had no doubts about her story. It was past the point of laughing, she wouldn't even have been offended anymore, at best she would have thought it idiotic. We don't know anyone who can lend us $1,550 on a Sunday with no questions asked.

– D. E.: Marie said. But D. E. had left the country this morning. She'd forgotten. Now she was about to cry. Then she raised her head. Her face was resolute once again. Her gray-green eyes were very large between her ruffled lashes. The lashes were only a little damp. She didn't care if we believed her, she cared that we hurry. Which people where have how much money in the house on a Sunday.

Dmitri Weiszand. 110th St., but $30 to $40 at most.
Amanda Williams, also only half an hour away, $90. Her paycheck had come only four days ago.
Mrs. Ferwalter, three blocks from here. $9.00.
Mr. & Mrs. Faure. $12.00.
Mrs. Erichson. Three hours away, across the Hudson. $700. Maybe.

– Can you give us a lot of money, D. E.?: Marie said into the phone, not shy at all, and naming a figure of $2,000 straight off. For D. E. had told us the wrong departure time again, ostensibly so that no one would be able to pester him with an airport goodbye, but we're not so sure about that. D. E. restored Marie's spirits, almost. She answered him in a brisk, mischievous tone; with D. E.'s help she could see a possible way out of the woods. I hadn't been able to give her that. She said "Yes" three times, then the call was over. She brought me my coat, pushed me out the door. Everyone else believed it.

But D. E. didn't make it seem any more real. Nor did the racing subway trains, empty on a Sunday. Even someone like D. E. can't get a personal check cashed on Sunday. A family was sitting on the West Side express, pressed close together, father mother son and little girl, all brushed and spruced up, the girl with tight braids braided for her half day at the movies on Forty-Second Street, the most affordable outing for the unemployed, for the Negroes. At least they could believe where they were going. The cavern under Times Square was empty and as quiet as a small-town market square. As we ran for the shuttle, a group of schoolgirls helped me by taking half the looks of amazement that had been aimed at me upon themselves. Then it wasn't amazing at all, the doors banged shut on this train too and it was off. In the Grand Central concourse, all the homeless people and policemen seemed to wake right up. For a moment I saw myself from the height of the blue dome, a tiny figure running from the General Electric corner, across a piazza, veering around the axis point of the information booth, until the escalators whisked the figure up into the Pan American Building. There were British people with golf bags in the offices of New York Airways, startled shabby old men who made way for us. The elevator shot up as though it meant to break through the sixtieth floor into the sky. On the flat roof above the other rooftops, the sea wind battled the gusts being thrown off in all directions by the helicopter blades. Even when eye to eye with the top of the Chrysler Building, a thousand feet up from the street, no simile occurs to us for the half-rounded, overlapping surfaces; how could we ever have been reminded, from down below, of slices of an onion? Southern Brooklyn was buried under identical square flat roofs, each surrounded by leafless hedgerows. To the south, the Atlantic crocheted wispy fringes onto the shore, arms behind levees, eyes separated by seawalls behind peninsulas, curved marks like writing in the marshlands. A streak of sunlight flitted across the cemeteries, flipping the pages of the gravestones like a sped-up top-secret film. After nine minutes, Kennedy International Airport compliantly composed itself under the copter. Our only fear was for Marie. If Karsch wants to play games with Mafia people, why does he have to give them our phone number!

Our meeting was set for here at the southwesternmost corner of the Pan Am Terminal. Who'd ever believe it. The fourth helicopter to come bouncing in through the stubborn wind was from Newark Airport. With his blue cloth hat perched all the way up on the top of his head, like a joke,

D. E. looked as if in disguise. But his expression was grim; he looked around downright ferociously. It was the first time we'd ever seen him anxious, confused, worried.

– Thanks for the great weather too: D. E. said.

Am I doing this for you, Gesine?
No, and thank you for asking, D. E.
I just wanted to say I'd be happy to.
I'd believe that more if you didn't say it out loud, D. E.

The whole time in the bus to the SAS Terminal, he told us about his obstacles getting here, and not in his usual quick jokey way. He spoke slowly, with bad-tempered pauses, as if thinking in a writing rhythm. The other passengers might easily have taken it for a goodbye conversation between a bored married couple. So: On the way to the airport he'd stopped by Oscar's, to get something he'd forgotten. (Oscar ran the "booth" at the junction and has often illegally sold D. E. alcohol on Sundays, and will likewise have lent him cash.) D. E. had also filled up his tank "where we always get gas." (That's another one of his friends, who would cash a personal checks. In other words, unmarked bills, above suspicion.) He had, unfortunately, parked his car rather carelessly at Newark Airport and really needed someone to go get it. On the sidewalk outside SAS check-in, D. E. handed us an airmail envelope to mail and a key ring with car keys. He wouldn't leave without giving us a hug, which he did in the Russian way, like a quotation, but he took more time with it than a quotation needs: both arms around my shoulders, one cheek, the other, the first again. – Take care of the kid! D. E. said grumpily before heading off joylessly to Copenhagen, a powerful man laid low with his dislike of traveling. He always says Copenhagen; he says Reykjavík too; it's probably more like Baffin Island, if not Greenland. Come back soon, D. E. Have a good trip, D. E. No one answered at SIX-AUKS, Manhattan. Marie picked up only after the fifth ring. She was speaking easily again, impetuous and excited, like a child. – I'll be waiting for you at New York Central Railway, third window from the left: she said and hung up before I could give the answer she didn't want to hear. She wants to come too; we'll have to get that idea out of her head. The helicopter back to Manhattan had few passengers. Concealed by the seat backs, I opened the flap of the airmail envelope. It was a wad of bills, all fifties or lower, most of them so dirty they might have been used to wipe the floor. It was not $2,000, it was $2,400. That's D. E., too much of a good thing every time.

– We'll mail it to ourselves: Marie said in the Grand Central concourse, a jittery kid who kept looking over Gesine's shoulder, looking sideways for anyone watching, and wishing she had eyes in the back of her head. – An airmail envelope from New York 10017 to New York 10025? I said. But Marie wouldn't let herself be distracted. She said: – If I don't tell you the address then your Karsch is in the soup, as D. E. so rightly says.

– You're trying to blackmail me.
– I want to come with you.
– Be brave!
– I can't be brave sitting home alone waiting. With you I'd be a little braver. I promise.
– All right, promise.

It hadn't cost much at all: two subway rides, $15.00 for the flight to Jamaica Bay, now $3.00 for the taxi to the helicopter terminal on the West Side, $5.00 for the shuttle bus to Newark Airport. In Newark we sent the extra money home by telegram. D. E.'s Bentley took some getting used to. The first address was a coffee shop in a service center on Route 1, just past Elizabeth, NJ. There really was a slip of paper waiting for us in the phone book. From that point on, it was a compilation reel from the last third of every single kidnapping movie: they sent us back to Newark, wanted to see us in Passaic, needed us to go to East Orange, made us park in front of Newark Airport for half an hour. After a while they decided to phone us at the various meeting points they'd ordered us to. These meeting points were dingier and dirtier each time, more like in the movies. Even Marie started getting a little bored. The men apologized: they hadn't believed their eyes when they saw the Bentley driving up. They still didn't know our name. But tomorrow they'd know whose car it was. This went on until early evening. Meanwhile, Marie asked about a christening in Jerichow thirty-four years ago, and the special features of the Portuguese language, and even seemed to be listening to the answers. In Roselle Park we had to go into a bar where female patrons stood out. The barman not only wiped down a table for us but the chairs, too. Disbelieving, confused looks kept coming at us from the bar, where men were hanging fat, stubborn rear ends off their barstools, which they didn't like having a woman and child look at. Then someone stood up and stalked over to the telephone, stiff as if from riding, then someone stood up listing a little and stared at us, maybe it was him we were there to meet, it wasn't clear. When the barman whispered a new address to us and we left the watering hole, everyone seemed extremely relieved. In Newark's riot neighborhood a man climbed into the back of the car. At first he couldn't believe he'd been dealing with Marie. Then he called her a "fast kid." How would you say that in German? I wish he weren't right. It was dark enough that we couldn't see him clearly. He didn't speak slang, didn't even speak ungrammatically. If the voice were on tape, we would have been able to tell that the speaker had been raised by Italian parents; in the flesh, aimed at the back of our necks, the voice was nondescript, unremarkable, like any other from the neighborhood. The man had been sent by Mr. Karsh. It was a real transaction. No, Mr. Karsh hadn't been kidnapped, not at all. He had gone to where he was now of his own free will, on his own two feet. He hadn't even been specifically invited, and had since had his impolite, practically improper behavior pointed out to him. Mr. Karsh had asked permission to make up for the discourteous impression he'd made. A figure had been named. Mr. Karsh had accepted the price. It was a one-time transaction, which couldn't be carried out without the consent of all parties.

– Do you have any problems with that, lady?
– None at all: Gesine said.
– How about you, young lady?
– Of course not: Marie said. – But I wish you'd hurry up. Tonight's a school night.

When the man in the backseat had counted out the bills, he stuffed them into the envelope, tucked the flap in again, and said: Not enough.

– What do you mean not enough! Marie said. She acted outraged. Earlier, she'd had her doubts about whether the situation would all work out. To her $2,000 seemed too low a price for a living person, and she's right, such piddling sums are unusual in this line of work. Now all she showed was anger at someone not sticking to an agreement.

– We had expenses: the guy said. Phone calls, gas . . .

It added up to another $13.00. Then he gave us a key and a location. The place was a half-burned-out row of stores in Newark. The fires during the riot had eaten away the plastic blinds, the store signs, the neon tubes and surfaces with the names of the stores, and had blackened the facades. The door was to a barbershop between a coin-operated laundromat and a smashed-in liquor store. The key fit. The smell of ashes and charred wood had revived under the dampness of the evening. Inside there was nothing recognizable. We were walking on shards of glass. When Marie ran back outside the glass crackled as though someone else was there. She relies completely on D. E.: if she needs a flashlight, he'll have one for her. When the light went on in his car, its outline seemed to give a comfortable stretch and look bigger. The only functioning car on the whole desolate street, it looked undefended, undefendable. Marie came back with, yes, D. E.'s flashlight. She found the door to a back room. Here the windows weren't broken yet, and the air was stuffy from heat turned up too high. Here, in one of the two barber chairs, someone was lying tied with straps around his chest, waist, and legs. They had leaned the chair back as far as it would go and raised the footrest. It may not have been too unbearable for some-one used to sleeping on his back, if not for a whole day at a time. It was one of those situations where for a moment I can't move. I want to keep moving, but that makes no difference. The person in the room wasn't moving, and our entrance hadn't been especially quiet. Marie, in her rage, was not at all careful when she tore the blindfold from his eyes. That woke Karsch up.

He was ridiculously shamefaced during the whole drive back to Newark Airport and the Manhattan bus terminal. When we parted, he tried to apologize. We couldn't accept that. He tried to thank us. Marie couldn't accept that.

– I didn't do it for you! Marie said.

Now it's almost eleven the next morning, and now it's over. Now the Newark police are looking for D. E.'s car, which Mrs. Erichson reported last night as having been stolen from Newark Airport. The airport is not where the police will start looking.

Now comes Karsch's call from London. Karsch is calling from a hotel on Gloucester Road, near the train station through which the line to Richmond upon Thames runs. Not only Karsch would be safe there.

Now the chauffeur from the Italian delegation comes and talks with Amanda to arrange a personal meeting with Mrs. Cresspahl. Again he gives no indication of being accustomed to entering entirely different sorts of buildings. He shows no sign of recognition. His gestures are so formal that he gets in his own way. He holds his cap under his arm in the vicinity of his heart, which makes it hard for his other hand to pull the impressive-looking envelope out of his left pocket. Amanda, outside, can follow the scene perfectly from her sideways-facing typewriter desk. Her eyes blink and twinkle with amusement. The envelope contains a personal check from Dr. Pompa for $2,000 and not a penny more. Gentlemen pay their debts.

Now the clock in the Commerce Department in Washington, which records a new citizen of the United States of America every 14.5 seconds, advances a step. Now it's up to two hundred million.

November 21, 1967   Tuesday

The New York Times praises the reaction of the nation's financial markets to Britain's currency crisis, speaking of a remarkably cool and orderly performance. Chicago's largest bank has raised its minimum rate by 0.5 percent, to 6 percent.

It wasn't eleven o'clock yesterday after all when the clock in Washington counted the 200 millionth US citizen. Officials slowed the count by three minutes to make sure that the president would be on hand at the right moment. In any case, the number was already too low. Since 1960 at least 5.7 percent of the population have been missed, among Negroes probably closer to 9.5 percent. To be on the safe side, *The New York Times* also alludes to the 790 million mainland Chinese.

So, it was Potsdam Day, March 21, 1933, a Tuesday, when a madman named Hitler humbly bowed and accepted the German Reich from an old field marshal, and when Cresspahl returned to Richmond in South London. What a fool. Hopefully he realized right away what he was leaving behind.

– People aren't supposed to insult their own father: Marie says.

– You've seen Richmond.

– I didn't think it was all that: Marie says.

We've seen it. It was a London November. What else do we remember? We arrived from Geneva, and Marie let her pleasure in being back among English speakers distract her so much that at Heathrow she tried to board the bus to the Air Terminal from the right-hand side. It was then explained to her. In the city, we searched Victoria station for the spot where Lisbeth Cresspahl dealt with an English baggage handler for the last time, in January 1933. D. E. offered to ask the station manager for information and was already on his way when we called him back. I didn't need to know it that precisely. We had lunch on the first (the second) floor of the station, and again D. E. tried to help, by dragging Marie into a discussion of the British coinage system. I had all the peace and quiet I needed to look for my mother in the dining room. I didn't find her.

What else do we remember? Marie compared the London Underground to the subway system she thinks of as hers. She thought these escalators went down too far, and she felt claustrophobic on the trains because the tunnel arches are so close to the roof of the train car. The next evening, D. E. flew in from his radar conference in Brussels and moved us into one of his hotels, an American one. There we saw Herr Anselm Kristlein face-to-face for the first time. We had long thought that surely the British give poor foreigners a place for the night only when the queen is out of the city; otherwise how could she enjoy a peaceful night's sleep! But the queen was in the city.

We rode the District line to Richmond, first through an open stone cutting alongside brownish dusty cables that looked as if they'd been laid out in a calmer time, sixty years ago, and not patched up of necessity after a German bombing. Then the light from above ground came into the train, etched black and brown in the colors of an English November. The sky-scrapers had to be thought away; my parents hadn't seen those. The posters rode stiffly next to the changing pictures in the windows: Barclays and Midland banks carrying on a stylized war against each other with their just barely ethical promises. Were those barges on the Thames? Fog. I could have had the order of the stations memorized: Ravenscourt Park, Stamford

Brook, Turnham Green, Gunnersbury, Kew Gardens, Richmond, and back to Upminster. Instead I had to buy a street map in Richmond; I didn't even know whether Cresspahl had turned left or right from the station. The woman in her kiosk called me "Dearie." Cresspahl had turned left, crossed the railroad bridge to the Quadrant, then turned onto Sheen Road, possibly taking a shortcut through Waterloo Place, past the frugal old stone cottages where he could have awaited his death. Lisbeth Cresspahl could have waited in one of the little houses on Sheen Road, all identically two-story with the same double bay window requiring a roof of its own; if worst came to worst we might have found her in William Hickey's old age home, just before Manor Road branches off to the left and to where her husband had once had his workshop. Cresspahl never grew older than seventy-four, we know that, but she could have survived him here, and one of these red columns with the handleless pot lid is where she might even now have been mailing letters to New York: Dear Daughter.

The English would've stuck us behind barbed wire before we knew it, dear daughter.
Only for seven years.
When they came to get Herr Mayer a second time, to send him to the internment camp, he excused himself for a moment and went into the next room and
I don't want to hear that.
Because that's what I did?
Would you have done it in Richmond, too, over a few years in an internment camp?
I didn't live long enough to find out, daughter. I can't know that, and I can't promise that.

We were traveling not alone but with D. E., and at first he turned the expedition into a thorough sightseeing tour of Richmond, showing us around the Green, to Maids of Honour Row, the Old Palace, Ham House, all elegant sites for the nobility and for culture. My parents would have avoided such places. So then he stuck to the middle-class parts of the city. He didn't ask his questions out loud, he only inspected me sidelong as though by now I knew all about the restaurant in the Tower House by the

bridge, so weather-beaten that it looked as if it were unsuitable for customers even thirty-five years ago, let alone for customers like my mother. On
the river path he took Marie and walked up ahead, hand in hand, occupied
with each other; he turned half around as if only to make sure I was still
with them. It's possible she walked here, in the winter of 1932, carefully
shepherding her heavy belly through the excited children watching a diver
at work. The river path was totally empty, the shrubbery bare. There was
still a Gosling's department store, on the corner of King Street. The Wright
Bros. shop had the same phone number as back then: RIchmond-3601. I
would have preferred to keep walking past Short's Greyhound Restaurant,
but the address, 24 George Street, had been recommended to D. E. All the
postcards of Richmond show summer conditions: clouds of lilacs on the
steamer landing, dollops of foliage bursting forth from the grand houses
on the water side of Hill Street, old people in beach chairs on the sunny
lawns beside a greenish Thames, Sundayish bustling around the Castle
Restaurant building, as colorful as a circus on the other side, but in reality
standing bare in the wind, huddled shivering under its threadbare colors.
I didn't see any of that. What Marie remembers best from Richmond is a
large barnlike dollhouse in a store on the corner of Paradise Street and
Church Walk, and it wasn't easy to stop D. E. from buying it and sending
it to America, for many pounds, $220. Wherever we went, the locals took
us for tourists from the US of A. Two elderly women, retirees, were sitting
by the window of a Chinese restaurant on Sheen Road and bantering easily with the owner, who was carrying a two-year-old boy on his hip. She
might have tried Chinese food in her old age, too. She might have sat by
the window like that, eventually with friends in Richmond after all, whil-
ing away the day. She would have learned to pronounce *tea* as "tiyee." The
Parish Church might have worked out, in the end. I would have had the
same red knees from the constant river wind as all the other girls walking
to school in the city, in knee socks even in winter. I would have been a
different person, except for my name. I wouldn't be German; I would talk
about Germans in the plural, as foreign, distanced. I would bear the guilt
of a different nation.

At first it was hard to find. Reggie Pascal's workshop couldn't have been
on Manor Road. Single-family houses dawdled behind neatly separated
front lawns all the way to the rail line, barely startled by the cars driving

past. Chicken-wire gates with large red circles in the middle, going up and snapping down like a trap, barricaded the street from the rails. A narrow footbridge had been put up over the rails, and from there you could see it. Reggie Pascal's workshop could have been in the triangle of land formed by the District line, the Southern Railway, and Manor Road, across from the gasworks. Maybe everything from before has been torn down. When Cresspahl gave up the business they tore down all the old buildings and yards where the Baltic Timber Company now sells hard and soft woods, by the yard too, inquiries welcome. If I'd grown up here it would have been in the odors of wood and gas, not mixed together, each in its place. At fifteen I would still have been jealous of the people who could live in the tiny "Railway Cottage" on the other side of the tracks. This would have been one of my most tenacious memories: standing on the footbridge over the Southern Railway, above the rattling trains, spitting affectionately onto the roofs of the train cars. I would come back and I would have to look every time to make out the gasworks boiler that had seemed so enormous to the child. They've painted it in the meantime. I would come back to Sheen Cemetery, very grassy in the northern part. There would have been places there among the flickering white of the skimpily carved crosses and figures. If they had died here, then here is where I could have visited my parents. If they had lived here, we would have spent more time together alive.

– I didn't think Richmond was all that: Marie says.

November 22, 1967 Wednesday

The American commander in chief in Vietnam, General William C. Westmoreland, predicted a steady decline in the strength of Vietcong guerilla forces but did not want to forecast a military victory "in the classic sense"; in the battle for Hill 875 near Dakto, he has lost 239 men since early November, the North Vietnamese 1,181 (estimated). And Mr. George Stroup of Tulsa, Oklahoma, has disowned his son for defying the draft; he would prefer that this young man no longer go by the name that his father bore as a fighter pilot in World War II.

Hippies have a house in east Denver and call it "Provo," meaning to suggest that they are provoking the Establishment. There, Carol Metherd, twenty-four, cut the heart of her two-year-old son, William, out of his body and inserted into the cavity a soft-drink bottle with a broken neck. She was said to be under the influence of drugs; she wouldn't talk but only stared at the wall.

A trip with D. E. runs smoothly, like clockwork, including the one to England and Ireland and back, in a year before this one. Give him your plane tickets and he'll recalculate the fares, and it has been known to happen that an airline had to cough up $2.00 in reimbursement. Let Marie mention something about an evening in "the Rainbow" on the sixty-fifth floor in New York, and the next day will find her high above London having lunch in the restaurant in the Post Office Tower without having suspected a thing even at the foot of the building. The child likes to be surprised. While Marie was still busy with her friends in South London, the breakfast conversation turned to Cresspahl's time in the Netherlands, and three hours later we were walking down Amsterdam's Brouwersgracht; not once had we felt rushed; and he paid not with his credit card but by changing tickets that could be changed only with true generosity. Let slip something about a hotel near St. Stephen's Green, neither whose name nor whose address you can remember, and there we all were in Dublin the next morning with the porter greeting him by name. He gives tips, not too extravagant. And that is how we traveled through Ireland, and the suitcases were always on the platform, the trains about to depart, the taxis waiting at the door. D. E.'s way of doing things is not even expensive. He doesn't rent a car to take us from Cork to Cobh, he avails himself of the little railroad plodding along the River Lee to the international port—the thing is, he knows it exists and its schedule too. (A foreigner disappeared while we were there, and *The New York Times* reporter described not only the search efforts carried out under the supervision of Detective Thomas Shean but the Lee, "which provides a scene of romantic beauty.") In Limerick, we had our third morning free, and D. E. took us to a place called Kilkee, built around a green bay harbor on the Atlantic, and still we got to Shannon Airport in time for his two bottles of wine over lunch and a conversation with a customs official about the prospects of a Third World War (the man would bet on it). Then we took off, and the plane was in fact a DC-8, and there were only five passengers on board besides us, so a crash would have hardly been worth it, and nine hours later we were back home. Marie likes his style of taking care of others. Someone else, even if tricks like this fulfilled their unspoken wishes, would rather be permitted to watch how it's done.

At the main post office in Richmond I asked for a form to send a telegram abroad and sat down at one of the tables facing George Street and then didn't know what to write or who I could send it to. D. E. simply observes such occurrences. It's a single glance, barely perceptible, since he deflects it at once into a careless, pensive attitude. And yet he'll conceal that he's troubled. In such moments, he sees in me not the person he wants to live with but someone at risk of going insane. And wants to live with me anyway.

> *Write it down, Gesine.*
> *Mijnheer Hendrik Cresspahl, Amsterdam, 1925?*
> *Write it.*
> *That'd be evidence against me, D. E.*
> *I'll protect you against such evidence.*

It is not his will he's asserting; it's my expressed request. We do live together, in different places. This too he has turned into an arrangement, where his need for perfect solutions overrides my mistrust of settled finality: what was planned as loose has become fixed, and moreover he is ever ready and able to show me that actually it hasn't become fixed. He does make suggestions, though. One was the excursion to Kilkee, that horseshoe of mostly one-story buildings with rustic facades ringing a patch of captured ocean, with one or two seasonal hotels, a low-lying village with perpetual wind for a neighbor, Europe at its back, the Atlantic before it clear across to the coast of America. At the western end of the horseshoe, on Marine Parade, there was a house standing empty behind its proper middle-class front stairs, walls neatly built around five rooms, protected by the Duggerna Rocks from the full force of the storms. For D. E. it was possible. He could afford to buy it and in less than a year he would turn it into a system of machines serving the occupants' every need; the local tradesmen, if no one else, would have had nice things to say about us moving there. It would have been forty-five minutes to Shannon Airport, where I would wait once every eight weeks, a wife to whom her husband comes home from work. Marie would have gotten used to a school in Limerick. It's a quiet place in the fall, in winter, in spring—not even fifteen hundred people live there. A path over the cliff leads from the New Found Out bathing area, a grassy spot from which you can jump almost fifty feet down into the ocean, past the bay, where the *Intrinsic* was wrecked in January 1836, to Look Out Hill, two hundred feet above sea level. There the seasons would once again teach me the changing colors of water. The winter nights would be very dark and clear. I would come home chilled to the bone from nighttime walks, as I did to Cresspahl's house. The cities would be very far away; the world, almost. That's what D. E. thinks: that I need a house of my own. He doesn't speak the question out loud; we'd simply taken one last side trip before flying home. He undoubtedly wrote down the names of the real estate agents in County Clare, Ireland, and the phone numbers at which they can be reached; maybe he's still waiting.

Similarly (I need only say that it's what I want) he would find us an eight-room apartment on Riverside Drive, facing the Hudson too, on the top floor in fact, and buy it, with whatever necessities Mrs. Erichson is accustomed to. He is free with his money, which is after all sold work—free in a way that is not at all hurtful, although also not unobjectionable. When Marie, after the assassination of President Kennedy, couldn't find her bearings again in everyday life, he whisked her away from a lunch onto a commuter flight to Washington and came back with a placated child, who now had at least seen the grave. In one of the antiquarian bookseller catalogs that the GDR mails him, I saw a picture of a map that showed Jerichow as a church tower and shipping insignia, and asked for it; I'd meant the black-and-white page of the catalog, but D. E. later hung the expensive colorful and medieval original on our wall. These aren't gifts. He gives what he gives on condition that it be used and consumed with him, with him there.

He wants "to live with us." We are not even from the same place anymore. His past, the people, the country, Schusting Brand the cobbler, Wendisch Burg—he in no way regards them as real. He's converted his memory into knowledge. His life with other people in Mecklenburg, only fourteen years ago after all, has been tucked away as though into an archive, where he continues the biographies of people and cities down to the present, or else closes the file in case of death. Yes, everything's still there, and he can call it up at will, only it's not alive. He no longer lives with it. He'd been in the States only a few years before he started using four dots to indicate ratios in his lectures instead of the German two, a diagonal line for division instead of a horizontal one, as though that was what he'd been taught to do in Wendisch Burg; when he wrote on the blackboard his letters came out the way they do here, fluent, anonymous characters. He is not a good teacher. His lectures fooled the students with their chatty tone; whoever tried to write down what he said instead of thinking it through was lost. D. E. had no desire to commit to anything beyond communicating that this was the known extent of physics knowledge, with the unspoken addendum: That's the best we can do for now. He endured his students' questions, their slowness, with a pleasant look on his face, he acted happy to help, but the delay pained him. Incidentally, he had forgotten that there was a guest sitting among the students during the lecture; he had to think his way back to me, even though he'd recognized me. He was respected at the college, and was friends with two or three especially gifted students, who thought they could pick his brain in strictest privacy in the cafeteria. In his field he is most at ease among his peers. His peers not only share his technical know-how and way of thinking—*exempli gratia*, about whether D. E.'s listening stations in Alaska and Greenland might be designed for other than defensive purposes—they also accept that the weapons systems of the USA are in a different category from those of the USSR, and from that point on his peers are no longer susceptible to any lines of moral questioning. An occasion involving morality was one of the few times D. E. almost flew off the handle. He didn't quite shout, but his way of speaking turned nasty, arrogant, meant to express contempt. In his view, morality is the business of those who hold power, who are always blathering on about it, and nothing for their subordinates to concern themselves with: their concern is survival. There are people who visibly work for Defense, even if only in the bakeries on army bases—and everyone else is working for Defense, too; the distance between the groups is purely subjective, objectively insignificant. His peers are nonetheless capable of using the case of Klaus Fuchs, the atomic spy, to discuss not the phenomenon of loyalty but the psychological knots of the traitor. In addition, they rely on the beautiful certainty that none of them will ever be treated as a war criminal, they all will be handled as specialists: that makes a person more comfortable expressing himself. At the same time: all D. E.'s friends in his field are interested in what the deal is with Socialism. For them it is a theoretical exercise, playing a game with an unavailable alternative; in them the roots of it are not biographical. There must be some marriages among them that were contracted at an age when young scientists join a political party; surely D. E. has analyzed the protests he arranged on behalf of Ingrid Babendererde not only in terms of their consequences but also in terms of the feelings they produced; fundamentally, though, these people want to be presented with a total revolution in the abstract, humanely carried out and humanistic in its effects. This comes out rationally as a longing for a Third Way; it is also no less sentimental than something three of these friends did concerning the Second Way currently on offer: for a year, they divided up among themselves the memoirs written by survivors of Stalin's gulags, on a quest to find out whether the Soviet secret police had killed the actress Carola Neher themselves or let Hitler's secret police take care of it. They wanted to clarify for themselves a bit more precisely how they felt about certain claims and a certain silence on the part of the poet Bertolt Brecht. The Carola Neher Club. One of them was Danish. The other lives in England, Prof. Dr. Dr. Harry Wittenberg, from a Jewish family that fled Nazi Germany in 1934; he is named in D. E.'s will. It's an attitude that has long since given up on individual protest and thus on any fundamental change in social conditions; it can live very nicely off its proofs and is actually quite a lot like what used to be called "petit bourgeois" thinking, which D. E. jokingly accuses me of.

He does it jokingly. He doesn't presume to know me. When I do something he thinks of as particular to me, he smiles in recognition, but openly, not taking observations and secretly tucking them away for later use. If he does have a mental picture of me, it is of little more than my needs (as he understands them). He reveals a lot—all of it acceptable, much of it delightful. He doesn't discuss Marie's father with her, or even with me, but he knows everything about Jakob's life that you can learn from letters to and from friends in Mecklenburg. He spends $70.00 a month on alcohol, damn right, and if you don't like it you can lump it, and when he drinks alone he punishes himself by serving his Beaujolais chilled. He too has his quirks and prejudices that he offers up as careful observations or unquestionable facts: for example, he calls the DC-8 the most efficient plane in the world, when all he knows about flying is what you need to get a license to fly a single-engine propeller plane. He plays the game you're supposed to play here, of showing off your money: he shows off a house, a Bentley, but he's paying for the house in installments and the car is used and he does his flying in borrowed planes. He likes keeping his real assets secret from his neighbors. His behavior is steady and consistent; he doesn't fly into rages. He has arrogated no habitual rights from his visits to us; he comes as a guest, every time. He's not jealous: it's only what goes on in my thoughts that he wants to be the only one, or at least the first, to know. There are many things he is the only one to know. What else does he want? Can't he rest on the laurels of his famous affairs, and conveniently acquire a family that already has a child, one who already understands him too? He says: No. Am I supposed to do at my leisure, financed by him, what he can't do: live for one person alone? He would say: If it were up to me. He would even spare me the endless acting of "social life." He doesn't even want children from me. If I ended up in a cage with him, at least it would be a cage made to my measure and furnished according to my requirements, down to whatever discretionary bank accounts and credit cards I wanted. The only thing is, why does he need someone in his life?

Marie could do it. She could stand to live with him in one apartment, in one house. On the Thames promenade in Richmond they were walking on ahead of me like they always do, side by side, without a care in the world. She was not only proud of the black coat with the fur collar that he'd bought for her on Regent Street, she was happy to be seen in the company of this elegant gentleman. They were laughing as they talked, and even the tilt of Marie's head toward him showed how much she appreciated their banter. Marie walked with her hands clasped behind her back, because that was how he was walking.

That I believe. The other thing I don't believe.

Today D. E. called from the north, on a suspiciously high-bandwidth line that brought his voice right into the room as though he were standing there. He's in another time zone, and still he caught the exact quarter hour during which our household has been put to bed but Marie not yet. He took his time. He frittered away the minutes with questions about Karsch, about the weather, and the surveillance agency will scarcely have noticed that by the end of the conversation we'd gotten a good scolding. It was a mistake to report the theft of his car to the Newark police, because the license plates were false, obviously, he'd had them changed "where we always get gas." – Happy Thanksgiving: D. E. says in a friendly voice, while he's scheduled a holiday trip for us to a gas station across the Hudson. Marie, who ends the conversation, comes in to inform me that in radio lingo *Amen* is just as correct as *Over and out*, both with God and with people. Again he's taught her something new, and something she can use only with him.

It's true, we hadn't looked at the car's license plates. It's true, the Mafia has friends in the New Jersey police force. It's true, yet again he's thought of everything, and we'd doubted his superintelligence. All of it true, and almost unbearable.

The government finally admits the truth: that it was keeping twenty-five thousand soldiers ready for the demonstrations last month, to prevent riots in the capital's slums. There were not only troops to clear people off the streets but giant bulldozers ready to be deployed for that purpose.

November 23, 1967 Thursday

It is the fourth Thursday in November, Thanksgiving Day by law in America for the 327th time. But we had things to do in New Jersey and drove in a hurry under the streets upon which, as every year, Macy's department store has sent its parade marching from Seventy-Seventh Street on Central Park West to Herald Square: enormous inflatable characters of American folklore, from a duck named Donald to a bear named Smokey, held and swayed by children in harlequin costumes, to the accompaniment of loud, raucous music, in order to thank in this fashion the Lord God.

The Mafia was apparently still dazed by a tax agents' raid on a phone bank in Brooklyn yesterday, where "Butch" (Joseph Musumeci), under the protection of "Kid Blast" (Albert Gallo), took bets on football, baseball, and New York horse-racing results, to the tune of an estimated $11 million a year. Now those involved have been indicted for failing to purchase a $50.00 federal gambling tax stamp, while D. E.'s car was sitting untouched in Newark Airport, with, yes, false license plates, a bit dirtier and still wet from this morning's rain. And neither Karsch's business partner nor the honorable police of the state of New Jersey stopped us as we drove to "where we always get gas." An old mechanic was expecting us, constantly wiping his shovel-like black hands with two rags yet offering us neither. His main concern seemed to be that we not explain anything to him; he also didn't let us watch him. After fifteen minutes he drove the Bentley with D. E.'s genuine inviolable plates back out of the repair shed, and even refused to accept a tip for working on a holiday. So much dignity, gravity, and patience in his face—we once took these things as signs of honesty; it's how he's reached the age of seventy. When we left he shook Marie's hand, with a somewhat embarrassed smile, as though wanting to warn her about something, and Marie actually began a curtsy and thanked him seriously and called him "sir." Sometimes, when I'm not watching, she is liable to treat Negroes in a haughty, imperious way; she doesn't dare with a friend of D. E.'s. When Mrs. Erichson came to Newark Airport to locate her son's stolen car with witnesses present, she was a little worried about the lie she was planning to tell the honorable policemen of the state of New Jersey over the phone, because it's not as natural for her to lie in English as it is in Plattdeutsch, and we didn't ask her about what this must have recalled to her mind from the early summer of 1933. – It's always a pleasure to be of service to a true gentleman: the attendant had said about D. E., perhaps as a greeting meant for him. There is no question but that D. E. keeps secrets from us, so now we'll keep some from him. Mrs. Erichson, in her nervousness, keeps calling us "child," but the term also applies to her son, the professor and military consultant. By the afternoon we were back on Broadway, the part of it where we live.

We came up out of the subway on the east side of Ninety-Sixth Street, and I recognized Francine from before. I didn't know her name. She was standing pressed against the window of a junk shop, looking somehow persistent, as though planning to spend the whole day there, on strangely stiff legs, arms hanging down, not at all relaxed. She kept her eye on the stairs, indifferently, as though just counting people, one by one, uninterested in their individual differences. When she recognized Marie her gaze latched on at once, and her rigid tired face loosened up, prepared to smile. But she waited until Marie nodded to her, and then nodded back cautiously, as if afraid of being pushy. I recognized this look. Often, in the afternoon, around when people are returning from work, this girl had stood at this entrance, almost as tall as Marie, a "colored girl," and she'd looked at me every time as though she were expecting me, and then immediately turned her face away. She walked after me once, keeping a great distance, from shopwindow to deli window across Ninety-Seventh and Ninety-Eighth Streets and across Broadway, and then disappeared, as though she were headed somewhere else after all. Then I forgot about her, and only a few details about her face remained in my forgetting: the color, usually called "chocolate"; the hair, not allowed to grow natural but twisted into strange little braids; the eyes, with a kind of absent look in her open gaze; markedly protruding lips that might indicate sadness, or might not. – That was Francine: Marie said.

Marie said:
– She stands there half the afternoon.
– Because she can't go home.
– At home she's stuck in one room with three other children, and her mother.
– Two brothers, fifteen and one and a half, and a sister, who's fourteen. They're all only half siblings. Her father's different too.
– None of the fathers lives there. If any of them did the mother wouldn't get welfare, that's the law.
– She's probably there today because it's a holiday.
– On holidays her youngest brother's father sometimes comes over and brings some wine and drinks it with her mother and sleeps with the mother in one bed.
– She doesn't mind anymore, except maybe on holidays. Turkey, pumpkin pie, maybe she doesn't want to see how they don't have it.
– Her allowance is twenty cents every two weeks, when the welfare check comes.
– There was also one time when she was standing by the subway station waiting for her own father. She doesn't know what he looks like, he's never been back since she was born. She knows his name is Benjamin, and she's sure she'd recognize him.
– Her mother doesn't tell her anything about this father. But she blabbed once, so Francine knows that twelve years ago he had a hotel room on West 102nd Street.
– At home she has to do her homework on a tea tray on her knees.

– Her little brother bothers her the most, the one from the fourth father. She has to change his diapers, carry him around, put him to bed.

– Her mother doesn't take care of the children. She keeps the TV on from morning till night.

– At night, when her mother doesn't have any visitors, she and the oldest brother sleep in one bed and Francine sleeps in the other bed with her sister and the baby.

– There are only two beds in the room. The older brother has to share a bed with his mother since he tried to do it with Francine's sister.

– You know.

– He tried to again with her, and his mother beat him. That was a week ago. He hasn't come back home since then.

– Maybe Francine's waiting for this brother at the subway.

– But she doesn't stick poison in her arm like he does.

– He started two years ago when he was twelve and a half.

– Most of the boys are in a gang, they sit on the roofs and do it together.

– Then he taught Francine's sister how.

– She's scared now.

– She's scared because she thinks she's going to have a baby.

– At first she did it with a friend in the bathroom a lot of times, so she'd have a baby. She wanted one so she'd get her own welfare payments and could live apart from her family, alone in her own room.

– But now she doesn't want a child anymore. She's decided she doesn't know enough she could tell the child.

– Francine says she doesn't shoot up.

– Francine says there's a gang of girls in her building that hold a knife to your throat if you don't want to shoot up with them.

– That's why Francine likes standing on Broadway, where there are policemen around.

– She goes upstairs only when there's a grown-up she trusts on the steps.

– But there aren't many she trusts. There are a lot who're addicted to drugs, or vermouth, or... I don't know the word.

– It's on West 103rd Street, right around the corner from us.

– All the apartments have been converted to rooms, with a family like that living in each one.

– The landlord sits in his apartment with the door open. It's like an office, with a counter. But there's not a window over the counter, there's chicken wire. They have to pass him the rent through that.

– I didn't go with her any farther than that.

– I'm not afraid to go up to her room. We have cockroaches too. I'm not afraid of the older brother either. I'm afraid that the mother won't be nice to me. That she'll act like everything's my fault.

– Francine is doing a lot better in class now.

– I showed her the public library on 100th Street and went there with her because she didn't want to go alone. The librarian gave her a card right away and said she could read there and write there too whenever it's open. It isn't always.

– Now Francine is grateful to me again: Marie says.

"One paratrooper, wounded, fell across the nozzle of his flamethrower, and was set afire," *The New York Times* reports from Vietnam. Someday will we have forgotten that we could read this in the newspaper? It is even still real today?

November 24, 1967 Friday

The dollar is taking another beating. In London and Paris they're buying gold like crazy. Incidentally, *The New York Times* estimates that America's private capital invested in Europe since 1958 totals $10 billion, and she describes the spread of American consumer habits from Sweden to Spain. As examples of European influence in the other direction, she mentions the enjoyment of a Château Mouton Rothschild or Spanish Riscal, as well as a certain appreciation for the European obsession with bidets.

After the definitive American capture of Hill 875 in Vietnam, the country's losses since January 1, 1961, now stand at 14,846 dead and 93,227 wounded, of whom admittedly only 49,312 required hospitalization.

The first documented case of the effects of LSD on a human fetus was reported today. A girl was born in Iowa whose right leg is shorter than her left and attached to her hip at an odd angle; her right foot is also too short and has only three toes. The mother, nineteen, took the drug only four times during the pregnancy.

The Cyprus crisis is important enough to *The New York Times* for the front page, column eight. She's put the picture of the Greek tanks above the picture of the Turkish troop transports. Clearly we should pay more attention to what's going on over there.

Marie does not condone Cresspahl having spent eight more months in Richmond, Greater London. She insists that once people have gotten married they need to live together. Here she has ideas about the way things should be.

Cresspahl had eight months to watch from a distance as the Nazis established their state. He must have followed the news. Ever since he moved to a city he'd read the papers, if in a rural way: only after the day's work was done, only when he was sure there was no more useful work left to do, slowly, as recuperation almost, with a deep-rooted mistrust that reserved for his own eyes any conclusions about the truth of what he'd read. But he had in fact seen the things that the reports from Germany were telling him. Anything he'd missed in March, the London papers brought him thoroughly up-to-date on. On March 21, the president of the German Reich decreed that Nazi crimes would not be punished under the law. On the same day, he instituted the death penalty for misuse of the uniform or insignia of Hitler's private army and established special courts. By that point Hindenburg had signed enough; now Hitler could go after the real power of the state. For the Nazi state was not yet finalized when Hitler was named Reich chancellor on January 30, 1933—only his followers thought it was. Others prefer to mark its beginning with the March elections, but Hitler received only 43.9 percent of the votes then, less than half. We would date the introduction of total dictatorship to March 24. On that day, the German parliament, insofar as it was not in jail, passed the Law to Remedy the Distress of the People and the Reich, with which the German parliament renounced its rights and transferred them to the new government. From then on, Hitler could give the force of law to whatever came to his mind, and so he began, already in March, by dissolving the state governments and introducing hanging as a means of execution, effective immediately, and by October 1939 he had increased the number of his laws to 4,500 and was using the parliament as nothing but a glee club, the most costly one in the world, its repertoire consisting of a total of two songs: first, the national anthem of the time, and second, a hymn to an SA functionary who had died from having snatched a whore away from her pimp, that is to say, had laid down his life for Germany. These were the added attractions that the government of the German Reich offered in March 1933 to Mr. Heinrich Cresspahl, Richmond, England, in the event of his return.

When Perceval realized that the master's wife was not going to be following him back from Germany after a couple of days, and not after a few weeks, he quit. He offered no reasons but also didn't want to look Cresspahl in the eye. Once he had his reference in hand he simply stopped coming to the workshop from one day to the next. During the three preceding weeks, Mr. Smith had kept him hard at work so that the remaining orders could be fulfilled without him if need be; still, Cresspahl began to miss the boy. Even fifteen years later, he could still tell stories about how Perceval was one of those people who, for all their height, for all the food they ate, kept an angular, bony appearance. Huge ears. Extremely pale skin on his face, through which the blood would rush. When he was lifting something heavy, his whole body looked contorted; he often forgot to use more than strength in his work. His work had to be checked. Maybe he didn't have what it takes to be an independent carpenter. He enjoyed the work itself less than the praise for having done it—but he had to have the praise. Cresspahl asked around town sometimes, but Perceval hadn't applied for any jobs in Richmond. His parents came to see Cresspahl and knew nothing of his whereabouts. Perceval never came back. One night in mid-April, though, one of Cresspahl's windowpanes on the second floor (where Lisbeth had had her sitting room) was smashed in, not without a certain care, but Cresspahl didn't want to believe that of Perceval. Silent departure suited him better: Cresspahl thought.

In April, the Reich government passed the Law for the Restoration of the Professional Civil Service, which Cresspahl didn't pay attention to because it didn't, he thought, affect his line of work. On April 1st, All Fools' Day in England, the Reich government stationed sentries from its private army outside Jewish businesses in Germany, tried to prevent customers from entering the stores, with boycott posters or by physical force, and photographed them when they came back out. In Jerichow there was a store on Short Street, owned by a Jewish couple (Cresspahl didn't know the name), which sold work uniforms. Couldn't he just picture the people in Jerichow standing in a semicircle around the scene, with two unemployed men in uniform at the door and Ete Helms standing between them, making sure, as a representative of the city police, that everything proceeded properly? True, Cresspahl hadn't been in Malchow for some time, certainly not to go shopping; there might be some Jewish businesses there he wasn't recalling. Could he have thought that maybe the large photographs in the London newspaper were true only of Berlin, not of Mecklenburg? Attractions of this kind were what the government of the German Reich presented in April 1933 to Mr. Heinrich Cresspahl, Richmond, England, in the event of his return.

Mrs. Jones came from Brixton, unasked, and offered to take over the household, at least until she could find out why the young Mrs. Cresspahl had failed to return with her husband. Cresspahl bade her farewell and put a pound into her hand so nakedly that she never did come back. He went through the rooms with a broom once a week. Wherever the broom didn't reach—in the curtains, under the cushions—the dust settled in and congealed with grime. It sometimes pleased Cresspahl to think that he could always just chop everything to pieces. Even the windowpanes he'd installed in place of the smashed ones had streaks—he had never wiped off his puttied fingerprints. Cresspahl ate lunch in the kitchen with Mr. Smith, sandwiches from a pub and beer for Mr. Smith, water for Cresspahl. In his younger years Mr. Smith had gone to sea, and one time the crew had forced him to step in for an incompetent cook. Invoking the fact that he had survived the journey, he occasionally tried to do something along the line of bacon and eggs. But he hadn't learned how to wash pots and pans, and when he ran out of unused receptacles he gave up cooking. It sometimes happened that Cresspahl would ask him to stay after work, for dinner he said, although what he had on the kitchen table was gin. With half a pint in his belly, Mr. Smith lost all his shyness and started talking. He always referred to Perceval as T. P. He said T. P. had actually talked more about the master's baby than about his wife. – Young blokes like that wanna family: Mr. Smith said, so slowly and clearly that Cresspahl realized how often he must have had the thought. It sometimes occurred to Cresspahl to offer him one of the empty rooms. But Mr. Smith didn't need a family, and he would get to his feet at around ten, leaving a little something in the bottle. He held it well, at such moments all you could see was that he was compelled to say out loud everything he was planning to do. – Guess I'll be going now: he said. – Time to be off then: he said. Then he left. At the door, he said: Glasses. Then he straightened his dull metal Health Service frames on his haggard little face. Cresspahl would hear him still talking on the stairs, and it sometimes happened that he would be saying to himself: That's all right then, Mr. Smith.

In May, the German government repaid the German industrialists' donations to Herr Hitler with various payments in kind. The government had the holiday of labor celebrated as a Day of National Work, then on May 2 occupied the union buildings. On May 10, it transferred the confiscated funds into its own institution, a thing known as the German Labor Front. The Communists had already been given the boot, now it was the Social Democrats' turn to get what was coming. They were the only party not to have voted for Hitler's Enabling Law. Now their having hurried to approve the Reich government's foreign policy on May 19 availed them nothing. On May 10, their offices were occupied; on May 22, their party was outlawed. That's how you do it. These were only some of the proposals the government of the German Reich made in May 1933 to Mr. Heinrich Cresspahl, Richmond, England, in the event of his return.

In May, Cresspahl asked Albert A. Gosling, Esq., to the workshop. He tried as hard as he could to tempt Gosling into a fight. He practically shoved the sparse entries in the order book into Gosling's face; by May, he was already no longer accepting new work. Little Gosling with his big gestures was happy to offset the losses with the savings in Perceval's salary: What a businessman. Even Mr. Smith, with his morning headache, felt a grin creep over his face and exchanged his wood plane for a very delicate rasp so he could eavesdrop better. Cresspahl pointed out to Gosling the trunks he'd built for himself, waiting next to the door. He didn't tell him that the costly and elaborately worked chests were meant for Lisbeth's belongings; he claimed outrageous allowances for the cost of their manufacture under the category: master's personal needs. Gosling liked the trunks. He ordered one for himself, but made of redwood, with brass fittings and handles. Cresspahl brought up certain things Gosling was known to have said, in front of witnesses, directed against Cresspahl's way of conducting the business (this he invented on the spur the moment). It turned out that Gosling had in fact been slandering not only the Germans but this one in particular, for Gosling took off his black hat. He hung his slightly overlarge umbrella on the workbench. He held out his hand to Cresspahl. He apologized. He saw the error of his ways. He was truly sorry, especially now that the German nation was showing the world what it meant to put one's house in order. It was a crying shame, he said, that England had underestimated Mosley. This Mosley was the leader of the British Fascists. Cresspahl gave up on picking a fight with Albert Gosling.

If he could have gotten Gosling mad enough to terminate their agreement, he would have been free then and there.

A week later, Cresspahl terminated their agreement at Burse, Dunaway & Salomon. Now it would be another six months before he could leave. If he was looking for time to reconsider, he'd given himself plenty.

Right, Gesine?
Or was Lisbeth being given time to reconsider?
Right, Gesine?
You still had plans in Richmond, Cresspahl!
Right, Gesine?

November 25, 1967 Saturday

Today *The New York Times* informs us that yesterday, in Hirschenhausen, West Germany, Field Marshal Eric von Manstein, who planned Germany's 1940 blitzkrieg against France, marked his eightieth birthday. The notice appears at the end of the daily war news from Vietnam.

A coffin from Vietnam was delivered to a Chico, California, couple containing the body of a stranger, not the one they were told it would be carrying: their son's.

Yesterday at lunchtime, two congressmen went shopping in Harlem and easily confirmed that the supermarkets there do in fact raise prices on the days after welfare payments go out, repeatedly change the dates on unsold packages, and claim that spoiled meat and frozen food that had been allowed to thaw are suitable for sale. Representatives from the chain stores in question claimed again and again that such mistakes were due to "human error."

What difference would it make if we stopped shopping at A&P?

At the end of April 1933, Dr. Berling told the young Mrs. Cresspahl she could now return to England. He spoke as though he had never advised her husband to stay in the new Germany. He was washing his hands behind her so all she could see of his face were his heavy bluish jowls. She couldn't prove that he had been so bold as to give advice to a married daughter of an Albert Papenbrock. She was so dumbfounded that anyone could see the opposite of her wishes as reasonable that she didn't give him a piece of her mind, not even when he said: And give my regards to the old Swede in Richmond! I've been to Richmond myself, you know. Bushy Park, the tame deer... *You're young, Fru Cresspahl. Make the most of it.*

Still, now at least she had something she could put in her letter to Cresspahl. Not the whole conversation, just the regards from Dr. Berling.

She didn't find much material in the child. She was busy with the baby many times a day, she could spend quarter hours watching this dumb Gesine indefatigably trying to heave her head from one ear onto the other, or blindly clutching with helpless hands at the space above her; on paper this turned into nothing clearer than "she can move more than last week" or "her eyes are sometimes green, sometimes gray." And the writing made her stumble upon the desire to have Cresspahl see the child growing up with his own eyes after all, and the fact that he was busy severing business ties and breaking up a household in England for her. It wasn't as if she turned these desires of hers into a conscience; it was just that writing to Cresspahl made her feel uncomfortable.

She could have reassured him about the Tannebaums on Short Street. They'd had a much less exciting time of it than the Jews in the stories that kept coming out of Wismar and Schwerin and reaching Jerichow. The Nazi District Committee in Gneez had stationed out-of-town Storm Troopers outside Jewish shops in Jerichow, like elsewhere in their domain: otherwise the sentries, with friends or relatives talking to them, might have gone soft. District Committee Chief Prause was not very familiar with rural areas. Long before second breakfast at midmorning, it was already all over Jerichow that Ossi Rahn and Max Breitsprecher were stationed in front of Oskar Tannebaum's Work Pants and Milking Aprons like an honor guard, and after a while there was indeed a semicircle of rubberneckers standing around them, just wanting to verify the rumor with their own eyes. Breitsprecher, a Gneez saddler, was unhappy about it. First of all, he didn't like standing next to Ossi Rahn in public. Ossi Rahn was so well known in the Gneez courts that he no longer had to give his name and personal information when he was brought in yet again for assault or nonpayment of alimony. Ossi Rahn called himself unemployed; Breitsprecher wouldn't have hired him to sweep his yard. Ossi Rahn had been living in a vagrants' settlement on the outskirts of Gneez since 1930; still, he had money when he went to the bars, and he'd had the SA take up a collection for his boots. Secondly, Max Breitsprecher had joined the Nazi Party as the owner of a small business, to whom it was promised that the power of the wholesalers and department store chains would be broken; now here he was standing with this fine Ossi outside Tannebaum's store, depriving not only another small business owner but also himself of Jerichow customers. After a few hours he let Ossi wander the sidewalk alone with his slogans to the Germans, telling them to defend themselves and not buy from the Jew. When Breitsprecher came back out of the store, the shade on the door went down with a note pinned to it: CLOSED FOR THE WEEKEND. Ossi Rahn tried to refuse an order. Ossi Rahn was chewed out in front of the assembled civilian citizens. Max Breitsprecher walked through the crowd alone, somewhat dazed, incredulous at first when Pahl said something to him, then greatly relieved. (Pahl said: Nice material, that uniform. *Custom-made it'd look even better on ya.*)

Lisbeth Cresspahl could have written to her husband that Oskar Tannebaum had reopened his store on Monday morning, and business was exactly as bad as it always was, but then she would have had to write what had happened to her sister during the Jew boycott. There was a relative of Tannebaum's in Gneez who was more scared, and he'd marked down everything in his store to get as much money as he could fast, to flee. A used fur coat was in the window that Hilde Paepcke could not resist. It was a steal even for Gneez, and in Krakow she could pass it off as bought in Berlin. A Papenbrock daughter doesn't let some people in uniform, shouting rhymes about this and that and waving cardboard signs, stop her from shopping. Inside, under this other old Tannebaum's nervous chatter, she lost the courage to actually buy the fur coat. Outside, she was met with a chorus of voices calling her a traitor to the German people. That by itself wouldn't have bothered her. But one of the SA sentries also seemed to be taking her picture. Now Hilde was afraid of old Papenbrock; her fear sent her back to Krakow, where her husband, Alexander, had already sold off a good portion of the equipment. Papenbrock had started by bellowing in fury over possibly ending up in the newspaper for an impropriety, and at a time when he didn't yet want to show the new government his true colors. In the end, though, he was mad at Hilde only for not having trusted him, and he didn't even need to take the trouble to talk *The Gneez Daily News* out of publishing the picture, but Lisbeth Cresspahl didn't want to put that in a letter to England.

As for the rest of April 1 in Jerichow, she hoped she'd never have to even *talk* to Cresspahl about what happened then. For Ossi Rahn, instead of heading back to Gneez, had marched to Jerichow's local Nazi headquarters. He'd not only denounced his superior, Breitsprecher, to Griem as a coward and Jew-friendly in the line of duty; he'd proposed the notion that a veterinarian's practice was not entirely unlike a business. Griem cleared four people to march to Dr. Semig's property with Ossi. Griem would have recognized the Rammin carriage and pair in the courtyard and withdrawn; Ossi Rahn couldn't tell one horse from another, and Ossi Rahn posted guards outside Semig's gate.

Baron von Rammin left Semig's office down the garden steps; he hadn't really noticed the racket from outside the house. In truth he was so angry he could barely see straight. A few weeks previously, a good friend of his from Austria, Count Nagel, Beatus Nagel, had written to him for a German medicine to treat canine aurock and he, von Rammin, had copied out from the letter what Beatus had heard from his veterinarian and passed the request along to Dr. Semig by postcard. Dr. Semig had called to confirm the symptoms of this dog in Austria, and von Rammin had described how Beatus's Weimaraner couldn't stop pitifully pressing its head against the ground. – Aha. Ear canal pain: Semig had determined, in his obnoxiously expert way, and he'd tracked down the medication the dog needed and ordered it from a provisioner in Württemberg and would presumably have sent it to the Beckhorst estate with his bill if von Rammin hadn't found himself with something to do in Jerichow that Saturday anyway and, moreover, been curious what "aurock" could mean. Semig, with his usual obnoxious tact, had handed him the package without a fuss and not even blinked an eye when von Rammin had started asking his question regarding the outlandish name of the dog's ailment and then broken off when he saw the word *earache* on the label. The baron had made it through the goodbyes passably enough, but when he clambered onto the coachman's box in the carriage in Semig's courtyard the feelings called up by the incident almost made him pass out. It didn't matter that he didn't breed dogs, only horses; thanks to Austrian pronunciation he had shown himself to be illiterate, if not an imbecile, in front of a university graduate (Jew or no Jew). He found it particularly intolerable that this Semig would never show the postcard around, the stuck-up prig, so honorable you could strangle him. Baron von Rammin's horses, which he'd set moving in the direction of Dora's vegetable garden, understood without the help of the reins that they would get out of this yard only with a half turn, and they accommodatingly pulled the carriage toward the exit. Baron von Rammin saw men in brown uniforms in the street, busy with an old woman who was refusing to hand over a basket tied shut with a cloth. Then they noticed the carriage and took up their post outside the gate. They shouted something. They distracted the horses. Now von Rammin's baronial blood boiled up various words behind his brow, in a froth that almost blinded him—the humiliation brought on by the Austrian dialect, combined with the unsubmissive conduct of the vassals of that Austrian, Hitler, and with the Weimaraner dog breed mixed in with his rage at the Weimar Republic—and the two horses accepted the strange fact that this time they were supposed to run people over, and they galloped at full speed out into the street. Ossi's subordinates saw what any child could have seen; they hurled themselves to either side. Ossi Rahn had once seen somewhere that you could stop a horse by grabbing it somewhere or other, but he didn't remember where, and in its confusion von Rammin's right-hand sorrel lashed out like any good-natured person would in self-defense. Then Ossi Rahn saw nothing more, a well-aimed lash of the whip having closed both his eyes. The witnesses later recalled the horrible crack that the whirling carriage wheel had made from banging against Semig's cornerstone, and also testified that Ossi, lying on his side on the ground, was only making a fuss as if the carriage had run over his left leg. Baron von Rammin's pair burst down the road between the quiet lawns of the Bäk like the embodiment of a thunderstorm, and slammed the carriage against the curbstone so hard as they tore around the corner of School Street that the carriage tipped up onto two wheels and quite some time passed before the other two landed back on the pavement. Then von Rammin had his horses back under control. During his ride back to Beckhorst he reflected on a face he had recognized among the onlookers. For he'd had two moments of clarity, one when he'd caught Methfessel's eye and the other when he'd lashed out at one of the faces that he'd always looked down into from up on his horse, with the sharply defined thought: Fall in, rabble! Back at home, he was calm enough for a letter to Beatus Nagel, about aurock and the Austrian nation from which he was hereby formally taking his leave.

Ossi Rahn was still on the ground when Dora Semig shut the gate with her own hands. He was holding his leg and whimpering. His subordinates helped him up and leaned him against Semig's garden fence; they held him for only a very short time and stepped aside at once. Ossi Rahn slowly realized that he had lain in the dirt at Mrs. Semig's feet. He wanted nothing less than to smash the Jew's house to pieces. But no one there was paying any attention to him, they were all listening to Grandma Klug, who was brandishing her empty basket and screaming for her cat and expatiating in an inexhaustible whine about the why and the wherefore and the kind of people who steal cats, sick cats, cats walking on three legs, cats the last and best friends in the world to an old woman! Methfessel found the cat in a bush on the front lawn. It was a perfectly ordinary gray-and-black cat, with a lot of scratches and scrapes and a sore rear leg.

On Sunday the Semigs were invited to lunch by a family named von Plessen.

Methfessel the butcher lost three estates as customers within a week. He went around Jerichow swearing to anyone and everyone willing to hear it again that on the day of the boycott he had only taken the detour through the Bäk out of curiosity, the same as everyone else, that he'd only watched for a couple of minutes, the same as everyone else, that he'd only looked for the cat the same way anyone else would have done for an old woman. He hoped his protestations would make their way back to the ears of his insulted customers. This they did not do. Methfessel went back to serving in the butcher shop himself. Then business in the shop fell off. He didn't know what to do: If he took up the brown uniform he would have a stable clientele too small to live on. A public apology in *The Gneez Daily News* would bring the SA down on his neck and not even gain any sympathy from the nobility. Sometimes he was so flustered with all his mulling it over that he had to force himself to remember that he hadn't done anything wrong, he'd done nothing, nothing at all, absolutely nothing! The only thing he got from all his talking around was that even his wife stopped believing him.

In Gneez, the Law for the Restoration of the Professional Civil Service threw a district court judge, two railway officials, and three teachers out of their breadwinning jobs; in Rande, the manager of the resort; in Jerichow, Dr. Semig, who as the meat inspector for the northern part of the Gneez district had been a civil servant. Up until that point Semig had been able to live off his meat inspection work as though nothing were wrong. He went up to Gneez and paid a visit to the district administrative office. It was pointed out to him that as per paragraph 3 he had been automatically retired due to non-Aryan descent. Semig pointed out that paragraph 3, subparagraph 2 overrode subparagraph 1 for civil servants who "had fought at the front for the German Reich or its allies in the World War." He had deliberately worn his Iron Cross to Gneez for the visit. It was pointed out to him by the district veterinarian that the position of meat inspector, having been left vacant for an entire day, even if erroneously, had had to be filled. Semig pointed out that an oversight had to be rectified by the authorities who had committed it. It was pointed out to him that an official position, once occupied, could not be reassigned. Semig pointed out the utter lack of legal grounds underlying this information. The district veterinarian pointed out the door. Semig returned from Gneez feeling that the whole thing had been a personal intrigue, directed against him as an individual. Lisbeth Cresspahl did not want to put that in a letter from Germany to England.

In May 1933, Avenarius Kollmorgen, in the name of and with the power of attorney of Reichsbaron Axel von Rammin, Beckhorst Estate, filed charges in the Gneez district court against day laborer Oswald Rahn, Gneez Vagrants' Settlement. It was alleged that the defendant had frightened the plaintiff's horses, creating a hazardous traffic situation, and was responsible for an injury to the leg of one of the horses, Hildegard von Etz, and also for the damage to one carriage wheel, and also that he had threatened the plaintiff with danger to life and limb, using derogatory words. When Ossi Rahn was taking a stroll with his Storm Trooper friends late one night on the Beckhorst Estate, a group of workmen had been waiting for him in the shadow of the barns and they drove him and his cronies off the von Rammin property with bludgeons; the baron, incidentally, was away on a trip to his properties in Thuringia. The next night, Ossi was caught attempting arson; at least that's what all the witnesses testified. Now he'd been thrown in the basement under the Gneez courthouse. His comrades set out to pay Herr Dr. Kollmorgen in Jerichow a visit, but Geesche Helms's sister answered the door, and Geesche Helms was married to the Jerichow police, and incidentally Dr. Kollmorgen happened to be out of town at the moment. Avenarius was staying at the Netherlands Arms Hotel in Schwerin, on Alexandria Street, and spending evenings at Uhle's, at Wöhler's, at Heidtmann's, and at the Golden Grapes with his friends from the Justice Department, spreading among them the wisdom of drinking fine wine. After a week, Avenarius was granted his audience with Reich Governor Hildebrandt, whom the Austrian had placed in charge of the good state of Mecklenburg, and the audience turned into a copious lunch with Mosel wines brought from Uhle's according to Avenarius's instructions. When Avenarius got back to Jerichow, the baskets of food and beer for Ossi suddenly stopped being accepted at the prison wing of the courthouse, and then they stopped being sent, and then Ossi stopped getting even the slips of paper from his loyal Storm Trooper comrades with suggestions about how to behave. That's how loyal they were in the Storm.

With Reichsbaron von Rammin's permission, Dr. Kollmorgen also undertook to represent additional joint plaintiffs, because now Ossi's whole life was on the table. Ossi, it turned out, had lashed out not only for political reasons but sheerly for the fun of it; that explained the mountains of reports. Ossi was safe behind bars; that explained the level of detail in the accusations. How Ossi had tried to strangle a hired hand's girl during sexual congress. How Ossi had sold a complete game-preserve fence as kindling to the Castle Hotel in Gneez. How Ossi had regularly extorted cash sums from prostituted women in the Castle Hotel. How Ossi beat his wife, how he let his children go hungry. It all came out, or almost all, and Avenarius, short in height as he was, stood fearlessly before the judges and spoke of the honor of the German nation, as embodied, for example, in its most select groups, such as, to take but one example, the Reich chancellor's Storm Trooper units, which, according to explicit statements to that effect, were determined unflinchingly to cauterize out such a stain on their brown uniforms root and branch! and where anyone else might come to a stop, Avenarius would rise lightly on the tips of his toes and look around the courtroom with his solemnly shining eyes. Ossi's demeanor was described in *The Gneez Daily News* as broken (like a cow's, when there's thunder in the air).

Two and a half years in prison sounded good to a number of people. The nobility thought it only proper that it had been defended against the insolence of the mob, and thought that this reflected well on the new government, all things considered. Dr. Semig had accepted at once that he was not the appropriate party to submit the official report on Hildegard von Etz's swollen leg, a professor of veterinary medicine had to be brought especially from Rostock instead; he felt in some way protected by the verdict. The upper and lower middle classes breathed a sigh of relief, since the court's decision seemed to promise that the SA wouldn't be allowed to get away with absolutely everything after all. The SA itself was almost pleased at the chance to show itself in public as enemies of injustice, opposed to filth, and it requested from the regional leadership new application forms for entry into its ranks. Not everyone was satisfied. For the farmworkers, this lone defendant was not enough. Kollmorgen gradually started to have misgivings—first for his dignity, then because several other courts were requesting he take on very similar cases but without his being granted any further audiences with Hildebrandt. And what had the big to-do of the trial done for Methfessel the master butcher? Nothing, if you asked him.

Not quite all of Ossi Rahn's activities had come out. For instance, the favor that Ossi had done for a high-ranking SA leader in Schwerin was not revealed. Instead of being transferred to an ordinary jail, he was handed over to the SA to do his time. The SA sent him to a "concentration camp" just outside the southeast border of Mecklenburg. It was said in Gneez and Jerichow that he was working there not as a convict but as a supervisor of convicts. Then his family left for Fürstenberg on the Havel, from one day to the next, and Roswitha Rahn had paid for the tickets with money from her own purse; now the rumor was considered proven.

Methfessel had started hitting the bottle somewhat, and one night he let himself be overheard in his cups expressing opinions about justice in the new Reich. Methfessel was taken to Fürstenberg to see for himself.

When he came back after a month, he refused to say a thing about it, not even whether or not he had seen Ossi Rahn. That was not something Lisbeth Cresspahl wanted to put in a letter from Jerichow to Richmond.

Come on, tell me, Methfessel.
Can you keep your mouth shut, Frieda?
I'm your wife arent I. Silent like the grave.
Then dont dig yourself one.

Young Mrs. Cresspahl knew that no one from Jerichow was writing to her husband, if only so as not to use up any of her material. She knew that Cresspahl needed news from her if he wasn't to rely on the papers. She realized he would ask for explanations after he got back, if nothing else because of this mystifying curiosity of his about everything she thought and did, when even she couldn't figure herself out. Then people came to see the Papenbrocks, bringing the latest news from Field Road, and she couldn't put that into a letter, she had missed the chance to begin at the beginning. When Papenbrock passed her a letter from England across the breakfast table, she sometimes winced. She thought no one could see it until the old man told her to stop being so jittery. He didn't look any closer than that. Like the others, he saw her as a married woman pushing her baby carriage around Jerichow and claiming from people a new kind of respect. Everyone actually called her Frau Cresspahl, and by now without stumbling over the new mode of address or adding a fleeting smile to it, and almost no one could imagine how confused she was.

She was so out of sorts that she caught herself doing things she hadn't meant to. Once, in the middle of the day, she took off every stitch of clothing she had on and adjusted the large mirror in the sitting room so she could inspect herself from head to toe. There were no more visible signs, almost, that she'd had a child. She had borne the child for Cresspahl—that was one of the promises she'd kept. Why wasn't that enough?

She had let Cresspahl have Semig as the child's godfather. Why wasn't her consent enough? Now Cresspahl was sitting pretty in England and he wanted her to defend the Semigs for him. Yes, since April 11, the day of Semig's dismissal, she had shown up at his door only once. It wasn't that the looks from his neighbors in the Bäk bothered her; it was Semig's house.

It had always been quiet. Clearly the Semigs preferred not to have children; now, in addition, there was no more bustling from the maid in the kitchen, no more knocks on the door, rings from the telephone, clatter of carts and carriages driving into the courtyard. And Semig had a way of coming out of his consulting room to the parlor for ten minutes, to be polite, and then sitting there without saying a word, gazing absentmindedly at his knit fingertips. He looked strange, too, since he'd shaved off his little rectangular mustache. As for Dora, the Köster side kept coming back out, however benevolently the visitor tried to shrug off the injustice against Semig as an injustice; she averted her gaze like an old schoolmarm deciding not to notice a child's unimprovable behavior. Meanwhile, they could hear Semig pacing back and forth in the empty office in the next room. Lisbeth had only hinted that Cresspahl might buy the car that had just been delivered to Dr. Semig and that he now had no use for. The Semigs interpreted everything as pity, whether a visit or an offer to help. They were so focused on their misfortune that they didn't even listen to you. Cresspahl imagined it would be easy to continue to deal with them, and simply the right thing to do. He had no idea how hard it was for her.

Earlier, praying had helped her. Now she had her St. Peter's Church right there and could sit in her usual place, and still she didn't come home comforted afterward. Her requests were specific and disheartened. She prayed for Pahl to stop throwing himself at the Nazis with his tailored uniforms at discount prices for friends. She prayed for Edith to be able to stop stealing from Louise Papenbrock's pantry. She prayed for Käthe Klupsch to stop bad-mouthing the Jews so blasphemously in the shops. She prayed that she wouldn't have to use words with Cresspahl anymore, that he would once again understand her nonverbally. She prayed for help, prayed to be able to do what she wanted to do.

And that you'd live, Gesine.
You think I don't have an answer for that? I do, you know. I just won't say it.

If she'd known Brüshaver, the new pastor, better, she could have gone to him and asked him outright whether the church perceived sufficient wrongdoing to justify living in another country. Then she would have forced herself to think: Brüshaver says so too. Brüshaver had been preaching repeatedly in recent weeks about a Christian's duty toward others as toward oneself; she didn't catch the hint in that. She would have gone to see Methling, but Methling had aligned himself with the new regime. And it was too hard for her to think of Methling and the church as separate.

She didn't mean wrongdoing in a civil sense. Even Papenbrock might wander aimlessly around the house muttering to himself about bankrupts getting rich on other people's property; that was wrongdoing on the part of the authorities, hence justified. She meant injustice, the wickedness that the commandments prohibited and the Bible said would be punished.

And Cresspahl had such the upper hand! His opinions about the Nazis had been proven right, one after the other. Except that they would start a war. That was just crazy, carping about the militaristic name of the new union, the Labor Front. It's just that Cresspahl wanted to sit out the wickedness in that England of his solely so as not to share the guilt for it. Was that not selfish? Could a person leave his own country just to live in safety? How could she have put that in a letter to him?

She sometimes managed to work herself up into feeling angry at Cresspahl. Whenever she'd gone to other men with her wishes, whether possible or deliberately unthinkable ones, she'd always been able to choose, then and there, between renouncing either her wish or the gentlemen's future company. When she'd told eager young Herbert Wehmke, all of eighteen years old, that he should just abduct her out the third floor of Papenbrock's house, she knew he would make his exit in a hail of sparks. From Cresspahl, too, she had demanded something he couldn't easily do, but Cresspahl had listened to her and dragged her by her own wishes into a situation she was partly responsible for. He refused to accept sole responsibility himself. Maybe that was respect for her, but it was too much to ask of her. Cresspahl wanted from her no more and no less than that she wring the neck of every last one of her reasons and come to England with the child. Sometimes she felt like it was possible, and not even the Jerichowers' talk could have held her back; then it occurred to her again that she would have to swallow some of her pride.

They had agreed, of course, to a separation until November; she had insisted on it herself, so that she too would have a sacrifice she could point to. But for Cresspahl actually to not come for a single visit in the meantime, that was something else. Maybe there were business reasons and whatnot; to her it seemed like pigheadedness.

By late June, Papenbrock had gotten into the habit of shaking his head in any situation and saying: Nah. The first few times he had brought conversation around the dining table to a halt. Then his family came to understand that it was merely a way for him to collect his thoughts. For Papenbrock was no longer part of the power structure. The offices of the German National People's Party had been occupied by the police and searched, exactly like those of the Communists and the Social Democrats; on June 21, the party dissolved itself, and on the 29th, Hugenberg left the government. Papenbrock's talking to himself, his distracted behavior, made Louise very worried. She tried scolding him, in a playful way she had long since unlearned, and sat there stiff as a board when he unexpectedly stopped behind her chair, put his hand on her shoulder, and moved it back and forth a little. He stared into space, ignored the others at the table. The gesture had signified more than the usual consideration. It had seemed almost tender.

In early July, Papenbrock got a phone call from Schwerin. In Berlin, in the River Dahme near the Grünau ferry, several bags of dead bodies had washed up. One of the bags had contained a man by the name of Johannes Stelling, beaten to death. Johannes Stelling had previously been the governor of Mecklenburg-Schwerin.

Papenbrock didn't promise to attend the secret memorial service for Stelling; he did call his children in from the street.

Horst Papenbrock showed up to lunch and his suitcase was standing in the hall, packed. Horst was ordered into the office. Papenbrock screamed at him for half an hour, just as a precaution. That afternoon Horst was on his way to Hamburg and Brazil. He hadn't put up much of a fight. When he said goodbye to the family, he'd seemed strangely relieved.

Lisbeth wouldn't have minded if Papenbrock had ordered her to leave for England. But Papenbrock never thought about his daughters' wishes he had already granted. Lisbeth had things the way she'd wanted them. And he had no intention of meddling in Cresspahl's affairs.

That left Hilde. For the time being, Hilde's place was here in the Papenbrock house. She was too frivolous for these times, and Alexander Paepcke needed something substantial to show for himself before being allowed to come take her away again. Late that afternoon, Papenbrock had telephoned Krakow; the next morning, Hilde was in Jerichow.

– *Y'learn somethin new every day*: Papenbrock said over breakfast to his two daughters, a bit sheepishly. He wasn't entirely happy to realize that his children would rather be given orders than make decisions for themselves. But he was content at least to know it now and willing to accept it as part of who the children were. He considered it a characteristic of theirs; it didn't occur to him that that was how he had raised them.

"Hilde and the baby and I went to Rande for a swim": Lisbeth Cresspahl wrote to her husband in England. "They had some unemployed people shoveling new sand onto the beach, it's almost like Travemünde there now...": she wrote.

November 26, 1967 Sunday

Yesterday morning James Looby, twenty-two, a college student from Bayonne, New Jersey, went for a walk in our neighborhood. On Amsterdam Avenue, at Seventieth Street, he was approached by three young men who asked him for a cigarette. He was a nonsmoker and didn't have a cigarette to give them. As a result, he got a six-inch knife in his belly. He had wanted to be a teacher.

This morning the subway started running eight of its thirty-six lines differently, and Marie left early this morning to try out the new routes and signage, at least in Manhattan. Unlike the South Ferry, Marie has hardly bothered with the subways. She never reported train dreams; the gray train cars didn't turn up in her letters to Düsseldorf or even in her pencil drawings from 1962. When she left the house a little while ago she didn't show any signs of anticipation, just the stoic indifference of New Yorkers who will need to take the subway tomorrow and prefer to familiarize themselves with the new lines today. There may also have been a certain pride in the distinctive qualities of New York, a claim to share in the ownership of this city. Someday, she promised herself, she would travel every subway line— all 238 miles, all 482 stations, day and night—with the single token coin you need for admission into the system, "if I can get up the guts"; this, too, at a point in time that she reserved for herself the right to determine.

When we got here six years ago, her experience with the West Berlin U-Bahn was just enough that she was willing to go underground with me, and also just enough that she didn't notice the differences between the two systems. The platforms here, which often serve trains on both sides (express and local), at first seemed much narrower than the European ones, so that the newcomer preferred to stand in the middle, out of a ridiculous fear of falling onto the tracks. The stations here have tiled walls, as we were accustomed to, but between the tracks, even where the trains go in opposite directions, there are steel beams, close together and not braced near the ceilings, which at the same time seem to weigh more heavily. The platforms were emptier here; not only did they lack the little cabins for the dispatchers, and thus the dispatchers themselves, but also the city maps and even the timetables, so that the subway schedule seemed plunged into an incalculable arbitrariness and one's wait for a train was an endeavor without any guarantee of success. Marie, not even four years old, didn't care about all that; still, she heard the sound of her first train and held her mother's hand tighter and shut her eyes for a moment when the heavy column of train cars rolled out of the tunnel past her. Then the only things left to learn were that because of her fare category as a young child she had to duck under the turnstiles at the entrances, which she didn't like doing because she had to let go of her mother's protective hand, and that the train doors could slam shut without an announcement and without warning, so that a child would have to quickly yank her careless mother in after her. It didn't take long before she preferred the corner seats, not only because they were near the doors but also for reasons of comfort. And she started correcting my pronunciation of the word *subway*, as if its fourth letter had never had anything to do with the German *w*.

We got used to it quickly and had various judgments, or maybe prejudices, to help us too. People had come back to Düsseldorf from trips to New York and had called the conditions in the subway "inhuman," in general and especially during rush hour. This was not true. Certainly it did happen sometimes that we ended up not only at the edge of the platform but also right in front of the door of an arriving train, and that the people waiting behind us shoved everything before them like some kind of superhuman fist; but the people in the train car gently stepped back and Marie was always given a greater amount of breathing room than she needed, and

in any case it was really only in the short rush of getting on or off the train
that the riders were tightly packed, not during the ride, when everyone
kept their distance, be it ever so slight, even the unhelpfully overweight
women, among whom the black women, taking a deep breath and catching
and keeping all the movements of their body in a kind of gyroscopic system,
were the most graceful. (Amanda is sure that she once ended up with some
sperm on the lap of her overcoat in the pushing and shoving. Nothing like
that ever happened to me, so her opinion of the subway isn't something
I'm able to share.) For six years now I have spent the minutes shortly before
nine in the morning and shortly after five in the afternoon in the subway
every workday, and there were only a few occasions when I had to miss out
on reading at least something in *The New York Times*. Let's hear it for the
New York subway system.

Marie calls home the first time from Chambers Street (so she says). It
is, in fact, true that the Transit Authority is no longer grouping the subway
into the three organizations out of which it was created: the IND, BMT,
and IRT, definitively consolidated in the possession of the city in 1940.
Our system was called Interborough Rapid Transit; now not even the abbreviation remains, nor the black or dark blue color of its individual lines
on the maps. Our favorite trains, earlier named the Broadway and Seventh
Avenue line after the streets it passed under, are now called merely 1, 2, and
3 and are indicated on the revised map with the colors orange, light blue,
and bright red, easy to confuse, by the way, with the E train in Queens, or
the 8, the elevated line over Third Avenue in the Bronx, for anyone who
does not have the relationships between the various parts of the city firmly
in mind. About Marie, it is safe to say that she has them firmly in mind.
"Now I'll try the Sixth Avenue," she says.

According to another prejudice carried to West Germany, New Yorkers
were always in a terrible hurry, whether on the streets or in the subway.
This too was not the case. There is not a single public clock hanging in any
of the subway stations, so everyone has to mentally work out his own hurry
for himself, without the help of the Transit Authority. Even on the most
crowded platforms, people move as though surrounded by a personal radar
system, never touching the people next to them; it is so unusual to see
someone running that when such a person does approach, a path opens up
in the middle of the crowd. In the low-ceilinged passageways under Grand

Central Terminal, when thousands of people are making their way to the subway tunnels deep underground, everyone's slow inching ahead is unpleasant at first, even a little creepy, but soon their patience and discipline make an impression and win one's trust. And if the streams of walkers under Times Square ever do get tangled up with each other, despite the barriers separating them, the conductors shout only "Step lively!" not "Hurryup hurryup," and the unruffled black man in the loudspeaker room is as considerate as ever and happy to pronounce his words of wisdom:

Walk, don't run!
A fall is no fun!
Step lively, ladies and gentlemen!
Watch your step, please!
There is a train due on track 3.

One other prejudice was homegrown, nourished on the hope that possessors of money riding the train, exposed to the calls pleas instructions suggestions offers and threats of the advertising industry as defenselessly as they are in a packed subway car, might cease to turn down the repeated advertisements. I, for one, no longer see the posters. I remember only my first one, from 1961, which asked riders whether they have nine lives like a cat or actually only one life, and then to think carefully about that fact. I do see, though, the embellishments the ads get from the riders themselves, who find the toothpaste smile of a model beautiful only after it has received spots written in marker over the front teeth, or who prefer their photos of aristocratically upturned noses with bushily splayed-out mustaches added underneath.

I call my bank president Henry. What do you call your bank president?
I call him an ass and a son of a bitch.

The hotel we stayed in when we first arrived in New York handed out a subway map, compliments of Union Dime Savings Bank, and for six years that map has hung on the wall above our telephone. It's a bit like a brochure for a nature park. The rivers, the bay, and the Atlantic surround the pieces of land with a dirty pale green; a lot of cheerful forest green is daubed wherever there are parks or even airports or cemeteries, as well as under the compass that indicates twenty-four directions. Across the islands and half islands and over the water, however, run subway lines that are now no more, red and dark blue and orange, prettily knotted together in southern Manhattan and near Jay Street in Brooklyn, awkwardly rounded into curves or even sticking out sideways, almost jerkily, like footpaths in the forest. The sightseeing attractions of the city are almost always printed right in their actual locations (at the time, there was still the electric ferry from Sixty-Ninth Street in Brooklyn to Staten Island—we missed our chance); across the river from us, the map gives not only the state of New Jersey but a place called Edgewater; the approximate shapes of the bridges are sketched in over the rivers; clumsy airplanes hang above the two airports; the statue named Liberty is standing on a sharp-pointed advent star; and, yes, there's a South Ferry actually setting out from Battery Park, trailing a delicate wisp of white smoke above it. Two extra elements in yellow indicate the offices of the bank that is providing all this information, and wherever the subways and parks leave any free space, the bank has put in cute little mailboxes, in case anyone wants to transact financial business by mail. All this generosity and thoughtfulness has earned the bank not a dime from our household, while we have been given an indelible image of the subway system in our memory. Many thanks, Union Dime Savings!

The sun has withdrawn behind the river and now it illuminates the buildings on the shore from far below, so that they appear like lovely, if unidentifiable, vegetation. Now it's starting to be too long that Marie's been gone. Now Marie calls home. The news is that it's a hard blow for the patrons of the former IND and BMT: their trains stop in stations that didn't used to be there and don't stop in stations they always used to stop in and some of them travel on lines they never used to travel on before. There are people standing in front of the new maps in the stations under Times Square and they can't find a route along which they might get out again and make it home; it's not only that the trains have been given names like Q J and QB but that you can't catch them at Times Square anymore, only at DeKalb Avenue in Brooklyn, never known as a transfer point before. A man is standing there in a blue uniform and he is a conductor and his name is Ossi Bell and between one and two o'clock he has given information to forty-three people to try to help them out of their deep confusion.

Not that Marie needed any information from him: she has already figured out on her own that the express to Brighton Beach, which used to go via Broadway as the Q, now comes from the Bronx as the D and now we'll have to catch it at Columbus Circle, and also that the trains to Rockaway Beach, whatever they're called, still go express only in Manhattan and stop at every station in Brooklyn, and they should have changed that, Marie says. Marie thinks next summer is likely to come around, she is making plans for trips to the beach even if it's only late November. Now if she wouldn't mind getting home before dark. If she departs from Times Square now she should be at our front door in fifteen minutes.

For there is one prejudice about the subway that feels truer, namely that subways are not for unaccompanied children, even a ten-year-old male child, even if he's been toughened up in the roughest corners of Harlem or the Bronx. This is something Marie doesn't want to admit. She refuses to acknowledge it and points out that there hasn't been an accident in the subway due to subway traffic for almost forty years. When I encourage her to be a little more precise, she rattles off the things she's learned in an exaggeratedly patient voice, sometimes with a snippy uptick of pitch at the ends of her sentences: She knows how to recognize a junkie. She can tell a drunk without even looking. She will never ever enter a train car that has only three people in it. If there's a policeman she'll stand near him. She doesn't think it's possible that even one of the two and a quarter million passengers a day who ride the subway might be dangerous, nor that she isn't brighter and cleverer than all of them put together. She doesn't see herself. What I see when she's riding the subway is a skinny little girl in braids and a windbreaker and white pants perched on a corner seat with her head leaned back against the wall of the train car, taking in with her eyes everything that moves—people, views out the windows, doors, policemen's truncheons—in such a comprehensive, almost spellbound way that she looks like she's dreaming. At the very least like she couldn't defend herself. She doesn't want to admit it, and even if she does phone home punctually in the intervals agreed on beforehand, she doesn't want that to be taken to mean that the warnings are in any way justified, but rather that, with infinite pity, she is willing to go along with the whims that overanxious grown-ups can't break free of. Plus, two years ago it caused a fight between us when she went to Flushing (to see where we'd almost ended up living), of her own accord and without saying anything first, and called home, happy as a clam, from somewhere named Queens Plaza only at a quarter past five. Now we have to speak gingerly on the topic of her trips, in passing, so as not to tear a hole in our domestic peace. Sometimes I almost wish she simply accepted it when someone told her not to do something.

Marie walks through the door now, eighteen minutes after her call from Times Square, with a copy of the new subway map. And now we'll see whether or not this is a child who respects tradition.

Hanging above the telephone is our old map, donated by Union Dime Savings. It is defaced around the edges with scribbled phone numbers, it is admittedly about to tear at the rips it received back when I carried it around New York in my coat pocket while looking for an apartment. But there are also the little symbols on the map that Marie used to mark the stations she'd been to, and circles around the transfer stations, and a few words written in the Hudson, or the Atlantic, or Central Park, in her awkward kindergarten handwriting. Will she sacrifice the old map to the new?

The new subway map is bigger—an elegant thing, mostly white, sprinkled with a well-chosen mix of eight colors. The shorelines are traced a shade deeper than the blue of the rest of the water, as in a dream, one not entirely devoid of danger. All the routes are laid neatly alongside one another in parallel lines or regular angles or textbook curves, and in proportions that falsely promise balance and completeness. Only the GG line, Queens–Brooklyn, has an unsightly angular bulge sagging out too far to the east-southeast. There seems to be something easy to misunderstand at Grand Concourse on 138th Street: the box indicating the trains that stop there conceals the fact that the 2 curves off to the right—we will have to look closely there many times in the future. Granted, the map is in accord with the reigning graphic-design trends of the moment. Will it end up on our wall? What is to become of the past?

Marie takes the 1961 map off its nails, lays it carefully in its folds from 1961, smooths the 1967 map against the wall, and pushes the corners until the nails come through. There it hangs, the new one.

– The other one is to keep: Marie says.

– To keep for whom? For you?

– For you, Gesine, good grief: Marie says.

November 27, 1967   Monday

A new political party has been founded in West Germany. Its platform calls for West Germany to quit NATO, a plebiscite on recognizing East Germany, and the abolition of incomes not earned by work. *The New York Times* sees little future in the undertaking, and gives it eleven and a half lines.

The US ambassador in Vietnam explains: The war in Vietnam is misunderstood.

Yesterday morning in the Bronx, James Dennis forced his way into the apartment of Wilbur Johnson, made Mrs. Johnson tie up her husband, raped Mrs. Johnson, and took the valuables in the apartment and his leave. Out on the street, he heard his name, looked up, and saw Johnson shooting at him. Apparently he had missed the shotgun in Johnson's closet. They may not have known each other.

That was Thanksgiving weekend.

But in Richmond it was July, and Cresspahl was happy about a large tree in his yard. It was an elm. He'd been worried about it since spring, because it was sprouting a thick covering of leaves in the lower branches, was downright obese around the middle, but the crown had stayed sparse, looking a bit like a shamefaced bald head, and it was too young for that. Then he realized that the tree wasn't sick, the crown was just exposed to the wind while lower down it was warmed on all sides by the walls of the surrounding buildings. As late as May he'd still been able to see through the branches, but now the tree was in fine fettle and had put forth leaves everywhere. That was the kind of thing my father worried about in the summer of 1933.

That was in July, and already refugees from Germany were finding their way to the Richmond gasworks. They arrived with greetings from Erwin Plath and a message for Cresspahl's ears only: *When the cow loses her tail, she realizes what it was good for.* Pained and dismissive, they cut him short, not wanting to hear why Cresspahl hadn't paid Social Democratic Party dues for the past eleven years; what they wanted was a bed in a room with a door that locked. Later they told him about a "concentration camp" near Fürstenberg, where a guy by the name of Rahn was known as "Kind and Good Ossi," because that was how his victims had to thank him for the beatings and punishments they received; one of them knew for a fact that

Posner, the pediatrician in Rostock, had hanged himself just the other day, on July 8, "because he was a Jew." Once they'd managed to sleep off the SA basements and the escape from Germany and the arrival in England, they stood around awkwardly in the hot courtyard, elderly gentlemen mostly, stiff from sitting at the Mecklenburg desks of the Social Democratic Party, and awkward too when Mr. Smith tried to give them his idea of English. They didn't stay long. They felt uncomfortable in this Cresspahl fellow's house—not just because guests start to stink after three days, especially strangers, but because there was no woman there. A woman wouldn't have put such outlandish food on the table, cold; with a woman, one could have talked about one's own wife and family back in Germany. Clearly one wasn't allowed to ask after wife and children in Cresspahl's house. He was equally vague and grumpy on political topics, be they the British Union of Fascists or the Irish Republican Army. And in the long run you couldn't just stand around watching him and this Mr. Smith work. Even the noise of their work followed you the whole time you were there. They soon found their way to the North Sheen station around the corner and went looking for their own people in the city, and they came back maybe once, with an entirely different kind of English, and then didn't come back again. Only one of the first arrivals, Manning Susemihl, never left the house. He had been a courier for the Social Democrat district office in Schwerin—a young man, twenty-five, in whom you could still see the trusting and touching child, a better look for him than the welts across his chubby cheeks that had now healed into whitish scars. Manning chose a different room every day and straightened it up for his comrades, not because he felt any special need for order and cleanliness, not merely to pay for the roof over his head, but to belong under that roof, at least a little. He picked up a broom and swept his way stroke by stroke from the yard into the workshop, which he reached in the nick of time to do something that the master, with the worst will in the world, could find no fault with. It turned out that he didn't know much about wood but did about colors. They took him on for staining and basically could use him for the mass of orders that Cresspahl had started accepting again so as not to waste all his time until November. Cresspahl paid him something for the weekends. But then he realized that Manning Susemihl had had enough dangerous trips to last a lifetime and was perfectly happy to have found both a countryman and long-term employment among the English (for, unlike what his surname said, he didn't like new places). Cresspahl forced himself to tell Susemihl not only when he was leaving but also for where. He thought for a while that he could avoid losing this young man. For Manning had given him an accommodating look, with his shining, naively trusting eyes, and walked off with a nod, as if there were at least something about the decision he could understand. He was quieter on the following days, and it was no longer silent contentment. When they sat down together for a meal, he picked at his food, but the bread wasn't that dry. He turned his face away a little when Cresspahl spoke to him and didn't look him in the eye when he answered. He left the house in the evenings. Once he'd found another place to stay, he didn't duck the goodbye. He was embarrassed. Cresspahl saw in him the accusation that he was embarrassed about but couldn't let go of. – *I've tried it. No way. I dont get what you think youre doing*: Manning Susemihl said.

– *Yeah*: Cresspahl said. Back then he still had a way of retreating into his thoughts in the middle of a conversation, standing quietly, head to one side, as though he'd forgotten the other person was there.

Cut your losses.
They were your losses, Cresspahl.
Thats what I'm saying: Get out, cut your losses.

When Cresspahl went to North London one Sunday in July 1933, someone walked and boarded and rode after him, a little gentleman with an umbrella, his summer suit fitting so badly that it was as if he had borrowed it along with its elegant accoutrements. The news that Cresspahl was terminating their contract had hit Gosling like a ton of bricks, or at least the proverbial one brick said to be unjust because it fell on one's head without warning. By that point Gosling had learned how to add two plus two, and even some odd numbers. He'd imagined Cresspahl safely on the leash that his foreign origin had tied around his neck. He had almost grasped that owning premises and machines, even if he was personally unable to live there or operate them, yielded less cash when simply sold than when people were employed to work there and on them. Sometimes he'd felt himself on the thinnest of ice, namely when he thought of times

in which an even smaller number of people might be able to (or want to)
buy the products of such labor, but never had he dreamed that the workers
themselves, acting on their own faithless accord, might be able to do him
out of these regular, and pretty nice, transfers of money into his bank account. At first he had pooh-poohed the letter from Burse, Dunaway &
Salomon, income having brought out a certain arrogance in him. Then,
with a cold shock of horror, he was forced to realize that this was not the
day and age for taking a high-and-mighty tone, at least not for him; not
even his wife believed his show of confidence. Apparently it was permitted
by God and man, in the midst of plentiful, excessive, practically overflowing unemployment, that the wrong people might lose their source of income.
Not only did he now have to expend time and effort dealing with the inheritance from Reggie Pascal, which he'd never had to before, and in a
most painful way, namely by thinking about it; he also had to pound an
unpleasantly extensive number of London's pavements with his tender feet,
from labor agencies to guild halls to union offices, and the purchases he'd
had to make in the surrounding pubs did as little good to his taste buds as
to his wallet. It turned out that any master carpenter worth the money had
a business of his own, however encumbered in debt, or else had escaped
into the furniture manufactories, where no matter how sales declined he
would always be the last to be let go, and he did not then want to go back
into public commercial life, especially not under the aegis of Albert A.
Gosling, Esq., and he told him so too, looking down into his admittedly
aristocratic face. He was free to hire any carpenter on the market; any one
of them would have been able to use Reggie Pascal's things to throw together
some furniture that could be sold more cheaply than that at the department
stores and would fall apart quicker too. But that wasn't what this business's
clientele were looking for! They wanted their furniture saved, refurbished,
improved! And they were capable not only of not paying for bad work but
of taking him to court over it.

It was irritating, insolent, insupportable for this German to take the
noose off his neck when it had seemed so firmly in place; it was degrading
for a personage such as Albert A. Gosling, Esq., to have to come cap in
hand to a man like that. Now the money saved every week on young
Ritchett's former salary no longer seemed like such a good deal. (Every
now and then T. P. had slipped Gosling some information about what went

on in the workshop, or what Cresspahl had wanted him to think went on there; in fact, T. P. wanted Gosling to finally get the clobbering he deserved.) This Mr. Smith played dumb; he was perfectly capable of accepting one gin after the next, with thanks, and then ultimately losing the ability to speak. (Mr. Smith had listened to Manning Susemihl's baffled questions about Cresspahl's mental state in the same sleepy fashion, interjecting an unflappable and uncomprehending "Yes" in inappropriate places for so long that Susemihl finally gave up on him.)

Cunning as a big game hunter, Gosling tried to encircle his prey by going to Salomon, not to Cresspahl directly, and asking Salomon what these "personal reasons" the German had put forth for giving notice might be. Salomon leaned his head on the inlaid lions on the back of his chair and stared at Gosling with as much amazement as if he were naked, or cloaked in animal skins. Gosling hastened to explain that it wasn't that he'd wanted to know anything personal about Cresspahl's reasons, and naturally not the reasons themselves, but only whether his abandoning the lease was in any way due to the person of Albert A. Gosling. Salomon let his simultaneously admonitory and wounded gaze rest for a while yet on the hairs under Gosling's nose and, suddenly cooperative, proclaimed himself willing to make inquiries. After another while Gosling once again took his seat in Salomon's visitor's chair, uneasily stretched out his legs and yet at the same time tried to sit up perfectly straight. Salomon sat comfortably and informed his client that the answer was in the affirmative. He'd put a consoling expression on his face, which Gosling didn't trust. The client was eager to learn whether and that this misunderstanding could be overcome. To this question: Salomon informed him: the answer was in the negative. Gosling had him repeat the information several times and now was standing at the desk leaning on his umbrella in such an inner paroxysm of rage that it looked rather like a toy bow. It made no difference, he had no choice but to leave, harrumphing copiously.

Gosling felt certain that this Jew was in bed with the German, was cooking up something, was of one mind and heart and soul with him, and anything else Jews are capable of. He didn't dare go see Cresspahl; he didn't like the idea of having to sit through an afternoon-long reprise of the objections and difficulties of the past few years. He decided to take Cresspahl's decision as meaning that he wanted to go back to his own country because and ever since that Hitler fellow had started taking such forceful actions, like now with a Law for the Prevention of Offspring with Hereditary Diseases, according to which individuals meeting certain criteria were required to register in person for their own castration. Then again, he didn't understand this version of Cresspahl with the outlandish idea that someone could give up an economic livelihood for the sake of a patriotic conscience.

And Gosling was curious. He saw the German waiting at the Richmond station for a train into the city and boarded and went north to Seven Sisters Road and followed him into a side street where the German rang the doorbell of a single-family house. The German came back after such a brief exchange of words that Gosling didn't expect much of a haul when he went up to the door himself. A woman opened it, someone renting out a room who might well have earlier lived alone in the once stately building, and Gosling always thought people in trouble were the easiest prey. At first she refused to answer his questions. Gosling gave her to understand in no uncertain terms that hindering a police action would make her punishable by law. Now the woman was positively eager, and if she did hesitate, Gosling had only to take his accent up a notch and snarl a little more sharply.

The foreign stranger had asked about a Mrs. Trowbridge. It was the first time he'd come here. Mrs. Trowbridge had taken two rooms upstairs in September 1931. She had moved out when the other lodgers complained about her baby's crying. A lady, a considerate, unassuming person, but with a baby that did make a fuss sometimes. And Mrs. Trowbridge's husband? Mrs. Trowbridge was a widow. And where had she moved out to? To relatives near Bristol, but she'd left no address, and why would she, she'd kept to herself so much when she was here.

Gosling would have been less disappointed had his criminological skills sufficed to prompt him to ask about the German's reaction to this uninformative account, which was not in fact uninformative. As it was, he didn't find out for the time being that Cresspahl, clearly stunned for a moment, had said: What baby? What do you mean a baby?

That was in July, while the light was still pure white, without the brownish tinge that August's withering vegetation imparts to the landscape.

November 28, 1967 Tuesday

The New York Times still can't let go of the cataclysm she understands the changes in subway service to represent. On the front page, admittedly at the bottom, she presents no fewer than three photos of confused-looking passengers, each with an intentionally humorous caption, for instance the one in which a train driver can give other people information but has to think twice about his own route home. She quotes a senior official of the Transportation Authority who's pleased that there are now only 105 to 110 riders per car in some trains, where before there had been 180 to 212. That's not the only reason she quotes him. He also invoked the concept of "a comfort level" of 180 passengers. What might that mean? A "comfort level" in the subway is "when a man standing can read *The New York Times*": so reports *The New York Times*.

Yesterday a representative of the Dow Chemical Company, speaking to an audience of students in Washington Heights, defended the manufacture of napalm and the act of supplying it to the US government. First of all, the spokesman, Dean Wakefield, does not consider the war in Vietnam to be, "on the whole," a moral problem. Dow Chemical was merely fulfilling its responsibility to the national commitment of a democratic society (in Vietnam). In any case, the chemical agent is so simple to produce that the army could make it itself. (*The New York Times* explains what napalm is.) When asked his views about the Krupp family, who made munitions for Nazi Germany, Wakefield called them "bad people." To the question of where he gets the moral standards by which he can pass moral judgments on businesses, Mr. Wakefield replied: From history. "From history."

It's been a long time since we've bought any household products made by Dow Chemical Company. But are we supposed to stop riding the railroad since it profits from the transportation of war materiel? Are we supposed to stop flying on airlines that take troops to Vietnam? Are we supposed to not buy a single thing because that generates a tax, and we don't know what that tax money will eventually be used for? Where is the moral Switzerland we can emigrate to?

The mail today consists of a letter with very large stamps. Depicted on each is an oak tree along with a man holding a book. The Jerichow postmark is missing the *w*. I lived there for ten years. Is that a possible place to go back to?

"WORKERS' SEASIDE RESORT—RANDE
Municipal Council
35 National Unity Street
Telephone: JErichow-2-55
November 24, 1967

RE: Your inquiry dated August 20, 1967—Number of Jewish guests at the resort in the years preceding 1933

Dear Fräulein Cresspahl!

We are compelled to begin our response to your inquiry by clarifying that we know you are a citizen of the German Democratic Republic. You are the daughter of Heinrich Cresspahl (deceased) and the owner of the property at 3-4 Brickworks Road in Jerichow where he lived until his death. You are still registered with the police as resident there, having failed to file a change of address with the authorities, as we can clearly see from the file on our desk.

Surely you understand how unpleasant it is to receive a letter from you from the United States of America, a country that is conducting a ruthless war of extermination against the brave Vietnamese people—a letter from a citizen who has not only abandoned her homeland, at a time when it was forced to fight grimly for its survival and the efforts of every individual were vital, but also betrayed Socialism.

This is the background information we must take into consideration in evaluating and responding to your inquiry.

We must first remind you of the special conditions under which the German Democratic Republic lives, labors, and ensures peace. You no doubt know that our country now ranks eighth in the world in industrial production, after almost twenty years of the hard work of reconstruction; you surely realize that deep-reaching social-revolutionary upheavals have proceeded hand in hand with such efforts and that now, for the first time on German soil, in the one and only Socialist state of the German nation, men and women find themselves face-to-face with a life of human dignity. However, one cannot lose sight of the fact that we share a common border with a social system of the capitalist type, in which all the old generals and Junkers, revanchists and warmongers, and needless to say the capitalist Flicks and their cronies have seized power and continue to plot day and night, as is their nature, about how they can damage our new State, now that their efforts to wipe it off the face of the earth have met with such humiliating failure. Such a common border, however, exists not only along the frontier of the territory of the German Democratic Republic but anywhere our enemies attempt to penetrate, even in the superstructure.

Under these circumstances, we find ourselves with the following question to put to you: What is the purpose of Citizen Cresspahl's inquiry? What can someone who has deserted into the class enemy's camp want with certain information from the prehistory of the German Democratic Republic, stemming from a time before she was even born? It cannot possibly have to do with any manifestation of nostalgia or personal recollection. The presumption of an objective intention is therefore justified. Our concern is with the possible transformation of this particular data, when seen from a simple social-critical perspective even by the non-Marxist-Leninist-trained eye, into actual occurrences involving the participation and collaboration of actual persons. It would take no special effort, and would acquire a certain fundamental plausibility, for an enemy of our State to undertake to create the impression, by manipulating various pieces of information factual enough in a limited sense, that the persons who exerted through their active actions or omissions an influence on the number of seaside resort guests of the Jewish faith in the years subsequent to 1933, and the persons working shoulder to shoulder today to build the most advanced form of life yet known, that of Socialism, are the same individuals. This in itself would be tantamount to the baseless accusation of latent anti-Semitism in the German Democratic Republic. No support for any such assertion can or will be offered here.

This mentality betrays a lack of the most basic understanding of human psychology, inasmuch as it disregards the thesis of the determination of Consciousness by Being and the principle of dialectical development. A human being under the inhuman Fascist hegemony who succumbed to the temptation to perpetuate discriminatory acts against Jewish citizens is no longer the same person once he has consciously worked through the fact of this temptation, entirely aside from the fact that in our current system such people are barred from the path to leading functions in the State and party. This is in accord with the policy of our State, which guarantees to all minorities, whether national or religious, treatment in accord with the principle of equal rights. This fact is itself the best proof that the German

Democratic Republic is justified in its unrelenting defensive struggle against the racist, supremacist, and colonialist forces of Zionism, which raised its treacherous bloody head not six months ago in the Middle East.

In addition, we wish to inform you that Gneez District Council Department of Statistics regulations prohibit the releasing of isolated statistical information to private individuals, even should that information exist.

Finally, we would like to remind you that your unlawful departure from the territory of the German Democratic Republic fourteen years ago has not released you from the duties and obligations of a citizen of the German Democratic Republic, and that the People and the Government, in accord with the principles of our constitution, expect you to work for peace and mutual understanding among nations, and against the imperialist warmongers.

Yours in peace!
Schettlicht. Klug. Susemihl. Kraczinski. Methfessel.
German Democratic Republic
Gneez District Council
Municipality: Rande."

Sometimes Marie says about Sister Magdalena: "I wish she were in Jericho!" It never even occurs to her, so firmly does the local language do her thinking for her, that Jericho is a very faraway place, and not a nice one. In English "Go to Jericho!" means "Go to hell!," and when you merely wish someone were in Jericho you want them to be in the back of beyond, far far away, anywhere but here.

November 29, 1967 Wednesday

Dear Marie.

Today I'm going to try for the first time to tell you some things on tape, "for when I am dead." You asked me to, seven weeks ago, when we were driving up to Annie's in Vermont. Remember?

I read the *Times* today / Oh boy.

Now you have it on tape that I can't sing. "Like crystal, with a tiny crack in it," Jule Westphal used to tell me. Then she let me stay in the school choir after all. Second alto.

Eisenhower, if they'd give him another chance, would march into North Vietnam, into Cambodia and Laos too if necessary. He wouldn't call it an invasion of North Vietnam but "removing a thorn in our sides." I'm telling you this because you used to think he was cute.

Now I'll read you something from *The New York Times*: "Within an hour of sundown the first tremors of trepidation rise in the West 60s, 70s and 80s. Stores are closing by 7 p.m. and within two hours such thoroughfares as Riverside Drive and Columbus and Amsterdam Avenues are only fitfully alive or almost deserted." It's like that in the West 90s, too, where we live.

As a child I spoke with a slight lisp, and that's a big help to me now with tee-aitch. Should I try it again? "Removing a thorn in our sides." Can you hear it?

In Jerichow in the fall of 1956 they treated me like a child, like a crazy woman. As if I didn't understand their situation

Sometimes I'm so tired I talk exactly as muddled as I think

I don't think in a very organized way, if you ask me

Where I come from it's not there anymore

There are still some books from there, you won't be able to read them. The ones in the glass-front bookcase. Of all the sayings, my favorites were the ones with "*sä de Jung*": "... said the boy." The fox and the cat and the hedgehog and almost all the birds could talk too. My very favorite was the one about the boy who sat on his bed and was so tired he couldn't lie down, so he called his mother and said, "Knock me over." But *de Jung* was a kid who had a hard life.

None of your ancestors could write their name. Cresspahl was the first.

The only horses you know are mangy, with flowers on their heads and rotten rags around their feet. We've never taken a horse-drawn carriage through Central Park, initially because of money and then because we thought it was for tourists.

In the beginning, you wanted to go back to Germany, believe me. But after just six months you stared at the supermarket girl's mouth the second time she showed you a one-dollar bill and asked you if you knew the name of the man on it. And you said: George Washington. And she said: *Do you like him?* And you said: *Yes ma'am.*

When I drop a plate or a bowl, you say sternly: *Watch your language.*

Sometimes, when you switch from something you think to something you know, you talk like a horse who sees the door to its stable, and when you talk it's like you're going home like a horse with no one at the reins.

Back when you were learning to write you would take the letters I wrote out for you to copy, which I didn't always close, and turn them into carefully closed ones, extend diagonal lines to join downstrokes, complete loops until the ends met.

Yesterday I explained a photograph to you: Ratzeburg, 1960. – Yes, I can picture it: you said. You sure know how to lay the manners on thick. When I was a girl I wanted so much to increase the surface on which love for one's mother might grow. I carried around a picture of her from when she was a child. 1913. – Was that her? I asked Cresspahl. In a long long dress. The picture had a very brown tint. I didn't believe him. She committed . . . She did something to herself.

Your father died before he had any idea of the meaning of the word *death*. I only know the most necessary things about your father.

And I don't trust what I do know, because it hasn't always been there in my memory and then suddenly it turns up as a thought that just came to me. Maybe my memory is only creating from within a sentence that Jakob said or maybe said, might have said. Once the sentence is all finished and there, my memory constructs other sentences around it, even the voices of totally different people. That's what I'm afraid of. Suddenly my mind is having a conversation about a conversation that I wasn't even there for originally, and the only truth about it is the memory of his intonation, the way Jakob talked

Today that sentence is . . . that I won't say it. It's harmless, no secrets no feelings. It's the saying it out loud that would make it unbearable, horrible

All I know about your father is what a person can know about the dead. Handball player, Socialist, lodger. After a while things take their places in front of a person and leave only a little space in which the person supposedly lived. I have to reconstruct what he cared about. He cared about his mother, but he left her to me and went away. Your father was good with girls. He was good with old women, good with Cresspahl usually, with cats, with all his friends. Jakob was the only one Wolfgang Bartsch could work a whole shift with in peace. Jöche needs to just keep his mouth shut, Jöche only happened to be there, Jöche was much too young. (In 1956,

Jöche spread the story that Cresspahl had been in Jerichow for forty years. You see what I mean.) Jakob could even get along with people who'd totally run out of patience—salesgirls at the end of the day, freight-train conductor women. He was better with me than I am with anyone

If I, . . . Listen Marie.

If I let myself get involved with someone, their death could hurt me. I don't want to feel that pain ever again. So that means I can't let anyone in.

This proviso does not apply to a child by the name of Marie Cresspahl.

Sorry.

You know I don't talk during the day.

November 30, 1967 Thursday

The North Vietnamese army announces: The battle of Dakto in southern Vietnam was a victory for them.

The Mafia used to do it like this: The family buys a normal bar that's losing money, redecorates it, and brings in a couple of homosexuals to lure the others. For more than a year, however, it has no longer been a violation of the state liquor laws for a bartender to serve a known deviate, and the city's drinking establishments for sexual minorities have been generating ever more interesting profits. So now the Mafia is starting to sell off the bars to regular operators and invest the proceeds and capital in private clubs for homosexuals who have good disposable income, and it's enjoying not only greater but quicker profits. It's easy to recognize plainclothes policemen among these customers. Things are well in hand again, it's business as usual.

Cresspahl did it like this: He went back to Germany six weeks after the Law to Guarantee the Public Order of October 13, 1933, was passed, which threatened with death or life in jail or fifteen years in jail anyone who acted to introduce into Germany for the purpose of distribution any (treasonous) printed matter with knowledge of its treasonous content, or who distributed such printed matter after its introduction into Germany, or who otherwise abetted in Germany any criminal act of high treason performed abroad.

In his coat pocket he was carrying a newspaper, clearly recognizable as printed matter, which contained the verdict given at the London trial conducted as a counterpart to the Leipzig proceedings concerning the

Reichstag fire. One step outside the customs zone in Hamburg and they could have proved it all against him: introduction, distribution, high treason. Not a great way to start providing for the care and maintenance of wife and child, Cresspahl.

I just forgot I had it on me, Gesine.
Thats what you wouldve said, huh, Cresspahl?.
Theyda believed me and the police would have too, and the neighbors cat.
You know that.

Cresspahl came within an inch of traveling down the Elbe with three hundred pieces of printed matter in a hidden compartment in one of Lisbeth's wooden chests, not one piece in his pocket. Susemihl had come to Richmond in all seriousness with the suggestion—innocent, jittery with excitement, enraptured with his clever idea. But he hadn't concealed the fact that such an errand would be a way for Cresspahl to redeem himself somewhat in his eyes, and he'd shifted too soon from the tone of a younger man to that of someone giving orders, so Cresspahl felt treated like merely a convenient opportunity, someone Susemihl didn't really care about. Then an argument started, confined to politics because neither of them wanted to get personal. Since it hadn't helped the SPD that they'd voted against Hitler's Enabling Law, it made perfect sense that they'd move their central headquarters to Prague plus expel every Jewish member of the central committee. Susemihl refused to believe that. Cresspahl could prove to him that the decree was dated June 19. Susemihl wanted to know why Cresspahl now cared about the Jews. Cresspahl now cared that it was shitty to hang victims of persecution out to dry. Susemihl heard from Cresspahl's tone, imperturbable and final, that he hadn't maligned the party inadvertently. He tried to say, with a pale face and strained forgiveness: Cresspahl really didn't understand anything about politics, fundamentally. This was supposed to lead into his goodbyes, and Cresspahl hit him precisely between his shining, suddenly outraged eyes, and didn't leave him lying in the kitchen doorway but threw him out into the yard, and the fact that it was raining was fine with him too. There's a kind of sudden, wide-awake onrush of rage that comes over a person when they're losing something, when there's something to be lost, don't you think, Cresspahl?

*Right you are, Gesine. And you dont just know it from me. Youve got some
a that yourself.*
Do not.
No?

It's true that Cresspahl missed his chance to personally approve the
German Reich's exit from the League of Nations in the November 1933
plebiscite, and add his checkmark to help the Nazi Party to their 92 percent
yes votes in the simultaneous Reichstag election—he happened not to be
in the country. He didn't even bring a child into the world to show his
confidence in the Nazi future, like the young parents of 1934; his child had
been meant to grow up in England. But the thing is, he did leave her with
the Nazis. And when he pulled into Jerichow at the end of November, who
was it who'd been named the chief of the political police of Hamburg,
Lübeck, and Mecklenburg-Schwerin?

Heinrich Himmler.
Didnt you see that coming?
Nope.
*The orders to triple the size of the army within five years came in April.
The first Employment Battle was in September. In October the German
delegation left the Geneva Disarmament Conference. In October the army
prepared for sanctions from the League of Nations. You'd been in a war. You
didn't want to be in another one. Why did you go back to where there was
going to be a war, Cresspahl?*
No one could see it coming yet, Gesine.
Yes you could.
Nope.
*Really? Simple as that? Suddenly there was capital punishment for po-
litical offenses, but you were planning to stay out of politics anyway? They
were heading for another war, but you wouldn't be called up, you were already
forty-five? Maybe they hated the Jews but nothing would happen to them
when you were around? They banned all the political parties, and you used
to be in one, but maybe it was better with only one party after all?*
Something like that, Gesine.
I dont believe it.

Hindsight doesnt just give you 20/20 vision it makes you a totally different and better person, doesnt it. Someone who cant understand other people anymore. What about you, Gesine? Where do you live? Cant you see your own war? Why dont you leave so that you wont be guilty? You know good and well what its like for growing children. Whatll Marie say when she realizes?

That the dead should keep ther mouths shut.

Its not enough for you that theyre dead?

If Im not supposed to say anything, why are you talking?

I dont want to scare you, Gesine.

You just dont want to say it.

You say it.

You had your wife in Germany and other than that you didnt really think about it.

Other than that I didnt really think about it.

Cresspahl went for walks with Papenbrock's younger daughter, not only at night on the rocky coast near Rande but down the street in broad daylight, arm in arm, and again the people in Jerichow were saying they went together like glue and gloss. One night these Cresspahls couldn't even wait to get back inside Papenbrock's house, they were standing in a doorway not a hundred feet away, kissing, and when Ete Helms's footsteps had fallen silent for too long they let each other go, in no hurry, and calmly wished him a pleasant evening. Ete Helms almost felt like telling them to keep going: he said back home. The stories were good-natured, the curiosity not malicious. Maybe there existed a man and a woman in this world who could do it—live together in a way that was ultimately not possible.

– Why won't you go on with the story today: the child eventually says.

– Czech tired me out, Marie.

– Say something: she demands.

– *Jen dou vode mně dál*
   láska mi vobešla

– More!

– *Šaty měla podzimkové*
   a vlasy měla podzimkové
   a oči měla podzimkové . . .

– Okay! Marie says. – I just wanted to see if you've been doing your homework.

December 1, 1967 Friday

Yesterday's snowstorm cloaked the trees outside our window like sparkling white strangers, cleared the sky, and set a blinding mirror in Riverside Park for the now unobstructed sun. It left behind a wind that wrote on everyone's bones that it was colder than six, no, six and a half degrees below zero (20°). The brightness, the cold clarity of the air had given the city a neat and tidy new suit, like a hardened juvenile delinquent trying to make a fresh start despite it all. On Broadway at the subway entrance, an alcoholic had slipped on yesterday's frozen slush and fallen fast into a peaceful slumber. The people, hurrying though they were, stepped carefully over the prostrate unfortunate's legs, like a horse stepping over a rider he's thrown.

Today *The New York Times* gives the names of the soldiers from New York and the surrounding area killed in the line of duty in Vietnam, but doesn't say how many war dead there were from the country as a whole.

About Admiral Roy L. Johnson, the retiring commander of the Pacific fleet, she reports: He is going to Virginia "to live."

John "Sonny" Franzese, on trial again for the murder of Ernest "The Hawk" Rupolo, yesterday impugned a chief state witness as much too criminal to be credible.

Near us, on Amsterdam Avenue and Seventy-First Street, a run-down hotel, the Sherman Square, is set to be torn down to make way for a luxury apartment building more than thirty stories high. The entrepreneurs hope that the poor and disreputable (the "small, sleazy elements") will leave the Upper West Side when their homes (their "haunts") are torn down. "This is the only way the city can grow."

Instead of a letter, Karsch has sent us a blank check "for whatever a new phone number costs." That was written in German, and Marie could read it, and she thinks it's only right and proper. But it cost nothing to get a new number. Our telephone company is driven by private considerations and would rather we make use of their services than be mad at them. Two days after our request we were "back in business," as the technician who installed the line put it, a man chatty about his work routine who went on and on trying to convince us to go duck hunting in the marshlands of New Jersey. So what are we supposed to do with a check from the Bank of the Holy Spirit in Milan, to be filled out with any sum we want?

There are two proof sheets stapled to the check, apparently the end of an article Karsch wrote about his trip to America. So, Karsch is one of those people allowed to work in peace and then to reread what they've written one last time before it's too late to correct any mistakes. But here he omitted any handwritten explanation, and the article is in Italian, which Marie can't read, and which Marie wants translated, right now, on the double. Every word.

So, before he came to New York, Karsch had paid a visit to see the Mafia in New England. He's less familiar with that part of the country and doesn't know as many people there as his colleague, Bill Davidson, who two weeks earlier published a similar article in *The Saturday Evening Post*, but it looks like the FBI let Karsch too read from the material their surveillance devices had lip-read from the Mafia fathers and lieutenants in the mafiosi's own offices, and it reads like Karsch too paid a call to Raymond Loreda Patriarca, the head of all the branches of the family in the Boston area, and saw with his own eyes the old man sitting on the stoop of one of his properties on warm afternoons, elegantly clad in a white sweater, white socks, and alligator shoes, playing with a fat cigar, wearing the benign expression of someone who knows his bodyguards are nearby and can see them too. "But when someone feels he's the Godfather, how can he not believe in his own innocence?" in Karsch's words.

True, he describes the different sources of Mafia income, from money-lending to fixed football games and horse races, to manufacturing LSD, to transporting drugs for and paid for by allied families, but then, as he writes, his gaze falls once more on Boston Harbor and *Old Ironsides*, the ship named after the American Constitution, open for sightseeing, and Karsch writes: That day it was closed. It's almost like he's just chatting with his readers, sure of being able to carry out their assignments. He doesn't include as much from Patriarca's CV as Davidson had, but to make up for that he has the life stories of Patriarca's parents, immigrants from Italy, from Sicily. Karsch puts the rumor that the New England Mafia wants to bump off their Godfather—because of his age and possible weakness under police questioning—in such a way that it just barely escapes turning into an aspersion on the leader. He doesn't omit the story of how Patriarca once got around a personnel shortage by hiring non-Italians, without however initiating them into the practice and ideology of the Cosa Nostra, especially the Mafia oath of omertà, and so now there's no mystery about why the structure of his empire is beginning to crack. Karsch offers up some sociology: how the Boston Mafia has sunk to the level of bar brawls and uses noisy dustups on the street and easily found bodies to do what Chicago can do quietly, discreetly, without leaving a trace; how nowadays Mafia families in other cities often send for "the Boston boys" to do their dirtiest work. His way of portraying the relationships between the Mafia and New England politicians instantly makes the reader outraged; but Karsch is already standing in Harvard Square, Cambridge, looking friendly, describing the confluent streets and the subway kiosk and the newspaper stand where next to the *Literaturnaya Gazeta* from Moscow are displayed the papers from Italy.

Mostly, though, he has a thing for children. The first is a girl he observes in the Italian neighborhood of Boston, a nine-year-old lady behind a vegetable stand expecting exactly the same restrained and respectful behavior from her customers that she gives them—dark eyes, almost black, mostly kept hidden behind their eyelids, charming sweeps of dark hair on her brow, gulping motions in her sinewy throat, maybe fear after all.

So, in Providence Karsch was trounced by Mafia specialists. He doesn't go the least bit easy on himself: he admits defeat, he doesn't act proud of having survived the beating.

The second child was a four-year-old Swedish girl in the Copter Club on top of the Pan American Building in New York, to whom it was increasingly inescapable that in a few minutes she would have to go up to the roof and board a helicopter to Kennedy Airport. Scared as she was, she sat down with the man alone at the next table and comforted him about the fact that she had to abandon him, she was about to fly off with her parents to "where our family was born from." When the announcement came, it took her by surprise after all. Pale but determined, she dragged along a heavy carry-on bag because that was what one did, but just before she got to the up escalator she turned around again and waved at the stranger so that it wouldn't occur to him to be sad about her departure.

So, Karsch went to New Jersey because of another rumor. He'd heard so often about a giant grill, prepared to order, on which the New Jersey Mafia would roast unfaithful members or intractable enemies, that he couldn't not try to see it for himself. Not only did he find the compound, a magnificent mansion surrounded by large grounds with sports fields, but he was invited in by the lord of that manor, a first-generation Italian immigrant who was delighted to practice his native tongue again with Karsch, happy to show him around the property, and moreover asked him, over impeccable cocktails, to send his greetings to his relatives near... He even had two of his bodyguards accompany the guest to a PATH station for the train to New York; along the way, the bodyguards decided to fleece this European a little, for their own benefit for once, and they detained him for two days, as politely as one could wish, in the back room of a Newark barbershop. It was basically ridiculous, filling the role of victim of a sideline of two foot soldiers, and things got a little wobbly only when the bodyguards realized that if this foreigner told their boss they had gone against orders, it might pose a risk to them. All the same, two days in the position of someone getting a shave was still ridiculous. Karsch was rescued from this situation by the third child.

The paragraph on this child—which he hadn't even marked—does not describe the child's appearance. It says only that the child, another girl, was a fourth grader who couldn't believe that a grown man could care more about how embarrassing his situation was than about what had caused it. The girl had told this correspondent that he couldn't have avoided the incident even if he had been carrying a gun. The correspondent was completely cured of the romanticism of the crime thanks to the child's behavior. He understood in the end that the child didn't want his thanks; solidarity fared better when simply noticed.

– *A tua disposizione, Fanta Giro*: the article ends.

– I don't mind if he calls us again: Marie says.

December 2, 1967 Saturday
Yesterday Lord Russell's tribunal for war crimes in Vietnam, seated in Roskilde, near Copenhagen, found the USA guilty on all charges, including

genocide, use of forbidden weapons, maltreatment and killing of prisoners, violence against prisoners, and forced movement of prisoners, and also aggression against Laos and Cambodia.

Jean-Paul Sartre, a member of the international tribunal at Roskilde, has already punished the USA once—refusing an invitation to the country two and a half years ago because its government was waging a war in Vietnam. Sartre's reasoning made every foreigner traveling to or living in the USA an accomplice.

In 1933, the Italian state railroad system lowered its prices by 70 percent to attract foreign tourists to the country and to an Exhibition of the Fascist Revolution. Sartre bought himself cheap tickets and visited Pisa, Florence, Bologna, Venice, Milan, Orvieto, Rome, and other cities. In Rome, the philosopher satisfied the requirement for buying the tickets and paid a visit to the Exhibition of the Fascist Revolution, taking a look at the glass cases displaying the revolvers and rubber truncheons of the "Fascist martyrs."

Back then, Sartre used to read the newspapers "not well but assiduously." In the fall of 1933, he went to Germany and spent a year at the Institut Français in Berlin.

The winter of 1933 was not a good time for Cresspahl to settle into Jerichow. Back then bricklayers didn't yet know how to work in cold temperatures, and he could tell that his daughter's property wouldn't be ready to live and work in until next spring at the earliest. Yes, he was with his wife again under one roof, but that roof was atop Papenbrock's house.

On the other hand, the separation from her had been good for triggering the process by which deprivation and longing scrape and retouch and paint the remembered image of the other person until anticipation suppresses everything inconvenient and the desirable qualities and behaviors are so firmly in mind that the dream can occlude the reality of the other person for days on end; for Lisbeth the separation had been maybe a bit too long. True, he'd arrived in Jerichow at an hour when everyone was already asleep, and his knocking on Papenbrock's door might have sounded like someone bringing bad news, but why was she totally unable to recover from the shock, unable to stop crying, until Louise Papenbrock brought her back to bed? Old man Papenbrock had been ready to keep Cresspahl and two bottles of Rotspon company until the wee hours of the next morning, with pleasure; to Cresspahl it seemed that she wanted to put off being alone with him. Her behavior made it seem like his arrival was something she'd been dreading, now come to pass. He had tried to forget that first night, and by the next morning he saw what he was hoping to see, and her way of looking at him, teasingly, head to one side, fit so seamlessly shadowlessly into his expectations that he once again thought to himself that yes, he would make an honest go of life here in this Jerichow. But then it bothered him to have the child referred to again and again as "your daughter," in a tone of voice that implied something besides what he could see. Nor could he always tell what it was that sent her so unexpectedly from a fun-loving mood into gloomy brooding; he asked her once, and her answer had been almost a reprimand: she had no idea what gloominess in her face he was referring to, she said, and he didn't ask again. Sometimes, too, she was so moody, touchy, impatient that he looked at her to see if she could stand to hear about Elizabeth Trowbridge. He put it off until later, reluctantly.

Whats wrong, Lisbeth.
What do you mean whats wrong, Cresspahl.
I wish youd cheer up.

The child. The child's face was red from all the beets she was eating. When she was full she was friendly to everybody. The child seemed to know every person in the house and accepted Cresspahl as another one. The child bleated her squished throaty noises as excitedly on Papenbrock's lap as on his. When the child was brought in to the grown-ups it was Papenbrock who walked her up and down the room and made sure that nothing colored blue was in sight, since the child thought anything blue was the Delftware bowl she was fed from. Everyone had their routine with the child; Cresspahl could only look on. When the child was alone she put one hand next to her head and turned her head toward the hand and observed her hand and moved it and curled it up and tried to understand what it was and why it was doing what it was doing. Cresspahl sometimes stood there and watched the child and waited to see if the child would turn toward him. But he had come into the room too quietly, and no one-to-one discussion ever quite got under way.

Old Papenbrock was somewhat confused. It wasn't easy for him to make his way among the new things and new words being sent down from Berlin to Jerichow: the Reichsnährstand set up to regulate food production, the State Hereditary Farm Law, the Winter Relief Program. In every law from Hitler's government he found something to object to, though they did have their reasonable side too. He thought it was a practical idea not to allow entailed farms to be divided or mortgaged, while also pointing out that the eldest son was not always the best farmer, and that for him there had never been loans without collateral. As for the Winter Relief Program collections, Papenbrock found it quite humane what the Austrian had to say about fellow members of the German people suffering from hunger; Papenbrock did not, though, feel that he had done anything to cause that hunger, and to be honest it went against his conscience when he finally coughed up a five-mark coin so as not to look bad. He still hadn't gotten over the fact that the new government had killed an actual governor of Mecklenburg-Schwerin; he decided that just maybe the Reich government had done so unknowingly. For in the end, though worried, he had attended the memorial service for Johannes Stelling, had shown himself quite openly there in his black suit, and had they come and arrested him? Had they dared to even warn him, an officer in the First World War and a pillar of the economic system? By no means, my dear Cresspahl. These are people who know what's what, after all. And in terms of property rights there was nothing to worry about now. This Hitler had announced the conclusion of his National Socialist revolution on June 6, hadn't he. So that was that. Not such a big deal. You probably couldn't see that so clearly from England.

Louise had fixed up what was basically a self-contained apartment for the Cresspahl family in the part of the building that had been a gabled house of its own before Papenbrock had bought it because he needed the storage space in its attic. There were two rooms with three windows looking out onto Station Street, and a room for the child with a window and a door onto the balcony on the garden side. Louise didn't entirely manage to respect her daughter's new rights and dignities, though, and was liable during a meal to send Lisbeth to fetch something she'd forgotten, and Lisbeth would stand up from the table like a child. The first time, Cresspahl let her go. The second time, Papenbrock noticed and called for the maid.

Lisbeth's sister, Hilde, was still at the Papenbrocks', waiting to see whether her Alexander would find his bourgeois footing once more. When the sisters were together Hilde wasn't like she'd been in March. She was still the more self-assured of the two, carefree, lively, even-tempered, but she didn't pay much attention to Cresspahl. She succeeded more than once in bringing the conversation back around to the mayoral election next October and attributing to Alexander Paepcke the necessary abilities, if no more. Then old Papenbrock would tense up his face, disgusted and amused, so you could read from the tip of his nose what he didn't want to say out loud to Paepcke's charitable wife. Maybe he liked that Hilde was gradually coming to see Alexander's clients' "missing" funds and his burned-down brickworks as something amusing, in any case long since forgotten. Here Papenbrock had not fulfilled one of his daughter's wishes. Paepcke in charge of the Jerichow city treasury—that made Cresspahl laugh too, as long as it didn't actually happen.

Papenbrock could have been. For Papenbrock had his finger in more than one pie when it came to Jerichow city planning. He'd spoken up in a public council meeting to say that the town should be developed to the south and the west, not up where Dr. Erdamer had proposed and pushed through a neighborhood of single-family houses but down at the other end, on the other side of the railway line, away from town, where up until now the land had been used by townsman-farmers, as well as on Brickworks Road, which petered out into nothing past the brickworks villa. – Once this street is built up and the Bäk is built up too and they're connected, Jerichow will have a complete western ring road! Papenbrock had cried. Past the Cresspahl property Brickworks Road was just sand, and where it met the Bäk there was also nothing but sand, and the houses on the Bäk stood at a good and proper distance from the intersection. Since the councilmen had already decided against the development of Granary Street, the workmen soon got busy on Brickworks Road and tore it up and laid gas pipes under it. The pipes stopped behind Cresspahl's barn. Lisbeth had grown used to cooking with gas in Richmond, and Papenbrock wanted to make his daughter's life that much easier, especially if the town was paying for it. (Actually, two-thirds of the gasworks belonged to the neighboring nobility, but Papenbrock had presented it to them as though they would pay only a third of the construction costs at most.) Cresspahl didn't like it. Papenbrock saw only the profit in it; in his scheming he'd overlooked that he was thereby taking his son-in-law's business into his own hands, making it look as though Cresspahl were unable to fend for himself.

Cresspahl had a hard time putting down roots in Jerichow. It wasn't that the terrain was all that different from around Malchow—a little colder, barer, relatively treeless. It wasn't that he was an outsider—he'd been an outsider in Malchow, too. In the Netherlands too, in England too. He had no need to know who was living behind every window, the way Lisbeth did. Foreignness had always been good for him, if not always to him. But something was missing here. Was it that the town was so small, so alone on the wide flat countryside? Was it Avenarius Kollmorgen, with his indefatigably reiterated "All's well, Herr Cresspahl?" and his conspiratorial facial expressions meant to allude to enormous reserves of secret knowledge? Was it life in the house of, obeying the rules and habits of, Albert Papenbrock? Was it that here you had to raise your right arm when you saw someone walking down the street with a flag?

All December long Cresspahl kept thinking about what to do if someone here should try to give him an earful. He thought he'd decided to pick Lisbeth and the child up under his arm and leave the country. He thought that's what he would do.

Then it was Christmas.

December 3, 1967 Sunday

"QUOTATION OF THE DAY: 'Cardinal Francis J. Spellman, Archbishop of New York, has passed away on this day at St. Vincent's Hospital at 11:45 a.m. May he rest in peace.' Message sent over the Police Department teletype.

. . .

The spokesman said that the Cardinal earlier had been feeling fine and had even discussed the possibility of going off again to Vietnam for Christmas visits to American troops there.

. . .

The Cardinal's brick and mortar, valued at more than a half-billion dollars, was spread over an archdiocese of 4,717 square miles. This includes

Staten Island, Manhattan and the Bronx in New York City plus Westches-
ter, Putnam, Dutchess, Orange, Rockland, Sullivan and Ulster Counties.

. . .

The Cardinal traveled hundreds of thousands of miles, many of them
as the head of the Military Ordinariate. This was, in effect, a second archdiocese that extended all over the world, wherever American troops were
stationed. Beginning with World War II, the Cardinal visited training
camps, fleets at sea, air forces at their bases, fighting fronts.

. . .

The Cardinal was a gregarious man, at home with a great variety of
persons. This characteristic puzzled some of his friends, who could not
understand how he could enjoy, seemingly equally, the company of a serious intellectual and that of a fun-loving, yacht-owning lawyer.

. . .

He enjoyed listening to songs, Irish ballads in particular. A favorite was
'Danny Boy,' and a monsignor on his staff, possessed of a good tenor, was
often called upon to sing it and other sentimental lilts.

. . .

But what was memorable amid the opulence of the Cardinal's garb was
his face. It was round, benign, shining, almost cherubic. The forehead was
high, the ears large, the nose a mite pointed, and the dark blue eyes peering
through old-fashioned rimless spectacles, were steady. The face conveyed
a sense of cheerfulness that even long hours of ceremony rarely seemed to
dull.

. . .

His father had a dry wit. 'Son,' he used to tell the boy, 'always associate
with people smarter than yourself, and you will have no difficulty finding
them.'

. . . when he traveled to South Vietnam at Christmas time. Addressing
American troops, he asserted: 'This war in Vietnam is, I believe, a war for
civilization.' He went on to say that 'less than victory is inconceivable.'

. . .

The President, recalling the Cardinal's visits to South Vietnam at Christmas, said that his 'grace of goodness touched all manner of men and nations.''

© The New York Times

"PUBLISHERS COMPETING FOR THE RIGHTS TO CHE GUEVARA'S DIARIES
Ernesto Che Guevara, the Latin-American revolutionary who published only one book during his lifetime, has posthumously become the center of a literary struggle.

Since the Bolivian Government announced on Oct. 9 Mr. Guevara's death and the capture of his campaign diaries, a number of American and European publishers have been competing for international rights to the documents.

. . .

Negotiations for world rights to Mr. Guevara's Bolivian diary are under way between Magnum Photos Inc. and the Bolivian Government. The Government claims ownership of the manuscript on the ground that the diary is a 'captured war document.'

Magnum, a cooperative of internationally known news photographers, began the talks six weeks ago in La Paz on behalf of a consortium that includes The New York Times. The price offered for the diary was reported by reliable sources to be about $125,000."
© The New York Times

"MANILA NEWSMAN FINDS REGIME IN HANOI IS FATALISTIC ON THE WAR
At cock's crow every weekday, factory and office workers in Hanoi assemble in courtyards for 15 minutes of calisthenics.

This ritual is one of the war, which, according to offi-
is bracing its people for what their leaders call the 'supreme sacrifice' of a long war.

There is little question that the North Vietnamese have conditioned themselves for such a war, which, according to official Hanoi predictions, may last 10 to 20 years.

Planners in Hanoi tend toward the most pessimistic and fatalistic estimates. When North Vietnamese leaders talk about a 'protracted war,' they take into account the complete leveling of their cities, including the capital and the nearby port of Haiphong."
© The New York Times

THE 20TH CENTURY MAKES FINAL RUN

"The Twentieth Century Limited, known to railroad buffs for 65 years as the world's greatest train, pulled out of Grand Central Terminal for the last time last night. There was no fanfare and the train was only half full.

...

At exactly 6 p.m., Herbert P. Stevens, a brakeman, signaled the highball, and the historic train slid down Track 34. 'It won't be the same,' he said. 'I've been with the line for 42 years, and with this train for 10. We'll all miss it.'

Among the passengers there was a sprinkling of mink stoles and sparkle. Older men and women who rode the Twentieth Century in its heyday were a little sad. As usual, carnations were given to the men boarding the train, and perfume and flowers to the women."

© The New York Times

December 4, 1967 Monday

When Guevara the revolutionary was dead, his murderers lashed him to the landing sled of their helicopter and flew him to Valle Grande.

The cardinal who loved the war is lying in state in an open coffin in St. Patrick's Cathedral in *The New York Times*.

Yesterday it rained from early morning through late afternoon. The snow has been washed away.

Yesterday I gave dying a try.

The dream knew the day of my death in advance, whether by calculation or prophecy. I did have a hard time waking up, but I could recognize the sounds in the apartment on the street and of the elevator outside our door. You would have to put a coffin into the elevator tipped upright.

You have to put your papers in order before the burial. You don't wash on a day like this. I was so busy planning that Marie had to call my name twice before I helped with the coffin. Marie seemed to be carrying the heavier end. We slowly, laboriously put the box on a folding cot that was suddenly there in front of the door, put it under the soft brown blanket. The coffin was so heavy that I could have been in it myself, but since I was carrying it from the outside, and could see Marie at the other end, I was only a little nervous.

The straightening up consisted of organizing large clippings from newspapers, mostly pictures. The clippings were dated by hand, and as each one was set aside it had to be put to the left, facedown, to preserve the sequence in reverse. This was happening in a room that the apartment hadn't had before: on the side, behind the long wall of the living room. In the living room people were moving around, there were footsteps and conversations, enough of a disturbance to make me mess up five pages. As I retraced my missteps in the papers, I saw a young man wearing the uniform of an American sergeant in the doorway on the displaced sofa. I didn't know him. His wife was next to him, a frizzy-haired brown-eyed woman with crazy lips who maybe I had gone to school with, not in Jerichow; what bothered me was something Marie said from behind the sofa.

– Should I wrap you in a blanket?

Now I could see the dead woman on the guest cot, a shorter and thinner figure than in real life, in a limp and helpless position, her head already half wrapped in hair. The figure was wearing a brown dress I didn't recognize. I've never liked wearing brown.

I knew the next thought but I just couldn't think it: I was dead, ever since I'd heard the elevator if not longer, probably since the night before last. I could still tell that much. But now I had to go view the body before I lost all my strength, and be the body.

The child told me to get to work. Marie was standing at the gray window, in the morning, at dawn, and holding up a handkerchief by both ends to block the meager light. The handkerchief was strangely square and unusually bright. I went and stood carefully behind her. Pictures appeared on a radiant patch of light between Marie's fingers—never before seen, never before photographed, in cold, precise colors:

Lisbeth Cresspahl in her coffin

Lisbeth Papenbrock, six years old, with long hair, lying as though floating, in profile

the barn before it burned down

a chicken pecking off a strawberry from beneath

the Baltic from a very fast very long flyover

the corner ripped out of the Empire State Building

but you weren't allowed to want anything, or tilt or otherwise move the handkerchief, or say anything.

– Give me the handkerchief, Marie.

She turned around. It was someone I didn't know, half a head taller than me, with long, sand-gray hair. Her face was in shadow. She folded the handkerchief up and politely pressed it into my hand. It felt soft and dirty, like a rag for cleaning, and it left marks on my hands and gradually got warm and it was the blanket I was being carried in. It wasn't unpleasant.

What remains today is the feeling of being carried and the numbness. Sometimes I had to tell myself things: This is what people call a candelabra, this is a fire alarm, Marie's geography notebook, the number 5 bus. Then it was all right again. On the north corner of Forty-Second Street and Third Avenue the rain is allowed to form ankle-deep puddles, so that many thousands of people have to swerve around them onto a part of the street that the red lights have cleared of car traffic, surely that is well known. The way one crowds to the right at the same spot every evening, at the entrance to the Flushing line, submits anxiously to the blast of air through the swinging doors, lines up in the lane into which the crowd enters three steps before the turnstiles, the way one then pivots left toward the stairs, the way once you get down to the platform you push ahead to the exact center of the newsstand, at the front door of the very train car that will stop two stops later exactly across from the foot of the staircase that leads to the West Side line, surely that is well known. That the IRT platforms seem emptier on Wednesday mornings than on other days is known. That the IND platforms at Fifty-Ninth Street being more crowded in the morning than in the evening is due to the people who work in the Garment District in the Thirties and have to punch in, anyone can figure that out. That Riverside Drive makes an *S* outside our building, with an infinite worm of light creeping toward us on it, has been thought so many times.

The lamp illuminating the main entrance seems new.

December 5, 1967 Tuesday

US DEFECTOR IN MOSCOW IS PICTURED AS A PARANOID IN WIFE'S TESTIMONY IN FLORIDA DIVORCE CASE

ENEMY BATTALION SMASHED IN TRAP
WEEK OF PROTEST AGAINST THE DRAFT STARTED
SCHOOL HEAD TURNS IN SON ON $81,000 BANK THEFT
FIRES KILL 9TH CHILD IN CITY IN 36 HOURS
BROOKLYN DRUGGIST IS KILLED IN ROBBERY
DEAL FOR A WITNESS IN FRANZESE TRIAL
MADRID STUDENTS RESUME RIOTING

By December 1933, it was already being said around Jerichow that this Cresspahl was a stubborn bastard.

No sooner arrived from England than he'd retreated from the eyes of Jerichow to the property he'd wheedled out of old Papenbrock and went to work on his barn. Came out of Papenbrock's house bright and early in the morning, showed his face in Market Square, and disappeared. Instead of turning onto Town Street, now called Adolf-Hitler-Street, he'd go the long way, past the school, down the Bäk to the end, then back again on Brickworks Road. Never came to Wulff's pub in the evening now, didn't stop to talk in the market, who knew what was on his mind.

Some were saying that the Cresspahls' marriage wasn't exactly hand in glove after all. No sooner'd the husband gotten his barn windproof than he started sleeping there, with his wife still under Papenbrock's roof. Then again, they said they'd do the same if they'd had their tools stolen one quiet night, like had happened to Cresspahl. Just sayin'.

To which others said you had only to look at them. Look how Lisbeth comes out Papenbrock's front door every day at noon with that covered basket of hers and carries it like a maid down Town Street, uh, Adolf-Hitler-Street. She could let Edith do it, couldn't she. But she doesn't, she wants to watch her husband eat, the way a wife should too. People said, in fact Inge Schnürmann had seen it one morning, with her own two eyes too, that Cresspahl would stop by Semig's house on the way to work and that the two of them would drive down the Bäk in Semig's new car, the few steps to the brickworks. Could Arthur be teaching him how to drive? He already knew how to drive. Was it possible that an educated and licensed veterinarian felt like joining Cresspahl in his construction work? No, impossible! But Cresspahl had put a new door in the gate opening onto the road, sturdy as a church door, enough to break even the hardest knife, and he made up for the loss of light by putting glass panes in the southern gate, just where someone taking a walk would be noticed and asked to explain his business. That was a bit much. That wasn't real nice. Especially since there'd be two people standing there staring at you, Cresspahl and Arthur Semig.

That's why people were also saying that this Cresspahl was a British spy, out to get Führer and Reich Chancellor Hitler. Others said that His Royal British Majesty George V was no Jew and was close friends with the Austrian. And anyway, Cresspahl had gotten in touch with the woodworkers guild in Gneez and registered in the guild rolls in Schwerin, it said so right in the papers. Well, there's a lot that the newspapers are saying. Some people didn't buy it and thought it more likely that Cresspahl was building an enemy radio transmitter so he could talk to his English buddies at night. Why else would he mount all that wire on the barn roof? It wasn't your usual lightning rod. Just the other day, two rolls of wire had arrived for him at the station. Why would someone need that much wire, it's radio, I'm telling you. Nah. He needs it for a fence so that you can't get too close when you want to throw a rock through his windows. Okay, okay, I'm not talking about anyone in the room. Anyway, that Cresspahl's a stubborn bastard.

Just replaces the panes himself, with his own hands. No way he'll give another tradesman the chance to earn a little money unless he has to. What was Heine Freese, Jerichow's glazier, supposed to do? He didn't get any work but still had to sell the glass to Cresspahl, to make at least that much. Go ask the painters, ask Köpcke the building contractor, they'll tell you straight out they haven't made a penny off him. Does it all himself. He can do it all himself. You'd do the same thing. I would too. And it's not like he's watching his money because he doesn't have any. Käthe Klupsch knew for a fact that young Mrs. Cresspahl had been looking at an electric refrigerator on King Street in Schwerin. Santo they're called, keep a temperature around forty degrees. Well Käthe Klupsch was just jealous; no husband for her, never landed one. Now Methfessel needed a refrigerator, anyone can see that. But even Louise Papenbrock got along fine without one. Cresspahl probably bought the thing to be nice to his wife. Next thing you know your own wife'll be coming to you asking for English nonsense like that! Aside from that, he'd put more work into his workshop than into his house so far. He didn't want people to see the kind of money he had in these terrible times, economically I mean!, he wanted to show that he needed business. Well, Elsa'd tried, she'd taken her aunt's old sewing cabinet to him, heirloom you know, not much left of it anyway. Not to help Cresspahl out, she was just curious. And he shows up with Semig's flatbed truck and carries it into the house and you could knock her over backwards with a feather! He'd turned it into a jewel! If you saw it in a shopwindow you'd be sad how you couldn't afford it. How much did Cresspahl charge? Oh, not too much. It was fair. But delivering it right into the house! That's no good. Suppose I went around to everyone's house delivering the shoes I'd repaired! Corrupts the morals, practically. But the chests, you've got to admit, those chests he'd made for the move he could have sold them on the spot in the station freight room the way they looked. Just beautiful. They'd go right in your front parlor. Paint em and put em in the parlor. You know what, Cresspahl'll paint em for you himself and charge you ten marks and put em in your parlor for you.

Stubborn bastard, that Cresspahl. Somethin sneaky about him! The minute you hear his furniture's come from England Swenson's already drove it out to him, in a closed truck too, on a sunny April day! Cresspahl mustve told him to. He'd had to let an electrician into his house, he had no choice, and thats all very well for Johannes Schmidt but really, he couldve taken a better look around now couldn he! Comes back sayin the walls are painted plain white and Cresspahls probably leavin the wallpaper for later and the furnitures a bit new-looking, the whole place doesnt look lived-in yet. That Johannes, no eyes in his head. And one fine May morning here comes Lisbeth out of Papenbrocks house, with Cresspahl, and Cresspahl has the kid innis arm ands wearing his Sunday best and this time they do go down Town—I'm saying downtown, not down Town Street, otherwise I'da said Adolf-Hitler-Street now wouldnt I!—and by lunchtime theyre still not back and the kid isnt back and thats all you ever saw of the move! Now they live there. Now he's there.

And they said he did it alone, without Papenbrock's help. Papenbrock had other things on his mind. You heard what Hilde Papenbrock, Hilde Paepcke, got for Christmas and for the baby, dincha? Right, the brickworks lease. You got it. He's a Papenbrock, looks after his kids. Had a leg up on us. Not a soul knew the brickworks lease was up, and while we're all whis-tling in the breeze Papenbrock pays a visit and talks his way into what he wants. Paepcke, Hilde's husband, he'd gotten himself into some trouble. Well, no jail no foul. Just you wait. Just wait till the brickworks burns down in Jerichow too. I didn't say anything. I didn't hear him say anything. Heil Hitler. Piss off. Sometimes Papenbrock does things like that just for fun, take it from me. Well, there's always something in it for him. But the gas line under Brickworks Road, he woulda gotten it next year anyway without having to work for it like that. He only did it so Friedrich Jansen would know the score, he might be mayor and head of the local party and a law-school dropout but Papenbrock's Papenbrock. Even now. Damn right. Always will be. Jansen probably didn't even realize he'd been steamrollered. He's got plenty of other things to worry about. Nah. Yes sirree. He knows we know we're doing Jansen Senior Esquire in Gneez a favor by letting his dropout son be mayor, and mayor of Jerichow, that'll probably be Pappy Jansen's last try for him. Yeah, Friedrich Jansen is a party veteran, member since '27, that's why we elected him, but we also remember him as a little boy standing on one leg in Gneez Park not daring to go home because he'd done it in his pants. And now he's after you like the devil, going after the poor city employees for their questionnaires about Aryan ancestry and not a single damn fool'd finished filling it out. Stoffregen was pissing his pants. Stoffregen, that doesn't sound Aryan. It sound Aryan to you? Stoffregen. Lucky for him Kliefoth knew. That Kliefoth. What Clay-Foot? Kliefoth, Dr. Kliefoth, the English teacher, the guy who bought Erdamer's house, Berlin, no, Malchow actually, that's where he's from I mean, he's teaching at the Gneez high school now, takes the train every morning. That one. Oh, him. So he hears about it and goes to see Stoffregen and tells him. And Stoffregen, Ottje, he shouldda known it himself don't you think, he's a teacher too isn he, and everyone wonders about their own name dont they? Not me. Yeah no kidding, Hünemörder, you wouldnt. So Dr. Kliefoth tells Ottje: It's Middle Low German, used to be pronounced with a long *o*, comes from *stôven*, speeding past, refers to the weather when he was born. Easy-peasy. Middle Low German is Aryan, so now Ottje's Aryan again. No, Stoffregen can't thank Kliefoth for it. That's not the whole story! Think about it! What does "Stoffregen" mean now! You won't guess. A round on me for anyone who can guess. Well? "Cloudburst." That's what it means, a sudden downpour, *Platzregen*. See what I mean? Ottje Suddenshower. And with a name like that he went chasing after Lisbeth Papenbrock, wanted to marry her. Lisbeth Stoffregen. Lisbeth Suddenshower, I don't know, I dont like it. Good thing she went for that Cresspahl. Lisbeth Cresspahl, that's all right then.

That's what people were saying, and that's how they were saying it.

The New York Times puts a picture on her front page, under the dateline, of the young people who sat down yesterday morning on the sidewalk outside the army induction center. She did not choose a moment when the police were standing in front of the sitters with friendlier looks on their faces. She has specially made a drawing of where in the city the protest took place. Anyone who wants to go to the one today can find the location with the help of *The New York Times*. That probably wasn't her intention.

In Springfield, Missouri, there is a former Secret Service agent, Abraham W. Bolden, who claims he was sent to prison because he'd wanted to tell the Warren Commission on the Assassination of President Kennedy that the Secret Service knew about the planned murder attempt before it happened.

Twenty-five years hard labor for a GI who pleads guilty to spying for the Soviets. Nikolai Fedorovich Popov of the UN, to whom the sergeant was worth spending $1,000 on, has long since left the United States.

The court in Queens still can't prove that Sonny Franzese was there when The Hawk Rupolo was loaded down with blocks of cement and dropped into Jamaica Bay. He was not even present when his three friends took The Hawk, still alive, out of the trunk of their car in the rear parking lot of the Skyway Motel near Kennedy Airport and snuffed the screaming man with four last plunges of a knife.

What sorts of things did Cresspahl want from 1934?

That there be some truth in the lore that mosquitoes don't go near walnut trees. He'd realized there were two walnut trees in front of his house, and somewhere without mosquitoes would be good for the child, wouldn't it. The child could sleep with the windows open, later.

That Lisbeth would stop scaring him. She was impossible to understand sometimes. When he went to take care of the old stove in the house, tear it out, she'd wanted to keep it. Denied ever wanting a gas stove. She could say such confused things, like: If we're not in England we shouldn't have things the way they are in England. He didn't like that, it wasn't clear. Was she sorry she'd made the family leave England? Or happy? Now they had a gas line to the house and never used it except to run the refrigerator.

That Lisbeth would start telling him again what was going on in her mind. She had a way of shutting her face up so tight that it looked furious, and you couldn't reach her. And she'd gotten into the habit of standing at the stove for several minutes at a time, staring into the flames. He didn't care about the wood being wasted in the open burners; the thing was she clearly didn't know why she was doing it, or when she was doing it, or that she was doing it. When he came into the kitchen she'd move like someone just waking up. She'd give a start, put the kettle she'd had in her hand the whole time on the fire, and turn to Cresspahl with a little shake of her head and a smile, meant to chide her own behavior.

He wanted her smile in some other situation, any other situation, not in front of the fire. He wanted her to always be the way she was when, as the younger sister but experienced mother, she gave Hilde advice about how to handle her baby, Ulrike. It was such a funny way she had, using just the outward form of teasing, conveying things it's impossible to put into words.

He wanted her to go back to not being so sensitive. A bucket put down too hard, a door that the wind slammed shut, and she acted like she was being shot at. If she felt someone was looking at her coldly then a cold look was what it would always remain, no reassurance or explanations made a difference, she rejected them all. It took her half the day to recover. And now that they'd moved as close to the church as it was possible to live, praying didn't seem to help her either. He wanted her to be the girl he'd known on the spot he wanted to marry.

> *There's plenty a man who sings with pride*
> *When brought to him is his new bride.*
> *If he really knew what they were bringing*
> *He'd likely cry instead of singing.*

That everything would turn out all right.

Cresspahl wanted to get back to the point, and soon, where he could live off income instead of savings. He needed new machines, too. He'd acquired from Heinz Zoll a milling machine, a combination planer and jointer, a band saw, a slot driller, and a table saw, all in the same shape—the planer was really the only one he'd have anything nice to say about. And they hadn't been cheap. And he couldn't get good use out of them. Who in Jerichow in 1934 was going to order a new bedroom set, a dining table? A stepladder at most. And this Kliefoth from Malchow had actually thought you had to go to Wismar to get a good desk. He'd have liked to make him a desk. On the other hand, the orders couldn't come pouring in too fast either because the assistants from the guild didn't work the way Cresspahl was used to, and he couldn't ask too much of the apprentices. It was hard to believe, but just try to find a good woodworking assistant. It's no problem to find a master, but a master employed by another master, that never works out. Sometimes he secretly wanted to bring Mr. Smith to Jerichow. True, Mr. Smith might be a bit dull-headed some mornings, from his gin or vermouth, but once he'd sweated the alcohol out the work practically did itself under his hands, and you didn't need to check it, much less fix it.

He couldn't hope to make a name for himself in Mecklenburg. He couldn't hope for a business like Kröpelin's in Bützow, Strobelberger's in Rostock, Schmidt's in Güstrow, Liesberg's in Schwerin—neither the income nor the reputation. This backwater couldn't support it. He would have to go on for some time making the kind of furniture you could buy at the department stores. No chance to practice the art of woodworking, no way. All he wanted was to get along in this Germany and stay in one piece.

He wanted Papenbrock to keep Louise at home. At least if she could come over to his and to Hilde's houses only for the children! But she came to spread her pious sayings. For each and every injustice, she knew a biblical injunction to patience and a promise of eventual rectification through the workings of God's justice. Such homilies left Lisbeth calm and composed, so happy and serene that you couldn't believe it would last; it didn't last. All it did was help her not listen when he told her the name of the person who'd committed one these "injustices" of hers, and approximately how much profit he'd turned doing it. But in this respect Papenbrock let his wife do whatever she wanted.

Cresspahl wanted his brother-in-law, Paepcke, not to get up to any mischief with that brickworks lease of his. A friendly guy, a good neighbor, but no businessman, Paepcke. His books were in a state that would make your hair stand on end. It was entertaining, of course, the way Alexander would gather his family around him on the lawn, sometimes right after lunch, and while away the livelong afternoon until evening, drinking coffee under colorful sun umbrellas, then Mosel. He played with his child— Cresspahl had never had that much time with his. And the brick workers only needed to walk past the gate and look across the street to see their boss's work ethic. That didn't bother Alexander one bit. He would go to Gneez for a game of tennis. And when Cresspahl put up a new flagpole for him, he wanted to pay for it. It was only right to offer money among relatives but not to insist on paying. Alexander should have saved the money. That never crossed his mind. It was nice to watch the two of them, living as carefree as children; it was troubling that they'd already forgotten how desperate their situation was before Papenbrock saved them. Cresspahl wanted, in other words, not to see the brickworks suddenly go up in flames.

He wished the Jerichowers would just tell him what they wanted from him, in words, not in stones thrown through his workshop windows.

He wished Dora and Arthur would come to their senses and leave the country. He was now almost close friends with Arthur, to the extent that one could be with an educated man, and if Arthur wasn't an honest-to-God Mecklenburger then he himself wasn't a Malchow man. He didn't want Arthur to leave. It's just that he should go live among people who had nothing against him, and who'd give him work. It wasn't nice seeing Semig shriveling up without work to do, like blighted wheat. And Dora was getting quieter and quieter, she was herself only when holding Gesine in her arms. He wanted them to be safe. He couldn't tell them that.

He wanted to be wrong about the war he saw coming.

He wanted the three more children he and Lisbeth had agreed on.

He wanted all his children to live until after he died.

He wanted his family to be safe from economic hardship, political danger, fire, and lightning.

And that is why, in early June 1934, he went to the Jerichow town hall and asked Friedrich Jansen for an application form to join the Nazi Party.

And the following day, Avenarius Kollmorgen buttonholed him at the freight window at the station, arched wrinkles onto his brow the way a cat arches its back, and nodded, significantly, and said, with the smile he considered a delicate one: *All's well, Häärr Cresspahl? All's well?*

December 7, 1967 Thursday

Since going back to Jerichow is not allowed, the dream has to invent a relative in Wismar, a lie, and the dream has to brazenly lie wooden stairs, worn down from all the rain, into the passport office, in a courtyard with wild vines on the walls. Anyone who knows this courtyard must have relatives there. Then it no longer matters that it's forbidden to leave the Wismar district. You just go with some dead person or another. The best would be Pius Pagenkopf: when he was alive, he was a general in the Soviet Air Force and drove an old Studebaker from the Lend-Lease Act with the USA. Driving in an old Studebaker down Town Street in Jerichow: people will stop and shake their heads. Then all you can do is hurry to take refuge in the cemetery. Nobody'll find me at the cemetery.

So, off we go. The bus from Rostock to Barth is empty, but I've never ridden that route and now really it's going to Newark through the Hudson Tunnel. At Newark Airport the plane is standing there all by itself, far out on the runway, alone, and it's about to start. I have a feeling it's called TRANSALL ILYUSHIN. Sitting in the plane on fish crates are down-and-out men in crocheted Norwegian sweaters. When the plane banks after takeoff, one of them leans over to me and, as I recognize him, he says: Gesine, don't be like that. Don't act like such a stranger. You're just as doomed to crash as us.

– What about the pilot?

– It was his choice. They left it up to him. In the sky he can freely decide for himself. But that's nothing to do with us.

December 8, 1967 Friday

Dear Marie. I'll tell your tape about today.

This morning a man was slumped against the wall in the elevator, totally limp, and after the cabin had hurtled fifty feet through the building he woke up a little and said to me with a kind of amazement "Gee-sign," and I addressed him with his title, to wake him up. But he still couldn't recall that he was the boss in control of a significant portion of the American millions, and in this defenseless state another of his underlings ambushed him with the question of how he'd liked his picture in *The New York Times*.

365 Friday · 365

For de Rosny had let *The New York Times* photograph him at home. – That's real fame, getting onto the women's page: he said, and he probably lay right down on the carpet behind his padded doors and went back to sleep.

Forty-five minutes later one of the vice president's secretaries called me. We've been invited to dinner. I was ready to accept right away but she is so used to fitting de Rosny into the most various times and places that she insisted on offering me three possible dates to negotiate over.

The New York Times has a description of how the president came to the city in secret to visit the dead cardinal: in his airplane to Floyd Bennett Field and by helicopter to Sheep Meadow in Central Park, so that he'd only be on the city streets for a mile. And he left the cathedral through the back door. The antiwar protestors have accomplished at least that much.

It's hard to tell stories about the office. Life there goes like this: "People whose only job is to initial a checklist, verify the accuracy or the wording of an invoice, can never keep from reviewing the whole procedure in depth, and as a result they leave in the errors they're supposed to catch! Sometimes it's caught in time, but the firm should really have been on the road to ruin a long time ago." You need to picture all this said with pride.

One of the managers, whose way of fulfilling his responsibilities is to make the rounds of the cubicles and individual offices, fills the air with the smell of farts whenever he's called upon to stop and consider something. His goal is to become a vice president someday, and no one can bring themselves to tell him why that will never happen.

In one of the elevator cabins, one of the digits is missing in the building's number set into the floor. That's something you notice, and I still wonder some mornings if maybe I went into the wrong building and only realized it from a glance at the floor. In the corner of the bathroom there's a crack in the caulking an eighth of an inch longer than it was last year. That's something you notice.

Amanda, you know her. You know how she likes to flirt all the time with the men from sales passing through: "Oh, this horrible rainy weather! A *man* doesn't mind of course but we girls can feel things in our hair, practically makes us want to tear it out...!" That's how she talks. She doesn't mean anything by it, and I'm sure she realizes it's nonsense, but she can't help it. And the men stand there at her desk in a total daze and think long and hard about what her words might mean and can't figure it out, and then blame themselves. One of them today slunk off "like a sheep": Amanda said.

At lunch today I saw a construction site filling half a block between Park and Lex. They don't do this in Germany but here they cut windows into the wooden fence for passersby, so the sidewalk supervisors stand there leaning on the fence and looking at the rough plot of land where you can no longer imagine a building, or buildings, standing, except as a canned memory called up by the sign saying a restaurant is moving. Two crane-like cranes, that's why they're the same word in English!, were at work above the rubble field. One of them was lifting two steel-and-concrete staircase parts that ran in opposite directions, still joined at the seams: it let them swing in the air and then dashed them to the ground, and still they weren't broken apart. Maybe that wasn't how it was supposed to go. A topic the men could discuss among themselves. The other crane was lifting a square of T bars the welders had cleanly cut free of the steel framework of a former building at the edge of the field. It swung them off to one side, high above the workers' hard hats. The murdered building's skeleton was almost stripped bare by now. It won't be coming back. After a while, they'll have separated the valuable parts of the wreckage out from the rest, cleared away both, and smoothed the ground flat, and the future will be ready to go.

But I never want to live in Germany again. There's a Nazi Party in West Germany now, and the Nazi Party has organized a goon squad and gives press conferences about it. And the press shows up. The abbreviation for the men keeping order at the event is SG, for *Schutzgemeinschaft*, and the head Nazi cannot understand, absolutely can't for the life of him see why anyone would think that this had anything to do with Hitler's SA, who also started out as security guards. And they're already talking about "bonds of common blood" again, *Blutsverbundenheit* if I'm understanding the English. I wouldn't want to live in Germany ever again.

In the afternoon there were three workmen kneeling and lying on the floor in the bank lobby, one of them almost flat on his belly, smearing some kind of polish on the yellow metal and the base and the belly of the six glass doors (and the kind we used for faucets and nameplates on doors in Jerichow was so proverbial it was like an intrinsic part of life itself, and I've forgotten it. Maybe I forget one second and a drip later all that's left is the interpreted second, which memory fails to catch too). They were rubbing away. There were only three hours left until the end of the workday, when the packed elevators come hurtling down, protesting their heavy loads with anxious creaking. By the time I got downstairs the afternoon's work had already been smudged by eight hundred hands.

Sometimes they cover door-size areas of the lobby's marble with a skin that looks like plaster. Your father would have known exactly what they were doing; I don't even want to ask.

I wanted to tell you about Mrs. Agnolo. Her son is stationed in Saigon as a pilot, and she's counting the days of his year of service in Vietnam. I know because she tells us. She says it so eagerly, without being asked, as if the magic of speaking the words might help her son. She dresses as young as the girls she works with in our secretarial department, and tries to adopt similar behavior, whether casual or chatty, but if you know about her son you can see her age in her face, can see that the makeup isn't doing its job. You can see her sitting at her typewriter not working, occupied with more than just filing her nails.

Last night a package addressed to Cuba blew up in the post-office branch on Ninth Avenue that handles foreign mail. Eight people were injured and other boxes went flying, in one piece or smashed. Be glad you don't get Christmas presents from Europe anymore, so you didn't lose any there.

In the year that I'm saying this into your tape recorder, you were a child proud of things like the fact that more Christmas parcels and packages are delivered in New York than in all of Belgium—as many as in France. For you, New York was the greatest, from the Upper West Side to the Lower East.

There's a picture in *The New York Times* today of the new Madison Square Garden arena, a gigantic oval for 20,000 people under an enormous sky, lit up very festively. The seats are still empty, or not ready yet, and I'm very glad that you will have memories like this from your childhood, and maybe I wish I had some like them for myself.

Then in the subway I saw a Negro boy, eight or ten years old, with a bulky shoeshine box between his legs. He'd fallen asleep on the crowded train, trustingly letting his head drop onto the arm of the lady sitting next to him. So she moved her shoulder forward a little, to support his head.

That's everything I saw today.

December 9, 1967 Saturday

Former vice president Richard M. Nixon suggested in New York that the struggle against racial injustice was more important than the war in Vietnam. "The war in Asia is a limited one with limited means and limited goals," he sez. "The war at home is a war for survival of a free society." Maybe he thinks he'll be getting the presidential nomination from Santa Claus.

Anyone with a soldier in Vietnam can call the Red Cross at 362-0600, and record a three-minute phonopost message for loved ones in the field. And it's free, since it's Christmas.

Yesterday, at Irving Place, Times Square, and Rockefeller Plaza, young people protested against the war. At 45 Rockefeller Plaza, Dow Chemical, the company that makes napalm B, has one of its headquarters. Dow Chemical has absolution from the secretary of defense: private industry, he says, has no influence on how the military uses its products. And in any case, napalm B accounts for only one half of one percent of Dow Chemical's profits. Police with billy clubs "weeded out" the protestors from the Christmas shoppers and tourists, as *The New York Times* sees it. At Rockefeller Plaza, under the giant, the shining, the colorful Christmas tree.

By Christmas of 1934, Lisbeth Cresspahl was long since back in the bosom of the church. She helped out in Sunday school, took part in putting up and decorating the Christmas tree across from the altar. She and Pastor Brüshaver's wife had become close. With her own sister's family living across the street from her, Lisbeth's most neighborly interactions were with Aggie Brüshaver. She crossed Brickworks Road, walked along the fence around the Paepcke property, past the back of Hilde's house, then through Creutz's gate and down the path between his beds and greenhouses to the back gate of the pastor's garden. That was fine with old man Creutz—he liked having dealings with a young lady, a little conversation at least. And Homuth, who'd rented the church land behind the garden, didn't object. The two women were careful and had beaten only a very narrow path along the edge of his field; at least the boys weren't coming for his beets as long as the women were walking there. Cresspahl wasn't concerned. Maybe it did Lisbeth some good to be something like a teacher. Brüshaver had met his second wife in the Rostock hospital where he was getting a second operation on his shoulder injury from the First World War; Aggie had been a deaconess, she knew more about helping in other people's households than managing her own, and at least when it came to cooking she'd learned more from Lisbeth in six months than in the three years during which she'd had to read her success or failure on Brüshaver's face. The husbands were not included in the women's friendship. Cresspahl remembered the other man's education and already had enough formality and stiffness from Arthur Semig; he also wanted nothing to do with anyone in the same line of business as Methling. If Brüshaver felt rejected, he showed it only with a little smile when they met on the street, an amusement that looked a bit secretive. Lisbeth didn't do anything to remedy the situation, because she felt that Brüshaver should remain the pastor, the authority; Aggie thought Cresspahl was a grouch, to be honest, hard to get along with, and also she blamed him whenever Lisbeth had a depressed day. Cresspahl was happy to have the two women in his kitchen; he liked to see Lisbeth cheerful, cooking so eagerly that she brushed her hair from her face with her forearm, or trading stories about their children, Gesine and Aggie's Martin, Mathias, and Marlene. Cresspahl thought: They're talking about children and cooking. And they were too.

But Lisbeth heard from Aggie more about the Protestant Church's conflicts with the Austrian than any other parishioner in or around Jerichow could know. The people listened when Brüshaver preached in his serious, reasonable, boring way, and thought it was very appropriate for him to point out the Christian duty to one's neighbors after the Jew boycott, that was the man's job, that's why he was there and what he was paid to do. It hadn't done Arthur Semig any good, and Brüshaver himself didn't go to Tannebaum's and buy anything there. Lisbeth, though, heard about the church's squabbles with the state in the same tone and level of detail that the pastor and his wife used in discussing events among themselves. She had noticed on her own that Hitler's SA had held Christian services for consecrating the flag or for troop musters, through mid-1933; she knew that Methling had been made SA chaplain with the rank of Sturmbannführer z.b.V. by the SA chief of staff in Berlin, in late 1932. From Aggie, though, she learned that there had been a "dictatorship" in the Evangelical Church of Mecklenburg, since April 1933, when Governor Granzow appointed a state commissioner to put the church administration in Schwerin under police observation. Next Rendtorff, the regional bishop, was driven out of office, and in his place came Schultz, the regional head of the "German Christians," with such a radical Thuringian background that he wanted to perform christenings with soil instead of water, since he, like all the other Nazis, had fogs of "Blood and Soil" in his head; during Holy Communion he actually invoked the Austrian and interpreted the symbolic blood of the Lord as the blood of the martyrs of the Fascist movement. These were not harmless news items for Lisbeth Cresspahl née Papenbrock. The German Christians wanted a single unified Reich Protestant Church, but she didn't want her Evangelical Church of Mecklenburg changed in the slightest, much less dissolved. In January 1934, Brüshaver had read to the congregation the declaration from Niemöller's Pastors' Emergency League: We must obey God more than man. That was the kind of talk that really struck home with this daughter of Louise Papenbrock. Whether it was a question of refusing to fill out the questionnaire with the paragraph about Aryan ancestry or a church wedding taking place under the non-church motto

So far from fear,
To Death so near,
Hail to thee, SA!

or the purity of Gospel message—for her the church was always right. The church must not be slighted. The church was being slighted. In March 1934, Brüshaver was summoned to have a talk with the high consistory in Gneez; Lisbeth heard from Aggie that he had been "given a stern warning" because he'd still refused to withdraw from the Pastors' Emergency League. That was too much for Lisbeth. Her agitations could be happy excitement, when, for instance, it was about a struggle and victory for the right side was assured; her agitations were sometimes more panic-stricken, desperate, when this Austrian's government agencies had no intention of acknowledging their injustice; at still other times they were hysterical, half crazy, such as when she could spend half the day singing one of the Pastors' Emergency League's slogans over and over, to a tune of her own, whether pumping water or peeling potatoes:

One People, One Reich, One Führer, One Fuss

She looked so stupid doing it. Cresspahl didn't like that she was letting the problems of the church weigh so heavily on her conscience. He didn't think she even understood what she was singing to herself. He would have felt ridiculous warning her about the secret police. Surely she realized that.

And he was afraid she would answer him: Everyone has to stand up for what they believe.

> *Were you that cold in church, Lisbeth?*
> *What do you mean, Cresspahl.*
> *You were shivering, child.*
> *When was I shivering.*
> *When Brüshaver was telling the Christmas story.*
> *I wasn't shivering, Heinrich. You're imagining things.*

December 10, 1967 Sunday

Hanoi's newspapers report that their National Liberation Front has killed, wounded, or captured 40,000 enemy troops in October and November, including 20,000 Americans and allies. So it says in *The New York Times*. With no hint that *The New York Times* had ever said anything different.

Publishers have lost confidence in the Bolivian government's claims to own the rights to Che Guevara's posthumous papers, and negotiations have broken down. When it comes to the interests of *The New York Times*, *The New York Times* reports that *The New York Times* is "reviewing the new situation."

Next week, four writers are to go on trial in Moscow because they had let it be known that they weren't happy about the trial of two writers, Daniel and Sinyavsky. Three of these writers wrote something, and the fourth, Vera Lashkova, allegedly helped type it up. That suffices for Article 70, crimes against the state, up to seven years in prison, up to five years in internal exile.

Someone's gotten married! The president's daughter got married! Lynda Johnson got married! She got married in the White House! She married a marine corps captain! A marine captain with marching orders for Vietnam! All right, calm down.

And Allen M. Johnson, of 54-09 Almeda Ave., Arverne, N.Y., wants the world to know that he will no longer be responsible for any debts contracted by his wife, Betty Johnson.

There was very little meat eaten in Jerichow in the fall of 1934, and it was Arthur Semig's fault. It was Methfessel the butcher's fault. It was the Nazis' fault. Now whose fault was it?

It started in September when August Methfessel paid a visit to Dr. Semig. He came not in darkness but right in the middle of the day, and he didn't go through his office door but stood right outside his garden gate and rang the bell. And since Dora Semig was now taking her time before opening the front door to the house, he stood there for quite a while, letting himself be seen by everyone living on the Bäk or walking by. He had something thick in his hand, pointed at one end and wrapped in white paper, maybe a bouquet of flowers?

Dora Semig thought it was, and anyway was surprised enough to show Methfessel into her living room. But he wouldn't sit down, he stood there awkwardly among the Köster Biedermeier and held what he'd brought with him firmly at his side. He was still standing like that when Dora came back with her husband.

Then Methfessel stood up straighter, faced them like an usher at a funeral parlor, and said his piece. These were times, he said, when nobody even knows what kind of times these are, and often something said about someone was taken as something that someone couldn't have possibly meant or, by the way, done at all. He didn't look at Arthur and Dora as he said this; he kept his head slightly bent forward and his gaze to one side, as though reciting something written on Mrs. Semig's polished floor. And so, what he was saying now and for all time was that he hoped bygones could stay bygones, that is, in the first sense, and especially in the second sense. Semig had no idea what he was getting at. Mrs. Semig couldn't figure it out either. Methfessel sat down with a heavy sigh, placed the wrapped object on his knees, and told a story involving Baron von Rammin and Grandma Klug and her cat doing things entirely with and to and among one another. After a while, Semig showed signs of having caught a hint of what Methfessel had on his mind, offered him the expected drink, took his first demurral as final, and stood up, so as not to delay Methfessel's departure from the living room. Methfessel shot up with surprising speed out of Dora's armchair, whose thin legs under his large frame may well have been making him nervous, shook hands with the lady of the house, and walked to the door—but the door that led to Semig's central hallway and office. Arthur apparently followed him like an obedient sheep.

– Here: Methfessel said, behind the office door: – Here! he said, and quickly unwrapped by way of hello the piece of meat he had with him. – Take a look at that! he said, and for a second he was once again the wily and confident man he'd been before his trip to Fürstenberg. It was as if a load had been taken off his shoulders and put in the best possible hands, but in any case not in his. He sat there ready to help, at least with information. Dr. Semig had put on his white apron, to show Methfessel that all the proper procedures were being followed. He also did him the favor of carrying the sample over to the table by the window, where he had his microscope, his scissors, needles, pipettes, chemicals. But even if he had been able to undertake a bacteriological investigation there, he wouldn't have done it in Methfessel's presence. He stayed standing next to his swivel chair, so that Methfessel wouldn't put down roots. But Methfessel didn't want to leave. He also didn't want to start, before a question helped get him going. How's business? From the topic of business, Methfessel could finally move into his other topic, and now Semig had to listen to a long and roundabout harangue about the veterinarian who had recently taken Semig's old regional inspector job. It did not the slightest bit of good to try to keep him from slandering a colleague (Semig didn't care whether the colleague in question was Aryan or non-Aryan). After a while, he had his hand in front of his mouth, as he usually did when thinking or reflecting, and a little while after that he sat down, to listen better. This Dr. Hauschildt certainly was interpreting the legal requirements rather idiosyncratically. He apparently preferred to conduct his inspections of livestock by phone. He would ask Methfessel over the phone to state the general condition of the delivered animals, and it seemed that by this point in his life Methfessel found it hard to come out with a particular opinion or firm statement. It seemed Methfessel was now quite sensitive to being shouted at, even over the phone. Then this Hauschildt would say: Carry on, Methfessel!, all the while without having ever seen, even from afar, the animal's posture or lips nostrils stool vulva vagina udder breathing. Now it's true, Semig too sometimes used to get to Methfessel's stall after dark, if he didn't have any other time free, and make do with rounding the animals up and prodding them awake. But he'd been practicing for fifteen years in this neck of the woods alone, and what he saw with the naked eye was not likely to be much different under a microscope. While this Hauschildt was just out of veterinary school, where he'd apparently found plenty of time left over from his studies to organize a National Socialist Student League, and word was also going round that he'd been stumped and stymied by a case of prolapsed uterus at von Meyer's. And Dr. Hauschildt's inspection techniques as Methfessel described them were not in the textbook, and in the short time it took him to call with the findings of the trichina test he could barely have made it home! This Hauschildt had clearly given himself special permission not to have to do the trichina inspection at the slaughterhouse. And now Methfessel was both scared of the law and afraid of his conscience. It was disgusting how cringing and submissive they'd beaten this man into being. Methfessel refused to lodge a complaint personally in Gneez. – I'm not in the party: he said, and he knew for a fact that Dr. Hauschildt was in the party and that he and the district veterinarian were constantly in each other's pockets, whether it was about neighboring seaside properties or shared sailboats or in the Ratskeller wasn't clear, and it made Methfessel visibly anxious to know even that much. Semig should take the meat to Gneez, not him. – My dear Mr. Methfessel: Semig said, and August should have been able to hear that this wasn't the condescension of years past, with which Dr. Semig used to brush aside stupid questions or naive expectations of a reduced fee. But Methfessel had no time for anyone else's helplessness. He thought now this problem was out of his hands and off his neck, and left with the grave words: *It's on your conscience now, Doctuh!* In the yard he made a cautious detour around Rex, who had practically offered him a paw. Rex was the German shepherd the Semigs had had since spring.

At first, all Methfessel got out of this were rumors around Jerichow that he'd been willing to part with a whole joint of meat to get back in the Jew's good graces.

The veterinarian would have liked to think it over for a few days, but if his idea of professional ethics weren't enough to push him over the line, the warm weather would have been. He wrote a relatively personal letter, which just might escape being filed with the business correspondence, and sent it to Schwerin that same evening with Methfessel's meat, registered and express, and in Schwerin it turned out he still was seen as Dora Köster's husband, and in the official notification sent to the district veterinarian in Gneez his name was not mentioned. Everything was "according to the representations of Mr. August Methfessel, master butcher, Jerichow." And

Methfessel was summoned to Gneez and signed a statement and thanked the officials there, somewhat comforted to find that law and hygiene maybe still did count for something in Germany today. And at the Gneez station, SA in civilian clothes jumped him.

Now Methfessel was not happy. On his return to Jerichow he found his cold storage cleared out, since the bacteriologists in Schwerin had found *Salmonella dublin*, a contaminant, in the liver that he'd submitted. Compensation? Forget it! And by now Methfessel was to the point of thinking that of course Semig hadn't had to bear the brunt. He was a university man, the gang stuck together, simple as that. He also didn't want to begrudge Semig his peace and quiet until they sent him to Fürstenberg where Ossi Rahn was waiting for him. After a week Methfessel had almost entirely recovered and would have been strong enough to start butchering again, but he no longer wanted to. Dr. Hauschildt now came very punctually and screamed about every minute he was kept waiting, and inspected the livestock not alone but with a student assistant who could certify that all the regulations had been followed. And since the veterinarian no longer skipped a single incision in his carcass inspections, he spent a long time doing them, real teaching sessions for his student, and that was not what Methfessel had had in mind. Now it was Methfessel who had to call Gneez to get the test results, and Mrs. Hauschildt was often unable to say where her husband was at the moment or how the tests had turned out. Dr. Hauschildt was now quite fond of using the square inspection stamp for Methfessel's meat, indicating Suitability for Limited Uses, and it sometimes happened that he picked up the triangular stamp, Unsuitable, and by this point in his life Methfessel had no interest in trying to prove that livestock farming in this neck of the woods couldn't possibly have gotten so much worse from one week to the next. The round stamp had always been the rule with his meat. Methfessel had turned melancholy. When the cattle trucks arrived on the morning of slaughtering day, Methfessel would be standing in his yard holding his head like a deaf person, as though he, not the bullock being brought to him, had been given a blow to the head.

And what a fellow he'd been!
That red red face, that blond hair. Well fed.
Blonder than the whole S. Å-Å-Å. put together.

Then the cars with the pigs would pull up. The pigs would be drowsy from the ride, happily nestled up against one another, and Methfessel would stand there and watch as his assistants drove the terrified animals to the slaughtering room's door with their brooms. Since he didn't help it took the men longer, and the pigs had time to scent the blood of their comrades flowing across the threshold, and Methfessel's neighbors complained about the pitiful shrieking. At first he'd still gone in with them, even if he went last, and it quickly fell silent again after a couple high sharp shrieks. But then Methfessel would come right back out the door, as if in a trance, a big strong man with sturdy arms, heavy shoulders, squat head, holding a bloody knife in his hand. He would shake his head, chew his blond mustache, he wasn't himself. And he wouldn't go inside, he'd hide in the woodshed, and after a while the men gave up trying to go get him. One of Elsa Pienagel's windows looked out on Methfessel's large yard, and that fall she often had visitors who came just to stand at the window when it was slaughtering day at Methfessel's.

So for quite some time there was not much beef and pork eaten in Jerichow, because Methfessel didn't have any and Klein the butcher had been known for too long as the second-best butcher in Jerichow and the prejudice was hard to dispel. Many chickens lost their lives earlier than they were meant to, and rabbits too.

Only at the Cresspahls' was there yet another reason. Lisbeth had noticed something about the sides of pork when Methfessel still had some to hang on the hooks in his shop. The backs were so bent. There were little dimples over the vertebrae, like on people. Like on Gesine, too. From that moment on Lisbeth had an aversion to meat.

We eat animals, and we kill them to do it. It's not right.
Really, Lisbeth? Tryin to save money?
That wouldn't be the worst idea, Cresspahl.

So there was meat on the Cresspahls' table only when he insisted, and she didn't eat any of it.

Now *The New York Times* is starting up again with her own brand of charity. Everywhere she can and some places she really can't, she inserts the appeal: REMEMBER THE NEEDIEST! and what she wants is money for her charity fund. It's not every news story that goes with a refrain like that: Remember the Neediest!

Marie cut three pictures out of today's *New York Times*, to keep:

The first, from the front page, brings into our home the merry widow of President Kennedy, because she went to a dinner for the Democratic Party at the Plaza Hotel.

The second gives us Lynda Johnson's wedding party, arranged in a semicircle, all with bowed heads, one person even kneeling. Yet they are not at prayer, they are watching a recording of the ceremony on television. The article ends with the refrain: Remember the Neediest!

The third is an artwork showing a humbly clad woman with a small child in her arms, in a room almost completely bare. The floor looks broken, the window too, as if it's letting in not only the light from the back court-yard but the wind too. "Many New Yorkers, such as this Puerto Rican mother and her child, face a long, cold winter with little hope, little money, and oftentimes no heat."

Edmondo Barrios, Marie's first friend in this country, grew up in an apartment like that in East Harlem.

He didn't come up in the first stories she brought home from kinder-garten. Instead, she complained about child-rearing in this country. From Düsseldorf, she was used to being allowed to cling totally and completely to another child, so here too she'd picked her favorite and sat down next to her and watched her mouth and followed her around (the way I go walking after D. E. when he gets up to go to the refrigerator for a new bottle and comes back to the table: just so I can see him while he speaks the sentence that I could have heard no less clearly if I'd remained seated). Pamela Blumenroth was this child's name, and Marie didn't want anyone to take her away. But Pamela had to be taken away because the teachers held that forming a bond with only one peer was risky for a four-year-old, and at snack time Marie was seated next to someone else, Mark the kisser, and she was supposed to play with him now, and she didn't want him, she wanted Pamela. The goal of such child-rearing was for everyone to get to know everyone else in the class, and the word for it was *togetherness*, but for a long time Marie thought the word meant "forced separation." She kept it a secret in school that the one she invited over to play for the afternoon was docile little Pamela, who back then had a face like an Irish farmwife, not Mark the kisser.

So that Marie would learn to change friends like shirts, she also ended up with Edmondo. She had earlier spoken of him as "the boy who hits." Then she realized that it was a particular category of children in the class that he regularly attacked, namely boys "who have skin like me," and that's how it came out that he was one of the "colored" children. Apparently this Edmondo needed no reason whatsoever to start a fight, he would just throw any random pink-skinned boy to the ground and sit on him and start punching. The victim's classmates usually assumed that there must have been some reason and stuck to their rule of not interfering in a one-on-one fight. Up came Marie one day and put her hand on his arm and said, *Lass das* in German, *Stop*, and not as an order but as a wish, and to be absolutely sure he would understand her she shook her head in a kind way. Edmondo, in unutterable amazement, forgot about the fight that he'd felt was necessary just a moment ago. He followed this remarkable person, speaking her strange language, and from then on considered her his friend, and not like the black girls in the class, to whom he continued to behave like a merciless sultan, but like someone you genuinely want to understand, please, protect. It might have been even easier as Marie's protector to get into situations requiring shoving and hitting, but Marie restrained him by giving the impression that she was there for him alone, as if that David Double-U wasn't even in the room. She also had no fear of Edmondo. The teachers looked on in astonishment at this friendship between the black and the European, and in relief, too, because now it happened less often that Edmondo threw building blocks in order to hit someone's eye, and now they almost never had to drag him out of a fight that could easily have ended with a broken bone for the loser, because Edmondo was eight whole years old and was in Marie's class only because of the four-year delay in his intellectual development. Edmondo was attending the kindergarten with a stipend from the church itself and was seen as the first subject of an experiment, and aside from that his skin color protected him from expulsion. The church would not appreciate seeing its goodwill impugned unless absolutely necessary. Now that the difficult black boy was with the little German girl, the lessons went by almost like in a normal class, without extra work and commotion, and this isolated partnership, however little conducive to "togetherness," was not broken up.

Marie also went to visit Edmondo in East Harlem, and life in the Barrios family was full of every imaginable stereotype of the ghetto. Edmondo's last name was not his father's but that of his younger brother's father, the one who had ventured to marry Mrs. Barrios. Then he left too, and Edmondo's father, a man whose first name was Rodrigo, probably would have wanted to live with Edmondo's mother except that his presence would have meant an end to her welfare payments, and there was no way for him to support the family because he couldn't find a job.

When you gotta mop on your head instedda hair, you cant getta job.

He came by occasionally, but not since Mrs. Barrios had gotten pregnant by another man for the second time.

Mrs. Barrios readily told all of this to the foreigner, since Edmondo had told her so much about the foreigner's daughter. She was a very pretty, slightly plump woman with lips of the kind that in this country are called Caucasian. She wore her hair short, like a man's crew cut, and in profile with her head held high she could look fun, mischievous. Like her, every object in the apartment was absolutely spick-and-span. The apartment consisted of two and a half rooms, one behind the other. The back rooms got their light through the single window in the front room. Mrs. Barrios was proud of her apartment, which did look fully furnished since the one big bed for all the children took up almost all the space, and a picture of the Holy Mother of God cut out of a newspaper and glued onto a cardboard frame turned even a scratched-up wall into something more. Mrs. Barrios felt fortunate to live as she did. The expected, prefabricated mental picture one had of an East Harlem apartment was completed by the fact that the sole window really did look out on the aboveground tracks of the New York Central Railway, parading commuter trains to suburbs in the country past the residents here, and luxury trains too, even the 20th Century Limited.

Except at night, Edmondo lived on the street and under the tracks, and he explained the street to Marie. When he told her that a man walking unsteadily was a "junkie," he said it not objectively but with visible hatred.

There was something there. It was not a usual thing for someone who lived on this street to turn up with a "white" friend and then go into the house with her too, and it was probably on these steps leading up to Mrs. Barrios's apartment that Marie first heard reference to human sexual relations. That embarrassed Edmondo, and his pride in his "white" friend was spoiled. Mrs. Barrios could not adjust quickly enough to the middle-class custom of sending one's child out to visit a friend, and had, in addition, no room for them, not to mention toys, so she took something out of her welfare money and sent the children to the Apollo movie theater on 125th Street. This was Marie's first feature film, a very sad story of a lady on the sofa and a sailor "who shooted," and actually the whole thing took place in a car, or on a plane, Marie was confused about that part, and it got completely mixed up in her dreams. That was Marie's first visit to Edmondo's, and she often wanted to talk about it, in detail, but did not insist on there being a second.

There was a second, but she preferred having Edmondo over to her apartment. The babysitters who had to bring him home from kindergarten with her and then be responsible for him for five hours made it very clear that the next time he came over was the day they'd quit. You could see it. That night Marie's room looked as if it had been searched in a desperate hurry, like in the movies, and panes of glass in Marie's door were broken, and only Marie was in one piece and cheerful and a little dazed. One of the sitters reported that Edmondo could put a person in a "Noah's Flood kind of mood," for instance when no suggestion or command got through to him and he just lay on the floor and refused to move and awaited the adult's reaction with the limited pleasure of a two-year-old: then you were in the middle of a tidal wave with nothing to grab hold of. Edmondo genuinely hadn't understood. He was waiting to be hit, he would have stood up for a beating. One time I saw him disobey his mother, and Mrs. Barrios, ignoring the white middle-class parents on the field trip, blindly grabbed for something she could hit him with, anything, and got hold of a jump rope and tried to break it on the boy, who didn't defend himself either. The educated, the liberals, the whites looked on very thoughtfully and seemed particularly struck by the fact that Mrs. Barrios stopped without warning from one second to the next, as though done with a job.

We could have asked Edmondo questions. His contempt for the junkies, there was something there. His desperately wanting to know whether

Marie looked like his sister under her skirt, that might have helped him. D. E. was the first person to look at the boy for five minutes and say that he needed medical help, and Edmondo, in the presence of an adult, a white man, had been behaving very quietly and properly too. He was hard to understand. A boy who attacked anyone and everyone, often with no thought for the power relations involved, why was he so scared of dogs? Someone in Riverside Park was playing with his dog, a friendly boxer, and the dog was far away from us, and his barking showed no sign of anything but tremendous fun, and Edmondo hid behind my skirt and begged and pleaded for us to turn around and walk somewhere else. Are there dogs like that in East Harlem? Do the police use dogs like that? We didn't ask him.

We only knew him for a year and a half, and then something happened at a summer camp for single mothers and their children. Edmondo wore the sweatshirt printed with the camp logo every day, as a shirt. He apparently did something there with a knife. He was nine and a half then, and strong. The psychiatrists transferred him to a special school. The school was more like a clinic. Apparently he had picked up some kind of sickness from life that the doctors didn't often come across. Mrs. Barrios didn't have to pay a cent for his housing and the attempted cures. At first, we were still allowed to visit him. He didn't know who Marie was anymore. Marie acts like that visit never happened. Then we weren't allowed to visit him anymore.

Even today, Marie says: He never hit me. And he was so strong he only had to touch you and you'd be falling down the stairs. He never did that to me.

Blessed be forgetting. Only she hasn't forgotten.

The weather is so rainy. After all it's almost Christmas.

December 12, 1967 Tuesday
"THE GLOW OF CHRISTMASTIDE LIGHTS CITY STREETS
. . .

In Manhattan, happy throngs of children and adults are drawn to the newly lighted Christmas tree in Rockefeller Center and to the spectacular window displays that line the midtown area's sleek streets.

Lord & Taylor's windows are an animated phantasmagoria of scenes from Christmas in Vienna, with tiny figurines dancing in Schoenbrunn Palace; a conductor and a diva performing in the Vienna Opera House of a century ago; the door of St. Stephen's Cathedral opening and closing, and children romping and bell ringers playing in an Alpine village.

The windows of B. Altman are a cornucopia of great art drawn from the Metropolitan Museum and depicting, in photographic slides, the themes of joy, beauty, the festive board, children, treasures and pageant.

Saks Fifth Avenue, which for years has ushered in the Christmas season with a display of choir boys and organ pipes, this year has emblazoned its facade with a tall Christmas tree.

...

It is quiet and warm in the Columbia Florist Shop at 200 West 231st Street. In the back of the small store, a woman prepares red Christmas candles for sale, putting little ribbons on them and setting them in their bright green bases. The busy time lies ahead, says Nick Dennis, the store manager.

'It's a little early yet,' he explains, pointing to Dec. 15 on a calendar. 'That's when business picks up.'

Outside the night has turned cold and the lights twinkle everywhere in the city and for a moment, at least..."
© The New York Times

Today Francine came over to visit Marie. When I got home from work Marie's double door was closed tight, letting through only the muffled sound of the guest's voice. It was high-pitched, and sounded surprised, and next to it Marie suddenly seemed like an alto.

– And you and your mother really live alone here?

– In three rooms?

– Are all these books yours? Not even a couple of them borrowed?

– I don't believe it. You don't have cockroaches. There aren't roaches in an apartment like this!

– Is that a picture of your father?

– Which way do you sleep on the bed? With your head by the wall? Or so you can see the trees and the sky and the river and the Palisades as soon as you open your eyes?

– Why do you say England's not part of Europe?

– May I touch this book?

– You mean he gives you a typewriter just like that, because you want one?

– Is he the man your mother... sorry, I meant to say: He must be a good person.

– 'Cause he visits you guys.

– No one gets in the building if Mr. Robinson doesn't let them in?

– Not even through the basement?

– If a water pipe breaks... I'm sure that doesn't happen in a building like this.

– It does?

– The same day? The same day?

– And all you have to do is say thank you?

– Your carpet looks comfortable to sleep on.

– Really, you went to summer camp in Maine, on Orr's Island? They teach sailing? I went to Green Acres once. That's still in New York State of course.

– Say something in your language.

– Your mother's language, I mean.

– And those five words mean: The more time you spend working on something, the harder it gets?

– *De Leng hett de Last?*

– So she speaks three languages—her own, and German, and ours!

– More? Wow!

– What's your mother like, really?

– All mothers are like that. I mean: is she dangerous?

– I'm afraid mine is sometimes. She doesn't mean to be, but she is.

– You and your mom are just staying here for Christmas? But you could go to Vermont, or England... to Italy too?

– I'd go to Italy if I could.

– And you're doing all that for your mother for Christmas? That must cost a lot of money.

– I could too? I could never do that.

– That's great that you want to show me. That's out of sight. But there's no point, my mother's never had anything like that.

– And she'd sell it.
– Yeah, the lighting. I don't know how you'll do the lighting.

But at this point Marie stuck her head out the double door and saw me sitting at the table reading the paper. The door shut again at once, just after I caught a considerate nod and a smile from Marie. She has declared her room off-limits: everyone else is allowed in, D. E. and Shakespeare and Esther, but not me. Marie is doing something secret in there. I told her she wasn't allowed to give me any surprises for Christmas, and she said: It's not for Christmas. It's for New Year's. It never crosses her mind that I could just walk in against her orders and see what it is.

Her plan involves more than just work, but it sounds like hard work too: blades on wood, hammers on nails, sanding, scrubbing. She also has to make her bed and deal with her clothes and take care of her room, and every night she takes the garbage bags out and leaves them by the freight elevator so that the trash and scraps give me no clues about what she's done that day. She has said that it may not give me pleasure but she's promised it will satisfy a wish I don't know I have.

The voices in Marie's room became unintelligible once they knew I was home. I could tell only that they were whispering, one in an eager stage whisper, the other shushing apologetically. They came out unexpectedly, and while Marie with her hands behind her back pulled the doors closed on her secret, Francine stood in front of me and took care of her Hellos and Goodbyes at the same time. She waited to see if I would hold out my hand for her to shake, and she kept her eyes lowered so as not to see whether the expression on the face before her was welcoming or something else. She made a curtsy and said: *Good night, ma'am.*

Already she had her coat on, schoolbag in hand, she was at the front door. If she was confused before, it was worse now. Mr. Robinson was standing in the open elevator, and he heartily wished me good evening, like a close friend of the family, which he is. Jason and Shakespeare were standing in the lobby inspecting, carefully and professionally, the tile that now was not only cracked but finally split into little unrepairable pieces. Francine knew that the one who liked to be called Shakespeare had an apartment in Brooklyn (a black working man with his own apartment) containing at least one cupboard secure enough to hold his collection of the stamps from our letters from Europe, and that he fixed problems in our apartment in exchange for nothing but kind words. But here was a second, and Jason was the third, "colored" man wishing us a nice day as if he genuinely meant it, as if we were all good neighbors, as if we knew each other personally and that that was how we wanted it. The little black girl ran out the door like they were after her. So fast that again I didn't take in her face properly, and all I know is that she struck me as a child who reads a lot and afterward isn't given much help thinking about what she's read.

– She acted like she was scared of me, Marie.

– Well of course she's scared of you! Sometimes you ask questions, Gesine... You know, Gesine, the kind of question...

– Don't trust anybody over thirty.

– That's not what Francine thinks, that's what I think. But I mean something different. You know what I mean.

December 13, 1967 Wednesday

During the 1966–1967 fiscal year, with fewer than half a million soldiers in Vietnam, 748 persons were convicted for draft-dodging; in 1944, with 11.5 million under arms, there were 4,609. Now do the calculations yourself, and DON'T FORGET THE NEEDIEST!

Last Tuesday the Vietcong massacred 200 members of the mountain tribes, and Senator Percy of Illinois came to see it, and so on, and DON'T FORGET THE NEEDIEST!

The New York Times has also taken another look around East Germany and found the regime more jittery than ever, more mistrusting of its people; the people would like to get out sometimes, consider their government the least liberal of all the Socialist countries, and see Communism as the superior social system, and DON'T FORGET THE NEEDIEST!

In 1935 they would still have let Cresspahl out of the country. They wouldn't have used force to keep him there.

– But he'd tied himself by that point down with his money seems to me: Marie says in German, or what passes these days for her German.

– Right. When you consider that an English pound was worth twelve marks thirty pfennigs in those days, there can't have been much left.

– *And he'd made a life for himself there*: Marie says in English.

He had made a life for himself.

At first the Gneez guild hadn't exactly abandoned him, but they had left him alone where he was, which was way up north on the coast. Any work that came to the carpenters in Gneez they needed for themselves. No one had asked this Cresspahl to come back to Germany. They were the ones who had spent the bad years driving around from village to village, town to town with their furniture samples, and people hadn't been able to place any orders, or pay for them in the end if they did, and all the while he was sitting pretty abroad, making money. Plus he was Horst Papenbrock's brother-in-law. It served him right to have to stoop to wheelwright work and fixing wagon shafts. If worst came to worst he could always go to his father-in-law, and where could they go? Not to the bank to dip into savings, more likely to bankruptcy court. You got that right. Cresspahl had paid his courtesy call to Willi Böttcher, the guild master in Gneez, and nothing since. Böttcher's part in the conversation had been limited to numerous sighing *Jå, Jå*'s, which added up to conveying that he didn't trust the new guy, not even enough to discuss whether or not times were tough these days. And Cresspahl hadn't liked Böttcher's son. The kid was sixteen years old, always bragging about his "service" in the HJ, which stood for Hitler-jugend, Hitler Youth. And about his friends in the regional HJ leadership and his nighttime shooting practice in Gneez Woods. Apparently that was another way to end up with the Nazis: sitting next to the Knoop kid in school since 1932. The Knoop kid was the son of Johannes Knoop, considered the biggest man in Gneez out of all 25,023 inhabitants—coal merchant, carriage trade, import and export. Johannes Knoop had an exclusive hunting license, and junior, Emil, had free access to the gun cabinet, and already by 1931 Emil Knoop with his father's guns had brought his whole class, members of the Christian Boy Scouts one and all, into the HJ. From sitting next to Emil in high school, Klaus Böttcher had ended up something like Emil's adjutant or staff sergeant. Then Johannes Knoop had had to send his brat off to boarding school, and the HJ in both Gneez and Jerichow were under Klaus Böttcher's command. He went to school in the uniform, he went to the dentist in the uniform. In his father's workshop, though, he had two left hands. And he had such a frivolous way of talking, this Klaussie. In June 1934, when the Austrian had half of the SA leadership shot, the Böttcher kid had said: Well, the Führer doesn't know everything. Such comments were accompanied by such an exaggeratedly cocky look that it was like he was trying to make the other person laugh, or like he had no idea what his words meant, and Cresspahl didn't care to take the time to figure out which. It hadn't escaped him that the scamp wanted to know how come Cresspahl had the rank of an NCO, and it wasn't just because he was curious, nor that his questions about Cresspahl's life in London were ultimately grounded in respect, but this didn't seem like the best strategy for getting into Willi Böttcher's better graces. So however friendly the boy's "Good morning" to Cresspahl might be, even from a military distance, Cresspahl's response was curt. He'd noticed all the same, though, that Klaus didn't use the Heil Hitler with him, the way an HJ group leader was especially required to. For the time being he chalked that up to the silly behavior that children so often have.

Then Cresspahl had to drop off his papers proving pure Aryan descent at Böttcher's, and the kid was waiting for him. He was again in full uniform, with a kind of thin leather knot in his tie and a braided cord dangling down his chest, and Cresspahl acted as though he were reviewing the child's clothing for its compliance with military requirements. – *Jå*, the Youth Federation's all through now: Klaussie said, in his cheery, fake-sophisticated way. – Yup: Cresspahl said, half opening Böttcher's door. Böttcher's entrance hall was as wide as half a street so that a truck could drive right up to the workshop. Klaussie, talking away, managed to steer Cresspahl back into the courtyard. It sounded like this time he really had something to say. It was about a hiker's shack that the Youth Federation had built on the south shore of Gneez Lake. In 1931, the HJ had been illegal and had often rented the hut for secret meetings.

– We were illegal too, you know: Klaussie said in his obnoxiously worldly-wise way.

– 'n' now we're gonna occupy it for good tomorrow night, and Heine Klaproth'll have a fit!: the guild master's brat said.

– You just wait 'n' see the look on 'is face day after tomorrow! Klaus said. Heine Klaproth was an apprentice with Cresspahl and had previously been a Christian Boy Scout. – You won' tell 'im anything, will you? Klaus said, and he looked genuinely worried, and he could barely contain his glee at his Nordic cunning.

That night Cresspahl drove Arthur's truck very slowly, as quietly as he could, down Adolf-Hitler-Street to Gneez and then on Schönberger Street all the way around Gneez Woods to the southern shore of Gneez Lake. It was October, and when he turned off the headlights he couldn't see his hand in front of his face. The lake was pitch-black. Lantern light was reflected in the water only on the lakeside promenade, far away. On this side, the shore seemed very crowded, and Cresspahl couldn't believe that the Boy Scouts had had so many members. – They're SAJ: Heine Klaproth said, Socialist Workers Youth. Apparently they'd rented the shack too sometimes. So in the dark, without making a sound, they dismantled the building. There were only three carpenters and two carpenter's apprentices among them, and even so by around three a.m. all that remained was the smooth soil where the hiker's shack had once stood, and from the boat landing not even the pillars. Someone had brought a rake, and someone had swiped a sign from the Rose Garden in Gneez, and what they left behind was a neatly raked piece of shoreline with a plaque in the middle saying: KEEP OFF— FRESHLY SEEDED. And early that morning when Cresspahl drove around the north side of the woods with his share of the lumber, he passed a tired crowd of Hitler Youth coming back from nighttime exercises, and this time Klaus Böttcher greeted him not with Heil Hitler and not with Good morning and not with the slightest sign of having seen him at all.

The stunt yielded more than some free wood. The SAJ had been the youth group for the Social Democrats, and now all of them from Gneez to Jerichow knew for certain that this Cresspahl was only pretending, just like they were.

Heine Klaproth started acting like a member of the family. The boy had always worked hard, but now Lisbeth could hardly stop him from doing favors he thought he read in her eyes that she wanted. When the woodbox was barely half empty he was already on his way out to chop more.

Lisbeth would probably have forbidden Cresspahl from doing this kind of night work and accused him of endangering the family, but since she only heard about it the next morning she thought it was pretty funny and merely regretted not being able to share the story with anyone, even Aggie Brüshaver.

And now Cresspahl was expressly included with the carpenter's guild regulars when they went out drinking. They told him the lay of the land. For one thing, he shouldn't be taken in by the Nazis' German Labor Front. In the first place, they'd stolen everything they had from the unions. And it wasn't their pay rates.

Just don't raise up any new masters, right, Cresspahl?
How does someone become a master, Gesine?
By marriage.
Gesine.
All right, how?
By working hard and being good, Gesine.
By working hard and being good. Fair enough.

They were nuts anyway, with their "beauty of labor" stuff. Flowers in the workshops! Have you ever seen a flower that can stand carpenter's glue? Enlarge the windowpanes! Are we gardeners? Places to sit during breaks! I sit on what I'm making, that's the only way my lunch tastes right. Put in lawns! Where's Gertrud supposed to grow her radishes? But the worst, the lowest down dog of a plan was for those idiots in the Regional Home Improvement Office of the German Labor Front to standardize the orders. Standardized furniture cranked out by the thousand! Those are jobs for factories, not craftsmen. We don't even get the bones from that fish!

And you need to watch out around Irene Loohse, she's got a brother-in-law, le-gal ad-vi-ser to the Labor Front, you might as well go straight to the police. Now ya know, Cresspahl.

And they said, around the end of 1934: Hey, Heinrich, something's going down. When it happens, we'll cut you in.

At first Cresspahl had wanted only to adjust to life in Germany and keep his integrity. It turned out not to be as bad as all that. His guildmates, you could get along with them, drink some beer, talk about machines and material and workmen, play some practical jokes on the Nazis—live your life. Not bad.

Shut yer trap, Gesine. Keep yer trap shut.

December 14, 1967 Thursday

Dear Anita Red Hair.

Dear Doctor of Oriental Archaeology!

Dearliest.

(Does the old man still say that?)

Thank you for your letter and for actually sending Henri R. Faure's passport back by November 15. Shakespeare sends his thanks for the Swiss stamps. Shakespeare, real name Mr. Shaks, first name (as I'm sure you've guessed) Bill, is an inexhaustibly nice black gentleman from Brooklyn, a plumbing virtuoso with the manners of a hotel manager. And he has given in to his name and not only knows half of *Hamlet* by heart but *Richard the Fourth* too. Collects our European stamps.

It was nice of you to have your "Henri R. Faure" write a thank-you letter to Henri Faure. Now the old Faures are convinced that they haven't been taken in by any shenanigans. Henri turned his passport around and around in his hands and found no trace of anything and couldn't believe that such a small thing could be the ticket out of a country that doesn't want to be left.

The Faures still think we did it for Judaism, and they greet us on the street, even from a distance. They are truly of the old school—he doffs his hat with a firm, elegant flourish and they stop and converse with us every time. My French now has a slight Belgian accent.

Meanwhile the GDR has lost a young "Zionist" who doesn't want to go to Israel at all, it turns out, but to Canada. If only you had time to explain to your Workers' Party how a certain part of the world works.

Dear Anita, it's terrible that you've lost your apartment. I'm sorry.

I liked that it was so close to the roof, up with the birds and the planes and the treetops. I liked that it had three exits, as the poet mandates, and three steel doors that closed like a bank vault. Life was safe behind them. I liked that it had two sides. The gray side, with the slanted north-facing windows, with the rooftops beneath it all the way to the broken tooth you call the Gedächtniskirche, from a safe distance too. I liked the other side, the one that caught the sunlight and even in winter the smell of the dry wind. I remember how the floor sloped a little. I liked that planes flew in over the city and could see you down on the balcony. It was a birch whose top branches reached your balcony, wasn't it? I liked about the apartment all the time you let me live there, and Marie remembers it too, if only the 125 stairs to your light switch and doorbell. I've lost something too, and Berlin won't be what it used to be.

I know you don't have time for research and excavations on this continent at the moment, but it makes me sad. I could have used someone like you around at Christmas. Someone who knows how to recite the fishes' night prayer, *exempli gratia*. I can't stand Christmas. I don't know what it is about it. I have no deaths from this time of year but I can't stop dreaming about death. And Marie expects the holiday routine, *and I have to go through all the motions*. Someone was asking about you here just yesterday: as the poet says.

Today is the day that *The New York Times* can finally report that the young man on the Greek throne has misplayed his hand and left the country. Sometimes I'm not sure that you and I would agree about such events. It's been five years since we've seen each other after all.

Actually, yes, I am sure. The other articles say, for instance, that Control Data Corporation has sold and delivered its 1604 computer to the Warnow Shipyards in Rostock, "because it is going to be used for commercial purposes." And the Pentagon has almost finished a "bomb bus," a spacecraft that drops off thermonuclear warheads stop by stop all over the world, just so the Soviets have a little less joy in their FOBS ballistic missiles, Fractional Orbital Bombardment System, you remember. The unemployment numbers are down to 3.9 percent, and were so high earlier because the statistics were fooled by the strikes. There are 200,000 addicts in New York, "people organizing their lives around the use of drugs," and three of the detectives who work this beat are suspected of selling narcotics to peddlers themselves, and at the bottom of almost every article it says DON'T FORGET THE NEEDIEST, because Christmas is right around the corner. Yes, we'd agree.

You can't come see this country for yourself but I can tell you about it. How your letter came. Around nine in the morning, a postal van stopped right outside our building and the driver carried a little armful in to Mr. Robinson and chatted with him about union wages. By around nine thirty, Mr. Robinson had sorted the mail and was taking the elevator up to the top floor. From there he walked downstairs floor by floor, and in fact went down every hallway twice. The first time, he threw the printed matter onto the doorsteps. It's a plopping echoing sound, which is what first announces the mail has arrived. You've got mail when your apartment door softly shudders from a gentle thump. Then he stuck the real letters between the door and the doorframe, at the height of the lock. There, you see, they are more taboo than the advertising left on the floor. Sometimes he comes by a third time, with a parcel or package, and rings the bell, and says: I've got NEWS for you! Not our door, it would be in vain for us, because I've long since left for work and Marie is already in school. I have never once seen Mr. Robinson do this, but ever since I heard the sound of it once, on a Saturday morning, that is how I imagine it and I know that that's how it is. Incidentally, Mr. Robinson knows all the tenants' daily schedules and he would keep a parcel for us in the staff room, and only start bringing it up and down in the elevator with him around four o'clock, so that he can present us with it as soon as he sees us. Now for how I can send off this letter to you. There are the ordinary mailboxes, blue with red hats. But they aren't hanging screwed to the side of the building, they stand on their own on the street corners, and when you pull the handle under the domed brow they open their shovel mouth. They have olive green siblings but those are stepchildren, for their heads are entirely closed, and they have to announce to all the world: We do not accept mail. They do, though, from mail carriers. In the magnificent buildings of Riverside Drive, there are bronze panels, similar to coats of arms, set into the wall and displaying a slot and telling you your zip code. In our lobby the box is only old cast iron, not elegant, but still, for our building alone. And I don't have to go to it. For in both office citadels and apartment buildings, flat glass shafts run from the top to the bottom, opening into mouths on each floor. In them the letter flutters downward, but as little as one floor down a passerby will already be startled by a racing spot hurtling through the corner of his eye down to our venerable receptacle, which the man from the post office visits several times a day in his truck, for example now, at nine at night. The truck, which I can see beneath my window, is blue and white, and shining red eyes turn on when it's reversed, and it can give off shrill warning tones. The driver steps out of his roomy cabin and goes around to the door of the stowage, grabs a sack, enters the building, comes back out with his sack, gets into the stowage, and this time turns on the light, which to us, from above, looks yellow in the night-gray roof of the truck. And now for the post office itself. The mail carrier's uniform is a light blue-gray shirt whose badge on the upper arm takes the name of the job literally: The man inside this garment is a "Carrier": it says. We all know what Herodotus had to say about them. They wear gloves and even so can manage a large number of tiny keys that they have hanging on a chain from their belt or in their pants pocket. Since the mail is sacred, its offices are modeled on classical temples, and since it belongs to the federal union of states, wanted posters hang in its branch offices. A postal vehicle has right of way, even over a fire truck in action. In the city, post office windows are protectively clad in lattice grates; in the country, the desks and counters are open. Well, we don't live in the country. But we'd be glad to drive you out to it.

Marie requests your attention and says that she knows who you are.

I would not be so bold, but would remain, Affectionately yours, G. C.

Your letter will have a postmark from the Grand Central post office. Only the best for you.

December 15, 1967 Friday

There is one matter in which *The New York Times* shows herself to be the elderly lady she is: typos. Today she mentions a "Wost Important Target," Longbien Bridge near Hanoi. May the pilots' hands be as fluttery as those of *The New York Times*.

She still considers the Greek king news. The man has moved out of the embassy in Rome, to a cousin's place.

These narcotics detectives apparently stole $2,783 from a suspect during a narcotics raid. And underneath appears the refrain: REMEMBER THE NEEDIEST!

The New York Times prints one story especially for Marie. The Honorable John Vliet Lindsay, seeing an empty cigarette box come flying out of the cab of a truck on Forty-Eighth Street near Fifth Avenue, ran after the truck and flung the box back at the three men inside the cab. – I'm the mayor: he said angrily. – I'm trying to keep the city clean. You ought to be ashamed of yourselves.

– Yes, sir: said the men in the truck. They almost tipped their hats.

But there are always people who refuse to treat an occasion with the seriousness it deserves. One passerby said to the mayor: Finders keepers, Mr. Mayor.

And Marie is utterly guileless. She falls for it. She says: John Lindsay is totally right! He's right! I don't understand what you're laughing about!

Weather: Mostly fair, windy and colder today, tonight and tomorrow.

– Time for a test: Marie says. – I want to see where you get these pasts of yours from. Enough lying. Tell me about Gesine as a child, when she was two!

– Gesine as a child, when she was two, could sit up, stand, walk, talk a little, and she already read the newspaper.

– Got you already!: Marie cries. – That's what I did! You got that from me!

– You, Marie, read the *Frankfurter Allgemeine Zeitung* when you were two, that's right. But you weren't allowed to put the least little rip in it, not even accidentally, and you learned that fast. You respected the printed word almost from the beginning. But the child in Cresspahl's house read *The Lübeck Gazette*, the free newssheet for Lübeck, Schleswig-Holstein, and Mecklenburg. Her grown-ups watched with pleasure when she tore the paper in half, with a big swing of her whole arms, because at least that was one way to rid the world of lies, and at least in that state you could use the paper to start a fire with.

– One–nothing: Marie says, sulking. Then she gets an idea that makes her look extremely crafty, her whole face lights up in an anticipatory smile, and she says: And Gesine as a child held the newspaper upside down.

– She did.

– Ha, like me! Marie says. – Like me!

– One–one. Kudos, Marie.

– I'm not done yet! she says. – What did the child say, when she did talk?

– The child felt that the most important words were: *Cresspahl, bear, buttermilk, cat*. Those were the ones she tried to copy. And if her father's name came out *Esspaw*, you can imagine the rest. All in Platt, by the way.

– Not the word *mother*?

– It's possible. Most likely yes, so let's assume so.

– What about me?

– That was your second word, and you used it in the form of my first name. You said: *Ina. Ina.*

– No score: Marie says, disappointed.

– No score.

– And the bear? she says, as casually as she can.

– Cresspahl's daughter pronounced *der Bär* as *d'Bä*. She'd already realized you're supposed to leave certain holes in what you say, she just didn't know what exactly to put in them. She said all the articles in all the cases in one way, and all the forms of "to be," "to have," "to come" just by adding an *s*.: *Wo ist der Bär?* became *'O's'd'Bä?* The vowel in *Bär* was more like the English "bear."

– And this bear didn't happen to be named Edward, living under the name of Sanders in gold letters *in a forest all by himself*?: Marie says. She is talking very fast, she is sure of victory.

– He was, and in other circles he was known as Winnie-the-Pooh.

– Now I've got you: Marie says, cool as a gherkin. – You got that from me. We have the German translation in the glass bookcase, right there, and it says Copyright 1938. But we're talking about March 1935. It didn't exist yet. You took that from my life, so now it's two to one, my lead.

– Not so fast. There's another book in that case, and if you look up Milne, Alan Alexander in it you'll see: *Winnie-the-Pooh*, 1926 (*Pu der Bär*, 1928).

– Dammit: Marie says. – Sorry. But it's frustrating, isn't it? By the way, I think we should subtract a point when someone makes a mistake. So now it's one–zero, your lead.

– You couldn't have known that, Marie.

– Anyway, it's a rule, starting now.

– Agreed. A rule.

– So why do we have the German edition from 1938? It must be yours.

– Because I got it in 1939, as a birthday present from Hilde Paepcke.

– Then how did the child Gesine already know about Mr. Sanders, Winnie-the-Pooh, in 1935?

– From Cresspahl. Cresspahl told the child stories.

– Aha.

– She didn't know the name Edward Bear lived under, in a forest all by himself, nor the nom de guerre he adopted in company. She only knew that her own stuffed bear was named Bear, and that the bear Cresspahl had in mind was this Edward he'd met through some English children in 1929.

– That was a trick, Gesine.

– Yes, maybe. A point for you?

– I earn my points fair and square. And here's one. The child knew the bear's English name. Like me.

– I read to you from the book I got from Hilde Paepcke. In 1959 we were living in Düsseldorf, and you still knew your mother tongue. German.

– Tripped myself up there: Marie says, now almost confused. But she's brave. She says: All right, minus one to plus one. Your lead.

– I really am against subtracting points, Marie.

– You are a very good mother, Gesine. Every other mother I know would laugh. But it's okay, you shouldn't treat me with kid gloves.

– *A tua disposizione, Fanta Giro.* Minus one to plus one. My lead.

– How did I say my name, Gesine?

– *Meh-ee.*

– And Cresspahl's child?

– *Gay Zina.*

– No points.

– State of play unchanged.

– It's not a game, Gesine!

– Point differential remains as it was, Marie.

– All right. I assume there were things Cresspahl's child didn't like.

– Getting her hair cut.

– Like me! Like me! One–nothing, still your lead.

– But she cried only once over losing her hair. Then Cresspahl thought of something and took the child by the hand and they went for a walk down Town Street in Jerichow.

– Down Adolf-Hitler-Street. No points either way.

– Down the Austrian's street in Jerichow, and he bought a leg of lamb from Klein the butcher, and some heavy corduroy pants at Tannebaum's, and a postcard at the post office, and the child trailed after him the whole time, into one shop after another, and then also into Fiete Semmelweis's, Hairdressers for Men and Women, Also Shaves. The child watched as

Cresspahl, at not quite the right time, only two weeks after his last cut, let some of his hair be taken off. Cresspahl had murmured something to Semmelweis, to make sure he wouldn't end up bald or anything, and Semmelweis was touched, charmed too, and the child saw that the business of cutting hair could be a pleasant, even fun affair for both men, and next time she let a little bit of her own hair get robbed from her without making a fuss, and she probably thought of it as a present for Cresspahl. Because she ran away from Lisbeth's scissors, it was Cresspahl's scissors she went to.

– Minus one to plus one. Your lead.

– I didn't mean it that way, Marie.

– I do. I started this.

– But think about cutting your fingernails, Marie.

– So that you can lie that Cresspahl's child cries when she gets her nails cut too, and then I'll have a point? No cheating please.

– It's not a fair *contest*, Marie! I mean: *Wettstreit*. There's no way I can not win unless I cheat a little.

– I've got something. The child didn't talk much.

– The child, even at two years old, was rather stubborn about keeping quiet. She listened to the grown-ups but rarely answered questions. Quite the diplomat. If Aggie Brüshaver asked the child how she was doing, she would have to guess the answer. When Heine Klaproth invited the child to come see his rabbits, he had to wait and see whether she was following him or had unexpectedly run off, with only a lone wooden clog showing she'd been there at all. Methfessel might stop her in the square and ask, in his conspiratorial voice, with his gentle lopsided smile: Do you want to be a lion? Eating everything again? But maybe she understood that he was beyond needing answers. She gave him a friendly look and then tugged a little on her father's hand so that he'd look at her, and Cresspahl did and understood that she'd finished her parley with Methfessel and was ready to go now.

– Hm. Like me?

– Like you. You were still like that when we came to New York. Zero– one. Still my lead.

– And Cresspahl's child loved to take walks.

– With him. She went with him to buy wood, to pay taxes, to the barber, to Wulff's. Cresspahl had told her Wulff's pub was an apple-juice store, and she must have understood. And she learned something else there: that she preferred apple juice to soda, when she shook her head Wulff took away the Fassbrause and brought the apple juice. None of that at home, none of that would ever happen with Lisbeth. The child liked going to "the apple-juice store," and knew all the "apple-juice stores" in Jerichow. Lisbeth realized that one morning when she was out shopping and the child wanted to go into the Lübeck Court. Lisbeth didn't understand and tried to keep walking. The child lay down on the dusty sidewalk in front of the steps of the Lübeck Court, flat on her belly, and had to be taken away by force, screaming. She expressed her defiance by refusing to walk, and Lisbeth had to carry her home through the whole town, and the child was screaming until inside Cresspahl's door, and that was the first time people in Jerichow began to talk about Lisbeth's abilities as a mother. The child was always doing things with her father—on walks, on drives, working in the garden, swimming in the Baltic, always, everywhere, whenever he wasn't in the workshop, and because you never had any of that I am giving you a point right now and it can't be taken back and if you refuse it there'll be consequences, one–one, game over.

– Don't cry, Gesine. Stop crying. Should I get you a glass of D. E.'s whiskey? Please, stop crying, Gesine!

Yes, sir: said the men in the truck.

One morning when the sky was gray
In mid-whiskey
God came to Mahagonny
God came to Mahagonny
In mid-whiskey
We noticed God in Mahagonny.

Looked at each other, the men of Mahagonny:
Yes: said the men of Mahagonny.

One morning when the sky was gray
In mid-whiskey
Come to Mahagonny

Come to Mahagonny.
In mid-whiskey
Get started in Mahagonny!

They looked at God, the men of Mahagonny:
No: said the men of Mahagonny.

December 16, 1967   Saturday

Today is a bad day for the Union of Soviet Socialist Republics. Not only was Sergeant Ulysses L. Harris of New Jersey convicted of espionage yesterday and sentenced to seven years hard labor but today *The New York Times* had to broadcast that fact to the world. In Italy, moreover, the Union of Soviet Socialist Republics lost its spy Giorgio Rinaldi for fifteen years in prison, Angela Maria Rinaldi for eleven, and Armando Girard for ten. Will they get compound interest on their continuing salaries?

The air force reports having heavily damaged two spans of the Longbien Bridge near Hanoi and hit a third. The comedian Bob Hope is off for his annual Christmas tour for the soldiers in Vietnam, Cardinal Spellman is dead after all, and DON'T FORGET THE NEEDIEST!

In the Morgan post office, primarily devoted to handling foreign mail, there was a second fire, but this time in all ten floors, destroying Christmas mail by the ton.

And justice has taken its course with Sonny Franzese and his three friends. Justice let another man, Mr. Walter Sher, who was sentenced to death for murder, write a letter stating that actually it was Mr. John Rapacki who'd helped Ernest (The Hawk) Rupolo into Jamaica Bay on August 24, 1964, with six bullet wounds and seventeen stab wounds in his body. Now the governor is commuting Mr. Walter Sher's sentence to life imprisonment, and Mr. John Rapacki says that's a lie and he can prove it. Either way, Franzese and his friends have been acquitted, and *The New York Times* observed that Franzese's wife, trim and blond, was sobbing, and knows why: with emotion and relief. Have a nice Christmas, Mrs. Franzese!

Marie doesn't find it especially out of the ordinary when the Cresspahl family is picked up from Riverside Drive late in the afternoon and taken to Connecticut by chauffeured limo. To judge by her behavior, she expected nothing less. Now the Cresspahl family not only has a friend who'll share his big car and house in the country with them, which might be pure co-incidence, if not just deserts; now there's someone else inviting them to enjoy such luxuries, the boss, His Majesty the Vice President himself, and Marie feels safe living in a world where hard work and ability are rewarded as they deserve to be. While the car was still in the city, she may have been sorry that its windows were tinted a discreet dark green, not giving any of the kids in her class the chance to see her partaking of this stylish trans-portation; on the highway, she started experimenting with what the proper behavior might be for a conveyance of this kind. She decides on a stiff, upright posture in the plump padded seats. Then a hidden chest of drawers built into the front wall of the passenger compartment is too much for her. She considers it possible that there's a bar inside it. She pulls one of the richly polished knobs in the most casual way she can manage. Heavens to Betsy, it is a bar, with a cooling unit too! There's a wireless phone in this car! And here there's a TV folded up to the size of a shoe box! Marie is so busy with her discoveries and her behavior that she doesn't even notice that Arthur is only waiting for an invitation to lower the dividing glass and begin the conversation he now seems to think Employee Cresspahl, eleventh floor, is worthy of. But Cresspahl, eleventh floor, is talking to her child. Cresspahl, eleventh floor, has other things on her mind.

De Rosny's house is a stone's throw from the Long Island Sound in a parklike neighborhood where even the streets are private property. The area begins with a little rise built into and crossing the street, meant to inform drivers from elsewhere, with a bump to the wheels, that they are now entering a new land where special rules and customs apply. The house has no fewer than five columns, white, in front of its two floors, holding up nothing but a pediment jutting out from the roof. The wrought-iron gates open themselves at a radio signal from the car. Marie is only a little embarrassed that Arthur holds the door open for her, head bent, cap in the vicinity of his heart. She thinks such customs are natural when they are respected and performed. She has time to give him a grateful sidelong glance. She thinks that all this is due to her mother's hard work.

She doesn't understand a thing. She sees de Rosny, this gangly hardy man, as simply a nice person with especially believable manners. She doesn't grasp that we depend on him. Even though she's been told this many times. She lets him lead her through the lower floor, living rooms filled with inflatable furniture, rustic cupboards, hanging chairs, walls covered with reproductions of comic strips and ads for canned soup. So this is where *The New York Times* took photographs. Since then, Christmas preparations have been made here too. De Rosny has hung from the chandeliers the biggest and brightest stars you can buy from New York's paper stores— practically morning stars. If you believe him, he set up the old Italian nativity scene especially for Marie, and Marie does believe him. He so thoroughly envelops Marie in the behavior one has toward a lady that she cannot help but conform to it. There's nothing for it but to say "please" and "thank you" and "may I" and "but of course." She would never permit herself an eyelash flutter like that with just me. Even her voice sounds different.

To Marie the whole evening is a friendly visit. She thinks it's possible for people to have power over one another at work, due to chains of command and differing salaries, but nevertheless to fraternize like equals in their spare time. She feels so unconditionally welcome there, due solely to her beautiful eyes, that she puts the whole de Rosny family into her inner circle at once, and the first thing she'll ask me after we leave is why Mrs. de Rosny spent the whole time on the second floor, wandering through the rooms there with a rather heavy tread. *The New York Times* won't have taken any photographs there. Marie thinks Arthur's metamorphosis into a servant is just funny, and bats her eyelashes at him when he wheels in cocktails on a converted baby carriage, Paris 1908, and she takes the orange juice Arthur has called a screwdriver as precisely the joke he'd intended. Marie sees the conversation before dinner as carefree stories of work in the distant city, and doesn't realize that it's actually a lightning-fast, merciless test of whether I fully and accurately understand the finance system of the Czechoslovak Socialist Republic, how much the Czechoslovakian government plans to raise the GDP by with its new 1966–70 Five-Year Plan, and even in which areas, for example by 50 percent in the chemical industry, and also whether the Czechs and Slovaks will succeed in meeting these goals, and if not then why not. What Professor Kouba had to say about the ČSSR's New System of Economic Planning and Management in the February 1966 issue of *Mirovaya Ekonomika i Mezhdunarodnye Otnosheniya* comes out of my mouth so fast that I wouldn't be able to think of the

402 · *December 16, 1967 Saturday*

German words for it, much less the thought behind them. It seems like I've passed the test, B minus maybe. All Marie has noticed is that once again her mother knows lots of things, and she displays her pride with big shining eyes.

It's by no means a sure thing yet, however, that the gentlemen in Prague seriously want to nudge their economy to health with credit in Western currencies. Still, it wasn't a Western banker who made a personal appearance at the Státní Banka Československá, it was the latter's president who paid a visit to Karl Blessing of the West German Bundesbank. What a blessing there's a Blessing. The question for me isn't whether it'll happen nor whether I'm willing. I don't know of a single company except Revlon, never mind a bank, where a woman is even an assistant vice president, and de Rosny won't change that. That's one thing.

All Marie notices about the dinner is how formal it is. A housekeeper, a cook, and finally Arthur each played their part in making it so. Marie sees only that Arthur really and truly pours some wine into one of her three glasses. She takes de Rosny's inquiries into my background for the pure expression of interest that one expects among friends. What he's conducting is an interrogation. He can do that, he's the boss, he's investing money at his own risk so he assumes the right to ask questions, and his most courteous way of expressing himself and his most winsome face don't make any difference. He wants to know quite simply everything I haven't told the personnel department, from the Mecklenburg tradesmen's guilds to my current feelings about the basic principles of Marxist dialectics. De Rosny can't understand how Cresspahl was the mayor of Jerichow, and maybe he thinks it's funny, in any case he wants it explained to him. With respect to Jakob, occupation and cause of death are enough. You are ever so thoughtful, Mr. Vice President. It comes out, though, that Jakob never did represent the German Democratic Republic at a European Railway Timetable Conference, in Lisbon or anywhere else, which is a blow to Marie. She'd been so sure of that. Oh well. And what would the Czechs and Slovaks think about me? How should I know? What he means is: the government and party of the Czechs and Slovaks. Most likely they aren't mad at me. I don't have to shove it in their faces, after all, that I passed through their country with a passport in which only the photograph was actually mine. But there might be something. The ČSSR is on very good terms with the German Democratic Republic, and they might decide to share the latter government's pain over the fact that I tried living under them for only three and a half years, and then left for the back of beyond. That doesn't bother de Rosny. On the contrary, he considers it an advantage, maybe. It's true, I don't have to put in writing for de Rosny, or the Ministry of the Interior of the GDR, or its Foreign Ministry either, the fact that I have a friend named Anita, Anita with the Red Hair, who helps private individuals out of the GDR, and that so far I have not been able to refuse her anything. Then there's the job with NATO in the Military Maneuver Damages Compensation Department in the forest outside of Mönchengladbach. De Rosny considers that a fillip, if anything making me more trustworthy. Could be, but what about how I got the job? Well, if he doesn't ask then I can't answer. And for de Rosny it's enough that I haven't heard from Dr. Blach again since Captain Rohlfs handed him over to the East German courts, not even since they let him back out onto the streets. And so the second order of business this evening is taken care of. Apparently, all in all, I have adequate knowledge and an adequate life for the haul our esteemed boss de Rosny has planned in the Eastern European credit market. So now I'd like to go home.

But Marie has one more question. She has followed the examination of my biography like a bloodhound, and in fact did hear quite a few things for the first time. But now it turns out she'd been thinking about something else the whole time, and so now the moment has come to interview de Rosny. She brings out her question a little timidly, with lowered eyes at first, and stays on a general level, not mentioning de Rosny's particular firm by name: Is it true that the banks are making money off the war in Vietnam?

De Rosny hasn't opened his mouth yet and already Marie believes everything he's going to say. Because he didn't let himself be tempted into a disconcerted sidelong look at the mother raising her child with such Communist idées fixes; he even refrained from any look betraying amusement at the childishness of the question. He sits up straight in his chair, he leans forward, he rests his elbows on his damask, he lays, almost folds his hands over each other, and he gives Marie a serious look. He is making the effort of an actor playing a doctor at a seriously ill patient's bedside. His voice is deeper, even. – We: he says, and he pauses, as though compelled to consider everything once again, for the sake of total diligence. Now Marie is a little frightened. Money itself is speaking to her, and Money is looking at her with steady, concerned blue eyes while it talks to her face-to-face.

– We wish, with all our hearts, that the conflict in Indochina could be brought to an end, whatever the outcome, or at least that our country were no longer involved in it. We don't believe that there will be peace with an American victory, not even in two years. And the peace in Indochina we could have in two years without a victory for our side, we want it now. Because war brings and increases inflation. Inflation, young lady, is a terrible thing for a bank. In the long run, a war puts the government in a position to tie the banks' hands, dictate what they can and can't do, down to the smallest details. Already it's going to take a terrible effort to repair the sicknesses lurking behind our current economic bubble. I'll tell you, young lady. If Mr. Johnson were to announce defeat in Vietnam, that we were cutting our losses, the market would jump fifty points. What am I talking about! Sixty points, on day one. And then there's the human side, the most important consideration of all, my dear Mary. Bankers have human feelings too. *Believe me*: de Rosny says.

And Marie believes him. She gives her mother an astonished look, accusing her of having presented things in a very different light, but since her mother doesn't speak up and contradict de Rosny, that's that as far as Marie is concerned. Marie should never have been allowed to come to this house.

When we leave, there's something else: a box covered in a white cloth is carried out to the car, and the Italian nativity scene is no longer where it was. Should an employee prove to be a thoroughly suitable person for a profitable assignment, one might well decide to tie her tighter to the firm with a gift worth, let's say, a thousand dollars, even if it goes to her daughter.

– *We all wish you a pleasant Christmas*: de Rosny says, and he actually does stay standing at his ancestral portal till the car has left the driveway. Marie is still waving through the back window when there's no longer any possible way he can see her.

And Marie gets something else, too. The false gifts just won't stop coming tonight. De Rosny wants to start his fishing expedition on the quiet. I'm learning Czech to make a vacation in Prague that much easier. The next time I happen to be asked about the bank's stance on credit to Eastern

European countries, the more intelligent answer would be: The bank's policy in this direction can be described as not aggressive, repeat: not aggressive. Strange that Dmitri Weiszand should have spent a whole evening and dinner at St. Wenceslaus drawing Mrs. Cresspahl out with this question. And it would be better if even Marie acted like we'd spent this evening over juice and popcorn at the Riviera Theatre. As expected, Marie is thrilled.

– *A real secret?* she says. – You mean a secret even *The New York Times* doesn't know about?

That kind of secret all right. For Marie that's exciting.

December 17, 1967 Sunday

Either it's Christmas approaching or else old madam *New York Times* is in serious decline. Because here she is, claiming unashamedly that there is a West German author by the name of Günther Glass. Even the "th" is wrong, and the rest simply beggars belief. Surely *The New York Times* knows that it's another author who has given life to the Glass family—Jerome D. Salinger, of Westport, Connecticut?

The New York Times was back in East Germany once again, and she looked around to see what's what, and found it. Hans-Dietrich Dahnke's the name, professor of German literature at Humboldt University in East Berlin is his game, and he tells *The New York Times*: "But people cannot see everything that is printed in any case. It is better when the party makes the selection for them." All right then, and DON'T FORGET THE NEEDIEST!

And the Air Force is dumping everything it has on Hanoi and even members of congress feel that the Vietcong are doing a better job of land distribution than the Saigon government and a charred package containing $44,000 in cash was found in the burned-out post office and the city's burglars are now going out to the suburbs and the common cold may be caused by psychological depression not a virus and Sonny Franzese is back home with his wife, Tina, and Hannah Arendt has said in public that "To oppose the government in the United States with violence is absolutely wrong" and, what else, REMEMBER THE NEEDIEST!

In 1935 my father started two things.

The first was he started planting a garden. Behind the house, from the back door to the front of the workshop barn, was untilled, weed-choked land, and one Sunday evening in March a whole group went to work turning over the soil, which had grown dry and hard. Each with his or her own spade, there were Hilde Paepcke, Alexander Paepcke, Aggie Brüshaver, Creutz the elder and Creutz the younger ("to be good neighbors"), Arthur Semig, Meta Wulff, Albert Papenbrock, Louise Papenbrock, the two assistants, the two apprentices, Lisbeth Cresspahl, Cresspahl, and the child. That was a long front against the land, and they dug in, they turned the soil, they threw the stones neatly into a pile, and people had fun, for Louise broke her spade, and Heine Klaproth was leaving a large and growing mound in his wake, and there was laughter, for Louise Papenbrock didn't want to let anyone help with her share, and after a few hours they were done. Lisbeth was given the honor of beating the paths between the beds. The others were given beer and pea soup from the very biggest pot in the house. Creutz had brought over ten fruit trees but he didn't want to plant the first, that wasn't how it was done, and so Cresspahl walked over and planted a tree and watered it and hoped for good apples. Then he paced off Lisbeth's paths again and made sure everything was in order, and the people standing at the windows laughed and laughed, because he didn't realize that the tiny child was walking behind him with her hands clasped thoughtfully behind her back, just like him. And in cold cold May the patch of land was a garden. That was something he started, meant to last.

The other thing came from the guild in Gneez. They had promised they'd cut him in, and they did. What they'd foreseen was the arrival of an order from the Reichswehr, which was now called the Wehrmacht, and written on that order was construction and road-building and jobs for carpenters and plumbers and glaziers and roofers and chimney makers and gardeners on dozens of acres north of Jerichow, halfway between the town and the sea, where the elevation is high above the water. Before they cut Cresspahl in, there was one last detail that had to be taken care of.

I hear you have ten thousand marks in the credit union, Cresspahl.
If you say so, Böttcher. Im not sayin that.
Even fifteen, Cresspahl. That's not what Im saying.
Aha.

Jå. Cant have that. Take it outta there and put it in Wismar, Lübeck,
wherever you want. I need to be able to say: Cresspahl has no more than eight
hundred in the credit union. I need to be able to say that in good faith.
Well thats what we'll do then, Böttcher. And thanks.

Then they cut him in and asked him into the guild master's living room
and divided out the batches of work, because the Mecklenburg Reichswehr
was known to prefer dealing with small tradesmen over big companies and
the Gneez guild wanted the whole contract. The tradesmen in Gneez
district did in fact keep the construction of Jerichow-North almost entirely
for themselves. Specialist firms were brought in from Berlin and Hamburg
only for the concrete work and the steel construction. And that meant
there was something for the hotels too. There was something for almost
everyone. There was something in the air, there was something you could
feel, and more than one person said it out loud: *Here we go.* Köpcke the
building contractor had so much reason to be happy that he started greeting Cresspahl on the streets again, even though Cresspahl hadn't sent him
a penny of work on his own renovations. Now there were pennies enough
for all, and no one had any complaints about the marks either. Not that
everyone got exactly what they were angling for. Cresspahl, for instance,
had especially wanted the officers' mess. He'd had his heart set on it. A lot
of people go to the officers' mess, and they talk. People with money. What
Cresspahl wanted to put on display there were massive brazilwood bays on
three walls. He pictured three tables for the middle, easy to push together
so people could gather around a large table, easy to remove to make a dance
floor. That was how it used to be, there was dancing in the officers' mess.
But the interior design of the mess went to someone else, and Cresspahl
couldn't push for it, because the man who got it was Wilhelm Böttcher,
master of the guild, since he'd landed the big one. In the end Wilhelm
Böttcher wasn't to be envied for it, because the Reichswehr, or Wehrmacht
as they called themselves now, sent him some guy who scribbled all over
his drawings like he owned them. So Cresspahl made do with the beds,
the closets, the sentry boxes, and the duckboards sentries need so their feet
won't get cold. And now he had almost more assistants and untrained
workers than he had room for in his house, he had to quickly convert the
old fodder room in the barn into a dormitory. And when Elsa Pienagel

came over and wanted a dining-room chair fixed up as nice as her sewing chest had been, he couldn't say for sure when it would be ready, and she'd have to come pick it up, since he didn't have time for home deliveries anymore. And there was something to show for it all, some real money coming in. By the time 1935 was over, he'd been able to buy another belt sander and a chain mortiser and a veneer router and a corner finisher, and say what you want about the German Labor Front and that drunken pig Robert Ley, but Dr. Erdamer wasn't too good for a high post with them, and Dr. Erdamer had worked out an arrangement for Cresspahl to buy new machines from the German Woodworking Co. in Schwerin, and the whole lot cost him just 9,500 reichsmarks. They'd've been a good 11,000 otherwise. Not rentenmarks anymore, reichsmarks. And Lisbeth had so much to do, with cooking for all the workmen and the house and the child. She did have two girls helping out now, learning how to run a real Mecklenburg household, and even so it was sometimes late in the evening when she stopped working, because it was often she who had to go to Gneez and get forms from the Army Construction Office on Station Street.

> *You can't ask me to do that, Cresspahl.*
> *What can't I ask you to do, Lisbeth.*
> *Go get the forms.*
> *I certainly can. The maids dont need to know everything thats in em, and the child cant take the train by herself yet.*
> *But then I'll be guilty too, Heinrich!*
> *Guilty of what.*
> *Of the war! The barracks are for war.*
> *Lisbeth, I cant help you.*
> *Can't we . . . can't you get out of the contract?*
> *Whatll we live on, Lisbeth?*
> *Ach, Heinrich. Live. What about the guilt!*
> *You wanna go to England?*
> *No!*
> *Then I dont know what you want, Lisbeth.*
> *Cresspahl.*
> *Can't you hear the child crying?*

And the roads in Jerichow-North were built strangely wide in various places. And behind the wall of barracks buildings there was more land fenced off than you'd need for a drill grounds. The fences ran for miles to the west. And the wide roads went on and on, they never stopped. And for a long time the children of Jerichow would learn the wrong word for *airplane*, they learned: *fighter*, and they learned: *bomber*.

In 1935, at the German Reichsbahn booth at the end of the steamship dock in Rande-Baltic, you could still buy rail tickets to anywhere, to Lübeck, to London. Maybe Cresspahl had stopped thinking about it because the government of His Majesty George V had disappointed him. The Austrian had gone ahead and reintroduced universal military service and every soldier had to swear an oath of personal allegiance to him, but did the English have to help him out with permission to expand the German fleet to up to 35 percent the strength of the British? They were in for a surprise from the twelve German U-boats put into operation in late June 1935, that's for sure, and from the ones to come too. And maybe he thought he'd no longer be welcome.

Brüshaver's church wouldn't have let him flee the country, and Brüshaver apparently didn't mind the son from his first marriage serving as a pilot in the air force of the Austrian who was trying to dissolve the church. Brüshaver probably asked how work was going in Jerichow-North because he wanted to try to get his son transferred there. As the commander maybe.

No one could expect the old Papenbrocks to go anywhere at this point. As ever, Papenbrock found in every suspect act of the Führer and Reich chancellor something that wasn't so suspect after all. It may have been a bitter pill that the guy had banned the Mecklenburg flag, along with the flags of all the other German states, but then again the two Mecklenburgs were once again united, for the first time in three hundred years, even those snooty Lübeckers with their Free Hanseatic City included. And the re-incorporation of the Saarland into the Reich, that was a stroke of genius. It was still annoying that he called himself a writer, of course, and that he hadn't stuck it out as a member of the Braunschweig delegation to Berlin a little longer, for appearances' sake if nothing else. But he, Papenbrock, hadn't had anything taken away or destroyed by the Austrian yet.

– Actually, why *did* Papenbrock go to Stelling's memorial service? Had he been in Papenbrock's party too?

– Johannes Stelling had been a Social Democrat, but in 1920, as minister of the interior for Mecklenburg-Schwerin, he hadn't lifted a finger against the Freikorps, safe in their Mecklenburg estates and going after the workers. If it weren't for him, Papenbrock could easily have lost his Vietsen lease a lot sooner. Stelling had been governor of the state from 1921 to 1924. And a Reichstag representative. Papenbrock probably wanted to pay his respects to him, even if they were his last.

And in late 1935 Arthur Semig was still in his tasteful house on the Bäk in Jerichow, continuing to receive his official pension, and he thought that was only proper. True, it was no longer even legal for him to hire a maid for Dora, there was no longer anyone in Jerichow he would legally be permitted to marry or conduct extramarital relations with, and his German citizenship had been revoked as well. In exchange, he had the right to fly the Jewish colors on his flagpole, and the municipal police would have been obligated to protect this flag from damage or defacement. Arthur simply couldn't bring himself to leave a country where everyone spoke like him, even if in many respects they didn't think like him.

And Peter Niebuhr was serving in the Eiche school for NCOs near Potsdam, and he'd been in the Berlin-Friedenau Communist Party! Was he trying to take revenge on Comrade Stalin, who now had his dead friend Kirov just like Hitler had Röhm, and who was taking his sweet time putting down the putsch while continuing his liquidations? Did he disapprove of the USA itself finally entering into diplomatic relations with Stalin's state, and of that state joining the League of Nations in these circumstances, albeit over Swiss objections? Peter's relatives didn't understand him. Ever since Peter had gone to university in Berlin, he'd become very hard to understand.

And even Martin Niebuhr realized by now that the Department of Waterways would never offer him anything bigger than the sluice at Wendisch Burg. And Gertrud Niebuhr would have wanted to adopt a child at least. And Lisbeth had had to promise her to come visit the lock for at least two weeks every year, with the child, Gesine.

And Horst Papenbrock had not only come back from "Rio de Janeiro," he had actually brought back his brother, Robert. Jerichow didn't see much of Robert, he'd been living in Schwerin for some time. And there was still almost no military presence in Jerichow, but Pahl was doing well with his made-to-measure uniforms for officers. The trades complained a bit louder, and they were doing well. The urgent demand for building material for Jerichow-North had even made a businessman out of Alexander Paepcke, who spent his days in the brickworks, in the office, not on the Gneez tennis courts. And the Paepckes had their second child in August 1935, a boy, Eberhardt Paepcke, Paepcke Junior. The brickworks still hadn't burned down.

And only Methfessel hadn't found his footing again. Methfessel had had to give up the business, to his oldest assistant, his sons were still children. It was disgraceful, seeing that big strong man wandering the streets of Jerichow and looking for children and asking them: Do you want to be a lion? That was supposed to be funny! And Dr. Avenarius Kollmorgen had closed his practice, he was showing his face outdoors more rarely now, and only asked very few people these days if all were well. And Dr. Hauschildt had developed into a well nigh capable veterinarian, ever since he'd had a sharp eye kept on him. And Methling had laid down in Gneez and died, having done his part for race and Reich, and he wanted to be buried in Jerichow, and had actually managed to force Schultz the state bishop to put on a more nationalist ceremony. A flag with a swastika was draped on his coffin, and six SA men carried it out of St. Peter's Church, and the schoolchildren were given a day off so that they could sing. Dr. Berling had found relatives living in Sweden, while off looking for his Aryan ancestry there, and now spent vacations in Scania. Swenson was operating two taxis now and an omnibus line from the Jerichow train station to Jerichow-North, and battling the German post office for the concession for a public bus line to Rande. Erich Schulz had not come back for the Jerichow expansion—he was said to be in the navy. The von Plessens and the von Bothmers and their peers had let themselves be absorbed, along with their whole equestrian clubs, into the SS. And Friedrich Jansen had been the mayor and Nazi Party district leader of Jerichow for almost two years now and had learned to listen to Kleineschulte and old Papenbrock. There were still a couple of people he hadn't quite taken care of yet. Johs. Schmidt was still asking for money when the party requested the use of his Musikhaus loudspeakers for national and National Socialist events; he'd soon learn. Another one was this Englishman, this Heinrich Cresspahl behind the church. Came to Town Hall and asked for a party membership form and didn't bring it back and claimed the form was for one of his assistants. The assistant had gone to Wismar, he'd actually been a party member since June 1934, Friedrich Jansen had figured out that much, something fishy was going on there. This Cresspahl didn't admit he'd had second thoughts when the Führer had cleansed his SA of traitors and bastards, he only said: He was still thinking it over. And then said it again, and again. There still wasn't anything you could hang on him, and still no way to get past old Papenbrock. But one of these days this Cresspahl would fall into a trap laid by Nordic cunning. Or into an open grave.

Cresspahl had taken out a second life insurance policy, with Allianz. Cresspahl could now be reached by phone, JErichow-209. It was always his wife who answered, though, he probably didn't have time for the twenty steps from the workshop to the house. Now it was 1935, and they still didn't have their second child, or a third. You wouldn't have guessed that of Lisbeth Papenbrock to look at her. The thing about the walnut trees had turned out to be true, their oils really did keep mosquitoes away. They had only the one child, Gesine, who by Christmas 1935 was a little older than two and a half. She still didn't talk much, but she kept her eyes wide open.

Hang on to your fence, don't reach for the moon.

December 19, 1967 Tuesday

Oh, *The New York Times* when she really lets loose! It wasn't anything exceptional, just the city's commissioner of the Department of Water Supply, Gas and Electricity resigning last week because he and Antonio ("Tony Ducks") Corallo from the Mafia had been running a scheme involving the private distribution of, for example, an $835,000 city contract. Two articles, starting on the front page and filling all of page 52. And another article on page 1! continued on page 53! And she does not neglect to offer in addition "A Glimpse at City's Corruption Over the Last Century." And in the commentary on the editorial page you can hear her voice shaking, and still she doesn't lose control of herself—she advises us to see the situation in its proper context and instructs us how to do so.

And who thanks her for it, other than with ten cents?

We want to thank her, because it's Christmas.

Thank you very much, dear lady.

It must be because it's almost Christmas that people are acting so strange. It can't be anything else.

It started with Marie, wanting to explicitly give thanks for an apartment from which in the morning she can see a wintry river and the brightly sunlit cliffs on the other shore. She does so in a roundabout way, putting on a patronizing tone to say: *Nice apartment you have here.* Anything more might have betrayed emotion. Then she said: Some children really do have it lucky.

And Shakespeare and Jason were downright exuberant, inexhaustible in describing Mrs. Cresspahl's outward appearance, and it may have something to do with the fact that they are soon to receive envelopes with a little green paper inside, but it can't be entirely about that.

The black mechanic in the middle garage on Ninety-Sixth Street, the serious man who goes over to a broken car like a doctor on a soap opera, waved with his whole hand to Mrs. Cresspahl, in a brotherly way, and it might mean: Take care of yourself, sister. Look out for yourself. Hope you have a good day now. He can say all that without smiling.

And again on West End Avenue, outside the liquor store, there was one of those tattered men each of whom has a sick aunt in New Jersey, which is why he needs at least thirty-five cents for the fare to see her, and Mrs. Cresspahl remained hard of heart and gave him not cash but a disdainful subway token, and he really and truly said: God bless you, lady. Impossible.

The old man at the newsstand practically wouldn't let Mrs. Cresspahl go, he talked to her and asked: Don't you want your *Der Spiegel*? It's just come up. He's always acted like people were a burden with their constant requests, and today he looked up at the sky and looked the customer in the face and told her: *Nice day.* And it wasn't just a statement of fact, it was not too far from a wish. Had someone given him a drink?

And at least on the eleventh floor of the bank they couldn't get over the fact that it was thirteen degrees (55°) on a 19th of December. Apparently that hadn't happened in decades. Apparently the last time was in 1931! Everyone's greetings are a hairsbreadth away from hugs. And no one pays attention to whether Mrs. Cresspahl answers a compliment on her appearance with a compliment in return, as the rules require. They may have meant it. Can it be true?

And all day the weather was clear and mild, or as they say here, like a balm. Total strangers smiled at Mrs. Cresspahl on the sidewalk, in the subway even! The light in the air felt solid. You could throw yourself against it with your whole body, not just your eyelids.

And in the cafeteria in the building, Sam himself intervened after I'd read his menu for the second time. – Get the pot roast, it's delicious, I promise! he said, kissing his fingertips with pleasure. Then the waitress took what Sam felt was her time, and he admonished the cook personally through the hatch: One pot roast for the lady here with a smile on her face!

And everyone else I ran into—Amanda, James Shuldiner, Mrs. Kelly, Mrs. Ferwalter, Marjorie—they all wanted to know how Mrs. Cresspahl was doing, and every last one wanted a truthful, honest answer!

And Marie broke the rules and called me at work to report that we'd gotten mail from Kliefoth, from Karsch, from D. E. And the man who sells us cheese would like, after approximately two years acquaintance, to ask Mrs. Cresspahl a question. He usually has a sour expression on his face, or else his pale complexion makes it look that way once it's brought out by a black growth of incipient beard well before the eponymous five o'clock. His store is so crowded that the customers have to take a number to be served in their proper order, and he has never once given the slightest sign of recognizing us. But this evening he was alone.

– So, ma'am, I have a question for you.
– Go ahead.
– You sometimes come in here with a child.
– I do indeed. Sometimes with two.
– I mean just the one.
– The one with the braids?
– Yes. That's the one I mean.

– And what's your question?
– Is she your child?
– She is my child.
– I see.
– Yes.
– In that case, I would like to ask you one more thing, if you don't mind.
– Yes?
– Umm ... Are you married?
– The answer is affirmative.
– Hmm. All right. Then that's that.

Das war es denn wohl. That takes care of that.

And Marie had asked Mr. Robinson to let her have the elevator, and she was riding it up and down in the building, waiting for the elevator doors to open in front of the Mrs. Cresspahl I am taken to be, Mrs. Cresspahl who wasn't expecting her child there, Gesine who I am for Marie.

The day will come when she looks like me at first glance, but the world will like her at second, and not even she will know that she smiles back like Jakob.

PART TWO

December 1967–April 1968

December 20, 1967 Wednesday

THE WATER is hidden deep underground where the street has to pass over a mound of rock—chlorine-green, lukewarm water packed tight in a tiled box beneath the Hotel Marseilles on West End Avenue, Manhattan, Upper West Side, New York, New York. The water is loud, it cracks and splits open under the swimmers' dives, sloshes against the sides, gurgles in the overflows, hurls the patter of walled-in echoes wildly this way and that. Tiptoes. Arms out. Ankles up. Head between arms. Soles flat next to each other. Now the water hits the top of your skull. The rapid passage under the water, following your hands, is through half-blind twilight.

The children in the shallow end of the pool are already greeting the head that pops up in their midst. – Nice header, Gesine: they say. But they say Gee-sign, and what they very well might mean is that that wasn't how they learned to dive. *Curious header, Mrs. Cresspahl.*

The children of West End Avenue and Riverside Drive fill the Mediterranean Swimming Club at this time of day, between the end of work and dinnertime. They endure the presence among them of the old ladies bravely paddling away in their flowered swim caps; they keep an eye on the young athletes trying to forestall the decay of their bodies with underwater forced marches; it is quieter in the corner where a lone mother is standing still, conscientious, shy, with a toddler on her lap. But the children like to clear the diving lane only for their own kind, letting the grown-ups wait on the board, and boys like David Williams make a game out of unexpectedly plunging down into the middle of the doggedly flailing musclemen.

They learned to dive differently. The jerk of the whole body, down to the ankles, from abruptly raised arms—missing. Look at this Marie Cresspahl, been in the country only six years: she glides into the water from the edge of the pool in a single unbroken movement, like a fish returning to

420 · December 20, 1967 Wednesday

its proper element. It is as though she simply lets herself drop, so lacking in visible kickoff is her jump. Marie is practicing diving with her friends— Pamela Blumenroth, Rebecca Ferwalter—but they don't throw coins onto the bottom of the pool, they throw locker keys, whose dull color camouflages them. Without keys they won't be able to leave the pool, so there is some fear in their giddy competitive screams, and when Marie comes up holding the rescued key in her outstretched hand, there is real relief in her small, wet face, shining with happiness. Later, when she pulls the tight swim cap off her head, she will look older than her ten and a half years amid her long-since winter-blond hair. In the white frame of her cap, the still-growing curve of her eye sockets is exposed under her abbreviated forehead, as though stripped of all protection.

Above the noisy water, halfway up the blue-tiled walls of the room, a balcony runs around two sides: the back of Bar Marseilles, where there are tables for two. That's how old this hotel is. For the customers of 1895, it was still enough to look down from far above at the swimmers, the barely clad; in a building today, the drinkers would want stools at the edge of the pool, or alongside it behind a clear panorama window. Still, Mr. McIntyre up there hardly ever comes to a stop in front of his ninety-nine bottles of firewater: there are enough people living in this part of town who like to meet up amid the redwood walls, spend a little time every day sitting on the shiny worn leather and polishing with their elbows the massive bulge of the mahogany bar, already gleaming with age. Up there, six years ago, a Gesine Cresspahl sat too long and tried to use Irish turns of phrase to find a false entrance into the local life, often next to Mr. Blumenroth, who at the time did not look like a father of Pamela. The Jews haven't given up on the Upper West Side yet—Jews are welcome here—but never once in six years has the head of a dark-skinned fellow American shown up at the delicately fretted balustrade, and just as, up there, it is not Mr. McIntyre's prices that keep the blacks from a visit to the Marseilles, so too, down below, it is not only the $60 annual fee that keeps the whites in the water among none but themselves.

On this particular evening, it's two hotel guests who are trekking back and forth in the pool along the south edge, stubbornly keeping to their lanes—two young foreigners. They stop, almost as if offended, before the old ladies who prefer the shorter swim across the pool; they swallow water and their rage at the children plunging into the depths right in front of their noses. Maybe they're Germans, technical trainees at their company's New York headquarters, because they are speaking German, despite the fact that not only Gesine Cresspahl but the Jewish swimmers too, if pressed, can understand their rather bewildered comments and cries. They have no sense of where they are; they speak openly, and loud. It's not clean enough for them here. They have a newly built pool at home. Many of the swimmers here look like they wouldn't be out of place in Europe. And finally Marie comes up, with smooth soft strokes under the water, to report, triumphantly: They're talking about you! They said you're the right size! That your bustline is too low! That maybe you haven't had children yet but you don't need any pumping up! With your hair, your cheekbones, you must be from Poland—*from a Slavic country!* she says. Because the Cresspahls speak German only when no one else is there to hear it, Marie insists on that, this Marie whose gray-green eyes are now full of affection, believing she has relayed a compliment to her mother, something agreeable.

And if you have kids, let's hope they don't have your bones, Cresspahl! I mean, if it's a girl, hope she gets Lisbeth's legs.

The pool of the Mediterranean Swimming Club, sixty-five feet long, eight lanes, may be bigger than the "Mili" in Jerichow, where Gesine Cresspahl learned to swim, the child who I was. The one there is bigger in memory—say those who have since returned. I am not allowed back. It's a long way from here, more than 4,500 miles, and even after an eight-hour flight you have to travel on until dark, and you still won't be there. That's more than 6,000 kilometers. That's Wendish country, Mecklenburg, on another coast. I lived there for twenty years. "If you cross the sea you may find yourself / Betrayed, sold out, in an American woods. . . ."

The rain shelters on the Mili in Jerichow-North were put up thirty years ago by my father, Heinrich Cresspahl, born in 1888, who left for the Netherlands to get away from the German wars, then went to England, and yet came back to Mecklenburg with my mother so that I could come into the world in Germany, a few years before the next war. She was so miserable already, my mother, Lisbeth, née Papenbrock. The airfield on the high Baltic coast near Jerichow, which my father helped build as a carpenter, was for a modern war, so a puny creek was stopped on its way to the sea and diverted and made to replenish the water of the military facility's pool. The facility was given the nickname Mili by schoolchildren, only after the war, when the Soviet occupying forces blew up the Jerichow-North complex, razed it to the ground, and forget about the pool. In 1953 Cresspahl's rain shelters had long since passed through Jerichow's stoves; only a few rotted stumps remained. It was February, the pool drained, the bottom neatly carpeted in white snowdrifts. Jakob came clambering down after me without a second thought. We walked up and down the bottom of the pool until all the lanes were filled with our footprints. No picture of Jakob's face on that day comes to mind, I would have to invent one. We were invisible, sheltered by the walls of the hole in the earth, hidden under the swirling sky, in the whistling silence. And he could tell me only how life abroad was for him, not how it would be for me.

The White House has now permitted the air force to fly with relative freedom through the so-called buffer strip along the Chinese border in Vietnam. Fourteen American scholars assure the nation that accepting a Communist victory would likely lead to larger, more costly wars rather than to a lasting peace.

Here is Mrs. Cresspahl, waiting at the edge of the swaying board until the diving lane is free. She lives around here, on the corner of Riverside Drive and Ninety-Sixth Street. Thirty-four years old. Her neck is stiff, she sucks in a belly. It won't be long before she's buying her shoes for comfort, not style. As she prepares herself for the dive, her eyes narrow, lips tauten. The sharp impact of the water on her head gives her a moment of numbness, blindness, absence; not for long.

– Quite a header, Gee-sign!

December 21, 1967 Thursday

In the Senate Foreign Relations Committee, some members are skeptical about whether the administration and Joint Chiefs of Staff told the truth in 1964, when they claimed that the destroyers *Maddox* and *Turner Joy* were attacked by North Vietnamese ships on August 4 of said year. According to Mr. John W. White from Cheshire, Conn., who was serving at the time on the *Pine Island*, a nearby seaplane tender, and who heard the radio messages sent by the destroyers at the time, they were "confusing because the destroyers themselves were not certain they were being attacked." Numerous signals were identified as incoming torpedoes, but then no torpedoes came. Was the radar actually picking up a number of small craft? Evidence of antiaircraft fire, flares? Could planes make out such small wakes from the air at night? At the time it was all considered true and sufficed to authorize the president to take the foreign war seriously.

– A president can't lie: Marie says: He'd always get caught!

She is standing in the kitchenette near the entrance of our apartment, in an apron too big for her, a dishtowel over her arm, turning meat in a pan, pushing her hot hair from her brow with a bent forearm the same way her grandmother and grandmother's mother did before her, not like a child helping out with the housework but like a member of the household who understands and accepts her role. Photographed like this, in ten years she would interpret herself as a child who grew up in fortunate circumstances, in a time of peace. She has taken her time, with a lower lip half tucked in and narrowed eyes, and when she spoke she was no doubt trying to show her mother that she was listening, but still reproaching the adult for her needless misgivings. It is a time of peace for her because she doesn't see the war in Vietnam.

She cannot see it. She has heard too many details from me about how war looks. She doesn't know anyone from school whose family has been sent a full coffin by the government. She's familiar with the ruins between Amsterdam and Columbus Avenues, but they were caused by the wrecking balls of land speculators from here, not by the bombs of an enemy from elsewhere. The small businesses on Broadway die out not because the heirs are casualties but because of the high rent and Mafia dollars. The government doesn't confiscate cars; the gas stations reward the purchase of gas with free gifts. Marie doesn't need to remember to lower her voice when a policeman is nearby. She can't imagine Mr. Weiszand being woken up at six in the morning by four plainclothes officials and dragged off to jail simply because he'd incited and led an antiwar protest at Columbia University. What she knows about railroads, ships, and airplanes is that to travel on them takes money, not a travel permit from the authorities. I would have a hard time naming a single item that wasn't for sale somewhere in New York. Our phone may be tapped but that doesn't take a war. There would need to be an army occupying Riverside Park across from our building and blocking the entrances to the Hudson River promenade with grenade launchers for Marie to be halfway convinced. Possibly, when it comes right down to it, she considers everything I tell her about Germany as nontransferable. That may be how they wage war in Europe, not here. She is here, though, and has enough to think about.

Marie is against wars because people can get hurt in them. Plus, she can't go against what I say outright; she doesn't even want to hurt my feelings. She started an argument with a teacher in class once, over the justice of the hostilities in Southeast Asia, but she sounded her friends out beforehand—Marcia, Pamela, Deborah, Angela—less to lay in a stockpile of solidarity than to not risk any friendships. Around Marcia's parents, Mr. & Mrs. Linus L. Carpenter, she wouldn't even let the topic pass her lips: the Carpenters give money to civil rights groups and want dark-skinned fellow Americans to have decent housing everywhere except in their own building, and they think the situation in Vietnam is old news, talking about it is tactless by this point, if not downright unseemly. Mr. Carpenter III—Georgetown, Harvard, colonel of a copter battalion in the reserve, the Carpenter of Allen, Burns, Elman & Carpenter—has explained to Marie that in a democratic form of government everyone is responsible for handling their own duties and responsibilities, and war is the president's. When Marie brought that home, cautiously, to test the waters, it also came out that she'd worn her GET OUT OF VIETNAM button only as long as it was fashionable in her class. She is as disingenuous as I have raised her to be.

She can't stand up against this country with the tools I've given her any better than I can. This is a country in which President Johnson is allowed to exploit Christmastime sentimentality with a televised interview promoting his policies at home and abroad, and can talk about "a Kennedy-McCarthy movement," and *The New York Times* will speak in a not dissatisfied tone of that "deadly hyphen" likening Senator Kennedy to the various peace groups more closely than he probably wants. Marie watched Johnson's dignified, devious appearance last night at the Carpenters' house, and came back outraged that the president could describe her senator as an unduly ambitious man who merely coveted his, Johnson's, job. She didn't notice that Kennedy was being denounced for wanting peace. She has been living here six years. She doesn't want to live anywhere else. She doesn't want to live in a country she can't trust. She trusts this one.

Her politeness is well nigh limitless. While setting the table and serving dinner she was still thinking, and before the first bite she said: You're saying that when a president's lie comes out, it's too late for us, and late enough for him?

She can look like such a little sophist sometimes. Chin on folded hands, head tilted amiably to one side, that's how she gazed at me, having proven that she listens to her mother's every word. She has added a second answer to her first one, and neither one shocked her in the least.

December 22, 1967 Friday

What a newspaper we have in this town! *The New York Times* reports that, according to real live astronomers, the sun in the northern hemisphere will be above the horizon for the shortest period of time and that winter officially arrived at 8:17 a.m. today.

It reports, too, that in August 1964 four crew members of the *Turner Joy* really did see the wake of a North Vietnamese torpedo in the Gulf of Tonkin, three hundred feet off the ship's port side; that the government, however, had already prepared contingent drafts of a full declaration of war, long before August 1964.

And Marie says, in a rather tense and snippy voice: – I can't live the way you want me to live! I'm not supposed to lie because you don't like lies? You'd have lost your job ages ago, I'd have been expelled, if we didn't lie like three American presidents in a row! You didn't stop your war and now you want me to do it for you? When you were young they were preparing their war all around you and you didn't notice anything!

– No one told me anything, Marie.

– But you could see it! *Apologies are in order, Mrs. Cresspahl.*

– Stop crying, Marie.

– Say *sowwy*, like I used to when I was a baby.

– Sowwy, Marie.

My war was well hidden. Even the name of the town of Jerichow was remote in Germany. Vacationers driving by on the road to the Rande seaside resort, what did they see? A quarter mile of rough paved road, making the cars hop and curtsy. Barns. Yards. The red eastern wall of the brickworks with its two real and fifteen false windows. Cool gravestones in the shadows. One street, narrow like a village's, with low buildings on either side, two-story, semi-decrepit plaster on the fronts, timbered sides. A monstrosity of a church with a bishop's-miter spire towering over it all, beclouded with treetops up to the start of the projecting gables. Lots of shops with display windows that used to be living-room windows. Karstadt's bunker-like box, a country general store. Or else they came by bus from the train station, and started with the market square, its almost regal buildings. Papenbrock's house, like the Lübeck Court, less modest than the town hall. Horse-drawn carts on the way to the weighing house. Hardly any local cars. Holiday quiet. Where the out-of-towners expected the actual town to start, they found themselves scooting down the smooth country road to the Baltic. To the left, a ways off, clusters of new construction, perhaps a workers' settlement, why not, as it said on the signs: "New Land North." Just where a strangely generous concrete road branched off, the main road dipped and behind the hotels of Rande thickly covered in bushes stretched the sea striped with sunlight. Off to the west, behind, forgotten, was the Jerichow-North Military Airfield. 1936.

But it wasn't called by its name in Jerichow. For more than a year now, the town's merchants and tradesmen had been working on it, making money, yet the site was called Mariengabe, after the village that made way for it. This had always been a customs border control area, so the new restricted zone didn't stand out. Vacationers looking for the abundant hiking trails mentioned in their out-of-date guidebooks were met with, and warned away by, army patrols at a good distance from the construction site. The local nobility had kept their regular table in the Lübeck Court; topics of conversation included the Olympic Games in Kiel, when necessary the 1934 drought, and still more reluctantly the Four-Year Plan. For Friedrich Jansen, mayor of Jerichow and district leader of the ruling party, had set up a regulars' table of his own, at the windows overlooking the stable yard, where he spent long evenings, mostly with out-of-town visitors. Oftentimes these were gentlemen from the secret police in Hamburg, in black uniforms, some had literal heavy leather coats to hang on the pegs. The workers in "Mariengabe" had refused to work for half a day in September 1936; there was talk of Communist leaflets. Herr von Maltzahn had found one in his forests and zealously pressed it into Friedrich Jansen's hand, "unread." Nowadays von Maltzahn was talking not about an airfield but about "our revenge for Versailles." Herr von Lüsewitz had received satisfactory compensation for his land holdings in what used to be Mariengabe, and since then liked to bring up his "sacrifice." Friedrich Jansen simply brought out his phrase about "Nordic cunning" and clearly knew "a pack of wine-guzzling aristocrat trash" when he saw it. In Peter Wulff's pub, people used expressions like "the big dog" and "a bloody miracle" to avoid mentioning the airfield, but not when anyone from out of town was drinking there, even if they were sitting out of earshot, no matter how good their Plattdeutsch sounded. Stoffregen, the head teacher, also tended to change the subject from the airfield right away, in his case to the Jews and the assassination of the head of the Swiss branch of the NSDAP abroad, which he described as an "unmasking." Kliefoth, the senior teacher, was widely understood to have left Berlin for a region in which the Nazis had come to power a full six months sooner than elsewhere for a reason—he would be forgiven here, but for what?—and word was that Kliefoth had interrupted a conversation about "the construction work" among fellow passengers on the train to Gneez with the comment: I'm warning you. Apparently he hadn't explained this notion of his. Swenson had made such a "modest" profit from his omnibus line between the station and Jerichow-North that he'd been able to buy a second van, and he called his participation in the construction of the airfield "doing his duty." Pastor Brüshaver attempted an outright joke, describing the thing as the "Reich Mission for People's Sport," after the signs set up at the western end of the construction zone; Pastor Brüshaver's son was in Spain flying missions against the forces of the legal government there and had a good chance of earning as his reward the command of an airfield, all they had to do was finish it. And my father had the saws in his workshop going morning till night, and at lunch tried to get the noise out of his ears by shaking his head, and he had a bank account in Rostock and one in Lübeck and received payments via a giro account in Hamburg too for the work of eight employees and had dutifully joined the German Labor Front and faithfully gave Heine Klaproth time off to serve in the Hitler Youth as the law required and had twenty ears listening to him around the lunch table, mine included, and he talked about Mariengabe.

He thought it was a good name, he said. Mary's Gift. Where someone was giving, someone wouldn't mind taking. Water was harder than stone, and anything that fell from the sky into the Baltic wasn't something he'd care to take. He'd seen airplanes in England. Lisbeth had even flown in one. She couldn't deny that now. Jerichow wasn't famous for anything yet, except Friedrich Jansen, but that would surely change with the bombs the English were going to be unloading here first. Jerichow and the English had a date, you might say.

Heinrich, your talk'll get us killed! Heinrich, the child!! Heinrich Cresspahl!

My father didn't talk about bombs, he talked in Platt about "*dropping shit,*" and these and any other unexpected thoughts he saw fit to voice— calmly, slowly, almost casually—they all found their way not directly to Friedrich Jansen and his fine leather notebook but first to the next-door house and across the yards and into the lawns and over the fields and only once Jerichow had been taken care of was it Friedrich Jansen's turn. Party Comrade Jansen passed them on word-for-word to the Gestapo in Gneez. That was a mistake. A stern official document was sent to his mayoral office, complete with national emblem and seal, from a Hamburg air force office, advising him in no uncertain terms to stop pestering them. By including his own name he had revealed that he had personal fish to fry, and the German air force was not interested in being the one to flip it for him. Moreover, it was proven scientific fact that water did do more damage to falling planes than land. Finally, not even a person with the rank of district leader was permitted to presume to insinuate that the air force command might be underestimating the potential enemy. As for the fundamentals of the situation, the relevant circles of the air force command tended to share the conviction that certain tradesmen were contributing more, and more effectively, to the expansion of the German air defense than certain timeservers in the ranks of the party and local administration. Heil Hitler! Friedrich Jansen had to sit there and keep his mouth shut now even when someone showed him how this Cresspahl shook his head during his speeches. As if he had water in his ears. Or when someone sat at Friedrich Jansen's regulars' table for a while even now, to cheer him up with Cresspahl's insinuations, and also because it really was annoying the way this Cresspahl talked so openly about war, like it was a foregone conclusion. It wasn't *necessarily* gonna happen. He was acting like a real spoilsport, to tell you the truth. He really was.

– Mariengabe: Marie says, upset and brooding. – I hope the English unloaded there plenty. 'Twould suit me fine.
– Sowwy, Marie.

What a newspaper we have in this town! She recognizes even us as customers, and takes the trouble to remind foreigners that we have to report our address to the federal government in January.

And Marie heads over to our post office on 105th Street that very afternoon to get the forms. Because what if we were deported! It's unthinkable!

243 Riverside Drive, New York, N.Y. 10025
December 23, 1967

Dear Dr. Kliefoth,

Many thanks for your kind inquiries after my child. Let me tell you a little about her.

Marie is ten and a half years old, four foot eleven, considered tall for her age. I don't have any recent photographs of her; in older ones, she generally liked to strike a pose. She thinks of herself as someone who observes the person behind the camera in a curious and at the same time solicitous way. A passport official would note her head shape as LONG/OVAL, but it's not as long as an egg; in truth it seems rather spherical in profile. In winter her hair is almost sandy-colored, especially her eyebrows. Eyes gray and green, depending on the light. Clear. Long, fanned-out lashes, not from me. I can see her father (whom of course you never met) in her face; my friends see me in it. I can also see several typical Mecklenburg qualities in it: a certain irony in the tilt of the neck, the upturned gaze from her lowered brow, the stony secretive mien, in general the trickiness, the plotting, the mischief. All in a foreign language. It is middle-class American, disciplined by a traditional school, standoffish against slang. But what she speaks, she lives. I, with my interpreter's certificate, often have to look things up. *Serendipity.* She currently has a thing for circumlocutions: *I scorn the action*, for instance, referring to an unpleasant task. A new way to apologize: *I stand corrected*, spoken in the accent of the Upper West Side of New York, which you would not find it so easy to grade.

She speaks German like she has a sore throat. She probably had to sacrifice the language she brought with her to get fully comfortable on the street, in the school, in the city. Düsseldorf, Berlin, Jerichow—for her that's geography. Germany, not *Deutschland*. She remembers more about vacations in Denmark. To take her back to the German language now would be more catastrophic for her than the move into American was. She would be happier if we had a real passport, an American one.

I can't give you as much information about Christmas in New York as you need. The visual assault starts unjustifiably early, up to four weeks in advance. Businesses attack first, and not only with targeted decoration. Acoustically, too, stores hammer into their customers' heads why they're supposed to hand over their money this time: Christmas music and Our Lingerie Guaranteed Imported Direct from Paris. On the streets, the Salvation Army has emerged from its lairs: trumpets and handbells. Finally, even the shabbiest bar will put up an electric runt of a Christmas tree between the bottles. The rich on Park Avenue, whose traffic islands in the summer are filled with flowers watered from "sources lying outside the city," set up large and lavishly lit Christmas trees, but not all the way to Ninety-Sixth Street, where the poor neighborhood, the black neighborhood, starts. We have Christmas trees near us on Broadway too, chicken-wired together at night into thick clumps, by day standing free, each in its own stand. Like luxury goods. They're on sale for the first-generation European immigrants—their children have already adopted the holly sprigs. Since Marie is in charge of the decoration in our house, we have holly. That's the word for *Stechpalmenzweige*. Other accessories considered important are the holiday postcards that the recipient can put up on the mantelpiece, to show how many correspondents he or she is loved by, and how many of that number can announce the prosperous course of their respective lives by means of lavish printing and graphics. We don't have a mantelpiece. Marie was also quick to move the dispensing of gifts from the night of the 24th to the American date, in her scorn for European customs. You also need a stocking to hang on the chimney. We do have a stocking. Then it's the job of an individual named Saint Nicholas, alias Santa Claus, alias Santa, to fill the stockings with gifts in the night. You'd recognize this *dispenser of gifts* because

> *He has a broad face and a little round belly,*
> *That shakes when he laughs like a bowlful of jelly.*

For Marie this is how it all has to proceed, because she considers it a required ceremony. She would probably prefer to celebrate (in a more technical sense) "Chanukah" with her Jewish friends. I don't know how to spell that in German. She's found out everything she can about this holiday: that it is celebrated from the 25th day of the month of Kislev through the 2nd of Adar, in commemoration of the rededication of the temple by the Maccabees after their victory over the Syrians under Antiochus IV. Your almanac no doubt has that much. Marie's holiday is over and done with on Tuesday morning, but this year her friends Pamela and Rebecca only start theirs on Tuesday evening, and children get presents on all eight days! You may also be aware that Chanukah begins with the lighting of the menorah, the nine-armed candelabra. But even though we're friends with Jewish neighbors, even if we count as exceptions to the Germans of the Twelve Years, to them we're still goys and Marie will never be allowed to watch Mr. Ferwalter light his menorah. Incidentally, the Jews reproach the so-called Christians for all the Christmas hustle and bustle, while the latter counter that Chanukah is if anything even more sentimental.

Perhaps you can gather from all this what status the birth of Jesus Christ has in the commercial realm. Yes, in the bank where I work there are gigantic wreaths of pine branches hanging on the wall between the elevators, with elaborate red ribbons, discreet, not cheap; customers as well as visitors are meant to see from them how the firm sees itself, and not only financially. But if tomorrow were a weekday, not a Sunday, I would have to go to work.

That's all I've seen. That's all I've been told.

This afternoon we got caught in an antiwar demonstration on Fifth Avenue—"afternoon" not in your understanding of the term, it wasn't one o'clock yet, but it was after twelve. Such sentences were called "real Klief-oths" in probably every one of your English classes, did you know that? There were about three hundred protestors at the demonstration and definitely at least that many policemen. We were trying to go to Dunhill's at Rockefeller Center, to buy you your morning tobacco, and the police were standing serious guard on the mall, the promenade there, because Rockefeller Center is, after all, private property. The policemen were making an effort to act calm, they were trying to keep the protestors on the sidewalk with *bullhorns*—how do you say that in German?—as though all they cared about was directing traffic, and the protestors had forgotten their megaphones. Only after one of them trumpeted a word into my ear three times did it register. LOVE is what he wanted, *LIEBE*. They called themselves Santa's Helpers and were unconventionally dressed, half from boutiques and half from the army surplus stores. What's more they had long hair, and the general public, loyal, patriotic, loaded down with their last-minute shopping, in inner turmoil from the large sums of money they'd just spent not to mention the outer sweat—this public shouted things about baths and hygiene. And that outraged Marie. She has learned that everyone should have the right to express their opinions in public; now here came people trying to impose their own clothes and hairstyles on others.

The leader of the protest was a young man with a mane of blond hair carrying an American flag and a sign in the same colors, reading KILL. The last I saw of him was when he tried to invade Saks with his friends, Santa's Helpers. Meanwhile the Salvation Army tootled calmly on, and fellows in hooded red coats and fake beards still waited to have their pictures taken with the kids. Finally the crowd pushed us out to Madison Avenue. The police were not openly angry, just exasperated from their prolonged effort to seem calm; they did still call me "Lady," but criticized me for bringing a child through their event with Santa's Helpers, telling me firmly to "go home." Now for a second time Marie was outraged. There might be moments when she still feels like a child—this wasn't one of them. In her anger, she forgot herself and called the policeman, admittedly in an undertone: a pig. *Ein Schwein.* I wasn't familiar with the term. Then she apologized for her ill-advised choice of words.

Forgive me for asking a favor of you, but could you please go to the cemetery and see if the Creutzes have covered my three graves for the winter? It's not that I care so much about the custom of tending to graves, it's that even if Erich Creutz decides he wants to do something for my money, Emmy Creutz tries to stop him, and I don't want to give her the satisfaction of putting one over on the daughter when she couldn't put one over on old Cresspahl.

My dear Herr Kliefoth, I wish you a happy New Year, your eighty-second, and an *otium cum dignitate.* Yours very sincerely, G. C.

December 24, 1967 Sunday
Right under the dateline on the first page, *The New York Times* publishes two pictures, as though they go together, are neighbors or family: President Johnson pinning medals on American soldiers yesterday at Camranh Bay, a huge base in South Vietnam: left. President Johnson with Pope Paul VI at the Vatican yesterday, glancing past the gesturing pontiff, his face in jovial laugh lines: right.

Because it's Christmas?

As the quotation of the day, she offers: "We are ready at any moment to substitute the word and the vote for the knife and the grenade in bringing honorable peace to Vietnam."

Because it's Christmas?

On Christmas in 1936 my mother wasn't dead yet. Even in 1937 she was still alive for Christmas.

Our Lisbeth. "Fröln Papenbrock" the Jerichowers called her to her face, later "Fru Cresspahl," but among themselves they talked about "Lisbeth," even if Lübeck folks have a different idea of what counts as showing respect. Respect for the family, that was something for Rostock, not Jerichow, where it was *Our Lisbeth* ever since old man Papenbrock ("Albert") spent the 1922 summer holidays there with his family. Not in the fancy hotels on the Rande beach but in Jerichow, in the Lübeck Court, they didn't go swimming too much but took lots of vacation-y carriage rides on the nobility's estates in the area, surveyor-y walks through town, and paid pointedly casual visits to the mansion off Market Square that the von Lassewitzes kept as their town house once they no longer had estates to spare. Papenbrock was thought to be someone looking to replace, in Jerichow, the estate lease he'd given up in Vietsen by Lake Müritz. No one thought his stay with his wife and son and daughters would give the entry in the Mecklenburg guidebooks the second line that Stoffregen the teacher thought St. Peter's Church and the Lindemann stable yards deserved. Still, these out-of-towners were something to behold, even if Papenbrock clearly thought he was the cat's pajamas. Ex-officer. Well, ex-captain. *Big guy.* Belly sometimes hung out past the curve of fabric he'd had tailored in Schwerin, well that's what holidays are for, right? He had a familiar way of setting his eyes on narrow, of shifting his teeth in the corner of his mouth—lots of people did that nowadays, even if he'd seen a few more of his marks make their escape into dollars. Albert. Next to him in the carriage, equally impressive, sat his wife, Louise, but there was something fretful and complaining in the tone she was using to try to keep the two girls sitting across from her under a thumb that hadn't been given her. Sonny Boy, Horst, was crabby mostly because he had to sit on the box next to the coachman, forced to be polite. Not much chance of him turning out to be a Papenbrock like his father. Hilde, the older girl, was a little condescending, when she asked for something at the table or was told she had to answer a local's question; she clearly thought the Papenbrock name was magnificent. Lisbeth moved and sat among them calmly, didn't grumble at the long family marches, nodded to the Jerichow children, plus she was her father's darling and didn't need to win him over. Maybe it was because she was the best rider of all three of them, constantly fearlessly jumping the paddock fences. She wasn't even of age yet—just sixteen. *We'll call er Lisbeth if we want to*, and to her face too, at the time.

All this noticed for future reference, and then in the summer of 1923 the Papenbrocks didn't come back. Someone left. The von Lassewitzes packed up in the spring, the way they always did when the time came for their trip to Cans or however you say that French word, and if the nicer furniture was put into storage in Schwerin this time that must have meant it was finally time to redo the house. The house did need work. The sea wind had eaten away much of the flower work from the plaster garlands above the double row of front windows, the cats could apparently no longer handle the mice in the attic, and the parquet floor, people said it was like walking on the frozen Baltic. Calls for bids were put out, for repairs, even renovations; not by the family, instead by Dr. Avenarius Kollmorgen, who hadn't been their lawyer before. It was misleading that Dr. Kollmorgen ("Avenarius") was somewhat short; he didn't answer questions, he just pursed his lips and brandished mysterious looks left and right and offered up sayings like the one about time eventually telling. He was probably keeping up with inflation. Still, he did assign contracts and paid in advance, not with the galloping German mark but in kind—in oil, in Finnish wood, in fertilizer, to be picked up at the harbors in Wismar or Lübeck. This was someone who wanted the work done fast but not shoddily. Avenarius had no complaints about the Jerichow workmen, except Zoll the carpenter in one instance, and in December 1923 the von Lassewitz furniture came back from Schwerin, sent not by a storage warehouse but by a restorer. Two days later there it was, the empty von Lassewitz mansion in pomp and splendor like a fairy-tale grand hotel, and up they came—the Papenbrock family by car, their servants by train, the household goods in a furniture truck from Waren on Lake Müritz. Lights on till late at night in all the windows. It was a good start. Albert had certainly diverted whole flocks of the post-inflation rentenmarks into his pockets, but what he hadn't paid for in rentenmarks were the properties, and more Jerichowers than usual availed themselves of their right as citizens to examine the entries in the land registry office. Not the von Lassewitz place: there was another quarter block on the south end of Station Street, and the adjoining garden and house belonging to E. P. F. Prange, along with his business, now folded, selling fertilizer. There was Schwenn's Bakery on the other side of the house, on Town Street, with the whole plot behind it, and a barn that everyone had forgotten all about, and this Papenbrock had the barn converted into a stable and granary. More than twice what anyone had expected, all in all. But it wasn't a great start. Papenbrock had kept the von Lassewitz coat of arms on the gable—out of modesty: some said; others said: theres another word for it now isnt there. But anyone who wanted to meet Louise Papenbrock, considered a grand personage, could just walk into Schwenn's Bakery any time it was open; it might belong to her, but still she stood behind the counter and cut the three-pound loaves in front of her breast so cleanly in half that weighing on a scale couldn't do it any better. She knew how to work! And Sonny Boy, the kid, Horst, his dad shooed him into the granary yard to take care of the horses, like he was destined to grow up to be a coachman. The nobility could order their fertilizer from E. P. F. Prange's shop, as always, although Prange himself had slunk off to his sons in Lauenburg. They only gradually started talking about how a different owner's name was printed under Prange's on the receipts. That was fine for the elder daughter's wedding, some time around 1928, and the von Malt-zahns came to the wedding too, even though Hilde's husband was not from the nobility and not a doctor of law, which he was still studying. Alexander Paepcke. And by 1928 it was no secret that the German Railroad was send-ing its cars for wheat and sugar beets to the Jerichow station not on orders from the Lübeck or Bremen dealers but on account of Albert Papenbrock, Captain, ret., or maybe in the end he'd made it to Major, ret.? What else could explain it? It must have been before 1928! The railroad had already laid a track to Papenbrock's granary in 1926, so he could negotiate his purchases deliberately, not on the spot. Clearly Albert'd made more money with his warehousing than you could tell by looking at him. And none of these princely manners! He got rid of his car, sold it to Knoop in Gneez, and drove the family around in the bakery delivery truck, and not too often neither. It was certainly safe to say that Papenbrock acted nice as could be when someone went to him to borrow some money. It wasn't him personally who came to the meeting when the interest hadn't been paid for the third time, it was the state bank. Papenbrock couldn't do anything about how the bank chose to act. And never in living memory opposed to a little schnapps, not in the office, not in the woodsmen's pub where the benches were neither covered nor wiped. One, sure.

He didn't feel Jerichow was good enough for the girls, not even Gneez was. Sent Hilde to a girls' school in Lübeck. Lisbeth had to learn science in Rostock, and home ec too. She came back home for good only in June 1928, not even twenty-two years old, and she planned Hilde's wedding and the social gatherings that the Papenbrock house was more inclined to in-dulge in than before, and she wasn't the same Lisbeth as the one known round Jerichow.

Rich men's daughters and poor men's calves soon find a man, and Lisbeth was meant to marry into Lübeck, and she wanted to wait. Papenbrock let her. How could Papenbrock go against his favorite daughter in anything?

And he gives her to a carpenter from Malchow and lets her go with him to Richmond, in England, in 1931, to get her out of the bad times. Brings her back so she can have her baby, Gesine, in Jerichow, keeps the husband here with a workshop in the country, 1933, times don't seem so bad anymore. And he watches for three years with his daughter living in the same town as him like an invalid, and he can stand it?

She doesn't look thirty. If you didn't know her you'd add five years on.

Always been pious, but now, when the kids come home from her Sunday school classes, they're bringing a conscience that there's no way you can use in everyday life.

Papenbrock has talks with the husband, Cresspahl, but on good terms, not as if he holds him responsible. Likes him better than his own sons.

Always such an open book. Now you don't want to look at her.

Pinched. *Pissed.* No, not pissed—like she's cooped up. As a girl, when she prayed at the mirror, she knew why she was doing it. Her eyes so big now, that's what you recognize her from. Not her look—she looks at you like you wasnt there, like shes in the middle of having a bad dream.

Papenbrock stands with her outside church after Christmas service and wants to tell her something and can't and crumples with such a sigh and walks off bent over like he just doesn't know anymore.

How can Papenbrock not know?

Can it be that Papenbrock went about it wrong with Our Lisbeth?

December 25, 1967 Monday

Christmas. Still a day to be celebrated, and not even *The New York Times* can count on more than forty-four pages worth of attention.

On the first day of the Christmas celebration in 1936, Lisbeth Cresspahl was taken from her house to the county hospital. It came as such a surprise to Cresspahl that only later that day did he realize it was intentional.

He'd seen her for the last time early that morning, sleeping next to her long outstretched arms, her breathing shallow, her brows fiercely furrowed as if she had to defend the beneficent numbing of sleep and dream. She looked like herself, as she often did when she wasn't awake. He still thought of her as the woman he'd married five years ago, young for him, happy to be alive for herself as well as for him. He even overlaid her words from back then onto her silences now. On many mornings he'd had the feeling that she was only pretending to be asleep; by this point he no longer wanted to ask her.

My father was in the kitchen, lighting the stove for the child sitting enthroned in a pile of pillows and blankets on the high chair from Vietsen, watching him in anticipation, happy, trusting. She had often had breakfast with him. The kitchen had kept the warmth of the previous evening, the big south-facing window was like a mirror before the morning-dark sky. The glow from the hanging lamp sat low over the table and made the Dutch tiles shine. When Dr. Berling arrived, it was barely light out.

Dr. Berling may not have realized that Cresspahl didn't know about his wife's phone call. He walked in through the front door, announced his presence by stomping up the stairs, was in the kitchen, walked right past the father with an aggravated greeting as he was spooning warm milk into his child's mouth, clearly unalarmed; he pulled the bedroom door shut behind him, and closed it again when Cresspahl tried to follow him. Came back, suddenly solicitous and gentle, moving quickly for all his bulk, and sent Cresspahl scurrying with one instruction after another: get blankets, prepare hot-water bottles, pack a set of clothes, call ahead to the Gneez county hospital but don't ask for an ambulance, get something waterproof for the bleeding, *go on, go on.* The child only started screaming when she was left alone in the kitchen, and Cresspahl carried his wife across the snowy yard to Berling's car, a limp and awkward bundle. Her head hung back, it looked painful, but he couldn't manage to jut his elbow out any farther while carrying her. With pupils so rolled back she couldn't see a thing, much less him.

The Berling who took his leave from Cresspahl that morning was no longer the one from 1933 who used to clap people on the shoulder "as a preventative measure," the one with the playful turns of phrase, who infected patients with his health, who cut short complaints almost as if insulted. Today's looked at you just as closely but not with the same vehement encouragement, listened more patiently, even nodded, his fat fleshy face impassive, even gloomy on occasion. He no longer drank where someone might overhear him; he spent his evenings at home. So many capillaries had burst in his cheeks that he was nicknamed "the blue devil." A big man, six and a half feet, two and a quarter hundredweight, sturdy like a butcher, grown sad over the years that were supposed to have been his best. And

Jerichow didn't hear from Berling that young Mrs. Cresspahl had just lost a child, only what he'd recommended and decreed to Cresspahl with a last nod before driving off: *Se hett wat ætn. She ate something.* Something you shouldn't.

For a while, Cresspahl thought it was an accident; he was also glad that the accident hadn't come at a bad time. It was the quiet season, between the holidays. The workers had gone home; he had no one to take care of but the child. And after all, Lisbeth's last strength, for the call to Berling, could have been what she'd had left, not what she'd saved on purpose. He didn't even have to tell the Papenbrocks anything right away if he didn't want to, or the Paepckes across the street. They were still asleep, Jerichow was still asleep. Later he didn't understand everything Berling tried to explain to him from Lisbeth's feverish talking: the carpentry work was in gear again; Lisbeth was long since keeping the household running again, tired, unyielding, and, yes, pale in the face like someone who'd been poisoned by something she'd eaten.

Dr. Berling said:

My mother had wanted to lose her own life along with the second child, to escape her guilt.

She knew many kinds of guilt, on that drive through the snow and during the operation, and some weren't hers at all, and yet were, in the end, part of hers.

She was guilty of going to England in 1931 with my father, secretly knowing that though she did want to live with him she didn't want it to be abroad. My father, of course, was guilty of having believed her. So much belief and trust is more than a person can bear.

She had wanted to flee this guilt and she came back to Mecklenburg for the birth. But a Christian should not flee from guilt, and Cresspahl was guilty of letting that happen.

Her guilt had then acquired numerous offshoots and relations. Not only had she returned to the manifold guilt of her father, who loaned money to poor people and demanded their houses in repayment, so that now they worked for him. (She might have meant Zoll the master carpenter, whom Papenbrock had "bought out"; but who else?) She had then wanted to stay in a country whose new government was oppressing the church, with a family who certainly could be accused of profiting from the new regime, with a brother who was accused of Voss's murder in Rande. Cresspahl, for his part, was guilty of not putting a stop to the increase in hers. He had given in to her about the move. But the husband should decide. As the Bible says. He had decided, wrongly, as she wanted.

Cresspahl was guilty of her guilt not being enough for him. He wanted to bring a share of it into the world, not only for the one child, Gesine, but three more. As she had promised him. But doesn't the New Testament say you should forgive the poor sinner his debts? Cresspahl was also guilty of not explicitly releasing her from her promise, while of course it was hers that she couldn't express her need for him to do so. But he made her feel her guilt, by spending the evenings writing and drawing over a bottle of Richtenberg kümmel until he could forget her promise.

She was guilty of not living with him the way she had vowed to do in church, hand on the Bible. But didn't the Bible also say: men should "crucify the flesh with the affections and lusts"? Galatians 5:24. Cresspahl was guilty of being unwilling to accept this from her; she remained guilty of doubting the words of the Holy Scripture.

So as not to retain so much guilt, nor multiply it, she had tried to commit a greater sin: protecting an unborn child from guilt, yes, but giving away her own life. It's true, God doesn't make deals. Still, it would have represented a kind of repaying of something. For Cresspahl's guilt too.

Which, fundamentally, remained hers: for she hadn't wanted to let herself be saved. She had not obeyed her husband. Back in early 1935, when he had wanted to go away and leave the Germans' new war. Why hadn't she taken it as an order?

Out of weakness, hence guilt.

Guilt was not talk for a doctor's ears, even if he was the last person she talked to. And she asked his forgiveness for that. For if her latest, her biggest sin reached the ears of the church, she would have to forgo the last sacrament. This way, though, dying in secret guilt, she could be sure of a Christian burial.

That left the guilt of deception, but not of malice. One of the smaller sins, venial, the kind a child has. And this was the only way Cresspahl would not learn of his guilt and would be able to live until his death, at least, free of the guilt.

And Dr. Berling said:

She doesnt remember any of it. People talk in a fever. Not one remembers a thing.

And he said:

Always this mawkishness around Christmas. Candles! Singsong! It's to blame for a lot, old Swede. You can bet on it.

He said:

She'll recover. Just wait a couple years, old Swede. After two years she won't be able to stand it without a second child.

And:

Godet Niejår, Cresspahl! Happy New Year!

December 26, 1967   Tuesday

Christmas is over, and *The New York Times* once again feels she needs sixty-eight pages to bring us all the city's shopping opportunities as well as the world's news: The air force has resumed bombing in North Vietnam. Fire on a Norwegian freighter in the harbor. The Free State of Bavaria sees itself as a bridgehead to Eastern Europe. Peking is silent on its atomic blast. Mayor Lindsay regrets errors, promises improvements, and by the way has a hidden television camera in his home office that allows him to appear live on six New York channels. Now we know that; who knows why.

One day, Marie will also say about me, among other things: My mother used to read *The New York Times*. Not as an indiscretion; as a description. She will compare me to Cresspahl in London, who wanted to hear the Labour Party speaking through the *Daily Herald*; to Lisbeth Cresspahl, who not inadvertently brought the Manchester *Guardian* back from the city but who in Mecklenburg was perfectly happy that there was only the *Lübecker General-Anzeiger* to subscribe to, not the *Lübecker Volksbote*, Social Democratic, banned, plundered.

Marie, that's not how it was. In April 1961, when we arrived in New York, we had other papers to choose from: the *News*, the *Journal-American*, the *World-Telegram & Sun*, the *Post*, the *Herald Tribune*, *The Wall Street Journal*, the *Long Island Press*, and the *Times*. I bought the *Times* for its British ancestry, and didn't even know that it was part of the minority that had endorsed John Kennedy for president against Richard Nixon. In the

442 · December 26, 1967 Tuesday

bank, they'd advised me to read the *Times*: for the rental listings every day, not only on weekends. We found our apartment in New York with the *Times*, five windows looking out on river colors, on Riverside Park, on open sky. I first realized *The New York Times* was a habit when they were out of it on Lexington Avenue and one day a polite child, not yet four years old, indicated with a jerk of the head on Seventh what I was looking for: a newsstand, with newspapers, though not the *Times*; and I didn't feel like buying the *News*. You saw yet again that grown-ups are strange, and still you couldn't let go of my hand in a place where the language, the colors of the cars, and the height of the buildings were strange, to say nothing of your mother.

Say what you want when you're over thirty: My mother fell for the conservative appearance, while imagining she hadn't fallen for inch-thick reporting about nothing, embarrassing photos of nobodies. You can say: My mother wanted to learn an educated, propertied American English, more than the one the workers spoke and the cops and the robbers. It may even be true. But if I did need such language to fool anyone, then I also needed it to pass muster with bosses who'd gone to universities. Make fun of it if you want, that I learned New York from the *Times*: not only who our senator was but how he'd obtained the vote; not only the mayor's name but the limits to his authority; what qualifies as misconduct, as misdemeanor, and as felony, and what the letter of the law permits you vis-à-vis the police. Say that at only twenty-eight I was giving age its due—that may have been true: No. 4,230, Lincoln's assassination, seems to me worthy of respect, due to tradition; as does today's: No. 40,148 in Vol. CXVII; but don't say I respected tradition unthinkingly. It wasn't: to hold up a new authority to replace the one I had lost. If that were true, I'd have had to think of the paper as a father; but I think of the *Times* as an aunt.

That might be admiration. The mirror of daily events, fogged over in only a few and often unavoidable places. The thoroughness of many of the articles. The scoops, the accomplishments: in the 1906 San Francisco earthquake, the 1912 sinking of the *Titanic*, the ten pages (out of only thirty-eight) on the dropping of the atomic bomb on Hiroshima, as early as August 7, 1945. Here I may be deferring to the *Times*'s praise of itself more than it deserves. Perhaps I am giving her credit for things that only I think are worthy: calling Barry Goldwater's candidacy a "catastrophe," explicitly; bringing news of the killing of John Kennedy to the people in headlines across all its eight columns, three or four days running. But I have also been in the lobby of the Times Building with you and I know the motto on the wall above the bust of the owner who made the *Times*, Adolph Ochs, and if it's common currency in our home, it's hardly used with a straight face.

"TO GIVE THE NEWS IMPARTIALLY,
WITHOUT FEAR OR FAVOR,
REGARDLESS OF ANY PARTY,
SECT OR INTEREST INVOLVED"

These are the flags that the city of New York flew at half-mast when this most loyal nephew of the *Times* was carried to his grave in 1935; this is her self-understanding as an "honorable human institution." During work hours, though, the aunt still does have a business to run, involving the procuring of news reports and their dissemination by means of sales; this was made clear to me, if it wasn't already, by the strikes of 1962 and 1965. With a one percent share of *New York Times* stocks, we would be sitting pretty in the Social Register of New York, Marie!

What struck me as auntlike (as soon as I could read her) was her inability to do something good without also discussing it. When the *Times*—never one to support a particular political party—supported a politician, it was expressly because she felt his party's position was correct, not that, say, Kennedy felt that. The conscience of the USA one would want: she was its caretaker. How insulted she was by Robert Kennedy right after he was elected senator, and how dreadfully she retaliated, accusing him of not writing his own book! If she described a people's representative's candidacy step by step, and had a friend of the candidate do it, it was not to support him but to instruct the public in the nature of the political process; a murder in the *Daily News* may be sheer pandering, but in her own paper any such item is sociology. The epitome of auntliness is her indomitable need to instruct: countless is the number of times she again and again mentions the fare on the South Ferry as an amazing five cents, which the locals as locals already know as a wonder of the world, and the tourists know from guidebooks. Eventually even I noticed the careless repetitions, came to mistrust the old-fashioned turns of phrase, mentally sought out more exact expressions that were by no means vulgar. (If I hadn't learned

American English from the *News* too, I would hardly get by on Broadway.)
These were signs of age and as such not worthy of laughter, or of contempt.
It was if anything rather touching how shocked she was at the death of the
Herald Tribune, what a body blow the swallowing of three papers at once
by a competitress was, and how she tried to wiggle her way out of the di-
lemma of trying to educate and entertain her readers at the same time!
How bravely, chin raised, she took a historical explanation of an event and
wrung present-day functional relevance from it, like it was nothing!

*We tell the public which way the cat is jumping. The public will take care
of the cat.*

Who, at her age, undergoes rejuvenation treatments like this? No longer
merely sending her people to stake out the mouseholes of the police, the
government authorities, the embassies, the wire services, the maternity
wards and crematoria, waiting in comfort and dignity for her people to lay
out their catch so she can conscientiously inspect it and then, aware of her
responsibility, describe it! No, instead she takes a seat, crosses one leg over
the over, sips her tea spiked with rum, chews on her world-famous cigarillo,
and thinks it over. Now she's got it. Before, she had by and large given
precise reports from around the world, small towns, large metropolises,
down to the last dapple: what happened, who did it, in what weather, and
what happened next. But there was something more, something missing,
wasn't there...? Right! What people were talking about in these cities and
towns! And there in a flash it is, for the taking—*The number one topic of
conversation in Hanover*...or: *in Moscow*..., to give the forty airmail
subscriptions a day sent there an entirely unexpected relevance. In addition,
from now on she'll have at the ready: The Man in the News. His biography,
main occupation, sidelines, hobbies, goals, enemies. And as if that were
not enough, she goes in search of things she presumes her readers have
insufficient knowledge of, in their own city! And then lectures tersely,
briskly, but still charmingly: on the life habits of various disadvantaged
groups, Upper West Side, Lower East Side; the mixture of structural and
real-estate problems in White Plains, "Stranger, come to White Plains...";
the emotional bonds among members of the non-white ethnic groups in
the ghettos, not only in Harlem but also in Williamsburg and Bedford-

Stuyvesant, now *that's* interesting—and she sits up straight and gives this news that is not really news the status of news! It's not so much that she's perfectly willing and able to prove the facts, it's about how it was old Auntie Times who found them in the first place. You always think that the time has come at last for the youth of today to stop trying to shirk their duties and responsibilities, but no, you have to do everything! Granted, she had her reputation to consider, and she put all this not right on the front page but near the top of the second—perhaps with a hint of apology—but the moral exemplarity was indisputable. Once again she has done the right thing and pointed out in the most delicate tone of voice that no one else would bring themselves to do it: suddenly, what we hear about the police is not only their arrests, releases, corruption, and preferments but how at the bottom of their hearts they feel about it all, about who has to faithfully obey whom in what circumstances, what rights those suspected by them actually have, and that at least 800,000 readers of the *Times* are most kindly requested to elect politicians who truly intend to subordinate the police to civilian oversight commissions, promise.

That one didn't work out, maybe because the other seven million inhabitants of the city think in a language that *The New York Times* refuses to countenance, live their lives with things that a lady of the world will not permit her customers to encounter even in the words of her ads: nudity, homosexual, carnal lust, naked, nothing on, panties, perverse.... Don't you see that there's no other way she could fulfill her role as aunt, Marie?

She spares me astrological nonsense, Marie. She's not entirely stuck at the level of enlightenment handed down to her in 1896 in a Geneva finishing school.

No comic strips for you, I'm sorry to say. Do you expect her to live like an ordinary citizen of the USA, with parents instead of ancestors, letting things happen in his home, and even enjoying them, which....

The old-fashioned, indispensable fairness that leads her to renounce political cartoons, because a cartoon can only say: On the one hand. Never: On the other hand.

Marie, your mother was someone who read the *Times* of New York.

With respect. Without respect. You figure out the synthesis. (I'll give you a hint: Defenseless.)

I leave it to you to prove that my upbringing forced me, via the *Lübeck*

Gazette, the Nazi *People's Observer*, the Soviet Union's *Daily Review*, the *New World* and *New Germany*, via the *Frankfurter Allgemeine Zeitung* and the *Rheinische Post*, to spend an hour a day chatting with an old aunt.

For when the Free State of Bavaria sees itself as a bridgehead to Eastern Europe, she'll pass that along. She'll remind me that as of January 7 the post office will demand more postage for our letters. Irrespective of whether or not I believe it she'll tell me what she heard an American soldier say in Vietnam: "Christmas and war are a contradiction in terms." Finally, she doesn't even keep from me that President Johnson's family had "a wonderful, wonderful day" yesterday.

And when I'm done with her I go wash my hands.

December 27, 1967 Wednesday kinderglut

It is the Wednesday between Christmas and New Year, known in New York as the kinderglut. Marie has never seen this word in writing, only heard it and said it, so she has no suspicion of any relationship to the German word pronounced "gloot," blaze or glow. She does, though, know the rights of a New York City child on this day: to no school, to Wednesday matinees, to run wild in the city, through the stores, through the subway, a right to have fun wherever she can find it. She will find it, among elsewhere, in a present for me, so small that it'll be as if it were stolen. Marie has kinderglut, the thing—she has no need to understand the word. I should, and don't want to.

I feel like I'm sick. I don't want to know.

The park is black and cold. A year ago, the New Jersey shore was white, bundled up high behind the bright icy blue river, and it brought back a winter morning on Lake Constance, the memory of snow-covered gardens, children on the railway embankment with their hoods up, the church-tower tuber on the water, foreland and mountain range rising up through the headlights there, along the water here, and the Säntis massif imaginable as hidden behind the new snow in the air. The moment of recall, the fact of bringing it into the present, corrodes both at once: past memory and present view.

Wet wind against the windows.

The New York Times has tracked down the inventor of napalm. (*The New York Times* explains what napalm is.) The inventor is a professor emeritus from Harvard University, Dr. Louis Frederick Fieser, pronounced the German way, "(Feeser)." In the fall of 1941 he received the contract from the National Defense Research Committee. By mid-1942 he'd finished. What he says is:

– You don't know what's coming. – You can't blame the outfit that put out the rifle that killed the president. – I don't know enough about the situation in Vietnam. – Just because I played a role in the technological development of napalm doesn't make me one iota more qualified to comment on the moral aspects of it.

Is there such a thing as anti-Fascist napalm?

The door to the back staircase, our fire stairs, is held open with a string tied around a heating pipe. A sign on the door is still clearly readable: THIS DOOR COULD SAVE YOUR LIFE IN CASE OF FIRE. IT MUST BE KEPT CLOSED AT ALL TIMES.

Marie plays Taking My Mother to the Subway. The metal steps of the coiled staircase sound xylophonically under her jumps. On the streets she walks at a downright polite distance behind me, hands comfortably stuffed into the pockets of her London coat, telling me all about her plans for kinderglut: she could go get her ice skates sharpened, she might take the subway to Queens Plaza again, could stop by Macy's to see the new arrivals from Lesney of Britain, Limited. . . . She's being tricky: what she's actually going to do is go back to our apartment and work some more on the "secret" she's promised me for New Year's. She walks on my right and so scares off the old man waiting at the entrance steps down to Mr. Fang Liu's laundry, a former gentleman whose current disarray is for now visible only in the frayed legs of his pants. He retreated as soon as he saw Marie.

He's tried it before. He's not practiced at it, he always has to start by saying "please," with an echo of his former days, then breaking off: Please. Ma'am. I'm sorry to bother you, You're very kind, ma'am, Thank you ma'am: Thank you. This morning he has to doff his hat and say hello, because he's ashamed in front of the child.

– Twelve more years and then I'll go to work for you: Marie says, suddenly dejected. She's embarrassed to be hugged on the street, even if it's just for a second, cheek to cheek. Today she wanted to.

In the rattling, racing, camphor-scented subway, *The New York Times* reports in her composed, ladylike voice that on Sept. 26, 1967, Mr. Gostev of the Moscow KGB posed the following question to the physicist Pavel M. Litvinov: Could you think under any possible circumstances that now, in the fiftieth year of Soviet power, a Soviet court could make a wrong decision?

Can you imagine it?

The Christmas decor and advertisements have disappeared from the parts of the bank open to the public, the wreaths from the halls, the cards from the desks. The teletype clacks as if it had never fallen silent. Employee Cresspahl has until eleven to prepare two letters to the Deutsche Bank in Frankfurt, one to the Bank of the Holy Spirit in Turin, one to Giovanni Agnelli's private office. A draft of an Italian/French contract is expected at noon, she has an appointment with the vice president at twelve thirty. And in the afternoon she's supposed to help the South America Department get through the backlog of credit letters, if she can, as a favor. I'd be delighted, Guarani. The vice president is sorry to have to cancel our meeting, he's off to Mexico. No, on a hunting trip in Canada. Actually, no, he's helping buy Xerox today.

Blind with repetition. In one shop your name is Antipasto, in another Gauloise, in another Coffee-Large-Black. Sitting comfortably at a child-size table in the Thousand Deli, continually jostled by the hurrying line of lunchers, were two men, Italian looking, who'd just agreed to something and were toasting each other with beer in paper cups, with rather loving smiles, trustingly. Because shooting, not poisoning, shooting is the custom of the country.

Dear Sirs: We hereby establish our IRREVOCABLE credit in your favor, available by your drafts drawn at 90 (ninety) days sight for any sums not exceeding a total of about US$80,000.00 accompanied by commercial invoice describing the merchandise as indicated below.... Dear Sirs.

And now you've learned something new, Gesine.

There is a message for you, Mrs. Cresspahl. Gesine, it's for you. Your daughter called. She said you looked so run-down we should send you home.

Fattish drops of rain, it should be snow, coming down into the evening crush on Third and Forty-Second, the people are crowding into the subway entrance, wind is jabbing the backs of their necks, and a chipper voice addresses them from the left, where a man is standing at his newspaper stand, hurling emphases into the air while swallowing the less important words: *GOOD EVEning! It's a PERfect EVEning! It's a PERfect EVEning for a NEWSpaper! We have the LATEST NEWSpaper in NEW YORK here!* He can still be heard on the descent into the cavern of the Flushing line. No one's strangled him yet. He's not from around here, this guy in a good mood. They'll kill him.

In the produce shop, the seller (from Galicia, spent four weeks in Berlin in 1923, Berlin has the best ice cream in the world): Nice stuff you've bought today. Because the bill comes to $3.85.

Amsterdam, the city proud,
Is built on posts of wood.
If it ever comes falling down,
Who will make it good?

Now it really is snow, a thin watery substance that doesn't stick to the sidewalk. Ninety-Sixth Street looks like water has been poured down it. But the ground in the park is almost completely covered in white.

Marie was upset that her disobedient mother stayed at the bank until the workday was over instead of coming home. She has politely left her kinderglut present on the table: a record by some people from Liverpool with questions to ask of life. But the note says she won't be back till nine. So she's out for kinderglut after all. The apartment is empty.

It's a PERfect EVEning to be FEVERish.

December 28, 1967   Thursday

In Prague *The New York Times* can't hear which way the wind's blowing. She has to learn via Frankfurt that Antonín Novotný addressed his party's Central Committee last week and leveled criticisms against Antonín Novotný, no longer considering him worthy to head the Czechoslovak Communist Party. *The New York Times* gives this Czechoslovak wind only twenty-seven lines, albeit on page 5; she must consider it a mild one.

Later, Cresspahl thought that Lisbeth's life with him had been known to the people of Jerichow like a story whose opening they'd been there for, whose developments they'd seen, whose every step they could predict in advance, whose twists they'd bet on, which they might be able to deflect but couldn't stop, which was no longer any of their business, which they knew good and well the end of, long before he did, Cresspahl, the person living it.

The idea of anyone trying to talk to him about his marriage would have so dumbfounded him that he would have forgotten to listen. Later, he understood that it was thus due to him if people brought it up so casually, so cautiously, in the break-time conversations of the master carpenters at the airfield, in halting exchanges of words keeping such a distance from one another that the answer came as a surprise when it did come and a storyteller had to face suspicious looks however sure he might be that his memories were welcome. Cresspahl hadn't lived in the area long enough, he couldn't join in the stories, only sit and listen; there was no reason he would realize that they contained information he might find useful. There was one about a horse trade in Gadebusch, then the story wandered off to a turnip cutter in Rehna, lingered for a while at a courtyard in Gneez, a man who'd tried to set fire to a home-wrecker's woodpile, and finally ended up back on the horse to Jerichow, took a glance at *our Lisbeth*, and wandered reluctantly off into the Countess Woods when lunch break was over. They didn't say *yer Lisbeth*, not even *his Lisbeth*, which meant he had to keep quiet and listen like someone being told things he'd never heard before.

> *The tantrums Papenbrock's Lisbeth had as a child!*
> *And all because of a horse someone'd beaten too hard.*
> *Her eyes would get so dark with anger!*
> *And always: "I," not: "My father."*
> *She wanted to show em on her own.*
> *Yes; but she did seem a bit crazy.*
> *Yah, always was a bit churchy.*

This was new to Cresspahl; he also thought he heard a warning in it some-times, an apology. And yet they were all things he knew, just seen from another angle, new from new seeing. He had already known most of what Dr. Berling had relayed from Lisbeth's feverish talk in the hospital, too, only said differently, put together differently; now this too was unclear, ungraspable, unexpressed.

It was Dr. Berling's comments more than anything that made him brood darkly, throw himself into monotonous work as though possessed. He didn't want to accept everything Berling said. And as for strange talk, Berling should just listen to himself. He called every halfway sturdy guy "old Swede," long before the Nazis gave him reason to dig up his relatives in Scania. Clearly he had read local-history tracts before moving to Jerichow, and too much about a certain Oxenstierna, under whom the Swedes in the Thirty Years' War had literally laid waste to the region. Another old Swede. He'd started in with his dark hints at "cancers in the heart of the nation" only after his wife left him and went to live in Schwerin with another man, and one in a peacocky uniform, an interpreter between Reich Governor Hildebrandt and the army. Berling probably should have picked another time to badmouth the Nazis, or at least another reason. Now he spent his evenings at home alone with the Rhine wine he had delivered by the case and trundled from the station straight into his cellar; he had too many drunken evenings behind him to mentally arrange Lisbeth's words for Cresspahl's use. That was eight weeks ago now, and what did he call Cresspahl? "You old heartbreaker": that was it, though he also said: "So, old Swede." In this neck of the woods, what was strange didn't come across as strange. The part of Mecklenburg Cresspahl knew best was Malchow, and things were different there.

Really it was only that Lisbeth took church too seriously, and that in the long run no one could live with both the teachings of the church and the demands of the Nazis. She'd learned it as a child, and in a house like Papenbrock's a child could grow up for years thinking like that.

He asked her once about the chaplain Louise kept when they had the estate near Crivitz, and later in Vietsen. He approached the subject casually, asking as if about something that had slipped his mind. Did she remember him? And Lisbeth, Lisbeth laughed, she half turned away from the stove and took a half step back too, until she could reach him and stroke his brow and cheeks like a child who needed comforting. If you believed her, she didn't even remember that clerical candidate's name. She laughed quite naturally, looked him in the eyes, happy, openly, and also as if she had secretly guessed something he didn't even know if he'd hidden. They still had such moments of understanding, even around other people sometimes. In such moments he was so glad to at least be living with her that he didn't need to be happy himself too.

He sat in the kitchen at night and got himself drunk until all he felt was tired. Didn't even have to go looking in the pantry, the bottle of Richtenberg stood right at the front of the counter, as though set out for him.

So it was Louise Papenbrock, whose blind pious child-rearing had prevailed with none of her children except this one. He couldn't make Lisbeth stop seeing her mother.

He could force Lisbeth to leave Jerichow, maybe not go all the way across the water but at least to Holland. But she hadn't managed with the foreign church in Richmond. The Dutch one would hardly be any different. And he didn't want to force her.

He blamed himself too and by 1937 was finally willing to admit that he should never have married a girl with an elite education and culture, when all he could offer was what he'd learned in grade school, in his craft, and on the streets. He could hear Lisbeth's voice from 1931: I don't want to quiz you, I want to live with you, with you and the children, four kids. You take care of your business and I'll keep up my end.

Sometimes he was almost at the point of knocking on Pastor Brüshaver's door in the middle of the night to wake him up and confront him over this Paul who'd apparently believed it was good for people not to touch women. Brüshaver with his three young children. What was left from these impulses during the day meant that he drove right past Brüshaver as though he didn't see him, only sometimes touching a finger to his cap, at the last moment, grouchily; on Sundays he sat in the pew next to Lisbeth with his arms crossed, marveling at this strong, not even narrow-minded man who decided to earn his living expounding a book that prescribed such rules for man and woman. Cresspahl had looked it up, this Paul had written it in an open letter.

And often there were times when he could almost forget Lisbeth's idiosyncrasies. Mornings when she woke him up, not inattentively, in a dull voice, but cheerfully, with jokes, from their time in England no less; days she made it through with regular work, totally normal behavior, even up for a little joking and teasing, so that the group sitting around the dinner table, suspicious at first, would feel easier and lighten up almost to the point of hilarity. It could last months.

There was something about her he didn't quite trust in these moods, however much he wanted her that way. He had told her, back in Richmond, about one Mrs. Elizabeth Trowbridge; Lisbeth hadn't asked for a full confession, just listened calmly and nodded afterward, as if she'd expected as much, as if she were satisfied. In Germany he'd had to add something: an admission that some of the money saved up in England would go every month for a boy that Mrs. Elizabeth Trowbridge had brought into the world without his knowledge. He had been waiting a long time for the chance to tell her, deciding only after dinner whether it was a "good" day. On such evenings, work done, house and child taken care of, they talked to each other as though they had grown up together—fast, almost carefree, always on guard for the other's teasing, never at a loss for a comeback, in half sentences the other person answered before they'd finished, enjoying each other, not looking past the other person for hours at a time. For Cresspahl these were memories of the early years, when she hadn't yet known about guilt and the parts of the Bible impossible to live with; they were also a performance, an act, because the end was always the same, she went to bed first, and alone.

She had wanted to know the other child's date of birth. May 1932. She didn't seem to mind. Then she'd said: Heinrich, they should live here; not too close to Jerichow but not too far. You could live with her, and with me too.

And no matter how often he kept track and cross-referenced and took mental note of how her moods shifted, he never figured out what set her off, or whether or not it was him. The episodes appeared from one day to the next, and by nighttime she was praying at the child's bedside over the war he'd predicted something about at lunch. He knew by this point that anything he said now would have no effect on her, and that she would reemerge from her isolation only when she could, and could show it.

> *Pray, child, pray!*
> *Tomorrow is the day*
>   *That the Swede is coming,*
>   *Oxenstern's coming,*
> *Tomorrow's the morn*
> *You'll be speared on his horn.*

December 29, 1967   Friday

Today at Maxie's produce store we spent:

Potatoes	5 lb.	$0.39
Beans	1 lb.	0.35
Cucumbers	2	0.25
Chicory	1 lb.	0.69
Rhubarb	1 lb.	0.39
Apples	2 lb.	0.29
Oranges	5	0.35
Turnips	1 lb.	0.10
Onions	1 lb.	0.15
Lettuce	1 head	0.29
Celery	1 bunch	0.29

At Sloan's or Daitch supermarket:

Coffee	1 lb.	0.81
Apple juice	1 qt.	0.41
Butter	8 oz.	0.46
Milk	2 qt.	0.56
Bread	1 lb.	0.33
Ital. oil	16 fl. oz.	0.85
Peeled tomatoes	8 oz.	0.27
Eggs	6	0.27
Buttermilk	1 qt.	0.29
Matches	10 bxs.	0.10
Detergent	3 lb.	0.78
Mayonnaise	8 fl. oz.	0.29
Tomato puree	1 lb.	0.25
Bottled water	2 qt.	0.41
Aluminum foil	25 ft.	0.25
Sweet cream	1 pt.	0.69
Beans, dried	1 lb.	0.24
Bitter lemon	6 bottles	1.15

At Schustek the butcher's:

Pot roast, beef	3 lb.	4.95
1 chicken	40 oz.	1.55
Teewurst	8 oz.	0.74
Imported cervelat	8 oz.	1.00

And a snowstorm. The sun came out only around noon.

December 30, 1967 Saturday

The Ministry of Health and Social Welfare of the People's Republic of Poland has thanked the Jewish aid organization Joint for its generosity in the support and vocational training of Polish Jews, and for the pensions paid to Polish Roman Catholic families whose members helped save Jews from the Nazis. "The letter said that such aid was no longer needed now that Poland had sufficiently recovered from the Nazi devastation during World War II, which among other things reduced the Jewish population in Poland from 3.5 million people to perhaps 30,000 today."

In 1937, Cresspahl was still not sure who he was in the little town of Jerichow, what he represented for the other inhabitants, who by that point numbered two thousand four hundred and ninety.

He was not seen as Jew-friendly, even though he still associated with Semig the veterinarian, a Jew, as if no one had filled him in on the events of April 1, 1933. It could be taken as stubbornness that Cresspahl stopped outside Dr. Semig's stately villa on the Bäk in Jerichow several times a week and carried something inside in baskets, but then stayed in the house much longer than was needed to simply drop off fruit or game. Possibly he did it for Dora Semig, born a Köster, who was no more "non-Aryan" than he was. And, when you think about it, Arthur Semig was just *one* Jew. Maybe that was something people learned in England, how to treat Jews as if they were friends too.

In Jerichow Cresspahl was called "the Englishman."

That was fine with him, it was as much as to say they didn't begrudge him Lisbeth and forgave him for Lisbeth's family too. He wouldn't have wanted to answer for the Papenbrocks. For one thing, they'd been in Jerichow only fifteen years, and hadn't started out properly. Papenbrock set up house in the villa that had belonged to the von Lassewitzes as if he bore their name too, and acted all chummy with the nobility of the region, who had not only the countryside but the town in their grip, with rentals, leases, interest payments, mortgages. But if he wanted to be the secret King of Jerichow then it was time he stood up and made himself known, not let someone like Friedrich Jansen be mayor; the town hadn't done much to be proud of, but they didn't deserve that guy. Papenbrock would rather rake it in quietly. Shrewdness counted for something in Jerichow, but that wasn't enough. Meanwhile Papenbrock's Louise acted like she owned the town and like St. Peter's Church couldn't keep its spire up in the air without her either. His girls were fine, at least while they were girls. They'd given away clothes as presents, toys too. And their Plattdeutsch, maybe it had a southern ring to it but it was their first language, learned from poultry girls and farm boys. Our Hilde'd sometimes been a bit too big for her britches, not all the way but you could still feel it. Our Lisbeth, gentle as a lamb to excess from church, was the best of the lot. Lisbeth, when she took a child with her to play in Papenbrock's garden, never asked whether it was the mayor's or a cobbler's. Papenbrock had brought up both of his daughters almost as an example for what children (in Jerichow) should be given and permitted and what not. You could hardly envy children, even if yours didn't have what Papenbrock's did. Once the old man had married them off, it yet again became clear that he wanted to secure his property by dividing it up. Hilde's Alexander Paepcke didn't stay the busted lawyer in Krakow am See for long, Papenbrock got him the lease to the Jerichow brickworks. In a way it was almost fitting that things went wrong for him there, Paepcke'd managed to end up in the red even with an insatiable demand secured for bricks for the Jerichow-North airfield, for another year at least—red spots in his books, red oceans actually—and with his tail between his legs moved to the easternmost tip of Military District II, into the Stettin Military Ordnance Department, and Papenbrock in his rage may have secretly slipped Hilde some housekeeping money but Alexander knew only about the strict wage he brought home. Podejuch. What kind of a name was that for a place. If it even existed, if it wasn't another "Rio de Janeiro."

And from the very beginning Cresspahl had no desire at all to answer for Papenbrock's Sonny Boy, Horst. Where the old man had tried to hold him back, he had tried to throw his weight around with that Storm Trooper group of his. Past thirty, and driving a truck around the countryside, barking at the trees along the country road with his comrades, because he'd sworn something to a foreigner by the name of Adolf Hitler. Tried to wear his shit-brown uniform to church for Cresspahl and Lisbeth's wedding. Well, he was keeping pretty quiet since he got back from his overseas trip. The Jerichow SA had to positively remind him he'd been their leader. Since then he joined drills and marches now and then, but he hadn't insisted on being rewarded with promotions and medals for his part in the Nazi victory. They'd been handed out while he was gone. He'd relearned how to work in his father's yard and granary, ruined his brown boots doing it. He'd been away for more than a year, came back broader in the shoulders, not so much the eager beaver, now when he held his head high it was relaxed, not stiff. Maybe he'd turn out a Papenbrock like his father wanted after all. Maybe he couldn't accept that his Hitler had had half the SA leadership gunned down like rabid dogs. Maybe he'd seen something in America. When he insisted on marrying that Elisabeth Lieplow, Papenbrock suddenly agreed, and he couldn't even hold against him that he spent half the week in Kröpelin; Horst had done himself out of his inheritance in Jerichow.

What he now refused to give the Nazis they got from Robert Papenbrock, the alleged long-lost brother Horst had gone looking for in "Rio de Janeiro." Robert had gotten himself found, and by this point he had a job in a confiscated villa in the state capital. Rumor had it that along with his brown "officeholder" uniform he had another one, in SS black. Another in-law.

About him Cresspahl said: *Dont know him, none of our business, I thought he was dead.*

It wasn't necessary. On the day of Horst's wedding in Kröpelin, Cresspahl was putting in windows in Jerichow-North. You never saw Cresspahl in the Lübeck Court where the nobility went, or in the station pub where the Nazis went boozing, at most you might see him in Peter Wulff's pub, which Regional Group Leader Jansen called a Social Democrat rat's nest. He got all the work he needed on his own, didn't want and wouldn't take anything from old Papenbrock. Bit quiet, he is. Middle of a conversation he'll be staring off into space, not there anymore. Englishman.

458 · December 31, 1967 Sunday

They knew full well that he'd worked in Holland only since 1922, and in England after that; that he'd been born in a village on Lake Müritz and made a master carpenter in Malchow am See, the same cloth-making town that Kliefoth the schoolteacher came from, and Kliefoth had moved to Jerichow more recently than Cresspahl. Him they called Klattenpüker, tangle-picker, after the tangles the Malchowers had to pick out of their sheep's wool before they could start making their cloth. Cresspahl was the guy from England—not in a bad way, sometimes as a joke, occasionally in confidence. (He knew all about the English. In case the English won the war.)

You had to admit that he usually knew about English things from the same *Lübeck Gazette* that they subscribed to. Guess he spent more time reading it.

It was true he'd been known to let rip with a kind of contempt, if not rage, about the cowardice of the English who'd let the German army occupy the Rhineland. Probably ashamed of these English.

You couldn't deny that he dismissed the visits of the Lord Privy Seal Lord Londonderry, of Lloyd George, of the Marquess of Lothian as childishness. Clearly he wanted something more, or something different, from the English than that they cross the Atlantic on their *Queen Mary* in four days for a blue ribbon. Couldn't hold that against him.

It was a fact that the Law Concerning the Reconstruction of the Reich had invalidated his Weimar Republic passport. That he'd had two years to go to the state offices in Gneez and request another one, with a swastika. And that he hadn't done it yet.

And along with that, that he wouldn't leave the Jew Semig in peace until he'd gone to Gneez and come back with a passport for himself and his wife.

It may be that Cresspahl would rather they called him something else.

Well, Klattenpüker?

December 31, 1967 Sunday

Pot roast. Lay strips of bacon around the meat of a well-aged rump (beef), rub in salt and allspice. . . .

Married life, Marie won't learn it from me.

She gets to see it playacted, but not even realistically. These performances are the visits from D. E., aka Dieter Erichson, Professor of Physics & Chemistry, adviser to the US Air Force on matters of radar technology, guest and host of this Cresspahl family for five and half years, and by no means the man of the house that the neighbors think he is when they see him coming with elaborately wrapped presents, with a suitcase from a trip, with longstanding stock phrases he uses as long as he's in the open doorway.

Once through the door, he may act completely at home, know the layout of the apartment almost without looking, offer casual passing signs of affection that Marie barely notices. Still, he won't entirely unpack his suitcase today either, and before he puts it off to one side in the south bedroom, he makes sure with a glance that he's permitted to enter. He won't stay long, not past tomorrow night, even if Marie asks him to. Which she might.

And she likes it like this. She likes how he sits at the table between the two windows, like a guest, and asks her how school is going because he genuinely wants to know, not because he's responsible for her. They have all sorts of little private codes, whether skeptical sidelong glances up from below, or trying to lie with a straight face, or sometimes having to say: *Which I undertook solely to help keep New York clean*, or whatever it is these days. She would like to live with him for good, in his house, and yet it would have to be on her terms. It never occurs to her to compare D. E. to the husbands who pay her friends visits in the evenings as fathers; for her he's a friend, her mother's but more clearly her own. She's the one who gave him the name D. E., from his initials, although it might also mean Dear Erichson, she shows her affection not with his first name but with the other name, the one everyone uses. – Well, D. E.? she says. – How's business in your business?

So that he'll tell her, cheerfully, patiently, about the US Air Force's Greenland radar installations, about the ritual phrases people are saying nowadays at the start of a meal in Thule, with stubborn reversions to the history of the Goths, which Marie doesn't always recognize, even though she's been hanging on his every word like a bloodhound. Kneeling on her chair, rocking back and forth on her elbows, not taking her eyes off him, his carefree expression, his playful lip movements, his skin taut from the cold, his gray hair at forty, his sober callous look, the Mecklenburger who's become an American. With their easy English, their suppressed laughter, they were acting happy.

Meanwhile the housewife stands at the stove and tends to her tasks: Coat it in flour, brown it in butter, slowly pour in simmering water until it's two-thirds....

He is never entirely happy. In his elegant winter coat from Dublin he sits on our chairs as though we hadn't bought them years ago from the Salvation Army; he would be only too glad to buy us others, whether named after Thonet or Morris. We still haven't gone to live with him in his house in New Jersey; he wishes he could at least do something for us in ours. He doesn't permit himself suggestions, but when he mentions the reputation of a "police lock," a metal bar propped into a hole in the floor and against the door, he has just voiced his opinion that our lock and small chain do not provide sufficient security. If it were up to him, we would have a leaking radiator removed and replaced by the building management and who knows what else; it's not up to him. These are gifts I can't accept. At first, while drinking, he would come out with cost estimates; in recent years, Marie has teased him over his ways of running a household, and mentioned the Plaza Hotel, not entirely to be nasty; we haven't discussed it for a long time.

I don't need to live in higher style, D. E.
I just wish I could do something for you two.
You do enough, D. E. And anyway, what do you really mean?
I just wish I could show you....
We know.

...add a couple stale bread crusts, some roots (i.e., carrots), 1 onion, 1 bay leaf, some peppercorns, and simmer together 2 1/2 hours; while D. E., like a paterfamilias from the old days, has taken the child out for a walk in the already dark evening, in the wet snow in Riverside Park, to work up an appetite. Married life, Marie won't learn it from me. An exception for a holiday, once, not always. When we have something to celebrate.

– What do we have to celebrate?
– The date, Gesine. Even if it's not entirely accurate from an astronomical point of view.

– Yes. That the year's over. That we survived it.

– October went by too fast for me.

– Everyone says why they're celebrating, Marie.

– Okay. Because this year Senator Kennedy caught up to the president. Because he's going to end the war in Vietnam.

– Bugs Bunny? Against the will of more than half the population, who want the war continued? Bugs Bunny?

– Senator Robert Francis Kennedy.

– *I stand corrected, Marie Cresspahl.*

– *Marie Henriette Cresspahl, at that.*

– Sorry, M. H.

– The astronauts who burned to death in January. The Soviet astronaut who crashed in April.

– Your summer dress, the yellow one with the tortoiseshell buttons.

– The Negro riots this summer in more than a hundred cities; the Ford strike; the New York school strike.

– The dress with the collar that's . . . how do you say it, *nackenfern* or *halsfern?*

– It's yours.

– Another 203 days and I'll be eleven.

– That we have that to look forward to.

– That none other than brothers from the CIA saved a comrade of Che Guevara's from death by shooting.

– That Che Guevara might have lived if he hadn't slapped a Bolivian officer during an interrogation.

– And long live our dear old Auntie Times!

– Now the New Year's resolutions. I resolve to keep my A average with Sister Magdalena, even if the monster never once gives me credit! Now you.

– To stay in New York, and that we can make it here.

– That's not a resolution, Gesine, that's a wish! You're only allowed to say something you have control over.

– To not turn out like my mother.

– You have a fever, Gesine.

– Fever or not, now I want to hear how Professor Erichson plans to improve in the New Year.

– By getting you two to marry me in the New Year.

– Wrong! Another wish.

– For me it's a resolution, *Mary Mary quite contrary.*

– *Which I undertook solely to help keep New York City clean.*

– Right. *Once upon a time, when wishes still came true, there was a woman who had everything, she was young and healthy . . . .*

– *So now she hangs in St. Mary's Church in Lübeck and is tiny as a mouse and every year she moves a little bit more.*

– She wished for eternal life, Marie.

– *What a stupid thing to wish!*

– Happy New Year to you, D. E.

– *Godet Niejår*, Gesine.

– *Happy New Year! Happy New Year!*

January 1, 1968 Monday

Three inches of snow. Twenty-four degrees Fahrenheit, smeared onto the windows by a wind that's even colder.

Marie manages to hold out all the way through breakfast. She lets D. E. distract her; he's trying to make her believe that her picture is in *The New York Times.* The *Times* has in fact printed an elaborately narrative image of two people, one smaller, the larger one at least similar in stature to D. E., both under umbrellas, walking down some stairs into snow with patches of slush and spindly park branches. She has to grant him the umbrellas, but she no longer believes herself to be the smaller person to his right, and now there's no point in keeping his thumb over the caption "Central Park," she knew right away that there weren't any such stairs in Riverside Park, even if she did take some similar ones last night, with a lamppost on the right, too, but never these.

– You'll never fool me with New York: she says, confident and certain and contemptuous.

For the new year, the Protestant Church of the City of New York informs us that it thinks there is no doubt that religion will be a failure in 1968 as it was in 1967. "There are so many things it doesn't do that it should do. . . ."

But then Marie can no longer contain herself, she has to reveal her present for me, her little New Year's gift. I don't know what it is. For more than six weeks her room has been off-limits; the only clues have been the sounds of sawing, hammers, and drills, much of which she's masked with the record player. In early December I saw her coming out from one of the side streets in the Hundreds onto Broadway, carrying slats and boards with holes sawed out; maybe the present is made of wood. She said it would satisfy a wish I didn't know I had. D. E., dressed first thing in the morning and on a holiday the same as for his restaurants and conferences, is leaning against the wall by the window, a comfortable observer, arms crossed, talking about his day. Back in his day, he says, children who did fretwork projects sometimes produced a light fixture for the hallway.

And watch yourself, Gesine. She's nervous.

If Marie's nervous, I'm the one who should be nervous.

The gift, set up under a sheet between the wings of the double door to Marie's room, is as big as a dog, bigger than the chow chow that used to live under Dr. Berling's desk. But a white sheet is draped on the dead, on what is written off, what will never come back.

– It's our house, Marie.

– It's not trying to be your house, only what I've heard about it!: she says, while pacing restlessly back and forth next to me, as if to force me farther away from the model.

It is the house that Albert Papenbrock signed over to his granddaughter in the spring of 1933 so that Heinrich Cresspahl would do what Lisbeth wanted and come back to Jerichow from England. It is a squat structure, a weather-beaten red under a low-hanging mossy red roof, complete with the sloping eaves on both sides. There are the three white crosses of the window frames to the left of the front door, one to the right. She got the door right, set into its beveled frame, with mitered corners, a wood bottom panel and the top half glass. Both halves are on hinges; each has a knob and a latch.

– It's not my fault, in our only photo the walnut trees hide the front of the house and half the door!

– You even remembered the doorstep.

The entryway had red tiles, like this one. Anyone who came in this way would head through the door to the left, leading to the room that the farmers before Cresspahl had used as a front parlor. Cresspahl had gone for something similar, with a table that could almost seat eight, which he'd brought back from Richmond and set up in the middle of the house as a table for special occasions. By the time the house was finished, the yard and garden redone, they were no longer celebrating any special occasions. So the table was placed crossways, head next to the window. It was where he kept his tax records, order books, drawings, folding rulers. Lisbeth's desk from Papenbrock's trousseau stood at the other window, with her books in the hutch. But Lisbeth never came here to read, and she no longer had letters to write. Cresspahl had cleared out the chairs and the dresser and put them in the workmen's rooms. Because he was sleeping in this room now, on a leather sofa against the wall, it was bare enough.

In the next room, not as big, warmed by an extension of the tiled stove, slept the child.

– Did the child's room really have only one door, to Cresspahl's office?
– You never mentioned any other.

So it was Cresspahl who used to check on the child at night. Without Marie I would have forgotten that.

He could go from his desk through the door at the end of the long wall, into the room with the large bed that he'd made to Lisbeth's specifications, in which she now wanted to sleep alone. From there straight into the kitchen. But when Cresspahl went to breakfast he took the long way, through the entryway and the back hall into the kitchen, to avoid seeing Lisbeth asleep. Meals were served here, at the long tile table, even on Sundays now.

– It's your fault if the other half of the house isn't right: Marie says, still a little anxious about whether she should really have tried to reconstruct the past.
– Because I never told you about it.

Why not? Why didn't I say anything about Paap, Alwin Paap, who had the front room to the right of the door? He lived there until 1939, the foreman. That was why he went into his room via the detour through the back hall, punctilious as he was about his position. Marie has divided the rest of that half into two rooms, the way it really was. The first, across from the kitchen, they still used as a large pantry. The second was fixed up for two workmen in 1935. They stayed till the start of the war. Then came the French, the prisoners of war. In three years they'll be sleeping there in bunk beds.

– A carpenter's daughter, Marie.
– Granddaughter, *at that*.
– Granddaughter. And the proportions are right.
– Really? Right? That's how it was?
– That's how it still is. It's still there in Jerichow, you'll inherit it.
– I don't want it. I was only trying to see what you were talking about. How it looks.
– You did a good job, Marie.
– In that case I'll do the loft conversion. For what's coming next.

January 2, 1968 Tuesday

On December 8, Leonid Brezhnev, General Secretary of the Communist Party of the USSR, once again helped out Comrade Novotný, General Secretary of the Communist Party of the ČSSR, one leader to another, and saved his position. Now Antonín Novotný is making promises and not mentioning that he may be making them in his successor's name. It struck him over New Year's that the overall economic development of the Slovakian region must be fundamentally of equal importance to that of the Czech lands, and that he would now permit any progressive ideas as long as they proved useful, even in culture and art, even if originating in the West. *The New York Times* would not want to withhold credit where credit is due, and she shows him to us photographed as a well-meaning man full of understanding for the plight of others.

The temperature is still stuck at minus four Celsius; in the subway hacking coughs were at one point louder than the train, runny noses and red eyes are a clear enough weather report, and yet this is not the conversation topic of greatest interest to the ladies of the sauna of the Hotel Marseilles. Sweating and sniffling, gasping and grunting, they crouch and lie in the dry smoky air, in the half dark, and they are talking about the rapes that are a part of life on the Upper West Side of New York. The tone is businesslike, sometimes outraged, generally unashamed, even though almost none of the naked women know Mrs. Cresspahl even by sight from shopping on Broadway, only Mrs. Blumenroth and a girl named Marjorie are acquaintances. Maybe it's enough that this side of the pool is rigorously barred to men. Many of the women are around forty, have two or three kids swimming in the adjacent pool, frenetic voices or gentle voices, belly fat or waistlines that haven't melted away. Only Marjorie is seventeen, tall, she alone still has a perfect body, and people think she's older than she is. When Mrs. Cresspahl stoops to enter into the uncertain light, the talk has just turned to the police.

Calling the police! Waste of time.

Not only that. Even if they believe you they ask you about the height and the weight, and you know what's coming next.

Whether the weight felt nice.

Right! Whether I came.

With me it was: whether he came.

The precinct sent someone to investigate the back stairs where it happened, and he expected me to offer him a whiskey.

Exactly! Then invite him to dinner.

You too?

When they caught mine, they let him go.

Because a man can't be convicted on the basis of an unconfirmed statement by the victim. Article 130, Penal Code.

By the alleged victim, if you please.

They never even try without a reliable witness.

And since I knew mine from when he used to deliver my groceries from the supermarket, the policeman dropped it then and there. Shut his notebook and forgot about it.

Of course I know the plumber. Who they keep sending.

Plumber, that's a good one. They're telegraph messengers too.

Magazine salesmen!

And they really stick to tradition. They use a knife, you never hear about drugs.

Right.

Followed me from the bus to the door of my apartment. Talking to me the whole time, everyone thought we were a normal couple.

That was the wrong thing to do. Keeping quiet is dangerous too.

You have to say as loud as you can: Fuck off!

Then he screams something about a disgusting whore who doesn't deserve him. Well, I survived.

He slammed me into the wall with one hand on my neck, with the other he pulled down his pants. "Three sizes too small."

That could have backfired.

It did. Scratches didn't heal for three weeks.

I always carry a police whistle.

Air pistol. Pepper spray.

Not allowed. It's illegal to carry a concealed weapon.

Again, not for the man.

Disarm him. Castration.

No.

No.

Change the laws.

I have a friend, she teaches karate, and if anyone wants I can get you a discount price. Karate!

That's no good either.

You remember the sixteen-year-old abducted and raped by three men in Bushwick last week? One of them was an applicant to join the police force.

In the showers, speaking through the wet curtain of her long black hair, Marjorie, the gentle child, says what she would do to defend herself, and acts it out, by stepping cheerful and naked under the streaming water like a tambourine girl in a parade, her knee delightfully shooting up.

– The things they don't tell us on TV: she says.
– And what would you do?
– I'd ask for money first.
– Tell me how that goes!

January 3, 1968 Wednesday

In the early-morning darkness today, enemy forces attacked the United States air base at Danang with about thirty rounds of 122 mm rocket fire, wrecking an F-4 Phantom fighter-bomber.

Three other planes were damaged in the eleven-minute attack on the base. Military spokesmen said that three air force personnel and one marine were wounded and about a dozen other servicemen hurt as they ran for cover.

It hadn't gotten to that point in Jerichow; the airfield was far from finished. Before that happened, Jerichow wanted to get at least one Jew out of the way.

So that's what they did for Arthur Semig, doctor of veterinary medicine, homeowner, bank account holder.

They didn't for Oskar Tannebaum, who lived on Short Street in two rooms off a courtyard, the store bell rarely summoning him to make a sale these days. Rubber boots, blue jackets, green caps, you could get all that in Gneez, in Wismar, in Lübeck. Tannebaum paid his taxes like Semig but he didn't have friends in the better families, he let his children leave the house in clothes that had been mended too many times, his wife was so frugal with her shopping it was like she was scared of being cheated. He used to have rich relatives in the county capital; he had not been presentable enough for these relatives to bring him along to Hamburg or Holland or wherever they'd ended up. Oskar was not from Mecklenburg, and his wife was from the lost eastern territories. Finally, the Tannebaums had only been in Jerichow for ten years at most.

Dr. Arthur Semig, on the other hand, came from western Mecklenburg, you might almost think Ludwigslust and the grand duke's residence; his wife was a Köster from Schwerin and moreover Protestant by birth. Arthur had opened his practice in Jerichow seventeen years ago, was invited to the coffee tables as well as the stables of the Bülows (the "Upper Bülows"), of Mayor Erdamer—he had belonged, by reason of property, of education, of his confiding little stories, his discretion, his countless rhymes for any and every child who ran past his legs. They couldn't let anything happen to Arthur. He'd understood something when he'd shaved off his little square mustache; now he had to be made to understand that he needed to leave.

Papenbrock started it. No, this time it was Axel von Rammin who started it. Or maybe it was Avenarius, Avenarius Cold Morning? It was Cresspahl.

They came at him from all sides, ignoring his exasperation, they listened to his excuses so patiently that it was always he who had to say the next word. He couldn't very well throw a von Rammin, barons for centuries, out of his house when he'd turned up for advice about rebuilding the cow barn and driven his carriage up not through the yard but on the Bäk, hitching the horses right in the middle of the street for all to see. Von Rammin actually sat there for half an hour listening to what Semig had to tell him about the latest in hygienic cattle breeding. Then, without relaxing his craggy face in the least, he turned the conversation to a friend in Austria, Count Naglinsky, known as Nagel, Beatus Nagel. Semig had had occasion to help him once before. Beatus was still grateful for his Weimaraner's quick and complete recovery with Semig's medicine. Beatus had ample estates at his disposal, and was, incidentally, above any of this Hitler's insanities, never even thinking of the German Reich chancellor as a true countryman. And now Naglinsky had had an idea. Along with his dogs he had his dairy cattle, he kept horses, he had suffered losses among his pigs as well as his chickens, and for all of these things he had to send for a doctor from the city. It was thus not a matter of economy, it just made sense, to keep a private veterinarian on-site. He had no objection to this doctor offering his services in the village on the side. He often had professional men over to dine, to stay in apartments in the castle. Baron von Rammin requested that a bill be sent to the estate for the consultation, gave Mrs. Semig his fond regards, and left with an additional personal remark from the heart about the climate in Lower Austria. It was Semig, not the baron, who had to run his hands through his hair as he stood in the doorway watching the man and his unsolicited advice ride off.

Papenbrock wanted no part of it. Papenbrock refused to have the money in Semig's account transferred into his own as the repayment of a loan; that would be lying, and immoral. Papenbrock balked at buying Semig's house; he had enough of those in Jerichow, and he needed his cash liquid for a security he'd promised in Lübeck.

Papenbrock was scared. The old man sat there bent over, laid aside his suddenly nauseating cigar, chewed his knuckles, and finally got to the point where he was cursing the Jews, in a shrill, almost nagging voice, with contemptuous waves of the hand, longing desperately for an end to the discussion. He was too embarrassed to look at Cresspahl.

Semig was satisfied where he was. He couldn't be persuaded that way. He'd grown used to living without the phone ringing. The drives around the countryside, the night work, had been hard for him; now he had time to read. Dora was managing better too, with the regular hours. He had no problem forgoing the games of skat with Dr. Berling; Cresspahl was a better player anyway, and they'd find a third. He was not going to let himself be sent away from Jerichow.

Then Dr. Avenarius Kollmorgen, attorney at law, came by. He did not walk down the Bäk; he invited Arthur and Dora Semig and Heinrich and Lisbeth Cresspahl over for an evening with red wine and, if it came to that, skat.

Avenarius had troubles. It rubbed him the wrong way to have to condone the humiliations his fellow lawyer Friedrichsen was going through in Güstrow, not only regarding his Judaism but even affecting his social standing. He hadn't been able to help Friedrichsen, but he found himself still in a position to give a helping hand to a university man in Jerichow.

Friedrichsen, 's he baptized?
No.
Is it on there?
His sign says "Dr. Jur."
Put on he's a Jew.

Kollmorgen gave his maid another evening off and led his guests into the parlor personally, with outstretched hand, and said his piece on his feet, teetering on his heels, his massive head held high atop his short stocky body. He discussed the relevant laws. It came out that he needed a loan, among other reasons to purchase a house on the Bäk "with which we are acquainted," and also that, since he wasn't fully up to snuff on the dictates and prohibitions of foreign-currency law, he had left all these matters for lo these many years in the hands of a "trading house" in Bremen, which he recommended. He arched his eyebrows in courtroom fashion, just as in the most famous moments of his cross-examinations, he looked Dora Semig in the eyes almost tenderly, he was really trying. Then he drank, rather too fast, before long was out of commission for skat, staring glassy-eyed at his guests, the corners of his mouth drooping. To Cresspahl, who had come alone, he looked like an overgrown child who can't swallow a setback.

For Semig refused. He forbade anyone's interference. His tone drew a rebuke from Dora. He let Dora say her piece, and Dora looked at him, pursed her lips a little tighter, and nodded. She hadn't even sighed.

Cresspahl offered Semig his balance at the Surrey Bank of Richmond in exchange, and Arthur wouldn't hear of it. Cresspahl said: We'll keep it all faithfully for you, not a penny'll be missing; Semig said: My dear Herr Cresspahl! If I'm not good enough for you....

Axel von Rammin had duly commissioned letters from his friend Beatus and was now insulted that a veterinarian was presuming to hesitate in a matter that after all a person of no ordinary standing had set in motion.

And Avenarius, when he ran into Cresspahl, occasionally forgot to raise his head with a graceful twist and say with mysterious significance: *All's well, Cresspahl? All's well?*

Lisbeth Cresspahl said: Christ was a Jew too. That means we all are. Leave Semig alone.

And Papenbrock said: If you all want to get rid of him and the nice way doesn't work, try the hard way!

January 4, 1968 Thursday

Back in the spring of 1961, Gesine had found a three-room apartment in New York, with five windows looking out over Riverside Park and the Hudson River. It was such a relief—she felt settled in, accommodated, at peace.

She knew it wasn't exactly a personal accomplishment; still, she almost convinced herself it was, though she had no one to brag to except perhaps a certain retired English teacher in Jerichow. She was proud of the fact that, beyond her wildest expectations, she was able to rent an apartment on one of the most famous streets in the world, Riverside Drive, noted in guidebooks not only for its beautiful old trees and the view of the coastal cliffs of New Jersey but also for its architecture and monuments—from the house of the worthy Charles M. Schwab, who helped Carnegie betray

the government with defective armor plating for its tanks, up to the tomb
of the eighteenth president of the United States, Ulysses S. Grant, who
died in misery describing his Civil War victories. She liked that this street
was gradually losing its teeth of wealth, unlike Central Park West and
West End Avenue with their bastions of affluence, and canopies outside
the doors to further protect their tenants, and liveried doormen to whistle
for taxis. She preferred to stick it out on her own when it rained, rarely
took trips that needed a taxi, and firmly refused to forget that the salary
from an office job was enough for Riverside Drive only because the law
still protected some rents from the market. If she could stay there, she
would act like a guest, left in peace at least at home.

It didn't take long before Mr. Cooper and Mr. Rider came along and
showed her that she'd happened to find a place in a building that itself was
worthy of mention in a book. Wasn't that just perfect?

There is a frieze of snakes and other animals, in sandstone that's still
white, near the bottom of the leather-colored yellow building on Riverside
Drive above Ninety-Sixth Street, on the third of its twelve stories. She'd
paid it so little attention that even well into late summer she thought it
was Egyptian, even though her windows were under, and in fact in, the
frieze, and she looked up at them often enough, to make sure they were
still there, not smashed in. Now America had caught up to her through
the very building where she lived.

For this building is known not only by its number, 243, but by name:
Cliff Apartment House, after Arizona's cliff dwellers. The mountain lions,
rattlesnakes, and buffalo skulls are meant to commemorate the forefathers
of the Pueblo tribe and in general the Indian people whose country was
taken from them—meant as a memorial, as if for the dead.

At first, the double coincidence did seem fitting. Marie was already in
school, spending mornings in the Rockefeller's church, called Riverside
Church, and she'd gotten to the fairy tales that were supposed to introduce
her not only to the country's language but also to a period in its history
that Gesine didn't trust the school to handle properly. All the Indians in
the stories they read at that school were descendants of a stumpy old man
with thick braids of black hair parted in the middle, a forehead covered
with pockmark-like nicks, a sharp nose, a lively mouth protruding from
the taut flesh of his face, expression completely friendly, eyes dim with

memory in their cavernous sockets—exactly the way an Indian from the Pueblo tribe had been depicted in the Papenbrock family encyclopedia on the lower left corner of the page. The red-skinned cliff dwellers prayed to the sun; a new page in Marie's understanding of religion. They raised livestock and knew now to irrigate their fields; Marie had never imagined a life of that sort of work before. The cliff dwellers' greatest accomplishment, in Marie's eyes, was where they lived: high up in caves, set neatly into the steep cliffs of the *cañon* and hard for the foreign conqueror to reach, or else in fortified villages built from the soaring *casas grandes* (stone towers) with neither windows nor doors down below, so they could be reached only by ladders, while stairways likewise connected the different families' spaces in the multileveled interior. Marie recognized these ladders in the rusty thicket of fire escapes on the south side of our building, and was grateful that the ceremonial halls for the Indians' councils and ritual dances were missing in our case, because otherwise she'd have had to deal with more unfamiliar people than she felt up to at the time. Back then she was sure she knew where the Indians had lived: on the other side of the river, where the sun is still brighter than the dark red it has when it sets for us.

So you wanted to stir up hate in your child against the country she was supposed to live in?
I couldn't even make inroads against the language.

It started off harmlessly enough. Marie brought home from school the information that the name "cliff dwellers" had been taken from them and was now applied to this country's tenement dwellers. So not even our building remained a memorial to them.

Then she said, in all seriousness, to reassure me of something: *Honest Injun!*, meaning a reliable Indian and also suggesting a suspicion that Indians are dumb by nature, if honest. She learned "peace pipe" for occasions of reconciliation, "war paint" as an expression for each new fashion item, and I couldn't tell her to mistrust the language she now needed for school. Marie gleaned from various passing know-it-alls that the surviving Indians are good for nothing except urban construction projects, since they never feel dizzy; then she doesn't want to hear that it's they who are building more buildings in New York, while she expected to hear that white construction workers drink coffee during their lunch breaks while the Indians fill up with liquor, sold to them under the guise of "firewater." From there it was just a small step to the view that Indian territories within the borders of the US are rightfully called "reservations"; they're not really "camps," since after all Indians can't live any other way. And then it was too late. She obediently accepted correction but was unable to think differently. Now she recognizes Indians not only by their facial features but also from their insecure manner, their vague, uncertain expressions, their failure to fit in that extends even to their clothes; she calls them, not to be cruel, purely as an observation: *Vanishing Americans*, as though it were simply the way of the world that those of her own skin color should survive.

As for what she might have said about the Indian leaning senseless on a stairway under Times Square this evening, I wouldn't have wanted to hear it. He didn't know where he was or how he'd found himself there, he definitely couldn't see straight, yet even in his drunkenness he lacked contentment, release from knowledge, the combination of giving up and trusting in others' help. He was somewhere far away, yet there to be grasped. His eyelids were trembling slightly. The fashionable cut of his coat wasn't going to protect him—not against the cold, not against the police on the subway. Marie was capable of saying: Sitting Bull, or: Chief Rain-in-Face, and only then, all innocent, would she have felt the nudge in the ribs from me, the warning grip on her shoulder that no longer reaches her where she now lives with her language.

Surely she must understand what you've told her about equality and human rights, Gesine.
But she doesn't believe it. She can't see it.
You are not raising your child properly, Mrs. Cresspahl.

The weekly summary of casualties listed 185 Americans, 227 South Vietnamese, and 37 other allied servicemen killed in action last week.

.... American and other non-Vietnamese forces reported killing a total of 623 enemy soldiers; the total reported killed by the South Vietnamese was 815.

American losses through Dec. 30 brought the death toll for 1967 to 9,353 and the total killed in the war to 15,997.

"Six members of a 25th Infantry Division unit were killed and 13 wounded yesterday in a 90-minute skirmish only 14 miles from Saigon. A few hours later 4 other Americans were killed and 21 wounded when their positions were mistakenly bombed by American and Vietnamese planes.

The 25th Division again raised, to 382, the enemy death toll from its battle Monday 60 miles north of Saigon. Troops searching the jungle near the artillery base that elements of the Vietcong 271st and 272d Regiments tried to overrun also found 75 automatic rifles, 11 light machine guns and 18 rocket launchers."
© The New York Times

"The Defense Department will continue selling great quantities of arms abroad to fight the gold drain. Pentagon sources said that sales were expected to reach a combined total of at least $4.5 billion to $4.6 billion over this and the next two fiscal years. (See page 1, column 4.)"
© The New York Times

"Newark, Jan. 4.—LeRoi Jones, the militant Negro writer, was sentenced today to two and a half to three years in the New Jersey State Penitentiary and fined $1,000 for illegal possession of two revolvers during the Newark riots last summer.

The sentence was virtually the maximum—it could have been three years—and allows no probation.

It was handed down by Essex County Judge Leon W. Kapp after he said one could suspect that the 34-year-old poet and playwright was 'a participant in formulating a plot' to burn Newark on the night he was arrested.

The riots, in which 28 persons died, lasted five days.

.... The judge indicated that he based the severity of Jones's punishment to a large extent on a poem published last month in *Evergreen Review*, a monthly magazine. He read the poem in the courtroom this morning, substituting the word 'blank' for what he termed 'obscenities.'

Addressed to the 'Black People!' the poem, as read by the judge, listed the merchandise in some of the city's larger department stores and in the 'smaller joosh enterprises' and continued in part:

All the stores will open if
you will say the magic words.
The magic words are: Up
against the wall mother blank
this is a stickup! Or: Smash
the window at night (these are
magic actions) smash the windows
daytime, anytime, together,
let's smash the windows drag
the blank from in there. No
money down. No time to pay. Run
up and down Broad Street
niggers, take the blank you
want. Take their lives if
need be, but get what you
want what you need.

Dressed in a striped African tunic and wearing a small red cap at the back of his head, Jones stood with his hands behind his back and laughed frequently while Judge Kapp read the poem.

Several times, however, he interrupted the sentencing statement.

When the judge said, 'You are sick and require medical attention,' Jones replied: 'Not as sick as you are.'

And when the judge noted that the prisoner, who has been free on $25,000 bail, had failed to appear several times for recommended examinations by the county psychiatrist, the writer interrupted: 'Who needs treatment himself.'

After Irvin B. Booker, Jones's lawyer, had appealed for a probationary sentence and a nominal fine, the playwright was permitted to make a statement. He rose and told the judge:

'You are not a righteous person, and you don't represent Almighty God. You represent a crumbling structure . . .'

'Sit down!' shouted the judge, loudly rapping his gavel.

At one point, after the sentences had been pronounced, a tall, slender Negro teen-ager among the spectators rose to protest. When he failed to respond quickly enough to an order to sit down, he was ushered out of court by several attendants.

'They're going to beat him,' cried Mrs. Sylvia Jones, the writer's wife. Mrs. Jones, who was holding their 7-month-old baby, was taken from the room.

As Jones was being led from the courtroom, he called back over his shoulder, 'The black people will judge me.'

. . . . would be filed."

© The New York Times

January 6, 1968 Saturday

Senator Kennedy deplores the poor education of the Indians and the Viet Cong are said to have killed 3,820 civilians last year and President de Gaulle didn't mean to insult the Jews with the expression "an elite people" and there was a fire in the Alamac Hotel on Broadway and the Christian Democratic Party of West Germany is attacking the Social Democratic Party for their appeal to the United States to end its bombing in North Vietnam and

Antonín Novotný is no longer General Secretary of the Czechoslovak Communist Party, he had to step down in favor of Alexander Dubček, a Slovak even, after a thousand years of Bohemian-Moravian domination, *The New York Times* did the math.

In Jerichow, a persistent rumor held that it was old Papenbrock who would free the town from the Jew Semig after all; another one had it that Papenbrock would acknowledge his found-again son, Robert, as his own only as long as Reich Governor Hildebrandt had a say in the state of Mecklenburg, not a day longer. That he wasn't him.

Not even the family could swear to who exactly the Robert Papenbrock of 1935 or 1937 was. He had come to Jerichow exactly once, maybe only because Horst insisted; he stayed Saturday and left for the regional headquarters in the state capital that Sunday and sent a postcard from Berlin and since he hadn't married the woman he had in his Schwerin villa he couldn't send an announcement. He was hard to visit, because if he didn't have visitors already then he was away, doing a job that required travel. First-class, sleeping car.

He might be him. The Robert who'd run off from Parchim in May 1914 had looked to be turning into a lanky sort of guy; this one was tall, heavy-set, fat in the face. He was the right age—Robert would be a little over forty now. The Robert who'd grown up in Vietsen and Waren had been quick and sharp; this one was mellow, sedentary, not a fast talker. It was really quite odd that he'd never even asked about the child he'd fathered with the French teacher's daughter. The Robert the Papenbrocks remembered had had no qualms about scattering debts all over the town of Parchim; this one had come to an agreement with the estate owner whose two horses he had borrowed, in a manner that even today counted as theft, instead of delivering to Schwerin: maybe the aggrieved party had lodged a complaint against Robert with his party. Robert acted puzzled about the whole business and had obviously expected Papenbrock to be honored to pay for these horses on top of everything else. He tended to pussyfoot in talking about the old days. Who knew you could unlearn Plattdeutsch to such an extent in a mere twenty years. A Mecklenburg child? Well, maybe foreign languages have something corrosive in em. What Louise Papenbrock had the hardest time accepting was his bald head, not even the old man had such a rounded forehead. When she thought back to Robbie's childhood hair, those way-ward tufts he used to have . . . well, overseas there were diseases worse than anything they had in Mecklenburg. That's it. *Just tell me, Robbie, why didnt you ever write?*

Robert spoke in his easygoing new way about the pride one had, and Louise on the sofa suddenly couldn't remember whether she'd enclosed eternal curses with the two hundred goldmarks she'd sent the "poor boy" in the rough-and-tumble alley district of Hamburg. In the ad she'd placed in Hamburg's *Fremdenblatt* she'd expressed herself differently: "Come home, all is forgiven, Your mother née U. from G——w." Papenbrock had parked himself in his chair so that his belly sat comfortably on top and he could give all his attention to the big lethargic man squirming his mouth around a wooden toothpick. Papenbrock was thinking about a pride that hadn't been enough to bring a German back home when his country was at war against half the world. Cresspahl sat at the table next to Horst and tried to catch his expression other than from the side, but Horst stayed leaning too far forward, looking at his hands, as if he had to get through something unpleasant. Cresspahl kept his eyes on Lisbeth, who was searching the newcomer's face, her chin propped on folded hands, benevolent but even more taken aback, and in no way the erstwhile little sister; what mattered to Cresspahl was how much he liked her, and how their child wandered around the table, now stopping next to him, now next to her mother, in a serious game. Sometimes everyone would glance quickly and secretly at Horst, and all he gave back was a nod that seemed to confirm something more to himself than to the others. Horst was probably regretting the loss of his inheritance to the firstborn, and in the end Horst hadn't been around at the time, had he.

All right. Robert had had his pride. But really, he'd bought false papers and shipped out, working his way to Montevideo on an American boat? That's what happened in too many books. And always upholding the honor of the German nation, our glorious Kaiser, proud Mecklenburg-Schwerin, and if anyone had something to say about it he'd been quick to say *You wanna piece of this? Let's step outside.* In German, not Platt, what do you think.

It was because Robert was passing himself off as a Norwegian, then as a US citizen, then as someone with a Mexican passport. That was why his brother'd had such a hard time finding him. Much later, Horst repeated this first afternoon of stories from his perspective, but not to his parents, and only when no one could accuse him of resenting the hit to his inheritance anymore.

The family knew about Montevideo from a former comrade of Papenbrock's from the regiment, since fallen, whom Robert had hit up for money. No word of Robert in Montevideo itself. In Porto Alegre, Paranaguá, Santos, Rio de Janeiro, there were lots of people passing through who maybe could've looked like the kid in the photograph once. By that point Horst's Portuguese was up to the task of fending off the greediest offers of information, and since he handed out Papenbrock's money not a little defiantly, his hotel addresses recommended him to the German communities. Robert had kept his distance from the Germans.

Robert had been an inspector on the hacienda of a family of German origin. Five-hour drive from Salvador, also known as Bahia.

In Vietsen Robert had learned no more about agriculture than you could pick up by watching other people work. That Robert didn't know how to drive.

Five hours with a chauffeur was what he meant. Ditto when he managed a factory in Colón. On the Panama Canal. Where he first learned English.

Learned Spanish as a taxi driver in Mexico. Mexico City. The ups and downs of life.

At this point, around four in the afternoon, Robert asked for a schnapps, and Lisbeth took the child by the hand and went off to do the household chores that she'd thought up for this time of day.

Canal Street in New Orleans—if you haven't seen that! The surging yellow waters of the Mississippi. The noble Indians of Arizona.

How Robert had helped build the Golden Gate Bridge. Wheeling a barrow of stones across a narrow plank. The sneaky Negro who bumped him. A Mecklenburg boy, how could he go down like that, in the San Francisco Bay?

And always saving his money. In a pouch across his chest when he rode the freight cars east. A hobo. The others lying on the roof with him, their resentful looks. Some tramps used to go rolling off the edge, and if the rails were running along a mile-high cliff, so much the better. And all that time, never dishonoring the image . . . the memory . . . the faith of our dear mama. The main thing was to survive.

Bought up a trucking business in Hoboken with the capital. Three employees. Lost it all in the Depression. Then, with the overpowering might of Manhattan constantly before his eyes, there had to be a way. Longshoreman in the port, and even so a down payment on a house in Long Island City. Part ownership of a restaurant with an old member of the Schwerin rowing team, on Broadway in the Nineties. Then Germany's rise from the ashes of democracy. By the time Horst found him he'd already applied for his passport. Practically. Horst just had to swear on the spot he was a Mecklenburger. *Just a technicality. You know.*

Jewed and niggered top to bottom, the Americans are. This war we'll win.

Learned to stand on his own two feet. Not be a burden to the family. Give his all for the victory of National Socialism in the rest of the world.

On the postcard with the New Reich Chancellery on the front, he'd written: They were putting him through the wringer in Berlin, but they'd definitely take him.

In September 1936 he was already giving a speech in Erlangen, at the Reich conference for NSDAP organizations abroad, "in front of 5,000 Germans from every corner of the world."

In Jerichow, though, they were talking about how Pastor Brüshaver's sermon the morning after Robert's arrival made no mention of the happy turn of events; the Papenbrocks could have requested it. It was said that Avenarius Kollmorgen would have to know if Papenbrock had changed his will, but that whenever the Erlanger speech came up, Avenarius always only mentioned his time in Erlangen and what used to count as proper in those days. It made sense that Papenbrock wouldn't try to show him off, this Robert. Always been a clever one, the old man. They never called on his services, and even though Robert had been back almost two years by now people almost never thought of him in connection with the Papenbrocks. What difference did it make if it was him or not.

Lisbeth hadn't liked that the stranger had wanted to hug her after more than twenty years as if she wasn't his sister. But Lisbeth had had a thing about being hugged for a while now.

January 7, 1968 Sunday

The underpass beneath Henry Hudson's parkway was stuffed so full of sparkling light that Marie expected the river to be a frozen, smooth mirror for the sun. But under the cloudless illuminated sky the enormous current was on its powerful way to the Atlantic, glittering with countless ice floes, no longer Hudson's river, so poisoned by industrial wastewater that the fish have already died far to the north—the memory of a river. Across the deep plain it cut into the land, a wind raced faster than a car would be allowed to in residential neighborhoods, and the ten below zero Celsius had so infused the railings of the promenade that the iron held fingertips fast. Marie happily stomped ahead through the slippery snow, melted and refrozen many times over, towards the sun feigning warmth more or less over Hoboken. She gave the promenaders coming toward us such a cheerful look that she seemed half inclined to share with them some of the fun she was carrying around with her. When she talked, the wind sometimes let little clouds of breath hang in front of her face for a moment, before the cold whipped them away. – Hoboken!: she said, and literally looked up as though trying to see the wool she wouldn't let anyone pull over *her* eyes.

– A trucking company in Hoboken, four salaries to pay, what else? City councilman at least!: she said, playing indignant in her amusement at the idea that Robert Papenbrock could have attained a middle-class income and status in our part of the world, just across the Hudson. She calls him "your uncle," as though inoculated against any family connection herself.

– In the twenties the transcontinental steamers still docked in Hoboken, Marie. There was trucking to do.

– I'll give you that. It's not a bad story he came up with.

– What makes it seem like a story to you?

– His excuses are too perfect.

– Still, it's possible.

– As possible as the restaurant "on Broadway in the Nineties"! In 1930! *In the Depression!* When he'd have been lucky if the guy he knew from Schwerin let him wash dishes, and if he didn't have to wipe the scraps away first with his hand!

– You don't believe him because you only see him from a distance. You don't like him.

– That's how you told it.

– I was only trying to say how it was. How it might have been.

– It sounded like you thought he was disgusting.

– Cresspahl did, at least.

– And you're on your father's side.

– No. Whenever I do understand him it shows.

– Second piece of evidence, Mrs. Cresspahl: Mrs. Cresspahl doesn't like that her whole family signed on with the people in power in Mecklenburg at the time (and in Germany, yes, I know). This "Robert Papenbrock," or his killer, didn't even start at the bottom with them, he parachuted in at the top!

– You don't believe for a second that he's the real him?

– Should I?

– I only said how it seemed at the time.

– Why not how it was?

– Because whether his story was true or not only came out years later. Should I tell you the story out of chronological order?

– No. Although I don't keep track of this Jerichow of yours chronologically.

– How do you?

– By your people. What I know about them. What I'm supposed to think of them.

– Okay. Go.

– Okay. He wasn't at first, but now Albert Papenbrock is almost my favorite. First of all he's my great-grandfather, not many people know theirs, at least in my class. Maybe because I feel sorry for him. The Nazis won't let him be king anymore, not in the town and not in his own house. Let him brag about supporting his family in high style; at least he wants to take care of them. That's a different feeling, and it's not nice to lose it.

– Did you learn that from your dealings with Francine? "The exemplary fashion in which Schoolgirl Cresspahl gives a helping hand to a black classmate, disadvantaged by race and family circumstances"?

– I don't brag about it, but *thank you for the apologies, Gesine.* Anyway, I can recognize Albert's situation.

– Okay. Now Louweesing.

– Who? Louise, Albert Papenbrock's wife? *No comment.*

– Because she didn't practice what she preached?

– *No comment!*

– Any *comments* on Lisbeth?

– She's your mother. So I've almost always made excuses for her when you tell me things. Now she's sick, and no one will help her. In a country like ours, in New York, she'd have gone to a shrink a long time ago and been cured. She wouldn't be trapped in her church, she'd be able to see it from the outside. And she's going to be the next one to die. Even you're going easy on her.

– Next?

– See what I mean? The tradesmen—Böttcher the carpenter, Köpcke the mason, Pahl the tailor—I don't hold it against them. They didn't understand the first war, what else should they do but work toward the next one. The guy who sawed my planks for your house, in the Nineties, he was

in Korea. Wounded too. You should have heard him talk about Vietnam!
Your educated men, though, Dr. Hauschildt, Dr. Semig, Dr. Avenarius
Kollmorgen, Pastor Brüshaver, Dr. Kliefoth, Dr. Berling, Dr. Erdamer—

   – *Hi, Mr. Faure. Mrs. Faure.*

   – *Oh certainly. It's a perfect winter day.*

   – *Take care on the steps.*

   – You can take Brüshaver off the list. He got the son from his first marriage back from Spain in a sealed casket.

   – *Sorry.* Still, an accident. With Semig, I try to keep in mind that he
couldn't have believed it was possible, what we now know was possible.
But the others, with their university diplomas, *those professionals*, just talking out their ass!

   – *Nice language, Miss Cresspahl.*

   – I'm not even bothering to insult them!

   – Cresspahl.

   – Him I'd despise if he weren't your father. I'm sorry. Sorry! I didn't
mean it. *I take it back. And I did mean it.*

   – Your own grandfather?

   – Yes, him. He was the only one with his eyes wide open, he'd learned
his lesson from the first German war—doing what, actually?

   – Bayonet charge in honor of the Kaiser's birthday on the western front.
He'd learned you can stab people and like it. And that gas attack at Langemarck.

   – Right. If he'd at least tried the Netherlands, they didn't look like they
were going to be in for a war. Trying that would have entered him into my
good books forever, how do you say that in German? And he had a child,
a Gesine, and he let her stay where he was expecting bombs to start falling.
I think it's horrible, a lot of the time, how you can think all these people
in Jerichow made you who you are, it's horrible that you think you're the
way you are today because they were the way they were!

   – If Cresspahl hadn't accepted the house from Papenbrock the Cresspahls would have been in England in 1945, maybe behind bars, but still,
and Jakob would have looked for a place to stay with some other family. If
Dr. Berling had understood anyone else's moods besides his own....

   – Okay. So that's why we're in New York?

   – That's why.

– And it was all decided back there, thirty years ago you were programmed to prefer the feel of a dime in your hand over a half-dollar?

– Yes. Maybe because there are Dutch coins that feel like dimes.

– I can't think like that. And you think that's true for me too?

– It does happen. Oh, we forgot one. Horst.

– I pretty much get him. Don't laugh. He'd made a mistake. Then he realized something. Because whoever it was he found, at least he'd been in New York.

She walked comfortably next to me in the cutting wind, cozily bundled up in her heavy coat from London, in her hat with earflaps, in herself. We had the sun at our backs, and she tried with every step to step on her shadow. In the winter, when the buildings on the cliffs of the Jersey shore are hidden in the snow and the blinding reflected light, Henry Hudson might have recognized his river after all from the mottled white cliffs. Marie thinks it's possible. And she knows for certain that someone in this city of hers, even way downtown where Broadway starts and not on Park Avenue where the West Germans cluster nowadays—she is convinced that anyone who comes to New York thereby comes to his senses.

The things she believed as a child, someone ought to write them down for her.

January 8, 1968 Monday

You can count on *The New York Times*, even we haven't escaped her notice: "And residents of Riverside Drive found the Hudson River glutted with more ice floes than they had seen in many years at this time of the winter." As though she'd seen us, asked us.

There is a quantity of family occupying the Cresspahl apartment that it would be too small for even without us. Marie decided that we were good enough friends with Annie Fleury and her children to live with them, just the way they were, showing up out of the blue, of the far north, of Vermont, of the Greyhound bus. Marie explained the subway route from the bus station to our Ninety-Sixth Street station so clearly over the phone that even though they'd arrived not long before the bank closed they'd been in the apartment a long time already, the three children all in Marie's room behind closed doors and Annie on the sofa, anxious, an uninvited guest, hurriedly standing up and already out the door to a hotel. You won't rush off to the Marseilles, Annie. You're so agitated, Annie, why are you sitting there with your knees clamped so tight together, what's making you lean forward so uncomfortably, kneading your hands! If you're not laughing, we won't try to make you. We'd rather see you here the way you used to be, with your coloring of wind and woods some help to you, your farmer's-daughter brow smooth, fun sparkling in your eyes, but we'll take you the way you are. Don't look around the room as if no one could help you. We can help you. We'll get Mr. Robinson, from the elevator, Mr. Robinson will bring up cots from his inexhaustible storage area in the basement, we'll bring the suitcase in from the hall to where you'll be sleeping.

You're here now, Annie.

Because I had no one else I could trust, Gesine.

None of your suitors from only five years ago, just because one of them would have something soothing to say about the news, and another would still try to get you to move in with him in his official residence at the Finnish consulate? Not F. F. Fleury, who wanted to live with you as in Thoreau's time? It'll hit him hard, having to stay alone in a house cracking with the cold in the snow in the mountains, abandoned by his Annie, who spent more than four years working to create a life in the country, with three children and venerable splintery floorboards, his transcriber, his secretary, the admirer of his genius as a translator from the French, finally run off one early morning to the Plymouth Union bus station, three children in tow.

How should we start, Annie? With tears, with division of property, with wailing and lamentation? We don't want to start at all. We can see that we have a serious problem on our hands, and that we should share it to the extent we can; not in front of the children. We and Mr. Robinson, we can get a TV set from his hideaway, for the kids, for Frederic F. Junior, for Annina the apple girl, for Francis R. too, aged two and a half, if they wouldn't be happy without one? We won't tell the children that you're not just taking a trip to the city. Should we hide you too? Not say over the phone where you are? *Happy to do it for you, Annie.* You're not here. No. You're not here.

Because I knew you wouldn't pressure me.

The things you're saying, Annie, think for a second. You're in New York, ships are sailing past on your right, the subway's running on your left, the 1, 2, and 3 trains, behind you your children are tired from the trip, sleeping like freight, Marie is sitting in front of you, a child of not yet eleven, and you want her to hear it? All right, tell her along with me, if you think it's educational. So Marie should hear that Annie Killainen wants to flee her marriage with F. F. Fleury because of Vietnam? Because of Vietnam. You're both over twenty-five and each reciting your scripted lines—his on the theory of the domino effect, China's greed, the honor of the USA in Southeast Asia, the continuation of the French legacy in Indochina, human freedom, and peace on earth; yours on the Seventh Commandment, re: foreign markets, the honor of the USA, the right to self-determination of even the smaller nations, human freedom, and peace on earth. How did you do it? Over breakfast? Whenever the children weren't there. Which was often. Or in French. Annie, it was like that forty years ago in Mecklenburg, you can't go back to that! And now F. F. doesn't want a wife who signs antiwar petitions, who's a member of antiwar groups, he doesn't want to drive to the store and see his wife standing there with a hand-painted antiwar sign; he wants his wife at home, with the kids, in the kitchen, in the bedroom. He says you're disgracing the Fleury name. And where you insert a pause in your story, Marie's not supposed to not know something is possible but I'm supposed to imagine it. I know, Annie.

Because I knew you'd understand, Gesine.

Yes. No. Annie, stay here. Stay a week, stay two weeks, make him sweat. Spend a day in our apartment and it'll be so spick-and-span I won't even recognize it. It'll be great for me. We'll go to the opera, to movies, to concerts; Mr. McIntyre at the Hotel Marseilles bar will marvel at us. Marie also knows the fairy tales of your, our Baltic that your children expect at bedtime; she'll take them to the park, to the zoo in the Bronx, to see

Broadway. It'll be fun. Three weeks, if you want. And then talk to him, to
F. F. He'll be taken down to size, short even with a hat, Annie. He's always
lived with someone to take care of him; he can't cook, he doesn't know
what to do with a washing machine, by now he's forgotten how to get a
typescript ready for print. He won't only realize he wants you, he'll realize
he needs you. I'll explain the Vietnam thing to him if you insist. But go
back. The children. Five years together. I think you should let him ask;
that'll be harder for him than if you do. But then let him come get you. It
doesn't matter to me either way; you matter to me.

*You live in a marriage part-time, when you feel like it, like putting on a
play, Gesine. You don't know what it's like to be really married.*

Fine, Annie. We'll find you an apartment in New York, and won't push
Riverside Drive. We'll find you a job in New York; I won't recommend too
strongly the bank that has me. Or go back to the United Nations, they still
only take the pretty girls there. Don't do that, take a ship to Liverpool and
Hamburg and Stockholm and Helsinki and Kaskinen, or Kaskö. What
kind of Finnish is that your kids are speaking. Francis R., his is the best,
Annina can get by. But F. F. Junior, you can hardly get the English out of
his mouth with a crowbar. Don't write to your parents yet. Stick around
for a while. *All right.* Five days. If at the end of the week you're still talking
like you are now I'll go with you to buy the steamer tickets.

Because you're my best friend, Gesine. Didn't you know that?
No. Sorry: I did. I meant: Yes.

January 9, 1968 Tuesday

Last week in the freezing-cold city 165 persons died of pneumonia, 70 more
than expected, and there is a shortage of blood for operations. Charles
Gellman, executive director of Jewish Memorial Hospital: "The Vietnam
war doesn't help either, because there is a lot of blood sent there."
The playground by Pier 52, bounded by Hudson, Gansevoort, West
Fourth, and Horatio Streets, is now, since yesterday, named after John A.

Seravalli. He used to play basketball there as a teenager. On May 26, 1966, the army drafted him. On February 28, 1967, twenty-one years old, he was killed on patrol near Souida.

In the summer of 1937, Horst Papenbrock wanted to enlist in the army voluntarily.

When he went to tell Lisbeth, he found her polishing the silverware. She had laid out towels on the kitchen table and the work seemed to fly through her hands as she swiftly turned three knives between her fingers, dabbed the cork in the water and then in the emery powder in the opened drawer, rubbed the blades clean, and put them in the basin to rinse off later. It was a warm afternoon in late July. The garden light, divided in rectangles by the window, was already slanting. Nearby, the starlings were on the hunt and above the ripe cherry trees. From a distance, Paap could be heard restacking boards. It was Saturday, the work week felt over already. Horst didn't want to start in right away so Lisbeth thought it was a normal visit and started telling him about the trip she'd had to take to the military construction office in Gneez that morning, and about the conversations on the train. She was thinking to herself about how her hair needed washing and was annoyed that now Horst too was an eyewitness to what people were saying around Jerichow—that she wasn't taking care of herself. Horst was thinking about his imminent departure, and he looked at his sister more closely than usual, probably did notice the loose, unkempt braids, but he still thought of her as the girl, the younger sister, whose reputation for prettiness he had often prided himself on. Then he told her, ever the big brother with his mysterious and amazing decisions, and saw her start as though she'd cut herself and was trying to choke back the pain behind pursed lips. Then he forgot what he'd seen once she started acting as he'd expected. He heard the innocent girl asking how far the garrison was from Jerichow, the little sister who felt bad for him over the blowup Albert Papenbrock was going to have. – *You dummy*: she added, the way she used to when they were kids, except the mutual understanding that used to underlie the teasing was gone. Horst must have noticed that the silverware was flying to the side a little harder now, but he thought she was in a hurry, and saw that Lisbeth was now wearing gloves because of the black from the silverware polish, and that it was the Güstrow family silver she was putting dents in. Horst was surprised when the child snuck away from the table and finally trotted off down the back hall. Lisbeth probably wanted to endure in silence the fact that her family was once again helping Cresspahl hang guilt around her neck, but she wasn't patient enough to do it.

You told him to, Cresspahl!
Come on, Lisbeth. The boy wants somewhere to hide. The armys not a bad place to hide.
For now. What if theres war?
I never tell your brother anything, Lisbeth. No friendly advice, no unfriendly advice. Besides they wont take him anyway.
Heinrich.

Papenbrock didn't bring off his blowup. He had the necessary fury at his disposal when Horst announced after the meal that he was leaving the family business, but he didn't know what to do with it. He had already sent the boy after the eldest; now he couldn't make him work for an inheritance he would not get most of. He hadn't made an effort to bring this Elisabeth Lieplow from Kröpelin into his house, even though she was now a Papenbrock; could he hold it against Horst that he was living with his own wife? He had raised his son with the precept that a real man was a soldier; what the boy was doing now might even be obedience. Albert was hit—bull's-eye. Words failed him. Earlier he would have had recourse to blows. He started several times: "You...you—," but Horst just waited calmly to see whether the old man would call him an oaf, and shrugged his shoulders more with regret than anything else when his father walked over to the door as though wanting to slap it, then slipped out muttering something indistinct. Horst hadn't even shown defiance. He was now as old as his thirty-six years. Papenbrock lashed out blindly the next day in his helpless rage. He summoned the Schwerin son to Jerichow, who thought nothing of driving up in a big chauffeured car in the middle of the harvest; he summoned Avenarius Kollmorgen, who walked in with shocking submissiveness, briefcase held importantly in hand, brows furrowed significantly but helplessly; he summoned Cresspahl as a witness. Who didn't come. Who probably realized that the old man could ease his conscience more readily if Cresspahl was willing to help carry the burden—he didn't have that much compassion. Dr. Berling was willing enough to come. After he'd draped the limp ribbon of subsequent letters onto his stolid B, the group in Papenbrock's office didn't know what to say to one another; even Avenarius admitted to himself that drinking Mosel like this didn't usually make him tired. But no suitable remark occurred to him, the moist dark cave of Market Square outside the windows did not lure him out of the house, and before he managed to take his leave just to be safe, he heard Horst say before witnesses what Lisbeth Cresspahl had overheard last Saturday on the train, at the Wehrlich station, from the conversation between Hagemeister the forest ranger and Warning the farmworker, something about the dealings between a certain highly placed party member and a certain Jewish veterinarian before the Nazi takeover. Horst hadn't meant to do anything but fill in a gap in the conversation, and the brother from the Americas contented himself with a bored shake of the head, as if he'd had enough of this stupid gossip in or between small towns. In addition, this Robert had acted amazed and embarrassed, and when the time came to shake hands his emotional look hadn't come off or rather had, practically slipping off his face.

In late August, Horst and his wife, Elisabeth, had moved to Güstrow. Sure enough, the army hadn't taken him. They could have appointed him a lieutenant in the reserve, since he'd come out of the war in 1919 as an NCO, but at nearly thirty-seven he would have been a bit old for a lieutenant. Horst may have suspected his father's fat fingers of pulling the strings behind his rejection; he did not come back to Jerichow. The settlement of his inheritance had been enough for his Lisbeth to set up a respectable apartment in Güstrow, not far from the new housing for the Reich Farm Bureau where he soon had a job managing the allocation of seeding material in accord with National Socialist principles. Alexander Paepcke had gotten him the job, through various Leonia fraternity brothers, so Papenbrock hadn't been able to prevent it. The old man actually had to look for a new warehouse manager, just as he'd wanted in March 1933, and couldn't speak his mind about the one he found, Waldemar Kägebein, who knew things by heart out of Aereboe's *Handbook of Agriculture* that Papenbrock had to look up. Robert Papenbrock, meanwhile, was serving the fatherland by means of a work trip abroad, this time not to Rio de Janeiro but to Chicago, Illinois. At least that's what the postmarks said.

And in Jerichow it was taken as proven fact yet again that no one could put one over on the Papenbrocks. Because the local SA was stuck with its suspicions, no one would try to go chasing after Horst anywhere firearms were being used in earnest. And Horst having a job at the District Farm Bureau wouldn't exactly hurt the family business.

It was too bad, of course, that the old man was now acting so unlike himself—gloomy, quiet, hardly ever with time for the cunning, circuitous, clever conversations he used to be so good at. But bars and pubs weren't safe in times like this anyway.

In September, Lisbeth née Papenbrock, 3-4 Brickworks Road, Jerichow, received a summons to the Gneez district court as a witness in the Warning/Hagemeister trial. The accusations included, among other things, defamation of a National Socialist officeholder by suggesting that he had derived unlawful profit from his dealings with a Jewish fellow citizen.

The summons was delivered to the Cresspahls on the day for which the Mecklenburg *Christian Family Almanac* recommended paying heed to verses 1 to 5 of the fifth chapter of Paul's Letter to the Romans.

Lisbeth could not be talked out of the fact that she'd heard it. She had heard: Hagemeister saying: Just look at Griem and his lot. Then Warning had said: He and Semig used to be thick as thieves, you couldn't even stir the pot. Now Griem is head sergeant or whatever with the Reich Labor Service.

Dr. Semig said: What kind of profit could a veterinarian have procured for a townsman-farmer! And Griem of all people! My dear Herr Cresspahl—!

Griem was surveying the Great Friedländer Meadow for land improvement, and it looked like he wasn't receiving his mail.

Robert Papenbrock, who had brought the charge, was not expected back from the States before early 1938.

Avenarius Kollmorgen was prepared to remember nothing. Papenbrock was more than happy to say he'd been seriously drunk. But Dr. Berling still hadn't gotten over the man his wife had run off with, and all August long he was busy spreading the story among his patients, whom he credited with understanding the "moral cancers" in government and party leadership.

Lisbeth heard it all right.

Our Lisbeth, under oath, before the judge—what would happen then?

January 10, 1968 Wednesday

Mr. James R. Shuldiner has decided to get married.

Mrs. Cresspahl would not have thought James Shuldiner capable of opening a conversation this way. She has known him since he'd paid a visit to someone in the office next door to hers in the bank, then from chance meetings on the way to the subway, eventually from hurried lunches in restaurants in the Forties; it was always he who called her, Mrs. Cresspahl paid for her own meal every time, and never did the talk turn to what he might have hoped for or gotten from these half hours. Perhaps he wanted to add a German to his circle of acquaintances; maybe others didn't lend the ear he wanted to his concerns about statesmen's behavior; possibly he keeps coming back due to the early-summer afternoon when he ran into us at a concert in Central Park and Marie respectfully asked him to explain certain mathematical calculations to her. Marie has long since forgotten that she didn't count him among her friends for long, and Mrs. Cresspahl should have thought a bit more carefully about what being sociable might lead to. For if today was like usual, the topics of conversation would have been that the Pentagon is once again trying to cover for the president with its statements about August 1964 in the Gulf of Tonkin, or that de Gaulle really was trying to compliment the Jews when he called them an elite people, "sure of itself and domineering." But no, we're now supposed to turn our attention to Mr. Shuldiner's nuptials, and he's in such a hurry about something that he can't wait until tomorrow at lunch, he has actually come to meet us in the Hotel Marseilles bar. Sits there with his body a bit twisted, elbow on the railing above the swimming pool, pleasure involuntarily shining in his eyes, yet by no means a radiant bridegroom: his brow is still tense, as if weighed down by some burden.

Mr. Shuldiner is asking us for a favor, as a friend. His wife would like to live in this neighborhood, and could we help? Another Bloody Mary, Mrs. Cresspahl?

No thank you, and sorry, no. Mrs. Cresspahl is not in a position to do that. For her the Upper West Side as a neighborhood has disintegrated into more and more particular sights and scenes the more she's gotten to know it over almost seven years—she cannot give an overall judgment. Mentioning her address has usually drawn a vague nod, an unseeing look fading into incomprehension. Greenwich Village to the south is well known in the city, at least as a myth; Riverdale in the Bronx instantly calls up a mix of recollection and fearful fantasy. What surrounds the Upper West Side is familiar, but it itself isn't. To the north, Morningside Heights peers over at Harlem, from a safe distance; Columbia University snatches building after building, street after street, and pulls them under its venerable cloak; there's the Cathedral of St. John the Unfinished and the church of Rockefeller, called Riverside, and then St. Luke's Hospital, where New Yorkers by no means on their last legs go too. The neighborhood south of ours makes it onto the culture pages of even European papers, with its opera and philharmonic, the subway there stops in an actually new station, the buildings there are not only renovated but genuinely renewed. So the fringes of the area are famous, but what lies between them, the Upper West Side, is a gap, an unknown hole, a different kettle of the most indigestible fish. Anything can happen there, Mr. Shuldiner. Why don't you and your girl stay in New Jersey.

That's just it. She doesn't want to live near the Orthodox relatives.

But does the girl want to fall in with heathens and Christians, Mr. Shuldiner? First of all, this is a white neighborhood, with at most thirty thousand Jews among twice that many Anglo-Saxon Protestants, Irish and Italian Catholics, and the two nondenominational Germans on Riverside Drive. There are some Jews who do their laundry on the Sabbath and some who are their rabbis' pride and joy; you should see Mrs. Ferwalter. And they're not, like the future Mrs. Shuldiner, from Rapid City, they are from Western Europe, from the Slavic countries. Will a young bride from South Dakota be able to cope? And what about the other fifty thousand, the Puerto Ricans, the blacks, and the pinch of Japanese and Chinese? The other, unknown ethnicities? They may all be Americans, but each group clings to its own language, they don't like to mix; the confusing, highly variegated blend is not even constant, the people here move so unexpectedly. Wouldn't your wife prefer an area where the people are more like one another and have reasons to get along?

Still, Mr. Shuldiner could offer his wife something special here. The metropolis does come at a price, after all.

Of course, Mr. Shuldiner. Central Park West, West End Avenue, and Riverside Drive—fiercely defended, substantial, old-fashioned heirlooms— still offer a life of comfort. Central Park West will probably look out for some time yet over the extravagant artificial landscape, manmade lakes, reflected clouds, rolling snow-covered meadows; at the leisurely winding paths; through the open sky toward the even haughtier addresses on Fifth Avenue crouching confidently under their water towers that are lit by sunlight delivered every evening, their subscriptions are paid up. Or, closer to the Hudson, take West End Avenue, that dark ravine between brick monsters but the cages in the windows are not for birds, they're for air conditioners you have to pay for yourself. Maybe there, between all the old age homes, you'll find a place for a young woman used to open country. Or in one of the numbered side streets, where single-family houses are still kept polished like precious gemstones. There, as on Riverside Drive, the sidewalks are swept clean, heavy vehicle traffic is prohibited, it seems desirable to live there. In this neighborhood it is easy to find a building built before February 1, 1947, in which the rents are frozen; there is not much new construction in the area. You'd only have to pay fifteen percent more than the old rent; Mr. Shuldiner can afford that. Of course.

Right. And he would know that his wife was safe.

Hardly, Mr. Shuldiner. The opposite is just as true here too. There are slums on many of the side streets. Where the poorest of the poor have to live, the fire department is even less strict about its regulations; why wouldn't those streets start burning the way Harlem is already? Why wouldn't the sidewalks collapse there, like in Harlem? There are plenty of buildings there where the people, whole families in a single room, have to bang on the pipes because the landlord is trying to save money on heat. The ones who complain to the city with a phone call every two minutes, they live here too. Why shouldn't they snatch your wife's purse, hold a knife to her throat? And don't believe Mrs. Cresspahl. She spent a whole year thinking that two apartment buildings on Ninety-Fifth Street were pleasant places, due to the movement in the hallways and windows, due to the Spanish greetings and singing she heard, the life on the sidewalks she saw; she hadn't understood why her child always wanted to walk on the other side of the street. The child had recognized the buildings as poor, as bad; only later did Mrs. Cresspahl see the evidence, such as the pots and bowls that these citizens have to put on their windowsills in cold weather because they can't keep their food safely inside.

Give it to me straight, Mrs. Cresspahl. You live here.

We can recite the statistics for you like a geography textbook, Mr.

Shuldiner: You are located on the northwest part of the island of Manhattan, between 70th and 110th Streets, between Central Park to the east and, to the west, the river that Henry Hudson managed to discover before his crew abandoned him to starve. Avenues run north-south, such as Riverside Drive, it's easy to get that wrong. You should see it from the air, Mr. Shuldiner. An irregular conglomeration of towers and shacks, hemmed in by high-rises. Almost a thousand persons per block, few of them singly in apartments, too many of them crowded together more closely than the law allows. The Upper West Side doesn't even have a name. The Dutch once founded a village here and named it Bloemendaal, Bloomingdale, but it never did turn into a valley of flowers. When the locals discuss the neighborhood among themselves, they call it "the area," as if it's nothing but an arbitrary grouping of buildings, a senseless juxtaposition of people and not a community, a neighborhood. You will sometimes have to enter the area through the park on Broadway where Verdi stands with pigeons on his skull, now known as Needle Park, after the syringes, Mr. Shuldiner. If you go up Amsterdam Avenue, you will see the resemblance to the bombed-out streets from the World War....

– And I admired you so much, Mrs. Cresspahl: Mr. Shuldiner says. He's been sitting bent nearly double for quite some time, elbows on the table, shoulders hunched, turning his glass around as if an answer were written in the sloshing mirror inside.

– I don't know my way around here, Mr. Shuldiner.

– That's not what I wanted. I was hoping you'd be able to help my wife.

– Give her information?

– And the other little things one does for a friend, Mrs. Cresspahl.

Later that night, Annie née Killainen said: Your second client in only three days. I can see why. You must've been that way in school too.

And then she wouldn't believe Mrs. Cresspahl's protests to the contrary. You're responsible for what people see in you: Annie says.

January 11, 1968 Thursday

Deep down on the front page, next to the continued news of deaths due to the cold in the city (so that we believe it), *The New York Times* brings us a photograph from the harbor, a stubby tugboat, tiny amid the densely packed chunks of ice floating down the Hudson yesterday afternoon. The water is so full of poison that a person can die from just swallowing a little too much of it, the cold isn't necessary.

When Cresspahl acquired the yard behind the Jerichow church, it was almost entirely open onto Brickworks Road. Now it was long since closed.

The farmers who came before him had put an entrance in the middle, to get to the open carriage house to the left and the cesspool, manure heap, and stable doors to the right. Cresspahl had dug it up and planted fast-growing bushes, filling in the gaps in the elderberry hedge with lilac all the way from the maple on the corner to the side driveway, which he'd built up like a road. You could see through it, but the way was blocked by a slatted wooden gate, even if it only latched shut, and anyone who tried to go through the bushes would find a chicken-wire fence, pointy ends up, in the middle of the leaves and branches. He had let it all grow wild, and anyone who didn't know about the house in back would think the path ended there, since beyond the brickworks it petered out in the sand to just fields. It was no longer a property from which a small child could stray onto a motor road; no chickens got out either. It wasn't until Cresspahl added a lock to the gate, in the summer of 1937, and Lisbeth hardly ever set foot in town anymore, that the people in Jerichow started talking about a prison he was keeping his wife in. Even though the gate was locked only at night. You could move the latch during the day, but it unhooked with such a loud bang that it scared you. He'd thought of everything! And even when it was loud in the workshop, the uninvited guest could only get as far as the third door, and there was Paap coming out of the fourth, or Cresspahl, or some other sturdy guy who didn't need a dog. Just try and explain that you were only wanting to get into the workshop, and why you didn't go through the barn door with the sign outside. There was no way to get to the house door, and no point in trying, since now it was always locked. Anyone Cresspahl let through to see Lisbeth was taken inside by Heine Klaproth; anyone else had to stay there with Cresspahl, with nothing to look at but the curtained windows, the empty yard, the little grassy lawn for the child, until the smell of the freshly cut wood made you dizzy. This Englishman, Cresspahl, would stand there so deceptively, like some harmless craftsman, sweaty, in dusty work clothes, neck bent, and then suddenly raise his head and aim his suddenly hard eyes right at you with unexpected precision, you'd remembered them as being just a watery blue. And if you preferred to leave the yard, you wouldn't even get a story to tell.

It wasn't only Warning's and Hagemeister's relatives who came, trying to talk Lisbeth into having a conscience. Avenarius Kollmorgen turned up too, and rapped his walking stick against the workshop door, and wouldn't stop brushing imagined lint from his broad shoulders while he proclaimed amid the running machines that whether or not a person named as a witness chose to testify was entirely at his or her discretion. Him Cresspahl brought into the house, to his desk, and when Avenarius said his goodbyes at the gate half an hour later, he beat so intemperately at the dusty hedgerow with his walking stick that the chickens came bursting out of their sandpits. Papenbrock was let in to see his daughter alone, and on the way back he preferred not to show his face in the workshop. Cresspahl came out to the driveway anyway, and the old man looked baffled. He'd tried out on his favorite daughter what always worked with Louise, and Lisbeth hadn't stood for it. She'd never been screamed at like that, and so what if he was her father, he'd better watch out for Cresspahl! Papenbrock couldn't fathom how someone wouldn't scream at his wife, but all the good advice went out of him when he saw his son-in-law's sidelong look, attentive, almost friendly. Others came too, like Brüshaver. Cresspahl poked some fun at him before letting him into the house, asking him about the Christian significance of an oath, and as a result Brüshaver started out less forcefully with Lisbeth than he'd planned, phrasing as a request what he'd intended as instruction. He got Lisbeth to the point of agreeing to lie if her mother said she could. Old Mrs. Papenbrock had more or less grasped what her husband and Cresspahl told her, but then felt too self-important in the affair and caught a wrong train of thought that only stopped at Romans 5:1–5. When Lisbeth told the story back home, she sat leaning to one side as limp as she'd been at her mother's, hands feebly in her lap, nodding so submissively that a chair back broke under Cresspahl's hands. Couldn't glue it back on later either. Warning's wife promised Cresspahl that God would visit twice the punishment upon Lisbeth's head. Hagemeister came in person, made no attempt to leave the workshop, asked rather casually about the trees in the garden, talked about shearing sheep in Rande, and appeared to have nothing else he wished to discuss. When Cresspahl let him go, it looked from the workshop like he was promising him something. He'd sent word to Warning that he had no time for people running their mouth off about Shitbrowns in a public train, in broad daylight, in this particular year. Criminal stupidity, if you ask him. A sheep had more brains than that. And a sheep didn't know enough to drink up a bucket of water in a whole year.

Then Arthur Semig, Dr. Vet. Med., practicing veterinarian, who had fought in the First World War and been awarded an Iron Cross, was arrested in Jerichow and taken through the streets to the station and held in the basement under the Gneez courthouse.

It was late September, off-peak season but good weather for swimming, when Lisbeth Cresspahl dropped her child off with Aggie Brüshaver. To her, as to Cresspahl, she said something about a trip to the dentist. She did go to the bus stop on Station Street, but got on the bus to Rande.

When the sun was down behind the land and the Baltic Sea water was cold and looked it, too, a fisherman heading out to sea noticed a bathing cap far from shore. Two and a half miles out in Lübeck Bay, far past the fifty-foot line. The water was seventy-five and eighty feet deep there. She was already too weak to defend herself when Stahlbom and his son dragged her onboard.

Stahlbom headed back to shore, because she was shivering so hard and not even three blankets got her warm again. He was thinking about the missed catch more than anything, because back in August 1931 a young woman, kindergarten teacher, had already swum a mile and a half out, although in that case it was because the dreadnought *Hannover* was lying at anchor there and she had already turned back. When Cresspahl arrived in Rande that night to fetch his wife, he asked on the spot how much he owed Stahlbom to make up for the day's take, and Stahlbom would probably have forgotten the whole thing if he hadn't been asked to.

– That was my mistake, the swim cap: Lisbeth said the next morning, lying in bed almost comfortably she was so tired, with a playful, absent-minded smile that quickly disappeared behind lips taut with anger.

– It was vanity. And I was punished for it: she said.

Dont ever do that again, Lisbeth!
I wont, Cresspahl, I wont do it again. Not like that.

January 12, 1968 Friday

Annie Killainen and her three children in the Cresspahl apartment, they
are easy to live with. The rooms aren't big, and the middle one with its four
doors lacks privacy, and still the little Fleurys aren't whining for their lost
cavernous halls in Vermont, even on the fifth day, and Francis R., Knock-
knees, has already set up places where he can be alone—at the Dane's desk,
in the mirrored armoire. Maybe at home they had to be even more quiet
than they are voluntarily here. Marie gets along with the big family too,
because we've set things up so that she's voluntarily offered her room to
the visiting children, and also because she is often treated as the household's
governing body, regularly asked "how your mother does it." It hasn't yet
struck her that Annie goes out with the children—to the freezing cold
park, to go shopping, to the Hotel Marseilles swimming pool—whenever
she gets home with homework to do. She has noticed that I am treated as
a breadwinner, with breakfast served hot almost as soon as I get out of the
bathroom, WQXR turned on punctually for the morning news, my coat
and scarf held ready for me, as though Mrs. Cresspahl were a man, a father.
I hope she won't insist on copying that later. In the building, too, Annie
has made her usual good impression: Mr. Robinson knows her children's
names and can tell them apart; Jason has hinted to her that an apartment
like ours might be opening up on the twelfth floor. A stranger would have
to drape one green piece of paper after another onto the palm of his hand
for that. What Annie imposes of her housekeeping is inconspicuous; suddenly the metal window frames have been scoured to a shine with steel
wool, the bookcase gleams as if fresh from the restorer; she doesn't draw
attention to it, it's not a reproach, not even compensation. It would never
occur to her to meddle with presents for the silverware drawer or linen
closet; all she has added is an extravagant stockpile of candles, because
"New York can get so dark." Said while drawing her head down into her
shoulders in mock alarm at her prejudice, until everyone's about to laugh,
and then she laughs. The tape player's counter remains staunchly at the

number from the night before, no letters are looked through; she may wipe away dust, or polish the drawers' strike plates. A lot of what it meant for Annie to be here we'll notice only when she's gone. But of course we don't want her to go.

> *You cannot stand living with her, can you, Gesine?*
>
> *I like it fine.*
>
> *It's almost unbearable?*
>
> *I see her and hear her, and it's fine.*
>
> *But when you're sitting in the bank thinking about her?*
>
> *Then it's not so good.*
>
> *Admit it, Gesine.*
>
> *These interrogations all the time! Just because you're over and done with everything!*
>
> *We have an assignment for you, Gesine.*
>
> *Yes, okay.*
>
> *Think it through more carefully. Don't spare yourself so much.*
>
> *I couldn't do it.*
>
> *There you go trying to dodge again, Gesine. That's not what we were asking for.*
>
> *Like it's nothing! Running away after five years living with someone, and no letter, no forwarding address, three children in hand! If I had five years of habits could I give them up? So easily?*
>
> *You're twisting things around, Gesine. You're exploiting your own objections to marriage.*
>
> *All right, you start.*
>
> *You can't stand it. You don't even want to imagine it. Annie marching with her antiwar sign in a ridiculous little procession on a small town's main street, the bank president stares at her and the mayor's grandmother and the soda jerk, and suddenly she's no longer the respectable Mrs. Fleury but a foreign Communist hussy.*
>
> *I chose not to enter a prison I would want to break out of.*
>
> *But the real prison, where Annie spent the night next to the town drunk and the local shoplifter?*
>
> *What she shoplifted, she must have needed, or else advertising made her do it. How does spending a night in jail next to her promote peace in Vietnam?*

Gesine. Annie did something.

With no results.

She didn't do nothing.

I'm a guest in this country.

Annie wasn't born here either, if it's about that.

I've gone marching with signs in the cold too, back and forth, back and forth, outside Cardinal Spellman's mansion because he'd blessed US soldiers in Vietnam.

You did it out of curiosity, and only once.

I didn't do it again because I don't want to be kicked out of the country.

How can you want to live in a country like this, Gesine?

Because it's Marie's life now.

The child, the child. Your emergency parachute, your inviolable excuse.

I want her to have what I never had.

And not what the children in Vietnam get.

Prove it to me! Prove it! Show me how I could actually know I was helping one single person! Go ahead!

If you don't start small then in five years you'll still be at war.

And if I don't just use words, if I go for a walk in Riverside Park with a sign and wave a Vietcong flag around in the bank and send checks to Students for Peace?

Better.

You guarantee peace in five years?

You know the answer. That's impossible.

You're impossible!

This is how we like you, Gesine, all worked up. So this isn't your everyday marital conflict after all.

I wouldn't like this kind either.

You wouldn't like it, you wouldn't let yourself be slapped in the face at a birthday party in front of your guests, at the table laid with the family silver, in the candlelight, and all because you called the president's policies toward Vietnam murderous?

I wouldn't let any F. F. Fleury from Boston slap me in the face.

You're jealous, Gesine.

Embarrassed, sure.

Well that's something.

If she wants to fight her husband she doesn't have to use that as a reason. She can disguise it.

Stop it, Gesine. You're accusing Annie Killainen of not fighting her fight at its source . . .

She's been in New York for five days and she still hasn't gone to where the students are collecting money to end the war, or where the fliers are being printed, or where they're being distributed.

. . . but there's never any doubt with us! "Papenbrock didn't want to help the Jew Semig get out of the country, it was enough for him to have a low opinion of himself too." Period. Not a word about the rest.

Isn't that how it was?

Even if it was, you're still making it up!

I straighten things up to make them comprehensible.

And you we're supposed to believe. But a living person, an Annie Killainen, you don't believe.

I'd be very happy if I didn't have to feel that.

But you do, because you know yourself.

It's not because I've caught myself in unintended lies. It's because I don't trust my own beliefs.

And now Annie's supposed to finish what she's started just so she can meet your criteria for logical behavior? She's supposed to act out the consistency you lack?

I'm not telling her what to do.

Yet you sit there in your empty apartment and something feels wrong and you're just waiting for her to come back without having done anything against the war?

Yes.

And all she has to do is open the door, pushing children before her like a mother hen her chicks, with lovely pink cheeks from the cold and from her memories of the Finnish countryside, bubbling over with the encounters she's had on the street, which in her all turn into friendly stories, occasions for laughter—you're not jealous?

That's when I'll remember why she and I get along so well.

And yet you resent getting sucked into her mood, her games, her stories, the fun of the big shared meal, as though you have no choice?

It makes me uncomfortable.

We feel sorry for you, Gesine.
You won't make me feel sorry for myself.
You'll regret that, Gesine.

January 13, 1968 Saturday, South Ferry day
It's South Ferry day once Marie announces over lunch their departure for the Battery.

Marie wanted to show off her New York City to the children from Vermont; she also wanted to share her possession with them, including the ferry to Staten Island. She didn't invite Rebecca Ferwalter,

– How many times do I have to tell you she's Jewish, Gesine?
– A ferry across the harbor isn't travel, Marie.
– Like you know more about Orthodox Jews than me! Ferwalters!

but she did invite Pamela Blumenroth, also a child of Jewish parents, but parents who would travel on the Sabbath without a second thought, although preferably on Israel's airline, if they didn't keep their planes grounded on Saturdays. Pamela and Marie ordered the grown-ups out of the apartment with them, and Annie was more than happy to spend a while away from the phone over which we are supposed to tell the now quite meek Dr. Fleury that she's not here.

From that point on, Pamela and Marie were the tour guides leading the out-of-town children from the zigzag subway platforms under the ferry terminal up to the escalators, both looking very tall in the middle of their charges, holding the little ones' hands, looking around, paying attention, real parents. In Pamela, all of eleven, you can often catch a glimpse of how she'll be at nineteen: solicitous to the point of tenderness, proud of what she's been entrusted with. She will one day push her own children through and under the turnstile as strictly and kindly as she now does Annina S., so that they'll learn after one time. F. F. Junior was mad that the rules said he was supposed to duck under the turnstile, and he stood bitterly off to one side for so long that Marie gave him five cents so he could go back out and come back into the waiting area standing tall, pushing hard against the truncheon, as if he were a big kid, and now he's really unhappy.

– Just like his father: Annie said, surprised, as if unwillingly, and pleased.

– You'll talk to him soon.

– Oh, Gesine. I wrote to him yesterday, just not the address.

The Fleury children were given thorough instruction, Francis R. Knock-knees too, who took turns sitting on Pamela's and Marie's laps. They were not spared the cars driving onto the lower deck, nor the search for the shoeshine man in the smoking room, nor the gruesome pointing out of life jackets in the ceiling—only then came rewards from the snack bar. They mustn't miss Ellis Island; they were presented more indifferently with the Statue of Liberty, who looked rather bored holding her torch away from her body, its flame gone out. Pamela stressed quite firmly that you could tell the ferries apart by their captains, some bring their boat into dock imperceptibly and others battering-ram style. The water was calm, the air temperature around freezing, the gulls had survived. The water towers, warehouses, piers, and chimneys of Jersey City and Bayonne look so innocent in the snow it's as if they had nothing to do with the region that hangs a curtain of rusty smoke before the sunset during the summer. That's how clear the air was.

It's even colder where I come from. *The New York Times* has had the snow on the Mecklenburg coast of the Baltic measured and reports drifts piled up 2.13 to 2.74 meters ("seven to nine feet"), cut-off villages and townships. This was news, in her view, only because four Soviet tanks, three as steamrollers, brought a pregnant woman from "Beidersdorf" to the hospital in Wismar, *where she gave birth to a healthy boy.* "Macklenburg," says *The New York Times*, the scatterbrained old lady. And this Beidersdorf is the town of Beidendorf, pop. ca. 800, located between Mühlen Eichsen and Wismar, where the land heaps up some 90 m. (300 ft.) above sea level. Had she paid a visit there in person, this trusting Auntie Times, the world would now know about Beidendorf Pond and its distance from Gneez, and Jerichow.

– You're leaving something out, Gesine.

– Maybe we should leave Mecklenburg alone while Annie is staying with us.

– No, there's something you don't want to tell me.

– What do you think I'm leaving out?

– On Thursday night you stopped when Semig was taken to Gneez under armed guard, with his Iron Cross on his jacket.

– Sergeant Fretwust took it away from him and gave him a receipt.

– But there was one of Lisbeth's stories that you didn't finish.

– Lisbeth tried to . . . She . . .

– Wait, here come the others.

Then we pulled into St. George Terminal and the children led us through the corridors of the ferry building to the turnstiles to Manhattan and we took the next boat back.

This is the coldest winter since 1917: an old man assured the children as they leaned into the wind. He said it not as someone who remembered it personally, more like a short-tempered schoolteacher—eyes flashing, hands gesturing severely at the surroundings, white mustache wet with zeal. Ships froze in the ice in the middle of the harbor, by the Brooklyn piers! Massive ice all through Long Island Sound! And in the first year of the war against Germany! New York had no coal, the ships couldn't bring soldiers or weapons to the European front! F. F. Jr. came over and asked us what kind of monsters exactly these "Huns" were. Annie hesitated, snuck a look at the German standing next to her, who was amused and wondering only about which lying technique would be employed, and said: They were so strong that the Great Wall of China was built to stop them. And Mrs. Cresspahl said: Once upon a time in a country called Germany there was an emperor, Wilhelm the Second, and he wanted his soldiers in China to take no prisoners and to make a name for themselves that would last a thousand years. You should see yourself looking at us. You look like a tennis umpire!

Then we pulled into the dock on Whitehall Street in Manhattan and the children conducted us down the ramp and back into the terminal and onto the next ship to Staten Island.

– That, over there, Mrs. Killainen, is an ordnance warehouse for the god-dinged US Marines: Marie said.

– Aha: Annie said. She hadn't really looked, and maybe she didn't realize what she was answering.

Then we arrived at St. George and walked through the gate to the boat back to Manhattan, and F. F. Jr. had managed his fourth little doggie, hot, and Annina had orange juice not just around her mouth but on her ear, and still Pamela and Marie did everything the little ones could think of, whether pacing off the length of the ship, or playing catch, or betting who could stand the wind the longest. If Francis Knock-knees hadn't fallen asleep we might have taken the round trip yet again. It was like—

– yes: Annie said.

– when I was a child and learned how to dive. I couldn't stop doing another one.

– when I ordered a steak in Italy, and then another, and then a third!

– For me it was a potato-and-bacon omelet after a walk with—

– Near Beidendorf.

– Don't laugh! Not far from Beidendorf, yes, Annie!

– *We were very tired,*

– *we were very merry,*

– *we had gone back and forth*

– *all night on the ferry.*

– Edna St. Vincent Millay!

– Edna St. Vincent Millay.

January 14, 1968 Sunday

Gaetano Gargiulo has a store on Farmers Boulevard in Queens. A young man, Nellice Cox, tried to hold it up and pointed a pistol at Gargiulo's son. Gargiulo ducked out the back door, borrowed a pistol from a nearby hardware-store owner, confronted the holdup man, and fired once. Nellice Cox won't be going back home to number 109-82 on 203rd Street in Hollis, and Gaetano Gargiulo is in custody for violating the weapons law.

– Listen, Gesine: Marie says. – Here's the last thing you said on Thursday night:

– "But Fretwust didn't include Semig's Iron Cross in the list of personal effects. He didn't think the Jew would be getting his medals back. Fretwust hadn't been a constable for long; by all rights he should have been vacuuming out sludge from the Gneez pumping station. And Fretwust wasn't embarrassed about his name, on the contrary, he was proud of it."

– Okay. That's not an ending?

– Not to the other story, Gesine. That's what I'm trying to show you. At 266 on the tape counter you said:

– "Even if the maids hadn't yet learned how to shop for proper meat, Lisbeth would rather see people at her table chewing and gnawing than show herself on Town Street in Jerichow."

– That's the *start* of the story, Gesine!

– Can I play?

– Annie, you wouldn't understand.

– Mrs. Fleury, we can't explain this to you. You'd never understand.

– I'm from a small town too, you know.

– Okay. What do you think about a veterinarian arrested in 1937 for having allegedly broken a law before 1933?

– Isn't that past the statute of limitations?

– Exactly, Mrs. Fleury.

– He was taken into custody as a witness, Annie.

– That makes sense. Risk of collusion, or whatever you call it.

– We don't call it anything. His wife had parents in Schwerin, a mother with friends in the ducal family, a father with close colleagues from his time in DEPO, the Mecklenburg Deposit and Exchange Bank. That's who the Kösters were. The Kösters made sure that their son-in-law was taken into custody.

– Prudish crowd.

– They did it for their daughter's sake, because it wasn't the criminal police conducting the investigation.

– Aha. The secret police.

– The Gestapo in Gneez probably didn't even know, at first, whether they wanted to clear the Reich Labor Service leader Griem from any suspicion of having accrued illegal pecuniary gain with the help of a Jewish professional man, or pin it on him.

– That depends on the evidence, doesn't it?

– Oh, there was more than enough evidence. Go track down everywhere a veterinarian went in almost twenty years of practice, from one estate to the next, Farmer X to Cottager Y to Granny Klug—you can find anything. One Baron von Rammin talked to the investigators in his courtyard, hand on his horse's bridle the whole time; the Bülows, the "Upper Bülows,"

invited them into the house. The Bülows had a son in England who apparently would rather study there than do his military service in Germany.
And if some farmer lost a head of cattle in 1931 because he didn't want to
miss out on Saturday night at the bar and didn't call the vet until Sunday
morning, what did he remember six years later? Maybe he didn't mind
making it Dr. Semig's fault at this point, the guy was in jail already anyway.

    – And Griem?

    – At first Griem didn't want anything to do with it.

    – He couldn't recall anything?

    – He knew there was nothing to recall. And he didn't understand why
the Gneez people wanted a trial; before he did anything, he wanted to
know who was gunning for him and why. He had attained his rank not as
a reward but because he was a good farmer, a townsman-farmer's plot in
Jerichow wasn't enough for him. He actually had a real gift for thinking
in large areas, planning work years in advance, training workers. Of course
he had accepted money when he'd taken a soggy meadow in the nobility's
private possession and had it improved at the Reich's expense, as land
critical for the people's agricultural economy, but since he could justify his
decisions his conscience felt clear. Still, if the Gneez district court wanted
to put him on the witness stand with a Jew, it wouldn't be long before they
were looking into his bank account.

    – Semig could've kept his practice, as far as he was concerned?

    – As far as he was concerned not even the Tannebaums would've had
to flee Gneez. Griem wanted his peace and quiet. He didn't do anything
for the time being except reject the rumors as "a cowardly attack on the
party."

    – Prudish bunch.

    – Meanwhile, the Blackshirts had time to hit pay dirt. They could go
house to house in Jerichow. Albert Papenbrock, grain wholesaler, had re-
mitted fees to Dr. Semig that would have been lower for comparable work
done by a day laborer. Heinrich Cresspahl, entrusted with deliveries of
materiel critical to the war effort, had bought a car from Dr. Semig and
had no bill of sale to show for it. Mrs. Methfessel was convinced that the
health department wouldn't have confiscated all their meat if Semig hadn't
sent a certain letter to Schwerin. Dr. Semig had treated his own ailments
but sent his wife to Dr. Berling, and Berling was in and out of the house

constantly when Dora had a broken ankle, but the bill he'd sent was what you'd have to call a friend's price.

– Never mind all the other things they stumbled across while looking into Semig.

– Berling's speeches about the fatherland in danger. This Cresspahl, apparently suspected of English tendencies.

– And Kollmorgen had wanted to buy the house on the Bäk.

– They hadn't discovered that yet. But they did hold it against this Jew Semig that he'd rejected an offer on the house from a deserving longtime member of the National Socialist movement, a regional group leader in the party: Friedrich Jansen.

– And the files on Kollmorgen's appearance before the court in the proceedings against a member of the SA?

– Proved very convenient.

– So now there's the trial?

– In mid-October the trial still hadn't started. What the Gestapo couldn't find by way of evidence was delivered to them in anonymous letters. And Griem hadn't been softened up enough yet. Griem sat in his headquarters, Gau District II, and talked. He knew that bullheadedness was a badge of Mecklenburg honor—pigheadedness not so much. He acted like he had no idea that the secret police didn't need anything but two men and a car to take him away.

– Did Papenbrock hire a lawyer?

– That would have felt to him like admitting guilt. And aside from the Cresspahls and him there were five other people in Jerichow who could expect a summons to Gneez; with so many witnesses, there was no way the truth would not prevail.

– So this Semig of yours…

– Of "ours"?

– Okay, Marie, fine. Of mine.

– …must've been happy as a clam.

– In the basement under the courthouse.

– He was safe there until the trial, and the trial was being prepared carefully and properly, not at all like what you always read about those times.

– He wasn't even accused of anything, Annie.

– Now you're both looking at me like I haven't understood a thing.

– There's nothing to understand, Annie.

– D'you know what, Mrs. Fleury? Sometimes I think I understand it, and I can't believe it. And yet it's from my own mother's life.

January 15, 1968 Monday

You were curious why there were so many loud bangs in the street. *The New York Times* has figured it out for you. Not only did last night's rain and today's thin driving snow catch you in the neck, the water also seeped into cable shafts, mixed with the salt that had been sprinkled on the streets during the recent snowfalls, causing short circuits and setting off gas explosions. It was the sound that the manhole covers made: *Pop.*

And whether you were curious about it or not, she informs you that you had failed to be present last night among the fifteen hundred people in Town Hall at a rally against the draft. You could have signed your name and address on the scroll, promised to counsel, aid, and abet young men who refused to fight. If you want to rectify the omission, you can find the group at 224 West Fourth Street. Will Annie do it? Will you do it?

You were always curious about your child's new doctor, his background, who he actually is, this man who shines a light into Marie's mouth, listens to her breathing, asks her about her sleeping habits in deliberate American English and nimble German with a Polish accent. Who is this worthy gentleman in his sixties, his back stiff down to the waist with age? What lies behind the friendly, slightly deaf expression on his plump face? Do you really want to know? Be satisfied with the diplomas in Latin on the wall, as long as Marie trusts him.

– The one on the left is from Bratislava, the one on the right from Warsaw. The one in the middle from Germany: the old gentleman says with somewhat strained politeness. You shouldn't have looked across the room like that at the solid frames, as if curious about something. Now you won't get out of the first-visit conversation, the formalities of an initial consultation. – Cresspahl, that's a German name, isn't it?: he says, half turned away from his desk, head to one side, paying close attention. The impassive, smooth face, the thin gray hair combed back over his ears in two billows, we wouldn't recognize it if we hadn't seen how carefully he deals with a child, how carefully he talks, so as not to frighten.

Cresspahl is a German name, Dr. Rydz.

– Germany wass a goot place to live, back then, Frau Cresspahl.

Back then was 1931. Germany was Berlin, when he was working at the Charité hospital and "the hospital on Reinickendorfer Street." He lived on Friedrich-Wilhelm Square in Friedenau. Took the 177 tram to Berlin Zoo Station. What did it look like back then?

Friedrich-Wilhelm Square in Friedenau was a charming place to live, at that time, Mrs. Cresspahl. Two west-facing windows, dry in the mornings from the sun and fogged over at night from the thick foliage outside. Friedenau was a nice place to take walks, the little streets with the old country houses, the stately apartment buildings, the bushy trees. Niedstrasse, Schmargendorfer Strasse. The clouds of chestnut blossoms right next to each other on Handjery. Some city council member must have been addicted to chestnut trees.

The people were polite and friendly in the beer garden by the post office, obliging, even to foreigners. It was a lovely year, Mrs. Cresspahl. After work you came back to the quiet parklike square as if coming home. The streetcars were boxes—ugly, crude, efficient. Do you know Berlin, Mrs. Cresspahl?

We get letters from friends in Friedenau that say they're building a subway through the square.

– What a shame about the church!: Dr. Rydz says. He has put his pen and paper aside and turned to face the visitors fully, talking in a lively voice, fingers comfortably interlaced. The church was a touch too small for the square, it looked somewhat deformed, like a little red-brick hunchback. Ugly, crude, and efficient—the empress's creation. She used to dedicate a new site to her God every three months. Her name will come to him in a minute: Auguste Viktoria von Schleswig-Holstein-Sonderburg-Augustenburg. Doflein was the architect's name.

– They say the church will stay, unfortunately, Dr. Rydz.

But that comes as a relief to him. At least one piece of the past still standing. It wasn't easy to choose between Berlin and the other European capitals, back then. Trips to Paris, Vienna, Prague, and no complaints when you got back to Friedenau, to the Church of the Good Shepherd, from which rather stuffy comments about Dr. Felix J. Rydz, MD's nightlife reached Frau Rabenmeister, *who, as a landlady, was—*

Dufte, Dr. Rydz? Swell?

Knorke, Mrs. Cresspahl. Spiffing. That was the word for it back then. Knew how to enjoy life, you might say. Anyone who left there to go back to a small if prosperous country town in Poland, to open a private practice, he'd seen his share of life and knew for good the country where his annual vacations would one day turn into a right to permanent residence.

Not so curious anymore, are you, Mrs. Cresspahl?

The Berlin girl who wanted to spend the 1939 holidays with him but not in Charlottenburg said that Cannes was fine. (You didn't ever happen to meet a family named von Lassewitz, did you, Dr. Rydz?) Four years at a French military hospital. 1943: escaped across the Pyrenees. 1945: ship to America, where all his degrees counted for nothing and it took him five years before he could practice medicine again, on the Upper West Side of Manhattan straight off, to get at least some benefit from his not just fluent Polish and German but Czech, French, Spanish, and English. Pediatrics only. It became clear in New York that he understood children best, better than grown-ups at least.

Now you know, Mrs. Cresspahl. The conversation ran so smoothly because you saw him as a European, and you think you understand them more easily; now you're pretty sure that he's Jewish. What happened to the girl from Berlin-Charlottenburg? Don't say that. Ask him something else, anything. If he's ever been back to Poland.

– No. Never.: Dr. Rydz says. His answer comes out unexpectedly fast, clipped; his soft face tenses, his gaze goes sharp and then off into the distance. He will never set foot in Poland again. More gently, he must have a forgiving temperament, he adds: All the Polishness I need comes right to my door on the Upper West Side, Mrs. Cresspahl.

No need to ask him if he's ever been back to Berlin-Friedenau. Why would he want to go visit the Germans who wiped out his family in Poland as nonhumans. Cresspahl, that's a German name, isn't it?

– Mrs. Cresspahl, are you sure you're feeling well yourself? Is there anything I can do for you, ma'am?

– Are they going to take him away from me too and send him to Vietnam?: Marie says.

– He can't even walk properly, Marie.

– Even if the war expands?

– He'll stay here, Marie. We won't lose Dr. Rydz.

– Gesine, did you see that they're rebuilding the burned-out building on Ninety-Sixth Street? They've set up a big crane, you should see it go! They've finally realized our area can't go to pieces, we need to be able to stay here.

– What if we left, Marie?

– Never! Never! Don't even think such a thing, Gesine.

January 16, 1968 Tuesday

In the low, blinding sun coming down Ninety-Sixth Street this morning, into which it was hard to walk with your eyes open, something was missing on Broadway. It was the bright yellow pack of taxis, whose drivers are on strike, and their passengers were stuffed into the subways, most of them men in sober business suits, looking around uncomfortably, nauseated by the crush of other people's proximity

Herr Dr. Walther Wegerecht, head judge of the district court in Gneez, forty-eight years old, considered outspoken and clever, admired for his glittering career and rich wife, was not happy to be placed in charge of the proceedings against Warning/Hagemeister. He'd had pretty much enough of such cases, if only because they were hard to get a handle on. Or so I imagine it. Friends from the university, now in office in Schwerin, had dropped hints about a possible promotion; Wegerecht the assessor had married up, a Schwerin girl who never let him forget how boring it was in the provinces and never felt that, say, an official residence overlooking the Berlin Tiergarten was out of reach. But by this point, he had started to wonder if his advisers truly were his friends. At first, the Mecklenburg Reich governor's chancellery had let it be known that the honor of the party and its associated organizations took precedence over all else, etc.; that was easy enough to arrange, especially for such a reward. When he first took over the case, he'd expected to find that it was ultimately directed

at Dr. Semig. But now he'd been forced to recognize that it was actually
aimed at Griem, with the Jewish veterinarian a mere detour. If the police
commissioner assigned to the Gestapo was to be trusted, these fellows had
a link to Schwerin too, but one with a further connection to the capital of
the Reich. At the Hanseatic regional supreme court in Hamburg, on the
other hand, the whole affair was dismissed as a bagatelle, and he didn't
want to ask around at the RSC in Rostock.

Wegerecht—body type pyknic, Mecklenburg round head shaved bald—
had joined the party relatively recently, almost too late, and more dutifully
than not. He came from the German National People's Party, he'd read
Berlin's *Deutsche Tageszeitung* with greater relish than the *Mecklenburgischer
Beobachter*, he would have preferred to see the restoration of the Kaiser's
(and duke's) house, and he didn't like what he was hearing from the army
about these Hitlerians gaining ground. What he retained from his old
party's orientation was an aversion to the Jews in Berlin, for national-
economic reasons, but not to a Jew who had fought on the German side
in the World War, who owned property in Jerichow and spoke good
Mecklenburg Plattdeutsch. He wanted only to teach a lesson to such a
person, so that he'd come to his senses at last and leave the country. That
would be the patriotic thing to do, the one worth a promotion. That was
also a side benefit the state prosecutor, Kraczinski, was willing to accept.
Otherwise, though, Kraczinski acted like he could easily spin out seven
more cases from this one, a real Jerichow nexus. On top of that, he was all
for going after Griem; Wegerecht wasn't sure about that. It was so hard to
get a clear look behind the scenes at the Reich Labor Service. It was like a
forest at night, where someone might be standing behind every tree, with
a truncheon. What Wegerecht was most sure of was that he had to get
through this situation with flying colors, so that his stand on the Zentner
case might soon be forgotten (D. Eng. Zentner, industrial business mgmt.,
traveling with a mean dog, mistakenly harassed as a Jew despite his warning that the dog was dangerous, v. SA, seeking compensation for injuries
suffered). Riding high, that's how he had to come through, and any false
move might end up in a broken neck.

Walther Wegerecht was well aware that his wife, Irmgard née von
Oertzen, cared less for who he was than for what he meant for her. His
good mood meant that the money would show up in the bank on the 30th;

his cares and concerns were, she felt, a reckless endangerment of their lifestyle. He couldn't discuss them with her, and in such phases he didn't see Irmi much, and she didn't even give him credit for turning a blind eye to the now more frequent male visitors from the garrison. She wanted him to be independent, confident, slick—that was the only way he could be sure of her. Plus the kids, and Wegerecht was a doting father. It wasn't because he'd lost a bet that he'd shaved his head; it was because his four-year-old girl, the latecomer, liked feeling the thick rug of stubble on the palms of her hands. He was not well. His ruddy cheeks made him look "in the bloom of health"; he preferred not to think about the listlessness, mild depression, downright unbearable impulses he felt for as long into the night as his work kept him up; his doctor chatted with him over Friday skat games at the City of Hamburg Hotel, but not about essential hypertonia. He sometimes had dreams about driving in a car with the windows closed, running out of air, being too weak to turn the window handle; now and then in the light of day it was like in his dream. He was not inclined to go to the doctor with ideas like that. If it wasn't wise to go after Griem, Irmgard would never come back to Schwerin, or if she did, it would be without him. If he started something against Papenbrock, Irmi would lose quite a few social contacts from the Jerichow area, and as for Gneez affairs, he was left to stumble around in the dark. If it was only about sending a message to Warning/Hagemeister, he should have closed the case sooner, and people might remember his former reputation. But then there'd still be this annoyance of the Jerichow Jew to take care of. And Irmgard wouldn't leave him alone, no doctor's note would help with that.

He knew he was losing his grip and decided to pay Ramdohr a visit. He hadn't felt entirely comfortable about having moved up the ladder while Ramdohr had had to step down from the bench due to his Social Democrat friends; he'd been using a heavy workload as an excuse for four years now. Ramdohr, no longer Judge Ramdohr, came to meet him at the door, introduced him to everyone in the family—his wife, all four daughters—as though their friendship had been in continuous use since 1933, and then kept his family there. The group sat outdoors, on a warm October evening, with a view of Gneez Lake, over a Mosel that hadn't been poured out so generously by Judge Ramdohr, and they talked about maritime law, one of Dr. Ramdohr's newer acquisitions. It was clear from the Horch parked outside the house, from the new furniture, even from the wallpaper, that his colleague Ramdohr ("former colleague," Ramdohr interjected) was earning more than enough money from his Hamburg consultations and, annoyingly, was in no way suffering the punishment his dismissal had been intended as. Late that night, when Wegerecht was seen out onto Gustloff Street, not pleasantly but annoyingly drunk, he hadn't made an inch of progress on the Jerichow situation, a relaxing evening of reconciliation and companionship had slipped through his fingers, and he couldn't even blame Günti Ramdohr for taking his revenge.

A chance to relax, or at least to get away and take his mind off his troubles, was what he was counting on from the Mecklenburg army maneuvers in late September 1937, to which he'd been invited thanks to Irmgard's friends in Schwerin Military District HQ, and yet even the first day was ruined for him. He stood and watched a senior head of the Labor Service pick a fight with some army officers, one of them higher ranked than he was. It was about a wooden walkway that the infantry wanted built, contrary to their own instructions and drawings from the day before, and they wanted it by tomorrow, 22:30 sharp. Wegerecht saw the brawny, thuggish fellow get the apology he wanted, and get it by nothing but stubborn, persistent, bellowing insistence that he was in the right, and Wegerecht hoped he'd never end up on his bad side, and then he found out the man's name, Griem, and that the name Griem enjoyed admiration and respect. (The following night, at eight o'clock and zero minutes, there was a wooden walkway across the moor, with a kind of handrail even, which the army had no right to hope for.) (On top of everything else, because Wegerecht had let this scene detain him, he missed his chance to see Mussolini, who'd passed through a couple miles farther west. He had been more interested in seeing Mussolini than his escort, the Führer and Reich chancellor. At least Mussolini'd made something of himself in his own country.) Then there was another dinner, at an estate on Krakow Lake, which Wegerecht didn't attend once he saw Head Sergeant Griem standing on the outside staircase—a boorish roughneck who had learned by that point to offer his arm to the ladies and tell stories so that active officers listened with obedient laughter.

Shortness of breath, heart palpitations, dizzy fits, decreased performance, irritability.

Was there some connection between Robert Papenbrock, who had filed the charge, and Walter Griem? The NSDAP foreign organization versus the Reich Labor Service?

If he knew Papenbrock, the old man would get his daughter to refuse to testify. Tone it down. Minimize. And then Wegerecht would be left holding the bag.

What about if he charged this Lisbeth Cresspahl with failing to notify the authorities? With spreading a rumor inimical to the state? Aiding and abetting? Under the Treachery Act of 1934? Article 1, Par. 1, premeditated? Par. 2, gross negligence? Minimum three months in jail. Up to three months, or a fine.

What about that?

January 17, 1968 Wednesday

Stalin's daughter, his little Svetlana, just can't keep her mouth shut. She's sitting pretty in Princeton, New Jersey, and still feels the need to respond to the protests against the conviction of four young Moscow dissidents for writing without permission. Does she imagine that a Soviet judge gives greater weight to a defector's voice than to anyone else's? Or maybe she wants to defend her father's intellectual property rights over the Socialist justice system he invented? Under it, countless men and women lost their lives; here the longest sentence was seven years. "We must not remain silent in the face of suppression of fundamental human rights wherever it takes place": Svetlana Hallelujah told Columbia Broadcasting System News; why doesn't she tell Dial-A-Flower to send their products to the graveyards where her father's comrades are buried? If they were buried. "We must give all possible support to those who remain honest and brave under unbearable conditions": struck her as worth saying too. Next thing you know she'll be surprised that Isaac Babel's daughter or Osip Mandelstam's widow isn't thanking her for her help. She sees "a wild mockery of justice" as having taken place. She's got that right.

Wegerecht was saved.

He couldn't believe it, to the very end. His Schwerin friends (especially Theo Swantenius, the lawyer among the four brothers) turned out to have a direct line to a Reich ministry, and everything came through loud and clear but was anything but, so everything looked just as treacherous as before, without even a promise of promotion in it. By this point it was too late to drag née von Oertzen into the situation—he had Gisela bring his breakfast as early as he now woke up, so that he'd still see his children but not his wife. One time his mind wandered and he thought the maid was his wife, and sighed; but Gisela was from Thuringia, so she couldn't circulate news of the district court head judge's condition to any interested parties in the Jerichow area, or even in Gneez.

The first clue came in the form of a reprimand: Could the presiding judge please bethink himself of the names of the accused. Since when are witnesses taken into custody while the accused are left running around, etc.

Wegerecht couldn't work up the nerve to send Semig home. He decided this meant he should lock up Warning and Hagemeister. That was in the last third of October.

Things with Kraczinski went as expected. The prosecutor had only wanted to give Wegerecht time to get on board with the charges, and he quickly, almost contemptuously, dismissed the judge's new ideas regarding how to conduct the investigation. Kraczinski was confident. Wegerecht didn't like that, nor his fat pursed lips, his crafty looks, his contented humming. There was something calculating about Kraczinski. He had worked something out in that sixth-form head of his under his schoolboy's part.

Wegerecht wanted to get it over with. He opened the proceedings on October 29.

He pushed the bonnet back on his sweating head, gathered up his robes, took his seat. His face was bright red, he looked healthy, like a spoiled child, but resentful. He was paying very close attention. Couldn't see well that morning.

His eldest son had told him something over breakfast: first period was canceled at school. To honor the birthday of the Reich minister of Public Enlightenment and Propaganda, the Berlin gauleiter Dr. Joseph Goebbels. One day earlier and the verdict could have been handed down in honor of Erasmus of Rotterdam.

While the criminal charges for transgression of the Treachery Act were being read out against Paul Warning, agricultural laborer, and Siegfried Hagemeister, forestry employee, Wegerecht searched the courtroom for unfamiliar faces. He found no visitors from the state capital, neither in uniform nor out. That was good. Unless it meant he was already written off to such an extent that a local observer was enough. It was hardly a consolation to have seen the Jerichowers sitting in the witness room like sheep in the rain.

The denunciation, submitted by a patriotic citizen filled with a sense of duty to the party and the state and presented by the prosecution, had been properly drawn up, sworn to, signed. Someone had helped, advised, filled in the cracks. But who?

Warning and Hagemeister were completely carried away by their eagerness to admit that they had expressed themselves in the terms described by the indictment. Both were shaken at having been taken down to the basement with the Jew Semig, as though not only he were in trouble but their own skins were on the line too. Hagemeister was calm, dependable, so like himself that what he said didn't sound like a recitation but like the start of a new conversation: – Just look at Griem and his lot.

– Yeah: Warning said. – He and Semig used to be thick as thieves, you couldn't even stir the pot. Now Griem is head sergeant or whatever with the Reich Labor Service.

The prosecutor had no further questions. Dammit.

Dr. Wegerecht was surprised that his palms weren't even wet, though his whole body felt hot. A headache like something inside his temples wanted out. He pressed his belly against the desk as though he could hang on that way. The District Court Head Judge Wegerecht of earlier days used to wave his arms with gusto as he talked; this one kept his hands flat on his papers. Seen from below, he was a stern and wrathful representative of the law, when he asked: What were they thinking of.

Warning hadn't been thinking of anything.

Hagemeister had thought there wasn't anything worth listening to. And it was so quiet behind the other walls of the train compartment that it seemed like the whole car was empty.

Now the prosecutor had a question, but it was so unexpected and proper that Kraczinski might as well have just woken up, or maybe it was that, with the best will in the world, he'd forgotten a firm intention. How had Griem come up in the defendants' conversation? What statements were made before the remark that was witnessed?

First: Hagemeister said. Kraczinski waved him to stop, as if he'd just thought of something. Hagemeister had gotten to the point where Warning was working for Griem in his townsman-farmer days, and Warning was eagerly trying to confirm it, but before they got to the point both men's gazes had strayed in confusion over to Wegerecht, since Kraczinski didn't seem to be listening.

Wegerecht called the witness Mrs. Cresspahl. Kraczinski seemed surprised.

Lisbeth was not the tradesman's wife Dr. Wegerecht had been expecting—whether the slow-witted, eager, or stubborn variety; the woman who walked in, sure of step, with face unbowed, wearing a black fabric coat with a velvet collar, was a Papenbrock daughter, undaunted, in fine clothes with fine behavior. Which form of the oath, Mrs. Cresspahl, the secular or the religious?

The religious. And Lisbeth had not only remembered but also reread what the Mecklenburg *Christian Family Almanac* recommended for consideration on October 29, 1937: Matthew 10, verses 34 to 42.

She had heard it at the time. (*Think not that I am come to send peace on earth: I came not to send peace, but a sword.*) By "at the time" what she meant was that she only knew the exact words from the policemen's allegations. (*He that loveth father or mother more than me is not worthy of me: and he that loveth son or daughter more than me is not worthy of me.*) She wasn't trying to deny anything except that she literally remembered it; if her brother, Horst, said that that's what she'd told him, then that's what she'd heard, and that was the truth. (*And he that loseth his life for my sake shall find it.*) On the contrary, the circumstances were extremely well suited for hearing properly, a Saturday in mid-July, noonday silence, the train from Gneez to Jerichow almost empty, and when it stopped in Wehrlich the wind was blocked by the Countess Woods. She could even hear the stationmaster's chickens scratching. (*And he that receiveth me receiveth him that sent me.*) Sorry, she couldn't understand the question. Why hadn't she filed a report herself? Because it's all twaddle. Nonsense, hogwash, *malarkey.* Not right in the head. Only someone who'd never set foot in Jerichow could believe for a second such crazy ideas about Dr. Semig or Griem, and Hagemeister knew it as well as she did. (*And he that receiveth a righteous man in the name of a righteous man shall receive a righteous man's reward.*)

It's nothing to do with protecting Jews, just the truth. (*And whosoever shall give to drink unto one of these little ones a cup of cold water only. . . .*)

When Wegerecht thanked her, she stayed standing before him for a moment. She had to be led back to her seat. Suddenly she looked like someone who had prepared for a long journey, for something uncertain. Her gesture, when she pulled her scarf out from under her coat collar, had something puzzled about it.

Griem—beefy, his pudgy weatherproof face making him look almost cheerful, state power personified there in his uniform: Not that he knew of. Idle chitchat. Poor slobs like that, he could only feel sorry for em. No, he would not bother filing a complaint. Let it be a lesson. A warning. Not that he was trying to anticipate the court's decision.

The prosecution moved to reprimand the witness Griem for offering unsolicited advice to the court. Now that was the Kraczinski of just ten days ago—sharp, rapacious, merciless as a hawk. The Kraczinski who then had no further questions didn't match.

Dr. Semig, Vet. Med., came into the courtroom with head lowered, looking not meek but like a grown man who'd let himself get caught in a childish mistake and who needed no accusations from others to add to the ones he was leveling at himself. He chose the religious form of the oath. After which he sat up straight, looked the jurors in the eye, turned unhurried to face Kraczinski. They'd given him back his Iron Cross. He spoke a bit slowly, because he had spent such a long time alone.

Did he continue to maintain that he had not procured any unlawful pecuniary advantage for then townsman-farmer Griem, when, in his capacity as veterinarian, he had evaluated a sick cow and sent it to be destroyed, for which the aforementioned Griem would receive a sum of 800 then rentenmarks from the cow fund (Mutual Cattle Insurance), more than he would have been likely to realize in a normal sale? And without Dr. Semig as the abetting party even receiving a portion of the profit from the abetted party?

Semig stroked his shock of gray hair as if embarrassed to have to repeat to an educated man what any child should have grasped the first time. Hepatitis was hepatitis. At no point had it ever been in his power to have the Bacteriological Institute in Schwerin falsify his findings. Not even in 1931 had his financial circumstances been such that. . . .

The rest couldn't be heard properly because Griem had started shouting as soon as Kraczinski had asked his first question, wild snarling half sentences interrupted by violent blows wherever his hand happened to land, on his knee, on the armrest, it was like he could feel no pain.

Dr. Kraczinski had no further questions.

Griem was given a fine for insufficient respect for the dignity of the court.

Semig was released, in a subordinate clause.

Warning was given 120 days in prison, for unwarranted suspicions directed at a party officeholder and hence at a party organization.

Hagemeister was fined two hundred marks.

Dr. Wegerecht went home, so stunned at Dr. Kraczinski's sudden change of heart that he invited him along for lunch. He sent Gisela to get wine, in broad daylight, and the joy swelling his heart from the resolution of the affair, and the first glass, was only slightly spoiled by Irmi von Oertzen's flirtatious behavior toward the new guest, and her asking why such trifles had even come before the court.

Hagemeister came by to give his thanks. He insisted on shaking Lisbeth's hand. – *That was one 'spensive conversation*: he said.

Cresspahl mumbled a response that might have turned into an offer.

– *What!?*: Hagemeister said. He was more than willing to pay a hundred to learn his lesson. He'd get the other hundred from Robert Papenbrock, that guy'd come crawling to him! – *Nothin personal, Fru Cresspahl!*

– I don't like it: Marie says. It's clear from her voice that she's lying on her back; since the Killainen family came she's been sleeping in the Swiss woman's room, with Annie and me. Her voice is slow, thoughtful, dissatisfied.

– Because everyone got off so easy? It's not over yet.

– Because you set it up to turn out badly and then it didn't.

– Bait and switch?

– Right. And that there's no ending. And no explanation for what happened.

– Marie, how could people in Jerichow find out who'd put in a call for Griem, and who against him?

– You mentioned ministries.

– They were far away, and even from up close Cresspahl couldn't see behind the curtain, and Papenbrock couldn't anymore. The Jerichow witnesses—Dr. Berling, Avenarius, a lawyer himself mind you—had heard so little that someone had to go get them from the witness room because the bailiff forget all about them. There they were still practicing their lines, evasions, excuses.

– Okay, Gesine.

– Now what if I tell you something about Peter Niebuhr?

– Whatever. Peter Niebuhr? An in-law on both Lisbeth's and Cresspahl's side. Young man. He has nothing to do with this story.

– Ah, but what if he does, Marie? What if he'd long since left the NCO academy in Eiche near Potsdam and was working in an office under Eugen Darré, head of the Reich Agricultural Corporation, and what if, while he was there, he'd come across a Nazi who'd been taking bribes and accepting other signs of gratitude, one from Jerichow no less, and had imperceptibly dragged his superior to the telephone, maybe his superior's superior, with the honor of German agriculture, so that at least in the vicinity of his relatives by marriage up on the Baltic *one* Nazi would get what he deserved, until it dawned on Peter that the denunciation had been filed by a Papenbrock, and that he wouldn't be giving his brother-in-law Cresspahl or sister-in-law Cresspahl the pleasure he'd wanted to give them, and now the instructions for Schwerin had to be reversed, between various different interministerial departments, and then he was given warnings he had to swallow, not only from himself but from friends who would have praised him and trusted him even more if the scheme had worked....

– Yes: Marie says. – Yes: she repeats, her voice deep in her throat, appreciative, convinced. – I'd believe that in a second.

January 18, 1968 *Thursday*

The New York Times doesn't let anything show in her face. Adroit and incorruptible, she holds forth on attempts to shore up the British pound, the gold cover of the dollar, and also the church's goodwill with regard to the Negroes, in which regard Henry Ford II himself refuses to be outdone. Our reliable old auntie brings us President Johnson's account of the State of the Union ("seeking, building, tested many times this past year, and always equal in the test"), in her own transcription, energy undimmed by her all-nighter; nor does she neglect to mention that Prince Sihanouk of Cambodia condemns the United States for a breach of promise she moreover quotes him as calling "cynical." She has the latest on the Mafia scandal in the city waterworks, arrested tax agents, stolen credit cards, the narcotics raid at SUNY Stony Brook; she informs us, almost consolingly, that Pavel Litvinov, if he's not happy with Socialist justice in Moscow, will not be allowed to work there as a physicist. All this on the front page, with no sign of anything missing. Such honest furrows on her brow.

If only we'd stuck to the continuations and not the new story tucked away on page 28! Such a seemly old lady, letting herself get caught in such embarrassing circumstances! She'd be ashamed to report such things about anyone else. But it's herself. It's . . . it's . . . confidential.

The opening, if not entirely innocent, is not too surprising. Yesterday afternoon, a federal commission studying discrimination against Negro and Puerto Rican white-collar workers met again at Foley Square and charged the news media with giving a false image of these minorities: just like that, in the *Times* headline, no quotation marks or sign of doubt. And surely our tried and true supplier of reality is above such suspicions.

The commission finds that the communications industry is giving Americans a false image of the society in which they live, and in addition giving Negroes and Puerto Ricans a distorted view of themselves. Of course. But not *The New York Times*, right?

Want to bet?

Come on. This industry holds a place of awesome influence in the nation, and it is these employers who in less than no time could create an intellectual climate for significant social change. *The New York Times* is in a position to do so, no question. If some may have shirked their responsibilities here, our upstanding old auntie—just, helpful, an ethical figurehead—won't number among the guilty. She knows what it means to be among the opinion and tastemakers "in a grave period of our national history"; she will do her duty. And right away she gives the percentages of these minorities in New York City (Negroes: 18 percent, Puerto Ricans: 10 percent), so that we can get down to business well-equipped with the facts.

The competition—the lesser competition, the *New York Post*—well, you know. Caustically, no other term will do, the commission addressed the *Post*: so *The New York Times* tells us, again in her sweet-and-sour way. Out of a total white-collar workforce of 450, only 24 Negro or Puerto Rican employees: 5.3 percent. Tsk tsk. Does it bother the *New York Post*, as a basically liberal newspaper, that there is a virtually segregated press in New York City?: the commission felt compelled to ask. And the *Post* could only reply snippily, as you'd expect: Any type of segregation bothers the *New York Post*. Har har. And only four black reporters out of all fifty-three. 7.5 percent. Humph. There you have it. Not one black editor. Those hypocrites at the *Post*.

This really demonstrates why we have riots and explosions of despair in our cities: the commission says.

Anyone wanting to scoop *The New York Times* had better get out of bed earlier. She has already paid a visit to the police in Los Angeles, Detroit, Virginia, Philadelphia, Chicago, Atlanta, to weapons factories in Memphis, in Springfield. Orders have been placed for Vietnam-type military helicopters, even. Next time the police will use the chemical called "banana peel" that makes the streets so slippery that it's difficult to walk on them, let alone riot. The New York City police have ordered five thousand helmets, $20 each—that's $100,000.

That's on a different page.

And now for the *Times*. A flourish of trumpets for the favorite!

All honor to the truth. The *Times* didn't come through unscathed either. But the commission was not so caustic with her, so cutting, so biting. It was critical, sure. Maybe to protect her. Spare an old lady the humiliation, sitting there before the judge in her little black dress, her tastefully preserved youth, the dignity of age, wringing her hands in her lap, anxious after all, and now she has to admit that out of her 200 reporters, no more than three were Negroes. 1.5 percent. That's right.

We picture a stunned silence.

The New York Times, née Ochs-Hays-Sulzberger, hurries to add: That refers only to the New York office.

Which doesn't help. The same was true for the *Post* too, wasn't it? And the old lady fails to show that the proportions in the Washington or Paris offices would be any better, though she implies it. Might be true. Right? Could be.

Then she regrouped. Held her head high once more, looked the commission straight in the face, said firmly: She wasn't proud that only 7
percent of her white-collar employees were from the minorities upon which
these hearings were focused. At least she gets credit for her attitude.

Then she squanders her moral gains and trips herself up with her manic
addiction to completeness. She says: A year ago it was 6 percent.

Oh my. That's less than the *Post*. And its number is only "about" 7
percent. Does *The New York Times* have a single black editor in its employ?
She may have told the commission, but she isn't telling her readers. We
better not ask.

There the old lady sits, humiliated, unmasked, with no respect paid to
her age and merits. Is she staring down at the tips of her shoes? Blowing
her nose? It doesn't help; the commission has a question for her.

Does she perhaps wish to retract part of her prepared statement? Where
it says that the *Times* is trying not only to preach but to practice accordingly?

–No, I don't want to: she says.

Does *The New York Times* see herself as a leader in the newspaper field?

– Possibly: she replies. We can just picture her, chin held high once
again, her proud gaze on the unachieved goal, her haughty schoolgirl tone.

That's a good deal of modesty: the commission responded. One could
only hope that someone like the *Times* would extend its leading position
into the field of equal employment.

– We are vigorously attacking the problem: *The New York Times* says.
This is the last thing she reports about herself: a promise. Is it a promise?
But the tears watering down her voice, those we could hear.

Time for a quick getaway. To *Time* magazine, Columbia Broadcasting,
American Broadcasting, Doubleday & Co., the J. Walter Thompson Agency,
Grey Advertising. They must have their own dirty laundry. They don't
come off much better. But anything to draw a veil over the horrible, intolerable scene that has just happened! Anything that's true. And then it's
not enough. So she turns to the Jews.

But the Jews aren't even the focus of the hearings!

Doesn't matter. There's enough there for at least two paragraphs, all
facts, and therefore justified: 25 percent of the city population is Jewish,
but only 4.5 percent of the 2,104 officers of 38 major corporations are Jews.

Yup. Speak of the beam in my eye and I'll speak of your mote. It's especially banks, insurance companies, shipping concerns, and law firms that take a hostile attitude toward Jewish executives. There you have it. And the hearings will continue today, and we'll see what else comes out!

I can hardly even recognize her.

A nagging treacherous old bag with a bad conscience. She's the one you let tell you all about what goes on in the world when you're not looking? And most of the time you can't be there to look, Gesine.

Doesn't it count for anything that she publicized her own scandal?

It seems she'd rather be accused of lying with euphemisms than of lying by suppressing anything.

But she didn't hide it, did she? She lists it right in the table of contents.

Look closer, Gesine. There's nothing there of what's in the headline. She couldn't resist one last try. It doesn't say anything in the contents about a false image of society, just "False Image."

If I throw this aunt out of the house, who will take her place?

You're saying you expected as much?

If I admit that today's story came as a surprise, what would that say about me? No thank you.

January 19, 1968 Friday

Fifty ladies were invited to the White House yesterday to discuss crime in the streets, among them *The New York Times* and the singer Eartha Kitt. Miss Kitt had an answer to the question of why young people rebel in the street, take drugs, and cut school: "Because they're going to be snatched from their mothers to be shot in Vietnam." "You send the best of this country off to be shot and maimed."

The president's wife did turn pale but she stood up and said, voice trembling, tears welling: You can't solve every problem with violence.

Eartha Kitt: The other guests knew the ghettos from visits, but she'd lived in the gutters.

Mrs. Johnson: I cannot understand the things that you do.

Miss Kitt: Then they'd missed out on something.

The *Times* tells the story almost first thing. Do we want to be friends again?

Lisbeth Cresspahl now felt she was in a fight too, with all of Jerichow, wherein were more than two thousand persons, and also much cattle. She had no desire to be forgiven for testifying against others before a judge; this way she could hold on to her guilt. Meanwhile, she preemptively forgave the Robert who had caused the whole to-do, and forgave Cresspahl in turn for cheerfully saying that he'd throw the denouncer out of the house right through the barbed wire. With that she reaped yet another tribulation.

She did not look depressed after the trial, and Cresspahl for his part expected a reasonable period to come next (he didn't want to think about sickness). Instead, it was more like Lisbeth could no longer keep her confusion and peace of mind in separate, alternating phases; there must have often been a mixture of both in her head. She was even more resistant to setting foot in town. To be judged by others' glances too, no, she didn't want that, no matter how much it would have added to her stockpile of suffering. For errands that with the best will in the world she couldn't entrust to Louise or Aggie Brüshaver, she didn't stop in Gneez, she took the connecting train to Lübeck, and a first-class compartment too, thereby avoiding any conversations with people she knew from the Jerichow area. And earning a reputation for extravagance. She didn't have to worry about many chance meetings in Lübeck, not in the shops, not in the department stores. She often stayed longer than she needed to, and had stories to tell back home about the new facade of the Holsten House, to which the Nazi building authority had added some new gables, or the old Gothic buildings on König Strasse, Meng Strasse, Schrangen, as though that proved the construction in Germany was less about the war than Cresspahl knew to be the case. He didn't fall for this gambit; he had learned to mistrust this bantering tone; he looked at her. Then he thought back to their time in England, her leisurely, carefree walks through the strange city, the clear-eyed look she'd had when she'd walked right past him in Richmond once. It was the look of someone who knew she was alone; now it was more fixed, more eccentric, clouded with brooding. There was still that soft line of the eye sockets from brow to cheekbones, and anyone who saw her in the padded first-class seats, possibly occupied with a silent smile, would more often

than not pull open the compartment door and address her as ma'am, before
realizing that the young woman in question was not in as friendly a mood
as she looked, and that actually there was something wrong with her smile.
Then Lisbeth would pull her coat around her, stiffen, turn her face to the
window, all so that no one would go after her for Warning's hundred and
twenty days in prison.

Not that that would have happened even on the line from Gneez to
Jerichow, where none of the trains had first-class compartments. People in
Jerichow saw things very differently. *Our Lisbeth.* Our Lisbeth had done
the right thing. Our Lisbeth wasn't a man, after all, and perjury's men's
business. What could Lisbeth do about a fake brother like that. The anger
was directed at Warning: both for not having the brains to keep his trap
shut on the train and for putting Lisbeth in such a bind. Talk generally
then turned to the fact that Warning was one of those people who'd rest
his chin on his spade handle while the cow's bleating next to him, and that
behind his amiable, in any case quite enjoyable grumbling, there was no
real get-up-and-go. People helped out his wife by giving her odd jobs and
sometimes money in exchange for nothing; he would face a different
homecoming to Jerichow than the one he was probably imagining in
Dreibergen near Bützow. And what about Hagemeister. All he'd wanted
was to hear that Griem had grown fat as a prize sow, or that *top hats sure're
nice but you cant wear em properly if youre not used to em.* Then Warning
opens his big mouth to bring up ancient history. And Hagemeister liked
to say, now in his usual half-asleep way, now with genuine feeling: *Cresspahls
wife saved my ass. Lisbeth Cresspahl saved my ass.*

That's how far things had gotten in Jerichow. Lisbeth wasn't Papenbrock's
daughter anymore, she was *Cresspahls Lisbeth.*

Hear she's sick. Never see her around anymore. All the more credit to
her that she told a real live district court head judge to his face that he was
asking about twaddle. Nothing but the truth. That's what she said: *Twaddle. Nonsense.* You try that.

She didn't hear about any of this, and it wouldn't have helped her if
she had.

– And now the story about the water butt: Marie says.
– What water butt? You don't know anything about that.

– I know that James Shuldiner was at the Mediterranean Swimming Club three days ago and he told me: Your mother wouldn't let *you* fall into the water butt.

– No!

– All right, Gesine. Start.

– For one thing, it was the summer of 1937, we're way past that.

– What's a water butt, anyway?

– Annie probably has one in Vermont.

– Annie's not here.

– A *Regentonne*, Marie . . .

– Yes?

– You usually find them in the country, freestanding is best but you want to make sure that leaves and pollen don't blow in. It's a rain barrel, there to collect rainwater because that's the purest kind you can get in nature. It does contain nitrogen, carbon dioxide, ammonium nitrite, and whatever else it picks up from the atmosphere, but not the calcium carbonate and salts that come from the soil. It's basically just condensed steam. Feels soft, that's why it's called soft water. Country rain is the purest. We had more ammonium because we got saltwater spray from the coast. Ammonium makes water softer. It lathers better that way. For the laundry, I mean. If the barrel's wooden, the water can turn brownish because the ammonium picks up trace organic substances. In England they call it a water butt.

– Wow, you're avoiding this story even more than you do Robert Papenbrock.

– You'll wish I hadn't told you.

– You treat me like such a little kid sometimes. I'm ten years old. Ten and a half.

– Cresspahl had set up a water butt next to the barn. That made it farther to carry the water, but the rain couldn't come down any purer. The fact was, until 1938 every part of the property was put together and maintained perfectly, like a textbook illustration. No iron cramp was left loose for long, the spring water didn't run back down into the ground but into a wooden tub where the child could sail little pieces of wood or cool her feet. It wasn't finicky either; after the new window was put in over the back entrance, a pane was taken out again so that the swallows could fly into the hall the way they were used to and build their nest on their ancestral beam. While they were there the red tiles were simply scrubbed more often, since the birds didn't always hit the *Lübeck Gazette* laid out beneath the nest. The water drum that the previous owners, the Pinnows, had set up by the kitchen window under a pipe running down from the roof was the same kind of thing. Cresspahl left it there. It would probably have fallen apart if he'd tried to move it. It wasn't watertight, which was why it was always surrounded by lush high grass and blooming weeds. I liked seeing that. But since the rainwater from the roof carried the debris of moss and wind dust, it was hardly ever used for washing and the lid was almost never taken off. But the lid was new, Cresspahl had made it so that I wouldn't pull a footstool over and then climb up and fall in the water.

– If the lid was missing, it could have been a mistake.

– A stranger's mistake maybe. But everyone who lived there knew about me and the cat. It was a big gray beast, fat and lazy. When Cresspahl was turning the Pinnow barn into a workshop and sleeping in the stalls next to his tools, this cat had come to visit him and stayed. Lisbeth and the child were still living in Papenbrock's house, and when they moved in the cat insisted on its preexisting rights. It didn't like me. I tried to get it to play with me. But it only wanted to lie on the inside kitchen windowsill and look out at the birds. It was old, too, not just sluggish. The child used to stand outside there a lot, head back, looking up at the cat and talking to it, and the cat looked back at me as though it knew a secret and still wouldn't say it.

– Negligence. Your mother couldn't keep you tied to her apron strings, and I know how it is with four-year-olds, they disappear like baby rabbits.

– You see.

– And now you have to climb up on the lid to look at the cat's face, and fall in the water, Gesine!

– Exactly.

– And your mother, she was standing right there?

– Yes. No. When I think it out of the corner of my mind I can see her. She's standing outside, by the back door, drying her hands on her apron, or wringing her hands, either one could be the other. She's watching me in amusement, the way grown-ups watch children's antics waiting to see how they turn out; she's looking at me seriously, approvingly, as if trusting me to make it all turn out right. When I try to remember, I can't see her.

– And she didn't move.

– I was underwater by that point. I could still see her in my mind; only then did I realize that all I could see in the round shaft of the barrel was the sky.

– Then she pulled you out.

– Then Cresspahl pulled me out. He'd come around the corner of the house behind her and saw her looking on. After the war he didn't want to tell me too many details about what had happened, he just said she stood there "as if paralyzed" while he carried the dripping bundle, me, past her into the house.

– Cresspahl taking off a child's wet things, washing her, drying her, getting her dressed, I can't see it.

– She did that, he went to get her for that. And when I had a new dress on, and was cheerful, had forgotten being underwater. . . .

– He hit her.

– Never. He let her watch him beat me. He didn't try too hard to soften the blows; he wanted me to remember that water butt once and for all. That was the only way he could protect me from Lisbeth.

– And she didn't grab his arm to stop him?

– Please. Now she had the unjust suffering of her child to offer up to her God too.

– Did you ever hit me?

– No. What I found so horrible about the beating wasn't the injustice but that my father was mad at me. That's why I spent the whole lunch looking for something I could do to atone, and under the table, too, so I was safe from his looks. Then I saw the cat coming back from a walk outside the house, and going under Cresspahl's chair, and lying down on his foot and clog. And I said: *Daddy, the cat!* And he said: *It can sit wherever it wants.* And he looked at me like he was surprised about the cat with me, and he was back together with me like before.

– She tried to kill you!

– She wanted to let me go, Marie.

– She must've hated you.

– It would have been pretty quick and painless, drowning.

– But she tried to get rid of you!

– "He that loveth his child," Marie. . . . She would have known that her child was safe, far from all guilt past, present, and to come. And she would have made the greatest sacrifice a person can make.

– You're trying to say that she loved you.

– That's what I'm trying to say.

– Next time you don't want to tell me a story, Gesine, don't tell it.

– Now you don't trust me.

– I trust you. You're your father's daughter, aren't you?

– Yes, Marie. I am Father's daughter.

Lisbeth I'll kill you
Kill me Hinrich. Theres no help for me now.

January 20, 1968 Saturday, South Ferry day
What does this mean, Gesine. What does this all mean!

Nuttin. "Nüchs," as Grete Selenbinder used to say.

When she didn't want to answer.

Just like I don't.

But you're learning Czech.

Československo je také velmi krásné.

It's not for a trip, it's an assignment from the bank. Every Thursday you get off two hours early, and Mr. Kreslil is paid by the bank too.

He doesn't know that.

The way no one's supposed to know. Where are you planning to go with this?

Nowhere. Nothing will come of it. They have never once let a woman work on the floors of the building with wooden floors, practically genuine carpets, practically genuine pictures hanging on the walls. Except as a cleaning lady of course.

And yet you have the fourth Five-Year Plan of the ČSSR almost memorized.

De Rosny has gotten an idea into that big head of his. And he seriously thinks the bee was sent bonnet-ward by the Státní Banka Československá.

You're doing something you don't believe in.

Isn't it enough that I work for the bank? Do I have to have feelings for it too?

Employee Cresspahl has been given some extra motivation. A more recalcitrant employee would be marked down for the next time personnel costs need trimming. Is that it?

That's it. And if in the end the Czechs and the Slovaks can't rebuild their Socialism with credit from de Rosny, Employee Cresspahl will still be sitting in the Foreign Sales Department, and the vice president will write off the investment.

You as an investment.

As part of the workforce, a cog being preemptively repurposed for another machine. Just so the bank won't have to feel bad later about not covering all the bases.

For de Rosny, Employee Cresspahl is a person.

He treats me like one. He's keeping the cog oiled and polished. The personal side of it is that de Rosny can write in his annual report to the stockholders: He has taken steps to reach out to Eastern Europe. That's to his credit even if nothing comes of it.

Let's assume that you actually do make it upstairs to the carpets, with the young men in their dark suits, and you have a rosewood desk like them, with a whole country's business passing across its surface. Maybe your colleagues will let you live, but it'll only be because they don't envy your Mission: Impossible.

A woman bank executive. The seven-headed beast. Now that would be news for The New York Times.

Never mind that, Gesine. De Rosny believes the show of loyalty to the bank you're putting on; he thinks it's lucky you actually lived in an Eastern European country. . . .

For three and a half years in the GDR. As a teenager.

Never mind that, Gesine. The Czech lessons, the economics you bought from Columbia University. . . .

To please you all. Okay, let's assume all that, weather permitting.

That's what the forecast shows.

That the ČCP actually wants to "democratize and humanize" itself? I know the words. Real worn-out shoes they are.

Then why wouldn't they hide their new boss in a rumor (some mummy past seventy who wants to sacrifice himself), why would they put him in all the nation's newspapers, Alexander Dubček, forty-six years old, with his complete biography?

It looks new.

And that they haven't passed the law about building new residential housing, and even admit that it wouldn't do the job?

Yes, sure. And decentralizing economic decisions. The rentability discussion. That rents which are too low make it impossible to maintain the buildings.

You see, Gesine. And then the Petschek family's life history on Czechoslovakian state TV.

That's a bit of a stretch. "The Rockefellers of Czechoslovakia." Shown as oppressors.

Yes, but with respect too, Gesine. With admiration: they never fell victim to a stock market crash. And when 1938 came to the world and Hitler to Czechoslovakia, the Petscheks sold off most of their mines and pulled out of their banks and emigrated to the USA. You think this Dubček government doesn't watch its own TV station?

It permits a story about capitalist cunning.

No, Gesine. A piece of the truth. As if these were people it was possible to learn something from.

I didn't watch it.

But you know that they even showed the buildings the Petscheks owned. Now serving as the Soviet, Chinese, and American embassies. The Petschek Bank, which was turned into the headquarters of the German Gestapo and then into the Ministry of Foreign Trade. This was a piece of buried national history dusted off and shown how it really was.

I wouldn't say that. Next you'll tell me that Češi a Slováci jsou bratři. *Liberty, Fraternity, Equality.*

Start with just one.

Okay. They'll be able to fix their economy faster and better with foreign credit.

And you'd work for that.

Assuming that Socialism would be left in place. Or put in place for once. You'd not only be paid to do work like that, your heart would be in it.

Yes. Now that's enough.

No, Gesine. There's something else. But here comes Marie, up from the car deck. Není to pěkné dítě?

Ano, je vskutku velmi pěkné.

So now if the Czechs and Slovaks united in brotherhood want such a thing, from de Rosny, then where will he set up this person's office? Where will the employee responsible have to transfer to?

. . . I didn't think of that.

Where would you be if you didn't have us, Gesine.

The bank has a branch in London.

And one in Frankfurt. Which is closer to Prague?

No. Not Frankfurt. Not again.

No one's asking your preference, Gesine. Is there a South Ferry in London? Where is the Frankfurt harbor you can take ferries across?

Marie.

Employee Cresspahl takes business trips to Prague and Marie spends her life in the Alcron Hotel.

She can't.

But she'd have to come with you, and she would go with you.

She'd lose three years before she learned how to live anywhere but New York. And you don't want to see the scars it'll leave.

No.

You see, Gesine. So now tell us again: What does this all mean?

The New York Times, this moralistic auntie, refuses to let Eartha Kitt off the hook for having talked back to Mrs. Johnson. The *Times* speaks of a "rude confrontation." And of what a credit it is to the first lady that she candidly replied that she could not understand the things and the life Miss Kitt understood. And that we can learn from it. Understand it. After centuries of psychic wounds the accumulated venom of the ages comes pouring out, often rude and irrational, often self-destructive. But it is there and it must be faced with compassionable understanding.

Clearly it'll be a while before we're reconciled with Auntie Times.

January 21, 1968 Sunday

The New York Times has once again sold a whole page to herself to inform her readers about her own progress. Since May she has owned the

Microfilming Corporation of America, she brags about her niece Halle-lujah, she has gotten fatter, but the most important thing to her is no doubt that she is losing the 117-year-old period after the title on the front page. It wasn't, she says, the $41.28 in annual ink costs for the dot, but the desire to make Auntie easier to read and enjoy.

Other than that, nothing seems to be missing. Not even that the ad-ministration sent a deputy secretary of defense to Senator Fulbright shortly before Christmas. The time had come for the senator to stop having his Foreign Relations Committee ask questions about whether US destroyers had actually been attacked in the Gulf of Tonkin in 1964. The administra-tion had conclusive proof and the three-and-a-half-year-long bombing war was justified. Senator Fulbright remains unconvinced.

Dr. Semig, him they convinced. In the first week of December, he took a trip.

Even then, it wasn't fear that made him do it. He hadn't been treated any worse in the basement under the courthouse than a thief not yet proven guilty. Dora had been allowed to bring him reading material, and out-of-hours visits had not been refused either. He'd been allowed out in the prison yard for half an hour at a time on many of the days, though alone. He'd been questioned only twice. He'd felt safe the whole time in jail, not only because Dora's bribes had softened up Alfred Fretwust but because of his certainty that what was happening to him wasn't possible. Since it wasn't right it had to be a mistake.

He did it for his wife.

When Dora came she told him about the progress she'd made getting their passports stamped. She did not tell him what the authorities promised her if she divorced him. They talked about the Jerichow house, about what she'd sold, about other things that Fretwust could barely understand. She didn't tell him that Friedrich Jansen had occupied the house for several hours with his gang of thugs, to measure the rooms. One time, she arrived without her coat, in late October, and he forgot to ask her about it. Frieda Klütz had spit on her in the Gneez railway station and she had taken off the sullied coat and placed it neatly in the shrewish old maid's arms. Arthur saw, though, that she was short of sleep, that she seemed thinner every time he saw her. He saw her large, burning eyes. He did not want to spend many more mornings waking up without her. He gave in. Among his quirks he felt he had to cling to the stubborn insistence that they call it a trip, not an emigration. Even Fretwust could tell that there was no difference, and he wrote in his surveillance notebook: Plans to leave German Reich. Fretwust avoided Arthur's name whenever he could in his notes, after Dora snapped at him once that anyone speaking of her husband had to use the word "Doctor." This had confused Fretwust. It was because he had gone to university, and that wasn't something anyone could take away from him. He had been an officer, and if you called him by his first name he surely remembered that that's how he'd addressed subordinates in the war. A Jew, yes, but a Jew in addition to that. The veterinarian's wife still carried herself as one of the people to whom he used to doff his cap. She could stop at a door so abruptly that a court constable of the New Greater German Reich might find himself positively running to open it for her quickly enough. When she gave him instructions about how her husband was to be treated, he tried to grin and couldn't pull it off; not even from his mother would he have accepted such a strict tone, such unrelenting looks. When it was time for a visit to end, Fretwust would, contrary to regulations, stand and face the wall for a few seconds. And then when he glanced back over his shoulder they would be sitting across from each other the same as before, they may have tried to pass each other something but he couldn't catch them in an embrace. When Fretwust later, over a beer, told stories about the horny old couple, his conscience would trouble him, but still he was almost sure, when he thought back to the afternoon, that Mrs. Semig put her hand on the Jew's as if attempting to comfort him for something. That was when she'd brought from Schwerin the suggestion that life in Germany would have been easier for the Semigs if they'd had children.

Semig wanted to spare his wife, and the people still talking to them in Jerichow, from what he thought was a mistake. It wasn't his fault but it was, nonetheless, because of him that the police and the Gestapo had paid them visits. He had exposed them to that, which was no way to thank them; thus he now had to leave them. That meant paying two visits.

First, to go see Cresspahl; only Cresspahl immediately suggested coming to see Semig instead. Once again Lisbeth didn't feel it necessary to let all of Jerichow know that they were on their way to the Bäk. But she lay in Dora Semig's arms like a child who'd cried herself out.

Kollmorgen came to see Semig too. The little man had prepared a speech, and insisted on holding Semig's hand in both of his as he gave it, with the result that he had to look a bit too steeply up and Semig too steeply down. The oration started well, with the occasion of farewell, but quickly veered off into the weeds, never to return. It was almost precisely four hundred years ago that Jürgen Wullenweber, the mayor of Lübeck, was hanged, and from this date, September 29, 1537, Kollmorgen proceeded directly to December 20, 1712, the day on which the Swedes had won a battle against the Danes near Gadebusch, and even if both dates were somehow tangentially relevant to the topic of surviving in difficult times, in the end even Avenarius himself didn't venture to draw the connection, and his listeners couldn't help but notice that this was not what he had wanted to say it. He was very embarrassed, and he stood there afterward with his back to the others whenever possible, trying to look like he was examining the Köster family Biedermeier. His hands clasped behind him, his helplessly intertwining fingers, were thereby clear for everyone to see, he probably didn't realize that.

That was the last case Avenarius Kollmorgen, Dr. Jur., ever argued.

Dr. Semig did not take his leave from the Tannebaums, Jewish clothing merchants in Jerichow. He had never had any dealings with them, not even as a customer.

Both Dora and Arthur refused to let anyone bring them to the station. They were planning to take the first train to Gneez, the milk train.

It left at two minutes past seven; at a quarter to seven the Semigs were standing outside Cresspahl's kitchen window, Dora in the light, Arthur farther back in the dark, by the milk rack. When he came into the kitchen, his face was still the familiar one—the once-happy wrinkles, the slightly pursed lips, the formerly tranquil eyes that had always brightened when he had an amusing thought, even if he refrained from saying it. But it troubled Lisbeth, she had already let his face go. Now Cresspahl had to drive them to the milk train after all, in the car that had once belonged to Semig.

– What did they forget?: Marie says. She had already asked about the mechanics of the move, interjecting questions about what was done with the used sheets, the china, the house keys. For her, after the goodbyes the night before in Semig's yard everything had been taken care of.

– They'd wanted to see the Cresspahl child one last time.

January 22, 1968 Monday

And here's Eartha Kitt in *The New York Times* yet again. Why won't this Negro simply accept that her comment about the war in Vietnam was a breach of etiquette because it was addressed to the first lady? But Miss Kitt calmly told radio station WEEI in Boston: "I don't know why. I am very surprised. I raised my hand and was called on to explain my views. That's what I did."

Eighteen Americans killed, at least twenty-five Vietnamese found dead after attacks on Hill 861 at Khesanh. Twenty-one South Vietnamese wood-cutters were killed in an attack by American artillery and tactical aircraft in Tayninh Province because they were working in a zone where anyone is regarded as a fair target.

Marie gets mail from there.

It's from Dr. Brewster, her first doctor in New York, who was called up for reserve duty last September and is now serving as a doctor in children's refugee camps in Vietnam. It is a totally unsurprising postcard, with a Japanese postmark, wishes for Christmas and a New Year with Peace on Earth, addressed to "Dear Mary" from her "Wm. Brewster." There's a rough spot on the back of the cardboard where it looks like something stuck on has been peeled off, maybe a photograph. For Marie's correspondence with her prodigal friend goes via Mrs. Brewster in Greenwich, Conn., "the wife," who may want to keep the exotic stamps for herself or else read what her husband has to say to this patient of his.

– Military mail is just stamped like that, I think: Marie says with a stubborn scowl. She takes back the card and puts it in her school folder, instead of setting it up behind the bookcase glass. Clearly she doesn't want to talk about these holiday wishes, or at least not in front of the Killainen family, who have problems of their own with the war. Marie would have rather been left alone with this piece of mail.

William B. Brewster, MD, was one of the first Americans she let into her life after being forced to accompany her mother to this foreign land in the early summer of 1961. He didn't have his practice on Park Avenue yet, he was working as a junior doctor at St. Luke's Hospital and was one of the people that Countess Seydlitz recommended to helpless Europeans who found themselves with a limping child.

Employee Cresspahl had, in the last days before the irreversible resumption of work, spent a day on the Atlantic with her child, at Midland Beach on Staten Island, to console the child for all the strange new foreign things, and even on the subway back the child was hobbling a bit, and the next morning she was walking with a limp.

She limped without the slightest impatience; she was not even four years old and she buckled a little as skillfully as an old woman, straightened up, buckled, straightened, considerately trying not to betray too much through the hand with which she was holding mine.

She sat on a bench in Riverside Park, under trees lit up by the summer sun, calm, tired, and she didn't want to show her foot. She denied feeling any pain.

Today, in a photo from back then she looks mischievous, confident. At the time she was scared. The pudgy little face from 1961, the narrowed eyes, the helpless lips struck passersby as traces of danger. She had short hair then, inexpertly cut. There were plenty of grandmothers in the park who wanted to take a shot at straightening out that pale windswept tangle. Marie had her head behind her mother's back before her mother could even see such meddlesomeness coming.

But she couldn't see what was wrong with the child's foot. Out of the eight million people in the city of New York, Employee Cresspahl knew maybe five. She hardly trusted her English at the bank, much less to interpret between a foreign-language child and a doctor. The friendly camaraderie from one park bench to another, the exotic trees and bushes, even the feel of the summer wind, the consciousness of a nearby river, of vacation, now constituted a hostile environment. That's when it started: If she let Marie see any uncertainty in her, even for a second, Marie would never even try to make a life here.

Marie's excuses were meant to protect her from a doctor like the one in Düsseldorf, who thought a gruff manner conveyed trustworthy warmth, and now from a doctor in New York. But at St. Luke's she ended up with a man who was if anything rather shy with new clients. Once his face brought the words *Thuringian* and *boy scout* to mind, you couldn't get them back out of your head. He didn't look summa cum laude, more like a farmer's son—a boy who thought school was hard, who even now stares off into space like he's repeating a checklist to himself. But nothing whatsoever was hard for Dr. Brewster, and he knew his business by heart too. He took Marie's right hand and shook it. She let him; she knew that this custom was not one you could avoid. He took her left hand and shook it, gravely, starting over with a totally new formality. She thought it a credit to him that he treated both hands equally. Then he took her healthy foot. She'd already accepted that her limping foot had to be as unclothed as her hand. He had made her curious. Back then I was happy. Back then peace still reigned.

Marie examined the balls of her feet, where this person without glasses or a white coat had found black spots, and Cresspahl the foreigner was afraid of her prejudiced idea of American medicine, which she thought they were now about to be subjected to. But Dr. Brewster came out of the side room with a gauze bandage, not a syringe, and he could wet it himself without summoning the nurse. The advice he gave in such a trustworthy way was grandmotherly: Keep the foot moist. Berta Cresspahl would have said the same thing.

And Dr. Brewster knew more than he'd learned in school. He made sure that the child was busy enough with the Lego set by the window and then asked the mother, who was not especially inclined, neither in her maternal capacity nor personally, to call her child stupid or ugly: She's a bright child, Mrs. . . .?

The mother didn't know what to say.

He watched the child for a while longer as she snapped some animal figurines together and apart; he was perfectly unhurried, his hands in his lap, and then he declared as an incontrovertible medical finding, serious and definitely teasing too: I do believe so. A bright child.

That cost ten dollars, and he had us so hooked that we went back. He remembered our names too. After three days the foot was how it should be. He didn't want to hear it over the phone, he wanted to see for himself. This time Marie held her left hand out first, to test him. He took it with his left hand, and she offered her limping foot first. She couldn't pronounce his name yet, and didn't manage to be more than annoyed when he slipped the tetanus shot hidden in his cupped hand out of his pocket and into her thigh. She was about to open her mouth to scream when he'd already said something to her and she preferred to hear what it was. He'd insisted on none of the vaccinations our prejudice had assumed he would; life in New York without a tetanus shot, though, was not something we would advise. Marie said: If that's what he wants. Then yes.

And he brought his client back through the waiting room and down the stairs to the exit onto 113th Street, here a one-way street running west, and he stayed hidden in the shadowy lobby, watching like a spy to see how the child was walking on her foot. He saw his work out the door and then gave it a final inspection.

We followed him to the practice he later bought on Park Avenue, refusing to let Miss Gibson the reception lady stop us, neither with her high-class manner nor with her doubts about our ability to pay. We had even learned to almost completely understand how he talked, the quiet murmur barely above a whisper, the vowels just breathed out; Marie can talk like him, so that only the aspirates remain audible—from "adhesive" just the "h"—but she doesn't perform him, she only imitates him, with affection, teasing, when he comes to mind. This is who they've now hauled off to Vietnam, and no one knows if he'll come back alive or be accidentally bombed by his own military. We needed him, in case anyone tried to tell us it was impossible to raise a child in New York. *Thank you very much, doctor.*

That night, after Marie put the Killainen children to bed in her room, she asked: What would it be like? If someone, not a soldier, got permission to visit the war zone, which I admit is not very likely, then what would it be like. A flight to Saigon, what would that cost?

January 23, 1968 Tuesday

– Is this the lady who called ten minutes ago, asking about the weather in North Germany over Easter 1938? Crassfawn? Do you have a pen handy?

Flensburg

4/17: 8°C, high winds, freezing rain

4/18: Morning: 1.5°; high of 7°; snow showers

Putbus

4/17: 5°C, no overnight frost, no precipitation

4/18: Same

Königsberg
  4/17: 5°C, snow cover
  4/18: Same

We don't have anything on Wismar or Stettin. Does this give you a general picture? How nice of you to say so, Mrs. Cressawe. The bill will be sent to 243 Riverside Drive, #204 . . . is that NY 10025? Not at all. You know what, while I was looking this up for you I found out that March 1938 was the warmest March of the century in that region; that's definitely not something I'm likely to forget. Yes. This is Herbert H. Hayes speaking. The pleasure was all mine, Mrs. Crissauer!

So the daffodils, snowdrops, and forsythias in Hilde Paepcke's garden would have been killed in the frost, and no leaves in sight, when her younger sister came to visit Podejuch from Jerichow with husband and child. Lisbeth had turned down invitations for Easter '35, '36, '37, like onerous demands; now here she was in the middle of a second such winter, and she'd insisted so strongly on coming that Alexander had to cancel plans with his friends from the department. Was there anything to the rumors that Lisbeth had turned unununderstandable, as they'd heard from one person in Jerichow after another?

The Cresspahls arrived in Gneez on Saturday morning on the postbus, he with a light-colored leather suitcase that stood out among the bags and baskets of the other passengers, the child at his side with a hand on the suitcase handle, not at her mother's, who stepped down onto the platform after them empty-handed and absolutely unenthusiastic. They took the second-class car, not third-class, on the Hamburg–Stettin express, which went past the Gneez housing development a few minutes after ten. Barely a quarter hour later, they stopped for three minutes above Schwerin Lake and could see the north tip of the island of Lieps nearby in the cold water, not completely bare but covered with matted brownish branches. Here they could have transferred to the Rostock line and would have been in Copenhagen by their usual dinnertime. It was the father who explained these connections to the child, and the child stayed next to him, sitting patiently, quiet, under her dark-brown cockscomb hairstyle that looked as if it had been turned down and tucked in by the child herself. The other two passengers in the compartment, an elderly Hamburg couple, occasionally snuck a look at the young woman who let her head lean back as if exhausted from something; who often closed her eyes as if that way she was free from having to listen too, or else looked indifferently out the window to escape from the prying eyes. To strangers it looked like a marital fight, but then again not, when Lisbeth suggested with an encouraging, solicitous smile that the child and Cresspahl take a stroll through the train. A little while later she too left the compartment, after being asked about mutual acquaintances between Hamburg and Schwerin, but she walked in the other direction.

Cresspahl was glad that for once Lisbeth had asked for something it was possible to do—though he could have used the Saturday for work. He told himself Hilde's questions would surely take her sister's mind off things; he was almost looking forward to seeing his brother-in-law and getting the chance to drink for pleasure, for once. Cresspahl stood at the left-side window and showed his child the Warnow River, which the train had been running alongside since Warnow: a little river dawdling over stones and broken branches. Then, on the other side, the canal between Bützow and Güstrow, which at one point had been meant to go all the way to Berlin. In Güstrow the station name was painted on the sides of rectangular lamps. The child wanted to know why they had to wait five minutes here. Cresspahl said it was because of the connection to Neustrelitz, then Wendisch Burg, where other relatives lived, the Niebuhrs. He forgot Horst in Güstrow. Then it was already 11:30 and they were passing through the forest east of Güstrow, the Priem Woods, where Army Ordnance Depot, North District, was being built behind a thin wall of pine trees. He knew that Schmidt from Güstrow was doing work for them. Kröpelin from Bützow too. For someone an Englishman could ask, Cresspahl sure knew a lot of state secrets. When they were passing the tall forest near Teterow, the Hamburg couple chatted with a new passenger about the annexation of Austria into the Greater German Reich, grumbling a bit but basically in qualified agreement, and Cresspahl told the child about the pike that the people of Teterow would throw back into their lake because they were sure they could find it again from the notch they'd cut in the side of their boat. At a little past 12:30 the Cresspahls headed over to the meal car, and at Malchin the child caught a glimpse of a little harbor with jacked-up boats and boatbuilding sheds. They were already on their way back by the time the train passed the Leuschentin Forest, because the meal car was too crowded, mostly with soldiers who had clearly been sitting over their beer and wine for a while already. The train stopped at Neubrandenburg for five minutes, and Cresspahl could buy the child a lemonade to go with Lisbeth's sandwiches. By then it was quarter to one; they passed through Pasewalk on the Uecker and, just before two, crossed the Pommern border between Grambow and Stöwen. At two thirty the train stopped in Stettin, and fifteen minutes after that they had the five miles on the Greifenhagen line to Podejuch behind them, and there Alexander Paepcke was at the station with little Alexandra and Eberhardt, and Alexander said: *Well, Hinrich, lets celebrate.*

Hilde, who had stayed home with baby Christine, just one year old, hugged her brother-in-law Cresspahl at great length while keeping an eye on her sister; Lisbeth did not seem bothered, if anything her expression was rather encouraging. Hilde thought she looked pretty much the same, aside from her tiredness. The work flashed through her fingers as expertly as before, only now without enthusiasm, without pleasure. Hilde may not have noticed that Lisbeth was watching Alexander's mouth practically in terror that night when he told them about the Stettin Ordnance Depot. Alexander was a major in the reserves now, *who wouldda thought!* The house in Podejuch was only rented, and expensive, but still impressive, *you gotta admit!* Yes indeedy. After Austria it might be Poland's turn, he said, or maybe Czechoslovakia was next in line to fall in with Germany. Of course that'll be a real war, Lisbeth! What didja expect? And you couldn't be too careful about planes, he agreed with Heinrich there. It wasn't so bad if you lived near an airfield, like in Jerichow, they'd try to land there in one piece, but the things you see in open country! The holes they left in the ground were big enough to fit this whole house in! Complete with cellar and chimney. Explosives that powerful were better transported by train than plane, doncha think? Y'know. Yeah. Cheers Hinrich! Lisbeth had retired upstairs very early, and since Cresspahl wouldn't accept the Paepckes' bedroom either, Hilde found nothing unusual about his spending the night in the back room of the widow Heinricius's house, three doors down, and Lisbeth in an attic room with the children.

In the morning Paepcke shouted for Cresspahl through the backyards, so loudly that all eight surrounding houses now knew that Paepcke was shaving and had visitors. After breakfast, Lisbeth insisted on going to church, so finally Alexander decided, with an irritated laugh, that in that case they'd all go. Over grog in the Forest Lodge in Podejuch he started heaping praise on Lisbeth's sister for everything he could think of; he was unable to get Cresspahl to talk about Lisbeth. (– We're both strangers among these Papenbrocks, aren't we: Alexander said. – Yup: my father said. He still didn't know that time was running out.) They went for a drive on the heath, Buchheide, and in a damp clearing between pitch-black pines they suddenly came across some cleverly hidden, gaily painted Easter eggs—Alexander Paepcke strikes again, the magician, who knows how to live. The edge of the heath was strangely elevated above the river valley and the new barracks. Another evening over beer, Mosel, and the prospects for the coming war. Hilde banged each new glass onto the table a little forcefully; that wasn't something a Paepcke would ever notice. Cresspahl had no chance to talk to Lisbeth alone; he would have tried to downplay what Alexander was saying. And then Alexander was standing at the window again, early the next morning, with shaving foam on his chin, shouting for Mrs. Heinricius, the state councilman's widow, to wake Cresspahl up. A walk along the East Oder. Hair of the dog and lunch in Stettin at the Terrace Hotel, with the stepped tower, at the foot of Haken Terrace; the Hamburg train left at three; at eight thirty that night Cresspahl carried his sleeping child home from the Jerichow station. Cresspahl was pleased with how the trip had turned out, and Lisbeth had gotten what she wanted.

You were seeing if there'd be a place for me there.

And wasn't there one, Gesine? Alexandra was four months younger than you, so you'd have had an advantage over her. She had the soft blond hair, you the dark, so she would have always been considered the pretty one and wouldn't have gotten jealous of you. You let loose with her more than you ever did at home—how you chattered away! You could have lived with her. Ganged up with her against that shrimp Eberhardt. You could have won Christine over. There was a place for you there.

Then why didn't you do it right away? What made you wait so long?

I didn't want to do it. Taking precautions doesn't mean you want to. I wanted to stick it out, if I could.

And if your sister hadn't wanted to take me in?

She would have taken you from Cresspahl, Gesine. You're your father's daughter.

Peace does not come easily to those
who once the wrath of Auntie Times incur.

Eartha Kitt has had to defend herself yet again for characterizing the war to Johnson's wife as the underlying cause of crime in this country, thus bringing tears to Mrs. Johnson's eyes. Miss Kitt still doesn't understand the problem. Whether as an actress, a Negro, whoever, she was entitled to her opinion, particularly when it was asked of her, she said. Meanwhile *The New York Times* remains unyielding and ends by mentioning the telegrams sent to comfort the president's wife, not those supporting Miss Kitt.

Well, Miss Kitt?

January 24, 1968 Wednesday

The roving cultural critics who indefatigably bring home news of the death of New York would be delighted to hear that the city's telephone network had collapsed or, for completeness sake if nothing else, that the postal system was in its death throes. If only this were true at least for unwanted phone calls, and the only letters that came to our door were the ones we could honestly say we were happy to get!

We would have been just fine without the one that came today from Boston. In it, a former football player who has since put on some weight tried his best to present himself as oh so delicate, accompanying what he says with gingerly gestures, and if he does have to seize hold of the problem after all, he means to do it gently, so that no one can blame him for any resulting injuries.

F. F. Fleury, away from whom Annie Killainen has run with three children, has, in full consciousness of his French manners, submitted a clean manuscript to the post office, third draft, no typos, probably with a carbon copy deposited somewhere. So now you see how polite F. F. Fleury can be, Mrs. Cresspahl!

He did not want to open with accusations of lying and malicious deception, the letter said. So much the better, Dr. Fleury. After all, maybe it's a coincidence that the Cresspahls' phone in New York was occasionally answered by Fleury Junior, right? Point for you there, Fleury. Thanks a lot, Junior.

He claimed to conclude from this only that Mrs. Cresspahl knew where Annie was staying or, perhaps, was keeping it secret on her request. The chivalry of the man. Right? Nothing was further from his mind than to meddle in such a friendship or try to prevent it. All right, Mr. Fleury, here we go.

As proof of this intention he would refrain from bringing up bygones with Mrs. Cresspahl. And what kind of bygones might those be, Mr. Fleury? Things like the undermining of friendly trust simply by refusing to accept the use of first-name familiar linguistic forms. That's true, Mr. Fleury, it was an evening last April, after dinner by candlelight and fireplace, Annie had left to get some ice cream, and you doubtless did mean it as more than just a change in forms of address. Still, you might see such things as a natural rigidity, a stiffness natural to a German, rather than as a rejection. There's a certain something about you, Mr. Fleury.

In addition, he saw no need to reiterate, even to Annie, what there was to find off-putting in Mrs. Cresspahl. This would include: the deliberate parading of housewifely virtues in a hostess's own kitchen; behavior that emphasized achievement even in manners and invariably privileged intellectual aspirations over interpersonal relationships; finally, a pedagogical system that had turned Mrs. Cresspahl's daughter if no one else into a browbeaten automaton. Marie, you robot, go knock him a new one!

He hereby formally withdraws these accusations, along with any others that Mrs. Cresspahl might find unpleasant. Since Annie hasn't told us anything about them, are we supposed to ask him what the rest might be?

To the matter at hand, the letter goes on. Yes, indeed, Mr. Fleury.

It had been thoughtless of him to doubt Mrs. Cresspahl's account of Henry Cabot Lodge having suggested, as early as 1965, when he was the US ambassador to Saigon, that America had oil interests in South Vietnam and Southeast Asia. Did I really say that? I can't be sure anymore. Furthermore he should have believed that the USA was financing seismic tests for future oil drilling in Vietnam via the UN Economic Commission for Asia and the Far East and had bought the results. He had gone and looked it up, and H. C. Lodge actually had made that statement; the ECAFE actually did exist and had carried out the assignments as claimed. Nor was the invocation of David Rockefeller's name in this context unjust. You see, Mr. Fleury. No, really, never again would he dare to argue with Mrs. Cresspahl on such matters, or refuse her all due respect. Hooray for that, Mr. Fleury.

And yet he did feel compelled to deny that Mrs. Cresspahl had the right to conclude, from the existence of business interests, that the American role in the war was criminal. That would be, if Marxist, vulgar. First of all, the country had properly paid the price asked for its investments in underground South Vietnamese oil and was thus legitimately entitled to defend this investment. This in no way infringed upon the right to self-determination of the Vietnamese people, if anything American participation in the development of a national oil industry promoted it. Anyway, our country had to pursue its own right to self-determination, which naturally included covering its own need for petroleum. There are moral justifications for courses of action besides refusing to go to war. Such as a nation's drive for self-preservation, for instance, a nation that moreover bears the additional responsibility of being a world power. We don't know how to answer that one.

Exactly. It will therefore come as no surprise to Mrs. Cresspahl when he once again takes the most vigorous exception to her reference to the role of the CIA. Undoubtedly this organization is technically in a position to embroil the South Vietnamese government in a putsch, which would enable the US to terminate the war on the grounds of breach of treaty obligations. Why wouldn't what had enabled one invasion after another in South America be just as good a trigger for a withdrawal from Vietnam? By no means, Mrs. Cresspahl. The USA has long since given its word of honor, and it is not a foreigner's place to pass judgment, out of a misguided sense of world citizenship, on the nation where she is a guest.

One hopes that this brings the discussion to an end. It certainly does, Mr. Fleury.

If he might be permitted a concluding remark. Go ahead, Fleury, don't be shy. Mrs. Cresspahl is clearly making every effort to lead a life of faithful friendship, political consistency, and complete awareness. I'd have to be crazy, Fleury. He will not be so indelicate as to measure how far Mrs. Cresspahl's efforts fall short of perfection. Very nice of you, Mr. Fleury. He does, however, feel compelled categorically to insist that all this represents merely her own version of perfection. And yet she derives from it criteria for other people, too—in brief she demands from her friends that they live the way she does. No. No. It's impossible to live with someone like that, spreading mortification and hurt wherever she goes with her rigid and yet ultimately only pretended exemplary behavior. That's not me. That's not me.

But there is someone who might indeed see you that way, Mrs. Cresspahl. When it comes to Annie—

This can't be his typewriter, Annie. It may use the same font but he didn't write this letter. He can't have.

But he called the office, your F. F. Fleury did. Said you should come home. Said the key's with the neighbors. The bank account has enough in it for six months. He won't be there and he won't come here.

Don't be so scared, Annie, it's not that. He did volunteer for deployment to Vietnam, but they didn't take him. Too old, what do I know. He was able to convince a Boston paper to send him to Saigon as a correspondent, only long enough to write a series of articles for the time being. He wants to see how things look from there.

Why should I say what I think of that, Annie! Say what you think! I'm just sitting here reading the newspaper!

The electronic net that the USA has cast over land and sea, the atmosphere and outer space, has acquired a hole. On Monday, North Korean patrol boats seized the USS *Pueblo* in the Sea of Japan, in its view an armed spy boat, according to the Defense Department a barely armed navy intelligence ship, or maybe "an environmental-research ship." Sighing, quite as if she had asked D. E. himself for his view, *The New York Times* adds that in the current art of war, "environment" often means the electronic surroundings, rather than more tangible phenomena, and "research" is directed toward the energy emitted by the enemy's electronic devices, in the interest of intercepting and blocking enemy radar and other electronic signals. But she can't understand it. She asks no fewer than five questions: Where was the destroyer escort? Was the *Pueblo* actually working for the navy or ultimately for the NSA? and other things we never quite learn. She hid the other questions, like Easter eggs, in her clever reports: According to Radio North Korea, the *Pueblo* was less than twelve miles from the coast, thus within territorial waters. The State Department says: Clearly outside the twelve-mile limit. A rear admiral in Panmunjom: Sixteen nautical miles, more than eighteen statute miles. The Pentagon: Twenty-five miles. Some military sources: Less than twenty-five miles. The game gets boring, and more than eighty men from on board have to wait it out.

Although they might be safer than some of the five thousand marines concentrated as reinforcements at Khesanh, together with four thousand pounds of "body bags": rubberized, zippered sacks for transporting the dead.

Which Dr. F. F. Fleury wants to see with his own eyes.

January 25, 1968 Thursday

So it wasn't the Leningrad Philharmonic that the Soviet Union had sent into space in 1961 but a recording by the 110-member Pyatnitsky Choir, to trick their Western counterparts. The Soviets think this such a good joke that they don't want to keep it to themselves.

The apartment is empty. The Killainen children's beds have disappeared back into Mr. Robinson's basement, the TV too. All the furniture is more or less where it was two and a half weeks ago, when the fatherless Fleury family landed. It's as though they were never here, except for a hint of the perfume that Annie cooled her brow with still hanging in the warm air. What happened, Marie?

Private Robert W. Meares of Fayetteville, N.C., nineteen years old, who had refused to wear his army uniform, was court-martialed, sentenced to four months hard labor, and fined 4 x $68. At that point he volunteered for Vietnam service. The jail sentence was suspended but he still had to pay the fine.

Marie thinks it was like this: Annie no longer wanted to stay with us after she read a letter that wasn't addressed to her. She can't face herself because the letter wasn't even hidden, making the breach of trust that much greater. She can't bear that G. Cresspahl must now think that Annie talked about her with F. F. Fleury as a difficult person obsessed solely with Vietnam and tormenting children. She is unhappy with herself because she didn't even want to stay long enough to deny it.

Yesterday the wife of President Johnson was harassed between her

554 · January 25, 1968 Thursday

limousine and a club entrance by young people with signs reading: WE
SUPPORT EARTHA KITT. "The First Lady pulled her mink coat around
her, threw her head back and made no response." She doesn't speak to such
people.

Try again, Marie. That doesn't make sense. All right: Annie can't stand
that you didn't admit the letter was from her husband. She knows she has
no right to hold it against you, but she does, that you decided behind her
back what she should and shouldn't be allowed to know about you. She
holds it against herself that now you'll think of her as someone who reads
other people's mail, but she didn't want to accept that she knew that you
didn't know she knew. So I had to go hail a cab on West End Avenue and
she and all three children got in and took it downtown, and since West
End isn't a one-way street, maybe she did turn uptown. Understand now?

The State Department in Moscow immediately rejected the US request
to intercede with the North Koreans regarding a seized spy ship. Deputy
Foreign Minister Vasily V. Kuznetsov did not even accept the American
piece of paper, not even as an aide-mémoire.

No. Can you try one more time, Marie? If you insist: She's offended
that by not telling her about the letter you prevented her from reassuring
you. She would have been happy to tell you that you're not the way Fleury
describes you. Especially that you're not perfect and that you have no desire
to be anything so horrible. So now she blames herself for putting herself
in a position where she can no longer tell you that. She blames you for not
even hiding the letter. She blames herself for not being the person you
think she is. Now I don't understand it anymore either.

A young woman mugged by a man with a knife at her mailbox on
Seventy-Fifth St. between Fifth and Madison, while a policeman a hundred
feet away didn't hear her repeated screams and the doorman blowing his
whistle, sums up the incident with one question: If the police don't help a
citizen here, what do they do in the slums?

Annie probably said some things in Finnish, Marie. No: She was upset
from the wait, because I got home from school later than usual, and that's
why I only really understood that she was mad at you for not wanting to
give her advice. She blames herself for blaming you even though she knows
that after a letter like that you couldn't discuss going back to Fleury's house
with her. She's mad that you never even tried to stop her, as if you knew it

was already decided. She blames herself for letting you think that she's going back not only to Fleury's house but also to his opinions about you. She blames you for not going to Vermont with her, and herself for having used you, for help finding a job and against fear. And if you don't take this $85 without another word then she never wants to see you again. She likes you, though, and she hopes you do come visit. She thought I wouldn't understand what she was saying and wouldn't be able to explain it to you. And so what does it all mean?

And what are we to think of a moralistic Auntie like *The New York Times* advertising for a studio where you can take photos of naked girls?

January 26, 1968 Friday

Last night, in the crowded bus terminal on Eighth Avenue, a man threw a nineteen-year-old coed to the ground on the landing of a stairwell to the lower level, threatened her with a pistol, and set about raping her in full view of several people, who made no move to interfere. Then along came a man named William Williams who freed the girl.

In April 1938, Wilhelm Brüshaver, the Protestant pastor in Jerichow, heard from his wife that Lisbeth Cresspahl had claimed that there was nowhere in the Bible where suicide was prohibited. Aggie Brüshaver found that hard to believe: Was it really true?

The recollection crossed her mind while her husband was taking off his mud-encrusted boots in the kitchen, after a visit to a sickbed, and she mentioned it in passing while doing the kids' laundry, so he half forgot it by the time he got to the door. He had his sermon to think about; he wasn't trying to be surly when he left the room without answering.

By this point, Pastor Brüshaver was writing out his sermons. He would sit by his lamp late into the night on Friday and Saturday, and look gray in the pulpit on Sunday morning, face puffy, and he no longer spoke like someone who had seen something and was simply reporting the truth of it—he looked as if he doubted his memory. It was not only reading from a page that made him stumble; he was in fact reconsidering, before some of the sentences, whether he had hedged enough. There was at least one person in the congregation before him who was listening to these sentences not for himself but to write them down for others. Then one of the friendly gentlemen from the Gestapo in Gneez would turn up, order a coffee as though in a commandeered restaurant, help himself to a cigar as though it had been offered to him, and inquire into the significance of his sermon on Judica Sunday. It was not enough for them that in the Gospel of John, chapter 8, Jesus really did accuse the people of seeking to kill Him because He had told them the truth; they wanted to hear which specific cases of death Brüshaver had had in mind. The fact was, he had half been thinking of Methfessel the butcher, beaten senseless in a camp over a few words, and of the executions in Hamburg he'd read about. He felt uncomfortable excusing himself after the fact by explaining that what was meant was divine truth, not worldly truth, see verses 40–41. He would rather have been brave, stood his ground, but he hadn't yet gotten over not being allowed to open his son's coffin. He had not been permitted to have the body taken to the cemetery in Lalendorf where his first wife lay buried. Then burial was not authorized in Jerichow either, it had to be at the Gneez main cemetery, so that the cortege would be smaller, and in the end not only were there strangers in attendance working for the police but a pastor summoned from Berlin and working for the police too. It did Brüshaver no good to remind them that he had sacrificed his son for the fatherland. Not even his having been an officer in the 1914–1918 war raised him above suspicion. Thus the visits from these gentlemen, the reproaches for his having gone to see Alfred Bienmüller who hadn't wanted to send his son for confirmation. Brüshaver had talked to Bienmüller like someone seeking information, and Bienmüller had politely laid the tongs in the fire and stepped outside of the smithy with him to give his answers. First of all, he didn't have the money. Second, not for that. Third, the boy's Hitler Youth troop had told him he wasn't allowed to. Could Bienmüller have possibly filed a complaint of harassment afterward? Or had Bienmüller told someone about Brüshaver's visit, and someone had overheard, of whose business it was none, and had turned it into a complaint? On the day after Palm Sunday, Bienmüller was working in Creutz's greenhouses and had given a rather perfunctory hello over the pastor's fence but not as if there was any bad blood between them.

The gentlemen had had no compunction about sentencing a pastor, Niemöller, who had been a navy officer and Freikorps paramilitary fighter, voting for the NSDAP in every election since 1924. Brüshaver remembered him well from the days of the Kiel mutiny after the Armistice. On November 30, 1918, Niemöller had pulled into port with the war flag flying. He'd had no intention of letting his ship be handed over to the English. At the time it was forbidden to wear the officer's dagger in public, but Niemöller wanted to defend the honor of the Kaiser's uniform by sticking his dagger between the ribs of anyone who jostled it. Brüshaver had not been on the U-boats, or on a destroyer. But he didn't like that these new gentlemen would sentence a comrade, a Kaiser's officer, to jail. He hadn't agreed with all of Niemöller's statements during the trial. Niemöller's sending Hitler a telegram of congratulations on Germany's exit from the League of Nations did look a bit scheming. He might have taken a different stance on the Aryan question in the church—that he found the Jews alien and distasteful was his own business, not the church's. From Brüshaver's point of view, Arthur Semig had been a member of his congregation, not a Jew. He had given Semig communion as late as 1934; after that, it was Semig who'd stopped coming. Brüshaver could subscribe most honestly to Niemöller's opinion that it was not in accord with the Scripture to replace baptism with a family tree. Jesus Himself had appeared in the form of the Jew Jesus of Nazareth. Right. But unfortunately Niemöller had then spoken of "this embarrassing and serious annoyance" that had to be accepted nonetheless because of the Gospels. Idiotic. What was really embarrassing was his story about going to see the Führer. At the end of the visit, the Führer had shaken his hand and said something. Niemöller had said something too. He thought the Führer and he had understood each other. *Captatio benevolentiae*, on a generous view. But then, on March 2, they had neither set him free nor thrown him back in jail but sent him off to Sachsenhausen concentration camp, and Brüshaver had read out the pulpit declaration: This act was not in accordance with the judgment of the court. It is written that: Justice must prevail, and: Righteousness exalteth a nation, but sin is a reproach to any people. Brüshaver had prepared himself for a visit from the Gestapo and was ready promptly to show the gentlemen where it stood written; that time they didn't come.

Now, for Quasimodogeniti, the Sunday after Easter, it was time for John, chapter 20. He could leave well enough alone with Mary not allowed to touch her son. But there was Thomas, too, who would not believe except that he see and touch the print of the nails in His hands. Writing out the sermon didn't help either. If two people swore it against him, it would be taken as proven that he'd said what he hadn't said.

No ban against suicide in the Bible. He was quite prepared to believe that this Lisbeth Cresspahl had read every word of both testaments of the Holy Scripture from cover to cover. But it was a bit ridiculous, wasn't it, this businessman's daughter, Cresspahl's wife, engaged in theological hairsplitting. To be sure, Samson had pulled down the temple not only over the lords of the Philistines but over himself as well. Abimelech had arranged his own death to avoid the shame of being slain by a woman. Ahithophel and Judas had hanged themselves. See also Acts 16:27; Rev. 9:6. Zimri set his house on fire and died, and this was explained as a consequence of his sins against the Lord.

In short, nine places, which Brüshaver noted down on a slip of paper instead of continuing to work on his sermon for April 24. He fell asleep over his work, and when Aggie came to bring him to bed, after midnight, he had forgotten what he had learned in seminary: that suicide was not wicked in the eyes of man or for moral reasons; it was a falling away from God.

If Lisbeth had heard that there was this fence, she might have not thought to cross over it.

When someone does what he's going to do
Then there's nothing he can do but what he does.

Vigorous lady approaching the end of her 117th year, well-off, dignified appearance, seeks....

The New York Times is looking for sympathy.

It is worth all of page 14 to her, despite the several department stores that would have liked to display there what's available for purchase today until 5 p.m. *The New York Times* has her priorities straight and shows us, on one of her factory floors, a few of the people who work for her: twenty-nine of its seventy-five copy editors, two of them women, sixteen with glasses, eighteen in short sleeves, two or three with beards, all respectfully or cheerfully polite, and no Negro man, no Negro woman among them.

You see here: *The New York Times* says, and we can just hear her surprisingly elastic old-woman voice, can just see the severe jabs of the pointer with which she indicates one face after another in the two crooked rows, the industrious disorder, the tables between the people, the boxes of index cards pulled closer in the back-left corner, the half-blocked fire extinguisher, the ancient TV set, the old-fashioned typewriter, the issue of *The Statesman* in a generous trash can:

You see here a curious assortment of people. Curious not in the funny sense. Nosey. They ask questions. Sometimes they drive reporters crazy with questions. But because they do, they make *The New York Times* just about the most useful newspaper you can read.

So that's who they are. And not only are they all wearing ties, each tie is knotted precisely under the collar button. Their training has been assiduous; they neglect no proper formalities. What kind of questions?

Questions such as: Is this name spelled right? Is that figure correct? Is this the right date? Shouldn't there be a phrase here explaining this fact? Is the meaning of this statement clear? Wasn't someone else involved?

Only the best for *The New York Times*. Such technique, such dramatic flair, what other department can compete? Any other kinds of question?

This kind: These people crouching there on the edges of the tables, daintily or distressed, willingly or hemmed in, they are oftentimes a little batty. Trying to get all the facts sorted out, all the questions answered. They do this because they have the funny idea that they're not copy editors at all. They think that they're us, the readers. They're asking the questions they imagine we'd ask. But they ask them before we even think of them, so that we won't even think of them.

Will these seasoned men, and the two women, be happy to see their employer describe them in public as a little batty? Or that they're portrayed in a frame of mind that "batty" does not even suffice to cover? We'll find out.

Questions such as: When they've got the answers to every question they figure you might ask, and maybe even some sneaky ones they think up themselves, then . . . they write a headline for the story. Then. . . . Questions. Answers. That's what a copy editor's life is all about. No bylines to gloat over. No public glory to bask in. Only an inner satisfaction to soothe the ulcer. The satisfaction that when we've read the story in *The New York Times*, our every question will have been answered.

As Countess Seydlitz says: Auntie Times is sure she knows us.

Do we have any questions?: the *Times* asks.

As a matter of fact we do. Why do they tuck away the fact that, according to the Fulbright Commission's report, the incident in the Gulf of Tonkin was not enough to justify the Vietnam War in its current scope? That the American ships involved had been spying that August 1964, and at least once had violated the territorial waters of North Vietnam? Unlike what the government and Defense Department claim? Why does that get just thirty-one lines buried on a page far from the front one?

That's the wrong question. Any others?

One more. Why do the twenty-two official war dead from today only get a tiny scrap of thirteen lines. Why are eighteen of them not given any names, and only Roland A. Galante from Ridgewood, Queens, Ernest P. Palcic of Staten Island, Peter L. Lovett from the Bronx, and Frederick A. Pine from Trenton appear in the paper for the last time by name. Does someone have to come from the New York metropolitan area for his death in Vietnam to be recorded individually in the most useful newspaper he could have read?

That's not the right way to look at it. Any other questions?

Any questions?

Fit to print?

January 28, 1968 Sunday

John Ramaglia, of 211 N. Sixth St. in Newark, announces via the *Times* that he needs an attorney, in a matter of life or death. His phone is tapped. Then he gives his number: (201) HU5–6291.

In the Jerichow post office, a watch list was pinned up on the sorting cabinet, over the repeated objections of Knever, the senior postal clerk, who had continued to cite the professional honor of a German postal official until Edgar Lichtwark had to hint at removal from service and loss of pension. When Knever gave in, the personnel department punished him with a demotion, and he was no longer deemed worthy even of telephone communications or registered mail—he now had to sit in the back stamping the outgoing mail and checking both it and the incoming mail for the senders' and recipients' names. His official phone calls now consisted solely of reports to the Gneez Gestapo, whenever mail to or from someone under observation turned up. Berthold Knever put up very faint resistance these days. For instance, he listened to Party Comrade Lichtwark with an attentiveness meant to express scorn at having to take orders from someone he saw as a good-for-nothing senior letter carrier from Berlin-Lichtenberg. Knever wrinkled his nose so much that he looked like a parrot with its plumes sticking up, and so received for his pains not the promotion he was five years overdue for but a nickname. Besides, for him it was a matter of principle, professional dignity, he would never withhold any letter due to be submitted for opening out of consideration for the recipient, especially when he felt he was being watched by one of the two apprentices whom he now had to teach how to hold the stamp hammer—loosely, subtly—so that the Jerichow postmark would land right on Hitler's skull. Monitoring the mail was a professional secret, in Knever's eyes, and that was how he brushed off Papenbrock, who was trying to ask him why some letters now took two days to get to Hamburg.

Papenbrock was not on the list. Cresspahl was not on the list. Semig was, as a sender, and only at the instigation of Friedrich Jansen, whom the Gestapo had to reward for his willingness to help. The first letters from Dora had made Jansen's blood boil. This Jew was supposed to go down, and now he and his wife were sitting pretty somewhere in Lower Austria where Jansen would never in his life get to go, even for a vacation. They were living in a castle, permitted to take their meals at a count's table. And the letters betrayed nothing. Not a word thanking Lisbeth Cresspahl for any favors—so once again nothing to prove against the Cresspahls. And Friedrich Jansen would have so loved to know where the Semigs had left their money. He didn't believe they had crossed the border with ten marks each in their respective pockets. They must have owned more than just a house and a stable and a practice! When Jansen tried to occupy the house, he found himself faced with a furniture truck, and the movers showed him documents stamped in Schwerin, according to which that disgustingly clever Jew had signed over the property with all its furnishings and chattel to his wife's parents. Friedrich Jansen had made a rental offer to these up-pity Kösters and received a two-line answer: The house had been rented to the air force, ten-year lease. He couldn't prove that Kollmorgen the lawyer hadn't in fact found a young veterinarian in Erlangen who wanted Semig's equipment. Every opening Jansen thought he found was walled up; he practically felt under surveillance. Dora Semig wrote about deer in the snow, snowy peaks, soil conditions, Alpine streams tossing out "gravel and pebbles," shopping trips to Vienna! Pebbles. And the non-Aryan left it to his wife to send their greetings, so Jansen couldn't even charge the Cress-pahls with associating with Jews. The letter he was waiting to see after March 12, 1938, didn't turn up.

The letter bore a Greater German stamp, under a postmark from Pirna, with the now obsolete added message "Your Vote for the Führer!": not the foreign stamps Knever was required to look out for. It's possible, though, that Knever had deliberately not paid attention this time, since the sender had given her name as Dora née Köster, living on Ad.-Hitler-St., Radebeul. Lisbeth didn't open this letter when it came but left it lying on the table for Cresspahl. He, not she, was to read it aloud, even though it was ad-dressed to her, no longer to the both of them.

It turned out that only the first three weeks with Count Naglinsky had gone well. Then Dora no longer felt safe in the village, and ventured on walks only in the forests that Beatus had barred to outsiders. In the village, Arthur had been given work only twice, then he was recognized as a Jew, and his wife too. "Which is true enough." People had spat on her. "In Austria they smell it." Naglinksy had pretended not to notice, and the evenings with gramophone music and conversations about people such as Galsworthy had become unbearable. In the first week of March, Arthur gave up the position that wasn't one, and Naglinsky, in his relief, gave them their money even though he hadn't yet gotten the equivalent of any of it from Germany (from "Raminsky," which maybe meant from Baron von Rammin—that was just a guess). In Vienna they had lost almost too much time, because "my husband" couldn't make up his mind to go to France and there were dangerous rumors going around about the customs officers at the Swiss border. On March 10 she had finally managed to get him to Bratislava. Arthur had put his faith to the end in the Austrian plebiscite and the Treaty of Saint-Germain. The Czechs had let them into the country, but "in an Austrian way." All the reports from Vienna were true: the enthusiasm about the annexation, the looting of Jewish businesses. The Jews forced to scrub the sidewalks with toothbrushes—there were photographs of that, of course. Prague was a more reasonable city than Vienna, she said. Dora could do sewing jobs for the richer émigrés, Arthur had found a position as an orderly in a veterinary clinic. "We don't need help." The only problem was finding a place to stay; one hotel room after another slipped out of their grasp, maybe because "we are Jews," maybe because they had to save money. Arthur didn't want to learn Czech. The letter was dated the end of March and had taken more than four weeks to get to Jerichow.

Lisbeth spoke of the guilt Dora Semig was trying to saddle her with.

Cresspahl had a talk with Kollmorgen, but even with two pairs of eyes they couldn't find any address hidden in the letter.

The Kösters in Schwerin, both in their late eighties, whatever the letter to them might have said, killed themselves with sleeping pills.

They were cremated by the police, in secret, no witnesses permitted. In Jerichow it was said that the two coffins had been tiny. In years past, Privy Councilor Köster had spent vacations by the sea near Jerichow.

January 29, 1968 Monday

In the Twentieth Precinct, between Sixty-Sixth and Eighty-Sixth Streets on Manhattan's west side, in ten months, residents have reported: 14 murders, 37 rapes, 552 robberies, 447 felonious assaults, 2,200 burglaries, 1,875 grand larcenies, and 371 car thefts. These are false numbers. The true numbers of rapes, burglaries, and assaults are more like two to three times higher, because many victims do not report the crimes to the police, perhaps out of fear, of lack of trust.

Would a foreign visitor coming to see Cresspahl in May 1938 have been able to tell that the country was in the hands of criminals?

Would Mr. Smith have noticed anything?

When Cresspahl thought about the workshop in Richmond, with the elm tree, his mind went back to both England and a time when Lisbeth still took pleasure in her own life and in one with others; he thought too about Mr. Smith, his small taciturn face with sawdust lodged in its rough wrinkles, this thin quick man who got through his days in order to get to his evening's drinking—thought about him if not as a friend then at least as someone he could count on across the Channel, without it going so far as to require Christmas cards or letters. If he decided he wanted Mr. Smith to pay him a visit, it wasn't for any particular reason, just so that someone might see what life was like these days in Jerichow, in Mecklenburg, in Germany. It wouldn't have been for the conversations.

Mr. Smith as a tourist abroad?

Mr. Smith in a dark suit, with a hat on his head instead of a cap, as a subject of His British Royal Majesty, on holiday: he wouldn't have looked poor or out of place. Mr. Smith could keep his gaze as impassive as you'd like, the five-and-dime glasses could have been just a whim. The rough skin on his face, that might be from the sea air. Surrounded by a foreign language he would have been even more close-mouthed than usual, and the customs officers at the Hamburg port would have taken him to be if anything rather dignified. He would have heard in their use of English continued courtesy and respect for his nation. And since Mr. Smith was capable of paying attention to people other than himself, he would have noticed that these officials were treating his German travel companions, who had still been treated as equals on board, rudely and suspiciously, like escaped prisoners turning themselves back in to their wardens and not exactly with a light heart.

Mr. Smith would have said nothing about this in Jerichow; he would more likely have come out with the question: What's all this about dogs? Was it a good idea to travel with a dog in Germany, if you wanted to be met with goodwill and good service? A foreigner, interested in the native customs.

Cresspahl would have said, cheerfully and easily, in response to such an opening remark: *Quite, Mr. Smith. Oh, quite.*

Mr. Smith would nevertheless have suspected a garden path up which Cresspahl too did not wish to lead him and, on the boardwalk in Rande, as well as in Jerichow, would have kept an eye out for passersby with dogs, to see whether they incarnated the kind of German that one could not detect in Cresspahl in England.

Cresspahl did by this point have a dog, but he would have introduced it to Mr. Smith even more passingly than the feline members of the family sleeping in the shavings from the night's work. He would have said: I'm just looking after this dog for someone.

What would Mr. Smith have brought with him for Cresspahl's child? Something to use. Not quite a pocketknife, but a sailor's cap.

The child would have imperceptibly gotten used to him, because he wouldn't have been tiresome with questions or attempts to play games with her, his presence would have been only noticeable as a cautiously observant gaze, quickly hidden away again, as though this foreigner were embarrassed.

Lisbeth would have wanted to hear all about George V's Jubilee procession through the streets of London on June 14, 1935—the outriders in their red livery, the heralds in their yellow uniforms with their trumpet, and finally the king in his red field marshal's uniform, with his graying goatee, raising and lowering his hand in military salute like an overworked machine, busy preparing, in the height of summer and the midst of cheering crowds, for his death. At first Mr. Smith would have taken her detailed questions to mean that Mrs. Cresspahl missed life in London. He would have made an effort to get past her halting English, and so would have failed to notice that in places where she was unsure she occasionally used phrases one can find in the King James Bible.

Cresspahl as tourist guide?

He wouldn't have been allowed to bring Mr. Smith to see the Jerichow-North zone; he could have talked about it. The number of inhabitants in Jerichow had fallen by at least four hundred once the air force construction battalion had withdrawn and the cleaning and straightening up of the construction site had been left to the local workmen. Mr. Smith would have easily deduced from the description of the barracks and the number of buildings meant to house civilian employees the existence of an airfield to be used for more than just meteorological observations. He would not have indicated to his former employer that he preferred Cresspahl's work in England, when he was still handling wood piece by piece instead of, as now, assembling it with powerful machines and a team of assistants; Mr. Smith would have decided to leave earlier than expected.

Mr. Smith would have raised his hand to an SA troop and their flag with the same gesture he saw Cresspahl make, and every time he would have glanced back over his shoulder to see whether everyone was laughing at him for it.

Then again, he would have compared the flag that Cresspahl sometimes hung on the barn door with the one flown outside the villa across the street from the property—a kitchen towel versus a bedsheet.

The evenings with these Cresspahls would definitely have left a sour taste in Mr. Smith's mouth. Some were bearable. On them, Mrs. Cresspahl would have sewing work out at the table, Cresspahl his cold coffee, and there would be more than water for the guest. In May the sun didn't set until after eight, and it stayed light out much longer. The mistress of the house looked more like her thirty-two years in the lamplight than during the day, when she toiled her way through the housework as though driven, knowledgeable and experienced in everything she did, nervous and jumpy when a visit or a delivery came out of sequence. Mr. Smith's initial shock at her appearance would have faded when he saw how the couple treated each other, heard their patient, often teasing tone. In Mr. Smith's presence they would have managed to bring it off once more. Mr. Smith would have grown used to his corner of the kitchen table and would already have been almost safely under way to sleep and to dream, what with the alternating "kümmel" and "Kniesenack," and would have crashed painfully out of this gentle flight when Lisbeth again brought up George V's death in January 1936, at Sandringham, and was suddenly out the door, in tears. Mr. Smith would not have understood that. Then he would have decided to feign fatigue.

Where would Mr. Smith have slept? On the leather sofa in Cresspahl's office, and Cresspahl next to his wife again. There Mr. Smith would have found Marine Sport brand cigarettes and a bottle of schnapps, thoughtfully opened, so that the guest would be all set until well past midnight. Maybe he would have reflected on marine sports, which in this country too were not generally affordable to the average cigarette smoker.

On evenings alone with Cresspahl, when Lisbeth did not reemerge from her room, they would have had conversations. Mr. Smith, in his new amazement at German greeting customs, would have recalled that George VI had been dreadfully shocked when the German ambassador had shot out a hand right under the king's nose. Brickendrop, they called him, because he put his foot in it every time. And George VI had enough problems already, with his stutter. He would have mentioned that there'd been a lot of talk about the persecution of Jews, the jailing of clergy too, but still, it had all remained polite, nothing insulting to the German government. Except for the *Daily Worker*, but that wasn't even sold on newsstands, just by volunteers on street corners. And slanderous movies like *Professor Mamlock* had likewise been banned. And when Ann-Mari, Princess of Bismarck, sent her children swimming in Sandwich wearing bathing suits with unobtrusive swastikas embroidered over the heart, well, self-confidence like that spoke for itself.

And no: Cresspahl would have said. Hopefully Cresspahl would have talked about the seven pastors from Mecklenburg who were in prison or camps in 1938. Hopefully Cresspahl would have said something about the dog still roaming around the yard, confused and lost, unwilling to settle on any fixed place to sleep. This was King, formerly known as Rex when his job was to guard the house and yard of a Jewish veterinarian in Jerichow— a dog who had lost his masters. If only Cresspahl had told the story from the beginning to where, for now, it ended.

But still: Mr. Smith might well have answered: the booming economy.

And no: Cresspahl would have said. He would put the number of skilled manufacturing jobs lost in Germany at over fifty thousand. And with every tradesman now having to pay into a compulsory insurance fund, it seemed that the government wanted to make money from the bankruptcies too. And now you already couldn't get steel frames for your machines anymore, what with rearmament gobbling everything up; Mr. Smith should just try to picture that, a planer on a wood frame.

That yes: Mr. Smith might have answered, stowing away what he'd heard behind his low wrinkle-shrouded brow, showing no sign of whether it was now lost forever or just hidden away. He would have smoothed the graying dark hair on the top of his head with eight fingertips, pushed his cheap glasses up his nose, and gone off to bed without Cresspahl being able to keep him. For Mr. Smith knew how to pass off goodbyes as acts of consideration.

Mr. Smith would not have stayed long in Jerichow. For if it was May 1938 by that time, the Germans would have already marched to the Czechoslovakian frontier, and the ČSR government would have ordered a partial mobilization, and Mr. Smith would have been needed by his company if his government decided to keep its promises to the Czechs and Slovaks.

Mr. Smith would have once again been visible in a window of the second-class car of the milk train, a short, wizened man who removed his hat to reveal a narrow face so impassive that it might have been concealing distress at leaving or maybe relief that the visit was over.

And where would Mr. Smith have gotten the money for a dark suit, a hat, new shoes not scuffed in the least? Who might have paid him?

(It wouldn't have been Mrs. Trowbridge.)

And what aim and purpose might Mr. Smith have been hoping to accomplish in Jerichow? What could he have been thinking?

And yet even he would have seen something.

January 30, 1968 Tuesday

Here we have Mr. Weiszand, Dmitri, who has proposed using first names with us so many times so that he could say: Gesine. – Gesine: he says, planting himself so firmly in the middle of the herd of pedestrians starting across to the south side of Ninety-Sixth Street that it's hard to get around him. – Gesine!: he says, and naturally we would like to take his surprise, his warm smile, for pleasure at seeing us again, but he runs into Mrs. Cresspahl on Broadway quite often, and typically contents himself with three words about the weather and Marie's school. – Gyezinneé: he says, he will never learn how to cloak his Polish-Russian linguistic heritage with an American overcoat, he will hug Mrs. Cresspahl in front of the shopwindows and passersby if he can, one Slav to another, because to him Mecklenburg is Slavic. Better to invite him into Charlie's Good Eats for fifteen minutes, for a coffee and whatever else he has on his mind. Hi, Charlie!

I know, right, Charlie? Such wet weather. Black coffee, from this morning. Call Marie, will you, tell her I'm held up. This is Mr. Weiszand. Professor Weiszand? All right, not professor. And this gentleman in the short-sleeve butcher's apron, with the quick arms, the theologian's face under a severe crew cut, this is the Buckwheat Pancake Champion of New York City, Charles, Charlie himself.

This isn't what Mr. Weiszand is interested in. He clearly considers it more important to tell Mrs. Cresspahl in confidence that she isn't looking too good. Not sick, exactly, but tired, overworked, eyes dull. What a way to start a conversation, Mr. Weiszand!

Lot of work at the office, Mrs. Cresspahl?

You know, it's work.

What kind of work, specifically, it is, is what Mr. Weiszand would now like to know, propping his head so firmly on a supporting hand, looking so faithful, so solicitous, as though he really wants to hear that Employee C. takes the subway for ten minutes from here to Times Square, needs another five to get to Grand Central, and after twelve minutes on foot removes her typewriter cover at just before nine a.m., five days a week too, until five in the afternoon, until this very minute, when she is still unable to go home, Mr. Weiszand. It's an IBM Selectric, with a type ball, if that's what you meant.

It was not.

And why are you growing a beard from ear to ear, Mr. Weiszand?

If Mr. Weiszand is to be believed, it is not because he has lost a bet; the mass of red stubble is sprouting due to worry. So as not to hear more about that, we will give him our job to think about: foreign language correspondent. Well?

German, French, Italian—?

And American, and English, Mr. Weiszand.

He fails to see why a bank would fill such a position. He sips a little of Charlie's black coffee, puts the cup down in bewilderment, adds some sugar, tries it again, puts it down with a shake of the head. He just cannot figure it out.

The coffee?

The bank.

To a French bank Mrs. Cresspahl writes her employer's wishes in French. To an Italian company in—

As a courtesy?

As a service, Mr. Weiszand.

And the psychological gains actually outweigh the personnel costs—?

That is not exactly a professional secret, but the one who knows it is he who receives the benefit, not she who does the work. Ask my boss, Mr. Weiszand.

Vice President de Rosny. Mr. Weiszand brings this out casually, to keep the interrogation rolling, not realizing that he has betrayed having known something.

Not de Rosny. A vice president and a secretary! No, the department heads for Italy and France, less often for West Germany. Most of them there speak American English pretty well by now.

And there's no one to check Mrs. Cresspahl's formulations?

There was, Miss Gwendolyn Bates, Vassar class of 1918, saved from the Depression and the marriage market by the bank, so devoted to the bank that she made work for herself when there wasn't any. Liked to call the translators into her office and draw lines with a long pencil and a raised wrist through the French that had not been spoken like that in her day, not maliciously, just domineering, out of sadness. Then one day at a meeting in Bern she insisted on one of her formulations too stubbornly, all in the firm's best interests of course, and for her retirement got the President's Medal in silver, no banquet. Lives with relatives in Colorado now, writing proud letters steeped in longing. She still hasn't realized we can get by without her, just as they always managed to do in the Scandinavia and Spain departments. If you ever go to Denver, Mr. Weiszand, take Route 25 toward Pueblo, turn left at Greenland—

Nor is this what Mr. Weiszand is after. Doesn't Mrs. Cresspahl speak Russian, too?

Ah, Mr. Weiszand. Six years of Russian in school, and not a single Russian in the whole town we were allowed to talk to. They were housed behind high green fences, the officers didn't take public transportation, and when a private climbed over the slats looking for just a bottle of booze—

Mr. Weiszand knows that. Whenever some fact can be understood or misunderstood as anti-Communist, he forestalls it with a short, snippy nod, pretending agreement and administering a reprimand. And does he want to hear yet again that this New York bank is not eager to do business with the Soviet banks in Europe, but would rather wait until they come to it, whether Vokshod in Zurich, the Moscow Narodny in London, or the Banque Commerciale pour l'Europe du Nord in Paris? The firm's policy in this regard is to be understood as not aggressive, I repeat: not aggressive.

But surely with respect to Czechoslovakia. Mr. Weiszand sits leaning as comfortably as before, his gaze pleasant, childlike, face shining with goodwill, openness, warmth. He has heard that Mrs. Cresspahl is taking Czech classes with Kreslil, from our Mrs. Ferwalter, oh perfectly innocently, nothing makes him bring it up but sympathy, an interest in the truth, the privilege of friends.

I'm just taking a private trip to Prague this summer, Mr. Weiszand.

Mr. Weiszand finds that exceedingly thorough, to learn a whole new language just for a vacation. Even now intrusiveness can't be proven against him; only, his eyes have become a shade more attentive, almost triumphant.

If you were not allowed back into your own country, and you had to meet your friends in a foreign one, and wanted to know what was going on around you for those three weeks, what would you do, Mr. Weiszand?

Mr. Weiszand would learn any language in the world if he could get a friend out of Poland with it. All the same he is taken aback, his guard is down for a moment. The solicitous look has slipped off his face, like someone caught lying, and he needs a little while to reapply it, with a nodding motion, a deep breath, an expression of admiration. He finds it wonderful.

This not said out loud.

Mr. Weiszand says he understands completely, wants no less than a handshake, loses himself in compliments in his embarrassment, says he was mistaken, Mrs. Cresspahl in fact looks radiant this evening.—Gyezinneé: he says.

Here we have Mrs. Cresspahl, tired, with no desire to work, eyes dull, half deaf in the middle of the long-winded detailed conversation between Charlie and his customers, cheerful broad-shouldered men chowing down as thoroughly as if they had just gotten out of bed and were starting their day. The voluptuous skill with which Charlie flips his steaks and burgers on the charcoal grill, the spicy smell of the meat, the cozy warmth—it all feels very far away. The next five minutes are almost unbearable, until Mr. Weiszand steps forth on Broadway into the wet twilight, alone, in his gorgeous trench coat of British manufacture, his high bare brow raised, brooding and annoyed, on his way to his sociological studies, not those of international finance, a man of emotional greetings and farewells, a friend who has become unrecognizable.

– What did Dmitri want: Marie asks. She had waited in the pool under the Hotel Marseilles, disguised in her tight white swim cap.

– Not to have a coffee alone.

– Has he found more Nazis in West Germany?

– No. This time it was that thirteen cents of every dollar in the federal budget are spent on education and social services but fourteen on the war in Vietnam and forty-three on defense.

– He'll be having another demonstration at Columbia soon: Marie says, taking her key off her wrist, throwing it into the pool, and diving after it in one smooth forgetful motion.

We're sorry, Mrs. Cresspahl.
I don't care about finesse.
But we do, Gesine. We wouldn't have started off like that.
And what if I'm wrong?
Well then you're wrong, Gesine.

January 31, 1968 Wednesday

The New York Times portrays Senator J. W. Fulbright as a serious, thoughtful man, who knows what he's asking. Now he wants to call Secretary of Defense McNamara before the Senate Foreign Relations Committee, too, to ask him: whether the destroyers in the Gulf of Tonkin three and a half years ago weren't attacked by North Vietnamese ships, if indeed they were at all, because they were crossing in and out of foreign waters on a spy mission. He does not want to get any answer other than that the war could have been avoided then, the war in which today American troops have to attack their own embassy in Saigon because it has been occupied by the Viet Cong.

Friedrich Jansen, upon the theft of the Sudetenland, called his Führer a statesman of true distinction, and Cresspahl agreed with him.

My father wasn't joking. He only pulled the legs of people who would not only notice but also not mind, so they could share in the fun. There would be no point with this regional party leader and mayor, and, moreover, Cresspahl had no desire to show or put himself in such a position. By then, 1938, Friedrich Jansen had been the mayor of Jerichow for five years and Cresspahl had had quite a good look at who he was dealing with. He would have described him as a pig. Not in the derogatory sense of the German word *Schwein* but based on personal appearance. There was his pinkish height, with whitish hair on top too; the heavy thighs, not sturdy but flabby; the massive arms, impressive at first sight and soft at second; and the delicate quivering fat on his whole body collected over thirty-six years without proper labor. But that wasn't enough to make Cresspahl call him a *Schwein*, and maybe he didn't want to waste a Mecklenburgish word on him. He called him by his full name, with a certain seriousness. That was a bigger insult for the representative of Hitler's party, and less costly.

The misuse of this animal's name common in German would have not fit Party Comrade Jansen badly at all, even if Cresspahl considered only what he personally had to endure and expect from him. There was the goatskin leather notebook Jansen liked to brag about so much that he sometimes flipped through it while out boozing with his buddies; the notes in the section for the letter C had already devoured half of the D section, even though there was only one other last name in Jerichow with the same initial as the Cresspahls'. There were the eager reports to the Gestapo headquarters in Gneez, about which Cresspahl learned not only from requests for further information but also from warnings. There was Jansen's speech on May 1, 1938, about how Jerichow needed to be cleansed of not only the Jews but also their friends. There were the sanctimonious inquiries into the application for party membership that Cresspahl had requested for an apprentice three years back, and yet still not for himself. There was nothing you could call enmity, only petty little underhanded efforts to trip him up for their own sake, and there were times when Cresspahl was glad he was a head shorter than Jansen. That way he didn't have to look him in his shifty eyes, pious like a lamb; he could look away from that broad, shapeless, pleasantly blood-reddened face, and at least have the man's pompous jovial behavior in only his ears. Cresspahl never even stopped to wonder why he found this guy so repellent.

He did not even give Friedrich Jansen credit for openly proclaiming his beliefs with full force and feeling; Cresspahl regarded that as mere life insurance. If Jansen ever reached the point when he had little to eat for a week and nothing to drink, had to work perhaps with a shovel, his back bent, it would finish him off in a hurry. Now whether or not Jansen suspected that in 1933 he'd been saved from a life of starvation wages or in a house of correction by the skin of his teeth, by this point he could no longer wean himself off his new life of breakfast at almost noon, office hours as he pleased, drives around town, and nights of drinking. He had been unable to put what he learned in civic office to use either. He had no idea how the various parts of the city fit together, how much of its tax

revenue it could recoup from the regional authorities and district administration, how much he'd have been able to get out of the Jerichow airfield
construction if he'd had a plan in place. The mayor's office was run by the
civil servants Dr. Erdamer had trained, and for the time being it worked
out fine for Friedrich Jansen, whose idea was that buddies in a few key
positions were enough and all the rest would take care of itself. So far it
had. And Cresspahl was sure that the fat lump was scared of the war he so
often carried on about. When he came back from voluntary defense exercises, during which he couldn't simply relax near the front but had to
clamber up walls in person, in heavy cumbersome person, he was so nice
to people for a few days that it was like he was asking for pity. It had gone
that badly for him. There was only one military matter he understood:
When he was in the Gneez Woods teaching his Storm Troopers how to
scout a terrain, he could plant himself with feet apart and say that this was
precisely one meter. I saw him like that myself, legs apart, rear end awkwardly sticking out, leaning forward from the hips, while a subordinate
measured the distance between his brown boots with a ruler. It was incon-
trovertibly exactly one meter, and Jansen could raise his crimson-flushed
head up high again.

Lisbeth said: Friedrich, as if speaking of a child who never learns and
is always getting in a mess; or sometimes: Friederich, after the incurably
horrid character in *Struwwelpeter*. The lines about the brute—"That Friederich! that Friederich! A naughty, wicked brute was he!"—were ones the
Cresspahl child knew by heart, although she wasn't afraid of him. When
Lisbeth recited them, she meant a kid who gave himself airs but none of
whose threats and wriggling came to anything.

When the Semigs left the country, Friedrich Jansen had wanted to buy
the dog the Jews used to keep in their yard. There he stood, outside Cresspahl's gate, sweating in the brisk sea wind, innocent as can be. When he
refused to accept that Cresspahl was looking after the dog, Cresspahl
whistled for King. Out he came running from behind the house across the
yard, he took his place next to Cresspahl and looked up at him, not yet
blindly devoted but friendly and obedient enough. He was six years old,
his whole body taut, fast and strong, with nice shiny white teeth. – Well
now, Rex?: Jansen said from the other side of the fence, all but squeaking
with bonhomie. The dog opened his mouth just enough to let a warning

growl escape and kept a close eye on this stranger. – Rex!: Jansen said re-proachfully, and again his voice was too high, the vowel frying. Since Cresspahl didn't move, the dog snarled again in his booming bass but stayed sitting. Now more than ever Jansen wanted to own this deviant dog, who had betrayed the Aryan race to the Jews, and Cresspahl had to sell him sooner than the child would have liked to an engineer in Berlin who had also taken a liking to him. After the dog was long since safely away and living in a garden in Grunewald, Jansen came by again and demanded to at least see his pedigree, and Cresspahl told him again that he had only been looking after the dog. So many different questions raced into Jansen's head at once that all he could manage to say was: I thought—

He didn't want to start cursing outright. By that point he was Cresspahl's neighbor. He had no more acquired the Jew's house than he had the Jew's dog; he'd had to spend five years renting Dr. Erdamer's house on the Rande road and now he was finally living in the brickworks villa, one of the most desirable addresses in town, because it had been built by a Schwerin banker as nothing but a residence, before the turn of the century—a spacious building, not at all blocky, with generous windows, high garden gates, an immaculate brick roof, in a watertight white oilskin. In front Friedrich Jansen now flew the flag with the Hindu symbol of good luck. With the villa came the brickworks, and the von Zelcks had given up possession only so they could reunite a feuding group of heirs under a single roof of cold hard cash. That was what they said. In the years since Paepcke's lease, orders had declined since by that point almost every building in the area that the Greater German Reich needed for the war had its high brick walls, and the rest of the construction was due to be done in concrete. This they did not tell Friedrich Jansen. As for the villa, Jansen gained possession of not much more than the bill of sale, the mortgages took up so much room, and to acquire the brickworks he'd had to go in together with various party comrades, for as much he would have liked to use his office to pocket a fortune he wasn't clever enough. Now he sat up late at night over the numbers his trustee extracted from the books, and he found them depress-ing and thought anxiously about his party friends. In 1933 Jansen Senior, a lawyer in Gneez, had accepted Friedrich's contempt over his mistrust of the new regime and suchlike sonly rigidities, and now he refused to speak to the regional party leader in Jerichow, never mind answer any appeal for help. But a party at the height of the summer harvest, with festive lights and crowded picnic tables on the respectable lawn, with singing and shooting contests and toasts until after midnight, there had to be one of those. The von Bobziens (the same ones who refused to let the SA use their Countess Woods for maneuvers) owned a breeding bull by the name of Frederick the Great: Friedrich der Grosse. That was how he appeared in the official stud-book list, and since the regional breeding office hadn't objected to the name, Friedrich the Jansen couldn't either. The Bobziens liked showing him off even to guests who hadn't brought a cow in heat at the end of a rope. It was a huge beast, lazy, spiteful, with a kind of stupid look in its eyes. "That's how bulls are." The sense of the German word *Bullen* that I learned just before Christmas as the English word *pigs*.

This Jansen remembered the two film reviews he had been permitted to submit during his student years, just as a test, and he spoke of "brilliant direction" as he listed off the stages of the Czech crisis in his fussy high-pitched voice. For him, the Henlein putsch of September 12 was more "Nordic cunning." He had repeated his leaders' phrases so often that he no longer thought about them and sometimes forgot a previous sentence by the time he got to the next one. He would try to fill up the resulting pauses with quick question debris: "Hmm? Well?" In Jansen's view, Hitler's September 26 speech in the Sportpalast was "genius" and other similarly adolescent words—precisely because it announced that he would soon break his word. For if "the Führer" wasn't thinking about territorial demands, then why did he talk about them, even if to deny making them? – The world has been warned: Friedrich Jansen said darkly. He had caught up to Cresspahl on Brickworks Road and circled around him at once to keep him from walking away. He sounded scared sometimes, as though he himself were in danger if his listener refused to believe him. A tall pink fellow swinging his arms; an awkward dancer. So it was no loss that the Poles had been allowed to occupy the Teschen area and the strip of Slovakian borderlands from the Sudetenland haul, you had to chalk it up as a gain, psychologically speaking. Use a sprat to catch a mackerel. At this point Cresspahl looked at him. He came across like a drunken child, but his breath didn't smell of liquor. By signing the Munich Agreement on September 29, the British had made themselves look foolish to all parties (a complete disgrace, to be honest). Cresspahl nodded again, several times, sincerely, and Jansen started to think that maybe he'd been wrong about this guy. Maybe there were special reasons the air force had for protecting him all the time. It was on the evening of October 1, when Hitler's troops had marched into Czechoslovakia and Jansen was delightedly holding forth about the haul of forty thousand square kilometers, that's four million hectares! four hundred million ares! Convert *that* to English measures, Cresspahl! All the border fortifications! A third of all the businesses! It was at this point that Jansen proclaimed his commander a statesman of true distinction, and for Cresspahl that was someone he had no connection with, who robbed him blind, who never thought of his gain but always the good of the state, a sheer enemy. And so he said, to Friedrich Jansen's delight: No one can deny that, even if they wanted to.

Then he walked on, turned around after a few steps, and already he had Jansen at the point where Jansen would not only reemerge from his front yard but literally come running after him. Cresspahl had one more question, a philosophical one. Included with the territorial gains were human beings, yes?, upward of five million of them? Jansen spoke of a liberated borderland people and suchlike, at great length, even though he was already on his way to his hair of the dog. Cresspahl wouldn't let himself be put off. There were other countries with German-speaking citizens, no?, what about Brazil? or Switzerland? How were they to become part of Greater Germany.

– Switzerland: Friedrich Jansen said: We've got our eye on that too!

February 1, 1968 Thursday

Yesterday, Mrs. Anne Deirdre Curtis, a slender young woman, five foot one, was seen by a neighbor at around four p.m. when she was coming home from shopping with her thirteen-week-old baby. When her husband, a twenty-seven-year-old medical student, returned to their apartment at 297 Lenox Road in Brooklyn at five thirty, he found his wife sprawled across the bed, covered in blood and clad only in a blouse and bra. The towel she'd been strangled with was wrapped around her neck. Her wrists bore marks indicating that she'd been tied up. Bits of broken glass and a broken clock lay scattered around the body. This suggested to the police that Mrs. Curtis had put up a struggle before being raped and killed. The baby was lying unharmed in his carriage. The bag of groceries was in the baby carriage too.

February 2, 1968 Friday Groundhog Day

The day that the Mecklenburg *Fox and Hare Almanac* called Candlemas. The almanac said: In Candlemas week if the badger sees sun / He'll go back to his hole for the four weeks to come. Here they have the *Waldmurmeltier* or *Erdferkel*, a *groundhog*, and if he comes out in Punxsutawney or Quarryville and sees his shadow and retreats back into hibernation then winter will last another six weeks; if he doesn't see his shadow, spring is coming. What we have here, though, is fog and steady rain, and the doorman comes out onto West End Avenue under the baldachin of an umbrella.

Plenty of new arrivals to the Hotel Marseilles must be shocked when they get to the elevator and it takes them and their suitcases down to the basement, not up to their rooms, merely because one of the passengers is someone the man at the lever wants to drop off first, and to whom moreover he says goodbye in a well-practiced manner. He calls her Mrs. Cresspahl, he mentions a child in the water, and only then does he shut the door and the scissor gate and start the journey up to the floors above ground level.

A dry hallway carpeted in green felt leads from the window of the Mediterranean Swimming Club past magnificently varnished benches to the "Women's Area." The door shuts tight, and behind it damp air sheathes the bather like a second skin. A lot of noise is trapped in here—the sound of flowing and swashing water, children's screams from the pool, casual conversations between cabins, the murmuring behind the hot walls of the sauna. Was it like this in Germany too? Did they walk around naked in the changing room, so uninhibited—schoolgirls, matrons, old women— eyeing one another at leisure under the spattering showers, with occasional compliments for a bosom or sympathy for a scar still red from an operation? The memory is gone. Forgotten. How was it then?

– Whatever you don't know you'll leave out, and I won't know the difference: Marie says quietly. She is squatting on the stone bench under the clock, knees pulled up under her chin, pleasantly tired and so a bit preoc-

cupied. She's already been swimming for half an hour. Still, she keeps slipping out of her crouch into a run-up and a lizard-like dive from the edge of the pool whenever a lane is free for eight yards in front of her; she turns around when she surfaces and keeps the lane free for her mother to dive. She comes right back to the bench, and every time the conversation continues as if there'd been no interruption. The bench is safely out of earshot of the other swimmers, and Marie deigns to speak German.
– Whatever you don't know when you're telling the story you fill in with other stuff, and I believe it: she says.

– I never promised the truth.

– Of course not. Only your truth.

– How I think it was.

– Come on, Gesine, there are some things you know.

– Friedrich Jansen's leg-span meter. But I don't know why my memory preserved that. Why not another view of him, or a more meaningful conversation?

– Memory the Cat, as you put it.

– Right. Independent, incorruptible, intractable. And yet a pleasant and beneficent companion, when it does show its face, even if it stays out of reach.

– In September 1938 you were . . . five and a half.

– And by the time I was eighteen I'd forgotten things I never wanted to lose and kept things I don't need. How Cresspahl used to clear his throat, and not what he said.

– Doesn't what Cresspahl did in 1951 have to fit the Cresspahl from 1938?

– More or less, Marie.

– Who knows that better than you?

– Let's go in the pool.

– I don't mind that the only thing you know for sure is how Friedrich Jansen stood in the Gneez Woods, and that the rest of the story grew up around that later. I just want to know how you're putting it together.

– Even though Jansen's story is only possible?

– It's the possibility that no one but you can get to. Whatever you think about your own past, that's a truth too.

– You're the one setting the assignment here, Marie.

– *Right.* How do you do it?

– Water butt—

– Murder attempt.

– Rex the dog, and what Cresspahl said about Dr. Semig after the war—

– The Semigs' emigration.

– Books, you know.

– Old movies. The exhibit at the Jewish Museum.

– Letters from Kliefoth.

– Yes. But are you stealing things from this year too?

– No.

– The rain in January 1968, you didn't use that. All the fires in Harlem—

– If I need a burning building for 1938, I don't need to go looking for one in New York, Marie.

– But the plane with the H-bomb that the air force lost eleven days ago, near Greenland? That same day, you told me about the plane crashes near Podejuch, the gigantic craters.

– That was a family story, Marie. It got locked into place after the rocket testing in Peenemünde, later.

– But the way Cresspahl's child pulled herself around the kitchen table with her arms up, hand over hand, until she learned to walk—you got that from a different child.

– From a child I know personally, and quite well.

– What else from now?

– Things I couldn't see then. Things I didn't learn and have to make up for. Take today's pictures from Saigon in *The New York Times*—

– Don't start that again!

– Don't worry, I'm not trying to pester you with the war. I'm just trying to answer you.

– Which pictures? The one of the officer carrying out of the building his child who's been shot?

– No. The series.

– The shooting.

– (The murder. I don't want to argue about it.) I mean the three-part event. In the first picture, a marine is marching a young man somewhere. The man's hands are behind his back, maybe tied. He looks like someone out enjoying himself, because of his checked shirt, and because he's wearing it untucked. His mouth is open, as though talking earnestly, but not angrily, to the soldier who has his face turned toward him in a friendly way, even if it's in the shadow of his helmet. The American seems to be leading him by the arm, not forcing him anywhere. The caption says this is a Vietcong officer, and he'd been carrying a pistol when captured. Part One.

– Two.

– Title: "Execution." On the left stands a man seen in profile from behind, wearing an obviously non-civilian vest, sleeves rolled up. This is Brigadier General Nguyen Ngoc Loan, South Vietnam's national police chief, and he is holding his right arm out with a revolver a hand's-breadth away from the prisoner's head. The prisoner is still standing, but his head is rather sharply tilted toward his left shoulder, eyes half shut, mouth gaping like a wound. Otherwise the head seems intact. Hands behind his back, surely they're tied. "The prisoner's face shows the impact of the bullet." That's Part Two.

– Three.

– The victim is lying in the street, his bare legs at unnatural angles. The brigadier general is holding the holster on his waistband open with his left hand, putting the gun away with his right, looking not at the dead man but down in front of him, as if mentally reviewing what he's done. In the background are storefronts and, unexpectedly, a man in an American uniform, wearing sunglasses, stopped mid-stride and turning slightly but not as though he wanted to interfere. After all, the man had been handed over to the brigadier general.

– I know, Gesine, I know that already.

– No. I've never seen anyone being shot. The second picture shows the moment of the prisoner's death.

– So now if someone gets shot in your story, you don't have to describe it to me, Gesine.

– There are other ways it can go, Marie.

– But if you have someone in your story get shot, I'll know what you're thinking about and I'll think about it too. Is that what you wanted?

– Partly.

– Okay. Now will you show me the dolphin dive again?

– Now I'll show you a dolphin dive again.

> *February 3, 1968 Saturday, South Ferry day*

– What did Cresspahl look like in September 1938?

 – Fifty years old. One meter ninety centimeters tall. (Six foot two.)
Erect posture when seen from afar, slumped shoulders when seen from up
close—from work or dejection. Longish face, a full head of hair: coarse,
stone-gray, curly. His face when he's not talking: so impassive that the
impression of attentiveness can cover any other expression. When talking,
when working: attending to the matter at hand, severe, searching, sharp.
Eye color: light blue to gray to green. Lips no longer slightly protruding as
in the early thirties, now pressed tight, making them look thinner. Deep,
jagged wrinkles at both corners of his mouth. Expression of the mouth:
no more hopes and expectations, only vigilance and slight disgust. But
unsuspecting. Clothes: usually blue work overalls, clogs in the workshop.
These used to be called the best years of a man's life.

 – Gesine, I mean what he looked like!

> *February 4, 1968 Sunday*

Senator Fulbright's committee has now discovered that the destroyer *Maddox* was encountering technical difficulties with its sonar, too, before it
reported a torpedo attack and gave the government a reason to escalate the
war against North Vietnam. In the new offensive, 376 Americans and
14,997 of their foes have died so far; 4,156 people have been detained as
suspected Vietcong. The soldier who delivered a victim to Brigadier General Nguyen Ngoc Loan was incorrectly identified as an American; he was
in fact a soldier of the ARVN. The dead man is famous, and his name is
not known.

 On October 15, 1938, a Saturday, Herbie Schäning, Jerichow's mailman,
brought the Cresspahls the *Lübeck Gazette* (Lübeck Advertisements, Lübeck's Latest News & Business Daily, Local Paper for the Hanseatic City
of Lübeck and Western Mecklenburg), volume 57, number 242, 15 pfennigs
on weekdays, 20 on Sundays, subscriptions 1.90 marks per month plus 30
pfennig delivery fee. And also a death notice, postmarked Bad Schwartau.

 Lisbeth would have been glad to go along to the funeral, even though
it was to take place on Tuesday, in the middle of the work week, and the

household could hardly spare Cresspahl. She was so animated, talking about the black dress Aggie Brüshaver would lend her and an old pair of stockings that was good for nothing but dyeing black—to Cresspahl it seemed like excitement. Then she saw in the printed matter accompanying the notice that it was not going to be a church ceremony, and she put the notice next to Cresspahl's cup. – Oh: she said, as though she should have known that this too would defeat her wishes, never mind the lost time. But Cresspahl could see that she was disappointed. She had taken to giving off a kind of sigh that came out very high-pitched, like her breath was being squeezed out. Secretly he was relieved. He hadn't known quite what to tell her about who exactly this deceased Anna Niederdahl was. He could only guess. Erwin Plath's name was on the envelope as the sender, but he lived in Lübeck, not Bad Schwartau.

– These Englishmen are utter scoundrels!: he said, for there was an article saying that the London *Times* had come out strongly against the proposition that the newly drawn northern border of Czechoslovakia far exceeded the terms laid down in the Munich Agreement, and to Germany's benefit; and Lisbeth said, not in an I-told-you-so way, but satisfied: *Y'see, Heinrich?*

In the paper, which flew into the woodbox next to the stove, there was also talk of two traitors, from Trier and Ratibor, who'd been hanged in Berlin. One was supposed to have been a "dangerous spy." Sold himself to a foreign intelligence service.

Then came Sunday with its morning haze and fog, steady winds, and during the sunny afternoon the Hitler Youth was collecting money for the Winter Relief Program, and got from Papenbrock not the five-mark coin from earlier days but a single penny, and Franco's troops bombed the Tarragona train station, and talk returned again and again to the mysterious dead woman retrieved from Preetzer Lake—who she might be, why the newspaper didn't mention her—and on Monday she was mentioned in the paper after all; *y'see, Heinrich?*

On Tuesday morning, Cresspahl walked down Town Street carrying the wreath old Creutz had had to make for him, medium-sized, nothing too extravagant, and between the wreath and the suit and black coat he was wearing no one stopped him, especially with little Gesine walking at his side holding his free hand, a subdued child in wooden clogs who remained on the platform long after the train had moved off behind the brickworks. Now the child wished she were standing at the crossing gates, so she could see her father one more time.

Come to me when you get back?
Even if midnight's hour has struck?
You needn't bring anything with, but come?
I'll come, Gesine, I'll come.

Anna Niederdahl was the old woman whose parlor Cresspahl had spent an afternoon waiting in a few years back. In death she looked more severe than the friendly fussy person who'd scolded him in a worried, solicitous way when he tried to leave, and because she'd reminded him of Berta Cresspahl he'd taken her by the shoulders, which didn't entirely displease her. Now she lay there displeased, chin stuck up high, making her look stubborn. Cresspahl did not go outside to wait for the others; he took a seat near the open coffin.

The mourners gathered around the grave were busy with matters other than what the occasion seemed to demand. Five men and a woman in obviously borrowed mourning clothes who seemed to be the only relative—around forty, tired, and even more exhausted by the night trip from Breslau. Cresspahl didn't know her. Of the others, he knew only Erwin Plath. The eulogist, a retired schoolteacher who handled such tasks professionally, tried to tell the story of Anna Niederdahl's life. A fisherman's daughter from Niendorf. A fisherman's wife in Niendorf. Husband discharged from the navy, crippled, supporting his wife with a vegetable garden in Lübeck. One son who remained at sea, one daughter gone missing in Hamburg, the other daughter exposed "to the persecutions of fate." At this the woman from Breslau raised her head with a look of outrage, and as soon as the hired speaker had gotten through the first sentence about immortality Erwin Plath stepped forward. When Lisbeth had wanted to come along, maybe what she was looking forward to were the two minutes during which the guests looked down on the coffin in silence. Then Erwin said, lightly, conversationally: *Auntie Anna. We wont forget. Not you and not what you did. We want to thank you, Auntie Anna.*

Now the woman from Breslau was crying. She clung to Cresspahl's arm as she stepped to the graveside and threw her three handfuls of sand at Anna Niederdahl's foot end. Then Cresspahl pulled off his glove and grabbed the moist dirt and thanked the dead woman for an afternoon and a plaice cooked in very little butter.

The gravedigger didn't mind letting the mourners shovel the dirt into the grave themselves—he'd already gotten his money. Only after they'd all left did he realize that they hadn't been very careful with the Niederdahl husband's mound. The boxwood border had been thoroughly trampled.

The wake was to take place at Plath's house, since the dead woman's two rooms had already been emptied out. But the house was full of men in dark suits, at least eight of whom hadn't been at the cemetery, while the woman from Breslau was not at the table. The meat and beer and schnapps that Gerda Plath served was consumed very slowly indeed. The meal seemed more like an obligation. Out of the eight people who'd been waiting here, Cresspahl knew two. He'd met them five-and-a-half years before, in an apartment on Kronsforder Allee. The man who had led the discussion back then, staggering under the blow of unconditional demands, was not here: the Nazis had beaten in his bald skull in Fuhlsbüttel concentration camp. The man in charge today was a reckless youngster, barely over twenty, who knew how to be implacable and amusing at the same time. Every now and then he ran his hand over his short hair, as though there used to be an unruly sandy mane there to push back out of his eyes. He knew Plattdeutsch and his High German had a Danish accent. They were discussing whether to support the Social Democratic Emigration Committee, which had moved from Prague to Paris early that summer. The Stockholm group insisted that now was the time for unified action with the Communists. The Paris executive committee had rejected their proposal again in August, and yet again in September. Then it was time to read their September 14 appeal "to the German people." Cresspahl listened, but paid more attention to the behavior of the people in the meeting—they were all in agreement, they were practically friendly. He felt at home here.

– We as comrades: someone said in the discussion, and caught Cresspahl's eye. – Yes well not you: the speaker said: You not as a comrade, you as Cresspahl!—and it felt right to Cresspahl that his dispute with the party was acknowledged but had been downgraded from something harmful to something you could bring up almost jokingly. The way these things are brought up among friends. Cresspahl helped himself to a beer after all, even though it was only late afternoon.

The group decided to give its agreement to the Paris committee, reject cooperation with the Communists, and await the downfall of the Hitler regime only after a war and the help of the Western powers. Cresspahl kept his hand down, since he had turned in his party membership book, and they said: *Hinrich now cmon.*

When it was his turn, they first listened to what he had to say about Jerichow-North and the airfield. It meant the war he'd been predicting since 1935; and yet he couldn't get rid of a slight sense of unease, maybe because they had counted his vote with the others'. He offered money without hesitation. They asked him whether it was possible to take people in, and he indicated with his finger on the tablecloth how his property was located next to the brickworks and across the street from Friedrich Jansen's place of work and residence. So that wouldn't work. Would he be willing to travel to Denmark? Cresspahl was more than willing to travel to Denmark. In that case he needed to break off contact with Peter Wulff, preferably via a loud argument with witnesses present, and Bienmüller had to get what he needed. Through it all Cresspahl was relaxed, even cracking jokes, and the others decided that marrying rich Papenbrock's daughter hadn't done him any harm after all. On the contrary. There was something cheerful and friendly about the man now, thanks to her. You could see it in his face.

Before the mourning party went their separate ways that evening, in small groups, only a few of them out Erwin Plath's door and the rest through the courtyard and the other buildings' exits, the woman from Breslau came in once more, and the gathering thanked her for lending them the death of her mother.

Cresspahl had promised the child to come look in on her in bed. But he spent the night in Lübeck and was back in Jerichow only the next morning. The tracing paper he'd brought with him as a present was not enough to console her.

February 5, 1968 Monday

Once, when the city lay covered in snow, de Rosny was showing two Western European visitors around two floors of the bank and stopped outside

Employee Cresspahl's office, and said: All we need now are a couple of wolves and it'll be just like your homeland!

Employee Cresspahl had stayed sitting, since she was only being shown to the visitors, not introduced, and she'd made up some lie about foxes and the henhouses way out in Beidendorf, and was amused all the way until lunchtime by the ideas a vice president had about Communist countries in general, and about Mecklenburg in general.

Today he offered Employee Cresspahl his sympathy because he'd seen a photograph of West Ninety-Seventh St. in yesterday's paper: full garbage cans and mounds of garbage bags piled on top, the result of the sanitation workers' strike. He doesn't know that in our neighborhood, alongside the neglected buildings, there still remain ones whose management takes care of the trash disposal; he is driven into the city on cordoned-off highways and knows at most an eighth of it. This exhilarating skepticism about a senior superior's omniscience, however great a relief it may be in private, must not be expressed or revealed, of course. Employee Cresspahl has been summoned to give a report.

In de Rosny's office you feel like you're in an apartment building, not above hangars of typewriters surrounded by closely set work spaces where people are shut in with their tasks. For himself, de Rosny has furnished a salon in the bank: Scandinavian sofa next to captain's desk from the age of sailing ships, intimate lighting from gold-and-green lamps, heavy royal-blue curtains with a patio outside. De Rosny moves among these things like a hotel guest, lounging around in a basically alien environment, on call, alert, with unshakable faith in his own orders. He likes to mask his orders, even if only behind a delicate hesitation. His lined, weather-beaten face relaxed and comfortable, his blue-eyed gaze kept lazy: this is how he performs invitation and welcome, discussing not only the effects of the sanitation workers' strike on the Upper West Side but also the war in Vietnam, to make his subordinate think he has taken an interest in what he regards as one of her quirks.

On TV de Rosny saw Brigadier General Nguyen Ngoc Loan shoot a suspect whose hands were tied and now he declares himself won over to Mrs. Cresspahl's view. (Mrs. Cresspahl has not expressed a view.) The fundamental brutality of war. And when you could see for yourself what the Vietcong were doing, right there on screen: de Rosny says: and hear

Washington calling their offensive a failure, it hardly narrows the credibility gap.

Definitely, Mr. de Rosny. That's just what *The New York Times* says, in a TV review. Now about my assigned duties—

At the end of the day, the *Times* is actually against continuing the war: de Rosny says. He is not inclined to give up a topic of conversation once he's settled on it; he lingers for some time over his disbelieving headshake, and anyone wishing to venture a guess might conclude that he was deciding Employee Cresspahl really was concerned with the events in Vietnam. Enough to find a similar remark on the second-to-last page of seventy, by morning. Now what was Mrs. Cresspahl about to say?

In regard to the ČSSR, it seems that at least the tail of the cat is out of the bag: someone by the name of Dmitri Weiszand may have been trying to catch that cat, Mr. Vice President.

– Aha: de Rosny said, with relish, as though gratified by a plan that had worked. All of a sudden he was no longer the suave host but a hunter, eyes narrowed, selecting his next snare with cunning furrows of brow. – Thank you: he said earnestly, and then said it again, with something like emotion, but he remained lost in thought, massaging his temples with his knuckles. The secretary who brought in the coffee hurried to hand out the spoons and milk and sugar and was back out the door so fast that it was like she was fleeing an unseemly scene.

And then de Rosny said:

– You'll never guess, D. E.

– That he knew, Gesine.

– Right. Squirmed in his seat, it was a bit awkward for him, and then he thanked me—

– For telling him voluntarily.

– I let him think so, but—

– first Employee Cresspahl stood up to him, insofar as one can while sitting down, and gave him quite the lecture: She refuses to be spied on! At the very least she needs to be told; she has a right; she has half a mind to; et cetera.

– I managed just fine sitting down, D. E.

– And he was duly entertained.

– How'd you guess!

– It's not a guess, Gesine. I've been in the working world for quite a few years myself; I have to live with bosses just like you.

– Now you want to show off how you're better at that too.

– When did Weiszand try to see the cat, Gesine?

– Tuesday. Six days ago.

– From what you've told me about de Rosny, I'd have thought he'd be quicker than that.

– Why don't you ever want to meet the men I tell you about, D. E.? F. F. Fleury, D. W. Weiszand, de Rosny?

– You'd feel watched, Gesine.

– No.

– No?

– The long, long leash, D. E.

– Does de Rosny believe it?

– Do you believe it?

– You yourself called the Council for Mutual Economic Assistance, the RGW, Comecon—you called it a kindergarten, Gesine. Will the kindergarten teacher like it if one of her children suddenly wants to keep a cat? Won't Moscow's International Bank for Economic Cooperation at least want to know whether the ČSSR is secretly trying to get an American loan?

– Yes. But that can't happen to me.

– What happened to you when you were in Mönchengladbach with NATO, then?

– That was personal, D. E.!

– And how did you get that job?

– Through an ad in the *Frankfurter Allgemeine Zeitung*, D. E.

– In 1955?

– In 1955, D. E. And now we're here in New York, and it's 1968.

– Exactly.

– This Weiszand's a sociologist, D. E.!

– So what, Gesine?

– A Pole, a Jew, the Soviets made him sit on the back bench in school before they handed him back to the Germans to put in their camps, why would he lift a finger for the Soviet Union?

– He may not want to.

– And so now we get to the psychology of the traitor, Herr Professor.

– No. To the hypothesis that personal misfortune means nothing compared to the victory of Socialism.

– Dmitri Weiszand wouldn't betray me.

– He wouldn't call it betrayal. Maybe he's trying to help you.

– "Anyone who organizes antiwar demonstrations is an agent of Soviet corporate espionage"? Your equations were more elegant than that, D. E.

– I didn't know anything about his connection to Vietnam, Gesine.

– You think it's possible?

– Based on what you've told me, Gesine.

– That de Rosny is having me watched.

– He would say it's about protection, and he would mean protecting his investment, not you.

– Oh no. Not again.

– Quit. Take the child and come live with me.

– I'd like to see that. You'll eat every last word, D. E.

– What would de Rosny say if you quit?

– I can't quit now, D. E.

– He's invited you to dinner.

– At the Brussels.

– Brown damask on the walls, soft lighting, *waterzooi de volaille à la Gantoise*. But bankers don't go there.

– *Selle d'agneau rôti à la sarladaise*, D. E.

– You must have looked quite the couple. So now D. W. Weiszand can see that you're being promoted too, on a trial basis, two floors up, to a new desk, it won't be called "ČSSR Department" but "General Contacts," with a telephone number not listed in the staff directory. Mrs. Cresspahl as a protégée.

– But you'd loan me out, Erichson.

– You'd loan yourself out, Gesine.

– Would that be so bad? This time it'd be a Socialist system that I was helping.

– No it wouldn't.

– Well then.

– And it won't work, Gesine.

– That's what I'd like to wait and see.

– It's a deal. And if it doesn't work out, and you escape in one piece, you'll marry me.

– Is this a bet?

– An agreement.

– If this doesn't work out either, then I give up, D. E.

– That's not what I want.

– *Gotta take me as I am.*

– *No winter's cold enough to kill the weeds.*

– Good night, D. E.

– I mean it that way too.

February 6, 1968   Tuesday

In West Germany there is a millionaire who was a member of the West German Free Democratic Party and the East German Communist Party simultaneously; according to news reports, he "wanted to keep a hole in the wall dividing Germany" by supplying intelligence through it. *The New York Times* also reports that the East German military intelligence service tipped off the West because the man would work only for a rival agency, the East German State Security Service.

In Warsaw the author of an operetta faces a closed-door trial because in so authoring it he disseminated "false information," according to a law enacted in 1946.

Lisbeth Cresspahl had already had to endure listening to her husband's words about the coming war; in the fall of 1938 she had to watch him act accordingly. She could no longer pretend that he'd been talking just to convince her to move back to England; she saw him preparing to stay in Germany, as she wanted, but in a Germany at war. Cresspahl went shopping.

He'd drawn up the first list on his own. At the top came the items made of steel, iron, brass: saw blades, nails of all sizes, axes, files, planer blades, rasps, clamps, shovels, fittings for furniture, for doors, for windows. These were followed by belts for the machines, gas, oil, grease. He actually bought a motor that didn't run on electricity, took it apart, packed the parts in waxed paper, and carried everything down to the basement under the former living room, putting it behind a newly built wall that looked like a partition for a junk closet. His purchases attracted no attention in Jerichow, because he bought these supplies in Lübeck, Hamburg, Schwerin, and also because there was nothing suspicious about a master carpenter buying fuses by the hundred when he had a dicey electrical system to work with.

Lisbeth tried to stop him, because it made his expectations for the coming years so much more real, so Cresspahl brought up October 19, the door-to-door collection of what was supposed to be every last bit of scrap metal in people's houses, for use in rearmament. Cresspahl had prudently prepared a lot of metal for pickup—considerable in weight, limited in use—and carefully put the receipt somewhere safe afterward. Lisbeth wanted to say that at least there was no need to have two petroleum lamps as backup, so Cresspahl said something about a single bomb hitting the Lübeck-Herrenwyk power station, which supplied Jerichow with electricity. All this work, too, Cresspahl did in his methodical, calm, implacable way, no matter how much time it took—so she couldn't even chuckle at his making a fuss.

She found it even harder to draw up her own list, as he'd asked her to. That would mean admitting to herself that the town of Jerichow, her house and household, her own child were facing times in which they would lack for shoes, clothes, even kitchen knives. She was so reluctant to do it that Cresspahl had to spend a whole evening interrogating her to find out what she would need in these exasperating circumstances of his, and it was only when she'd come across large boxes of candles, tobacco, and shoe leather in the pantry that she found herself ready to comply. She did it, complaining of headaches to make Cresspahl feel bad, but then he wasn't satisfied with linen and cotton, he insisted on sewing-machine needles as well.

When she went shopping herself, she often came back from Lübeck or Schwerin happy enough. She liked giving presents and would bring home an extra apron, or a shawl, for the Labor Service girls; she amused herself by buying a fancy pair of embroidery scissors or a patent lemon squeezer she would never use. At times she felt a bit like she had in the days before her marriage, when Louise Papenbrock was completing her trousseau; she was reassured and reassured again by the displays in the shopwindows, where she saw no shortages, no signs of impending war. On Sundays the

Lübeck Gazette brought her sixteen pages of ads, with Underberg Schnapps, Mercedes Typewriters, Attica Cigarettes (genuine Turkish tobacco), Junker & Ruh Gas Stoves, Karstadt's, Securit Glass, and other firms offering everything imaginable, as though they couldn't unload their wares fast enough, or bring new ones to market. Maybe this really was all just a tiresome mistake on her husband's part, harmless enough since after all he was only putting in a somewhat exaggerated stock of supplies; even Cresspahl looked amused when she brought home a hat that she'd only be able to wear the following summer—he seemed to realize she was making fun of him.

There were other days. Days on which she was exhausted before she started. She didn't want to shop, she might sit in the restaurant at the Lübeck station for half an hour before letting a movie poster divert her from her task. She felt ill at ease in the movie theater, as she walked from the ticket counter into the auditorium, and during the wait in the dim light, but her headache would disappear as soon as the pictures started moving. All the way through to the evening when she got back to Jerichow, she would be dazed and distracted, but rejuvenated, by the hour and a half of forgetting she had enjoyed—an hour and a half of losing herself in a world of play and make-believe without a hint of Cresspahl's war.

These were the movies shown in Lübeck in the third week of October, 1938:

Mazurka, with Pola Negri, rated 14+

Covered Tracks, with Kristina Söderbaum, adults only

13 Chairs, with Heinz Rühmann and Hans Moser, general admission

Little Sinner, with Rudolf Platte and Paul Dahlke, adults only

A Girl Goes Ashore, with Elisabeth Flickenschildt

The Jungle Princess

Petermann Is Opposed, with Fita Benkhoff

Dancing Lady, with Clark Gable

Clark Gable?

We had Coca-Cola too, daughter.

The same as today's?

The same as your daughter Marie drinks, daughter.

Did I drink it as a child?

Of course, daughter. On Schüsselbuden Street in Lübeck. You didn't like it.

And you went to the movies the way I did during my first year in New York?

Just like you in New York, daughter.

As an anesthetic.

It was a stupid feeling. But as long as it lasted I felt safe. As long as I was there no one could find me, not even I could.

Did you take me with you?

I tried sometimes, and did something nice for you after all. Don't forget that, daughter.

I won't.

She told Cresspahl about the trips to the movies, the wasted time. She wished he'd criticize her, not only so she could hold his injustice against him but also to help her resist these derelictions of duty, these attempts at escape. But Cresspahl didn't begrudge what he thought were her pleasures. As long as she led him to believe she had no secrets from him, he was almost not worried.

February 7, 1968 Wednesday

Dear Mary, *liebe Marie, dorogaya Mariya*—

I have something to say that I don't want you to hear for eight years.

One reason is: We have only three hours a day together after I get home from work, and today when we were going over your day at school, you were busy.

You were busy with the pictures you'd cut out of *The New York Times.* The first was of the Chinese Quarter in Saigon. The bombs, fires, and street fighting have left a relatively smooth layer of rubble behind, and since the photo also isn't very clear you didn't take this to be the remains of human dwellings but of a garbage dump, with fire and thick smoke rising from something like a forest behind it. And again you told me that this couldn't happen to us in New York—and already it was less real to you.

The second picture shows a machine shop after a bombardment, also in Cholon, and a bucket brigade of small children trying to put out the fire. You're generally opposed to child labor, as I've taught you to be, so you told yourself that the children weren't working at a job, they were trying to save their fathers' jobs. To you that constituted a difference.

The third is something *The New York Times* calls a street scene, even though at first sight there's no one moving about in the picture. In the foreground, lying on a smashed street next to a wooden handcart on two bicycle wheels, there is a person, motionless, in a position he wouldn't be able to maintain for a second if he were asleep. He is recognizable as a person from a clear face and from the limbs that are still there. The thing that's been thrown into the dirt behind him, a sack of coal or crumpled blankets, you don't recognize as a dead body until you read the caption; you wouldn't even have noticed it. Likewise the third body, on the right, in the background, behind a jeep, a piece of meat with outstretched legs or, if the head is missing, arms. Next to the jeep, an American tank takes up the rest of the street, with a soldier's head in a helmet sticking up very small out of the turret, so that's why she can call this a street scene.

The fourth is of a hospital corridor with patterned tiles, filled past capacity with a line of people who've been shot and burned. The accompanying article discusses the two to three people per bed, stretchers squeezed in wherever there's room, and another ward that is mostly empty, for patients who can afford to pay for treatment, such as Jim Morris, from South Pine, N.C., Marine Yeoman 2d Cl., insured. You, though, are looking for the name of your old Dr. Brewster.

You put only one of these pictures in your folder, the third. The others you've left on the table as though they would disappear on their own. Tomorrow morning you won't find them there.

When I was alone, I could still say "for when I'm dead" into your tape recorder, but now I'll write it so that there's no way you'll learn about it any earlier than 1976. On tape you might hear it too soon, and I find it hard to take the dazed expression of understanding you put on when you don't understand something. You nod, and I can see that you are repeating what you've heard over and over again in your mind, as though you could grasp it better that way. You think you're being polite; really it's nothing but what's left of your fear from 1960, when you realized you couldn't switch me out for another parental unit—that you were stuck with me come what may, your one and only mother, and for the time being at least you couldn't afford to lose her. What's left of that fear is the way you still put on a show of paying great attention to what you consider my eccentricities, but never say that's how you see them, to be safe. This started in a playground in Remagen eight years ago, and in another eight years you can try to deny it.

What you could have heard from today is what I'm trying to tell myself the latest news about the death of Charles H. Jordan means. Charles H. Jordan: an executive of the Jewish relief organization AJJDC, the Joint, found in the Vltava River on August 20 of last year. On August 16, Mr. Jordan left his hotel in Prague to buy a newspaper. Friends as well as colleagues ruled out suicide. A Belgian scientist visiting an Eastern bloc country some time later was kept under constant surveillance, and when he complained about it he was told that it was so Soviet agents wouldn't do to him what they did to Mr. Jordan. Or maybe it wasn't the KGB, it might have been Arab agents. On December 10, Ernst Hardmeier, the Swiss pathologist whom the AJJDC tasked with performing an autopsy on the dead man, was found several hundred yards from his locked car in a snowy forest near Zürich, frozen to death; he had not completed his investigation. That was how things stood until now.

Now a Socialist government of the Czechoslovak Socialist Republic has given the American government a report on the death of one of its citizens. It is an interim report—perhaps the investigations will be pursued further. As of now, the Czechoslovakian government maintains that Mr. Jordan died on August 16 between 11 p.m. and midnight, and that he fell into the river from a certain place on the First of May Bridge in downtown Prague. The cause of death was determined to be drowning; the body showed no signs of major trauma; the word choice does not rule out a blow with a sandbag or the like. The report is accompanied by photos of the place of death and drawings of the river currents, as measured by conducting tests with a dummy of Mr. Jordan's size and weight.

So if it once again starts to be the case in a Socialist country:

that a death cannot be justified by reasons of state;

that if there's a murder there must be a murderer;

that a dead man has at least the right to the truth about his death;

that murders in the night, in secret, behind closed doors, are forbidden and, if not prevented, condemned:

then this might really be Socialism—with a functioning constitution, with freedom of speech, with freedom of movement, with the freedom for even an individual to decide how to use the means of production.

There are still some things missing here. No, they haven't answered whether the dead man was in fact killed, and if so by whom, on whose orders, and why, for what?

Still, *dorogaya Mariya*, it might be a start. I would work for a Socialism like this, and I would want to.

I am sitting here alone, at the table with your pictures from the *Times* on it, alone with the lamp and your sleeping breaths that are louder than my pen, and alone with a crazy belief that this year might actually turn out all right. That's what I have written out for you, so when the time comes you'll understand what I may be starting to do this year, at age thirty-five, dear lord, one last time. So that you won't have to guess, like I do.

Sincerely yours.

February 8, 1968 Thursday

Yesterday the American-led camp at Langvei, near Khesanh, was assaulted by Soviet-made PT-76 amphibious tanks. Street fighting in Hue. The city of Bentre destroyed by shelling and bombardment from the southern allies; this was "necessary in order to save it," a US major said. And in Hue, Captain Bacel Winstead, at the sight of marines zipping off to battle on motorcycles they had "liberated" from recaptured middle-class homes, said: The American military is the damnedest military in the world.

Around October 20, 1938, in Dassow near Jerichow, a man was sentenced to eight months in prison plus legal costs. He was not a member of the Nazi Party but had worn the insignia of the party anyway, to express his "inner conviction." To the court, his behavior seemed "all the more reprehensible" in light of his long criminal record.

When an idea came into Lisbeth's head, Cresspahl generally picked up on it quickly. Once, when Lisbeth heard that the Hitler Youth had started waiting outside church after services with their collection boxes, she pinned to her hat the badges with pictures of prominent Nazis that the Winter Relief Program gave out for donations, so that she'd be able to tell the collectors, daintily pointing a finger to her head: *Already got one.*

Cresspahl talked her out of that, but liked seeing that she could still joke around and yet also see reason, even if this wasn't the right occasion for it. Similarly with the old gold coins that everyone was supposed to turn in at the Reichsbank: Lisbeth went to Ahlreep's Clocks and had a five-mark coin set as a brooch and wanted to send her little Gesine to a children's party at Party Comrade Lichtwark's wearing her new pin. Cresspahl talked her out of that.

It wasn't always a joke. When the Sunday *Lübeck Gazette* ran a full-page report on the London messenger boys, she got so caught up in reading it, seeing the children in their uniforms—their shoulder straps, caps held on with chin straps and pushed back on their heads, numbered badges over their hearts—that it ended in smothered tears, and by evening she'd already finished the first three lines of a letter to the editor in which she planned to denounce the inhumanity of English capitalism, though really it was all about her own memories of London and her need to punish herself. Cresspahl picked up on that too, as hard as she'd tried to keep it secret. He talked her out of that.

One thing he didn't pick up on for a long time was that Lisbeth was starving her child.

By this time the child would still be asleep when he got up; he ate breakfast alone, and in any case didn't have the time that the bigger Gesine wanted to spend on her first meal of the day. He now had to leave the house as early as he'd had to back in his own childhood when he'd gone out into von Haase's fields with the other day laborers—he had to catch the milk train to Gneez to make the connection to Lübeck, he had prep work to do at the airfield, or else in the hour before breakfast he had to replace the flagpole in Friedrich Jansen's front yard that unknown persons had skillfully sawed partway through during the night. When he got back to the table, Gesine was up too, and he probably liked how attentively she watched him eat. If he'd asked, Lisbeth would have said that the child had already had something, and Gesine wouldn't have been able to contradict her, except to say that it wasn't enough.

That's how it went during second breakfast; that's how it went at dinner. Cresspahl made sure that Paap and the workmen had meat on their plates; the meat on his was also as it should be; the child was sitting next to Lisbeth, two stools away from him. Why would a five-year-old doubt that her mother was giving her portions with the best will in the world, to the best of her ability? How could she appeal to her father for help when her mother had repeatedly warned her not to bother him? During the Easter visit to Pode-juch, the Cresspahl child had eaten with the Paepcke children, and Hilde seems to have noticed that this Gesine was quietly, secretively putting everything she could onto her plate and into her apron pocket—she mentioned it later. The Labor Service girls knew perfectly well that the mistress's and master's child had an unusual appetite, and that she'd have stolen the soaked pieces of bread from the cat's bowl if she dared; Lisbeth kept her pantry locked at all times, and if she caught the girls slipping her daughter anything, she was liable to put on a truly withering look and forbid any meddling in her child-rearing. Later the girls used to say: When she looked at you like that, so coldly, her eyes so steady, it was scary. It wasn't only laymen who noticed; Dr. Berling saw the Cresspahl child on Town Street: a not quite emaciated thing but certainly skinny, who seemed not to have grown in the past six months and who looked around at the world somewhat dazed. Louise Papenbrock was no longer working in the bakery, and the child couldn't go begging from the salesgirls; nowadays old Papenbrock only occasionally slipped her a candy, in strict secrecy, after Lisbeth had given him a pointed speech about sweets being bad for the teeth, yet again in the severe and distant manner she had adopted. When the child stuffed herself full of unripe apples, her stomachache was a reason to keep her in bed. The first time the child was allowed to lick a bowl of cake batter she was six years old, but Lisbeth had scraped it out with a white rubber spatula that left nothing behind. She wanted to deny the child not only food but pleasure. If she couldn't sacrifice the child, she at least wanted to do her good by making her suffer. There were exceptions, like the bottle of Coca-Cola on Schüsselbuden Street in Lübeck, when Lisbeth took pity on herself as well as on the child dizzy with hunger—there were not many. By October 1938 this had been going on for almost a year.

In October 1938, Hermann Liedtke complained to Cresspahl that he'd found his lunch nibbled at, as if by a cat, more than once. He had started bringing in sandwiches from home, preferring to take the money than eat at Cresspahl's table. Cresspahl nailed the cat flap in the workshop door shut, but Liedtke could still show him bite marks in the bread, and they really did look like a cat's. Cresspahl was on the point of handing out padlocks for the clothes lockers—some kind of fight among the workers was more likely than a cat, he thought—until one day he ran into the child in the empty workshop. She had pushed her chair back from the breakfast table, had seen Liedtke leave, and was now standing by his locker, gnawing carefully on his bread, so scared of being found out that she folded the wax paper back together with both hands after every miniscule bite. She was barely over three feet tall then, and she started in terror when she looked up and saw Cresspahl there. She held the little packet out to him, which was too awkward for her fingers, and said cringingly, sighing, eyes downcast: *I didn mean to.*

Lisbeth looked kindly at the child, who had been so ashamed to confess; but Lisbeth didn't want to discuss it further. Cresspahl sent the child out of the room; Lisbeth didn't want to discuss it. Looked him straight in the eye, undaunted, head held high, with the hint of a smile at the corners of her mouth, as if Cresspahl wouldn't understand her anyway, where she now was. He could have gotten it out of her by force: I've been fasting too, Cresspahl. He didn't try to use force.

This time the silent treatment came from Cresspahl and lasted more than a week; he started taking the child with him to go shopping, or to the airfield, and when they ate at home the child would sit next to him, in Lisbeth's place. He was deeply embarrassed when he held out food to the child and was given a shamelessly grateful look in return. In Jerichow people started talking about how he wanted to take the child away from *Our Lisbeth*, and after only three days Lisbeth asked him to leave the child with her, promised him "whatever you want, Heinrich," but now Cresspahl liked having the child with him all day, especially liked talking to her, explaining his work to her. He went ahead and added locks to the lockers, and Hermann Liedtke had one more cat story to tell and never suspected the child, who now spent half the day patiently waiting under the workshop awning until the machines were turned off or Cresspahl stepped outside. Cresspahl kept the child with him, even though by that point he believed Lisbeth's promises; later, he admitted he'd wanted revenge and said he wished he'd given in this time too.

Thank you, daughter
There's nothing to thank me for.

Yes there is. For not telling Marie. Its almost like you can forgive me now I forgive you. I forgive you! I forgive you!

Sold out! Closed! Done for the day! Mrs. O'Brady says, bent down behind her counter and knowing only that she has another customer, not which one.

– Out of matches?

– No! Oh, it's you, Gesine. Those goddamn pictures!: Mrs. O'Brady says, her coarse vigorous face flushed and pounding with blood, and mad about that too.

– No. Never filtered.

– Here! Here you go, something that can be damaging to your health! It was like the issues were going up in smoke—people were tearing them out of my hand!

– You can tell me, Mrs. O'Brady.

– *Time* magazine, Gesine! With the photos! That's how some people get their kicks!

– Do you have the *Time*, Mrs. Williams, Amanda?

– Here's the *Time*, Gee-sign! It's unbelievable!: Amanda announces, so worked up that she slams rather than places the magazine on the table. She too is red in the face, talking in a higher pitch than usual, and faster too. But these aren't naughty pictures, they are several pages of color photographs taken after the Vietcong attack on the American embassy in Saigon. Dick Swanson, working for *Life*, caught the moment when Ambassador Bunker in front of his bunker, a dignified white-haired gentleman with his hand in his pocket, was inspecting the enemy dead with his soldiers and staff. On his lawn lay two locals, one on his back looking almost relaxed, the other contorted, in a blood-soaked shirt, blood over his whole face too, not as red as the band on his right arm. Blood has flowed out onto the low round wall of the gigantic planter, a lush stain, with spatters at the edges. It's a typical war photo, but Amanda can't recover. – It's against all good taste!: she says.

– It certainly is, Amanda.

– Isn't it? Everything in its place, the war over there and home over here! If I'd seen that over breakfast I'd have spat out my food!

– Shouldn't we know what the war is like, Amanda? Not just in black and white?

– That's what you have to say, Gee-sign? You? I've known you for years, Mrs. Cresspahl, and I've never once heard you say something tasteless! You're all about tact and reserve, it's almost English, and now you're telling me this?

– Not so loud, Amanda. The others will think we're having a fight.

– We are! Imagine a woman with a son in Vietnam seeing that! Mrs. Agnolo seeing that! She'd practically collapse! And you're all for it! Gee-sign!

– It's calculated precisely!: says David Guarani, a proofreader, the elegant gentleman of his department, not much older than twenty-five but so confident in his technical knowledge of banking and in his inevitable promotion that he wasn't even taken aback when de Rosny walked through his department and realized with utter amazement that Employee Guarani was comfortably draped over one and a half chairs reading his magazine while a man kneeled in front of him, salving his ankle boots. But even Guarani isn't interested in discussing the fact that Barclays and Lloyds banks in London are planning a merger, perhaps tired of the war between their posters in the Underground, which would be a proper topic for an expert like himself. Martins Bank is involved too. No, Mr. Guarani has adopted his thinking posture, left hand behind a head held high, eyes veiled with relentless analyzing and classifying, right hand as though ready to write out the results.

– You think it's innocent, Mrs. Cresspahl: he says charitably.

– I don't think it's innocent at all, David.

– Precisely. You hear me? Precisely. If these photographs are being published in this layout at just this moment, it means something!

– Selling more copies.

– No. Yes. Well. But. If dead Government Issues are being stacked on the tailgate of an armored vehicle in the middle of Saigon, all tangled together, arms and legs sticking out, heads hanging down, with the blood on them black as ink—

– Does that mean more than what it already is?

– That's what I'm trying to say, Mrs. Cresspahl! It means that all the money behind *Time* magazine doesn't believe what the government is saying about victory!

– It means that the Tet Offensive was a victory?

– And not just a psychological one, like the military commanders are saying! It means we're not going to win this war, Mrs. Cresspahl.

– That would mean support for Kennedy then. That's what he could run on.

– What do you mean, Kennedy. Our Kennedy? Robert Francis? Bugs Bunny of New York?

– Our senator from New York. Yesterday in Chicago he denied "any prospect" of a military victory.

– I didn't know that.

– *New York Times*. Front page. Article on page 12.

– I guess I should read the politics section sometimes: says Mr. Guarani, finance expert. He says goodbye distractedly, remarking that it's strange how much farther and faster your thoughts can go when you talk things out.

– If anything of the sort happens again ... !: Mr. Shuldiner says in a threatening tone of voice. Today he cares even less about how Gustafsson's fish salad tastes. He holds up his loaded fork for a minute at a time, contemplating, observing its cargo from various angles, until the whole of his next sentence finally comes to him.

– I do think it's useful: he says.

– Sorry, Mr. Shuldiner?

– Well, this poor dog of a GI hasn't even realized he's dead, his hand is still clutching his gun, and his two buddies are dragging him by the legs to the ambulance tank, without turning him over, his face is scraping through the sand and the rubble, and all this right in the middle of Saigon, at Tansonnhut Airport, where civilian airlines land too, you know. You just need a visa, Mrs. Cresspahl, and now you get out of the plane....

– True, Mr. Shuldiner.

– This Mr. Guarani, this colleague of yours you told me about, isn't he due for a tour in Vietnam?

– Half orphan. Only child.

– Ha!

– Weren't you glad to serve in the army, Mr. Shuldiner?

– Only now do I realize how glad, Mrs. Cresspahl. Because I served my time when we were at peace. Or let's say, half peace.

– And if anything of the sort happens again, Mr. Shuldiner?

– Ah. Sorry. I have days when I'm very confused, especially since the engagement.

– Maybe it wasn't that important.

– Yes, it was. Do you know what I'd do then?

– No.

– That's what I always say is so European about you, Mrs. Cresspahl. You pay such close attention to people's words. It's funny too.

– You "think it's useful"?

– Yes. Now whoever wants to dodge the draft will take this issue of *Time* into the courtroom and enter these pictures as Exhibit A for the defense. And, if anything of the sort happens again, I'll sell my war bonds, believe you me!

– You buy war bonds, Mr. Shuldiner?

– No. My fiancée is getting half of her dowry in war bonds. My new in-laws are very patriotic Jews.

– Doesn't bother me: says Sam. His restaurant is almost empty by now, and he has time to chat with a fat, sour-faced guy in a leather jacket; they treat each other with such familiarity that they must be friends. The new issue of *Time* is sitting under the customer's elbow, opened to the color pages, already heavily crumpled. Sam doesn't like that John Stewart depicted a Government Issue who'd been shot, a black MP built like a bull, kneeling like a gorilla, glaring dully "at the enemy" from under his pink blood-soaked headband. He's glaring at the camera, isn't he, Sam points out. And instead of waiting out the seconds until the man keeled over dead, John Stewart could have been shooting with something other than his camera, now couldn't he.

– If you're going to do something then do it: the other man says. He seems extremely talented at keeping a conversation going without actually saying anything. It sounded like he was agreeing, but he could easily deny it.

– And anyway it's fake: Sam says. He half pulls the magazine out from under the other man's elbow, looks at the pictures, then puts them down. He gazes blearily, kindheartedly, at his bald friend, the gray wrinkles in his brow even closer together than usual, and says: The colors aren't right. Ever seen a color photo with natural colors?

– Nah: the other man says. – Well, everyone's got their own idea of what's natural: he says.

– That's right.

– Could still be true maybe.

– But it's just one vivid second of the truth.

– And a vivid second of the truth is not just marketable property—

– it's hot property: Sam says, clearly pleased that one of their pings was yet again answered with a pong. Then he notices Mrs. Cresspahl, who has come to pick up her afternoon tea, and he gently, affectionately, starts heaping abuse on her. The solitary customer buttons up his shabby leather jacket and, without turning around, slides off of his stool and heads out to the street.

– Seeya, Sam: he says.

– Take care: Sam calls after him; and now here it comes: I can't believe you didn't say anything, you turkey! Just stood around waiting till we were done gabbing! If I don't notice you, gimme a good smack in the head! Thems the rules! Starting now! Tea, with lemon. Twenty cents! Thank you, Gesine. What a day, today.

– These Fridays.

– Right, Gesine. And now you go back to your cube, sit right down, and don't do another thing. You've had enough for today too.

– Sleep well this weekend, Sam.

– You too.

– Hello?

– Mrs. Williams, Foreign Sales.

– Oh, I thought this was Cresspahl's number.

– One moment, I'll connect you.

– Hello?

– Yes?

– It's Eileen.

– Eileen?

– See? You've been buying your damned cigarettes from me for two years and you still don't know my first name. Eileen O'Brady.

– I didn't want to intrude, Eileen.

– Quite all right, Gee-sign. Listen, I called around and got a new batch of *Time*. Should I set one aside for you?

– No thanks, Eileen, it's all right. Wait! Eileen! Actually yes. Please do.

February 10, 1968 Saturday, South Ferry day

Eugene J. McCarthy, the Democratic senator from Minnesota who plans to run against the sitting president this fall, has been rebuked by the White House and the Pentagon for claiming that the military sought nuclear weapons for use in Vietnam.

Mr. McCarthy denies he said that; at most he said that it wouldn't surprise him if *some* generals *had* been asking for nuclear weapons for use in Vietnam. A tape of his Boston TV interview includes these words: "Well, I expected that there would be a demand for the use of tactical nuclear weapons by someone. [Pause] As a matter of fact, there have been some demands for their use already."

George Christian, the White House press secretary, was asked whether President Johnson had received a request from the Joint Chiefs of Staff to authorize the use of nuclear weapons if it became necessary.

Mr. Christian said that Mr. Johnson had considered no such decision.

Senator J. W. Fulbright, the Arkansas Democrat, asked Secretary of State Dean Rusk if he had any information about a report that a specialist in tactical nuclear weapons traveled to South Vietnam last weekend.

A spokesman responded that there was no substance to the report.

The *St. Louis Post-Dispatch* described reports that the United States has stockpiled tactical nuclear weapons in South Vietnam for use if the Communists threaten to overrun the allied forces at Khesanh.

High-ranking United States military officials said that the United States stockpiling nuclear weapons in such an unstable environment as Vietnam would be ridiculous and utterly foolish. If the United States ever did want to use atomic weapons, these officials said, the devices could be brought in with little delay.

On October 26, 1938, a Wednesday, the Luftwaffe took over Jerichow-North.

This time Johannes Schmidt of Johs. Schmidt Musikhaus did not request reimbursement for costs. He blared the rules and regulations for the day through town at his own expense, from a van specially fitted with loudspeakers. He wanted this to be seen as his contribution to the national honor. He spent all afternoon Tuesday driving up and down the streets in person, out into the villages too, proclaiming in his clumsy High German that all houses were to be beflagged, and that the thing would initiate at ten a.m.

At ten a.m. the number of people standing in Jerichow's Market Square exceeded the town's population. In the middle was a long rectangle of blinding white flagpoles wound around with garlands of fir. A police delegation from Gneez held back the throng from a weak fence, but old Creutz kept squirming through to admire his handiwork once again. Even right before the celebration began, he tied a loose garland back in place, openly cursing at the lunkheads who'd tried to damage his craftsmanly reputation. By which he meant the policemen, who hadn't been all that careful, and since they were less carried away than he was, they reacted with smiles instead of a warning.

The Luftwaffe troops didn't take the train all the way to Jerichow. Jansen had decided that Station Street was too narrow for an entrance of properly thundering magnificence; the soldiers got off unobtrusively in Knesebeck, a station a mile or two outside of town, so that they could arrive as though out of nowhere. When they got to the brickworks, the band struck up the first march, "Der Hohenfriedberger." There, where a path met the road, a man of about fifty was standing, holding a child's hand, observing the newcomers without much excitement, with disdain if anything. Spurs on boot heels crashed and flashed on the surface of Town Street, and already local boys behind the parade were hunting for ones that had come off in the cobblestones. Girls in BDM uniforms were throwing flowers at the soldiers from the sidewalks. Papenbrock's maid Edith craned her neck and sometimes tried to jump; she was laughing and cheering wildly and kept grabbing Stellmann's arm. – No! No!: she cried, ruining two of his photographs. Behind the troops the windows slammed shut and the townsfolk came running out onto the street, to the market square, leaving the neighborhood deserted.

At thirty seconds to ten, the Blues arrived on Market Square in a square formation with the SA, the National Socialist Reich Veterans Association, and the Naval Storm Troopers. Friedrich Jansen, on the flag-draped dais, was the only one who knew why he was opening his mouth as if to give a speech, then shutting it, then opening it again. He had suddenly realized that Pastor Brüshaver actually dared to not ring the bells of St. Peter's Church. In his fury, Friedrich Jansen pulled himself together and got a first word out of his mouth, though what it was remained unknown, for now the Catholics were pulling at their bell rope. However laborious it sounded, the effort produced little more than a tinkle that stopped at once, as if shocked. In just a few sentences Jansen worked himself into a frenzy. He spoke (measured; firm) of the happiness felt by the town at having its own garrison. How in the past they'd had to beg for soldiers (full of self-pity; threatening)! Now, though, the Führer, foreseeing—no, knowing—the wishes of his people, had bestowed them as a gift (preacherly, humble). When Jansen quoted from the National Prize winner Heinkel's Rostock speech, he misspoke in his sacred awe and gave the current maximum possible airspeed as 900 kilometers per hour when Heinkel had said 700. – *An next time a cowardly foe tries to take up arms agains' the German people* (pitying). – *We wont turn a hair* (Grand Hotel). – *Dont give a fig about* (university man, down to earth). – *Then we'll just say: Down, boy!* (dog owner with Graves' disease). – *Sit! Stay! Silence!*: he cried. Whenever he expelled the word "Luftwaffe," spittle poured inexhaustibly forth, and he himself didn't know what he was saying. When the time came for Georg Swantenius from Gneez, somewhat bittersweet with envy, to thank the Führer for this proud day in the name of the local party branch and district leadership, Jansen was still red in the face and panting. The next day, Stellmann sold more photographs showing Jansen in this condition than of any other subject.

When the commander of the main unit stepped forward, the crowd fell silent, like students in a classroom not daring to try on a school inspector what they do with a bumbling teacher. The lieutenant colonel spoke in a normal tone of voice, calm, relaxed, practically civilian. He introduced himself by name. He looked around, so that many people had the feeling he had looked straight at them. He thanked the crowd for their welcome; as he should. The troops would make every effort to earn their right to live in this community; he knew the rules of hospitality. This day made him very happy; no weightier words were needed. When the Catholics tolled their bell, he composed his face and bent his head forward slightly; he showed respect for the church. He spoke with a Hanover accent, like a neighbor. The way he paused, with his mouth hanging good-naturedly open, he might have been from the region. Long bones, thoroughly developed muscles, left shoulder jutting from a wound. When he ordered the men to present arms for the playing of both national anthems, his syllables were clear and distinct; it sounded incongruous, and uncomfortably peremptory. You couldn't figure this man out, and for the time being the people of Jerichow saw that as a point in his favor.

Among the photographs of the ensuing events that Horst Stellmann developed, Cresspahl is no longer to be found—not at the handing over of the keys outside the guardhouse, not at the laying of the wreath at the cenotaph honoring the dead from the First World War, not at the outdoor air force and SA concert on Market Square. Cresspahl stayed on his property, tidied up the workshop, and did his books, uncommonly irritated by the squadron of airplanes flattering the town's residents with their loud circling overhead. He did leave the house and look up at the line of aircraft. He stood in front of his barn and observed the flag hanging down over the path from the north gable. He wandered all over the property, chin in hand, through the empty rooms, and through Lisbeth's.

It's all my fault, Cresspahl.
Now it's my fault too, Lisbeth.

That night there were celebratory balls in the Lübeck Court, in the pub, in the Rifle Club, in the Forest Lodge. The Cresspahls went to the one in the Rifle Club. For two and a half hours *Our Lisbeth* sat out not a single dance. She was so cheerful, laughing, relaxed, totally different from the way people described her. When she did sit down, it was always next to Cresspahl, with a hand on his shoulder as if absentmindedly, but firm.

I wanted to sleep with you again, Heinrich. Before it's all over, I mean.

610 · *February 11, 1968 Sunday*

February 11, 1968 Sunday

Since yesterday afternoon, a black girl has been living with the Cresspahls, and not everyone thinks it's all right.

We took the girl, Francine, out of a chaos of police cars and ambulances and strewn garbage on 103rd Street, away from a knife fight and battle for authority involving police, welfare workers, and supers, took her away from the indifferent bystanders around her bleeding mother and the screaming baby. The ambulance drivers took the baby; the police sergeant wasn't happy about letting Francine go with white people.

– Are you sure you know whatcher doing, lady?: he said.

Mr. Robinson, who once again had to bring a bed up from his secret vaults, was not as happy with the new lodger as he'd been when the Fleurys came. He set up the bed, placing it neatly in Marie's room the way she wanted, but during the goodbyes he remained standing in the doorway, puzzled, not feeling his crisp waves of hair with his fingertips as he usually does during moments of doubt but with head hanging, genuinely scratching it in puzzlement. That way his eyes were hidden. – Oh, well: he said at last, now unhappy with himself too. – I guess you know what you're doing, Mrs. Cresspahl.

How does Francine feel about it? She called us. She's known Marie for almost six months, from school, she knows the apartment from having come over to play. During her visits, when she was alone with Marie, she seemed confident, cheerful, virtually on equal footing. Yesterday afternoon, almost as soon as we'd shut the door behind her, she was as shy with Marie as she'd been all along with Mrs. Cresspahl—and she used to literally run past her to avoid any look or word. She sat down only when asked to, and then as far away as possible, her long spindly legs pressed tight together, hands clenched on her knees, looking at the floor. When giving thanks for a mug of hot chocolate, she spoke to the teaspoon too: – *Thank you*: softly, hopelessly, as if even this wouldn't mitigate the danger. One time, when Marie was talking about D. E. and Francine thought no one was watching, she ventured an incredulous look that she just as abruptly aimed elsewhere. She had come with what she had on when misfortune struck—a shabby lumberjack coat—and it was a long time before she was willing to take it off, as though she didn't want her visit to turn into a stay.

It probably wasn't because of her mother. When we finally reached a nurse on the phone, Francine didn't want to take the receiver. When she was told her mother would fully recover from the stabbing, she nodded without relief, more out of politeness than anything. She nodded at the news that her other siblings were still missing, and that the youngest was now in a children's home, as if there was no reason to remember this information. And then there was one more thing, a message Francine's mother wanted passed along to Mrs. Cresspahl: God bless you. We can't possibly feel all right about that.

It was a mistake to try to distract the black child with a game—Francine didn't know how to play pick-up sticks, obediently learned it, and was so unhappy at her clumsiness that she accidentally broke a stick in two and was then inconsolable. – Now we'll always think of you, when we're missing this stick: Marie said, but Francine heard this as anger, not friendship. It was a mistake to serve a dinner not eaten with the fingers, and it didn't help that Marie casually laid her knife aside and went at the cutlet with the side of her fork like Francine. It was not a good idea to send Francine to take a shower—she inferred suspicion of dirt and vermin. – We take one every night: Marie said; Francine heard not information but an order. Maybe it was a good idea to give her a pair of Marie's pajamas and a complete set of clothes for the next day; it was not a good idea to put all her things straight into the laundry basket as if they couldn't be worn another day. Francine was very relieved when it was bedtime, now she no longer had to face the dangers of this strange household, and she pulled the covers up over the tightly wound braids sticking out from the top of her head; she lay there stiffly, took a long time to fall asleep, on the lookout for some other danger she hadn't anticipated.

Rebecca Ferwalter didn't like that her friend had taken in a black girl, and from a street, a building, she had been explicitly warned to avoid. Rebecca, the smartly dressed little Jewish girl in a jacket dress made from a reduced-size pattern for adults, Rebecca of the ladylike manners and masklike doll's face, felt as if someone had sprung a trap on her, and during a truly awkward conversation she made up an order from Mrs. Ferwalter according to which she could stay at our apartment for no more than ten minutes. Rebecca hears what is all right with her mother several times a day, and, even more often, what isn't.

It was not all right with Francine that we assumed a mother with stab wounds in the chest and shoulder would of course be visited by at least one of her children. Every time we asked for information, at the hospital entrance and in the corridors, she stood to one side, so seemingly uninvolved that people at first thought it was the Cresspahls who were visiting a black woman. Francine did not go in to her mother happily, and she opened the door to the ward for us after only a very few minutes, at which point she started acting as if she had even less of a connection than we did to this woman lying there awkwardly bundled away under money-saving green blankets, wrapped in an extravagant bandage, half unconscious with medication, her fat gray face covered in feverish sweat. – She's a good chile: she said with effort, and perhaps from conviction, not as a request, and Francine suddenly stared off past her, stubborn, downright hostile. And the fact that we couldn't stick it out for long amid the beds set so close together, the smell of poverty more than illness, the guarded looks from the black neighbors—that was not all right with us. Francine stayed at the door until Marie turned around. Now she had a cowardly, mocking look on her face, very much up at us from below, and Marie innocently asked what was wrong. Francine didn't answer, her defiant look unchanged, as if it were Marie who had something she needed to own up to. Maybe it was a good idea to take her shoulder and steer her out of the way of the other visitors, but Francine hadn't expected that she would be brought back to Riverside Drive again.

> *Now you've seen it, Marie.*
> *I didn't see anything. A woman in a hospital.*
> *Now you're lying, whitey.*
> *My lies are none of your business.*
> *This one is.*
> *You won't get me to talk about it, Francine.*
> *I'll come with you two, but I don't believe you.*

Being left alone with a pile of comic books was all right with Francine, and she pushed one of Marie's double doors shut as if by accident, to be shielded from sight. She took pretense to the point of pretending to be asleep when Pamela Blumenroth came to get Marie for a trip to the Mediterranean Swimming Pool. But then she did fall asleep, and her little black face came out from behind the door looking very scared, eyes black with shock surrounded by huge whites pointed at the strange woman blocking the exit in a strange apartment. Then, waking up, trying for an obliging meekness, she said eagerly: Should I take your newspaper down to the street for you, Mrs. Cresspahl?

Then she didn't understand that people in a building like this can leave their trash in bags by the freight elevator at night, instead of sneaking it out to the city trash cans on the corner. She took in, as yet another unbelievable thing, the information that Mr. Robinson goes through the building at ten at night, floor by floor, and takes the trash to the incinerator, and then I had to explain the incinerator to her too.

It was impossible to explain to her why Marie had circled in red one of the photographs on the front page of *The New York Times*: a wounded marine in Danang and next to him a military chaplain in fatigues, with a cross on his helmet cover, staring upward, on the lookout for God and evacuation helicopters.

– Vietnam: Francine said, unmoved, incurious, as if about something totally unconnected to her. As if about the moon.

It will be less all right with Marie as soon as tomorrow morning. She didn't mind in the least that she could go swimming without Francine, who might have been the only black person there and hard to defend. Tomorrow, when she and Francine arrive at school together, she will run over to her white friends, with relief.

It would not have been all right with one of our great German poets. He described a similar refuge in a book, and challenged his readers not to put down the book even so.

> *I hear that in New York*
> *At the corner of 26th Street and Broadway*
> *A man stands every night during the winter months*
> *And finds shelter for the homeless gathering there*
> *By appealing to passers-by.*
> . . .
> *Don't put down the book, fellow man who reads this.*
> *Now a few fellow men have beds for the night*
> *The wind will be kept from them for a night*

The snow meant for them falls onto the street
But this won't change the world
It will not improve relations among men
It will not make the age of exploitation any shorter.

And there is one person it is impossible to tell whether Francine's stay is all right with: D. E., who arrives from Kennedy Airport around six in the evening, just back from Europe, bringing two dresses from Copenhagen for Marie, now one of them for Francine, since

– I know all about it: he says, and Francine believes him;

– *though I am a stranger here myself*: he says, and Francine laughs, naturally, spontaneously;

– *which I undertook solely to help keep New York clean*: he says; and Francine looks at this white man with shining eyes, eager to hear him talk about such mysterious things as a "Magasin du Nord" on a "Kongens Nytorv" in "København," and jealous in advance of the moment when she will have to share him with Marie.

D. E.—he would accept being a father even to a black child. But again, only on one condition.

February 12, 1968 Monday

These were the movies shown in Lübeck in late October 1938:

A Night in May, with Marika Rökk

The Day After the Divorce, with Luise Ullrich and Hans Söhnker

Code LB 17, with Willy Birgel

Cargo from Baltimore, with Hilde Weissner

Premiere, with Zarah Leander

Red Orchids, with Olga Chekhova

Between Love and Hate (His Brother's Wife), with Barbara Stanwyck (USA, adults only)

What kind of movies were these?

"Red orchids are the favorite flower of a great singer played by Olga Chekhova. Red orchids play a role in the plot of the film, which is about industrial espionage and uncovering the real criminal, because they are the hiding place of a secret code that Nica, an engineer, is desperate to find. With this document, he can prove that he and his friend and comrade are innocent. He has already been sentenced to death for treason. He succeeds after many difficulties. The singer remains at his side, even if, at a moment when her belief in Nica wavers, she almost ruins everything. . . . Camilla Horn plays a dangerous spy and Ursula Herking is striking as always." (*Lübecker General-Anzeiger*)

Fog in London.

Cresspahl had stopped earning money from the airfield construction. Klein the butcher supplied meat for the garrison, Papenbrock baked the bread, the restaurants had business from the soldiers on weekends. The hotels in Rande, long since mothballed by this time in past years, were packed: training courses, wives, National Socialist film nights. Pahl the tailor placed his ads in *The Gneez Daily News*, in a different spot every day, and waited for them to catch an officer's eye; he had his fabric ready. Jerichow's merchants had gone in together on an ad welcoming the arrival of the troops. The church sold one plot of land after another around Jerichow. Köpcke the architect had orders for vacation homes on the bluffs, he could hardly keep up with them; the carpentry work went to Böttcher in Gneez. Cresspahl now had only Alwin Paap and one assistant working with him; Kliefoth hadn't looked to Wismar for his new bookshelf after all. The other contracts were for piddling little jobs.

Cresspahl had time to go for walks. In the evenings, he and *Our Lisbeth* were sometimes seen on the seaside promenade in Rande—walking in silence, keeping their faces turned toward the rummaging sea. This was not held against them as citified airs, it was thought to be nostalgia for 1931 when they'd walked there in secret, as people in love, about whom not many reports reached Louise Papenbrock.

The Japanese had captured and occupied Hankou.

The sea wind had long since plucked the trees bare, not only along the coast but in Jerichow as well. Sometimes old Creutz would be there leaning against his fence when the Cresspahls returned to the light in their house. Had they taken their dahlias down to the cellar yet: he asked. The Cresspahls had almost completely finished preparing their garden for the winter: they said. October always has to have twelve nice days, just like

March: Creutz said. Hadn't March had only eleven this year: Lisbeth Cresspahl said, and Creutz heard her quiet laugh. He could barely see the two of them in the darkness, but he stayed where he was, unconcerned. They would wait until he was ready. The Cresspahls had always been agreeable neighbors.

In August, the Jews had been banned from working as brokers or traveling salesmen. Arthur Semig no longer had to get worked up about that. Now they were to be forbidden from working as lawyers, and their medical licenses revoked. Arthur Semig had been spared that.

It was perfectly all right with Warning that his shovels kept breaking, as if naturally, without a trace of having been sawed. What difference did that make, when his fence was almost more gaps than pickets at this point; a piece of wood like that can always be put to good use, burns well. The latest, though, was that the leather O-ring had been nicked from his pump. Not even his guard dog would do anything for him these days. Jailbirds. What he'd said about Arthur Semig, only jailbirds did things like that.

Your leather should not just shine, it should live. Erdal extends the life, and the beauty, of your shoes. Lordy lordy. The leather should live.

Bums who don't want to work get sent to the house of correction. That's how it is.

The good things the airfield did for Jerichow. Some of them came out only later. Of the sixty-four children Brüshaver had baptized so far this year, thirteen were illegitimate. But better to pay taxes for that than for— *hey, sommuns comin.* Oh, 'sjust Cresspahl. Tanglepicker Cresspahl. Brings is wife along when he goes out fer a beer. Next thing yknow your own wife will wanna come. These English ways. Well you cant talk to him about illegitimate kids and whatnot. Wont do fer *our Lisbeth.*

On October 27, Ernst Barlach, sculptor, draftsman, and dramatist, died. Because he was taken for a Jew, people in Güstrow had spat on him in the street. They had hounded him by banning his work, his exhibitions, until he just lay down and died. The people of Lübeck had made a certain Alfred Rosenberg an honorary citizen, but hadn't allowed Barlach's sculptures onto the walls of their St. Catherine's Church. The *Lübeck Gazette* hadn't felt like printing anything of its own about his death, they had preferred to reprint from the *Berlin Daily* that Barlach had remained a problem for a new breed of men now traveling other paths. Lisbeth spent a long time puzzling over this line: The writer had wrestled more over God than with God.

> *With God, but you can't do that.*
> *Yes Lisbeth.*
> *Over God—that's what you're supposed to do.*
> *Yes Lisbeth.*
> *You ever see him when you were in Güstrow?*
> *I didn't, Lisbeth. I know Büntzel. Friedrich Büntzel, Lisbeth, now theres a guy who knows about wood. This Barlach took advice from him. But first he had to say about a block: Itll split; and Barlach said: It wont split.*
> *And then it split.*
> *And then Barlach listened to what Büntzel the carpenter had to say.*
> *You'd've known it too.*
> *Not anymore, Lisbeth.*
> *Heinrich, it's a bad time to die. If only it were August. When the soil is light.*
> *Yes Lisbeth.*

February 13, 1968 Tuesday

The Union of Soviet Writers has likened Alexander I. Solzhenitsyn to Joseph V. Stalin's only daughter.

And to whom does President Johnson liken himself on Lincoln's Birthday? To President Abraham Lincoln.

The New York Times has a comparison of its own to make, now that sanitation workers have begun to pick up nearly two weeks of uncollected garbage: "This time the city was Saigon and the crisis was the Vietcong disruption of the city at the beginning of the month." The *Times* means the New York garbage crisis. The *Times* means the losses of human life in Vietnam. The *Times* likens them.

On this day, Employee Cresspahl was repotted like a plant, repacked like freight, repositioned like a workbench.

The new pot, new warehouse, new factory floor, new office—it's certainly bigger. Amanda Williams says: grand. It is a grand domain, the sixteenth floor, not far beneath the executives. Here the light comes not only from fluorescent tubes set in the ceiling but from reading lamps perched under expensive Swedish glass, and above the typewriter two shaded white tubes fully illuminate the pit for the typewriter ball. Here the desk is not of the manufacture provided to such pitiful lower depths as the Foreign Sales Dept.; it is an artfully designed slab with smoothly gliding jewelry boxes built in. This room does not await the sort of visitor who is content to sit on a usual chair—the VIPs here shall sit on a sofa. Here there's a plush wool rug underfoot, not wall-to-wall carpeting, and the office is in a corner of the building, with windows on two walls, nearly six square yards of light behind the venetian blinds, though admittedly all dark clouds today. It is a promotion straight out of an American fairy tale.

And yet Employee Cresspahl is sitting on the generous upholstery near the door, ready to leave at any moment, like a visitor, not the proprietor, without a glance at the papers and writing materials she is meant to be putting away in the safe and the open drawers. It didn't happen like a fairy tale at all.

The announcement of her move had been without notice, offhand, half forgotten. Then, unexpectedly, in the middle of the workday, in broad morning, the envoy of Fate appeared at the Foreign Sales door, more startling than a window washer sliding into view out the window.

– A very good morning to you!: Fate wished her.

The young man dispatched to her was slim and curly-haired, wearing light gray overalls with the bank's logo embroidered over the heart. He sized up Mrs. Cresspahl with a casual nod and pushed a squat cart on casters into her office, blocking the exit. He gripped the cart's handle like a hospital stretcher or funeral bier.

– Stop, I beg you! Whoever you are!

He was a little startled, not having been in this job long enough to know the tone the employees affected here. Still, he was not to be kept from his appointed round. He turned and reached around the left side of the door and slid the plastic nameplate out of its slot, holding it up to me not quite like a doctor but still like a nurse who has seen more than enough cases like this and knows his way around. Mrs. Cresspahl felt herself nod, and he tossed my name into one of the trays built into the top deck of his cart. And it was gone.

– Says so right here on this paper: the young man calmly announced, like an executioner clearly taking no questions. He had grafted the laconic speech patterns of Western movies onto his Puerto Rican English; the violently clipped rhythm sounded strange with his dark skin, that of the loser, and his guileless face, long practiced in ingratiation. He seemed shy as well, overwhelmed by the remorselessness to which his checklist held him. The list remembered every last inventory item, from calculator to ashtray, and a tray for personal effects had been sent along too. This was the one part of the terrain where the list suffered a defeat. For Mrs. Cresspahl merely took a thin slip of paper off the base of the desk calendar—and it fit in the smallest pocket of her suit. The young mover had never seen anything like it. It baffled him. The only personal item was the name next to the door. He clearly wanted to ask for an explanation but he remembered his supervisor and took the room apart in barely twenty minutes. When he was done the metal shelves of the file cabinet were gleaming, the bookcase was empty, the corkboard was bare, the chairs arrayed between the naked work surfaces might have been in a shopwindow, the keys swayed slightly and then the office was empty, ready for the next person.

The young man took his leave by thanking her. – Some folks make it harder than it needs to be: he had said. His cart piled high, he withdrew, as if with a coffin followed by no mourners.

The old office was lost. The new office was a foreign land. With no room to work in and no equipment to work with, she had no business being there at all.

Employee Cresspahl sat outside the office that had just been hers; sat, though, next to Amanda, who was phoning around the whole building, nagging delightedly, downright ecstatic that yet again something had been ruined by overorganization. – You can't run a business like this!: she said. – Don't go running round after the kid, you're a lady! – On behalf of Mrs. Cresspahl, I am appalled!: she shouted into her telephone, and in less than fifteen minutes she had found out that the memo had been lying in the outer office of the Personnel Department since yesterday morning, substantially compromising a secretary's reputation for efficiency, and finally the head of personnel himself, Mr. Kennicott II, came onto the phone. Every time he said something, Amanda put her hand over the receiver to signal the latest state of battle. – He's wavering: she said. – He's weakening.

– He's giving in!: she concluded, having won. The excitement had done her good. She was now talking in a very deep voice, felt pleasantly flushed, and patted her mane of black hair back into place with delight and both hands. She'd made up for Friday's fight, and come out ahead; now she could say: I'll miss you, Mrs. Cresspahl.

– I'll miss you too: Mrs. Cresspahl lamely replies.

– Sweet Jesus, don't take it personally!: Amanda said, the same request Mr. Kennicott II made when he came to Foreign Sales to fetch Employee Cresspahl and accompany her to the new office, skillfully and illogically explaining that any action, having been split into three simultaneous component parts, stands or falls with the intentionally steady or unsteady flow of information, all with his most personal and abject apologies. When he ran out of things to say, he inquired into the origins of the name Cresspahl, began describing an uncle of his, of German descent, who had changed his name from Junkers when World War I started, not to renounce his Germanness but on account of the neighbors, in a small town in Michigan . . . and after he finally said goodbye, with secret relief, his face slipped immediately into oblivion, only his pleasantly creaking voice remaining in memory.

That wasn't how it should have been either. From now on he's going to expect to be greeted in the halls, won't he? He can't possibly imagine how forgettable he is. Send me a photo of yourself, Mr. Kennicott II, please.

Then de Rosny walked into the new office, Mr. Vice President himself as he lives and breathes, a jolly godparent wanting to share our joy at his gifts. Everything all right, Mrs. Cresspahl? He didn't believe it was, he had his doubts about the desk placement and helped move it with his very own vice-presidential hands so that it no longer stood at an angle between the windows but squarely in front of one of them. In the process, he came across a drawer protruding a miniscule amount, and opened it, and hurriedly shut it again, the look on his face conveying that he wanted to pass over an indecent matter in silence. Then he realized that Employee Cresspahl couldn't possibly have had time to put her things away yet, and he pulled the drawer open again.

– Shoes: he said, aghast.

Of course, Mr. Vice President. A pair of women's shoes, white pumps, hardly worn.

– I ask you, just for the record—: he said, already heading into the punishing storm he planned to hurl down onto all the floors beneath him.

Employee Cresspahl wears a smaller size. Who in this country wears white shoes in February? No, Mr. de Rosny.

Employee Cresspahl was given the rest of the day off, with the justification that the telephone in the new office had not yet been connected to the right number.

What must you think of us, Mrs. Cresspahl?
Am I supposed to think something?
Now you have something on me!
That's not the way I see it.
That's because you haven't spent enough time on the sixteenth floor yet!
Besides, white pumps in the desk, no one will believe me.
Well then there's no reason to tell anyone, is there.
Is that a deal, Mr. de Rosny?
Done, Mrs. Cresspahl.

– You don't look well, Gesine. What's the matter?
– You wouldn't believe me.
– Tell me, Mrs. Cresspahl. Tell Francine.
– This afternoon I went to two movies, one after the other. It must be that.

February 14, 1968 Wednesday

In Darmstadt, in a small dingy courtroom, a trial related to the murders that took place in 1941 at a ravine near Kiev known as Babi Yar has been under way for four months. *The New York Times* now gives the number of victims as more than thirty thousand Jews and around forty thousand others. The eleven defendants, former members of the SS, put on interested, bored, amused, or abstracted expressions. None seems worried or distressed by the evidence. One cannot recall, the next was not responsible, the next had only heard about it. When the walls of the ravine were dynamited and the debris was shoveled over the bodies of the victims, some were still alive.

One defendant was told that a previous witness had testified he was a specialist in stringing up little children by the leg, shooting them in the head with a pistol, and throwing them into a prepared ditch. This defendant got upset. It must have been someone else with the same name, he said. It wasn't him. It's a mistake. *The New York Times* counted the number of spectators at the trial on February 13. There were four. Yesterday, Bernd-Rüdiger Uhse, of West Germany, one of the prosecuting attorneys, explained the lack of emotion at the trial to *The New York Times* as follows: "If you see a car accident today and look at the bloody victims, you are horrified. But if you talk about the same accident five years later you will not get very upset about it."

In early November 1938, Herschel Grynszpan, seventeen years old, shot and killed the German embassy attaché Ernst vom Rath in Paris, "out of love for my dear father and my people, who are enduring unimaginable suffering." He was very sorry to have harmed anyone, he said, but he had no other way to express his protest to the world.

In early November 1938, there was panic in the USA—about outer space. Orson Welles broadcast a radio play on CBS, in which a spaceship landed in New Jersey and men with death rays attacked. Orson Welles's listeners took it to be a news report and fled the cities. Praying women knelt on the streets of New York. Other people ran around with their heads wrapped in handkerchiefs and scarves, to protect themselves from poisonous gases. The highways were jammed. Princeton University dispatched a scientific expedition, with student volunteers and death-defying professors. That was November 1938 in this country.

In the other country...

In Jerichow, Mecklenburg-Lübeck, in early November the party's regional film office showed two movies at the Rifle Club: *Sword of Peace* and *Jews Without Masks*. The former attracted an audience, even from the country-side, first because it promised to include recordings from the prewar period, second because it denied that there was a war to come, despite all the re-armament going on. The latter film, *Jews Without Masks*, practically emp-tied out the auditorium by the end, to the dismay of Prasemann the restaurateur, who had planned to sell the audience beer and schnapps af-terwards, and to the fury of Friedrich Jansen, who decided to post SA guards at the doors during the next screening. Whoever the regional party film warden might be, he clearly had no idea of country people's mentality. The film was assembled out of snippets of earlier motion pictures made by formerly German Jews, and it unveiled not "the disastrous effects of the Jewish influence on our culture" but the fact that the scenes depicted could only take place in the big city—try to picture Oskar Tannebaum alone in a drawing room with some lady! The Storm Troopers in the front row had stayed in their seats, though, and they went on buying rounds until midnight, enough to console Prasemann somewhat.

On November 5 and 6, the Hitler Youth were out and about again, with their second Winter Relief Collection Effort, and they not only accosted people on the streets but rang doorbells. Papenbrock, whom they had woken up from his afternoon nap, cursed them under his breath and boxed one of the boy's ears, who, considering his misdemeanor sufficiently punished, then held the collection box out to the old man after all. This was Otto Quade, who got smacked on the head again back home because August Quade, plumbing and heating, had a loan out from Papenbrock. There was a picture in the newspapers of Edda Göring's baptism—the very same person who is in a court battle today over her rights to a Cranach painting of the Madonna that the city of Cologne had had to give her father to mark the happy occasion—and the Gestapo in Gneez had received a denunciation of several persons who had failed to answer the call for donations for the baptism; the inquiry later revealed that the boy in question had held out his collection box to a group of chatting beer drinkers, that the offensive comment had been entirely unrelated, and that Alfred Bienmüller, who had already decided not to have his son confirmed, was surely justified in expressing the intention never to pay for any baptism whether or not his fifty-year-old wife ever bore him another child. Lisbeth Cresspahl was outraged that the second Winter Relief Collection Effort didn't even respect the sacred festival of Reformation Day. On November 8, the *Lübeck Gazette* published the news of the shooting of vom Rath, adding that in National Socialist Germany not a hair had been touched on a single Jew's head, let alone his life being threatened. Lisbeth seized on the bit about the hair, since Spiegel the lawyer in Kiel had been shot in the head, not that she was in any way condoning the murderous intent. Cresspahl saw anxiety flare up in her face for a moment—"like fire from a struck match," he would say ten years later—then serenity returned, almost amusement at how drastically the Lübeck newspaper had failed to get at the truth. Then the child, Gesine, who by that point had learned to tear the *Gazette* into pieces for toilet paper, was called into the room. Cresspahl had not taken his trip to Malchow and Wendisch Burg over the weekend, since Lisbeth had wanted to go to church on Reformation Day; he did not want to postpone it further. It didn't occur to him that things would go differently this time than they had two years ago when David Frankfurter had shot the Swiss Nazi Wilhelm Gustloff. He wanted to check that his parents' graves in Malchow were being maintained properly, to go see Schmidt and Büntzel in Güstrow, and to stop by Wendisch Burg so as not to hurt his sister's feelings. – Take the child with you: Lisbeth said. The child was standing by the coal scuttle, tearing the newspaper into strips, proud and serious as she was whenever she did the chores she had learned to do—feeding the chickens, picking berries in the garden. – Gertrud will be happy: Lisbeth said, not urging him, not trying to persuade him, and since Gertrud Niebuhr had once again not received the promised visit from Gesine this year, he and the child left to catch the eleven o'clock train.

– Gesine: she called out when they were already past the gate. She stood in the front doorway, leaning against one of the doors, her arms loosely crossed under her breasts. She waved, several times, until the child too raised her arm and moved her hand a little. But the child was tugging at Cresspahl with her other hand, and later he could only assume that Lisbeth had been smiling as she waved, and that she would have let herself be hugged.

My mother was seen two more times the next night.

It remains a mystery why she wanted to go to Gneez. The movie showing at the Schauburg Cinema was one she'd already seen in Lübeck, *Covered Tracks*, with Kristina Söderbaum. *Heroes in Spain* was playing at the Capitol that evening, preceded by *Festive Nuremberg*, which would only have reminded her of the war Cresspahl thought they were rehearsing for in it. The Gneez synagogue stood along Horst Wessel Street, which led from the Capitol Cinema to the station. When Lisbeth was seen there, the roof of the house of worship was already on fire but downstairs people in tattered clothes that looked like Methling charity were hauling shiny things out the front door, and things in sacks. The street was bright from the fire, and from the light in the synagogue, but the windows of both the adjacent houses were dark. A line of police ran all the way across the street from one firewall, and another line of police jutted out from the other wall. Lisbeth Cresspahl was noticed as she tried to cross the cordon to get to the far end of the street. The officer didn't even ask her what she was doing there; he advised her to go around the block and try from the other direction. The onlookers, a dark silent group, made room for her, but apparently she didn't move. She was still there when the fire truck came from the far end of the street and began setting up. By that time the fire had spread down to the ground floor of the synagogue, and the looters' trucks had left. The firefighters acted with urgency, precision, as if carrying out a drill, except for only one thing: they took up a waiting position instead of trying to put out the fire. Lisbeth may have still been there to see Joseph Hirschfeld come running up Horst Wessel Street, shoving the crowd aside with sweeps of his powerful arms in spite of his sixty-nine years, and how the same officer who had given such polite advice to the Papenbrock daughter ran the rabbi back through the crowd. He was holding the old man tight by the arm, and, also because he was taller, he looked like someone disappearing down Horst Wessel Street with a victim, not with a prisoner. Then the fire brigade did start spraying water from time to time, onto the corners of the buildings adjacent to the one on fire. When the roof of the house of worship collapsed and exploded into the air, burning sparks sprayed onto the street and the onlookers stepped backward. By that point Lisbeth was no longer there. Maybe she'd left to catch the Jerichow train, eleven thirty departure.

It seems that some of the people who'd set fire to the Gneez synagogue might have been in Jerichow too, in Oskar Tannebaum's shop, and if so she might have recognized them. The Jerichow police didn't have enough officers to cordon off the street, which was why Friedrich Jansen—sentry, mayor, police chief—was there too, revolver drawn. The SA, dressed up for the occasion, took their time with Tannebaum's shop. It was such a tiny opportunity, they had to draw out their pleasure as much as they could. It was like amateur theater. Prasemann the innkeeper held a finger to his lips, and only when the narrow street had fallen almost silent did he raise his ax and break the glass in the shop door with it. Then they recuperated with suppressed laughter. Oskar Tannebaum still didn't turn on the lights. Next they painstakingly hacked the door to pieces. The onlookers in Jerichow were more excited than the ones in Gneez, commenting on the spectacle, praising or deprecating the various blows. – *Here e goes there e goes, here e goes there e goes*: quoting Reuter in Plattdeutsch, or: *Well at least this doesn cost any money, said the farmer, as he beat his son.* Pahl said that one, for whom the Jew had been poor competition. It was meant not so much maliciously as pedagogically—it was time for this Jew to learn his lesson once and for all. When the SA were in Tannebaum's store, they discovered that they'd forgotten the shopwindow, and threw chairs and shelves through the panes from the inside. There's not much that's hard in a fabric store but they managed with the cash register, which sprang open when it hit the sidewalk. There was money lying on the street, not many bills, a few coins. – *Its not right*: a woman's voice said, clearly spoken by an old lady, distressed and appalled. – *And now we're off, said the mouse, as the cat ran across the floor with it*: said Böhnhase when Oskar Tannebaum was thrown out onto the street. He fell on his knees but stood up again at once. Demmler didn't like that (Hansi Demmler, Jerichow housing development), he'd liked it better seeing him on his knees. Tannebaum had to gather up the money on his knees and bring it to Friedrich Jansen. Friedrich Jansen waved over Ete Helms, and Ete Helms stood at attention before him but refused to take the money. Jansen, bright red in the face, threatened him with punishment for refusing an order, and Ete clicked his heels together and didn't take the money. For Jansen then to have tucked the money into his own jacket pocket would have been as bad for his reputation as what he did do, which was throw it on the ground and stomp on it. Only Peter Wulff, standing quietly off to one side until then, heard the first shot. Now he called for calm, in a businesslike military way, totally ignoring the representatives of state power. Then came the second shot. Friedrich Jansen ordered the street cleared for the fire brigade, and the old-fashioned vehicle was pushed up to the jagged hole in the building, even though there was no fire. Then Frieda Tannebaum came out of the building, slowly, without anyone pushing her from behind. She was carrying her eldest child in her arms. She stopped and stood, like Oskar, with her back to the wall. They looked at each other across the child. The child was Marie Tannebaum, eight years old, a wild, secretive little girl, who used to ramble around in the Countess Woods ever since Stoffregen hadn't let her come to his school anymore. She had long black braids that now hung almost down to the sidewalk. When she got too heavy for her mother, her mother slid down to the ground with the child in her arms, still obediently keeping her back against the wall, and collapsed on top of her. She was still holding her child as if the child were just asleep and mustn't be woken up.

Apparently Lisbeth Cresspahl arrived when Friedrich Jansen was stomping on the money. She had slowly pushed her way forward through the crowd and had just reached the front when the second shot was fired. After that she'd stood still, silent like everyone else. Only when Mrs. Tannebaum slid to the ground did she step forward, around Friedrich Jansen, so that the first slap in the face surprised him. But she hit him several more times, even though she couldn't seriously hurt the big heavy man. She lashed out at him the way a child does, clumsily, like she hadn't learned how. Friedrich Jansen simply grabbed her wrists.

Ete Helms pulled her back into the crowd, and because he had his hand on her shoulder Friedrich Jansen probably assumed she'd been arrested. Friedrich Jansen now took command of the fire department, and the fire department now had to shoot water into the building for half an hour, even though it was not on fire, because Jansen was standing behind the pump with his gun.

Ete Helms had let Cresspahl's wife go as soon as they were out of sight of the crowd. It was outside Papenbrock's house, and he put his hand to his cap in parting. Helms remembered her as going into the house, but he didn't actually see her do it.

– Is this another story you don't want to tell me?: Marie says. – Would Francine not understand it?

– She wouldn't.

– Like the rain-barrel story?

– Something like that.

– Don't tell me, Gesine.

February 15, 1968 Thursday

The question was a broad one. Would the use of nuclear weapons be considered in Vietnam. General Earle G. Wheeler, the chairman of the Joint Chiefs of Staff, answered it narrowly: Not in Khesanh.

There is also news about the people who consider me one of their own. Three East German girls were expelled from the Winter Olympics in Grenoble for warming the runners of their luges (sleds). But they said it was the West Germans' fault.

And once again *The New York Times* gives the mayor, the Honorable John Vliet Lindsay, a good hiding. Does he seriously think he should lease out the subway loudspeakers to carry commercials? A sample: "Times Square. Change for the BMT and IND. And stop at Nedick's for an orange drink and a hot dog." To a captive audience! On top of the cacophony of clank, screech, and grind under the ground! – It's incredible!: cries *The New York Times*, and down rain the blows on the mayor draped across her knee. An unpleasant sight, an excruciating sound.

Cresspahl traveled south with his child, through Blankenberg and Sternberg and Goldberg, the last leg from Karow to Malchow on a line that no longer existed after the war. The child learned: Blankenberg am See, "on the Lake," and Sternberg am See, and Goldberg am See, and Malchow am See, and to this day the name Karow exists in her memory as a dry place. There was nothing there but the station and a street and the Habben Inn. They had lunch on the train though, sandwiches that Lisbeth had packed and that her husband cut against his thumb into more manageable strips for the child. When he held the Mahn & Ohlerich beer bottle up to her face and let her open the flip top, she made a face but then did try a wary sip of the burning bitter stuff. They looked like old hands at traveling together. One time, somebody asked Cresspahl where he was going with "the little girl," and he gave the girl a long look and then said, sadly: *She doesn't wanna say*, and silly Gesine thought that here too he was respecting her pride. Cresspahl wasn't asked often.

At the Malchow cemetery, the graves of Heinrich Sr. and Berta Cresspahl were as neat and tidy as any paying customer could possibly want, and he didn't bother checking in with the caretaker first. The couple shared a gravestone, and Berta had had her name and date of birth chiseled into it at the time of her husband's death, so the year of her death stood out gleaming in the dim light.

Thats my dad and mum.
Cant they come out?

Theyre shut up in there for all time, Gesine.
Mommy says the dead come back.
Not here, Gesine. Not in our world.
Im never gonna be dead.
Thats right, Gesine. Dont be.

Gesine Redebrecht had the name Zabel now. Her father had fallen in the war, in 1916, her grandfather hadn't been able to get the woodworking business through the inflation. By 1924, neither building nor property was left from her inheritance, and she'd married a man who didn't take long to drink up the rest. Now Gesine Zabel was a maid in a hotel on Malchow Lake; Cresspahl took a room there because he didn't know that. (Three marks, child's bed one mark extra.) Cresspahl left the dining room as soon as the child got tired and sat with his pipe by the open window, near the black water, smeared now and then with the remains of the full moon. Other than that, not much light pitched and tossed on the water. Gesine Zabel didn't come out until just before midnight. She was now forty-nine years old. Her long thick blond hair had gotten thin, and sandy, and was too short for braids. She'd had to work hard for eighteen years now and hadn't been brought up for that kind of life. Countless frightened looks had left crow's-feet in the corners of her eyes. While serving the food she'd seemed harried, defenseless, annoyed, her expression preemptively apologetic. She was too tired after her day to be able to spend more than half an hour outdoors. In the morning, a plate with an apple and a knife was sitting on the windowsill, her excuse for visiting a guest's room.

Youre drinking, Hinrich.
Im drinkin, Gesine.
Peter Zabel wasnt bad.
Never heard anyone say he was.
Its not like I couldve married you.
We were just kids.
Why didnt you just stay in England, Hinrich!
My wife wanted it this way
Is she a good woman?
Shes a good woman, Gesine.

Is the child hers? She doesnt look like you.
She takes after me, I think.
And now youre drinking, Hinrich.
Is there anything I can do to help you?
No, Hinrich. Try to help yourself.

The next morning Cresspahl's child was shocked when told to shake hands with the woman who'd brought her breakfast, but she obediently stood up. She had also tried her best to get dressed and washed by herself, without her father's help, so as not to spoil the trip with him. She shook the woman's hand, made the Papenbrock curtsy, and thanked her in High German. It was only later that she dared to ask if the woman had been crying. That was on the way to the station, by a school with a chorus of children's voices coming out of an open window, and Cresspahl gave her a two-mark coin as "trip money" so that she would forget the tearful eyes of the strange woman, just as in the instructional verses of the children's book.

You Can't Trust the Fox in the Grassy Dew!
(Or any promise from a Jew!)

From Wendisch Burg they took a branch line running southwest from Neustrelitz, and then a postbus to the Niebuhrs. The driver dropped Cresspahl off in the middle of a mixed woodland. A low red roof in sluggishly creeping fog was visible between the leafless tree trunks. This was the Havel Sluice, Wend. Burg.

Already at the sluice-keeper's house with Cresspahl's sister and Niebuhr were Niebuhr's brother Peter and Peter's wife and child. It was with this Klaus Niebuhr, not quite five, a Berlin child who could barely speak Plattdeutsch and understood it not much better, that Gesine was sent off to play behind the house. There was a swing there, and the childless Niebuhrs had built a sandbox too. – But I don't live here, I live in Berlin!: said the boy....

Martin Niebuhr led his brother-in-law around the property with modest pride, showed him the sluice, the office, the two phones, the beehives, but for the rest of the afternoon Cresspahl was alone with Peter Niebuhr, who was trying to fix up a boat in the shed on the other side of the river. It was a wrecked H-Jolle dinghy with a broken mast that had lain out all through the previous winter too. Peter Niebuhr had bought it cheap, but he didn't know enough about boat-building, so the conversation with Cresspahl started out rather uncomfortably.

Peter Niebuhr, thirty years old at the time, took cautious stock of the older man. He could not comprehend a life story like his: Mecklenburg, emigration, return to the Nazis. He couldn't grasp the patience with which the other man held back what must have been his own questions: why a card-carrying member of the Communist Party had gone to the Eiche school for NCOs and from there to Darré's Reich Agricultural Corporation. After they'd been working side by side in silence for a while, Peter started with Dr. Semig, not without a certain defiance, prepared to make only minimal apologies. – *M'boy*: Cresspahl said after a time, and the man of thirty, university, graduate degree, employed at a ministry in the capital of the Reich, not only accepted this mode of address but also the calm, testing look in the eyes of this relative he barely knew, nothing more than a master carpenter in a tiny Baltic town. Then Cresspahl recalled the other man's education and said, in High German: It worked out well, just the way you probably had in mind. If you hadn't done it we couldn't have gotten him out of the country.

Cresspahl liked the kid. He had gotten all the stamina, strength, and horse sense of both Niebuhr brothers, leaving the elder, Martin, with nothing but muddleheadedness, dillydallying, and complacency. Cresspahl liked that Peter felt uneasy not only about giving up his party but about going over to the other side to feed his family. Cresspahl saw something of himself from fifteen years ago in it. And Peter could hardly have gone abroad with his career, unlike Cresspahl. He also liked the woman Peter had found to marry, this Martha Klünder, from Waren, still a girl, shy with everyone except her husband, not a trace left of the civil servant's daughter she'd been when he met her. Cresspahl looked at this marriage, not much more recent than his, with a certain envy. He thought about Perceval too, T. P., whom he'd lost in England, and of Manning Susemihl. Maybe he wanted to take one last try at something like that. He let Peter tell his side of the Griem story, then told him how it had looked from Jerichow. He didn't interrupt when the younger man started going into

632 · *February 16, 1968 Friday*

details about his superiors, who hadn't wanted to take his side without a Nazi pin on his lapel. After a while, they quit work and walked down the river as far as the next village, and came back for dinner almost totally of one mind. As for the boat, Peter should send it to Jerichow, he wouldn't pay for anything but the transportation. In return, Cresspahl wanted to learn how to sail.

The children were sent off to bed next to the living room. They'd spent all day telling each other about their parents, their houses, their neighbors, and they went right to sleep despite the murmur of voices in the next room, full of laughter, pleasure, an eagerness to be friends. Gesine had never in her life met so many new people in one day.

It was Gesine who heard the phone ring the next morning. Not the one connected to the Department of Waterways internal network but the regular one from the Reichspost. She had just reached the door to the office when Martin Niebuhr handed the receiver to Cresspahl. It was about six in the morning on November 10. My mother had already been dead for an hour.

February 16, 1968 Friday

The average woman industrial worker in Czechoslovakia is 5 feet 3 1/2 inches (161 cm) tall, weighs 139 pounds (63 kilos), and has a bust measurement of 35 inches (89 cm). These statistics are said to be important in helping industrial designers build machines better fitted to workers. Is this a mistranslation? Sometimes work follows Mrs. Cresspahl home to Riverside Drive.

– Gesine, I'm having problems with Francine.
– In school?
– There too.
– Are your white friends making you pay for having a black friend?
– They don't see her as my friend.
– Because you avoid her in recess every day?
– Because Sister Magdalena has separated us.
– Is this more *togetherness*?

– No. Francine feels so sure of me now that she isn't being careful.

– You were talking to each other in class?

– Almost never. It's like this: when she doesn't understand something, she relies on me.

– Are those Sister Magdalena's words?

– More or less.

– Do you believe her?

– Yes, Gesine. I believe her.

Secretary of State Dean Rusk has written an angry letter to Senator J. W. Fulbright. The latter's questions about the possible use of nuclear weapons in Vietnam did a disservice to the country. The letter does not explicitly rule out the existence of plans to deploy tactical weapons in Vietnam.

– Why is that a problem for you?

– You're saying it's none of my business, Gesine?

– It's Francine's more.

– I helped her.

– She thanked you.

– I helped her into a situation she can't handle.

– Give her a little time.

– Gesine, in fifth grade she has to learn the things she'll need for sixth. *Right?*

– *Right.*

– So she'll always be behind the rest of us.

– You're talking like Mrs. Linus L. Carpenter III. "With all our hearts we want the Negroes to be able to live in apartments like ours. It's just, maybe we won't start in our particular community, with its complicated arrangements that have developed along other lines."

– Gesine, I'm not handing out apartments, I'm stuck being owed something I don't want!

Twenty-four Soviet writers, including Konstantin Paustovsky and Vasily Aksyonov, have asked the chief prosecutor to grant to Alexander Ginzburg and his friends, convicted last month of anti-Soviet activity, a new trial that would not "evoke gloomy recollections" of the Stalinist trials in the 1930s. Could you think under any possible circumstances that now, in the fiftieth year of Soviet power, a Soviet court could make a wrong decision? Can you imagine it?

– Why isn't Francine here?
– I don't know.
– Where is she?
– I don't know.
– Does she have a key?
– I have to stay here because she doesn't have a key.
– What did she say when she left?
– That she'd had enough.
– Of you? Of us?
– Maybe. Or else maybe she can't stay cooped up in an apartment for so long.
– That's because of the one she came from.
– Of course, Gesine. I know. I don't blame her either. But why would she run away from her homework when this is maybe the first time she can do it in peace?
– It's too soon, Marie.
– I know how she is with reading too. If it's a comic book or a Western, you can't get it away from her. She's like someone who doesn't want to wake up. But not with a textbook.
– Teach her.
– Listen, she's out on Broadway, or 118th Street, people-watching or looking at shopwindows. Or cars.
– She's waiting for the brother who disappeared. Or she can't break the habit.
– And I'm supposed to go running around after her with *Mathematics Five*? Should I keep her here by force?

For two days, the Vietcong dug into Hue's Citadel have been bombarded and shot at from planes, artillery, and ship's cannons. Yet the US marines gained only 200 yards over the course of a day. As of yesterday American losses in combat since the official start of the war stood at 17,696 dead,

109,922 wounded, and about 1,000 missing or captured. Military authorities reveal the number of investigations into marijuana use by servicemen in Vietnam, but not the number that have yielded positive findings.

– You don't like Francine, Marie. Maybe your room is too small for the two of you.

– That's wrong, and that's not the point.

– You think she's ugly.

– I do not!

– You've said so.

– I may have said so when I didn't know her. Now I know who she is. It's not that.

– What is it?

– She can't live like we do.

– She breathes totally normal air, it seems to me.

– I know, Gesine. And she thinks nothing of going into all the drawers without asking. And when she gets curious about my photo collection, she doesn't put the pictures back the way they were. Do you like when she plays the tape recorder you leave out?

– She doesn't understand it, Marie. It's in German.

– And what if she erases it?

– To do that she'd have to deliberately hold down one button and then push another.

– It can happen by accident.

– Oh please.

– Look, I'll show you.

– Then I'll just take the battery out.

– And what'll you do if she opens the locked shelf of the bookcase, just because it's locked, and messes up all your Mecklenburg stuff? Or sells it?

– She doesn't steal, Marie.

– I'm not saying she does. Say: she takes it.

– Because she used to have nothing, and now still has almost nothing.

– She sometimes has more money than you give her. Count our grocery money.

– She knows where we keep it?

– I showed her.

– Objection overruled, Marie.

– No! It was so I could ask her not to unlock that drawer.

– And now if she does it, it's theft, and you've helped her do it. Is that it? That's how we'll kick her out? Or some other way?

The army has stockpiled equipment to control future summer riots, put it in secret depots across the country, and drawn up a central plan, complete with maps of sewer, water, and electrical systems. In addition, immediate airlifts of the National Guard to any potential trouble spot have been preplanned. Special Weapons and Tactics (SWAT) teams have been formed, each consisting of a rifleman whose weapon has telescopic sights, a spotter, and two officers with shotguns and hand guns to provide cover fire. For this summer.

– I suggest you apologize, Mrs. Cresspahl.

– If you want me to.

– And now tell me. What if Francine does learn from us that she needs to leave other people's things alone. That nothing dangerous is being kept from her. That you discuss money first, not just secretly take it. What will she do with all that when she goes back to her people?

– She's going back?

– People go back to their mothers, Gesine. How will she get along there with our ways?

– We need to think that far ahead?

– That's what you've always taught me to do. Two steps ahead.

– Why do you want to be responsible for more than *a bed for the night*?

– You don't get what I'm saying, Gesine.

– I don't get your jealousy. You know what de Rosny would say: Jealousy, *young lady*, is a terrible thing for a bank. *Bankers have human feelings too. Believe me.*

– Is that why you're holding that newspaper up in front of your face? Because I'm jealous?

– Hi, Francine.

– Hi Francine!

– Nice to see you, Mrs. Cresspahl.

February 17, 1968 Saturday

"REFUGEES FIND HUE PROVIDES NO HAVEN

By Thomas A. Johnson, special to *The New York Times*

HUE, South Vietnam, Feb. 16.—When the Vietcong's Lunar New Year offensive started here 17 days ago thousands of South Vietnamese refugees fled to Hue university on the south side of the Huong River for safety.

Today, there are more than 16,000 people cramped in the three main university buildings, about half of this city's new refugee population, and safety is nowhere in sight.

Several refugees have been killed and many wounded during artillery, rocket, and mortar duels between the enemy forces, along the southern end of the city's historic Citadel, and American forces directly across the river.

'Several South Vietnamese leaving the university have been shot by snipers just a few blocks away,' one American doctor said. A Vietcong sniper, posing as a refugee, and firing at American soldiers from a university window was shot to death yesterday by South Vietnamese policemen, also posing as refugees.

And this morning, tear-gas fumes dropped on North Vietnamese and Vietcong positions in the Citadel, drifted across the river to choke and irritate the refugees huddled in family groups in scores of university rooms.

The duels across the river continued sporadically all day. Several started when enemy gunners fired on naval landing craft ferrying supplies along the river to United States marines fighting in the Citadel. At other times, it was American artillery, jet fighter-bombers, or the 5-inch Naval shells from a ship offshore that caused enemy forces to retaliate at the only target within their reach.

After most of the duels, refugees can be seen carrying a wounded friend or relative to an aid station.

One man rushed to a concrete wall on the university grounds to watch a duel about 2 P.M. today. As soon as he crouched there, an enemy mortar exploded about 20 yards away and the man fell to the ground, blood running down the side of his face. He got up and ran quickly to a university building, almost knocking down a woman who carried a limp and bleeding child. . . .

The health, sanitation and food situations have changed for the better during recent days. American and South Vietnamese medical teams have inoculated 12,000 people against typhoid and cholera and have set up a permanent station to continue the inoculation. At least two cases of cholera have been reported here.

Work crews have cleaned up the hospital and have dug up latrines on the university ground. Tons of rice, vegetables and frozen sides of pork are distributed from each of the buildings.

But this improved situation has its own problems, an angry American civilian official pointed out. 'They're selling the rice,' Dr. Herbert A. Froewys, the deputy chief medical officer for the pacification program here, complained yesterday. 'The rice was sent to feed these people—they're selling it.'

The doctor hurrying through the compound, refused to tell just who was selling the rice. But he shouted: 'It's going to stop! Believe me, it's going to stop!' "
© The New York Times

"3 DEAD ENEMY SOLDIERS REPORTED CHAINED TO GUN
Allied Officers in Hue Assert the Bodies Were Discovered When School Was Taken

HUE, South Vietnam, Feb. 16 (Reuters).—Allied officers said today that three North Vietnamese soldiers had been found here, chained to a machine gun and left to die defending their position.

The three men were shackled around the ankles to the stock of a Chinese-made light machine gun. They held their position with other enemy troops for two days in a school until they were overrun yesterday by the South Vietnamese Fifth Marine Battalion.

The allied officers said the chained men were all privates. The men were barefoot and their bodies riddled with bullet holes.

'They were little men, same size as me,' a South Vietnamese marine only 5 feet tall said.

Maj. Paul Carlsen of San Clemente, Calif., an adviser with the South Vietnamese marines, said the chain binding the men to their gun was like a heavy dog chain and had links about half-an-inch wide.

The machine gun, which has a circular magazine and is commonly used by both North Vietnamese and Vietcong troops, can be operated by one

man. It was apparently intended that after the first man was killed the two others would operate the gun until all three were dead."
© The New York Times

"GERMAN POET HAILS 'JOY' OF LIFE IN CUBA
MIDDLETOWN, Conn., Feb. 16 (AP).—The German poet, Hans Magnus Enzensberger, has left a fellowship at Wesleyan University with a blast at United States foreign policy and praise for Cuba, where he said he wants to live.

Mr. Enzensberger took off from New York City today for California and a trip around the world, according to a friend on the Wesleyan campus.

The 38-year-old poet told a university audience this week that a three-week visit to Cuba had convinced him the Cuban people have 'a sense of joy, meaningful and significance.' He viewed United States foreign policy as an attempt to impose the will of the United States on smaller countries throughout the world."
© The New York Times

February 18, 1968   Sunday

My sympathies, Mr. Cresspahl.
Hello.
When did you hear of your wife's death?
This morning around six.
From whom?
Jansen.
The mayor and regional party leader?
Jansen.
In what form did you hear?
In no form. Over the phone.
What were his exact words?
"Good morning. Your wife is dead now."
In what tone of voice?
Jansen.
Are you and Jansen enemies, Mr. Cresspahl?

Jansen's no enemy of mine.

Your wife slapped Jansen in the face on 9 November 1938, 23:55 or 24:00 hours.

Am I under arrest?

Why would we arrest someone like you, Mr. Cresspahl. Look at all the rabble running around free.

Then I want to go see my wife now.

Of course, Mr. Cresspahl, right away. Just a couple more questions.

In that case I have something to ask you, Herr Commissioner—

Please, call me Vick.

How did she die. Of what.

That's what we are trying to find out from you, Mr. Cresspahl.

I haven't been in Jerichow since Tuesday morning. You were the one who came and picked me up from the Güstrow train.

And which train did you take to Güstrow?

The Berlin–Copenhagen.

And before that? Where have you been since Tuesday?

In Wendisch Burg. With family.

The whole time?

Before that in Malchow am See.

Can you prove it?

I have a hotel bill.

With whom did you have contact during this time?

I was checking on my parents. Their graves.

We'll find everything out, Mr. Cresspahl. We'll find everything out.

How did she die?

You had a fire, Mr. Cresspahl.

Yes.

So, you already knew that?

No.

Your in-laws live in Jerichow, you have a telephone, JErichow-209, and you want me to believe that—

My line was dead.

Ah, right. The fire truck drove into a telephone pole.

Yes.

How did you know that? You can speak freely.

February 18, 1968 Sunday · 641

You just told me, Mr. Vick. No one answered at the Papenbrocks'.

They couldn't. They'd long since left for Brickworks Road.

There was no phone on the train, no time in Güstrow, and I was going to try them from here in Gneez but you had me picked up.

I said "You had a fire" and you said: Yes.

Yes.

It doesn't surprise you in the least.

All that wood on the premises, it burns easy.

But it didn't start in the workshop. That didn't go up until later.

Where was my wife.

At midnight, in Jerichow on Market Square, and before that at the Jews' place when the accident happened.

What was she doing at the Tannebaums'?

Don't treat me like a child, Cresspahl. I'm a two-hundred-and-twenty pound man. Don't you read the newspapers?

Yes.

But not today.

Not today.

I see. And nothing struck you as out of the ordinary in Wendisch Burg. Your family lives in the middle of the forest.

My sister lives with her husband who operates a sluice, in the forest.

I want to tell you something, Cresspahl. What happened last night, across the whole Reich, is not what we're here to discuss. I don't want to hear anything about it.

What kind of accident was it, Mr. Vick.

A Jew brat got shot dead.

Walter? Marie?

Marie, Mr. Cresspahl. Marie Sara Tannebaum. Your wife—

My wife doesn't even have a gun.

It's none of your concern who the culprit was. Who made the mistake. Your wife was merely there.

And then she slapped him in the face.

That's right. Ah, here we have the report from Wendisch Burg. You were there. You might have said up front that your other brother-in-law is with the Reich Agricultural Corporation. Here. Look at this. We have no secrets here.

Then the fire started.

We don't know when the fire started.

Where did it start?

The fire department was called this morning, 4:30 a.m. The fire had just broken through the roof.

Through the roof of the house?

Of the barn. Where you had your workshop. Do you have enemies, Mr. Cresspahl?

Was it arson?

We don't know. Everything was burned to the ground, everything west of the former stalls. The fire burned through three of the four doors leading east from the workshop. The fourth, at the southwest corner, was locked and bolted. The fire got there last. The ceiling had only just started to smolder, but the oxygen must have been used up.

It used to be the fodder room.

That's where your wife was.

Was she dead?

No. She died while being carried out.

Did she die from the fire?

She wasn't burned to death, *if that's what you mean, Mr. Cresspahl. As of now the doctors have declared the cause of death to be asphyxiation.*

Yes.

Explain to me, please, how the workers in the house could have not heard anything. Or seen anything.

All the windows on the east side have shutters. If any panes broke there the glass would have fallen inwards, not out onto the stone. If the fire spread from the threshing floor and the barn stalls, through the workshop and the jobs in progress, then all the light would have gone up or west. No one lives to the west. If the fodder room's still standing then the glass in the south door must've been the last to go. Alwin Paap must have heard that.

Like you were there in person, Mr. Cresspahl.

Yes.

Alwin Paap was not who called the fire department.

Then it was Friedrich Jansen from across the street. He might have noticed the light when the north gate started burning.

It was indeed Jansen, Mr. Cresspahl. Does that make anything come to your mind?

Mr. Vick, can I go see my wife? It's three hours until the next train.

You won't need a train, Mr. Cresspahl. Now tell me something. Earlier you spoke somewhat disparagingly of Jansen.

I said that I had no quarrel with him.

You're too good for that.

I'm a carpenter. Jansen's a regional party leader. What would I have to fight about with him, Mr. Vick?

Let us say, for the sake of argument, arson.

Impossible for someone from the outside. Anyone who tried to break into the workshop wouldn't get far without making a lot of noise. It's not like a fire, contained by the walls and the roof. My wife would have heard something. Paap definitely would.

Your wife hears it, gets up out of bed, pulls on a winter coat—

A blue housecoat. Padded. London label.

As if you were there, Mr. Cresspahl. She surprises the intruder at the door—

At which door?

That's just it, we have no evidence! Of course we don't! That Jerichow fire brigade of yours seems to think you open a lock by swinging an ax at it!

Yes.

Since they couldn't put out the fire.

The fire department couldn't put out the fire.

They tried, Mr. Cresspahl. They found the hydrant in the courtyard and hooked up the hoses and rolled them out, all of which took some time, and then the pump wasn't working. They'd used it to make trouble at the Jews' place.

Who had?

Jansen, Mr. Cresspahl.

Yes.

Nothing occurs to you.

So all the wood in the yard burned too.

All gone, Mr. Cresspahl. Everything. The machines are nothing but melted scrap. And then the walls collapsed on them too, and the roof. You could say you were lucky not to lose the house.

Yes.

The intruder, the arsonist, now takes your wife's keys, drags her into the workshop, hits her over the head—

Did my wife have a head wound?

We don't know. She has a spot on the back of her head that might be from a sandbag.

I know who works with sandbags.

My dear Mr. Cresspahl, I will pretend I didn't hear that. We're not the Gestapo here, we are the criminal police, but I advise you not to try to take advantage of that. So the guy takes your wife, unconscious now, and locks her in the fodder room—

The fodder room has a double bolt. A child could get out of there.

But there was no key in the door.

We keep the key in the door on the outside, and never lock it.

There was no key there, Mr. Cresspahl. Now he can take his time to start the fire, lock the door again, and get away. He may not have had far to go.

It would have to be someone who didn't like the work the shop is doing for the Mariengabe air force base. Or was doing.

Mr. Cresspahl, if you are trying to get someone cleared just so you can take revenge on him personally—well, fine. But that's no use to me.

So I can leave now.

You're not leaving, Mr. Cresspahl. Will you please take a close look at this rope.

That's not a rope. It's a piece of clothesline.

Perhaps one of your clotheslines?

Why not?

Do you recognize it?

My wife kept her clotheslines in the house, to keep them dry.

And what about for the little everyday items of laundry?

They put up one line, usually, and it's not always taken down at night. Along the garden fence.

We found it cut, Mr. Cresspahl. Don't touch the end, that's evidence!

Some folks steal a cow in one place and a rope for it somewhere else.

He wasn't stealing a cow, Mr. Cresspahl. But he knew what he wanted. We won't know whether this piece matches the rest of your clothesline until the report comes back from the lab. But we do know that your wife was tied up with this piece of clothesline.

It doesn't look burnt at all.

But it smells like it's been hanging in smoke for a year. It was tied around her ankles, and also pulled through a ring in the wall and knotted. There was another piece on the ground next to her, she'd obviously managed to get her wrists out of that one.

So I'll be going now.

One more thing, Mr. Cresspahl. Did Friedrich Jansen actually say, "Your wife's dead now?"

"Good morning" and then that.

Not, for instance, "Your wife has committed suicide"?

No.

And so what do you think of the fact that Friedrich Jansen is telling everyone in Jerichow who'll listen that your wife committed suicide. What do you say to that?

I say it's none of his business.

Mr. Cresspahl. You don't understand what I'm saying. You are trying to not understand me. You are here at the police station. The criminal police, not the secret police.

I haven't forgotten.

And now I have something about you, too, that I don't plan to forget, Mr. Cresspahl! You may go now.

Is my wife at home, Mr. Vick.

Your wife is not at home. The body has been confiscated due to suspicion of foul play. There will be an autopsy tonight. You may report to the Gneez hospital tomorrow, Mr. Cresspahl. If you want to know what she died of. My sympathies, Mr. Cresspahl.

Goodbye.

February 19, 1968 Monday

This victim is named, Ngo Van Tranh, and yesterday morning in Saigon a South Vietnamese marine suspected him of being a member of the Vietcong. Ngo Van Tranh, already seriously wounded, said that the Vietcong had taken him from his home in Thuduc the previous night and forced him to carry ammunition. He is offered water, he's clearly trying to drink it; he is lying half under some boards. Then he's questioned by another marine and threatened with a rifle. Then a third marine knifes him and finally kills him with a rifle burst. Three times the Associated Press takes a photograph, and in the last one he who had once been Ngo Van Tranh is lying in the rubble almost completely under the boards.

Cresspahl didn't try to find answers. He found them.

On Thursday night he'd stayed in Gneez. He went to see Wilhelm Böttcher, the master of the carpenter's guild in the Gneez district; after he left, Herbert Vick came round to question Böttcher. If Böttcher was to be believed, Cresspahl had bought some of Böttcher's best wood off him—light oak, aged five years. – You realize, don't you, that I am here from the police, not the Gestapo: Vick said, in that confrontational way of his that he thought won people over, but Böttcher refused to say whether or not he thought Cresspahl was being a little too businesslike, going around making purchases when his wife wasn't even in the ground yet. Vick left with a renewed appetite for the next incomprehensible piece of information.

Vick spent the evening in the dining room of the City of Hamburg Hotel, where Cresspahl had taken a room. Sat there over his official beer— a short fat comfortable man, kneading his plump chin and staring off in the direction of the door whenever his nose wasn't buried in his thick notebook. Vick didn't discover what Cresspahl ordered from room service because Alma Witte wouldn't be cowed. He did better with the hotel employees he waylaid in secret. Cresspahl didn't go anywhere for quite some time, as if he wanted to stay hidden from everyone, stay where he was. After a while Wegerecht, the district court head judge, invited Vick to join him at his table; Vick felt somewhat exposed sitting there with his beer and chaser but couldn't bring himself to join the gentlemen in drinking their red wine. Finally, the bellhop peered into the dining room as though looking for someone, and Vick made his way out to the lobby. He stood next to the telephone girl and read the slips of paper on which Cresspahl had written out his telegrams, handing them to her one by one. They were ordinary death notices, to be sent to Timmendorf, Wismar, Wendisch Burg, Neustrelitz, Schwerin, Berlin, Lübeck. He had her translate the one to London. – Mr. Cresspahl requests the recipient's presence at the funeral of his wife: Elise Bock said pertly, happy to show off her knowledge of foreign languages, indignant about the snooping, and Vick told her, too, that he was from one particular department and not from a certain other particular department. It came out sounding unusually harsh because he was irritated at the certainty with which Cresspahl gave the date of the funeral, as if he knew the body would be returned to him by then. Smith, in Richmond—that sounded a bit suspicious. Meanwhile, the questions from the gentlemen Wegerecht and Rehse made it all too clear that Vick was good enough to sit with them only as long as he kept feeding them tidbits about this latest Jerichow affair. Vick pleaded the late autopsy and left earlier than he would have liked. On the corner of the market square he turned around, but Cresspahl's windows were still half open, and dark.

The next morning, he waylaid the man at the Gneez train station. The man had gone to the hospital at seven a.m. and they hadn't shown him his wife. As Vick could have told him. – I wouldn't advise it: Vick said. – Yes: Cresspahl said. – I mean, looking at your wife: Vick said. – Yes: Cresspahl said. He didn't look too exhausted but his eyes wouldn't quite focus, and they were redder than they'd been the day before. Vick let him leave on the train to Jerichow and then got in his car, but got stuck behind some very slow trucks on the long narrow climbing country road, and he had no desire to pick a fight with anyone driving vehicles with air force plates. So now Cresspahl was more than half an hour ahead of him.

The Jerichow fire brigade hadn't been able to put out the fire completely and had posted a fire watcher by the smoldering ruins. The workshop building had collapsed, except for the eastern outer wall with the stubs of the former stalls still attached, and the almost untouched box of the Pinnows' fodder room to the south. Where there'd been a machine, you could still sometimes see a little smoke rising out of the rubble. They'd pulled apart the burning woodpile in the yard, and charred black boards and beams lay scattered all the way to the remaining workshop wall. They'd ripped out the barbed-wire fence in the bushes and dragged it across Brickworks Road, like a barrier. The house hadn't been this visible for a long time—now it was hidden by nothing but the bare walnut trees. Dazzling white window crosses in the clean red walls. The sky, sunless, was a bright white. It was so quiet that it was like no one was there, Cresspahl thought.

In the kitchen there was a fire under the kettle, like every morning. The door to Lisbeth's room was closed.

Her dress lay draped over the foot of the bed. She'd meant to hang it up in the closet and then go to sleep. The blankets were thrown back. She'd sat on the edge of the bed, not for very long. The air here was almost free of smoke.

In the kitchen she had taken the hurricane lamp off its hook. She had opened the door to the hall very quietly, so that the workmen in the west rooms wouldn't hear. Walking barefoot.

Some kerosene had been spilled in the storeroom. She was already hurrying by then. From the back door on, she probably ran.

She had so little time that instead of untying the clothesline she'd hacked through it with a knife. You should always untie every knot was what she'd always told the Labor Service girls. The pruning knife had been stuck into the top of a fence post, so that someone would notice it and it wouldn't be ruined.

Where the path started to slope down by the pump there was an impression in the wet ground, as if she'd fallen there, onto her knee. But there were a lot of footprints overlapping there, and yet no sign of bare feet.

The south gable of the workshop hung down at an angle. The door was now only the frame. The doorpost had been hacked away with axes. The debris on the ground was black and greasy with smoke. The two panels of the door were still joined in the middle by the lock. Here she'd gained herself a little extra time.

When she'd entered the workshop on the night of Wednesday to Thursday, it had smelled of cut wood, stain, varnish, machine oil, work. She hadn't turned on the light because the big bright patch in the night might have woken Alwin Paap. She'd blocked the glow of the lamp with her body and then set it down in the middle of the old barn's threshing floor under a machine, so that the building would again look dark from the outside.

Then she faced another choice. She could unhook a ladder from the wall, lean it against one of the crossbeams, climb up, kick the ladder away, tie herself to the beam with the clothesline, and jump. That way she wouldn't have needed three hours to die. But maybe she didn't want to be seen with her head dangling sideways from a broken neck, not by anyone. She decided she shouldn't be found at all.

Then she dragged the clothesline back and forth across a saw blade and cut it into short pieces, unsuitable for hanging. Now all she needed to do was knock over the lamp. Everything here would burn.

In five years the Pinnow barn had become a solid, windproof building.

It was dry inside, even in winter, and slightly warm on even the coldest days. She didn't need to do much to help the small fire along. It was enough to lay down a path for it from wall to wall, from one long end of the building to the other. By then the walls were already hot and clothed in bright colors.

When a flickering sheet of fire came down from the third crossbeam and draped the north door, the fire was already pushing into the room where the oil cans were. Then she was surrounded on all sides, except for one permeable place near the south door where the flames kept parting. She'd have been through it in a single bound.

She hadn't been trying to escape. She'd locked herself in the former fodder room so that people wouldn't find her easily or soon. She'd decided to wait there.

In jumping through the door she brought hardly any fire with her. She'd shoved the key down into a crack between the floorboards where no one would find it. The fodder room, turned into the workmen's room, was empty, with no tools she could have used to get the key back out of the floor. The window had iron crossbars set into the wall. There wasn't even a way for her to let air in—there were also the heavy shutters covering the window and bolted on the outside. Now she was safely locked in.

The fire hadn't come up to her from the floor, it came through the wall of the toolroom and down from above. At first the walls just creaked, then the heat charred them black. The floor stayed intact until the end. Then she'd bound her feet, knotting the rope to the ring, so that she couldn't run away. When she was totally stupefied, she tried to tie her hands. Cresspahl didn't believe that. When she fell over, maybe she hit the back of her head against a protruding beam; maybe she was dazed from that without realizing it.

The firefighters hadn't found her right away because the fire was blazing too high, and roaring too loud, for there to be anyone left inside to save. They'd knocked the first door on the right out of the wall, with its frame, because it was locked. The damp debris lay on the ground. In the debris was a push broom, its handle broken off, otherwise almost clean. Cresspahl, kneeling, brushed off the spot where he conjectured Lisbeth. The chalk outline showed a shape lying on its side, arms stretched out near the body, like a sleeping woman's.

They'd been in no rush to get her out.

They'd put out the fire around the fodder room with bucket after bucket of water from the pump, to secure the evidence.

The interior walls had already burned thin by that point but they were still standing, and the roof hadn't yet come down. So they could pick her up and run out the south doorway where they'd broken the door in, down the path between the workshop and the lumber pile, which was just starting to burn.

Then she'd lain on the ground until she was dead.

– A complaint from you, Mr. Cresspahl, that's all I need!: Vick pleaded. He was standing on Brickworks Road as if he'd sprung up out of the ground, but could only look over at Cresspahl, not trusting his short legs to get him through the snarls of brush and wire. He lifted one foot halfway over the barrier, then put it back down. He'd caught up to Cresspahl after all, but now it was of no use.

February 20, 1968 Tuesday

– Don't you want to wake up, Gesine?

   – I can't.

   – Just a little, Gesine.

   – You're Marie.

   – Not necessarily, Gesine.

   – But you are.

   – Yes. But I'm not scared.

   – Am I in the hospital?

   – You're in your room, Gesine.

   – But it's dark as the grave in here.

   – That's because we've shut all the curtains. You're not supposed to have any bright light.

   – So I'm only sick?

   – Dr. Rydz wants to check on you.

   – Dr. Rydz?

   – He doesn't just know about children, Gesine.

– You have the flu and a fever, Mrs. Cresspahl. It's practically an epidemic in the city.

– So you did make it through after all, Dr. Semig.

– It's no trouble at all for me to come see you, Mrs. Cresspahl.

– But you need to register at the Hamburg district court, Herr Semig.

– Of course, Mrs. Cresspahl.

– If you don't you might be declared dead, Herr Semig.

– Everything will be fine, ma'am.

– No.

– 39.2.

– What's that in Fahrenheit?

– 102.6, Miss Mary. It's not dangerous.

– This morning she was 103.6.

– 39.8. It won't get that high again.

– But she's not eating.

– Until tomorrow, Mrs. Cresspahl.

– Don't forget! The district court, Hamburg!

– *D'y'wanna drink some?*

– You're not Marie.

– *I don't get you, Mrs. Cresspahl.*

– *You are not Marie.*

– *Of course not. I'm Francine.*

– Marie.

– *Mary!*

– You can go back to sleep now, Gesine.

– I have to go into the office.

– I already called to excuse you.

– You can't do that. Nobody can do that.

– Mr. Kennicott II says you should stay home until Monday. With best wishes.

– I don't know him.

– But he knows you, and even your shoe size. No, sorry, the size of some shoes that aren't yours.

– Marie, I have to go to work.

– You have to sleep, Gesine.

– And what'll you live on?

– I can cook, I can bake—

– and then tomorrow / the child / I'll take. *And there will be / an end of me.*

   – *Of him*, Gesine. Rumpelstiltskin.

– What day is it today, Marie?

– *Tuesday.*

– But it must be Friday.

– On Friday you came home from work with a headache. On Saturday we had a South Ferry day, and I'm sorry. You've been in bed since Saturday night, and Dr. Rydz came the first time on Sunday. Since then you've been asleep, and talking in your sleep.

– I don't talk in my sleep, Marie!

– I know. Dr. Rydz explained it to me. It's part of the sickness. You don't always know who you are.

– I do too.

– And what's with 1906? November 12?

– That's when Lisbeth Papenbrock was born.

– You were talking about that. For a long time.

– I want to go to the hospital.

– You can't go to the hospital. Mrs. Erichson is coming tonight.

– I don't want her to.

– She'll sleep in your room so you're not alone if you wake up in the night. It's no trouble for her, she doesn't sleep much anyway.

– But I don't want Louise Papenbrock sitting at my bedside at night.

– There's nothing you can do about it, Gesine. D. E. sent her, she must be in Bayonne by now.

– And you called a Jewish veterinarian too!

– A Jewish pediatrician, Gesine.

– You see!

– It's the fever, Gesine. Dr. Rydz explained it to me, and now I'm not scared anymore.

– Marie. Did I say anything else?

– Yes, about a fire. In Brooklyn and a man and his child burned to death.

– In Brooklyn?

– Yes, in Bedford-Stuyvesant.

– When was that?

– This morning.

– This morning you were in school. You yourself said it's Friday.

– It's Tuesday. And we didn't go to school. You're still contagious. Maybe you heard us talking about the fire in Brooklyn.

– Who was here before, Marie?

– That was the doctor, Dr.—

– I know that. I'm not asking about that. Sorry.

– It's the fever, Gesine.

– But there was someone else here. A girl. Back from somewhere.

– That was Francine. I'm also sorry I had a fight with you about her.

– That wasn't so long ago.

– Friday evening.

– You see! Friday!

– Francine has been with us since the Sunday before last.

– All right, Sunday. And there's no child here.

– Francine went to the pharmacy.

– Marie, but, there are more people here, I just can't see them in the dark.

– You were dreaming, Gesine. You dreamed about people in black suits and dresses.

– Yes. On Sunday.

– And now you need to sleep.

– I want a sleeping pill, but it has to be the kind where you don't dream.

– I'll get you one tomorrow.

– I need it now.

– It's the middle of the night, Gesine.

– You're talking to me like I'm a child. And calling pediatricians! Anyway you're right, I am one.

– You are one, Gesine. You're asleep.

February 21, 1968 Wednesday

On Friday morning, after Cresspahl left for the train back to Gneez, Pastor Brüshaver went to work on his funeral sermon.

Cresspahl had not requested a sermon.

He had come from the scene of the fire, face sooty, coat streaked with dirt and debris, and listened to Brüshaver's account. Sat patiently on the visitor's chair, his unseeing eyes on the man across from him, hands held loosely in his lap, not folded. He'd washed his hands. His eyes were screwed up, tense with remembering, and Brüshaver realized he was the final eyewitness Cresspahl wanted to hear from.

She had lain on the north side of Brickworks Road, by the Creutzes' fence, reposing on the coat from a brown uniform. There'd been a lot of people standing around her—Friedrich Jansen, Alwin Paap, the Labor Service girl, old Creutz, Amalie Creutz, Aggie Brüshaver, Brüshaver, and others whose names Brüshaver didn't know. It was still night, dark, the light from the fire only flickering this far. He decided not to mention Lisbeth's clothes. Cresspahl asked. Lisbeth had had on a blue housecoat but it was open, and he'd noticed spots where the nightgown underneath had burned through. Brüshaver had gone over to her just as Berling slipped his hand out from behind her head. He continued to kneel, though, and he'd closed her eyes before Brüshaver kneeled down. He saw no damage to her face except some fresh blood from her nose and a patch of open skin under one eye. The right eye. Berling had later called the blood under her nose "pulmonary blood," from the asphyxiation. Then Aggie had covered her with her own coat. Friedrich Jansen got the phone number for Wendisch Burg from Alwin Paap, then left. At half past six, the police from Gneez had arrived. They'd brought an ambulance and by seven, after inspecting the house and the scene of the fire, they'd driven off.

Cresspahl also wanted to know who had laid the body onto the stretcher, seemed satisfied to hear that it was the two orderlies from the ambulance, and stood up. Brüshaver had suggested Sunday for the funeral. Cresspahl said: Monday, at three. Brüshaver had had a church funeral in mind, and Cresspahl said: She doesn't need to go into the church. Brüshaver asked about the text for the graveside ceremony, and Cresspahl pulled the page that was now missing from the City of Hamburg Hotel Bible out of his coat pocket. It was Psalm 39, with some verses crossed out. Cresspahl placed the page on the desk, as if not sure the pastor would find it in his own Bible.

What remained for Cresspahl to ask came easily, he had thought about it so many times. The request wasn't for him at all, it was for Lisbeth. Brüshaver felt like he was being asked for a casual favor more than anything else. He knew it wasn't customary: Cresspahl said. But his wife shouldn't lack for anything at the grave.

And thou shalt not want.

This Cresspahl had requested: invocation, lesson, prayer, Lord's Prayer, consecration, benediction. That was three items more than the Church of Mecklenburg allowed to suicides.

Brüshaver followed Cresspahl into the kitchen, where Aggie had set up a washbowl for him and was brushing his coat. After Cresspahl had dried his face, Brüshaver asked him about the blessing in the house. – *Nooo*: Cresspahl said, and Brüshaver already understood that this man did not want the church in his house anymore, now that he was alone there. Cresspahl hadn't needed to drape the hand towel so neatly over the back of a chair, like something he had now used for the last time.

Then Brüshaver had to watch his own wife throw herself on the other man's chest, as if seeking forgiveness for something.

His wife put fresh coffee on his desk every two hours, even brought him his meals so that he wouldn't have to get up from his work, not even for fifteen minutes. A woman in the house with eyes red from crying, and three children creeping past the door as though beaten into silence, how was anyone supposed to work like that!

Aggie wanted the Sunday sermon to discuss Lisbeth. That went against every rule and custom. She could be mentioned by name in the religious service for the congregation on the following Sunday, when she was in the ground. The woman knew that. He didn't want to lose face with her. This Cresspahl wanted the church to acknowledge partial responsibility for the death of his wife. Brüshaver would never see him in church again whatever he did; still, he didn't like the thought of spending his life next door to someone who didn't respect him at all. That's vanity, Brüshaver. You don't want to put up with someone refusing to say hello to you in the street for as long as you live in this town. That's not vanity.

Brüshaver hadn't gotten three words down on paper when someone came to bother him. Vick, from the Gneez police (not the Gestapo). Wanting to hear about conflict between Friedrich Jansen and Cresspahl. He didn't understand that in Jerichow the two men might as well have been on opposite ends of the earth, and that it was the town's other inhabitants who'd whipped up any conflict between them and kept it going. Was Jansen capable of seeking revenge? Jansen was capable of seeking revenge, but only when in his cups and with Cresspahl out of town—sensing a trap, Brüshaver said nothing. Why would a man like Vick suspect a, let us say, worthy champion of National Socialism? What did he need this denunciation for, was he trying to get Jansen safely locked up in jail before saddling him with irregularities in the Jerichow city finances? – Because we have to purge the rabble from our ranks! – Because I am a faithful National Socialist!

There is no passage in the Bible that explicitly forbids suicide. Young Mrs. Cresspahl had asked about that, when she was still alive. If you looked at it properly, this was an unmistakable cry for help. There may have been other people in the town from whom she had sought reassurance, support, information; they were under no obligation to admit it. The pastor had a duty to confess it. But you can't start a sermon for the twenty-second Sunday after Trinity like that.

On Thursday at around noon, Brüshaver had gone to see the Tannebaums after they hadn't come to see him about Marie's funeral. Brüshaver had planned to offer them a burial (a "quiet" one) in his cemetery, assuming Oskar had final say and his wife didn't want to take the child to the Catholics. He found the family in the wagon shed in the yard. They had set the coffin on the ground and were sitting on chairs around it. It was a mass-produced coffin, with shiny black varnish. The Gestapo had sent it from Gneez, and Swenson was to bring it back to Gneez that evening for a nighttime burial. The child looked very tall stretched out inside it, head tilted sharply back, arms at her sides. The blood that had run out of the hole in her temple had been dabbed away so cautiously that the traces were still visible, and they had avoided touching the wound itself. Oskar stood up in front of Brüshaver as though wanting to block his way to the body. He said, in a stubborn but not hostile voice: Now that shes died like a Jew, shes gonna get a Jewish burial. When Swenson drove up in his hearse that evening, the house was empty, as messy and waterlogged as the SA had left it. The von Bobziens owned the house; that was why Jansen had wanted to prevent the fire that wasn't there. The Tannebaums had left town on Field Street, with the coffin and the dead girl's little brother on a farm cart, the parents on foot, wife next to the horse, Oskar next to the boy, who sat facing backward. If they were trying to get to Lübeck, they had many miles of sodden roads ahead of them before they reached a main road. Now it was Friday afternoon, and no one had seen them in any farm, in any village. Brüshaver had thus been spared the fuss with the church authorities and the Gestapo over giving the little Jewish girl a Christian burial. Now, for Lisbeth Cresspahl, he was about to risk much more than a warning.

True, the Bible does not explicitly forbid suicide. But in place of the prohibition there is the reminder of God's mercy offered to those in despair. Now it was also the case that suicide made it impossible to repent, and thus be forgiven. He certainly couldn't stand up before the congregation and deny forgiveness to Lisbeth Cresspahl. Brüshaver took up his book and read. He sought proof that God reserved to Himself the right to end a life, because He alone knew the end to which He was directing that life. Reading like this gave him a fleeting, uncomfortable feeling; it was excused by the task, it was an excuse to avoid the task.

Late that afternoon it occurred to Brüshaver that he didn't know for certain whether Lisbeth had deliberately and premeditatedly taken her own life. It was only Cresspahl who had admitted it, by asking for the exception; Cresspahl had been far from Jerichow on the night of Wednesday to Thursday. Word around town was of an accident, and Jansen had started rumors of murder by so stubbornly insisting that it had been suicide. Brüshaver took the six o'clock train to Gneez. He found Cresspahl in Böttcher's workshop. Böttcher brought the Jerichow pastor only as far as the door. Böttcher could understand that Cresspahl wanted to make his wife's coffin with his own hands; it was still a bit embarrassing, though, and he didn't like having anyone watch his colleague do this work.

Cresspahl gave Brüshaver a pleasant look and rested his arms, laying them along the bottom part of the box, which after eight hours work he'd finished. Brüshaver asked his question. He heard his voice take on a pleading tone, and on top of that Cresspahl was looking at him the way a teacher looks at a pupil who even after a simple explanation still hasn't understood. – *Yesss*: he said patiently, with something like amusement in the corners of his eyes. Brüshaver repeated his question. Lisbeth had, after all, believed in God. Now Cresspahl filled himself a pipe, lit it, clapped the cover shut, spat at the match. – Now maybe he'll believe her too: he said.

He stood up, not because Brüshaver had found nothing to sit on but to stretch, his pipe held high in his fist. He waited for the next question. Brüshaver looked with a kind of horror at this man who could impugn his own wife with such a death and accept the loss of the insurance money for the workshop and machines so that she could keep this death of hers forever. He let Cresspahl wish him good night and left, but stopped again out in the yard. Cresspahl had sat back down next to the coffin, hunched over, letting his hands hang into the box, still holding the pipe. Clearly he wanted to use this burdensome interruption at least as a work break. He didn't look the least bit out of place in the other man's workshop.

If God does not forbid suicide, does He not guide the desperate person's hand when He permits such an end? If God arrogates to Himself the right to let live, is it not also God's purpose when that life ends? Now Brüshaver had only Saturday left, and less than half a page written.

On Saturday Cresspahl's notice appeared in *The Gneez Daily News*. It was signed by the Papenbrock, Paepcke, and Niebuhr families, but Cresspahl had written it. There was no mention of tragic fate, of God's (inscrutable) wisdom, or of Lisbeth having been taken (snatched) from life. It said: Lisbeth Cresspahl has passed away.

The police had released her. Early that morning Swenson brought her to Jerichow, but before the news had gotten round town, there was new barbed wire strung up around Cresspahl's property. Anyone passing by, as though just by chance while out for a stroll, probably saw Cresspahl, Paap, and Heine Klaproth clearing a path to the house door through the piles of charred wood and broken bricks; no one dared go up to the house. Clearly Vick, too, no longer considered the yard a crime scene. And Aggie Brüshaver went to her husband in the study and told him that people had been pestering her all morning about when exactly the Cresspahl funeral was going to be, more eager than grieved, and that Frieda Klütz was going to have a new black dress made for herself in the two days left until Monday.

After that, the words came to Brüshaver quickly and easily. By noon Aggie could sit down at the typewriter. He paid visits that afternoon, and everyone who saw him so relaxed and cheerful couldn't believe it the next day.

Twenty-two weeks after Trinity Sunday was, as decreed by the government in Berlin, one of the monthly "stew Sundays," when the money for

Sunday dinner was to go instead to the Winter Relief Program. But Fried-rich Jansen was out, on something he called a matter of honor, and without him the SA didn't dare to make social calls as a pretext for checking whether a household had a roast on the table after all. The church was no more crowded than usual. Cresspahl was not there.

Brüshaver opened with Matthew 18, the requirements for entry into the kingdom of heaven: Except ye be converted, and become as little children. Then there's talk of he who offends the child, and it were better that a mill-stone were hanged about his neck and he were drowned in the depth of the sea. (Brüshaver left out the part about the necessity of such evil in the world, and the misery threatened to those who commit it.) Then came the bit about the hundred sheep. If one of them goes astray, doth a man not leave the ninety and nine behind and go seek the one? And if he finds it, that one is most precious to him. And you should forgive seventy times seven.

Then he gave the people of Jerichow the speech that Cresspahl hadn't wanted to hear at the grave. He gave it for Louise Papenbrock, who even now couldn't keep from showing, with her stiff back and raised chin, pride that in the end it was none other than she who had lost her youngest daughter. He gave it for Albert Papenbrock, who at first stared rigidly at the pulpit, as though performing a duty and a scandalous one too, then thoughtfully, as though pondering a suggestion. He gave it for people like Richard Maass, who saw going to church that day as more of a rebuke of improper behavior than anything else. He gave it for the man who took transcriptions of his sermons to the Gestapo. He gave it for Hilde Paepcke, who was crying. He gave it for Lisbeth, and he apologized to her. He gave it for Cresspahl.

It was none of the Jerichowers' business how Lisbeth Cresspahl had died. Suicide was not reprehensible before man or on moral grounds. It was a matter between Lisbeth and her God that she had expected more from Him than He had been willing to give. She had been as free to die as she was to live, and if it would have been better to leave the death to Him, she had at least offered up a sacrifice to atone for another life—a murder of self for the murder of a child. Whether that was a mistake or not would not be decided in Jerichow.

On the other hand, it was very much the Jerichowers' business *that* Lisbeth Cresspahl had died. They had contributed to the life she could no

longer bear. Now came the catalogue that formed the basis of the verdict
against Brüshaver. He started with Voss, flogged to death in Rande; he
omitted neither the mutilation of Methfessel in the concentration camp
nor the death of his own son in the war against the Spanish government;
until he came to Wednesday night outside Tannebaum's shop. Indifference.
Acceptance. Greed. Betrayal. The egotism of a pastor, too, who was concerned only with the persecution of his own church and who had, in violation of his mandate, kept silent—who had let a member of his community
seek her own, implacable, unhallowed death before his very eyes. Where
all had rejected the Lord's everlasting offer of a new life, one woman alone
was no longer able to believe in it. Benediction. Final chorus. The End.

And you typed it up for him, Aggie.
It was like he had seen the light.
But you knew the price.
Brüshaver wasn't vain, Gesine.
And if he'd thought of his family?
He didn't need to anymore. What Aggie was was proud of Brüshaver.
Because he'd stopped living a lie?
Enough of the theological claptrap, Gesine. I was glad he did it.
And you weren't doing it for yourselves.
We did it for Lisbeth, Gesine.
As if I should believe the dead just because they're dead.
Believe us.
You have to let people say their piece, cause geese cant talk.
Just believe us, Gesine.

February 22, 1968 Thursday
In 1938, St. Peter's Church in Jerichow charged ten marks for a pastor's
services at a burial, six marks for a full ringing of the bells, five marks for
the participation of a cantor, five marks for the use and cleaning of the
church, thirty marks for bell-ringers' wages (two hours), twelve marks to
dig the grave. Fees to be paid in advance. Everything from this catalog,
except for the closed room and the embarrassing singing, was ordered for

Lisbeth Cresspahl, and when the bells, just recently rehung by Ohlsson of Lübeck and converted to electrical operation, started chiming their D F G B, work was laid aside in many houses in town. The air force had obviously taken seriously their goal of earning the right to live in this community, and in the daily orders for November 14 they mentioned that pedestrians as well as horse-drawn or motorized vehicles were to stop on encountering a funeral procession; and today the acoustic signal was enough for everyone because Lisbeth did not pass through town.

When the bells announced the start of the funeral at three o'clock, the coffin was carried down the path neatly raked between debris and burned wreckage from the fire. The coffin was bright, smooth, unvarnished. It looked very durable. The pallbearers were Alexander Paepcke and Peter Niebuhr, both in army uniform; Horst Papenbrock and Peter Wulff; Alwin Paap and Mr. Smith. Cresspahl walked behind the coffin with the child, then old Mr. and Mrs. Papenbrock, then the invited guests. When Lisbeth was carried through the open funeral parlor to the cemetery, the waiting crowd started to push their way through the six-foot-wide gate; more people were already standing among the crosses and gravestones, dark, quiet, like hidden ghosts.

Our Lisbeth.
Lookit the child.
Nothins less healthy than bein sick.
Ottje Stoffregen is already wasted.
Can ya believe they havent come for Brüshaver!
Wont dare do the blessing. Wont dare.
The one who doesn dare is you, Julie.
No use layin arms an legs on the fire, its gotta be wood.
Dying in November, I wouldnt like that.
Fog Moon.
Fer a Jew brat.
Maybe itll help Marie though.
And it's not right, they can't do it! If she killed herself she belongs in the corner with the suicides, where they put the unbaptized!
Hope I get as nice a funeral as this someday.
Our Lisbeth. And our turn will come.

When Lisbeth was set down on the Cresspahl family plot, a boy in an attic window far away started waving, and another boy ran into the north portal of the church, and the bells stopped so suddenly that the silence hurt. Now everyone ran at once from where they'd been standing off to the side and gathered around the open hole.

Brüshaver pronounced the invocation. That was permitted by the regulations of the Church of Mecklenburg. He spoke in the same voice as in the sermon the day before—calm, matter-of-fact, like a doctor prescribing. A little louder.

– In the 39th Psalm, we read: Brüshaver said. This was the lesson, and it was not permitted for this death. Brüshaver had memorized Cresspahl's deletions so well that he didn't stumble once. He began with the fourth verse, which speaks of the purpose and measure of my days. Cresspahl had cut the pangs of death beforehand, and the heart hot within, and the fever that burned. From the fourth verse he skipped to the eighth; after that, Lisbeth's promise to keep silent, her plea for an end to torment, and her confession that she was consumed by God's blows were omitted. Hear my prayer, O Lord, and give ear unto my cry; hold not thy peace at my tears: for I am a stranger with thee, and a sojourner, as all my fathers were. *O spare me, that I may recover strength, before I go hence, and be no more.*

This was when the funeral speech should have been given, but Brüshaver took half a step back to clear more room for the lowering of the coffin. The child looked up at Cresspahl, amazed that he was allowing her mother to go into the ground.

Then followed the prayer and the Lord's Prayer, both permitted. While Brüshaver transacted his business with his God, he emphasized that He alone knew what had transpired in the soul of this woman we are burying today. Mr. Smith, trying to replace the unintelligible words with English ones, was confused by the fact that in this country men covered their faces when praying, but at the Amen he was relieved that they had all held their hats in front of their faces.

Lisbeth got her consecration. Brüshaver threw soil onto the coffin three times, raised one hand above the grave, and said the: earth to earth, ashes to ashes, dust to dust; in sure and certain hope of the Resurrection to eternal life through our Lord Jesum Christum (dubious declination); who shall change the body of our low estate that it may be like unto His glorious body, according to the mighty working, whereby He is able to subdue all things to Himself. What does that mean, the mighty working? They must have pumped that out of some emanation theory. In the consecration the person being buried is addressed in the familiar second-person singular, and Brüshaver talked to Lisbeth naturally, kindly, the way one promises a child that it will never die. Amen.

Then Brüshaver pronounced the final benediction, which Lisbeth was also not allowed to receive. Now he had transgressed against both worldly authority and that of the church.

Now the boy at the attic window waved down at someone again, and that someone ran into the church. Then Ol' Bastian pressed the button for the tolling that would hang over the town for the next two hours. Pauli Bastian was not happy with this new electric way of doing things; before he'd had four assistants to help him. And this way he still had to stand there. And even after almost five years he was still not pleased with Pastor Brüshaver's calm, businesslike manner; now, with a full ringing, Brüshaver had finally put his foot in it, tripped himself up, and *when that happens ya fall on yer back an break yer teeth.*

Brüshaver took his time putting the biretta back onto his head. He stood in front of Cresspahl and simply stayed there until Cresspahl had his face under control again.

I'm doing this for you, Lisbeth. It's for you. Do you even see it?

They were standing in the receiving line in this order: Gesine in front, next to Cresspahl, then Mr. and Mrs. Papenbrock, the Paepckes, the young Papenbrocks, the Niebuhrs from Wendisch Burg and Berlin. Cresspahl looked so intently at those offering their condolences that they couldn't get off with an unclear mumble, and some contented themselves with a silent handshake. Wulff said: *She didn deserve tha'*, and he meant not only the death but what Cresspahl had let the pastor risk. Wulff would have to spend seven long years thinking that this comment was why Cresspahl no longer came to his bar, said hello to him on the street, or even looked at him. But he didn't know that yet. Käthe Klupsch stepped into the slimy mud like a chicken into a puddle, she was so worried about her shoes. Mr. Smith said, embarrassed, helpless: *You know*—; and him Cresspahl answered, saying: *I do*. It lasted probably twenty minutes before the procession of hand-shakers had passed down the whole line.

Gesine had positioned herself pressed up so tight against her father that her right hand was hidden. When she realized that this meant everyone would take her other hand, even though it wasn't the "nice" one, she put both behind her back. Then they stroked her head. It was very annoying. She didn't understand why Martin and Mathias Brüshaver bowed to her and Marlene curtsied. That was for grown-ups, wasn't it. The child was tired. After three days with new people at the sluice she'd left Wendisch Burg early in the morning. The Niebuhrs hadn't wanted to say anything to her, and she'd put up with their dejected air, their pitying caresses, only out of obedience to her father. Her father had waited a long time before taking her to her mother. He'd also forgotten to tell her that the fire had been in their own yard, not just anywhere, and she had a hard time recognizing the property, the naked house. When Cresspahl brought her into the cleared-out office, it was dark with people in black clothes. These were the relatives; I have so many relatives; but she didn't recognize them all. On the big table in the middle of the room was a box made of pale wood, with something inside it, because some people were looking into it, some at her. Cresspahl had lifted her up. Someone was lying in the box. The child took a step in midair, and another, until Cresspahl set her down on the table next to the coffin. It was nice that he didn't let go of her. She had been told that her mother was lying in there, and she tried to picture it. The one lying in there was bigger than in her memory. She was covered up in a funny way, up to her middle. She knew that black jacket and white blouse with the ironed ribbons at the neck. The face was unrecognizable, so brightly colored. And like it had slipped into itself. She didn't know this kind of smile. The hair, so full, not tight, looked fake. She tried to walk farther along the edge of the table, at least to the folded hands, to take them. Then Cresspahl took her arm and brought her to the strange hands. She looked at him, and his nod gave her permission. The hands weren't hot, though, as if from a fire—they were cold, like a shovel handle in winter. Then she'd been put in a corner of the room, and Cresspahl had put a cover on the box. Then the little bells started ringing outside, as always at funerals. Now she had to stand in the cold, stuck to the wet soil, and her mother was being shut up into the ground for all time, which was not at all what she'd said. When Cresspahl picked up Gesine and put her over his shoulder and walked away from the open grave, she was already asleep.

At five in the afternoon, they still hadn't come for Brüshaver.

Brüshaver stayed for a decent interval at the Papenbrock house, where Louise had set up a large table. He didn't stay long. Louise Papenbrock no longer felt so sure about her condescending way with the pastor and was trying to be extra obliging, which didn't quite come off. She was also stuck switching back and forth too quickly between being the grieving mother, silent and devout, and being the bustling housewife, trying to keep some twenty people served with food and drink while needing to keep close watch on the mouth the fingers the eyes of the cook the maid in the kitchen on the stairs in the dining room. Brüshaver also noticed that the mourners were gradually recalling their everyday lives, and he took advantage of the first gentle prompting from Aggie to leave.

The silence around the long table was not stubborn, nor, when it fell, especially extended; still, there was conflict and hostility crossing the table this way and that: Papenbrock at his son Horst and Horst's wife, who wanted to get back to Güstrow that evening, which meant that there couldn't be a conversation to settle things; when it came to wanting revenge, the old man claimed that as his prerogative alone. Papenbrock at the Robert who hadn't even sent a telegram from overseas, forcing him to fake Robert's condolences with a counterfeit wreath ribbon. Louise at Cresspahl, because she'd had to yield the place of honor at the burial; at the Wendisch Burg Niebuhrs, for sitting there so quiet and downcast as if they knew more about grief than their hostess! who in any case had heard more than enough on the subject; at Lisbeth—how could she do to her what she'd done to herself?; at Alexander Paepcke, for being on his second bottle of Rotspon already. Horst at his father; Horst at, especially, Peter Niebuhr, because this young guy, one of the proles at Lisbeth's wedding, was now with the ministry in Berlin, and presuming to instruct him in seed selection, and competently too. Hilde at her mother, for her endless bustling about, and at Cresspahl, for making such a fuss over his child and not sending the girl to live with her in Podejuch. Alexander at Cresspahl for spending so much time at the lower end of the table with those Lübeck strangers, including one named Erwin Plath—Alexander would have much preferred drinking with his brother-in-law, not these Schmoogs, who couldn't keep up. Alexander at himself because he'd worn his uniform out of vanity and everyone had recognized him as just an administrative officer anyway. Alwin Paap felt uncomfortably like an employee, and wished he wasn't there. The Schmoogs, the Niebuhrs, Heinz Mootsaak were taken aback that Mrs. Papenbrock had made up the finest rooms for the Paepckes, while their rooms still had laundry baskets standing around, or no sink, but they weren't angry. Peter Niebuhr felt no hostility at all, only that he'd have liked to get out of his conversation with Horst Papenbrock and would've most liked to go for a walk with Martha outside of town. He stayed, though, for the sake of this Mr. Smith from Richmond who took so much pleasure in Martha's high-school English; now he could be proud of his wife, that too. No one at Cresspahl.

After the first evening bells had rung, everyone in Papenbrock's house stood up. Then Ol' Bastian pressed the button again, and now came the bells rung especially for her—the woman who had been buried that day.

They came for Brüshaver in the night, four hours before dawn.

– Gesine, wake up.
– Why.
– You're talking in your sleep.
– I don't talk in my sleep.
– I'm supposed to wake you up if you do.
– What did I say.
– Don't hit! or something like that.
– Thanks for waking me up. What day is it?
– Thursday.
– Hey, I need to go into the office.
– It's February 22, Gesine.
– Right. I need to go to work.
– It's Washington's Birthday, Gesine! The stock market is closed, the banks are closed. Day off from school!
– I'd like a day off too.
– What are you dreaming about, Gesine.
– That I'm asleep, I think.

February 23, 1968 Friday

To spare Stalin pain, the USA kept from him the fact that as early as the spring of 1943 his son, Yakov, had been shot and killed by the Germans in Sachsenhausen prison camp at his own request; today the news is out. Janusz Szpotanski, in Warsaw, will have to spend three years in prison for his unpublished operetta, and a fine of 600 zlotys it will cost him too (25 dollars). The secretary of defense, McNamara, assured the Senate Foreign Relations Committee that he could prove that there were attacks on US destroyers in the Gulf of Tonkin three and a half years ago, with highly classified and unimpeachable information, while not doing so. In Cuba, no milk is being distributed to anyone over thirteen years of age; hopefully this isn't one of Enzensberger the poet's favorite drinks. Brezhnev was in Prague to help celebrate the twentieth anniversary of the coup. In West Berlin, 150,000 marched for the Americans in Vietnam and 10,000 against them. A bomb went off in the Soviet embassy in Washington, and yesterday the statistics felt it was too cold, with icy gusts of wind and temperatures around minus 10 degrees Celsius, and the *Times* calls Brigadier General Nguyen Ngoc Loan controversial. That was the week we missed.

Today we lost Francine.

She was only in our apartment for twelve days, and it could have been longer as far as we were concerned. She was almost at home here.

For Francine it was good that Mrs. Cresspahl had been in bed since Sunday, sleeping off a fever day and night, occasionally semiconscious, talking in her sleep, supposedly. *Allegedly.* This was something for Francine to do, she knew how to handle it, it probably felt like a chance to earn her keep. She gave real thought to what she could do to help and when it was her turn to go shopping she came back with ice cream, she kept putting fresh glasses of ice water next to the bed, she always walked on tiptoe. Marie tells me. This morning Francine came in with a gray bitter brew of tea, and not from the pharmacy—she'd bought it from an old man way up in north Harlem, a wizard with herbs, and she said, with total certainty: If the medicines don't beat that fever, this is the one thing that'll help. It wouldn't do to take a polite sip, Francine's long journey and the trouble she'd gone to demanded that the patient drain the cup to the dregs. There were no dregs. The patient's throat opened right up. – When you wake up, it'll be gone: Francine said, earnestly, and she came along for a while into a dream where she was wearing a delicately crumpled lace handkerchief between her braids, and it made her skin look slightly darker. She didn't trust the white woman, for a long time wasn't even comfortable being around her, and tried to bluster through her nervousness by talking like a nurse: "we" need to do what she says, "we all" want to get better soon, Francine's voice very high-pitched, firm, but with a tinge of playfulness since it was, at the same time, a game. She'd changed.

She was no longer the child who sits on a chair as if protecting her territory, who defends her possessions with fortifications on all sides, even when what she possesses is merely the new privilege of being listened to one minute longer than the competition. She could now consider even Marie's clothes not to judge whether she could acquire them, with compliments, flattery, requests, but simply to decide whether she liked them. Once she'd realized she had the right to ask for things, and that the response might be Yes, she no longer felt the same need to ask. When she felt sure that her share in the use of the apartment was really hers, there was less envy for Marie, and less admiration too. She could see Marie for who she is, not what she has. Meanwhile, Marie drew much of her own flexibility and forbearance from what she knew Francine didn't have at home and never would. There could be no real rivalry.

When they suddenly had a sick woman in the apartment, they'd had to set up a strict division of labor, each depending on the other's work, and Francine was more dependable at some things than Marie. When the meal is over, a Francine goes and washes the dishes, industrious, uncomplaining, because it needs to be done; a Marie puts the dishes in the sink first, to enjoy the reprieve. Mrs. Erichson came expecting a mess in the kitchen like the ones in the other rooms, but found a tidy apartment running smoothly, almost up to her Mecklenburg standards—except for the excessive supply of TV dinners and the frozen chicken, which left her momentarily speechless.

For Mrs. Erichson, the days in New York were not a chore but a vacation in the city; she liked giving the children instruction

If ten're milkin then one has to stand by the bench an rattle the buckets or it wont work

and was soon quite taken with the little black girl, who might say, so like a maidservant: Yes, ma'am; Of course, ma'am; but who wasn't timid and often looked her right in the eyes in a spirited way that might have been provoking to the old woman, but a Mrs. Erichson does not let herself be provoked, that's what all her sayings are for—*From little scuffles grow big fights.* When she left for New Jersey again, she was almost on the point of inviting this Francine to come visit with Marie—she didn't say so out loud this time. Mrs. Erichson saw this household up and running without her help, and wanted to get back to her own; when the patient no longer required her services, she got in her car and by now is far past Bayonne. The fever came down around noon, and it's stayed down.

Before dinner, Francine and Marie sat at the table in the big room and tried to catch up on as much of the schoolwork they'd missed as they'd been able to phone around for. They were half visible from bed—the fair head next to the dark one, Francine's back a bit more hunched, Marie leaning far back in her chair as she does when she's thinking about something, chin high, a pencil in her mouth, looking at the ceiling. Then the bell rang, and the door to the patient's room was quietly pushed closed, but in their hurry they left it open a little. The patient was supposed to sleep more, and now she woke all the way up.

The visitor's voice was that of a young man, sluggish, with a tenor's sharp vowels, around twenty-five years old. This stranger might have a university education but he switched easily into slang, and when he did the words sounded quoted, and his cautious, suspicious, roundabout approach sounded well practiced. At first the conversation was between him and Marie; even later, Francine didn't say much.

    – If this is the Cresspahl apartment then I'd sure like to come in.
    – Is this how you always do it?
    – It is.
    – Then you can leave now. Don't think we're here alone.
    – I'm from the city, little girl.
    – You can go look for your little girl somewhere else. I suppose you have an ID.
    – You're really something else, kid.

– From Welfare?

– So, you can read!

– We have nothing to do with Welfare. My mother has a job.

– And so how does she make sure the family is supported?

– She works for a bank in midtown.

– That must be Chemical Bank?

– It's not Chemical.

– Do guests get offered a chair around here?

– Well, since you're a gentleman.

– Children, children, I didn't mean it in a bad way. You try running around all day in buildings without elevators.

– You do it for free?

– All right, so you want to talk business. I am looking for a girl named Francine, eleven years old, colored. I have a picture of her.

– Well?

– That's her.

– And if she is?

– Then I've come to the right place.

– It's completely legal that she's living here with us. The police know about it, Francine's mother has the address too.

– Who else would I have gotten it from.

– Do you understand what this is about, Francine?

– I'm supposed to say hello from your mother, Francine.

– We were going to visit the hospital again tomorrow.

– Francine's mother isn't in the hospital anymore.

– We'd know that.

– Apparently you don't. Otherwise you'd figure out that because of the cold spell there's an even bigger shortage of beds than usual. She's been discharged.

– I just need to pack my things.

– You can't just send Francine's mother back into a pit like the one on 103rd Street, after an injury like that!

– It wasn't me. What's your name, anyway?

– M'rie.

– Well then, *dear Mary*. (Okay, you're not my "dear Mary," now I know.) I am handling this case. I heard the story during a routine visit. And I made a decision: If she does come back, then it won't be to that pit. As you so accurately put it.

– That is extraordinarily nice of you, Mr. Feldman.

– I've moved this case into a hotel.

– One of the ones where the city pays the rent?

– You've got to admit, it's better that way.

– That hotel probably is a little better than 103rd Street.

– Now the mother is there all alone with her baby. The older daughter has run away from the juvenile center, they can't find her.

– And the older brother's gone too.

– That's the kind of family it is.

– I don't think it's their fault.

– *My dear Mary* (Okay! I know!), if I started thinking about it that way I'd never get anything done.

– And now you're taking Francine with you.

– If she doesn't want to come, I can also have her picked up.

– So that's how it is.

– Mary, don't you think a family should live together?

– Yes. And Francine should take her mother's place watching the baby so that she.... Nothing. I didn't mean anything. Never mind.

– Maybe her injuries aren't entirely healed yet. Francine's mother says she wants her there.

– Why doesn't she call us?

– That I don't know. But obviously she doesn't want to. Can't bring herself to. Something along those lines.

– And you've got a letter from her.

– I can leave it here for you. And anyway, it's for the best.

– For whose best?

– Mary, if your Francine has known for two days that she's supposed to go back to her mother, and known the new address too—

– I don't believe it.

– Francine, do you know a Mrs. Lippincott? She lives in your old building.

– Yes, mister.

– Didn't you run into her on Broadway the other day?

– Yes, mister.

– Did she tell you where your mother is and that your mother wants you to come back?

– Yes, mister.

– Francine.

– It's true, Marie.

– Francine!

– So. Now when does this Mrs. Cresspahl get home from the bank that isn't Chemical?

– She's here. She's sick.

– Bloody Jesus, you're a weird generation. Now I have to go through everything with her all over again.

– No you don't.

– Maybe I should introduce myself to her.

– You can't go in there. If Francine wants to say goodbye.

– No, Marie. I don't want to tell her.

– You see.

– Even you didn't understand. It wasn't a lie.

– So now you're going.

– We can go now, mister.

February 24, 1968 Saturday

Public Notice. Louis Levinson, age seventy-five, brother of Sam, Isidore, Tillie, and Pearl Levinson, wants to be contacted by some member of family. Tel. INI–6565.

When my mother was a child, a doctor said: The child's got a weak heart. And have her walk with her stick more often.

Children used to have to walk with a stick across their backs, held in the crooks of their arms. To learn good posture.

My mother had narrow hips. When she was sixteen, she was still called "weak." She always walked slightly stooped, with sloping shoulders. She tired quickly, even after a half-hour walk. Then she learned to ride horses.

When she passed a mirror, it was: *I cant help it, I think Im pretty.* She was teased about it her whole life. (Because one time, when she was ten,

she'd spent so long combing her hair that she was fifteen minutes late.)
Dont you think youre a little too pretty? If I may say so myself.

At eighteen she was the chives on everyone's soup.

As a child, she'd said: I know a girl who doesn't believe in God.

God, who invented the atomic bomb, also shoots at sparrows so they shall fall on the ground from the bush.

She walked so softly her shoes never wore out.

Her dresses all stopped at the knee when she was supposed to marry the man from Lübeck.

Papenbrock to Cresspahl, in 1931: I am sure that you'll be able to make my daughter happy. I say this man to man.

A sentence written in secret, in English, in Richmond, in August 1932: *You know, I have secrets in my head, but I do not know them. Only my head can get at them.*

Had a manic sense of responsibility, even for the birds in the garden.

When the doctors found out what she'd died of, they washed her hair.

Outside the north portal of St. Peter's Church there was a lectern, with a page for the funeralgoers to inscribe their names. Pauli Bastian usually stood beside it and asked: Viewing? Viewing? This time he couldn't say that. This time people asked him: What! No viewing? No viewing?

A Protestant. "Protestants decide for themselves what is most important."

The noise of the beach stones scoured by receding waves. She could tilt her head listening to that for a long time. She liked it best in the fog.

When she took out stove rings, she sometimes forgot that she had them on a hook in her hand, she would be so lost staring into the fire.

She always marveled at her long neck. As a child she'd had almost no neck at all.

She was gone so suddenly; she wasn't spoken about.

Invisible.

February 25, 1968 Sunday

Many senators on the Foreign Relations Committee do not want to hear another word about this Tonkin business from the government, and the chairman, Fulbright, calls Secretary of Defense McNamara negligent in his duties, for having failed to give the committee important information. Calls him "derelict."

Derelict: wouldn't that word apply to Mrs. Cresspahl's English, too, despite her trying to make a living in an English-speaking country? As it does to a ship adrift without captain or crew. It's not enough that *derelict* makes her think of her Latin classes, seventeen years ago in Gneez: of *linquere* and *depart*, of *relinquere* and *relinquish*, of *relictus*, relic, abandoned thing, plus the prefix *de-* meaning not "down" but "down to the bottom"— thoroughly, completely, finally. *De-relict*: the country its inhabitants flee, the land the housebuilder rejects, the alluvium the sea leaves behind, the silted water, the abandoned wreck, the house beyond redemption, the ownerless property, the article willfully cast away, and just when the meaning seems contained behind a fence of knowledge it's already slipped away, and her next step onto what she thought was safe ground meets thin air. For Cresspahl studied English English, not American English; and for a hundred years American English has been wont to transfer the sense from the passive *Relikt* (relic) and *derelict*, via *dereliction*, neglect, to a person who does (doesn't) actively perform their duties: the delinquent, the culprit, a liar, as well as people whom both the police and the *Times* take as not merely down-and-out but willfully turning their backs on society, now standing on the Bowery unshaven, in rags, swaying with hunger and alcohol, beggars, bums, tramps, *derelicts*.

Mr. Fulbright told Mr. McNamara what he thinks of him; Mrs. Cresspahl has listened carefully to what the gentlemen had to say. Were she asked to explain on the spot what she took it to mean, she would hesitate. Maybe she owes her image of McNamara on the Bowery to the subhead in which *The New York Times* prints the word "Derelict" in bold. It's not so much that she'd be embarrassed to admit a mistake—she'd be worried about the consequences of not being fully able to do what she's paid to do.

This will not do, Cresspahl. If one were not to call Comrade Stalin's English classical, one would have to say it's as simple as can be. C minus, Cresspahl. Sit down. Baumgärtner, your turn.

After the war, Dr. Kliefoth served as the principal of Gneez High School with little time to teach English. Frau Dr. Weidling took his place until Soviet counterintelligence found out that her husband had been a captain not in a tank division but in intelligence and sabotage, and that she owed her mastery of the language to the trips abroad that Capt. Weidling had taken her on with him. Kliefoth was soon removed from his post, as teacher too. Then English through twelfth grade was taught by a young man with the first name Hans-Gerhard. He had never been to England, and explained to the silent class that his professors at the University of Greifswald had accepted certain deviations in pronunciation from him when he couldn't exactly copy the British language LPs. His justification had been: he heard it differently. This was his first teaching position, and his first mistake. He then made reference to his youth and asked the students if he could address them by first name, despite their having reached the age where last names are customary; he mentioned the New Spirit of the New Schools. Lise Wollenberg spoke up. – Of course, Hans-Gerhard: she said. Heinz Wollenberg was still considered a pillar of society at that point, and Lise got an apology from the young man for his fit of rage. After this third mistake, he no longer called his students by their first names. "The Gold-Bug" by Edgar Allan Poe was not read in his class, instead he went through "Is War Inevitable?" by Josif Stalin. Cresspahl, the student in the center block, front row, on the aisle, didn't get a good grade for that one. There was no prospect of private lessons with Kliefoth, since he would have accepted neither money nor favors in return for them. H.-G. Knick moved his lips as though chewing when he switched into a foreign language, his voice changed too, and several times a month he had to hear from his students that they "heard it differently," even though his vowel sounds probably came out as close to British as he was capable of making them. Cresspahl got an A in English on her Abitur exams, and her bumpy essay on the prospects of a Communist Party in a parliamentary democracy was enough to get her admitted to the University of Halle. The Saxons too were taken with the New Spirit of the New Schools, but they didn't leave it up to the students to decide how they heard it. Professor Ertzenberger would have liked to use her for demonstration purposes in his seminar. He was delighted to have such an example.

Miss Cresspahl, please pronounce a cluster of k *and* l.
Tackle. Shackle.
And now in a German word.
Mecklenburg.
Do you hear it?
No, professor.
Please say: "Wesel."
Wesl.
Your articulation is Make-len-burgish to the bone, Miss Cresspahl! You can't separate the l! *"M, e, ckl, e, nburg." That has got to go.*

She started talking. During her second semester, she understood the passenger on the Leipzig–Rostock express who'd spoken to her in English after noticing the English paperback in her hand, though only after he repeated himself. Anyway, Englishmen on the East German railway were not the rule in those days. In Frankfurt, when she was studying translation, she still couldn't manage the English of the children she had to babysit at night in the American quarter, and at the US Army radio station in West Berlin she still wasn't at the point of pronouncing "either" with an *ee* sound or "fast" with a short *a* or the word for *Künste* like the one for *Herz*, "arts" as "hearts." In New York, people think she has a New England accent, in New England it's thought to be a New York mishmash. Now after almost seven years in New York she can call a dollar a *buck* (deer, *Bock*), but she hears the British pronunciation in her mind and uses the idea that a deer is something you can own, sight, hunt, and bring in to help her remember. Speaking Italian or French, on the other hand, is a perfectly harmless activity, fully planned and always conscious; in American English, she no longer has to plan out the grammar on all sides, but then occasionally falls into a confused pause as if from a great height.

Called McNamara *derelict*.

Where other offices have family photos and flowerpots, she has put up a thin slip of paper (not enough by way of "personal items" for the Puerto Rican mover). On it is written: THE CUSTARD APPLE IS THE FRUIT O' THE SWEET-SOP. Which means nothing more than DIE FLASCHEN-BAUMFRUCHT IST DIE FRUCHT DES FLASCHENBAUMS. The bottle-tree fruit is the fruit of the bottle tree, you might say, but don't. She cannot understand it. For the CUSTARD she sees on the poster at the Times Square subway station twice every workday has nothing to do with bottle trees, it is an egg pudding. The fruits of American bottle trees are egg-shaped, there's that. Then again, whipped egg whites aren't *Eierschnee*, egg snow, but named from a French word for a pastry. The bottle tree, named thus after the shape of its trunk, is in any case called sweet-soaked, sweet-sop, and another name for its fruit is *sugar apple*. She cannot understand what these words know about one another, and the slightly nose-diving dizziness she feels whenever she sees this sentence warns her away from the thought that she will ever be able to live on the English side of language.

That thought is what she needs to go in to work with, tomorrow.

February 26, 1968 Monday

– They called it *Reichskristallnacht*?: Marie says.

– Yes.

– Like "Washington's Birthday"?

– Yes.

– Okay, Gesine, start.

– Because among other things the Jews had their windows broken or their crystal smashed or stolen.

– You told me that Jews lost their lives, their businesses, their homes. A billion-mark fine. Expelled from schools. Their pensions gone. Their insurance canceled. And the government called these measures harsh but fair.

– Yes, Marie.

– And "Kristallnacht," this was a government word?

– No. It came from the governed.

– I'm trying to believe you. Explain it to me again.

In the week after Kristallnacht, Cresspahl was still in Jerichow. It was a perfectly ordinary week.

On November 14, Monday night, the NSDAP held a social gathering for party comrades at the Beach Hotel in Rande. The Beach Hotel stood opposite the harbor bridge, on Street of the SA. The Gneez Music Academy took part, performing instrumental pieces, and a group of Jungmädel sang

"The Red Flags Burn in the Wind." Jungmädel was what they called the girls who were still too young for the BDM. Friedrich Jansen gave the opening speech in a quiet, almost docile voice. The Beach Hotel's large hall was full except for a few seats, and Jansen thanked the county head of the party for his presence. Swantenius, from Gneez, watched him with a suppressed smile, which the other man might have taken for comradely if it hadn't reminded him of the services Swantenius had provided for him before the party tribunal. Jansen cried "*Sieg Heil!*" three times, and three times the auditorium answered him with "*Sieg Heil!*" Then the Jungmädel in Mecklenburg folk costumes performed some folk dances. The National Socialist Women's Association had rehearsed some songs. Finally there was a play performed in Plattdeutsch to much laughter, and the marksmanship and dice prizes were handed out.

The dance went on until midnight. When the Jerichowers came back from the party, the city was dark except for two windows in Papenbrock's house. There sat the old man, who didn't want to let Cresspahl go home. He was tired from drinking, and roused himself only seldom, with loud sighs. Cresspahl stayed until Papenbrock no longer noticed that he was being put to bed on the office sofa.

On Tuesday, the bag for the pound collection was dropped off at Cresspahl's house. Printed on the bag was a stylized Reich eagle perched on a swastika. Later Mrs. Jansen came over to apologize on behalf of the BDM girls, who had thoughtlessly followed their list, but the bag was standing ready, filled with semolina. The Labor Service girl couldn't tell Mrs. Jansen where Cresspahl was. Cresspahl was with Koepcke, the head of the construction firm, and that afternoon the first trucks arrived with the workers who would finish demolishing the barn and carry off the first loads of debris.

On Wednesday, Richard Maass put a globe in his window. He noted on a sheet of paper that this globe showed the new borders of Germany. It was only a sample, to his customers' disappointment, but Maass received twenty-one orders.

Head Teacher Stoffregen borrowed the sample for one of his classes. More debris was hauled off of Cresspahl's property. The child was not in Papenbrock's house, and apparently their maid had been strictly warned not to gossip. It was impossible to get out of Edith why Gesine was still living with her father instead of her grandmother. Meanwhile, more people than usual were standing in front of the parish bulletin board, but it still hadn't been announced whether Brüshaver would be back for the Sunday sermon. Brüshaver's eldest son had not come to school.

On Thursday, a lot of people from Jerichow went to Gneez. Stoffregen had reserved one and a half train cars for the school. In Gneez the new recruits were being sworn in. With the coming of the air force, Jerichow now had all the same delegations that Gneez had, except for the National Socialist Brotherhood of Hunters. It was generally thought that the Jerichow celebration had been more uplifting. It was also said that it was Brüshaver's fault if the Jerichow celebration hadn't quite come off. In Gneez the church bells rang before the swearing in. There was a Protestant chaplain and a Catholic one, each making points about the significance of the oath to the flag. Then "Now We Gather to Pray" was sung. The "*Sieg Heil*" had come in more punctually on the Jerichow market square, and the echo had been better too. That evening, the building that had been Cresspahl's shop finished being leveled to the ground.

On Friday morning, two of von Zelck's harnessed teams arrived and started plowing the area where the barn had once stood. Cresspahl and Paap put up fence posts along the line of what had been the east wall. If you imagined the line continuing, it cut off a third of the garden. It looked as if Cresspahl was planning to sell or rent out the strip of land. By late afternoon all the charred wood was gone from the yard and the teams were plowing up the soil of the yard. Then Koepcke came with his steamroller and turned the fresh furrows in the yard into a neat, flat surface.

On Saturday morning, the air force invited the population to a Christmas display. It consisted of broken toys that had been fixed and were meant for the children of needy fellow Germans. Gneez might have its army, but Jerichow could be proud of its air force. Even the Royal Eagle had a different look than usual, with wider wings and an elongated neck. It looked elegant, even on a wreath ribbon. One such wreath ribbon had been stolen from the Cresspahl grave. Stoffregen the head teacher surprised three boys making a deal to resell it during recess and forced them to give the piece of fabric back to Cresspahl with their apologies. They came back and reported that Alwin Paap hadn't let them on the property, and that Cresspahl wasn't there.

Anyone who called JErichow-209 in the afternoon always reached Alwin Paap. He refused to answer questions, was so businesslike it was downright unfriendly, Cresspahl must have arranged things with him. So now people had to wait until Monday morning. But neither of the Labor Service girls came in to do their shopping. They'd both driven off with their suitcases. Had Paap learned to cook, then? No, he'd started boarding at Creutz's, but he didn't go to their house, the food was brought to him at Cresspahl's yard so he wouldn't have to leave. Papenbrock, in his treacherous way, asked into the phone what the reason might be why the caller was asking him about Cresspahl. Koepcke had made arrangements with Cresspahl to not be paid until December 31, but still it worried him that the man had left town. Koepcke didn't want to tell Papenbrock that he had any doubts about Papenbrock's son-in-law's payment ethics, and said nothing more. No one wanted to get on Papenbrock's bad side.

So presumably Cresspahl left Jerichow on Saturday morning. With the child.

February 27, 1968 Tuesday

The White House says that President Johnson is satisfied that Congress had been given the full facts before it approved the Gulf of Tonkin Resolution authorizing the expansion of the war. Senator Fulbright still doesn't buy it.

A Pentagon spokesman in Saigon said today that the new censorship policy would have no effect on the Defense Department's daily and weekly updating of totals of killed and wounded.

Louis Schein, a Bronx real estate man, is supposed to tell a grand jury if he was either threatened with death or beaten up by John (Buster) Ardito over a loan of $5,000. John Ardito is said to be a major power in the Mafia family of Vito Genovese, and Louis Schein doesn't want to say anything. He would rather face the penalty for contempt than the penalty from the Mafia. He won't even say if he knows Ardito.

At the end of December, two days after Christmas, Cresspahl returned to Jerichow.

– You can't do this to me!: Marie says. For four days she has not wanted to talk about Francine. She sees Francine in school, she dodges my questions with a scowl as though they're tactless. So now we need something else to fill our evenings. She seems eager, attentive; she's trying to push something aside.

– He brought the child.

– Where was he, Gesine! Where was he!

– There was a branch office of the HAPAG, the Hamburg America Line, at the market square in Lübeck. They had an express service from Hamburg to New York via Southampton and Cherbourg.

– You're kidding me. Cresspahl in New York?

– Adult tickets started at 605 marks, which included a six-day stay in New York. Don't you think he would have done it?

– Gesine, is this another water-butt story?

– No. And we're not talking about my mother anymore. She's dead by now.

– Did she, in the fire—? Okay. I don't want to know. I promise.

– So you don't think Cresspahl would've wanted to see New York?

– That wouldn't feel right. It would fit too perfectly. First a random Robert Papenbrock in New York, then your father, and thirty years later here we are. It would be too contrived, like a novel.

– Well, that's 905 marks less for HAPAG.

– You're trying to test me, Gesine. You said something not too long ago about a transfer to Copenhagen, on some lake, with a view of an island, and before that there was a British consulate in Lübeck. On Schüsselbuden Street. On *that* Schüsselbuden, you said. So there must have been a Danish one too.

– On An der Untertrave. But if he went via Rostock, he could pass by Grosse Mönchenstrasse, the Danes were there too, and the German Railroad had connections every day, on the Schwerin or the Mecklenburg, to Gedser forty-two kilometers away. To Denmark.

– I don't understand. Wasn't Germany a dictatorship?

– That wasn't what I said. It was ruled and administered by criminals.

– A dictatorship lets people out?

– The majority of Germans were happy with Hitler and Company. No one suspected them of wanting to leave the country by the millions. So

682 · *February 27, 1968 Tuesday*

yes, there was even an excursion ticket you didn't need a passport for, Warnemünde–Gedser. A visa was enough, and you could buy one on board for twenty-five cents. The crooks kept their eyes peeled only when it came to money. Travelers could take only ten marks with them, and in coins, not bills. Then they could land in Denmark, and it's true, the Danes would by no means force them back onto the Nazi ship.

– Warnemünde?

– The mouth of the Warnow—where the *Warnow mündet*. One of Rostock's peripheral harbors at the time. The express train from Berlin went onto a ship there. If it was the *Schwerin*, twelve years old, not much over three thousand tons, 106 meters long....

– A South Ferry! A *North Ferry*!

– With smoking and nonsmoking lounges....

– I like it, Gesine.

– Sleeping cabins, bathing cabins, balconies, promenade decks, and a grand restaurant, since the trip lasted two hours....

– You're making our South Ferry look bad. It can't have a restaurant for a twenty-minute trip! Or sleeping cabins.

– Marie, that was the ship that the Schwerin head of the German Railroad had in service. I didn't make it up.

– Cresspahl was carrying the illegal money under his hat. He might have done that.

– He had the child carry it, sewn into her bedtime doll. He might have done that.

– He was doing some business for Erwin Plath in Denmark.

– That I don't know. I don't even know if he went to Denmark.

– But you can prove it. You have his passport.

– I stole his passport in 1951: the GDR one, not the one with the swastika. There's no one left in Jerichow who knows anymore, and after the war I didn't want to ask him what he was doing at the end of 1938. What I do know was told to me in bits and pieces, but this wasn't.

– So let's assume Denmark. A man alone with a child.

– Later in my life I took a lot of train rides—from Mecklenburg to Saxony, from Bavaria to Italy, from Wales to Scotland—and I didn't have to get used to it. I already was. Maybe I learned it when I was five. I sometimes dream stretches of line running hundreds of kilometers, dense mixed forest next to the second track until the exact spot where the grassy fields start, and it's not a line I recognize, even when I'm awake. When I came to New York with you, I didn't have to learn what a large ship is like; I already knew.

– It's not like that with me.

– With you it didn't last six weeks.

– All right, then, Denmark.

– Maybe. When you and I took the train from Copenhagen to Esbjerg. . . .

– Déjà vu.

– That's too intellectual for me, Marie. Maybe it was a fake memory when I recognized the landscape on either side of the train, the islands in the Great Belt, the Middelfart Bridge, and finally the ferry to Harwich. But your déjà vu doesn't just mean what's been seen before, it means what's been experienced, and I don't have that, or a premonition of what's about to happen. And two years ago I *really* wasn't turning my attention away from life, so that the present moment would be immediately dismissed as memory. . .

– I was just showing off with "déjà vu."

– . . . because we'd just been to see Ingrid Bøtersen in Klampenborg and were on our way to England.

– You just recognized it, that's all.

– And I didn't realize I did. I couldn't. At the moment of seeing, what was seen got snapped into a preprepared place in my brain and became real; the moment it stopped being seen, it was forgotten. That's what happened to me with Nyhavn in Copenhagen, with Amaliegade, with the main station; not with the Museum of Danish Resistance in Churchill Park, Kastrup Airport, or Klampenborg. The other feeling, déjà vu. . . .

– You don't have to rub it in.

– But I also had it in a school hallway in London, in Victoria Station, in Glasgow on the right bank of the Clyde, in the town center. Why. . . .

– You were there, Gesine. Cresspahl was there. He went to take another look around in England, in Denmark, maybe even in the Netherlands. To see if there was a place for him there. He wanted to emigrate, Gesine!

– I wish.

– A man, alone with a child, traveling for six weeks.

– It's unclear. Lots of nights alone with him in bare rooms. As if I woke up and he wasn't there and I went running through lots of rooms, none of which I recognized, and turned on the electric light, wailing pitifully, and when I had people around none of them understood me. Not because they were laughing too much. Because I couldn't tell them what I wanted. That might be a dream. I also remember something about a thatched-roof house with rounded dormer windows, and four children I was handed over to— I've never consciously seen a house like that in my life, and yet we were near the water. Little waves, bright clean sand in the rain. But as if I'd never been unhappy, because Cresspahl had promised to come back, and did come back. And that we were almost never in the same place for more than a day. If you want to imagine that you can believe it too.

– Believe it, Gesine!

– But there's no way to prove it.

– I'd rather have proof of why Cresspahl went back to Germany, to Jerichow.

– I don't know.

– Gesine, the town hadn't become what Richmond was. The relatives would be fine without him, his friends too. And fifty yards from his house there was a mound of dirt with his dead wife under it.

– Maybe Cresspahl had given up.

– Do you think he had?

– Not yet.

February 28, 1968 Wednesday

And still West Germany has as president an old man said to have signed construction plans for a concentration camp in 1944. He doesn't believe that he did, but he couldn't swear to it under oath. An American graphologist recognized the 1944 signatures on the plans as the president's. A Bonn student who added "concentration camp builder" after the president's name on an honor roll in the rector's office has been expelled. The Christian Democratic Union (CDU) party, in the ruling coalition with the Social Democratic Party (SPD), responded to demands that the accused step down by saying: Those demanding it are only trying to pressure the coalition and switch tracks for another one. That's how much West German politics cares about concentration camps; that's the kind of country it is; and Mrs. Ferwalter says: I'm sure he had to do it, he must have had a wife.

Mrs. Ferwalter lost part of her life in the Germans' concentration camps; she knows that and speaks of it casually, the way other people talk about their Abitur exams. She is a squat woman, broad-shouldered like maids from the country who used to work so hard they never got a chance to live and who fell into bed at night like a sack of potatoes; Mrs. Ferwalter should be able to get a good night's sleep. But she can't. Since the Americans found and freed her in southeast Europe, she's been anxious—in her sleep, running the household, when she talks, she can't quite lose an expression of horror and disgust no matter how friendly a face she's making; she keeps her eyes narrowed, though they are big and gentle and capable of great tenderness. In the middle of Broadway, in the middle of hurried evening shoppers, she carries herself as if encircled by hidden dangers. This Cresspahl, the German, is no danger to her—she plants herself carelessly in her path, laughs her awkward laugh, walks with her a bit, looks sideways at her every so often as if at something horribly repulsive, in an affectionate, friendly way. Hello, Mrs. Ferwalter.

Mrs. Ferwalter is coming back from the Bronx with Rebecca, where they went to see a relative who works as a barber. First, he does it for them cheaper; second, he knows how to cut Rebecca's hair in layers so that it looks more European.

What counts in Mrs. Ferwalter's eyes is not that Cresspahl is German but that she's European. You can talk to this Cresspahl about Austria and she'll know where it is. Mauthausen's there. Mrs. Cresspahl doesn't go blank even at the mention of České Budějovice, she knows the lost old country, even the lost tip of Slovakia now occupied by the Soviet Union. Were they the ones who handed the Jews over to the Germans in 1944, before their uprising? We can't ask about that. And Mrs. Ferwalter doesn't care, what she cares about are the other woman's boots—yellow leather, lacing all the way up on hooks. Are they European? They're from London, Mrs. Ferwalter. She is very pleased. One of the things she appreciates about Cresspahl is her familiarity with other kinds of style than the American one, and her understanding that Rebecca's mother must be insulted that her child's birthday wasn't acknowledged even if it's because she was sick.

Yesterday Marie did go and deliver a gift, as one should in Europe. And it was a pencil case from Switzerland! Rebecca doesn't get to use it, though; it will be shown to guests and then put behind glass in the cupboard as a sign that the Ferwalter household is still upholding European values. – From Saks Fifth Avenue!: Mrs. Ferwalter cries. – You must always shop there? Denial is useless, Mrs. Ferwalter will believe it anyway. She considers Cresspahl someone from "a good family," she's said so to Prof. Kreslil; such origins probably help in the friendship. The point is that the pencil case is from Zurich; that Cresspahl has to do a lot of writing in her job and so she knows what's good to write with. Of course it would have been even better if the present came from Germany, the workmanship there is the best anywhere.

Mrs. Ferwalter refuses to hold it against the West German president that he is suspected of having built concentration camps. For her, the good Germans are automatically excused. "They didn't know." It makes her uncomfortable that the head of state of West Germany knew. The dignity of the office makes it hard for her to believe this. She doesn't want to be convinced. In any case, she doesn't let anyone swindle her out of one penny when she goes shopping.

She admires people who are tall and good-looking. There's a North German woman in her building, from Hamburg, married to a policeman, with a strict code of conduct for herself. Wakes up at seven even though she doesn't have to, things like that. This German is almost six feet tall, with a long neck and freckles; she wears her hair back; she's twenty-four. She likes to talk about her disciplined lifestyle, and Mrs. Ferwalter admires her.

Now Mrs. Ferwalter would like to know if it's true that Cresspahl, with such a European background and everything, actually took a black child into her home.

She nods with satisfaction when she hears that it was temporary; she took it to mean: it was an aberration. She nods only to herself, not putting it on for Cresspahl; she won't allow herself to criticize. She has no tolerance for Negroes and believes in all seriousness that God made them to live in squalor, poverty, and sin.

Not even her religion, for whose sake she got sent to the camps, is enough to make her think of the Germans as anything but goys like the rest. She has such a harsh covenant with her God that she can see only Orthodox

Jews as her equals, whether poor or not poor. She can't help but prefer the not poor ones slightly, out of respect for God's decision in this case. She rigorously observes the holidays; Rebecca and Marie are often separated. On Saturdays, Rebecca is categorically not allowed to even take a walk or come over. On Friday the house is cleaned and the meals are cooked in advance and kept warm so that they won't have to light the stove the next day. Rebecca is not allowed to bathe on the Sabbath. She has to go to the synagogue with her father and brother, and if she forgets and has an ice cream at the snack bar, she is less afraid of God than she is of her mother. Rebecca has been raised under the dark principles of the Old Testament: Chasten I not my child? do I not show that I love him? Mrs. Ferwalter looked on, appalled and suspicious, at the freedom with which Mrs. Cresspahl let her child grow up; only lately has she relented a little. Mrs. Ferwalter is so firm in her principles that the Jewish community of the Upper West Side of Manhattan is not up to her standards. There are actually religious services held in small shops on Broadway here. After the holiday, the faithful stand in the middle of traffic and crowds of pedestrians the way other people do outside a movie theater! Mrs. Ferwalter also has a bad conscience for not going to synagogue often herself. It's the money issue. With great frugality and hardship she can scrape together enough for Jewish summer camp for Rebecca, who should lack for nothing when it comes to her Jewish upbringing. Mrs. Ferwalter is hurt when Cresspahl sends her child to an out-of-town summer camp, because otherwise Marie could have played with Rebecca, who has to stay at the P.S. 75 school camp to save money for the Jewish one; the unpleasant feeling connected with this can be concealed by a show of being insulted. But it's fine to have a German playmate. What the Germans did to the Jews was God's will.

Now that the Cresspahls don't have a black child in the house, Rebecca is allowed to come over again and be friends with Marie. Was it that, Mrs. Ferwalter?

It was. Mrs. Ferwalter once went to a movie that showed a European landscape, a castle in the mountains, a nobleman with many motherless children, there was lots of singing, and at the end there was a marriage. Mrs. Ferwalter cried. She doesn't want to hear it called kitsch, though she does admit that it did show reality in a pleasant light for a while. "But we deserve that, don't we?" Besides, such things do happen. In Jerusalem, a chief rabbi got married, he was seventy, the bride was forty. Such a pious man, beard down to his belly button. There's still romance in the world.

– You're not blind in that eye too, are you? *Or have you given up, really?*

On her journey, in her flight from the German camps, Mrs. Ferwalter lost her language. At home they'd spoken Yiddish, which they'd called *das Deutsch*. In school she'd learned Czech, which she now speaks not quite as brokenly as the German she learned in the camps. In Israel she learned Hebrew, and the family spoke that language with one another until they came to America. Then her son started answering Hebrew with English, and so she had to learn English. Since then she's spoken Yiddish with her husband and English with her son and Rebecca, though an English that the children couldn't always understand. Then Rebecca started learning Hebrew in a New York school, and Mrs. Ferwalter felt she had to learn it anew. She has three different languages for her husband and two children.

– You not take it wrong way?: Mrs. Ferwalter says. For we've now reached the building on the side street off Riverside Drive where this family has lived for nine years, four people in three-and-a-half rooms with all the windows facing a courtyard, and clearly Mrs. Ferwalter has made up her mind to do what she has to do on the street, not invite the German into her apartment. Home is for the family; leave the outside to the outsiders.

What she has to do is give a word of advice. She's older; it's permissible among friends. Maybe it's nothing serious, but it won't end with a breakup from Professor Erichson, will it?

It was a summer Sunday morning not many years back that D. E. came down to the park and sat down far away from the Cresspahls, like a stranger, with a paper cup of coffee and a newspaper under his arm for breakfast. Mrs. Ferwalter was sitting next to Cresspahl, saw him look over, and felt reminded of people she'd gotten to know only too well in the camps. She almost ran away, and it took a while before she could even endure the presence of this big strong German man in the same room as her without sliding her chair back, shifting her feet, working her lips, more than she usually does. Now she's trying to be on his side, and what has made her do that?

Because Mrs. Cresspahl has started something with a top executive at her bank yes? After being conspicuously singled out by him yes, with more money, a promotion in office, everything.

And where did Mrs. Ferwalter hear that?

From Mr. Weiszand, Mrs. Cresspahl. Dmitri Weiszand. Whenever you run into him at Columbia University, he has time for a chat, even with a humble Jewish lady from the ČSR. Actually it was he who started these conversations, around three months ago. Such an approachable person, so gracious, even though the Germans did beat him in their camps.

Now Mrs. Ferwalter is very anxious with worry. – I not try to interfere!: she cries. – You not take it wrong way!: she says, and now it's an order, not only the words but also in her voice.

– Who knows what's for the best, Mrs. Ferwalter.

– That what I always say: she says, not exactly beaming but happy with herself for having made an effort in what she thinks is a good cause. Now her mouth is relaxed, she looks pleased, untroubled, a young woman all of a sudden.

I just like you, my German friend. Can't you understand that?

No, Mrs. Ferwalter, I can't. But it's something for us to be happy about, and we like you too.

is the day after the evening when a West German journalist in the New York Hilton Hotel took part in a discussion of the latest prospects for German National Socialism. Herr Klaus Harpprecht opened by saying that he'd been a young soldier under Hitler but now was married to a Jewish woman who'd been in Auschwitz.

Explain this to us, please. You're German too, Mrs. Cresspahl. Try to tell us what this means.

Is the day on which it can be reported from Bonn, West Germany, that the government is banning an illustrated weekly that raised questions about the signature of the country's president on blueprints for a concentration camp. The official justification for the ban were an anthropology serialization and a series of photographs showing Brigadier General Nguyen Ngoc Loan executing a young man on the streets of Saigon. The government fears that these photographs might "brutalize" youth. The government expresses no opinion at this time about the effects on young people of being in concentration camps.

Explain this to us, please. These are your countrymen, Mrs. Cresspahl. Try to tell us what this means.

This is the day on which the German writer Hans Magnus Enzensberger publishes an open letter in *The New York Review of Books*, "On Leaving America."

Explain this to us, Mrs. Cresspahl. You're also German, aren't you? Try to tell us what this means.

Mr. Enzensberger wrote publicly to the president of Wesleyan University to say that he was resigning as a Fellow of the Center for Advanced Studies there. He begins with a few elementary considerations.

He publicly admits he thinks the class that rules the United States of America (including the government) is the most dangerous group of people in the world. "The most dangerous body of men on earth." Paul Goodman said the same thing last October in a speech to military industrialists: "You are, at the present time, the most dangerous body of men in the world." Well, who wants to quibble over a quotation being exactly accurate. "In the world"—that sounds so blah. No: "on earth." Solemn. Resounding. Downright biblical. "On earth."

Because Mr. Enzensberger was unaware of this fact three months ago, he now, three months later, intends to publicly leave this country.

This West German has heard from many Americans that they are deeply troubled by the state of their nation. When Mr. Gallup goes forth among this nation, he can ask a very large number of people questions. How many Americans has this West German met in twelve weeks? Belonging to what social classes, or class?

In any case, this West German's result does correspond with the Gallup poll from yesterday. He doesn't presuppose much knowledge on the part of those he is writing to.

Well, these many Americans have told him that they feel the crises in this country, not least the undeclared war in Vietnam, are accidents, mismanagements, "tragical errors." To this interpretation Mr. Enzensberger cannot subscribe. Obviously the obvious reaches new obviousness once an Enzensberger says it.

The ruling class of the United States has ruined so many countries;

nobody can feel "safe and secure" anymore, not in Europe, not even in America itself. No one has claimed otherwise. But at least this gives him the chance to tell us that he needs to feel safe and secure.

Mr. Enzensberger admits that he is wasting our time with his truths; he would like to present them "in a scientific way" but just doesn't have the space.

How absolutely horrid of *The New York Review of Books* to refuse him the necessary column inches. And the editor of the journal *Kursbuch*, Mr. Hans Magnus Enzensberger, cannot possibly be sufficiently condemned for his horridness in closing its pages to the truths of Mr. Hans Magnus Enzensberger.

Moreover, others have already treated these truths at great length; Mr. Enzensberger says so himself. He gives the names of these American scholars: suggested reading for the readers of *The New York Review of Books*. He apparently feels these readers have some reading to catch up on. Baran and Sweezy, in fact.

The academic community in this country does not think much of these other scholars' work on the topic Mr. Enzensberger does not have the space to discuss scientifically; it has called their work old-fashioned, boring, and rhetorical, or so Mr. Enzensberger has gathered, and he wants to get at least that much straightened out.

He discusses our society. It "has become permissive about the old taboos of language," the "ancient and indispensable" words of four letters, *fuck* and *shit* and *piss*. The whole society came to that decision, and Mr. Enzensberger was there.

But there is another society: polite society. This is where Mr. Enzensberger has gotten to know his ninety-eight million Americans. By common consent, they have banished other words: *exploitation* and *imperialism*. These words have "acquired a touch of obscenity" in Mr. Enzensberger's polite society. Among the like-minded, needless to say. However, to do away with the word for a problem is by no means to get rid of the problem itself. So true.

Mr. Enzensberger then turns to the notion that "bank presidents, generals, and military industrialists" (Paul Goodman, q.v.) "look like comic-strip demons." He wishes to correct this misapprehension. They are in fact well-mannered, nice, "possibly lovers of chamber music with a philanthropic bent of mind"—the same kind of people the Nazis had too. All right then. Now we know. Their "moral insanity" derives not from their individual character but from their social function. After these astonishing, original insights, surely no one will go on thinking that the President of the USA is acting in his capacity as a private individual. You have to say what has to be said.

Nor is Communism what Mr. Enzensberger's analysis is giving voice to. He has no reason to fear this time-honored indictment. Fearless as he is. For the word *Communism*, used as a singular, has become rather meaningless—it has many meanings now, conflicting, some even mutually exclusive. So there's not much to fear there, and Mr. Enzensberger fears not. But just in case this is not sufficient to cover his back, Mr. Enzensberger also has Greek liberals, Latin American archbishops, Norwegian peasants, and French industrialists at his side—his whole polite society. American industrialists are "the most dangerous body of men on earth," Paul Goodman says so too, but French ones aren't. And these auxiliaries of his are moreover not Communists, at least they are not generally thought of as being in the vanguard of Communism. So nothing can happen to Hans Magnus Enzensberger. He has stated his claim in public; now it's our job to back him up and not take away his sense of safety and security. Otherwise it would turn into a real shitshow (all branches of society have become permissive about taboo words, since they're indispensable).

Which means, which logically entails, from which follows: a fact. That 125 million people ("most Americans") have no idea of what they and their country look like to the outside world.

No! Inconceivable! How can it possibly be true! How, then, *do* they look to the outside world without knowing it? Without having the least idea?

Mr. Enzensberger has read the answer in the look that follows American tourists in the streets of Mexico, soldiers on leave in Far Eastern countries, businessmen in Italy or Sweden. Sweden seems to be an alternate. What's more, the same look is cast on embassies, destroyers, and billboards advertising American products, from General Motors to IBM. An international look, the same in every country. Wherever the look is not looked, there and only there will you find the territory of the US of A.

Enzensberger recognized it easily, this look. And by God he'll tell us why. It's a terrible look, one that makes no distinctions and no allowances. Mr. Enzensberger has felt it on himself, because he is a German.

In 1945, the Germans had to answer to the world for fifty-five million dead, plus six million more victims of the death camps.

In Mr. Enzensberger's eyes, American citizens carry the weight of a comparable guilt.

Never mind about the dead. The dead can be counted on to keep their mouths shut.

What follows is an analysis of this international look. The attempt to analyze it. Modestly denying that he is the favorite, then crossing the finish line first after all. And then the laurel wreaths of victory too. "Try to analyze."

This modest, timid schoolboy—who manages to figure everything out in the end—says: The look consists of a blend of distrust and resentment, fear and envy, contempt and outright hate.

And anyone who doesn't believe it is welcome to come meet him in Rome in the summertime and see the proof for himself by the fountain at the foot of the Spanish Steps.

For you see, passersby in Mexican, Far Eastern, Italian (or Swedish) streets have already analyzed American foreign policy. It is only in America, and especially in the pages of *The New York Review of Books* and the groves of Wesleyan University, Middletown, Conn., that people don't know what's what. But here at last is Mr. Enzensberger to tell us.

This look hits President Johnson. There's hardly a capital city in the world where he can now show his face in public.

Here many of Mr. Enzensberger's listeners will no doubt audibly sigh: If only.

Because of all the heads of state in the world, the President of the USA is the only one protected by security measures whenever he appears in public.

Since that's not true, Mr. Enzensberger moves quickly to the "kind old lady" across the aisle from him on the flight from Delhi to Benares. That look hits her too. Bad news for the airline, isn't it. All that money spent on advertising and now Passenger Enzensberger is undermining it, maybe the flight attendants too.

It is an indiscriminate, blind, undistinguishing, unallowing look, lock stock and barrel.

It is "a manichaean look." That is to say, it comes from followers of a doctrine of dualism between the Lord of the World of Light and the King of Darkness between Spirit and Matter, with the World and Man created from an unseemly and deplorable mixing of the two. According to this doctrine, the World and Man can be saved only when the portions of Light are extracted from Matter once more and returned to the World of Light. This process continues until the final purification in the Fire of the World. Initiates can hasten it by simply abstaining from sexual reproduction. It is also greatly assisted when the Elect renounce the pleasures of meat and wine. They are advised to avoid work. Possessions should be cast aside to the extent possible. However, anyone who lacks this elite wisdom—who has children and eats meat and drinks booze and works and does so using his own means of production—will receive a look from these Manichaeans: like *this*. "Manichaean."

Mr. de Rosny, vice president of his bank, jaunts carefree around the world, and in Mexico, in Bangkok, in Rome (or Stockholm), the locals look at him, and all these locals are childless old people, monks and hoboes, owning nothing, vegetarians, teetotalers. Manichaeans.

Mr. Enzensberger does not like this look.

While he feels obliged to tell us all this, he still feels sorry for us.

Mr. Enzensberger sees a connection between the blind gaze of the Manichaeans and the fact that he does not share President Johnson's beliefs. Someone might secretly suspect a certain something; he is going to put a stop to that. Actually, every last thing the president says about collective graft and collective guilt is *not* the view of Mr. Enzensberger.

Anyway, he does admit that other countries exploit and pillage the third world too. In case his readers are unfamiliar with this process, he describes it.

What Mr. Enzensberger admires in America: the work of three political student groups. Hardly comparable with Europe.

And he does "resent the air of moral superiority which many Europeans nowadays affect with respect to the United States" just because their own empires have been shattered. He knows such Europeans, and he can't stand them. They seem to regard it (that is, shattered empire) as a personal merit.

There certainly are Europeans like that, and they are deeply abhorrent to him. All this hypocritical nonsense.

However, he does want to insist on such a thing as personal responsibility for what your own country's government is doing. He cannot spare us that, for he has not been spared it himself. We've been looking for someone like this for a long time! Someone willing to take responsibility for a West German president suspected of signing concentration camp blueprints.

When Mr. Enzensberger thinks about it, it all seems familiar to him. Conditions in America today are like they were in Germany "in the middle Thirties." Respectable statesmen visited Berlin and shook hands with the Führer; such things happen in America.

For example, most people refused to believe that Germany had set out to dominate the world.

Just like in America. Here Mr. Enzensberger's many Americans have told him that they refuse to believe that their government is trying to dominate the world.

In Germany, there was a lot of racial discrimination and persecution going on. Just like in America.

It's, oh, some three hundred years back that German square-rigged galleons set out from the African coast loaded to the gunwales with black men and women that they planned to bring to market in Hamburg and sell off as cheap concubines or bargain beasts of burden. Just like in America.

Where people constantly parade Negroes through the streets with shaved heads and signs around their necks saying they'll never file a complaint with the police about the Storm Troopers again. Just like in Germany in the middle thirties.

Lastly, Germany had "a growing involvement in the war against the Spanish revolution." Just like America.

Vietnam is the Spain of our generation! That's what such people say.

But they don't ask their friends the French industrialists for discreet donations for the side they hope wins.

They give public speeches, to make sure that no one might think they're secretly fans of America. The friends of the legal Spanish government sent shiploads of medical supplies, brought big checks, took weapons in hand and fought in brigades against the military clique, and one at least went to see what was happening so that he could write a book about it.

Only at this point, after the Spanish Civil War that stands in for the war in Vietnam, does Mr. Enzensberger see his analogy break down. For instance, there's the destructive power wielded by Mr. Enzensberger's present masters. Power of which the Nazis could never dream.

And if they did anyway, if they dreamed of a rocket that could reach New York, so much the worse for dreams.

We have also today reached a degree of subtlety and sophistication unheard of in the crude old days, says Mr. Enzensberger. Verbal opposition today is licensed, well-regulated, and even encouraged by the powerful. So that's who's encouraging him.

It is a precarious and deceptive freedom for Mr. Enzensberger. He pictures censorship and open repression, direct and hard; but no, he doesn't want that either.

Dear Mr. President, he writes, to the president of Wesleyan.

It took him three months to discover that the advantages he was being given would end up disarming him; that in accepting an invitation and money, he had lost his credibility; and that whatever he might have to say would be devalued by the mere fact of his being in Middletown, Conn., on these terms.

He'll probably manage to defend himself just fine against West German money, but he's not up to taking on the dollar.

A piece of advice has been given him: To judge an intellectual it is not enough to examine his ideas; it is the relation between his ideas and his acts which counts. Mr. Enzensberger has now decided to act. He is leaving a small town north of New York and going to San Francisco and from there on a trip around the world. Not really. Around the earth.

For it is one thing to sit in comfort and study imperialism (there it is again, that obscene word). To confront it where it shows a less benevolent face—yes, peasant, that is quite another thing.

He's been to Cuba. The agents of the CIA in the airport of Mexico City were taking pictures of every passenger leaving for Havana!

No other country anywhere has its foreign intelligence service take people's pictures!

Nor do they invade other, smaller countries and leave traces; their respective economic systems never leave "scars" on "the body and on the mind of a small country." No way.

Mr. Enzensberger has seen it for himself.

Mr. Enzensberger has made up his mind to go to Cuba and to work there for a substantial period of time. Maybe three years.

This is hardly a sacrifice, he writes.

He just feels somehow that he can learn more ("joy") from the Cuban people than he could ever teach the students of Wesleyan University about political attitudes.

He wants to be of use to the Cuban people. He, himself, personally, wants to be of use to an entire population.

The transformation of Mr. Enzensberger into an asset of the Cuban people, live on stage, step right up. No tricks, no double curtains, no veils!

This letter is a meager token of gratitude for three peaceful months.

It was three peaceful months anyway.

He realizes, of course, that his case is, by itself, of no importance or interest to the world outside the university.

Then he goes and gets his letter published in *The New York Review of Books.*

Because his case does raise questions.

That it does.

Which do not concern him alone.

Definitely not.

Which he therefore wants to answer in public.

No, not so confident. Which he therefore wants to *try to* answer.

As best he can.

As best he can, yes. And are these the right questions?

And now let's see how he signs off to the university president who tried to disarm him with advantages, make him lose his credibility, devalue whatever he might have to say. How, according to Hans Magnus Enzensberger's teachings, should we treat an enemy?

With sincerity and devotion.

"Yours faithfully,

Hans Magnus Enzensberger,

January 31, 1968."

– This countryman of yours, had he never been to this country before?

– He's been here many times, and for long stays too.

– Mrs. Cresspahl, why is this German treating us like children? Elementary-school children.

– He's proud of being such a quick learner; he's just trying to show us his progress, Mr. Shuldiner.

– So now we're supposed to go to Cuba too? Doesn't he have anything to do in Germany?

– You should never read other people's mail, even if they show it to you.

– But he must have been wanting to set an example for you, since you're German.

– Naomi, that's why I don't want to live in West Germany.

– Because of all the hot air from people like that?

– Yes. From good people like that.

Last night the fog hung twilight over the river early, and this morning there was a thick haze left over. Even the fourteenth floor was invisible in its wrapping. This afternoon there were heavy rain showers rattling the window, into the evening.

March 1, 1968

At six in the morning there was snow in the park. In the city it turned right to slush. At lunchtime, Lexington Avenue was almost dry, with bright sun.

Mr. Greene has given up. Twenty years ago he opened a tiny jewelry store on Lexington Avenue between Eighty-First and Eighty-Second Streets, one of the many stores we went to all the time as though there weren't such businesses on upper Broadway too. His store was kept locked in the middle of the day, and he would scrutinize his customers through the grate before he released the catch with the push of a button. His eyes, almost cornflower blue, look and see precisely; he tried to recognize the customer by sight by the second time. Marie got her first ID bracelet engraved by him. His work desk was neatly stocked with many instruments. – Don't throw out that watch: he said, when he could have tried to sell us a new one. – It's a good watch. Made in Ruhla, now where's that? In recent years his store had been held up seven times and cleaned out once, and now the insurance companies aren't interested. His policy has been canceled and he's closing up shop. His store gets a burial of honor in the *Times*, with a slice of the personal and statistical story and relevant social-critical commentary from an insurance agent, such as: "Years ago, the hardest thing to find was customers. Now, the hardest thing to find is underwriters." And since the police decline to comment on the subject, the *Times* remarks that the police decline to comment.

The Jerichow police department, three men strong now that the air force had come to town, was spared having to help the Gestapo with the expulsion of Aggie Brüshaver. Aggie left of her own free will.

As a rule, pastors' wives keep the right to live in the pastor's house when their husbands are in jail. But the state felt Brüshaver had gone too far with Daniel's penitential prayer the day before Lisbeth's burial. Rather than dispute the assertion that the devil (your adversary) walketh about as a roaring lion (1 Peter 5), he handed his interrogators the citation for that passage as well as the others that an attentive member of his congregation had been writing down since 1936. After serving his sentence, he was to be put into protective custody in a concentration camp, until a point in time not yet determined. The high consistory of the church likewise felt that the funeral ceremony giving the Cresspahl corpse equal rights had gone too far, so there was no help to be expected from that quarter, nor any chance of a renewed posting to Jerichow. He was not only officially suspended; the authorities were not above a sentence of complete expulsion. The illegal church authorities, the National Council of Brothers, could have used its money for Aggie. People like the von Bobziens weren't shy about sending her potatoes and game without charge, leaving their car parked outside the pastor's house even in broad daylight; after Aggie Brüshaver left town, Baron von Rammin left the German Faith Movement "for National Socialist and religious reasons," giving public notice. It did not escape Aggie that the people of Jerichow were also pushing her to leave. Her children were left in peace in school—here Head Teacher Stoffregen made one of his unfathomable distinctions; people continued to greet and talk to her on the street. But no one came to visit, and Aggie noticed from the, as it were, surprised and questioning glances that the Jerichowers felt it was a burden to stick by her and Brüshaver. When she'd been allowed to visit him at the detention center in Rostock, she had also visited her hospital, and the hospital had been happy to take her back as a nurse. Now she and her children lived a good distance away, in Rostock old town, near St. Jacobi Church; her eviction order didn't find her at home and wasn't forwarded after her.

By that point the Jerichow congregation was in the care of a vicar who didn't want to abandon his assistant pastor position in Rande either, so religious services were held in Jerichow only every other week. Vicar Pelzer said let us pray for the persecuted and oppressed, in general, not for Brüshaver by name, partly out of caution and partly out of disapproval for Brüshaver's lack of caution, and Jerichow didn't like Pelzer. That was how things stood. Then Wallschläger arrived.

Wallschläger the resplendent. Wallschläger the savior. Wallschläger, herald of the joy of standing with Adolf Hitler while simultaneously being a Christian. He was a little wild, and the church authorities had already had to remove him from other positions; in Jerichow he stayed six and a half years. He didn't look like much. Nothing stood out: partly bald, hooked nose, wide mouth, nothing. Maybe you hardly saw him because he didn't seem possible. In Jerichow, joy was never shown so forcefully, with a raised and also wavering voice. Not even if you'd finally had a boy after seven girls, or had a secret stash of money. Wallschläger could go there, even about the Jews.

Wallschläger seriously believed he could still save the congregation of Jerichow from the ethical coarsening caused by that Brüshaver, and he cheerfully reviewed what he saw as the man's errors. He did it theologically. What is the Christian faith anyway? Well? Nothing that came out of Judaism! Jesus made a Jewish understanding of the Old Testament impossible, and anyone calling Him a Jewish traitor who poisoned His own faith better look out! Luther and Bismarck and Hindenburg were German, and what Germans they were, and they were Christians. Now let us pray. He did it historically. He told some story about a raid in the heath near Mölln in 1638, and even a local historian like Stoffregen had to shake his head. Already, three hundred years ago, the Jews had concealed and employed marauding soldiers! And now let us turn to the book of Judges. He understood that most of his congregation lived off the land, so he did it locally. The famine in Schleswig-Holstein during the war was the Jews' fault! And a group of Jewish professors had brought about the slaughter of a million pigs in 1914!—because allegedly there wasn't enough grain and potatoes to feed them. They would not be allowed to prevent the victory of German arms again!: he cried, and he asked his congregation to thank God with him for the deliverance from this accursed people (God knew what He was doing when He hadn't sent Jesus into the world in Germany). They didn't want to hear this in Jerichow, though. They were done with the Jews. Anyway, people from elsewhere had taken care of Tannebaum. Hadn't they tried to keep Arthur Semig on the down low for as long as they could? They didn't want any lessons about that. It was their business. None of a newly arrived special pastor's.

Wallschläger didn't stop with the Jews; after them it was his own race's turn. The number of people leaving the church did not decline. In one year, four; the next year, ten. It wasn't worth the church taxes, ten percent of one's income tax plus two marks. It wasn't worth it for the kind of communion where the wine no longer meant the old kind of blood, it meant that of the National Socialist martyrs. Wallschläger still shouted a fiery *Heil Hitler* whenever he walked into a room where people were standing around a bed in which someone had just died. He was called out to the estates only for emergency baptisms. Not even Pauli Bastian liked the new pastor. He played the gentlemen where Methling had made a kind of comradely bluster and Brüshaver had prayed politely. Pauli Bastian gave notice for January 1, 1940, and afterwards came from Rande to the Jerichow service a few times, sitting in the second row, arms crossed over his chest, gravely observing the pastor, a thoughtful expert, an independent man. Bastian had augmented his salary with farmwork, the weather had given his face truly dignified furrows, and people around Jerichow occasionally said that when you came right down to it, Pauli's appearance and demeanor was more like a pastor's—as long as he didn't open his mouth. Pauli was so exalted by this talk that he forgot the second half of the comment. What they said about Wallschläger was: Wool-whatever, don' care where he pulls the wool, that's not his job.

Cresspahl didn't leave the church. He stayed for Lisbeth's sake, and if Wallschläger was the church then so was Brüshaver.

With Alwin Paap's help Cresspahl had turned a corner of the house into a small workspace, enough for repairing furniture. Alwin Paap had liked his six weeks as master of the house and grounds; he felt less like an employee, and now automatically greeted customers with firm confidence, as Cresspahl had told him to do while he was away. Alwin had succeeded in finding a girl as well—once someone knew about the strength in his body, a slightly crooked jaw wasn't too bad. Alwin had moved into the main house, the east gabled room. Its windows couldn't be seen from the cemetery, much less from the pastor's house. Still, Wallschläger couldn't resist getting involved. He went into the house, paid a visit to the man who looked at him like a stranger on Brickworks Road and said hello to him as if by mistake, if he did at all; it's not like he was interested in discussing his wife's death with him. He was flabbergasted, he couldn't believe that the two men barely looked up from their work, let a squared board fall at his feet, neglected to offer him a seat, and were clearly even less interested in having a conversation in the living room. In his resplendent, exalted voice, Wallschläger cried that he, he too had been young once. He was over fifty, with gray skin, often with foam on his lips. But he could not endure that Cresspahl—! Cresspahl half turned and looked at his visitor. – *Izzis your house?*: he asked, not bothering to wait for an answer, and Wallschläger had to put up with an apprentice carpenter taking him out into the hall and to the stairs and slamming the door behind him. Alwin Paap now held his head high and looked as tall as he actually was. Cresspahl had let him bring the girl into the gabled room, and now this pastor wanted him to go lie outside with Inge Schlegel on the wet ground in the cold spring! Alwin was no longer in the habit of letting other people meddle in his business, especially not when it came to setting a date for a wedding. – *Yer comin along*: Cresspahl said when he got back, and this was one of the few occasions when Paap actually turned red.

After that, Wallschläger had to send a request in writing for every delivery in kind around Michaelmas, and at the other holidays too, and likewise for the cash payments for the sacristan's benefice. A lot of people in Jerichow did the same, and the question did sometimes occur to Wallschläger of whether he might have not gone about things quite the right way.

– Bit heavy on the church stuff: Marie says.

March 2, 1968 Saturday, South Ferry day
Yesterday the West German president, Heinrich Lübke, appeared on his country's TV. He stated that he could not recall having signed blueprints for concentration camps in the Nazi Reich. Nor not having signed them.

The secretary-general of the Christian Democratic Union, the party of which Mr. Lübke is a member, attacked the man who had once again brought up the matter in his mass-circulation magazine. He too had been an impassioned follower of Hitler.

I forgot to ask when Cresspahl started it; by September 1939, he had already been working for British counterintelligence for several months.

– I don't like it: Marie says, stubborn, indignant. It is so cold and windy today that she has paced the length of her ship without going outside. Sits there reluctantly, bored, watching the shapeless clouds above the harbor. She doesn't like it.

– Because he was betraying his country?
– That too.
– But wasn't his country in the wrong?
– Gesine, isn't this country in the wrong? Can't you talk about how for hours, and that's just the list? Is that enough to make you go betray it?
– We're guests here.
– We live here.
– Okay, Marie. If I decide to do that, I'll ask you first.
– There's no way I'll help you.
– And what's your other reason?
– Everyone in your family worked hand in glove with the Nazis. Cresspahl most of all. Now you want to save the honor of at least one of them, and of course you pick your father.
– I have proof.
– This is a totally ordinary *halfpenny* with George VI on the back.
– Look at the year.
– 1940. Maybe you found it in England just recently and brought it back.
– They mailed it to me from Jerichow when my father died. That was in 1962, and he'd never set foot in England since the start of the war.

– Tell me! Tell me! Why didn't you tell me sooner!

– Would you have understood it?

– No. And I don't understand it now either. Tell me.

– Life insurance with Allianz Bank....

– Listen, Gesine. I thought you'd made it up. I've agreed to your making things up, I've signed on, but I'd rather that this was the truth. Is it true?

– It started with money.

– You really know how to hook me. You're at such an advantage, Gesine, you know me.

– Cresspahl took out life insurance only for the child's and Lisbeth's sakes; now Lisbeth's death brought in no money. He hadn't even reported to the fire-insurance company in Hamburg the loss of the workshop building and machinery; then they noticed they hadn't received a December payment. In January they sent a warning, but still no money came. Jerichow, from Hamburg's point of view, was in the flatlands, possibly the hinterlands, in any case not a place where written correspondence was worth much. In mid-February, then, they sent someone in a car with HH plates, left parked in the middle of town as though the driver had gotten out merely to have lunch at the Lübeck Court. Cresspahl later said: a tennis guy, so I imagine him like Dr. Ramdohr—tall, gangly, with a small head, a kind of sleepy expression, but wide awake, not easy to catch off guard and not a chance to browbeat him. Maybe because Ramdohr had so much business in Hamburg then. This other man attracted no attention in town, even with his briefcase; he didn't walk to Gneez Street but through the churchyard like a sightseer, walked out of the chapel gate onto Brickworks Road, and was on Cresspahl's property with almost no one having seen him. Now comes something I don't know.

– So imagine it, Gesine!

– I imagine: They knew each other from Denmark in November (or England in December); that way the conversation could have opened with a memory. I also imagine: that this was the first request. That way the man might have made the suggestion naturally, casually, like something obvious; not as if it could cost him his neck. And Cresspahl might have said no less calmly that he wanted to think it over. Or: think it over a bit more. Then the man might have showed him the police report on the fire he had in his hand and said: It's easy for a lamp to fall over in a wooden building storing wood.

– But Cresspahl was owed the money!

– Not if it was suicide.

– Suicide, what?! Okay. I know. Sorry.

– Cresspahl wanted to test them first. He took the train to Lübeck and asked around among Erwin Plath's friends, but they were busy with Franco's victory over the legal government of Spain, and when they did talk about England they cursed the British government, which had contributed to starving out the People's Front. And at that point the Social Democrats were beginning to dig themselves in. Then the visitor came again, and this time Cresspahl found it easy to believe him. Because this time what the man brought with him was a page with the Foreign Exchange Control Law of February 1935 on it. That law threatened anyone who failed to report foreign assets with ten years in prison. Cresspahl had failed, for three and a half years now, and a court could have proven: deliberately.

– Why is it the government's business where I keep my money?

– Listen to you, you American. The government was in the hands of crooks, and what they wanted was to get their subjects' foreign assets into their own pockets. Sorry—a law like that with a ten-year prison term had already been passed in 1931.

– Wasn't your father careful?

– He certainly kept an eye on the law. But why should he follow this one, when only Salomon, of Burse, Dunaway & Salomon, and the Surrey Bank of Richmond knew about the rest of his English account? And by the end of 1938, it would no doubt have already been emptied, with the monthly payments to Mrs. Elizabeth Trowbridge. She, though, had decided to raise her child without the help of someone who'd decided to marry another woman, and sent the remittances straight back until Salomon gave up.

– And wrote to Germany?

– Salomon did not entrust his clients' secrets to the mail, especially not the German mail. There were enough fugitives in London by then who could have warned him not to. Besides, Salomon could afford to ignore the laws they had in Germany—he respected the English ones.

– So Mr. Smith betrayed Cresspahl? I don't believe it.

– Not him, and not Perceval either. T. P. had wanted to get so far away from Richmond and memories of Mrs. Cresspahl that he had to join the Royal Navy. It was Gosling.

– Hence "Gosling the patriot."

– Gosling couldn't get over the fact that the German had stopped managing Reggie Pascal's workshop for him, without permission, of his own free will. It hadn't been a cash cow, quite, but he had managed it so that Reggie's nephew could live like a lord. Gosling had found Mrs. Trowbridge outside of Bristol and nor had he failed to notice the child. He could only suspect that Cresspahl was paying for the child, that it was his; he denounced him as a stab in the dark, who knows why. He wanted the German's money to go to the English state at least, and maybe a nice reward for him crossed his mind.

– And they sent him packing like a lunatic.

– Right. Then a few weeks later, the government he'd been trying to help paid him a little visit. Represented for the occasion by two sinister gentleman, one of whom kept softly sniffling, as though it smelled unpleasant when Gosling was there. When they left, Albert A. Gosling, Esq., had firmly and most fearfully decided to forget the whole affair and, especially, with a solemn oath, forget about the money.

– So the British could blackmail their man in Jerichow, Cresspahl.

– And he didn't mind.

– I'm glad I don't have to write an essay about this one.

– It's simple, Marie. As long as they thought they had him by a rope around his neck, ten years in prison, they wouldn't know the real reason he wanted to help them.

– He didn't trust them. They were blackmailers.

– And he hadn't told them he had a score of his own to settle with the Nazis. On the balance sheet stood his wife, Voss in Rande (he hadn't even known him personally), Brüshaver, the war.

– The war hadn't started yet, Gesine.

– As long as the Nazis hadn't started the war yet, Cresspahl did sometimes feel uncomfortable. Once they marched into Poland, he felt sure of himself and furious with the inaction of the English on top of that.

– Would the Nazis have strung him up?

– Oh they would have loved to.

– So a child meant nothing to him.

– He didn't feel like he could raise a girl anyway. He had money hidden away in the country for the child; he trusted Hilde Paepcke, and not only because she was Lisbeth's sister.

– And you forgive him for that.

– I forgive him for that. And now he could call the English "utter scoundrels" in another sense. Except that Alwin Paap knew hardly anything about Cresspahl's time in England, and the wife who might have listened to him wasn't there.

– Okay, I'll accept that.

– And Cresspahl, again, didn't mind. As soon as he accepted, the fire insurance money came. When a lamp falls over in a woodworking business it could be an accident. Or nothing but clumsiness. It was a lot of money. German money was still worth a lot then.

– So now they'd bought him off too.

– Blackmailed, bought and paid for, safe and sound. But in fact he'd decided for himself, and kept his freedom.

– Y'know, I'd keep all of this to myself if I were you.

– I agree. Jakob knew; D. E. knows. Now you know.

– It's like a skeleton in the closet.

– Not for me. It's just that it's my father's business, and I don't care to tell it to everyone.

– Five years we've been taking the South Ferry and we've never once caught a storm! Yesterday's could've waited till Saturday. Taking the South Ferry in a storm—I wish I could do that.

March 3, 1968 Sunday

The West Germans have released Robert Mulka—the former adjunct commandant of Auschwitz, convicted of helping in three thousand murders—from Kassel prison, for health reasons. The *Times* came into our apartment with two inserts of Greek advertisements. In New Haven, Church Street and the university campus were swept bare of pedestrians by a harsh wind, eighteen degrees. Now a thin bowl of moon is lying on its back above Riverside Drive. The sky is almost black.

"Dear G. C.,

Handwritten, for you. That's how you like your letters, you daughter of Cresspahl. This one wouldn't get written any faster on the typewriter anyway, and maybe not at all, because the standardized font would imply an objectivity the letter doesn't have. Whatever the reasons, handwriting softens things. That's not what you mean.

I won't use the word. Not because it would be too imprecise for me but because it's already had its day with you. By now it's so contemptible to you that you use it only when you're wanting to play in your foreign language, and etymology is playing too. For in English it has Latin forebears, *lubēre*, *libēre*, trying merely to suggest a pleasure, a delight, a favor being performed. For instance, you might say to a not unpleasant suggestion: *I'd love to.* You'd say that; the other thing you won't say. I like that.

It's not that I'm trying to cop out. You tease me for liking precise words; in my mind I do use the word that you don't want to hear and that I have no other opportunity to use. Like you, it bothers me that it fits into the HaveHaveHave Syndrome, whether applied to consumer products, persons, or life. I can live with it when it secures the past. I accept it in a literary book when it's applied to a dead man who is no longer there to reap the reward, who is free from the need to repay it, whether in money, affection, or words themselves. It's better if it's an old book. To make a long story short and insufficient, I can use the word for the sum of the relations between one person and another—relations that contain a history, that are kept up, whose quiescence shuts down a part of the person. There certainly is a need involved, but mere self-interest couldn't survive there; a coupled system of person and person requires sustenance from all sides, reciprocal, a feedback loop.

This detour around the word has cost me twenty-nine minutes. I write that down too, and you laugh.

You shouldn't marry me—you should live with me. You're the one who talks about 'should's: what I mean is that's what I want.

It's attachment. Not the way Klothilde Schumann meant it. She was my landlady in East Berlin, and she accused me of that once, because one time she came into the room without knocking and Eva Mau and I fell off her sofa. It's that kind of attachment too. But it's more that I can tolerate G. C. in any and every situation. That is not a generalization, that's the sum of almost six years of addition. (And don't tell me that I feel this way simply because you're so tolerable.) There was only one time that I couldn't stand your face. It was last week, when you had a fever, when you let a pediatrician treat you and even in your sleep issued orders against hospitals and against where I'd have wanted to have you taken. I did like your stubbornness, you've bundled up good reasons in it often enough, but I didn't like that you were in danger and wouldn't let me do anything to ward it off. Incidentally, that's the occasion for this letter. Since I wasn't permitted to do anything about your possessed burning sleep, go against your unconscious orders, I didn't come back. Only now do I set foot in your apartment again, with a bow from the waist, the way little boys are taught to make on the Misdroy boardwalk so that they know how to express deference.

I'm not asking you; I'm explaining a suggestion.

This is what you think my life is. When you observe it you politely mock me, but you do create a certain distance. You've seen a lot; I don't deny anymore that this is how it looks. That I'm not really present in my work—only my ability is, not the whole person. That I've long since given up trying to justify my career. What the Soviets did in Mecklenburg after the war, that's not enough; what the Americans are doing in the world, now that the phase of consumption is over, that's not enough. I would have a function in this intertwined system no matter what my job was; this is the job I have. I wouldn't be of any use on either side above and beyond the use of my employer. The other side: it wouldn't work there. At least I'm indifferent to this side. Even my lack of biographical motivations infuriates you—I have no biography, just a CV. In such situations of ennui, one can make a lot of noise with planes and cars and the machinery of the job; that may fool other people but not oneself. And not you either. If I stayed alone, I would only be watching to see what happens in the next twenty years, not especially hoping that my prognosis comes true, just curious; there's not much else left. Call it waiting.

You don't live like that; for you there are still real things: death, the rain, the sea. I remember all that; I can't get back to that place. What feels real to me is you.

Where I have an old woman with her eccentricities, because she's still alive, you have a past that's alive all around you, a present that includes the dead, and your Marie knows more about who she is too because she's learning where she comes from. There's something there I can't put into words. I will never be able to say of my own mother that she was anything more than what I saw in her, heard from her, heard about her; you on the other hand go right ahead and say: My father wasn't out for revenge, he just didn't want to get his hands dirty with the Nazis. Which is really an incomprehensible claim since it can never be proven. And from you I believe it completely: as a truth that you use to get through life; most of the time as the truth. Of course I know living people where they're doing their jobs, turning into their functions; there are some of those people I'll miss. That sounds nice, and friendly, and behind it are a few hours of companionship without giving or taking offense, and then again all it really amounted to was a little more wasted time. You, though, don't pass a horse without looking it in the eye, touching it, until the horse knows who was there. That's not why you're doing it, but that's what others get from it. I wish you would live with me.

You can talk; I can't. You say, about Amanda Williams: She's flat on the floor with her soul. From anyone else I would take that as a clumsy remark, and either argue it away or leave it there naked—from you it suddenly illuminates the whole sum of relations that go to make up a person, including the unexplained or still-unrecognized part. You also said about her once: She's not heated all the way through; this should go against my systems engineering but instead it expands it. I laughed when you said it, and it delighted me for days. I hope you've reheated her by now. Whatever I say, even if it's something new and newly described, is already in quotation marks the moment I say it. An actual event in Wendisch Burg that really happened not many years ago: from me it turns dry, maybe amusing but nothing more than an anecdote. While you tell Marie about one named Shitface, 'and the other one was named Peter,' and she sees before her eyes a cat and another cat, because they've stayed alive in you. In me they've turned into words. All of these are things I can't explain. They are the kinds of thing I don't even want to take apart; I only want to be around them.

You haven't given up. Needless to say, I would find that unbelievable in myself. I agree, you're right. Even now you haven't gotten tired of taking the promises of Socialism at their word; you stubbornly challenge the imperialist democracies with the noble values of their own constitutions; to this day you refuse to forget that the church, in blessing the recruits in the barracks yard in Gneez, included their instruments of war. If it were naiveté, I would eagerly take up this perennial pedagogical task too. But no, it's hope. You don't say it out loud, and not only for the usual Mecklenburg reasons. Forget that I originally tried to talk you out of your Czech business; now all I want is for those people to come to their senses so that for once you won't have to bear the brunt. Forget our bet.

The child won't be taken from you—that's a promise. Anyway, she will never be mine, she will always be your Marie.

If we meet again someday, then maybe we should be together.

I've written you this because I'm being loaded into a Scandinavian Airlines plane again. And because I wanted to write it. The undersigned prefers not to talk about it. Neither snow nor rain nor heat nor gloom of night stays these couriers from the swift completion of their appointed rounds, and if Herodotus still counts as one of the pillars of society then the courier should reach your door with this letter at around eight o'clock on Sunday. Otherwise, we will have the inscription chiseled off the brow of your central post office.

Sincerely yours, D. E. A child who was not in your class."

March 4, 1968 Monday

If we do convict four citizens on charges of expressing views other than those of the Soviet government: says the Soviet government, via *Pravda*: that will be equally justified as the purges in the 1930s. So now the state itself has confirmed that the thousands of dead from that era enjoyed a good name for a period of only twelve years, now ended.

Sometimes it seems possible. Yesterday, in fact, *The New York Times* mentioned Czech hopes for long-term West German credits. The price would be "recognition of West Germany." De Rosny could get it for them cheaper than that.

Sometimes it seems impossible.

Maybe de Rosny hasn't found the right employee after all and was badly advised. Not only must Mrs. Cresspahl tilt her head back even farther now to see the glass of her cell in the tower of the bank, and she rarely finds the right corner; she must also fight off a shyness that she hadn't expected in herself. She often presses the elevator button for the eleventh floor, as though afraid of the higher one, and only then the "16." Then the cabin might stop at the old place and the doors slide elaborately open and no one steps out, unless maybe someone invisible. In the higher realms the elevators are less crowded, and even if the occupants don't observe one another more closely as a result, it still seems that way. Since Employee Cresspahl prefers to keep her eyes pointing upward for the time being, at the panel above the door that shows the floors, she has also found herself greeted in fatherly fashion by a gentleman whose face she couldn't remember, Mr. Kennicott II, and he said: Settled in nicely, Mrs. Cresspahl? She said, beaming, helpless: Thanks very much, sir.

What's proceeding nicely are the lies, not what the head of the Personnel Department calls "settling in." It starts with the extravagant furnishings in the corridors. There are carpets. The neon tubes are not covered with simple glass but contained in expensively patterned plastic boxes, and they illuminate not bare walls but printed posters in gallery frames. Down in Foreign Sales the doors were of green-painted steel; here they're substantial mahogany slabs moved by brass knobs the size of a child's head. Downstairs she could sometimes skip the large trial smile at the entrance to the department; here Mrs. Lazar is sitting or, if she's away from her post for the moment, a deputy is. No visitor passes without signing in, unlike downstairs where there's less to hide. Mrs. Lazar, an older lady who carries herself like a rector, invariably stares at the new woman stiffly and encouragingly, and along with the time of day she offers a broadly unfurled smile, as if, along with the question of how it's going, she is being given a daily birthday present. Employee Cresspahl moves rapidly on, past the expensive desks in the spacious, salon-like hall, as though wanting no one to disturb her; what she wants is to avoid talking to anyone.

It's not fear of her new department—she misses knowing how she stands in relation to other people. When de Rosny presented her to his subordinates, the introductions went off with downright delighted looks from the men, and she has gradually learned their names, which she didn't catch at the time, from the triangular bars that each has placed before him: Wilbur N. Wendell, Anthony Milo, James C. Carmody, Henri Gelliston.... The nameplates on the eleventh floor didn't include first names. The name "Cresspahl" is still missing from next to the door of the new office—this nameplate clearly won't have the addition of "Miss." Anyone permitted to work up here has the right to be addressed as a married woman. She would love to know what people thought of her in these splendid dungeons. Does Mrs. Lazar see her as one of de Rosny's whims? Do the irreproachable encounters with colleagues in the open room not actually conceal skepticism about the newcomer's knowledge, or outrage at having a woman stationed at their side? Not even conversations about work are allowed; Mrs. Cresspahl has her own sphere, as do the others, and she is asked no questions about it. Now and then she feels glad not to have to sit in the open room; she has a door to sit behind. These doors are allowed to be closed. And yet she's more uncomfortable now than she used to be with her door open, because a knock would be more startling.

No one knocks. How to manage writing her memos is left to Mrs. Cresspahl's discretion; she could lie on the sofa for a long time if she had something she needed to read. These strange new surroundings, the distance from the others, ties her more unforgivingly to her work—suddenly she can't even decide to take a break. Downstairs, when putting off a tricky passage, she could bring a coffee or cigarette over to Naomi, Jocelyn, or Amanda Williams, and spend fifteen minutes chatting; it looked properly official and left her refreshed for the next hours of work. Here the rules are less strict; for all intents and purposes she can decide for herself when between nine and ten she'll arrive, whether to take an hour for lunch or an hour and a half, as long as she's still to be found in her place until five o'clock. She has not yet had the chance to learn such freedoms.

She often finds herself sitting in the middle of her new work, surrounded by maps, diagrams, journals, books, without having had a thought in her head for minutes at a time, leaned far back in her swivel chair, arms hanging down, mute blind deaf and tired. And yet she can deliver a file folder to Mrs. Lazar almost every four days, and every time Mrs. Lazar takes a new courier envelope, addresses it to de Rosny, and staples it shut, since clearly the usual closure with a string around a button will not suffice.

But compliments are obligatory. After nine days, Mr. Milo has come up with a new one. An Italian man who no longer speaks the language of his mother—brown-eyed, brooding, with forgetful lips, dry brittle tufts of hair—today he stops Mrs. Cresspahl in the hall as if he had something urgent to tell her, something he hadn't managed to say two days ago: You type better than I've learned to in ten years! At least then there was a conversation about the keystroke storage capacity of the IBM Selectric 72.

No one comes by. Amanda did once, to supervise the move and the new arrangements, called the new office glorious, and didn't come back. Everyone still says hello to her in the elevator, asks how it's going, smiles as though glad to see her, but they do so from a distance. On Friday afternoon Mrs. Cresspahl dropped by Foreign Sales and wanted to use Amanda Williams's calculator to compute some numbers for her 1967 taxes, and everyone was dumbfounded at the visit, like it was indecent. As though what they'd had in common was gone now and they were no longer working on the same plane. Mrs. Cresspahl's temporary successor is a writer from Switzerland who wants to make money in the city for a few more months, and because he mentioned difficulties with his Italian, Mrs. Cresspahl promised him she'd help out. He will ask Amanda what he should do, and will send Mrs. Cresspahl nothing. If the phone ever rings it's a wrong number or, once in a blue moon, de Rosny, handing out praise and good wishes the way you give sugar cubes to a horse.

It's so quiet. When the workday has ended, what she misses most is a soft click. That was Amanda, downstairs, outside the open door, wrapping up her coffee cup for the night and placing it gently on a shelf of her metal cabinet. That click was the start of the free rest of the day.

It's so quiet that one day Employee Cresspahl didn't leave work till half an hour after the end of the day. She had lost track of time. She didn't like that, and the smile of recognition from Mr. Kennicott II in the elevator didn't help either. Downstairs people used to look out for each other, help each other to some extent; up here everyone has to take care of themselves.

Sometimes it seems impossible. And have a good trip home, Mrs. Cresspahl, take care of yourself. *Take care.*

March 5, 1968 Tuesday

When people in the bank talk about the joint next door collapsing, it sounds hopeful, delighted. Today what they're saying is that it could just as easily have happened here before it did at Chase Manhattan Bank—namely, that a small group of conspirators used an accomplice in the wire department to request precisely $11,870,924 from a Swiss bank with a fraudulent cable authorization. One single word had saved Chase Manhattan. The gangsters requested the transfer in dollars instead of Swiss francs; that was the only reason why the Swiss bank cabled Chase for confirmation. It could have happened here.

And yesterday when the vice president decided he needed to take his dictation machine apart, he found a nest of cockroaches in it. Why does he have to keep a fridge in his suite? The little monsters smell food twenty floors away. This place is clearly falling apart.

If the city does collapse, the roaches will survive.

We got our apartment from a Danish woman and a Swiss woman, and at first we couldn't believe it. In the mornings, brown husks of wings on the floor as if shed by tiny bugs. Brown creepy-crawlies gathered in the dark sink, running off when the light's turned on, trying only to get away. They looked so single-minded. In Jerichow, a *Schabe* was a tool—a scraper; in New York, a *Schabe* is a roach. I thought it was some kind of mistake and stomped at the first roach I saw on the floor, with shoes on. It was no use—it disappeared into a crack invisible to the naked eye. And it was dangerous to try: they can cause all sorts of allergies, from asthma to eczema, even death, and even throwing away the shoes and socks I'd been wearing wouldn't have helped. Anyway, they are too fast to die like that. The air current caused by the moving foot is picked up by the roach's tiny hairs, the message is transmitted to its powerful back legs (without any stopover in the brain), and before the shoe reaches the floor the beast has scooted away. They were everywhere—in the spines of books, in seat cushions, in lamp sockets—each with five eyes, six legs, two highly sensitive antennae, and this time I applaud the supermarket for selling spray cans of poison without making you ask for them specially.

Mrs. Cresspahl was so ashamed that once, when Marie asked, she told her a roach on the wall was a fly. Why shouldn't a fly be half an inch long. Marie wasn't yet four and accepted it; she had already found various other things bigger in this country than she was used to.

Then, in the broad daylight of 1961, Marie was sitting on the floor and watching something next to her, discreetly, practically like a friend.

It was a female cockroach on the floor, heavy with pregnancy. Maybe she was too weak to hide, or else her self-protective instincts were no longer paramount. Marie could describe it later: the sacklike vessel sitting on the lower body from the waist down, packed firm like a feather pillow, long and narrow, releasing a quick succession of little white threads from an opening in the side, almost like quickly unspooling snippets of ribbon, and the maggot-like nymphs emerged, unfolded, swelled, acquired a gray shimmer, and were recognizable as bodies, all in tiny clear blocks of time, countless numbers per second, and while the mother still lay on her side producing babies, the first ones were already running off, complete adults in miniature except for the wings, and Marie asked. Since the word *children* came up in the course of the explanation, she offered money as rent for these new additions to the human race, and watched with horror as they were swept into the bags that the super incinerates in the night. Mrs. Cresspahl was so ashamed that she told the child not to ever talk about the scene again, even in the German that other people couldn't understand.

Then, during that summer of 1961, on benches in Riverside Park, the newcomer from Germany was given her first lessons in the science of cockroaches. She already didn't count for much there, because she was only a "part-time" mother, since she worked, and because she was therefore unable to keep up in the precise cataloging of bowel evacuations (quantity, coloring), loose kneecaps, and ingrown toenails, and also because she didn't have any knitting with her. But she was permitted to sit and listen, and so she learned that it's always the Year of the Roach in New York.

The most common kind is the German roach.

It was discussed as a completely normal, ordinary, respectable topic, and if a housewife tried to deny that there were roaches in her apartment, she gave up soon enough, under pitying or mocking and always disbelieving looks. The roach was spoken of with respect, hate, comic despair, systematic expertise, and absolutely, unquestionably as something invincible. For they eat everything, from dry furniture glue to the inflammable tips of matches; if a poison does manage to get rid of them for a while, they develop a resistance to it within a few years and what's supposed to kill them turns into their dessert. When one of the older matrons brings up the happy year of 1940, when chlordane still worked against cockroaches, it was heard not as folklore but as a piece of American history. Theses were put forth, such as the theory of cyclical waves, or that the critters survive because reproduction is their first priority, not, as with, say, rats, third. This latter theory was discussed more eagerly and at greater length than the one about cycles. Horror stories were told, like the one about the dignified old lady who was sitting in a darkened room in a Mexican hotel, watching an old home movie in which she was fingering a brooch on her chest. "Suddenly I realized I hadn't worn a brooch." *The New York Times* heard that one, too; indeed, this January the *Times* was willing to devote a practically academic article to the cockroach, with facts such as that its escape mechanism functions within 0.003 seconds, a world record. Such a respectable topic the cockroach was and is in New York.

When the German started describing her own first experiences—full of embarrassment, ready to beat a rapid retreat—she had given the ladies on the benches a pleasant thrill. Now the whole story of roaches could be told to her again. This time the fact that cockroaches probably came to America on German ships was casually dismissed. There are Americans among the creatures, and Orientals. A long list of spray poisons was written out for the newcomer, passing rather swiftly back and forth as each housewife championed her own favorite. Then came the advice: Always wear a mask over your mouth and nose when you spray, because even if the chemicals don't do anything to the roaches, they're harmful to people. Don't wipe up with water too often—that's what the Oriental roaches like. Shake out clothes after every time you wear them, and before you wear them. Turn everything you buy around and around, carefully, before you put it in the refrigerator. Triple these security measures whenever your neighbors are painting their apartment, because the roaches will come over to your place. Then came more horror stories: How one desperate woman put a whole pan of roaches into the oven and blasted it at 300 degrees for three hours, and afterward they all cheerfully got up and went their way, except for one, which wasn't dead, only stunned.

It remains in memory as a pleasant hour, full of good cheer and helpfulness. Still, Mrs. Cresspahl would not want to admit to a visitor from Denmark or Germany that roaches are hallmarks of this city, much less give them a talk like this one.

The topic of roaches does have its horrifying aspects. They are the oldest winged insect still extant in the world, 250 million years old—it was their Age, really, not the carboniferous Coal Age, and still is. They are useful to science, for their powers of resistance and terrifying fertility. They can starve for months and then, once they've understood that no food is forthcoming, go about their business. They can understand, they are intelligent, they can learn. What science can't understand is why they bother to live for five months since their only goal seems to be to reproduce. But there they are. They live with the poor and the rich alike, and now Francine believes it; they live in airplanes, on the South Ferry, in the tallest glass skyscrapers; they are the lowest common denominator of New York; it is highly possible that they will have walked on the moon before people. They're a cunning bunch.

For three whole months we cherished the belief that our apartment was almost free of them, and we made do with the strip of powder that the super's exterminator laid down outside the apartment door every month to secure the borders. Then the heating went down over the weekend, and on Monday when the heat suddenly came back on they decided to try out a new tactic for such eventualities, daring to go out entirely in the open, stinking with fear when attacked. The kinds of comment about societies for the prevention of cruelty to animals that pass our lips during these few days are strictly emergency measures. When Marie is reminded that she once wanted to pay rent for these creatures, she lashes out against the monsters all the harder, all the more bitterly with her spray can, cursing unchallenged.

De Rosny quietly cleaned out his office, without putting up a fight or punishing someone else whose fault it was. It wasn't anyone's fault, not in the bank, not anywhere. De Rosny knows when he's beaten. This time he's given up.

March 6, 1968 Wednesday

When asked who he was, Che Guevara reportedly said his name and: Don't kill me. I'm more valuable to you alive than dead.

The New York Times gathers information in Munich, too, but has brought specially from Prague the news that the new Communist leadership no longer wants Jiří Hendrych as secretary for ideological matters—the same Hendrych who so vehemently cursed rebellious writers and students last summer and autumn. The ČSSR is also said to soon be allowing the sale of foreign books and newspapers the same as normal ones.

For the official notice of people from the New York area killed in the line of duty in Vietnam, the *Times* today no longer uses the normal type size but the very smallest one.

Cresspahl had taken his child to the Paepckes. Once the Paepckes left Mecklenburg, they were known in the family as the "Berlin-Stettin relatives," and to the child too they seemed very far away from Jerichow, from Cresspahl. It had been a safe night journey, and even though Cresspahl had explained it to her as a move, and her clothes and toys had come along in a suitcase, she still didn't believe that her father would leave her there. There were two navy servicemen sitting at ease across the aisle in the train car, stretched out, giving each other a tongue-lashing out of boredom. – *Stop it, Ill tell my mother*: one of the two adults said, in a very thick Mecklenburgish accent. It sounded like he couldn't even speak High German. They were two voices, two red cigarettes aglow. For the child, these were the very first "sailors." The fact that she couldn't be sure what they were laughing at stayed with her. She fell asleep on the train, and when she woke up the next morning she immediately clenched her eyes shut again, with the shock of having different people around her. Then she jumped up and ran through the Paepcke house, got lost, finally found the front door. Cresspahl had already left.

The two older Paepcke children kept a close eye on the Cresspahl child, to make sure she didn't deprive them of anything. She didn't. Alexandra kept her place next to her mother, chubby Eberhardt didn't lose his next to Alexandra, Christine's on Hilde's other side was safe too. This Gesine sat at the foot of the table, kept her eyes on her plate, and ate her bread in a particular way: first all around the crusts, then into the soft middle in careful, slow bites, as though it were something precious. The Paepcke children could eat however they wanted, and if one of them licked the pat of butter right off, Hilde unflappably spread them a new one. The new child was not recalcitrant after breakfast either, she obediently went along with everything, said yes to every suggested game, didn't act the eldest. After a while she went off to the attic and looked for a new place to cry. That afternoon she let the others tell her everything they had to say about

Stettin—the cinemas, the harbor tours; clearly her Jerichow gave her nothing to brag about.

That evening it turned out that the new girl had acquired something after all. Her place was set next to Alexander Paepcke, who would've been happy to sit at the foot of the table by himself with enough room for his paper and his glass of beer. Tonight he practically forgot to eat, with all his questions for the child from Jerichow. Did Methfessel still ask people if they wanted to be a lion? Had Cresspahl given her an allowance yet? Did she want to see how to balance a cane on your nose? He showed her how to, and handed her five pfennigs more "pin money" than Alexandra's, going strictly by age, and the Cresspahl child talked to him even though she didn't like looking up. She remembered the obligations of a guest, which her father had impressed upon her, and tried to be well-behaved. Eventually Paepcke gave up. When it was over he wanted to stroke her hair, but he caught Hilde's warning look in time. Then his own kids claimed the right they'd never had before. Paepcke's face now looked practically fat, he hadn't looked that exhausted before, he was slower—but he only had to try a little, he was a magician with children, a maker of jokes and the butt of jokes in one. That night he tried a lot, laughter filled the kitchen, but the Cresspahl child asked quite early if she could go upstairs.

That night, at great expense, Paepcke put through a call to JErichow-209. He wanted to appeal to Cresspahl's conscience. It was only right and natural that Cresspahl not want his child in the clutches of Grandma Papenbrock's religion, if only because he felt it had taught his own wife how to die; it was only right that Louise had to hear this without the old man or Hilde taking her side. She had sat there like a big fat bird, insulted, feathers ruffled. And she'd cried; the family was used to her tears, whatever the occasion. But Paepcke did not want an unhappy child under his roof, and he didn't think he'd be able to console her because she took after Cresspahl and would stay stubborn even in grief. – *A dog'd take pity on er, Hinrich*: Paepcke said. There was a long silence from the other end of the line, but Paepcke didn't think he could hear any sighs. Then Cresspahl said: Alex—, in a determined way, utterly devoid of hope, and Paepcke didn't pester him further. He was unhappy, and that night Hilde didn't once say: *Stop drinking so much!*

Around ten o'clock his daughter came downstairs because she'd found the Cresspahl's bed empty. Alexandra didn't say where the other girl was, though—she didn't want a sermon about hospitality—and Paepcke had to search the whole house until he found Gesine in the attic, crouching in the dark between baskets and suitcases, where she could cry in peace. Paepcke was so upset that he screamed at everyone, not just the child, and fetched the maid out of bed to see, and the next morning the state councilman's widow, Mrs. Heinricius, told everyone in the general ("Colonial Goods") store that Paepcke had wanted to kill his wife in the night, shots had been fired, the fire department had come.

Paepcke sat there at breakfast and said, with a glance at the Cresspahl child: If you only knew what some people have to go through. And he was the head of a Military Ordnance Department by then. It didn't seem right. That night he didn't come home, he stayed in the Podejuch station pub until midnight. Paepcke couldn't bear to see children unhappy. It's true; it would eventually lead to his death. And if there was drinking he had to do, he'd rather do it outside the house.

You shouldn't forgive me for that, Gesine.
I forgive you, Cresspahl.

March 7, 1968 Thursday
Cuba has received an offer from the United States. Two conditions for resuming trade in nonstrategic goods are on the table: severing military ties with the Soviet Union, and cessation of "hooliganism in the hemisphere." The third condition, a settlement of claims resulting from the Cuban government's expropriation of US government and private property, should go without saying.

As the *Times* understands it, a Czech general is now in this country because it was no longer possible for him to support President Novotný. It's not quite clear how we should understand this, since back home the official case against this general was limited to charges that he'd misappropriated $20,000 worth of state-owned alfalfa and clover seed (even though he wasn't a party secretary in the Department of Agriculture—he was in the Defense Department). Back home, they hoped the general wouldn't meet with a fatal accident, and here they hope to get some of the defector's valuable military intelligence.

– You're trying to make Cresspahl out to be better than he was: Marie says. She says nothing about Francine. In school she looks right past her, never talks to her. She can't imagine that Francine wouldn't want to go back to her own mother. It's like her understanding of Francine is broken, there's a crack or a scratch in it that she has no Band-Aid for. It looks like Francine has insulted her. – Gesine!: she says.

– You don't believe it?

– I don't believe it of him. A carpenter, and if he's living next to an air base. . . .

– He was employed at this air base, as a carpenter. The base commander had asked the Gneez guild for a recommendation, and most agreed that Böttcher should give him Cresspahl's name. The man had just lost his wife, his workshop too. He needed work, otherwise his marbles'd be next.

– He doesn't get any farther into the airport than the door he's supposed to fix. . . .

– The first of those doors was in the officers' mess, where a party official in his cups had tried to shoot a swastika into Böttcher's sturdy woodwork with his revolver. Really.

– You see? And maybe he adds a porch onto the civilian personnel's vacation homes every now and then, as a side job . . .

– and in Semig's house he had to build a whole new office, with six-foot-high wainscoting and a gap left for the safe Lieutenant Colonel von der Decken wanted built in. It was Cresspahl who made a door to hide it.

– You see? Now your father was a safecracker.

– He didn't need to do that.

– Fine. But this lieutenant colonel of yours, a von der Decken no less, talked to tradesmen like dogs. "Good job, good boy." You say so yourself. So maybe he saw a few planes from afar.

– From up close, Marie. And even from a distance he could have counted them. It was already quite a lot that he knew the number of civilian employees, and knew their job descriptions.

– So now you want to make out he had technical military knowledge too.

– No one's making out anything. I'm just trying to tell you a story.

– Okay. Now the Brits know how many planes there are at Mariengabe Airfield near Jerichow.

– And which ones live there, and which ones are only visiting, and which ones are bringing deliveries or taking them away. The trucks of fuel or bombs, Cresspahl could see those just on Town Street. Of course his bosses, or the people who thought that's what they were, would've much rather had someone like Professor Erichson, who would have been able to draw the airfield from memory that night. They had to make do with a tradesman who could memorize type numbers like HE 111 P and enough of the plane's appearance that it could be identified as a fighter. That was enough for the Ju 52 transport, or the He 59 hydroplane, a little double-decker like that. As for the Ju 87, that beast, it wasn't exactly the talk of the town around Jerichow. . . .

– I would have believed you, Gesine. Now you're exaggerating again.

– The Ju 87 was a "Stuka," a *Sturzkampf* plane. Dive-bomber. When one of them plunged down at a target, built-in sirens gave off a hellish shriek. That was the psychological side of warfare in those days. They were called the sirens of Jerichow.

– After the trumpets some priests blew while they marched around some city walls until they collapsed?

– That worked only on one city: the Jericho in Jordan. Joshua, chapter 6. And the account of that city's destruction is a legend, by the way, you can ask our friend Red Anita about that, she helped excavate there to get her PhD.

– The sirens of Jericho. Now that's one coincidence too many for me.

– And what should the people in the other Jerichow say—the bigger city near Magdeburg?

– I don't like it when something comes together so perfectly. You're telling me sirens of Jericho in Jerichow, that's not made up.

– Not by me. Cresspahl also knew that the Ju 87s had machine guns on their wings, and that the DO 17 P long-distance reconnaissance planes had earlier been called DO 17 Fs, during the Spanish Civil War. That could come up in a conversation a harmless workman happened to walk past in town. It was also useful when he could add where the airplane fuel was hidden underground—that was already a target on the map in London.

– Harmless workman! He was someone who'd lived in London!

– And someone who just nodded when asked whether he'd stopped wanting to live outside the German Fatherland after its glorious rebirth. That made him reliable enough. The guy looked a bit slow, actually. Hadn't done too well in England, had he. Anyway, he still had his work, that's what counted. And his stories from London were pretty funny: *In London therere bedrooms where you lie on the bare ground. Just a rope up at the top end, an you put yer head there, and in the mornin they let it drop and thats yer alarm*: he said. He was having his fun with them.

– You know, when you talk in Platt, I sometimes feel like I understand a word or two.

– Say: *Kattdreier.*

– "Caterer"?

– You see? And Cresspahl wasn't limited to the airfield. There'd suddenly be new people in the Forest Lodge or Rifle Club, in army uniforms, not from around there, who couldn't resist showing off with their parachutist knives. That was not long before the offensive planned against England. So he also picked up that the paratroopers had schools in Stendal and Wittstock, that their day's pay was fifty cents but every jump brought in twenty-seven marks, which was why they were sitting in the Forest Lodge drinking beer and trying out the bit about one last time before we die on anything with a skirt. Cresspahl didn't have to do it alone either. Erwin Plath was in a bit of a tizzy that the national soccer team under Reich Coach Sepp Herberger would be playing against Hungary, Sunday the seventh of April 1940 was the historic date, but he was puzzling over why the motorboat *Hanseatic City of Danzig* had moored at the East Prussia Quay in Lübeck-Travemünde, now painted gray but still unmistakably familiar from the days when it still carried Baltic tourist traffic, not navy military. It had also docked in Rande, outside Jerichow. On Sunday they screamed and shouted over the heroic 2–2 in the Berlin Olympic Stadium; that night the *Hanseatic City of Danzig* sailed from Travemünde with the First Battalion of the 308th Infantry Regiment of the 198th Infantry Division in her belly—the division recruited in the collapsed Czechoslovak Republic, in the "Protectorate of Bohemia and Moravia," mostly Swabians and Sudeten Germans. Many had hoped that their annexation would be in the last act of war of the century. The day had begun with frost on the ground, then it warmed up to nine Celsius, the sky stayed clear. It wasn't the start of spring, though—it was the start of the occupation of Denmark. The grunts could only guess at that, just like Cresspahl, for the orders weren't opened until the 9th, by which time the *Danzig* was sailing through the Great Belt. Still, it wasn't too late for London to get intelligence about which troops had been sent to Denmark, or a memo that such outings started not just in the Kiel and Swinemünde harbors but in Lübeck's too.

– You mean there were more people like that in or near Swinemünde and Kiel? Who betrayed their country... ?

– They betrayed the Nazis. And as with Cresspahl, there was nothing special about them, they didn't stand out. Cresspahl wasn't in the party, of course; this counted as a point in his favor, if anything, as far as the air force was concerned—that swastika of bullet holes in the officers' mess, remember. Cresspahl didn't have a Blaupunkt radio (with the magic eye) like Alexander Paepcke, which it was forbidden to listen to since the start of the war since it could pick up foreign stations; Cresspahl had a thing named the People's Receiver, *Volksempfänger*, VE 301, seventy-six reichmarks including the antenna, "manufactured in memory of the People's Uprising of Jan. 30, 1933." Cresspahl was hardly talked about in Jerichow at all. Maybe it was said that he'd gone a bit funny after his wife's death. Held his head like an ornery horse, got in the habit of a nod that looked deaf, a titch too obedient. It was often taken for stupidity, too; sometimes an order was explained to him twice, as though he hadn't understood it. Then it turned out he'd understood just fine, but he nodded again anyway. And some people in Jerichow had their own reasons for keeping their mouths shut—more than a little that was still usable had been stolen during the fire at Cresspahl's workshop, Alwin Paap couldn't be everywhere at once. There were mornings when tools labeled C were thrown over the fence. Maybe it wasn't only because the C could betray them. And it was better, it was healthier, to keep your distance from someone who'd been that unlucky—

Go away, black blackbird,
If I am so black
It's not only my fault,
It's my mother's too,
Because she didn't wash me

When I was little,
When I—
and having blackbirds in a tree behind the house, that didn't attract attention either. There were a lot, and many of them were braver than he was.
 – That's not what I meant, Gesine.
 – Many were braver than he was when betraying their country.

At seven, the darkness was perfectly clear. The skyscraper across the Hudson is lit up as if for a party. From New Jersey, our Riverside Drive looks lit up as if for a party.

March 8, 1968 Friday

The New York Times is delighted that students at Harvard have now parodied her too. On the joke front page, among other news, the Parthenon collapses; there is a two-column headline on the top left about a failed airlift to Khesanh: since the parachutes didn't open, Tanks, Heavy Guns Fall Mercilessly on Men Below / Marines Crushed....

Longshoremen in New York have refused to load onto a freighter a ketch belonging to Dr. Benjamin Spock, who'd intended to sail around the Virgin Islands on it. Some months ago Dr. Spock took part in an antiwar demonstration in Lower Manhattan, and the dockworkers remember it.

As of midnight on Saturday, 19,251 Americans have fallen in Vietnam. Have died.

And the Czechoslovakians, invoking the extradition treaty of 1925 (supplemented by an annex in 1935), want their fugitive general back: Antonín Novotný's supporter. Alfalfa and clover seed.

Cresspahl's child spent a long time in Pommern with the Paepckes, more than six months; still, it wasn't too long.

There were evenings like the ones in late May 1939, when the strawberries were ripe and released juice into the sugar. They were eaten with silver forks, at the table out in the garden, and Hilde kept piling more and more piles onto Gesine's plate. The child was so rapt as she ate that only after she stopped did she notice that everyone had been watching her, helpless with silent laughter, no envy. By then the child had long since stopped feeling watched, suspect, unmasked. She could laugh along with them.

At the Paepckes', a child had no duties, no cares. When Gesine and Alexandra offered to walk to the store, Hilde acted like she needed to think it over and often said no if she'd thought up another new game for the children instead. – May I turn the roast potatoes?: Gesine asked. Gesine had learned a lot of High German by then. – All right, turn the potatoes!: Hilde would snap, in a put-upon tone that threatened terrible punishments. She couldn't keep it up for long, and soon laughed. But she'd rather keep the child away from the stove. A child can burn to death after all.

The way Hilde carried on with Alexander—I've never seen anything like it since. Alexander would come home and hang up the coat from his uniform; Hilde would come up next to him and put her arms around his neck. – You're not feeling well!: she would accuse him, and he would shiver as though having swallowed some bitter medicine. – *What WOULD I do without you and the li'l potaters*: he'd say. Hilde could tell from a distance if it was an evening on which he would brook no delay, even with words; then all Hilde cared about was getting dinner over with, the big girls had to look after the little one, they all got a stroke on their hair, their back, then Hilde would follow her man to the bedroom and not be seen again for the rest of the night.

Heard from afar, without looking, when very tired, Hilde's voice was my mother's. That voice taught the Cresspahl child how Lisbeth had stopped talking to her. With a long, ringing second vowel in the first name—not as an order or a warning, the way people did later, but with affection, always taken by surprise with new delight.

Hilde stood at the stove and Alexander looked her dreamily up and down. After he'd thought it over for long enough, he said: I used to think you had pretty legs. 'S'not true though.

Hilde looked at him questioningly, slightly sad really, and Alexander decreed for all time: FEISTY legs, that's what you have!

Neither of them cared that the children could hear. What remains is a feeling of infectious enthusiasm, of pleasure in being part of such a life. (The other side was jealousy; that was kept from the children.)

When Alexander let loose with long rants about the "Nazi pigs," then too Hilde watched him closely, agreement showing in her mouth. Lisbeth used to interrupt with frightened accusations. (Heinrich Cresspahl! Think of the child!)

Alexandra and Gesine were supposed to go to the doctor for shots, and Hilde wrote them an excuse note: My children cannot come on March 21, because we are celebrating the first day of spring.

My children. Gesine had no doubt about it. She knew she was Cresspahl's child and that she had to live with him—that was an inner certainty. From the outside, she was one of Hilde's children.

Whether the first day of spring or one of the cats' birthdays, events were celebrated in style. Even if the sky threatened rain, Hilde helped Auguste the maid string up lanterns in the garden. She invited over enough children to fill the garden, every time, except never the children of SS Commander Bindeband, even though he had six to offer, with names like Gerlinde and Sieglinde and Brunhilde and Kriemhild. There was tiddlywinks and musical chairs and Squeak Piggy Squeak, and Hilde would shamelessly cheat if a child was at risk of losing too often. As she shoved the pot closer to the blindfolded child with the helplessly waving stick, she would look at the others conspiratorially, and everyone would agree to forfeit some of their own chance of winning. The writer here may not want to say so, but it really was true of Hilde: she had a beautiful (crossed out).

Then Mrs. Bindeband invited Alexandra and Gesine over to play. The Bindeband children had braids all the way down their backs. They wore sackcloth clothes, burlap aprons. The games, though, were the celebration of a heathen Easter festival in a villa that used to belong to a Stettin Jew. The Persian rugs, the oil paintings, all seemed preserved intact. Along with a bad conscience came the sensation: My God we're poor. When they came back home, Hilde wasn't mad but she was disappointed. From that point on, the children never let themselves get tempted into the Bindeband house.

Hilde had lost a maid over a Hitler picture. Her name was Frieda Lämmerhirt, she was from Berlin, and she'd cut a photograph of Hitler out of the newspaper. She received a harsh reprimand, and later another from Alexander. She'd messed up the newspaper! But no one had ever saved *The North German Observer* in this house. She gave notice on the spot, packed her things in silence, and left, taking with her the Hitler picture she'd so carefully pinned up on the wall of her room. Bindeband heard this too about the Paepckes, and afterwards less.

In the Stettin Military Ordnance Department, Paepcke had in fact found people he didn't have to include among the "Nazi pigs," and he often brought three or four home with him, without warning, and those were long nights for the children too. No one paid attention to the children— they just joined the fun of the grown-ups. They knew they were not unwelcome. Alexandra sat next to her seriously pontificating father (We're gonna lose this war too; at least we've learned how it's done) and pushed him until he finally toppled over in a harrowing pantomime, like a night swimmer plunging from a great height into a bottomless sea.

There were evenings when Alexander would read to them. How King Henry found the Fair Rosamund. Sometimes he lost his place in the book and happily read the same passage several times, one that Cresspahl as a student later found in Fontane: "There is nothing so crazy that it cannot seem thrilling for the moment, or even correct, when a certain artistic light is shined upon it, but it is all an illusion. No one starves in Mecklenburg, hundreds starve in London, and yet England is the pride and model of all nations and Mecklenburg cuts a comic figure. One is the very image of higher things, the other of lower!" – Remember that, Gesine! He quickly bethought himself and included the others, and threatened them with "the pit" if they failed to think on it for the rest of their lives. Then he went on reading.

And no matter how often he threatened to refrain from stroking their hair, never once did a child have to "go to bed bareheaded."

And when they went to go swimming in the Oder, Alexander never failed to sing on the ride there:

> To horse! We ride to Linlithgow,
> I and you by my side;
> There we will hunt and fish, with joy,
> As in the days gone by.

Giant picnic baskets were brought on these trips, full of bread and cakes and hard-boiled eggs and milk and fruit. Children at the Paepckes never stopped getting fed. When someone was by no means hungry yet—when he or she just barely sensed a minor creeping idea of hunger in the distance—more food appeared. Sour milk with sugar.

The Paepckes had a bellows camera to take photographs with—an article of faith for them. The subject had to be precisely two meters away, the sun at the photographer's back if possible. Hilde kept the thing in the kitchen cupboard; no sooner had Christine torn down a curtain than she had her picture taken. (Am I two meters away?: she asked the tiny little Christine.) The big kids had a costume ball with the remains of the curtain; they too had their pictures taken.

When the children wanted to go swimming, a tin tub with elaborately curved edges was set up in the garden that morning. But only in the afternoon they could swim: by then the water was sure to have gotten warm enough.

At the Paepckes', a child would be sitting there painting, or cutting up fabric, and Hilde would never walk past without praising the work, and not with fawning but with detailed questions. At the Paepckes', the children learned to feel who they were.

Hilde knew that the neighbors expected her to show her husband's occupation and rank with her clothes; she preferred to wear her hair wrapped in a scarf tied in back, like the farm women. She did a lot of her own sewing, wore pants, and answered reproachful greetings with innocent, friendly replies as though she hadn't noticed a thing.

At the Paepckes', you could lie around on the property as if in a forest, beneath the pines and acacias, on ground soft with needles. No one would come bother a child there. If the child came back inside from the solitude, Hilde would have a ribbon in her hand and tie it around the child's forehead, and she wasn't wrong: the child really had been out among the Indians.

In the summer the Paepckes took the children to Fischland on holiday. The war hadn't started yet. Evening on the Shoreline Cliff looked strangely different than it did on the north shore near Jerichow. On their last day in Althagen, Cresspahl came. He looked old, shorter than they remembered, emaciated. Without warning there he was on Border Road, and Gesine knew he'd come to fetch her.

Since she knew the Paepckes were standing behind her, she felt too embarrassed to run up to Cresspahl. Then she heard Alexander saying something in a very loud voice about bird nests, and she realized that none of them was looking at her, and she ran.

The next morning, nothing could be more right than to leave for Jerichow with him. But it was already wrong to leave the Paepckes behind.

*Gesine, if you'd written all this down it would've been be a real thank-you
letter!*
As it should be.
You grieve for us too?
I do.
We wouldn't have believed it of you when alive. When we were alive.

Cloudy, mild, twelve degrees (53°)—not a South Ferry day. Marie got dressed
as though for the ship, in pants and a parka with a hood, and for bad
weather, where the clothes need to be old and not too valuable. Marie
had picked a non-school day to try to clear things up with her friend
Francine, but she couldn't reach her by phone in the city homeless shelter.
So now Marie wanted to go looking for her on the streets, in the slums of
the Upper West Side. You don't wear a coat from London for that, she
might get curses hurled at her for that, and not just curses.

Our slums are around the corner, and a foreign country. *Elendsquartiere*
is what they're called in German, but the slums in our neighborhood are
not "housing" meant especially for the "destitute," unlike the blocks thrown
up for workers by the land speculators in the German big cities: a *bidonville*
in Paris, a *Barackendorf* for refugees, a *shantytown*. The slums in New York
weren't built as slums; here the slum is like a jellyfish in society, it moves
around.

On the side streets between the avenues, they're now in a lot of the
brownstones—the four-story buildings named for their original facades of
reddish-brown sandstone—and after the Civil War they were in fact a sign
of bourgeois prosperity. The spacious lobbies were made for dignified
entrances. The four floors were meant for a single family, plus servants—
richly furnished interiors with fine wood wainscoting, oak parquet floors,
marble fireplaces, carved doors, lathed banister posts in the stairways. They
held salons, splendid parties, with fancy carriages stopping outside. These
were luxury residences, and even though now the fronts have started to
peel off or else have been sloppily painted over, the buildings themselves
don't seem to go with the dirt on the front stoops, the rotting furniture

and mattresses, the uncovered garbage bins, the smeared windows, the remains of the sanitation workers' strike, the scattered garbage that will remain if it can withstand the rain and is too heavy for the wind.

These buildings have been given up on. They were built for whites, Anglo-Saxons, Protestants. The Irish, who began moving here in large numbers in the seventies of the last century, gathered in the apartment buildings along Columbus and Amsterdam Avenues, but many of them saved up for one of these fashionable brown houses and took advantage of possession by renting out rooms. The Irish were the most powerful political group in the neighborhood before the Jews arrived from Harlem, unable to cope with the growing proximity of the Negro. Then came the Negroes from the ghettos of New York, and the wave of Puerto Ricans after World War II; the white-skinned immigrants, long since accustomed to the scale of values they'd encountered on these shores, gave up one street after another. Not entirely, though. The owner can turn one of these single-family houses into four apartments first, one per floor, and make up the lost property value with higher rental income. The landlord can then turn these small apartments into single rooms. Now he makes many times the old rent. Since his renters see even such living conditions as an improvement, if they come from Harlem or Brownsville, and the Spanish-speaking ones are incapable of resistance to begin with, the landlord is free to delay repairs, save money on heating, not bother with a super. The laws are specific and impose fines on all such acts of negligence, but people without education or sufficient knowledge of the language rebound off the bureaucratic system, and the courts are inclined to treat the slumlord mildly for it is he who embodies the concepts of income and property.

Income and property are what created the slums in the first place: the ugliness and permeability of the dividing walls, the unreplaced window-panes, the defective door locks, the broken mailboxes, the slippery encrusted dirt in the hallways, the rusted kitchens, the cells infested with vermin and the rats about which the representatives of the people laughed out loud last summer. Mrs. Daphne Davis, in Brownsville, Brooklyn, got to the point last summer where her daughter was playing with a rat. It was so big the child was calling: "Here, kitty, here kitty." When it gets to that point, the city inspectors give up, whether they're supposed to come for the plumbing or the fire escapes, and the sanitation workers get the picture too. The garbage here is picked up less often than in middle-class streets, and in a perfunctory way that knows nothing of sweeping up. But Income and Property are not the ones to whom the riot act or the book of Leviticus is read.

When a family like the Carpenter III's on West End Avenue wishes all the best for the Negroes—an apartment in their own respectable if not elegant apartment building not included—then Liz Carpenter III if not her husband brings up, with no doubt in her mind, the slums as proof that these blacks simply would not understand how to live in a civilized community. As if such understanding were an innate gift of nature. Scarcely any of the arguments intended to forestall a reasonably equal distribution of property in society bothers to try to be cogent or have even the appearance of logic; this one, moreover, ignores the fact that not all Negroes live in slums and not all slum dwellers are Negroes. The prejudice of the American nation against a long-established tenth of its members may be incomprehensible, but what this prejudice is used to defend is perfectly tangible and concrete: jobs as a means of income, education as a means to a better income, the right to rights that safeguard income. It's known as a race among rats, and handicapping some competitors can certainly help one's own chances of winning.

No group has had to battle for their rights as long as the Negroes. The freed and escaped slaves who came to the more easygoing, less conceited North last century were still isolated, in designated neighborhoods; still exploited by "white" homeowners and businesspeople; still excluded from equal education; always fired first, always hired last; while one group after another immigrated from abroad and found their footing before their eyes. The Germans, the Italians, the Jews, in the fifties the Puerto Ricans were recognized as citizens. It's been eight years and the classic numbers John F. Kennedy cited still hold true: "The Negro baby... has, irrespective of ability, statistically one-half as much chance of completing high school as a white baby, one-third as much chance of completing college, one-third as much chance of becoming a professional man, and twice as much chance of becoming unemployed." John Kennedy said that in a 1963 TV address. Whatever the roots of this traumatic exclusion by the whites, the consequence is that Negroes as a group must accept the greatest losses in the struggle for work, and as a result they represent the highest proportion of

734 · March 9, 1968 Saturday

citizens who have given up hoping to find a job, who were never in a position to have that hope, who let themselves fall into the slum.

The slum is a prison into which society deports those whom it itself has mutilated. These are apartments in which bedbugs and roaches cannot be kept under control by even the most patient efforts, in which the refrigerator functions not to cool food but as a safe that the bugs can't crack. When whole families have to live in a single room without any money for recreation or escape, the children witness inevitable fights and get to school tired and haggard, their homework unfinished; their accomplishments necessarily lag behind the demands of the curriculum, they leave school as soon as they can, they "drop out" and start working in lesser jobs, which will be obsolete with continued technological development; they are educated for poverty. If two-thirds of the Negroes on the Upper West Side are single men, this is because families abandoned by the breadwinner thereby gain the right to welfare support; sociology has dutifully invented a "single-room occupancy factor." The Negroes in the slums feel neglected by the police—their streets are more sparsely patrolled; break-ins are met with more boredom than anything else; in a brawl they are more likely to arrest the dark-skinned man than the light-skinned; still, the Negroes wish there were more police, more reliable protection (while the whites can afford to demand a civilian supervisory board for the forces of law and order). (The Communist Party of America is a nonstarter.)

Resistance is useless. If the residents of the slum attempt a rent strike against the building's owner, the court will be on the owner's side. If he doesn't manage to evict the tenants, he'll let the building fall to pieces. If nothing else, he can always count on the cold. Then the city shuffles the tenants into the armories and they're not his problem anymore. It's worth paying a little tax on the property so the city doesn't take the building, staggering as it is under mortgages and Brother Wind; there's always the hope that the city will eventually condemn the property to public use. If stubborn tenants stay, they'll be hounded by rowdies, junkies, vandals, and metal thieves, not all of whom are neighborly enough to turn off the water before they steal the pipes. When it's dripping from the ceiling and the doors have all been broken in, the last tenants move out, and the property soon finds itself in proper condition again.

Where there's no longer any question of restoring order, the garbage will come flying out the windows, and if it lands in a back courtyard then it might be a message: "air mail." The whites as a group do not get the message; maybe the isolated white passerby hears something, a bottle exploding next to him on the sidewalk. When I hear "the whites," I often think of figures in sheets, ghosts, corpses on their way to the cemetery. Since the whites as a group refuse to help, why not stick a knife in an individual white person's heart and get what you need from his briefcase, his cash register, his apartment. Since people trapped in the slum have all their ways out to a worthwhile life blocked, why delay escaping into the illusions and sickness of drug addiction? Since society has put up a fence around this life, why follow the norms of that society, why treat a social worker as anything other than someone bringing a check, why not send kids out to beg, why live under a roof. Since the bonds with society have been broken, why not rip out public phone cables; why leave a forwarding address when you go somewhere else, under a bridge, onto the Bowery, into jail, off to the war in Vietnam?

The word *slum* is also a verb, meaning to stroll around on run-down, dangerous streets, and the New York police has ordered five thousand helmets in advance, for the coming riots.

The mayor, the Honorable John Vliet Lindsay, is reasonably sure of his ground here. He often mentions the ghettos in his speeches, and one of them, Brownsville in Brooklyn, he calls Bombsville.

Mrs. Cresspahl and her daughter went slumming this afternoon, and in our slums the children were out on the streets. These included children who needed to use the streets to answer the call of nature, and ones who would prefer a bath but had no water to bathe in. Ones whose clothes have been washed and patched so many times that they don't dare set foot in school under a teacher's judging eyes. Ones searching a long since eviscerated car for any sellable part that might have been overlooked. Some ran wild, playing baseball with a broomstick. Others didn't have a game to play and stood around like unemployed grown-ups—bored and hostile. They had all learned how to recognize a junkie, a homosexual, or a drunk on the street, and to expect them, as everyday parts of the neighborhood; the dog barked at the tottering figure with the bottle, though, and could barely be placated. We saw it. We live here.

Francine was in none of the places where she usually spent the day. But the man at the counter of the Mediterranean Swimming Club, a curiously soft man in his white T-shirt—one of the men with a mild voice, a tone defensive in all directions—had news for us.

– Can I see your card again? How do you pronounce that name: Crisspaw?

– Most people say it like that.

– Might a Negro girl have been asking about you?

– Yes. Someone named Francine?

– Mhmm.

– Did she leave a message?

– What message could she have had for you, Mrs. Crisspaw? She wanted to know if you were here in the pool. And it turned out you were. Then she left.

– I don't understand, Mr. Welch.

– Me neither. Usually it's only the police who ask questions like that and then leave so that you have no idea what they're up to. She came back again this afternoon. Of course anyone can get the number wrong.

– Oh, of course, Mr. Welch.

– So I said by mistake that you and the young lady were here in the pool. This time she wanted to come in.

– Is she still here?

– Whatever are you thinking, Mrs. Crisspaw. The wilderness of the streets has swallowed her up.

– Mr. Welch, if she comes back we'll pay the daily fee for her. Whether we're in the club or not.

– But she's a black.

– We know her. She's a friend.

– Does that mean you'll guarantee for her?

– That's what it means. Here's a dollar.

– A dollar's a dollar, Mrs. Crisspaw, but I hope you know what you're doing.

Since the new Czechoslovak government ended censorship two weeks ago, *The New York Times* has run into unexpected difficulties in Prague: Is it the government speaking or just him when a television journalist warns on television against hasty purges along the old Stalinist lines? If Alexander Dubček wants to carry out his economic reforms, will he manage without a settling of scores in the bureaucracy? "He is said to be against any vendetta." These uncertainties, once a Communist stops treating its national television as its private property!

March 10, 1968 Sunday

In Prague someone is allowed to say on the radio that the nation's future must be decided by the entire population, not just the Communists. The Communists are meeting in sixty-six regional and local party conferences and debating among themselves how they can get rid of President Novotný without using Stalin's means, with which Novotný was so familiar. The *Times* hears unease among the functionaries of East Germany: over the economic ties with the ČSSR, but not, for instance, because liberalization there has any prospect of changing life in their own sphere of power. In Warsaw, students are acting out for the second day in a row; they are demanding more democracy!, an honest press, and the like.

We went over to some friends'.

In the American sense of the word, Jim and Linda are *friends*. They let you go in with them on renting a house on the Jersey shore, they like having meals with you, they come over at the drop of a hat, they insist on knowing how you're doing, they tell you relatively intimate details about their children, parents, aunts, and as a result they remain very firmly in our minds even if we haven't seen them for five months. Maybe our visit was too dependent on a polite reason for it. The O'Driscolls have moved out of the Upper West Side and only now are they firmly enough settled into a basement apartment in Greenwich Village, now the Cresspahls too should come check out their new place. Jim has gotten even heavier—sometimes he can raise himself from his armchair only with a mighty heave—but he painted the walls himself, added woodwork and moldings to the rooms, a whopper of a man, now with a new red mustache hanging sadly under his nose. He still watches Linda with pleasure, and secretly pats himself on the back not only for having found her, five years ago in Greece, but for having brought her back to New York. Linda has acquired his version of

English—New York English with a heavy Irish accent—and ideas such as that she and a friend will run their own kindergarten if the public one isn't good enough. Linda with her peasant braids, dark jealous looks, stunned expression when catching sight of one of her own children, as if her Patrick and Patricia were miracles she had worked. At the O'Driscolls', the children act like they have to win their parents over every day anew; they come in from the little backyard so often, drape themselves around Jim's neck, lay their heads in Linda's lap, so as not to be forgotten. Toys are scattered everywhere because Jim works in an office where he puts his degree in psychology to use inventing ever new sales possibilities for the toy industry. The visit felt comfortable, familiar, welcome, as with friends.

Mrs. Cresspahl was greeted with the pleasantly anticipatory question: What's the good word, the good news?—to which one is supposed to answer that Ireland is now free, or that President Johnson has stopped an old lady on the street, obviously a widow, and urgently pressed her to surrender her lamb; it doesn't come off without a half hug either, without thorough cheek kisses from Linda, and Marie is addressed as the new babysitter who's been awaited with trepidation for days, and who now turns out to be not an old blunderbuss but an educated young lady to whom one can hand over Pat and Pat with a sigh of relief.

In the kitchen. Everyone prepares lunch together at the bar-high table. Slices of bread with lox and ham and cheese. Sherry and whiskey, from Ireland, between the salad bowls.

Conversation. About how America is turning into a police state. Jim is convinced that the government has set up *detention camps* for the coming Negro riots—prison facilities into which citizens will be sent summarily, strictly on the basis of skin color. Whether the O'Driscolls should go back to Ireland; it was only Jim's father who'd been the first to come here. A rambling argument about Linda's Greece, to which she cannot return. About the choice between Nixon, propounding unclear war plans, and Rockefeller, who has no peace plans on offer. About Hans Magnus Enzensberger. About Jim's father. About mail from the family in Nauplion. Careful noise from the kids in the backyard.

Maybe it was simply too long since we'd seen the O'Driscolls. In a pause came Jim's brooding remark: What we did to the Indians is basically what Himmler did to the Jews.

Now it was no longer "Gee-sign" who was supposed to explain Himmler, it was "the German woman."

The awkwardness continued, no matter how many funny stories Jim told from his office, or how much he reported about his physical condition. Ten days ago he came out of a bar on Third Avenue and slipped and fell under a car. Drunkenness was ruled out, it had only been five gin and tonics. It was more like fainting. His heart . . . ? When Jim talks about himself, you get the sense that many things about him are a mystery to him. Even the act of raising his glass to his mouth seems to amaze him.

The awkwardness was also enough to discourage taking a walk. Instead the decision was made to go to a film club. So much was said, and in such detail, about the nature of the venue, the donation system instead of tickets, and so on, that Mrs. Cresspahl missed the name of the movie. I missed the title of the movie.

It was *Night and Fog*, and another one.

I left after the first one. It was in Brooklyn.

The air was as thick as fog between the *brownstones*. Children behind a screen window were discussing the lone passerby. The end of Second Street seemed to run straight into the port. Foghorns. On Seventh Avenue the Irish bars were full, the delis filled with Sunday customers, children were teasing the sales clerk by reaching their chins up onto the glass counters. Gray-haired drunks were standing helplessly on the corners.

We'd missed the beginning of the movie. The French narration was disconcertingly insistent on being elegant. The images of hunger, humiliation, death on the electrified fence, the children's home, the gas chambers, the industrial exploitation of the remains. The footage shot after the war, tinged strongly red from the bricks of the walls. Again the dreaded image with the shiny wide plowshare of the Allies shoving and shoveling the bodies into the grave into the ditch. The fields of bodies. The stacks to be burned.

Picking up the child from the O'Driscoll apartment. "Didn't you like the movie?" The auditorium had been rented from a church. In the light, the decorative inscription visible on a crossbeam: *The Place Where We Meet to Seek the Highest Is Holy Ground*. In the darkness the sweat felt so heavy that it was like the skin couldn't breathe.

These are good friends of several years. They look at me and they think of the crimes of the Germans.

Without meaning any offense. To them it's obvious, natural. So it goes.

March 11, 1968   Monday

The amount of annual aid to Cuba from the Soviet Union exceeds $150,000,000. More than $400,000 a day.

In the opinion of the NBC television network, the war in Vietnam is lost. In the opinion of *Newsweek* magazine, President Johnson's strategy for Vietnam has run into a dead end.

It looks as if the ČSSR really does want to clean house. In party meetings there are secret ballots. Antonín Novotný is urged to, yes, ask the Czechoslovak people themselves if they trust him. In the trade-union newspaper the rector of Charles University, noted neurologist and psychologist Dr. Oldrich Starý, declared that many people in Czechoslovakia suffered from split personalities caused by fear and by a system in which people were manipulated like cogs in a machine. At the grave of the foreign minister Jan Masaryk, who jumped or was pushed from a window in his official residence twenty years ago, three thousand students were permitted to gather. The president of the Supreme Court is making plans to correct the errors of justice made between 1955 and now. It is stated in public that innocent people are still in jail.

If Cresspahl had left his child with the Paepckes, she would have long since been dead. If he'd sent her to Aggie Brüshaver, she would have longer since been dead. He thought of Jerichow as a dangerous place, with the airfield so nearby, but decided to bring his child to live there because of Hilde Paepcke's letters. With her long and detailed descriptions, she'd tried to make him see that Gesine was lacking for nothing in Podejuch; what he took from them was how much he was missing without the child. Maybe he didn't care that she might die as long as he would be with her.

He still didn't think he was up to raising a daughter, and he asked Avenarius Kollmorgen to suggest a woman who could keep the house in order and who understood about girls.

Avenarius suggested Grandma Klug, Frieda Dade, Grete Selenbinder, and Amalie Creutz. Louise Papenbrock, in her big house on the market square, was happy to hear about every time Cresspahl sent another one away, but she felt insulted before the whole town by Cresspahl not giving the child to her, and Albert didn't help.

The first woman to turn up, though, was Käthe Klupsch. Cresspahl hadn't used the fire insurance money to build anything, he lived humbly in his house and walked in shabby clothes through town to the station where Swenson's bus departed for Jerichow-North; some in town saw him as a "match"—barely fifty, owner of both property and an insurance payout that rumors put at around a hundred thousand. Cresspahl barely knew Klupsch by sight. He looked indifferently at this old maid, who'd brought a shamefaced Geesche Helms with her as a chaperone. Klupsch was a hefty, bony person who wore her hair up in a plump little nest. Whatever those custom-made clothes were supposed to be, they made her whole body look angular. But everything she said was meant to deprecate and minimize herself. Her tone wasn't far from whining, the words running into one another, words like "blow of fate" and "test" and "charity," shot through with little insinuations and rumors. Cresspahl sat at his table, apparently deaf, he was trying so hard to find a pretext to get rid of this churchy old hypocrite. Geesche Helms sat stiffly on the sofa, trying to show that she was sorry she'd offered to help. When Käthe Klupsch wasn't making use of her big pious upward gaze, she kept looking around—at the floor that hadn't been swept for some time, at Lisbeth's open desk, at the three doors, as though taking measurements for her future empire. She mentioned, not without pride, the maids Cresspahl would hire for her. Maybe her voice was the reason why no one had wanted to hire her. Or the la-di-da manners, meant to demonstrate her education and Christianity. Cresspahl never found out. Gesine came in and freed him. She walked in from the yard in a carefree, downright Paepckean way and found herself so forcefully clasped by this suitoress that she tore herself away. – You poor child! Käthe Klupsch had said, but then, in unthinking annoyance, she reprimanded the improper behavior. For quite some time she would say around town that for all her charity she wouldn't have lasted long in a household as uncultured as that one; she often thought back, though, to Cresspahl's calm reply: Poor? The child's not that. Was she supposed to take that in a religious or a financial sense? Jerichow could only laugh.

Grandma Klug approached life in Cresspahl's house as a kind of well-earned permanent sinecure. Then Alwin Paap was called up into the army too, and she couldn't manage the heavy work. She would've loved to spend longer on the chair she'd moved into the sun outside Cresspahl's house, pleasantly numbed by the sunlight. She liked that there were two cats in the house. She told the child fairy tales at night, insistently, with eyes closed. She scared the child too. When they found a wreath in the pillow, she was out. Grandma Klug died in the Gneez hospital in October of '39.

Frieda Dade came because an air force soldier had gotten her pregnant and she didn't think he was going to marry her. She couldn't go back to her family and now she wanted a place in Cresspahl's house. Twenty-one years old, home ec degree. Thick bulges of fat beneath narrow eyes. High-handed, out of fear of being criticized; as strict with the child as with an adult. She was the one who got the kitchen back in gear, but after four weeks she was married after all and went back to Dade the barber in Gneez.

Grete Selenbinder stayed longest. She was a widow with a son in the navy; she had the time and she wanted the money. Around forty, an indefatigable worker, absolutely insistent on obedience, praise, and propriety. Propriety required that she hang out the swastika flag before Cresspahl forgot to again. She was the one who got the whole house back in gear—down to the basement, down to the ground. Cresspahl suspected her of looking through his papers, of having a key to Lisbeth's desk. Grete Selenbinder wanted to dominate. Whenever she could, she would shut a door someone had left open; she carried a little basket of keys with her wherever she went. When she failed to receive praise, she burst into tears. It wasn't tactical, like Louise Papenbrock's crying—she enjoyed it, she brought about occasions for it on purpose. Churchgoer. Obedience was her undoing. At the end of her first year, she'd made porridge for the child, who didn't want to eat it. – If you haven't finished every last bite in three minutes ... !: she said, and left with her little basket of keys. Cresspahl came into the kitchen, saw the child sitting in despair in front of her bowl, gulped down the porridge until the bowl was perfectly clean, then Grete Selenbinder came back in and accused Gesine of having poured it out. Since she called it lying, she had to go.

The room she'd furnished with a low chest of drawers and big brass bed was then used for the French prisoners who'd been sent to live with them. They were given their meals in the brickyard, as was the guard posted to Cresspahl's house.

After that, Amalie Creutz still came by two days a week to clean, but no one cooked at the Cresspahl's for a long time.

Cresspahl took care of breakfast and the evening sandwich, and when Gesine left school at noon she took Swenson's bus to the airfield. She ate there with Cresspahl, in the canteen for the civilian employees, and that was where she did her schoolwork. She was only eight years old but Cresspahl brought her along when he went for a beer at the Beach Hotel in Rande. Sometimes Kliefoth sat with them, and every two weeks there was a stranger there too, someone the child didn't know at first. Now Cresspahl was raising the child himself.

He taught her:

What I see, what I hear, what I know is mine and mine alone.

Even if I know that a name is false or a place is wrong, I must stick to the false one.

What my father does and knows belongs to him. Only he is allowed to talk about it, I'm not.

It's not wrong to lie as long as that protects the truth. It's funny that other kids learn something different, but not dangerous.

We have a different truth, everyone has his own; it is only with Cresspahl that I'm allowed to share mine.

March 12, 1968 Tuesday

Around eleven in the morning and again at one thirty in the afternoon, snow rustled against the office windows. The flakes burst apart on the street, melted on the warmed sidewalk. At five, when the people were let out of their glass cages onto the street, fat rain was coming down. The upper floors had disappeared; they'll be waiting tomorrow morning, good as new. Grand Central and the trains for Times Square were strangely overcrowded and some of the transit cops had grown hoarse from shouting. The trees in Riverside Park had been strangled by something white.

When German troops occupied Prague in March 1939, there were snowflakes floating in the air.

Cresspahl had sure been right about his war. That same year the Germans marched into Poland. The following year they took Denmark, Norway,

Belgium, the Netherlands, France. In August 1940 they tried to clobber England.

This was one of Cresspahl's worries. A German could never go back to England again.

In 1941 it was Bulgaria's, Greece's, and Yugoslavia's turn. He sometimes knew it a day in advance, occasionally a week. But he didn't know if the information reached London.

Meanwhile the Latvian, Lithuanian, and Estonian states lost their independence. The Soviet Union was represented in Slovakia by an embassy. East Poland came as a bonus. Finland came at more of a cost. On August 20, 1940, Leon Trotsky was murdered. And the Soviet Union said nothing.

On June 22, 1941, the Germans attacked the Soviet Union, and it ceased to say nothing.

Papenbrock: That'll be the end of us.

Meta Wulff: In times like these, Cresspahl. Can't we be friends again?

Mayor Tamms, June 1941: The resplendent flag of National Socialism. . . . February 1942: He hadta go an try that too. . . .

From Papenbrock's calendar, February and March 1942: Meeting of the horse insurance union, Rehna. Regional farm-holders meeting in the Archduke Hotel, Gneez. Heroes' Memorial Ceremony at the Schönberg Monument. Members' meeting for the cattle insurance union. Entering cattle into the 1942 stud book, Gneez parade grounds.

From Friedrich Jansen's diary: Death penalty for Rostock enemy of the people. When it comes to the winter collection we know no mercy, not even for a pair of gloves! *Battle Squadron Lützow*, what a movie. But shown from the regional film car! Pathetic! Jerichow needs a movie theater! They're starving in Leningrad. The Communists are using bras as earmuffs in Lemberg. Java capitulates! Malta in a hail of bombs. Litvinov's call for a second front is met by deaf ears in London!

Käthe Klupsch's, Frieda Klütz's, and Elsa Pienagel's proof that victory is inevitable: Bananas are an enemy invention; bananas cause polio. How can Germany be facing defeat if there are still medals for the Reich street collections, the bird medals: blackbirds, bullfinches, chaffinches, titmouses, orioles, robins; I need one a those misself. You can buy People's Gas Masks at the NSV, but you don't have to; if there was any danger you'd have to.

The final drawing for the Sixth German Reich Lottery is on the 9th—oh if I could only winnit this time.

Tamms's official proclamations: It is forbidden to operate bath boilers, flow-type water heaters, refrigerators, gas heaters, or cooking stoves, because the transportation arteries are overloaded or frozen. The following reductions are hereby in force for the 35th ticket period of food rationing: As of 4/6/42 children between the ages of 6 and 10 will receive 350g of meat per week instead of 400g, still 266g of fat. Blackout in force between 8 p.m. and 7 a.m. I reiterate: Anyone traveling for pleasure will be fined, or in serious cases sent to a concentration camp!

Everyone in Jerichow was worried about the Poles. At the Schwenzin farm one Pole had thrown the payroll book in the inspector's face, screamed at him, hit him with a pitchfork. In Granzlin, one had thrown a pot of hot coffee at the farmwife's head. They'd been dependably sentenced to death but that wasn't enough to reassure anyone—something must've come along to give them the courage to put up a fight. What that something might be was not said out loud. And now a Pole named Henrik Grudinski had thrown Police Commissioner Engelhardt down the stairs in the Wismar paper factory on March 19 and was later seen near Proseken. He must've crossed the ice in Wismar Bay and come through Jerichow, imagine! right through my backyard! Cresspahl had worked things out to his own advantage again—he had Frenchmen in the house, and a guard too.

Cresspahl's daughter had few worries. On Air Force Day in Jerichow-North, Cresspahl had pocketed a paperweight made from an enemy aircraft before it could be auctioned off with the other war booty; now, for the past three weeks, Gesine had more friends in school than usual and had to take the thing out of her satchel and show it around again and again.

She did have one minor worry. The song that Head Teacher Stoffregen drilled into them refused to get out of her head:

Adolf Hitler is the Leader.

Adolf Hitler loves the children.

The children lo-ove Adolf Hitler.

The children pray for Adolf Hitler.

It wasn't having to learn it that bothered her, it was the fact that it came back to her in moments when she didn't have to say it. It felt so firmly lodged in her thoughts. How does that work, when you don't believe something and you can't get rid of it anyway?

Cresspahl had a different kind of worry. The halfpenny with George VI on the back hadn't been enough for him, even if it was dated 1940.

– I was about to say that the Saturday before last! An English fighter pilot who'd been shot down might have had it in his pocket because he'd forgotten about it, or as a good-luck charm. And it was the Germans tempting him with it! Maybe he was working for them the whole time, not for those utter scoundrels the English: Marie says, not entirely certain, but hopeful. She's been saving this objection up for ten days, for the moment it would have the maximum effect. She doesn't like people betraying their country.

– It wouldn't have taken *him* ten days to figure that out.

– Okay. He figured it out right away.

– And pretended that that was enough proof. He didn't insist on any more; he brought up the subject again only once.

– He was scared?

– It wasn't that bad. Anyway, he did want to get out in one piece, maybe even for the child's sake—

– A child meant nothing.

– . . . and at the end of March he got an answer. It was at a meeting to which he was supposed to bring the letter that Werner Mölders, a fighter-plane inspector, had supposedly written to the provost of Stettin before he crashed in November 1941, near Breslau. This letter made the Nazis so mad that they threatened to throw anyone distributing copies of it into a concentration camp; the British wanted it very much for their leaflet propaganda, whether it was a fake or not. Cresspahl hadn't been able to find a copy; occasionally at Jerichow-North airfield a silent toast was drunk to Mölders.

– Doesn't everyone say the Germans didn't know anything about the concentration camps?

– Maybe the Germans who didn't read *The Lübeck Gazette*. Cresspahl had told Gesine about Alexander Paepcke's radio with the magic eye, and on March 25 he took a trip, basically for pleasure, even though a camp was the penalty for that.

– A man with a child!

– It didn't seem like a serious infraction; it might have looked necessary. Anyway, it wasn't only a pleasure trip—he was supposed to have a look around near Rechlin, see what was up with the nightly booms and explosions. Sounded like rockets. From there it wasn't far to Wendisch Burg, so Gertrud Niebuhr could get her annual Gesine visit too. When Cresspahl was sitting in front of Alexander's magic eye in Podejuch, Dr. Kliefoth was on leave from the Russian front in Jerichow, and listening to the BBC, and was very surprised indeed at the story he heard on the broadcast after the opening four Beethoven notes. He remembered it differently.

– Alexander was risking his neck.

– Alexander was with the Military Ordnance Department, you see what I mean. Who would mess with him? The children were probably sent out of the room, he probably stayed next to the receiver, ready to shove the needle to another station immediately. But if Heinrich wanted to know what it was like to hear London, he would do him that favor.

– Go ahead, Gesine. You win. I believe you again. I'm a sucker every time. Go ahead.

– *"The memorable hero Robin Hood—"*

– I knew it.

– *"having been unjustly accused by two policemen in Richmond Park, was condemned to be an outdoor and went and lived with a maid who was called Lizzie Pope near a brook where there was no forest. . . ."*

– "Lizzie Pope near a brook." *Lisbeth, Papen, Brock.* They could have spared him that.

– Actually they couldn't. They were proving they knew about him.

– And what had the policemen in Richmond Park wanted him for?

– Only he knew that. In the summer of 1931, before he married Lisbeth, he was out for a walk in the park in Richmond at night, at a time when the police were on the hunt for a purse snatcher. "Would you mind being of some service to us, sir?" Half an hour on guard at the church square. Do you remember the blue plaque?

– Yes. And there was no forest in Jerichow.

– There were the Countess Woods near Jerichow, to the west, far enough away. And now he was condemned to live on the outside, outside of England's doors. *Outdoors.*

– They thought of everything, like friends.

– It did have sentimental value.

– Dammit! I believe you, Gesine.

– So now that's enough for you? Do you need yet another story, about an English pilot shot down in Germany and making his way to Cresspahl's house at night and living for a while in the attic, behind an impenetrable wall of stacked-up firewood, until Gesine can take him by the hand and bring him to a certain address in Gneez, again a man with a child . . . ?

– It's enough for me. I don't need any more, Gesine.

– And when the Royal Air Force hit Lübeck on the night of March 28 to 29 with two hundred and thirty bombs, and as it were inadvertently blasted to pieces a hangar in Jerichow-North, Cresspahl was safely far away in southeast Mecklenburg, at a sluice, in the forest.

– You're overdoing it again. Again it all fits together! You and your exaggerations, Gesine!

– That one was a coincidence, Marie. It wasn't worth it to send someone like Cresspahl away from a location the RAF was planning to *drop some shit on*. He wasn't that important. He was one little thread in a net, not even a knot. He was replaceable. The net was easy to repair.

– Gesine: If. Then.

– If it was treason then at least it should have been impressive?

– Not minimized.

– Treason's boring, Marie.

– Now that I don't need to believe.

– Gestapo! – Gestapo!: cry the students in Warsaw at the militia beating them with billy clubs.

March 13, 1968   Wednesday, Purim

Since sundown, the Jews have been reading in their synagogues and temples the story of Queen Esther, who saved them from the Persian tyrant Haman, viceroy to the Persian king Ahasuerus. Mordecai told her about Haman's dark plot and so the Jews didn't have to die on the Purim days, "the fateful days" appointed for their death. When children hear the story, they whirl their rattles so that the noise drowns out Haman's name whenever it comes up, and the children get treats that are only for that day.

It's a celebration that not only Rebecca Ferwalter takes part in; Pamela Blumenroth, too, is missing from the swimming pool under the Hotel Marseilles this evening. So Marie has time for a vague reconciliation with Francine. The reconciliation is not a success; they don't want to be alone together, they avoid touching each other, sit far apart. Francine has adopted a general demeanor—negligent, inattentive—as though we weren't really worth the trouble.

This country that I—

As the West Germans say: where I sleep well, that gets the job done, that's got my number, cross my heart—

—where I sought hospitality after the first time I came back here from Europe, the moment I caught sight of the blurry nighttime colors over Idlewild.

All it takes is whitefish for me to feel put through the wringer.

You want that for gefilte fish? (Whispers)
(Whispers) But that's one of the others. Looks German.
Oh, you want it for fish dumplings. Very good, ma'am. Get out!

– Gesine. Gee-sign. You've been talking to the recorder all night.
– It has to be typed up right at nine, Marie. *This is work.*
– *Don't be offended.*
– 'Night.

Riverside Park is on city maps, and the people here say it, and I believe it. But they all have a secret, and among one another they say: Shabbas Park.

Giving me a shock, yet again, yet again.

March 14, 1968 Thursday
More than thirty-five hundred students and one hundred faculty members refused to attend classes at Columbia University yesterday as a protest

against the draft and the Vietnam War. Most faculty members canceled their classes rather than force students to cut if they wanted to join the boycott. An astounded administration official remarked: "Goodness, I've never seen so many of them with ties and jackets. They are being gentlemen."

What do the students in Warsaw want from their government? Respect for the constitution, especially its guarantees of freedom of speech and assembly; the release of all students arrested since the first demonstrations last Friday; punishment for those who called the police onto the extraterritorial school grounds; guarantees against further persecution....

"D. E., to live with you.

To stand me.

You wanted to avoid the positive form but the negative form is an admission.

At school in Gneez, along with the unforgettable schoolyard sayings, there was also a dumb one, about who you'd marry: 'If you can stand his (her) face *en face* but not in profile, forget it.' Advice like that, passed on among girlfriends (or groups of male friends) and from the upper grades in the school to the lower: these were rules for a summer crush. I've tried it, now and then, and it's true, I feel a slight shimmer of vertigo when his profile tells me something different than his face purported to. A dumb saying. Is saying you could stand me that much smarter?

If you take the face, seen from every angle—I'm not that face.

You see a space bordered or divided as usual, by forehead eyes mouth nose; in it are continuations of Cresspahlian or Papenbrockian bone structures and sculptural forms, news from great-grandparents, remains of their possibilities, which I don't know and which you don't know. What you see might be perceptible but surely not comprehensible. When you carefully remove your gaze, look aside in a shocked or concerned way, and try to seem merely pensive: I understand more or less what you're thinking. It arises from the situation, maybe from the history of your judgments— whatever the face expresses, it is not entirely you. Not you. And not me.

You won't see uniqueness as anything worthy of praise; the typically unique visual juxtaposition of rarely unique facial features whispers to the observer: 'individuality.' This observer thinks he sees signs of relationships. Faces are described as expressive surfaces. I've tricked you here, D. E.

You would have to presuppose infallible communication between the cerebral electrical system and the facial musculature—you're the chemistry professor, you tell me the right words. Also presuppose that impulses in nerves appear to be more expressively reliable than those in electrical measurements, by virtue of being visualized in more appropriate material: a medium as superior as it is amenable to those impulses, almost creative where the movements that enter it need to be varied (in intensity at least). In a literary book, the author can say: a more emphatic grin. What that really means is a more visible grin. When I notice the intention, though, I have fallen out of any natural expression; I am no longer presenting myself at all, just the grins I am thenceforth taken to be.

I'm not exaggerating. I do this every morning at the bank—the smile of greeting, the American smile I can't pull off.

You should see it sometime. Maybe you wouldn't be able to stand it.

Everyone seems old enough to use his or her face. Does that mean any more than having it within his or her power?

A face's reactions to stimuli seem recognizable, if not exactly comprehensible, if you assume that those experiences are like one's own—comparable, analogous if not identical. The observer identifies with the universal, by perceiving the universal.

Don't be shocked—it's taken me half an hour to get to this point.

D. E.: If someone wants to see another person's face, with all these possibilities, every morning of every day from now on (i.e., live with it): does he mean the consciousness it signifies or what he's worked out in his mind as the system of consciousness he can recognize? His counterpart, sure, a different person, but Difference itself?

What would it mean if, behind this arbitrary intersection of general forms, what consciousness thinks and is really were hidden? What would it mean if consciousness uses contemporary or biographically cultivated models, and expectations of certain images, along with breakdowns of mimicry in these respective modes, for purposes of deception?

(I don't consciously intend any deception toward you, with you.)

What the observer feels he can stand is not, in any case, the idea of a consciousness—he likes a look, he considers it pure, sees no ulterior motives, finds it 'beautiful.' And so he rewards the bearer of that face: considers possession as service.

It's the same with me as it is with you, only I have my doubts about what that 'it' is.

Maybe you haven't drawn up one of your lists of pros and cons for me; maybe you've made a map, though. You're going to have to change it. Because I want the freedom to live like you: not vulnerable, while attentive to others' vulnerabilities. Untouchable, unreachable by childish dreams of twenty years ago that I'd unlearn if I were smart, or at least not naive. With nothing left for me but what you call waiting.

And you were exaggerating: I don't know anything about any cat named Shitface, 'and the other one was named Peter.' Marie's sleeping and I can't ask her. Have I really told any stories about that?

My dear D. E., maybe they haven't hustled you off to Stockholm at all and they'll forward this to you somewhere else. But if you are in Finland, have dinner for me in Kaskinen and tell me when you get back about the Killainens, who've lost a daughter to America.

The Czechoslovakian Socialist thing, against your predictions, seems to be going smoothly. Since the East Germans have started to see 'counter-revolutionary forces' in the ČSSR, and are issuing express warnings against 'spontaneous democratization' and calls for 'sociopolitical changes.' Let me see it through to the end.

Live with you. . . . On Scandinavian Airlines too? So that you can come home not to my apartment but to 'ours'?

And when you do come back I hope to get a lecture, the seventh, about the defensive nature of your line of work. I recently read something about simulated flight patterns that counterfeit airspace infringements to still-not-yet-enemy radar systems, so that the resulting radio alarm transmissions can reveal something about frequencies? I know you think it's of purely psychological importance how close a person is to the war machine, and I know my place in this system as well; even so, I do prefer a certain distance, even if it's just optical.

When two thieves fight, the honest man gets his cow back.

This letter is written by someone like our Mecklenburg *Hein Fink, so stubborn he was supposed to go to the gallows and didn't want to.*

D. E., I mean it the way Marie does.

Sincerely yours."

March 15, 1968 Friday
The deputy defense minister of Czechoslovakia, one General Vladimir Janko, shot and killed himself today. According to one story: in the staff car bringing him in for questioning about his role in the military plot supporting Antonín Novotný. According to the other: in his apartment after he heard that the cabinet had discussed his involvement.

In Bentre, the city in the Mekong delta destroyed by the Americans "in order to save it" during the Vietcong offensive, the South Vietnamese government has provided not one brick, not one sack of cement for rebuilding. Twenty-five hundred families are homeless. Four hundred and fifty-six civilians were killed, and two hundred additional applications for death certificates are still being checked.

Cresspahl came back from Wendisch Burg to Jerichow on Sunday evening, in time to make it to his meeting at the Beach Hotel in Rande; he waited there one and a half hours, twice as long as planned and permitted. Afterwards, he decided that maybe his courier hadn't lived in Berlin after all but was in Lübeck with his radio the whole time, until the English bombing caught him there. The man had remained so vague to him that he couldn't even quite imagine him dead. What with the man's forbidding manner, his abrupt dismissiveness as a university graduate, and his constantly roving eyes, Cresspahl could sometimes barely believe he'd heard and memorized all the names and numbers Cresspahl gave him. The party medal on his lapel sometimes seemed crafty, other times creepy. In Rande people seemed to know him, they called him Fritz. Fritz sounded too boyish, too easygoing for this upright fifty-year-old, and too familiar for Cresspahl's taste as well, but those were the terms they were on, Fritz and Heinrich. Whenever anyone walked past the table, Fritz would be in the middle of a long disquisition on birds or wild animals; maybe he'd been a teacher. Cresspahl would have liked to ask him why he was working for the English; the man avoided such discussions with a formality bordering on arrogance.

On the following day, March 30, 1942, the Polish POWs from throughout the Jerichow area were taken to the airfield to clear the rubble that had once been the hangar. All the panels of the walls had fallen out, the roof fallen in, but the steel frame was still standing, even if on bent, jaggedly broken stilts at one end, like a dog holding its hurt leg off the ground. The parachute mine had shattered windows in a wide radius, and Cresspahl helped Freese with the glazing. Freese's stock on hand wasn't enough for all the windows, and he was disgruntled at having to put up cardboard. The tradesmen barely mentioned what had happened to Lübeck between eleven forty five on Saturday night and three thirty on Sunday morning; Lübeck wasn't many miles away, and that accidentally dropped bomb could've just as easily hit Jerichow itself. In the canteen, Gesine told stories from school in answer to Freese's questions. Head Teacher Stoffregen had cast it as a villainous trick of the English to choose a brightly lit full-moon night for the attack. – What don't they teach kids in school nowadays . . . !: Freese said with an embarrassed shake of the head and an inviting look at Cresspahl. But Cresspahl had his head bent over his plate, as the child had for some time.

That evening, Mayor Tamms came to see Cresspahl. Jansen had resigned, "due to overwork," and had turned the brickyard over to a Lübeck manufacturer just to pay his bills, and the regional party headquarters was now located in Oskar Tannebaum's old store. In three weeks, Ed Tamms had cleared out Jansen's legacy from Town Hall and proceeded to make himself welcome on his own merits. Favors were no longer handed out from Town Hall, permits were issued strictly according to need, and under Tamms no one could convert building repairs into a new building. Now that Ete Helms knew he had someone like Mayor Tamms behind him, it wasn't so easy to intimidate him with a party badge, and if someone didn't pay a fine, Tamms was prepared to follow up with a summons. Maybe it hurt, but it was the old way of doing things. The large swastika flag on Town Hall stayed; Tamms flung out his hand when greeting someone; Tamms was considered a "National Socialist true believer" but rarely talked about it. Late thirties, studied national economy at the university, no degree, married, three children. In conversation calm, not slow, no evasions. It bothered some people that he didn't take the time for the usual Mecklenburg circuitousnesses; still, they felt like he was saving them time, not just sparing his own. He was from Mecklenburg, from "Olden Mochum," so called for the formerly numerous Jews in Alt-Strelitz. Witticisms like this did not go over well with Tamms: he would give the speaker a cold look, obliging him to hurry if he still wanted to get to his original business. He was more than capable of holding the door open for a visitor.

On this day, Tamms had confiscated the unused bedrooms in Jerichow—politely, inflexibly, without any talk of community spirit, deaf to complaints. The resistance was halfhearted once he'd spared neither Papenbrock nor Avenarius Kollmorgen, although he had contacted them first and remained in contact afterward. Louise Papenbrock hadn't wanted to prepare ten rooms at once for total strangers; Tamms had said: The Führer expects from us . . . ; from Jansen it would have sounded like a threat. Tamms simply presented it as a fact, and since Louise secretly saw him as a gentleman, she agreed to set up her laundry room as a first aid station too, in the interests of a public reputation for Papenbrock charitableness, and Tamms thanked her just the way she wanted: surprised, a little touched, and yet for something that of course she would do.

Tamms came around the back of Cresspahl's house and met him in the kitchen, where he and the child were not alone but in the company of two of the French prisoners, who preferred not to eat their cold meals while crouching on their bed frames. It was forbidden to sit at the same table as POWs during their sentence; Tamms didn't bring up the infringement, and while it's true he didn't shake hands with the Frenchmen, he did wish them good day, in their language. The house was full, and Tamms accepted what Cresspahl said even though Cresspahl had offered to show him. By then there were prisoners even in Lisbeth's old bedroom. During the war a lot of people moved in and out of Cresspahl's house. Tamms was at the end of a workday; he took a seat once the Frenchmen had taken their leave. Monsieur le Maire didn't curse the English. He talked about Germans (not: "our national comrades") looting in the Lübeck ruins or selling food at inflated prices. He talked about people sentenced to death in a sullen accepting tone. Tamms said: It's war.

On March 31, a Tuesday, *The Lübeck Gazette* came to Jerichow again, with three pictures of the destruction of the city. The main headline said: "Rash U.S. Efforts to Secure Position"; the subheadline, "Outcry Against British Desecrators of Culture."

On April 2, there was no more *Lübeck Gazette*—Charles Coleman Publishers had been "coordinated" with the Wullenwever NSDAP Press, which the Nazis had stolen from the Social Democrats. It was called *The Lübeck News* now, and so sure were they of victory that it was announced for seven issues a week.

Train tickets to Lübeck required presenting an authorization from the police, the authorities, and the party, and anyone who didn't buy a return ticket was liable to end up held in the city. Cresspahl was told to look at the news in the paper. The merchants quarter below St. Mary's Church was almost completely destroyed. The spires of St. Mary's Church were still standing, burned out. St. Peter's was a ruin. Two-thirds of the old town was destroyed as the fire spread. The bombed-out people had arrived in Jerichow on Tuesday morning. Louise Papenbrock couldn't understand that she wouldn't be able to get them to work, or even talk. It was up to her to make sure the children were washed, the food was prepared, and she liked being so busy, running all around the house; she did it in a pious, lamenting way, and it wasn't easy to be grateful to her for it.

On April 5, Wallschläger preached in a church with almost every pew full, about the desecration of Palm Sunday by the unconscionable, heathenish English people, sworn to the side of the Antichrist.

On April 5, the first notice of a mass grave appeared in *The Lübeck News*. Cresspahl noticed in private the way the survivors explained the events to themselves and their readers:

We still cannot grasp the misfortune that. . . .

The British attack, in violation of international law. . . .

An inexorable fate has snatched from us. . . .

On the fatal night of March 28–29, fate decreed that. . . .

In the barbaric British attack. . . .

In the treacherous enemy attack I too lost. . . .

In the enemy action. . . .

In a tragic twist of fate. . . .

At the airfield, Cresspahl gathered:

That the antiaircraft defense hadn't managed to shoot down a single plane. On top of their rage at now having to look on helpless as new waves of bombers continued to swarm through the sky, the teams in Jerichow-North felt angry that *The Lübeck News* described twelve lost British planes, knew about a captured crew, and called the bunglers in Lübeck heroes.

That Lübeck itself was to blame. Lübeck had never gotten over its incorporation into Prussia in 1937 and hadn't wanted to be in the vanguard of the Reich in air defense measures either. With its crowded city center, too, under wooden beam roofs. An untrained populace had run for it, enabling the fires to spread. Among the officers, additional outrage at Minister of Propaganda Goebbels, whose ranting about the desecration of culture had failed to prepare the population for the attacks that were still to come.

Aggie Brüshaver wrote from Rostock describing high schoolers jealous that Lübeck had come first yet again, not Rostock.

On April 6, *The Lübeck News* gave the official death toll at 280. On April 11, the number of victims reported was 295.

You were responsible, Cresspahl.

I was responsible for Coventry too.

And you could stand it?

It was on November 14, 1940, that they'd attacked Coventry. The Germans. Four hundred fifty bombers. There was a cathedral there too. From November 19 to 22, they flew over Birmingham three times, more than eight hundred people bombed to death there.

And that offsets it?

No, Gesine. But the Germans did start it. They made a word out of it: coventrieren, *"to coventry a place." What they do is against international law only when the other side does it.*

You didn't like the Germans anymore, did you.

Not those ones.

Not the ones in Lübeck either.

Gesine, think about Rostock, think about Wismar. Lübeck could now sleep easy every night. The Red Cross set up its transshipment point there, and no more bombs fell.

They showed their gratitude, Cresspahl.

They handed out another one of their honorary citizenships, this time to the head of the Red Cross. What they were celebrating may not have exactly pleased the other cities.

Or that Churchill went to the mass grave of Birmingham, and Hitler didn't go to the one in Lübeck.

That was Churchill's duty, Gesine.

What if Tamms had put refugees from Lübeck in your house?

Our house was under the same sky as Lübeck, Gesine.

And what if the refugees had lost children in the fire? Or a wife lost a husband?

I'd already lost a wife, Gesine.

Now you really are saying one thing offsets another.

No, Gesine. I was past that. I was somewhere with no comparing, no accounting. No one understood me back then n you dont now.

I do, Cresspahl.

Lettit go, Gesine. We're past that. *You don't need to lie anymore, Gesine.*

March 16, 1968 Saturday

is the third Saturday of the month, and Countess Seydlitz is throwing a party.

We met Mrs. Albert Seydlitz as an old woman feeding the pigeons in Riverside Park in the exact spot where the city, by means of a cute little plaque, states that it is forbidden to do so. This was six years ago, across from our building, and Marie stared at her in such bewilderment that the woman started talking to her. But who Countess Seydlitz is—that we do not know. She's an older lady, gaunt of face like an eighty-year-old, with a student's center part in her white hair as was the fashion sixty years ago; she has lived in New York for forty years, and tends to call people around thirty "Child." Her manners aren't those of a countess—she's more careless, like someone who's had to invent her manners herself. She was once a German, is disconcertingly knowledgeable about the estates around Schwerin and may well have come into the world there, but it wasn't on Jungfernstieg in Schwerin itself. She has ice-gray eyes, thin lips, like a man. Nothing is known about any Count Seydlitz. Some say she was born Emma Borsfeld, others give Erna Bloemdorf as her maiden name. This old lady explained to Marie that the laws of the city don't apply to everyone, and after we'd taken strict instruction from her several times without once pushing back, the invitation to come by on the third Saturday of every month (except in the summer, which she spends in Cannes) was extended to us as well.

Countess Seydlitz's apartment sits on the roof of a building off Riverside Park, in the Eighties. It has two floors, built around a main hall with a skylight, and a roof deck facing west with a panoramic view of New Jersey's skyscrapers. Whoever it was who consoled her for matrimonial disappointments with a noblewoman's title also left her money, now long gone. The

furniture is a hundred years old, built for a prosperous family in Mecklenburg—Empire, Biedermeier, highly polished pieces upholstered in austere
striped patterns—and Countess Seydlitz has maids working for her who
make sure no traces of ashes, rings of glasses, or drops of alcohol are left
behind after her parties. Both students and professors of the more aesthetic
departments are received here, along with art dealers, Communists, employees in diplomatic service, German émigrés; emissaries from the Kennedys are said to have come. Jews, while invited, remain a minority, don't
stay long, and tend not to come back. Countess Seydlitz inevitably addresses
her as "Child." Tonight Countess Seydlitz is wearing an ankle-length dress
with gypsy fringes and a chain of brightly colored wood around her gaunt
neck: a flower girl amid all the painstaking suits and formal black and
white. At nine p.m. the parquet is packed, and the din of conversation
bounces back down from the night-dark glass of the skylight like heavy
surf. – You know everyone, yes?: Mrs. Albert Seydlitz says, and as usual
Mrs. Cresspahl knows barely two guests, one of them only by sight.

– It's too stupid, Georgie Brown resigning like that. What are we
supposed to do in England now?
– I don't know. Give Madame de Gaulle a kiss. . . .
– Herr Kristlein, this is Norman Podhoretz. *Norman, meet Anselm.*
– Just between you and me: Who's our hostess? I know the Seydlitzes.
– I couldn't tell you.
– Did you come by plane or by boat?
– *How do you like America?*
– Never ever take the subway in New York. These ritual murders, you
know. . . .
– Kennedy's running. He'll split the party in two.
– The Irish are mad though. They should have gone to Fifth Avenue
this morning!
– Quiet.

A dark-skinned man, addressed by most of the people there as Joseph,
though that isn't his name, is handing out drinks. Rumor has it he'd been
a boxer, Countess Seydlitz's lover, a platoon leader in the marines, a bartender. He tends bar at these parties, holds his taciturn thoughtful face

high above his broad shoulders, wears the requisite white jacket like an elegant thing, and does his work with such confident, expert hands that you could probably blindfold him without causing any problems. Guests often try to recruit him for their own events; none has ever succeeded. He answers friendly remarks with a precisely calculated smile, which remains in memory like the Cheshire Cat's. Ever since Mrs. Cresspahl observed him a bit too thoughtfully once, he has handed her her glass first, even if she's in the very back of the crowd around his table. His expression as he does so may be mocking, or it may be loyal. Even for the half wasted he mixes the drinks precisely, down to the drop—it won't be he who neglects the proper forms.

– The CIA has a computerized index with every American of African descent....
– Computers can't do that.
– You don't know Hoover.
– Anyway, New York will just be transplanted across the Hudson. The camps'll have the same names they do here: Harlem, Brownsville....
– I'm writing a book about the CIA.
– Finally, something new. Not another book about the Kennedys.
– About how the CIA killed Kennedy.
– Shares in Swedish steel.
– Since I've started investigating I've been followed everywhere I go....
– You didn't know? Call MUrray Hill 6-5517.
– I don't take planes anymore, or taxis. If there was a subway to Dallas....
– Who is our hostess, actually? Seydlitz, Albert—?
– What we did to the Indians is basically what the Germans did to the Jews.

The New York Times has written de Rosny a letter. De Rosny is one of the bankers who was trying to get President Johnson to promise he will send no more troops to Vietnam, so that the dollar will make up its recent losses. But de Rosny is out of town—he went to Washington yesterday for a meeting with Europe's leading central bankers. They want the valuation of the dollar against an ounce of gold changed.

– I'm still on Zurich time.
– You must be exhausted, Mr. Kristlein.
– What do you give a man like that?
– What is a "Bloody Mary," actually?
– Tomato juice, vodka, pepper—
– Pepper? That's very unhealthy. Damages the kidneys! You mustn't take another sip!
– Born Blœrstadt, I think. Related to the Karstadts.
– No, to the Brenninkmeyers.
– Oh do come to Vassar too, Mr. Kristlein! *We are dying to hear you speak!*
– It is the nightingale, and not the lark: No, Shakespeare didn't write that, I did.
– What do you give a man like that?

The other person Cresspahl knew was Dr. Weiszand. He had managed to express his amazement at encountering her here, in this apotheosis of a rotting society. After she'd listened at the edge of the group around him for a while, she left the apartment, went out onto the street, back home.

– Socialism is invincible.
– Do you mean that statistically?
– I'm not against it. I just think it's unseemly.
– These are my students!
– But you can't go around with a hat collecting money for the Vietcong. It's just not done.
– You should tell our hostess, whoever she is.
– Take the example of Czechoslovakia. There they've fired an interior minister and an attorney general because they didn't support rehabilitation forcefully enough!
– You can't bring back the dead, can you?
– These Stalinist purges after the end of the war—they really happened, you know.
– We're a cozy little family here. Come join us.
– Your glass needs refilling.

– Do you want to bet that your Czechoslovakian thing, or whatever it is, doesn't work out? Should we bet? Right here in front of witnesses?

– I know him. He always looks exhausted like that.

– Socialism purifies itself.

– It used to be that it was only at night you couldn't walk in Central Park. Did you hear about the forty-seven children who were almost drowned today, in the middle of Central Park?

– The Soviet Union has other things to worry about.

– We believe it.

– That would suit you perfectly—for the Soviet Union to end the war in Vietnam for you!

– Is this your first time in New York? For God's sake, don't ever take the subway!

– I'd like another Bloody Mary after all.

– Bravo, Herr Kristlein!

– New York isn't what it used to be.

– Take Le Pavillon.

– Take Manny Wolf's Steakhouse.

– Take the Waldorf restaurant.

It couldn't be helped, Gesine.
Couldn't be helped.
If you're going to go at all, why do you stick by the walls the whole time?
So I can see better.
You should open your mouth, Gesine!

March 17, 1968 Sunday

President Johnson has decided against the bankers. True, he isn't sending to Vietnam the 206,000 soldiers that his general, Westmoreland, requested, but still, he's sending 35,000 or 50,000.

In Prague, for the first time since the Communists seized power, former soldiers who served in the Spanish Civil War or on the Allies' side have been allowed to gather in public. For twenty years, what had mattered about them was not their service against the Fascists but the fact that as a result they had international connections.

In Poland, the Communist Party explained itself to the workers thusly: They, the party, had "very often" made "difficult and unpopular decisions," but "we are not a party for the weak." And is it conceivable that students decide of their own accord to demonstrate in Poland? Not for the party, which has decided there must be Jews lurking behind it, set on handing Poland over to West Germany and Israel.

When Alexander Paepcke traveled, he always prepared for his trip. He sought out the shortest travel time and best connections, and from the moment they went out the front door, his family had to follow no time-table but his. When he went to Fischland, in the wet June of 1942, the train to Stralsund didn't follow Alexander's timetable—it arrived there later than the train to Ribnitz could wait. Alexander was miffed at the two-hour delay. By that point he was serving the war effort in the civilian manage-ment of the occupied French territories, but he didn't recognize the war in the form of a late train, because the train that had done this to him was a German one.

That was why the Cresspahl child spent such a long time in the Ribnitz train station, standing under the poster advertising Schachenmayr Wool, refusing to believe that Alexander could leave her in the lurch like this. She roused herself to look for the way to the harbor almost too late. They were just pulling up the gangplank on the Fischland steamboat ferry. The boat was sitting there like a fat black duck in a hurry. She sat down facing the stern. Her father had sent her away even though the school year wasn't over in Mecklenburg. Behind the steamship there was still the Ribnitz church tower, then that of Körkwitz, then the Neuhaus dune. She might never find Jerichow again.

She spent half the afternoon standing in the Althagen harbor, a nine-year-old child in a dress that was too long for her and had been washed too many times, her cockscomb of hair awry. She had no ticket for the ferry or train back. Her pocket money for the trip had almost all gone to the ferry ride here. She had nothing to prove that she was from Jerichow. She was afraid she might not be able to find the Paepcke summer house after three years. She stood on the right side of the bay, which even then was a little overgrown with reeds. The ship's propeller had torn up plants in the water.

Then Paepcke arrived on the steamer bringing workers back from Ribnitz. He was decisive and happy now. Straslund had turned out to be a good place for toy stores; he'd bought presents. He was back in Mecklenburg, not pissing on the corner in Stettin. Paepcke was wearing white pants, a white hat. He thought the child Gesine must be consoled because he'd apologized to her with a present, but the pocketknife he gave her was exactly like the one she had already, except for one little scratch.

Paepcke asked about Jerichow, about Methfessel, about Gesine's French, about Aggie Brüshaver. And the Brüshaver kids, with their mellifluous names: Martin and Mathias and Marlene Dietrich. Gesine said: They're dead.

Alexander didn't understand. How could such little children suddenly be dead!

They had lived in Rostock, on the street alongside St. Jakobi Church. On April 25, when the Royal Air Force came to Rostock, Aggie had night duty at the hospital and her children were home alone when they burned to death.

Paepcke, somewhat embarrassed, made Gesine promise not to tell his children. She didn't understand why not. They hadn't even known Marlene.

Village Road was shady. When light came through the courtyard entrances, it was white. The houses were sheltered from the wind by high hedgerows. When the two village boys with their wheelbarrows stopped by a gap in the thick bushes, Gesine recognized the house. It was a long brick cottage under a cane roof, the west wall painted white and then yellow. There was a semicircular dormer window in the roof (not two). The way in went down from the hedge so steeply, onto a floor lower than the doorstep, that you felt like you were sliding into the house.

The garden was totally overgrown. Painstakingly laid out, with one terrace for flowers and another, lower one for vegetables, it was now a tangle of grass, weeds, and surviving flowers surrounded by bushes. A gate opening onto a likewise surrounded field led east to the lagoon; the Maypole was still intact. When three children grabbed the ropes dangling from the top and started running, they would soon be flying in a circle high above the bushes. That was when the vacation truly started: when all the children came down safe, none banging into the iron pole.

The rooms had names. Hilde and Alexander slept upstairs, in the Lagoon Room. The Prince Room, the great-uncle's domain, stayed locked. The children's beds were in the Atteljé. When they woke up, a regular dull sound could be heard through the windows—it came from the coastal artillery batteries, shooting down at the sea from the Shoreline Cliff for practice. Alexander's voice rang through the house. He cursed the military for being here too, the dirty pigs.

A great-uncle of Alexander's had bought the house back around 1902, from a painter who had added a studio onto the cottage. There was the mandatory tiled kitchen in the basement, and a dumbwaiter, and a pump for the kitchen. But the Paepckes preferred to get their water from the well in the yard with a rope and bucket. I've never seen such clear water since.

From the East Room upstairs, you could look sharply down at the lagoon, white in the morning light, and at the grasslands that spent weeks on end underwater. The water came up to your knees. It was nice walking there, for the splashing feeling under your feet, and also spooky, because it was like the marshes in books, the bogs, the moors. There were often fishing boats, local *Zeesenboote*, floating motionless out near the thin horizon, without their brown sails after their night's labors.

To the west, where the sea was, the land rose sharply. Even today, when a path climbs sharply I expect to find the Baltic that the child of that time would suddenly be looking down on.

A west wind blew in our faces, as usual. To the left of the path were the Nagels' fields; to the right was a single house, bundled up tight against the sea with thorny brambles. This house had a sundial. Since the ram had slept in this first morning, or was busy somewhere else, we got to the edge of the cliffs unchallenged and clambered down to the water. The ground broke off under our feet. By then Hilde was far behind, we couldn't hear her calling because of the constant wind blowing in from the sea. We were reprimanded severely, first because Hilde had been scared and second because we'd damaged the Shoreline Cliff. "Dumb as a vacationer!" was a phrase that summer, and so it has long remained. The swallows dug enough holes in the crumbly shoreline cliffs.

Paepcke was determined to be on vacation. No newspapers. Forget the radio! He swam way out and when he came back, puffing with pleasure, Hilde said his name several times, accusingly, as though she had only just now started calling it. Alexander taught the children how to swim, partly by convincing them that they already knew. He said there was a "sandbank" ten feet out from the beach, and once he got the children that far they would keep swimming after him.

The beach was dotted with canopied wicker beach chairs. It was quiet, for not many of the Althagen cottagers rented out, plus Althagen was seen as a village while Ahrenshoop, the next town over, in Pomerian, in Prussia, was a "resort." Althagen had one lone hotel, named after the Baltic, which was just across the street from it. It spelled its name with a circumflex accent on the "o," and Paepcke wanted to explain that to Gesine, but unfortunately she already knew all about it from "her" Frenchmen in Jerichow, so he had to think up something else on the spot for the other children so that their feelings wouldn't be hurt.

By then yet another child had joined them: Klaus Niebuhr, from Friedenau in Berlin. He was very proud of having come all this away ("into the flat country") alone, but Eberhardt Junior, who'd spent too long with three girls, had adopted a new worldview—rather than taking the male side, he pointed out that Gesine had come by herself too. Klaus the man was hurt, and at being outstripped by a girl too, but now at last she had the chance to give away the pocketknife.

Alexander could have sat with his buddies in the Baltic Hôtel, but they didn't like the beer there. At the Kurhaus spa resort in Ahrenshoop, the clientele was too high-society. Paepcke saw himself as society, high too. He sometimes went to the Sea Mark with Reynard Fox, but expressed his suspicion of the place by calling it *Setzeichen*, "Placemat Mark," instead of *Seezeichen*. Their favorite establishment was Malchen Saatmann's pastry shop. A place for locals in the winter, it was an outdoor café in the summer. Malchen was a tidy woman, solid, brisk; I can't remember a thing about her face and would recognize her at once. Malchen never said one word too many, not even to children, but even children felt they were being treated fairly.

Nowhere did the cooking smell as good as it did at Malchen Saatmann's. Fischland was poor in smells—there's the smell of salt water, of fish, of

rotting seaweed. After the war, I never found the old smell again at Malchen
Saatmann's. The children's favorite thing to buy were *Schnecken*, the snail-
shell-shaped morning buns. When they were sent to get bread after hours,
they were allowed to walk in through the gate in the back part of the
building. It was vacation, with special events every day.

When it rained, Alexander played with "his" children the game known
in German as Now Don't Get Mad, but he called it *Pakesi*, which was how
Cresspahl had brought it from London, named after the Hindi word for
twenty-five, *pachisi*, and because it was something British it was played
with its own special rules: that two pieces of the same color could be on
the same space, forming a blockade; that a piece on any color's exit space
is safe ("Home Rule"); that three sixes in a row is too much luck and means
a trip back to Start. Alexandra couldn't stand seeing her pieces sent back
to Start: the flush shot through her whole face, and then she'd have that
to be embarrassed about too. No one busy losing would look too closely at
why their luck suddenly took a turn for the better. But Paepcke's good
nature was harder to keep up; by the end he'd be staring, wordless and
angry, at his lost game—he'd become Someone Who Got Mad.

The house hadn't stayed as regal as Alexander's great-uncle had planned
it to be, with antique furniture and bare walls. Alexander had hauled in
discarded pieces from his earlier households, half broken, with torn upholstery—perfect for children. There were flowers in every room. A child
could be alone in any room. There, on a wobbly sofa with gently rearing
sidearms, I read my way into the Orient, strode down marble steps into
the water where huge fish had moored, and was Harun al-Rashid.

Alexander had spent his vacations in Althagen since he was six years
old, spoke Fischland Plattdeutsch like a Fischländer, and was on a first-
name basis with everyone in the village—now everyone insisted that his
children not act like foreigners. The villager who eventually married her
captain stood outside her door and brought us in to her dinner. Where the
hallway widened she had her kitchen, the old kind, with a stone oven on
which things in many pots were sizzling: people were going in and out,
taking a sip of water from the bucket with the ladle, sitting down to eat,
being served a drink, only dropping by to have a word. She wasn't offended
when we didn't want the bacon, she spread tea sausage on bread for us, and
then, when there was still a look of suspicion on our faces, she sent us home

with the sandwiches and Alexander took pity on us and ate them all. It had put a dent in his Mecklenburg reputation, though.

In the evenings, coming back from the sea, we would run into children our age herding cows home. Nights on Fischland were too harsh for milk cows. Alexandra stared wide-eyed at Inge Niemann, whose cows were walking so calmly ahead of her stick, and Paepcke asked Inge to let his child have the cow and the stick for a bit. He was forgetful that evening and kept walking. All the other cows kept walking too, while Alexandra's stayed where she was. She took the liberty, too, of nibbling a little from the side of the road. Alexandra looked at me but I didn't want to suggest that she hit the animal. In desperation, Alexandra gave the beast a friendly shove, and the cow looked back in amazement, straight into our eyes. Alexander, having had a moment while walking when he remembered the children after all, saved us from this unfortunate situation.

And never to bed bareheaded.

Be wise then, children, while you may,
For swiftly time is flying.
The thoughtless man, who laughs to-day,
To-morrow will be dying.

Cresspahl, who'd said he would not be coming, came in late July. Alexander looked forward to a whole week's evenings and said: *Y'r a good man, Hinrich!*

One time, Paepcke did have something he needed to take care of at the post office in Ahrenshoop, so he took a couple of his children with him and went for a walk on the embankment by the lagoon, past the Dornen-haus, to the windmill that's not there anymore, to the old fort. On Ahrens-shoop Street he saw Cresspahl walking with a man one had no choice but to classify as a spa-resort type, high-society. He looked like Berlin, civil service, party insignia. Paepcke noticed the party lapel pin when he caught up to them, and he heard that Cresspahl was in a hurry somewhere with the other man. "Fritz," Cresspahl called him. Cresspahl arrived at the post office right after Paepcke. – *'E took me fer a vacationer*: he said, without being asked, and Paepcke decided to believe him. But it didn't seem like Cresspahl, letting a stranger take him for a spa visitor and then going for a walk with him too, in conversation, hands comfortably clasped behind his back.

Alexander didn deserve that, Cresspahl.
An if I'd told him would he a deserved that, Gesine?
You didn trust him.
I didn want him to hafta trust me.

That night the Allies bombed Hamburg. You couldn't see Hamburg from Fischland.

That summer, after a long time being embarrassed, Alexander dared to ask Cresspahl something. It was just a couple thousand marks more he owed than he could come up with right at the moment. Cresspahl wasn't thought of as stingy, but frugal, yes, and Alexander, to his disbelieving amazement, found himself free of all his debts on the spot. Cresspahl didn't even ask him for details. They briefly, in passing, mentioned repayment. Cresspahl trusted Alexander to make over a share in his Althagen house to Gesine when Alexander inherited it from his great-uncle. Alexander didn't have to but he stuck to his word and put it into his will in Kiev. Hilde never knew. Cresspahl used to tuck away money for his child like this in lots of places all over Mecklenburg: in case they got him. Killed him.

It was a very quiet summer. There were no planes in the air the way there were in Jerichow. The morning booms from the coastal battery were forgotten by day, as was the nightly foghorn, also not visible.

Then Cresspahl had to settle an argument between the Paepckes: Was the beacon fire you could see from the Shoreline Cliff Warnemünde's or Poel's?

Then Alexander Paepcke told some vague stories about the civil administration of the occupied zone in France. He was not looking forward to the Berlin–Paris furlough train, and he gave an exaggerated sigh when he brought out a little leather suitcase that the children hadn't noticed until then. In it was a kepi for Paepcke Junior. Christine got a Breton doll in folk costume and slept with it for the rest of her life. For Alexandra it was a set of dollhouse china, gilded. For Klaus Niebuhr there was a ruler with French markings, and the suitcase, a high-status toy, went to Gesine. *And what did she get, the soldier's wife?* The children almost couldn't believe that they were getting even more presents for Alexander's departure, and Alexander, in his pleasure at their happiness, casually said, about the doll-house china: Took it from a hotel. The gold was a very convincing color, and his daughter asked, outraged: You can do that? Paepcke said, in his broad, delighted voice: *Yeahhh*; he noticed Cresspahl's look, and added, embarrassed, every inch the major in the reserves: *Hey, I paid for it, yknow!*

One time, Hilde tried to ask about the night Lübeck was bombed. Cresspahl got out of it by saying he'd been in Wendisch Burg.

He did tell her, though, the story that was going around Jerichow: It had looked like a peaceful bonfire in the bright night. Luckily it had been so loud, despite the fifteen-mile distance.

And again Gesine faced a choice. She could stay in Althagen. Summer break lasted until September 1 in Mecklenburg, and she could go back to Pommern with the Paepckes until then. Cresspahl didn't look at her at all, he held his hand over his eyes and looked for something in the evening sea. She looked up at him and could hardly see his face, and said, without thinking: *I wanna go back to Jerichow. Take me with you.*

It was lucky that the fire in Lübeck was so loud?
The bombs, Gesine. You imagined them less that way. The noise took that away.

March 18, 1968 Monday
Dear Marie. I'm telling you this on tape so that you'll have to believe it.

"The old bum with the tattered brown bags has shaved and now he looks like an ordinary Jewish man."

You said that. You were wanting to tell me the latest about the neighbors, that I miss during the day.

He's not a bum: he begs. He is one of the ones I give to. I shouldn't.

Remember the beggars in the *subway*. There's a man who rides the IRT in the morning or the Lexington Avenue line in the afternoon, when it's not rush hour: black, about thirty, unable to look anyone in the eye, maybe due to a sickness. He moves in a dazed stagger, leans against the door however he's landed there, grips tight to the straps or poles as if hanging on them, and sings—yowling notes in which you can only occasionally make out anything like words, and none you can understand. He always breaks off very suddenly, holds a sign up in front of his belly—he'd been carrying it carefully under his arm after all—and walks with a little tin cup very close to the seated passengers, asking to get paid for his music. His neat purple lettering begins with the words: *My mother has multiple sclerosis. . . .* —with no spelling mistakes, written out like a doctor's finding.

Another one, also black, around fifty, and actually blind, wearing a blue cap, feels his way through the car with his white cane and holds his cup close to his body, showing no sign of whether he's heard a coin clink into it.

The rule is: Since "charity in small things and reform in large" do not work to change or rectify society, they should be avoided as sentimentality and wasted effort.

Occasionally someone gives them something. Black passengers reach into their pockets and show solidarity, or else that there are blacks who have money like normal people. Pink-skinned housewives feel entitled not only to give nothing but also to put on an act as upstanding citizens who have no need of such things, praise God, they have to make ends meet with the harsh (honest) wages of hard work. Some men, if they're wearing suits and ties, feel from the looks of other passengers that it's really they who should be the first to act, and so they comply with the general judgment. The contempt that is actually a defense mechanism is directed at the taker. No one is unselfconscious.

There are glances back and forth. These glances mean: scorn for anyone that gullible; contempt for the one who brags with his quarter where a dime would've been fine; condemnation of the black race, which does after all have money too.

Marie, I wish I were indifferent—that I could give and forget.

Then there's the mistrust of the asker. They are seen in the subways too often, it's as if they had an office there. The way they work their way through the moving trains has something professional about it. They can live off their takings, sometimes even have a little extra to spend on life's pleasures. But they're too sick for that, too broken. They may have let themselves drop out of society, but why don't they make use of the admittedly meager emergency assistance set up for them? Have they arrived at this mode of employment on their own, or are they being sent out by a foot soldier or low-level boss in the Mafia, who repays the day's earnings with nothing but a place to sleep? Is their pitiful decision to throw themselves upon the pity of strangers enough?

The woman I was once shut the door in an old man's face, very slowly, embarrassed, before giving him the chance to explain how things stood with his lunch. That was back in Saxony, when I was a student and still believed what I'd learned in school—that in an already almost entirely Socialist state there were no beggars.

In the subway I have my hand in my purse when the beggars are still four steps away. I don't give them quarters, not even dimes—I know the rules.

But I do drop a subway token into their cup, so that they can keep riding.

You will be able to say of me: My mother was a rather inconsistent person.

What you're hearing now is more rain.

I would've liked to be more consistent, though, untouched by the influence of biography and the past, with the right kind of life in the right era, with the right people, working toward the right goals, at least a right goal. I know the rules.

"The old bum with the tattered brown bags has shaved and now he looks like an ordinary Jewish man." Thank you for the report.

March 19, 1968 Tuesday

The Communists in the ČSSR do and don't want to force out their president, Antonín Novotný. They describe him in the party newspaper with merely a Mr., not the party title of Comrade; they refuse to let him go on TV; but they're waiting for him to step down on his own.

Yesterday Robert F. Kennedy began attending to the business of being a candidate for president, calling the current president's policy in Vietnam "bankrupt." Then he even said to college students in Kansas: I will work for you and we will have a new America.

Don't forget, spring officially starts tomorrow morning at 8:22!

In June 1942, life ceased to have any appeal for Dr. Avenarius Kollmorgen, retired lawyer, Jerichow, and he gave it up.

Until that point it hadn't been known around Jerichow how he'd spent his last year. His practice had closed its doors for good in 1935. Since then he had sometimes been seen on walks around town, but he preferred roads where he was safe against running into people. Anyone who did want to hear him ask, yet again, All's well?, encountered a distressingly disturbed person shuffling impatiently back and forth, desperate to end the conversation, and not even once did he ever again raise himself on his tiptoes and dispense his brand of opinions with earnestly shining eyes. At first he'd taken the walks for his health in the morning, by 1941 it was after lunch, and eventually they took place near twilight, before stopping altogether. The light from his windows, though, would creep out onto the market square ever later into the night; both it and the slowly moving shadow had looked professional.

During these nights, Avenarius had been preparing for his death. Most of the books no longer stood on the shelves with their spines facing out: they were in piles of equal height, lined up and ready for packing. Written in each book was the date when he had last read it; there were only two rows he hadn't gotten to. In his desk there were lists that inventoried the whole household, with a column for who was to be the future owner, every line filled in. Geesche Helms's sister, who had now worked for him more than twelve years, got all the Kollmorgen dishes, as well as the furniture. What wasn't given away was to be converted to money and given to the University of Erlangen, as was the library. There was an index to the library. Dr. Kollmorgen had destroyed all his personal documents—he wanted nothing left behind but the Mystery of Avenarius. In the open desk drawer Ilse found, as she had been told she would, the page with instructions in the case of his death—from directions to Dr. Berling's and Swenson's to requests for the funeral. He took his leave from certain people with old-fashioned printed notes, but he didn't need them, everything had been decided and paid for in advance. "Do not allow the participation of the church" stood there in painstakingly arabesqued handwriting. In this, in all the judicious arrangements, Dr. Kollmorgen's voice could once again be heard, now no longer the pleasantly dozing one but stubborn, disappointed, not without contempt. Ultimately he hadn't liked that the town had satisfied his need for solitude. There were not many people who came to his salon one morning to see him one last time. In life he had shrunk, children had to be told they mustn't laugh; in the coffin he looked substantial and as if seeking approval and respect. He was dressed for a party in a bygone era, with his arms at his sides as if he were standing, an observer, an examiner. Around the eyes he looked softer, not very different from someone sleeping. Almost eighty years old he was, had been. Swenson looked in several times but the funeral guests continued to stand around Kollmorgen, not impatient, solemnly whispering, as though trying to make up for all the missed visits. Then, at the open grave, a lawyer from Hamburg said something in Latin that the Jerichow mourners couldn't understand, while none of them wanted to say anything. It was Avenarius's business, living alone and dying alone.

Ilse had taken the bequeathing of the china as a hint from Kollmorgen that the time had come for her to take a husband, and in the fall of 1942 she married a fisherman in Rande, who had waited five years for her. Ilse Grossjohann was her name now, a respected housewife, envied for her furniture. Now when she came to Jerichow to go shopping she no longer had the face of a helplessly marveling girl.

For Gesine Cresspahl there was a sealed package, "With compliments, to be opened on March 3, 1954."

In November 1942, because Avenarius was dead and buried, Cresspahl had to bring a letter to Dr. Kliefoth. It was a French letter, postmarked in Leipzig, in Dora Semig's handwriting. *"Chers amis,"* Cresspahl could figure that much out. And it was urgent.

He didn't like going to Kliefoth with it. Kliefoth was from Malchow, a tanglepicker, an educated man. He had lived in England, but at universities. They had World War I in common, but by 1918 Kliefoth had long since been made lieutenant. He'd subscribed to French and English newspapers to the end, from a different *département* or new county every eight weeks, but he'd volunteered at once for the war against France after they hadn't taken him for the one against Poland, due to certain blots in his Berlin file. Since then he'd been on continuous active service, reaching the rank of general staff officer in 1C (counterintelligence) under Baudissin, until finally they'd sent him home for reaching the age limit, and the whole time he was making his reconnaissance flights over the Soviet Union his wife had hung the swastika flag out for him. Cresspahl couldn't get a handle on this man in a hurry.

The evening was a long one, lasting almost till midnight. Kliefoth came to the door in full uniform, invited the carpenter in with casual but unmistakable politeness, saw the other man hesitate, and started right in, revealing who he was.

Kliefoth kept saying: Army. The army. As though that was all that mattered.

Before long they found a sector of the Russian front where they might have both been at the same time in 1916.

Cresspahl couldn't decide.

Kliefoth told him about his flights over Jersey, as a member of the Second Army Corps, "at the King of England's expense." He'd been the only one who liked the English breakfast, "Bring on the porridge!," and the Italian waiters were as delighted as the French ones were impressed when he'd revealed his familiarity with the national specialties. Bring on the porridge!

That didn't help Cresspahl. He had heard from Böttcher's son, Klaus, the world traveler, that during the march into France Kliefoth had driven past the marching columns in truly gentlemanly style, relaxed in the backseat, with a leather-covered silver bottle of cognac at his lips.

Now Kliefoth tried again. Told him how in 1940 he had sworn that a student with a Jewish name was Aryan.

Katzengold, something like that.
Don't tell me her name!
No?
Right, Mr. Kliefoth. That's how it is.
And even if it was lying under oath, it was God's work and I'd do it again.
She's still alive then?
Living in Hamburg! It's about time you learned to trust me too, ya ol tanglepicker.

Then Kliefoth translated Dora's letter. Arthur, too, was still alive. After the occupation of Czechoslovakia they'd tried Switzerland but were only allowed to stay two days on straw in a camp. They had run out of money. They'd spent it in Paris. When the Germans came to France, they'd actually managed to escape into the unoccupied zone. During these seven days on foot and in overcrowded trains, Arthur had "woken up." Not that he'd let himself be talked into Marseilles and trying get overseas—but he'd found an apartment near Cannes, arranged for false papers, and found a job, all within just over a week. Arthur hardly felt his sixty years even though he was working as a butcher. Having studied veterinary medicine turned out to be useful after all. He chopped up the animals clean and quick, the same way he'd learned to heal them. Impossible to give an address due to illegality of work and apartment. "Please pass this news along to my parents, too, who haven't answered our letters. We think with warm love in our hearts about Lisbeth and the child. We really should have switched to informal pronouns before we left; Arthur is sorry not to have done that, it was his responsibility as the elder. Thank you too. Lisbeth, don't always take everything so to heart. D. S."

Kliefoth was sorry there was no address. He had people in the German Army who could have helped the Semigs, even now that the Italians had occupied the Riviera, and would have wanted to, too. Cresspahl believed him.

Kliefoth advised Cresspahl not to bring the letter back home. Kliefoth praised Dora's French once again; his own, he said, was "grade-school" in comparison. The letter was tucked into *Chambers's Encyclopedia*, at page 467, "Vetch" and "Veterinary Medicine."

Kliefoth was right. The Gestapo turned up at Cresspahl's door the next morning and he could tell them in good conscience that he'd been unable to read the letter so he'd thrown it into the fire. Then they tried to nail him for not having reported it.

And why didn't you ask your French POWs?
How could you not have recognized the handwriting?
Oh, it was your wife who always took care of the correspondence? Then we'd like to talk to your wife. On the double!

March 20, 1968   Wednesday

Word comes for Employee Cresspahl from West Berlin, Germany: at least she occasionally garnishes reports from Vietnam with unfriendly adjectives, "which is the least one could expect."

So apparently there are people in Germany concerned about whether I'm acting properly. I'm supposed to be ending the Vietnam War, for them.

Which would surely be more than the least one could do.

I could write a letter to the editor of *The New York Times*; I could spend my life in prison for a failed attempt to assassinate President Johnson; I could publicly set myself on fire. Nothing I can do will stop the war machine, not by one penny, one soldier—nothing.

And yet there are people in Germany who expect it of me.

March 21, 1968   Thursday

A West German actor, formerly an East German actor, has returned to East Germany because he is sure that the powers that be there play no part in the oppression of the Negroes in the United States or the American war in Vietnam. He didn't know that before. When a country's crimes lie heavy on one's conscience, one simply moves to another country.

There are also critics of the war with the rank of former marine commandant. General David M. Shoup estimates that up to 800,000 American troops would be required just to defend South Vietnamese population centers against Communist attack. The only way the United States could achieve military victory would be by invading North Vietnam. The Vietnamese war was not worth the cost, he said.

School in Jerichow had gotten Cresspahl's child to the point that in November 1942 she did her homework with the People's Receiver whispering next to her; she turned the volume way up after every victory fanfare announcing a "special report." She was waiting for the Soviets to lose Stalingrad. First of all, she wanted it over and done with; second, she was on the side of the German troops. Cresspahl had his own reasons for giving her the biography of Reich Air Marshal Göring, or books like *Stukas* or *Mölders and His Men*—the child should show innocent enthusiasm for the German military at school, and especially for the air force. Cresspahl got his playacting; the child got her injuries. (Cresspahl consoled himself with the hope that the war would be over by the spring of 1943.)

Back then, school in Jerichow had eight grades. After fourth grade, children were divided into those meant to attend school for only as long as was legally required, and those whose parents could send them to the lyceum and gymnasium in Gneez. Gesine didn't know that she was meant for Gneez starting in 1943, and she had come to terms with the Hermann Göring School as one did with a home, a homeland, with living in Jerichow.

The principal was Franz Gefeller: Sudeten German, Henlein putschist, party speaker in Gneez district. He had realized that if he pulled back his mouth he looked almost identical, his whole face did, to Reich Minister of Propaganda Goebbels; he liked to put on this expression, especially when punishing children. In his normal state he was easy to take for a cocky short man. When screaming he often slipped into falsetto. When he flung his hand out high for the Nazi salute, it seemed too short, surprisingly short.

Yooo are a child of Gerrmanny,
So keep always in mind
What the cruel enemy forced on you
In the Treaty of Ver-sall-eye!

In first grade, when Gesine learned the old German Sütterlin handwriting, her teacher was Prrr Hallier and there was no doubt that his class epitomized the school as a whole. He didn't start teaching until he had drilled into his class how to sit down and stand up in unison. Whoever wasn't synchronized was the first to be called on. He was one of the men "they hadn't taken." He had put up a little shelf under Hitler's picture, with a vase, and considered it an honor to ask a student to buy fresh flowers for the idol. He suffered from how hard it was to make friends in a small town and would often announce that he was planning to drop by for a visit. Gesine had thought he was "her" teacher and felt betrayed when she wasn't allowed to be in the room during Cresspahl's first conversation with him. He was called Prrr because he interrupted children the way you tell a horse to stop. He handed out grades in the school's sandy courtyard, after the children had come in and sung. He betrayed the Cresspahl child once again by not giving her an A in Conduct, having never once called her attention to any problems. He'd observed her all year long, never warned her, and pushed her right into the trap. Then "they" did take him after all, and in June 1940 he was shot and killed.

Cresspahl was also upset by the B in Conduct. It impressed upon him the fact that diligence in this subject was supposed to make children submissive and obedient for later life.

Then came Olsching Lafrantz, proud of her last name, bitter over the first name the children had hung on her—*Oldie* in Platt—for she considered herself still marriageable, since even at forty her hair could be called red. Freckles, scraggly, like governesses in books. For Gesine, she no longer merely epitomized the school, she was an individual, and they clashed with each other. Oldie Lafrantz was upset that the Cresspahl child stood out; the child was upset that she wasn't allowed to stand out. She moved around, she stood up without being asked, she talked back because she wanted her teacher to notice her. Miss Lafrantz, to supply a vivid concrete example in math class, used Storm Trooper columns in rows of three and groups of six. She taught the Latin script instead of the German, giving as justification that the Germans had to write like the worldwide empire they were about to conquer. ("So that other peoples can understand our Führer's orders.") She was a good-natured person, who sometimes complained as though harried by something. Gesine Cresspahl didn't understand how she could call children a burden. Conduct: B.

In third grade, little Cresspahl underwent her first entanglement. She had noticed a boy named Gabriel Manfras because he seldom spoke. His face was taciturn too—Slavic of cheekbone, slanted of eye. He could talk when the teacher wanted him to, though. The Cresspahl girl wanted this boy to notice her, and she swung on locked, outstretched arms between two desks, until her shoe slipped off her foot. She fetched it from under the blackboard, told the other kids to look, and repeated the trick. This time, in an unbelievable swerve to the left, the shoe went flying through the closed window. It was during break, and at once it was totally silent. In those days children were awed to the point of inner terror by the hierarchy starting with the teacher and reaching its pinnacle with Adolf Hitler; many of the children came from farming families too. Manfras was among the most frightened. Oldie Lafrantz had never in her life had to endure such criminal behavior. She didn't even trust herself to punish it properly. Little Cresspahl was sent to the principal's office.

She felt it wasn't fair to be punished for a mistake. If she'd deliberately flouted the rules then fine, she'd have answered for that. She left the schoolhouse wearing one shoe, got the other from the snow, and ran to the only public phone booth on Market Square to call Cresspahl. For Gefeller to take off his tinted glasses and look at her with his strained dark eyes— that was punishment she didn't deserve. She was accused, per Olsching Lafrantz, of damaging state property and wasting material essential to the war effort, such as glass and wood. Cresspahl ordered her to the airfield, repaired the damage that evening with glass from the stock in his basement, and did not bring her to his meeting with Olsching Lafrantz. Conduct (pained): B.

The next teacher was Ottje Stoffregen. By that point he had accepted what Jerichow had done to his first name, Otto; had reconciled himself with the Nazis' suspension of all local history magazines; considered himself prudent. When he did bring himself to resist, the resistance took the form of practicing the old German Sütterlin script, "so you can read your grandparents' letters." There were not many grandparents in or around Jerichow who wrote letters. Ottje Stoffregen hit. Anyone who arrived late had to walk slowly past him and get at least three painful whacks with Ottje's cane in the soft spot between the neck and the shoulder. The first time it happened to the Cresspahl child, she said then and there that it didn't hurt, to minimize her shame before the other children, and Ottje repeated the ceremony. Ottje didn't forget that this was Lisbeth's child— the Lisbeth whose hand he had sought in marriage, with poems and letters, until he'd made himself ridiculous throughout Jerichow; his behavior toward the child alternated between harsh and indulgent. Alcohol had made him liable to fits of melancholy, and he sometimes looked at the child with what seemed to be tears in the corners of his eyes. He had become short-tempered, too, and sometimes hurled Cresspahl's notebook from his desk all the way to the back wall of the room, over four rows of desks. She had written "Better Betimes." Stoffregen never forgot that by all rights he should have been the principal, not this "phony German" Gefeller, "foreign war booty"—but he followed Gefeller's orders, even when he scheduled him for two hours starting at eleven and then a sewing class for girls at two. Cresspahl's child didn't come to school on those days, bringing excuses from her father like: "My child has to eat," and: Was Stoffregen saying he wanted the air base canteen to change their hours? Cresspahl had heard only vaguely about Stoffregen's courtship of Lisbeth, since it would have upset him; Stoffregen took Cresspahl's notes as deeply mocking. Stoffregen harangued Cresspahl's child in a way he secretly thought of as "cutting," and brought up Cresspahl's demands for "special treatment," for *an extra sausage*, in such sincere outrage that the child actually had a fleeting vision of a fat, lightly browned sausage. You can't listen to Stoffregen when he's like that. Maybe that's how a person looks when tasting something extra special. Conduct (in mawkish fury): B.

The discipline Gefeller imposed was consistent and predictable. In the spring of 1943, a farmer complained about a boy who'd supposedly startled his horses. Gefeller took the trouble to interrupt Stoffregen's class. The boy was one who'd had to repeat several grades, who was bigger than the others and scared of school. Gefeller had him step forward. He tried to defend himself against the principal's tirade. The farmer's horses had bolted on their own, probably because they saw the boy's span approaching. The complaint, though, was that he had tickled their ears with stinging nettles. Because of his lie, the boy had to pull down his pants and stand there in front of the whole class in his hand-me-down farmer's long underpants. Then Gefeller took the boy in one hand and started beating him with the cane in his other, bellowing the whole time about crimes against the German People's agriculture, and about prison. Since the boy was strong from working in the fields he could twist and turn, pulling Gefeller in a circle around him, all the while wailing as though the blows from the cane were hurting him. Gesine Cresspahl knew full well that she was about to do something dangerous, but she couldn't stop herself—during the next recess in the schoolyard she spat on the ground at the principal's feet. That's how much she trusted in Cresspahl's protection. Conduct: D.

After she'd learned all this, Cresspahl sent her to the Gneez girls' high school. She didn't mind spending every day alone, with twice-daily train rides, as long as she no longer had to go to school in Jerichow.

As far as Gefeller and Stoffregen were concerned, those grades in Conduct should have sent her straight to a special school—better yet, the Rauhes

Haus institution for boys in Hamburg. Dr. Kliefoth, though, a bearer of High and Highest distinctions with his dissertation on the French word *aller*, a prince in the kingdom of the Gneez inspector of schools, swore another oath: that the child was well-behaved.

March 22, 1968   Friday

"ARMY HELPS POLICE LEARN ABOUT RIOTS
By Homer Bigart, Special to The New York Times
Fort Gordon, GA., March 20

On a piney knoll some 60 city and state policemen and National Guard officers gathered yesterday to watch the testing of 'nonlethal agents' that may be used this summer to disperse riotous mobs in the nation's cities.

It was unseasonably warm, a lazy, hazy Georgia day more conducive to spring fever than to incendiary design.

Robins sang, coffee and cookies were served and the post band played 'The Stars and Stripes Forever' as the sixth class of the Civil Disobedience Orientation Course climbed out of an Army bus to begin a 20-hour course on the anatomy of a riot.

This was the setting for a weekly exercise at the Army's riot control school, an institution hurriedly conceived a few months ago to teach the grim lessons derived from the Detroit and Newark riots, and from other racial disorders of last summer.

Army Manual Revised

Each week since early February, a new class of police officers, guardsmen and occasional Secret Service or Federal Bureau of Investigation agents has completed the course, directed by the Army's Military Police School....

Deadly serious, yesterday's class sat in a covered stand and awaited the demonstration. Out front of the spectators, down a gentle, sandy slope at ranges of 50, 100 and 150 yards were clumps of black silhouettes, representing mobs.

These 'mobs' were to be assaulted with tear gas hurled at them by foot troops or sprayed on them from a helicopter.

First, the members of the class saw a squad of military policemen approach the nearest mob under a protective smoke screen. The squad, an eerie gas-masked apparition, emerged suddenly from the smoke to confront their assailants.

Next, the M.P.'s shot off smoke grenades designed, the instructor explained, for signaling or perhaps just to determine wind direction. The grenades came in reds, greens, yellows and violets. Shot off together, their smoke combined in a bilious psychedelic cloud.

Wind Direction Vital

Wind direction was important, and many in the audience kept a nervous eye on the weather vane, knowing that two types of tear gas, so-called CS and CN, would be demonstrated next. It was recalled that on a previous occasion the stands had emptied suddenly when an errant wind sent a cloud of gas billowing up the slope.

CS is the type of tear gas now favored by the Army. It is more devastating on a mob than the gentler CN used by the civilian police.

CS, as described by the Army, 'causes an extreme burning sensation, a copious flow of tears, coughing, labored breathing and tightness of the chest, involuntary closing of the eyes, stinging on the moist skin, and sinus and nasal drip.' Nausea and mild vomiting may occur if a heavy concentration is used. . . .

The high point of the demonstration came when a helicopter swooped over the range, emitting a white cloud of gas that was forced down on the mobs by the downdraft of the rotor blades.

Tomorrow, the class attends another outdoor show, this one involving a simulated battle between militant civil rights demonstrators and the National Guardsmen. Both the rioters and the Guardsmen are enacted by the Army's 503rd Military Police Battalion, one of the units that defended the Pentagon against the peace marchers last October.

The clash is staged in a Hollywood type mockup of a community called Riotsville [*Aufstandsstadt*], replete with the normal targets of a looting mob—a liquor store, a television and appliance shop, a sporting goods store that sells guns, and a drugstore.

'Baby,' a firebrand militant portrayed by a 22-year-old Negro sergeant named Bob Franklin, harangues a crowd, charging police brutality. The crowd waves signs denouncing war. One sign reads, 'We Shall Overcome.' Bricks and rocks made out of rubber, but hefty enough to be realistic, are thrown at the 'Mayor' when he tries to placate the mob.

But here comes the National Guard. Using tear gas, bayonets, an armored personnel carrier, and classic antiriot tactics, the troops prevail. 'Baby' is seized and taken off in the armored car, a prisoner.

The class spends the rest of the study hours in a classroom dominated by a huge table model of a city that presents in miniature not only a slum area but also a downtown district with 'skyscrapers,' an industrial center, a port area, hospitals, schools, a city hall and critical facilities such as power stations.

The class studies problems relating to the defense of these installations, the containment of mobs and the detention of prisoners....

The course examines just about every conceivable device that might be used by rioters, including sewers and underground storm drains.

An instructor warns his class: 'When troops are on a slope or at the bottom of it, dangerous objects can be directed at them such as vehicles, trolleycars, carts, barrels, rocks, liquids and so forth.

'On level ground wheeled vehicles can be driven under their power toward troops, but the drivers can jump out before the vehicles reach the target. This target may be used for breaching roadblocks and barricades.

'In using fire, mobs may set fire to buildings and motor vehicles to block the advance of troops, to create confusion and diversion or to achieve goals of property destruction, looting and sniping.

'Mobs may flood an area with gasoline or oil and ignite it as troops advance into the area.

'They may pour gasoline or oil down a slope toward the troops or drop it from buildings and ignite it.

'They may place charges of dynamite in a building, timed to explode as troops or vehicles are opposite the building, or be exploded ahead of the troops so that the rubble blocks the street.

'They may drive dogs or other animals with explosives attached to their bodies toward the troops. The charges may be exploded by remote control, fuses or a time device.'

Troops must be trained to ignore taunts, the instructor says. Troops, he says, 'must be emotionally prepared for weird mob actions, such as members of the mob screaming and rushing toward them, tearing off their own clothes or deliberately injuring or maiming themselves.'

But the need for stringent fire discipline is stressed. Only that force

necessary to control the situation is to be exercised 'in consonance with
our democratic way of life and military teachings.'

The revised Army manual expected April 1 will contain new sections
on the control of arson and looting."

© The New York Times

March 23, 1968 Saturday
Every additional soldier that President Johnson sends to Vietnam costs
the national budget between $20,000 and $40,000. (The family of a killed
soldier receives a $300 allowance for funeral costs; that's what an army
funeral costs.)

Now it's in *Pravda*, too, that students in Poland have been disorderly
for the last two weeks. Now it's true in the Soviet Union too. So true, that
"anti-Soviet agitators" are said to be behind the disturbances.

Antonín Novotný, since his party doesn't want to touch him, has resigned. (His son has resigned as well, if only from a sinecure.) The Communist Party's presidium estimates the number of victims of the Stalinist
judiciary system between 1952 and 1964 as 30,000.

Today Mrs. Cresspahl was where the men of America live.

It was one of the bars D. E. calls "his," this one on Third Avenue, Irish
by name and by nature, and a sign had recently been hung in the window
expressly inviting ladies to visit the establishment. It was hanging on a
dainty little chain, written in black and gold, elegant and old-fashioned,
and it means that business from male clients tails off at around seven o'clock
and has to be pepped up by admitting prostitutes; unaccompanied women
are welcome as well. That's why D. E. said, the moment we sat down: You
know my wife, Wes.

Can you forgive my letter to Stockholm, D. E.?
Let's not talk about it, Gesine.
It was self-defense, but I was just lashing out blind.
All is forgiven. Let's pretend we're married for Wes.

– What a pleasure Professor to meet your wife as well congratulations:

Wes said in one breath, carelessly, without even bothering to look at her. He is the boss of two bartenders behind the forty-foot bar, the man of the house with a householder's rights, but he does all the work himself—serves the ten or more customers sitting in front of him, each one waiting for his very own personal conversation with Wes. His diplomatic talents also extend to pouring and refilling the right drink for his silent customers, unasked; never failing to hear a goodbye; and, lastly, keeping spaces free for friends who are stuck in another zone with strangers until Wes summons them over with a significantly raised finger. In addition, he is a private bank—cashing customers' checks, guaranteeing personal loans, holding on to money won in bets, all without a fee. Wes is a registration office who knows that a missing person is staying in Galway or Lisbon and who gives or withholds information following his own unerring judgment, just as he imperturbably says into the telephone perpetually shrieking for attention: Your husband's not here—but not before having held out the receiver to the hunted spouse and waiting for his desperate shake of the head. Once Wes has walked his beat between the customers and the seventy bottles twice, he has woven a thick net of handshakes, looks, and conversations. Today, he scrutinized the lady next to D. E., sometimes openly, before finally deciding to assume that the professor wasn't pulling his leg.

Wes is a big strong man of around fifty with an almost expressionless firm mouth and gray eyes. All his looks are silent examinations, and the secret to his enormous revenue might be that a man may want to lose his wife's respect but doesn't want to lose Wes's. Wes doesn't show much of his face, keeping his eyes on his work with the glasses, bottles, strainers, sinks, and when he has to combine two substances by shaking, he stands off to the side so that he can be seen in profile, a serious man carrying out a fixed ritual. His hair is in tight curls, like Cresspahl's, only strawberry blond instead of gray, and thanks to his distant way of holding his head, his fixated listening, the image of my father in memory has now lost a little bit more of its sharpness.

Wes filled D. E.'s glass and solemnly informed him, so as to do what must be done: I like your wife, Ericksen. Looked at the lady out of the corner of his eye, to see if she was insulted or anything, and accepted, serious and satisfied, D. E.'s answer: So do I, Wes.

And now D. E. got his very own personal conversation with Wes for the evening. During it, Wes prepared drinks for other people, took one customer's money, put coins back down on the bar in front of him, wiped the counter, stacked glasses in an artful construction next to the cash register, but it was D. E.'s moment and the other customers pretended they weren't listening.

    – I like your wife, Ericksen.
    – So do I, Wes.
    – The Aer Lingus thing is on again.
    – I could use a ticket in August. For one giant, same as usual?
    – One giant, no extra charge. Not that I want you to think I don't like your wife.
    – You know what you're doing, and thinking, and feeling.
    – It's a free country.
    – Once you pay for it. *See you later, alligator.*
    – *In a while, crocodile.*

D. E. didn't talk much. He greeted people he knew with a measured raise of his glass, looked around, patiently took auricular confession from a drunk next to him, made sure with occasional glances that I was appreciating his enjoyment, and invited me to enjoy myself too.

In this home away from home, men and women aren't judged by the color of their skin. If someone doesn't bother the people next to him, if he's looking for a little relaxation from the drink and not to get wasted, has money to pay with and maybe a little inside information about the horse races too—that's enough. In that case he is an ordinary guy, and welcome. Here a man's a man: a white rowdy will be thrown out onto the street while a calm black devotee of firewater will be addressed respectfully as: Sir.

One of the men thought I was one of the women here to earn money. – Are you a stewardess, or something? he said. – I mean, because of that, that winged wheel on your pack of cigarettes. That was why, I thought: he said, then caught Wes's disgusted headshake, felt bitterly reprimanded, took his money, and tamely departed.

The men here treat each other with consideration, thoughtfully, even affectionately. One is having problems with his eyeglasses. Can't see well.

Wes goes over and hands him a napkin. Makes a wiping movement of the hand. He doesn't want to get involved in another man's private business, of course. The man wipes his glasses, gratefully. Gives the napkin back, exhaling. If it weren't for you, Wes.

Another customer has just gotten a refill of his Canadian stuff. There's a bottle of soda water next to his glass. He could pour it in himself. – Mix it? Wes says. He who is heavy laden should be spared at least that labor.

One fat little double-chinned ventriloquist's dummy answers the question of how it's going with: I feel like I'm going nuts. Wes answers, carefully tipping the full measuring glass over the rocks: You look that way too. This is what the sad fat man wanted. At least there's one person in the world who understands him. He repeats: I'm bout ready for the funny farm, that place in Nutville where they grind down all the rough edges. Now he really does look like a hurt child, overwhelmed, about to start crying. Wes has just leaned forward with a sympathetic look on his face but now he barks at him, callous and rational: Be sure to leave me your address, then, in case I ever want to visit. Because Wes has things to do: now he has to extricate a tiny onion from a narrow jar with the point of a little knife (– Oh just use your fingers: says the customer, who couldn't care less); now he suddenly has to pick up an ice cube and throw it bull's-eye into the cash register of the western zone twenty feet away, and George is astounded, and the customers entertained; Wes is busy. Someone has knocked over a soda bottle by accident. Wes picks up the half-full bottle, holds it high above the bar, and calmly pours the rest out. – Is that how you wanted it? Now the sad little man feels better. – You know what, maybe I'll get a round-trip ticket after all: he says.

Quiet conversations, relaxed. Not a word about the war. A warm bustling night on the street outside the windows. As if we were at peace.

I come here every so often to enjoy myself, Gesine. You should try it some-time.

I am trying. I am trying.

March 24, 1968 Sunday

The East German Communists have twice refused an invitation from Prague, as though that would help soothe their concerns that democratization in Czechoslovakia might play into the hands of West German capitalism. Alexander Dubček didn't act like a stubborn child; he boarded a train to Dresden and tried to explain things to his comrades. They have already reached the point of confiscating newspapers from their Socialist brotherland.

In the fall of 1942,

the von Bobziens near Jerichow no longer had any trouble keeping unauthorized walkers out of the Countess Woods. Two men had hanged themselves on trees there, with money in their pockets.

the Reich minister of propaganda, Joseph Goebbels, called the wartime Winter Relief effort a "unique ledger of German Socialism," but *The Lübeck News* was full of an unusual number of for-sale and trade-wanted ads. Böhnhase the tobacconist was picked up in Jerichow and taken in because he'd sold products for payment in kind. Seven years prison.

almost every villa behind the Rande embankment was expropriated, confiscated, a third of them rebuilt. "Air force residential needs war-critical." Now the officers were trying to burn in their stoves the driftwood they had so zealously collected on the beach that summer. The wood stank, refused to burn, went smokily out. The officers, who prided themselves on their country know-how, had neglected to let the rain wash the salt out of the wood.

The Reich governor of Mecklenburg, in a public proclamation, warned against spreading rumors about events that took place during the bombardment of "a" Mecklenburg city. And so the carousel of stories about looting and corpse-robbing went around faster.

Leslie Danzmann was now living in one of the villas on the Rande embankment, as a "housekeeper." She was left almost completely alone, since the owner had his own phone to attend to in the Air Force Research Office in Berlin and traveled to the Mecklenburg Baltic coast only now and then, on weekends. Cresspahl was a guest at the villa on these occasions, and not a guest of Leslie Danzmann's. He brought the child along, and Danzmann darned the child's clothes back into shape while Cresspahl sat and drank with her employer, Fritz, in the study. She saw nothing but the bottles left late at night after the meetings were over.

The serial novel in *The Lübeck News* was called *G.P.U.*, after the Soviet secret police—

Grauen (horror)
Panik (panic)
Untergang (downfall)—

and the double eagle atop of the front page was now even more stylized, perched to the left of the lettering in its new blocky typeface, and carrying the same shield but now it bore a swastika in place of the old coat of arms.

Leslie Danzmann's Fritz might be unassailable in Berlin, but he couldn't help her in Mecklenburg. Since she had a high-school diploma she was conscripted into the Gneez Labor Office, not the munitions factory. It took almost an hour to get from the Baltic to Gneez, along with the women from the countryside working in the arms industry. And they still had children, the house, and the barn to take care of at night after work; she could take her shoes off and put her feet up. Yet this was the most lethargic and exhausted period of her life. She was not used to working.

The newsreels were offering a new service. If someone recognized their fallen son in the reports from the front, they could order a still, as perhaps the last photograph of the soldier in question. All they had to do was precisely describe the scene from the film, or even the scenes before and after it. This service applied only for the dead. Horst Papenbrock, fallen near Stalingrad, had not been seen in any newsreels.

His brother, Robert, was stationed in the Soviet Union as a so-called *Sonderführer*, a "special unit commander." From there he'd sent a girl to the Papenbrocks—twenty-two, blond, and tall—for his parents to look after for him in Jerichow. Louise treated her like a maid. ("On August 12, the birthday of the mother of our Führer, the Medal of German Mothers will be bestowed." That was how Edith had been forced to get married. Edith was gone from the Papenbrock house.) The Russian girl was named Slata. She spoke enough German to do the shopping in Jerichow. She didn't act like a prisoner of war, and no one could tell what the Papenbrocks were up to this time, so people were polite to her, even friendly. The annoying thing was that she accepted this as her due.

Cresspahl was approached on the subject of this future Russian sister-in-law. She reminded him of Hilde Paepcke, and not only because she wore her hair in a head scarf the same way, albeit a white one, and he tried to speak in her favor. But more often he talked about how a *Sonderführer* might mean this or it might mean that, but if you went by the Dutch word, *zonder*, it meant just: "without" or: "ain't nothin."

On Monday, November 2, 1942, the clocks had to be turned back an hour.

Dr. Kliefoth was waylaid while walking to the Jerichow train station. District Leader Swantenius found it improper that a certain someone was not in the party and that in the end it was he, Swantenius, who would be held responsible. The vague and scanty news from Stalingrad was depressing him, and he mentioned the eastern front reproachfully.

What, you were on the eastern front?
It's just that I no longer have a full set of teeth in my head, otherwise I'd be doing my bit in Italy now.
Hmm. All right then. Well if someone like you doesn't want to join the party.
No time.
All we've got joining the party are the riffraff.

In those days, in the place for "War Decorations" on questionnaires, Kliefoth would write: Iron Cross 1st Cl. & 2nd Cl., WWI; Iron Cross 1st Cl. & 2nd Cl., WWII; "etc.," because he'd run out of space. "The things you pick up in two wars."

Leslie Danzmann in the Gneez Labor Office was supposed to advise the foreign forced-labor women, and she was scared of the *Black Deffil*. This "Black Devil" was a Yugoslavian woman who owed her nickname to her wild dark eyes and her dangerously insistent criticisms of the Mecklenburgers. The men were more afraid of her than the women. This Dunya didn't see why she had to live abroad and work there too. She stayed in a job for four weeks, sometimes six, but didn't let anyone talk sharply to her or restrict what she ate, and if a request was expressed to her as an order, she would dash whatever she was holding onto the floor. Then Leslie would have to find her a new position, and she was good-natured enough to be scared of Dunya's idle threats to have her friends beat Leslie up. She had such thoroughgoing contempt for the Germans that she didn't even try to learn their language.

Leslie Danzmann occasionally managed to get the head of the Labor Office to give her travel permits, not filled out. She wondered why Cresspahl wanted to travel by train on so many weekends. Still, Leslie liked to do her friends favors.

In the death notices from the front it didn't always say that a young man "gave his life in faithful performance of his duty to the Führer and the Reich"; sometimes it was that he lost it, or at least "found a hero's death in the highest fulfillment of a soldier's duty"—found it, like something he was looking for.

The air force had had Cresspahl build a new workshop at the airfield, pitiful compared to the one he had lost but enough to assemble the "dispatch boxes" from knotless pine and the beechwood ammo boxes, 25 mm thick minimum. Since Cresspahl had the stamp of the airfield commander on his applications, the Hamburg-Altona district guild office occasionally granted him an iron permit. Iron permits authorized the bearer to order frames for machines. By that point a lot of the carpenters in Gneez had to make do with wooden frames. When he could do it without attracting attention, Cresspahl would pass along an iron permit to Böttcher. He had gotten a metal saw for making box and case linings and a disk sander.

The head of the Gneez Gestapo branch, he doesn't need a name, claimed to have gotten home one night and found his wife murdered with an ax, and he started a panicky investigation—targeting himself, Herbert Vick thought. Sergeant Vick, of the criminal police (not the Gestapo), drove around the Gneez countryside questioning people in his menacing way, in Jerichow too. ("National Socialism must remain pure!") Had anyone seen a girl at around two a.m. on the night of the crime, standing in the alley, wailing? Had anyone seen, through a gap in the curtain (charges already being prepared for violating the blackout law), two men and a lady talking at the window table in Café Heidebrecht? Did anyone have any information about the motorcycle found totaled the next morning outside the police station? Who had invited a member of the air force into a car at the approach of a police patrol and driven him off without turning on the headlights? Here Herbert Vick did manage to purify his National Socialism. The head of the Gneez Gestapo branch shot himself in the head two and a half years earlier than his colleagues.

Article One of the Mecklenburg Constitution used to go like this: *Everythin stays the way it is.*

How many more times.

What the member nations of the Warsaw Pact expressed to one another in Dresden was their shared belief that the proletariat and the working people of Czechoslovakia "would ensure further progress of Socialist construction in the country."

How many more times will hope lay foundations of strictly rational stone before erecting with irrational walls the room where disappointment will later live so comfortably. Why doesn't repetition make it fireproof.

Children like repetition, precisely because it's not perfect. The new is not yet the same.

They are urgently expected, and they desperately want, to learn sameness: how to manage a spoon, a face, a life, the way grown-ups do, who laugh at the child's deviations, which promise the existence of possibilities besides repetition.

The woman who puts the kettle on the stove in the morning is Papenbrock's daughter, not me. The person straightening up an apartment in New York at night is Cresspahl from thirty years past, and not him either but the discipline of grandfathers across the centuries, and not them either but the social arrangements forced upon them.

Deviations feel refreshing, almost precious: someone's apparent independence or idiosyncrasy; the gentle shock when an elevator in Copenhagen needs to be operated differently than the elevators in New York; the first year in a foreign language.

March 25, 1968, is a day in spring—in spring since 1938.

Cresspahl, in a quotation of his English employers, had his child do things: in less than no time! Marie is told, with the help of a quotation from British employers: You've done this, forgotten that, in less than no time. And the norm is repeated.

Justification: Unconsciously ingrained norms save time.

Repetition spares consciousness, starves it.

Living and forgetting a whole day—forgetfully reinserting oneself into a long since written-off time, the Monday feeling of working people seven days ago and seven times seven days and seven times that.

Repetition may be enough to inculcate certain principles—Socialism, capitalism, order, chaos—but to sustain them takes authority. They persist for the sake of the father; to please him; out of fear of school or other agents of society that threaten expulsion for disobedience.

What remained of this day was not its evening but the Friday evening during which a plane tree in Riverside Park had been cut down and sawed to pieces, branch by branch. The motor sounded like a small motorcycle, enough for a dream escape in a secret trip along the river in the fog. But now there's a place missing: The tree, and not the tree but its repetition.

How many more times will I be carried through the tunnels dug into the stone beneath the city of New York for its subways and arrive between the forest of pitprops at the station and intersection of Ninety-Sixth Street and Broadway?

When will Marie be caught and trapped in repetition?

How many more times?

March 26, 1968   Tuesday

De Rosny, the ideal man for these times.

The East Germans and the Soviets have suggested extending a substantial credit to the new Czechoslovakia, so that the West Germans can't give it—a suggestion in the form of an ultimatum.

De Rosny, on the phone, his vocal cords perfectly relaxed: Sounds like good news to me! Whose nose is that skin off of, Mrs. Cresspahl? We'll just keep going!

It is not exactly he who does the keeping going.

He can set a company's policy in simple terms: He sees it from above.

His first line of defense is: The West Germans tried to demand that the Czechoslovaks reopen diplomatic relations in exchange for their hard cash. Well, de Rosny is de Rosny and all relations with him are diplomatic in nature.

His main line of attack is: The ČSSR needs money from the zone of the dollar, not the soft money of the Council for Mutual Economic Assistance. In this realm, he is the Palatine Prince. Nothing is likely to happen against his will.

Sleeps well. Is instantaneously present again upon waking, with no desire for the protective miles of the dream. For him, sleep is the pause between battles, dreams the defects he makes sure are repaired. He drops himself into the day as though into cold water, uncomplaining. Enjoys the massage. Radiates friendliness, so that his staff will bounce it back to him. Enjoys his breakfast, alone with the plans that have wonderfully developed and ramified and blossomed in his sleep.

Anticipation makes him impatient. He could get from Connecticut to New York City by helicopter!—were it not a statistical risk for a life like his. A game like his life.

He knows about other ways of life. Alone in the car with his man Arthur, he enjoys his contact with Arthur's way of life, and the tall black man, dignified with the practiced gestures of service and gradual aging, tells his boss about his wife's health problems, children's academic progress and setbacks, neighbors' parties and conflicts. De Rosny sits in his box seat, watching the children play far below.

Arthur has saved for more than ten years and hoped that de Rosny would pay him in something other than his salary and health insurance. Then he asked for one single hot stock tip.

De Rosny tells the story complacently. His chauffeur approaches him, thinking him pleasantly disposed, and asks him about money left lying on the street. A de Rosny doesn't bend down to pick up such money. (He doesn't talk about money, he talks with money.)

When the story doesn't get quite as much of a laugh as usual, he adds: Anyway, he gave Arthur a raise, instead of a hot tip. The afterthought comes out so obviously belated and contrived; a fact might have made it there faster.

Why shouldn't de Rosny supply the Soviets *for* the ČSSR? He has his secrets too, rarely discussed with enemies, like elegant schoolboy schemes.

Arthur's work might be a game of Parcheesi (Now Don't Get Mad); de Rosny's subordinates' might be chess; his own is probably more like poker but with incomparably higher stakes.

So he sits down and loses thousands at a time—he's not in a position to get mad. His repetitions are experience, as he sees it; he suffers setbacks to make room for the triumphs. Both, for him, are the feeling of being alive.

He doesn't need to worry about manners: they were instilled in him by family tradition, private schools, universities. The machine that takes care of his life automatically, imperceptibly supplies him with money (cash and symbolic), clothes as convention requires, apartments in world capitals, houses on coasts. Since he's doing it, what he does is right. His place in the restaurants of the world is undisputed, and he sits there alert beneath his friendly demeanor, bored beneath his epicurean mask, waiting. The moment a pastime invades his privacy, he breaks it off.

Among equals, he is not so equal. De Rosny, of the de Rosnys. First among second chief executives, to keep his hands free. Counts his victories, only then his dollars. Not vulnerable. Dangerous. Generous.

Terrible, what happened with his wife.

Untouchable. Sympathy prohibited. Unapproachable even that way.

When he spends a night in the city, it's to work.

Chooses secretaries for their unobtrusiveness. So they won't bother him.

Firm in his belief that where he has given orders, something happens.

Leaves his exterior to others' doubts whether his handicap refers to golf or bluffing; uses his own doubts not for self-reflection and enlightenment but to fall asleep in amusing fashion.

Sleeps well. Knows how to wait.

March 27, 1968 Wednesday

When Stalingrad fell back into Soviet hands, Wilhelm Böttcher had his son home on leave: the same Klaus who had been trying since 1934 to escape from the paternal woodworking shop—first into the Hitler Youth, then into the Reich Labor Service, until finally in April 1939 the army relented and "took" him. In February 1943 he came back, twenty-two years old, slept for three days, and on the fourth spent an evening in the City of Hamburg Hotel in Gneez with Dr. Weidling, one of the teachers to whom he owed his defeat in the Gneez high school. Now the two men were on

equal terms. True, Weidling was there as a Tank Corps captain from somewhere or another, but he was not allowed do discuss his counterespionage
assignments; his student had pinned to his tunic an Iron Cross 1st Class,
Wound Badge, Attack Badge, and all the other hardware so necessary to
his male pride. Only five years ago, Klaus Böttcher had been too skinny,
runty, and weak-lipped for his soldierly bearing; now it fit him like a glove.
Later that evening Dr. Kliefoth joined them, another of little Klausie's
former enemies, but all Kliefoth could tell Cresspahl was that Klaus
Böttcher the clever talker had kept quiet, using the two older men merely
as drinking companions and to get the name of a doctor who could extend
his leave.

Whenever Klaus had run into Cresspahl on the street, he'd stopped
him and reeled off stories in a shrewd, self-satisfied way. They were stories
about things that had taken place far away from Gneez, from the paternal
hearth. Cresspahl thought of his colleague's son as one of those people who
wouldn't dig potatoes in the middle of a field but preferred two rows along
the edge so that they'd have something to look at while they worked and
would be distracted visually at least. He no longer thought the kid was
trying to pick up unguarded remarks, just that he liked flexible back-and-
forth situations that allowed him to make amusing suggestions, and liked
to talk about them. Cresspahl listened to him now as a harmless, even
mildly amusing ne'er-do-well.

In 1938, in the Labor Service, Klaus was in danger of having to do the
same work as everyone else. But he'd escaped needing even to learn how
to hold a shovel—when no one else said they were a tradesman he reported
for carpentry duty and from then on lived as a free man. The quartermaster needed to replace thirty stools his predecessor had burned or sold, and
must have regarded Labor Serviceman Böttcher as a miracle worker. Undeterred by the absence of wood, Böttcher stole a load of railroad ties from
the Schwerin–Ludwigslust line, sawed them up in a little woodworking
shop twenty miles away, and built the quartermaster his thirty stools, plus
twenty for his own inventory, to give himself greater flexibility in his business dealings. That was how he became the head of the carpentry division,
could get his friends who had figured out Klausie's strategy to place orders
with him, and could get out to Neustadt-Glewe whenever he wanted.
– That's probably not how it was in your day?: Klaus Böttcher had said, in

his provoking way, meant to solicit from Cresspahl not annoyance but appreciation.

How someone like Klaus Böttcher lived in 1940, in Bromberg, Poland: Avoiding ethnically German girls whose fathers worked in the party. He found the German civilians quite unappealing on the whole: "down and outs" living in Jewish villas, arms traffickers, confiscation profiteers, currency speculators. Instead, Klaus—

What? Sounds like a vacation, Klaus.

You got that right, Mr. Cresspahl. 'Cept that there was summer school, you know?

No.

Learning Russian, in this officer-level school there.

Whaddaya want with Russian, Klaus!

Cause it's off against the Russians next! Next year.

What's your division's insignia again?

Yellow braid on the right shoulder. Nothin special, Mr. Cresspahl.

—he went out at night with a Polish girl, showed up every morning in the barracks at six sharp, responsible for training and instruction. It was easy with Pervitin. (– "Pervitin"?: Cresspahl asked.) The leave regulations had been relaxed since the regiment was from Schneidemühl and the men's names were enough to identify them as relatives of the locals. Still the men had to go out in pairs and no Poles were allowed on the street after ten. So Klaus got his girl a military coat and cap and strolled through town at night with her like that. Army personnel had to keep their weapons with them even in restaurants; Klaus gave his girl a little lady's pistol so she could defend herself against any ethnic Germans who gave her a hard time. He celebrated Christmas with the girl's friends and taught them the German way: it's important to have a good time, but no boozing under the Christmas tree. Then Klaus was ordered to report to the commander. On his desk lay Klaus's letters, photos, all taken from the Polish girl. The first lieutenant knew Klaus from their training together, from nights in the Residenz Café in Schwerin, called him by his first name, bawled him out for therapeutic purposes when Klaus tried to ask about the girl. – So now are you going to denounce me for racial defilement?: Klaus had ended by asking Cresspahl, in his sly, amused, almost desperate way. – If only I knew if she's still alive!: Klaus had said, for once not the man of the world, not proud of his deeds, not sure of his life plans.

The second-to-last day of his leave, Klaus had one more story to tell about his life. People were sitting in Böttcher's parlor, ill at ease. Every person there may have known the secrets they themselves shared with Böttcher but not why all the other people were there. But first they had to discuss things like hairdressers no longer being forbidden to give perms. It was true, but would it last?

Cresspahl and Kliefoth were the only ones there from Jerichow. The awkwardness was due not only to the presence of a party member from the Gneez tax office but also to Klaus's uncertain, hesitant manner. He sat hunched between his parents on the sofa, not a hint of the staunch upright staff sergeant but a boy who really wanted a longer vacation. Klaus brushed his hair back from his forehead, shook it forward again, tried to keep his distance from the group with gruff "No, no"s and strange looks, until Mrs. Böttcher walked over to the sideboard, opened the liquor compartment, and put the bottle of kümmel in front of her own cherished boy, to pour at will. – *If I cant go to sleep then I wanna know why*: she said.

> *I cant tell you anything. Theyll shoot me.*
> *Klaas,* dear, we're your parents. *Thats Kliefoth, thats Cresspahl—*
> *Dont be mad, I cant.*
> *Come now, Böttcher!* Pretend we're in school.
> *Allright. Allright. We were drivers, a bunch of us, fifty or so. Supposed to bring 180 Belgian cart horses from Bialystok to Smolensk, on foot, to the horse depot. Twelve miles a day. At night we put the horses into stables, or sometimes where people lived. There wasn't enough room in there for the animals, the drivers wouldn't go in with them. The horses would get scared and start kicking. And me in charge. What a shitshow.*
> *Klaas.*
> *The SS?*
> *Well there you have it, Mr. Kliefoth. The SS aren't hated, I wouldn't say that, but they fight to the last man, you have to give em that. But theyre Nazi, they should be the first to bleed. That doesn't bother us. Sometimes during an enemy approach I would park a couple trucks across the road, set em on*

fire, and then, with a badge I'd nicked from the MPs on my camouflage coat,
lead the SS Death's Head division right to the Russians.

> *You deserted, Klaas.*

Otherwise I wouldnt be sitting here!

> *You did the right thing.*

Um—

> *Go ahead,* my boy.

Well, I was wounded.

> *Oh, God! You were wounded. Klaas.*

Now stop it. I was in the military hospital in Schaulen, and I looked out
the window. There was a fence around something, shanties and whatever was
left of a town. They were keeping civilian prisoners in there. Dressed in kind
of rags.

> *What did the SS do to them?*

Nothin, Mom. *Not while I was looking.*

> *And then?*

Yeah, Dad, who wants to watch something like that!

> *Aha.*

You see what I mean.

Well say it.

Well in Smolensk we were immediately confined to barracks. No going
out. I didn't think they meant me too, as the guy in charge. So I went for a
walk outside of town with a friend—

> *Klaus!*

We didn't find what we were looking for! We found a heap of dead bodies
in a forest on the edge of town. Five, six feet high. Like this. Shoulder high.
Civilians. Stacked up, like for burning.

> *Partisans. Saboteurs.*

Children, Herr Kliefoth?

> *No, Klaus, no.*

Children. Women too. Like they'd been coming home from work. From
shopping.

> *You got a photo, Klaus?*

We were about to take one when a squad turned up, MPs, took us to the
SS. They were going to shoot us on the spot.

> *How can you put yourself in danger like that, Klaus!*

The danger was already there before we got there. Anyway. Report on the double. Marching orders. We had to swear.

Swear what, my boy?

That we didn't see it! That it never happened, Mom.

Impossible.

Is it?

How could they let you go on leave then? You're free to tell the whole story.

But the leave's the reward. For swearing it never happened.

Do you believe this, *Herr Kliefoth?*

The SS does things like that.

And not the army?

The army!

Klaus wouldnt have to do something like that?

No.

I can't believe it.

Wouldna helped me either way.

Children?

Children.

But they're Germans, the SS!

You got that right.

The children, they were civilians?

Gimme a break! It wasnt that dark. One of them, one of the girls, just a little bit different and she coulda been Cresspahl's!

Cresspahl, do you believe this?

Yup.

is the day, starting right after lunch break, for Professor Kreslil, the teacher from Budweis, Bohemia, who left his students behind almost twenty years ago and now tries to scrape out a life on the Upper East Side of Manhattan with Czech translations, writing documents in Czech, and giving occasional private lessons in his language. At first he tried to maintain a teacherly air, sitting behind his desk thoroughly prepared, surrounded by teaching material, as though he were responsible for not just one single student but the thirty at a time he once had. With his teacherly trappings it looked like he was trying to prove how indisputably he was earning every penny of his fee. For the old man needed the money. His America wasn't the land of reassuring fairy tales of success; all he needed it to be was somewhere far enough from Czechoslovakia. Where he lives, the Upper East Side, is no longer the closed community of the affluent but an unprotected herd of crumbling four-story buildings on the edge of the German and Hungarian neighborhood. Finally, the rendering of scientific or mechanical processes in another language does not come easily to him, since he used to teach languages, for as long as the Germans and, later, the Czech Communists let him. The moment of giving him the check at the end of each lesson was embarrassing for him, suggesting as it did the instant transformation of his efforts into mere money; yet it was a relief not to be cheated out of his money, and he thanked Mrs. Cresspahl in an old-fashioned, nearly worshipful way. – I am very much obliged to you: he was still saying in late November.

He was the one to turn their Thursday afternoons into social, even friendly occasions. When Mrs. Cresspahl walks in he is incapable of not standing up, walking over to her, making a bow, and kissing her hand; she for her part did not insist on beginning the lesson at once in exchange for her good dollars, so the occasion gradually deteriorated into trial conversations, then real conversations, after the first month taking place in Czech, which was no longer the sole rationale for her visits. Moreover, Professor Kreslil likes to offer a lady elaborate compliments instead of praising her like a schoolchild, however pathetically her throat may have managed to bring out the consonant-heavy syllables. It was Kreslil, in his courtesy, who offered to spare the lady and customer her walk deep into the East Nineties—suggesting walks, accepting invitations to Riverside Drive, and even showing up at the bank, a distinguished elderly gentleman, gaunt in his shabby, loose-hanging clothes, his carefully composed features held strictly in place out of sheer bewilderment at the sight of a sixteenth floor in a bank, until he walked through Mrs. Cresspahl's door with a solemn bow and a grave expression but one that has recently taken to showing signs of fun along with recognition.

It's not because of his increased fee, even though it amounts to two taxi fares per session, which he can pocket almost entirely by taking the bus and subway: the playfulness and complicity his face now offers is due to mutual understanding. His first time in the Lexington Avenue building he said: He had walked past Petschek Bank in Prague so many times, never dreaming that the lords of finance rested their eyes on paintings, or kept their feet cool or warm on tapestry-like rugs, or that their self-image required antique furniture. He spoke without anger, without rebellion, if anything amused, surprised, as if at foolishness. Mrs. Cresspahl tried to deny that she was guilty of, or part of, the splendor of her false environment; Professor Kreslil could not give even this his full and serious attention, and he looked her in the eye with such pleasure, as if wanting to acknowledge only her, not where she is.

You are Slavic, Mrs. Cresspahl. A member of the Obotrite tribes—close relatives.
Maybe that's it, Professor.
You say you are from the German Baltic? But there's no land in the Baltic.
What about Bohemia near the sea?
Still, you're definitely not a German.
I most definitely am, Professor.
Ne. Ne. Smîm se Vás na ně co ptáti?
Prosím.
If you would say "Anatol," I could say "Gesine."
You're older, Professor.
Perhaps then it might be my privilege. I've grown wary of privileges.
Whenever you want, pane Kreslil.

Now, under his supervision, Mrs. Cresspahl no longer reads solemn texts from the nineteenth century but *Študáci a kantoři* by Jaroslav Žák: *Students vs. Teachers: Strategies, Schemes, and Self-Defense,* a 1937 handbook in pseudoscientific style that pretends to give high-school students lessons in how to do battle in a hostile environment. It never ceases to delight Kreslil the teacher that we in Mecklenburg did much the same things as the students of the ČSR described here, from diverting a teacher's attention onto his favorite topic to dealing with snitches, and when it comes to finding equivalent student expressions for school authorities, Professor Kreslil is able to forget himself and try out a German term after all. Questions about the state of battle at the high school in "Meeklenburg" led to answers out of which emerged information about Cresspahl's position as mayor after the war, until gradually parts of our life stories began to intertwine. While I was supposed to be learning the Gothic German script, Anatol Kreslil the high-school teacher was hiding his wife and relatives and self in a village outside Vyšší Brod, near the former border with Austria. The schoolgirl Cresspahl was on vacation in Fischland; that summer, the Kreslils were betrayed to the German occupying forces by his father-in-law's neighbors and lived in hiding from that point on in the suburbs of Prague, with four families, who in Kreslil's stories do not appear as "Czechs" but as Alžběta and Bohumír, Viktorie and Jakub, Jiřina and Mikuláš, Růžena and Emil. While Cresspahl's child lay in her own room in her own bed and listened half asleep to her father's stories of Robin Hood's time on earth, the Kreslils in their hiding place overheard a Jewish neighbor visiting Růžena, wanting to buy with her last money a pair of boots for her five-year-old child's deportation to the extermination camp. When Růžena gave her the boots, knowing the child's destination, the Kreslils no longer wanted to stay with her, they'd rather starve with others, and Mrs. Kreslil died of hunger only a few days before the Allies arrived, and the Cresspahl child was neatly eating around the crusts of her bread first to save the tasty middle for last.

> *It's in the past, Mrs. Cresspahl.*
> *No it isn't.*
> *You hear how I tell you about it. Like something that was.*
> *Yes, something that was.*
> *Let me change the subject to something else, child.*

– Please summarize today's article in the *Times* about Czechoslovakia, Mrs. Cresspahl.

– The country's foreign minister protests to the East German ambassador for interfering in domestic affairs.

– Because.

– The East Germans criticized democratization in Czechoslovakia, for endangering the ties of friendship between the Eastern bloc countries and thus serving West German monopoly capitalism.

– Whereas,

– the Czechoslovak Communist Party newspaper said there was no reason for Czechoslovakia to pursue the same policy toward West Germany as East Germany does.

– Correct.

– Don't you ever think that maybe you could live there again, Professor Kreslil?

– *Ne. Ne.* Never again. Never with the Czechs.

This is what Thursday afternoons are now.

March 29, 1968 Friday

Antonín Novotný is unwilling to personally acknowledge that the party is always right, always, every time. Others might lose but he is unwilling to, and he pushes out of the way a radio newsman's microphone, into which he could have said so.

The new president of the Czech and Slovakian Socialist Republic is considered a friend of the Soviets. Holder of the Czarist St. George Cross, Hero of the Soviet Union, holder of the Order of Lenin, former defense minister, later deputy premier in charge of physical culture and sports until the Stalinist purges demoted him. Then along came Nikita Sergeyevich Khrushchev, asking to see his old friend. Novotný rushed to summon General Ludvík Svoboda from his work on a collective farm, and Khrushchev hugged him and gave him a seat on the presidium at his side.

The naming of Ludvík Svoboda as a candidate for president is seen as an attempt to placate the Soviets, and the Soviets furiously deny that they want to stifle democratization in Czechoslovakia. The only thing that's happening in the ČSSR, in their view, is an "activation of Communist Party organizations and the state administration apparatus," and they appear to be fine with that.

In Memphis, Reverend King marched with three thousand demonstrators, but there were youths who ran away from the protest, smashed windows, and looted stores. The police began using riot sticks and tear gas. A sixteen-year-old is dead.

In the summer of 1943, the Friedenau Niebuhrs wanted to spend their vacation somewhere other than the sluice in Wendisch Burg, namely on the Baltic, near Cresspahl. They asked Cresspahl to find them a place. He thought it was too dangerous in Rande near the Jerichow airfield and found them a place in Rerik. Plus Cresspahl preferred to remain alone, unobserved. In Rerik there was only Antiaircraft Artillery School I (lecturer in the antiaircraft commander training course: First Lieutenant Max Wachtel), and also he'd managed to get the Niebuhrs an air force officer's house for two weeks there, instead of just a hotel room for two adults and two children, including one, Günter Niebuhr, only a couple of months old.

Gesine was sent to Rerik for the second week. This meant trains from Jerichow to Gneez, then to Wismar, then to Neubukow on the Rostock line; from there the postbus did the eight miles to Rerik in half an hour. She wasn't happy about leaving Jerichow and did it only out of obedience. She was also confused by his telling her not to ask older people about "Rerik," instead to say "Alt Gaarz," as the settlement had been known until 1938, when the Nazis elevated it into a town and gave it a new name to recall the lost trading town from which only scattered rubble remained. At the Neubukow train station, right when she boarded the bus, the child asked if they were definitely going to Alt Gaarz, and the driver nodded at her, several times, reassuring, approving. Now this was a well brought up child. He gave her a seat in the front row.

Waiting at the Rerik post office was Klaus Niebuhr, unhappy yet again that this Gesine should be allowed to travel around the world without parents, but too much an expert on Rerik, after a week, not to appoint himself as her guide through a town with straw-roofed farmhouses in the middle, not at all like in Berlin-Friedenau. The church, with its massive spire, on high ground, could be seen from almost everywhere, and still Klaus disparagingly compared it to the church Zum Guten Hirten that he had back home. But he took his time, showed her the dolmens, told her they were locally known as the Giants' Tombs, walked her along the promenade on the shoreline cliff. The land was totally bare under the white sky, treeless. You could look down onto the Salzhaff spit, the roaring surf. To the west, though, was Poel Island, the coastal cliffs of Rande, Jerichow.

As in Jerichow, there were constant air-raid alarms, and Gesine didn't understand these Niebuhrs who felt safe just because the Wustrow peninsula wasn't Berlin. She got up from the table at the first howl of the siren, ready to run into the basement, and even though Klaus's parents had told him that he mustn't make fun of her, she felt their smiles. The Niebuhrs seemed strange to her in other ways too. Peter was acting like he had a hard time calling her by her first name. He treated her with a kind of distant politeness, asked her if she agreed to every plan they made, reprimanded Klaus but not her, as though he had an adult's rights. An unusually tall man, thin everywhere on his body. He had so little flesh on his cheekbones that his lips looked pursed, as if from something sour. Eyes behind dark glass. Played games with the children, but not like the games Alexander Paepcke played; he quickly left them alone and went to wherever his wife was. I didn't know at the time that he had ceased to be indispensable at the ministry and was going to be sent to the eastern front after his vacation. He'd invited Cresspahl's child to join them because he believed in fulfilling his obligations; he would have preferred to spend the time alone with his family. It was the last time. Cresspahl also said after the war that Peter would've defected to the Soviets the first chance he got.

Martha Niebuhr, that summer, was also showing a side of herself no one had ever seen. If you came upon her in the kitchen, you would find her crying. She was always impatient with Klaus, always after him. Klaus would look up, surprised, showing that he too didn't recognize her sometimes; he had reached the point of avoiding her. If she saw him fall down, he didn't care about the pain or the wound, he would only brace himself for his mother's scolding. She looks cheerful in photographs from other years, though—loving, happy, lips half open in anticipation, large dark eyes, head resting on Peter's arm at every opportunity. Gesine was counting the days until her return to Jerichow.

There weren't many. Maybe a rowboat trip across the Salzhaff to the Tessmannsdorf fir woods. Walks to the Bastorf lighthouse maybe, or up Diedrichshäger Hill in the Kühlung ridge. Then came Sunday.

The Sunday-afternoon sirens had been on for three hours. All the grown-ups had emerged from the air-raid shelter into the open, as had the bigger kids, Klaus first. Gesine stayed sitting inside with the baby, Günter, embarrassed because she was excluding herself, stubborn because she was following Cresspahl's rules. Baby Günter was asleep, half naked, breathing hard in the heat. Gesine blew air in his face from time to time. It was a pinched,

laborious face. She was alone with the child in the big, homey basement.
The house belonged to the air force and the shelter was built per German
Industrial Standards. There was a supporting wall under the middle of the
ceiling. Bunk beds fixed to the walls. A murmured voice from a radio
somewhere, giving the grid-square references for the Allied planes' advance.
At the top of the steps leading out was an iron door in a rubber frame, ajar,
and behind it a little anteroom with another airtight door, standing wide
open. This was explained to Gesine as a gas lock. She stood up and went
over to the steps, so that she'd be able to describe the gas lock to Cresspahl
better later. The grown-ups were standing in the garden, including an officer with a telescope. The planes hung in the sky, neat and orderly, like a
net, shining in the sun. Suddenly the officer's voice rang out, shocked and
alarmed. – They're releasing!: Gesine heard. She went back and stood in
the middle of the basement. She saw Klaus Niebuhr fall into the open gas
lock and slip down to the basement floor, strangely slowly. Immediately
after the first impact there was mortar dust filling the air like flour. There
was a hole in one of the side walls of the basement. The lights went out.
Gesine heard the baby screaming, felt her way over to him, and ran back
to the hole in the wall with him, holding the bawling creature up to the
air. She was very deep underground. But they went looking for the children
by the almost completely destroyed gas lock. The detonations had been so
loud that she only realized after a minute that people had been calling for
her, several times. Since she had the baby in her arms, she had to kick Klaus,
still lying on the floor, in the side to wake him up. She was the oldest child.
Then he crawled outside over the slanting surface of rubble, pulling her
after him. Now she had only one arm to hold the baby with. The baby's
head hung back at a horrible angle. She knew that wasn't right. She was
scared because the baby was only whimpering now.

Outside she didn't see all the adults because many of them were lying
on the lawn. The house—Air Force General Pirrmann's—looked intact,
but there were craters in the ground all around it. There were adults lying
in the street too.

No one asked the children questions when the buses came from the
antiaircraft school. They were loaded in, driven to Kühlungsborn, put up
in hotels. There was another alarm that night. This basement was not built
per GIS. She saw the walls full of water pipes, whispered to wake Klaus

Niebuhr up, and slipped through the crowd with him and baby Günter over to some stairs with the night visible at the top. Now she realized that she was scared. The next morning, Cresspahl was in Arendsee (which was now called Kühlungsborn. Arend Lake had been "Aaron Lake" in the years when Jews were still allowed to swim there).

The telegram to Cresspahl had said CHILDREN ALIVE, as if one of them might be missing a leg or something.

That was how Gertrud and Martin Niebuhr got two children they could call their own for ten more years.

That was how Gesine lost a little blue straw hat.

That was how Peter got to stay with his wife, Martha, in a shared coffin in the soil of Wustrow.

The child Gesine was familiar with funerals by that point. She knew all about the bit with the three handfuls of earth thrown onto the coffin.

March 30, 1968 Saturday, South Ferry day

It is now the case in the ČSSR that students can shout for the First Secretary of the Party to come downstairs at midnight, and that Mr. Alexander Dubček will come down to them.

– What are the guarantees that the old days will not be back? was one question asked, and the answer was: You, the young, there is only one path and that is forward, etc.

It is also the case there that the Communist Party newspaper is asking the United States to return 18.4 tons of gold to Czechoslovakia. This is part of the gold that the Germans stole from the country. In 1948, the United States returned 6.1 tons, but it kept the rest to this day because of the American property nationalized when the Communists took power.

On that topic, de Rosny is taking a trip to Washington and paying visits to various government departments not listed in his itinerary, trying to sort things out inconspicuously. But the Communists don't care about the message he's so carefully sent them, they just go public! On Monday he'll ask: Mrs. Cresspahl, is this the Communist mentality or the Czech one.... Explain it to me! and he will put on an expression of enormous curiosity.

But today he can't find us, today Marie has proclaimed a South Ferry day, and we are unreachable aboard the *John F. Kennedy* crossing the smooth New York harbor. The ships look like they're resting at many of the piers even though there's still a backlog of work from an almost eleven-day waterfront strike. Cold waves of air are coming in from the Atlantic, but Marie wants to stand in the wind, swinging thoughtfully by her elbows on the railing. When she sights Staten Island Borough Hall, she looks like she's examining it as meticulously as possible, checking whether the changes in the silhouette of the coast match her usual expectations. And yet she asks about a bygone time a quarter century ago, about a child.

– What were you like as a child, Gesine?

Waiting in the ferry terminal on the Manhattan side, the little glass circles in the doors looked like holes in a prison when the faces of arriving passengers appeared through them. Childhood fears always live on.

– What do you mean you weren't fit for school! she says, indignant, a little disturbed too. Now she'll have a harder time bragging that her mother may not have inherited much but she can still support her family just by selling what she's learned.

– Because I was one of the new fifth graders in the Gustav Adolf Middle School in Gneez, and from a backwater like Jerichow too, it was my job to stand in the hall and run into the classroom with a warning shout whenever the enemy approached, so the whole class would be standing with arm outstretched when the teacher walked in, ready to shout their Heil and their Hitler. This routine was new to me and should have been enough to keep me on my toes if only I'd understood it. Instead I stood daydreaming by the open door and the teacher clamped her hand onto my shoulder and dragged me into the classroom, where blackboard erasers were still flying around or a big question mark was being chalked on the seat of the teacher's chair. I got a thrashing.

– Did it help?

– What? You don't mind that they pulled your mother's pinafore up over her head and beat her mercilessly? You're supposed to respect your mother!

– I've been beaten in school too, without you warning me. And anyway, I'm supposed to love you! And respect you too.

– It helped scare me, but didn't make me reliable. So someone else got that job. They'd given up on me as too stupid.

– Sure, for that! But you were a straight-A student in other things.

– Yes, like Adolf Hitler's biography. They rammed that into our heads so hard that I could crank it out in my sleep. But when it came to anything that required thinking, like fractions—

– Gesine, your math skills are what pays our bills, never mind fractions!

– Marie, on the front wall of the classroom in Jerichow there was the line from his book about the German boys who should be as hard as a product made by Krupp, tough as leather, and something something. Even that I didn't understand. I knew about leather, it wasn't tough. We used to say "Tore off easy as sheepskin" to mean *off like a shot*. I had to console myself with being glad I wasn't a boy. In Gneez, they'd painted in thick brown Gothic script on the wall of the classroom:

> You are the Germany of the future
> and so we want you to be
> the way this Germany of the future
> should and must one day be. —A. H.

Center-aligned too.

– So?

– The thing is, if you have that before your eyes for hours on end, you start thinking about it instead of listening about fractions. Getting your ears boxed didn't help. I got one slap for having forgotten my math notebook again. That one still makes me mad, and, and, I'll never forgive Julie Westphal for it. She never thought to explain to me why we weren't allowed to leave our notebooks home. I had only fear for her, not respect. It wasn't because she got to come from Jerichow to Gneez only due to the shortage of teachers, not on merit. Cresspahl never slapped me, not even for forgetting things. So I spent the class drilling my pinkie into the cap of my pen and enjoying the smell of dried ink. Back then we had to go to the auditorium a lot, stretch out our right arms, and sing the two national anthems; I didn't mind, it used up class time. For an essay I didn't write out what the biology teacher had told us about *Felix communis*, I wrote what I knew about the Cresspahl cats: what they looked like, how many whiskers they had, their moods, where they put the mice, and "the house-cat has 32 teeth." F.

– Stop! I don't think I like that!

– *I* like it.

– Gesine. Were you punctual at least?

– Before long some of the teachers would smile when I arrived, partly because of the elaborate excuses I'd worked out thinking it was the polite thing to do. It wasn't easy. I couldn't even say the train from Jerichow was late, because Lise Wollenberg was on it too and she'd been on time. I got to Gneez on time exactly once, early in fact. Cresspahl had forgotten to change the clocks for daylight saving time, and I took the train to Gneez with a crowd of sleeping men who got off at Gneez Bridge as though in a dream, for the Arado factory. To me they seemed like a hidden army, and I knew for the rest of my life that they go to work unseen, unknown, and yet governments claim to know them. I was on the rough cobblestones outside the school an hour early and got yelled at anyway, this time by the custodian. I got to the City of Hamburg Hotel on time, where Elise Bock would serve me the daily special (without a ration card). I was on time for the trains back to Jerichow. I was often late getting to the air-raid shelter in the basement under the City of Hamburg Hotel. Since the bombing of Hamburg in July 1943 they'd been extra quick with their alarms in Gneez, because of the rocket factory of course, and I ran at personal-best speeds through the streets so that I wouldn't get shoved into a strange basement, always scared of the Hitler Youth kids behind me, screaming and ordering me to stop. Those kids were dangerous.

– Gesine, why did you even care whether or not a bomb got you?

– Out of obedience to Cresspahl. I thought he'd miss me. Forget it, I don't know. What do you mean with a trick question like that?

– You were living like a dog, Gesine. Lunch with strangers, no help with homework, getting up at six, you were only ten!

– That was the life Cresspahl had arranged for me. Had had to arrange for me. And so I didn't mind. Again I'd been asked to choose. Alexandra Paepcke would have liked to go to the Empress Auguste Viktoria School in Stettin with me, not by herself, because after the big bombardment of Stettin the school had been evacuated to Rügen and turned into a rural boarding school. I would have liked to make Alexandra happy; Alexandra was my favorite of all the kids. Cresspahl read me Hilde's letter, looked at me, and had me trapped. So I became a commuting student from Jerichow.

Lunch with Elise Bock wasn't as good as at the airfield canteen, but I did like being a guest in a hotel. Cresspahl did ask about my homework, and not in passing, and I could tell he didn't really like checking over my Latin homework so I'd tell him it was done. That was when he started speaking English with me. To help me. And every morning he sat at the table with the breakfast made, he waited for me, every school day he took me to the station for the 7:08 train, he made my school snack and gave me money too so I could buy a chopped-herring sandwich in Gneez on my own—

– Gesine, you lived like a dog.

– I had it good.

– Gesine, why aren't there photos of you as a child?

– Marie, your grandfather was a tradesman! If his wife had lived, she might have picked up photography from Hilde Paepcke. Even the Papenbrocks would bring in a "professional photographist," Horst Stellmann, and only for special occasions. And Cresspahl didn't need any pictures to help him remember. He could count on his own recollections. I was the first one to take pictures; I was the first in the family to be afraid of forgetting.

– The Paepcke photographs. Where are they?

– They were destroyed when the Paepckes died.

– Don't tell me about that.

– No.

– Gesine, what were you like as a child?

– I thought I was fat. I stuck out my lips. That makes you feel fatter. My problems were scraped knees and torn dress pockets; I'd learned how to take care of those on my own. I didn't look at people in an unfriendly way but I glowered so that they wouldn't stroke my head and call me poor. I wasn't poor. I had a secret of my very own, my father.

– And a D in Latin.

– An A, actually.

– Aha, Gesine. All right then.

March 31, 1968 Sunday

The light was so clear on the other shore of the Hudson that the buildings stood out sharply, closer, too close. Usually the pollution in the air paints a hazy zone of trees there, as if the river could prevent things from proceeding on that side the way they do in New York.

When the announcer on station WQXR states his job, he promises: *The news—prepared and edited by The New York Times.*

The news as the *Times* writes and splices it.

The kind of face Antonín Novotný made when his successor was elected? Stony. Vladislav Hall in Hradčany, in which the election of Ludwík Svoboda took place, had formerly been used for what? Jousting on horseback. Would you care for an impression of Party Secretary Alexander Dubček? He raises his eyebrows in what appears to be a state of perpetual surprise, peers over his horn-rimmed glasses, and reads in a rapid monotone.

It's all there: The Polish government shut down eight departments of Warsaw University. The Polish government alleges that Jews formed a ring in the Nazi ghetto, "the Thirteen," that collaborated with the Gestapo. The Cologne police force has arrested a Cologne police detective, Mr. Theo Lipps, for having played a part in the slaughter of Jews in southern Russia. The American nation now disapproves of President Johnson's handling of the situation in Vietnam to the tune of sixty-three out of a hundred, if Dr. Gallup is to be believed. Beginning today, you can't get the Sunday edition of *The New York Times* for thirty-five cents—it costs fifty, a half-dollar.

The station announces over and over that it will be carrying President Johnson's address to the nation tonight, in which he will speak of peace in Vietnam and Southeast Asia. Marie refused to believe that the message would be anything but: The war is over. Marie refuses to be sent to bed before she's heard it. Marie doesn't like that the Cresspahls don't own a TV. She would have liked to see the world being put aright with her own eyes.

It doesn't start well for Marie. – Good evening, my fellow Americans: the old man says. But tonight Marie, too, wants to be addressed that way, at least this time.

The first impressions fit together: The man speaking here is rural, rustic. He seems elderly. Seems a little bit sickly. Speaks awkwardly, sometimes almost stuttering. Here we have someone helpless, abandoned, alone. He can't do his job well, can't even avoid making a rustle when he turns his pages.

Before too many minutes have elapsed, the man has said that tonight he has ordered the nation's aircraft and naval vessels to make practically no further attacks on North Vietnam. Why wasn't it this afternoon?

As far as Marie is concerned a start like that can be followed only by marvelous things. But she can't imagine what that rest might be.

If the North Vietnamese government even now does not want to negotiate: the old man threatens: our common resolve is unshakable, our common strength is invincible. It sounds whiny.

This resolve and strength of yours aren't the poetic kind, they consist of soldiers and equipment. Now the president's voice gets stronger. Though he is breathing heavily.

He will send another 13,500 troops to Vietnam, to join the 525,000 already there, as well as artillery and tank and aircraft and medical units. That will cost an additional $2.5 billion in this fiscal year and $2.6 billion in the next.

To protect the prosperity of the American people and the strength and stability of the American dollar.

De Rosny won't like that. Marie doesn't like that.

When the president realizes the volume of his voice has dropped, he overcompensates and makes the speakers rattle. His plaintive tone is meant to tell the idle listener that he is hard at work.

It is his fervent hope: he says: that North Vietnam will now cease its efforts to achieve a military victory. That sounds like a request. Later whiny.

He wants to base peace on the 1954 Geneva accords, which his treaty partner, South Vietnam, has neither signed—not the cease-fire, not the commitment to neutrality—nor, of course, followed.

The president speaks of his thirty-seven years in the political service of our nation; of the state of the nation; of divided factions, parties, regions, religions, races.

– Whatever that was: Marie says. But you were there when history was being made. Will I ever be again?

Marie understands as historical only the fact that this man will not run for reelection as president.

That is how he wants to heal a divided nation. He thanks his listeners for listening. Wishes them good night. And God's blessing.

Almost everybody understood it differently. The telephone started ringing as soon as the broadcast was cut off.

What human grandeur.

That would never happen with your Communists.

Robert Kennedy'll be happy, won't he.

Downright philosophical.

How can you call it a cop-out, have you no respect for an old man!

McCarthy'll be happy, won't he.

We always hated him, Gesine; as of tonight, we revere him.

Genius chess move. Genius directing.

What moral greatness.

This moralizing, no.

He's reached the level of John Kennedy.

The war can't be going that badly.

What they used to call a good paterfamilias.

Sense of responsibility.

The greatest personal sacrifice.

Six months in the White House as a lame duck—you wouldn't do it.

We've sent him a telegram asking him to take it back.

He will always be seen as one of our greatest presidents.

We'll keep sending telegrams.

So Fate does exist.

And not even the telephone system of goddamn New York City is collapsing.

We'll remember this president.

   – Gesine: Marie says: sometimes you don't understand this country, even though we live here.

   – You're right, I don't.

   – That scares me.

   – Do *you* understand it?

   – Not always, when I try to learn it from you. That's when I'm scared.

April 1, 1968 Monday

The New York Times gives the President three big headlines across all eight columns for his sacrifice, as though he'd died. She observed tears in his eyes. And if she must express an opinion, she considers many possibilities: that he was even more determined not to lose at either the convention or the ballot box; that he didn't entirely mean it and a treaty with North Vietnam could still let him reemerge as the President of Peace; that maybe this move comes too late. What does the *Times* call the war? "Dreadful, cruel and ugly—the war that nobody wants."

In the ČSSR it is now the case that three thousand men and women who were imprisoned, tortured, and ostracized for not being Communists when the Communists seized power in Czechoslovakia are able to meet in the heart of Prague. Not only are they allowed to mourn their dead, they are allowed to seek compensation for the living, and with the full consent of the government and the party, too.

Moscow Radio reported the President's decision to stop bombing but not his abdication of office. Over there the truth is parceled out like medicine, at Moscow's discretion.

At the bottom of the pile of mail is a letter postmarked with the single word "Jerichow," with very large stamps—two oak trees, each with men holding books—and addressed in unfamiliar handwriting.

Don't accept it, Gesine. *Return to sender.*

"Jerichow, March 17th inst., Dear Gesine.

March 1968, for all the headwinds.

Gesine, you don't know who this is writing to you. But you know me. You wouldn't recognize me. I'm old now, fat and pudgy everywhere, with white hair, frayed around the eyes. All that tennis and it didn't help. Can you picture me now?

I don't live where you're thinking anymore. Not in a house either, just a room on Market Square in Jerichow. I could have gone to Berlin and lived like the maggots, or died in a Schöneberg basement. Now do you know?

What if you imagine me speaking with a Scottish accent like Mary Hahn's in Rostock: '*On the spur of a moment*'? The same English Lisbeth had?

I'm writing you posthaste, since you don't write me at all, and shouldn't. They have a watch list in the post office; you probably don't know what that is. I'm not scared though. If they lock up Gerda Wollenberg for going to Italy with a permit for West Germany—well she should have known better. Why should I be scared of sheep when I've got a dog in my pocket? It's just that I don't want to be asked why I'm writing you. I think I'm not supposed to.

Gesine, child, what have you done? Did you write a letter to the Rande municipal council? What was in it? Were you cheeky? You were never cheeky as a child. You didn't want to take off your dress when I had to sew it back together, and when I pricked you with a pin you stared at me and didn't say anything. I can still see your look. Those clothes, they were in tatters. You were an easygoing girl, tall for age nine, with a coxcomb of hair on your head, always crooked. It was just that you dealt with grown-ups as though their being older meant nothing. Except with Cresspahl. And of course Cresspahl's daughter is what you've become.

I knew Cresspahl too. People say I slept with him. He didn't want to. There. Now you know who I am.

If you did write a letter to the authorities in Rande, it must have been hard for the comrades to swallow. It seems you asked about a number, and it probably wasn't the year of the Founding of the Republic but something from Jansen's and Swantenius's Thousand Years. Methfessel won't say. I knew Methfessel as a boy, and now this boy is thirty-five and won't answer an old lady, just walks away! Methfessel and the party, that's the guild and the party, and he was the first who had to take an official interest. Schettlicht's a schoolteacher in Rande, from Meissen, I'm not going to ask him. Kraczinski is the regional headquarters in Gneez, I'm not going there. Same with the others. Whatever the information was that you asked for, they didn't like it. They put it on the agenda in the party meeting.

It's true. But that was a bad move, because now they can't shift all the blame onto one person, they all had to write you and sign it. Methfessel didn't want to. Went to school with you, after all. Schettlicht dictated the letter, probably wanted to show the comrades from the countryside what you do in his circles when you're looking the class enemy in the eye.

What was it, Gesine? Methfessel makes a face as if they've marked and branded you a child of imperialism, a warmonger, and whatever else you're up to in New York! Methfessel says: After getting a letter like that, *I* wouldn't show my face in Jerichow again.

But they want you back. They think you should come to Jerichow,

Gesine! All four thousand miles, and then across the border. For a couple of days. And why? I know why, I just don't believe it.

They thought: maybe it can all be patched up. Amicably, you understand. They go to see Kliefoth. The watch list in the post office, you understand. They want to know if he's writing to you.

You know that already: Kliefoth says.

So what's in her letters: they say.

You know that already: Kliefoth says. They say to tell them again.

Kliefoth: Do you have a warrant?

They can't do much to him, you know. Eighty-two years old. And in good with professors in England. Birmingham, I think.

Might he help them out in a delicate matter?

Kliefoth: I'm an old man, the only letters I write these days are about personal matters—you can imagine what he said.

Kliefoth talks about you like a friend, like an equal, and as if that pleases him very much. Did you know that?

They came to me too. The rumor about Cresspahl in my bed, right? Sorry, and it's not true anyway. They wanted to know if I'm writing to you.

Maybe they think that there's someone in the post office who forgets about the watch list sometimes.

They can't believe that we're not writing each other, and don't want to believe it. Because now they have no one who can write to you and say you should forget that letter and they'll make you a brand-new one!

I didn't even have your address. Kliefoth wants to ask your permission first, make sure I'm allowed to know where you live in New York. Emmy Creutz, they went to see her too, probably imagining all sorts of dastardly things. It really is a small town.

Gesine, you won't believe it: They're renaming Brickworks Road. As Cresspahl Road! There's going to be a plaque on your house, in bronze, and the kindergarten they've put in the building is going to be renamed Heinrich Cresspahl Kindergarten.

Your newspapers probably don't say what's going on here. What's going on is that the Soviet Union has dug up its man Richard Sorge. They're not called spies, though, they're 'scouts.' 'Heroes.' So now the GDR needs its own scouts. And supposedly Cresspahl was one. Not for the Soviets, that's too much to ask, but for the English, which is still against the Nazis. Gesine, is it possible? Child! I can't wrap my mind around it! Gesine, write and tell me it's not true!

Just so I know. (Don't write to me, write to Kliefoth. I can just ask him if he's received any letters with a 'No' full stop that he didn't understand.) That's all you can do.

It was in the papers, our *People's News*, which used to be *The Gneez Daily News* but now it comes out of Schwerin, they only deliver to Gneez.

The paper had something about Ludwig Krahnstöwer, for his seventieth. Hero of the anti-Fascist resistance, that kind of thing. Claims to have been a radio operator from 1943 to 1945, in Hamburg, with the handle Jürss, or JÜRSS, but working for the Soviets and the British at the same time, and says that most of his Mecklenburg reports came from a single man, and says: from Cresspahl. He admits he never met him in person. He says: Cresspahl.

I'd sooner believe Jerichow is getting a tram line to Wismar! That's the latest rumor.

Because if it's true, Cresspahl could've lived like a king after the war and been happy! Since the Soviets would have known about his reports! Gesine, keeping something like that secret, I don't believe any man alive could do that, and can't possibly be true.

Just imagine, unveiling a new street sign and a memorial plaque here!

Honorary citizen of Jerichow, maybe, how does that sound!

You won't do it, I know.

All I want to say is that I'm an old woman, I have my pride, never mind. I liked you very much, even when you weren't a little girl anymore. After all, you were Lisbeth's child. I would have loved to raise you; Cresspahl wouldn't give you up. You didn't notice an old woman walking by who'd once sewed your buttons on and pinned your hair up, you said a polite hello and kept walking. There were times when the town was laughing at me, too. And you had Mrs. Abs, she became like a mother to you, didn't she. I only want you to know that I would have been happy to be that too. Not for Cresspahl's sake, for you.

You know who's writing this. I won't see you again. It's maybe because of my former life that I want to at least be remembered. By you. Never had any children, after all.

—A friend and well-wisher!"

April 2, 1968 Tuesday

Justice in Mecklenburg during the Nazi war:

Fedor Wagner, Polish carver in Groß Labenz, said Germany was guilty in the war against his country. Arrested September 3, 1939. Transported from Dreibergen-Bützow penitentiary to Auschwitz. No trace.

Wilhelm Zirpel, from Michelsdorf near Belzig, riverboat man, had listened to Radio Moscow and made antiwar statements in Malchin. Arrested December 11, 1939. Five years hard labor in Dreibergen-Bützow, in Sachsenhausen concentration camp after January 26, 1945.

Johann Lehmberg, from Rostock, engineer, spoke against rearmament. In prison since 1939; transported to KZ Neuengamme on January 22, 1940; later murdered there.

Louis Steinbrecker, from Rostock, grocer, called to labor service at the Walther Bachmann airplane factory in Ribnitz, arrested on December 27, 1939, for "treacherous statements," sentenced to two years hard labor in February 1940, transported from Dreibergen-Bützow penitentiary to KZ Buchenwald where he died on July 31, 1942, "of pneumonia."

Eduard Pichnitzek, from Neddemin, laborer, talked to Polish prisoners of war in their language and had a beer with them. Sentenced to three years in prison on April 22, 1940. Detention in Dreibergen-Bützow gave him pulmonary tuberculosis, from which he died on January 25, 1943.

Karl Saul, forty-three years old, from Schwerin, plumber, repeated news reports from foreign radio stations. Sentenced to three years hard labor on June 4, 1940, his wife to two years.

Martha Siewert, twenty-seven, from Teerofen in Karow, sentenced on June 17, 1940, to two years hard labor for listening to the BBC and for disapproving of the war.

Hermann Kröger, from Schwerin, bricklayer, talked to two Frenchmen at Ziegel Lake on August 12, 1940, and gave them cigarettes. He said: Workers from every country need to stick together. He was sent to jail for eighteen months.

Harald Ringeloth, twenty, from Grevesmühlen Reich Labor Service Camp, got two years hard labor on August 14, 1940, for subversive statements.

August Spacek, from Elmenhorst near Rostock, milker, let four Polish workmen in his apartment listen to foreign radio stations, and was sentenced for that to four years hard labor on October 2, 1940.

Friedrich-Karl Jennewein, from Güstrow, workman, was sentenced to two years hard labor on November 29, 1940, for subversive agitation, transferred to KZ Mauthausen on July 3, 1942, and died in Güstrow in 1946 from injuries sustained during his imprisonment.

Otto Trost, grocer in Schwerin, had listened to the BBC and spoken with a customer about its reports. He was sentenced for these acts to two and a half years hard labor on August 8, 1941, and died in Dreibergen-Bützow on October 20, 1943.

A tailor, a short, hunchbacked man, and his wife dragged a bucket of water over to prisoners of war, half starved, half dead of thirst, in Neu-brandenburg. The following day, both the man and his wife were arrested by the SS and disappeared without a trace.

On October 9, 1941, at the Kröger dockyard in Warnemünde, sixty-year-old Erdmann Fünning, boatbuilder, was arrested. For having discussed news from the BBC among his fellow workers, ten years hard labor was decreed for him on January 21, 1942.

Paul Koob, worker in the munitions factory in Malchow (I.G. Farben), called Adolf Hitler a traitor and the Winter Relief a war bond. He was sentenced on June 9, 1942, to two years in jail.

Master baker Köhn, Rostock, sold approximately a thousand loaves of bread to Polish prisoners of war between fall 1942 and early 1943 without collecting ration cards from them. That cost him two and a half years hard labor and a thousand-mark fine.

Johann Schulz, from Warin, sixty-eight years old, employed in the railroad-car factory in Wismar, was arrested for a second time in December 1942. He was sentenced on March 8, 1943, to five years in jail for the spreading of facts detrimental to the war effort. He witnessed the liberation in May 1945 from the Dreibergen-Bützow penitentiary and died on the way home, in Zernin, on May 12, 1945, of injuries sustained during his imprisonment.

On November 10, 1943, four clergymen from Lübeck were executed: the Catholic chaplains Johannes Prassek, Herman Lange, and Eduard Müller for listening to and spreading foreign radio reports, and the Protestant pastor Friedrich Stellbrink supposedly for the sermon he'd given on Palm Sunday, 1942, after the bombing of Lübeck.

Walter Block, excavation foreman and Communist Party functionary in Malchin, was arrested again in May 1939 for illegal political activity, spent six years in KZ Sachsenhausen and KZ Neuengamme, and drowned on May 3, 1945, in Lübeck Bay, along with eight thousand prisoners the Nazis had wanted to remove by ship in April.

Wilam Simic, a Serb, worked as a cook in the Dornier Works, Ltd., in Wismar. For giving Soviet prisoners of war food in the factory, he was given a sentence of six years hard labor on February 25, 1943.

Walter Jahn, from Güstrow, master mason, called to labor service in Priemerburg, predicted a clear defeat in July 1943 and was given three years in prison on October 11, 1943.

Theodor Korsell, councilman and doctor of jurisprudence, fifty-two years old, had said in the Rostock streetcar after the fall of Mussolini: the leader of Germany needed to resign, too, since the Germans could no longer possibly win. "And we don't all want to burn ourselves on the pyre, do we?" He was executed on August 25, 1943.

Friedrich Schwarz, from Waren, fifty-four, workman, expressed satisfaction over the fall of Mussolini in front of fellow workmen. On November 16, 1943, the *Niederdeutscher Beobachter* reported that he had been executed.

Wilhelm Schröder, Schwerin, master carpenter, said on July 25, 1943, after the bombing of Hamburg: What, you still think we'll win? I don't believe it and I never did. Two-year prison term handed out on May 11, 1944.

Karl-August Grabe, from Grabow, sixty-four years old, cattle trader, said in the presence of others in late 1943 that Germany had lost the war. As a result, he faced the First Senate of the People's Tribunal on February 26, 1944, and was sentenced to death.

On March 21, 1944, at 11 o'clock, the Polish forced-laborer Czeslaw Nowalkowski, twenty-three years old, was hanged on the parish land of Stove village, near Wismar.

Otto Voth, forty-one, a farmer in Zeppelin in Güstrow district, was arrested by the Gestapo on March 29, 1944, for having stated that the defeat of the Germans was no longer preventable. On January 25, 1945, a sentence of five years in prison was pronounced against him, to be spent in Dreibergen-Bützow.

Karl Willführ, from Eldena, riverboat man, called to labor service in the Dömitz dynamite factory (Dynamit Corp.), had protested against the mistreatment of Soviet prisoners of war. In September 1943 he was arrested by the Gestapo, in 1944 sentenced to three years hard labor, and on January 25, 1945, murdered in Gollnow prison in Pommern.

Ella Kähne, from Beckentin near Grabow, gave a Soviet prisoner of war some rubber cement in 1944, to patch up his boots. One year in prison.

On November 30, 1944, the laborer Josef Molka, born in Poland, living in Germany since 1929, was arrested with his three sons for having given POWs on the Mörslow estate near Schwerin food and news from the front. It was considered additionally incriminating that he had urged his children not to go to war and get themselves killed. He was sentenced to death on January 15, 1945, and killed on February 6, 1945, in Dreibergen-Bützow.

In Ziebühl, near Bützow, August Schlee, farmhand, spoke in favor of giving his village to the Soviets without a struggle. An SS commander shot him on May 2, 1945.

Marianne Grunthal, from Zehdenick, forty-nine years old, teacher, heard about Hitler's death and shouted: Thank God, now this horrible war is over! On May 2, 1945, on the square in front of the train station in Schwerin, she was hanged from a streetlamp. Today the square is named after her.

The basement in the Dreibergen-Bützow penal institution where the executions took place is now a museum.

This was a whitewashed cellar. A steel beam had been mounted in front of the back wall behind one vault of the ceiling. Three hooks hung from it. Under the hooks are three low stools. Along the ceiling are two cords, along which two curtains can be pulled open or closed to make three separate death chambers. Outside the entrance arch a piece of dark cloth is hanging to either side, which could be drawn so that the victims walked into a dark narrow tunnel unaware that anyone was next to them hanging from a hook.

I sometimes dream about Cresspahl there.

April 3, 1968 Wednesday
– The Flushing line is out of service!: the invisible loudspeakers under Times Square say, and the passengers are standing five deep on the platforms of the shuttle to Grand Central. Today a lot of desks near Third and Lex-

ington Avenues will sit empty for longer than usual. *The New York Times* folded in thirds serves well as a defensive club in the crowd.

The paper contains a photograph of Dr. Jozef Břeštanský, the deputy president of the Supreme Court in Czechoslovakia. He was supposed to draft a law for the rehabilitation of victims of the Stalinist purges, and the Slovak newspapers had doubts about his suitability for the task, given that he had taken part in these false proceedings himself in Bratislava in 1955. He disappeared five days ago and was found hanging awkwardly from a tree near Babice, with a rope around his neck.

President Johnson, who has promised to bomb only a little part of North Vietnam along the demilitarized zone, has sent his planes to Thanhhoa. Now *The News York Times* can measure the "credibility gap" between the president and the country: two hundred miles (322 km) wide.

The stock market believed in peace. The trading volume rose to 19.29 million shares. Around the world the dollar is respected again; gold stocks are creaking under the pressure of declining prices. What should we believe?

Giant headlines pushed through the crowd in the subway that evening: HANOI'S ANSWER. HANOI'S ANSWER. Mrs. Cresspahl borrows the front page from a student who has long since turned to the sports pages. Hanoi has said that talks will begin only after the United States has proved that it has really stopped unconditionally all acts of war.

The young man takes the page back, wraps it carefully around the rest of the paper, tries to jostle it straight and make it look brand new, and gives it to her for free, all in silence, with an expression of relief, mockery, and pity on his face, even when the stranger shakes her head.

You're another one of them, aren't you, ma'am. Taken in by everything. We'll never get anywhere with them.

April 4, 1968 Thursday

The sky over the Hudson this morning is as overcast as it was over Ribnitz and the Saal Lagoon during the summer twenty-four years ago, when the Paepckes began their last vacation. This time they all met the train the Cresspahl child arrived on, Alexander in an unfamiliar uniform but still recognizable at once from his delight, his businesslike manner, his mock officiousness. Now the anticipated pleasures were replaced by the real ones. Alexander said: *Many children, many blessings: said the sexton, pocketing the fee for the christening.*

It may have been too late for the Althagen boat, or there may not have been room for six people with bags and suitcases; Alexander led his entourage diagonally across the station square to an ambulance that looked alarmingly official. Speaking to the children as if they were patients, he crammed them onto under next to the stretcher, enjoying their horror, amazement, and delight at this latest adventure. Now a vehicle of the municipal hospital was driving north along Fischland Road on very urgent business. Alexander was proud of an old Leonia friend's willingness to do him a favor, and even prouder that he'd thought of this one. He sang with the children the whole way, loud and happily, and no one suspected a thing.

The evening was a long one for the children, but Alexander wouldn't let them leave the house. They didn't feel under observation; he never let them out of his sight. Gesine had to tell them about Jerichow, and it took him fifteen minutes to teach her the fractions her school hadn't been able to ram into her head all year. Alexandra was sent off to the wardrobe and told to come back looking like the Queen of Sheba. Alexander had returned from the Soviet Union that morning and had seen his family again for the first time at the Stettin train station. He asked Paepcke Junior how school was going and taught him some new tricks for copying, "for when you're in over your head, my boy." For Christine, he demonstrated how she'd drunk from a cup when she was two. She used to hold it tight in both hands when it was full, carelessly let it drop when it was empty. Christine was now seven and excited to see how she'd held her pinkie elegantly away from the cup as a baby, before discarding it as useless, just like Alexander; she laughed even harder than the others, not hurt at all. Alexander was incapable of hurting a child's feelings. There was a lot of talk that night about the past, about Lisbeth too. Lisbeth's child realized that these people remembered her dead mother as a thoroughly delightful person, beautiful by the time she was eight, a friend to people and animals her whole life long, her mocking ways meant to hide her tenderness. Lisbeth's sister didn't say much, occasionally prompting Alexander with half sentences, sometimes pressing both forefingers against the bridge of her nose as though fighting off pain. To the children she just seemed tired, and no one suspected a disaster. Christine and Eberhardt went trustingly to sleep on Hilde's lap, their heads against Alexander's chest, and were carried out, put to bed, gently kissed, and looked at while they slept.

The next morning the Shoreline Cliff coastal batteries were firing at the sea, and after the first dull thud Gesine waited for Alexander's voice to come up through the ceiling and curse the Greater German Army for its unseemly behavior. But Alexander wasn't there anymore.

The morning was almost white, with fringed cloud-boats in the sky. The reflection of light from the lagoon was an exquisite pain in the eyes. The paths between the small farms were protected and warmed by the tall bushy hedgerows. There were painter ladies sitting around in the meadows, like every year, trying to get the Dornenhaus onto canvas even though the old cottage was barely visible under its hipped roof and hidden behind the rambling thornbushes so high that they hung down over the roof, at 45 degree angles from the wind, thick and impenetrable. The familiar slat fence still ran along Border Road, the coastal cliffs fell off steeply as ever right where Pommern started, and the children remembered Alexander's stories of the sea breaking through here. Border Road was bare on the Althagen side and densely built up on the Ahrenshoop side with buildings in splendid colors, in the famous blue, with the gardens sheltered from the wind and nurtured by the southern sun, way down below the steep slope up to the road, with hollyhocks in every color growing up to the roof. The children recalled Alexander's serious explanation that these houses had a back door to the north, from the days when Mecklenburg and Pommern were at war and the inhabitants were not allowed to set foot on Border Road. It was Fischland, but not the right one. The vacation didn't seem possible without Alexander.

By evening, Hilde could see that the children were at odds with her and the world. Alexander had not been on leave, he'd been ordered to southern France and had left the train against orders to help take the children to Althagen, to see the children one more time. It was more than he'd been capable of to openly say goodbye to the children. Hilde tried to make out that it was partly her fault that he'd had to go back to his post early that morning. Then she sternly ordered everyone to write letters to Alexander, and that way she salvaged the next day's prospects.

Hilde sent the children out into the fields with the farmers. On the narrow strip of ground between the two bodies of water, the children rode with the harvesters on the jolting carts, ran alongside the mowers, tried to help bundle the grain into sheaves, sat and ate with them; they came home parched, dumb with exhaustion, and thought they'd been working. On Fischland the stooks weren't sheaves leaning against one another like gables, as in Jerichow, but round cones perfect as pretend Indian teepees. In damp Mosquito Woods, separated from the Darss part of the peninsula by traces of inroads made by the Baltic, the children went blueberrying and were given for supper what they'd found, with milk, and they believed they were living off the work of their own hands. Hilde was capable of running all the way to the woods after a child who'd forgotten her sun hat. The Althagen house was surrounded with a solid gravel dike meant to distribute the rainwater from the roof evenly into the soil. It was an honor to be entrusted with the task of weeding the dike, called "plucking the dike," with the Plattdeutsch *puken*. The evening walk to the beach for a swim was like a reward. A path ran through a very high field to the Shoreline Cliff on the Niehagen side, between willows and poplars shielded from the wind, an ordinary cart path that kept unexpectedly stopping at an abyss plunging down to the sea. Letters were written to Alexander about the watchdog at the Nagel farm that refused to allow public access to the levee and Lagoon Road; about people they'd run into on the village street; about visits to Alexander's friends. It turned out that you could invent your vacation. They'd learned that from Alexander.

Today I know that this vacation wasn't like that.

Not far from Althagen, on the other side of the Saal Lagoon, was Barth concentration camp. It held prisoners from the Soviet Union, from Holland, from Czechoslovakia, from Belgium, from Hungary, who had to work at a branch of the Ernst Heinkel Airplane Factory Corp. A Czech doctor, Dr. Stejskal, kept a list of the women and men who were buried in the Barth cemetery and the mass graves. There are 292 names on it. The bodies of 271 prisoners were sent from Barth to the Rostock crematorium. The causes of death were "tuberculosis," "pneumonia," "suicide." There were people "shot while trying to escape," and if a woman persisted in refusing to work building planes to attack her own country, she was taken back to Ravensbrück concentration camp and murdered with gas. We didn't know that. Hilde Paepcke drove us to Barth, over the swivel bridge, to see the town. We saw nothing. The stretch of rails along which Cresspahl's child rode to Fischland passed Rövershagen. In Rövershagen there was a concentration camp whose prisoners had to work for the Ernst Heinkel Airplane Factory Corp. Now I know.

Alexander's family had arranged among themselves that Hilde shouldn't spend this summer alone, so they came for weeks or weekends—greatuncles, aunts, dignified older persons, dressed more for a funeral than for a vacation. The children didn't notice the worried advice being given in the house; the children played a game with the adults. They opened a flower shop on the front porch where they sold buttercups for a penny, daisies for two pennies, and the ladies and gentlemen waiting to buy stood in lines six or eight people long, snaking all the way to the dining room. The visitors had a long-practiced tone, formal and familiar in one, since every last one of them knew the whole family out to the great-grandfather and the fiftieth anniversary of a childhood prank. It was an overcoat of thickly woven, mutually recognized information, in which any individual person was barely noticed compared to the fact of their belonging, their compatibility with the others. Alexander's aunt Françoise had taken charge of the advice-giving, even though she had never forgiven him for being kicked out of the Mecklenburg bar association. She was severe, forbidding, dressed in black and white in the hottest weather; she was the first one to go along with the children's make-believe. The children were not to notice anything.

The presents Alexander had left for the children were white raincoats from the Soviet Union, waterproofed with a rubbery material. They felt unworn, smelled fresh from the factory, but there were sunflower seeds in the pockets. When Alexander had told stories about the reoccupied Baltic countries, it had seemed strange that the Baltic Sea was there too, in such thick, mighty forests. There the Baltic was like a shining snake in the forest.

From the postwar years I now know: Alexander was part of the Todt Organization. He'd had to put civilians to work from among the Soviet population, after the SS handed them over to him. One time, he had protested slightly against accepting a squad of fifty Jews because there were children in it. He got out of that one without a court-martial; the army took him back and sent him to NCO training. There was nothing else to be done. By that point, the war brooked no discussion. None of the Paepcke family connections were enough—not the Leonia fraternity connections in Mecklenburg, not the officers from the old army, not the connections from the Stettin Military Ordnance Department. It was unbelievable that the family couldn't get him transferred to a safe position.

At Althagen they played a game where Alexandra Paepcke sat on one side of a turnstile in the border fence, Gesine on the other, and they spun the gate and sang: Now I'm in Pommern! Now I'm in Mecklenburg!

Memory of that summer preserves the turnstile, the vacation. It wasn't like that.

April 5, 1968 Friday

I'm sorry they shot him.

You're not sorry, Mrs. Cresspahl. Ma'am.

We've been living in the same building for six years, Bill.

Martin Luther King was a black man like me. You're one of the whites.

Last night Martin Luther King was shot and killed in Memphis. It was around six p.m., seven o'clock New York time. He'd spent all day in his room at the Lorraine Motel. He'd chosen this motel for his stay because it was Negro-owned. He'd come to Memphis to support the sanitation workers on strike since Lincoln's Birthday, February 12. A week ago he led a march in the strikers' cause that ended in violence; the last rally had been on Wednesday. At about 6 p.m. he emerged from his room onto the balcony and chatted with friends standing in the courtyard parking lot.

– You mustn't believe this of our country, Mrs. Cresspahl. It's not like that.

– It is exactly like that. And worse.

– A Nobel Prize winner we shoot here in America must be a Negro, demanding equal rights for Negroes.

– Both the national and New York stock exchanges opened with a moment of mourning over the news. And there was another moment of silence at eleven.

– Do you know of a single Negro with a seat on the stock exchange?

– The riots are coming to New York tonight.

Dr. King was leaning over the railing. He was relaxed, open-faced, genial. He was dressed for dinner at a reverend's house in Memphis. His driver warned him it was cold outside and told him to put on a topcoat. Dr. King promised he would. A friend introduced him to the musician who was to play at the rally later. Dr. King had asked him to play a Negro spiritual: "Precious Lord, Take My Hand." He greeted the man, glowing, and repeated his request. Then the shot rang out.

– He saw it coming.

– When he was flying to Memphis all the luggage on the plane had to be searched and the plane kept under guard, because of him.

– Last night he was on TV, alive. They showed his speech from Wednesday night. That his people would reach the Promised Land, but maybe not with him.

– TV should be banned.

Dr. King collapsed onto the balcony floor. He could still be seen from below because the railing was only iron poles, painted green. Blood gushed from the right jaw and neck area. His necktie had been ripped off by the blast. He had just bent over; if he'd been standing up, he wouldn't have been hit in the face. Someone rushed up with a towel to stem the flow of Dr. King's blood. Someone else tried to cover him with a blanket. Then someone came with a bigger towel. The fire department took ten or fifteen minutes to send an ambulance. He was carried off on a stretcher, the bloody towel over his head. He had only been out in the open about three minutes.

– The other Negro leaders laughed at him for trying to attain equal rights without violence.

– Many of them hoped he might be right after all.

– Now they have no choice but to believe in violence.

– There's going to be white blood on our streets tonight.

– We're trapped here like in a cage.

– The Negroes will be able to block all the trains by tonight.
– No whites'll get out of this city alive.

The sound of the shot seemed to some of the people there to have come from a passing car. To others it sounded like a firecracker. A man in a nearby building, watching TV, thought it sounded like a bomb. When the perhaps fifteen people in the motel courtyard area, all Negroes and Dr. King's associates, turned around to look at where the shot came from, police came running from everywhere, especially from where the shot came from. First they cordoned off an area of about five blocks around the Lorraine Motel. Then four thousand National Guard troops were ordered into Memphis and a general curfew imposed. Dr. King died at 7:05 p.m. (8:05 p.m.) during emergency surgery on a gunshot wound in the neck, "a gaping wound."

– Well maybe they are overdoing it a bit.
– Flags at half-mast! It's not like he was Kennedy.
– The blacks need to be smoked out, block by block!
– Maybe it was one of them that did it themselves.
– My hairdresser has had to wear dark glasses since last night because a Negro hit him under the eye with brass knuckles. And he's French.
– What did he say?
– He just took off his glasses and looked at me.
– Do you really believe that there were no deaths in Harlem last night? They're just trying to keep us calm.
– One single headline in the *Times,* and half the news on the rest of the page was about other things.
– Well maybe they are overdoing it a bit.

The police say the assassin was a white man in his thirties, who was fifty to a hundred yards away in a flophouse. Dr. King's chauffeur saw a man "with something white on his face" creeping away from a thicket across the street. The police believe that a late-model Mustang was the killer's getaway car. A high-powered 30.06 caliber rifle was found about a block from the scene.

– That's gotta be planted evidence.
– Was he acting alone?
– Do you think Oswald was acting alone?
– Do you think it'll be like with Kennedy?
– They may find the killer, but they won't find who gave the orders.

After Dr. King was pronounced dead, his friends met in his room. They had to step across a drying pool of Dr. King's blood outside the door to enter. Someone had thrown a crumpled pack of cigarettes into the blood.

– If the bank is going to close early, they should have closed at noon.
– By now the Negroes will have mined all the bridges and tunnels.
– The Negro soldiers in Vietnam are sending weapons home. You wouldn't believe how many machine guns the mail delivers to New York every day!
– And hand grenades. And plastic explosives.
– They stabbed a white woman walking with her child on Madison Avenue because she was wearing a mink coat.
– And we send them to Vietnam, too, so that they'll learn close combat.
– First the Indians. Then the blacks.

I'm sorry they shot him, Bill.
You're very polite, Mrs. Cresspahl, I know that already.
I'm sorry.
And still, if the black people come here from Harlem tonight, I won't lift a finger for you, ma'am. Do you know what it means to be scared?
I do.
You don't know anything. You're not black.

April 6, 1968   Saturday

"Mrs. Martin Luther King
St. Joseph's Hospital
Memphis, Tennessee
Dear Mrs. King,

After the personal loss that you have suffered
that has befallen you
that the whites have inflicted on you, I want to express my—"

"Mrs. Coretta King
Lorraine Motel
Memphis, Tennessee
Dear Mrs. King,
In light of the loss that you and your children have suffered,
that the whites have inflicted on you and your children, and whose national importance the official sympathies of the government can do nothing to minimize,
it must feel strange to know that in your city, as in this one, people are walking around on Broadway, enjoying the weekend, pleasantly warmed by the sun. You know about the memorial march through New York yesterday, the dockworkers stopping work, Mayor Lindsay's visits to the ghettos. In our neighborhood there are some businesses closed, including Jewish ones, with the Sabbath gaining another meaning this time besides that of their religion, on handwritten cardboard signs in memory and honor of your husband. But there aren't many cars driving with lights on in broad daylight. And there are plenty of people in the street doing their Easter shopping, the sports events canceled today and tomorrow are just postponed, they might take place as early as Tuesday night, and I want to assure you that not everyone here agrees wi—"

"Mrs. Martin Luther King
Southern Christian Leadership Conference
Atlanta, Georgia
Dear Mrs. King,
First I want to apologize for the telegram my daughter sent you last night, but I should tell you that the child is only ten
that in fact I share in the impulsive, hotheaded tone of that telegram, in a spir—"

Why can't I do it! Tell me!
This is real, Gesine.

It's not just another death.
It's a death like ours. Predictable, likely. And yet unlikely.
Because he wasn't Kennedy?
Because he was a Negro. Whether he preached nonviolence or violence.
He'd gotten too visible.
That's why I thought I should send a—
No, Gesine. What kind of country are you voluntarily choosing to live in?
A country where black people get killed. So what is there for you to say.
You're right. Nothing. Nothing.

April 7, 1968 Sunday

The news photos of the riots in Washington show dirty smoke, balls of it in the streets, spread wide over the city. It obscures the White House: the caption says. Another photo shows a low line of close-set buildings with half-collapsed facades, some already burned out to empty boxes. There's still something left for the fire to devour in some of them. These are American houses, recognizable from their flat roofs and vertically divided windows. This is what a war in American cities would look like.

In Mecklenburg, at the middle school in Gneez, they were still saying in January 1945: You get orders first and explanations later!—not without a certain military element, as if the teachers were all amateur army officers, every last one. They sometimes made it more literary and said: Leave the thinking to the horses, their heads are bigger! whenever a child had said: I thought. . . .

The Cresspahl child didn't say what she thought, she sat there mildly watching and taking good note of how the teaching staff handled a child who'd thought something. The Cresspahl child had a secret. She knew that the war was almost over. She'd told Cresspahl what she'd heard in school, something about the V-2 rockets laying waste to London, and her father let slip a surprised then hearty laugh that looked a bit like he was choking. But the secret meant it would be all over with this school in a few weeks.

A child could see it. There were still families in Jerichow that believed in the community of pure Germans and refused to buy food on the black

market—families with starving children. The farmers and tradesmen had
gone back to a barter system. Cresspahl didn't have problems finding a way
to fill his pipe—his French prisoners of war took care of that; Lise Wollenberg, though, walked through the whole train on the rides to and from
school looking for an unconscionably discarded butt for her father, because
the smoker's ration cards again had only ten cigarettes in each of six sections, to last for four weeks. The children saw it in the Gneez station.
Public express and semi-express trains had stopped running; only people
with business away from home, and schoolchildren, were allowed to ride
the locals. The Allies had broken the German rail system. The Gneez station had fallen silent. Only very rarely did a ghost train for official trips
pass through, with few people waiting on the platform for it. Only postcards
could be sent to Wendisch Burg, and the mail carrier in Jerichow had more
letters in her bag to bring back to their senders as undeliverable than letters
arriving from elsewhere. The Cresspahl child had been stopped on the
Rande country road because she was going to the Baltic for pleasure and
there was a regulation, applied even to the Hitler Youth, prohibiting the
use of bicycles for distances of more than three kilometers. The Cresspahl
child had relayed the teacher's question to her father—When would the
girl finally join the Deutsche Jungmädel? She was eleven already!—and
Cresspahl had written a note excusing her on the grounds of being a commuting student, but privately said: *Nope. No more o that, Gesine.*

Among the grown-ups in Jerichow, though, there were conversations
about the waxwings that had unexpectedly come down from the north:
delicate creatures with reddish-gray, whitish, reddish-yellow colors, their
bodies a bit like crested larks. The grandfathers still esteemed these birds
for their ability to know the weather in advance, precisely because they
traveled around so restlessly—in general, their arrival was supposed to
mean a harsh winter ahead. For some people, this harsh winter was also
the defeat of Germany. Others said that a Germany still planning to run
a railroad line from Jerichow to Wismar (or Lübeck) couldn't be losing a
war.

Then the airfield fell silent. Takeoffs weren't worth counting, landings
barely. Mariengabe Airfield, the pride of Jerichow, was starting to die.

Ham-burg and Lü-beck and Bre-men,

there's no need to be a-shamed in;
the devil always shits on the biggest pile
so Jerichow's gonna stay clean for a while....

And Otto Quade got a slap to the head. For years the song wouldn't have gone like that—Jerichow had had the air force there.

Really, Mariengabe Airfield had been typical Jerichow-style all along. When it was still part of Air District III Berlin, it was meant to be just an operational base, one small node in an expansive network, a 500 x 1,000 meter airstrip aiming west with a perpendicular one added later. The fact that it took three and a half years to finish was due not just to inadequacies in the local construction industry but also to plans for a long-range bomber, later abandoned along with any sense of Jerichow's importance. That too was something of a blow to the town's pride. True, the number of troops stationed there increased past the three hundred who'd arrived in October 1938, for appearances' sake, but then the airfield was reassigned to Air District XI Hanover, just Hanover, under Air Force Command 2 (North) in Braunschweig, just Braunschweig, and Air Force General Hellmuth Felmy hadn't even bothered to visit Mariengabe, despite the celebrations that would have welcomed him in Jerichow, complete with a brass band on Market Square and a torchlit procession at night.

The first commander of Jerichow-North, Lieut. Col. von der Decken, left town before town could really get used to him. His home in what had once been Dr. Semig's villa was always quiet. The residents of the Bäk got to see him mornings and evenings, when his car and adjutant stopped outside the door—as if an airfield commander were an ordinary employee going to an ordinary workplace. He accepted a few invitations to the estates in the area, where he had relatives, but the town got nothing from that. Von der Decken's wife had what she needed brought to the house, and treated tradesman and contractors as though she couldn't quite see them. When Cresspahl installed a safe for her husband, she left him a bowl of stew in the kitchen. Her Hanover airs, trips to the Schwerin state theater, bored expression—that was all appropriate for Jerichow, but previous masters had at least showed themselves a little more, offered up more stories about their lives for public consumption. The two von der Decken girls remained in memory: fourteen-year-old twins, blond, very Berlin, sharp of feature like their mother. They didn't go to school in Jerichow but were taken in an air force car to the Gneez academic middle school. Nicknamed "The Dolls." Their horses were kept in the former veterinary stables; during the harvest, they would go for rides in the Countess Woods, or along the coast, often accompanied by a cadet, and Jerichow had another example of how to provide for children's entertainment—an even better example than the Papenbrocks. Then the commander was sent with his combat brigade to the eastern front, and the family moved to Lower Saxony; one and a half companies from the brigade came back, the numbers were replenished, they flew back to the Soviet front, and they didn't return. By that point Jerichow was on its fifth commander, what with transfers and redeployments. Each one was younger than the last and now they were all majors, who didn't bring their families and who lived at the air base, not in town. The last Air Force Day, when the base was open to the public, was held in 1940—after that there wasn't enough fuel, or money, and Mariengabe became Jerichow's secret: tightly fenced in; secured by guards, sentries, patrols; a sound often heard in passing that woke up the town only when the wind was out of the northwest.

That's how things stood until 1944. The unit that took over the base in 1940 had trained pilots until it withdrew to France; a battalion was left behind for basic training and a company added for air-signals instruction. The task of earning the right to live in this community, as von der Decken had promised to do, was now pursued, somewhat less ambitiously, by the airfield staff officers, older men from the reserve. The Gneez paper published a dramatic article about the events of the night of March 28 to 29, 1942, so that people near the airfield would know that it was more or less still in operation: how the crews with gas masks, steel helmets, and rifles ran into the bunkers and the ditches; how the medics, mechanics, and fuel attendants manned their posts so that landing fighters could be taken care of as swiftly as possible, "and, with engine thundering, the slender bird rises up into the night to face the British terrorists." This was not enough to produce any new children's games in Jerichow. One time, the upper grades of the Hermann Göring School were taken to the Archduke Hotel in Gneez to hear a holder of the Knight's Iron Cross with Oak Leaves describe his personal experiences; the number of men of serving age called up into the air force was increasing, as hoped. Since 1943, privates were housed at the base and stayed up all night with march music blaring from their standby barracks; they hurtled out across the Baltic in their Messerschmitts, or to Berlin, and not only the British shot them down, German antiaircraft fire did too. The airfield garrison still raced out into position, or to take cover, whenever the siren sounded, but their own fighters didn't come back to Jerichow-North, and the Allies soared high above the Baltic coast in broad daylight, heading into Germany, untouchable and proud.

Just as there had been Rostock schoolboys who resented that Lübeck got bombed first, the boys in Jerichow were annoyed that the British and Americans didn't think their base was worth even a minor air raid. All they got were the strips of tinfoil the Allies dropped to confuse the German radio system. In Wismar, in Rostock, there was a trade in antiaircraft fragments. In Jerichow they'd just gotten antiaircraft machine guns; in other places, there was already artillery.

Ham-burg and Lü-beck and Bre-men,
there's no need to be a-shamed in....

Cresspahl was asked about Mariengabe less and less often now that it was no longer a fighter base. The conversion of direction finders on VHF equipment and their repurposing for instrument flying and night interception was the last thing his employers were keen to have confirmed. After that they didn't even mind that he couldn't find any trace of the new bomb-sighting mechanism they thought Jerichow was testing. He occasionally reported which air force engineer had been put in charge of civilian airfield personnel, or who was looking after the day-to-day administration of the site; starting in early 1944, what he was supposed to do was take trips with Leslie Danzmann's permits from work or the air force stamps from Jerichow-North. Anyone who traveled near the Rechlin Air Force testing station needed relatives to visit there, or replacement parts and wood to look for; near Ribnitz there was not only the Walther Bachmann Aircraft Works AG but also a child to fetch from her vacation. Wherever relevant, he added information about the Mecklenburg concentration camps to his reports so that they'd hit the Heinkel factory branches but not the foreign forced laborers in Krakow am See, in Retzow outside of Rechlin, in Neustadt-Glewe, Rövershagen, Reiherhorst near Wöbbelin, and, especially, Comthurey near Alt-Strelitz. He had seen the prisoners there near the train station, being herded to work on SS Major General

Oswald Pohl's estate—beaten half dead, human beings trudging like starved beasts.

> *All the Germans knew, Gesine. The SS called them KL.*
> *The right abbreviation for Konzentrations-Lager.*
> *But the Germans made it easier on the mouth, from the beginning.*
> *KZ. "Concert Camp."*
> *Not even KZL.*
> *You still say you're not keeping score, Cresspahl?*
> *Nah, Gesine. I'm just keeping track of it all for myself.*

So Cresspahl was in the clear, still in one piece. The airfield commander had done everything he could to tighten security. But Cresspahl's doors on the base were always kept closed per regulations. One time, a 1C had come from air force headquarters, an elderly major, and Cresspahl felt under observation for two days. It turned out to be just that he knew Lisbeth's story, from the von der Deckens. Counterintelligence had infiltrated people into the base who said they'd been transferred, but they always asked random questions, made disparaging comments about the SS to encourage confidences, and gave up on him every time as a harmless old man, not all there—he'd gone a little bit soft in the head from a tragedy with his wife.

> *Maybe I had, Gesine.*
> *Yes. Well, no more than me.*

Once again, the word around Jerichow was that Cresspahl knew how to take care of number one. After the boys and the old men were called up to drills in the last-ditch People's Force, Cresspahl wore the uniform of an air force sergeant and had a proper service book in his pocket. At the airfield the war would come quietly to an end, and again he was one of the people who'd get through it without shooting, without being shot.

Jerichow-North had no more fuel and nothing happened there but some basic training, a new course every three months. The airfield was silent.

At the end of January, a collection was taken up for the army and the People's Force, things like laundry and clothes "of all kinds," knapsacks, shovels, sunglasses, and still the Hitler Youth came back to the party headquarters with their handcarts almost empty this time. Among the donations was footwear worth less than it would cost to repair it. Some people turned in tattered horse blankets just so Friedrich Jansen wouldn't come looking for anything. From Käthe Klupsch there was the belt from her father's World War I uniform, for Käthe Klupsch was superstitious and thought that *one* person's goodwill could make up for where others had given up. Cresspahl donated nothing.

You knew how to wait, didn't you, Cresspahl.
I'd given up waiting, Gesine. There was nothing left, just you. Someone like me had nothing to wait for.

April 8, 1968 Monday

Yesterday Martin Luther King's family was photographed by the open coffin: Yolanda, Bernice, Martin Luther III, Dexter, and their mother. Their father's head is lying strangely low. The youngest daughter, Bernice, whose chin barely comes up to the edge of the coffin, tries to look away over him. The other children know that they have to look at the body. But they aren't used to looking down like this.

The attorney general has declared the murder a federal crime. The justification for this exception is based on a law stating that the Department of Justice has jurisdiction over crimes that violate a person's civil rights, in this case that of Dr. King to his life.

In our neighborhood, on the west side of Broadway at Ninety-Sixth Street, a clothing store next to Charlie's Good Eats has been robbed, its windows broken in, for the second time. Stuck to the planks where the shopwindow used to be there are pieces of paper with clumsy, handwritten complaints. A few passersby stop to read them, to sign the petitions. They are watched by Negroes standing there in a waiting posture.

On one of the pieces of paper, the store owner asked the question: What's next?

Written below that in red ink, in another ductus: Next we kill you. You'll see. You're soft.

April 9, 1968   Tuesday

Martin Luther King was buried today.

Families and lovers were sitting on blankets on the lawns in Central Park, having picnics in the sun.

Schools, banks, and stock exchanges closed.

The four thousand seats at the orchestra clamshell in Central Park were packed, with many more people standing behind police barricades. Leopold Stokowski's hair kept falling into his face while he was conducting. There was a girls' choir in red robes and the American Symphony Orchestra. When we got there they were playing excerpts from the German Requiem and the St. Matthew's Passion, then the Ode to Joy.

The zoo, the carousel, and the stables in Central Park were full of children intending to enjoy their day off school. The park was in full spring bloom, green dotted with red and yellow flowers, and brightly colored bicyclists, too, and girls with dogs, and people walking. From the transistor radios came reports of the progress of the burial.

At Columbus Circle a hot-dog vendor had run out of sauerkraut and kept apologizing. He hadn't done business like this all year. In the subways the seats were almost empty. Maybe the Negroes among the workforce hadn't all come to work because of the TV broadcast from Atlanta.

Young people, mostly students, were keeping a silent vigil outside City Hall, bareheaded. They've been standing there since ten and they stayed until the clock struck noon.

The signs in the closed businesses, no longer all handwritten, said: We are mourning Martin Luther King. Some of the signs, with printed, embossed, or neatly painted letters, now inform those who see them that this store is not only honoring the dead but doing so in respectable fashion.

People standing behind us occasionally say something about Negroes having threatened store owners who didn't want to close voluntarily.

We often heard: It's like with Kennedy. All the bells in the air. . . .

Females are allowed to have lunch in Wes's bar if they don't ask to be served at the bar themselves. We had a good view of Wes from our booth. One time he went over with his arms outstretched to a girl who was standing and waiting behind a group of male customers. Welcoming, delighted, he held his arms out—come to me—until the girl said: Two bottles of such and such. – Ah: Wes said, disappointed, hopes shattered. As he handed her what she'd ordered over the men's shoulders, he invited the men to share a secret grin.

Some of the conversations from the bar reached us:

– Why aren't there any tow trucks here today! The traffic hasn't been this normal in a long time.

– They're all in Harlem today. Otherwise things'd get out of hand there.

– At least *something* good.

– So, Wes, what's the good news?

– Yes indeed, sir! The country's in flames!

He didn't notice us, and Marie didn't ask why we came here.

In the afternoon the big department stores on Fifth and Lexington reopened. In the morning the streets had looked like the day after a holiday, quiet and almost empty, but now the cars were crowding one another again, horns honking, pedestrians were bumping into one another with their shopping bags.

At around five o'clock we found ourselves on Third Avenue at the window of a store selling TV sets. The business advertised its wares by having all the sets in the window on. For a long time, the color pictures showed only the coffin in Atlanta, glinting in the sun, resting on an oxcart stuck in the crowd of people, unable to move. The camera tried panning to the brightly colored US and UN flags above the mourners' heads then swiveled hopefully back to the cart, but the coffin still hadn't budged. The only difference was that the sun was gone and now the coffin looked dull.

Tonight, before the theaters begin their performances, they are supposed to have a minute of silence. Then the play can start.

– Talk to me, Gesine. Listen to me!

– Okay.

– If you don't buy a TV set now then I'll ask someone to give me one— D. E., Mr. Robinson, I don't care!

– No. We can rent one.

– At least that!

– But for what? King's funeral is over.

– For the next one, Gesine. For the next one they kill. For the next one!

April 10, 1968 Wednesday

The assassination of Martin Luther King unleashed violence in a hundred and ten cities. The whole city of Washington was shut down: banks, restaurants, businesses, stores—all closed. The Chicago jails held nearly twice the number of people they were built for. Across the river in Newark it's still burning. Dr. King has been buried, and *The New York Times* is concerned about the future of the American soul: Nothing of irreplaceable material value has been lost, but....

Baseball season opens today.

The Czechoslovak Communist Party has now completely staffed the government with people who were not the Stalinists' accomplices. The interior minister, General Pavel, has many years' familiarity with the country's prisons from the inside. In addition, the party is demanding of itself that the state security organ only protect the country against hostile acts from abroad, not be used to solve questions of internal policy. It sounds like something out of a textbook.

In March 1945, a forgotten crocus came up in Lisbeth's garden. Colonies of bees flew in the sun, cleaning themselves. The tree behind Cresspahl's house was black with starlings. The first lapwings were making noise in the marsh.

In March, a Stettin Military Ordnance Department truck on a country road in Vorpommern was strafed by low-flying Soviet planes and went up in flames. Everyone in it was killed except for the driver. Cresspahl got the telegram only after Hilde Paepcke was already buried with Alexandra and Eberhardt and Christine in a single grave that we couldn't find after the war.

April 11, 1968 Thursday

It begins again. The questions are like the ones following the assassination of John Kennedy.

Why did the Memphis police, shortly after the killing, broadcast an alert for a white Mustang, adding that it was equipped with a radio antenna similar to those on cars with citizens band radio receivers and transmitters?

Who was "police car 160" that put out a false report on April 5 at 6:35

p.m., thirty-four minutes after King was shot, saying that they were following a white Mustang in an easterly direction through north Memphis?

Is there someone in the Memphis police force who wanted to divert the Memphis police force so that King's killer could escape west into Arkansas or south into Mississippi?

Why did the police radio report at 6:36 p.m. that a blue hardtop 1966 Pontiac had joined the chase for the alleged escape car, and at 6:47 p.m. that someone in the white Mustang was shooting at the blue Pontiac?

Why were there no more broadcasts about the three cars? Because headquarters had diverted enough police cars in the wrong direction by that time?

Why did the driver of police car 160, Lieut. R.W. Bradshaw, say yesterday that he hadn't seen and didn't chase any white Mustang that night, and say today that any comment would have to come from his superior officer?

Would the information about the false police report have ever come out if a local radio-equipment dealer hadn't been monitoring police radio calls and heard it?

How could he hear it, since his monitor was unable to pick up a call from the area where police car 160 was actually located at the time?

Then again, how could the message come from a private car with a citizens band radio as if the message were coming from a police car? That would require extensive modification of the radio equipment done by someone with expert knowledge.

Why did the police know about a second man involved in the assassination and yet claim for days, along with the FBI, that the killer was acting alone?

Why is the FBI following up on evidence suggesting a conspiracy to commit the murder only five days later?

If a government committee ever files a report on the assassination of Dr. King, it'll no doubt clear everything up.

In the revised history of the town of Wendisch Burg published in 1965 for the eight hundredth anniversary of the town's founding by the Committee for the Jubilee Celebrations in the Regional Headquarters of the Socialist Unity Party, the city was said to have been saved from bombardment and artillery by two men, Alfred Wannemaker and Hugo Buschmann.

Both were members of the then-banned Communist Party and today are senior officials in the Rostock regional headquarters and an East Berlin ministry, respectively. The book states that on the night of April 28, 1945, the two men and a Polish forced laborer snuck through the woods south of town until they reached the vanguard of the Soviet troops and were taken to the commanding officer. Mention is made of justified suspicions, wasting precious time, but A. Wannemaker apparently had a map of Wendisch Burg with him and he marked on it, for his Soviet comrades, the German troop positions complete with numbers of men, quantities of vehicles, supplies of fuel. The discussion was interrupted by a skirmish with isolated German forces, and H. Buschmann had to take cover on an office floor in the village school while telephoning with the mayor of Wendisch Burg and arranging the terms of surrender. The Pole (as interpreter), the solidarity of nations (in the class struggle), and the Red Army marched into Wendisch Burg on Old Street between undamaged timbered gables.

Cresspahl started his story with a memory: You know how he is; as if his listeners were as much in a position as he was to call to mind in an instant an image of Martin Niebuhr—a stooping, long-armed man in blue mechanic's overalls, who exerts his strength without haste, is slow to speak and slow to come to a decision, almost sleepy, but then suddenly "wakes up" and acts both judiciously and quickly, devious and deceptive when need be, and, in the end, rightly. What woke him up was an SS Storm Troop leader having decided to blow up the Havel River sluice in Wendisch Burg and flush out the Soviet troops to the south with all the water above it. First of all (spoken in an almost not even scandalized voice but contented, knowing he's in the right:) First of all, this was Martin Niebuhr's sluice. His superiors were solely the Department of Waterways and perhaps Berlin, but in Berlin the front lines currently ran past the Halle Gate and Alexanderplatz. The SS plan violated the chain of command, it was totally illegal, and civil officer Niebuhr was of no mind to condone or support an action running contrary to official regulations. He had worked on the damming of the water since he was a child, whether by stacking branches or apprenticing as an assistant sluice keeper, and it went against his acquired nature to flood the Strelitz countryside, his own handiwork, with the Havel. In addition, the explosion would also blast the official building, his house, across the region, and he knew full well that the Department of

Waterways would never give him anything but this Wendisch Burg sluice and not even that if it ever was rebuilt. It was Cresspahl who expounded to us Martin Niebuhr's considerations and motives; what Niebuhr actually said, brief and final, was: *Can't be done.*

He thought that this official statement would take care of it. Luckily for him, he was faced not with the SS but with two military engineers sent by the SS and not terribly happy about it, since the SS was comfortably dug in just outside the South Gate of Wendisch Burg and these two were alone in a completely cleared area, half a mile or so closer to the enemy. One of them is apparently an architect in Hamburg today, so he might have known something about construction and felt averse to destroying a sluice facility. As for the other, the SS was still too close, he was afraid of a court-martial and being shot, he set to work busily unloading the dynamite from the sidecar of his motorcycle and seemed determined to blast a big hole in the ground just there at nine o'clock sharp the next morning. (This was on the evening before April 29.) Gertrud Niebuhr had overheard the time set for the detonation, but first it was time for dinner. There were two children at the table with them: a ten-year-old boy and his two-year-old brother. Since Gertrud Niebuhr was in her own house, not someone else's, she expressed herself freely about this plan to inundate her own neighbors' houses in the villages to the south, and while she listed the names at great length Martin Niebuhr had time to work out his plan undisturbed. He sacrificed two untouched, unopened bottles of liquor, with which he'd been planning to make a down payment on a cow; he left nothing undone. Then he came out with his view that blowing up the sluice, if it was a military action at all, was one directed more against the civilian population than against anyone else. He could sketch out a contour map for his guests, if they wanted, showing the Mecklenburg rises

Go on an call em mountains. Even if theyre Mecklenburg mountains, come on, theyre mountains!

behind which the Red Army could advance to the north unhindered, even if the Bolter sluice on the Müritz were blown up too, they wouldn't have to rush in and occupy a big wet patch south of Wendisch Burg! And a patch is all it'd be, too! There were many times, after the war, when I was

848 · *April 11, 1968 Thursday*

visiting the sluice house, when I looked at him to see if he was capable of

visiting the sluice house, when I looked at him to see if he was capable of shouting, and found him quietly good-humored, patient, more of a grand-father than an uncle to his brother's two children. And yet the Niebuhrs had a young tank soldier hidden in their attic that night, a deserter, and Karsch said he could hear the old man's voice loud and clear through the ceiling. The older boy, Klaus Niebuhr, secretly brought Karsch's share of dinner upstairs, and Karsch realized that there must also be a telephone at the place the Russians had reached by that time. No use denying it, Karsch.

At this point, Cresspahl would imitate his brother-in-law Niebuhr on the phone as if he'd been there in person. Holding a pretend receiver to his ear, exaggeratedly astounded at the lack of dial tone; holding the receiver out at arm's length like something disgusting, then putting it down. His normal telephone was connected to the main network and the SS had disabled the switchboard in the post office. Niebuhr had wanted to show he was brave enough to talk over a line the Gestapo might have been listen-ing in on; it was harder for him to use his other telephone, connected to the Department of Waterways private network, for a purpose that would surely have to be called private. But he was in a hurry; he couldn't count on the two engineers staying alone with his wife and cognac for too long without getting suspicious. The first lock south of Wendisch Burg came on the line with a serious: *What a business! Man, what a business!*

– Ya got that right: Martin Niebuhr said. He was also hampered by the cover story he had planned to use on the open line. – *Theyre right here*: said Ewert Ewert. I went to see him in 1952, near Strelitz; he told it the same way. Niebuhr didn't even have to initiate his act of high treason. A Soviet officer took the phone from Ewert and asked to hear the situation in Wendisch Burg. Since the officer spoke German almost without an accent, Niebuhr had to ask him to say something in Russian. – I can't understand you; please speak proper German: the Russian said in Russian. Niebuhr still thought it might be an SS trap and asked for Ewert again. – It's'a Russians allright!: Ewert confirmed. And then, after these justified suspicions, wasting precious time, the Soviets got their picture of the enemy situation. The SS had marched into Wendisch Burg on Hitler's birthday and promptly told the town to supply a gift for the occasion. The townsfolk had had to dig tank traps in a semicircle around the South Gate. The street looked untouched but was mined. The gate looked invitingly open, like a monument, just like the guidebooks said, but there were rails laid behind it down which they could push a wall of solid rocks. Here, on either side, the SS had set up machine guns on the town walls. There was a company of men in town guarding the high school, where prisoners from the dissolved concentration camps were being kept once they couldn't be marched any farther. The guards were supposed to shoot the prisoners the moment a German victory in Wendisch Burg was in doubt. Martin Niebuhr confirmed to the man on the other end of the line, in great embarrassment, that Soviet citizens were among the prisoners marked for death in this way. The SS had forgotten about the harbor—the town lay exposed to the whole lake. The army was to the north; they had wanted to move on before the SS took them under their command. – I thank you for your service in the fight for peace: the voice told Niebuhr in its strange, meticulous German, so that he was shaking his head when he returned to his guests in the living room. He told them he'd been on the phone and the Soviets would be there in half an hour.

The Soviets entered Wendisch Burg from the north, when it had just turned dark out; on the lake side of town they met the units that had crossed the lake right before midnight, and there was shooting only around the high school, and not for long. Not until they had freed the prisoners did they turn their serious attention to the SS at the South Gate, and what was left of the SS then drove past the sluice at top speed and took the first turnoff to the west. The engineers at Niebuhr's place took their uniforms off, sold him the dynamite and motorcycle, and headed out on foot through the woods, toward Müritz, to a village where Martin Niebuhr knew some people.

The next day, the Red Army officially marched into Wendisch Burg, flag flying, between undamaged timbered gables. There were certainly a lot of phone calls made that night.

Cresspahl finished his story with the saying that's carved into one of the timbered beams of a house on Old Street in Wendisch Burg, three doors down from the post office, and maybe it's still there today: ONLY / A FOOL / TRIES TO PLEASE / ALL.

I dont wan you makin this all public, Gesine. Cresspahl shoulda kept his trap shut.

It's true, though, Uncle Niebuhr, isn't it?

Truth. Truth. Whatta loada crap.

April 12, 1968   Good Friday

Yet the bank's open.

And de Rosny's friends in the Treasury Department seem to have been less reliable than he might have hoped. The United States doesn't want to take the initiative in returning the $20 million of Czechoslovak gold, but insists that any initiative must start from Prague. One justification is: So as not to compromise Mr. Dubček's reforms.

– A teachable people, you are: Mr. Shuldiner said on the phone last night. One of the leaders of the Socialist League of German Students, Rudi Dutschke, who does, however, prefer (according to a quotation) arguing for change to the use of force, was shot three times yesterday afternoon by an unknown gunman in West Berlin. Mr. Shuldiner was trying to be nice to Mrs. Cresspahl. The German shouldn't hear the news from Germany any later than necessary. The Germans, eager to learn. That's how it looks from the outside. *The New York Times* adds, practically shocked: Mr. Dutschke had no police protection. That's something they still need to learn, it seems.

President Johnson has called up 24,500 reserves to the Vietnam War. A few days ago he was still talking about 13,500.

On Easter twenty-nine years ago, Cresspahl sent away a Jewish refugee from Berlin. He had escaped from a concentration camp, was dressed in normal clothes again—white summer coat, Tyrolean hat—and his gestures, too, fit him so loosely that it seemed like they could fall right off him at any moment and leave him standing there with nothing but fear: he is remembered, still present. Gronberg; I don't remember his first name. A tobacconist from Schöneberg in Berlin. He was looking for a fisherman to take him to Denmark. Cresspahl kept him in the house only long enough to pretend he was telling him the best route, maybe he gave him a meal; he didn't, though, go to Rande with him, help him find and convince a fisherman. The man had a forty-five-minute walk to the sea, after his long trip, and Cresspahl sent him off alone. After the war he told me that he hadn't wanted to endanger his business with the English (against the Germans) for the sake of this one man. I often think I understand that. I wish, how I wish, I could understand Cresspahl in this too.

For the Jews, tonight is the beginning of the festival commemorating the exodus from Egypt more than two thousand years ago, and at the Ferwalters' the dishes used on only this one occasion a year will be out on the table with the baked goods and wine that symbolize the stones and mortar of the Egyptian pyramids, and Rebecca will ask the four questions to start the celebration, the Ferwalters will drink wine four times—to their release from bondage, deliverance from servitude, redemption from dependence on Egypt, and finally their being the Chosen People, selected— and once again Marie will not be allowed into her friend's apartment. Marie feels only curiosity.

The Ferwalters' Pesach dishes are from Germany. We asked Karsch for help, and he did get them cheaper than we could and sent them in separate packages, each below the minimum for New York customs. They're valuable, with cobalt-blue rims, in upper-class style, but we've never seen them. When it's not Pesach they rest in the Ferwalters' linen closet, packed in linen and plastic. It's a Rosenthal service because Mrs. Ferwalter thinks that this is a Jewish company, because of the name.

Louise Papenbrock had a Rosenthal service, with lots of green fish swimming through reeds, and the Papenbrocks called these plates "the Rosenthals," including on the few occasions when the Semigs were there.

Our bakery on Broadway has turned into a Jewish one today. They have no bread other than the unleavened kind, because in the hasty flight from Egypt the dough had to be taken in that state, and instead of pastries there's the stuff made of nuts, raisins, apples, and cinnamon that Mrs. Ferwalter calls charoset. For Mrs. Ferwalter came into the store after us, stood happily next to us, and again and again encompassed us in her affectionate, disgusted look.

What did Dora Semig mean when she described herself as Jewish, "which is true enough"? Did she convert to the Jewish faith among the Czechs, or the French? Did Semig try, at the end of his life, to live how the Jews live?

Mrs. Ferwalter doesn't know how salt can be kosher, or why the super-market doesn't stock products stamped simply "kosher" these days, only products certified by a rabbi as "Kosher for Passover." Is it because no flour is used for the Pesach cookies? How can salt be kosher? She doesn't know. She shrugs her fat shoulders, shakes her kindly, nauseated face back and forth, as much as to say well, what's the difference? The customer in front of us puts a large box of matzoh down on the counter by the register and says as she does so: I'm sick of matzoh!

Mrs. Ferwalter, with a big eavesdropping smile, pointed out this un-orthodox person, as though raising a finger in front of schoolchildren to show them how they are not supposed to do things. Then she paid for her own matzoh, a small, thrifty box.

Walking down Ninety-Fifth Street, it came to her. She knew after all: People just want to make money!: she said. – *Everything is business!* she repeated, happy to be playing the role of the wise elder, more experienced, able to teach young Cresspahl and her daughter something about the ways of the world. When we say goodbye on West End Avenue, she lovingly hugs Marie to her giant hips, like her own daughter. Then, having shared her holiday cheer with us, she walks laboriously off on her oversize legs that the German SS broke for her.

There are posters in the subway stations that show an older Indian, with a weather-beaten face, black pigtails, black hat, eyes twinkling with the delight of biting into a product of a Jewish firm:

> You don't have to be Jewish
> To love Levy's
> real Jewish Rye

There tend to be swastikas drawn on these posters. It's true that they aren't drawn correctly, following the template, but tonight I saw one more of them than I did this morning.

April 13, 1968 Saturday, South Ferry day
but we kept going, taking buses from the St. George terminal onto the Verrazano Bridge, far above the open neck of the harbor, raised high into the pale blue warm surrounding sky, and then through south Brooklyn to

Coney Island, where people in brightly colored shirts and dresses are anticipating the summer on the wooden boardwalk, and finally to the Stillwell Ave. subway station, in front of which you can get what Marie says are the best hot dogs in New York, the only little sausages that aren't poison, and we rode back underground for another hour, under the East River and across Manhattan, to our Ninety-Sixth Street and Broadway, and that night we were tired as if from a vacation. On the way, Marie kept wanting to have her mother lose the war.

 – How did the Russians treat you?: she asked, looking not a little suspicious. She was prepared to discount at least half of any normal stories I had about the Russians, because I don't consider the Soviets beneath discussion, as she does. I don't consider them "the others." She has picked up her anti-Communism like something breathed in with the air.
 – It was the British who came to Jerichow, Marie.
 – The British, of course. Since Cresspahl was involved with the English, it had to be the English who came to him. Everything in your stories always has to fit together, link up with no snag, not the tiniest little mousehole of a gap!: she said. It was her last try. I had one final chance to admit that Cresspahl's dealings with the English were more likely, given their entry into Jerichow, but still not true. For the last time, Marie tried to clear her grandfather's name of treason.
 – It was the British, and Cresspahl couldn't care less, Marie. He was done with them. His work was over. In January 1945 he'd gotten word from Hamburg that he should go undercover as completely as possible, not endanger himself any longer.
 – Decent people, the English.
 – Decent, and not talkative. Not once did they bother him again, until Ludwig Krahnstöwer ran off at the mouth just because he'd turned seventy.
 – Cresspahl couldn't have not cared whether his daughter grew up under the Russians! Gesine!
 – He didn't try to get me to Holstein. He had a cousin there, on a farm, who could have seen us through. The commander of Mariengabe—
 – I wish you'd say "Jerichow-North." It's like you're trying to draw me in by using my name.
 – The commander would have handed him travel orders to East Holstein,

no questions asked, stamped safe as could be. But all he wanted, along with the rest of the civilian airfield personnel, was to be formally discharged from the German Air Force, backdated to mid-April. Kutschenreuther even offered the soldiers discharge papers, but so few of them wanted to leave that even on the morning of May 2 there were operations as usual at the air base, hoisting the flag, drills and exercises, equipment training.

– Why was Jerichow safer than anywhere else?

– Because it was in the middle. On April 29 the British entered Bremen and the Soviets occupied Wendisch Burg. From Jerichow you could wait and see who got to Wismar first. If you went west too soon you would end up in the fighting. Even so, an old woman on School Street was doing brisk business as a fortune-teller. And one night there was a break-in at the town pharmacy, because Dr. Berling refused to prescribe deadly pills, not even if it did turn out to be the Russians who came. There were no more sleeping pills to be had, the NSDAP leadership had confiscated them for their own use after the party officials had to give all their guns to the fighting troops.

– And Cresspahl was still building "dispatch boxes" at the airfield for the German victory?

– He borrowed a team of horses and got his machinery and drove it to a brick shed next to the house. I feel like he just unloaded the machines, covered them, locked the door, and that was that. Sat in the sun, pipe comfortably slanting down from between his teeth, and warmed his hands. Waiting.

– He didn't want to abandon his property.

– Well, legally it was my property, Marie.

– You know me too well, Gesine. You know I'm a sucker for fathers.

– He hadn't even been letting me go to Gneez for school. The first time I came back and told him that we only had to recite poems, "Archibald Douglas" and the like, so the school wouldn't lose face, he sent them a note from Dr. Berling and another of his own: "My daughter is needed at home." Those were happy days.

– You lazy student, Gesine!

– True. And I sat on the milk rack with "our" Frenchmen and taught them the forbidden song. In the army they would punish you for singing it; in Jerichow-North you'd break off in the middle if you saw a superior coming, but Cresspahl just stood there pleased, listening to Maurice and Albert's clumsy attempts. Zherman eez deefeecult languewich.

– Sing it for me.

– Everything is finished,

Everything is through;

In March, it's, Hitler's turn,

In May the Party too. . . .

– Boy, you really can't sing. Sorry.

– And here come the English, Sixth Airborne Division.

– Excellent. White parachutes filling a sky like this one, drifting down onto the Jerichow-North airfield.

– The Sixth Airborne came through Gneez on May 2 and hurried off toward Wismar. All they sent to Jerichow were a couple of men in a truck.

– Not even tanks?

– The Eleventh Tank Division entered Lübeck. Why would they need tanks in Jerichow?

– You never make the war exciting, Gesine!

– For your sake?

– Well. Kind of. Yeah.

– They accepted Kutschenreuther's surrender of the airfield and ordered him to continue to run it. They removed Mayor Tamms and ordered him to continue to serve in a provisional capacity. Then they went looking for a new mayor.

– And Cresspahl showed them his halfpenny minted in 1940!

– It wasn't like in the movies, Marie. They thought of Kliefoth first, but he felt it necessary to report to them in full uniform, with all his medals of honor and decorations pinned on. Next in line was Papenbrock. The officers were billeted at his house, and Papenbrock slipped back into the old days, tried to wangle something, hand out this, get back that. They had a look at the strange old guy's son-in-law, and since he could actually talk to them in their language they made him mayor, with Tamms as deputy.

– Gesine.

– If you insist. In the first week of June, intelligence officers from the Second Army came following the combat troops and questioned the mayors. They had Cresspahl on one of their lists. For them he took out a piece of wood that had once been a level, unscrewed the brass in the middle, and showed them the coin.

– I can't picture that without a manly embrace. Or some fine words.

– These were officers, Marie. Career military men. By doing his work on time and acting dumb, Cresspahl had gotten along fine with Kutschenreuther, who in the end was only reserve, a shoe manufacturer from Osnabrück, hardworking and prudent enough, a little man who gave orders as if he didn't quite believe they'd be followed. The men who'd come to see Cresspahl were different: the kind who thought they stood apart from the rest of society, single-minded about their work as a sacred duty, their gaze turned inward. And they really carried their batons clamped between their elbow and lower ribs, just like I'd seen in pictures.

– What did they say, Gesine.

– *Thank you for taking the trouble to see us.* We're dreadfully sorry to be taking up any of your time.

– And Cresspahl?

– That he'd rather keep it a secret. They took that as a faux pas, as if he were doubting their professional honor. Nodded to him, drove out of the courtyard. They'd walked right past the refugees in the house without seeing them.

– Was Jakob already there?

– Yes.

– Not now, Gesine.

– Whenever you want.

– And really, nothing else touch-and-go with the English? Shots in the night? Attempts to blow up Jerichow Town Hall? Anything exciting at all?

April 14, 1968 Sunday

– You dialed West Berlin, Mrs. Krissauer?

– Two minutes ago. Eight-five, five-three, five-....

– West Berlin is on the line.

– Seat reservation.

– Is that your code for today, Anita?

– It is. Gesine. Where are you? At the airport? Tempelhof or Tegel?

– I'm at home.

– I know you. You're in the Hospiz Hotel in Friedenau two blocks away trying to trick me. Come over right now!

– I'm on Riverside Drive. It's seventy degrees here, Fahrenheit.

– It's not true.

– Anita, listen. I just wanted to ask you something. Whether you're still alive.

– Ask me something easier. Why wouldn't we still be alive, Gesine?

– Last summer, during the riots in Newark, you called me to—

– These aren't riots, Gesine. You know what it usually takes to make a revolution.

– It says in *The New York Times* that several thousand students blocked traffic on the Kurfürstendamm for more than two hours last night, that the police used horses and water cannons—

– That's right. Today too. Almost four thousand. I saw it. The police charged like mad into the crowd clubbing anyone within reach. The students fought back with sticks, with cans of spray paint, firecrackers, even apples!

– Were you there?

– As an old lady, you know, thirty-five....

– I am too, Anita.

– Yeah well I can't do it anymore. They run at the police chanting "Ho! Ho! Ho Chi Minh!" My feet don't join in and my mouth doesn't open.

– We really are alike. Why Ho Chi Minh? Isn't it about the killing of Herr Dutschke?

– It's about Rudi Dutschke and Herr Professor Doktor Springer, said to have brought about Dutschke's murder with his newspapers.

– *The New York Times* says: The murder was inspired by the assassination of Martin Luther King.

– It was!

– Then I don't understand it, Anita.

– The president of the Republic of North Vietnam as a symbol of the revolutionary war of liberation, and a newspaper publisher as a symbol of the powers of oppression. Something like that, Gesine.

– There's a quote here: Not with violence but through the force of the argument....

– Dutschke?

– Yes.

– Well maybe we're not supposed to understand it, Gesine.

– *Don't trust anyone over thirty.* So it's not an uprising.

– No, it's just that you shouldn't go down the Kurfürstendamm, Gesine. We built a little protective floodgate....

– Hey, be careful.

– Just a piece of sugar for the horses listening in.

– With their little ears and big heads.

– Nasty creatures when they get scared. Feel bad when they kick out. Peace March, that's what they called it. At the head an older man, with a wooden cross—

– Celebrating Easter there too?

– and the police aimed six big jets of water at him, thicker than an arm. At one point a Negro appeared, an American apparently, and the police were suddenly gentle as doves. Photographers everywhere, from the papers, the TV stations, the student organizations keeping track of police contact. The police beating a citizen of the protecting power, America! Then they arrested him after all. The police have 350 people in their bunker now.

– And you a proper matron on the sidewalk.

– Hey, I'm a society lady! My dress is gone, my back needs a plumber. Those are some serious water cannons, you know! You'd have gotten knocked over too.

– "Anita, my child!"

– Yeah, I wouldn't bring my grandmother to something like this. Soaking wet in the tram. Which is free today. If you look like a student going to the march, the East Germans will let you ride for free.

– Since they're not allowed to meddle in the domestic affairs of West Berlin, right.

– In theory, no. What have you been up to?

– We went all the way to Coney Island yesterday afternoon just to have a Nathan's little-sausage, oh you really should come. I'd show you everything. Everything. We left around seven thirty, and at twenty past eight the Negroes attacked the area, the corner of Surf and Stillwell Avenue, youths, children!, broke windows and fought with the police. One patrolman was hit over the head with a bottle, he needed six stitches. Then the trouble spread into the subway station, into the trains, the Negroes were racing through the trains, knocking whites to the ground, robbing them, breaking more windows—

– Because of King's assassination.

– Because of Martin Luther King. And it was very hot. But now everything's back to normal in the city.

– What's wrong, Gesine?

– You think they canceled their Easter Parade on Fifth? Complete with a fashion show—Nehru jackets, bonnets—everyone bouncy as a puppy?!

– But it's only a week since they shot Martin Luther King!

– That's the kind of country this is.

– Were you two at the parade?

– No.

– Still, Gesine, don't come back here. We're not getting anywhere here either.

– What do you mean, Anita.

– Gesine. What we wanted, as children.

– Socialism and all that.

– Right. You know, I was at a teach-in at the Technical University yesterday and the young people actually didn't kick me out. They discussed why they were still being beaten and dispersed by the police. How it happens that only twenty cars were there to block the distribution of the Springer newspapers, when they'd expected six to eight hundred. Then a young man stood up, twenty-three years old, psychology student, and he explained it to them. He hadn't come to the last protest, he said, because the car belonged to his father. He can't put it at risk. He's perfectly willing to break with society, just not with his father. Destroying other people's property, sure, but don't let any harm come to his own. All with talk of the working class they're supposed to be convincing to overthrow society. Using a vocabulary that even a well-educated person would need a special course to understand.

– Don't get so angry.

– And you can get beaten up or shot just as well there too, on Stillwell Avenue, or Riverside Drive.

– Listen, I'm sorry about your back.

– Gesine, is it true about the plague? That it's being carried back to you in America from Vietnam?

– You can't expect otherwise with five thousand cases a year. One of them will infect an American.

– It says that in your newspapers?

– It does. What have you been doing? Besides business?

– Other than business we're still operating our business. And the old man is on a lecture tour in Poland.

– Sounds like you're both still risking your necks. How can you!

– We're a proper academic couple, Gesine, you should take a leaf out of our book. Who would ever guess that people like us run a travel agency for one-way trips?

– Not me.

– Why don't you come around anymore wanting someone brought from Rostock to Lübeck? We'd do it for you at cost.

– Most of my people are dead, and the children from my year in school have left. All the ones who wanted to.

– Look at all this treasure we're burying under the Atlantic. Pure gold.

– I know, right?

– What time is it there?

– Six in the afternoon. The park out the window is all colorful with people on the grass.

– Keep going.

– The sky above the Hudson is puffed clear except for a couple of fat white clouds. The Palisades are brown now, the skyscrapers above them flashing in the light. Shimmering between the thin trees, you know.

– And Marie?

– Gone swimming.

– Like it's peacetime.

– And for you it's the middle of the night. Are you in bed?

– In bed, with a bent back. The middle of the night, the mail plane overhead. Good night, New York.

– Good night, Berlin. Come visit.

– I will! And just to see you. Imagine that!

– Yes.

5:20 p.m.

Two Negroes are standing between the cars on the West Side subway line, singing something wailing, howling, a bit like a religious service. The Negroes in the car look serious and conceal their faces behind fatigue, suffer under the damp air that's crept into the tunnel. (Thin nets of rain had hung in the air around Grand Central.) A white tries to get the others to grin, by casting glances at the singing Negro, but in vain. All the passengers in the racing, swaying train are entirely indifferent to the danger that the black men will slip and fall. If the transit police drag them off the train before we get to our stop, we ourselves will definitely be late, and we don't want that, we want to get home, we're coming home from work, *rabotat', rabotat'!* The men are singing, they're trying to put some life into somebody.

The New York Times discusses the student revolt in West Germany indulgently, forbearingly, making an effort to be fair—an old lady who feels that she understands the youth of today. Her true concern, though, is that the East German Communists might exploit the unrest for their own purposes, and all of a sudden her opinion turns into a letter to the Soviet Union: May it refrain from encouraging Mr. Ulbricht on this dangerous course.

The Soviet Union had long since sent its Ulbricht Group to Friedrichsfelde, near Berlin—even before the German forces capitulated. But Jerichow thought it was safely British.

The British in Jerichow wanted to show that their mayor deserved respect, and they sent a jeep with a driver for him every morning, which was to take him to work, from one end of the tiny town to the other. They flew a Union Jack from Town Hall and stationed an armed guard outside his room. They helped him and turned his official pronouncements into realities:

The military court imposed a year in prison as punishment for stealing 30 kg of potatoes, and six months for 15 kg; nine months for using a motorcycle without permission from the military government; three months for being out after curfew;

and anyone who spit on Cresspahl would get nine months in prison for insulting a representative of the British Crown, which they would have to spend in the basement under his office. Cresspahl was the only German in Jerichow who was allowed to use electricity for anything other than operating a radio. For the counterintelligence officers who came to question Cresspahl had felt compelled to take Eduard Tamms off to prison camp after all, despite Cresspahl's asking them not to, so the uneducated mayor often had to stay up late in Town Hall, constructing official statements, out of words, with Leslie Danzmann at the typewriter, under electric lights.

And so Jerichow gradually came to look quite respectable. When Karsch snuck through the Soviet-occupied zone to Jerichow, the town seemed downright opulent to him. The shopwindows may have been empty, and even the tradesmen had signs on their doors saying that no one would answer no matter how long people knocked, and his bottle of kerosene from Wendisch Burg was enough to make him practically rich in cigarettes; but there were no lines of people outside the Town Hall offices, no refugees who had to sleep out in the open, and a stray soldier would be picked up right at the entrance to town, driven to the Jerichow-North camp, questioned, fed (officers ranked major or higher in accord with Air Force Daily Rations Class I, thanks to Kutschenreuther still managing the base), and after a few days driven west, even if he wanted to stay in Jerichow. The town lay small and peaceful under the white summer sky, as if in peacetime. On June 15, Montgomery canceled one of his orders from March: now British soldiers were allowed to speak to, and play with, German children. Every night at nine the town turned obediently quiet and dark; the children too had learned about hunger by that point. The one house that wasn't tidy and respectable was Cresspahl's.

He had split up half the house among refugees from Pommern, later from East Prussia; he didn't have time to keep it tidy there too. In his own house there were two children lying sick with typhus. He counted on Mrs. Abs and her groats to keep them alive, maybe even cure them. It was Jakob's mother's face I saw above me that summer—gaunt, parched, squinting; distressed when we were too weak to eat.

Cresspahl had put his child in the bed he'd built in London in 1931 for himself and Lisbeth; now I lay in it not alone but with a fourteen-year-old girl who, in my fever, I kept thinking was Alexandra Paepcke, and I wasn't scared even though I knew she was dead. She lay in a big nest of white hair, bright sandy blond like Alexa's; like Alexa's, it ruffled out over her forehead a tiny bit when Jakob's mother combed it; from the side her nose resembled Alexa's, and all she had to do was close her eyes to look like Alexa asleep. I could only see her from the side. At night I would start up out of a dream and cry for help, from Alexandra, lying next to me. In her dreams she cried out for her parents.

Her parents, the Ohlerichs in Wendisch Burg, had sent Hanna to Warnemünde, to some fisherman relatives, so that she'd be safely at sea during the last acts of war. That's what she talked about when she was awake. On May 1, she had set out from Warnemünde on her uncle's cutter, along with German U-boats. There were still German warships off the coast. At Rerik Reef, German planes came out of the sky and shot holes in the cutter. After three days on Poel Island, they had the cutter shipshape again. In the Timmendorf harbor, launches were still delivering conscripts. Then Polish forced laborers tried to ransack the cutter, and they set out for Wismar. German warships were still anchored in the roads. From a Wismar merchant ship the Ohlerichs replenished their stores and received instructions to scuttle their boat if Soviet craft got close. Hanna tried to figure out the time from the position of the sun, and how many hours of swimming it would take to reach the Danish coast. When they got to Gedser, they were shot at by British planes, which stopped only when the family hoisted a white sheet. It was still Greater Germany in Gedser, an army commander was in charge of the port and the SS in charge of him. There were relatives from Rerik in Gedser but they had set sail before May 2 and didn't know anything about Hanna's parents in Wendisch Burg. Refugees from East Pommern and East Prussia were living in the cattle-loading stalls, on straw. A German Railroad ferry was docked in the harbor, with an army general and his sister-in-law living in its saloon. His staff officers were camped out on the bridge of the ship. After the capitulation, people from the Danish resistance took charge of the port and the refugees were given food from the SS field kitchens, then butter and bread and cheese too, and because the food was distributed by Germans the butter was star-shaped. In mid-May the refugees were let out of the locked stalls and taken to a prison in Nykøbing; the fishermen were ordered to sail to Flensburg. The Ohlerichs went to Niendorf, where they'd had friends since the twenties, when they'd fished together, with seines. After five weeks, at Hanna's insistence, they went south, and from Travemünde they were deployed to Wismar, where the people were starving. The Englishman in charge of the town welcomed the fishermen. They were very valuable to him, and he sent patrol boats out with the cutters because by then the Soviets were already on Poel and trying to capture fishing boats for themselves. The patrol boat sped in circles around the ten cutters, you try gettin a fish out a the water like that. The Wismar commander realized that fishing in a group didn't bring in enough of a catch and the cutters were allowed to sail on their own, each with an English soldier on board. The Ohlerichs had to get their soldier out of bed in Wismar and then he slept belowdecks again until four. Then he made tea, and gave some to Hanna, with some sugar too. Just when Ohlerich was about to send his eldest boy to Itzehoe to buy nets, the news reached Wismar that the area was being exchanged. The Soviets were already stationed at the eastern border of Wismar and that night they came through the border zone into town. The Ohlerichs decided to go back to Warnemünde, they had a house in town there, and Hanna thought that was closer to Wendisch Burg. Off Kühlungsborn they were shelled despite their white armbands and the ticking on the mast. There were a lot of cutters on the water and women visible on board every one. It was a Sunday when they pulled into Warnemünde, the townspeople promenading along the boardwalk in their holiday best. The fishermen were taken off their boats by the Soviet military the moment they moored at the pier and led to a kitchen space on Front Road. The Russians shoved in a bucket of kasha and the Germans, afraid of poison, didn't touch it. At night they were taken one floor up, one at a time along a red coconut-matt runner, for interrogation. Two officers with plank-like epaulettes divided up the work: one wrote, the other frisked. From the other rooms you could hear Russians celebrating their victory. How could she explain that a wooden clothespin with a coil spring wasn't a murder weapon? Why did the victors refuse to believe that Hanna had ordinary scraps of cotton in her pocket because she'd had to clean machinery on the cutter, not to tie colored threads together into a signal? The next day, three of the boat captains were taken to the commander; the others had to march on foot, under guard, to Neubukow. Fishermen marching! In Neubukow, Hanna thought of Cresspahl, who used to come and see her parents in Wendisch Burg, and she ran away from the guard and came running, ducking left and right, down Road 105 through the Soviet lines to Jerichow. Hanna had avoided the war, like the Ohlerichs wanted; now she was lying sick in Jerichow and couldn't go back to them.

– Are these adventures at sea exciting enough for you, Marie?

– And Jakob?: Marie says.

– Jakob wasn't in the house. He'd taken the Abs horses and gone to work in a village on the coast, in exchange for part of the harvest. He didn't come to Jerichow much.

– Tell me how it started, Gesine.

– When the refugee carts from the east had been unloaded, Jakob took all the horses and rode out into the marsh. Cresspahl had told him where to find a watering hole safe enough to use as a horse pond. He was five years older than me. He was one of the grown-ups. He had a grown-up face, secretive, stubborn, severe. He had a bandage around his neck, and under it a wound from a strafer. I wanted to help him and I pretended I knew my way around horses. After leaving the pond the horses were frisky and Jakob asked if I knew how to canter. Again I said yes. He'd given me a sorrel to ride, a playful young thing, and I didn't have to bring it to a gallop, it started jumping when it saw its friend jumping. To the animal's amazement I flew headfirst over its head and landed in front of its feet. It had stopped so abruptly that it looked from below like it was about to tip forwards. Looking accusingly at me. After that I kind of avoided Jakob. Even though he'd been worried when he lifted me back up onto my feet, and he'd put me back on the horse only after a lot of reassurance, he stared straight ahead in such silence that I thought he was laughing at me on the inside.

– And then?

– Then I hid. The typhus had made my hair fall out and given me rheumatism in my shoulders and knees, my bones were all crooked. I didn't want him to see me like that.

– And when he did see you?

– He said: Itll grow back, *wacht man*. And I understood he was promising me new hair, but I didn't understand the rest. It meant, "Just wait."

He was from East Pommern. In Mecklenburg they say, *Töv man. Töv man, du.*

– So you still didn't know each other!

– No.

– And that was the first day of the rest of your life?

– Would you know on the spot?

– Of course, Gesine. I'm not from Mecklenburg. I'll know.

April 17, 1968 Wednesday

In the last week of June 1945, Cresspahl announced that the Western Allies had come to an agreement with Stalin about the date on which they would clear out of their occupied territories of Mecklenburg, Saxony, Saxony-Anhalt, and Thuringia, and in exchange enter the Western Sector of Berlin. The Soviets would be coming to Jerichow on Sunday, July 1, 1945. The British had long since lifted the travel restrictions in their occupied zone, the roads were open from Mecklenburg to Holstein, to Lübeck, to Hamburg, to the Lauenburg Lakes, to Lower Saxony. Should we go with the English or should we stay?

You couldn't take Brüshaver as an example. Brüshaver hadn't found his wife in Rostock; he thought she was dead back when the Royal Air Force coventried Rostock the first time, and then in the concentration camp none of the red preprinted cards came on which the survivors of air attacks could check off whether they'd survived. Brüshaver thought he would find his wife in Jerichow, if anywhere; he reached the town after three days on foot, cadaverous, covered with dust, found the pastor's house vacated by Wallschläger and his wife busy scrubbing the floor. After that, Brüshaver didn't think about fleeing the Russians, he thought about his Sunday sermon.

You would've expected the Papenbrocks to go. The old man had made his money with deliveries to the air force, among other things—they'd take that away from him. And the bakery. And the house full of refugees, he wouldn't get that to himself again. It was baffling that he stayed. It's true he'd missed the nobility's retreat from the area, he couldn't get a single horse-drawn cart for his things anymore—could it be that Albert was ashamed to go on foot? Was it possible that Albert, in his all encompassing wisdom, had neglected to squirrel away land and money in the British zone? Papenbrock hadn't aged well, when he turned up on the street his shoulders were bent, his flyaway hair sticking out under a bald patch that no longer looked elegant, it looked ill. When Papenbrock stayed, it was his first blunder.

A lot of people thought that one person would come back: Arthur Semig, Dr. Vet. Med.

They called it an act of infamy and betrayal on the part of the English to hand Jerichow over to the Russians! In their time under the British, the Mecklenburg soul had already manufactured for itself a right to be taken care of.

On the morning of July 1, the Soviet advance staff arrived in Jerichow, in two big American trucks. They didn't stop in town. At the airfield they found the remains of the British occupying forces. Any planes that had been left intact, the British had fueled up and flown into their zone; there were empty buildings and the runway that Kutschenreuther had been supposed to blow up. The British had taken their prisoners with them, down to the last man. These included a lieutenant general who had said in front of Papenbrock that the Greater German Air Force could never have become the Greater German Air Force without the technical armament assistance of the Soviet Union and the Lipetsk Fighter-Pilot School in the twenties. Clearly he'd decided to take his chances with the Russians. Then he let himself be hauled off to the west after all.

There was still time before the next morning.

Pahl the tailor had lost his relatives in the Hamburg firebombing. He didn't want to live among strangers, depending on the same charity from his fellow Germans that he had denied to homeless refugees himself. He and his family went out into the marsh and drowned themselves in the bog. Others tried it in the Baltic.

Dr. Berling swallowed the pills he hadn't wanted to prescribe to his patients. He had treated the forced laborers and POWs almost like human beings, even giving them sick leave when necessary; in Gneez there were doctors who put a pencil on their hearts, not a stethoscope, and said: Ah. Off you go! Dr. Berling had no reason to be afraid of payback from the Russians, and he took his life anyway, the big depressed *blue devil*.

There was no news of Robert Papenbrock except that the Soviets planned to kill him as soon as they got their hands on him. About Horst's wife, that she'd been taken prisoner outside Danzig as a truck driver for the army. The Böttchers knew about their son that he was in a camp in southern Russia; they'd gotten eight anonymous letters before his name was read out on the Moscow radio. Methfessel the butcher, who'd lost heart after a few weeks in the concentration camp, had been hauled off to a nursing home by the Nazis and, on the Führer's orders, been given a lethal injection as a creature unworthy to live. Friedrich Jansen had gone to ground in the Lauenburg area, where no one knew about what he'd done in Mecklenburg; the pistol he kept with him in case of emergency was discovered at a checkpoint and the British sentenced him to death for possessing a firearm and shot him in Lübeck, without any idea who he was.

A stray soldier had brought to Jerichow a letter from Alexander Paepcke. It was written in Kiev, dated early June 1944. In it Alexander promised his niece, Gesine Cresspahl, a share of his Althagen house if he should inherit it himself. In September 1944 he had reopened the letter and begged Cresspahl to convince Hilde to move from the right bank of the Oder to the left, or if possible farther west to Mecklenburg. Alexander asked Cresspahl to take his family in if he fell in the war. A Frenchman had written around the bloodstains on the letter that the possessor had died on September 29, 1944, but not where he was buried.

Maurice and Albert left for Lübeck with the English. (There was a third Frenchman with them, his name forgotten. A farmer's son from the Clermont-Ferrand region, who'd kept aloof from the city French as well as the Germans.) They didn't say goodbye to the Cresspahl child, and she was disappointed when she found other people in their room. They had taught her how to ask what time it is in their language. They had sung together. The child had believed that they weren't enemies, not hers.

On the night of July 1, many things were buried in the soil of the gardens and courtyards of Jerichow. Papenbrock brought the family silver to Cresspahl, who had to reopen the part of the basement he had already walled shut.

– Did Cresspahl stay because of Lisbeth's grave?

– He didn't want to travel the country road with two children sick with typhus.

– Wasn't he scared of the Russians?

– Why, Marie?

– Gesine, he left you in Soviet hands!

– It was a good education, I wouldn't have missed it. And after eight years I could leave.

And after eight years I could leave.

The walnut trees in front of Cresspahl's house were still standing. Gun stocks are made of wood like that.

Hanna Ohlerich still didn't know why she'd been sent off to sea. Her parents had hanged themselves in Wendisch Burg as soon as she was out of the house. Karsch hadn't wanted to tell her when he saw her lying in a fever.

On the morning of July 2, the Soviet occupation forces marched into Jerichow on the Gneez Road, the men in low clattering horse carts, the officers in American jeeps. The city commander was installed in the brickworks villa across from Cresspahl's house. There they raised the fourth flag of the century. And that one stayed.

That evening, the green picket fence around the headquarters was almost finished.

That evening, Cresspahl was driven there from Town Hall. The commandant wanted to see how his mayor lived. He saw the refugees' cramped quarters in Cresspahl's house, and that the mayor slept in the room that was also his office. He offered to have the house cleared of strangers at once, and wasn't happy with Cresspahl's headshake of refusal. Whenever he could, Cresspahl avoided talking to the Russian—there was so much observing of him to do.

The Soviet major was an old man, stocky, burly, sad. He sighed a lot. He didn't realize he was doing it, but whenever he sat down or started talking, a heavy breath with a slightly throaty tone came out of him. He asked Cresspahl to clear off the table. Then he had his orderly put three bottles of vodka on the table, sent him out of the room, lowered himself into a chair with a sigh, and began the process of getting to know this German. – Pleess, Meeyor: he said, and pointed at the other chair.

It was still light outside. Since night refused to fall, Cresspahl's child crept up to the door to take a look at the stranger, and he tolerantly called her in and had her stand before him.

– You, Fascist: he said teasingly.

The child had wished him good night with the Papenbrock curtsy and was confused that this wasn't enough for him. Her shoulder hurt like it was being beaten. She was embarrassed about the cloth on her head. She was dizzy from fever again, half deaf. Cresspahl watched her like she was facing a test she needed to pass and he wasn't allowed to help. She could barely keep her eyes open. The man looked at her like he was trying to have some kind of fun with her. She wanted to go back to bed and lie down, so she obliged him. This clearly pleased him, and he repeated the game.

– You, Fascist!: he said, in a voice of threat and delight.

– Me Fascist: the child said.

April 18, 1968 Thursday
The New York Times is feeling generous toward John Vliet Lindsay today, and mentions only in passing that he has rejected the proposal to broadcast commercials on city subways as "an invasion of privacy." The passengers' privacy is the fierce withdrawn silence of people trapped, solitary, driven back into themselves.

In the ČSSR, the party newspaper can now report that district organizations representing thirty-one percent of the party's membership were in favor of an extraordinary congress to elect a new Central Committee. According to party statutes, thirty percent is enough. Then the editor of *Rudé Právo* shows up before a session of the presidium and leaves the article out of the second edition, as though it weren't true. On radio and television, however, it can still be reported as the truth.

There were 746 murders in New York City last year, most on weekends, the fewest on Wednesdays. The most common reasons were domestic disputes and insulting comments. Always be polite!

If de Rosny doesn't want it to happen then there's no Thursday afternoon, Professor Kreslil won't get his check, and Employee Cresspahl is invited out to a ball game at Shea Stadium. The employee's child's presence is requested as well. De Rosny wants to be seen in female company.

It's a work occasion, because on Long Island, halfway onto Grand Central Parkway, de Rosny tells his driver that during the game he needs to go fetch a deity named Rutherford from the Regency Hotel and bring him for a meeting in the stadium. Arthur swallows his anticipation and affably replies: The things I won't do for you, Chief. De Rosny can't stand being around anyone not in a good mood—it might dampen his own—so he says: I'll make it up to you with box seats in June, just for you, all right, Arthur? Arthur knows that now he has to give a deep sigh and say, as though dismissing the whole thing: That's all right, sir.

De Rosny passes the time by inventing a dialogue between a teaching robot and a student, with Marie. Clearly he's not interested in buying Xerox after all; he's getting to know computers. As the car drives up to the stadium, a giant enormous three-layer bowl with an eighth of it cut out, de Rosny finishes the game by saying as the robot, in a slow robotic voice: *You did re-al good.*

And Marie says, once again in the role of the courted lady, not just the robot's schoolchild: *You mean "well," don't you?* and they are proud together at having made and corrected a mistake together. He lets Marie walk in ahead of him.

The ushers give him the royal treatment and pull cloths from their back pockets to wipe down the yellow box seats one more time for his benefit. Each compartment is labeled with a plastic sign bearing the name of the season ticketholder. Here is that of the only lord and master above de Rosny—the bank president himself—and de Rosny settles, makes his guests comfortable with affable, careless gestures. They have to change seats twice, so that they'll be sure to think their desires are being catered to, and to let him have his fun.

The flag is still at half-mast.

The crowd is excited, yelling, hooting, celebrating, in their mighty rows of seats, the top ones light green, middle ones bluish, the lowest ones orange. Fifty thousand people want to have a good time.

Finally the words of the national anthem are projected on the scoreboard. Enthusiastic screams at the end. This anthem ends with a question mark.

De Rosny gives appreciative explanations: That ball goes ninety-five miles an hour. If it hits you, you can't complain, Marie! Read your ticket.

Most of the players walk like they've shit in their pants. Sometimes one of them charges a catcher like a tank gone berserk. When someone's injured, the music immediately changes to something more soothing.

– It's a gentleman's game! No violence!: de Rosny shouts excitedly. I guess it looked different from where he was sitting.

Every two minutes, airplanes take off from LaGuardia, thundering. When it's quiet, sellers cry: Peanuts here! Getcher beer here!

De Rosny enjoys not only the game but the opportunity to explain it to Marie. She knows the rules of baseball; she listens to him with wide, obedient eyes, following his pointing finger with them. He describes the *home run*, where the hitter can run around all the bases at once. De Rosny twirls his finger, brings out various comparisons with ballet too.

What, we don't know why there's a green shield hanging behind the flag? It's so the catcher isn't blinded by the sun when he looks at the pitcher.

Then, as he talks about Willie Mays, de Rosny is transformed from a man of the world into a little boy staring intently straight ahead. He's watched Mays since he was a child, his heart pounding every time. At nineteen, Willie Mays still used to go back to Harlem after the game. The self-same man, Willie himself, who wrapped in holy sanctity is swinging his bat down there on the diamond! Used to play ball with the Harlem kids, with a broomstick. *Stickball.*

Where the boss lives they don't know that radical Negroes see Willie Mays as a traitor. He refused to support the black athletes' boycott of the Olympic Games.

De Rosny has never spoken to Willie, only seen him from up close, and yet he talks about him like a friend, as if he shares his suffering, and always looks up to him, because in baseball de Rosny can't do what Willie Mays is famous for. So he says Willie has grown quieter now, but also sadder. A word that doesn't exist in the world encompassed by de Rosny's orders, but does applies to the black idol with the bat.

After hinting at Willie's somber marital history, de Rosny decides something. It brings in no profit, it betrays certain feelings, and yet it shall be. Firmly, defiantly, de Rosny promises his distant, bat-wielding, furiously running friend: Someday, when he can't do it anymore . . . he'll have a job waiting for him in our San Francisco branch!

The airlines tirelessly stamp their logos onto the minds of the people suffering from the noise, especially TWA and Braniff with its Easter egg colors. Next to the 727s, the lower-flying propeller planes seem antiquated.

In the outfield, Willie catches balls with his hands in front of his belly, that's his trademark: de Rosny earnestly explains to Marie, and she registers the information with a nod. Eager to learn. Can't she see that this soul mate of de Rosny's has just caught a ball with his hands much higher? Is all that counts of reality what de Rosny wants?

– Line! Someone's trying to throw across the line and can't do it. – That happens once in fifty years! You're getting everything today.

The batter comes up to the plate; the man on third can steal home. Mrs. Cresspahl is not the only person who wishes she weren't here. Two girls are sitting in front holding up one or another of their homemade signs, listlessly.

Something historic transpires. The coaches substitutes a pitcher, not trusting him with the bases loaded. The new pitcher is ceremoniously driven up to the plate in an open car, his cape taken from him like a gladiator.

At the top of the seventh inning, people stand for their team, de Rosny for the San Francisco Giants, so Mrs. Cresspahl for San Francisco too, not knowing why. Baseball with the boss. People all around them are still sitting.

– Bring 'em all home, Willie!

Near the end of the seventh inning, the fans of New York stand up. About thirty thousand of them, they're not surrounded by people still sitting, and de Rosny raises his chin slightly.

Then Arthur arrives with the deity, Rutherford, an upright white-haired old man without a glance to spare for the field. Golfer. The people sitting in this stadium don't read the financial section of *The New York Times* and fail to realize that a prince in the kingdom of the dollar—practically an archduke—is tarrying among them. The two men withdraw into an empty box toward the back, don't even look up at the resplendent diamond. Both put on glasses and read from little slips of paper for about twenty minutes. De Rosny raises his arm and Arthur is ordered to take the high personage to catch his flight to LA. But the discussion was apparently satisfactory, because now de Rosny doesn't want to watch the rest of the game, he's happy to hear it over the radio in the taxi. The whole thing was very profitable, for Arthur gets promised a second time that he can bring his whole family to the bank's baseball box "sometime this summer."

– Wasn't that a great afternoon, Mrs. Cresspahl?: de Rosny demands.
– Oh, yes, definitely: Employee Cresspahl says.

Don't you like this country, Gesine? Afternoons out like this?
I'm sure you want me to say I do.
Don't like this country? Go find another one.

April 19, 1968 Friday
"The New York Mets gave Willie Mays another chance with the bases loaded yesterday": *The New York Times* says: "and that was a mistake." You got that right. Five to three. Mistake.

Much obliged, Auntie Times.

No, not homesick.

But there is a waking up in the night, with a shock in the nerves, not wanting to recognize the thick gray light outside the windowpanes and looking for another window; even the April colors don't look right, the morning blue of the Palisades, the river dimmed by clouds, the hard trunks of the plane trees in the faint green of the park. Until what's been seen a hundred times finally slides into place above the expectation.

There are mornings when the glittering sun on the East River disappears in the shadow of the blinds, and Long Island becomes a different island. The smog turns the crush of houses in Queens into a soft rolling landscape, forest meadows, vistas of a church tower like a bishop's miter, the way I saw it once from the sea as the boat jibbed, obscured by furrows in the ground, eventually reachable not far past the shoreline cliff.

I don't want to go back there. I have lived in Jerichow, Mecklenburg, Saxony, Frankfurt, Düsseldorf, Berlin. The places are still there, not the dead, not Cresspahl, Jakob, Marie Abs. Not she who I was.

Nine more hours, one more day in front of the humming hacking typewriter, in a wedge of light slanting into the room that wraps the others' voices and the machine noises and my voice into a gray twilight that by noon will have many layers.

Then Marie will be standing on Broadway and 108th Street, next to the car she has picked out for the trip "to America." She has insisted on one condition: that it not be a Mustang.

Then we'll say hello to each other like strangers, and she'll scan my face for traces of work, follow me with her eyes—circumspect, concerned, secretly cheerful. As if she can't let her charge out of her sight.

She calls it: *I'm keeping an eye on you.*

– *Ick häud*: that's how Cresspahl would say *ich hüte*, I'm minding you, when asked about such things. I was still a child. I would stay a child for a long time yet, and someone else would say the same thing too—Jakob.

APPENDIX TO PART TWO

THROUGH CRESSPAHL'S EYES

Information given in the circumstances of 1949. In answer to a sixteen-year-old girl's questions. He was sixty-one.

Why did he, as a German—

He does not see himself "as a German." He's on the side of the Mecklenburgers, who talk about "Prussians"; even before he lived in Holland and Great Britain, he thought of "de Dütschen," the Germans, as the others. He has no desire to be held responsible for them—not their world wars, not their image in the world. Never once did any German ask his opinion about the laws they were imposing on him. What they said in his name cannot even be expressed in Low German. Or Dutch. He always paid his share for life in Germany, paid it punctually, from taxes to garbage-collection fees; even for that it doesn't especially seem to him he got his money's worth. And so he felt both obligated to and free to decide for and about himself, as the occasion demanded.

All right then, as a Mecklenburger.

For a while. As the son of a cabinetmaker on an estate in Müritz, Mecklenburg. As a cattleman's boy, and then an apprentice carpenter after all, in Malchow, Mecklenburg. But not anymore by the time he was in the Holstein Twenty-Fourth Artillery Regiment (Second Battery), in Güstrow; an NCO on the eastern front in 1917; definitely not by 1920, in the Workers and Soldiers Council, at Waren on the Müritz, Mecklenburg, because at that point the Mecklenburgish qualities of the estate owners didn't matter, only the degree to which they had helped, or not, the Kapp and Lüttwitz putsch. After that, in the Netherlands, in England, seen from the outside: a German, or: a Low German, or: Cresspahl.

Why had he gone to live abroad. The Netherlands—

The reason for that was a person, wearing a skirt. Or: He had once

I

practiced the art of woodworking, even if among the Germans he'd had to work for a long time with a hatchet.

To Amsterdam for a girl; to England:

for a girl. It was 1925. Elizabeth. War widow. Very young. Possibly wealthy. MRS. ELIZABETH TROWBRIDGE. Neither of them wanted to get married, they just wanted to come together voluntarily, occasionally, at prearranged times. She helped him financially, with a loan; he paid it back punctually. Unfortunately, the payment date coincided with his decision to marry another woman, from the Müritz region after all; he was willing to live with her suspicions. It had been Elizabeth who insisted on their each having the right to separate, no questions asked; she kept from him her desire for a little less independence, and also her pregnancy. He says he only learned about the child, born in May 1932, a year later, and against her will. HENRY TROWBRIDGE. Died with his mother on November 14, 1940, in a German air raid on the British Midlands. This might be a false report, but he's had to consider it true for too long by this point to want it any different. This would be what Mrs. Trowbridge would have wanted.

Doesn't he want to go back to England?

Not now, not ever.

Because of the German bombings?

That's the second reason. The first: memories. Even picturing a walk through Richmond in London brings back his situation between 1926 and 1933, too much familiar recognition to bear along with the renewed consciousness of his losses. Incidentally, he was familiar with such feelings from the winter of 1932, when he could still have hopes of staying in Richmond—there was nothing new for him to learn there.

His situation in Richmond upon Thames before 1933.

It had a different name then: Richmond, Surrey. Pascal & Son, Master Woodworkers, Renovation, Restoration (also new work) had their house and workshop near North Sheen station. The firm was already fifty years old, with long-term customers from the middle class and the aristocracy, but REGGIE PASCAL was the last, he had no son, and he wanted to leave the business to the Richmond guild. An old man, with curious ideas maybe, but determined to keep the inheritance out of the hands of his nephew, Albert A. Gosling. Buried at North Sheen cemetery. This workshop was, under pressure from Dr. Arthur Salomon of the law firm Burse, Dunaway & Salomon, against his partners' better judgment, given to a master carpenter of German origin to manage in trust.

ARTHUR SALOMON.

Jewish. He'd been stationed on the other side of the western front, as had many a long-suffering reserve lieutenant on the German side. You could compare landscape sketches from the war with him. Arthur Salomon had felt like a foreigner at university, in the army, and still now as a partner of Dunaway and Burse; maybe he wanted to give this German from "Michelinberg" a chance. He also helped by prohibiting Reggie's nephew from setting foot in the workshop, and taking on the headache of managing all business dealings with this Albert A. Gosling, Esq. By 1931 he'd long been a trusted friend, who sometimes came over to visit or for dinner to see Mrs. Cresspahl. He handled Cresspahl's personal business until his death in 1946, in particular the Trowbridge matter, despite his client again being one of the enemy.

Friends in Richmond?

MR. SMITH. First name not known. Carpenter, merchant marine, ship's cook, petty officer first class in the Royal Navy during the war, hard drinker. If he'd mustered up the patience to get his master's qualification, Pascal's workshop wouldn't have been too much for him to handle. A gifted woodworker. Helped Cresspahl run the business until November 1933. Then visited Germany once before the second war. The only person in England Cresspahl would have liked to see after 1945, without any fear it would be awkward. Killed, coincidentally, in Mecklenburgh Square in London, by German bombs, probably the first time in his life he'd set foot in it. Buried in North Sheen, on September 18, 1940.

ALBERT A. GOSLING.

Part owner of a fabric shop in Uxbridge, now able to have a much easier life off the income from Reggie Pascal's inheritance. At first he even wanted to sell the workshop; went along with Salomon's lessons in economic theory, more just to see than from any insight. Hence mistrust of Cresspahl's statements; thus spreading rumors against "the German" in the pubs of Richmond. The income sufficed for a real capitalist's wardrobe, though, and also an attempt at corresponding behavior. The little lord. Greyhounds, young friends. When Cresspahl gave due notice of his termination of trusteeship, Gosling felt justified in his earlier suspicions, bookkeeping-wise as well as economics-theoretically, especially after the German's representative refused to continue to run the work- shop under his own sovereignty. It was Gosling who discovered Mrs. Trowbridge and her child, and also that Dr. Salomon's law firm was sending her regular sums from Cresspahl's English account. In 1938, he uncovered the fact that she'd been returning the money for the past five years, and that Cresspahl thus possessed a sum in a foreign bank large enough to convict him under the German foreign currency laws. Gosling filed charges against Cresspahl, also hoping for a reward, and the British Defense Department, Air Force Division, forced Salomon to hand over the incriminating material. Gosling is once again part owner of a fabric shop in Uxbridge, London.

Why C. didn't try to marry Mrs. Trowbridge.

He doesn't have to answer that.

LISBETH PAPENBROCK.

A girl who took the ferry from Priwall to Travemünde in August 1931. They could have seen each other seventeen years earlier in Malchow, eleven years earlier in Waren, eight years earlier in Amsterdam, ten days earlier at the Schwerin train station. In the end, the Trave River brought them together.

Joining in matrimony: reasons against.

Age difference—she was born in 1906. Her acquaintance with art and higher education. Her addiction to Protestant Christianity. The Pa- penbrock family.

Reasons for.

The future. As he followed her from the ferry landing to the linen store to the garden restaurant on the mouth of the river, he knew for certain that she would come to England with him, for him; that whatever her background he would live with her, for her. They were of one mind about that, before they'd said it. He is not going to give a sixteen-year- old girl marriage instruction.

Married life.

They both spent seven more years trying to keep to the plan they'd agreed to, despite being aware of their various failings. Lisbeth had re- spect for, if not fear of, the spoken word, especially a promise. Disloyalty towards another was for her disloyalty towards oneself. He didn't insist on the four children she'd wanted to grow old with; he'd let her go back for the birth—back to her parents, to the Germans, to the Nazis; eventually he went back to Jerichow with her, for her. She understood her church better there. In Richmond, with four children and different religious services and without the Papenbrock family, she would have had a less easy time finding a reason to die. She'd be only forty-three now.

The meaning of the expression: ALBERT PAPENBROCK, KING OF JERICHOW.

From the beginning, Lisbeth's father struck Cresspahl as someone out of a book. Born in 1868, raised to be nothing more or less than an agrarian capitalist. Encumbered in debt like a general before marrying into money from Hageböcker Street in Güstrow, as well as into a distant relation to genuine nobility, the von Heintzes—neither an entirely insignificant matter when it came to rapid promotion in the Kaiser's war. The later loss of an estate lease near Waren on the Müritz was a dangerous setback. To this day, the old man doesn't know that Cresspahl was on the Waren Workers Council in 1920 and sent the detachment that would ferret out army weapons in the children's room at Papenbrock's house; there was no need for him to learn that so shortly before his death. It's true he gave up the estate only in 1922, perhaps because he, as a middle-class citizen, had given his word of honor like the nobility; perhaps because the guns were found in his house anyway—the scandal wasn't the broken word of honor but that he'd gotten caught. Cresspahl, for his part, inclined to the theory that a Papenbrock could bear up just fine under social condemnation reaching from the southern shore of Lake Müritz to the northern, but that he'd been caught at something else: failing to spend as much on draining the estate as was contractually required. The leaseholder would be no less vigorous before the court than his partner in profit, and when Papenbrock, in an incomprehensible lapse, also forgot to add a certain discreet thousand-mark note to his next offer of a lease, he had to move, straight into the inflation. Shuffling foreign currency and material assets around was more than enough, in 1923, for the von Lassewitz villa in Jerichow, E.P.F. Prange's fertilizer business, Schwenn's bakery, and firm control of the sale of all the grains and sugar beets that came up out of the soil anywhere near Jerichow.

He was the bank in person. He embodied in his own person the historical transformation from agrarian to merchant capitalism: he had, for instance, voted almost instinctively, though secretly, against compensation for the nobility. He was King of Jerichow until 1936, when the Nazis locked his businesses into their Four-Year Plan. Admittedly his comrades from the German National People's Party were still in the Schwerin government, only in rather lower positions than before. Loss of power and fear for the outcome of the war tamed him; by now, Cresspahl could even forgive Papenbrock for have given his mother's first name in the death notice as Grete instead of her real name; it was careless, just a way for the Papenbrocks to assert themselves on this occasion too. All the same, it was hard to believe that such a person was Gesine Cresspahl's grandfather—that she came from such a family at all.

Where did Cresspahl learn these formulations, only now being taught in the New School? "Agrarian capitalist"?

He had once been a member of the Social Democratic Party.

LOUISE PAPENBROCK.

Born Utecht. In 1871. Not often invited to the officers' parties in Güstrow. When the great Papenbrock required her inheritance, she must have been almost pleased. He got his way in everything, and only after the wedding did she start to take refuge in religion. Robert Papenbrock, born 1895. Horst Papenbrock, 1900. Hilde, 1904. Lisbeth, 1906. Successfully implanted the fear of God in the youngest, while the two boys shook it off and Hilde escaped it by living with Alexander Paepcke. She tormented Lisbeth with it the way a sick person tortures an animal. In his, Cresspahl's, view it was practically attempted murder. Louise had been unable to find solace in adultery. Papenbrock went off to Hamburg on important business and had a good time on Herbertstrasse; Louise kept a theology student as a spiritual adviser. The old man did bring fur coats back from Berlin for her, though they didn't always fit and felt ever so slightly used when she put them on; and yet Louise was never permitted to join her husband in the capital. So she wasn't exactly up to snuff when she did have to go to Berlin with a teacher's daughter from Waren, whom Robbie, Louise's fine boy, had gotten pregnant. An abortion proved compatible with her Christian conscience. No custom-fitted fur coat this time either. By then she'd come to be satisfied with Papenbrock's business successes, and she gradually came to enjoy keeping the possessions together, especially during the war of 1914–18, when she had almost sole control of the business and the farmhands. Once, for example, she caught the kitchen maids making a downright hearty lunch for the servants, with real bacon and the good smoked sausage. From that moment on, the *mamsell* had to butter the bread under Louise's supervision, and it occurred to "madame" that she could dilute the coffee too. During the grain harvest. She took Papenbrock's blows and passed them along downward. When he became King of Jerichow, she was out of her depth. Yes, Papenbrock demanded that she personify the power and the glory in their small town; she was never sure that he wasn't about to whistle her back. He stopped the beatings in 1933, when he first became scared of the Nazis, over his possessions. On the other hand, in the summer of 1936 a woman from the Waren region requested an audience with the Papenbrocks, and Louise did not find the stranger worthy of a personal discussion with the great Papenbrock. The woman, around forty, accompanied by her mother, had come for the certificate of Aryan ancestry. Louise didn't understand, not for a long time. What did it have to do with the Papenbrocks whether someone was of Jewish descent or not. She barely remembered the many nights Papenbrock had spent away from home in the 1890s, hunting deer, he'd said. Then she did have to go get Papenbrock from the office after all, so he could celebrate a reunion with his paid-off favorite from forty years back and the fruit of their love. Papenbrock pacified his wife with the same Christian tricks he'd learned from her. And when Lisbeth and Horst died, she not only wore the mourning but bore the grief, as pride, too, that the occasion belonged to none other than Mrs. Papenbrock. Incidentally, as late as 1945 it was still something to see Louise Papenbrock rule the roost in the former Schwenn's Bakery. People would line up for hours on Town Street when the Papenbrocks had baking day, women were fainting with hunger, and Louise, sturdy as ever, gave the customers short shrift and passed out the bread like a blessing, always happy to point to the sign on the wall: *Make it short. Or help me work.* With Louise, Cresspahl preferred to make it short.

Would he like to say anything about Lisbeth's death.

She. . . .

He didn't have to.

On November 9, 1938, an SA squad in Jerichow shot and killed Marie Tannebaum, a child. An eight-year-old girl. A Jewish girl. On the morning of November 10, Lisbeth died in the burning workshop building.

ROBERT PAPENBROCK.

"Robert Papenbrock." There may have been two of them. One was Louise's firstborn son, raised as a prince. He took whatever he wanted whenever he wanted, people as well as things. Old Papenbrock had to pay more than a few maids' dowries and find cottager boys who wouldn't mind raising someone else's child as their firstborn. Papenbrock had wanted to keep his young Robert out of the whorehouses; Louise was content to marvel at Papenbrock's generosity toward chambermaids who had somehow gotten pregnant while in their service. *Little Robbie, my good little boy.* Robbie ruined horses racing them against cars, Robbie aimed guns at village boys and even at his own sister, Robbie was too much for the strictest boarding schools, Robbie stole horses when he couldn't borrow them. This son disappeared from Parchim in May 1914, lived for a while in high style in the alley district of Hamburg, off the gold ducats he extorted from his mother with cheerful threats, and when the time came for able-bodied men to rally to the Kaiser's flag he set sail on a steamer in the South Atlantic. The family let it be known that he was studying import/export in Rio de Janeiro. This was the first Robert Papenbrock. He didn't write letters.

"ROBERT PAPENBROCK."

One of old man Papenbrock's bright ideas. In July 1934 he sent his youngest son away from Germany, with the job or busywork to go looking for the long-lost firstborn. Back came Horst in the summer of 1935 with a man of roughly the right age. He might have been him. Louise thought this was something Papenbrock wanted, and she accepted the stranger, although his easygoing chubbiness, bald head, sluggish manner, and skin coloring around the neck troubled her. His story fit with the one that had stopped in May 1914; he had, of course, spent a long time with Horst by that point. He claimed to have lost his Mecklenburg accent, and Louise decided to believe in his voice. Horst didn't interrupt the man's stories; only shortly before his death did he suggest that the only thing out of all these stories he'd be willing to swear to was a sleazy hotel in New York where the man he'd found had been working. But Horst had spent the years until 1914 with his brother, and Horst swore before the German consulate in New York that this was honestly he. This Robert Papenbrock didn't want to live with his family. He put himself forward to the Hitler government as a friend in the USA for the Nazis, and worked first in the foreign division of the NSDAP, giving speeches at meetings, translating for promotional speakers abroad. Then the secret police took him. First came a postcard from Berlin, in hard-to-read hand-writing; later, occasional letters typed from dictation by secretaries. In the so-called Russia Campaign, he saw action as the head of a special unit behind the front, and old Papenbrock has made it through several dicey interrogations from Red Army investigators. During the war, there were rumors of this special-unit commander executing hostages in Ukraine. He did send a girl from Ukraine to the Papenbrocks, maybe because he still had ladies living in his requisitioned villa in Schwerin, or else because he actually wanted to deliver a bride to his family. This was Slata, who worked for the Soviet headquarters in Gneez after the war, writing and translating.

"The Angel of Gneez."

Until she and her child were arrested and sent east into the Soviet Union. Fall of 1945.

HORST PAPENBROCK.

The old man tried taking a hard line with this son, so as not to lose another heir to overseas or jail. Horst first tried to escape in 1917, into the army. In 1919 he was discharged as an officer's candidate, but the old man still beat him over every mistake he made in the business, how-ever minor. Other punishments included being grounded on dance nights and being made to do estate work on Sundays. Horst's second escape attempt was into the illegal Freikorps paramilitary. The old man rather liked the soldierly side of it, and of course the anti-Communist activity; he could not accept that his son was evading his authority and used a threat of disinheritance to bring him back. Horst was one of the first members of the NSDAP and the SA in Jerichow, harassed and mocked by his father as ever, so during all their military drills the boy was tenta-tive, slack, weak. When he tried to show some energy, it came out jittery. What Horst contributed to the institution of Nazi violence in Jerichow was posting an armed guard over a flagpole in the schoolyard. He, Cresspahl, does not consider it proven beyond a reasonable doubt that Horst took part in killing Voss, in Rande—does not consider it probable even, since the boy had learned to be scared of violence and would've been too scared, if nothing else, to beat a man to death with steel bars. Unless there were a lot of people there, and he was very drunk. Papenbrock was worried that his heir apparent might come to harm in the conflict between the SA and the SS, and sent him abroad. If Horst found a brother there, thereby losing half his inheritance, Cresspahl does not think his motive was the love of truth. Papenbrock had just whipped the boy into indifference. His last escape attempt was to join the new army, and now that Papenbrock had threatened to disinherit him so many times, anger gained the upper hand. Horst lived a few years longer in Güstrow, a civil servant in the agriculture department, married to the Elisabeth Lieplow from Kröpelin who Albert Papenbrock hadn't wanted to let into his family. Horst apparently lost his life in the siege of Stalingrad, an older lieutenant to whom not even the death notice written by his superiors attributed bravery.

Why did people always call Lisbeth Papenbrock, Louise's daughter-in-law, Ilse?

Her full name was Elisabeth Ilse Friederike Papenbrock née Lieplow. She's called herself Ilse since she came to Jerichow to work for Louise, intending by this to show that she didn't want to remind Cresspahl of the first name Lisbeth. She thinks she's being tactful, while she's trying to imply that there's any chance of confusion.

THE NIEBUHRS.

PETER NIEBUHR, forestry student in Berlin, member of the Communist Party until November 1932, then voluntarily enrolled in the NCO academy in Eiche near Postdam. Transferred to the Reich Agricultural Corporation, a kind of department of agriculture. Peter Niebuhr, via a superior, initiated a lawsuit meant to curtail the private income of a Reich Labor Service leader but in so doing forced Lisbeth Cresspahl to give false testimony under oath at a time when what she needed was peace and quiet. A very young man, happily settled with his wife, MARTHA KLÜNDER, from Waren, if only his connection with the Communist Party hadn't remained vivid in his mind. In the summer of 1943, he was called up and planned to defect to the Soviets; in the summer of 1943, he and his wife died in Rerik in the attack on the First Antiaircraft Artillery School. So their children, Klaus and Günter, came back to Mecklenburg, to MARTIN NIEBUHR. Former supervisor in the Department of Waterways, promoted in 1933 to sluice keeper in Wendisch Burg, less as a reward than as charity. In 1931 married GERTRUD NIEBUHR née Cresspahl, the younger sister, the dithery person who'd decided to stay in Malchow with her mother, until her mother died and her own life was past too. No children; a play area in the backyard for children visiting from Berlin-Friedenau or Jerichow. Beekeeping, gardening, feels out of place in cities. Then they got his brother's children. Martin Niebuhr's civil service, which handed the SS a defeat in April 1945. Where the Havel now flows through a large dry area, Martin Niebuhr pulled the plug on the war. He is deeply embarrassed when anyone tries to point out his bravery, and it would be extremely rude to discuss it with him. He is well and properly hidden behind his doddering demeanor, and in the end he'll have been a better father to his brother's children, and Gertrud a not unskillful mother.

C.'s situation in Jerichow after 1934.

At first, subjectively hampered by Papenbrock's wish to sign over a property to the baby, so that his son-in-law would stay in Jerichow. Objectively inconvenienced by Papenbrock's drive to engineer advantages for this branch of the clan too. Nickname: "the Englishman." Accepted by the guild once he'd given in concerning price collusions (though not wage agreements). From 1935 on, with the start of the construction work on Mariengabe Airfield, disproportionately high workload and profits. When the airplanes arrived in Jerichow-North, Lisbeth disposed of the workshop building, perhaps as a precaution. After that, he survived on work for the airfield commander, eventually even in uniform so that he wouldn't be drafted into the People's Army. His installation as mayor under the British occupation may have wiped out all the goodwill he had stockpiled in ten years, and his removal from office and arrest by the Soviets was no doubt seen by many as proper comeuppance. He has a feeling he'd be doing better in Richmond, even now, as an enemy alien.

People he knows or owes something to, in Jerichow.

WILLI BÖTTCHER in Gneez, the guild master. The tradesmen he worked with in the dockyard crew: HEINE FREESE, glass; KÖPCKE, construction;

CREUTZ, garden maintenance, but Creutz had also been a good neighbor and tended to Lisbeth's grave above and beyond the call of payment. Later, to ALMA WITTE, City of Hamburg Hotel, Gneez, for feeding the child during the day. Still, he preferred to do his evening drinking alone. Beginning in 1943, when the black market started to replace the command economy, almost everyone in town got reacquainted with one another.

The first Nazis in Jerichow.

Horst Papenbrock. WALTER GRIEM, for whom townsman-farmer status was not enough, and his family too burdensome. In the SA, despite ranking below young Papenbrock, he nonetheless treated him like a whimpering dog. At first Griem hadn't had to hit anyone; after the Nazis seized power, he didn't go into the administration, he went into an area where he could expend his energy on physical work. Now, given his service in the Reich Labor Service, resident in a general's camp in the Soviet Union, or then again maybe head of a construction crew in the Soviet Sector of Berlin. When PAHL the tailor marched with the SA, it was for business reasons more than anything else; drowned himself before the Soviets arrived. In Gneez: MAX BREITSPRECHER, but only until the summer of 1934, after which he kept the SA and SS off his back with monetary contributions and so died in the navy, on a minesweeper.

KLEIN THE BUTCHER.

Jerichow's butcher used to be AUGUST METHFESSEL; he ended up in a camp for nothing but a little dumb talk, was beaten into an inability to work, was killed in medical experiments. KLEIN inherited his customers. His own anti-Fascist resistance struggle began like this: A lieutenant walked in with a private, and they said in a quiet, ugly voice: We're so-and-so, we're from such and such, and your business is now confiscated. By tomorrow morning you need to provide meat, sausage, lard.... To which Klein, proud of his reasonable reaction: *You cant do that!* Then they said such and such. Then they left. Then they gave him a packet of meat tickets with AIR FORCE printed across them. Then they swore him in, backdated to the start of the war. And Klein said, insulted by their doubting his professional honor: *If you ring the bell by noon, then by the next morning at seven sharp!* And that was how the butcher KLEIN's anti-Fascist resistance struggle ended. *"They threatened me with a concentration camp!"*

BÖHNHASE.

Tobacconist Böhnhase, German National People's Party, proved his oppression by the Nazis as follows: If in 1932 he hadn't carried Reds, the Communist cigarette brand, in his store and distributed them so vigorously around Jerichow, then the Nazis in 1942 would hardly have been so set on seven years of prison for him, just for having sold rationed tobacco products in exchange for smoked bacon.

Friends in Jerichow.

ALFRED BIENMÜLLER, horseshoer and nailsmith.

No further details?

No further details.

And Peter Wulff?

And PETER WULFF. He was in Jerichow in 1931, a barkeep and owner of a general store, member of the Social Democratic Party. Friendship to the point of reciprocal letter-writing. Peter Wulff was in a position to translate Cresspahl's English news about the Langemarck trial of January 1933 into a Jerichow thicket of whispers that ruined the celebration of the Day of the Founding of the Reich for Dr. Erdamer, the mayor, himself Social Democratic Party. Again and again Wulff had not been able to bring himself to leave the SPD—not after the Kassel party congress of 1920, not after the Görlitz one of 1921, not even after the Kiel one of 1927, in which they'd already made it be about "organized capitalism." That was one of the running conversations with Wulff; another was the friendship between Lisbeth and META WULFF, a fisherman's daughter from Dievenow; still another was what they could do to the first Nazi mayor, Friedrich Jansen. One of Wulff's educational efforts, in 1935, to a customer who wanted to leave the church with the excuse that Jesus was a child born out of wedlock: Wulff: Your mother wasn't married either, what should we do about *you*? In 1938, at the request of the Lübeck SPD, Cresspahl had to give up all contact with Wulff, publicly, so the townspeople would think there'd been a permanent break. Two days after the war ended he had found an opportunity to talk to Wulff, who didn't know the reason any better than Cresspahl did. The whole thing had apparently been forgotten, and Wulff too refused to forgive the SPD for such personal politics, whether or not the party was banned. In the years of the pretended feud, Cresspahl could only suspect that it was Wulff who sawed into the flagpole in front of Friedrich Jansen's house at night, if only to give Cresspahl the repair work. Wulff was delighted to admit it, and also that it was in fact he who, every March, to the admiring amazement of the Gestapo and the police, had smuggled flowers onto the grave of Friedrich Laabs, whom the Kapp putschists had killed in the cellar of the Archduke Hotel in Gneez. Until 1942, the Nazis' prime suspect was Cresspahl, who lived next door to the Jerichow cemetery and had easiest access to the grave. And now you can talk to Wulff about the SPD's role in battleship construction in 1928, or about the Social Democratic endorsement of German foreign policy in May 1933; he refuses to give an inch about the Kiel party congress, though, not even after a second bottle of schnapps. And since he neglected to inform the Soviets about his membership in the SPD, he didn't have to follow the merger with the German Communist Party and join the Socialist Unity Party either, and so he avoided the resignation therefrom that would no doubt have been required after being forced to close his shop. Cresspahl and Wulff have a good time together, and both regret having missed out on almost seven years of it.

FRIEDRICH JANSEN.

Mayor of Jerichow after Dr. Erdamer's resignation in March 1933. Papenbrock thought he was clever exerting his power behind the mask of money, rather than being forced to advance aims other than his own in the administration; Papenbrock's cowardice saddled Jerichow Town Hall with a failed law student as a successor to Dr. Erdamer—a favor for old Dr. Jansen and a disgrace for the town. The boy was so pathetic that he couldn't even manage to set up any crooked business with the brickworks lease. If the British hadn't shot Jansen by mistake for possession of firearms, there would've been more than enough people in Jerichow to take care of him. Hünemörder, for instance, who after Hitler's 1934 speech had merely said: I don't think so, gentlemen, and if we're not up to our necks in war by 1939, then . . . ! Hünemörder didn't get out of the concentration camp until 1936, and he moved from Jerichow to Lübeck solely to spare himself the sight of Friedrich Jansen. One example to stand for Friedrich Jansen's behavior in general: After Lisbeth's death, he liked to show around town a clipping from *The Lübeck Gazette*, from the spring of 1931. The article described Erich Ahrnt, a twenty-three-year-old stableboy, born in Berlin, who set a barn full of wheat and hay on fire in Hohenhorn near Schwarzenbek and waited for death in an engine case. Legs severely carbonized, upper body lightly burned. It cost people like Wulff and Kollmorgen no little effort to stamp out the rumor of a connection between the two cases. He has Wulff to thank for that too.

EDUARD TAMMS.

Jansen's follower and successor as mayor. The British forces arrested him not because up until 1945 he'd applied the laws that were valid at the time but because his wife was related to men in black uniforms. And he hadn't even used those connections to get himself transferred anywhere from Jerichow.

What about the nobility around Jerichow?

AXEL VON RAMMIN, Reichsbaron and all that, smuggled money to Austrian friends so that a Jew could emigrate from Mecklenburg with what belonged to him. The VON BÜLOWS (the Upper Bülows) refused to give in to the pressure to bring a son back from studying abroad in England. The VON BOBZIENS didn't let the SA use the Countess Woods for field exercises; they also made deliveries in broad daylight to the wife of the arrested pastor, free of charge. The VON MALTZAHNS let both sons enter the SS. The VON LÜSEWITZES were rumored to keep their Hungarian and Italian day laborers in stables, but not after 1942. Finally, Count FRIEDRICH FRANZ GROTE from Varchentin was the regional head of the Agriculture Department for Mecklenburg. When another count, HANS KASPAR VON BOTHMER, came back from the war severely wounded, he opened up his castle for use as a typhus hospital, helped with the nursing, and died relatively quickly of spotted fever.

Why wasn't PASTOR BRÜSHAVER a friend.

A university man, an officer in the Kaiser's navy, German National People's Party from way back. In Hitler's war against the church, he was a member of the Pastors' Emergency League, disobeyed the state bishop's instructions, but let the son from his first marriage fly missions against the legal government of Spain, secretly hoping this would yield a promotion high enough for a position as airfield commander, until he got him back in a soldered casket he was not allowed to open. This Brüshaver spoke about Lisbeth's death in a sermon that was enough to get him arrested, and also gave her a full church burial, against the wishes of both the Church of Mecklenburg and the Gestapo. As a result he was separated from the three children from his second marriage—who were incinerated in Rostock by Royal Air Force bombs—and from his second wife. The Nazis had wanted him to live in a concentration camp until 1960; when he came back to Jerichow in 1945, looking for Aggie Brüshaver, he was so malnourished he could barely talk. He, Cresspahl, knows full well that the man put himself in the hands of the court not only for Lisbeth's sake but for reasons of his own; still, he cannot respond in kind to the man's easygoing friendship. He can't manage that yet.

SEMIG.

ARTHUR SEMIG, DR. VET. MED. A Mecklenburger from the "gray area" in the west, near Ludwigslust, married to DORA KÖSTER from Schwerin. Groomsman for Lisbeth, godfather to Gesine. If there is such a thing as Christianity, he practiced it, in his orderly way. He wanted to do justice to his Jewish grandparents as well as to the Nazi laws against him; he left Jerichow purely as a favor to his friends, so as not to endanger them.

Did he—

All we know is how the KÖSTERS died. After a risky 1938 letter their daughter sent from Prague, Privy Councillor Köster and his wife took the trouble to poison themselves, both at an advanced age. Two very small coffins, burned in secret by the Gestapo.

Again: ALEXANDER PAEPCKE.

Alex. Who offered C. his friendship without hesitation, when all he was required to do with his new family was put up with them. One of the great and mighty Schwerin PAEPCKES. There was a banker in the family, members of parliament before the First War. The Paepckes went to the court with their archduke. The family came to an unexpected end with Alexander, born in 1898. He did have a sister, younger, but she could preserve the name only while unmarried, so not long enough. Inge Paepcke had been permitted to recite rhymed verses during a visit to the empress—it was that kind of family. The empress had thereupon rewarded her with a brooch, not the most valuable work ever made by H. J. Wilm,

Berlin, Jeweler to the Royal Court, but still with a blue *A* for Auguste and a *V* for Viktoria covered in some kind of glittering things. The family council decided that Inge could keep the reward for herself, but as soon as Alexander had a daughter the brooch was to be given to her, and so forth, down through the generations. At the time Alexander did not have a wife, never mind children. The Paepckes gave him time to look around for the right one. Alexander, however, already saw academia as the epitome of respectable life; he took his time with the looking around, paying off this and that pretty young thing from the Schwerin theater with a jewel or a dress. The family succeeded in talking him out of such marriages every so often; his condition was that they pay off his debts. (The family council behaved rather more indifferently toward Alexander's mother and sister, who spent money quite a bit less generously.) In the summer of 1928, Alexander went to see his aunt Françoise at the Graal Müritz resort on the Baltic, and he couldn't stand seeing a White Russian émigré pay court with princely dignity to a girl named HILDE PAPENBROCK. Alexander's great-uncle took the trouble to pay a secret visit to Graal, and before he even left Rostock he sent a telegram to the Pearl of the Sea Hotel: MARRY AT ONCE. The family was so happy with Hilde that they agreed to a wedding in Jerichow, instead of Schwerin, and within eight weeks. The Paepckes, too, wanted to make their peace with the Papenbrocks as long as they could get a bride out of them. And here began Hilde's great holiday from her parents, a life full of trips to Berlin, excursions from one estate to the next in the Krakow area, lavish parties in seaside hotels. Once, Alexander forgot to notify Schwerin of a certain embarrassing situation in time and was unable to pay one of his clients the money he owed him from a settlement. This client was a major landowner and a late payment was not acceptable. After his Leonia fraternity cronies dropped the ball too, Alex was actually disbarred from the Mecklenburg Legal Chamber, and from then on he got by with leases of brickworks. (Or had it been the notary's office?) Hilde couldn't stand to see her man Alexander in trouble and had no compunction about setting these brickworks on fire, and the first time it happened the insurance company was willing to believe in spontaneous combustion. In 1931, Papenbrock brought his elder daughter back to Jerichow and gave her husband the lease to the brickworks here; as old man

Papenbrock looked on in alarm, Alexander ended up in the red despite the new construction, practically next door, of a military airfield with an inexhaustible hunger for bricks. Alexander withdrew to the Stettin Military Ordnance Department, but for the Paepckes he'd done well. Alexandra came into the world in 1934, and the family council traveled to Jerichow to pass down the empress's brooch, and came again in 1935 for Eberhardt's birth, and went to Podejuch for Christine Paepcke's birth, and the baptismal gifts could be used to pay off Alexander's "obligations" almost every time. He, Cresspahl, wasn't bothered by Alexander and Hilde's disregard of rules and regulations; on occasion he regretted his own inability to be like that. And he doubtless wanted to give his own child a childhood like the Paepckes gave their children—he put that down in writing. He only rarely felt excluded on visits to Podejuch or the country house in Althagen, on Fischland, when the Paepckes' education and aristocracy shone through and the child Alexandra might say: *Pray some tea, said she.* Still, for him, Hilde and Alexander were.... Alexander met his death trying to help foreign children in occupied Russia. His own children died with Hilde in the spring of 1945, in West Pomerania, in a military truck strafed by fighter planes.

Still, Alexander didn't know about, you know? Only Alfred Bienmüller did, horseshoer and nailsmith of Jerichow?

Cresspahl didn't want to put Alexander in danger. Bienmüller was a last resort. Anyway, Alfred didn't know enough to piece together the whole story, not even a tenth of it.

But KLAUS BÖTTCHER is putting two and two together. He's come up with reasons why Cresspahl wanted to know even the smallest details about the army, down to a regiment's aiguillettes, as late as 1944.

Klaus can just stick to his father's woodworking workshop; he's looking at a full audit from the new government's finance office. No one brought him back from his forest camp deep deep in Russia before his sentence was up just so he could go around hawking nonsense.

Cresspahl brought...?

Along with others.

DR. KLIEFOTH.

Because he was an English teacher? He certainly liked to talk, almost brag, about his time as a staff officer on the eastern front—1C, coun-

terintelligence—about his reconnaissance flights across Soviet lines, maybe in a way that presupposed a certain unusual level of curiosity in Cresspahl. But Kliefoth was also nonchalant enough to not turn off the BBC just because someone came over to his house.

LESLIE DANZMANN.

A friend of Lisbeth's from her boarding-school days in Rostock. Around 1940, times got tight for her on only a navy widow's pension, so she had to work as a housekeeper at a villa in Rande, near Jerichow. She was the only one who might have realized that Cresspahl didn't come visit her "Fritz" to drink the night away but rather to pass him the latest information about Mariengabe Airfield or Barth concentration camp. Still, she was shy around "Lisbeth's husband," and there *were* enough empty bottles on the table by the end of each such night.

That doesn't make it any less true.

Now's not the time to say so out loud. Such English matters have to be dealt with at length in fictional form first, in films or so-called popular nonfiction books, to make them more bearable for the public; then we have to wait for the so-called academic books that get a foot or two closer to the truth every decade; in fifty years, when they open the archives, they'll be as close to understanding it as we are today to founding the German Democratic Republic. Or as far away as the moon is from Jerichow.

But—

He knows perfectly well that keeping quiet is harder for a sixteen-year-old than it is for a nine-year-old. He blamed himself enough when his child fell for one of Ottje Stoffregen's tricks.

OTTJE STOFFREGEN?

Head teacher at the Hermann Göring School in Jerichow. Local historian, former suitor for the hand of Lisbeth Papenbrock, if you believe Peter Wulff. And you can always believe Wulff. So it was Ottje's memories as well as his alcoholism that he took out on Cresspahl's child. In music class, Stoffregen played the first four notes of a Beethoven symphony on the piano, the call sign of the British Broadcasting Corporation, and asked the class who recognized it. It was Cresspahl's child who raised her hand.

Sorry. Sorry!

That's all right. But when the Gestapo gumshoes searched the house, they didn't find anything like Alexander's Blaupunkt radio, with its magic eye and automatic station finder, just what was called at the time the People's Receiver. *Volksempfänger.* And Cresspahl's child immediately recalled that she recognized the four notes from a record at the Paepckes, and with Alexander's sworn statement the Gestapo had to leave it at that. Alexander was glad to help; C. was relieved that the whole thing could be forgotten, down to today.

But Cresspahl *was* an anti-Fascist!

On the British side—an indigestible fact in times like these. You can tell your own child about it someday.

Am I allowed to tell Jakob now?

Jakob, yes.

Translator's Acknowledgments

MY ENORMOUS thanks to Astrid Köhler and Robert Gillett, Patrick Wright, and Holger Helbig for giving so generously of their time and expertise in reviewing much of this translation; to the organizations listed on the copyright page; and to the many editors and copy editors at NYRB Classics. All remaining errors and stubborn decisions are, of course, my own. I would also like to acknowledge the earlier, partial translation by Leila Vennewitz (Parts 1–3) and Walter Arndt (Part 4) of a heavily abridged version of the original, published as *Anniversaries: From the Life of Gesine Cresspahl* in 1975 (Part 1 and half of Part 2) and 1987 (the rest of Part 2 through Part 4). I referred to it often and borrowed some of their many inspired solutions to difficult passages.

NEW YORK REVIEW BOOKS
CLASSICS

ANNIVERSARIES

UWE JOHNSON (1934–1984) grew up in the small town of Anklam
in the German state of Mecklenburg-Vorpommern. At the end of World
War II, his father, who had joined the Nazi Party in 1940, disappeared
into a Soviet camp; he was declared dead in 1948. Johnson and his mother
remained in Communist East Germany until his mother left for the
West in 1956, after which Johnson was barred from regular employment.
In 1959, shortly before the publication of his first novel, *Speculations
About Jakob*, in West Germany, he emigrated to West Berlin by streetcar,
leaving the East behind for good. Other novels, *The Third Book About
Achim*, *An Absence*, and *Two Views*, followed in quick succession. A
member of the legendary Gruppe 47, Johnson lived from 1966 until
1968 with his wife and daughter in New York, compiling a high-school
anthology of postwar German literature. On Tuesday, April 18, 1967,
at 5:30 p.m., as he later recounted the story, he saw Gesine Cresspahl,
a character from his earlier works, walking on the south side of Forty-
Second Street from Fifth to Sixth Avenue alongside Bryant Park; he
asked what she was doing in New York and eventually convinced her
to let him write his next novel about a year in her life. *Anniversaries* was
published in four installments—in 1970, 1971, 1973, and 1983—and was
quickly recognized in Germany as one of the great novels of the century.
In 1974, Johnson left Germany for the isolation of Sheerness-on-Sea,
England, where he struggled through health and personal problems to
finish his magnum opus. He died at age forty-nine, shortly after it was
published.

DAMION SEARLS grew up on Riverside Drive in New York City,
three blocks away from Gesine Cresspahl's apartment. He is the author
of three books and has translated more than thirty, including six for
NYRB Classics.

ANNIVERSARIES

From a Year in the Life of Gesine Cresspahl

Volume Two

UWE JOHNSON

Translated from the German by
DAMION SEARLS

NEW YORK REVIEW BOOKS

New York

THIS IS A NEW YORK REVIEW BOOK
PUBLISHED BY THE NEW YORK REVIEW OF BOOKS
435 Hudson Street, New York, NY 10014
www.nyrb.com

Originally published in German as *Jahrestage: Aus dem Leben von Gesine Cresspahl.*
Publishing rights reserved and controlled through Suhrkamp Verlag, Berlin.

The translation of this work was supported by a grant from Goethe-Institut using funds provided by the German Ministry of Foreign Affairs. It was made possible in part by the New York State Council on the Arts with the support of Governor Andrew Cuomo and the New York State Legislature.

The translator and publisher wish to thank the John Simon Guggenheim Foundation, the Dorothy and Lewis B. Cullman Center for Scholars and Writers at the New York Public Library, and the Uwe Johnson Society's Peter Suhrkamp Stipend for their generous support.

Library of Congress Cataloging-in-Publication Data
Names: Johnson, Uwe, 1934–1984 author. | Searls, Damion translator.
Title: Anniversaries : from a year in the life of Gesine Cresspahl / by Uwe
   Johnson ; translated by Damion Searls.
Other titles: Jahrestage. English
Description: New York : New York Review Books, 2018. | Series: New York
   Review Books classics
Identifiers: LCCN 2018010220 (print) | LCCN 2018012166 (ebook) | ISBN
   9781681372044 (epub) | ISBN 9781681372037 (alk. paper)
Classification: LCC PT2670.O36 (ebook) | LCC PT2670.O36 J313 2018 (print)
   | DDC 833/.914—dc23
LC record available at https://lccn.loc.gov/2018010220

ISBN 978-1-68137-203-7 (boxed set)
Available as an electronic book; ISBN 978-1-68137-204-4

Printed in the United States of America on acid-free paper.
10 9 8 7 6 5 4 3 2 1

CONTENTS

PART THREE

April 1968–June 1968

THE WATER is black.

The overcast sky hangs low over the lake ringed in morning pinewood shadow, darkness rising from the muddy ground. The swimmer's hands push forward as if through heavy dye but are shockingly pure when they come up into the air. The shores are close on all sides; in the dim dawn an observer would think he saw two ducks moving in the middle of the lake, one with dark feathers, one light. But it's too early for anyone. The silence makes the lake gloomy. The fish, the water birds, the land birds don't want to live in this dredged-out basin, these stunted trees, this chemically treated landscape set up for paying customers. Sink two feet under the stagnant surface and you'll lose the light in a greenish blackness.

– How many lakes have you done in your life, Gesine?: says the child, says Marie, says the strange fish poking her head up after a long plunge. – This is your how-many-eth lake?: she says in her strange German.

Two voices above the water, in the murky silence—one an eleven-year-old soprano, cracked around the edges, the other a thirty-five-year-old alto, smoothly rounded, not especially big. The child doesn't let the Baltic Sea count.

It was there, in the Ostsee, that the child I was first swam: off Fischland in the Lübeck Bay near the maritime boundary of Mecklenburg, formerly a province of the German Reich, now a coastal region of the Socialist state of the German nation. I swam with children who are dead now, and with soldiers of the defeated German navy who called the great mighty Baltic "the flooded field of the seven seas." But in American geography books the Ostsee is called the Baltic Sea, and Marie says it doesn't count. It's not a lake. She's an American child.

How many lakes has her mother swum, taken in, racked up. What's the number.

Here in America, where people are starved for restrained, attentive, and well-behaved children, they call her a European child. Marie stood politely at the edge of the lake, still misty with the dawn, and patiently followed her into the bone-chilling water—Marie's mother, her partner for better or for worse ever since she was born, not yet dispensable. And she acts properly, as she's learned to from the nuns who teach at her school, carrying on a conversation during the swim. Much as she'd prefer to go underwater, she keeps her head up and tries for an interested expression on her determined, shiny wet face.

How many lakes in thirty-five years?

Gneez Lake: Fritz Reuter High School gym class after the war; the public beach on the Gneez side, where Gesine Cresspahl the child was supposed to be training for competitions. Gneez Lake again, again with others, on the south side, the kids' swimming hole in tenth grade, class A-2, eleventh grade A-1, twelfth grade A-1. At home, in the military facility's pool, forgotten by the German Air Force and the Red Army, with Lise Wollenberg, Inge Heitmann, and the boy from the Jerichow pharmacy. Never in Dassow Lake, less than eight miles from my father's back door and utterly inaccessible, its shore being the line of demarcation, the national border—the water was in the British zone, the Federal Republic of Germany, the West. With Pius Pagenkopf: in Cramon Lake, between Drieberg and Cramon, an hour's bike ride from the town where I went to school, in 1951. Alone, from Jerichow in northwest Mecklenburg to Wendisch Burg in southeast Mecklenburg: in Schwerin Lake to the island of Lieps, in Goldberg Lake, in Lake Plau, in Lake Müritz. With Klaus Niebuhr, Günter Niebuhr, Ingrid Babendererde, and Eva Mau in all seven lakes around Wendisch Burg, until 1952. In Leipzig, in Halle: lifesaving courses in indoor pools, through May 1953. The last time in Gneez Lake: end of May 1953, and Jakob held my impaled foot high off the ground like I was a young horse and the way he moved it sent a shiver up through my body with no pain at all.

Never with Jakob. Jakob would still be working in Cresspahl's house, in the villages, when we left Jerichow in the evening for six laps in the Mili, the military swimming facility that we all stubbornly called the Mili (Mariengabe air base now had a new name too: it would never be known as anything but Jerichow-North). Jakob left town to work for the railroad; a photograph was taken of him once on the Pastor's Pond ferry, in Schwerin (in the company of Sabine Beedejahn, Prot., twenty-four, married). Jakob used to go lake fishing with friends, coming back from the Mecklenburg lakes with buckets of live crabs, and I didn't know those lakes, and he went without me, with fishermen, with girls, with work friends, and I hardly knew him.

After leaving behind the East German authorities: almost every day for two weeks with Anita in Wannsee, West Berlin, as far as you could get from the border. In West Germany: public pools in Frankfurt, Düsseldorf, Krefeld, Düren. In Geneva. In America: Lake Winnipesaukee, Lake Chippewa, Lake Travis, Lake Hopatcong. Again with Anita in the Vosges, in France.

– Eighteen valid, four don't count, one unclear, and bonus for Lake Travis, Texas!: Marie says.

But the landing is now just a quarter mile away, and she immediately puts her head sideways into the water, so sure is she that the challenge to a race has been understood and accepted, and after kicking underwater for a long time she comes up into a crawl, strokes sharp and precise and almost silent. She wants to get back to the borrowed expensive house, all glass and mahogany beams, where there's a phone and news on TV and possibly *The New York Times* from the village store, and soon, as early as tomorrow afternoon, the return home to Manhattan, New York City, Riverside Drive and Broadway, the corner of Ninety-Sixth Street.

This lake is called Patton Lake, named in honorable memory of a general from this country. Here heavy tanks practiced until 1944 for the last assault on Germany, until the thick old trees were stumps and the ground so churned up by caterpillar treads that the area had to be turned into an artificial lake, with trees having nowhere else to go and high yields from vacation rentals. From here came the Sherman tanks that measured out the market squares of Mecklenburg, too.

– *And you came swimming all the way from Mecklenburg!*

Marie has been standing on the deck for a while; hand on heart she salutes the flag that's raised to honor the victor in stadiums, then welcomes the loser swimming up beneath her. She speaks the words with delight, because she can assume a teasing tone, and from the heart, because at last she has a chance to say something in English, the language of her own country, not the German she speaks so clumsily now.

Vacation in the country. Somewhere in upstate New York, but no more than three hours' drive from the city, and on the long leash of the telephone line the bank can tug at will to summon Employee Cresspahl back to work from her two-day break.

– I did, I swam the whole way here from Mecklenburg: I say in German.
– *And did the nineteenth lake in your life!*: Marie says in English.

Lots of heavy black Patton water for the afternoon.

Vacation in the country. This time it's a chore for Marie.
– You need your *New York Times*: she said the moment we were out of the water, thereby claiming the right to the mile's walk to the country store, the right to alone time in the woods. Our borrowed summer house was a model home, full of not only Finnish furniture but all the latest gadgets; in the afternoon Marie left again, for the two lemons we could have managed dinner without. There was still a long time before we had to go back but she'd packed up the car already, then she had something else to do outside, for a map of the area she was making as a gift for the owner. She announced her walks as if suggesting them; she took on the shopping duties voluntarily; she always found a way to get out; she wanted to be alone, once in a while.

For almost eleven years we've had only each other to depend on, and she's struggled to build her defenses. In 1957, for twenty-four-year-old Gesine Cresspahl, baby Marie had been part of her—for a long time Marie had to accept that. She met her grandmother, Jakob's mother, but Mrs. Abs wanted to live alone, didn't want to die near us; if any memory of a grandmother remains, Marie never mentions it. She had to deal with the brisk forceful women at the Düsseldorf day care center, but it was always entirely up to her sole legal guardian whether she would be handed over to them or saved from them. Cresspahl made one last visit to the Rhine— "to the West"—and wheeled the child around the Hofgarten, but he was wearing his black overcoat dating from 1932, kept slipping back into Plattdeutsch with Marie, and a grandfather like that might well have scared her. And then Cresspahl went back to Jerichow. Marie spent her early years waiting among strangers for the one and only familiar person to come back at last from these incomprehensible separations—work. In the morning she tried to ask if she had to share the day with this invincible "work" or if she and Gesine could stay together until the day's last bedtime—she had a hard time making herself understood. She was given her birthday breakfast with two candles, then stayed quiet. Gesine had plans for her child, parental intentions as inadvisable as they were stubborn. First, that there be no detours on the way to standard High German. It felt funny in her throat, and approximations were accepted gladly, but still the only way to produce true maternal rejoicing would be successfully combining letters into a single word, say *M* and *i* and *l* and *ch* into *Milch*, "milk"—which might in turn be a disguise for another word, named *Dust*, "thuhsty," to which a superfluous *r* had to be added in some baffling place. *Durst*, "thirsty." Marie was eager to please this person; at first, she resorted to watching her, pointing to this or taking that. But she had no desire to start a conversation or even try to. Because she was also supposed to deliver these words in an order she was rarely free to choose. And, if she'd understood aright, this woman was also trying to turn her into someone who deliberately refused to say anything about a dry feeling in the throat: whether in fun, from tact, or out of stubbornness; three proposed mimicries, three possible agreements, all reached through no intermediary but her own face. Admittedly, this was also the start of their shared secret: that Marie spoke to this woman in a way she never spoke to anyone else—not the teachers, not the babysitters, certainly not the cohort of others learning the job of being a child in their own ways. No one else even noticed the wordless understanding between her and this woman. And there was no one else around to make things easier, to whom it was even worth running—just this one partner, both there to help and no help at all.

Not having a living father, she for a long time lacked a word for fathers, lacked even the idea of one. At two and a half she didn't understand questions about mothers either. She didn't have a mother, she spent her life with someone named Ina, Zina, G'sina, a tolerable enough protector but way too clever a peer.

This person didn't insist on being obeyed; you didn't have to carry out her wishes on the spot. You could get her to change your bedtime, could have your way about destinations for outings, and after you'd asked her to take away a tree with lit candles on it you could count on her to hide how flame bursts out of a match too. And she so insisted on pushback that you had to think things over, try to remember things that would have been much nicer if they'd stayed passing feelings or sights you could simply forget. The only thing you were helpless against was the part of this woman called "Work" (an ally? an enemy?). "Work" required a plane trip to West Berlin, "Work" required staying in strange houses with people speaking an even more mysterious language; obedience wasn't enough, but curiosity came in handy, since there was nothing to be done without this woman or against her. The child could be reconciled to a trip abroad with the promise of return after a countable number of days, so she innocently came along on a trip to France and boarded a ship to America, but after a week at sea it turned out this woman had outsmarted her. The trip was a move—this friend or foe named "Work" blocked their return to Europe, and now the habit of morning separations turned without warning into an arrangement involving a preschool on the Hudson in an entirely new language. After two years in New York Marie could still describe the room by the Rhine she'd left behind. She had long since been getting around in German as if in a first second language, but still she would point to privileges left elsewhere, to a sense of injustice. She'd accepted New York as a gift and she defended her new-won city as a right.

Even before starting school she began catching up with this woman, faster than a child on the other side of the Atlantic would have. This woman's English hadn't actually been all it was cracked up to be. Didn't the child master the swallowed vowel sounds quicker, the imperceptible onsets of aspirants, the set melodies of the sentences here? It was the woman who listened to her and had her repeat certain words as though trying to learn them from her, wasn't it? And who was the one who made the Cresspahls respected customers in Maxie's grocery store, or in Schustek's, if not the child, tasting the products first, nodding to authorize purchase? Who was the first to realize that Rebecca Ferwalter was not just any child but one who called Saturday the Sabbath? Who made sure we walked on the north side of Ninety-Fifth Street, not past the Puerto Ricans and their reason for picking a fight that the child had already noticed while the woman kept going on about "happy homes"? In the subway, which of them knew how to say the names of the lines in American English, and it was the child who could find the quickest route to the Atlantic, was it not? The fact that in this country citizens had to call their policeman "sir," no matter how urgent the accident or fire—who'd had to explain that to her elder? The younger Cresspahl, the one in the lead.

Victories. And yet, in this terrain of competition, struggle, trials of strength, how slow it was in coming—the separation, the independence. How long it took for Marie to establish her standing in the eyes of this other person, always in control! By now this woman had become, for school purposes, *"my mother"*—said objectively or in self-defense. My mother is from a small town on the Baltic. But her father was a rich man. Mrs. Cresspahl's child was expected to address her mother by first name, or jokingly as "Gee-sign," and was allowed to give her, also jokingly, motherly advice. Mrs. Cresspahl's child didn't know many other kids in school whose mothers made their own money with their own jobs, and Marie decided to be proud of that. Little Cresspahl had a mother whose topmost accent sounded foreign, if British. During the 1964–65 school year, little Cresspahl read till her eyes were sore and her fingers cramped, not as a striving teacher's pet but because she had a mother who might take a child with unsatisfactory grades back to Europe. Mary Cresspahl, fourth grade, might take it upon herself to insist that her name was pronounced "M'rie"; her braids might have been her own decision too; she didn't snitch; she'd mastered school slang—but it was from her mother that she'd gotten her attitudes toward religion, and the Jews, and promises. European values, perhaps, but foreign. In the beginning Marie had met plenty of children who would innocently say they hated their parents; maybe Marie just wouldn't let herself say it out loud.

"Life with my mother wasn't easy": Marie might well think such a sentence, even if disguised in English and stored up for a future listener whom she hasn't found yet. This mother had brought ideas from her Europe that she wanted the child to apply here. All people were endowed, or were to be provided with, equal rights. Now what was Marie supposed to do with that? She could show her mother how she gives up her bus seat for a black woman with the same alacrity as for a pink one, she could go down to our basement and console Jason for the long long hours remaining until sunset, but to take the one black girl in her class, Francine, under her European wing—how would that work out with her light-skinned friends?

She had to leave things out when she talked about this at home, and the worst of it was that her mother simply wouldn't stop believing that a truth would emerge through this lie, and through other undertakings for Francine's benefit that Marie would really have rather avoided. This mother tried to teach her that there was a difference between just and unjust wars—but how is a child supposed to connect events from the year 1811 (Shawnee uprising under Tecumseh) to the American war in Vietnam when her very first attempt cost her friendships and almost got her expelled? She could speak out against today's war in private, at home, nothing binding—perhaps hoping her mother would assume that she was equally opinionated at school. But this was a vague hope, there was a lie inherent in the answer, and the question, and the silence, and it was precisely this lie that her mother was determined to ban. Didn't she get that her code of ethics was acceptable but was valid only in the other language, untranslatable into thought or deed? Anyway, she wasn't honest herself—she pretended to prefer the Socialist cause while working in a capitalist country, for a bank! While the child can't very well suggest that if that's what her mother wants she should move to a Socialist country to be consistent, because then that child would lose the whole city of New York, and all her friends and the subway and the South Ferry and Mayor Lindsay, so she has to make do with dishonesty, which she's told shouldn't exist. And then, if her mother does follow through—unopposed by her child—and leave New York for the Socialist cause, possibly as early as this summer, young Cresspahl really will be in the soup, which she's helped to stir herself. What Marie will say someday about her mother, Gesine Cresspahl (Mrs.), is: life with her was not an easy alliance.

Two days' vacation in the country. Variable cloudiness, occasional flashes of sun on the sluggish water.

Marie has lots of things to do near school, uptown on Riverside Drive, or around Broadway on the Upper West Side—and nothing to do at Patton Lake. In the city she only has to be with her mother for a few hours—by Patton Lake she sometimes perched on the landing so askew, looking like such a wreck, that it was as if she were waiting in the desert for some army helicopter to land and save her from the uninterrupted togetherness, and from the awareness of it.

– No: she said: Not an army copter. But I'd take one from Radio Boston.

(And then loyally upholding good manners she said it was her own fault she was bored.)

She read the bundles of newspaper she'd brought back. In Brooklyn they shot and killed Charlie LoCicero, a Mafia elder, in his corner luncheonette as he sipped a strawberry malted. Eleventh Avenue and Sixty-Sixth Street— Marie would have liked to go see the crime scene, and tomorrow it'll be too late. On the Hudson, five NATO warships dropped anchor at Pier 86, and New Yorkers will line up to see the destroyers, and Marie would have enjoyed walking around them too, with a fat black marker, leaving behind a Was Here doodle or Peace sign (– A Peace sign: she says). People from the rich suburbs have paid a visit to the city's northern slums to do a little sweeping, painting, and cementing up cracks there, while leaving the insides of the buildings, with the roaches and the rats, untouched. (– It's so their conscience'll be clearer when they drive through: Marie says.) Nevertheless, she too would have happily watched these visitors from prosperity, and been in New York, not on Patton Lake.

Now and then it was international news she brought outside to her mother, not without turning her mother's deck chair a little toward the sun and tucking her blanket in tighter. She actually does act like she's dealing with an invalid, the way she passes along the scraps. In the process you can leave your hand on the other person's shoulder a little longer than strictly necessary, without seeming needy, much less affectionate.

Yesterday morning in Bonn the air force marked the fiftieth anniversary of the death of Baron von Richthofen, the "Red Baron," who shot down eighty French and British planes. In Cologne's Klingelpütz prison, apparently, mentally ill inmates were regularly beaten to death. Marie takes the page back in silence, returns her mother's nod, withdraws into the house in silence.

That's the kind of country you want to go back to, Gesine.
I haven't attained honesty yet, Marie.
Maybe it's happening here too.
Maybe we'll stay.
See!

She doesn't go near our host's TV set. Six years ago Gesine Cresspahl concluded that American TV shows were damaging to children, and there's no TV in our apartment. When Marie needs to watch something she goes over to friends' houses, or down to Jason in the basement, but here she leaves even the radio alone. As a result, she can do two things: point out how true she is to a long-ago promise and show that she doesn't want to disturb a vacation in the country by making noise.

She's recently started getting uncomfortable about the fact that a certain someone is working forty hours a week not only for herself but for another person's livelihood and tuition, her own. She has promised me that in return I'll get a house in 1982, in the part of Richmond where Staten Island is quietest.

Every time Marie left the house for a walk she changed clothes. The nearby vacation homes are still almost all empty. She might run into the young woman at the gas station, and one or two dogs, and have the retired farmer at the store to talk to. Yet she trades her pants and sweater for an elaborate dress, suitable for churchgoing; she pulls her hair back into a neat ponytail, shines her shoes for the walk around the lake. She mustn't give the locals a chance to say that a New York child doesn't know how to behave in the country.

And after the first stranger has wished her good morning, she exchanges hellos with all the rest, for New York's sake.

She came back and puzzled over people in New York who'd met Mrs. Cresspahl once at a party and promised her the keys to their summer house on Patton Lake after half an hour of conversation. (She brought that up only in passing; it was meant as a compliment to Mrs. Cresspahl. She had to be considerate—tomorrow morning her mother was going back to work.)

She brought me an article from *The New York Times* that had been overlooked on Saturday, and handed it over in businesslike fashion, officially, as something for work: We have a reliable old aunt in the city who's looking out for us.

In thirty-six lines she covers the following: the foreign minister of the Czechoslovakian Republic, Jan Masaryk, fell out of a window in March 1948. Major Augustin Schramm, a security officer at the Foreign Ministry suspected in Masaryk's death, was murdered. Now another major, Bedřich Pokorný, assigned to investigate both deaths, was found three weeks ago hanged in woods near Brno.

Did you believe that he fell out a window, in 1948? When you were fifteen?
Last night we only just got to July 1945. Do you want us to skip ahead in
the story?
No. Anyway, I get it.
What do you get?
That you don't want to talk about it, Gesine.

Then she had to get through a half hour with Sergeant Ted Sokorsky,
the country policeman who looks after our hosts' keys. Mr. Sokorsky sat
himself down on the landing, shyly accepted a beer, and started bringing
out tactful phrases about the weather. He spoke softly, which Marie took
as a sign of his respect for Mrs. Cresspahl, a visitor from New York and a
lady. He was young enough, and Marie would've liked to ask him to take
her for a ride round the lake on his ungainly motorcycle but instead she
decided to display the ladylike reserve that certain mothers raised their
children to maintain. Mr. Sokorsky wasn't sparing with his *madams* in
addressing Mrs. Cresspahl, and he brought off a bow, from the neck, after
locking up the house; Marie will never see him again, and for years to come
when the conversation turns to the police she'll bring up one named Ted
Sokorsky, not brawny, almost delicate, and the deference with which he
treated my mother, here I'll show you.

But now the vacation in the country is over, we've long since reached
the Palisades Parkway across from Manhattan, and Marie already thinks
she can see the place in the finely sculpted apartment towers where the wet
lilac-colored reflection of the evening sun comes off the five windows behind
which she's about to turn on the lights, all at once.

– If it's okay with you, Gesine: she'll say. *By your gracious permission:*
she'll say.

April 22, 1968 Monday
In the morning a heavy fog hung over the Hudson, astonishingly bright,
and like a guest over breakfast it opened a white eye occasionally, blearily,
blindly blinking.

But someone who still doesn't get New York weather, even now, will end up caught in a sudden shower on the hill of Ninety-Sixth Street leading up to Broadway; she was already running from the newsstand down into the subway, and like many others she trotted to work down Lexington Avenue with *The New York Times* folded into a roof over her head.

Peeking up from under its edge at the traffic light on Forty-Fifth Street, she saw on the inside of the roof how the war had been waged this weekend: thirty-one Vietcong dead in battles northwest of Saigon on Saturday, another fifteen yesterday morning farther north... she moved forward with the crowd, hemmed in by strangers' elbows. Not until lunchtime did she review the details in the dried-out paper, for instance that *The New York Times* would characterize the battles around the foreign capital not as an American defensive action but rather an offensive.

The paper's weather forecast for today: Mostly sunny and mild. Not this slashing rain.

Bright, sunny days, shored up by steady heat—for Marie this was not enough, as the sole memory of the first summer of the New Era in Jerichow, never mind that it's almost ninety-one seasons ago now, almost four thousand miles away too. Lazy storytelling, she calls it. Squatting in front of the fireplace in the summer house, feeding the fire until, probing carefully, she finds the kindling that can light that other fire. – I gather the Russian victors didn't behave well: she said.

Tell her, Gesine.
I was just a child then. Twelve years old. What do I know?
What you heard from us. What you saw.
She'll take the wrong information and use it.
She's a child, Gesine.
It's easy for the dead to talk. Were you honest with me?
Do better than we did.
And also so she'll know where she's going with me. To whom.
And for us, Gesine. Tell her.

Jerichow, all of western Mecklenburg, was still occupied by British troops, cordoned off with lines of armed soldiers, but the Soviets had long since arrived—they were nowhere to be seen and yet there, in conversations, in suppressed fears: as rumor. They were no longer the vague subhumans that the Reich Ministry of Public Enlightenment and Propaganda had been importing into Germany since 1941; they weren't even the photos from East Prussian villages where German units had managed to beat the Soviets back and could snap their shutters in front of battered women's bodies or crosses of men nailed onto barn doors—the government had made up too many news reports with too many faked photographs as proof. There was a sick child at my father's house, Hanna Ohlerich, from Wendisch Burg, whose parents hadn't believed much from the government but they had believed this and so hanged themselves: prematurely, before they'd had a chance to see and hear the foreigners from the East with their own eyes and ears, said the survivors, including Jerichowers safe under British management. Then, by early May already, came rumors amounting almost to news reports—not from the fallen government but from friends and relatives in the rest of Mecklenburg, the part under Soviet occupation. In Waren, an enemy of the Nazis known to the very end as the "Red pharmacist" had celebrated all night long with his liberators from the Soviet Union until they'd forced themselves on all the women in the house anyway and everyone in the family killed themselves with the poisonous medicine they hadn't been saving for such a purpose at all—this news was firmly grounded in a specific name, a specific market square, a specific business on the ground floor of a specific gabled building. In Malchin, in Güstrow, in Rostock the rumored Russians had tried to wash potatoes in toilet bowls by pulling the chain, then threatened to shoot the hapless Germans for sabotage, for flushing the food away. From Wismar came the report that three Soviet soldiers had hauled a grandfather clock past British sentries one night and taken it to a clockmaker, telling him to turn it into thirteen wristwatches— much in demand in Soviet Mecklenburg due to the foreigners' habit of never winding wall clocks and then throwing them into the bushes or the water, as broken. A number of country manors had burned down because spectral looters didn't believe in electrical lights, even when the electricity still worked, and had lit spills of paper on fire to help them search. They used a microscope from the pathology division of a university clinic to buy two bottles of booze; they shot at pigeons, with live ammunition; they were reportedly incapable of singing their melancholy songs. All of this, along with the Russians' infatuation with children, was both hard to believe and widely known in Jerichow when the British withdrew, and again various locals and refugees in town hanged, drowned, and poisoned themselves, but not all of them out of fear of the new occupiers: Pahl hadn't known where to go next; Dr. Berling, MD, hadn't found a cure for depression in all his studies. The rest—an estimated three and a half thousand people in Jerichow on July 3—stayed.

– Out of curiosity?: Marie said the day before yesterday. She hadn't let herself laugh often enough; she'd kept her face hidden, near the fire, her gaze on the flames so unwaveringly that she seemed not to be listening, or maybe listening only to her thoughts.
– Out of curiosity.
– Curiosity backed by a sense of how much they'd lost?
– Not necessarily what they'd lost.
– Mr. and Mrs. Maass, 14 Market Square.
– Like them. Maybe nothing had happened to them personally, but they'd heard stories.
– So now they wanted to see if the rumors were true?
– Yes, and there was another reason.
– The children weren't curious though: Marie decided.
– Maybe not. Since I don't know the words for that curiosity, you're probably right.
– And because of your Jews. The six million.
– How can you say something like that, Marie!
– I can to you. They were waiting for payback.
– Yes. Though they didn't believe all the news reports.
– They wanted to see for themselves how the bill came due.
– Yes.
– Like always.
– Yes!
– So they *were* curious: she said.

People, whether locals or refugees, stayed in Jerichow because they had a roof over their heads, whether their own or borrowed. Besides, starting July 2 the British wouldn't let anyone with household goods cross their new border, the Trave Canal—now you had to swim without luggage.

Wulff stayed, not only because of his pub and general store but because he'd been a member of a banned party (Social Democrats), declared unfit for military service too, and if not exactly expecting a reward he still felt he could count on his business being treated fairly. (– He was curious: Marie said.) By this point it was fairly obvious what was keeping Papenbrock there. My father stayed because the British had made him mayor and he wanted to hand over his official duties properly. And the locals put their faith in Jerichow's outward appearance.

Because what could the Russians possibly see in this little town, far from the main roads, tucked away in the country near the Baltic but without even a harbor? Whichever direction they came from, they'd see nothing but a low clump of modest buildings. The bishop's-miter church tower, however tall it was, however densely surrounded by the leaves of six-hundred-year-old trees, was a sign of bygone prosperity, not current riches. They would likely have already seen the country seats of Mecklenburg, magnificent metropolitan showpieces surrounded by parks; they'd no doubt have marched down streets lined with commercial properties, tokens of imperial times, in various Mecklenburg administrative centers, the so-called fore-cities— but in Jerichow they found few buildings over two stories. Wartime economy had ripped open large holes in the stuccoed ones, exposing the bricks, while the wood in the half-timbered ones had gone far too long without paint or even Carbolineum. And what did the entitled victors come driving into town on? Not asphalt, just bumpy round cobblestones, and in Rande there wasn't even a blue basalt double line for a bike path (which went with the rumor that the victors didn't know how to ride bikes). There remained the brickworks villa, where they'd set up their headquarters. They'd retreated at once from the von Lassewitzes' town house, now the Papenbrocks', after finding all the rooms full of refugees (so maybe there was something to their alleged fear of epidemics). The English had set up their club in Lindemann's Lübeck Court Hotel, now the Soviets would put their own name on it. To the uninitiated, the market square might well have seemed a bit too big—some who owned three-story properties there could be facing confiscation. Aside from that, however, the municipality of Jerichow could only have seemed uniformly impoverished to the Soviets, with nothing to loot, at least nothing that anyone let them know about.

Up until the Sunday after the entry of the first Soviet troops—until the night of July 8—only one single rumor had become fact. A Red Army man had forced his way into the shop belonging to Otto Quade, plumbing and heating, and pointed past the low partition at a floor model dating from prewar times. – Faucet: the soldier had said to Bergie Quade in his thick, *h*-less Russian accent: *Wassergahn* instead of *Wasserhahn*. Bergie—who, following the then-current advice, was dowdily dressed, with a filthy face and a rag smeared with chicken shit under her skirt—had answered, with typical Quadish presence of mind: *Wassergehn?* I'm not going in the water. Don't need to. Are you wanting to know who from around here's gone into the water? You mean drowned in the marsh, in the Baltic . . . ? The Red Army hadn't waited to hear her whole list and marched off, shaking his head, which to Bergie looked reproachful, she couldn't help it. This was the only unaccompanied soldier seen in Jerichow that whole first week. The commandant had shut himself up in the brickworks villa along with the whole occupying force, communicating with the Germans via orders he had Cresspahl post outside Town Hall. No Soviet airplane had yet landed at the Jerichow-North air base, that unfortunate token of the town's having taken part in the war on the wrong side; even though the area, with its razor-wire fences, would have been perfect for a prison camp, the new right side didn't use it for that either.

So, which way was the wind blowing in Jerichow that first week of July in 1945?

All them rumors, seems real overdone (B. Quade).

And even if they are not exaggerated, the Russians wouldn't dare try anything among people with experience of the British occupation (Dr. Kliefoth).

Still, they really did rape Ilse Grossjohann (Frieda Klütz).

They're not running the town, they're not using the airfield—that won't last (Mr. and Mrs. Maass).

Looks like the British'll be back, Papenbrock (Creutz Sr.).

The things Cresspahl's doing, an he's not even embarrassed (Käthe Klupsch).

Maybe we'll end up back in Sweden. 'S just two hundred years back (Mrs. Brüshaver).

Papenbrock's in the elite, you know. Businesswise, I mean (Elsa Pienagel).

They're the ones scared of us. A curfew! They're scared! (Frieda Klütz).

Maybe they're driving round the country in the middle a the night (Frieda Klütz).

In the war, gossip like that was called latrine talk (Alfred Bienmüller; Peter Wulff).

Töv man, du (Gesine Cresspahl).

April 23, 1968 Tuesday

She was still on her own for a moment. Yesterday evening's sky, painted with broad brushstrokes, had crept into the last pictures in her mind before waking; in her clearing consciousness the dream remained, like a wall she could take shelter behind. Like getting up for the first time in a long while. She was no one—a field of memory in which strange grasses grew; a stormy sky over the Baltic Sea; the smell of grass after rain. Just a few glances out at the Hudson, and with the light in her eyes the sense of time would run faster, and in it her, Gesine, Mrs. Cresspahl, employee, a four-digit number in the 753- exchange, not here, midtown. Not yet.

There were further postponements. Was for a while still I, Gesine, still I, Marie, still we, the child and I, still the voices from the dream. Gradually the felted sensation of sleep crumbled into dry powder. Although woozy, she could nonetheless show pleasure. Marie had tied her hair up in a ponytail so high and tight that it stood straight up for a while. Our roles separated us. How an eleven-year-old pours tea for her elder. How Gesine pulls herself together into Mrs. Cresspahl, mirrored in the child's scrutiny: here's my mother, thirty-five years old, she doesn't see the one gray hair in all the dark ones. Disguised for an office, equipped for a day out of the house, less recognizable now. How a child sullen about school talks as if looking forward to the essay she has to write, to make it easier for her mother to go out into the world as a working woman. Marie's worried, un-American face once more, soft with sleep, in the crack of the door. Then alone.

With time to continue to drift along for a while, though on set paths, from one square of the board to the next, punctually advancing in time—but still, on her own. It was she who promised the newspaper man a good morning, and that she would never burden him with anything more; a real connection born from acquaintance, that's him. She was almost disappointed to find herself among strangers again on the express side of the subway platform, and relieved to see yesterday's lovers come running down the scuffed stairs just in time, inexperienced, unsure of each other, separated on the train as it shot downtown. She wormed *The New York Times* out from under her arm: Good weather over North Vietnam; 151 bombing missions. It was she who let herself be shoved so close to the tips of a transit policeman's shoes that he moved aside slightly, all but saluting her. On the Grand Central Shuttle she walked to the next car through the swaying doors, not to gain three seconds but to feel herself moving in something moving. She scanned the rows of underground store windows, satisfied to see all the products she could do without. At the ticket counters, again with fantasies of running away: that was her. And yet on Lexington Avenue she relaxed in the camaraderie of all the different people around her, the small-town brick buildings between the skyscrapers, the pizza chef she always saw, holding his large round disk up to her like a greeting. The low-ceilinged retreat for men, the wooden table with the breakfast beer right by the window—she's seen it so many times, she has not tried to understand it so many times. Between the facades with their many windows she looked up in search of the sky over the city, and sure enough the bulrushes swayed as they should in the drifting clouds. A few more steps and the stroll through the city of daily surprises has come to an end. The person flushed through the marble bank lobby, sucked out of one throng into a thinner one and then into the last elevator lane, that was no longer her, that was Mrs. Cresspahl, employee here for the past four years, formerly a foreign-language secretary, fourth floor, then eleventh floor, and now transferred to the sixteenth, integrated into the firm's operations though no doubt dispensably, provisionally, temporarily. – How are you! she is repeatedly asked on her ride up in the closed cabin, and she will answer: How are you! with a drawn, thin-lipped smile, the corners of her eyes not budging. That's someone else.

That's our German, that's our Danish girl. She's single, available; married; a widow. Engaged—Wes saw her on Third Avenue with some guy from Kansas. Nah, Nebraska. Has a foster child, two, no actually the kid's hers. Gee-sign. Has a sense of humor; she might say: You wouldn't find my village on the map, I'd have to write it in myself, but she also says: I was born in Jerichow, that's in Mecklenburg. Yerry Show. Looks taller than five four.

Has a thing going with the VP's son; only took her three years to make it into the tower with all the fat cats. She's allowed to eat in the bosses' restaurant but goes down to Sam's for lunch—bad move. Good move, goes back and visits her old departments, doesn't burn any bridges. Helps a friend a hers check his letters of credit; must be cause she used to be a Communist. One of the vice president's little games, de Rosny's like that. Special assignment. Don't get memos from her, her number's not in the directory. Yesterday she took a French heir out to lunch; she's just de Rosny's left hand. She has a corner office; the bank's given her a safe. Miss Cresspahl. No, Mrs. So she is available. Personnel won't say. Who is she? A girl on the sixteenth floor where men work. Won't be long 'fore she's transferred to the Milwaukee branch. Ten thousand a year. More like eleven. Cresspahl, name sounds Jewish. Celtic. In short: No one knows her. Maybe that's just what the fat cats on the sixteenth floor want. Bottom line: Unknown. Anonymous, camouflaged. Unknowable.

The sun beating through the unprotected windows takes her back again. Here in the spacious office full of functional and residential furniture is the same hot, semi-high eastern sunlight that ignites the haze over the low settlements of Long Island City to the color of a sea seventeen years ago. She was there once—held a sextant up to the sun. That was her once.

Cresspahl's in-box is stacked no higher than usual, but today for the first time there's newspaper in it: page 12 from *The New York Times.* An article is circled in big exuberant loops; her boss has put his URGENT stamp into the ad space next to it. He's even taken the trouble to dash off initials meant to denote de Rosny, and again they look more than anything like a prince's little crown.

"Memo
From: Cp
To: de Rosny, Vice President
Re: N.Y.T., 4/23/68; Czechosl.

With reference to the claim that subsidies in the Czechoslovak economy are distributed in accord with an 'arbitrarily set plan,' I refer to my report on the 1966–1970 Five Year Plan, memo no. deR 193-A-22.

The declared figure for subsidies in fiscal year 1967–1968, 30 billion crowns, is remarkably close to the actual sum, which according to my calculations amounts to slightly more than 15 percent of the net national income (deR 193-CD 48).

The Czechoslovakian ruble account in the Soviet Union, estimated by the N.Y.T. as ten billion crowns, may actually have since exceeded the nominal equivalent of sixteen billion dollars. However, in addition to the lack of USSR products worth purchasing, this also represents what may someday partially eliminate Comecon's leverage (deR 23-CF-1238).

The reform efforts are presented in exceptionally general and simplified terms. The N.Y.T. describes in detail the delegation of responsibility to the enterprises themselves and the plan for gradually withdrawing subsidies. More precise information about the leveling off of differential taxes on unprofitable businesses would have been useful (above-cited source not applicable here).

If functionaries of the Czechoslovak government are communicating with organs such as *The New York Times,* not only about personal political struggles in the background of the debates around reform but also to indicate the real possibility of the country's return into the International Monetary Fund and International Bank for Reconstruction and Development, this suggests that, more than wanting foreigners to think they are creditworthy, as previously assumed, they also want to publicize the advocates for reform in their own country. Would a further report on this topic be of interest?

Negotiations of loans from capitalist countries are here mentioned in print for the first time. I would like to assure you, for the record, that the leak did not come from this office. Still, the unofficial admission should excite more than the market (see prev. par.).

Best regards,
G. C."

What on earth did you do to my English, writer?
It wasn't yours.
It wasn't this miserable limping German you've translated it into.
Your English was as business *as it gets, Gesine.*
I wasn't insane when I wrote it!
But you were tired. Distracted too.

The employer has added delighted exclamation marks next to a paragraph in the *Times* report from Prague:

"The state of Czechoslovakia's economic health is like that of an injured man so full of morphine that he not only is likely to be permanently stupefied but he is unable even to tell the doctor where it hurts."

You can see de Rosny here, in his underlining: after such prolonged strain from peering downward a moment of refreshment has been granted him. This man full of morphine might get employee Cp. a new code number.

Later, day sinks into evening against venetian blinds tilted perpendicular to block the sun, sinks into the slow return trip to Riverside Drive, to us, where we live.

– This is what Mecklenburg looks like? Marie asks. She has stood up specially from her homework, is standing behind her mother's chair, even bringing her cheek close, to have a line of vision that's parallel at least.

It was nothing. Ragged fog drifting over the river. A gap in the always astonishing green of the leaves seems to open onto an overcast inland lake, behind which memory sees, again, and gladly, a bluish pine woods on the other bank's Palisades, sees the region of bygone times made again and again transparent and unreal by the stage-set trees.

– Hm: Marie says, reassured, reassuring, as if to a shying horse. Where would she be if her New York, river and riverbank included, were something different, or even comparable to something different! To her it's incomparable. Her time living here still stretches before her.

April 24, 1968 Wednesday

In the Czechoslovak Socialist Republic three employees of the judiciary have been dismissed—no mere bailiffs or janitors but three high-ranking deputy general prosecutors, one of them the chief military prosecutor himself. The new government's spokesmen provide no further explanation. It seems as if these guardians of the law in former times have now become guilty of crimes.

The Soviets had been occupying Jerichow for barely a week but by the second Monday in the first July after the war the locals had already decided that there was one man responsible: Cresspahl, my father. "The Russians are his fault," the verdict ran, and it covered more than just complaints about the foreigners. It really did a person good to say these words. As if without Cresspahl the Russians would never have come in the first place.

It had started with throwing Käthe Klupsch in jail, and Cresspahl hadn't done that. The British, while they were there, had threatened to punish anyone who spread rumors that they were going to leave Jerichow to their comrades-in-arms from the east. One bright June day, on the crowded sidewalk outside Klein the butcher's empty shopwindow, Käthe Klupsch, however impossible she thought such a fate was, couldn't resist giving herself a pleasant shudder by uttering the forbidden prediction. Two Tommies marched Käthe Klupsch off to Town Hall between them. The soldiers made sure not to get too close to this stout lady with the heaving bosom, and for her this was "bodily assault." The four-hour wait outside Cresspahl's office: that she'd felt was "a cynical effort to wear her down"—she'd been told only that she wasn't allowed to talk. After that, the process of determining the facts had been a "spiritual ordeal" and "brainwashing" too, since Cresspahl had been obliged to translate his British visitor's questions for her. Having admitted that she was able to read, for example typed public regulations, she was given a warning; because Cresspahl didn't have time to write out a special pass that night, the British held her in a cell under Town Hall until curfew ended. Käthe Klupsch now thought she'd "been alone in the building with Cresspahl until six in the morning," and probably got herself a bit mixed up with the two refugees in Rande who'd had to stay in jail until the Soviets took them as prisoners for the same offense. This was how Klupsch talked until the Soviets did move into Jerichow; afterward her only complaint about Cresspahl was his secret alliance with them. Cause in the end they did come, didn't they? And for that they'd turned a blameless woman into a political prisoner, didn't they?

The Russians were Cresspahl's fault.

No. It hadn't started like that.

The British had made Cresspahl mayor of Jerichow. While they could have seen him as just another German, one who'd betrayed his sometime British home even, they instead seemed to trust him, like a friend almost. The British intelligence officers hadn't found anything to worry about, they'd saluted him when they left! a military salute, too! Even Americans had come, from their area around Schwerin, and spent nights in Cresspahl's office, and if they had questioned him over his (Western) reliability there'd still been drinks and fine words. Then the Soviets had moved in and they let Cresspahl stay mayor. That was their military cunning—trying to hide their secret conflict with their Anglo-Saxon allies. Still, they hadn't exactly adopted Cresspahl, much less confirmed his official position. They'd installed him. Under the reign of the swastika, that word "install," *Einsatz,* had carried connotations of something irregular—manpower shortages, stopgaps, "emergency measures," whether putting a special unit to work "to help with" the harvest or deploying scattered troops or installing an unelected official, sometimes without even asking him first. Now Cresspahl had betrayed the British again, posting a notice on Town Hall that by order of the Soviet commandant he was henceforth a henchman of the Russians, a tool in their hands—"installed" as mayor.

In May and June it had been the American Eighteenth Airborne, as represented by the British Sixth Airborne division, under B. L. Montgomery— the people of Jerichow had gotten quite used to their old occupiers. No sooner had they left than Cresspahl was serving the new occupiers, the local commander K. A. Pontiy, the Russians.

Cresspahl had helped the Russians to an eighth of the town. Their fence around the brickworks villa had by no means been the end of it. On the fourth day after their arrival, it became clear why they'd merely run a few lines of razor wire through the golden rain bushes on the west side of the property. That morning, eight able-bodied men were ordered to report to Cresspahl's office in Town Hall, summoned by name, and Mina Köpcke had to come too, representing her husband's construction firm. And was their job to clean up the Lübeck Court, wrecked by the British, so that Jerichow would get its hotel back? No, they were to build a fence. A fence running due west from the commandant's headquarters, through the back gardens of the houses on the Bäk, then straight north to Field Road, east to the edge of the yards of the houses on Town Street, and back to the property they'd already occupied! Mina Köpcke had been managing the books and supervising repairs for her husband ever since he'd gone missing with an antiaircraft gun in Lithuania; now she was eager to show him what she could do with a project of her own, and was put in charge. Cresspahl yet again showed what a Russian stooge he was, by giving them his whole stock of wood, and when that ran out Mina was free to tear down fence boards anywhere in Jerichow she wanted and her enemies didn't. She had a requisition order with a Soviet stamp to prove it, to which she could add: It (the confiscation; the Russians' construction project) was Cresspahl's fault. Unlike him, she wanted to be patriotic, she didn't set the fenceposts as deep in their stone foundations as she would have for a fence of her own, and when she had the paint mixed thinner than it would have been for a German customer she thought she could use the harsh sea wind as an excuse. But now what did this Cresspahl do, this fellow businessman and protector of Jerichow's interests back in the day? He had one of her fence boards sent to her, as a sample; when her second paint job still turned out pale lime green, the barrel of synthetic resin was weighed on the town scales before her eyes and she had to sign a receipt. Then she came to Town Hall with her bill, and did Cresspahl file it away in good faith like a fellow victim of a foreign power? Late that night Cresspahl was seen with his buddy K. A. Pontiy pacing the length of Mina's fence, like two friends out for a stroll, one wielding a surveyor's rod and the other delighting in the wide swerving arcs the compass made. Köpcke & Co. was summoned back to Town Hall and Cresspahl calculated her chicanery out for her in square feet and cubic feet. He said nothing about fraud or even about innocent mistakes—he just asked for a revised bill. Sat hunched at his mayor's desk, elbows too close together, and however tired he was he could have looked her in the eyes more than just that once, from deep under his brows, so surprised. Mina Köpcke stuck to her numbers, signed her aggressive bill, and accepted a draft on the government bank for later payment. For now she received no money at all, and she attributed that to Cresspahl, as the Russian way of doing business and as his fault.

Not only was he betraying Jerichow to the Russians, he was taking his own cut! While Mrs. Köpcke and her seven men were fencing in a whole street, the Bäk, and a notice saying "Requisitioned" was being nailed up on one house after another, and since the construction was proceeding from both south ends, the Bäk was turning into a sack whose opening narrowed day by day. The Bäk had formerly been a residential street of respectable brick houses, less than forty years old and often with generously proportioned attics, among them Dr. Semig's practically princely villa, all with sizable gardens separating them from the narrow lots on Town Street, and now the homeowners in this prosperous area had to move out, into the overcrowded town, billeted where papers signed by Cresspahl ordered them to go. They were allowed to take only what they could carry; they had to leave every room in a condition permitting immediate occupation by the foreigners. And Cresspahl refused to let anyone come complain about the single room they now had at Quade's, or above the pharmacy, sometimes even shared with refugees! He would agree to see the refugees who themselves had been billeted in the Bäk, waiting so much more patiently now that they were on their third or fourth relocation in six months, and he allocated to them the rooms that the Jerichowers had been wanting to keep for themselves or their relatives, because he knew every building in town as well as the locals knew his. Then the north end of the fence was extended right across the Bäk, and that was the last time this street was ever seen in Jerichow, to this day. The people in houses adjoining the fence on Town Street complained about the shadows it cast on their gardens, the plants that didn't like so much shade. And whose fault was that?

Meanwhile Cresspahl's own house and property lay outside the fence, on the other side of Brickworks Road. He'd looked after his friends: Creutz's vegetable garden was within the fence and even though all its products had to be handed over to headquarters Amalie was allowed to go on using the path to Town Street running alongside the pastor's house, and the land the Creutzes leased from the church had been fenced in for them too, as though permanently theirs now. Pastor Brüshaver, once again a neighbor of Cresspahl's, could also stay in his house unmolested, though it occupied a strategic weak point that should have been fenced in to make the army enclosure a solid stronghold. And Cresspahl had secured himself, too, against looters and unwanted visitors, since the only approach to his property was on Brickworks Road but now there was a road sign, the first in its history, a board sharpened to an arrow, and it said: КОММАНДАНТУРА. Who would go down that road unless they had to? Cresspahl hadn't even arranged for a German translation. It practically looked like a call to learn Russian—they wouldn't put that past Cresspahl either.

And he'd forced Bergie Quade to come to the commandant's headquarters. The Red Army soldier she'd so glibly enlightened about "Wassergahn"

came back to her store with a boy, a refugee from Pommern who was staying in Cresspahl's house. About seventeen but broad shouldered. He looked
Bergie in the eye as if he'd long been a man, and a silent type too; she
couldn't put him off, talk him out of the store. The Red Army soldier looked
at Mrs. Quade as he talked, and she felt almost attractive under his remembering gaze. The boy didn't smile, he just translated. It sounded reliably
North German, even when he had to ask the Red Army for clarification.
Bergie Quade couldn't resist the urge to wash her hands again. By that
point she'd decided to be cooperative, so she invited the visitors into her
kitchen. She hid her satisfaction while walking down Town Street between
them, as if being led away, an upstanding German housewife under arrest,
she even managed the requisite look of grim determination. She followed
them across the Creutz property, stopped for a minute to talk to Amalie,
who was supervising the fence builders as they transplanted some gooseberry
bushes, and then really and truly set foot in the occupying power's sealed
compound. The Kommandatura. Over the next few hours the Red Army
learned swear words that would circulate for some time, a bit garbled, in
the Jerichow Soviets' vocabulary; Bergie Quade also complimented Jakob
Abs for following her instructions with delicate precision, like an expert
plumber. The last German owners of the brickworks villa had decided to
leave the Soviets with sawn-through drainpipes rather than whole ones,
and the kitchen and bathroom faucets looked to Bergie suspiciously as
though they'd been pounded with hammers, and secretly she couldn't
believe that people who were, after all, nobility could have treated their
house in such fashion. Then Bergie Quade had the choice between submit-
ting a bill to the government bank or receiving a half-liter bottle of unlabeled
vodka, she accepted her husband's balm, and had a drink on the house,
too, with Wassergahn the Red Army soldier, who'd helped with the repairs.
When Jakob brought her out through the brickworks villa's front door
onto the civilian Brickworks Road, she was tempted to check in at Cresspahl house, to see if he didn't need help after all, with all his refugees and
the child. But Jakob shook his head and Bergie walked the length of the
cemetery wall to Town Street like everything was normal—tool bag in her
fist, bottle under her skirt where she'd earlier had her shit-smeared rag,
deep in thought about who she could tell all this to. If she wasn't mistaken,
her tactics had cost Cresspahl time as well as effort. So that at least wasn't

his fault. But Mrs. Quade's unwillingness to give her neighbors a full report was enough to ensure that they had something to blame him for.

Meanwhile Cresspahl had had to post Order No. 2 from the military commandant of the town of Jerichow: All residents were to turn in their radios, batteries, typewriters, telephones, microphones, cameras, "etc." at Papenbrock's granary within three days. That night, Cresspahl explained what "etc." meant: guns, explosives, rifles, and firearms of all kinds; the following day, K. A. Pontiy's Order No. 4 demanded that all gold, silver, or platinum coins or bars, and all foreign currency, be handed in at the credit union, as well as documents pertaining to foreign assets, and again Cresspahl was seen as the Soviets' accomplice. For the townsfolk saw him going to Town Hall that morning with his telephone under his arm, and another time with two army Karabiner rifles someone had thrown onto his property overnight, even though the collection of People's Receivers and "etc." in Papenbrock's granary didn't amount to much. Then Cresspahl showed his fellow citizens that he hadn't lived among them for twelve years for nothing. He posted a reminder at Town Hall that the post office had a list of former owners of radios and telephones. Some people from that list turned up, but they were planning to throw their devices at that Russia-lover Cresspahl's feet, and they had to wait a long time at the granary gate because the mayor kept announcing every two hours that he was on his way, and never came. Finally, the commandant threatened with arrest the owner of any home where requisitioned property was found, and now the locals forced the refugees to go in and hand over what *they* had while they themselves burned what they didn't bury, including the genuine Russian rubles from prisoners of war that they'd saved to do business with after the British forces returned (or the Swedish ones arrived). At least they could still blame Cresspahl for their losses; it was his fault and they had the receipts to prove it.

Jerichow could see just how dishonorable a Soviet lackey Cresspahl was from his actions toward the Papenbrocks. He kept sending more and more homeless refugees into his very own in-laws' house, to the point where they had to spend their old age camping out in Albert's office. He'd done nothing to stop the Red Army from removing the von Lassewitzes' furniture from the Papenbrocks' house, carrying it onto Market Square, spraying it with Lysol for all to see, then driving it off to the Kommandatura. Papenbrock's yard and granary were confiscated, all the grain in them too, and they became the Red Army's supply depot, and Cresspahl could just go on living his life after robbing his own family of their property. Even if he lived to be ninety, how could he make up for such guilt?

The Soviets themselves didn't respect him. The British had had him chauffeured around in a jeep from morning till night; the Soviets let him walk, from Brickworks Road to Town Hall, from the hospital to the gasworks, from one end of Jerichow to the other, without even an escort— defenseless, alone.

– But now they weren't spitting on him anymore: Marie says.

– No. Not even shouting things after him.

– Did they take it out on young Gesine?

– It was meant for my father, wasn't it. Young Gesine didn't care.

– When you were sent to go shopping—

– Yes.

– and they shoved you out of the line. Accidentally stepped on your feet. There were parents who wouldn't let their kids play with you—

– It wasn't like that, Marie.

– They didn't see you?

– They didn't see me.

– And now I'm supposed to think about a Francine, a black girl in a white school, and in the morning when she comes over to me and says hello—

– Don't make that comparison. The child I was—

– Fine, Gesine. I dig you. You were trying to tell me a story, not teach me a lesson. Still, I can think something out for myself.

– There's no comparison, you can't think that.

– I can think what I want.

– Whatever you want, Marie.

We got home late, and heavy rain hung a flapping gray curtain of mist in front of the river and land beyond the park. Behind that curtain the world stops.

April 25, 1968 Thursday

The new prime minister of Czechoslovakia, Mr. Černík, has praised his
Czechs and Slovaks for their good work since 1948, as is only proper at the
start of a new economic program on the set list, and then proceeded to tell
them what that good work has achieved: a per capita national income up
to 40 percent lower than that of "advanced capitalist countries," delivery
of manufactured goods to customers often taking three times longer,
transport and housing and retailing in similarly poor shape, and he actually
mentions the $400 million foreign trade deficit with capitalist countries,
calling it relatively small but "very unpleasant and inconvenient" because
it involves short-term loans. Employee Cresspahl has already been calculating and summarizing all that herself, since December, for the bank files;
she has been useful to the company and has no reason to fear being fired
on the spot when she's ordered to report to the management's floor in the
middle of the workday; she can look down on two sections of Third and
Lexington Avenues without too much to worry about. From such a height
the people down there look not just foreshortened but distorted.

Twelve years ago the bank hadn't been here and would have been rather
nervous about handling a piddling $400 million. As for a female assistant
to a vice president, that was unthinkable.

It was a family bank, not only in terms of who owned it but of what it
did. Its name still reveals its beginnings in small Midwestern towns, giving
loans against wheat on the stalk, bribing the sheriff, and taking a man's
word the same way it took a promissory note. The name—with its country
ring, smacking of forefathers and filial piety—has remained.

There exists a photograph, in the brownish detail of around 1880, that
purports to show a village branch of the bank in North Carolina: outside
the big window with its garland of golden letters stand the justice of the
peace with the blacksmith and the shopkeeper, all chatting, all befrockcoated,
and the bank manager is leaning in the doorway, dressed as if for church,
eyes under his hat brim ingenuous and miscalculated, and every performer
in the scene is really and truly bisected by the wooden railing that actual
cowboys used to tie their horses to back in those days. The picture refuses
to stay fixed in the second during which the photographer ninety years ago
told everyone to hold their breath; it wants to keep moving, to the rattling
stagecoach pulling up in a cloud of dust, the relief driver on the box seat

shot through the eye, the horses frisky, the townsfolk pouring out of the neighboring buildings, ladies looking down from the top windows of the hotel, the strongbox hanging by its last strap, brutally pried open, and a shot rings out, and fresh horses are brought over, to chase the robbers—will they be bandits or Indians?—until finally, with a booming echo, the picture fades out and zooms in to the sign at the bank entrance: CLOSED FOR FUNERAL.

Not a few people in the company insist that the photo is retouched, or that all it shows is a movie set from a Western. Some claim to have seen the movie and swear they remember the scene. Anyone who dares to suggest the opposite—that maybe the film set was based on this photograph—is immediately suspected of being un-American, of mockery even. Mrs. Cresspahl doesn't say this anymore.

Around the turn of the century the bank made it to Chicago, to a little mansion inside the Loop it could call its own—narrow but noble of chest—and after 1945 it was practically rich. But the family in charge wanted to preserve its gains and increase them too, its cake should be kept in the pantry while nonetheless being eaten, a bearish attitude toward life. And so the family council believed the rumor of 1947, about the imminent death of New York City, and kept primly distant from that infamous region known to devour both men and money. They came to New York in 1951, too late. They wanted to move into the right neighborhood and found a old building five hundred yards from the Wall Street subway station; their decision to cloak it in marble and inscribe it in gold only diminished it further. And not only its appearance refused to gain in stature. They'd missed the Bretton Woods Conference, they tackled the stock market with less than stirring boldness, they couldn't find Chad on a map, probably thought it was a detergent. Headquarters was still on Lake Michigan, watching the sick child on the Atlantic with anger and defiance, yet continuing to send the little cripple ever more money. In 1961, when Gesine Cresspahl came to New York well acquainted with empires like Morgan Guaranty Trust, she barely knew this bank's name—she might have innocently called it a brokerage house or financial firm. And now she's standing high above ground level at a window in its new building, barely visible from the sidewalk, waiting for de Rosny to have a free moment—deputy chairman of the board, deputy CEO, deputy omnipotence: de Rosny.

De Rosny, too, once laughed at the idea that he might join his good name to that of this financial institution.

In the mid-1950s, more often than chance alone could explain, news came sailing out of the Bay with the Golden Gate: de Rosny was looking for something back east. Reason: the California climate no longer agreed with his wife.

It was a typical de Rosny reason, and if it made his partners smile for a moment, taking this for a familiar leg-pull, then what were lesser mortals, whose names probably struck him as belonging to harmless characters from the great American book of fairy tales, supposed to think? Not many offers came de Rosny's way, and the few that did weren't from that building near Wall Street. De Rosny didn't need them. If he felt like moving back east he could pick up the phone and ten days later everything in his house would have been rolled across the continent and set back up on Long Island Sound in a family property, precisely the same as he'd left it in San Francisco, give or take six inches. De Rosny hadn't worked or fought his way up into money, nor had he married money—he'd been born into money, his parents had given it to him and him alone, and he'd breathed through the aromatic, nourishing, protective shell of money ever since he'd known his own name, long before he'd started to learn the banking business in Singapore, because he was bored. So the word was: de Rosny wasn't available. Sitting behind phones on the fog-covered hills, he was paid whatever he wanted over and above what others were paid, simply because of his kinship with money, his descent from money, because he and money were one. De Rosny wouldn't waste his time on such a negligible problem, even if it could be rectified on the East Coast. De Rosny was considered unpredictable. He was prepared to risk a rift with Howard Hughes and publicly criticize Howie's business (not private) investments in Hollywood; de Rosny's vacations weren't spent there, they were spent with the aristocracy in Great Britain. And he had more than enough business with airplane manufacturers already, he didn't need Howie's inventions, particularly since they didn't stay in the air long enough. Others called him unserious. They didn't mean how he handled money. No, it was that he didn't know how to live. Evening meals—the blissful reward for a day of hard-fought meetings—bored him, and visibly. De Rosny didn't drink hard liquor, and he could have offered religious reasons as an excuse but instead he admitted just not being interested.

Shared confidences? Ha! Does anyone even know his first name? He once got a friendly slap on the shoulder and sent his suit out for dry cleaning! He invited almost no one into his home, and certainly not friends, and they left with no stories to tell. At home de Rosny served imported white wines from some unremarkable region in France where there's a hill—weak stuff, hardly loosened the tongue at all. While other people were happy to have their picture in the paper at a restaurant with Eleanor Roosevelt, de Rosny was sitting at Franklin Delano's fireside ages ago, and *not* having himself photographed, and F. D. had gone so far as to disguise the business nature of these chats with exchanges of boarding school memories. In the middle of the war against the Huns. No, de Rosny was given too much, too easily, it wasn't fair. He probably knows God's address and doesn't even bother to send Him a thank-you note. And this crafty rogue, this all-too-flexible fifty-year-old, his whole body trained by something other than tennis—you think anyone's going to discuss some trivial matter in New York with him, just because he wants to move back east? (Because his wife was not doing well in the sunny Pacific climate.)

De Rosny passed through Chicago, staying not in the city's luxury hotel but at the Windermere, and unfamiliar visitors graced the Windermere's conference room, and five firms in the distant south were narrowed down to two, and two to one, and suddenly New Orleans appeared on the market with a product that sold with childish ease, and a child could have thought of it, and is that what Matthew 18 meant? (Ask those Gideons.) (And the Windermere was practically buried in reservations for the next six months.) But de Rosny did deign to listen to some little eastern thing, and was annoyingly familiar with the matter already, and pointed out the considerable cost of solving it. In Chicago they thought he meant his salary, and they were wrong. De Rosny let himself be seen in New York, ostensibly back from inspecting his mansion in Connecticut, and the visitors he received at the Waldorf Towers included some who'd had to invite themselves. De Rosny brought no notebook listing his conditions, no secretary to relay them; apparently he wanted the time this little bagatelle was costing him to be made up in amusement.

Apparently his conditions were: That the board of directors would never try to make him president.

The compensation he felt was appropriate for a Vice President de Rosny, and the percentage by which it would increase annually—those are numbers that someone like Employee Cresspahl will never learn.

Then the horrible thing with his wife happened. All the better that he was moving back east, even if he had to pay for it out of his own pocket. Which he didn't. Chicago had preemptively taken care of these costs, and once again he'd made out better than he deserved.

Except for his wife. It was only four years later that her story came out, and even then as such a vague rumor that it's simply not worth telling.

De Rosny moved into the unfortunate shack on Wall Street, and for quite a long time nothing further was seen of him. Clearly the whole thing was some kind of practical joke on de Rosny's part. He even left the problem child's rustic name unchanged, although the marketing department had welcomed him with a chic, slimmed-down pseudonym. De Rosny insisted on reinstating the old-fashioned font, and replacing the comma with an *&* in the style of a year before yesteryear. He may have realized that he needed something to show, so he opened a branch office in California with his friends. (De Rosny loans de Rosny the following sum on the following terms...) The financial world found the part of his behavior they knew about disappointing, old hat even; de Rosny held internal meetings, not press conferences. Internally word was getting out about what all that talk of costs in Chicago had meant. It was an enormous sum. An outrage. This time no de Rosny was offering to contribute anything. His people in San Francisco had suddenly gone deaf too. They put it to a vote in Chicago. De Rosny would have been a very, very expensive ex–vice president; his only condition had a nasty catch to it, predictably enough. It was a challenge. They didn't mind picturing de Rosny picking up his hat; they couldn't bear imagining how the scene would continue: with him putting that hat on his head, turning in the door being held open for him, and saying goodbye to all the cowards. So de Rosny stayed in the boardroom, in his deputy's chair; in northern California the air force bought a bigger rocky plateau. In New York the talk persisted of a de Rosny failure.

In those years, although the elevated rail no longer hurtled by on its stilts above Third Avenue, that artery between Fortieth and Sixtieth was still mostly lined with low, four-story brick buildings, each one a box much like the others, built for classy renting and poor living. While scholarship was busy envisioning the death of New York City, the El generated more businesses on Third, the commuters walked on roundabout paths from Grand Central to Park and Madison, and the foot traffic called forth more street-level stores—bars, tailors, hair salons, little hideaways too—and on the upper floors many of the buildings were sealed off by dirt on the windows or blinds, with only a few monuments to prosperity hulking sheepishly between them. A gang of brokers swooped down onto one such block between Lexington and Third, bidding and underbidding, and no one could put a name to the purchaser, unless it was some superbroker. When a homeowner hesitated, the wrecking balls went to work next door and the plot of land was without form and void. One owner of a corner property still had a case moving through the courts while the steel frame of a new building was going up over his head, like a child's idea absurdly enlarged, and since the scaffolding was lit up at night, all the way up to the top, *The New York Times* remarked on it and backed its opinion up with a photo. You could look in at the construction site through generous ovals in the fences, even Gesine Cresspahl walked innocently by it, and stopped, and marveled that bricks were actually being stuck into the steel girders as a testament to tradition, from top to bottom as it turned out, leaving them hanging naked and exposed. The man on the corner kept tirelessly going from court to court, complaining to the construction firm, and the world, that General Lexington (or was it Washington?) had once spent the night at his establishment, which was why he alone from the whole block had let the wood from yesteryear remain, and painted it green and white, and de Rosny relented. It wasn't literally de Rosny, but he may have leased that part of the building from the construction company and apparently it was up to him to decide to keep the historic little building on the corner, under an umbrella of concrete, and again a venerable, ambitious bank from Chicago and Wall Street snagged forty-three lines and a photograph in *The New York Times*. Two gigantic towers went up, one on each end of the block, wrapped in blue glass, and even the part connecting them was fifteen stories high, and the workmen hadn't been shy about how deep they'd dug the foundations. The construction firm's name hung above the entrances in large, if removable letters, and the bank's ground-floor windows looked for the time being like a branch office, temporarily rented. De Rosny had a lease for the whole monstrosity and he sublet it out, to lawyers, to UN delegations who'd been waiting all this time not three blocks away for office space. In the end it got to the point where the bank was paying rent to itself, and now it was time to record the building in the land registry and *The New York Times.* The bank by no means wants to occupy its whole premises on its own, but it can evict at will and when needed, to make more room for itself, and the old-fashioned agricultural name with its *&* counts this milestone of uncompromising architecture as its property. Still, even this name isn't chiseled into the marble, it too is removable. For what de Rosny is truly proud of is that this building was built to be torn down at any time, within thirty days, and the empty lot sold to the next sucker at a tidy profit.

He'd been doing occasional work the whole time. The word *Chad* was now on people's lips in the bank, painfully familiar to some people, and de Rosny spread knowledge of other parts of the world too. Headquarters has moved from Chicago, the head of the family now lives on top of one of the towers, with a roof garden and swimming pool, wearing the emperor's new clothes while de Rosny is doing the work. All day long people come up out of the subways under Lexington Avenue, are swept north from Grand Central, and de Rosny has scorned neither their savings accounts nor their direct deposits. He made the building more than a few feet taller than Union Dime Savings's on Forty-Second Street, and he must have enjoyed seeing Chemical come after him, quite a bit later, and building on Third Avenue. And ads like the young lady with her lips softly, voluptuously open:

when she thinks of a bank,
her reaction is CHEMICAL

—none of those for him; he only barely accepted the marketing department's new logo of five lines derived from the company's initials, and the guards in the lobby may wear it embroidered over their hearts but de Rosny doesn't let his chauffeur, whose uniform is more in the British style. Everything in the building matches, every part of the machine fits together, from the square footage allotted to every workspace to the underground garage, but the template is not visible, it exists in de Rosny's head. He is considered strict, merciless even, in his role as boss; he's referred to in the building as D. R., dee-arr, in a respectfully amused undertone. The president, the head of the family, may make announcements over the company intercom in the cafeteria, but people pay less attention than they do to the rain rebounding off the sealed double windows; de Rosny's coldhearted utterances produce laughter, and one rumor among the employees is the almost

sincere wish that the damn PA system someday finally be converted to
television. This, they feel, will let them get at the truth, as if a de Rosny ever
lets the cat out of the bag before the deal is done. So far only three people
in the whole bank know what de Rosny has planned for the ČSSR, and one
of them estimates the plan's worth in the neighborhood of $400 million,
based on these bloodthirsty short-term loans he's been reading about in
the paper.

De Rosny seems puzzled. He rushes out his door to meet Employee
Cresspahl, hastily closes the door behind her, starts marching with long
strides up and down his spacious carpet. A man thinking hard. A man
thunderstruck. He could be a teacher, the kind who looks around the
schoolroom absentminded, thin lipped, even after ten years giving no sign
of his accumulated familiarity and friendship, just moving on to the next
item in the lesson plan.

De Rosny cannot understand these Communists, especially not the
Czech or Slovak ones. How could they go and count their money right out
in the open, in front of civilians! And then say what they plan to do with
it too!

Correct behavior, in Employee Cresspahl's view.

Against the rules, in de Rosny's. Not only are the Communists behaving
like Communists, they're ruining the market for the loan he wants to slip
them under the table, on the sly.

So that would be playing by de Rosny's rules. By this point Employee
Cresspahl is permitted such comments, in this room, harmless, knees
together, gaze fixed attentively on the bridge of de Rosny's nose—the
schoolgirl. De Rosny amuses himself setting a little trap. Would his faithful
and hardworking Gesine Cresspahl like to take a quick trip to Prague,
pretending to be a tourist, and share a bit of de Rosny's inner life with the
new leaders?

Employee Cresspahl doesn't want to be de Rosny's faithful and hardworking
tool, she would have to discuss such a trip with her daughter first, she has
a dentist appointment tomorrow, hairdresser's too. She doesn't want to,
and she has to say: Of course. I'd be happy to. Tonight?

No. The Communists wouldn't take a woman seriously enough. As
someone authorized to speak for a New York bank.

Employee Cresspahl begs to differ. Women's equal rights in Socialist countries.

De Rosny, with an unexpected twitch of his eyelid, reminds her of the statistics she's prepared on this topic too. Then he has her at his mercy and he starts by evaluating her report from Tuesday. He says: But with me, in the pay of us murderous man-eating capitalists, you'll get equal rights like you've never seen! Just wait four months!

– Very good. I can wait. Sir: Employee Cresspahl says.

So this is our life. This is what we live on.

April 26, 1968 Friday

Yesterday, in the middle of Times Square, New York observed the anniversary of the Warsaw Ghetto uprising twenty-five years ago, and we missed it. More than forty thousand men, women, and children died after a forty-day fight against German soldiers, and yesterday three thousand of the living stood on the sidewalk and traffic island where Broadway and Seventh Avenue diverge, and we weren't there. Fifty-five Jewish groups united to commemorate as well the six million people whom the Germans killed elsewhere, and we didn't know. Speeches were given, telegrams read, a tenor of the Metropolitan Opera wearing a yarmulke sang Yiskor for the dead, and we wouldn't have gone to that. But that doesn't help, the place where the rally was held is now, since yesterday, called Warsaw Ghetto Square, and we'll have to keep that in mind.

Cresspahl turned his town commandant's orders into regulations and behaviors in Jerichow, and would have liked to know what he was doing, and hardly once managed to understand K. A. Pontiy.

It wasn't the language. Since early July there'd been a Soviet Military Administration for the State of Mecklenburg and Vorpommern, in Schwerin, and it issued orders in German, signed General Fedyuninsky, countersigned Major General Skossyrev, and one after another they were brought to Cresspahl in the brickworks villa ready to be posted. K. A. Pontiy's German, too, may not have been good enough to teach the language but was good enough to make himself understood, at least in terms of what he wanted from the people of Jerichow. And yet Cresspahl didn't understand him. His child was given short answers

Thats how he wants it.
But he cant just do that.
He can.
Then why are you doing it?
Cause he won.
Thats what winning means, Cresspahl?
Times have changed, Gesine. Now—

and soon stopped asking questions. (The child was busy enough with other things.)

When Cresspahl tried to understand it in military terms, he got somewhere, sometimes. If he had to build a fortified headquarters in a small town, one that wouldn't be easy to see into, he would probably have started much like the Soviet commander. The houses on the west side of Town Street stood harmlessly outside the fence, betraying nothing. The mouth of the Bäk was closed off with painted wood, no barbed wire, much less a gate, and now that street was practically a blind spot in the town. Anyone wanting to get at the Soviet fort from the west would have to trample ripe grain. To the southeast the only access was a sandy turnoff into what looked like a back road petering out between the cemetery wall and the hop kiln, not like a military headquarters with armed guards, triumphal arch, and barbed wire. Cresspahl hadn't been promoted in 1917 to a rank involving officer training, so Pontiy's camp was a hideaway strictly by the tactical book as far as he knew.

By this point he'd had two weeks to observe his town commandant— in the middle of nights and early in mornings, charged with crimes and immune from prosecution at least for the time being—and whatever it was he managed to see, he hadn't been able to put it all together. K. A. Pontiy with his mussel-colored glances, no eyebrows, blunt naturally bald head, sluggish with age or from his shoulder wound, he might have been Cresspahl's age, maybe a little younger. His constant unconscious sighs might be due to illness, or grief, it didn't make him frail. Maybe he didn't stand up with

Cresspahl because then the German would be able to look down on his bald skull, and after a while Cresspahl was ordered to sit down, officially. He would walk in the door and K. A. Pontiy would be hooking the clasp of his uniform at the neck, especially for the foreigner, possibly for military dignity. Their discussions quickly turned into questioning, practically tribunals, for K. A. Pontiy would give a stretch with his numerous papers before him, and next to him there would be a lieutenant standing stiff and straight, hand on his pistol holster sometimes, adjutant and prosecuting attorney in one. Sometimes Cresspahl thought that Pontiy didn't want to lose something again, maybe his uniform, maybe his dignity. When angered Pontiy would stand up and put his cap stiffly on his head. He was suspicious of the Germans, and that was all right with Cresspahl, but he didn't threaten Cresspahl with removal from office, he threatened him with pieces of his life story. He was quite familiar with agricultural problems: Pontiy would tell him, his voice soft, sharp, and dangerous, accompanied by an unexpected wink. You couldn't pull wool over the eyes of an engineer like him: Pontiy would warn, contemptuous, but quickly shifting into an almost brotherly tone. As a sometime graduate of the Frunse Academy he stood up for the Red Army's honor! K. A. Pontiy revealed to his mayor, in obviously blind rage, right before sentencing him to arrest and execution, but then might take Cresspahl's measure with a satisfied look and dismiss him from the audience, like a badly raised child it'd be good to put a little fear into. Cresspahl couldn't figure him out, not even superficially.

If K. A. Pontiy had been to the Red Army's military academy, and was sixty years old, why was he a major with a little row of medals and nothing more? Why did his army assign him to a tiny town like Jerichow?

He'd said his parents were farmers, and marveled at charring the ends of fenceposts before digging them into the ground, and didn't know he could have demanded Carbolineum and tar oil? (He'd wanted a fence in Jerichow, and never in the Soviet Union?)

He was an engineer, and he tried to measure his fence's square footage with a field compass, enjoying the ingenious (if imprecise) instrument, like he'd never heard of a surveyor's tripod in his life!

He wanted to defend the Red Army's honor, as head
of the military branch

of the government bank
of the Soviet occupation forces
of the town of Jerichow
and his nation's representative to the German nation, and then he demanded, not from it, but from individuals, their gold and silver, and English and Dutch stocks, and every bit of platinum that turned up in Jerichow—whether the owners had come by such property during the war or not, whether they'd followed the Nazis or shunned them—and then didn't hand over these precious objects to his country, but kept them for himself, traded them for liquor, handed them out to guests or underlings. When Cresspahl was asked about Order No. 4, he might say things like: We're in the middle of the harvest, and he himself hadn't turned over much more than his out-of-date statements from the Surrey Bank of Richmond. He discovered the Red Army soldier known as Wassergahn making a fire with them in the brickworks-villa fireplace, so the Red Army and its government bank lost one or two pounds sterling. Cresspahl didn't say anything, he didn't want to get the guy with the inexplicable name punished, but he didn't understand the thing about defending the army's honor.

When the Red Army had put Dr. Kliefoth's coin collection into circulation as valid tender in Jerichow, Cresspahl put two Lübeck thalers, dated 1672, Schwerin, in his commander's palm, and K. A. Pontiy pounced on the coins like a chicken, examined the recent bite marks, and slipped the museum pieces into his breast pocket. He was head of the military branch of the government bank. Cresspahl was informed that the German Army had done the same thing in K. A. Pontiy's fatherlands, and what could he do but nod. In doing so, he had slandered the Red Army by comparing them to the Fascists and should have been shot at once, up against the cemetery wall! Cresspahl was freed with a passing question about the names of streets in town. He went to complain when the stupid child, Gesine, had obliviously worn a piece of jewelry around her neck that a nighttime looting patrol could tear off her. It was the five-mark coin from the Kaiser's time that Lisbeth Cresspahl had had Ahlreep's Clocks make into a brooch in October 1938, in defiance of the Nazis' robbery of everyone's gold, and at two in the morning Cresspahl had to explain to Major Pontiy the difference between coins and pieces of jewelry. K. A. Pontiy gave a grave nod, whether with fatigue or satisfaction; tried once with screaming; seemed relieved when the German didn't give in. He admitted he was right. Two days later, an abashed Red Army soldier walked into Cresspahl's kitchen, beckoned the child Gesine to come out, and handed her back the brooch, knotted in a silk kerchief. *Izvini pozhaluysta* means: "please excuse me"; *ne plakat'* means: "don't cry." Cresspahl went by the Ahlreeps to thank them for not having reported the hidden property, and K. A. Pontiy reminded him, days later, with a smile as pleased as it was mischievous, that he had restored the honor of the Red Army.

There were confidences exchanged. Cresspahl had wanted to know whether the commandant wanted a temporary or permanent fence, and K. A. Pontiy refused to tell him whether he would be handing the territory back to the British soon or the Jerichowers later. (The result was that Mrs. Köpcke had to set the fenceposts more solidly in stone.) What the Russian had answered, with an almost Mecklenburgish pleasure in a trap seen through and leapt over, was: For e-v-ver, Meeyor.

If only we could ask Cresspahl! From the child's point of view, the dealings between the two men often looked like hearty friendship, lurching between plain unconditional loyalty, murderous conflict, and stubborn-yet-heartfelt reconciliation. Would Cresspahl today be able to remember that far back?

When Cresspahl went walking through town with the two mysterious Karabiner 98k rifles, he didn't get home until late. K. A. Pontiy had had him picked up at Town Hall and escorted to the brickworks villa, and it turned into a party. Cresspahl was greeted with his very first handshake, given food and drink until midnight, and on the outside stairs K. A. Pontiy missed several times before managing to clap Cresspahl's shoulder, with feeling too.

Cresspahl turned in his telephone, and his Receiver for the People, because he and his house would be more severely punished than people who had only read the order. But that was the wrong thing to do. For all that his commandant spoke of the many telephones and microscopes that Germany owed the Soviets, he'd thought Cresspahl had more brains than that. Socialism had been promised, and Socialism wasn't life without telephones and radios, was it? For some it might be, but Cresspahl needed to be able to hear Pontiy, didn't he, whether by phone or over the radio. This time there was a parting handshake because Cresspahl had nodded about Socialism, and K. A. Pontiy sent him, from his personal stock, the eight-tube superhet that the refugees in Dr. Berling's apartment had turned in out of gratitude or superstition. Now the mighty blue-and-black thing sat silently on Cresspahl's desk, together with the memories of Lisbeth's first attempt and Dr. Berling's stubborn death too. Pontiy came by to see whether his mayor had consigned to the attic this proof of his trust in a select few.

Pontiy came by to see Cresspahl. Not at Town Hall, in his bed. Whether at midnight or two hours later he had him woken up, gave him two minutes to get dressed, and sat down beside him with a sigh for a chat about those nights by the sea when everything looks so low and yet the sky is the way it is over Leningrad, if not even higher. But Cresspahl had to play the host in his house just like Pontiy in the brickworks villa, which by this point included providing the vodka. (The mayor didn't have to trade on the black market in person—the one he had threatened with punishment in his official announcements—because Jakob did it for him. Jakob had brand-name liquor in stock, believe it or not, hidden somewhere in the house that no one else ever found, and Cresspahl preferred not to ask the boy questions. Only he wished the boy would tell him its equivalent value, not say that it was part of the rent for his mother and himself.) One morning, Hanna and I were woken not by the sound of birds but by the sight of two swaying men, dim in the dawn light, one of them saying, in an odd, surprised voice: *Deti, devushki.* The other confirmed: Children, girls: in a foreign, angular voice, like a mechanical dictionary, and it was my father and he'd spent the night drinking as though with a friend.

He didn't understand him. K. A. Pontiy, major in an army in possession of the science of atheism, appeared in church on Sunday with a four-man escort, waved kindly up at the organ that had fallen silent, annoyed until it started up again, then walked benevolently up and down between the pews full of singing people, gesturing like a conductor, until Pastor Brüshaver started his sermon. He did everything but sit at the front of the congregation. The uniformed visitation was over in eight minutes. Then the delegation went on to take a look around the cemetery, and K. A. Pontiy commented on the shady cave that the trees created as shelter from the July heat. In addition, he criticized the untended condition of several graves. On Monday the town commandant forbade, per Order No. 11, any future burials in the cemetery as well as parking the corpses in the chapel on Brickworks Road. Before news of these first strikes against the State Church of Mecklenburg had even reached the other end of Town Street, Aggie Brüshaver had a dapper, practically gallant visitor to lead to her husband's desk, K. A. Pontiy, military commandant. Brüshaver expected a ban on church services, and Pontiy asked for an explanation of the liturgy. He expressed how much he was looking forward to the next such performance. He noted with regret that the Nazis had indeed melted down the zinc and copper of the new bells to make cannons. A question about burials made him surly for a moment, as if his friendship were being repaid badly. When he left, Pastor Brüshaver was of the opinion that St. Peter's Church had been promised new bells soon, from who knows where. They said around Jerichow that the Soviets treated only pastors who'd been in concentration camps like that. But K. A. Pontiy paid his respects to the Catholic rectory, too, though the priest lacked those credentials (and he asked Böhm to give Brüshaver a bell after all, at least a small one). If there was to be atheism, then it would be a type with pious song and the tolling of bells from right next to the faithless commander's villa.

– *Public relations:* Marie says. – Clever guy: she says, if that's the right translation for *smart cat.* She thinks so long and hard about K. A. Pontiy, amused almost, as if she should venture to try to be friends with him (like the Gesine Cresspahl of back then. Like me!). She's having a harder time getting to sleep, stretched out under the blanket, breathing as if counting every breath. And yet what comes to her mind is public relations work.

– No, Marie. Here you're wrong.

– Okay, Gesine. Fine. I'm talking about people and times I don't understand. Presumptuous, precocious, foreign. You tell me how it was.

– No. That's not what I think of you. Who would ever—

– *Never mind.* Tell me.

– K. A. Pontiy's official attitude toward the church wasn't from 1953; East Germany was years away from being a country.

– Was the Pontiy from 1945 part of 1953?

– He wasn't in Jerichow anymore. We hadn't heard anything about him for a long time.

– So, he mostly wasn't. So, 1945.

– Cresspahl had Leslie Danzmann write up a memo about every *Vergewaltigung* reported to him, even the ones that didn't happen in Jerichow town, or Jerichow parish, the ones in the Rande military region or on the estates. There were a lot, and Cresspahl described more than where they'd taken place. That evening he'd hand them in at headquarters, to Mr. Wassergahn, and since the commander couldn't always read them right away

– there were lots of nighttime phone calls, meetings, serious accusations among friends.

– Right. At first K. A. Pontiy would have tried to be amicable. You know, young men, away from home too long, alone too long, Cresspahl's a man, K. A. Pontiy's a man...

– Man to man. Nudges in the ribs.

– Right. But no nudges.

– Cresspahl didn't go for it.

– So then came the stories about young German men, away from home too long, alone too long...

– And he had K. A. Pontiy shot for the comparison. Red Army and marauding Fascist killers.

– Right, you see? Sometimes it's okay, other times punishable by death.

– You don't understand?

– Cresspahl didn't understand.

– And so he was shot.

– Sentenced to be shot, if he ever brought another such memo without the name, rank, unit, and serial number of the perpetrator. Slanders against the Red Army that couldn't be verified were punishable by death.

– And slanders that could be verified?

– They'd be shot. He promised Cresspahl that, and

– out came the vodka again. Everything hunky-dory.

– And Cresspahl got a big sign on his front door, and another on the back door, and all the refugees under his roof got a special ID card

– Off-limits! Off-limits!

– And for a long time K. A. Pontiy would say, over and over, almost like Avenarius Kollmorgen, head tilted, remembering: Satisfied, Meeyor? Sat is fied?

– Gesine, what kind of crime is that exactly?

– *Vergewaltigung?* Never mind.

– Another water-butt story?

– No. But I forgot to leave it out.

– Gesine, I'm ten years old. Almost eleven.

– *Very well.* A man used violence against a woman to make her—

– Oh, that.

– When have you ever heard of *Vergewaltigung?*

– You mean *rape*, right?

– *I mean rape all right.*

– Gesine, what do you think is the number-one topic of conversation among every female person in New York? Don't you listen when the ladies trade stories by the swimming pool under Hotel Marseilles? You want me to imitate Mrs. Carpenter?

– Number-one topic of conversation in your class?

– Number-one-and-a-half. So admit it, K. A. Pontiy did care about public relations.

– I hope you don't get old in New York, Marie.

– You're in Jerichow, Gesine. In Mecklenburg. In July 1945.

– Right. During the first week, Pontiy asked his mayor: Why do the Germans see us, their liberators from the yoke of Fascism, and act like we're the devil?

– A negative theist then.

– Cresspahl didn't tell him that the English had tried their hardest to convince him to go with them, the night before they'd left. (That was Käthe Klupsch's night under Town Hall.) He wouldn't have been the only one they'd tried to convince. They left with loudspeaker cars and said no one but proven Nazis had anything to fear from their brothers-in-arms, but in secret they described their ally as the devil no less than the Americans did. A bunch of—

– Subhumans.

– The word was ready to hand. *Untermenschen.* Even K. A. Pontiy used it.

– For Germans. For some Germans.

– And in his innocence, he tried to get this sorted out with another order. He ordered, twelfthly, that the war was over, civilized behavior could rear its head once more. The custom of greeting one another, for instance.

Now every member of the Red Army in Jerichow was to be greeted properly, parked vehicles too, on spec.

– And the Jerichowers realized they'd forgotten the Austrian style of greeting. Something to do with the right arm, wasn't it? Ancient Roman?

– And Cresspahl didn't understand Pontiy.

– It's because he didn't help Pontiy understand the Germans. Or at least one of them, him.

– Or only this one.

– Anyone comes to their father's defense. I'd have done the same.

– But wasn't K. A. Pontiy another crook?

– *I like crooks.* As long as they just take their cut and don't do any other damage. *Don't you like crooks?* Didn't Cresspahl like crooks?

– Cresspahl could deal with crooks. He was clueless about them, he didn't do business with them—they got along just fine, like pals.

– Well, you don't have to understand someone right off, Gesine. *G'night.*

April 27, 1968 Saturday, South Ferry day
but we decided to spend our day off differently.

For this is also the day on which the Veterans of Foreign Wars show their loyalty to the nation with parades, in dark ceremonial uniforms, white puttees, white sashes around the hips and chest, kepis with badges on their heads, rifles over their shoulders, flags of club and state in holders on their bellies. Parochial-school bands and youngsters from drum-and-bugle corps will march with them, Fourth Avenue in the Norwegian neighborhood of Brooklyn as well as Fifth Avenue in Manhattan will be nationalistically decked out, the archbishop will lead and will end the march with the mayor. This year's parade, the twentieth since 1948, is also dedicated to the memory of the late Cardinal Spellman, one of the war's first and most enthusiastic supporters, and for the last two years the Loyalty Day Parade has been a show of support for American servicemen in Vietnam and a threatening fist to those who oppose the war. We could have gone to see that.

There was another option: *The New York Times*, on her Food, Fashion, Family, and Furnishings page, gives us a picture of the Scanlons and their daughters, Rebecca, five, and Caitlin, two, because someone bought an 1894 Brooklyn brownstone for $28,500 and didn't tear it down, they renovated it, and one of their delights is the third-floor bathroom with its original bathtub on claw-and-ball feet, the marble sink, stained-glass windows, and a toilet complete with pull-chain, in New York City. John Scanlon's Irish mustache could be one of ours, his Italian wife another, and the *Times* gave us their full address, 196 Berkeley Square. Subway to Grand Army Plaza. Marie doesn't feel like going there either.

She chose the peace parade in Central Park and dressed for the occasion as deliberately as a grown-up. There'll be police there, you have to wear something you can run in. Marie insisted that her mother take her dress back off and instead wear pants and an old blue cotton shirt (that could withstand a policeman's grip. That wouldn't hurt the feelings of any of the dark-skinned demonstrators from Harlem). In the end Marie, too, stood there dressed in self-defense, in sneakers intentionally left dirty, and looked in the mirror, learning from it that she should untie her braids and hold her hair in place with just a black hairband. (Shawnee uprising under Tecumseh, 1811.) And so we walked up Ninety-Fifth Street, white squaw and half-grown, wiry, blond-haired Indian girl.

On the corner of Amsterdam Avenue, we had to stop and scan the apartment buildings, the street, the corner store. Four children used to live here, friends if not great friends, and they let themselves be taken away from New York by their parents, to a suburb where the sapphire-green lawns are no more real than the imitation village streets made of plaster and aluminum. Marie can't understand a move like that, and maybe at least the children have come back to the Upper West Side of New York. Not today.

The streets were dry after a morning rain. The pale sun up ahead gave off some warmth, enough for a holiday.

On our zigzag path through the blocks, we often passed houses like the one the Scanlons had decided to save—once proud middle-class home for a life on three stories. A whole row of them had had their stairs and windows torn off; some of their brownstone comrades had been entirely gutted. The doors from inside the dead house stood around the bare lot where it had been torn down, some of them cracked apart, kicked in, weathered into various colors—inadequate fences like those surrounding a grave.

Marie didn't let the scars of urban speculation bother her; she looked the passersby carefully, intently in the face, unfathomable like an Indian. But when people called out Hey, Great Chief or let out the whinnying cry of the native inhabitants of this land she didn't give them the same closed-off expression she usually showed strangers. If she didn't actually say anything back, she did smile. These were New Yorkers, and she was going the same direction. Kindred spirits, friends of peace and of the Indians.

At eleven o'clock sharp we were on the corner of Central Park West and 101st Street, like the *Times* had told us to be, and the parade wasn't there yet.

The sky was cloudy by that point, letting the sun peek through only occasionally, grayly threatening rain.

The people lining the sidewalks didn't yet make them much more crowded than the usual pedestrian traffic, though they were waiting. Assistants of the parade committee were walking back and forth, trying to sell "original" buttons as souvenirs of the morning of April 27, 1968. Marie was disappointed that commerce had joined the march. She wasn't surprised; she probably expected it; still, the party now started on a slightly false note.

She took the free sheets of paper—the flyers in support of Senator Eugene McCarthy, depicting horrors of war. The Communist Party was handing out extras, too, but *The Daily Worker* offered her a language much like the one *Neues Deutschland* once offered me, and neither of us quite understood it. Lots of those sheets fluttered to the ground. Marie kept hers under her arm, as a favor to Mayor Lindsay (*which I undertook solely to keep New York City clean*).

Then she saw children holding balloons, green and blue and yellow, painted PEACE, but the dignity of her ten and a half years didn't permit her any more than a few kindly, slightly condescending glances at the littler kids. Then came adults with black balloons bearing the peace symbol. Marie clambered down the park wall and stretched so she could reach into her pants pocket. No more vendors walked by. She kept the dime in her fist anyway.

She watched the policemen, her eyes narrowed, Indian-style, under her black hairband. These guardians of law and order stood in small groups at the crossings, along the curb, familiar with one another. Their conversations looked private. Now and then they got their hands dirty, moving wooden sawhorses from the side streets to preemptively corral the parade. There were still a few cars driving down the street but the buses were already rerouted. Marie asked how many demonstrations her mother had done in her life so far. She was readier to believe a number over fifty than that we hadn't been allowed to just watch.

– You had to march?: she asked. – That's what we want to do too!

On the third floor of a building across the street, a young shirtless man clambered out onto his rented windowsill. He hung a stenciled banner across his two grimy bay windows, opposing the military occupation of the Negro neighborhoods. The black neighborhoods in New York are not in fact under military occupation. Then the agitator appeared with a telephone receiver at his ear, said some defiant and belligerent things to his distant friends, and sat down on the ledge for good. Marie kept looking up at this unathletic person, as if he were bothering her. She refrained from making any remarks; he was acting normal for New York, she couldn't tell him not to do it; she went looking for a place for us somewhere else.

But now the edges of the parade route were packed so full that any spectators stepping up to fill the gaps seemed pushy. In the soft hum of voices, the chattering of the police and network helicopters came down from overhead—none of the copters themselves did, though.

Ten minutes to twelve, and the parade got started with a group of men on motorcycles. The drivers were wearing brown suits with yellow stripes. The Magnificent Riders of Newark. Their bikes didn't roar (though the *Times* can't resist describing it that way), they whispered. The drivers had to keep putting their toes down on the ground for support, because of the slow pace. They were followed by the van with the famous people, under the protection of fifty sturdy bodyguards. Marie recognized Pete Seeger on the platform and waved to him ("Where Have All the Flowers Gone?"; "If I Had a Hammer"; "Turn, Turn, Turn"). Pete Seeger taking part in the demonstration made everything almost perfect again for Marie, but she was too shy to enter the parade right behind Pete Seeger's bodyguards. She let a bunch of other groups go ahead, mentally comparing her knowledge of New York with the neighborhood names on the banners they carried. Everyone was in a good mood, like on an outing. Instigators shouted happily: WHAT DO WE WANT?, and the chorus answered in syncopated pleasure: PEACE, NOW. Or: WHAT? PEACE; WHEN? NOW! When she decided to step off the sidewalk and join the kindred spirits, the show started.

The show was a row of young girls in Vietnamese clothing, black smocks under pointy straw hats. Short American girls dressed up as Vietnamese women. They wanted to show who the country was killing in their place in Vietnam. It wasn't their place. As if they might be killed here and now, on the corner of Central Park West and 101st Street. And as if even so it was just a game for them.

Marie could have gone with them, we would have found each other later. What spoiled it for her?

Then we saw the senior police officers walking alongside the relatively narrow column of marchers, one with a radio, another with files. Next to Marie on the sidewalk was a ten-year-old black girl with a steno pad, wearing a PRESS badge on her blouse, earnestly paging through what she'd already noted down. Marie turned in such a way that the other girl could have asked her a question, but the other girl acted like she didn't see her. Remarkably few signs in the parade that anyone had written and nailed themselves. People wearing crash helmets; in shabby military uniforms but with their shoes polished per army regulations. The occasional women tended to be wearing sunglasses; one of them, in a Pepita houndstooth suit, could have been me (in a photograph). By then we were walking on the sidewalk, looking for a subway entrance to escape down, neither of us admitting it to the other.

We also saw a tall young man from a school with an average sports team, his face strangely red. He was holding a teeny-tiny Chinese woman by the elbow, trying to be encouraging; she was desperately unhappy. (From afar, we saw the self-promoter fidgeting around on his outside ledge again; he was, as he'd hoped, greeted and applauded by several groups of people.) On Ninety-Sixth Street we found ourselves next to the unhappy couple again, she wearing his jacket now, but she still couldn't forgive him for something he couldn't suspect, at least not until later that night.

But it wasn't over at Ninety-Sixth Street, we were supposed to keep going until Seventy-Second and then into the park, to Sheep Meadow, where the rally with the speakers was to take place that afternoon. Mrs. Martin Luther King was scheduled to speak, Pete Seeger was there, Mayor

John Vliet Lindsay would come. Supposed to sit on the grass, sing in a group while waiting, chat familiarly with people nearby, about the weather, about the city.

– John Lindsay?: Marie said, disbelieving. – He was just on the platform at the Loyalty Parade!

Then she didn't want to accept that the mayor might appear in front of both the enemies and the supporters of the foreign war, equally a friend to both, wanting all their votes equally for the period after December 31 of next year. It was the first time she said, not in heralding tones, but pleading: It's still Saturday. Let's make a South Ferry day of it.

So we rode on the IND to the IRT, boarded the ferry *John F. Kennedy* at Battery Park, and traveled across the whole harbor to Staten Island. Marie braided her hair on the way, her head turned farther aside than usual and her fingers so slow that it was as if she were braiding in her thoughts. She cut up the hairband with the Indian symbols embroidered on it, with a shard of glass she found lying on the sidewalk, so that she could tie her braids. We took the bus from Staten Island over the Verrazano Bridge to Brooklyn and from there went back to Riverside Drive underground. Now it's six thirty and a yellow stripe is hanging over the Palisades, sharply outlined against the blurry bluish upper reaches of the sky. The sun has a yellow hole. Minutes later, the yellow cell dissolves into darker colors.

Marie knows not only her mayor John Vliet Lindsay's birthday, but the names of his children and what schools they all go to, she keeps photos of him from *The New York Times,* she has adopted his line about "the fun of getting things done"—she considered him a friend. She said something, as she tore his pages out of her scrapbook, but it won't get written down here, Comrade Writer. You can say that maybe she bawled while she was alone in her room, but nothing after that.

April 28, 1968 Sunday, Start of Daylight Saving Time
Sheep Meadow in Central Park: 522,725 square feet, divided by the minimal space required for one person to sit down comfortably—9 square feet—makes room to hold 58,080 persons (not counting a remainder of 5 square feet); that's how meticulous *The New York Times* is. When Mrs. Martin

Luther King arrived, the Meadow was only half filled. She read a decalogue of ten commandments on Vietnam, said to have been on Dr. King when he was assassinated, and the tenth said: Thou shalt not kill. Long, sustained applause.

Another protest took place yesterday, on Washington Square, unauthorized but justified with "The streets belong to the people." Someone who struggled against the police was wrestled to the ground by numerous plainclothes men, kicked, kneed, hit with a leather blackjack (a "sap"), and anyone who tried to photograph police loading demonstrators into a paddy wagon was arrested along with them. That doesn't make Marie feel better—she wishes she hadn't missed anything there either.

The day before yesterday, a doctor in Czechoslovakia committed suicide—a former physician in Ruzyně prison in Prague—and the new interior minister, Josef Pavel, says he was tortured by that same doctor. And wants an official investigation too. What the Communist sister parties agree to do among themselves, the Czechoslovakian one wants to break the silence on, and a "Club for Independent Political Thought" has sprung up, and not been banned, even the Socialists are allowed, who want to bring about an unrestricted democratic life. What will become of this country?

Cresspahl was now in his third month as mayor of Jerichow and still learning on the job.

He couldn't do much with his mirror image. If he tried to demand, as mayor, that the citizens of Jerichow do what he was expected to do as a citizen, that didn't work. He remembered when he'd had to pay taxes and preemptively set the deadline well in advance: August 10 for business taxes, August 15 for property taxes, September 10 for income and corporate taxes, and so on each quarter. Leslie Danzmann helped him realize, though, that most of the May and June payments hadn't been made, various people in Jerichow hadn't paid even under the Nazis, had decided to wait out the British, and had no intention of delivering either the current or past due under the Soviets. K. A. Pontiy had no suggestions except ruthless full enforcement, relying on one of his Orders and the excuse that the nonmunicipal taxes were still "Reich taxes," even if the Reich was no more (same as "German Reich Railway," which wasn't even run for Germans anymore either). Cresspahl had no one who could collect the back taxes; Leslie Danzmann had to calculate a collection surcharge of 5 percent of past due amounts, retroactive to the Reich's March and February, on every index card. The mayor's office might post it, could in totally flagrant cases send out notices—which only put the government bank in debt to schoolboys for messenger fees—but "Hitler's taxes for Stalin" did not materialize. Since the town didn't have any money it could only be in the townsfolk's pockets, and anyway it was worthless in the age of barter, but the townsfolk insisted in stubbornly seeing themselves as subjects of the Soviets, not of the municipality of Jerichow.

People like Peter Wulff authorized the town to deduct taxes from their bank accounts, for the time being. But the bank accounts were frozen, no one was allowed to make transactions—not Cresspahl, not the account owner, not even K. A. Pontiy.

K. A. Pontiy ordered Cresspahl to charge the Jerichowers an additional 5 percent of any withheld moneys, as a penalty. Now Leslie Danzmann could do her calculations in units of ten, that was easier. It stayed on paper, and K. A. Pontiy ordered Cresspahl to "take executive action" with respect to the defaulters' property if they didn't pay cash. Cresspahl asked what he meant by "executive."

Town Commandant Pontiy meant the confiscation of tradeable objects: machines, motors, tools. And the like.

Cresspahl suspected that if the means of production were taken away, labor might drop off, taxable labor included. K. A. Pontiy, with a sigh, bowed before the almighty power of dialectical materialism, and ordered such objects to be left in the owners' hands, but not as their property.

The mayor couldn't make him understand, he could only repeat, that then the work really wouldn't get done. Pontiy agreed to order the work. Sometimes Cresspahl even laughed, it looked like a coughing jerk of the shoulders, and Pontiy sighed. Strange country, this Mecklenburg.

Well, *khoroshó*. Here's an order: confiscate the real estate. All or part. Then they won't have to pay property tax.

K. A. Pontiy stretched in his seat as if he wanted to have the problem taken out and shot. It was formerly Papenbrock's office chair, and two inlaid lions were interlocked over Pontiy's shiny head. He turned around to look sternly at his second lieutenant, signaling he should take his hand off his holster. Then he ordered Cresspahl to secure the tax debt by confiscating furniture. As punishment and to set an example. Sat is fied, Meeyor?

Cresspahl drank the liquor meant to indicate mutual understanding (Pontiy had put his Mauser down on the table so that his mayor would drink), but was unable to return to Town Hall satisfied. Many, perhaps most of the houses in Jerichow had belonged to the nobility, only a few from that class had left for the west, and they didn't pay Jerichow property tax. But anyone who had left Jerichow after May 8 had had his property temporarily confiscated for the good of the town, and permanently if he didn't return within a year. Now the municipality owned a lot of its buildings, but had to pay property taxes to itself, and didn't have the money to.

(The mayor's office could have raised the rents on the town's property. Raising the rent was strictly forbidden. And the Jerichowers put aside the lease and rent money for the owners who had fled—in accord with the law, they felt, here too—and the government bank got nothing.)

Cresspahl introduced monthly payment of wage and revenue taxes, instead of quarterly. (The commandant hereby orders that a state of emergency is in effect.)

But Jerichow had been the workshop for the surrounding countryside; tradesmen didn't get enough work from the town itself. The estates and village precincts in the area, now divided into independent "Kommanda-turas," paid in kind whenever they could (or were allowed to) hire someone in Jerichow. The farmers compensated their laborers not with money but with food and drink and a roof and the promise of wheat in the winter. Was Cresspahl supposed to impose a tax on payments in kind?

Mrs. Köpcke, construction, ceded the government bank's debt to Mrs. Köpcke to the government bank, to offset against any city and Reich taxes she owed, in advance, until March 3, 1946. She wrote off these payments as made. Cresspahl signed. Receipt of one (1) fence plus cash-free tax payments, confirmed.

There was another nighttime fight with K. A. Pontiy. Pontiy placed himself on the side of the German Reich and pronounced all obligations toward the aforesaid valid past the date on which the German Reich had capitulated to him and the Western Allies. The freezing of bank accounts had no consequences of a legal or civil nature. The days of civil rights were over!

Cresspahl, then, took it that the Red Army was a force majeure that had rendered the financial institutions insolvent.

Pontiy didn't fall for that and dismissed his mayor with the order to institute dog taxes. Droll and devoted creatures, dogs. Don't you think so? Omitting to register: punishable. Per dog! Let's say: 150 reichsmarks.

Cresspahl canceled the corporate tax. There were no longer such corporations in Jerichow.

Then he seized the cash reserves of the credit union and paid the concerned parties at the hospital, the gasworks, the sanitation department the wages he owed them for the past three weeks ("since the Russians"). He partly offset the amount, though, with the remaining assets of the estate owners, whose accounts hadn't been frozen, but were now, since they'd left.

– A mayor like that always has one foot in jail.

– I know, Gesine. All ri-i-ight. But your dad wasn't a crook. Like John-Vliet-Lindsay!: Marie said. That was yesterday. She refuses to be consoled, and Cresspahl's inching toward Socialism had no effect on her.

April 29, 1968 Monday

If work awaits in midtown then you have to leave Riverside Drive at eight thirty, the same as before, but the sun is rising on a different timetable. The start of Daylight Saving Time has again moved it way over to the left so that it shines blindingly down from above as it did six weeks ago. Ninety-Sixth Street's canyon floor was still deep in shadow, though, and the lost hour gives us a real feeling of shady early mornings.

When Cresspahl's child woke up, the July sun was already surrounding the house, the shade cooling the room. It was so early, though, that she still couldn't hear any sound from the other people in the house, and everyone was really asleep in the commandant's headquarters across the road. In the silence in the shadows Gesine clambered out the window and crept through house and yard looking for traces of Jakob.

He wasn't easy to find, and suddenly he'd be standing there, where just before there'd been nothing.

Going looking for him was a bit desperate, and a twelve-year-old girl has her pride. Jakob wasn't always in Jerichow. He'd rented himself out with his horses, in a village far to the west, hours away on foot. Two open windows by the front door were a good sign—Jakob's mother kept them closed at night, despite the big notice proclaiming the house off-limits. Gesine Cresspahl walks past them now, almost without a sideways glance; she's just on her way to the pump. She is up to nothing special when she walks out into the yard, every inch a girl out for a stroll, she can casually turn around and check if the chimney is smoking, an even better sign. Because nobody cooks breakfast as early as Jakob. But that wakes Cresspahl, who pads to the kitchen in his socks (so as not to wake a sleeping child) and joins Jakob for coffee. And now the daughter of the house could walk through the door and sit down at the table, she too has the right to breakfast, but it would stand out, it's too early, the children in the house get their first meal from Jakob's mother, and the one time she did join them after all Cresspahl spoke differently, as did Jakob. As if she weren't grown up. Jakob's year of birth, 1928, subtracted from her own comes out to the same annoying difference every time. Five whole years. You can sit in the shade next to the rotted beehives and calculate the years, and suddenly there's Jakob standing at the pump, unwinding the scarf from around his neck. How could he walk barefoot so quietly! (There was sharp gravel on the path from the back door, scattered there years ago by Cresspahl to discourage his child from going out barefoot.) The wound on Jakob's neck had closed up but it still looked red and raw, and Gesine Cresspahl felt very embarrassed. She was hoping to stay hidden, and now he was calling her. Now she is standing at the pump like a child and helping an eighteen-year-old grown-up splash water over his neck and head and making a face showing how exploited and ill-used she feels. But since Jakob nods instead of saying thank you, the child can't say Don't thank me! Then he's off, without even a chance to ask him about the red fox, and everything's all wrong, it would've been better not to have seen him at all.

One weekend, late in the afternoon, almost evening, Gesine Cresspahl was sitting high in one of the walnut trees outside the house. Not to worry, she has things to do up there. She might be carving something into the bark with a knife. Or maybe, if she's perched right up at the top, almost above the branches, a girl might be counting the roof tiles. Or the ones with too much moss on them. Or looking for broken ones. In no way shape or form was she up in the tree because you can look west from there without anyone seeing you. You can't trust your own eyes when there's a little mark on the horizon, trembling before the setting sun, and a quick breath later the country road is deserted. He could also come out of the forest, at the bare spot where it's called the Rehberge. But to see that you have to climb up to the top of the tree, where it's dangerously thin, and it would sway, and betray a child, who's too clever for that. She had just decided that the figure at the corner of the Russian fence was a stranger, not Jakob, when she heard his voice. She was so startled her foot slipped and made a jagged sound. But that could easily have been a bird. Only she couldn't find Jakob. The Abses' windows were open but his voice didn't sound indoors. It was soft, but as if he were in the yard. The yard was empty. – *Devyatnadtsat':* said the voice, "nineteen," and down below she saw Wassergahn the Red Army soldier squatting by the tree trunk. He shook his head and started telling a long story: *Posledniy den'*... – *Ne yasno:* Jakob said pleasantly, "don't know about that," and now she saw him too. He was squatting there like Wassergahn, both of them staring over the green fence and up at the top floor of the villa, clearly not doing some kind of deal but working to improve the friendship between the German and Soviet peoples. Yet she saw a fistful of the blue-and-white Allies money, no one in Jerichow would accept it as payment, Jakob stuck it in his shirtsleeve. (In his shirtsleeve.) After too long a while Wassergahn stood up and stomped over to the gate in the green fence, where he belonged, and Jakob stayed crouching under the tree. He didn't look up, oh no, but he stayed there relaxing until Cresspahl's daughter was totally stiff from sitting without moving on one and a half branches.

That night she was back up in the tree, and someone really did come out of the house, tinkling softly. Apparently a very fat man, because he walked as if on eggshells and his pants legs were exceedingly stuffed with something. This unknown individual stopped at Gesine's tree and gripped it hard enough that the upper branches actually did shake a little, then said, in Jakob's voice, dreamily, appreciatively, in anticipation: I wonder when these walnuts'll be ripe.

Blushing is something you can feel happening to you; some people learn that as just a child, even on a dark night.

And he liked Hanna Ohlerich more, that was obvious. Probably because she was a couple months older. True, he brought Gesine an egg too, but he just put hers down, he put Hanna's right into her hand. She might say as casually as you like that Jakob was in the yard, she's known it for the last half an hour, maybe she's talked to him, and it wasn't her waiting for him, was it? And you had to sleep at night next to this Hanna Ohlerich, and it didn't matter how wide the bed was, you could never get far enough away from her. There she was, sleeping, *she* wasn't thinking about... people tinkling like glass in the night. Hanna sat next to him on the milk-can rack and asked him questions! Like it was nothing! True, he called her "child," and called Cresspahl's by her name. Because Hanna's parents were dead. She told him about when she'd worked as a machinist at sea, but it was only the Baltic, that flooded field, and she'd been allowed near the cutter's engine only to clean it! Another girl definitely needs to sit there too, just to make sure the bragging doesn't get out of control. Lurking there a ways off, not wanting to join the conversation or anything. So, Jakob was from Pommern? Gesine had known that for a long time, and the name of the village too, and that it had been on the Dievenow River. But some girls go on to ask about Usedom Island. So it hadn't helped Jakob in the slightest that the Poles hadn't taken it? Not at all. And so Jakob is planning to stay in Mecklenburg? And some girls hold their breath until he says: *We dunno yet.* How else is someone to hide her sinking feeling of disappointment than by asking if Jakob has ever been to Podejuch? Podejuch in Pommern. Jakob's never heard of Podejuch. If someone doesn't know what to say next she has to leave the conversation, and her whole body feels like it's lost a battle. It feels shriveled up.

And the grown-ups kept Jakob all to themselves, a child never got the chance to talk to him! If there happened to be any children who wanted to. Jakob was like the house newspaper. When Jakob said that the Germans were allowed to use electricity in Lübeck again, even if only to listen to the radio, there was no point in doubting him. Maybe he'd been across the demarcation line. Jakob said: Stettin's in ruins, and the Poles won't let more than forty thousand Germans stay—and so Stettin was rubble with only forty thousand German inhabitants; a child asking, rather slyly, about the Haken Terrace was of no use, cause look, he knew it. He sat there looking a little sleepy, friendly enough, eyes a bit veiled, too much dark hair. You hardly noticed him at all. Clearly that's how he got around so much. Or did he know all these things from the papers? He didn't, there weren't any.

Not long after that, Jakob was sitting at the table in Cresspahl's house, which was where he belonged after all, and yet the man almost never came to Jerichow. Jakob said something about nuts. When walnuts turn ripe.

It's a while before a girl can leave the kitchen without overturning the table or tearing the door off its hinges!

High up in the tree—the black market tree, not the other one—Gesine Cresspahl found a piece of paper tied to a branch. It wasn't a piece of paper. It was a newspaper! The British Military Government news sheet, published in Lübeck by the Twenty-First Army. Really and truly, a newspaper, with a price on it even.

Gesine Cresspahl would have liked to think Jakob had swum the Trave Canal or Dassow Lake to Lübeck for her sake. But that was too much. He must have had business to do there.

Still, Cresspahl's daughter now shared a secret with him, and she was the only one who knew. And that night, when Cresspahl said he wished he could read the news from Lübeck for once, she denied to his face that she'd ever heard of a Western newspaper.

And Jakob had betrayed her to the grown-ups again, because Cresspahl said: It was a secret, and can she keep a secret again, and the thing was in the right-hand walnut tree, fifth branch pointing east, top surface.

– That's what being in love is like, Gesine?
– That's what it was like for me.
– Is that something I'll inherit?
– Are you ashamed of me, Marie!
– No. Really, I'm not. It's just, I might do it differently.
– Go right ahead.
– Should I tell you when it happens?
– You won't.
– So just because that's what you were like as a child, I have to—
– No. That's not why. You are free, independent, not subject to parental directives, all of that.
– Did the British news feel wet?
– It had never been in the water.
– Good. So what was in it?
– Not much. Things I've forgotten. And also that at the end of July 1945 an airplane crashed into the Empire State Building.

– A plane? Gesine!

– A B-35 bomber, and it rammed the seventy-ninth floor of a building that was the tallest in the world at that time. Empire State Building, 350 Fifth Avenue, between Thirty-Third and Thirty-Fourth Streets. Well known to every documented New Yorker.

– You want to link Jakob to New York somehow, even if it's by newspaper.

– If I want him in New York, I always have you.

– Thank you for the information.

– About the B-35 bomber?

– That my father knew that New York State's nickname was the Empire State. And that we have a 102-story building here.

– It'd be 101 in his way of counting.

– Right. And also, I wanted to say I'm sorry.

– No.

– Yes, I've been horrible since Saturday.

– No you haven't.

– Yes I have. I've been sulking, I haven't been answering you properly, I've been horrible, just because of this elected official, Lindsay.

– Forget it.

– And if I ever forget what my father was like, let me know.

April 30, 1968   Tuesday

Now what might Employee Cresspahl be looking for in one of the top drawers of Kennedy Airport, and with a child, too? The restaurant is called To the Golden Skies, if not even higher; the management prices in the triple-filtered cool air, the tables are covered in genuine linen and laid with stainless steel pricier than silver, the berth-like booths are widely separated and to hell with the exorbitant rent per square foot, each is an island unto itself, under lamps specially made in Italy, and the built-in music is so genteelly restrained that it's almost silent in the room. It's almost not an American restaurant. Whether European tourists preparing for their return or natives getting accustomed to the strange manners people have abroad, everyone here has to pay a stiff price, and at first the waitstaff, in brightly colored livery after the fashion of forgotten royal courts, view the mother and child at window table three as a risk.

The lady, thirty or thirty-five years old, is dressed appropriately for the establishment, although people have been known to dress up in such suits who in the end are nothing but typing-pool girls from midtown. She's had her hair done by a professional but it's still not much more than a negligent skullcap reaching down to her neck, practically a man's cut, a salon in deepest Queens could have done it instead of one on Madison Avenue. She's not wearing jewelry, thinks a long bare neck is good enough. Thirty-five years old. No accent, but a European handbag. *No* white shoes. Who knows, maybe she just came from the East Side Terminal by bus, she might never have enough money for a plane flight in her life, much less dinner at the Golden Skies, and she'll pay for her dine-and-dash with a visit to the night court in southern Manhattan.

The management has nothing to do with such losses—the head waiter is responsible for them out of his own pocket. It wouldn't be the first time. Anyone in the world can book a table from Washington, through the Scandinavian Airlines system, window view, two and a half hours, calling themselves Professor Erichson. This lady's no professor.

The child, now. The young lady. Now that's a child who belongs in restaurants. She's in fourth or fifth grade, she's not scared of the money she breathes in when she's here, the money quietly watching her in the form of fine woods, sheep's wool, waiters' graceful footsteps. This is hardly the first time she has accepted a leather and vellum menu with an attentive smile and then laid it aside, as though time were not money. Orders water. But a pitcher full of water and mineral ice is standing right in front of her, so now she acts modest, lets her glass be turned right-side up and filled, like a present. Says "eh-hem," not "thankyouverymuch"; samples the free sample; nods to a waiter like a vineyard owner. Maybe a foreigner, this child. They don't wear their braids so long here, the clips might be from Tiffany instead of Woolworth's, hair that white blond with sandy shadows in it probably came to Kennedy on Scandinavian Airlines, that's for sure. The child doesn't put her elbows on the table the way children do, she keeps her hands loosely folded, and not around her glass either, supported by her forearms, like they taught her in finishing school. She keeps talking and talking to the rather silent patron, in a fun-loving soprano voice she keeps low in pitch—only occasionally does the tone rise sharply. That sounds childish. Or British. You walk past them without a glance, and your glance is drawn to them anyway, and you pour the young miss another glass of her goddamn free water and get an acknowledging look in return, a nod, downright chummy. Gray-green eyes, not like her mother's. Still, a lively face. Her lips aren't her mother's either. Doesn't let the presence of the waitstaff interrupt her in the slightest, just keeps telling her story about a suitcase full of dolls. Clearly a story about some totally different child—one that's just turned funny. She's trying to cheer the woman up without annoying her; can the corners of her eyes be laughing at the same time, at a waiter who wants to finally take their order? No, a child like that doesn't do such a thing, and when the doubtful table at last orders a bottle of Beaujolais you can give the child a discreet wink, plausibly deniable. Because only one of the pair at the table is using her glass, and the party is still doubtful, isn't it.

I was sitting that same way in the Düsseldorf airport eleven years ago, a month's saved-up money in my pocket and even so the staff kept an eye on me, as someone unlikely to be able to pay. I just wanted to look at the planes departing for points farther west, where I wasn't allowed to go. I wanted to go to England.

We were sitting that same way in early May seven years ago, at a picture window like this one, when the airport was still called Idlewild, and wishing we were in one of the planes scuttling into the air between us and the thickening ink of the sky—heading out over the Atlantic, away from here. We wanted to get out of New York, go back to Europe; Flushing, Queens, New York, 11356, had been too much for us. Marie let herself be talked into one last trip into Manhattan, since her toys were all back in the hotel. Seven years later here we are.

We've been back to Idlewild/Kennedy Airport, but when it was with luggage Marie always looked at the ticket to make sure it was good for a flight back home; since then we've picked up friends or cars or bosses here, once it was money to reinstate the constitutional rights of a certain Signor Karsch. And from year to year the child was ever more helpful, a credit to us. And now and then we come for a meal as if we'd missed our usual mealtime, but actually it's a date with D. E.

Aka Professor Erichson. Suddenly, as soon as they see him, the waiters enlarge their temporary politeness into hospitality. They think they are faced with an older gentleman, what with his gray hair—he is only turning forty this year. The fat in his face, purplish more from burst blood vessels than a cold wind, makes him look older too. He sometimes has a truly gray, distant look, and however agile he may be in moving his heavily weighed-down bones, it can still look elderly. He stops in the door as if he doesn't know what to do; he hands over his hat like a sacrifice; and yet they recognize him as someone who belongs here. It's not the money. They won't inspect his jacket—constructed especially for him, and in Dublin, and for more than three hundred; when they see his pipe they won't guess that it cost what someone else might fork over for a small car, and anyway he keeps it hidden in his hand like a small sick bird. He is dressed 100 percent like an American on a trip. It's not his habits: he doesn't carry himself like a frequent honorary guest at D'Angleterre in Copenhagen or the banquet halls of the allied Western air forces. He doesn't review the restaurant while standing in front of the maître d', neither by gentle sniffing nor visual scrutiny—maybe the subtly cool air makes him shiver slightly. We can't explain it and yet from the very first word and nod and footstep he is recognized as someone who knows his business. Restaurants such as this are run for him, and he takes it upon himself to dignify their labor, and to pay for it, with pleasure on both sides if possible. He's acts like the waiter's partner, and we believe it; we can't prove anything except that the man with the serving trolley stops and looks at the new customer in an objective, almost physicianly way, smiling to his equal. Now D. E.'s here and immediately we look like a family of three who haven't seen one another for a week or three, the type to observe one another without surprise, pleased, looking forward to later, and for now with wordless understanding. Maybe he'll offer a compliment: *Your wheat's in bloom, Gesine.*

Your Czechoslovakia's shedding its skin, Gesine.
Are all the dead the same to you, D. E.?
Not the ones from 1952. But when someone hangs himself in 1968 because he was a prison doctor in Ruzyně, Prague, in 1952, he is making a statement.
But twenty-six people in the ČSSR have hung or poisoned themselves this month just for having obeyed Stalin about torture and executions back in the day.

Were they forced to?
No. Maybe then.
They had the same choice then that they have today.
The Republic should do it.
Kill them?
Punish them.
Arrest them for their murders before they commit suicide?
Yes D. E., yes. Fair trials and all that.
For that the Communists first have to take power in Czechoslovakia.
You see. But a Stalinist, the former minister for national security, gets up and tells a Slovak newspaper: It was Stalin's orders.
It's not going quickly enough for him, Gesine.
But the Czech papers act like he'd been talking about the weather!
Your Mr. Dubček, he can't alienate his Soviet friends, even with the truth.
But the Soviets've sent shipments of wheat to Czechoslovakia for twenty years and now they're suspending delivery.
They'll pin another medal on that Stalinist for having spoken of Stalin's crimes.
These homemade dialectics.
You're going to have to learn them again, Gesine.
Okay. So we'll negotiate Canadian wheat for Prague.
It's just a detour, Gesine.
There's something I want to say about these detours. When Marie's ready.
Marie's saying something.

– John Vliet Lindsay's a ——: Marie says. She's waited until the reunion was safely underway—she's been watching her D. E. and not wanting to bother him in the brooding he's been stuck in since February, which he can refuse to discuss but can't conceal. Still, D. E. has to be notified of changes in the family situation. For her latest information about Mayor Lindsay, she really and truly sat up straight and took a deep breath and still her voice cracked.

– John Vliet Lindsay's a ——: D. E. says, overtrumping her bad word with one even worse, which not everyone knows in New York, which certainly isn't meant for the ears around this table and never, ever, for the mouth of a child. But it makes Marie feel better. She has watched D. E.'s mouth and looked into his eyes and mentally compared what D. E. used to say about her now abandoned friend, and she believes him. She laughs to herself, a little embarrassed at the unexpected word but delighted to have been answered like a grown-up. Now we can start.

– Your wheat's sure in bloom, Gesine: D. E. says: Your Canadian socialist wheat: he says.

This is how we should be, together. That's what he wants. It is too bad that he has to keep an ear out for the gently squealing sounds of the engines outside the dark window, listening for a plane that will take him away, and definitely not a commercial flight to Scandinavia. Another hour and half, maybe, and the waiter will bring him a slip of paper with a telephone number on it, or bring a telephone to the table, and it really is too bad. It would be different if we agreed to live with him. Marie would agree. He won't bring it up. All that's missing is one word, spoken out loud. Why can't I say it?

May 1, 1968 Wednesday

How's it going back in the West German homeland?

In Stuttgart, after 144 sessions and one and a half years, a court has sentenced some SS soldiers who kept the Jewish population of Lemberg (Lvov) as slaves before finally killing them in the Belzec death camp. (When someone didn't feel like shooting prisoners, his superiors did nothing to him.) In Lemberg some 160,000 people died of the Germans, in Belzec one and a half million, and now one of the guilty is going to spend life in prison. The other, according to the court, spent most of his time drunk and so he's getting just ten years, since mercy must prevail.

In Baden-Württemberg the New Nazis won 9.8 percent of the vote in the state election, which is 12 of 127 seats in the state parliament. Every tenth person on the streets of Baden-Württemberg...

The federation of West Germany has eleven states and in seven of them the New Nazis have representatives in the legislature. Chancellor Kiesinger is purportedly embarrassed, Nazi that he was himself, and Brandt, his partner the anti-Fascist, is said to regret the loss of trust. So they say.

A stiff price—that's what *The New York Times* calls what the Social Democrats are paying over there for joining the right-wing governing coalition. But she stays true to her principles, our staid aunt, and blames the restless left-wing students too. If they'd only kept their mouths shut after the shooting of their leader, the voting public wouldn't have gone over to the side of those who promise New Violence and severity. It should've been a happy Easter!

– What does that have to do with you! You only used to live there once!: Marie says.

– I only used to live there once.

– But we've got a revolution right here, twenty blocks from our front door!

– Did you see it?

– Today's the fifth afternoon! Even you should know that, from your newspaper. Your aunt must have told you something.

– She didn't say anything about a foreign child running around Columbia with the policemen and the students.

– Not running. I stood there and watched, like other people. To make sure the police wouldn't start beating people when they started arresting them.

– Then they'll beat them in their paddy wagons.

– You really are a spoilsport, Gesine.

– But at least the students saw that a girl was watching, and that she agreed with them.

– It's not much, I admit it. But maybe I'm learning how to do it.

– For when you're nineteen.

– So tell me what the problem is! You're responsible for my upbringing.

– Don't get arrested.

– Gesine, don't you agree with the students?

– Agree? Oh, sure, I agree.

– There. They're trying to make their university better, and after talking and talking they're doing something now, you can see it. You must be in favor of the university stopping construction of the gym in Morningside Park and ending its affiliation with IDA, the Institute for Defense Analyses, it does research for the Pentagon.

– Those are noble wishes.

– They didn't just write letters or carry signs around. They occupied buildings, you know that.

– And barricaded themselves in with bookshelves.

– Gesine, are you against violence? Since when?

– I'm against violence to books.

– Oh, that. They drank up the president's sherry, they slept on his green carpet, leaving only cigarette butts and empty cans.

– Almost half a million dollars in damage.

– Columbia's a capitalist enterprise, isn't it? If the capitalists won't comply they'll have to pay.

– And scare people off with the vandalism of the educated youth.

– Okay, fine. A tactical mistake.

– It didn't have to be. That's what the whites left behind, but in Hamilton Hall, where the dark-skinned students were, there was no garbage. They had their own sanitation teams cleaning the building every morning during the occupation, didn't they?

– They did. A point in favor of the Afro-American Society, and one against the SDS.

– Students for a Democratic Society.

– No?

– Definitely, Marie. And last night the police came in the middle of the night and removed them. Seven hundred arrests.

– A setback, a temporary setback. But it isn't true anymore that only success counts in this country.

– There's also the publicity.

– Gesine, you yourself would contribute ten dollars for the prisoners' bail, if anyone asked you.

– Fifteen. To be polite.

– Isn't it revolutionary to fight for something that helps other people?

– It isn't selfish, that's true. Is it revolutionary when the first demand is nothing but amnesty?

– If they want to go unpunished, maybe they think the punishment is unjust.

– They can only go to school once in their lives?

– If you insist, Gesine: Yes, they're white middle-class students. Maybe they're not exactly sure where they are. Any other objections?!

– Point 2 on your flyer there.

– Cease construction of the gymnasium in Morningside Park. Totally fine.

– Marie, the university bought the land from the city seven years ago, there've been plans drawn up since 1959, and even then Morningside Park belonged to the people from Harlem, the blacks, and a separate swimming pool for the Harlem community was part of the plan, and the spokesmen for the blacks were happy for their children. What's the difference in 1968?

– That it's harder to see.

– That the public part, for Harlem, would be at the bottom, and that the blacks could get in only from the eastern side?

– No, Gesine. Maybe the people of Harlem know who they are and what they deserve more now, maybe they don't want charity from the whites' university and don't want to have to enter through the back door.

– And that's why the university should build on its white side, Riverside Drive.

– Right.

– Out of respect for the people of Harlem.

– Right.

– And Harlem still has no swimming pool in the park. Is that the right price?

– It is, Gesine. The city should build them one. They deserve it.

– I agree.

– Are you just giving in or do you really agree with me now?

– I really agree with you.

– Anything else I can do for you, ma'am?

– Point 4 on your flyer. The IDA.

– They're working for the Joint Chiefs of Staff! They've got blood on their hands! They evaluate weapons systems, do research for the Pentagon, help the government think up ways to fight uprisings!

– They've existed since 1955 and the Massachusetts Institute of Technology helped found it. Why was it okay then? Columbia only joined it in 1960. Why was that the wrong time?

– Because now we're in a war, and they're working against Vietnam.

– Why weren't the students of 1955 and 1960 on the streets protesting the atomic bomb?

– Okay, you're right. The students were a bit late.

– And they're late again. Since March, Columbia as an institution has no longer been a member of the IDA. If Columbia professors did work for them, or consulted, they did so independently.

– How do you know that?

– Guess. From a future war criminal known in private circles around town as D. E.

– This grown-up know-it-all-ness, it's like a conspiracy you're all in on!

– Marie, why are the students demanding in late April that the university do what it did last March?

– Yeah, well. A little late.

– Is the university supposed to expel from its sacred garden any professor who refuses to give up his job with the IDA?

– Exactly.

– There's nothing about that on your flyer.

– Oh, Gesine. These tiny little inaccuracies—

– It is inaccurate.

– That's all it takes for you to be opposed?

– That's all it takes.

– It's like you're apolitical!

– Maybe I've spent too long studying politics and don't know how to put it into practice anymore.

– If I invited you to take a little walk around the Columbia campus, would you come with me?

– Yes.

– To show the students that you're on their side?

– Riverside Park, or the promenade along the river, would be fine with me too, Marie.

– And I wanted you to be lying. You're tricking me, you just want to challenge me.

– No, that's not true.

– If I didn't know that you'd had a hard day at work today...

– It's not that I'm tired from today, Marie.

– If you weren't doing something every day to try to help that Socialism of yours in another country...

– Then what.

– I don't want to insult you.

– Go ahead, say it.

– How's your business going, the Socialist wheat from Canada and all that?

– Say it.

– And it's your, what's it called, "alma mater" too, isn't it?

– It's a store where I once bought four semesters of economics. I was its customer, I paid, and I left unsatisfied.

– So how's your business going?

The Communist Party secretariat in Prague denies that their Soviet friends have stopped the shipment of wheat. A gross fabrication, they say. On the contrary, they've received from Moscow a credit of $400 million in exchange for goods that the Soviet Union normally buys from countries with hard currency. Truly. Except the wheat shipments due to arrive haven't come.

May 2, 1968   Thursday

Today *The New York Times* once again has news to report from her own family. She has visibly elevated two of her most faithful nephews in her undimmed eyes; one says that the paper has already become "lighter in appearance and more inviting to read" during his tenure to date. As if we haven't noticed? He reiterates, though, that our aunt's lofty intent remains unchanged: "To be the accurate, objective newspaper of record. To serve adult needs by being complete in our coverage. To explain, explain and explain again—not in the sense of a primer but in order to fill in the gaps for readers." We'll remember that, and not forget.

We will not forget the girl in the film strip above and to the right of the ticket counter in Grand Central, ceaselessly, perpetually, eternally combing her hair for the greater glory of a company.

The child that I was had lost her hair in the summer after the war, from typhus. She kept her distance from people; there had been a few friendly types who'd tried to cheer her up by pulling the beret off her head, as though her appearance wasn't that bad. Jakob acted like he didn't see

Maurice's gift on Gesine's head—with him she could forget it was there, remembering only from the sweat. He didn't use force to try to help, didn't even use words. He sent a stranger into the yard, head shaved like a Red Army soldier, and since he was wearing civilian pants, rolled up to the knees, and a shirt much too big for him he might have been a Red Army deserter, on the run, turning up unsuspectingly at a commandant's headquarters. This unknown individual didn't seem nervous, he just sat down on the uprights of the milk rack behind the house and waited. It was early in the morning, and even though it was during harvest time none other than Cresspahl's daughter was the first to see him. She went outside, went inside to report the beggar, he called after her. His voice was so much like Jakob's. She realized only when she came back with the mirror. He looked at himself in the mirror, its frame held firmly on his knees. She stood next to him. She saw almost no hair at all in the mirror, just a long, shiny skull with a bare face on it, vaguely familiar around the eyes. He looked into the mirror a bit grumpily, as if criticizing the work of the hairstylist who'd made him look like that. He didn't have to say anything; she understood the bet, the child that I was, and took off her beret. In the mirror she was in the lead, hairwise, although the sight was still a shock. And then my hair grew back.

May 3, 1968 Friday

Now that the Communists in Prague have their $400 million from headquarters safe in hand, almost, they can admit that it wasn't as bad as all that with the delayed wheat shipments from the Soviet Union. On the contrary. The latest reports have it that deliveries are coming in even bigger than requested—here *The New York Times* chides herself. The US government tries a different tack and speaks openly of its interest and sympathy in recent developments in Czechoslovakia, which "seem to represent" the wishes and needs of the Czechoslovak people; it is considering the transfer of gold to a Communist country, despite its own dwindling gold reserves, and in an election year no less. At the May 1 Parade, Dubček, unmoved, sends special greetings to the Soviet Union, "whence our freedom came and from which we can expect fraternal aid"—he doesn't want to stir up trouble, he wants to smooth it down on the other side. Maybe the ČSSR can use USSR dollars to purchase manufacturing licenses in the US. And as for the US government offer, that is irresponsible and unacceptable. All right, all right, playtime's over.

The town of Jerichow was surrounded by wheat fields, with Baltic fish nearby, but was short of food. The townsfolk of an earlier time could have helped one another out, tradesmen swapping with townsman-farmers; now that refugees were being put up in rooms, attics, and barns, there wasn't enough bread. The military commandant wanted to be not only a good father and provider but a proud one, and he ordered the unclaimed harvest brought in.

The mayor went about it differently, decreeing that:
Everyone who
    (1) owned a scythe
    (2) could use a scythe
should report to Town Hall, room 4, henceforth to be called the Labor Office. As of July 12, the office had been notified of eight scythes in all of Jerichow, most of them reported not by their owners but by malicious neighbors. Ten times as many people as scythes turned up for the mowing, almost all of them women, refugees one and all, and they all claimed to know how to mow, they'd brought little children along too, to tie the sheaves, to steal the grain. It was a motley crowd, dressed in rags, some intending to tackle the stubble in the fields barefoot, all of them gaunt and weak with hunger. A bottle of clear water and the prospect of a handful of grain—that was their lunch. Cresspahl remembered how a scythe tore a heavy swing from your shoulders. He mustn't sigh in front of these people. He led this heap of workers out of town on foot to a field that had once been part of one of the landed estates, mowed one length for them, along the side of a hundred-meter square, then took off his jacket and turned around to look at them. The mower women were a long way behind him, the children running around with sheaves even farther back, and now he lost a whole morning showing them, again and again, how to plant their legs against the ground and shift their weight so the swing of the scythe wouldn't pull them off their feet. And the children, including children from town, couldn't get how you can twist a skein of stalks under your elbow into a cord that you knot on the bottom. One of them, his Gesine,

was so eager she had two left hands. By midday he had little more from his team than the promise to keep trying. "Cresspahl's bunch of cripples," the people of Jerichow called them, but on the second day there really were too many sheaves to count at a glance, even if the stubble looked a bit like a choppy sea. And the dummies who'd responded to Cresspahl's decree were paid, half in cash and half in grain from the previous year's harvest, weighed out daily in Papenbrock's granary. For a while there were Jerichow townswomen who would have been glad to turn up with scythes they'd forgotten about, or just to tie sheaves.

Then some of the women were assaulted by K. A. Pontiy's comrades and didn't return. One was found too late, in a hawthorn hedge, with a shattered jaw, and she died while being transported to the hospital. *Transported* meaning carried in a horse blanket, a heavy load for four women. K. A. Pontiy refused to be responsible for men under other Kommandaturas— he was already having a fight with the commandant of Knesebeck. A soldier had come back to quarters there with wounds from a reaping hook all down his arm and on his back, and said something about a Fascist attack, but it had just been children defending their mother against him. Pontiy started a hunt for Hitler's Werewolf resistance forces in Jerichow, and Cresspahl was ordered to be shot several times over. Then came the reconciliation, and Pontiy solemnly declared himself prepared to give the volunteers an escort from among his men. Then the women refused to go to work under such protection. K. A. Pontiy ordered the harvest brought in at once.

There were still men on Jerichow's farms, and they had harvesting machines, but Cresspahl had trouble getting them onto the nobility's fields, this time for legal reasons. The von Plessens had sowed the fields, the estates had always managed them—wasn't it theft to reap the harvest there? In Jerichow, as elsewhere in Mecklenburg, it was considered a sin to let wheat rot on the stalk; the departed owners' anger was still more frightening. Finally Cresspahl was able to talk them into saving the wheat, for its owners as it were. So now they cleared the fields outside the leased areas, and guarded the grain that wasn't theirs at night with bludgeons and dogs (for which they didn't pay the new tax). Those who stubbornly refused had their machines confiscated by Cresspahl as soon as they'd finished their own harvest. And he had an easier time finding people to operate the machines once he stopped distributing ration cards to any family in Jerichow without at least one member working. (When the mayor arranged a card for Gesine on the grounds that she was working and Mrs. Abs got one for her son, this was seen as cheating.) The machines were felt to have been taken by force, and the work was not performed with the zeal promoted by ownership, so the equipment broke down more than usual. Cresspahl could talk all he wanted about benefiting the town—people felt it was being done for the Russians. It didn't help that Red Army soldiers could be seen racing their horses up and down the roads. Worse yet, a detachment showed up in a field in the Jerichow housing development and traded their two worn-out nags for a horse that was hitched to a cart, like during the war, at gunpoint. The cart could still be moved, if twenty people leaned against the spokes, but no more work was done that day. Gesine came back to town that evening leading the Russians' sick horses, which no one had wanted to bring in, and waited for Cresspahl outside the Kommandatura door. Cresspahl was already inside, busy negotiating the return of a tractor that someone from the Red Army had "borrowed" because the commander had needed it to take him to Gneez on official business and had forgotten it there. K. A. Pontiy was somewhat uncomfortable, there was also the matter of some cans of diesel oil, and he mentioned Ukraine, just in passing. In Ukraine, you know, people carried the wheat to the threshing together, they didn't need a vehicle, and women and children pulled plows there too, and you know what else, the milk production from the cows didn't markedly decrease until after four months, cf. the lessons learned from Swiss husbandry. After listening to this instructive cultural information, Cresspahl repeated his question. – Tractor? What tractor?: K. A. Pontiy said, confused for a moment, at a loss for longer.

He saw the horses Gesine had brought back as a sign of good faith—the return of army property—and he waved her around the corner onto the Bäk. But the child wanted new ones in exchange, – *Novye*: she said, scared though she was of making a language mistake, and Pontiy kindly explained to her that these horses weren't *novye*, nothing like the fine Ukrainian breed! Cresspahl tore the reins out of the child's hand and left the trampled front garden of the brickworks villa without saying goodbye. When it was dark, K. A. Pontiy paid his mayor a visit and threatened to have him shot if he didn't ensure that the town had enough to eat.

What troubled the commandant was the idea of anyone comparing the state of things under the Russians with that under the British. At one point he asked Cresspahl point-blank. My father decided to let Pontiy stew about this for a while and called English rule over Jerichow manageable, if not benevolent. They had managed things well because they knew when they were leaving. They'd lived on the supplies at hand, which were obviously enough for eight weeks. When they left there was no more coal for the trains, which couldn't take milk to Gneez or bring back potatoes. They'd forced Jerichow to shut down the gasworks, which had damaged the furnaces; its workforce had wandered aimlessly around the fields, unskilled there, depressed. Even the bakeries were without fuel. The British had generously distributed sugar and salt and oil from their warehouses, and the villages and farms had faithfully tried to deliver their quotas of beef cattle and milk. The British had given Cresspahl access to the government bank to pay whatever he needed to—wages, past-due bills. Even school had been open under them, two days after they got here. They were trying to leave behind a good impression of Western methods to make it harder for the Soviets to do the same. Even from a distance, they won hearts and minds by supplying electricity to Jerichow from their Herrenwyk power station, and Pontiy was not happy to hear this. Cresspahl half expected an order to build an independent supply of electricity for Jerichow, but first things first: his job was to supply the people of Jerichow with food, as well as the British had done, and, within four weeks, better.

The Jerichow mayor's office contracted with the Fishermen's Association in Rande, represented by Ilse Grossjohann, for the delivery of at least two crates of fish per day. (This was the old association that the Nazis had dissolved, reestablished by the kind permission of the British.) What Grossjohann asked in return often changed: sometimes the fishermen needed sailcloth, sometimes nails, sometimes lubricating oil for the engines, and Cresspahl couldn't always manage to find these things somewhere in Jerichow to confiscate. He told the town's commandant nothing about this trade, and Pontiy didn't mention it either, but after a week had passed Pontiy's jeep appeared in Rande one morning, and the Red Army soldiers demanded the "fishes for Yerrichoff." Ilse Grossjohann had learned something about the law from her time with Kollmorgen, and moreover she'd been a prosperous fisherman's wife for three years, and she insisted on the terms of their agreement, force majeure or not. Before Cresspahl could lodge a complaint, two bundles of fish—flounder, gurnard—were delivered to his door: his cut under Pontiy's socialism. He sent the fish to the hospital; he arranged a new loading point with the Fishermen's Association, though even so Pontiy beat him to it often enough.

Cresspahl was offered deliveries of both milk and beef cattle from the administrator of the Soviet Beckhorst farm (formerly the Kleineschulte farm). The farm needed baling twine, crude oil, and leather for machine belts. Cresspahl could picture the cows—tough old bags of bones—but he agreed to take them sight unseen. It was a complicated transaction. The town had to loan Alfred Bienmüller out to Beckhorst, so that he could repair the motor and combine, which needed the oil and the leather, but by that point Bienmüller's business was the Jerichow Kommandatura's official repair shop, and K. A. Pontiy's trucks took precedence, especially the one he was planning to exchange for a convertible, to the Knesebeck commandant's advantage and disadvantage, in the interests of reconciliation. Bienmüller applied for a *propusk* to go to Beckhorst for family reasons, and Pontiy had no choice but to sign it and have it stamped. Milk was in short supply in town because both the local cows and the ones confiscated from the refugees had been herded together onto seven farms, which made deliveries to the Red Army, not the district offices and the independent municipalities, and the Jerichow Kommandatura had a reputation, even among the well disposed, for being self-sufficient. Pontiy didn't get milk from Beckhorst. One night Bienmüller took a walk along the coast and the next day he repaired the farm machines and the night after that he planned to escort the truck full of milk canisters back to Jerichow. At the edge of the woods, the mayor of the village met him and told him that he was having an argument with the Soviet administrator and needed the milk for the refugee children in his village since the farmers were now tamping butter into barrels. Cresspahl did not invoke force majeure, he recast this part of the deal into a trade of salt for butter, and he sent the twine from Papenbrock's supplies. The cows got as far as the Rande country road, then the Red Army herded them into their little hideaway on the Bäk. At least that's where Klein the butcher had to slaughter them, not in his own yard where people might have seen them; his shopwindow stayed empty. In late July it had been a long time since there'd been the hundred grams of meat per person in town. Cresspahl couldn't even get the daily half pint of milk per child that he felt was essential (as did Pontiy. But Pontiy took as much as he wanted from the dairy, each time with the comment that he too had children in his stronghold). Cresspahl would have preferred it if the foreign commander had stolen the Germans' food out of hatred, as punishment, on his own account; he couldn't come to terms with the game Pontiy made of it, with his soulful *nichevo*s and gentlemanly *shustko yedno*s.

Cresspahl ordered every poultry owner to deliver one egg per day. These eggs would be handed out only in exchange for coupons from children's ration cards. All he got were complaints about stolen chickens, especially from the buildings whose backyards adjoined the Soviets' green fence. He didn't need to go chasing down the chickens, he could hear them on the Bäk, a street that had earlier been much too fancy for poultry keeping. Because the thieves sometimes left the hens' and roosters' twisted-off heads behind in the miraculously undamaged coops, the Jerichowers began to kill their own chickens without authorization. Cresspahl could forbid it. And Cresspahl could stuff his pockets full of hard-boiled eggs at Pontiy's banquets.

It wasn't so much that he was afraid of anyone "going a bit hungry"—it wasn't a hardship yet, that would come in winter. It was that he couldn't keep the talk under control, the vague, insidious rumblings, not even malicious, just resigned: that nothing made any sense, everything was falling apart, it was all for the Russians. This talk might flower into panic, enough to make the supplying of food to town collapse.

The mayor decreed:

> The town of Jerichow has sufficient potatoes from previous years'
> harvests to meet its current needs

and forbade the harvesting of new potatoes until August 15, 1945. This was taken to mean that he clearly expected a potato shortage and was actually trying to warn the town, in his heart of hearts he was a Mecklenburger after all, on the Mecklenburgers' side—and the Jerichowers stole their own potatoes under cover of night, hid them in their cellars, and introduced them as a new currency for use with the refugees. The Jerichow Kommandatura stopped a group of workers on their way to the wheat fields one morning and made them dig up new potatoes, and it wasn't even late July yet. Of course the mayor couldn't forbid the Soviets anything; he didn't begrudge them their enjoying the taste of fresh new potatoes; but he didn't appreciate their making him look ridiculous when he was trying to keep the town fed.

And so he started doing business on his own again, something that hadn't been allowed since the victors had arrived,

the US has been holding $20 million of Czechoslovak gold bullion since the end of World War II as security for the return of confiscated American property. The folks in Prague are offering 2 million as compensation and settlement. The US is demanding 110 million. Whose turn is it to bid?

and he turned one of Alfred Bienmüller's electric motors and a set of rubber tires in Knesebeck into a business transaction, equivalent exchange values with the help of a considerable addition of window glass and motor oil, and in Rande he didn't find the harvest truck he'd planned to make drivable again but he did find maybe a pile of freshly dug potatoes, the dirt still on them, and a couple hundredweight of wheat, in factory-fresh sacks. Civilians were not allowed to accept foodstuffs or items of daily use from Soviet soldiers. But he'd given his word for the window glass, and the workers who'd dug potatoes for the Soviets had been allowed to take home from the Bäk two big pots of rich meaty stew, and he hadn't been able to get any of that for the hospital.

Meanwhile he'd managed to accomplish one thing, to the considerable consternation of the military commander. When K. A. Pontiy acted yet again like the crazed Queen of Hearts and threatened *Off with your head!*, Cresspahl could now nod pleasantly, as if in agreement, but without giving an inch. It was like with the Cheshire Cat, whose head was to be cut off because it wanted only to look at the king, not kiss his hand. But only the cat's head is visible, and the executioner refuses to cut off a head when there's no body to cut it off from. The King insists that anything that has a head can be beheaded, and don't talk nonsense, while the Queen says that if something isn't done about it *in less than no time* she'll have everybody executed all round,

> *in less than no time, Gesine!*
> *is he going to shoot you, Cresspahl?*

and the cat's head stays up in the air and the executioner comes back and the cat has disappeared, head and smile and all.

May 4, 1968 Saturday, South Ferry day

The Cheshire Cat's grin followed me into my last dream, along with the sun shower from yesterday afternoon that lit the street from the side and made it black as the sound of the car tires suddenly picked up. Minutes later the sun vanished behind a thick bluish curtain, the same way the Cheshire Cat's grin did before I woke up.

Marie has left "Saturday breakfast" on the table: hot tea, toast buried in napkins, all on a tray for easier transport, and *The New York Times* fresh from Broadway. Maybe she would learn how to live in a Prague hotel.

What the students of Paris are having for breakfast are clashes with the police because some students want control over their education and want to overthrow the institutions of capitalism, the ones along Boulevard St. Michel, for example. In Prague the students are assembling at the foot of the statue of Jan Hus and thanking the Communist Party "for the present shortages in housing and transport, for bad worker morale, for legal insecurity, for a currency without value, for a low economic standard," and will the Communists think it's contagious? First of all they deny that they ever discussed a Soviet loan of $400 million with *The New York Times*. The truth is, rather, that Mr. Dubček has just now flown to Moscow to discuss the gold ruble, as well as such matters as natural gas and crude oil, possibly as payment for the Soviet debts of 425 million. The truth is, rather . . . and if they call Auntie Times, to her face, crowned in glory as she is, a lady who doesn't speak the truth, then she will have to relay the message to us. Feeble. And, incidentally, she adds that Comrade Dubček arrived in Moscow last night for a weekend. The truth is, rather . . .

Here we have someone chasing after her child—a person, a lady, you don't know who I am. Walking north up Riverside Drive, by the buildings whose entrances are separated from the big road by hilly tree-covered islands, walking as if she grew up there, and yet she once gaped from afar at the mighty colossi of the apartment buildings with their weathered ornamentation as places she would never reach. She has friends and acquaintances here, though: Good morning, Mrs. Faure. We're fine too. We're going to see a child. The trees in the park are full of leaves now. There are no evergreens there, it's bare in the winter. Foreigners insult the trees outside our windows by calling them *Bergahorn*, sycamore maples, when really with their mottled white bark they're sycamore figs, the tree from the Bible. Now, at 100th Street, she detours all the way around the Firemen's Memorial, she just wants to read the plaque again, the one that honors the lives of the horses, for they too died *in the line of duty*. The portals of the corner buildings are fancier, built to frame grand exits and entrances; some of them stand empty, though, dusty and double locked, and people use the entrances on the side streets where no one will catch them alone. As if muggers came out of the park at night. On 113th, where the Hungarians, a freedom-loving people, have put a certain Lajos Kossuth up on a pedestal, New Yorkers are said to have mourned after the events of fall 1956. We wouldn't have gone to that. And on 116th there's an evergreen after all, a spruce tucked into a grove. Will we see it in winter? But now we've climbed uphill enough, long since reached the elevation of Columbia University, and here, by the clumps of concrete and marble, obtrusive modest shoehorned into a row of town houses, blinding in the morning light, bare and inaccessible, there stands a sepulchre from the Far East, the much-admired marvel of New York modern architecture with a six-hundred-year-old stone from a Scottish monastery reverently set into its facade: Marie's school.

The school is having its spring art fair today—all the parents are invited, together with friends, yet the double glass doors in the gloomy passageway are closed. We too have to present ourselves at the porter's lodge first, to a sister who makes sure we don't have a knife up our sleeve or a gun under our jacket. There are strict rules in this building. A man without a tie would probably be sent packing. – Are you one of the parents, Mrs. . . . ?

One of the parents. Cresspahl, class 5B. That's who I am.

The art fair is set up in the lobby and one of the adjoining classrooms around the corner—a sizable event dedicated to the higher glory of the budget, over and above the exorbitant tuition, and it will yield not one single stipend for a child of poor parents. We didn't come to buy anything, we're here to see on behalf of a child. The underage sales personnel, predominantly girls, stand behind tables and are having a hard time running the business with such a small amount of change. Here we might have some batik, there a belt made of sack string, there a chain of bone rings, and whatever else you might be missing in your life. We like this girl, the one with the green eyes, the gray eyes, with the braids, with the strong shoulders in the jacket of her uniform, watching us so strangely, as if she wanted to throw us out of the sacred building. She goes behind the counter with us, shows us the homemade goods, names a price, points at "$1.20" on a head-band, and says: Twelve tickets—it's a steal, ma'am.

She brings us over to a table in the second room with a dollhouse on display, behind ropes on stanchions, do not touch. It's not a model of a city house, it's more rustic, built low under its roof painted brick red and moss green, mullioned windows carved neatly in. The child slips under the rope divider. She touches the house. She lifts off the roof, holds it upside down, looks invitingly at us. Well? The workmanship on the beams couldn't be better, we must admit. – The technical term is tongue and groove: she says, and now people come up to listen and ask questions, a real audience. Now there are rooms visible in the uncovered attic, one filled with toy firewood. Firewood in the house? – Maybe it would get stolen from outside: she says. There's a smokehouse in the building, too, but empty. In another room the bare walls suddenly have old-fashioned wallpaper on them, the floor is varnished, the room is furnished with table and bed and wardrobe. – Ser-vant's quarters: one of the people standing around says, proud and amazed; he gets a nod in return and looks like a horse that's just had its nose stroked. On the attic floor, in the corridors, stand wooden crates that don't look like suitcases—the refugees' luggage stored at Cresspahl's—and Marie explains, like a fact from the dimmest, most distant past: Clearly the people who live here traveled a lot, I mean more than the statistical average. The grown-ups nod at this. Lifting up the attic roof reveals the compart-ments of the various rooms: Cresspahl's daughter's in front on the left, which the child calls a guest room, and next to that Cresspahl's sleeping office, which our tour guide describes as a reception desk. She shows the furniture around in the palm of her hand, but these have been bought elsewhere, from the Museum of the City of New York, and she has a feeling they're more Flemish-style. She lies whenever she can, turning the Frenchmen's room into a sewing room, the pantry into a workshop, all in the dry, New England tone she brought back from Orr Island; it all comes off with a *Yessir* and an *I'm sorry, ma'am*? The spectators discuss the architectural style among themselves, one is in favor of Norwegian origin, he saw the same thing in Massachusetts, another claims to recognize it as Pennsylvania Dutch, and the child shrugs her shoulders, an expert, but beyond her competence here. Finally she's managed to bring one of the onlookers to the first question: What it costs. How much you can buy it for.

– It's obviously not for sale: the child says. – Maybe it'll be auctioned off this afternoon though.

– Not a Dutch auction, an American one: she says.

We won't place any bids on a house like that, we'll let it go. The child, on the other hand—her we take, fleeing the teachers sneaking up on us, and we ride the subway straight to the harbor where the ferry is waiting.

She herself was the child who built that house, and when they asked her, she shook her head, not knowing.

– One of us did: she said.

May 5, 1968 Sunday

Time to give up, Gesine. It might as well be today as tomorrow.

Oh, please. Because of "information reaching Paris"?

Information that reached Paris and made it into Le Monde.

Who is this General Yepishev?

Aleksei A. Yepishev is head of the political administration of the Soviet armed forces.

So now he's the politburo of the CP of the USSR?

Why wouldn't the Red Army want to go on maneuvers again? They are the military, Gesine.

They won't do it.

Yepishev says that faithful Communists in Czechoslovakia need only appeal to the Soviet Union for help. If they do he'll come and safeguard their Socialism.

Old Believers like that have been in the minority for a long time.

A letter's enough, come at once. "The Soviet Army is ready to do its duty."

They won't do it.

They marched into Hungary in 1956.

That's why they'll be extra careful now.

This time they say "other" Socialist troops are coming with. To spread around the bad press.

Possibly East Germans. They recommend their version of Socialism. German uniforms back in Prague again.

They may not use only their uniforms, Gesine.

They won't send tanks to Prague. Not in 1968, twelve years after Budapest!

You've only heard rumors about it until today.

That makes sense. The rumors paint a rather different picture.

Gesine, General Yepishev said it at a meeting of his party, on April 23. A French newspaper reported it yesterday. You read it today.

I've already seen denials in print.

And pigs can fly.

No! No! I didn't see it!

"A child doesn't count for anything."

The Red Army won't do it.

Because a certain Gesine Cresspahl doesn't believe it?

Exactly. That's why.

The military commander of the town of Jerichow, K. A. Pontiy, might shoot at birds with a rifle, might kick a cat out of his way as often as pet it, he might jump down Cresspahl's daughter's throat for not sweeping the path to his villa clean enough, but he didn't entirely forfeit her respect. In fact, she was downright grateful to him. He'd removed the corpses from her sight.

The British had made dead people public in Jerichow. They were the Nazis' prisoners from Neuengamme concentration camp, twelve miles southeast of Hamburg, along with its Mecklenburg branch camps, Boizenburg and Reiherhorst in Wöbbelin. At Neuengamme the Nazis hadn't managed to do it. When the German Reich had to clear out the Majdanek, Treblinka, Belzec, and Sobibor death camps in occupied Poland, it made squads of prisoners open the mass graves, dig up the bodies, and grind up the bones. The bone meal was strewn on the fields, the gas chambers and incineration ovens were blown up, and once the prisoners had leveled the camps to a plot of land smooth as innocence they were killed for their efforts. In Austria the Germans had had to leave the Mauthausen camp standing, and at Neuengamme they didn't manage it either. The Danish government negotiated for their countrymen until, in April, they could have the famous Convoy of Ninety-Two White Buses transport them to Frøslov and Møgelkaer. More than six thousand people were left behind in Neuengamme, under German command; to keep the British from finding them, they were evacuated. First, some five hundred died in the freight cars on the way to Lübeck via Hamburg, unable to endure any further starvation, lacking medical care. Four cars' worth of sick prisoners weren't even loaded onto the ships, they were screaming with fever, they were shot, and anyone who didn't hear that in Lübeck's outer harbor might well have heard the festive sounds of the German SS in the adjacent grain silo, celebrating final victory with the finest cognac and delicacies from stolen Red Cross parcels. The prisoners, whom the people of Lübeck knew absolutely nothing about, spent almost ten days waiting at Lübeck's wharf in their freight cars, German Reich Railway cars, out in the open, or else stuffed into the *Thielbek* and the *Athen*; more dead kept being buried next to the harbor. The *Thielbek* had been bombed in 1944, and not been repaired, and was hardly seaworthy: two tugs had to tow the ship down the Trave and out into the bay. The *Athen* could move under her own steam and she brought more and more batches of prisoners from Lübeck's industrial harbor to the *Cap Arcona* in the Bay of Neustadt. The three ships carrying prisoners were easily visible from land, and known to not only the fishermen. The *Thielbek*, 2,815 gross register tons, 345 feet long, draft 21 feet, had carried freight for Knöhr & Burchardt in Hamburg. The *Athen*, somewhat smaller, was also designed to carry freight, not people. The *Cap Arcona* was built for people— a luxury ship of the Hamburg–South America Line, 27,560 GRT, 675 feet long, draft 28.5 feet. Before the war it sailed to Rio de Janeiro, thirty-five days, first class only, 1,275 reichsmarks: avoid part of the winter and relax in the mild sea air under the southern sun! The *Cap Arcona* was designed for 1,325 passengers and a crew of 380; now, however, there were 4,600 prisoners belowdecks with the sick at the very bottom (with no medicine or bandages) and the Russian prisoners in the banana storage hold (with no light, no air, and for the first three days no food); the dead were piled up on deck. The ship stank of the dead, of the disease and shit of the living— a putrid heap and not even moving. For the *Cap Arcona* was not seaworthy either, not without fuel. There was almost no food for the prisoners, they were not given water, but roll call, with counting off and tallying, was mandatory. It took longer to die here than in the gas chambers, but it wouldn't be long before they were all dead. Then came freedom. Freedom came across the bright sunny bay on May 3 in the shape of a squadron of British bombers. At around two thirty they flew over the Bay of Neustadt and started in on the *Athen*. The Germans defended their prisoners with antiaircraft fire; after the third direct hit they hoisted a white flag. The British pilots may have seen it, because they left that ship and attacked the ones in the outer bay. After twenty minutes the *Thielbek* lay down on its side and disappeared altogether under the surface of the water, since it was almost sixty feet deep there. The *Cap Arcona*, with the captain's bedsheet on the mast, took an hour, then it tipped onto its port side, slowly, faster and faster, until it was lying on its eighty-five-foot side, twenty-six feet of it above water. Meanwhile death was proceeding more quickly, and in various forms. The prisoners could die in the fire, in the smoke (the fire hoses had been cut), from the German crew's rifles (the crew had life jackets), jammed in by hoarded food supplies, crushed in the panicking crowd, from the heat of the glowing *Cap Arcona*, in the lifeboats plummeting into the water, from jumping into the water, of cold in the water, by being hit or shot at by German minesweepers, and on land from exhaustion. The saved numbered 3,100, the dead somewhere between 7,000 and 8,000. At around five in the afternoon the English took Neustadt, so it was in the British zone, same as Jerichow, and contact was permitted between the two places, and that's how we knew about it.

The dead washed up on every shore of Lübeck Bay, from Bliestorf to Pelzerhaken, from Neustadt to Timmendorf Beach, into the mouth of the Trave, from Priwall to Schwansee and Redewisch and Rande, even into Wohlenberg Cove, as far as Poel Island and the other Timmendorf. They were found almost daily.

Too many washed up on the coast near Jerichow—the finders couldn't bury them all secretly in the sand. The British occupation authorities had issued orders that all corpses from the water be reported, and they insisted that these orders be followed. The British took a truck and rounded up men who had been members of the National Socialist German Workers' Party. These men were driven along the beach, and wherever a black lump lay on the white sand the British stopped. The Germans were given no gloves for the loading, not even pitchforks or shovels. The British drank their whiskey right in front of the Germans; despite this medicine, they too had to throw up. The British created no special cemetery for the dead from this watery camp. When the truck was full, they drove the load far inland, all the way to Kalkhorst, even Gneez. When they drove into Jerichow they lowered the sides of the truck. The MPs made the Germans leave their houses to look at the cargo as it was driven down Town Street to the cemetery at a walking pace. Slower than walking. The cargo was not easy to recognize. It had been damaged by bullet wounds, charring, shrapnel, blows. It was recognizable by the faded, split, clinging, striped clothes. The individual pieces of human being were often incomplete. There were limbs missing, or there were limbs on the truck bed without a torso, one day there was nothing but a piece of head. The fish had eaten a lot of that one. The British made the people of Jerichow gather on Market Square. In the middle lay the first load of bodies. The commander handed over to the Germans the Germans' dead. He made them their property. He allowed them to place the mortal remains from the sea into coffins. Then they were permitted to close the coffins and carry them to the cemetery. After the dirt had been shoveled onto the mass grave, the British fired a salute into the air. At the cemetery gate stood a sergeant, holding a box in front of him, and on this box he stamped the ration cards. Anyone who had not accepted the dead would not eat.

– It was their dead! Those English are utter scoundrels! Marie says. – You guys let them get away with anything, and then some!

– They were the Germans'. The Germans had held them prisoner, loaded them onto ships. If they'd kept them the only difference was they would have died slower.

– The British dropped the bombs. They saw the prisoners' camp uniforms and fired at them anyway. That's the truth.

– The British didn't want that truth. You could be thrown in jail for less than that. There were German U-boats above water all around the ships, and none of them were hit—that was too dangerous even to whisper.

– But you Jerichowers knew.

– It wasn't new information. You could already see prisoners like that in striped clothing in Mecklenburg (maybe not in Lübeck)—but they weren't to exist in language. Now the British were bringing in dead bodies and decreeing the cause of their death however they wanted.

– The Mecklenburgers may have been cowards, but the English weren't.

– By 1956 they'd put out five volumes on the air offensive against Germany through the end of the war. May 3 was before the end of the war, and nowhere is the bombing in Lübeck Bay mentioned.

– Official history. Stiff upper lip.

– It is also official history that the British came before the German submarines had time to sink the prisoners themselves. The monument in the Old Cemetery in Jerichow is official history too.

– And one in the British zone?

– In Pelzerhaken, near Neustadt. And four years later the British gave permission to the owners of the *Thielbek* to salvage any articles of value. The sea hadn't quite flushed out the whole ship—there were still some bodies, and heaps of bare bones—they had the ship repaired. Let's call it the *Reinbek* and put it back out to sea until 1961, until it's worth selling. Today, if you happen to see a *Magdalena* flying the Panamanian flag, that's the *Thielbek* of May 1945. The *Cap Arcona* was worthless except for the scrap metal. The *Athen*, though, that turned into the Soviet *General Brusslov* in 1946, then the Polish *Waryński* in 1947, and the Polish Line ran her from Gdynia to Buenos Aires and Rio de Janeiro. What's left of the *Cap Arcona* is the ship's bell. You've seen it.

– At the Museum of Danish Resistance in Copenhagen!

– In Churchill Park, in Copenhagen.

– And you still wanted to swim in the Baltic?

– We ate fish from the Baltic. The Germans eat fish from the Baltic to this day. There are almost three thousand prisoners lying at the bottom of the Baltic.

– And K. A. Pontiy stopped it?

– He stopped the education of the German people by means of the overland transport of bodies. This particular flotsam had to be collected in the cemeteries of the coastal villages, outside the territory under his command. That cost—

– and he made Jerichow pay for it.

– Tell it to the judge, Marie.

– No. I would've been grateful to him too.

The military commander of the town of Jerichow didn't manage to do it on first try—to keep the dead at a distance. For a while they came at him from the other side. They were the refugees, from far outside the parish, who died in the villages and on the farms surrounding the town, in early July already. They hadn't brought coffins with them when they fled the war; now that they were dying of typhus, they wanted to stay in Jerichow. Pastor Brüshaver was still notified of the first cart, so the little bell could be rung as it pulled up. As a result, Gesine no longer went behind the house; she did keep sitting in her walnut tree, even though that was impolite to the dead. It was a panel truck, with boards running down the sides and cross-planks at the front and the back. *Kretts*, Gesine called the frontboards and backboards. But language had run off somewhere, away from her. She thought: cabbages, beets. Outside the mortuary chapel the driver and his assistant raised the back *Krett* and pulled the topmost body down until it flopped onto the stretcher. Gesine tried to think that Jakob, in his strange Pommern German, called a *Krett* a *Schott*—she could feel her mind running off somewhere, away from this. The second time, it was too onerous for the villagers to have to dig such deep holes, and they offloaded the strangers into Jerichow's mortuary without Brüshaver hearing about it in time. That time it was a harvest cart, they were lying visibly one on top of the other between the ladders that the wheat was going to be brought in on the next day. A human arm like the one hanging out past the rails between the rungs, swaying alongside the wheel, seems alive. You couldn't tell where the dead had come from; K. A. Pontiy had nowhere to send them back to. He ordered sentries to keep watch the next day.

Another cart was pushed up to Pontiy's villa in the night, by hand, quietly, on rubber wheels. Hanna Ohlerich and Gesine didn't hear that one; at one point they woke up reassured when they heard one of the commandant's cars, which jolted into reverse after lots of loud rattles and shakes, making the horses whinny. Gesine was safe from any new arrivals; that morning she went outside without a second thought. When she glanced to the right she saw both of the chapel's double doors standing open, with something that looked like a shoe on the ground right outside them. She tried to tell herself that someone must have just slipped and fallen there, but she knew that now she wanted to see the bodies.

Maybe the living had brought lanterns in the night. The dead weren't piled on one another the way they'd been in the cart. They sat in the little mortuary hall as if alive, their backs leaned against the walls, most of them with their eyes open. Their dresses, pants, and heavy jackets had been left on, out of fear of infection, or else put back on—they were a bit crooked on their bodies, too high on the neck, too high over the knee. Some were touching one another, holding their neighbor seated, otherwise they might slip. There were two together in the northwest corner, as if they'd sat down next to each other on their own. It was a young man, who seemed to Gesine twenty-two years old, with black hair and long muttonchop sideburns, in a neat black suit with shirt and tie—a city man whose shoes had come off somewhere. His head was turned to the side, as if he were looking at the wall. Then, though she was right up next to him, a girl lay half slumped down—a blond with her hair up, all freckly—and she had slid halfway into the young man's lap, and her posture was so peaceful, his hand on her shoulder seemed a little embarrassed, and not there voluntarily. They looked posed.

There was also a chicken in the hall. It had escaped from the Kommandatura. It was feisty, fully alive. It had found some grain next to the corpses' pants pockets but in its confusion it was pecking at the bare flesh too.

The mortuary had its windows in the side walls. Morning sunlight slanted in from the right side and lit up the chapel like a waiting room—lit the loving couple most of all.

Gesine had taken only a half step into the chapel, for no longer than a couple of seconds. She felt watched from every direction, and immediately stepped backward. In doing so, she tripped on the body whose shoe she had noticed earlier. The jokester had forgotten him, he was the only one lying with his face in the gravel.

She didn't need to run back to the house. Walking, she considered at leisure what she was expected to do next. Now she knew she was guilty of something—she didn't know what. She refused her breakfast, and the rest of her meals that day, but it still wasn't enough to soothe her conscience. She could have eaten without getting sick, she even had some appetite, though she wasn't exactly hungry that night. It would have seemed like a betrayal of the gathering of the dead to her.

Cresspahl saw the staged scene too, and that afternoon he had it taken away and then nailed the mortuary shut. Jerichow has had its other cemetery for some time now, the one K. A. Pontiy ordered, on the Rande country road between the town and the air base, on the left, on land expropriated from the nobility. It didn't have a fence, but Pastor Brüshaver had stood there and done the things and said the words he felt necessary for a consecration. From the countryside you reached it by going around the town, about a mile and a half; it took maybe half an hour longer with a horse and cart.

Today it's called the Central Municipal Cemetery. Surrounded by a low fieldstone wall, and within that a ring of thornbushes.

The chapel, build in 1950 and much more massive than a garage, can't be seen from the road.

The old chapel, by Cresspahl's house, has collapsed and been replaced by part of a white brick wall between the red stones from 1850. The churchyard cemetery is considered an attraction, because it has been untouched for more than twenty years.

Later it must have been an honor to be allowed into the earth by St. Peter's Church. That's how Cresspahl ended up there, in a grave next to his wife, as a former mayor of the town. While he was alive, he managed to get Jakob a place there, near him.

And it's a Schott, *Gesine, that's what it's called.*
It's a Krett.
Schott.
Krett.
You laughed first!
You did.

May 6, 1968 Monday
Yesterday, on Karl Marx's hundred-and-fiftieth birthday, *The New York Times* took part in the festivities around the house where he was born in Trier. The students shouted "Ho, Ho, Ho Chi Minh!" when the chairman of the Social Democratic Party, which owns the house, sought to enter it. The East Germans staged an event of their own. In the West German one, Ernst Bloch contended that many errors had been committed in the name of Marx. "Some people not only do not know anything about Marx but they tell lies about him."

Dramatis personae:

MONSIEUR HENRI ROCHE-FAUBOURG, part heir to a French banking firm. Twenty-one years old, 136 lbs., skin color yellowish, race Caucasian, hair black with split ends and curling over his shirt collar. French, graduate of an elite school in Paris. Has begun to study law and economics. Serving one year in New York. A personage insulted by not being received at once by his father's New York colleague, instead being first handed over for a subordinate to deal with. At a meal at the Brussels two weeks ago he was capable, all the way until coffee, of refusing to believe that the lady with him really spoke French. Clings fast to his role as the sole person in New York who speaks and understands French, despite the waiter's proving the contrary. Considers his language to be his exclusive possession, and while he is unable to punish encroachments on this his property with a whip, he did make frequent use of a lack of comprehension. Then he kisses the hand of the lady paying his check, and says with a smile on his impatient red lips: What a charming remark! It was a remark on the enamel-like nature of typical American makeup and was, like all the previous remarks, made in French. He replied in the same language for the first time. Has thirty-one words of American English at his disposal, thirty of them English English. Long jackets, reaching down to the tips of his outstretched fingers, sharply tailored.

DE ROSNY. First name unknown.

The scene: A descending elevator, rear shaft. It's a normal elevator, not reserved for senior executives. Time: an hour after the close of business. The vice president is alone in the elevator with Mrs. Cresspahl. He is performing for her benefit the conversation he had with ROCHE-FAUBOURG, alternately as himself and as the young heir.

DE ROSNY: So what did you have in mind here?

ROCHE-FAUBOURG: Yes, well, my father left the decision up to me.

DE ROSNY: He seems to have turned into an American father. He used to be fine.

ROCHE-FAUBOURG: My father is in excellent health, thank you for asking.

DE ROSNY: I guess I'm about to behave like a German father—

ROCHE-FAUBOURG: *Pardon?*

DE ROSNY: Because there's something I want to tell you. You need to finish your studies.

ROCHE-FAUBOURG: Yes, I was planning to get an MBA.

DE ROSNY: An MBA! Please! You'll learn business administration when you take over your father's business, and if you turn out to be a dud at it, you can assign the job to someone else. And all the other jobs too.

ROCHE-FAUBOURG: I thought—

DE ROSNY: Your life is set in stone, isn't it? In a few years you're going to take over your father's business.

ROCHE-FAUBOURG: I flatter myself that—

DE ROSNY: So what you need to do is enjoy the free time you have left. Beforehand!

ROCHE-FAUBOURG: This American idea of enjoyment—

DE ROSNY: If you really want to, you can work here for a year. A forced march through every department.

ROCHE-FAUBOURG: Maybe for six months.

DE ROSNY: For that, of course, you would need to be interested in the condition of American workers.

ROCHE-FAUBOURG: Now that—

DE ROSNY: You could read a few books. But what you need to do now is live a little. How old are you?

ROCHE-FAUBOURG: Twenty-one.

DE ROSNY: You need to learn how to live a little. Get a sports car in June and drive around the country for two months. Go to a meeting of the Communist Party. Cresspahl will tell you everything you need to know about New York.

ROCHE-FAUBOURG: A couple of weeks ago she gave me the impression, in the most charming way—

DE ROSNY: There, you see? Just don't take up too much of her time, she's working for me.

ROCHE-FAUBOURG: Might I perhaps occasionally—

DE ROSNY: An MBA, what nonsense. That's all right for someone to study if they haven't got anything to take over. You are taking over the firm, aren't you?

ROCHE-FAUBOURG: If my brother—

DE ROSNY: When the year's up, you're to present yourself to me and I'll give you a test. Have a good morning.

ROCHE-FAUBOURG: Goodbye.

The vice president repeated parts of the scene as he walked, to the amusement of other subordinates walking quickly past him and trying to make their haste look like tact. The vice president is in a different kind of hurry—he has no train to miss, his black, air-conditioned limo is waiting for him. Still he keeps fidgeting with a cigarette between his fingers without ever managing to bring it to his lips, because his lips are busy saying: You have to picture it, me standing there in front of this young man, no one has ever talked to him like that in his life, and he came within a whisker of missing it. And people always think German fathers are tyrants, dictators really, and I as an American had to tell a French child: Here's your job, such and such. Get an education ...

– Marx won't be of much help to him now, Mr. de Rosny.

– Ah, there I go again, forgetting that you have a German father. Can you forgive me, Mrs. Cresspahl?

– No. I'll never forgive you.

– You're all right, *young lady.* If only everyone who worked for me was like you. If only they were all like you.

May 7, 1968 Tuesday

So, what has Alexander Dubček brought back from occupation headquarters in Moscow? "Understanding" of the process of democratization he has initiated in his country, "full respect of mutual rights," and a loan, almost, of hard currency from the leading treasury. He said he'd been happy to explain his Socialism to the Soviet comrades.

And the city of Cologne has gotten back the Cranach painting it had been forced to give Hermann Göring's daughter for her baptism in 1938. Edda G. wanted to keep it, not as her own personal property but to give it to the Free State of Bavaria, but now Bavaria has also decided to relinquish its claims.

In Jerichow's eyes Papenbrock got off easy almost when the Soviets came to get him. Maybe it wasn't exactly fair but you'd have to call it square, after all the money Albert made from Göring's air force. Now the former business king of Jerichow was going to have to pay back taxes.

That's what it looked like. One Sunday evening in mid-July the victors drove into Market Square in a two-ton truck, with no sign of K. A. Pontiy, so that it looked like orders from his superior. Three men strode into the house, all officers, not with weapons drawn but still like an arrest party. If they spent half an hour in there, they must have been searching Albert's office for his earthly gains, and the fact that they did so silently only made the ambush more ominous, that and the recollection that Albert was far from the only one whose friendly dealings with Göring's air force might rub the Soviets the wrong way. Only one person sent for Cresspahl, Bergie Quade, but her husband, Otto, was back on Town Street much quicker than the mayor; he came walking up so slowly that he seemed to be saying he couldn't do anything to help, especially not such close relatives. Papenbrock was already being brought out of his house, in a work shirt and worn-out regular pants, shoulders bent, eyes on the ground, arms hanging emptily at his sides. It was retold many times: how the old man tried to step up onto the tailgate, slipped, raised his lame foot again, and it scraped back down the side of the truck, this time banging his other shin hard, and how the officers had watched him like a sick animal there's no point in helping. Then Louise came running out of the house, wailing and wildly swinging a bulging travel bag as if wanting to hurt herself or one of the officers. Finally a Russian gave Papenbrock a gentle push, not exactly as though wanting to hurt him, and Albert stumbled and fell onto the truck's loading bed, the officers climbed in after him and latched the tailgate shut, the truck turned around and drove back south, maybe to headquarters in Schwerin, possibly an even bigger prison. They had taken the travel bag from Louise, but they hadn't handed it to her husband, they gave it to the driver, and even if Albert had a bit longer to live in custody it didn't look like he'd be coming back.

There hadn't been many onlookers, so the stories about what happened didn't end up fragmentary. The onlookers there were had kept a proper distance, so as not to be taken along on Albert's trip by mistake, but every one of them claimed to feel a shudder when Louise, still a big woman, tugged with both hands at the front door, which was sticking—clearly she was weakened by her sobbing—until she had it back in its frame and could bolt it from the inside. That spared the witnesses the expected expressions of sympathy, but when they stepped back and turned around they found themselves face-to-face with Cresspahl, the one they called the Russian lackey, the traitor. But from this close up no one wanted to tell him that now he'd let his father-in-law get arrested. They felt trapped in his silent, challenging gaze. Cresspahl had enjoyed the Russians' flight from Louise's tearful entrance, and so he seemed almost relaxed, head tilted toward the evening sun, checking the time. – *'Ts nahyin:* he said, reminding them of the approaching curfew, that Soviet lickspittle, instead of staggering under the misfortune befalling his family. They left him alone and he walked off down Town Street. He hadn't even given them any information. But anyway, it was nine o'clock. Suddenly you could smell the time—sweet, unwholesome, slightly greasy—from the scent of the linden blossoms.

If you think of Jerichow as the center of a clock (where the Hydrographical Institute puts its compass rose on its maps of Lübeck Bay), the village and seaside resort of Rande would be at approximately one o'clock. In the eight o'clock direction, but far past the edge of the clock face, was the Old Demwies estate, still southwest of Gneez, in the former Principality of Ratzeburg, far enough from Jerichow. Even if you'd hidden your telephone instead of handing it in you still couldn't get through to another number, the post office still had nothing to deliver, and the travel ban took care of the rest; and so, for some time, Albert Papenbrock was thought to have vanished without a trace. Only around the end of 1945 did people start talking in Jerichow about someone in far-off Old Demwies, managing the estate for the Soviets, by the name of Papenbrock. If you believed the reports, he wasn't acting like an old man of seventy-seven, he was bossing the farmworkers around like an old-time overseer, talking to his Soviet superiors like someone who'd never gotten his hands dirty with the Nazis. He sure wasn't shy. And if someone's only described to you in words, can you recognize him right off? He'd supposedly made his way there from the Müritz area, maybe he wasn't the Jerichow Papenbrock. You couldn't ask Cresspahl. Papenbrock's wife said she didn't know anything. Yeah it's not him. When Soviet counterintelligence came to Jerichow the translators almost always got back the same, plausibly indignant answer: You all arrested him a while back! Doncha even keep a list of who you put away?

In early August, returning from Lübeck to Jerichow, Jakob took an inordinate detour through Old Demwies so that he could tell Gesine something about her grandfather. She'd have trouble recognizing him. He now wore mended-up clothes all week long, a torn shirt, patched pants, and a black straw hat he never took off so people wouldn't know he was bald. The commandants of Old Demwies, known as the Twins, hadn't understood his name and called him the Pope; he didn't correct them. In the village they called him the Pastor, because he spoke so gentle and mild when assigning work in the mornings, and raged so furiously when they hadn't made their quotas in the evenings. As far as Jakob could tell the farm was running on textbook lines—they'd already brought in their wheat from the fields and had started threshing. The farmworkers respected the P. for it—he took care of them with extra allowances and right of residence just like the former masters who'd fled; they wanted him to be even more on their side. He avoided getting into fights with the Twins like any other employee. At night the Soviet men would go for a stroll through the farmhands' cottages shining their flashlights at the beds, looking for grown girls, but all they found there were small children—you could complain to this overseer and he'd actually send someone to the commandants, those two young guys never seen apart, but they just laughed at the nightly disturbance. One time, the soldiers had suddenly been moved by the sight of all those sleeping children right up next to one another and they stood there a long time, shining their flashlights on them, amazed at the little tykes lying there like peas, sleeping like little peas in a pod; this family was offered a room in the manor house, because the Twins decided to interpret the story as meaning a lack of space, while the Pastor could have told them otherwise. The Pope had convinced the Twins to station some Red Army soldiers to guard the farm, so that he could get the work done; at night he locked himself inside and didn't hear anyone knocking no matter how loud it was. The Soviets had put him in the foreman's cottage—the whole house, where the former Nazi regional group leader had lived with his wife and children before hanging himself and them. The Pope didn't want the privilege or the honor and took in two refugee families, putting them into the narrow rooms, as if he preferred not to be alone at night. Jakob had seen the old man only from afar; he'd seemed jittery, and Jakob didn't want to shock him with a visitor from Jerichow. Plus Cresspahl hadn't given him any message to take to the old man.

Papenbrock had hardly bristled at the deal. He was sure he could explain to any Soviet court, even a military one, what he had been doing during the past twelve years, but given that starting in 1935 he'd trusted Cresspahl

more than either of his own sons and had done so all the more ever since
Lisbeth's death, he was as good as submissive when in June 1945 he realized
that he was no longer up to making a decision of his own, whether it was
to hole up in Jerichow or flee to the British across the demarcation line.
Louise had wanted to keep the house, and if not the whole business then
at least the bakery. Papenbrock hadn't stayed for that reason, or for her
sake at all, it was just that he lacked the self-confidence to drag his Louise
away by force. Then Cresspahl came and told them that the Soviets were
looking for the father of Robert Papenbrock, who'd become well known
for executing hostages in Ukraine. So, the old man let himself get sent
somewhere right by the border. So, K. A. Pontiy could request certain
deliveries from the administrators of the Old Demwies estate—he'd sent
them an extremely skilled estate manager.

We'll be gettin this back, said the farmer, giving his pig some bacon.

May 8, 1968 Wednesday
The city government is armed and ready for racial violence this summer,
and city officials can better estimate the numbers now, after the arrests at
Columbia University. There are 196 detention pens in present court buildings and a special pen on Rikers Island that holds 1,600 prisoners. Altogether
the police can arrest 10,000 disobedient persons a day, and if there're more
they'll probably be able to handle it.
    Senator Robert F. Kennedy has cleared his first hurdle on the way to
the White House, winning the Indiana primary—not with as many votes
as he wanted, just 42 percent. Eugene McCarthy received 27 percent and
he can barely give his staff pocket money. Still, according to a poll of college
students, McCarthy is a good twenty-five points ahead of Kennedy, who
mentions his own money and his right to spend it on whatever he wants,
such as a win in Indiana.
    A young man is standing in the Cresspahls' doorway, with short hair
and, fervently devoted to tradition, a button-down shirt tucked into his
pants, blinding white thick-waled socks in shoes polished to a military shine.
Without being pushy he takes a friendly look at the set table, at the peaceful

family life by the evening windows, the darkening green park; he doesn't insist on being invited in, he can say his piece just fine while standing...

If only we understood this country where we want to live! After seven years. We heard news of the 1960 election as anecdotes that reached Germany—Nixon's heavy stubble that hurt him on-screen against John Kennedy in a once famous debate, this one not about kitchen technology; we arrived to find President Kennedy and at first wanted to give him credit for abolishing the line on the questionnaire where we had to say if we were planning to assassinate him. Then we learned. We learned what a party precinct is and what a county committee can do, how someone becomes a favorite son and how much a TV ad costs per minute until it's broadcast for free as news—the whole local folklore of capitalist parliamentarianism. Without much hope, just to know where we'd be and what we'd support if we trusted and believed in who we were for.

This time it's supposed to be Eugene McCarthy, if we listen to the new generation, now not flower children but ballot children. There hasn't been such an upswelling of student support since the 1964 civil rights march in Mississippi—the democratic process counted for nothing against the executive branch's arrangements with the Four Hundred Families—and then came the New Left, you could escape into the psychedelic embellishments and desolations of consciousness, into personal excuses, whether working for the Peace Corps in South America or another antiwar protest outside City Hall or the Pentagon, still we kept hearing the word *frustration*, the disgust at empty gestures that accomplished nothing but venting feelings so they no longer bothered you. Then, unexpectedly, in March 1968 they were back, from the posh schools and the poor schools on the East Coast—from Harvard, Radcliffe, Yale, Smith, Barnard, Columbia, as well as Dunbarton and Rivier—and a campaign following all the rules to the letter started for one Senator Eugene McCarthy. Why?

Fifty-two years old, born in the hamlet of Watkins, Minnesota, pop. 744. Is that why? Because he has Irish ancestors like Kennedy, is Catholic like Kennedy, but more reliably so on both counts? That's a reason he himself supposedly gave. Fine, they no longer set store in the fear that the pope might control the children of America, they are thinking more like Stalin, admittedly not bringing up the size of the pope's army right off;

but this prejudice is so powerful around the country that even we've heard about it. What else do they like about him? That he zipped through middle and high school in six years instead of eight, with straight A's except for in trigonometry, a hero on the hockey rink and baseball diamond? That helps a man's reputation hereabouts. Yes. He was one of the few to pick a fight over the radio with the other McCarthy, the sniffer-out of Communists, maybe they credit him with bravery for that. Still, five terms in the Senate as a Democrat and not one law bearing his name. Is it because he embraced the nickname he was given, the Maverick—the animal that doesn't run with the herd (qv. Texas rancher Samuel A. Maverick, 1803–1870)? But he worked with his party in 1960, supporting in vain one Adlai Stevenson just because he didn't like Lyndon Johnson and saw nothing but reckless spending and ruthless actions when he looked at Kennedy? In 1964 he went back to the well with LBJ after all, hoping for the vice presidency, and as a reward got mightily dunked. Is it because he was one of the first senators to come out in favor of pulling back in the war against the people of Vietnam? He hadn't said anything until January 1966. All right, well, he's more or less antiwar. He's picked fights with L. B. Johnson over everything, whether the crisis in the cities or that in agriculture. Both these things are true of Robert Kennedy too. Are they more true of McCarthy?

Why do we even want to understand the students supporting McCarthy? Is it because we secretly want to be one of them, not just in our opinions but also in age?

They first went over to him for giving long-enough speeches in a dry tone, professorial, with no tricks or appeals to emotions. Maybe they went over to him first because they were students, and only then because they agreed with him. They might have liked that here was someone demanding hard work from them, not a circus. But why do they now put on his severe, restrained airs and sobriety themselves, shutting the persistently bearded boys up in the back rooms to seal envelopes or lick stamps, wearing pencil skirts instead of minis on the streets where voters walk, forgoing men's jewelry, turning up clean-shaven, avoiding any impression of eccentricity, ringing the doorbell like a bank teller, in jacket and tie? And the press can report that they're sleeping chastely segregated by sexes, the boys in gyms, the girls in private quarters. McCarthy likes it that way, the voters like it that way, but this is the discipline and ethos of an earlier time, and one of these days the merely faked image is going to turn into the reality of "*law and order*," isn't it?

Eugene McCarthy drags his family into the campaign with him like everyone else, wife Abigail, Ellen Mary Michael Margaret, for touching appearances and intimate details; twelve-year-old Margaret, in seventh grade, is his "secret weapon"—aren't the students embarrassed? Don't they notice any problem with this national custom? Are we allowed to be embarrassed?

Are they with him because he's surrounded by stars? John Kenneth Galbraith, professor of economics at Harvard, has brought every one of his Americans for Democratic Action around to McCarthy. The poet Robert Lowell said for McCarthy that the Republicans cannot sink and they will not swim, whatever that means; McCarthy writes poetry himself. And then came Paul Newman, no less, the giant broad-boned actor oozing decorum and decency, who in his recent films plays the selfless, noble detective, or the advocate for the Indians guarding the bag of their money until he's killed, his heavy head with his blond hair tipping to one side, it's all over. Is it the people like this surrounding him? And they won in New Hampshire in March, with 42.2 percent of the Democratic vote against LBJ's 49.4,

Hey, hey, L. B. Jay!

How many kids did you kill today?

and the students said that if he'd gotten 10 percent they'd leave the country, with 20 they'd burn their draft cards, with 30 they'd go back to school, but with 40 they'd come along to the next primary in Wisconsin, and some were still with him yesterday in Indiana, though now deployed against Robert Kennedy, whom they'd earlier supported. Because of Kennedy, maybe.

Robert Francis Kennedy, Democratic senator from New York, stood up as recently as January 30 and promised his friends and supporters that he would not run against Lyndon Johnson "under any foreseeable circumstances." For the sake of party unity. Sat back and watched McCarthy proceed from state to state as the only antiwar candidate and didn't help him—inconsiderate, gutless. Then he saw the number of people in New Hampshire who were sick of the president, and Robert Francis wasn't there with them. How did he go back on his word? By suggesting that the president declare himself incapable of managing affairs involving Vietnam; the president declined to do so; the next day, Kennedy announced he was running against the president, "not out of any personal enmity or lack of respect for the president," or so he said. Stood up in the Senate Caucus Room in the old Senate office building on Capitol Hill, where his brother John had announced his candidacy eight years earlier. His tie clip a model of the PT 109 patrol torpedo boat his brother John had commanded with honor, on film, in World War II. His words were those of his brother John. With his wife, Ethel, and nine children he announced his candidacy as John's brother, to take votes away from Eugene McCarthy, for whom he'd done nothing—like a hungry dog who considers another's bone his own legitimate property. Paul Newman grumbled at the shame of Kennedy choosing to take a free ride on someone else's back; others said he was endangering the young people's new trust in democratic process, or called him a claim jumper, and one student for McCarthy concluded: Hawks are bad enough, we don't need chickens; finally, Kennedy was compared to the cowbird, which sits on grazing cattle, scans them for parasites, and lays its eggs in other birds' nests. Undaunted, three hours and twenty minutes after pulling the lever in the voting booth, Kennedy marched in the St. Patrick's Day Parade in New York with a green flower in his buttonhole, an Irishman among Irishmen, and that afternoon he declared his candidacy in Boston ("because America can do better"), the next day in Kansas. A choice between McCarthy and him would be one between fairness and underhanded tricks. So would we choose McCarthy, and why exactly?

He hasn't said what he'd do with the soldiers in Vietnam. It's possible he would handle agriculture and finance and housing construction differently from his predecessor, who now doesn't want to keep going; won't he have to accommodate himself to the Four Hundred Families, and everything they need for their money and power and more money? Why vote for this guy instead of for someone else? Why vote at all in this country?

Now there's one question we'd like to ask, concerning our personal circumstances. Two weeks ago McCarthy criticized the current administration for failing to realize that the dollar was a more important factor in world stability than military power. We have a boss, de Rosny, who understands what this means; it wasn't quite clear enough for us. Are we going to lose our job? And if it keeps us, where will it send us?

So what do we do with this young man ringing our doorbell at eight at night, holding a clipboard, asking us whether we are a registered member of the Democratic Party, and whether he could tell us a few words about McCarthy. Will we understand him?

May 9, 1968 Thursday
is the day we take Czech lessons, and at two o'clock on the dot Professor Kreslil ducks into Cresspahl's office, carefully pulls the door shut behind him, and only then adopts a more relaxed manner. Maybe the long walk through the tall building makes him uncomfortable—past the doormen, next to countless strangers—or maybe it's the opulent decor on this floor, the sixteenth, that intimidates him, and it only just now occurs to Cresspahl that she should wait for the old man on the sidewalk every week and escort him in. But there's no way she can apologize and suggest this, he would implacably refuse the help even though he wants it. *Čeština je těžká.*

Hellos, goodbyes, asking how it's going—all of this has long taken place in the foreign language; the lessons have dissolved into conversations, but the small stock of things they have in common has quickly been exhausted, and when it comes to their mutual friend Mrs. Ferwalter they can only pass on a greeting, not discuss, for instance, the source of her health problems. After that, the conversation has to be restarted using occasions that lead away from personal matters, usually stories from the day's *Times*, and once again there is not only a division into teacher and student but into a Czech Jew and a German daughter of German parents—Mr. Kreslil would, of course, deny this with his implacable politeness, were it ever to be expressed. So, the task is to retell the stories in our own words. It's just that Mr. Kreslil no longer likes hearing the latest news from Prague, ever since the police roundups that swept the country in the fifties now threaten to return, or other acts of cooperation with the USSR, we can't ask him about this part of his life story.

Truman's eighty-fourth birthday doesn't yield much. The street fighting between Parisian students and the police is unclear from where we sit. We've all but forgotten the reports from Cholon, Saigon's Chinese district, as if the war news weren't new every day. The jobless rate for the dark-skinned being more than double the rate for the pink-skinned—that too is a repetition. An ad on the front page announces Wanted: Former Professional Bank Robber to give advice on new film, call Thomas Crown, CIrcle 5-6000, ext. 514. In principle yes. But no.

So let's take the *Times* poll on the protests at Columbia University. It says that fifty-five out of one hundred adults in greater New York blame the students. Even more do in the suburbs, among those over forty, and among the non-college-educated. Fully eighty-three supported the decision to call in the police, and fifty-eight found the degree of force they used to have been absolutely correct. It's a hard article to paraphrase, full of numbers and more numbers and the temptation to duplicate phrases, and here come the first hesitations. They are what spoil the almost entirely correct sentence: there was no breakdown on whether the persons polled were Negro or white, because the polling organization presumed that most were white. "Simply because of the economic factor of having a telephone."

The sentence wasn't exactly prizewinning anyway. The student realized too late that Professor Kreslil can't afford a phone, for economic reasons and also because, in the part of the city where he lives, a phone in the apartment is often a tool for burglars. I'm still making mistakes. *Ještě dělám chyby, pane Kreslil.*

– *To nevadí. Ano, mluvíte poněkud pomalu*: says the old gentleman, for whom politeness to women takes precedence over reproach, and once again he looks at Cresspahl in a charitable if baffled way, as though wanting to put the Czech language into her mouth and brain and yet not understanding how he came to be here in this room with her, or what she wants that language for. And suddenly we're not sure either. He holds his sallow skull still, attentive; he lets nothing show in his blank face; he can't exactly be enjoying how we're trampling around in his language. That's not something you can make up for by repeatedly thanking him for his efforts, or even by bringing him out of the building onto the street. Today it didn't go well.

That was a warning, but this Cresspahl wants to try her luck again. She gives herself the afternoon off, starting that moment on Lexington Avenue— she doesn't even tell Mrs. Lazar she's leaving, she can pretend the absence is for work reasons. There's a Czech film playing at the Baronet, subtitled, not dubbed. She's been studying the language for six months, she wants to take a test.

In the Baronet, on Fifty-Ninth Street, across from Alexander's department store, in one of the three new cinemas on a New York corner persistently written off as dead, they're showing *The Fifth Horseman Is Fear,* "made in ČSSR," it starts at four o'clock, the people behind the counter are not ashamed to take two dollars per ticket, there's a seat free on the aisle in the smoking section so I can leave early if needed, all right, test me.

CARLO PONTI PRESENTS:

In Prague under the German occupation, a guy is dropped off at a Jewish lawyer's apartment. He's wounded and the Germans mustn't find him. Dr. Braun arrives in the attic room of a dusty, run-down apartment building, the prognosis is not good, he probably won't make it. He not only has this wounded man to worry about now, he also works in the bare (stripped bare) office of the Department of Confiscation of Jewish Property, where he has to say into the phone: *Ano.* Yes. Bravely, reliably, hopelessly. Everything drains out of his face as he listens to the other end of the line. Mrs. Cresspahl can occasionally understand clearly the specific things he says, but she doesn't always grasp the whole, so her gaze keeps slipping down to the annoyingly helpful subtitles. Now she's distracted by the differences between the original and the translation. Braun goes looking around the city for a place that'll take in the wounded man. The screen keeps showing furniture trucks with German on them: KIRCHENBERGER—why does the audience eventually laugh at that? Then there's the bar, the Desperation Bar, copious drinking in party clothes and dancing to pathetic jazz, probably drug use. There are Jews there too but they can't help. One shot begins with ordinary-looking shower nozzles that suddenly transport the audience to the ones in Auschwitz, the ones that the gas came out of. These ones are for water after all, because when the Nazi army operates a brothel with Jewish women it wants them clean first. They haven't been whores for long, they used to be the daughters of the middle class, the bon ton of Prague. The alternative is being sent to the gas. Another alternative is a quick slit to an artery, Dr. Braun sees someone there bent over a dead woman. Is it not just the wounded man in hiding, does he want to buy morphine for other reasons? Missed that. The crosscutting with the scenes of present-day Prague, what are they supposed to remind us of? of how locals acted under the Nazis? of forgetting? Some things stick in the mind, when there's no dialogue to hinder them: the boy on the bicycle in the suburban street who sees the Germans' car outside the door of his house. The start of the sequence at a similar point, the expectation set up for the audience and then disappointed. But is that in the original dialogue? that it's the lawyer suddenly breaking off his phone call which brings the police to search the building on the second day of the story? Does Mr. Fanta really say in the nightclub scene: "I did it, it was my duty"? Groveling Mr. Fanta with his stack of *Schulungsbrief* Nazi magazines. The caretaker protecting her bunny rabbit—of course she's hard of hearing too. The music teacher talking to the pictures on her wall, she's not very plausible. A butcher's wife who never stops humming. And then there's an ambiguous hero on the stairs with a dark, decisive look in his eye. If the German police in Prague can trace an anonymous call to a specific building, why can't they tell which apartment it's from? On the second morning, the wounded man has been removed from the attic room, by whom? At the end of the movie, there is talk of an approaching "confrontation." The subtitle says "a little talk." The long circular staircase, the tenants filing past looking at the corpse. So is the wounded man still hidden in the attic, just somewhere else, and Dr. Braun is trying to distract the police from this possibility by killing himself? Done. The End. *Konec.*

Test failed.

Cresspahl is sitting in the bar at the Hotel Marseilles, a regular for years, a member of the Mediterranean Swimming Club, a lady Mr. McIntyre will serve even without a companion. A conversation about the weather, so cloudy! in May!, wouldn't bother him a bit. But this Mrs. Cresspahl is sitting there dazed, as if something incomprehensible has happened to her, customers like that you just leave alone. And turn on the six o'clock news.

NBC's *Sixth Hour News* shows refugees in a storeroom. The sounds of gunfire. Stretchers being hauled down a hospital corridor. The bundles on them no longer look human. "The exact number of casualties is not known, since doctors are unable to reach most of them." Now Cresspahl puts down her glass, more sensitive than she usually is, and goes straight home, which she'd been trying to avoid doing.

She gets a glimpse of her second defeat when she's still on Ninety-Seventh Street, during the few steps it takes to get to overcast Riverside Drive. "The fifth horseman is fear"—what is that supposed to mean. The fifth knight, the fifth mounted soldier, fear. Aren't there four, for carriages, with the fifth coachman running alongside them? The declaration sounds like something from the people who wrote under the name of Shakespeare, but she doesn't recognize the quote. She had to buy her English from a translation school; there wasn't money for a university. But she's read her Shakespeare anyway, all twelve volumes! She may not have read her Bacon as well, or Longfellow, she doesn't even have him on her bookshelf. It's not good to be an autodidact, it always comes out eventually. She doesn't push the apartment door shut, she leaves her fate to chance, she goes straight to the books. Here's the *Oxford Dictionary of Quotations,* seventh rev. ed., 1959. Under "Horseman": one single entry, Calverley's ode to tobacco. Under "Fear," almost two columns, a gaze passing swiftly over them is held up not even the third time through, there's nothing to do with horseback riders or fifths. She is so confused that she swallows her pride and looks under that too. Nothing.

She's been living in New York City since 1961. There they are showing a Czech film titled *The Fifth Horseman Is Fear,* a phrase that is apparently so familiar in English, in American English, that Oxford's book of quotations doesn't even need to include it. Everyone knows it, except Cresspahl. She's not only failed in Czech, she's flunked English too.

Then out from the elevator comes a child with schoolbooks under her arm. She closes the door behind her, slightly surprised, and says, in her unthinking, unhesitatingly fluent English: Hey, Gesine! How was the movie?

May 10, 1968 Friday

The East German government never interferes in other countries' domestic affairs, and tomorrow it's sending a special train to Bonn on its German Reich Railway, with eight hundred seats for West Berliners wanting to protest the German Emergency Acts—round trips for foreigners costing less than standard rates. It never interferes in the internal affairs of independent states, and it publishes in the newspaper that American and West German troops are entering Czechoslovakia to take part in a war film; the embassy on Schönhauser Allee immediately denies the report, but there it was in black and white in the *Berliner Zeitung.* Now, true, it was only "informed sources" who'd heard the GDR's custodian tell his Soviet friends that this act of West German aggression demands a strengthening of the Warsaw Pact forces on the western border of Czechoslovakia. With East Germans among these new troops. Still, you can lead a horse to water but you can't make him interfere in it.

Meanwhile, for the twenty-third-annual time, the Communists in Prague are thanking the Red Army for liberating them from the Germans and once again promising friendship to the Soviet Union. Those who liberated the western part of Czechoslovakia got their wreath too, placed on the site of the destroyed monument to American soldiers in Pilsen. Plzeň. And the Soviet troop movements along the Czechoslovakian borders in Poland and East Germany, these really are supposed to be just training exercises. If you ask the Foreign Office in London, reports that they are meant to bring pressure on Czechoslovakia are "hard to believe."

The military commander of the town of Jerichow, K. A. Pontiy, had given his Jerichowers a new cemetery, and now he wanted one for his army.

Cresspahl told his commandant that he hoped none of his subordinates ever died under his command.

– A mighty race, the Russians!: Pontiy confirmed in all seriousness. Maybe that wasn't enough of a reward for the German's compliment, so he gave him a nod too, overly exaggerated as if to a child.

Cresspahl didn't respond further for now, considering this another one of Pontiy's passing whims. Admittedly he'd actually had a large flag with hammer and sickle flown on the post-office tower just because an officer was monitoring the telephone exchange there, but he'd forbidden the removal of the "German Reichspost" sign.

Pontiy cleared his throat slightly. His throat certainly wasn't sore. Maybe it was involuntary.

It was early one evening toward the end of July. Cresspahl should have been out in the fields checking the day's haul from his band of cripples, he had paperwork to do in Town Hall—and he was being ordered to take some time off, sitting down. Pontiy's office with the south-facing windows was dry and cool now. Cresspahl could see his own roof over the edge of the green fence, and one of the walnut trees too, its crown swaying a little, even though there was no wind. The chimney was dramatically lit by the western sun, its smoke turning slightly yellow as it emerged from the weathered bricks. The air was so thickly laden with a sweet flavor that it couldn't be coming from the lindens alone. Had the villa's garden ever smelled of jasmine? Had Hilde Paepcke planted jasmine here? It wasn't the golden rain. Now the top of the walnut tree twitched again. Like a cat's sitting in it.

What K. A. Pontiy wanted wasn't some ordinary cemetery but a field of honor! But he was past being able to scare his German, who shifted his shoulders a little, as if collecting his thoughts from somewhere else. – And put it where? he asked, not paying extremely close attention but coming across as obedient enough.

The Red Army, as represented by this commandant, had been thinking of Market Square.

During his first years in Jerichow, Cresspahl had been constantly struck by how big the market square was in this small town. And its spacious expanse, between the colorfully gabled buildings, had been crowded and lively even as late in the day as now. At harvest time the farm wagons would start coming in starting in the morning, to be weighed on the town scales; the waiting drivers got water for their horses from the town pump, stood talking to one another, hired a boy to watch the horses and popped off for a glass at Peter Wulff's pub. There were carriages on the square too, one- and two-horse hackneys and landaus for the ladies of the nobility when they came calling on the mayor's or pastor's wife. Once the wheat and turnips were unloaded, the carts would take a wide loop through Papenbrock's yard onto narrow Station Street, where the drivers talked to the horses since the wheels of the now-empty carts were clattering louder, and they'd reappear on the other side of the square. The fishermen's guild parked their little retail truck in the southwest corner, over the objections of Emma Senkpiel's egg shop; that was where Papenbrock liked to take what he called offense. The Lübeck Court porter would come from the midday train with his luggage cart, tired summer tourists behind him like sheep. There had been a time when a car had stood outside practically every other building on the square, even if no one in the building, or in Jerichow, owned it. When Swenson, the owner of the transportation company, was feeling lazy he would park his bus on the square overnight, where it would be seen. The east side of Market Square was too nice for shops, that was the one on the postcards, along with St. Peter's Church. Not at this time of day, but in an hour, the nobility's carriages would be pulling up outside the Lübeck Court, if the men were avoiding Schwerin or arguing with the innkeepers in Schönberg. Plenty of room on Market Square, no doubt about that. When the air force had come marching into town, you could see it would have been big enough for drills. Now it was empty, and all that space not being put to any reasonable use had an almost hypnotic effect, a person got strange ideas just from standing there.

– *Khoroshó*: the commandant said cheerfully, agreeing. It wasn't clear whether he was pleased with the once and future economic bustle of Jerichow, or the available space. Cresspahl thought he'd led this Russian away from his idea, but in fact it had him firmly in its grip. Pontiy was looking forward to putting the surveying tripod to use again, having the middle of the square measured, and possibly regretting that the dignity of his office would prevent him from marching around alongside it with the compass. So, the obelisk in the middle—marble, with a red star on top and tablets on all four sides.

Cresspahl reluctantly emerged from his dreamy recollections. Shouldn't the dead be amongst themselves, undisturbed by the gaze of foreign eyes?

On the contrary, every foreign eye only adds to the dignity and honor of the Red Army! Pontiy said it to be nice, to explain. He did not yet suspect what Cresspahl would be forced to tell him; for him this was still an enjoyable conversation, because it was going somewhere practical.

Cresspahl suggested the square outside the train station. They could remove the monument to the victors of the 1870–71 Franco-Prussian War while they were at it, and of course no one would be putting up any monuments to this war. Not as big a space as Market Square, obviously, but enough for a dozen graves. Cresspahl was in command of his thoughts again by this point, and added: Everyone in Jerichow has to go to the station sometimes, and would thus have to walk past the heroes' memorial.

This was one of the rare occasions that Pontiy did not let out a sigh. He had to give vent to his distress, and he was still rubbing his hand over his sweating bald head. Clearly he was very deeply committed to someone. It was also possible that he had not yet been notified of the official Red Army policy toward the dead of the Franco-Prussian War.

Cresspahl put forward a number of other sites—the Rifle Club grounds, a section in the new Main Cemetery, a gentle rise along the Rande country road with a view of the sea. Pontiy patiently rejected them all. Then they both realized that Cresspahl wanted to hide the dead away, Pontiy to put them on display. The question was who had more power.

Cresspahl had worked out that the Red Army dead would have to be brought in from the countryside around Jerichow, if there were to be enough of them to give their place of rest the necessary dignity. Cresspahl mentioned the cemeteries used by the nobility, and by the villages.

Now he'd made Pontiy mad, but good. He'd turned redder in the face, and his voice came from farther forward in his throat. He brought up things like craftiness, deceit. Again and again he had tried to trust this mayor of his and now he wanted single graves for *geroyam Krasnoy Armii* on the side of the road even! That was how dead Fascists were buried in Soviet Union, by stick with helmet on, like dogs!

Cresspahl gave the Russian credit for trying to convince him, not simply issuing orders. He didn't want their discussion to get to the point where Pontiy would leap to his feet, put his cap on his head, and start shouting— not in this breezeless heat. He asked when the first burial was to take place.

Pontiy ordered him, in a voice monotone with contempt, to have four workmen and a stonemason report to Market Square on the morning after next. Five would be better, since after all the cobblestones would have to be taken up before the digging could start. None of them should be forced laborers, forced to pay for their Nazi connections with more menial tasks— they should be real, genuine, honest workers.

Cresspahl thought about Pontiy's order to bring in the harvest and said nothing more. He would have to ask women to help with the burying, since there weren't any workmen who fit Pontiy's criteria; he would have to drop by Kliefoth's this very evening, and go with him to see Alwin Mecklenburg Gravestones & Ornamental Masonry (now run by his widow), and tell them how to go about building an obelisk . . . but he gave up. He'd wanted to keep this Russian from being tripped up by local customs, he'd tried often enough to give him a sense of the area he now commanded, but tonight he couldn't do it anymore. And it wasn't just weariness.

Pontiy had him read through a well-worn mimeographed copy of a memo. The memorial tablets for soldiers must be made of granite, those for officers of marble. Inscriptions in enamel, crimson red. The rear echelon had evidently caught up to their K. A. Pontiy.

The commandant felt watched, and knew that reaching for the vodka that night would not be taken amiss. The two men had often shared a wordless understanding of one another. This time Pontiy was mistaken. He ascribed to Cresspahl a hostility toward the Red Army. He invited neither the mayor nor the townspeople to take part in the ceremony.

It was a young man who was driven down Town Street in an open coffin, nineteen years old. He had died on the Rammin estate, no word as to how. His face had a vague, uncertain look above the collar of his uniform. He looked like he'd stumbled upon some secret, too much for his young brow, his totally inexperienced lips. Gesine had accidentally caught sight of him outside the commandant's villa.

When five people dig a hole on Market Square in Jerichow early in the morning, and two officers with eight men are standing there watching, a square of that size can seem pretty empty.

May 11, 1968 Saturday

From the life of D. E., aka Professor Erichson. In response to questions from Marie.

He resists giving these responses; he is almost ashamed, were he capable of it. The thing is that he considers his life an ordinary one, following the rules, a standard product die-stamped in overlapping punches by the machine known as Society. He has no stories. But he can't just sit here with us, the morning sun coming through the windows, playing at family life, and refuse to give information to a member of that family—a fact he recognizes with pained looks from under his sparse eyebrows, staring into the bowl of his pipe as if down into an abyss. At least it's only the Cresspahl child who wants a sample, the other Cresspahl has raised her newspaper in front of her face. She's reading. She's hiding her secret pleasure at the trap our crafty old fox has been caught in. Don't laugh, don't laugh.

As a child D. E. had to wear his hair in a side part.

It's not much, but Marie kneels on her chair and grabs him by the hair and divides the gray mass into a thick cloud and a tiny little narrow strip over one ear. Like that? He nods, unhappily. They both shoot quick looks at the edge of the newspaper at the other end of the table, but it hasn't moved an inch.

Here we have a child from Mecklenburg just coming into view and already he's started almost everything differently from how we did.

Born in 1928, grew up in Wendisch Burg. Yes, Wendisch Burg, who doesn't know where that is? Near Jerichow. People nod too hastily and start looking around the area near Genthin, west of Berlin, not up by the Baltic near Lübeck. Never one of Mecklenburg's fore-cities, but on the other hand not under the thumbs of the Dukes of Strelitz or other nobility— Wendisch Burg was part of the Hanseatic League from the beginning. Express trains used to stop there through the end of the war!

From your life, D. E. You can't put us off with the railway.

Northeast of Wendisch Burg the railway had torn up the countryside to make a switching yard for the freight-train connections with other countries. The cars with ore for the war from Sweden arrived to the very end and were routed west, around Berlin. International arrivals came in on the Königsberg–Stettin line, too—later it was booty from Poland and the northern Soviet Union as well as prisoners for the camps near Berlin. A high narrow bridge with a narrow walkway spanned the wide field crisscrossed with tracks. A boy used to stand on it, losing himself in the heavy clouds of coal smoke, the panting of the Doppler effect coming up from under the bridge. A lively child, his head rather thin, not easy to get a handle on. His hair in a part (blond). Light-colored sailor suit (Bleyle), dark-brown knee socks. With a special talent for squinting in family photos.

Son of a barber, scion of the established firm of Erichson, Quality Hair Salon for Gentlemen and Ladies, on Old Street in Wendisch Burg, next to the Three Ravens inn. (On Adolf-Hitler-Street.) The child didn't want to sweep up the hair on the green linoleum floor after he'd finished his homework, not even once it became material essential to the war effort— that's what a younger sister is for. Erichson senior wanted to be in charge of more than just one family and pushed to be taken into the army right away, in 1939; in 1940 they took him. The boy didn't like being told what to do. Would go up onto his railway bridge, or down to Bottom Lake.

Mother from the country, distantly related to the fisherman-Babendererdes in Wendisch Burg. They wanted to keep the child from any middle-class pretensions above his station, they cut their own hair, and the boy's too, so that Ol' Erichson could huff and puff over the blemish on his professional reputation. First escape from home, from the snooty town house: to the thatched lakeside cottages. Even as an adult D. E. is grateful to his relatives who taught him not to look down his nose at them just because he was forced to go to school; he studied his Latin by day and went fishing with them by night. Learned how to boil tar. How to coat a rowboat with the hot acrid tar. Sadness over a pike found floating in the reeds, white belly up. Freeing a finch from the fish traps left on shore to dry. A bucket of eels tipping over. Rowing into a west wind in the rain, working. But the fishermen also posed one another by the shore in the summer to have their picture taken, and the male children were given the grown-ups' brown caps, the SA caps, with the swastika, maybe because this band of robbers was going to break the shackles of high-interest loans. It was here that D. E. achieved his best squint, under the visor of the cap hanging down over his thirteen-year-old ears. The war with the Soviet Union had started already.

And the famous love affairs, D. E.?

First things first, his sister, five years younger. Heike would come with when he went ice skating with the fisher children. Hand in hand with a girl of eleven, yes, but they didn't say anything and now she's married to the head of the Wendisch Burg taxi cooperative. Nothing more than that? That was it.

But there was nothing wrong with D. E.'s eyes, and his father's fondest wish was for him to be trained in one of the Nazi Ordensburgs, as one of the Austrian's future generals or executioners. Mrs. Erichson mislaid the honorable invitation and the boy had no choice but to serve in the naval Hitler Youth, nothing more. There he learned how to row in a crew; he'd rather have been alone in his sailing canoe. That summer an H-Jolle dinghy was known to cross the two lakes, when not docked at the sluice. I never knew the Niebuhrs, Marie—never spoke a word with them. The troop leader received a report: Squad Leader Erichson seen handing out food at the Sedenbohms' (mixed marriage, no privileges, yellow stars).

Photos torn up, cut to pieces, burned. One may have been kept, in a drawer near the bottom of a small dresser in Fürstenberg. It showed the winter of 1943 and four young people standing in it, around sixteen years old, in a field north of Oranienburg with a thin copse of pine trees behind them, in the fog, in the dirty snow. Three were boys, dressed in the Air

Defense Hitler Youth uniform, blue gray. They didn't have the large swastika armband on their arms, as required by regulations, but they did have them in their breast pockets, in case crazy superiors turned up. All three have managed to get hold of air force belt buckles, now that as soldiers they are so superior to the regular Hitler Youth, and they wear the shirts of their uniforms belted over their pants, like how soldiers wear their tunics, not tucked in like children do. The fourth young person in the picture was a girl. Maybe it was she who saved the photo.

D. E., famous for his string of brilliant love affairs. It was only a week before the picture was taken that the searchlight battery had had to assemble behind a village tavern to receive instruction from their leader, a lieutenant, Iron Cross 2nd Class, suspected of sexual intercourse with a Polish forced laborer on the estate. He'd ordered the boys to "clean themselves" immediately after every such act, and this was how D. E. first heard of such diseases. He'd never gotten further than shy or overly bold letters sent via the air force postal service, Berlin office.

It certainly wasn't his steelworks he was guarding, he'd realized that much.

It's just that he'd only worked hard at two subjects in school, and he attracted attention in the antiaircraft course with his knowledge of the speed of sound at various temperatures and how machines function. He was withdrawn from his searchlight course and served during the Battle of Berlin as a flight observer at an antiaircraft telescope. Despite such perks, they hadn't forgotten the Sedenbohm affair; he was neither popular nor envied. "People from the capital of the Duchy walk like they've got a stick up their ass" (alluding to his birthplace, Neustrelitz). He sometimes forgot who he was working for—the B-24 Liberators floated in the viewfinder close enough to touch, narrow wings, thick bodies, large oval stabilizers on the tailplane, perfect machines. It had turned out that his eyes were more useful than other people's. The other people "helping" the air force were groggy when roused from sleep, despite the dim red light; he had good night vision and was quickly made "senior helper." He'd already learned how to use an RRH acoustic tracking device when he was moved to the latest "Fu-MG" short-range tracking device that Telefunken had built, the 41 T. They'd never heard the word *radar*. This device located enemy bombers from almost fifteen miles away and automatically relayed the changing altitudes to the artillery and missile launchers via a directional device—the guns adjusted with violent lurches as though operated by invisible men. The machine did the killing, there was no need to touch it. But there were some officers who had tried to kill Hitler, and since then the high-power battery had been fenced in, barricaded off, a prison camp. No matter how many men and airplanes they blasted into tiny pieces, they came down onto the field like hot hard rain. After all, Berlin was burning. In January 1945 they exchanged his red antiaircraft gunner's collar tabs for black ones and ordered him to the Oder; on the way there, he deserted.

For that girl from Fürstenberg? Sure, Marie. It's just that Ol' Erichson had gone missing back in February 1942, his mother was all alone with his sister in Wendisch Burg. He had to get there before Sokolovsky was done.

The conqueror of Berlin? Who died yesterday? That's right. General Sokolovsky, commander of the Soviet armed forces in East Germany, marshal of the Soviet Union, Hero of the Soviet Union, ran the Berlin blockade. 1897–1968. The one who thought Americans could never win in Vietnam except with atomic bombs, which would be World War III.

The deserter waited in a forest ranger's home on one of the farms by Top Lake, four miles from Wendisch Burg. The house was full of strangers. An SS tank unit was making the area unsafe, looting the last food supplies, seizing the men of fighting age. D. E. spent a lot of time up in trees there. Then, when the first Russians came to look around, in their low-slung horse-drawn carts, D. E. had to keep watch, not hide. He sat on the edge of a desk by the window and watched the road running past the woods to Wendisch Burg. As soon as he saw anyone from the Red Army he had to run through the house and warn the women so that they could escape out the back doors into the dense underbrush. He didn't continuously stare at the road, he relied on his ears too. There was a lot of luggage lying around the place, from people who had hanged themselves in the woods, and in one suitcase D. E. found a reprint of Albert Einstein's remarks in the *Proceedings of the Prussian Academy of Sciences*, 1915: Jewish physics. He read them slower than he had ever read anything in his life, while listening for hoofbeats or rattling carts. His fifth time through, he had to admit that he would never truly understand this theory of general relativity, although he could memorize it. His thought had run up against a solid wall, it was downright painful. Sometimes his efforts at understanding unexpectedly turned into a sense of flying, of effortless soaring motion. Then the autopilot crashed without any clear explanation of why. D. E. was not yet eighteen years old, and was forced to admit that there was truly a limit beyond which his thoughts could not go. That this would be his life. Talented, if you ask him, but no genius. In mid-May the rumor crossed the lake that the Red Army was going to reopen Wendisch Burg High School, with Sedenbohm as principal, and D. E. set out. And so he missed his sister, who had run away to join him.

– When you were keeping a lookout from the corner of the desk in the forest, that was because of the rapes? Marie asks. She is no longer kneeling next to D. E., she has leaned back away from him. They can watch each other as if in a contest, neither one yielding, neither one relenting. The older of the two nods glumly, now he'd probably have welcomed some assistance from the elder Cresspahl. She folds her paper, lays it aside, and now she too watches him, slightly curious. If you want to be part of our family let's see how you do at answering children's questions, D. E.
– It was: D. E. says calmly: because of the rapes.
– That was your job there.
– And in return I was given food and lodging.
– And the forestry people had relatives in Fürstenberg, and one of them was a girl who had gone into hiding in the woods near Wendisch Burg?
– Who brought up the subject of my affairs? Anyway it was hers too!
– And who did that one end up marrying?
– A surgeon in Hamburg, if you want to know.
– That was a risky trip for her if the Russians were already in Fürstenberg.
– She was shrewd for seventeen. She made it through in one piece.
– And: Marie says, as dismissively as him: did you take an oath to Hitler?
– Three times.
– Is it right to call him "the Austrian" so much, the way a certain lady of our acquaintance does?
– It is right, that's where he was from. The lady in question is probably also referring to the fact that many of his helpers came from there. She would also no doubt have preferred history to take a different course, branching off at, say, the North German Confederation, 1866–70.

– Don't bother trying, D. E. You won't trip her up. She won't fall into your trap.

– *Which I undertook solely to keep New York City clean.*

– And is she wrong?

– It wasn't an Austrian brand of insanity, if I'm to believe my doctors.

– What did you do with your steel helmet?

– Buried it.

– And when other people, farmers, found it plowing—

– the skeleton was missing.

– And your sister?

– Died in May 1945.

– How old?

– The same age as Gesine in July 1945.

– And you're not going to tell me any more than that?

– The rest, *my dear Mary*, I will hold back.

– And were there really Red Army cemeteries on market squares in Mecklenburg?

– Not in Wendisch Burg. In other places there'd be an obelisk with a red star on it, lit up at night.

– D. E.!

– The public utilities connected it by an underground cable to the street lighting.

– So, what'll we do now?

Finally D. E. can assume his other role: protector, initiator, maker of plans. – We could go to the amusement park in Palisades Park; but Marie won't spend a whole Saturday on such childish things, even if he's in the mood to. Any ideas in the paper? The *Times* has a picture of the Y Bridge in Saigon, taken from above, so that the street fighting can only be guessed at; that recalls our Triboro Bridge on the other side of Manhattan? Neither of them wants to go there. A trip to Boston is rejected as well; we've missed the train to Philadelphia; finally we decided on a trip to the Atlantic, Rockaway Beach. But not the way D. E. thinks. – On the subway! Marie says. – On the subway! Because that way his car will stay parked outside our building, that way he can't drop us off afterward on his way home, that way she has him for the rest of the evening, maybe even tomorrow.

May 12, 1968 Sunday
"QUOTATION OF THE DAY: 'We tried to go down one street three times and so far we've had 5 killed and 17 wounded in my company. I don't care whose birthday it is, we're going back to clean them out.' —S. Sgt. Herman Strader in Saigon, where the 2,512th birthday of Buddha was celebrated yesterday."
© The New York Times

"AIRLINES AND LAW ENFORCEMENT AGENCIES FOUND UNABLE TO COPE WITH FLOURISHING CRIME AT KENNEDY
By Charles Grutzner

The flood of recent thefts, including diamonds, blue-chip stocks, palladium and other high-value cargo, at Kennedy International Airport has focused attention on the activities of organized criminals at the city's airports.

One of the cases brought the sentencing last week in Federal Court of the nephew of the reputed Mafia boss, Joseph Colombo, to two and a half years in prison as a conspirator in the cashing of $407,000 in American Express travelers checks stolen at Kennedy Airport.

Twenty-three men and two women have been indicted, and all but four have pleaded guilty or have been convicted of transporting and passing the travelers, checks, which were stolen on Aug. 30, 1966. In all that time, however, no one has been arrested or indicted for the actual theft.

United States Attorney Robert M. Morgenthau has called the theft and disposal of the checks here and in Las Vegas, Dallas, Baltimore, Puerto Rico, the Virgin Islands and elsewhere the work of a gang familiar with air cargo handling at the airport.

The American Express case and the other thefts have raised serious questions about the ability of existing law agencies at the airports and the airlines' private guards to provide adequate protection of high-value cargo.

In 90 reported thefts at Kennedy Airport last year, the loot amounted to $2.2-million, two and a half times the 1966 total and nearly 50 times that of five years ago. The Port of New York Authority, which compiled the figures, did not include thefts of items valued at less than $1,000, nor did it include the $2.5-million in non-negotiable securities stolen from Trans World Airlines last Aug. 10.

Among those sent to prison in the American Express case, besides

Colombo's 34-year-old nephew, Maurice Savino, was Vincent (Jimmy Jones) Potenza, 40, who has been listed by the Federal Bureau of Investigation as a member of the Mafia 'family' headed by Carmine (Mr. Gribs) Tramunti, reputed successor to the late Thomas (Three-Finger Brown) Luchese.

Potenza and Americo Spagnuolo, who bought the stolen checks at 25 cents on the dollar and sold them for twice that to the passers, pleaded guilty to conspiracy and took maximum prison terms rather than identify the actual thieves.

One prospective Government witness, John Anthony Panarello, an ex-convict named in the indictment as a co-conspirator but not as a defendant, has been silenced by gangland guns. His body, with two bullets through his head, was found in a roadside ditch in the Catskills as his rented car burned nearby...

An official expression of concern over underworld influence at Kennedy came from S.I.C. Chairman Lane during the questioning of the hearing of Alvin C. Schweizer, regional director of Air Cargo, Inc., a corporation set up jointly by the airlines to hire trucking companies.

Mr. Schweizer had told of threats of labor troubles allegedly made by Harry Davidoff, an officer of Teamster Local 295, against National Airlines and Northwest Airlines when they were considering changing trucking companies.

BURGLAR AND EXTORTIONIST

Referring to Davidoff, a convicted burglar, extortionist and bookmaker, Mr. Lane asked Mr. Schweizer: 'It seems to me that one man could tie up the whole air freight industry in New York if he has that much control over the union—is that right?'

'Yes, sir, very definitely,' replied the witness. 'Because the drivers of the catering trucks and refueling trucks and the food processors who come onto the airport with food for the flights are either teamsters or other drivers [who] would respect any informational picket line that Local 295 or any other organization might establish.'

There was testimony also that a negotiator for the Metropolitan Import Truckmen's Association had threatened American Airlines with a shutdown of the airport if it hired a 'non-associated' trucker. Mr. Lane also charged that racketeers held key positions in both the union and the trade association.

Among underworld names that came up at the airport hearings were those of convicted labor racketeer John (Johnny Dio) Dioguardi and Antonio (Tony Ducks) Corallo, identified by law enforcement agencies as members of the Tramunti Mafia 'family'; Anthony DiLorenzo, an ex-convict described by authorities as an associate of the Vito Genovese 'family,' and John Massiello, a reputed Genovese Mafioso and convicted smuggler.

DiLorenzo, a convicted car thief, was on the payroll of the Metropolitan Import Trucking Association for $25,000 a year as a labor consultant. Massiello was also on the same payroll as a labor consultant.

Joseph Curcio, a convicted labor racketeer and strong-arm 'enforcer' who once shared the same cell in Atlanta Federal Penitentiary with Joseph M. Valachi, the Mafia member who later testified against the crime organization, was on the payroll of a trucking company as a salesman. The company's president admitted during the S.I.C. hearings that Curcio had never brought in any business.

Most of the underworld influence uncovered in the air freight industry has been at the 4,900-acre Kennedy Airport, which is as big as all of Manhattan south of 42nd Street. The airport is crowded with cargo buildings and heaps of unguarded freight are piled even on the aprons of the flying field. More than 40,000 people work on the airport...

FORGED PAPERS USED

Two men drove a panel truck on Feb. 27 into the cargo area of KLM Royal Dutch Airlines, showed forged papers marked with what resembled a United States Customs seal, loaded the $508,000 shipment of the rare metal palladium from the Soviet Union, smiled at a guard, and drove away. The airline was unaware it had been robbed until five hours later when representatives of the real consignee arrived in an armored truck to claim the shipment.

Port Authority police contend that the robbery might have been prevented if KLM, which had been robbed three times in the last two years, had notified them when the men in the panel truck picked up the metal. Lieut. John Lefsen, in charge of the authority's cargo squad, said:

'If we'd been called in to guard the loading of the shipment, we'd have known right away there was something wrong. Engelhard [the consignee] always uses an armored truck and this was just an old, battered green truck with floorboards missing.'

According to authorities, the thieves had known the flight numbers of the precious cargo, which had arrived in two shipments, and the exact number of items in each."
© The New York Times

"HAPPY MOTHER'S DAY / To Sylvia, the best mother in the world, from her children Ellen, Peter, Frank, and Amy."
(Public Notices and Commercial Notices.)

May 13, 1968 Monday
In the morning the park was so stuffed with gray light that the year seemed already to be tapering off into winter.

A senior member of the Institute of International Politics and Economics in Prague writes in a journal published by Columbia University in New York about the freedom Socialist nations have to make political decisions on the basis of their own needs, too, so why might that not include working together with capitalist nations. But the article was written before the Moscow Conference, and before the Soviet tanks entered Poland.

In Paris, on the other hand, the workers understand what the students are saying and want to help them oppose the government, by holding a general strike for one day and one night.

Employee Cresspahl is scheduled to learn something this morning, something from one of de Rosny's smaller drawers, and she obediently shows up to work in the kind of dress that a distant friend of the family might wear to a funeral. For the others at the meeting, though, it is a happy occasion—an annual stockholders' meeting of an allied company—and this time she is going to experience it up close, not see it in a movie, or guess how it is from the *Financial Times*. So that she knows how it's done. As if she would ever be allowed to take part in one herself someday.

– I'm only supposed to be managing an account for Prague: she told de Rosny over the phone. He could hear her embarrassment and resistance, but once again the boss was feeling like a benefactor and wanted to give her the gift of this experience. He started small too, you know.

The stockholders are standing in chummy groups in a windowless corridor on the twenty-eighth floor, chatting away, all in agreement that they'd as it were showed up for a dull gathering and were looking forward not to it but to when it was over. There is one man standing alone, with his back to the wall, wiry, gaze aimed inward as though memorizing something but distracted by keeping an ear out for the starting gun. Like before a gallery opening. It looks more like a class reunion around the CEO, a giant Viking who holds his blocky skull still, slightly tilted to one side, as though he were only listening, thinking about nothing but the boyish hairstyle he is reshaping with one hand, but it's precisely he who attracts a happy crowd and greetings cried from across the hall that he answers with short, salty teasing. Employee Cresspahl is supposed to get so close to this man that he'll shake her hand, but she keeps ending up at cold shoulders, blind looks. She retreats into one of the telephone booths furnished in fine wood and dials the numbers that spell NERVOUS on the dial. – The time is ten oh seven: a voice in the telephone says. But Cresspahl's assignment was to introduce herself here as a representative of the bank. Which isn't the truth, heavens above—a male executive is delegated to do that. It's just that she should secretly think: she's the host here.

For a company that buys and processes and wraps up and resells information, the meeting room is quite small. They want to make do with five chairs on the platform, only two microphones at the lectern to the left, the committee's table could hardly take a heavy turnover, and the rest of the room is full of ordinary metal folding chairs, not many. Clearly this is a frugal company. With its documents in hand Mrs. Cresspahl withdraws to a place near the back wall—that gives her the salaried-professional air she was trying to avoid, and a waiter bends down next to her holding a tray of coffee cups. She can hear the CEO talking in the corridor, relaxed, lingering over the secondary stresses of the words: How can you stand it, to have them keep taking blood out of you, they don't know what they're doing. (This to an executive who doesn't conceal his disease, he uses it.) – There is no. Way. I'll be taking questions: he says, and maybe this is a running joke because the announcement is met with laughter. Then the board enters the room, with the acting president in front, and he really and truly looks at every single person along the wall as if they'd drawn him into the room with their dutifulness. He is about to nod, and again he notices Cresspahl. But this time she can't escape out into the hall, she's trapped between the hard-lipped resolute matron and heavy, flower-patterned drapes with net curtains, meant to make you forget the view of the back lots that haven't yet been cleared.

On the agenda: Increasing the stock portfolio from three and a half million to five million shares so as to buy new companies. Hiring an accounting firm. Choosing executives for the coming fiscal year. Cresspahl listens hard to the formulaic way of speaking, tries to memorize it, maybe she will, and it's possible she'll celebrate the ritual of legalistic repetitions with more delight than the men at the directors' table, it being her first time. The CEO has now delivered his annual report like a story with more intimate family details than anyone wants to hear, and now he opens the floor to questions. He insists on getting the inquiries he'd said he wouldn't take, until a man in the bank uniform carries a hand microphone on a long cable over to a questioner. It's the anxious man from before, who has mentally rehearsed his scene so thoroughly that now he blows it. Stammering, with wide eyes, and then with words tumbling out on top of one another, he starts in on a complaint about the inadequate exploitation of a tax law that he's discovered and wants to insist on, with a look on his face that is begging for mercy, and the chair of the committee cuts him off, not impatiently, more like someone dismissing a child you can't be mad at. The questioner is referred to the section of the paragraph he'd just challenged, given the address and phone number for Allen, Burns, Elman & Carpenter, the mike has already been taken away from him. Now the unfortunate man stretches and Cresspahl could tell him that the committee is rewinding the tape with his valuable protest on it and erasing it. Now for the vote.

The committee's little men in black wind busily around and between the rows of chairs, distributing forms, to the exhausted questioner too, who'd tried to scare the gathering in the name of justice and honor but is now grateful simply to be permitted to write his name. Cresspahl has attempted an unfamiliar expression, not far from head shaking, and yet the functionary repeats his question: Are you a stockholder? Your name please?

– No: the employee says. – I'm here for the bank! With that she gets a motherly, worrying sidelong look from the matron.

The CEO is not happy with his employers' patience. He talks comfortably to himself, again as if in a family circle, at the dinner table, talking to his kids between courses. – I wish: he says: we at least had the lady here who voted against me in '67, with her five shares. I wish at least she was here today! Then he can finally put down his pencil, which he'd tried to sharpen with a Swiss Army knife in the meantime, and read the results of the vote. He shakes his head, concerned; he puts on a pair of glasses especially to be able to look reproachfully out at the people in the room over them. He says: One lone vote against me, what's that supposed to mean!

The names of the executives and employees present are again read out. The executives are obliged to stand up, the employees are allowed to merely acknowledge their presence with a nod. The disappointed boss has the last word—he has come here full of strength and fighting spirit, almost none of which he's had occasion to use, and now all he has to look forward to is yet another lunch. – So, until next year.

As they file out he waits to catch Employee Cresspahl and asks her her name. He comes across like someone painfully aware of how awkwardly he's behaving, but it simply must be done.

– You were the one vote against me, weren't you? he asks, confidentially, in gleeful anticipation. With his broad back he cuts this lady off from everyone else; only a few searching looks get through the barrier to her.

– No: Cresspahl says, and explains her status under the procedural rules. – I wasn't authorized to cast a vote: she says.

At around four o'clock she makes her report of this little gathering of de Rosny's friends to Mrs. Lazar, and ten minutes later, before de Rosny leaves for the day, she's put through to him. – I'm supposed to say hello to you too! he says, and today the connection is so clean that it's like the boss's squeaky pleased voice is right there in the room. – Apparently you were a knockout! he says. You were a seasoned pro, you're a natural!

Those are the views on human nature in this bank.

May 14, 1968 Tuesday

The new Economic Council of the ČSSR is discussing a plan to make the Czechoslovak crown exchangeable with other world currencies now, not in five years. This would be the first Eastern Bloc currency acceptable on the capitalist market; conflict seems inevitable. The country could then pay its debts or trade deficits with its own money, so it would no longer need loans in dollars, and Mrs. Cresspahl would not have to be transferred away from New York.

Cresspahl sometimes thought about moving away from Jerichow. It was he, not K. A. Pontiy, who would have to go to jail for the illegal acts by means of which he carried out the commandant's orders—from fudged bookkeeping to black-market barter while in office, sometimes to the town's advantage, sometimes not. But he couldn't imagine that Pontiy would forget himself to the point of removing his mayor from office, assuming that it still wasn't enough to get him shot. There wasn't much he needed to bring with him to the West, basically just his child and the Ohlerichs' Hanna, if she wanted to come. But before he left he should at least know where he'd be taking them.

Someone told him. It was a man my father's age but skinny like a boy of eighteen, though his hair was white, and not from the dust of the road; he was standing next to the pump on a Sunday afternoon as early as August 1945, as if he'd appeared out of thin air. He asked Cresspahl's daughter if he might have a little drink of water from the pump. She hadn't encountered such manners in a long time, and she claims she immediately took him for someone from Cresspahl's part of the world. She shook her head and went back into the cool stone house to get him a glass of water. He was standing there in the same place, and while he drank the water he looked at her as if his gaze had to jump off the end of his nose, he was crinkling it so much. For some incomprehensible reason he asked her what time it was, and when Gesine looked up at the sky he sat down on the pump stone, sighing at the aches and pains of age, which were not what he had. He was wearing his watch just above his ankle, he was clever, and he had made it, the whole long way and across the border too. Now she recognized him: Erwin Plath, not so much one of the guests at a funeral in 1938 as one of Cresspahl's wartime secrets. She brought him into Cresspahl's office without anyone seeing them and took off at a run for the fields; she couldn't bring him with her through Jerichow.

This was one of the few times that Cresspahl acted like the man of the house and told Mrs. Abs to serve him dinner in his room—he didn't want to miss even fifteen minutes of a visit like this. Then Gesine was sent for a bottle of Jakob's procurement, and when it was time for her to go to bed

Erwin Plath pulled her back onto a chair, solemnly explaining that he simply had to look at her a little longer. Cresspahl looked quizzically at his child, his eyes lost in a memory, and he didn't send her to bed, or Hanna either. The children looked at the grown-ups enjoying this reunion like children: eager, trusting, enjoying each other's company, continually happy at the prospect of more, and they kept telling each other how it had been. Then Cresspahl came out with his question.

Plath started nodding, but he pulled his lips back from his teeth as if he'd bitten into something rotten. He wasn't living in Lübeck anymore, he'd ended up in Itzehoe. He didn't get into specifics about his move, or about his new line of work along the Stör River, but was happy to do so about the British. Clearly they didn't care as much about how they behaved in occupied territory of their own as they did in places they were about to hand over to their Soviet brothers-in-arms, ideally not with a bad impression of British governance. Was Cresspahl familiar with the barracks in Itzehoe— the Gudewill, the Waldersee, the Gallwitz at Long Peter, the Hanseatic by the cemetery? Cresspahl was. The British were there and there wasn't nearly enough room for them. At the end of May they'd requisitioned the best residential neighborhood in town, the Sude, ninety-five houses, most of them mansions with modern furnishings; they gave the occupants three hours to get out, with nothing but valuables, clothes, and sheets. Now English families with one or two children were in these houses, while the Germans were crammed into every last attic, shed, even basement. And Cresspahl surely knew about Itzehoe's sewer system. That there wasn't one. He did. The Military Government had permitted one sealed room per house where the Germans could store their things; these things soon turned up on the black market, that was how much respect the British showed seals. They were in the Hammonia Hotel on Holzkamp Street, in the old covered cattle market, in both movie theaters; they'd set aside the sports grounds for themselves. A lot of the requisitioned living space was standing empty, but they held on to it anyway. Sude was off-limits to Germans unless they worked there. One morning the mayor walks into his office and sees that his desk is gone, along with all the other furniture—occupation headquarters had come and taken it away. The British went and raided German houses personally, too, taking furniture, pictures, radios, cameras, stamp collections, and other items essential to the war effort, not even bothering to hide behind orders. They drove their jeeps through Itzehoe like maniacs, they didn't care if they killed anybody. One division was called the Desert Rats, they were housed in the Hanseatic barracks, which they called the Richmond Barracks. Desert Rats.

Hanna asked about the net factory, where she had some relatives. Plath knew them, they were still living near the gasworks waiting for it to restart operation, they had no raw materials, they were producing nothing. Hanna thanked him, daunted. She was looking for somewhere else she might live besides Jerichow—now here was another one lost to her.

– Richmond Barracks?: Cresspahl said, confused, but what he was confused by was the behavior of the British.

Plath waved that off, suddenly intent on business. He hadn't come because of the British. Cresspahl had been given some kind of order to form political parties, hadn't he? The British didn't allow such things. But look, the Soviets!

– Yes and no: Cresspahl said, with a not entirely clear conscience. There had been an order from K. A. Pontiy, but he'd lost sight of it. The commandant was demanding a local branch of the Social Democrats, another of the Christian Democratic Union, and a Communist one. Cresspahl couldn't go around like God creating the world now could he? Political parties from scratch in Jerichow!

Now Plath woke the sleepy children up, by saying goodnight to them. He led them into the bedroom like sheep, so sweetly that they hardly noticed, and said something nice to each girl about her hair. When he got back to Cresspahl it was quiet for a long time, and the children fell asleep to gentle rustling sounds. It was the night creatures flying in through the open windows and hitting the globe of the kerosene lamp.

Plath reproached his old Socialist friend that he couldn't leave Jerichow without having a successor, assuming that he was planning to leave.

Cresspahl grumbled something. Maybe it meant that things would probably run better without him.

So, Cresspahl was supposed to set up a party to the commandant's liking. The Communist Party. And this Pontiy would get his next mayor from there.

Cresspahl couldn't even manage a Social Democratic Party.

– The SPD? What about it! Plath said, as if his own party left a bad taste in his mouth. Then it came out that he'd already been scouting around in Jerichow for former members. They'd all snubbed him, and one of them, Peter Wulff, apparently cited the views of none other than Cresspahl himself, who also thought that this parliamentary stuff was full of shit.

– All this shit all over again...: Cresspahl muttered, suddenly confrontational.

Plath had found only one man for the CDU, a guy named Kägebein.

Cresspahl was fine with an outsider doing his work for him. He couldn't repay him, not even with a joke.

At this Plath turned patient, and eager, and started talking indirectly. Cresspahl was reminded of his time in the SPD—the secret agreements reached before the meeting started, the prearranged interruptions or questions of order, until the results of a vote "stood" before even one hand was raised. The results had been little mice. And one battleship. Cresspahl just kept his mouth shut.

Plath ignored the reminder that he'd been Cresspahl's junior back in the artillery barracks in Güstrow. He put it to Cresspahl that the Communists only wanted a Social Democratic Party to exist so they could swallow it up in a coalition later. The stuff about acting in unity with the Communists, 1931, 1935. Erwin Plath had come to make sure that the right people got in on the ground floor with the Communists. Not just refugees hoping for new land, no, local people who wouldn't be accused of opportunism. Communists from the very beginning, but actually secret assets of Social Democracy. Alfred Bienmüller, the Jerichow blacksmith, was prepared to make the sacrifice. Why wouldn't Cresspahl do it?

It was for this that Erwin Plath had slipped over the "green border" near Ratzeburg, and Cresspahl managed to spin out the evening longer with Plath's reminiscences of bygone things and another half bottle of vodka, and he didn't even let his disappointment slip out. But it was there. He thought Plath had come to see him, not for the cause. For a moment he considered whether he could say yes, just for Plath's sake. The next morning he was relieved to discover that Plath had moved on in the night, to a new local branch. For the children, though, the visit had been wonderful, and Hanna Ohlerich asked Cresspahl to write out this friendly Itzehoe man's address for her then and there.

Meanwhile, K. A. Pontiy didn't once ask Cresspahl to become the

Communist Party chairman. His mayor was supposed to create parties for him, not join any. That's how it looked.

Rudé Právo, the party newspaper of the Czech and Slovak Communists, turns to its readers with a questionnaire, more than two-thirds of a page long:

Does the internal democratization of a Communist party provide a sufficient guarantee of democracy?

Should the Communist Party carry out its leadership role by devotedly promoting free progressive socialist development or by ruling over society?

Can you speak of a democracy as being socialist when the leading role is held only by the Communist Party?

Can you imagine that?

May 15, 1968 Wednesday

This morning the subway was even more packed than usual, and at Ninety-Sixth Street a young man kept pushing back against an old man who was trying a bit too desperately to force his way in. – Stop grabbin like that! he said, and he actually managed to get the old man back onto the platform. You could still see him cursing behind the closed door as the train pulled away. The old man tried to hide among those left behind on the platform, white in the face, avoiding all looks; from his accent, he seemed to be a Jew from Eastern Europe.

The East Germans have written a letter to the Czechoslovak Socialist Republic. In it, it says: "The victims of German fascism in Buchenwald, Majdanek and Mauthausen as well as Lidiče are a warning signal that should keep one from illusions about the possibilities of cooperation with German imperialism." Prague Radio felt handicapped by the millions of dead resting behind these names, otherwise one could describe it as downright piquant that the victims of the concentration camps are being called to mind in Berlin, of all places! That was the day before yesterday.

Today we hear from Moscow, again, that Thomas Masaryk, founder of the Czechoslovak Republic, paid an anti-Bolshevist terrorist 200,000 rubles to kill Lenin. In Prague they're wanting to rename a street after Thomas Masaryk.

Mrs. Ferwalter no longer cares about the news from Czechoslovakia. Back in March she already dismissed such matters with a gesture of throwing something away, and since she used both hands, it must have been heavy and dangerous too. Maybe it seemed that way because of the testy, disgusted look of her turned-down lips, even as she smiles. Today she catches us coming out of "her" bakery, and her face is entirely transformed in a happy grimace that's only a little rigid. – Mrs. Cresspahl! she cried. – Marie, my dear Mariechen! she cried, so pressingly did she need to share her happy news with us. She hasn't found another of her long-lost relatives, her husband hasn't been given a raise for his backbreaking job at the shoe store—she has her papers.

She has to tell us about it, we're friends of the family, and besides, we helped her. We would be sitting in the park and discussing the children's progress in school or the price of bread and suddenly she would turn her big friendly bulk to face us and say, with a sly wink: 1776? and we would confirm that that was indeed the year when the states declared their independence. We listened to her recite the amendments to the Constitution, tell us who General Grant was, and how someone becomes president, and she would keep switching to a different topic with every piece of knowledge that came back into her mind. She was often discouraged—an old woman, her brain harrowed with nervous twitching and insomnia, no longer capable of studying—and she let herself be comforted like a child. When we didn't succeed in doing so, she would leave with a protracted handshake, her face averted, walking off sadly and clumsily on the legs that the Germans and Austrians had ruined for her. But she also sometimes started in with concealed glee that broadened her lips into a smile until her whole obese face was kneaded soft with the joy of being an American citizen. Now, as of yesterday, she has been given her second, third, and fourth papers.

She was reluctant to admit her pleasure outright, so as not to jinx it; she mentioned tax benefits. But she could not hide that the prospect of an American passport was like a new protective shell, another bulwark against the past.

We were also supposed to improve her German. It wasn't easy—she may not realize herself whether any given one of her words comes from her stock of Yiddish, Czech, American English, Hebrew, or German; she rarely manages a whole sentence in one language. We have talked her out of "German Federation" to help her learn to believe in the Federal Republic of Germany; we've told her she can't say she has a *Liebelei* with her daughter Rebecca—a "flirtation"—or even a *Liebschaft,* a "love affair," even though these are actually the more precise words for the *Liebe,* or love, she feels for her last-born child. But we have let her get away with using a form of address that belongs in letters, *Meine sehr geehrte Frau Cressepfal,* which she says to express her friendship, and Marie allows herself to be called *Liebe Mariechen,* however much she despises that diminutive; Mrs. Ferwalter still makes mistakes with various other German forms of address. Hopefully the West German embassy won't demand such things.

For when our Mrs. Ferwalter becomes a US citizen she will be allowed to put in a claim for personal compensation from the West Germans; were she an Israeli citizen, as she once wanted to be, the money would bypass her on its way to the state treasury. We've gathered that much, and are reluctant to get into further details with her about offsetting murders with money. The survivor also has to prove that she once lived under German rule; apparently the American certificate of discharge from Mauthausen concentration camp is not sufficient. The corner of Ruthenia where her native village was has ended up now on this side of the border and now on that side, and were she ever to admit Hungarian sovereignty she would be directed to an as yet nonexistent consulate. That's what she says. She won't actually have to go to Park Avenue and say in German where on a map of Slovakia she was picked up. She'll have to write a letter. She came over and asked our advice about who she is. – Am I a *Hausfrau,* a house wife, Mrs. Cresspahl? she said. We agreed, although we know other words that would describe her. She so insisted on honesty that instead of taking the corrected draft of her letter back home, she copied it out at our table, perched uncomfortably on the edge of her chair, knees wide apart, awkwardly bent over the sheet of paper, writing swiftly, interrupted by sudden anxiety attacks. She considered this less fraudulent. If it was fraud, it's one we'd commit again.

Not only is she happy with her citizenship papers, she has already acquired pride in this country. – The government sends out checks all over the place! she says, not forgetting her solemn gratification that the government doesn't have to help *her* out with checks, only those whom God in truth has decreed must be poor: the Jews not deft enough to get by and the Negroes, every one alas doomed to blackness by Providence. And are we supposed to spoil her pleasure by arguing? Are we supposed to abandon her because she's gained citizenship in a country that wants to exterminate another country in Southeast Asia?

There's no choice, she has to tell us about her test after all. In the middle of Ninety-Fifth Street, next to the ominous chicken-wire schoolyard fence, she has to show us how she placed one foot in front of the other when she was finally called up to the front. It seems she tried to hold her head high, and she would deny that her chin trembled. Quaking and dignified she entered the room, unaccompanied, defenseless as a lamb, holding on to herself with two fingers on either side of her dress until her nails pushed through the fabric into her flesh. No, she didn't want it as a present, she wanted to pay for it with pain. Then the educated gentlemen in their dark suits realized that she was just an old Jewish lady, they wouldn't hurt her, and they didn't. She remembers only one question. Who becomes president if Mr. Johnson dies. – Gott ferbitt! she cried, and passed the test.

She has celebrated the occasion by going home in a taxi instead of on the subway. As she tells the story we can picture her, stretching out her arm in a way suggesting more equal rights than she'd had the day before, waiting next to the taxi until the driver reached back and opened the door for her, she's a citizen now isn't she? Leaning almost all the way back in the taxi, hanging her wrist in the looped strap just like she'd seen other people do, driven home high above the Hudson, a little sad about the waste of money, a little afraid of when the pleasure would come to an end, but entirely determined to keep it alive by telling stories about it, and now weren't the Cresspahls among the first to be told?

We are so glad, Mrs. Ferwalter, and we duly offer our congratulations.

This Czech film showing, *The Fifth Horseman Is Fear*, that's probably not right for celebrating, is it? Something about fear, that's not her thing anymore. On the other hand, if it's something from olden times, with music...

I don't think so, Mrs. Ferwalter. It's not from olden times, and the music is sometimes used to accentuate pangs of conscience and in most of the rest of the movie too.

– And how are you, Mrs. Cresspahl?

– *Ještě deělám chyby.* This is the sentence that's as good as my Czech gets: I still make mistakes.

– No! Never no! she insists. No friend of Mrs. Ferwalter's can be having a bad time of things on a day like this, and for the first time we are invited into her apartment, for a "shenuine jewropean" cup of coffee and a look at her citizenship papers. And would Marie like her cup of milk hot or cold?

So she has returned from her new status back to the bosom of her native land. She tells us the Jews in the western part of the Czechoslovakian Republic were assimilated, just like in Germany for instance. "Moritzes." Still, in Mrs. Ferwalter's village they lived apart, a separate group, but respected. What did they have to be afraid of under Thomas Masaryk? But that meant the Germans could avail themselves of a compartmentalized society, there was no place to hide. And she says she didn't even try to flee the Germans, believing they'd long since caught everyone they wanted. You couldn't trust the Hungarians. She will never go back to the Czechs, and never to the Slovaks, not even with an American passport.

This reminded her that she is now entitled to an American passport. Since Marie happened to be sitting closest to her, it was she who was given an extravagant hug.

– The joy: Mrs. Ferwalter said, almost in tears. – The joy!

May 16, 1968 Thursday

Last night FUCK THE JEWISH PIGS was still written on an advertising poster in the lowest walkway of the Ninety-Sixth Street subway station. Today the word JEWISH has been scratched off.

The New York Times is addressing economic need in Czechoslovakia, beginning with Moscow's attack on the memory of Thomas G. Masaryk and calling it disgraceful. She says this not as news but explicitly as her own personal opinion—after all, somebody's got to be the voice of manners and good breeding. She feels it's unlikely that the United States will play a role in helping Czechoslovakia overcome its economic woes any time soon, but she may be wrong. The old lady suggests various substitute actions the government might take, relating to tariff privileges and the Czechoslovak gold in American hands. The moral case for using the gold to put pressure on Czechoslovakia has always been weak, she says. Now there is also a political case for a reversal of attitude, in fact an overwhelming one. Is she trying to give the government in Moscow even more reason to be suspicious?

In August 1945, in the middle of the week, Dr. Kliefoth gave himself two days off. He had come to the office in Town Hall especially to do so. Cresspahl was sitting behind a mountain of paperwork, Kliefoth got his time off in passing, even Leslie Danzmann didn't really give him a good look. Later they both remembered Kliefoth's tiny moment of hesitation at the door, and then they realized what he'd wanted to say.

Dr. Kliefoth didn't have to go work in the fields. K. A. Pontiy had authorized a lifetime supply of food-ration cards, once and for all, without requiring proof of work. For Kliefoth had met the Red Army representative in the walking-out uniform of the German Army, wearing all his medals and decorations according to regulations, the same way he'd done for the British, only this time expecting to be arrested. The commandant didn't even have this headstrong man brought in, he paid him a visit himself, accompanied by a large number of soldiers. It wasn't an interrogation, more like a court of honor, and Kliefoth wouldn't call it anything else. The gentlemen discussed the First World War, in which Kliefoth had been a lieutenant, and the Second, in which he had discharged nothing less than the duties of a 1C staff officer on the eastern front. It apparently ended in a handshake. Afterward, while Pontiy didn't post an order of protection on Kliefoth's apartment—looters had already removed far more than a coin collection that was a byword in professional circles—the city was ordered to continue paying his officer's pension, and Cresspahl was not allowed to house refugees in Kliefoth's apartment, Pontiy insisted. Mrs. Kliefoth had flown the swastika flag on the days required by law, like all the citizens of Jerichow; now their hopes had been dashed and of course it reached Pontiy's ears. Pontiy threw out various anonymous letters too, and although they tried to convince him that Kliefoth had been a member of the Nazi Party, he trusted this adversary's word. Pontiy spoke of the great honorable militarist in his territory not without pride, and asked after him. He shook his head when the upstanding militarist voluntarily took in homeless refugees, into three of his four rooms, and when he went out into the fields with everyone else too K. A. Pontiy brooded darkly, emitting vengeful noises with his tongue, because this pure-carat militarist scorned to accept mercy from his gallant foe.

Dr. phil. Julius Kliefoth, high school teacher in English and geography, lieutenant colonel (retired) as well, reported to Cresspahl the third day after the scythe order. Cresspahl didn't want to dismiss him. This scholar, well traveled in the capitals of England and France, former lecturer at the University of Berlin, put forward, in his depreciatory, too-brisk way, that when it came down to it he knew how to use a rake. That was supposed to be his excuse. Cresspahl wanted to think that the scholar had come for the partial payment in kind; he had heard vague rumors that the man's wife lay sick in bed; he did need every hand he could get for the harvest. They kept the easiest work for Kliefoth, but the Malchow city boy was soon seen standing sheaves upright. Honing scythe blades with a hammer is something a person needs to learn how to do—he managed it. Then he did more than his work. The women had no idea that the use of a scythe didn't come naturally to him. He was almost sixty and they didn't call him Grandpa. After a while it was he who divided the work up. They came to him with their arguments and accepted his curt decisions, even if they came out as "Nonsense." They saw how exhausted he was lying in the shade of the sheaves, panting in the heat, they saw him struggling to force his bones to do this unaccustomed work; they let him say when their break time was over. He stalked from one end of the row to the other on his stiff legs, every now and then muttering something military to himself, it sounded encouraging, nothing to take exception to. *Go on! Go on.* Wherever Kliefoth was, work got done, and many a Red Army soldier retreated in surprise when an old man chewed him out, from above. He was a leader, and he brought up the end of the row in the evening, and he stood last in the line at the granary. He looked like a day laborer, gaunt, in baggy trousers hanging on stringy suspenders, a tatty collarless shirt stretched across his protruding shoulder blades—only his staccato stride didn't fit the picture, and his slim wrists betrayed him. Fatigue pulled his wrinkled face into a sleepy expression, but he could still make a child snap awake at the end of a long dry day, with a quick look meant to suggest renewed surprise, so that the child felt found out, watched. He didn't sweat, his whole face under his bristles of white hair was red, there was spittle drying on his thin lips—Cresspahl's daughter thought he looked brave. She liked hearing how he talked to a woman about to give up, he was so helpful and concerned, it was a deep voice, a bit like a turkey gobbling. By evening he could hardly get his voice out of his throat, but Cresspahl's daughter only showed him her water bottle, she didn't offer it; to her he remained the teacher, just as, to others, his punctiliousness made him forever the Dr. phil. She always knew where he was in the field; the rakes near him were swinging, work came easier. Now he'd taken two days off.

He must have gone from Town Hall to the Old Cemetery: Pastor Brüshaver saw him. (Cresspahl and Brüshaver had learned how to talk to each other by that point.) Kliefoth owned a grave site even though he had no one buried there—it was included with the house. He stood in the middle of the main cemetery path, to gauge the view of the gate and the commandant's villa from there. It looked like a strategic reconnaissance. Brüshaver stood at a window looking out onto Town Street, to catch him when he left; he didn't pass by there, as in fact he had never once come to the church for anything since he'd lived in Jerichow.

The next morning, before the birds started singing, he was pushing a rubber-wheeled cart out his front gate; the cart was half as long as the coffin it carried. He had a boy with him to do half the pushing so that Kliefoth could keep the load from slipping.

It was an imposing coffin, dramatically vaulted and fluted, with wrought-iron garlands, three bronze handles on each side, six feet, like a piece of furniture. He had unscrewed the crucifix figure from the lid and now the box was harder to keep control of. Miss Emma Senkpiel had wanted to pass over into another life under that cross herself, she had been very reluctant to give Kliefoth this piece from her stock. Moreover he'd had nothing to offer in return. She wouldn't take a can of oil, not even a pound of tobacco, and she didn't want Mrs. Kliefoth's clothes. So she took a couple of cooking pots and ownership of one of the cabinets with seven doors. She needed neither the cupboard nor the pots, it was only to give the appearance of an exchange, he was so timid. And the old maid was worried about suddenly standing naked before death. Her coffin was not one that Kliefoth would have chosen voluntarily.

They reached Market Square and the boy stopped pushing. Kliefoth looked south across the square. There was the Old Cemetery. The sun was much too high, he would not be able to reach the Kliefoth grave site in secret anymore. – *Go on!* Kliefoth said. He steered the coffin a little to the left, aimed it at the country road to Rande. The boy started pushing again and spit into his hands.

It took half an hour to get to the New Cemetery. Kliefoth had to wear his last intact suit, of course, even though it was a bit too light a gray, with a black armband at least, those were hardly clothes to work hard in, and soon he was gasping. The road was uphill. The boy didn't look at him when he stopped for a break. Twelve years old maybe. It was Gabriel Manfras, who never talked much, and even if he later described this morning as nothing unusual, at the time he'd almost dropped dead of fear. Kliefoth really was acting like he was out of his mind.

At that time the New Cemetery was just an open field. There were individual grave mounds here and there, most of them sprawling, not neatly defined, certainly not covered with flowers. They stopped at one such wide hole, still half open. It had been dug in advance, but for a body without a coffin. New mourners would have to extend the end of the hole with a spade. Kliefoth had forgotten his spade. The boy was happy to run back for it.

Kliefoth sat next to his coffin for a while. No one could see him from the road. He started poking around in the earth. Apparently he wanted to dig a private hole. When the boy returned with the spade he could still see the tracks of the rubber wheels. They led back to the Rande country road. There wasn't a cemetery for quite a ways on it.

The detachment of Soviets guarding the gates to the former air base stopped him and asked for his identification, *propusk*. Yesterday Kliefoth hadn't had to think about that. But now he was halfway to Rande, and this was the right place to go. Gabriel Manfras had caught up to him. To the boy, the teacher seemed feverish. Kliefoth put his hand flat on the coffin lid, right before the sentry's eyes, and feebly turned it palm up. This officer had never seen such transport on this road before and sighed at the crazy German. He pointed back to town, at the New Cemetery. Kliefoth indicated the way to Rande, toward the sea. Now the boy talked for a bit, just so they could get out of there quicker. He was afraid the Soviets would open the coffin and he didn't want to see that. The Soviets let Kliefoth go, with the comment that he should go fuck his mother, and the officer clapped him on the shoulder several times.

In Rande the boy sat next to the coffin for half the day, on a side road near the landing. They had taken the coffin down, since it wouldn't stay on the tippy cart, and put it in the shade of the hedge. It sat there in the sand like a forgotten piece of furniture.

Meanwhile Kliefoth was talking to one fisherman after the other. All he wanted was a crossing to Poel Island, to Kirchdorf, they could make it Timmendorf if necessary. He'd keep going from there. The fishermen didn't ask him about that. They wanted to know what Kliefoth could offer them.

Kliefoth had nothing he could offer them at the moment.

They knew him of course, he'd been a big fish in the army and a school principal in Gneez, sure. They knew his wife too—he'd gone for walks with her on the Rande promenade, sat with her at the outdoor tables of the Archduke Hotel. It wasn't that. But the Baltic, so smooth, just slightly ruffled, was a dangerous body of water nowadays. There were Soviet guards along the beach who wanted to see a *propusk*. Kliefoth didn't have one. What if they ran into a Soviet patrol boat on the water, with a coffin on board. With a German lieutenant colonel on board. And it could take four hours to get to Kirchdorf. And a boat would have to pass right by the Wismar harbor. Where cutters from elsewhere were being confiscated. Sorry, Mr. Kliefoth, meanwhile no hard feelings.

When Kliefoth got to the head of the Fishermen's Association, it occurred to him that he did have something to offer: the rubber-wheeled cart.

Ilse Grossjohann first let him finish his argument that a woman born in Kirchdorf on the island of Poel needed to be buried in Kirchdorf on the island of Poel. She agreed about everything. Then she offered him a cemetery plot in Rande. She could, she'd been head of the congregation since May.

She was the mayor too, but found no man willing to help Kliefoth bury his wife; ever since she'd led the work unit burying drowned bodies from the *Cap Arcona* floating concentration camp, the association hadn't been happy with her. It was two o'clock in the afternoon before they'd dug the hole. The woman and the boy were worried about lowering the coffin evenly, so Kliefoth went into the hole first. He caught the foot end, inched his back slowly along the wall below ground level. He had to tip the coffin diagonally after all, if he wanted to get out from under it. Then the woman and the boy pulled him up with the rope because he didn't want to step on the box. When the hole was covered, Ilse Grossjohann left alone; Kliefoth refused to listen to anything. Well, if he didn't want anything to eat, her children needed something. After a while, the boy left the Rande cemetery too. Again Kliefoth couldn't be seen from the gate, in his summer suit, between the bright hedgerows.

That evening Kliefoth was back in Jerichow. He didn't have his key with him; usually the refugees would have let him in. But they weren't there. Two Red Army men with their families were there. Kliefoth walked farther into his apartment so oblivious to their presence that one of them held his machine gun diagonally across his chest. Kliefoth had just realized that his wife wasn't in the apartment anymore, and walked meekly back out to the stairs.

On the street he noticed a pile of trash he hadn't seen before. These were the things from his apartment that the occupiers had no use for—an almost complete run of the *Yearbook of the Association of Mecklenburg History and Antiquities*, the *Papers of the Mecklenburg Local History League*, the seventeenth-century law books, the medieval poetry, the Merian engravings, the Homann and Laurenberg maps, the pewter. The copperplate prints and maps were punctured all over from the broken glass; the pewter plates had been gathered up by the neighbors. But they didn't come out of their houses to give him back what they'd rescued, they didn't help him gather up the debris, they let him crouch there alone in the gathering darkness, not long before curfew.

He found his wife's family *Mecklenburg Hymnal*, printed in Schwerin, 1791, His Grace the Duke's Special-Privilegio. This Example of Fine Printing with Gospels and Epistles unbound Costs 14 Schillings Courant. The Kirchdorf copy was a bound one, in shiny black leather, and the silver plates on the covers together with the corner fittings kept the book from being damaged. Only the clasps were broken. The plate on the front cover bore the initials J. L. with the year 1791; the tools of his trade were engraved on the back—a compass, a T-square, a protractor divided into degrees. On the last page his wife's ancestors had kept records one after the other. "My Son Friederich Gottsch. Johann, born on April 3 and baptized April 19, Anno 1794." "Father died on August 29, morning, 7 o'clock 1834, Buried September 3." Now Kliefoth had to add another line to the last page, and he could prove that his wife had belonged in Kirchdorf. At least he'd brought her part of the way there.

In such a hot summer, Miss Cresspahl. A person gets some crazy ideas.

I would've too, Dr. Kliefoth.

It was just an idea.

They moved her to Kirchdorf in 1950, though, didn't they, Herr Kliefoth?

You see! I would have forgotten about that.

Why do I keep picturing an apple?

That's how it is, Miss Cresspahl. She didn't look dead. When I came home from the field, she lay there as if she were alive.

Why didn't you let Cresspahl help? We would've come out to you.

Your father, my dear girl, already had his head half in a noose. I didn't want to bother him. Was I really hobbling when I talked to that woman during our agricultural activities?

Gobbling, Herr Kliefoth.

You mean I talked like a turkey?

From deep in the throat. "Oo-ah, get a hold of yourself, why wouldn't your husband be alive, we'll take a break in a minute." Wanting so much to help.

Then someone else can hear me.

Yes, Herr Kliefoth. I can hear you perfectly. Are you dead now too?

All someone needs to get into your club is a modest membership fee. And that I have.

When, Herr Kliefoth?

Sometime around evening, I should say, when it's afternoon in New York. Sometime this coming November, I should say.

The military commander received a report that the indomitable militarist took only one of his two days' vacation. K. A. Pontiy issued Order No. 23, making it punishable for any inhabitant of Jerichow to house a member of the Red Army without the commandant's written permission. He didn't try to put Kliefoth back in his apartment or restore the stolen goods. He wasn't omnipotent.

May 17, 1968 Friday

We want to tell you something, Gesine.

I don't want to hear from the dead every day.

Just listen, this will help you.
Do what?
Get back up after English ran you down.
It didn't, as far as I know.
Last Thursday, Gesine. The Fifth Horseman Is Fear.
Okay, tell me.

"And I saw when the Lamb opened one of the seals, and I heard, as it were the noise of thunder, one of the four beasts saying, Come and see. And I saw, and behold a white horse: and he that sat on him had a bow; and a crown was given unto him: and he went forth conquering, and to conquer."

The conqueror on the first horse.
Let Lisbeth do it. She has a clearer voice.

"And when he had opened the second seal, I heard the second beast say, Come and see. And there went out another horse that was red: and power was given to him that sat thereon to take peace from the earth, and that they should kill one another: and there was given unto him a great sword."

The war of all against all. But my English is just what Mary Hahn taught me, and Aggie learned hers at the Schnappauf und Sellschopp boarding school on Alexandrinen Strasse in Rostock. You go now, Aggie.

"And when he had opened the third seal, I heard the third beast say, Come and see. And I beheld, and lo a black horse; and he that sat on him had a pair of balances in his hand. And I heard a voice in the midst of the four beasts say, A measure of wheat for a penny, and three measures of barley for a penny; and see thou hurt not the oil and the wine." *The third rider, on the black horse, famine, starvation.*

Exploitation.
That's how you learned it, Gesine. Now it's Kliefoth's turn.

"And when he had opened the fourth seal, I heard the voice of the fourth beast say, Come and see. And I looked, and behold a pale horse: and his name that sat on him was Death, and Hell followed with him. And power was given unto them over the fourth part of the earth, to kill with sword, and with hunger, and with death, and with the beasts of the earth." *The fourth horseman brings death, Miss Cresspahl. That's the point.*

It's just the Apocalypse! The book with the seven seals!
Just the Apocalypse, Gesine.

Nothing but a piece of the Bible I forgot. I'd have failed a confirmation test, nothing else.

And English.

But if I'm counting correctly there are only four horsemen.

And The Fifth Horseman Is Fear.

There is no fifth.

There was for the Czechs. For them the Germans were all four plagues of the apocalypse in one, and more—more than conquest and war, hunger, pestilence, and death. The Germans brought with them a fifth horsemen of their own, especially for the Czechs, fear.

That's what they offer foreigners.

That's what they offer the Germans in New York.

The Nazis.

And the people talking about Mauthausen and Belzec. Remember? It was only Tuesday.

That's why I shouldn't go to Prague?

You can't talk there. Or work. Or live. Give it up.

May 18, 1968 Saturday

Yesterday the mayors of Moscow and New York were observed on a black leather sofa in Mr. Lindsay's office. How the other man deals with strikes by municipal employees, Lindsay wanted to know. – Strike? replied Vladimir Fedorovič Promyslov. – In fifty years of Soviet power it has not happened once.

Cresspahl had problems with his police force.

He needed someone a few years younger than him, someone who'd lived in Jerichow since before the Nazis, respected if not admired by the townsfolk, levelheaded, unbribable, and Peter Wulff had turned the job down. Cresspahl had caught up to this friend two days after the war, six and a half years after the quarrel the Social Democratic Party had ordered; they'd told each other who had smuggled flowers onto Friedrich Laabs's grave every March, in unsacred memory of the Kapp Putsch; who had watched from in hiding when the flagpole outside the Nazi headquarters was sawn almost through in the night. Cresspahl didn't mention his business with the British;

Lisbeth's death could not be discussed. As far as the SPD was concerned, they had reached a tacit agreement not to forgive them for their meddling in personal friendships. There were plenty of other things, for both of them liked spending their leisure time together, and soon it was not just for old times' sake anymore but with the joint intention of getting Jerichow back on the rails and moving it in a new direction. Wulff was glad that the British had made the other man mayor; under the Soviets he'd continued to help out with kidding and advice, but was not willing to back him up as the police. Wulff would rather turn up at the schoolyard each morning when work was being assigned and haul sacks of grain or help dig the holes for K. A. Pontiy's fence than go down into his fellow townsmen's cellars or up into their attics. He could see that Cresspahl was stuck with his job for the Russians and didn't want to risk getting caught the same way. He suggested Fritz Schenk.

Pontiy and Jerichow needed a manly figure.

Cresspahl would rather have Mrs. Bergie Quade at his side.

The war had left few of the men of Jerichow behind, and Fritz Schenk was one of them. Since 1939 he'd avoided conscription with an inexhaustible stream of attestations, petitions, and testimonials; to prevent the women of Jerichow from looking askance at him, he'd given the town numerous and thorough descriptions of all his abdominal complaints, sometimes without anyone asking. He had joined the Social Democratic Party in 1928 for his job as town clerk and registrar, was expelled (willingly) in December 1932 for conspicuous remarks criticizing a Reich government's refusal to use violence, reinstated under the Law for the Restoration of the Professional Civil Service, loud in his praise of his beloved Führer *and* Reich chancellor, coy about invitations to join that party, deaf to all such suggestions after February 2, 1943, and registered as unfit for military service all the way through to Total Surrender in 1945. Cresspahl was inclined to see all this as skillful maneuvering; he recalled some rather exaggerated congratulations he'd received upon registering the birth of a child in March 1933. He didn't trust his dislike of the man and recommended him to Pontiy. Maybe what bothered him about Fritz Schenk was his stay-at-home complexion, his long thin stick body, his smooth, affected manners, his lips too full for a man of fifty and pursed when he scented victory. Schenk was his name; Sourbeer would have suited him. And Peter Wulff suggested him mainly to watch him put his foot in it, not to mention keeping his own hands clean. Cresspahl tried to find someone else. He couldn't pick a refugee who wouldn't know the town's back alleys and back doors. He wasn't pleased—appointing Schenk as chief of police meant he had to pile more paperwork from the housing and registrar's office onto his own desk. Schenk took it as an insult, and Wulff's scheme slowly dawned on Cresspahl. Just recently a paper-pushing clerk, Schenk now faced the choice of filling in bomb craters or being Alfred Bienmüller's dogsbody. So he decided to work for the authorities, and spoke just as he had twelve years earlier of the sacrifice he was making for the new era. – I vouch for the files up until and including today! he said. Cresspahl recognized Schenk's anticipation of things finally going wrong for this carpenter turned mayor, this cobbler who hadn't stuck to his last. – You're the boss! he cried, carried away by his own obedience, taking this tack rather than responsibility for what he was going to be asked to do.

At the swearing in, Pontiy asked him, playfully, enticingly: You Fasceest? Schenk was unaware of the commandant's addiction to private jokes and, breathing heavily, rejected any such suspicion. He spoke of the German People's sense that when the war was over life itself would be over, and the German People's relief upon finding that it was not in fact over. Cresspahl watched Schenk's fussing in embarrassment; that kind of patter might be all right coming from someone like Wulff, but Wulff's lips would never utter such stuff. Pontiy was merely disappointed that his chief of police had concocted such a speech; he called him You Good Example, You Go First and You Become Communist, put his cap on his head, and swore the man in. Cresspahl still didn't know what Schenk was planning to get out of a job like this. And when Schenk was asked about the Social Democratic Party he had shuddered with such palpable disgust that in the end Pontiy decided to use him to found the German Communist Party, Jerichow Branch. Again Cresspahl mistrusted his own instincts. If Schenk had hated the Nazis as much as he now exclaimed he had, maybe that had been how it really was and Jerichow just hadn't seen it.

For his subordinate Schenk picked Knever, Berthold Knever, former senior postal clerk, demoted as a result of his indefatigable altercations with the head office to working behind the counter and finally to mail carrier. Cresspahl didn't object to his choice. If Knever chose not to believe that there would be a postal service under the Soviets, that was Knever's business, and he thought the old man might keep an eye on Schenk. Knever had always been a stickler, down to the gram when manning the postal scale, also in his attire, patched though it might be, and the shopkeepers could set their clocks by Mrs. Knever back in the day, so strict was he in demanding punctual meals. If Cresspahl was right in his suspicions, Knever could dispel them and keep tabs on Schenk's every last move—glowering, observant, bristling, perfectly fitting his nickname, the Silent Parrot. So Cresspahl gave Knever a uniform too, as well as a third man, from East Prussia, Friedrich Gantlik. These were German Army uniforms stripped of insignia, with the swastika cut out of the middle of the white armbands with a pocketknife and POLICE painted on instead, the seal of the town of Jerichow stamped underneath.

They'd begun their service on July 4, and right on their very first shift they failed to carry the Karabiner 98k rifles they'd been ordered to take with them. Pontiy was probably trying to let his man Cresspahl know that he really meant it about the Red Army's chivalry toward women, and that if a black sheep ever did turn up it was up to the German police to deal with him, armed. That struck Cresspahl's policemen as rather gruesome. He could hardly blame Gantlik for wanting to avoid an exchange of gunfire with the Red Army—he had taken the job with the town mainly to acquire residence papers. He was short but tough, a farmer without land, and maybe he'd lost his harmless appearance on the long trip from the Memel to Jerichow. Cresspahl sent the three men to Pontiy, to test their marksmanship, and they came back with good results and a stern warning from the commandant that the negligent wounding of a Red Army soldier would be, in his words, unforgivable. Schenk looked blankly at his mayor, his swelling lips pursed. Cresspahl spoiled Schenk's schadenfreude by appealing to his men's manhood. After that they sometimes made their rounds armed. But when the full-scale looting of Karstadt's department store was under way, half of Town Street overrun with people, strewn with bales of fabric and cooking utensils, the police hopped around the edges of the excited crowd, almost as confused as the crowd was, like chickens, never thinking even to fire shots into the air. Schenk fired a shot into the air when Hanna Ohlerich ran away from him after coming down from a cherry tree Amalie Creutz had pressured her to climb. The police took their guns with them when they were called out to an argument between Germans; when a Soviet assault was reported, they marched tamely out of Town Hall so as not to get there in time to do anything, rifles over their shoulders instead of at the ready, and Miss Senkpiel came to complain that they'd picked *her* shop to leave their guns in, just for fifteen minutes, and sometimes it was evening before they came to get them. So the squads of harvest workers lacked protection, few infractions against Soviet chivalry were reported to the commandant, and two Red Army soldiers with their followers could put eight people out on the street from Kliefoth's apartment.

Jerichow's police were conscientious in performing their lesser duties. Anyone digging up new potatoes in defiance of the law was reported. Anyone putting up a sign offering to swap baby clothes for a work shirt on his own gate instead of on the official noticeboard at Town Hall was brought into Cresspahl for punishment—he had actually needed to forbid the posting of such signs. After Pontiy thought it over and decided not to take part in a rally of former members of the SPD, the police appeared and ordered the group to disperse. A stretch of street not swept clean enough, that made them really mad. Dogs without license tags had it rough.

What Cresspahl's police liked best, though, was going into people's homes. They had enough orders to do so from the commandant or the town government. There was cattle and poultry to be counted, so that the deliveries to start August 10 could be planned. When a sheep was put to the knife on schedule, there was still the skin to be seen to. The children had to turn in their textbooks for German (anthologies and grammar books), history, geography, and biology; everyone had to turn in the books they owned in Cyrillic script—so here came the police again, to plant themselves in front of the bookcases. The tradesmen's businesses were required to report their supplies of raw materials and fuel, so the police checked, lifted floorboards, crawled around under the roof, rummaged around in water butts, to make sure the lists were complete. The hunt was on for Köpcke's motorcycle because it hadn't been registered with the mayor's office, until one day Mina Köpcke dismounted and showed her *propusk*, signed not by the Soviet Military Administration in Schwerin but by K. A. Pontiy in person so his fence would be finished faster, and the motorcycle had been turned overnight into a little truck. On their treks through the kitchens and parlors and stables of Jerichow, Mr. Schenk, Mr.

Knever, and Mr. Gantlik saw more than enough to amuse them. Their eyes would light on beanpoles only partly concealing a barrel; they'd say nothing for the time being and then report such discoveries to Cresspahl. He couldn't object, he needed anything that was in short supply for his deals with the Soviet Beckhorst farm or the Fishermen's Association in Rande, so he'd write out his request for permission to confiscate and send it to the DA's office in Gneez and hope for a good word from Slata in district military headquarters. The district of Gneez was a large one, it was up to Slata to present reports on emergencies in Jerichow and she probably didn't want to remind people too often of her previous life there; sometimes the form came back from the courthouse too late. Sometimes Schenk seized the property before it was authorized, "to avoid any risk of suppression of evidence," as he put it, snippy because unassailable. It wasn't Schenk who was cursed out for hauling off an eighteen-month supply of artificial fertilizer—the guilt was hung around Cresspahl's neck. He was happy as long as Knever didn't report him for embezzlement. Then, in one of the townsman-farmer's houses, which hadn't been thought to have a cellar, they found coal: the house was sitting on a mine of briquettes, enough to supply Jerichow with gas for five days, and next door lived Duvenspeck, gasworks superintendent, and so a brigade of women with handcarts had to go bring back the black gold; in the end half a ton was missing from the quantity Duvenspeck was willing to admit. That was more than the two briquettes each refugee had sneaked under her apron added up to. Cresspahl's police had gone in on it with the guy who'd revealed the storage space, and the loyal and faithful Knever, upholder of the law, hadn't reported the misappropriation because he himself has built a neat tower of briquettes in his pantry, edges lined up perfectly, elegantly tapering toward the top, camouflaged as a wall. Gesine had seen it when she'd gone to bring him a message; these days she couldn't take her eyes off pantries. For Cresspahl it wasn't just about upholding the law, it was that the district commandant sometimes came to Jerichow and hauled off things Cresspahl had applied for, and it didn't go well for him if there were shortages. He preferred not to have his policemen's apartments searched on the evidence of a child, so instead he went to the commandant and suggested he give his forces of law and order a little extra training in their jobs. Pontiy would not rest until he knew the nature of the goods in question. He was delighted to hear that there was coal in the gasworks for his winter. He invented on the spot the proverb of the ox which thou shalt not muzzle when he treadeth out the corn. – Yes, the ox: Cresspahl said. Pontiy agreed with an emphatic nod.

Meanwhile, there could now be found traveling through the countryside around Jerichow a young man, Gerd Schumann he called himself, formerly in the National Committee for a Free Germany in the Soviet Union, and dispatched, after a management course in Stargard, Pommern, to this out-of-the-way spot as a canvasser for the Communist Party. Cresspahl had talked to him and found him agreeable enough, if a little too High German for around here. Twenty-three years young, stocky and already running to fat, with an aggressive but at the same time withdrawn look, invariably dressed in a military tunic that, oddly, showed no signs of wear and tear, and he squared his shoulders in military fashion too. Redhead, he was nicknamed, even though his hair was somewhere between white and gray, with a silvery sheen. – From now on

the great flag
of the freedom
of all peoples
and the peace
of all nations
shall wave over

Europe! he would shout, oblivious to his listeners' aversion to any more flags. He brought out such proclamations in a carefully calibrated tone that rose and fell in a kind of singsong, and, again like Pastor Brüshaver in church, the young man could quote chapter and verse: Generalissimo Stalin, May 9, 1945. This manner of speaking had become second nature with him; he would work his way through the KPD's whole ten-point program like that, to an audience of tired day laborers and farmers that the village commandant rounded up and brought to him after work, and because the Communist Party of Germany was demanding things like a war against hunger, unemployment, and housing shortages, a few coins would eventually drop into his collection plate, and he would hand out his leaflets and membership applications. He had far more power than Cresspahl. He carried a very visible pistol in his belt, and with that and the Russian language he could defend himself against uninformed Red Army soldiers; he had a say in the allocation of housing, he had money, he could use bedsheets and red paint to make banners with slogans that stretched across village streets, and when refugees asked him about their old East Pommern territory he would simply bang his fist on the table and calmly expound the guilt of the entire German people for the war, in singsong paragraphs, reverberating pauses, and elevated pitch. By the end of June his party had almost a thousand members in Mecklenburg-Vorpommern; it had more than three thousand by the end of July, almost eight thousand by the end of August. Cresspahl probably realized that the young man liked his unfettered movement from place to place, and his evening performances, his ever-changing overnight stays, but still he invited him to stay in Jerichow. Once this able and fearless man had a place to live in the town, he could probably be offered the post of police chief. (Secretly, Cresspahl hoped that this rival king might succeed him as mayor.) The young man refused to even hold a meeting in Jerichow. – That's your business, Cresspahl: he said, in an unexpectedly Berlin tone—so mocking, so amused around the corners of his eyes, that Cresspahl thought the man must have seen through him.

The man demanded power and didn't take it. Cresspahl was stuck with the problems he had with his police force: *like the cuckoo's stuck with his song.*

Yesterday around noon the Soviet general Aleksei A. Yepishev arrived in Prague. He was taken aback when asked whether the Red Army really did stand ready to move in response to a call from Prague for help, and perhaps because it was a young lady thrusting the microphone in his face, a brunette in a powder-blue shirt, the short, plump man wearing many medals finally answered her with a slight smile: This is a stupid thing. What stupidity.

May 19, 1968 Sunday

Today in the column for Commercial Notices, under an ad for shipping your car, the American Society for the Study of the German Democratic Republic steps up to offer a lecture this Friday on European Disarmament and the Two German States. To ship our car we should call 227-6334; to study the GDR, MOnument 6-4073. That number might live right around the corner from us.

Where we live is on the park named after the river.

For seven years we have lived across from Riverside Park, this wide expanse of meadows, gentle hills, walking paths, retaining walls, highway cuttings, tunnels to the river, old trees, hawthorn bushes, monuments, and pergolas, we have walked almost every one of its 106 hectares, and because we didn't grow up next to it—because we had no right to it, even by proximity—we tried to earn it by using it, and reading about it too, the way only newcomers, foreigners do.

A hundred years ago there was no park, only the railroad Cornelius Vanderbilt ran along the shore of the Hudson: seven long-distance trains per day in both directions, plus seven slow trains stopping at every station from Thirtieth Street to Poughkeepsie. Then the landowners—the Martins, the de Lanceys, the Stryckers—campaigned for a park on their property, and the city had to buy it off them, strip by strip, for more than $6 million. By 1879 the inner edge of the park was finished, a civic playground with paths for bicycles and horses, with little temples and secluded, restful corners. The river was still closer to the buildings than it is today; in 1910 it was pushed back with stone excavated from the Catskill Aqueduct, in the 1920s still farther with the rock that had been in the IND subway's path. Even in 1930, there was still a lot of empty land between the park and the railroad tracks; in 1937 the tracks were built over, hidden inside natural-looking hills, and by 1940 the park looked like it had a hundred years earlier—mildly civilized with angular paths and other signs of artificial construction, but thoroughly disguised as a pristine landscape. Henry Hudson's parkway, hidden by mounds and hedges, is like a miracle, looking every time as if it sprang up naturally.

In summer the park is like the site of a continuous public festival, and we are among the attendees. The banks along the shoreline promenade are packed with day-trippers from the poorer areas, the tennis courts are in use, chess players are sitting astride the benches and teaching kibbitzers lessons, people with the day before yesterday's newspaper draped over their face are asleep as if in their own apartment (which the park may well be), on the field at Seventy-Fourth Street the walkers let their dogs run free and are happy to stand and have a long conversation about their animals, picnics are spread out on the grass, half-naked children are jumping and squealing under the glittering cool fountains in the playgrounds, or chasing after the swings, or crowding around the man with the ice-cream cart. Long-distance runners are on their way, a bike parade with balloons came by around two. In the city marina on Seventy-Ninth a child can see how a boat is rigged up, on Eighty-Eighth a clientele that always looks the same is busy holding their rods and hoping for fish with robust constitutions— they catch a pathetic eel every now and then, and the sport of it is enough for them. We can see what street we're at without needing to leave or even look outside the park: there are number plates on the lampposts, PL 38310 corresponds to Eighty-Third Street, and the fact that the lights were designed by Henry Bacon, who built the Lincoln Memorial in Washington, is one that we've looked up, so that we might be more at home here.

The park is built for use, and it has found favor with the police. They drive their patrol cars there for breaks and man-to-man talks, and at warm times of year the forces of law and order rest their horses in the deep shadows of the shrubbery. You can see them, and people on the benches don't need to know one another to start a conversation. The park seems to be a picture composed of nothing but peaceful occurrences, and in fact many of the inhabitants of Riverside Drive feel a sense of solidarity. They are like one another in their level of education, their incomes are comparable, they lack pink skin only in exceptional cases, they send their children to the same schools, they all have the same housing conditions to defend, they act as a bloc in political and parental meetings. Someone around here who waits for the bus in the morning holding a child's hand can be almost sure of going to kindergarten or to school accompanied by no one she does not know, at least by sight, and the bus driver, who has escaped from the traffic crush of the city into the swiftly flowing river of Riverside Drive, speaks to the people getting on here as if to a family that's nicer than the other families.

The dark-skinned parkgoers, on the other hand, come from neighborhoods where parks are not provided, or are less in favor with the police and now destroyed, the grass withered and trampled, the few trees damaged, the ground covered with shards of glass from bottles broken there in neat, clean, steady rage. On weekdays the dark-skinned children are a minority in Riverside Park, they play in their own groups, and the Negro woman keeping an eye on a pack of kids running wild is watching her white employer's boys, not her own. The Puerto Ricans are among themselves on the baseball fields, the Negroes practicing for themselves alone on the basketball courts, and the West Indians play soccer with one another. They are borrowing the landscape that is theirs by right.

We can take the Promenade along the Hudson from the narrow paths running alongside the highway, past the magnificent paved play areas and well-tended fences under lampposts, up to the unprotected grassy roads and to 124th Street, where a stone tablet has been placed in the shadow of a large-tooth aspen to honor the efforts of the Women's League for the Protection of Riverside Park. We wouldn't have been a member of that. We have the river. The river under the unobstructed sky pulls you in toward the nearby sea, presents slowly moving ships, foghorns at night, green and gray and blue colors mixed with those of the park, a holiday view, and so poisoned is the river by industry that people aren't even allowed to swim in it. The river gathers up from the sky both its light and its dirt, which helps give the sunsets their ominous coloring. The smell of the river comes with us back to Riverside Drive. The leaves in the park are already holding the lamplight under them in glowing caves. The goods trains are rumbling through the belly of the park, bringing meat for the New York markets from Iowa and Nebraska, the Maine and Canadian woods transformed into paper for tomorrow's *New York Times*, for the diary of the world. Above the sparkling terraces of New Jersey's lights, above the tangle of colors of the amusement park in the Palisades, above the gray river, that wide gateway to the north, there are white bulbs arrayed on nearly horizontal arcs of cables; above the double-decker shelf between the two piers of the George Washington Bridge, headlights and taillights grope their way along, and Europe's tour guides recommend the view. We can't recommend more than the view ourselves.

We live here.

May 20, 1968 Monday

Charles de Gaulle has found the word he was looking for to describe the general strike in France: "Reform, yes. Shit-the-bed, no." *Chienlit.* The Grand Old Man.

Near Manhattan Avenue and 119th Street, in the vicinity of Morningside Park, the following method has been noted: The bus driver sees a pretty girl standing at the bus stop, pulls over to the right, and opens the door. In steps not the girl but three or four gang members who have crouched down and crept up along the side of the bus, unseen by the driver. They hold a knife to the driver's throat, grab the money changer, and vanish. The whole operation takes less than thirty seconds. *The New York Times* calls the scene of the crime the Upper West Side, where we live; actually it's only near here.

Shifting clouds and white bursts of sunshine, like one more snowball a child throws onto the roof so that it'll roll off, leaving a thick track, bursting apart in the hand.

In winter 1945 one of Cresspahl's daughter's troubles was over.

She didn't want the two members of the Abs family to move. Jakob should stay; Jakob's mother should stay. She cooked my meals and showed me how to do my hair, she helped me in a strange land. I still remember the evening when I was standing with my hands behind my back, – Gesine: she said, lightly and politely touching my shoulder with her rough hard hand; I still remember her fast subdued voice. I remember her face: long and bony and far advanced into old age in the narrow dry eyes. I always had a mother. Always.

Mrs. Abs felt that in Jerichow she was in the wrong place, and the wrong house there too.

Her husband couldn't find her in this small town, tucked away near the sea, tucked away in the wheat fields. He hadn't promised to find her and the boy. When he was released from the military prison in Anklam and dispatched to the East Prussian front, he'd made a secret detour across the Dievenow in order to spend two hours in the middle of the night on the Bonin estate, to give her his last will and testament verbally. She hadn't believed it. She'd promised him she would go west, cross the Oder, cross the Elbe even, but so he could find her. That was only five months ago. When the Wolin regional party leader threatened anyone who set off for the west with death, von Bonin drove off with nine heavy covered wagons; all that was left for the wife of the missing estate manager was an open potato cart, an extremely old horse, and instructions to look after the estate. Long before the regional party leader ordered the evacuation west, she'd left the island. Near Augustwalde she found herself on the autobahn to Berlin and under fire from Soviet strafers. Jakob was more scared than she was, and she had blood from his neck wound on her face. After they laid the dead to one side there was an extra horse, the sorrel. She'd wanted to take the boy to the Podejuch hospital but he didn't agree to stop now that they could hitch two horses to their cart. From then on, it was probably him in charge. He held their course through Neubrandenburg and Malchow toward the so-called gray area in western Mecklenburg, and after passing the mouth of the Elde they were forced ever more to the north, no matter how small the roads they took, as far as Wismar, and they'd come to Jerichow because the road by the sea was so empty and seemed safe from army and party patrols. She'd stayed because for the first time they were offered a place to stay; because Jakob wanted to wait out the war, and then because of the British occupation of the town, and then because of the two sick girls in Cresspahl's house, and then to wait for the British to come back. But her husband wouldn't be able to find them in Jerichow. He had taken her from a farm in the gray area, the seventh child, the unpaid maid—a dairy inspector, educated at Neukloster Seminary, and he'd wanted her for his wife. She had not left her family on good terms, she couldn't go back there for some time; still, he would look for her near Eldena, if anywhere. She'd obediently learned the job of cooking in Hamburg, thirty years old already, spending three years there while her husband was in Brazil looking around for somewhere they could move to together, until at least he was forced to return to shattered Germany. She was thirty-eight when Jakob was born in an estate manager's apartment near Crivitz; that too was where her husband might be looking for them—in Crivitz, in Hamburg, near Hagenow. Once the post office started accepting postcards again she had sent Cresspahl's address to eleven estate managers, schoolteachers, and church offices, wherever her husband might think she was; she had even made herself write to her family. No answer had come back, and she didn't believe Cresspahl when he said he'd find the man if he ever turned up in Mecklenburg. Cresspahl was trying to comfort her. She was willing to believe that his offer of hospitality was good indefinitely.

There was so much about the house that she didn't understand. This Cresspahl didn't own it—it was the property of his daughter, a twelve-year-old girl, and if you didn't believe that you could go ask Papenbrock. Papenbrock as a father-in-law, with his mighty palace of a house on Market Square:

how did that go with the remains of a woodworking shop behind the cemetery. He had one dead son he was allowed to put up a memorial plaque for at the family tomb and another that couldn't be mentioned, he'd killed children in Ukraine, set villages on fire. Yet the Papenbrocks had a Ukrainian girl living with them, at first as a maid and starting in December 1944 officially as a fiancée, and the Germans would say hello to her on the street, because of the Papenbrocks. In Pommern, on the Bonin estate, the forced laborers were treated like cattle that could talk. This Slata hadn't been deported "to Siberia" by the Red Army, she was working as an assistant in district military headquarters, she'd apparently earned her nickname the Angel of Gneez and now the people in Jerichow were denying the rumors that she'd knelt at Pontiy's feet and kissed his hands. Now rich old Papenbrock had been ordered off to a Soviet farm south of Gneez, to work as a supervisor, and refugees and Russian soldiers had taken over the house from his wife and were turning the big parlor into a dance hall at night. Cresspahl was the mayor, he could have stood by his mother-in-law; she never came to ask for anything, he always walked right past her house. Cresspahl's child hadn't been allowed to visit her grandmother for several years. People said. Every now and then Mrs. Abs heard talk about someone called Our Lisbeth. Lisbeth could've pointed the mayor in the right direction; Lisbeth had been dead seven years now. "Our Lisbeth" came up in conversations outside empty shopwindows, during breaks in the fields. For a long time Mrs. Abs thought she was someone living in Jerichow, maybe sick. Jakob discovered that she had been Cresspahl's wife, and since November 1938 could be visited only in the cemetery. She had died in a fire, possibly suicide. Her husband didn't look after the grave, and Amalie Creutz hadn't been able to do much for it since early 1945, the mound had almost fallen apart. Mrs. Abs took Cresspahl's child with her and showed her how to replant and maintain such places; the husband averted his eyes now when the child set out for the cemetery with the watering can. But when Mrs. Abs set up a kitchen garden behind the house he was almost overcome with surprise, he even thanked her. He knew what people in Jerichow had been telling her for three months—about the house, his wife's death, the Papenbrock clan. He praised her cooking, talked about the weather, asked after Jakob, whenever his duties gave him time to come home. Plus the Soviets liked having him as mayor since it had been the British who'd appointed him.

Then again he'd since had any number of risky fights with the commandant, involving shouting matches and shrewd reconciliations; he couldn't count on a salary, or gratitude, but could on a hard time for years to come, what with the nasty ideas the people in Jerichow were cultivating. He'd said something on the topic once, which made sense to Mrs. Abs. Someone had to do it, didn't they? That she understood. Someone has to do it. But there was too much about him that remained baffling.

She wanted to repay him for the food and lodging so she kept the house in order. He'd taken in more homeless refugees than he'd needed to or than K. A. Pontiy had wanted him to, and now the stovetop was crammed with pots and pans and casseroles. Mrs. Abs couldn't stand the constant bickering, everyone hiding things, she had learned how to run a large kitchen, so after a while she had taken over cooking for everyone. The people staying in Cresspahl's house, even the schoolteacher from Marienwerder, bowed to the authority of this tall gaunt woman who would look at you so silently, talk to you so evenly yet firmly. And she did have the head of the house behind her, and had been there longer than most of the others. There was no more sneaking meals in the bedrooms, in the attic; meals were served at the big tiled table in the kitchen. There were still a few hidden supplies of grain or potatoes, but the rule was introduced that everyone had to contribute something for meals, and after a while the possessions that had been such sources of conflict sat out in the open alongside one another in the pantry, behind an unlocked door. When Jakob came home with his earnings he was allowed to slip the children an egg, an apple, but the piece of bacon or the rabbit went into the common pot. Mrs. Abs got her own share to contribute, sometimes a big hunk of meat, by doing the laundry for the commandant and his two officers. There wasn't always enough to make everyone feel full,

Mrs. Abs! Theres a horse lyin in the marsh path! A dead horse, Mrs. Abs!

How longs it been there?

Just today.

Who knows about it, Gesine.

Just me. But we cant eat horse!

Youll get somethin else. Can you keep quiet?

Quiet as a tree.

Then go get me the knife.

and the children would rather there'd have been a lock on the pantry door. But there were fewer arguments in the house, the grown-ups could go out with Cresspahl's band of cripples and earn ration cards, and the teacher knew that her baby was being taken care of. The children learned from Mrs. Abs how to keep their room clean, Cresspahl's too, and they were at least shown how to wash windows. She would have been happy to make dresses for Gesine and Hanna out of the ones hanging in Lisbeth's bedroom; she asked Cresspahl for permission and the next morning they were gone. Jakob traded the patterns Cresspahl didn't want to see again for parachute silk and uniform fabric, and a sewing machine came into the house, where it stayed for five days before it had to be converted into alcohol. There was work to do in Cresspahl's house and that was enough for Mrs. Abs. She could put ointment on the children's scrapes and scratches from the wheat and rapeseed stubble, she could treat swelling boils with an Ichthyol salve and send the children off to work with an ever-so-slightly thicker slice of bread spread with sugar-beet molasses. Sometimes the children felt like a reason for her to stay. She'd won Hanna Ohlerich over immediately; Gesine remained out of reach for a while, maybe because she'd surfaced from her fever in such hesitant baby steps and was able to recognize her only afterward. Neither of them called her Mother, but also not Auntie, and though they almost always stuck to calling her Mrs. Abs they did slip into first names often enough. Hanna Ohlerich was a guest of Cresspahl's too, and she occasionally betrayed her thoughts of living elsewhere with narrowed, unfocused eyes—already it didn't really matter to her who she'd have to live with. With Gesine, Mrs. Abs felt half welcome. She would give Mrs. Abs a faraway look, ask questions in roundabout ways, stand there mute and withdrawn when Mrs. Abs ran to meet the mailman and came back disappointed. When it was possible to hear Jakob with the children, Mrs. Abs pushed the kitchen window's flap open a little. She heard Gesine's sudden urgent questions about Podejuch, noticed how Jakob was pulling her leg, saw how Gesine slunk off and came back to the kitchen crushed. And if she ever smiled at such twelve-year-old misery, it was never in front of me. By the time I'd learned not to let it show anymore, she'd helped me.

In late August, Mrs. Abs was carrying around a clipping from a newspaper in her apron pocket, folded small. When she was alone she sometimes read about what Edwin Hoernle, cofounder of the old KPD and now president of the German Agriculture and Forestry Administration, had announced about land reform: "that what matters today is to fulfill the old dream of every German farmworker and small farmer, the dream of a little farm of his own. These people are linked to the democratic Germany for as long as they live," and while she didn't understand the word *democratic* she took the rest to be a promise. She wasn't a farmworker, she had worn a white apron in the von Bonins' kitchen, but she'd worked in the countryside until her thirty-second year. This time she felt the days until Jakob came back to Jerichow were even longer. She was fifty-five, she wanted to take a farmstead with him. Jakob was almost eighteen, he could run a farm.

She had a bad conscience and talked it over with Jakob only at the end of the day; she didn't want to do it in the house, she went out onto the marsh path with him. Jakob didn't like doing that, it couldn't help but seem to Cresspahl like they had a secret.

Then he started talking to her like she was sick. He didn't want to settle the land somewhere. He wouldn't be able to farm anything with two horses, and a seventeen-year-old farmer. He admitted that the land around Jerichow grew lots of wheat; he'd seen the manor houses that were going to be torn down as emblems of feudalism, they would have to rebuild there. With the rubble? With wood? They had no plow, no harrow, no mowing machine, and there weren't any to be had on the black market either. And you didn't get the land for free, you had to pay for every hectare with the equivalent of a ton of rye, sometimes a ton and a half, and sure you could spread out the payments in installments until 1966 but did she want to start off with a debt like that? Not to mention the delivery costs: 550 liters of milk per cow, twenty eggs per chicken, and they didn't have the animals yet, there was their liveweight too. He presented this all to her cheerfully, and his mother felt patronized, and even though she was shocked to hear the difficulties in such detail she thought he had ulterior motives.

She was almost angry at him. The boy should have property. Now isn't the time for that: he explained, again in a dry, dismissive way, and she was so at a loss that she asked Cresspahl to help get her unreasonable offspring's head screwed on straight.

Cresspahl sat on the front steps with both children, even though it was already dark, and they looked at the Abs boy as if they'd been waiting for this moment. Cresspahl stood up, put his hands in his pants pocket, and looked ready to stand there for as long as it took. He himself had thought about settling the land, whether with the von Zelcks' permission or not, and he hoped Mrs. Abs would come with him. The children and Jakob made five, Jakob's father would make six, maybe enough to get by on a farm, and even the loans didn't scare him off. But he hadn't expected Mrs. Abs to agree to it, and K. A. Pontiy certainly didn't.

– Y'see? said Jakob cheerfully, although he hadn't actually won the argument. It wasn't the first time that there seemed to be some kind of arrangement between the two. She grabbed the children and took them inside. She could still see Jakob sitting down with this Cresspahl. Out of the brickworks villa's gate came Second Lieutenant Wassergahn, pulling the shirt of his uniform into pleasant pleats, rubbing his hand over his chin, smelling his hand. Mr. Wassergahn was on his way to a dance in Louise Papenbrock's parlor, and now Jakob and Cresspahl discussed the question of whether "these brothers" could be trusted. They were far from used to talking to each other, and what we could hear through the windows late into the night sounded a lot like an argument.

Mrs. Abs didn't go back outside to them and kept her bedroom windows closed. She was outraged that such a proposal had been made to her, in front of the children. She wasn't unhappy about the fact that Cresspahl wanted to settle the land only if she would come too. She figured out what lay behind all these clever arguments of Jakob's. He didn't want her to work in the fields. She should work standing up straight, or better yet sitting, not bent over; things should be made easy for her. He thought she was too old. Cresspahl, even though nothing could come of his proposal— he didn't think she was too old. She disagreed with both, and agreed with both. A week later, she showed them both that she wouldn't let herself get tied down to Cresspahl's house. She started working half days, in the hospital, as a cook.

Gesine didn't like seeing Mrs. Abs get dressed to go into town and pack her black bag. It was a leather case you could go on a trip with. Someone who could leave the house to go to work for no good reason could leave town too. How was Mrs. Abs to be kept in Jerichow?

May 21, 1968 Tuesday

First the French Communists didn't see the general strike coming, then they didn't support it, and now they want an alliance with all the forces of the Left, a veritable republican regime, which they even see as opening the way to Socialism.

The Polish ones, on the other hand, have finally figured out why the Poles keep misunderstanding them: it's the Czechoslovak ones' fault. The way they keep letting themselves get questioned in public about their plans—that can only be damaging.

The East German ones have gotten caught in Sweden with buried radio transmitters and several fake mailboxes.

The Czechoslovak ones are still playing host to Alexei N. Kosygin. After two years of negotiations, they are helping to open a branch of Pan American Airways in Prague, eighteen years after it was shut down following the coup, and the airfare to London can be paid in crowns. In Karlsbad (Karlovy Vary), the Soviet prime minister strolls openly through the streets and takes the famous healing waters.

Today we decided to no longer shop at Don Mauro's.

Don Mauro has a shop on Broadway (take the last car of the West Side express, come out of the Ninety-Sixth Street station walking east and in the opposite direction from the train), a little trap with tobacco products, candy, and cheap stationery for teeth. A row of phone booths may lure in a few customers, but he doesn't carry newspapers, he hasn't even supplied a bench where customers could linger any longer than it takes to exchange some money for merchandise. It's a shoebox of a trap, thriftily partitioned off from the business next door, and the slowly circling fan blades in the ceiling seem like luxurious furnishings. But the truth is that Don Mauro is a pillar of the Puerto Rican community on Manhattan's Upper West Side—a jewel on the church council, a man respected by the police, the head of the citizens' association, and anyone intending to win an election in this district had better not try without Don Mauro's goodwill. When Don Mauro arrived from his island eighteen years ago he could barely afford an apartment and had a hard time finding work, but he started off differently from the Negroes. The blacks still say, even today: See? That's how they treat us. From the word go, he thought: They're not going to treat us like that. From the beginning, Don Mauro had more equal rights, was more an American citizen than other people; he was helped by his family's lighter skin and the "right hair." Don Mauro started in this very shop and soon he was teaching his first son how to deal with the police and simple bookkeeping; by now he's training nephews for the stores that he is going to find, stock, and lease to them. Those other people may still have to pay protection money to the guardians of law and order, at Don Mauro's said guardians have to pay for their purchases and a proffered box of cigars is already an honor (one cigar per uniform). Don Mauro stands behind the counter in the back, chewing the same cold cigar stump from morning till night, or maybe all week. Sometimes the stump shifts around in the corner of Don Mauro's mouth, transforming his thoughtful expression, as if he's spit something out, but actually something's just popped into his head. He monitors the nephew at the register, he runs the expiring lease of the laundry next door through the calculator in his head, he chews around at the hard nut of a rental clause, nimbly, delicately, until it opens under his clever bite. Don Mauro doesn't merely look contented, the ceaseless plans and discoveries are depicted so joyfully in his face that clearly there's real happiness behind them. When he goes back every other year to check on the Estado Libre Asociado de Puerto Rico, visit his mother, attend mass in his native village, and see which younger relatives are ready for New York, he'll tell them stories about this piece of Manhattan, willingly if a little moodily. There are some places there that look like home, with the shop names, the neon signs, the bodegas. The buildings may be taller, but there are holes in the bottom with the island's music wafting and swimming up out of them. There are churches there that have service in Spanish, theaters showing only movies in their language—the homesickness isn't bad, and it doesn't get worse. The family sticks together there, just like here, and so do families; on Sundays you can see the girls in the park, respectable, dressed nicely, still Spanish looking. If your skin color's light then a lack of English isn't too big a problem. And so a new young man is standing at Don Mauro's cash register every year, acquiring the English of the Yanquis, moving on with the rank of store manager, later he might own one himself. The ones who understand this can sometimes be left alone in the store while Don Mauro climbs the narrow stairs in the side of the building—the discreet entrance to a second-floor office where he talks on the phone (no one knows what he says), keeps his money in the safe, has his secret bottle of cough syrup. The stairs lead only to this office. Who's going to know about it aside from the super? You hardly see anyone on the stairs. The door in the alley is half covered by the bins and bags with the hotel's garbage—just a crack that opens and closes again before you know it. There's a lot to think about regarding that office and the dime-store padlock on the door, the customers seem like a dream, and just a moment ago there weren't any.

Is this one? A Yanqui, a man about fifty, in a white shirt but needing a shave, with razor burn on his neck, saying something about dimes. Is he wanting to exchange his small change for bills?

It's the supplicant's lucky day. He looks, concerned and paternal, at the youth behind the counter—a sixteen-year-old with a hard narrow head, a dreamy look in his eyes, kind of friendly beneath the furrowed brow and still childlike waves of ash-blond hair. He tries to repay the cashier's favor with politeness, and is moved by his own feelings, too, to try to do something in return, so he says, a little recklessly: I'm not really a bum, you know... and he turns for support to the lady standing next to him, and she really does smile, not in pity, she's trying to encourage him.

Enter Don Mauro. He sees the apprentice's fingers in the till and no sale. The group stands paralyzed as he very quickly covers the distance from the door to them, though they've all seen him come marching in—an old man, shoulders stiff, his dignity only enhanced by the fury in his face. The youth gets a whipping from some Spanish whispered in a monotone, that won't heal before Saturday. The beggar is driven out of the shop like an infectious cow, every one of his submissive gestures intercepted by Don Mauro with a thrust of the chest and hisses of abuse; he adroitly shifts his legs to maneuver his victim until the man manages to escape out onto the sidewalk: the beggar, the failure, the parasite, – *You bum! You dirty bum!*

Barely out of breath, Don Mauro steps up to the lady customer still in the shop, not triumphantly, just a realistic businessman who came up the hard way. The youth lurches aside as if shoved with two hands. Moody, menacing, demanding, Don Mauro snarls: *Yes, ma'am?*

He knows this customer, he knows what she buys. Now she apologizes. Says she's made a mistake. She doesn't need anything in this shop.

– You're trying to give up smoking, Gesine?
– Not this way.

– You want to change the economic structure of the whole city of New York?

– Not this way.

– You want to go ten blocks farther every time, to the next Don Mauro, Don Fanto, Don Alfonso?

– No.

– You give to beggars, you said it was a personal choice.

– I know, Marie.

– You taught me it's wrong.

– No I didn't.

– Yes you did. So now you've showed your true colors, Gesine.

May 22, 1968 Wednesday

The New York Times, educated lady that she is, not only interprets for us what Charles de Gaulle might have meant with the soiled bed of his nation. She wants to give us an all-round education, and today she presents us with a key to the language of the American armed forces. Light losses are those that do not affect a unit's capability to carry out its mission. Moderate losses or damages mean that the unit's capability has been noticeably impaired, and finally heavy means that the unit can no longer perform its designated function. Decoded: If an installation in Vietnam reports light losses, a good hundred men might have been killed out of three thousand. In this language, those hundred don't count yet.

Last Tuesday East German border troops tried to fence in five hundred acres of West Germany near Wolfsburg, basing their claim on an 1873 map showing the border between Brunswick and Prussia, which was supposed to be the demarcation line in 1945. The West Germans admitted that there had been deviations in their favor, but protested that it was the Soviets of back then who'd drawn the line in the first place. – The Russians can err, too: the East German colonel said. According to the recollections of someone living on that border, his friends hadn't erred unless a gold watch or a few bottles of schnapps were part of the deal; then they would draw the fateful line in a bar with their English associates, on a beer coaster or a cigarette case. Today it's a shooting matter.

By October 1945 the people of Jerichow had long since stopped believing in the arrival of occupation troops from Sweden. They'd halfheartedly resigned themselves to the Soviets' staying, and now my father was being greeted on the streets again, when he wanted to be.

The mayor was credited with making things so bad for the refugees that most of them had left town. A man who relieved the townsfolk of the burdensome duty of hospitality couldn't be all bad.

K. A. Pontiy, commandant, had helped him do it. In the week he'd arrived, Pontiy had had his police register everyone in all of the houses, locals and refugees on the same list, the actual hard-power capacity, how many ration cards were needed—and Cresspahl thought it was only a paterfamilias's duty. He would learn more about Pontiy during the registration process. Two weeks went by and Pontiy started to doubt the security of his vouchers. He declared them invalid as of August 1 unless they bore the commandant's stamp as well as his signature. Again the people lined up outside Town Hall, up the stairs and down the hall to the room where Wassergahn was wielding his stamp. (All while the main and supreme directive from the state was to get the harvest brought in.) The sanctification of the documents went badly for the residents who'd been kicked out of the Bäk, for Wassergahn found any change in the information once he'd affixed his seal inconceivable, and the "moved parties" had to come in yet again, with Leslie Danzmann, to have their emergency lodging, the address for their ration cards, recognized. Wassergahn did not like having such cases explained to him—he looked darkly from the supplicant to the mayor's secretary, with furrowed brow; he hadn't forgotten the reason for these moves, he just thought of it as in the past, hence not open to discussion, particularly since it introduced messiness into his neat clean documents. On top of that, Wassergahn, for all his clean-cut professional appearance, kept uncertain hours. Two days' work on the harvest was lost. Pontiy was counting on 3,224 hungry subjects and on August 1 Cresspahl showed up with a request for 3,701 ration cards. Patiently, pedagogically, threateningly, Pontiy told his mayor to cease the annoying custom of letting every refugee who turned up in town make it into the registration card files with the right to a stamp from the commandant. The "illegal arrivals" were to be presented to him in lists, twenty heads each; he was stingy with his permits, shunting whole families off to the country whether they were willing to work or not.

At the same time, he tackled his population from another direction and had them register for labor duty, in a separate card file, whose data nonetheless had to be entered into the main card file. The contours of Pontiy's economic power had gradually grown blurry, given the differences between citizenship rights, residence rights, and applications for new citizenship and for repatriation, and in late August he ordered another registration of all residents. They had to bring in only two of his documents, plus identification cards and birth certificates, and this time he threatened anyone who failed to report with either arrest or expulsion from the town. That same week, he issued an order looking for every member of the former German Army with a rank of major or above, and likewise for anyone who worked in the former arms industry, whom he threatened under martial law. That was the occasion on which 1C Kliefoth, with all his service and military papers, was not arrested, though leaseholder Lindemann was, for not having registered as a hotel owner, solely because the Red Army had commandeered the whole Lübeck Court and was now running it. Leslie Danzmann and Cresspahl worked whole nights through on the general index that Pontiy wanted in the brickworks villa, and if it wasn't ready by September 1 then it would be up to the governor of the state of Mecklenburg-Vorpommern what to do—he had set that same date as the deadline for the registration of all male persons over the age of sixty, all females over fifty-five, and all university graduates of any age, on penalty this time of withholding ration cards and prison and/or a fine. Among the refugees there must have been some who didn't want anybody to be able to look up their previous life in Pontiy's safe, and others who resented the time spent on registrations instead of working or standing in line outside shops; they went looking early for a place on a Soviet-run farm, or in a village, far from Jerichow.

The indefatigable counting and recounting of heads and limbs, of elderly, sick, underage, and subject to compulsory insurance, all helped but was not enough alone to make Jerichow unsafe for many refugees. The town's supply of food was exhausted. The harvest had eventually been brought in, and faster than usual—mostly during personal nighttime trips out to the fields, and in the form of single sacks of potatoes and private bags of ears of wheat—but this was not food the townspeople would be distributing over the winter. There was absolutely no work available in town, putting at risk the right to a ration card. The displaced farmers went first. (Officially, no one could be referred to as "displaced" or "driven out" anymore—only as "evacuees" or "resettlers.") Anyone who wanted a piece of land from the stock of expropriated land needed to hop to it with the winter tilling. The papers that K. A. Pontiy and Cresspahl had collected from every refugee in only three months were a treasure trove, in the eyes of the commandants around the countryside. (The term "refugee" was no longer permitted in spoken use either.) Out there, the city people had gone back to city jobs by that point and new laborers were welcome. Near potato clamps, getting paid wages in kind, refugees might yet make it through the winter. There were lots of reasons why Leslie Danzmann had to register the departure of resettlers, but first and foremost the people of Jerichow chalked it up to Cresspahl.

It was under Cresspahl's regime that the schools were reopened. Starting October 1, the children, who'd been running wild, were finally kept busy again, and each one was given a rye bun in school too.

It might have been Cresspahl who'd pulled off a real live train at the Jerichow station, three passenger cars in tow, every day since late September. It departed for Gneez in the morning and came back in the evening. Heinz Wollenberg was glad that his daughter Lise could attend her high school again, and had suggested that his daughter be nice to Gesine Cresspahl. Cresspahl was just doing his duty. – Hi there: Lise said on the platform, for the first time since June; this cheerful nonchalance seemed a bit fishy to Gesine, but she said: Hey.

Cresspahl was given one hundred and twenty marks a month, plus twenty marks as a housing allowance, for working from morning until late at night. He couldn't supplement his income with carpentry, having neither the time nor the opportunity to get materials on the black market. He was hitched to a wagon in which sat K. A. Pontiy and the Red Army. He took no benefit from his office; let him have his losses.

He may have introduced bicycle registration to give his buddy Pontiy an overview of who had what, but still, it helped reduce thefts a little.

No, Cresspahl was still needed. It was thanks to him that Jerichow got fish from the Baltic, even if only for the hospital; on ration-card coupon No. 10 there was an unexpected allocation of salt; he would keep pestering the Gneez district office until it released some coal to run the gasworks with. And those utter scoundrels, the Englishmen, had cut Jerichow off from their Herrenwyk power station, the town had gone dark, and Cresspahl had found a generator for the hospital in exchange for Mrs. Köpcke's truck and the last spare tires Swenson had left in his hideaway, and the two victimized companies had been compensated at peacetime prices and told not to make a fuss. Because who was going to get Jerichow connected back up to an eastern power grid, them or Cresspahl?

In mid-October when all male and female persons between the ages of sixteen and fifty were ordered to report for exams for venereal diseases, "by order of the commandant," the talk in Jerichow was that Cresspahl had won one against Pontiy. Older women came too, bringing girls under sixteen. Pontiy hadn't realized the consequences, but the mayor of Jerichow had. It started to look like Cresspahl was in charge now.

The Jerichow government bank had recently started collecting taxes again. The new city bank, formerly the credit union, no longer stayed open from ten a.m. to ten p.m. just because it was ordered to: the tradesmen were depositing their earnings there daily; word had gotten round that the money wasn't disappearing, it could be used to make payments, with forms and signatures, just like before. It was a meager economy, a hungry life, a barren town—but Cresspahl had helped get it on track.

On October 22, two Soviet officers who were strangers to Jerichow paid Cresspahl a visit. It was evening, already dark, the people's movements around the jeep outside Town Hall were unclear. Leslie Danzmann was able to say that Cresspahl had left without a struggle. Not even a kerosene lamp knocked over. Then Cresspahl's secretary was arrested too. Pontiy issued his Order No. 24 through Fritz Schenk:

In the interest
of stabilizing
the town's autonomy
and increasing
the productivity
of the municipal economy
and introducing
a stricter order
into the affairs
of the Town of Jerichow
I hereby relieve Mr. Heinrich Cresspahl from his duties as mayor, as of this 21st day of October, 1945.

May 23, 1968 Thursday

The West German government spokesman gives the number. Czechoslovakia's Socialist neighbors will send in ten to twelve thousand special troops. The intelligence services, along with well-informed Czechoslovak and Western sources, call the information nonsense. That's true, they didn't even name a date.

– Cresspahl trusted his man Pontiy one too many times.
– And for too long, too.
– Yes, yes, grown-up psychology. Not for children.
– Cresspahl had gotten some news in September. Dr. Salomon still considered the German a client. He had found Mrs. Trowbridge and Henry Trowbridge. They'd died in an air attack on the British Midlands on November 14, 1940. Cresspahl hadn't had the slip of paper from Lübeck long before he got into a fight with K. A. Pontiy about his order to bring in the harvest, and it was a long night.
– A drunken night.
– A night in a state where things weren't blurry, where you were anchored to a particular thought that seemed to grow bigger and bigger. Toward morning they were barely drinking any more, just taking longer and longer to answer each other, half an hour sometimes. And Pontiy said forgetfully, sighing, that his son had fallen in Germany in April 1945.
– And Cresspahl told him about his son in England, that he'd lost to the Germans too.
– No. It was just two words, he never forgot them, they were his two best words in Russian: *Ne daleko.*
– That *was* all it took? That Pontiy's son had died *ne daleko*?
– That was enough for a while. *Ne daleko.* Not far. Near Jerichow.

May 24, 1968 Friday

Since January 1, 1961, 23,500 Americans have died in Vietnam. Which the military calls light casualties. The Vietnamese victims are not included in this number.

The presidium of the Czechoslovakian Communist Party had something to say to newspaper editors, executives, and radio commentators: Stop talking about the Soviet Union's past crimes all the time. Don't insult the Union of Soviet Socialist Republics. Don't dwell on the new KAN clubs. The party presidium isn't giving orders to the press or anything. The leaders believe that a good Communist understands the need for self-censorship when facing dangers "both from the left and from the right," and that belief is good enough for them.

KAN: *Klub Angažovaných Nestraníků*. Even in English we don't exactly understand it: Club of Committed Nonparty Members. How would that go in German? A new party founded on the principle that its members are not in any party. *Bund der engagierten Parteilosen?* "Alliance of Politically Active Independents"? It could also be the Left with nowhere else to go, under a new roof.

8 p.m.: Dr. Laszlo Pinter, Hungarian Delegate to the United Nations, will be speaking at Church Center, 777 United Nations Plaza, as a guest of the American Society for the Study of the German Democratic Republic. Topic: "European Disarmament and the Two German States."

There's a table by the door where you can donate 99 cents, more if you want. We ask for our one penny back, despite the cashier's embarrassed opposition—we want to keep the coin as a souvenir. The flyers on the chairs give the society's address as 370 Riverside Drive. That's on 109th Street. Marie has definitely babysat children there. It's a nice place to live.

Most of the audience members are old and seem to be timidly acquainted. A gathering of party members in the audience of a gathering of not the party. Strangers are exposed to surprised and searching looks, as if they were uninvited guests.

The first speaker emphasizes that visas to visit the UN have been refused to representatives of the GDR. Pithy American English. *My-self*, etc.

The second speaker proves, in a swift, soft, professorial voice, that the study of the German Democratic Republic is desirable for reasons of culture, peace, and understanding.

The guest from Hungary is a tall man with a red face and bulging flesh, maybe thirty-five years old. Narrow-framed glasses, thick black hair. His English teacher taught him not to nasalize endings: he calls certain things *promissink*! He says: Yu-RO-pean. Probably learned his English closer to Moscow. He begins with the ancient Greek myths, Crete, Europe the cradle of ideas and colonialism. Two world wars. Germany is divided. NATO. Warsaw Pact. This is not my official position, please don't quote me on that.

The effects of atomic bombs. Not the horror movie the way it appears on-screen. Very, very crucial factors. The attempted putsch of 1953, which was not successful: snippier, haughtier tone.

The fire alarm keeps going off in the hall.

The Danube Federation. The Rapacki Plan. This brings me to the German question. *What do we have in Germany?* Five NATO divisions, a leading role in the Atomic Planning Staff, the Potsdam Agreement not in effect. The fellow isn't set on cigarettes from back home, he smokes the local brands, bright red-and-white packs, Marlboro or Lux.

The Nazis. Started in 1930 with 2.2 percent. All the things the emergency laws allow. He forgets the confiscation of cars, in front of this audience of all people. The demonstrations in West Berlin: putting the laws into practice for the first time. The demonstrations in Warsaw, Paris, and New York may have been at the same time. For every one of these facts I could mention a counterfact. If this was the proof, it is not complete yet.

The matter of peace. *Vesch' mira.* This is why we need dialogue. A statesman has made a proposal. He talks in long circumlocutions about this statesman, talks in worshipful tones. When the suspense has gone on too long, he gives up the name: this statesman was Mr. Kosygin from the Soviet Union.

Applause. Q&A.

– The East German attitude toward the developments in Czechoslovakia.

– Yes, well, you know… I have to tell you something. The Czechoslovak Socialist Republic would subscribe to everything I said, nearly word for word. I don't see the connection. I don't know anything about attitudes. Congratulations to *The New York Times* on its self-proclaimed promotion to spokesman for the GDR!

– (Examples:) GDR jamming stations, lead articles in government papers, a top television commentator's trip to Bohemia.

– Yes well if you want to change the topic…: counters the comrade from circles not used to being addressed in that fashion. He doesn't shirk from his argument, here it is: I can't compete with *The New York Times,* I can only rely on my own clipping service.

An older woman, long diagonally cut white hair hanging down to her neck under a kind of bonnet. She says something mild, something overindulgent about government credits for home purchases here.

– And how do you have a dialogue over a wall?

– Well yes. Of course. (Expected question.)

The government's credits when someone wants to buy a house are ...

– My comment on that, in a word, is this: It would be a damn good thing, if you ask me personally. ONE SHOULD ALWAYS ADDRESS A TOPIC FROM THE PROPER PERSPECTIVE. While West Germany had the Marshall Plan, East Germany started with absolutely nothing.

The mouthpiece does not have it easy among the curious, some of them readers of *The New York Times,* and he has no clippings from that source. One calls himself a genuine Communist. One is a clergyman, one is a West German immigrant worker, one

has been to the GDR. He is the president of this society, he has talked to the young officers at the Brandenburg Gate. White hair, too red in the face. Talks in a slightly complaining voice, looking sharply down to the right at the floor. The soldiers at the Wall are unarmed but people shoot at them.

Well then.

– Why did the meeting between the SPD and SED in Hanover fall through?

– Because it wasn't supposed to be a conversation between two sovereign states. The Hungarian guest has to get the right answer handed to him by the man taking the entrance money, who translates the word *Handschellengesetz,* "handcuff law," from East German propagandaspeak via American English *safe conduct* back into West German: *freies Geleit.* The East German speakers don't want a guarantee that they won't be prosecuted, they want diplomatic immunity. Bravo to the man at the entrance!

There was someone else with a question about West Berlin. Why does the East German press always refer to West Berlin as "on" GDR territory instead of "in" it, as both natural and political facts would suggest? We'd like to hear the answer to that one ourselves. How did the western sectors of Berlin find themselves on GDR territory before the GDR even existed. That question got in reply a gesture of helplessly raised arms, already weak from the flood of other questions: Hungarians can be so likeable. How dearly he'd love to answer this question, of all questions, if they'd only let him. The man with relatives in West Berlin doesn't raise his hand again. Cresspahl is afraid she'd offend him if she repeated the question. So we won't hear the answer from this man whose mind has been made up for so many years and will remain so.

The president of the Society for the Study of the GDR is, in conclusion, in favor of goodwill. Of appreciating the GDR, once it's been studied. And we're in the red to the tune of $250, which is why there's a genuine, antique, Methodist collection plate set up at the door. Thank you.

And just like on the old collection days, an assistant puts three five-dollar bills on the plate at once, to fool the later contributors. Mrs. Cresspahl unloads her cent there, wishing only it were a red one.

May 25, 1968 Saturday, South Ferry day

In the IRT subway line, the management—may they suffocate in the heat—have removed one of the pair of fans in every car! When the cars creep screeching in the tight squeeze up to the curved platforms under the ferry terminal, the passengers in the front cars first have to walk between dark tunnel walls, and inside the station there are ramps to the train doors. Only then are the doors opened, and today the sticky air intensified the fear that they wouldn't open at all.

– So both my grandfathers had criminal records: Marie said the moment we were aboard. She was trying to take this news of her forefathers like a devil-may-care desperado, but ancestors like that have always made her uncomfortable. Whatever she hears at home doesn't stand a chance against what she learns in school, which is that being arrested proves you're guilty. She wasn't supposed to learn that: white middle-class thinking. But that's how she thinks.

– Jakob's father was never put on trial, Marie.

– He was in a military prison, in Anklam, you admit that. Did he at least avoid the draft?

– You may not have liked what he did. And I don't know what he did.

– He could have been your father-in-law. It's my grandfather, Gesine.

– All I know about him is that he was born in 1889, Neukloster Seminary, Brazil in the twenties, jobs as an estate manager in Mecklenburg and Pommern, drafted into the army in 1943, and prison—what I picked up in conversation over those fifteen years with Jakob and his mother. I was in no hurry to ask questions and then Jakob died. I didn't want to press his mother and then she died. Neither liked to talk about Wilhelm Abs, and I only know his first name from the will. If I had to say his birthday, I could only say July, I'd have to look up the exact date.

– And where's he buried?

– His wife refused to believe he was dead until she was. He'll be seventy-nine in five or six weeks, if that's what you want to believe.

– In the Soviet Union. We wouldn't recognize him.

– You wouldn't mind a stranger, would you, Marie?

– Tonight I want to write down his birthday. Not to celebrate it, but so at least one of us knows it.

– And no criminal record.

– Make Cresspahl innocent, Gesine. Even if you have to lie a little.

– The officers who arrested him started off treating him like he was innocent. He wasn't pushed into the jeep, they patiently held the door open for him until he found his seat in the dark. He wasn't handcuffed. They gave him a blanket. There was a little chat about the chill in the air, winter's coming, hope the frost doesn't get the potatoes. When Cresspahl asked them to let him go to his house for five minutes, they didn't refuse rudely, it was more bemused, like he was someone new to a different world. They gave him some coarse *makhorka* for his pipe, like hosts. At Wehrlich station they locked him into a chicken coop.

– That was something he could never forget. He could never even speak of it!

– They did apologize. They didn't want to keep driving that night, one of them had a friend in the Wehrlich Kommandatura, there were no prison cells set up at the ranger station. Plus he wasn't supposed to be seen by the German staff. What else would you have done with a prisoner if you were them?

– Good, just keep on lying, Gesine. Then they brought him dinner on a tray.

– Maybe they forgot about that because they were so happy to see their friend again and the party was so fun. Cresspahl could hear their voices late into the night, singing, toasting, why would they think about a chicken coop.

– Now the escape.

– The lock was meant to protect the bygone chickens from both foxes and robbers on two legs. It was hard to pick in the dark. They'd moved the jeep in front of the door, he couldn't tip that over. There was no window, the walls were solid brick, the hatch was for chickens. He also might not have wanted to admit guilt straight off by running away. And in fact Soviet soldiers searched our rooms several times over the next few weeks, they were waiting for him in Jerichow. The chicken coop wasn't bad to sleep in; they'd left him the blanket. It's just that he banged into the low perches at first, and the stink of old droppings revived with the humidity of the night air. A sour smell, the legacy of three generations of chickens. Seeps into a person's clothes. Still, the Russians found their prisoner asleep the next morning. And now they were driving in a stinking jeep, trapped with the smell by the rain, and they all told jokes, every joke they could think of about roosters and chickens. Cresspahl got a hunk of bread, a sip of vodka, *makhorka*, like one comrade among others on a holiday trip, only he was the only one who didn't know where they were going. Where they were going was the basement under the Gneez district courthouse; his companions took their leave with encouraging if cautious claps on his shoulder. Ever since then Cresspahl thought that an arrest wasn't seen as anything to be ashamed of in the Red Army, at most it was a bit of bad luck that could happen to anyone. Good luck, they wished him. That was the start of the first phase.

– You walked to school above his head.

– The girls' high school in Gneez had been converted into a Red Army hospital. The lower grades were put in the Sacred Heart School—

– a parochial school, like me!

– a city school named after a convent and a chapel, long since burned down, commemorating the ritual persecution of the Jews in 1330. From the ruins of that pious quadrangle to the station I only had to cross two streets diagonally, and then I was right by my father though I never knew it. All I saw was the monument for the Franco-Prussian War, black and shining like a freshly polished train engine, and the two red flags like

tongues sticking out of the courthouse roof. That was where the German
police took the people dealing in food on the black market, gun owners,
members of the German Army arrested during the July registration, young
men under suspicion of being in the Werewolf resistance—it never crossed
my mind that Cresspahl might be locked up under that building. Language
dictated that anyone the Soviets picked up was sent "to Siberia," no one
had to tell me.

– And now we have the tortures, the water chamber, the starvation diet.

– Cresspahl felt like they'd arrested him just to put him away somewhere
and then they'd forgotten about him. The jailers brought food to his cell
twice a day, sometimes in the evening too—bread from their field bakery,
fish soup made of water and cod heads, leftovers from the soldiers' meals.
At school we learned to write and speak Russian but Charlotte Pagels
might have been using a book from the German Army's supply: she told
us kasha was cabbage soup,

> *shchi i kasha*
> *pishcha nasha*

when actually it was buckwheat or semolina groats with jam or a few shreds
of meat, my father in prison would have marked those days on the calendar
if he'd been allowed a calendar. When the cell door was unlocked he had
to stand at attention against the wall, head touching it, so that he couldn't
see into the hall. When he did this according to regulations they would
hand him the bowl. They didn't like it if he talked. They called him *otets*
and *durak*, Father and Fool, neither meant in a bad way, and gradually he
learned. Apparently they'd counted the inscriptions and drawings on the
saltpeter-covered wall and he wasn't allowed to add to them, so he got
himself a day with no food when he started a calendar. He found month
grids from spring 1945 scratched into the wall, final remarks before transport to Bützow-Dreibergen, the notes of the British national anthem accompanied by a blasphemous text, swastikas with entreaties for luck in
battle—those could all stay. It might have once been Dr. Semig's cell, but
he found no sign of him. To teach him about secret possessions they ripped
open his straw mattress every now and then and scattered the filling across
the cell; they praised him like a child when he'd reassembled a mattress
from it by nighttime. In December they noticed him shivering and stuck
a thermometer in his mouth. He wasn't allowed to see what it showed, and

his next meal came with a blanket. More horrible than the cold was the lack of light: it came in through a round tapered shaft terminating below a grate at the back of the building, for only a few hours a day. There were two or three voices in the next cell; he remained alone. His departure was quite a ceremony. The young men in their exquisitely spick-and-span uniforms had taken him to the washroom lots of times, with gentle nudges of his arm, because he seemed blind; this time they helped him remove his beard and gave him warm water. He was given parts of uniforms—air force on the bottom, army on the top—and for the first time in seventeen weeks he didn't smell like chicken shit. Sitting all alone on the bed of a covered truck he was driven south, and he learned to see again from the blurry spring green by Schwerin Lake. He was taken to the Soviet Military Tribunal in the capital, and now he was supposed to talk.

– The unauthorized withdrawals from the nobility's accounts.

– He'd paid those back as soon as enough taxes had come in (and as a result the Jerichow government bank stayed empty to the floorboards). Maybe he hadn't been able to bring himself to pay interest on the loans, and such transgressions were part of Phase One.

– Woken up in the middle of the night and made to recite numbers.

– In Schwerin the Soviets were working round the clock, the court calendar decided when it was his turn. For days on end they didn't need him for anything, of course, and in the heated cell, with the plentiful light from above, he almost relearned what it was like to have a place to live, then without warning they'd come get him in the middle of the night. The court ran like a machine, demanding trot and walk and gallop from a standing start from both defendants and prosecutors; Cresspahl couldn't blame the specific people in charge of his case. One of them seemed like a military man to him, the other an auditor, they traded off. They'd prepared their case, they had the Jerichow Town Hall files on the table, and at first Cresspahl only had to tell them about everything he'd done. If one of his stories pleased them, he was allowed to repeat it. They watched him uneasily; they were expecting him to defend himself, not agree to one judgment after another against himself.

– With a clear conscience, Gesine. He hadn't taken anything for himself.

– It was for someone else's benefit, not his. While K. A. Pontiy had bindingly abolished civil rights in Jerichow, he had not explained the new

kinds of guilt. So now the gentlemen of the Schwerin SMT read Cresspahl
Law No. 4 of the Allied Control Council, and took it to mean that the
laws in force on January 30, 1933, were valid for the time being. He hadn't
been able to follow them.

– What he'd done was its own defense.

– What an American! You and your truth! The truth can be used in
the service of anything.

– But it's what really happened!

– Cresspahl wasn't interested in going beyond his own truth. He did
find out some new information. He'd confiscated two bags of roasted coffee
beans from Böhnhase, with the permission of the Gneez DA's office, but
now in Schwerin the hoarded merchandise was described to him as originating
in an illegal act, and it wasn't even coffee anymore, it had magically transformed
into crude oil for the generator powering the hospital lights. In other words,
Cresspahl was supposed to answer for the hidden hands through which
the coffee had previously passed—for a past he knew nothing about. He
didn't see how he could do that, so he didn't sign. The two interrogators
found his rigidity amusing. They went along with his quirk of not naming
any names other than those on paper in front of him—they had names,
they helped him out. He was gradually led to believe that not only Leslie
Danzmann but Gantlik was in jail, and Slata, and Amalie Creutz, and
Peter Wulff, and Böhnhase, and the mayor of Beckhorst village. For a long
time the conversations stayed friendly—he wasn't kept standing, they
moved his chair from the edge of the room up to the desk, and when it
came to tricky memories he stood next to the interrogator like a colleague,
bent over the files, searching, turning pages. Since he was used to smoking
a pipe he was allowed to go pick one out from the seized-property room
and he found one of English manufacture, barely damaged, with a curved
mouthpiece, like the kind Uncle Joe used to smoke; it would be taken out
of a drawer at the start of each session and locked away again at the end,
like a medical instrument. Sometimes he even got Krüll instead of *makhorka*.

– Uncle Joe, I should know that one.

– You should, you American. Josif Vissarionovič was shown with just
such a pipe when he was introduced to the public here, back when he was
still supposed to be an ally. The photograph shows him with a mischievous
look in his eye, like a good uncle.

– The defendant with his resemblance to the supreme lord of the court.

– The interrogators didn't care. They were from another country, they might not ever have seen that picture.

– Did they also call Cresspahl "Little Father"?

– They addressed him in bourgeois fashion. They wanted him to feel competent, an adult who'd made mistakes while of sound mind and body. The mistakes had been established, now he needed to recognize the crimes. And to help him along they presented various bits and pieces the way they saw it: Slata had been taken to another court, in the Soviet Union. Her name had served only to prove Cresspahl's connection with a perpetrator of crimes against humanity. Amalie Creutz wasn't in jail at all. And why would she be, from Cresspahl's own statements he'd been perfectly willing to believe she was pregnant, his request to have an abortion approved had been found in the Schwerin Department of Health and countersigned by him as proof

of the goal

of the defamation

of the honor

of the Red Army,

they didn't need Mrs. Creutz as a witness anymore. And the gentlemen were certainly prepared to summon Fritz Schenk for a face-to-face confrontation, they were very interested indeed in such a thing, only Schenk was no longer in Jerichow, and the German comrades reported that he was indispensable. Even a Soviet examining magistrate has his limitations, you see. All that talk about omnipotence is greatly exaggerated.

– Whose side are you on, Gesine! You belong on Cresspahl's but you're not advocating for him.

– Why should I be on just one side? What I know has more than two sides.

– Would Cresspahl be okay with that?

– They covered everything with him all the way back to 1935. He had done carpentry work for the Jerichow-North air base, until 1938, and until 1945. He admitted it. He had, therefore, starting in 1935, with no evidence of coercion, helped German militarism up onto its feet and into the air. Although Cresspahl realized that the one implied the other, and that they were trying to cast him as someone who'd paved the way for the Nazis, he

didn't want to follow them across the bridge to economic sabotage in
Jerichow as a past and present Fascist. He wouldn't sign. They tried it again,
this time offering something in return. When he would ask about his child
in Jerichow, they would sternly refuse to say anything, shaking their heads
at his denseness; after two weeks, they revealed after all that Schoolgirl
Cresspahl had been transferred to the Bridge School in Gneez with a B in
Russian. He thanked them for bending the rules; he didn't deviate from
his own. They scolded him, not without a certain sadness; they had failed
in their goal of at least moving him to somewhere between the subjective
and the objective truth. By that point they had enough facts, they no longer
needed him. He was sent to a camp where the Nazis had once kept their
prisoners, he was supposed to help straighten it up.

– Was that his sentence?

– It was a holding camp. The gentlemen of the Schwerin SMT hadn't
threatened him with any specific punishment. Only once, when they didn't
know what else to say, had they asked: if he'd really rather spend thirty
years in prison than fifteen, or at most twenty.

– He was clever enough. You got mail from him.

– The camp was well guarded, with dog patrols between the two rows
of barbed wire, searchlights at night. He was there with other people but
they were quickly taken off to sentencing and other countries, they couldn't
take messages. Even in his work he couldn't smuggle out any messages—the
bedframes, the window crosspieces, the barrack sections, everything stayed
inside the fence. Anyway, he could only guess at the nearest town or village.
He might be anywhere in southwestern Mecklenburg. Other people knew
more precisely, Neustadt-Glewe they said; that didn't fit the route he'd
been brought on, as far as he could tell from the night transport.

– When are we up to now?

– August 1946.

– So now I'll be your guide, through Staten Island, New York, as of
May, nineteen sixty-eight.

The Czechoslovak Communists have had to pay. To avoid having eleven
thousand special forces in their country and a Cominform within the
Warsaw Pact they are now to permit military exercises on their soil in June.
The East Germans dismiss the stationing of allied troops in Czechoslovakia

as West German provocation, and have the following information about the plan to move Socialism into the present: "The wheel of history cannot be turned back." History as a winch that winds up the past, irrevocably, for eternity. Onward!

May 26, 1968 Sunday

The parts of Staten Island, borough and Richmond County, that Marie showed me yesterday. *Now you know, Gesine. I won't have to bring it up again.*

After the wasteland of single-story brick on the north coast of the island, finally some trees and landscape at Silver Lake Park—sheltering lines of trellises and windbreaks. Gentle rises and falls of the streets, uncomplaining, with the undulations of the land. Still some country houses from former times, ingenuously armed with columned porches, Greek antiquity in wood. Verandas in leafy shadow, windows dark in the heat, concealing quiet, creaking rooms. Boxes sheeted in bright Dutch brick with white frames precisely cut in. High branches stripped by the Atlantic's breath, corpulent whispering clouds of green. A gathering of gulls on the leeward shingle roofs. Electrical lines on rough-hewn poles that are often tilted, from an age of modest technology. Grass growing in the cracks between slabs of the sidewalk, weeds and shrubs high and rampant around the stairs. Lawns sloping down to the street, cool, hedges wild. Neighborhoods. What would it be like to wait here by the window, in the hazy overcast air of early summer, and later warm in bare damp November. *Here you'll have a country life. Mecklenburg, California. Stay here, Gesine. I'll buy you a house here as soon as I can.*

The trains of the SIRR crossing the island make less of a susurration than their name. They claim to be Staten Island's Rapid Transit, an offshoot of the Baltimore & Ohio Railroad—what they are is a jerky, rattling suburban line. Wobbly train cars from not long after the First World War, stopping every mile at narrow, barely roofed platforms. Nervous clanging at crossings; hollow howls when approaching stations; bravely onward drives the little train, as though heading straight to the Gulf of Mexico. A number, a year, catches the eye, engraved too formally in a concrete sill of one of the cramped little bridge houses: 1933. Ragged bushes right up next to the third rail. *Start here, Gesine; stay here.*

The Verrazano Bridge sends wide lanes of traffic shooting to New Jersey above the railroad tracks cut into the landscape. From Oude Dorp and Arrochar on, tiny airplanes hang in the sky, boarders at the aircraft field near Richmond Avenue by the creeks flowing into Arthur Kill. *You could get away here, and we could come visit you, by land, by sea, by air.*

The ferry building on the southern tip of the island is even more vacant now, the planks falling off it, walls of wooden pillars aslant in the putrid water. The water has burrowed right up next to Tottenville station, chewing on garbage, nourishing rust and sludge. Tottenville station was built to serve the ferry to Perth Amboy; that end of the station was now silent, wrapped tight in chicken wire, as though no boat had left for New Jersey in a very long time even though there'd been one since colonial days. The other shore lay there waiting, inert, with cranes, warehouses, a church, roofs flashing in the leaves, motionless in the midday heat. To the north, a bridge on stilts crossed Arthur Kill, frozen in midstride like a gouty cat. Construction rubble, oil barrels, junk on the beach, splintering posts in the water, and, farther out, backlit pleasure craft and fishing boats. Everywhere, vegetation reclaiming the sick land, covering the scars and wounds of the ground; *the externals of vacation, Gesine.*

In Tottenville, death passed by. In the white light laid out by the sun, two black-clad couples walked toward a building that looked like a fancy dairy or private school. The two women's skin was very warm beneath the transparent fabric. One man, in a business suit, shyly brought up the rear, as though embarrassed by the prospect of seeing the person lying there, or by the expectation that they would be carrying him in himself through the back door of the funeral parlor in a few years. (As though he were visiting his future home, with himself inside it, having not thought about his move at all.) *When you're dead, Gesine, I won't let the embalmers get you.*

In Tottenville, crippled houses huddled together, collapsing, draped with pieces of plastic. A little synagogue shack with a skin of asbestos shingles. Italian plaster figures on dried-out patches of lawn. A living cat, white, with deeply blackened eyes, wants to be noticed, there is something it knows. Children on porches, an old woman sitting with a book upstairs, watching. Swings and wading pools in the backyards. Hot wood smell, acacia blossom. One of D. E.'s love affairs, Wannsee, Berlin, 1949, long nights next to a girl leaning on the garden gate in the scent of acacias; by day the little white flowers stayed hidden in the green of the leaves; in 1949 what she wanted from a man with black-market connections was not chocolate or a phonograph record but a swim cap. *Or go live with the poor, Gesine.*

An unexpected wide field of high grasses, wild shrubs growing everywhere. A steam freighter so close to the shore it seems grounded. A white gable outlined against the horizon of leafage, a canting roof set in front of an almost cube-shaped wooden box. Behind the dark windows, on the long porch facing the Atlantic, not a sign of movement. A steep, overgrown path for the mailman. *Or that, if you want.*

On Raritan Bay. The Raritan Indians' name for the island was Aquehonga Manacknong, "Place of the High Sandy Bank," and they thrice succeeded in driving off, with fire, the invaders from the Delaware territories. Henry Hudson said he sighted land here on September 2, 1609, and at once named it in honor of his masters, the Dutch Staaten-General. Staaten Eylandt, lost to the British in 1664. Four years later, the Duke of York had a hankering for the islands in his bay, he wanted all of them that could be circumnavigated in twenty-four hours, and one Captain Christopher Billopp sailed around Staaten Eylandt end to end in the prescribed time, for which feat he was rewarded with 116 acres out of the roughly 37,000 he had procured for the king's brother. He did not have Dido's problem. In Billopp's house, around the corner here, General Howe met with a delegation of rebels after the Battle of Long Island for the first peace conference of the Revolutionary War, to no avail. William Howe read the Declaration of Independence here for the first time, and said: This here has been signed by rather determined men. *Your Mecklenburg was stolen land too, Gesine.*

On the sandy roads, covered with puddles of water, lonely cars drove as if cowed by field and thicket, so far from eight-lane highways and apartment buildings. Marshlands, no longer traversable due to broken bottles and rusty tin cans. A colony of summer houses falling apart. Children who stared at strangers walking by, giggled at the strange child's city airs. Near the water, a married couple sat in a car, helpless, ready to drive away. Look, real reeds. This is plantain, good for cuts. We made soup out of goosefoot. Rabbits used to like to eat this. A red maple. Chicory. Ribwort. Shepherd's purse, you could eat that. Nettles were good as spinach. Sunburn weather. *Don't forget why I showed you all this, Gesine.*

Anyone who sent Ho Chi Minh, the President and Enlightened One, many happy returns on May 19 has now gotten something from him in the mail:

> At seventy-eight
> I don't feel very old yet.
> Steadily on my shoulders still rests
> The country's burden.
> Our people, in their resistance,
> Are winning tremendous victories.
> We march with our younger generation.
> Forward!

© Viet Nam Press, Hanoi

A testimonial to Alexei Nikolayevich Kosygin. Premier of the Soviet Union. For our reading pleasure in *The New York Times.*

A quiet and retiring man of sixty-four, taking the waters in Karlovy Vary, seen going for walks with his granddaughter, cannot possibly mean the Czechs and Slovaks any harm. Hard currency from Moscow, that was the carrot. Military action, that was the stick. Both merely shown, for now.

He gained: troop maneuvers, tightened censorship, a ban on legal opposition.

If the generals continue to growl in the *Red Star* about an American finger in "internal affairs," he will have to cut short his visit to the ČSSR and go see them, and yet he is forgiven.

For what he explains to the Stalinist faction will shape Czechoslovakia's future—and the world's.

Placed on record, today's, in New York, Forty-Third Street, west of Times Square.

The Communists in Prague are taking their first steps toward a law, to be passed in July or August. Relief is planned for a hundred thousand persons who have suffered penalties à la Pontiy, such as expulsion from their homes, removal from jobs, and the like. Forty thousand prisoners from between 1948 and 1956 are to receive 20,000 Czech crowns for each year spent in prison, with 25 percent to be paid immediately and the rest over a period of ten years.

That would add up to about a billion crowns by the end of 1970. A dollar, the paper says, is worth seven crowns, or in special cases sixteen. Compare the exchange rate of the ruble. Factor in not only the $400 million from Moscow but the 20 million in overseas assets, plus the 5 million in pensions that US Social Security withholds from Czechoslovakian citizens. Will it be enough?

So that was work today. In forty minutes we'll be back on Riverside Drive, at home.

Anyone could come.

She just comes from Grand Central, lets the crowds push her toward the West Side line, finds her place where the third door of the first car stops.

As if New York functioned properly every day. The subway as sunset.

They didn't announce anything at Grand Central!

And you fell right into their trap, young lady.

No trains running here.

Even if they were, you couldn't get on.

That was always my place, where the third door stopped.

Well that's where we're standing now, you Caucasian, you pink child.

Oh, you big black man!

At least let her stay on her feet. Don't knock her down!

Me? Knock over a lady? There's just surges here underground.

What's the problem here?

That we're stuck standing here packed tight in the heat, as if they're planning to spray water all over us. Then put the lid on.

I'd sure like to move an arm.

No electricity.

Stay! You stay in your bag! Stop climbing on the nice lady.

She brings you home and then what!

None of us is ever going to get home.

Where's the problem?

Look. She wants to know exactly too. With a diagram and everything.

So, if you move my bag between your legs a little, there, you see what I mean?

I can move my arm from the shoulder—

If you block out this fat black man—

Aha. Probably better for him too.

There's almost something you can do to help, y'know?

It's an outrage, the subway system!

We know. New York'll always be New York.

Don't look at me like that! My hand's on the outside of your bag, not the inside!

Itchy?

None of your business. I've got a job.

And the two of us together?

When the little one smiles, she means me, you foreigner.

I'm not little.

Here comes a train.

Like a hobbling horse.

A power station's on fire in Brooklyn.

Hey, they're not getting out!

This is our train. We're not giving it up.

It's my train! I need to get home!

And even if we need to take it to the Bronx, the thing does *move.*

You can escape from the Bronx. Not from here.

They're looking at us like an enemy army.

Well this is a reason for war, isn't it? They're cooped up in their train, we're in this pit of a station.

We look at them like an enemy army. And then they ride off into the darkness.

If the train stops in the dark they won't know where it is.

Anybody else ready to give up? I'd be happy to give up, but not alone.

No one here's giving up.

You'll never make it up the stairs. More new people keep pouring down the stairs.

They don't know yet.

Anyone can come.

The place where the train's broken! New York is falling apart!

The system's been bringing in money for sixty-four years, why should they fix it?

For us?

That's how they treat us.

Well, the thing is, in a taxi this time of day...

If not I'll just lie down next to the rail and be under one fan after another. It was nice being able to breathe.

I bet I have money for a taxi.

We won't let anyone not with us through to the second row.

You see the train on the opposite platform? The batteries under the cars are glowing.

That won't get far.

None of us are getting anywhere.

You've already got one foot on the edge of the platform. Next time—

Push 'er in!

Turn around! Shoulders out!

Don't move! She's lost a shoe.

She can do this barefoot.

Two upstanding citizens like us and still we can pry the subway doors open!

Just stick the shoe in! Between their heads, they'll notice that.

Look, they actually put her shoe back in her hand.

Usually a train comes every two minutes and bites off a piece of the line. Now they're coming four minutes apart, and this one's been sitting here an extra thirty seconds.

We shouldn't have pushed her in after all. She's in and we're looking at empty rails.

Maybe she'll be stuck in there when she wants to get out. Or just stay like that, in the dark, somewhere under Broadway.

I don't envy her.

We don't envy you.

Have a nice trip!

Have a nice trip!

Did she thank you?

Just wrinkled her nose, like this. Wouldn't want to be pushy and actually give a smile, you know?

I know what you mean.
And there she goes. Hey, don't mention it!
See y'all tomorrow!
Sounds good. Till tomorrow.

May 28, 1968   Tuesday

This morning the train stopped in the dark, past the Fiftieth St. station. It was hard to judge how far we were from the lit platform. My memory keeps reporting that there is a bright spot next to this stretch of track, a hundred feet wide, two hundred feet wide, seen just the day before yesterday, an opening into the light, a staircase to the surface. The ever-returning search for a way out marked time, took up space, pushed thought aside. Fear of every additional minute grew and grew in the motionless silent crush of people until the train jolting into motion was unbelievable. On the stairs beneath Times Square the policemen were standing around, in a good mood, hands comfortably clasped on the billy club behind their back, and they looked at the scared passengers as if to say: Are they after you? Did they let you go this time? You're running like there's a prize at the end.

After Cresspahl disappeared, Jakob reluctantly took over his household.

His mother had tried to do it alone. The refugees in the rear of the house kept to the rules she'd introduced, both in the kitchen and taking turns to keep the halls and stairs clean; maybe they thought Cresspahl had given some last-minute instructions, but Mrs. Abs felt that this was dishonest since she hadn't been given any such authority. If Gesine and Hanna Ohlerich weren't there she would probably have packed up her things and sought refuge where Jakob was working, two hours from Jerichow, where she wasn't known as the housekeeper of a mayor the Russians had arrested. She wasn't afraid of being arrested herself, but she expected nothing good from any authorities, and she clung to that opinion until the day she died. She had difficulty dealing with the envoys from Warnemünde or Lübeck who showed up at the door in the middle of the night with business only Cresspahl could make heads or tails of. But there were the children. She had to organize Gesine's mornings and evenings like she had before her father's disappearance. She took Gesine to the Gneez train in the morning, took Hanna to school in Jerichow, and in the evening had to keep them both busy, in the kitchen, with mending clothes, with homework, and, not trusting herself as a storyteller, she relied heavily on the deeds of the famous medieval Wendish king. On one such evening, sitting around the kerosene lamp on Cresspahl's desk, the first squad that turned up to search the house came bursting through the door—two Soviets they didn't know, with Mayor Schenk and Gantlik as witnesses, a purposeful whirlwind that was soon gone again without leaving even an overturned chair in its wake. Still, she was so shaken that she spent the night on a chair next to the girls' bed. She left the chaos in Cresspahl's room alone until Jakob had been fetched. Jakob wouldn't do what she wanted. These arrests weren't only happening around his mother, he knew about some day laborers, and about the Lübeck Court. The wind was blowing the same way everywhere in Mecklenburg, and the border to the new Western Poland had been closed on November 19. His mother let him give all his reasonable arguments and he realized she needed an unreasonable one. He stabled his horses with his business partners at the border and stayed in Jerichow. For him it was the wrong arrangement. He still had a credit of grain from his wages but the sorrel and the tottery old gelding were eating it up. He got nothing but money for his work repairing the gasworks—out in the country he could have earned potatoes. It wasn't even that he owed this Cresspahl anything. He wanted to do him a favor.

It was because we couldn't get to Lower Saxony with the horses anymore, Gesine.

That's why you stayed?

What would people think.

That you two were going away and leaving me in the lurch. So you wanted those bastards to starve you slowly.

Don't forget, we were looking to grab that house of yours too, jung Fru Cresspahl.

You sure know how to make fun of me.

A younger sister like you was just what I wanted. Pure selfishness.

It was me who was selfish, Jakob.

How does a young man from the country who's landed in a strange town go about being head of a household that hasn't even been entrusted to him? This young man started by charging rent, retroactive to July 1—the coming of the New Order. He'd measured out the house in his head, and the people in it hadn't even been warned before he put a receipt book down on the kitchen table. It was no more than Mrs. Quade or the Maass family were charging but still it rubbed them the wrong way, because they weren't used to it. The teacher from Marienwerder threatened to lodge a complaint because he couldn't put a rental agreement down on the table. A light bulb went on in the others' heads when they heard "put down" and they started paying, after all it was only money. Now the Cresspahl child had an income at least, enough to cover the cost of boarding her friend Hanna. They were free to take up the matter with Town Hall if they wanted—the name Abs was known there, because when he'd applied for his ration cards he'd insisted he was someone doing heavy labor. That led to an argument over the 2,450 grams per week instead of the usual 1,700, but in the end they had to give those grams to the gasworks repairman; in the confusion, he'd accidentally been given a residence permit, and it was in the files, and irrevocable. It was also hard to dispute that he needed 0.43 reichsmarks for the 1,600 grams of bread for each of the two children too. And if that wasn't enough, young Abs had brought back forms for the latest registration of every resident's personal information, and it was his job to fill them out. "You are required to enter all persons forming part of the household as of December 1, 1945, regardless of whether they were present or temporarily absent on that cut-off date." The name Cresspahl, Heinrich, b. 1888 was staunchly put right at the top, as head of household. The Abs family put themselves down as his representatives, not as caretakers. "Do not include members of the occupation forces": young Abs might get in trouble because of course he'd included one Mr. Krijgerstam as a member of the household, since this ingenious survivor from the Baltic provinces did sometimes wear a Red Navy uniform. But he could also be found in Jakob's room wearing a dressing gown—a sallow-faced man in his forties, smelling of fruit. With a serious expression and the manners of a well-paid waiter, he would offer for sale ladies' underwear, some even silk, a private Soviet citizen. Jakob dried his hands on the same towel as the Russians did, as they say; he called them by first name and patronymic. He hadn't taken his stake off the black market when Pontiy's detachment was transferred. Even Wassergahn still came by to see him. Jakob had his own room, solely because he now and then conducted some German-Soviet meetings in it, and he hadn't hesitated to move his mother into Cresspahl's room, possibly to be a guard for the two girls' bedroom, but he had made sure that the Housing Office forgot to inspect the house he was in charge of. He might not escape punishment forever, but for now what he brought to the communal evening meals was satisfactory. By bringing little jars of milk for her baby boy he'd gotten the bewildered schoolteacher from West Prussia to the point where she said he was "a man of true sensitivity" (a doctor had prescribed it for Jakob). The two girls used to burst out giggling at such comments but he soon put a stop to that; not only did they learn to feel pity for the unfortunate teacher, they wanted to make it up to Jakob, too, and secretly kept their eyes on him when he relaxed at mealtimes. His face had turned blank; he liked to adopt a faraway look, then he'd drily swallow a smile. When he looked at Gesine she felt trapped, unable to escape; she was often reminded of his sorrel, who when drinking would always turn his eyes to look at the person holding the bucket. What the others saw in Jakob was that he'd spent ten hours mixing cement or shoveling coal in the gasworks, and for now they accepted him as the man of the house.

Jakob was dissatisfied with himself as head of the household.

He'd had to look through Cresspahl's papers with Gesine, whatever was left after the search, since she rightly viewed every decision now as one she needed to make—her own decision, to be made together with Jakob. Cresspahl's account books and drawings were left in Lisbeth's secretary, to catch future prying eyes, while the 1935 life history and two passports were tucked away down in the east corner of the basement, where there was no basement. Jakob watched his step carefully, but she still realized they'd put his papers in order like a dead man's. Her lips started quivering, because she didn't want him to see her actually crying, and he didn't know what to do. Whatever it was, his own words weren't enough and he had to go looking for his mother so that she could hug the child to her apron. That night he realized that there shouldn't be a place set where Cresspahl used to sit. She understood him in a quick glance, which immediately swung wetly over to Mrs. Abs; he could see her thinking about the chair that she used to pull out at the empty end of the table when she heard Cresspahl coming; it seemed to him that she knew another way and just couldn't tell him. Eighteen years old and not seeing what's right in front of his eyes because his mother doesn't want him to see it—and now someone like that is supposed to console people.

He was only doing his duty when he cut Amalie Creutz down from the wire around her neck; his mother had had to fetch him because old Creutz hadn't dared set foot in his dead daughter-in-law's room, after fifty years living next to a cemetery and supervising burials. Jakob lay the body on the bed, his mother washed her and changed her clothes, because Creutz refused to come away from his golden rain bushes along the Soviet fence and wouldn't come near the house until morning. That was all the Abses had in mind to do, they didn't owe this stranger anything more. That evening Cresspahl's daughter got back from the school train and acted calm. She asked about the coffin, the appointment with Brüshaver, how the body was to be transported. She also knew that there was a letter for Cresspahl, and Mrs. Abs admitted that she'd found one in the dead girl's jacket; it was put with Cresspahl's things under the floorboards. The child would have tackled the obligations of this family friendship on her own— unhesitating, oddly experienced—but here the Abses decided to help her. Jakob went to Gneez with some Schlegel brand liquor to see Kern the carpenter and came back with a coffin, Mrs. Abs wrote Gesine an excuse note for school, and together they took Amalie Creutz to the New Cemetery in Swenson's (Kliefoth's) rubber-wheeled cart. Jakob stood like a genuine mourner next to Creutz just because the old man needed a firm grip on his arm, and Pastor Brüshaver shook Jakob's hand too, then his mother's, then Gesine's. In the eyes of Jerichow, they were representing Cresspahl's house, but representing the Red Army too, and even if Cresspahl would've wanted them to, in the end it wouldn't help his cause.

Keeping Cresspahl's house safe didn't only involve knocking a broken lock back into shape and onto the door, or distracting children from their hunger or putting up shutters. Jakob could only guess whether or not Cresspahl wanted his daughter kept away from her grandmother so permanently. He would see this Mrs. Papenbrock behind the shop counter, she would look so weepy and bitter when she asked after Gesine. He had seen her in church at Amalie Creutz's funeral and noticed that her eyes were brimming with tears, though directed less at the coffin than at the left front pew, at the back of her granddaughter's neck. (Jakob couldn't know everything about Jerichow after only five months; he didn't realize that old Mrs. Papenbrock had a talent for tears until later.) She didn't send for the child, she didn't come get the child—Jakob could see her waiting, like a fat sad bird with ruffled feathers. Did Cresspahl mean times like Christmas too? His child nodded. Did Gesine? She looked at him clear-eyed, didn't stop to think, and said: Should I? She would do what he said, he had taken Cresspahl's place. Jakob shook his head, and again after Gesine left the room; he now answered Mrs. Papenbrock somewhat more curtly. He wasn't sure if that was what Cresspahl wanted.

How do they celebrate Christmas in Jerichow? In church? With everyone in the house? With just the two children? Another thing for Jakob to worry about. All he knew was the presents he'd be giving—a standing sled for Gesine and a bike lamp for Hanna Ohlerich. Then old Creutz brought his advent wreath over as he did every year, the children asked for a baked apple for their Christmas dinner, and prepared the party on their own. When they came to fetch him the table was all set and ready, and he felt he had gotten off easy.

And now what is a head of household like this supposed to do when it gets out after all that December 25 is his birthday, and everyone in the house shakes his hand and thanks him?

Cresspahl had been supposed to be shot too often, he'd gotten inured to it, he didn't think they could take him away, so he hadn't even made a plan for Hanna Ohlerich. Hanna knew that her parents were dead and buried in Wendisch Burg. She vaguely realized that she had inherited the woodworking shop, but the will was somewhere with her fishermen relatives in Warnemünde. Why didn't Hanna want to go to Gesine's school with her? Hanna was only going to go to school for as long as it was mandatory, then she'd study carpentry. With who? With Cresspahl. And if Cresspahl wasn't back by Easter 1946? With Plath. But if his trade wasn't carpentry then it didn't matter to Hanna if she went back to the fishermen. She walked next to Jakob on Brickworks Road, he thought she wasn't paying attention. He changed his stride. She took a short step, in the middle of the snow, so she'd be even with him again. She listened to him. She blew on her hands to fight off the cold, she sniffled in the cold air, she was obliviously doing her own thing. Maybe she was surprised at him. He was four years older than her, he was the head of the family. Who else was supposed to know what was to become of her!

At the corner of the cemetery, the other child came up to them, satchel on one shoulder. This Gesine walked right past them, indifferent, like she didn't know them, but it wasn't that dark on a January afternoon, in the glittering snow. She often did that when she saw him with Hanna, and Jakob didn't understand it. There were many times he thought that she wanted to show him something, then she'd cover it up again. In November she'd come to him with questions about the English. Whether the Soviets didn't want the same things as the English. Jakob granted that they used to, before. In that case would the Soviets help someone who'd helped the English? – Yes-and-no: Jakob said cautiously, he had become plenty Mecklenburgish. He no longer thought English connections were a positive in the Soviet zone but didn't want to say so too soon. The child understood perfectly and ran off; later she dismissed the question, said she was just curious. Why was she so insistent on taking it back? What was there to be scared of? And why was it enough to give her a bad conscience? Now he'd have to watch out for that child, still he couldn't figure it out.

That day he didn't need to call her back, she came back on her own, ran through the loose snow, one time she slipped onto one knee. – Jakob! she cried when he was standing right in front of her already. – Jakob! The English have made a trade!

Again these English. What did the Cresspahls have to do with the English? The child had totally forgotten to act aloof and dignified, she was beside herself with excitement. Jakob couldn't deny that the English had made a trade. It had been the talk of Jerichow for a week, again they were saying: This neck of the woods is going to end up in the West. Not in Sweden, dammit, but still, with the British. In December the British had ceded a large piece of land to the Soviets, near Ratzeburg, almost twelve thousand acres, in exchange for some four thousand acres east of the town so that the demarcation line wouldn't run so close to it and it would have some backcountry to farm. The villages of Bäk, Mechow, and Ziethen were granted to Schleswig-Holstein; Dechow, Groß Thurow, and the whole east bank of Schaal Lake along with the Stintenburg Holm now belonged to Soviet Mecklenburg. Around two thousand people were handed over to the British: the population of a small town (like Jerichow). If the border wasn't drawn properly in one place, then it wasn't in other places either—if territory could be found for a town like Ratzeburg, then just think how much space the Free Hanseatic City of Lübeck needed to stretch out in! The demarcation line at Schlutup and Eichholz hugged Lübeck a little too close for comfort too, and then if you factor in the strategic requirements of the British, you could probably draw a line from the north tip of Ratzeburg Lake, or from Dassow Lake, over to where Wismar Bay starts. And then Jerichow would be in the West.

– You knew! Cresspahl's child cried, and if it made her so mad and so miserable then Jakob wanted to make it up to her by making a guilty face. He didn't think Jerichow would be a morsel to satisfy England's strategic hunger. When he turned to look at Hanna, he noticed how awkwardly she was looking down at her feet, as if she were present at a bereavement, if not partly responsible. If Jerichow went to the West, Gesine would be separated by one more border from Cresspahl's prison.

Jakob should have brought up the rumor himself, so he could rid her of the idea that Jerichow was going to the West. Now Gesine firmly believed it was and took even the most vigorous denials as nothing but efforts to console her. Now it was for nothing that Cresspahl had been put down on the registration form as "temporarily absent," and she'd asked to see the form so many times, just to read that one section of it.

Jakob was not satisfied with himself as head of the family.

May 29, 1968 Wednesday

Cost of Living Index, taking 1957–1959 values as 100:

U.S.A.

	APRIL 1968	PERCENTAGE CHANGE FROM MARCH 1968
All items	119.9	+ 0.3
Food (includes restaurant meals)	118.3	+ 0.3
Housing (includes hotel rates, etc.)	117.5	+ 0.3

Apparel & upkeep	118.4	+ 0.7
Transportation	119.0	0.0
Health & recreation	128.8	+ 0.4
Medical care	143.5	+ 0.4
Personal care	119.0	+ 0.5
Reading & recreation	124.9	+ 0.6
Other goods, services	122.5	+ 0.1

NEW YORK

All items	122.5	+ 0.3
Food (includes restaurant meals)	118.8	+ 0.3
Housing (includes hotel rates, etc.)	121.1	+ 0.2
Apparel & upkeep	122.8	+ 0.5
Transportation	119.1	− 0.1
Health & recreation	133.3	+ 0.5
Medical care	145.2	+ 0.5
Personal care	115.6	+ 0.8
Reading & recreation	136.6	+ 0.7
Other goods, services	127.7	+ 0.2

This means that what cost $10.00 ten years ago is now $2.25 more expensive. Some workers lost thirteen cents a week in their purchasing power. The dollar is now worth 83.4 cents. Will we make it here?

If Jerichow had ended up in the West:

Town Street would be a ground-level canal, paved over between banks of plate glass and chrome. Even in the poorest houses the wooden window frames would have been torn out and replaced by display windows or double-glassed sealed devices that swing open both up and to the side. Two driving schools, a travel agency, a branch of Dresdner Bank. Electric lawn mowers, plastic household appliances, transistor radios, TV sets. Methfessel Jr. would have had his butcher shop tiled from top to bottom. The assistant's sports car, complete with roll cage, parked at the entrance.

Of course you would still be able to buy, maybe at Wollenberg's, wicks and globes for kerosene lamps, centrifuge filters, carriage whips, axle grease, the kind of chain laid out for the cow to step on so that it can't run away when the farmers pull up in their Gran Turismos to do the milking.

And there would still be bargaining over the counter, that would've stayed the same.

Jerichow would be part of the Lübeck Zone Border District. Representatives in the Kiel state parliament. Grousing about Kiel. The surviving nobility as CDU candidates.

Newly counted among the "good families": garage owners, drink distributors, army (Bundeswehr) officers, public works officials. Not Bienmüller—he wouldn't let his son join the Federal Navy. Though he wouldn't mind listening in on ship-to-shore phone calls via Kiel Radio. (Rügen Radio too.) Vacations in Denmark, TV from Hamburg, pop music and a TV station from Lower Saxony, Hanover Broadcasting Company. Officers of the Federal Border Guards would partake at the Lübeck Court, which would be called the Lübeck Court; enlisted men would drink at Wulff's pub. No one would set jeeps on fire here.

Jerichow would have five picture postcards for sale instead of the earlier two. The new ones: The red-brick addition to Town Hall (Hamburg-style). The rebuilt "Swan's Nest" (formerly Forest Lodge). The monument to "Divided Germany" (or to the prisoners of war) on the square outside the station.

A small town in Schleswig-Holstein. Maybe the farms would be reckoned in tons, in acres. There'd be a coastal road from Jerichow through Rande to Travemünde with room for three cars abreast.

Papenbrock would've gotten rich again by 1952, from managing the new great power: the nobility's property. He would have disposed of the von Lassewitz town house before he died. The town would renovate it, even bringing in stucco workers from Hanover for the garlands under the windows. Half the building would be a museum, the other half a cave for various offices. The sweet-tempered German Socialist Party, Gneez.

The town council would have laid sewer pipes under almost every street by that point. The brickworks would have turned into a factory for plastic household goods to keep a labor force in Jerichow. Lampposts even on the Bäk. A neon mushroom on a long stem illuminating Market Square at night. The hospital would have been turned into the gatehouse for a clinic with an operating room. In the station restaurant they'd have lowered the ceiling, the furniture that had been used for fuel would've been replaced by Gelsenkirchen Baroque, a refrigerated display case for cakes, wall-to-wall carpeting.

The old inn on the way to the Countess Woods would have been appearing in guidebooks for some time. Set on fire in the midfifties, rebuilt as a hotel and restaurant: a three-story L-shaped building. The swans wouldn't recognize the Forest Lodge, not reading its new name. A rapid turnover in the lease, with restaurateurs first surprised and then horrified by the lack of customers. Hadn't the brochure described a "pearl" of Nordic urban architecture, invoked the beauty of the countryside?

Jerichow would once again have submitted to the district capital. There'd be five buses a day on road to Gneez, to the greater glory of the Swenson family business. The front of the buses would read GNEEZ–RANDE (VIA JERICHOW), not JERICHOW. Gneez would attract and take from Jerichow: housewives, workers, civil servants, moviegoers, schoolchildren. In Gneez not only the movies would be as fresh and current as in Ratzeburg or Lübeck. In Gneez there'd be night schools offering language courses, slideshow lectures, readings from novels. In Jerichow people would be miffed at the new building for the Gneez Tax Office. Jerichow's best-known attractions: a rather old air force pool for swimming classes and a location slightly closer to the border.

Rande would have grown, with Jerichow getting little to show for it. The beachfront would've been built up to a depth of over half a mile with weekend cottages, condos, villas. Concerts in the pavilion across from the Archduke Hotel. Which might be called the Baltic. Even in Rande there would be products and entertainments unavailable in Jerichow. Rande would have a spa therapy center, a temperature-controlled seawater swimming pool, a more modern cinema than the one in the Jerichow Rifle Club, and many of the stores would stay open in the winter too. The Rande streets would have been torn up and redone two or three times. The signs on the roads approaching and leaving Gneez would say "Rande" more often than "Jerichow." Ilse Grossjohann would not have stayed mayor for long. Still, she'd have two cutters docked at the new landing, and a cozy little tourist trap dotted with shrubs and bushes, the Naiad Garden Restaurant, where the day-trip boats from Denmark dock.

The airport at Jerichow-North would be Mariengabe Airport, licensed only for private planes, competition for Lübeck-Blankensee. The runways were already more than a mile long, solid 1936 workmanship too. Mariengabe, annual mecca for international air rallies. Sporty, noncommercial, right near the border, and entirely peaceful.

A radar-monitoring station would have been built near Rande, on the coastal cliffs not far from the border, screened from view with hedges. (The Federal Republic of Germany would still not have sovereignty; in 1960, as a military partner, it would have been allowed to take over the facility from Great Britain.) Even now, in 1968, the three old naval barracks on the east side of the little sports field. They would still look temporary. The rotating radar dish can be rapidly taken off its support, disassembled, and loaded onto the three trucks parked in such a way that they seem waiting to drive off. Flagpole on the little square outside the exit. A lost dog (German shepherd) next to the sentry box. The sound of the Baltic ruined here by the droning of engines. Signs below the barbed wire on three corners: Military Security Zone, No Trespassing, Violators Will Be Shot, Barracks Commandant, Federal Defense Minister, Liable to Prosecution under §100 Subsection 2 Par. 109g. Jerichow wouldn't have that.

Sometimes, most of the time, the people of Jerichow would act like it was a real backwater, somewhere like Klütz. Shut down Town Street for three whole days just to change a cable. Let the tourists who're just going to the sea anyway take a detour! The excavator digging out the trenches is the latest model, and its driver can cut edges with it as foursquare as Heine Klaproth used to do during his labor service. He can even make nasty asides about how idiotic the staring tourists are. Maybe Heine Klaproth's his father. The deft orange-painted monster would have been rented from a company in Lübeck, though.

Because graves in Jerichow would still be dug by hand. It would've come too late for Amalie Creutz. Families visit the cemetery at Christmas. The blue spruce wreaths they bring might have been stolen, but not from someone the deceased didn't know—that could be taken as an insult. Then they'd go home and feed the cows a second time, as a Christmas treat. But they'd all have to be there. Evening church service. Brüshaver would be under the ground, though, not up in the pulpit. They'd know where to find old Papenbrock's grave. Cresspahl wouldn't want to go on. Let someone else live.

The out-of-towner in the pharmacy asking where she might find a dry cleaner would not only be directed to the building "opposite the Shell station," she would also get a verbal assessment of the duration and quality of the treatment. That would still be the same.

Legal advice: Dr. Werner Jansen. Real estate: N. Krijgerstam, working for R. Papenbrock Co. Taxis and buses: Heinz Swenson. Information on the names of fields and meadows, and local history: O. Stoffregen. They would, perhaps, have still been there.

Friends in Wismar would have to be over sixty-five years old to visit people in Jerichow. Transfer at Bad Kleinen to the interzonal train to Hamburg via Schönberg and Lübeck. They'd have become very different people from one another.

If Jerichow had ended up in the West.

May 30, 1968 Thursday, Memorial Day

On May 30, one hundred years ago, General John A. Logan gave an order. He was commander in chief of the Grand Army of the Republic at the time, and it was well within his rights to decree that this day be set aside to decorate the graves of comrades "who died in defense of the country in the late rebellion." It has expanded, the remembering is now supposed to include the dead in foreign wars too, especially the unknown soldier.

In our neighborhood they go looking for him around the corner, at Riverside Park and Eighty-Eighth Street, where there's the Soldiers' and Sailors' Monument. Outside the noble, unused little temple, modeled on the choragic monument of Lysicrates in Athens, they went marching this morning with drums, trumpets, and glockenspiels, men and children in uniform, so that even up by us the air is filled with drum rolls and fife whistles.

We were on our way to Grand Central Station when the remains of the parade swung onto Ninety-Fifth Street—we couldn't escape. It was parts of a women's regiment, fiercely determined ladies who in no way brought to mind office work or nursing during the Korean War, so erect did they hold the flag, so stiffly did they swing their arms and plant their legs. The two buildings of poor people on the south side of the street were covered

with flags. As many as three faces in each window. On our side stood the
alcoholics—woozy, defenseless, patriotic. One was holding a little child's
flag in his hand, unaware it was there. The parade was accompanied by
boys and girls running up and down alongside it, with toy plastic machine
guns and handguns: they looked similar enough to the real thing to fool
you, and the sounds at least were right.

The schools, post offices, stock exchange, and banks are closed for the
sacred occasion. The holiday lasts through Sunday.

Vacation in the country, on Long Island Sound.

Vacation with Amanda Williams, Naomi Prince, and Clarissa Prince.
Mr. Williams is waiting back in New York, Mr. Prince has gotten a divorce,
Clarissa Prince is five years old. Marie Cresspahl will have to work for her
vacation.

The house belongs to Naomi's father, an accountant who's worked his
whole life to pay for it. His loneliness is there in the living room and on
display in the study: yearbooks of the New York Stock Exchange and the
Collected Best Plays on Broadway, 1931. In 1931 he got married, in 1942 he
went off to fight the Japanese, in 1943 Naomi's mother moved to an unknown
location in New Mexico. Collections: pipes, mussel shells—both abandoned
shortly before achieving real stature. Leaves outside dim the rooms.

Today and the next two days: meals together, walks, until the big cleanup
on Sunday morning. On the screened porch, a boat's deck on stilts, it'll be
nice to watch the rain, if it rains. On Saturday night we'll watch the
presidential candidates debate on TV, McCarthy the workhorse against
Kennedy the high-strung foal. Or maybe we'll forget to. At night, before
we fall asleep, we'll talk, half honestly. That afternoon two young men turn
up, friends of Naomi's, maybe Mrs. Williams's. They're both named Henry.
They drink very moderate amounts, talk about job prospects in New York,
and direct every fourth sentence to the outsider, Mrs. Cresspahl. Oh yes,
this is just the kind of landscape I like. They come back in the evening and
pick up Amanda to go to a barbecue in a backyard far away; Mr. Williams's
call from New York misses her by minutes. Who is going to go pick up the
phone and lie to him? We all talk differently than we do in the bank, our
workday familiarity here broken up into caution, shyness, privacy. Amanda
has suddenly turned timid and afraid, hardly speaking up at all, even though
she's usually the chattiest. Naomi and Amanda know something about

Mr. Prince that they still need to talk about, but not till they're alone. It's as if Amanda is scared of the children, but a house with so many wooden rooms is supposed to be even more full of children. A cleaning lady came by and was sent away, Naomi doesn't explain. Do you like the rain? My father isn't exactly strict, but he expects you to behave a certain way. Did you have to raise a father too? I'm afraid I did try to do that too, Naomi. *Y'see?* The instant before night reaches the ground, the moment before we feel fear, we see the children coming back. They've been at the beach until now.

The beach is the shore of a bay curving out into the Sound. Hard sand. Expensive villas on the water in the bluish light. Motorboats anchored past the bathing area, a tiny sail heading northwest. Reeds, marshy meadows. Fifty acres of mixed woodland, narrow access roads. A marina on the other side of the spit of land. Not many boats out on the water. Elaborate, elegant revolving cranes, several floating decks. The water still, almost black. Fingers glow in the darkness. When you surface your face feels pulled, as if it's slid back into an earlier shape. On the middle jetty a blanket has been laid out under the open sky, there's a shower next to it—you can live here, by the water. Finally someone came walking up to us, he doesn't know any neighbors who'd go swimming at this hour. He stops next to the strangers, greets them warmly, starts a conversation about temperature and humidity. And he wishes us a restful night, a relaxing vacation. As if we'd come home.

May 31, 1968 Friday

Vacation in the country. Country rain.

A day trip in West Germany four years ago. We were on our way north from the Hamburg Airport, and in Grömitz there was a bus in our way. Marie was curious about "Holstein Switzerland," even if it came with explanations from the Holstein Swiss. We were tourists—and we bought two excursion tickets like tourists.

The bus was tightly packed with mostly women and children. We were crammed onto the seat that folds down in front of the rear door. Now that our way out was thwarted, Marie would've liked to escape. One lady, quiet, with an elegant hairdo, stepped hard on her foot and it wasn't enough to just land on the toes either—she put her full weight on Marie's instep. The child couldn't help but look long and hard at her. The lady stood next to us, pulling four rows of passengers in around us, complaining all the while about a child who wasn't grateful for a stomp on the foot, these foreigners, whatever will a spoiled girl like that do when she gets hip problems. Marie crawled so fast up over her mother's lap to the window seat that it looked like she was about to jump. But the door couldn't open, the bus drove off, we were trapped in the hostility steaming over at us from three sides. It's about respect for your elders! And what was infuriating was that this child showed no fear, merely wanted some distance.

The bus driver spoke through a microphone, selling us the region. His passengers' commentary about the new single-family houses, the lakeside property for sale, was tinged with good-natured envy: Well now! Isn't that something? Yes, but what it costs! The driver had dialed back on his dialect to accommodate his paying customers; some grammatical mistakes remained, of course, he'd learned them especially for the job. – This might interest youse. He pointed out an abandoned inn, reported the tragic death of its owner. The men used to really like to go there, there was no phone in the place. Explanations of the local economy: it was agricultural. Cultivation of grain, rapeseed, – you use 'atta make öil. And of course tourism, – it's you, ladies'n gentlemen, who're paying the bills now! After sounding the depths of tolerance in such fashion he would look expectantly into his rearview mirror and gather up the approving laughter of his cash cows. Stories about refugees from East Germany, with bedsheets as hoods, coming across the frozen Lübeck Bay into the channel, – break emselves off an ice floe n sail right over. This stuck in the mind and would turn into a dream of drifting corpses whose hands you brush with your hand while you're swimming, but he'd only been trying to show the blessings of the free market economy in the proper light. White, cheerful light, flowers in the front yards, bricks as if scrubbed clean, thatched roofs neatly mended, all as if the war had passed this place by. Before, in, and past Lensahn, the microphone explained the wealth of the Grand Dukes of Oldenburg, – but in Oldenburch now! estates, forests, whole villages all 'longin' to him! The passengers' silence briefly disturbed by respect. Views of the storks' nests must have been included in the price, the way every last one of them was pointed out. One village had won the contest for the title of Most Beautiful Village, the prize was a bronze chicken, – but the president of our district assembly lives there, he maybe helped out a bit. Obedient laughter at the human weaknesses of high officials, indication of a property far to the north of the road, – y'see that there man-see-on? a film was shot there, *Hochzeit auf Immnhof,* youse all remember it? Lots of ahhs and yeses, craned necks. We're supposed to picture a precipice in the Kasseedorf Fir Woods (actually a mixed woodland), hidden by trees: that's where Carl Maria von Weber got the idea for the Wolf's Glen! A little later, by the shore of Lake Eutin, – youse remember the four trees? That's the swimming scenes from *Hochzeit auf Immenhof.* Eutin, City of Roses, the composer's birthplace, Voß's house, no shortage of culture here. And Eutin Castle, that belonged to the Grand Duke of Oldenburg too, – but that's in Oldenburch! Coffee break between Lake Keller and Lake Uklei, announced as if giving an order, no doubt about his cut from the inn.

Marie, without a glance at the beauties of the landscape that had been paid for in advance, walked over to a jetty and lay down, pulled the sock off her foot, and put her mistreated leg in the water. She didn't complain, she did what needed doing. She was just seven that August, she'd been in New York only three years, she showed the discipline Castle Hill summer camp had taught her. She was limping visibly when she got back onto the bus. The lady, her hairdo the very picture of otherworldliness and grandmotherly elegance, turned in honest outrage to the mother of this child who had turned out so badly and wished her hip troubles in old age; she was almost weeping with rage. – *Vi forstår desværre ikke tysk*: Mrs. Cresspahl said.

As he started driving, the bus driver solicited some information. Look left, look right, is the person who was there before the break still there? He was unable to restrain his delight at the fiftieth repetition. The fact that his attention was split between chauffeuring and *conférence* sometimes sent his sentences into truly rustic pleonasms: Here in Malente there're some rilly beautiful w-walking paths, and there you can go on some rilly pretty w-walks. He announced the boat ride across five lakes and mentioned the one life preserver ring for a hundred and fifty people, – it's there for the captn! The owner'd splained it all to him: Captns are in short supply, see?, but you can always get more passengers. The passengers, instead of giving him one to the kisser, smiled thoughtfully.

There were three people who didn't want to take the boat, and the driver

took them to Plön by bus instead, continuing to explain the landscape.
– Yeah, that's where 'ey burn the straw-aw. Not done samuch these days.
They go right upta a stack of it n set it on fire. Now something about the
name Fegetasche: today it's the name of a famous restaurant, that's what it's
still called today. They rilly do clean out your pockets there, *fegen* the
Tasche, costsa lotta silver for your coffee n coke. Marie looked evenly at her
enemy, who even as the steamer was pulling into Plön was searching for her
obstinate victim on the lawn—she looked the old bag straight in the eyes as
she slipped by, but didn't finish her scrutiny, and still said nothing. She knew
that the only way we'd get back to our rental car quickly was on this bus.

On the ride back through Plön we were shown the castle and the former
cadet school: the superfamous boarding school! next year we'll be getting
some relative of an Oriental despot! The passengers were familiar with this
particular dictator and nodded understandingly. That's how it is. After
that, we got a stud farm for Trakehners, an old barn whose straw roof
reached down to the ground, more storks' nests, – for the children. This
innuendo, too, was met with a pleased noise. Satisfied and exhausted, he
slumped down and turned on a cassette of canned music—songs from
concerts by Greater German Radio and the Nazi army:

"But That Can't Rattle a Sailor" (to be sung after losses in the sea war)
"Dark Brown Is the Hazelnut" (light brown the SA)
"And That's a Sailor's Love" (...)
"In a Little Town in Poland" (lived the girl I longed-to-be holdin')
And a women-make-the-world-go-round operetta number: "Ganz ohne
Weiber geht die Chose nicht":

– *ganz ohne Gummi hält die Hose nicht!* the women in the back of the
bus sang along—wobbly, menopausal, dressed in discreet bourgeois style.
Their choirmaster took them through Neustadt, charmed them with the
funds that a bypass road would gobble up, made them meek just thinking
of the cost of building a new harbor. He did not tell them anything about
the seventy-three hundred prisoners of the Nazis who, in similarly pleasant
weather in May 1945, were killed in the sea off this city, not even of the six
hundred sailors and guards who died in the line of this kind of duty, so he
didn't need to show them the memorial on the beach near Pelzerhaken
either, even though it really is a point of interest, and quite possibly worth
the question of how much it cost and who paid for it. The passengers sang

along with the tape and were so wiped out with bliss when they got out in Grömitz that they no longer berated the foreign child, Marie, just felt sorry for her as a victim of deeply flawed child-rearing. Marie locked the car door as soon as she got in.

A day trip in West Germany. At midnight we were on the ferry to Bornholm. Marie denied she felt scared for one single second. Now we're in Connecticut across from Long Island.

June 1, 1968 Saturday

Marie was on an expedition, and she found no spare *New York Times* in the woods around the house, she would have had to steal one from the marina. It was lying open in a cockpit as if posed for a photo shoot. (Marie thought it was pretentious; since the day before yesterday she's wanted her own boat.) What she did find was a plump little duck in the general store. Since no one wanted to cook it—not Naomi, not Amanda Williams—it was time for Mrs. Cresspahl to show off her kitchen skills. The last time Naomi's father got a new stove was in 1937, a sturdy smoky thing where you have to guess the temperature. The task is to cook for five in a strange oven, and the two other women are warming up their appetites on the beach in the evening sun. There was once a girl in Cresspahl's kitchen standing next to Jakob's mother taking lessons: chop the liver, heart, and stomach very fine with an onion and mix in one egg, a pinch of pepper, salt, and a piece of white bread softened in broth. There's no broth. Luckily there's a girl standing in Mr. Gehrig's kitchen, watching the work: Then stitch the stuffed body closed at the top and bottom openings, melt two ounces of butter...

– You didn't have any duck to eat in 1946, Gesine.
– In 1946 we went hungry, strictly following the recipe.
– What were you like as a child at the New School, Gesine?
– It wasn't anywhere near finished. Even in spring we were the class from the old Girls High School. It's true, Eike Swantenius was dead, a Brit had shot her, driving by. Even Wegerecht's daughter came to class sometimes. The commuter students from Jerichow were still Wollenberg and Cresspahl,

same as before, and they still didn't sit next to each other. There was a quota of refugee children assigned to us, and they had to fit into our curriculum irrespective of theirs. Since we'd already started Latin, we and they had to continue it. The law said I wasn't supposed to leave Jerichow until I was done with eighth grade. One new thing were rye rolls in the break after second period.

– Couldn't you get your revenge on Julie Westphal now? Slapping you for forgetting your notebook, she'd been a real fascist!

– Julie Westphal had retreated before the wrath of Schoolgirl Cresspahl. She didn't even report for work at the beginning, under the Soviet occupation; since July she'd been second deputy chair of the Cultural Association in Gneez. There she held musical evenings, with seventeenth-century aphorisms; she apparently melted at the grand piano, neck held high like a gulping chicken, and because she was an artist she received the rations of a heavy laborer.

– What did they say when you transferred in Gneez?

– The same as here: Please keep clear of the platform edge. We had old ladies for teachers: Charlotte Pagels, with her sister, and Frau Dr. phil. Beese. Mrs. Beese had been given early retirement in 1938, Lottie and Fifi Pagels as the civil service law required, they all considered themselves victims of Nazi despotism and they held out their grievances to us like badly mended clothing. They felt they were doing us a favor by bothering with us, and hadn't tried to learn anything about how to deal with twelve-year-olds. What they wanted was a salon of well-behaved children, rather like Louise Papenbrock when she'd take the fine porcelain out of the glass cabinet but only to look at, not to touch. Fifi would sometimes throw up her hands in the middle of math and cry: You bad, bad children! She'd turned fragile and vulnerable under Lottie's lash, now a sketch of her in the dirt from the rain on the windowpane was more than she could take. Beese stuck to a strategy of contempt: silently averting her head when your handwriting slipped below the line, smushing her lips together and gravely stepping backward to the safest place, the lectern, the bridge of the ship.

– And Stalin on the wall behind her.

– No Stalin, no Marx. We were given objective lessons in the subjects we hadn't had to turn in our books from. The Soviet Union could never come up, so no geography. The rule of three in cross-multiplication, the

ablative, Friedrich Schiller—we covered those. Not biology. The new
textbooks weren't invented yet. Lottie, who we also called Charlie, learned
each day's Russian lesson in advance from one Mr. Krijgerstam, in private
lessons, not by taking his Cultural Association course.

– What could you get with an A in Russian?

– Nothing from these ladies. Anyone who could recite Goethe's "How
gloriously gleams / all Nature upon me!" well, which meant in sparkling
fashion, would get Lottie's nature gleaming upon her. Brigitte Wegerecht
was taken out of school with typhus on January 3 and came back on March
6 with a cap on her head. (She was teased for her half-bald head, and
Schoolgirl Cresspahl and she made plans to sit next to each other the following year.) Brigitte got a D in Russian, since she'd missed it—no crime
at all in the Pagelses' eyes. Getting a D in needlework, on the other hand,
was considered absolutely positively unforgivable. We were being brought
up for a bourgeois household.

– Not in an anti-Fascist way?

– Not in a pro-Soviet way. One of our assignments was to research our
name. This was the worst possible invitation for nicknames. Schoolgirl
Cresspahl didn't want to be pegged as "cress on a pole," but she'd also prefer
if the name didn't come from "Christ." Maybe from *chrest* in Wendish.
When it was her turn, she said her name was put together from North
German *kross* and Plattdeutsch *Pall.*

– "Pawl"?

– Yes. A sailor's term. The ratchet brace in a geared wheel that prevents
it from slipping back when you turn it, and a big, crude, crass one too.

– Just like the bread rolls in Germany.

– Exactly. Mrs. Beese said: Nothing doing! Cress, from the Greek *grastis*,
"green fodder," Old High German *kresso,* plus *falen,* as in "Ostfalen,"
Eastphalia. And now I had my nickname. Greenfodder.

– Did you put jumping jacks on her chair, or a needle, or a wet sponge . . .

– Jumping jacks! We didn't have those. A needle was a valuable property.
Anyway, she herself got rid of the name for me. To help the local children
and the refugee children get to know one another, we all had to share a
little of our life story—

– There, you see?

– No, she still didn't have a handle on the children from Stargard,

Insterburg, Breslau—the East. For her it was about their father's job. And here's where you get your anti-Fascism: Wegerecht's father was held against her as though he were her fault personally. Beese, with her graduate degree, had been free to do nothing. Wegerecht had stayed head district court judge until 1940; in 1942 he was shot and killed by partisans in Greece. Brigitte felt that was punishment enough for her father, plus it seemed to her that he had made her, she hadn't made him. She looked at me, afraid I'd go back on our plan for next year, and I nodded, especially now. Mrs. Beese cried: You've got it coming to you, Cresspahl!

– Did you pour ink on her hair from an upstairs landing? You could've done that at least.

– We didn't have any ink to spare. Anyway other people started in on Frau Dr. Beese. Lottie Pagels felt it just wasn't right that Cresspahl's own father had been dragged off by the Russians. Fifi at her sister's side, letting her lower lip droop with grievous disapproval. From that moment on I was a favored child, nobody cared anymore about a flaw in the needlework or a crossed-out number on my math homework. No one calls a kid like that Greenfodder, they look kindly and forgivingly at her. I never forgave her.

– Wasn't that as good as an apology?

– Now the whole class knew what had happened to my father, and what might happen. Would you have liked that? I always thought about him anyway, it's not like I needed particular occasions to think of him. The thought of him thought me. Now I'd be reminded of him in school all the time, by strangers. All that was missing was for them to ask me about him every week.

– Someone must have seen him—in Gneez, in Schwerin, somewhere.

– Marie, when the Soviets arrested someone he really and truly disappeared. Jakob didn't know the countryside and even Cresspahl's friends from Neustrelitz to Wendisch Burg to Neustadt-Glewe couldn't tell him anything. Jakob kept his Russian business partners as secret as he could—I wasn't supposed to notice anything at all about Krijgerstam's or Vassarion's visits. I knew he was looking. They were nice to him, but questions about Cresspahl made their faces go stiff. Too dangerous. Contagious. They didn't want to end up arrested by the Red Army. Comfort was one thing, pity was fine. Where he was stayed a secret. As if he was dead.

– You recently told me your Easter water story. You heard his voice. But he wasn't there, Gesine.

– He'd told me I wasn't allowed to leave the house in a dress. But if I wanted to get some Easter water and wash in it to make myself beautiful I had to go out in my best dress, the green velvet one. When I got back I heard his prohibition again. He wasn't there, and he was speaking as though through the door.

– In your head.

– Now you'll think your mother's crazy.

– I hear voices too, Gesine. Now don't you have to sprinkle some water on this nice bird here?

– You can take off his string.

– And may I stay up late to watch the battle between McCarthy and Robert Kennedy?

– You usually don't even ask.

– Naomi! Clarissa! Mrs. Williams! It's ready!

June 2, 1968 Sunday

We must have looked like a crumbling chunk of family, rough around the edges, on the Stamford platform—two children shivering from the rain, three aunts or mothers, with luggage as though snatched up in a quick getaway. Whether the adults in the group were relatives or trapped in some other kind of fight with one another, the passengers already on board the train made room in the nearby seats—maybe they were curious, maybe it was just because the new arrivals were dry, but they were rewarded with neither a continuation of the argument nor a reconciliation. They could see Naomi's thin face, pinched into the shape of a lovely svelte owl mask, pointed severely and joylessly at the wet scenery outside. The train swung back and forth, she remained stiffly at the window, even when the Sound disappeared in the fog, or behind the backs of houses. Amanda, our Amanda Williams, the delight and eye candy and terror of men traveling alone, still hid behind dark reflective sunglasses after it was half-dark in the train, brooding over what hadn't been said, lips pouting, as if imitating a sulking child. The children took no part in this game their elders were playing, withdrawing to a double seat at the far end of the car with their backs to them. The girl with the braids held up a newspaper page with comics for the smaller one, explaining to her some of the final acts. She didn't really take much pleasure in the latest news of Bugs Bunny or Li'l Abner, she clearly had trouble getting the point, and Clarissa kept her impish face impassive and mad, like in school, no resemblance now to the hopping olive from earlier today. And it wasn't only from the rain still hanging in her curly hair. Mrs. Cresspahl read, in many sections of *The New York Times,* what she'd missed on vacation, but her ears too were still ringing with the sound of three voices—Amanda's aggressive alto, Naomi's careful girl's voice, and the flat tones that had sounded so halfhearted in the bones of her own skull. It had been a painful session, over the rest of their break-fasts, cozily tucked away from the heavy country rain that pelted the roof and the lush greenery outside the windows. It was supposed to be a game. How all three of us could live in this house by the sea,

your Marie with Clarissa, Amanda, yours truly Naomi, and you, Gee-sign.

For the children?

Us too, we've never had such a fun weekend in the country. Couldn't we have a piece of vacation every day?

Would there be room for us?

One room for each of us, and for the girls. And one common room.

And we'll pack the husbands away in the bunkbeds in the garage.

Mr. Prince is banned from the house. I'll go by Gehrig again.

Mr. Williams can go jump in a lake, and not one near here either. Yeah, it's been in the air for a while.

Anyway, we'll need the garage for our cars.

Gesine, don't you have someone? Wouldn't he come?

He'd be glad to, Naomi. Just the man for you, Amanda.

The guy from Nebraska?

Not exactly . . . German, at least he used to be.

You won't have to tell us what he's like in bed. We know you don't like that sort of thing.

Okay, that helps.

Right. So that we wouldn't be a family, more like a club.

All the laundry together, all the dishes in one dishwasher, making one meal a day instead of three.

And someone to watch the children during the day.

And after work you drive to the station and pick us up from the New York train.

So who'd be the head of household?

You, Naomi, and the former Mrs. Williams.

Who'd be the housewife?

Whoever wants to. Do you want to, Mrs. Cresspahl?

She can't. She has something going on with de Rosny, she doesn't have to say what it is. You, Naomi.

I'd try it, for two months to start—if your Marie agrees to it.

You'd be perfect, Miss Gehrig.

Yeah but you know I could never make duck like you did.

So the kids would go to school here.

Where I went to school. Half the way runs through the woods, then on Main Street to the golf course.

Tell us more. Traditions. Curriculum.

Gesine, I'm another one of those children who was supposed to have it better. Your Marie will lack for nothing. Educationally speaking it's almost New England. With a ticket to Vassar College included.

What do you pay for Marie in New York?

$890 for tuition, 200 for meals, 150 for school uniforms, 300 for after-school activities. It comes to $1,600.00 a year.

You see. You see?

Now it's also true that Marie wants her own boat.

I can teach her to sail.

She knows how to sail.

You see. You see?

It's just, she won't give up the apartment in New York.

So keep it. We'll have a pied-à-terre. You'll have a pied-à-terre.

How long'll we do it for?

We'll try it and see. As long as it works out.

And the cost?

What do you mean the cost.

We'll open a pot. We'll set up a budget. We'll sign a contract.

The house.

I'll get the house, Gehrig Sr. would rather give it to me before he dies anyway. I'll contribute the house.

And if your father wants to come back, or when he comes for a visit, we'll stick him in a hotel?

Oh, Gesine!

We'll have to tell him.

Okay, Amanda, Cresspahl's right. We'll tell him.

Because of the neighbors.

They've known me since before I could walk.

I meant buying.

What do you mean, buying?

He'll give it to you. But we're not his daughters.

I wouldn't take advantage of him!

Okay. We buy it. If he puts the money in his will, I'll get even more.

Naomi, we're not going to talk about your inheritance. You started with the house.

Let him sell us his house. He'll have one more story to tell. I have six thousand. Your turn, Gesine.

We could get our hands on four. Amanda?

Does it matter if...I don't really want to take anything from Mr. Williams...two thousand, to start. My folks in Minnesota...

Twelve thousand in cash, that's enough. Henry'll get us the rest. Yeah, the guy from Thursday, who couldn't take his eyes off a certain Mrs. Cresspahl! His father runs the First National branch in the village.

In the village. In the village...

You see. You see?

Okay, how many shares. Five?

Three, Gesine.

But what about Amanda? She'd have to pay more than she should for just one person.

Amanda, say something!

It won't happen.

Because of money, Amanda? Mrs. Williams! Either you're over him or you're not ready to do business.

It's over. I'm done with him. Just, sorry.

Amanda pays one part, you pay one and a half, I pay two.

You pay two? Marie's not even twelve. I want to pay two if you do.

For the price of the house? For the household expenses? For the sailboat? For the two cars?

Stop it. Don't be so German, Gesine.

Should we stop talking about it?

What a ditz you are, Naomi.

That's right, I'm an idiot. A real pig. A ... Can I stop now if I say sorry?

Okay. Forget it.

You two would have to keep things a bit cleaner. How else are we supposed to live here.

Fair enough. Look, Gesine, I'm not Jewish. My grandparents were, and not all of them either. In my father the Austrian side is much more pronounced than the tribe of Israel. I'm no more related to the Jewish ones than I am to the other ones, Gesine. I don't have any personal thing against the Germans. And if your father was in a Nazi camp, on the wrong side—

No. No. Not that.

I'm talking about you. We'd want to do this thing with you.

Because you liked my duck.

Enough already!

Okay.

Be honest, du. I still remember that from high school, in German you can call someone by their first name but you have to not think the second-person singularis pronoun, it also goes with the second ... the third pluralis. Thou ... be honest, you!

I think of you in the second singularis. "Du," and "Naomi."

Now you two have to tell me everything.

See!

The housewife. Amanda, you start.

We'll need a schedule. Like on a bulletin board.

Like in the office. But we're trying to get away from the office!

I think work schedules are appropriate.

Okay, make us one, Amanda. But yesterday she wanted to watch something other than channel seven. You didn't care what McCarthy and Kennedy had to say, you just stayed to be polite.

Still, we agreed about Kennedy.

Still, we'll need a second TV. If you know what I mean. Gesine.

I'm trying to keep Marie off TV.

And that will be fully respected. No, I mean for what you don't like.

We've known each other since, what, 1963, 1964? If I were—

Gesine, don't be so . . . Okay. I saw you. And this morning you set the table again, I'm sorry. The milk in the carton would have been good enough for me but you wanted it in a little pitcher, and not a plastic one, porcelain. Am I right?

Well, if we have pitchers.

We'll have them. What else?

What about vacations.

Here it'll be vacation every night, every weekend!

She means vacations from us.

No! Amanda! It's just, I need to go to Europe in August.

Yeah, well, relatives.

Maybe you'd rather stay with us than visit them.

No, it's not that. A tourist trip, to Czechoslovakia.

You have to . . . ?

She can't get around it.

You don't need to explain.

You won't have to pay your household fee and Marie will stay with us.

If you convince her to.

You don't want her to, do you, Gesine.

On the contrary, this trip—

Something's going on here. If you don't trust us, get a separate lawyer. Are you afraid we'll steal your guy from Nebr—your guy from your bed? Or have you lost your mind after all, just because you're a few stories higher up than us now? You think you're better than us?

Amanda. It was supposed to be a game. Leave her alone.

If anyone's ruining this game, it's her!

Do you want to leave New York, Gesine?

No. No.

You don't know exactly what's going to happen come fall, right?

Right.

You know that, Amanda.

Right. And we'll need a room to cry in too.

until all three of us were sitting around the table as if we'd lost our language, moved to tears in the corners of our eyes by friendship, goaded into rage by disappointment. We were rescued by the children, who'd had enough of *East Side Kids* on TV—the merry adventures of gangsters back in the thirties, which Marie wasn't supposed to be watching though. She hesitated in the doorway, as if walking into an awkward mood like a headwind. The adults were duly ashamed of themselves, and so that Clarissa wouldn't get upset too we silently finished the big cleanup and took the village taxi to the 1:50 train from Stamford, although we actually could've stayed till tomorrow morning. Since then we haven't really spoken.

The New York Times describes again what we saw last night on channel 7: Robert F. Kennedy's right-handed gestures quoting his brother, his striped tie, his indefatigable smile. The *Times* reveals that he'd refused a public debate against McCarthy for many weeks, until he was too upset by the latter's win in the Oregon primary. The *Times* has heard Kennedy's wife say that she can't ever think of him except as having won, and the *Times* also prints as tentative ellipses what we didn't understand in the broadcast either, for the sake of accuracy. And what does she have to report from the home country?

In one Germany, the Communists blew up the Leipzig University church on Thursday, at four in the morning our time. First-semester student Cresspahl had been struck by the building for not being made of brick and for having been built to stand between other buildings, the Augusteum and the town house containing Café Felsche that had been totally bombed away. Completed in 1518, consecrated by Martin Luther in 1545, used since 1945 by both Catholics and Protestants—the child from elsewhere had learned these things about Leipzig, too, she was planning to stay awhile. Stud. phil. Cresspahl (first semester) was inside the church only once, for a concert, in a space divided into neither galleries nor naves, a bourgeois, almost domestic space from which the piety had been removed, and very bright, even though the rounded dormer windows scurrying all around the roof let in no light that made it down to the ground level. And now it hadn't been enough to, say, remove the ridge turret from the roof, or the top of the globe with the cross on it, the Wendish Cross; some students had to be arrested, other people protesting behind police cordons threatened with arrest if they "whipped up emotions against the authorities." That sounds like a bad translation. There were architects who sought to preserve the Leipzig church and include it in the university building project, but the "East German leader" said something about old teeth that had to be extracted by Socialism. *Mr. U. is a native of Leipzig.* Even a tiny piece of common sense like this has to be taught to people against their will; they need to be made—by threats, with force—to revise the picture they want their city to show the world. "Citizens, disperse or else you will be arrested": that's probably more like what the loudspeaker cars actually hurled at the people.

On the same page, p. 7, adjacent as if related, we are told something about the other Germany's lower house, no, Bundestag: 384 representatives cast their votes for the Seventeenth Amendment to the German Constitution. Now anywhere the government detects a state of emergency it can snoop into people's letters, packages, and telephone conversations, force them to do government work, at gunpoint too—all achievements that aren't exactly making West Germany less like East Germany. Then the Social Democrats promise not to permit any misuse of the law, as if there were guaranteed to be a Social Democratic Party for all eternity and as long as this state exists. The workers have understood that strikes under such states of emergency can be broken by armed forces; the middle-class citizens seem not to have realized that a state of emergency can confiscate their cars. The government wants gratitude—they claim they've extracted a little more West German sovereignty from the General Treaty between Germany and the Allied victors; the Allies have given up some of their dirty deals, a couple of ungrateful brushes with West German nationals, but in their barracks they remain rulers under their own laws, and it is they who decide about Berlin and about Germany as a whole, even if the Soviet Union has a word or two to say about it. This is what the Federal Republic calls sovereignty.

Explain this to us, please, Mrs. Cresspahl. You're German too. Explain to us what the Germans are doing.

And now it's homework time. On May 4 the Czechoslovakian defense minister announced a visit from Warsaw Pact troops for maneuvers. This General Dzúr let people believe that the maneuvers would come in, maybe, the fall. Last week he corrected himself and stated the time as June. And it was still just May 31 when the Soviet troops moved in anyway, across this most casual of borders.

Others wanting to join in the fun are expected from Hungary and Poland. But the East German Communists aren't sending their troops yet, for now they're just mad at their Prague comrades.

As the train pulls into the tunnel under the East River, Mrs. Cresspahl has disappeared from her taciturn group. As the light above the bare factory roofs of Queens returns to the train car she does too, unsuspiciously, from the buffet car, for in her hands she is holding three paper cups full of a brownish fluid. What's surprising about this tea is only that there are ice cubes floating in it. At this point Marie turns around after all and takes her mother's measure with a cool, instructional look. Because if a lady goes off to get double bourbons, however demurely disguised, Marie is sure that she could've learned such behavior only from long-lasting contact with Soviet military personnel.

What's left of the rain is sitting on the flat roofs outside. Again the train needs to duck into the ground and under the river, and then we'll be home.

– Have some tea: Mrs. Cresspahl says, and the friends accept their portions. Amanda W. can do so only by raising her head a little too impetuously, still ready to take offense. Naomi smiles a little off to one side and closes her eyes for a moment, as if wanting to indicate a secret that Amanda is now excluded from. The other passengers miss what they've been waiting for, because they have to stand up long before it's time and pull together their coats, bags, umbrellas, newspapers. The three women sit next to one another, comfortably unhurried, and one says once that this is some good tea, and another one answers, not bad as tea goes.

Then, in Pennsylvania Station, the other two don't want to take the subway with the Cresspahls, they go upstairs to Seventh Avenue with the disappointed screaming Clarissa to hunt down a taxi. What will the driver talk about? The murder of his colleague Leroy Wright, the demonstration crossing Brooklyn Bridge to City Hall, joined by no police presence except a new taxi partition made of bulletproof glass . . .

Outside the Ninety-Sixth Street station exit the air is heavy with humidity. Those who can sweat release pearls of it from their foreheads as involuntarily as breathing—Marie, on the other hand, promptly turns very red in the face. As soon as she can, right inside the Riverside Drive door, she's going to ask. She will say she approves of what happened: even a secret with de Rosny needs to be kept, Indian-style. She will say she doesn't approve of what happened, because someone who starts an extended family on Long Island Sound lives only an hour from New York, not nine with transfers on the other side of the Atlantic. She'll say: This dialectic of yours, Gesine, you could've left it behind in Europe you know!

June 3, 1968 Monday

Yesterday the mayor of Saigon went to inspect the main battle line in his city, along with other friends of Vice President Ky's, mainly police officers but also relatives. They entered a school, now converted to a command center. At which point the house was blown to bits, as if by a missile from an American military copter. Now the army says it wasn't using any helicopters in that area. Before, the US embassy prematurely apologized to the South Vietnamese government, and the victims' families, "with deepest regrets and condolences." His Excellency, President Nguyen Van Thieu, friends with still other Americans, suddenly has seven sinecures available for his underlings, and if he ever writes his memoirs in the West he will have a thing or two to teach us about the nature of the home front.

The new Communists in Prague both do and don't want to take the old ones to court over the murders they committed for Stalin. Removal from office, yes; investigative committees, definitely; "settling accounts within the party in public," no. Alexander Dubček is less eager to have a reputation for vindictiveness than his predecessors were, and is urging his comrades to protect their friends by not exposing Soviet involvement in the crimes of the 1950s, and his comrades are complying. As for those outside the party, what business is it of theirs, even if they do demand public probity? They are not being governed against their will, not yet, but this wish is refused to them. They were just bystanders, you might say, on the inside but not inside the party.

Hanna Ohlerich had wanted to wait until Easter 1946. By that time Cresspahl should have been released and back in the workshop and she an apprentice in his trade. She took his release for granted, and afterward had to find something else to do. She started writing letters—not even secretly, Jakob's mother was supposed to see even though she didn't let her read them.

She had turned to Mrs. Abs right away, but only as a mother-like person from whom she expected comfort, help. (You could more or less tell what kind of parents the Ohlerichs had been. The father dealt with whatever came their way; any outward steps to be taken were decided by him. The mother was allowed to run the kitchen, the cellar, and the home, albeit under his supervision. He had the last word, interpreted by his will alone, right up to the rope he gave her and the other one he took for himself. Strict, also affectionate, easy for a child to look up to. Just as Hanna's father had exerted authority in the home, he'd been a bulwark against the outside world.) She pinned her faith on Cresspahl for all this, not on a woman.

She still counted on Jakob and on many evenings followed him out into the yard so that he'd postpone his business deals and go off to the marsh with her, two leisurely saunterers in the damp May twilight, strolling along like a long-established and permanent couple (on which occasions Cresspahl's child didn't want to be seen as abandoned, bereft of the appropriate companionship she deserved, so she withdrew to the walnut tree, making very sure not to look west where the pair could just be made out in the haze with the setting sun behind it). Jakob was allowed to read the letters, which in fact were intended more for him than their addressees, the Warnemünde relatives. To him they seemed pleading, desperate, as if Hanna needed to be saved from a den of thieves growing more and more dangerous by the day. Cresspahl didn't return. "Get me out," she'd written. Jakob acted the big brother and merely explained the difference between Hanna's actual situation and her description of it; he talked her out of her mistrust for the Warnemünders and into a mistrust of Erwin Plath; eventually she pretended she'd only wanted reassurance. He was not satisfied with himself as head of the household.

He told Gesine she needed to be more considerate of her friend. Gesine wasn't aware that anyone had been inconsiderate to Hanna! They shared everything, didn't they? They shared a bed, neither wanting to go to sleep without the other; they did their homework together at Cresspahl's desk; they waited in the long line for soggy Papenbrock bread, in silent solidarity; people not from town thought they were sisters. Whenever Gesine asked

Jakob for some money over and above her weekly allowance, she held out her hand again for Hanna's share and they went to the market together, to buy a packet of grass seed each from Wollenberg, just to buy something, because Wollenberg wanted to make a sale for once, and then they watered each other's test plots. She treated her friend like a welcome guest, didn't she? Took Lisbeth's box camera, which Jakob had bought back from Vassarion and given her for her birthday, and gave Hanna a half share in it? She paid the forty-pfennig fee for Hanna's ration card herself, that was only right, and she didn't mind doing it. They shared their hunger, their pimples, once even a CARE package. Jakob knew that, what could he be thinking?

The package wasn't full by the time it reached them, it was just a lump of American lard, two cans of American corned beef, a pair of stockings, and a Waterman fountain pen, all packed together in an old flour sack and dropped off by a man from Berlin ("West Berlin") on a motorcycle, who also left behind an uneaten sandwich on unbelievably white bread as though it were nothing. Gesine couldn't think who might have sent it; only later did she realize that the photograph of three strapping German shepherds was news from Grunewald, from Dr. Semig's dog Rex. Anyway, it came for Cresspahl's daughter, but after contributing the foodstuffs to the pantry they cut the sandwich neatly in half and ate it together, and Hanna could choose whether she wanted the pen or the nylon stockings that suggested shimmering shadows of night on her legs. Hanna was free to give Jakob the stockings after trying them on, and Gesine couldn't think of anything more worth doing with the Waterman—were they not united?

Didn't they see, hear, think the same things? We witnessed the liberation of Leslie Danzmann's boots in such unity that ten years later she could still tell the story in detail and I could still recall every single still or moving picture of it. It was in early June 1946, Hanna had come to the Gneez train with me that day, and a procession caught up to us on Station Street. In the front strode Leslie, chin held stiffly high, eyes pointed straight ahead, which didn't help her on the cobblestones. She had worn out her presentable shoes during the war, and her one pair of "indestructible" shoes from 1937 may have survived her walks to the mayor's office but not her arrest by the Russians, so now she'd brought her husband Fritz's lace-up boots up from her hiding place, padded them, and was wearing them to work hidden under long pants. Would've said something about self-respect. Since she'd been arrested the Gneez Labor Office hadn't taken her back, but she had found a job in the Housing Office department whose mission was to protect the resettlers from the wrath of the locals, and she wanted to look like a properly dressed civil servant there—Hanna and Gesine saw this as vanity. Now this lissom lady having trouble walking was being followed by a young Red Army man, excited by the unfeminine heels he'd glimpsed under the masculine cuffs, and he was offering her a trade, making himself perfectly well understood despite using only personal pronouns and nouns, and doing so relentlessly, so that a pack of jeering children was running along after them, little brats who'd just reached school age, eager to see how the show would turn out. Leslie Danzmann made a beeline through the station and clambered up into the train, hand over hand, as if into a lifeboat, and thought she was safe. Her business partner in uniform was so merrily drunk that morning that the door hit him when it swung shut, he fell flat on his face, into the train car, not discouraged in the least, for now he had an even better view of the object of his quest. Both hands fervently clinging to Leslie's legs, he crawled on his belly like a crab back down the footboard onto firm ground. Our Leslie, stunned by the exclusively blank looks she was getting from the other passengers, slipped and landed on the floor of the train car, unladylike, legs sticking straight out, boots exposed. By that point the Soviet had unhooked the crisscrossed laces, neatly and not unskillfully, under a barrage of pleading remarks too. The Cresspahl and Ohlerich girls had had plenty of chances to squeal with pain at the gravel sticking into their own bare feet but they stayed in the shadows of the rotted bicycle stand, watching wordlessly. The man in the army uniform dyed to another color stayed where he was at the window of the station shop (which was the post he'd been assigned); he was not as out of view as he might have liked, and, with a gun in his holster, he was the very image of the "Volkspolizei" as depicted in the new newspaper, *New Germany*, that both Gesine's and Hanna's schools had gone over in detail. We saw the stationmaster in the train engine, far enough away from the scene; we heard him swear about the train car's door that was still open, in which we could see that Leslie Danzmann had sat up, her mouth in a tortured smile. We saw the Russian carefully wrap his foot bindings back around his feet and pull the former Danzmann boots up over them, not without difficulty, and as the departure whistle blew he pushed the door open wider, into Leslie's legs (knocking her over), threw his own felt rags in after her (in faithful observance of their agreement), and marched in elation over to the station exit with the band of little children timidly, excitedly dancing around him. That day we both cut school, fully understanding one another from the tiny wink that slipped from our eyes and tugged at the corners of our mouths—we were united. United against the adults, united in our pitiless suspicion of them (with Cresspahl secretly and Jakob's mother more vaguely excluded). Is that not unity?

But on June 30 the Soviet Military Administration shut the borders between their zone and the Allies'. Too many people had run away from their New Life (not Leslie Danzmann)—one and a half million going over to the British alone. Hanna might have recognized in this a law of political economy, but all she saw was that yet another possibility had been taken from her. Again she felt trapped with us. How could Jakob have talked her into staying in Jerichow?

For the harvest he loaned us out to the Schlegels. She went uncomplainingly. We'd had enough of waking up every morning with shriveled stomachs, walking around all day bent almost double with hunger, having to leave the table bravely every evening while the Marienwerder schoolteacher was still feeding her baby son. Besides, Jakob had promised to visit us on the weekends.

At the Schlegel farm we were greeted as "Jakob's girls" and put to work that same afternoon, but our only job was to eat thickened milk with sugar. We were allowed to accompany Inge on all her chores around the farm, but not help with any. She'd have let us pluck strawberries, but only as many as we could eat. From the outside the house looked like an ordinary half-timbered building under a thatched roof, standard Lower Saxony style that textbooks would call classic; nothing inside it was to be hidden from us. We could climb into the space under the living room and examine the still, we were shown the tobacco field disguised by the sunflowers planted throughout (more than two hundred of them), we even got to take a look at the collection of Karabiners in the bench next to the stove that looked so solid to the uninitiated. That's how good an introduction Jakob had given us. But we never did find out where he slept here. It wasn't a farmhouse anymore. Where the wings of a farmhouse would usually have open stalls for horses and cows and sheep and pigs, these had been partitioned off with walls between the roof beams, a carpenter had laid wooden floors over the beaten earth inside, and the stall hatches had been neatly enlarged into double-leaf casement windows, so now there were three nearly square rooms on either side of the hall and six doors opening onto the big dining table that reached almost from the front door to the kitchen. A sea breeze came in from the northeast, it smelled of warm clean wood everywhere, the walls were intact as well as the doors and the windows, as if the war hadn't passed through these parts. And Inge Schlegel wasn't nervous at all about being alone on the farm with one polite Doberman and two half-grown girls. The agricultural work all took place on the other side of the farm, in a brick building that looked like a factory only at first glance, before you noticed the moss-free thatched roof. Inside it, the ten-year-old Schütte-Lanz threshing machine looked more like two years old, all oiled and polished; there was a smithy neat enough to be in a museum; the shelves in the storerooms were fully stocked with boxes, kegs, and other containers; the stalls smelled occupied and active; the pigs were running free in their wallow; and again the girls couldn't shake their sense of peace, a false sense, for all this couldn't be explained by the semicircle of forest ringing the farmstead to the east and toward the sea. That evening, with the return of the mowing machines and harvest wagons, they realized that the war had passed through here after all, and settled down to stay. The rooms along the hall, once apartments for workers and sometimes summer visitors, were now occupied by refugees. But these weren't like the refugees in Jerichow—they had come to Schlegel's farm with their eyes open, they didn't immediately lie down and wait for pity but wanted to earn their keep with work. Even though it was work on someone else's property, not on their own which they'd lost in the East, most of them had nonetheless been here for more than a year and few of them wanted to move on. Johnny Schlegel had laid down rules for his farm; newcomers were given a share of the profits according to how many horses they'd brought and how much work they'd done, the same as when he'd been starting out before the war, going by the books about land resettlement until the National Socialists had outlawed it. Still, except for the estates left behind by the local nobility who had fled, there was only one large farm like this in 1946—not even Kleineschulte had left anything comparable behind—and the girls from Jerichow remained mystified. Later, as time went on, they started to understand what was going on, but on that first night Johnny treated them differently. They were happy to keep their heads bent over their plates, for once not because they were hungry but because they were almost frightened of the man who would be their employer for the next few weeks—a little worried about where Jakob had sent them. They noticed that no one said prayers at this table. From fleeting glances they got the impression of an older man (he was fifty-eight) who had worked outside his whole life: one-armed, ridiculously tall (in the evenings he was six foot three), oxycephalic, bald (though a little tuft of curly blond hair had sat high atop his turret-shaped head for many years), an educated man because he sometimes raised a pair of fabulously tiny oval-lensed glasses to his eyes. While the rest of the group, all equals, chatted harmlessly across the table, especially with their children, Dr. Schlegel said nothing; he looked like he was grimly calculating things in his mind, and the girls from Jerichow were scared of him. Nor did they see a chair for Jakob. Then they heard Johnny's booming bass voice, without any throat clearing or other warning, and they nearly jumped out of their skins. Because he was talking about them, and by name. They almost stood up out of sheer obedience. They learned that they were the children of *my friend Cresspahl* and of Gustav Ohlerich, *a good man, from Wendisch Burch.* They were *good Meeklnburg chilren our Jååkob's entrusted to us.* They *long to uur farm now.* That was all. It transformed their tablemates' friendly looks into something like encouragement, and now they felt welcome. Inge Schlegel was still wearing her engagement ring from Alwin Paap, she probably had quite a lot she could say about Cresspahl, and about where he no longer was, and Johnny most definitely knew more than he said about how Hanna's parents had died. In spite of their relief, they still felt their wages of hundred-weights of wheat were in danger, and they asked what their jobs would be. – *Jobs'll turn up*: Johnny said in an offhand way. What jobs? they shyly asked. Johnny'd imagined them as a kind of fire department maybe, or kitchen help when necessary, maybe pick some apples, churn some butter (nothing about tending geese). And didn't we protest together, practically as one, probably proud of our ages of thirteen and fourteen? We hadn't come here for a vacation! We'd come to do serious work in the harvest! We were instinctively of one mind, right?

Full work in a harvest. That's what we wanted? No mercy? Out to the fields we went. Johnny Schlegel's commune had wheat as far as the eye could see, fifty or sixty feet above sea level, gently rolling hills that at first we thought would make for a nice change. The previous summer we'd distributed the wheat sheaves across the whole field; here the latest science sent us to the edges, out of the dips, and we were constantly running, pursued by the magically returning machines and carrying sheaves not much smaller than ourselves. The days went by fast. Where we'd been the day before, the stubble was already being plowed over, deep for the seed and fertilizer drills, shallow for the sugar beets, because a day in July's worth as much as a week in August: as Johnny taught us on his frequent visits out to see if "Jakob's girls" were ready to give up. We would have been ashamed to look Jakob in the face if we gave up; what he'd brought back from Schlegel's farm were earnings, not presents. Sometimes Hanna was older than me—she said about the thirst: It's worse at sea. When the sheaf-binding harvesters had to be run without twine, those were bad days, because the straw rope didn't easily reach around the sheaves the machine could tie, and also because it was harder to tell when our work would be over. It gradually dawned on us that Schlegel might not have just cut some pages out of the land registry to save his nearly four hundred acres from confiscation; probably the Soviet officers from the Beckhorst farm had helped him out, the ones who often came by at dusk, greeted casually and without fear, like ordinary visitors. Maybe. But why was Johnny's missing arm inevitably the cause of such laughter, even from Johnny himself? We were equipped with pieces of truck tires that we tied onto our feet with gas-mask straps, as sandals, but still the ankle-high stubble found its way in, and at night Hanna would put balm and bandages on my feet, and I on hers. We dreamed gray and white and yellow, the massive clouds in the sky, the ears of wheat, the stubble, the firm sandy paths. Over breakfast there was a BBC program in which, again and again, the Austrian was made to scream out his thing about the last battalion on earth. We learned how to pack cartloads of wheat. Our skin hardened, much too slowly. Awns of wheat in our face continued to startle us. Grain is what the earth bears and everywhere in the world what's most important is called corn, *Korn*: maize in America, rye in Germany, wheat in France and Mecklenburg. *Triticum vulgare*: Johnny said. When the carts drove in, Hanna took the spot up on top of the wheat, I liked walking next to Jakob's sorrel and wanted the horse to recognize me. I meant it as affection when I took hold of the harness as if to lead him, but it was more like hanging on for support. When the thresher started up with its flapping belt it looked ingenious yet cruder than the simple trick nature might still have up her sleeve for exploiting the corn. The wheat. The other children spent the harvesttime in the orchard, or cleaning out the stables, or helping in the kitchen—Hanna and I were taught to operate the Schütte-Lanz. She was allowed to go onto the threshing floor before me, to cut the ropes around the sheaves and pass the wheat, fanned out in a flat sheet over her arm, to Mrs. von Alvensleben. The names on the farm were: Inge, Johnny, *Johnny sin Olsch* (his missus), Mr. Sünderhauf, Mrs. Sünderhauf, Mrs. von Alvensleben, Mr. Leutnant, Mrs. Lakenmacher, Mrs. Schurig, Mrs. Bliemeister, Mrs. Winse, Anne-Dörte, Jesus, Axel Ohr, Hen and Chickee, *the Englishmin*, Epi, and then the children under thirteen; there was an old strip of film in the drawer, but it was for a box camera, and that had been left behind in Jerichow and couldn't be fetched, so all but four of the faces are now forgotten. Anne-Dörte had stuck close to us out in the fields; back at the farm she pretended to be Johnny's goddaughter. We suspected her, if only vaguely, of having had something to do with our new clogs: newly carved, with an arched sole, padded with cloth under the leather, held together with real tacks and wire, they were hanging from our ladder one morning, and they fit, once our feet had healed up. Cresspahl's daughter reigned behind the threshing machine, leaning on the handle of a pitchfork, and every couple of minutes she would fork a load of the long straw onto a box wagon. If there was twine for the baler, though, the other children had to help out, the ones stationed by the chaff, the sack openings, the short straw. The whirling hum of the machine slowly peeled your brain away from the inside of your skull. Every hour Hanna and Gesine would trade places so that we could keep working, as a team. Anne-Dörte was nineteen and we'd never in our lives seen anyone so pretty—we would never be like that. The clogs couldn't be from her. Johnny crouched under the machine with us and taught us, there in the dark, the path that the precleaned wheat took through the bucket elevator. He was so pleased. When August 20 arrived he had actually done what he'd planned, forty double-centners of wheat had been driven off to the Soviet Beckhorst farm and he'd been given his receipts, bilingual, with stamps, and now the gentlemen there owed him twine and crude oil and a good reputation. When weren't Hanna and I together? We always sat together at the table,

at the same places, a flask of barley coffee would be sent out to the fields
for us and us alone, we were occasionally addressed as a single person, we
slept next to each other in the hay in the apple loft above the living room.
Of course we didn't tell each other everything. I was now sure that Cresspahl had slept like this, next to pears and apples arrayed on slats, at Schmoog's
farm when *Our Little Granny* had died; I wasn't going to bring up relatives
dying with Hanna. Though by this point she knew about her resemblance
to Alexandra, and asked about her. Where Alexandra might be now, if.
Whether Alexandra would've been strong enough to handle the wheat
harvest, if. On other nights we would decide—shyly, cautiously—that some
other adults might be exceptions. Mrs. von Alvensleben, definitely. Johnny,
with reservations. Hanna would fall asleep with a great sigh, as if sinking
down deep into something. Not a word about Anne-Dörte.

Yes, Jakob kept his promise and visited. Before long we could tell when
he was near the farm: Anne-Dörte's chair would remain empty at dinner,
and at around our bedtime she would reemerge from the woods and come
into the hall, her hair more carefully combed than usual, in her one, gray
knit dress. A few minutes more and there would be Jakob in the doorway,
relaxed, cheerful, not like he'd just been walking for two hours. Maybe it
was the wind off the sea that had tousled his hair like that. Then, before
disappearing into the living room for his business with Johnny, he would
talk to us. Have a little chat. Concern himself with the children. Like a
legal guardian. He'd never promised us any more than that. We never
followed Anne-Dörte, even though we'd see her on the footpath leading
to the sea between the pines. Sometimes her hair would be wet when she
came back, Jakob's too. Now we knew why we'd never found Jakob's bed.
On the nights of Jakob's visits we would lie in the moonlight shining from
over the sea, silently pretending to each other that we were asleep; neither
of us would be woken by the other one's tears, and we were too tired to
talk in our sleep.

That was also how we lay there the night of the rain that destroyed the
rest of the harvest across the whole region. It was on August 27, 1946, and
people said there'd never been a storm like it in living memory. The clouds
poured down with a violence that Johnny decided to describe as tropical,

like the torrents of rain a little while ago, at 2:45 p.m., filling the space
between the buildings on Third Avenue with such deep darkness. When

brightness flashed up, the racing drops seemed sharp. New darkness, now accompanied by thunderclaps, made the riverbed of the street look wintry, the slick pavement full of reflected light from the shopwindows, like at night. The thick panes rattled under the blows of a normal New York rainstorm

and people were assigned only work that could be done indoors. A thick sack folded into a hood would be wringing wet after the fifty feet to the farm building. Not even the animals calmly endured what was darkening their stall doors for so long. There were places in the farmyard that looked like deep lakes. Johnny taught us the average August precipitation in the region: 2.6 inches. That evening he said he estimated there'd been 7.5 inches of rain that day alone. The forced inactivity, the creeping damp soon emptied the hall; we couldn't stick it out any longer with Johnny either and lay down on our tarps in the apple loft. The thatch roof crackled and smelled more and more like a crushing weight. It was already dark, because of night, but we couldn't close our eyes. Worse than during our dreary monotonous motions in the wheat, a single thought kept turning around and around in our heads, returning again unchanged every time: It was not our fate to be a countess like Anne-Dörte. But someday we too would be nineteen, with faces as lively as hers, with visible breasts, firm bodies, aware too of our legs—just not at the right time. It would be too late. In our cave under the pelting rain it was so quiet that maybe Hanna thought I was asleep. The empty blackness woke to her furious voice: I'm not a child anymore! It sounded determined, unrepentant, and I hated her, because she wasn't suffering enough under the calamity I'd thought was as huge for her as it was for me. Again she was older than me.

"When the young fellows talk to you don't you answer them and don't look at them and don't turn around. If they still won't stop then get rid of them nice and quick: Yes. No. Might be. Don't know. I see.

When a young fellow's peeled an apple or pear and wants to give it to you, just let it be, don't eat it.

When the young fellows sit next to you and want to talk to you and want to hold your hand, just pull your hand right back and stick it in your apron, and then if they won't stop turn your back on them and don't give them any answer at all.

Then when the young fellows bring some musicians in the night or act crazy
some other way, like they'll probably do, and right outside your room too, say:
You think I'm here for you? I don't think so. You don't look the type to me.
Boys from next door are always the worst."

On the way back home, honorably discharged, thanked man-to-man,
we couldn't believe our eyes. In the forest one of us always walked ahead
of the other with her hand behind her back, ready to give the sign: Someone's coming (on the right or on the left); no one came, we thought we'd
just been lucky. The people in the village, who'd always given Schlegel's
people such grumpy answers or better yet none at all, looked angrily right
past us as usual—but we saw an open farm gate, and a box on undamaged
rubber wheels in the yard, with a long bar that you could attach to a jeep,
it was new, in five hops we could have had it and been long gone. It was
eerie seeing the gate open like that, unguarded. On the long walk down
the shoreline cliffs, the wind from the sea hid the smell of the motorcycle
that shot out of the Countess Woods and was right in front of us before
we could even start running; the Red Army men drove right past us, not
looking at us, looking mad, all officers, one huddling in the sidecar as if
sick. We were positive we recognized the uniforms. We couldn't believe it.
In Jerichow, though, by the time we got to the Rande road, the Germans
were truly taking it too far. We saw a girl in a skirt and a white blouse,
right there on the street, well within sight of the Soviets guarding the
airfield; from a distance she looked a bit like Lise Wollenberg, who knew
better. Then a woman passed us riding a bicycle in broad daylight, through
this area, and she had an honest-to-God canister of milk hanging on the
handlebars. Walking down Town Street we realized how many women
there were in Jerichow now, because suddenly they were wearing dresses
again, and we could see who was poor because they were still wearing pants.
Bergie Quade walked by as we were scouting out Brickworks Road, and
she had buttons open at her neck, her stocky arms were bare and immod-
est, and Bergie told us. We'd been in the country, we weren't up to speed
on Jerichow. No! The Russians were gone.

But we saw some on the Rehberge too. Are the Swedes coming?
Children. No. The Russians aren't allowed out anymore.

Like a kinda curfew?

No, seriously. Sokolovsky worked it out on his own with the party. "My dad is in the party / My mom is in the party..."

Marshal Sokolovsky? The commander in chief?

He's confined em all to barracks. They're living in their rooms. No more going out alone. Almost makes you feel sorry for em, locked up like that.

Is the commandant still here?

Yeah, not exactly, Gesine. But otherwise the last few days have been like living at peace.

Oh. Peace.

You two might wanna go pritty yourselfs up a little too. And they're going to be holding elections soon.

We're not pritty enough how we are?

You are. You both are. So its all working out. Everything in life comes in fits and starts

like when you're milking a bull.

What depraved little girls you've turned into!

Hanna promised us again that she'd stay. If Vassily Danilovič Sokolovsky could impose such order, then surely the next thing he'd do would be send Cresspahl back. Hanna could have her apprenticeship.

Meanwhile the Soviet Military Administration had increased the rationing. With our Card 5, Hanna and I could get three hundred grams of bread instead of a quarter pound. And we had our fat bags of wheat on top of that. We would definitely survive the winter.

Cresspahl's front door, previously sealed shut with the board of the protection order, now stood open late into the evenings. The Russians in the Kommandatura were ones we didn't know. This was apparently the third crowd since K. A. Pontiy.

– It's the Twins: Jakob said. We were sitting with his mother, telling her about the farm. We were back from a long trip. She'd kept us close to her while we talked, one arm around each of us, and she exclaimed in the pleading tone that she otherwise used to express disappointment at naughty children: Girls, what a sight you are! She was so quiet and hollow-eyed that she would have looked dead if she weren't moving. It felt totally and completely like Sunday evening in the house. We bragged about how much food we'd had and refused our dinner. Hanna politely asked who was looking out for Gesine's grandfather now that the Demwies Twins were in charge in Jerichow. Jakob, the psychologist, the appointed guardian, the expert on girls, let slip: Papenbrock's been ... transferred. They've transferred him.

Hanna finished it for him: – Arrested. Gesine was more shocked, but merely blinked. This house was a magnet for danger. It wasn't safe here.

And she wasn't given time to reflect. On September 8, the NKVD worked on Sunday. The following people were hauled away from their breakfasts in Jerichow: Mrs. Ahlreep of Ahlreep's Clocks, Leslie Danzmann, Peter Wulff, Brüshaver, Kliefoth. The rumors that wouldn't stop going around Jerichow were quite sure that a carrier pigeon had been sighted over the town. By this point Hanna had lived in Jerichow long enough and was more inclined to notice that all these names had a connection to Cresspahl than to think that the Red Army had gotten worked up over some unsurrendered pigeons or a banned club. That evening the arrested people were released, to avoid attracting notice in their places of work. Rumor had already put them in Neubrandenburg concentration camp, to keep Papenbrock company; in fact they'd been held in the basement under Town Hall. All had been strictly sworn to silence. Having started with Leslie Danzman, Jakob wasted an hour—she lied from fear. Wulff, Kliefoth, and Brüshaver assured him: during their questioning, there'd been maybe two questions about Cresspahl. One poking into Cresspahl's service on the eastern front in 1917, the other trying to link him to a certain privy councilor in Malchow named Hähn. Kliefoth had heard that name only once before, in connection with some arms deal back in the early twenties.

Hanna thanked Jakob when he came back from Warnemünde, but only as if he'd done his job. (In our new mode, we only talked to this person in the most cursory way.) Her fishermen relatives had gotten into trouble with the Volkspolizei during the municipal elections. Apparently they'd already sent for Hanna. Hanna was to board the boat in Rande, so that her departure for the British zone wouldn't attract attention.

Jakob wasn't to bring her there. While Hanna said goodbye to him in the house, Gesine stood outside the door, not wanting to see how Hanna and Jakob were going to leave things. In Rande, Hanna didn't want to board Ilse Grossjohann's cutter alone. Around midnight we were at the spot known as de Huuk, 11° 7' East, 54° 2' 4" North. Later Gesine realized that Hanna had hugged her as she would a boy.

For days she could still feel in her arms the sensation of pushing Hanna onto the other boat. She also found it easy to think that Hanna should have stayed with her after all.

When Gesine came back to the empty bed at sunrise, she found Hanna's wooden clogs next to hers, all four placed neatly in a row.

June 4, 1968 Tuesday

This country now has more than three and a half million men in its armed forces, almost as many as it had in 1953 during the Korean War; today the voters in California will tell Robert F. Kennedy something preliminary about his suitability for the presidency; today's armed robbery happened at 71 West Thirty-Fifth Street; the citizens of Czechoslovakia, with the permission of the new Communists there, can now know officially as well that the great and good Antonín Novotný was dishonest about political activities not only in 1952 but also in 1954, 1955, 1957, and 1963;

the East German Communists have released a Columbia University art historian even though "forbidden" buildings may have ended up in front of his camera during his dissertation research on Berlin architecture, and without the Americans having to give anything in return. "You could say it was done with mirrors."

That was something that Cresspahl the certified translator, living in New York for the past seven years, had to go look up—just to make sure she wouldn't feel too at home in the language: "done with a trick." Nine months in jail and then returned to the outside world without a trial. Sleight of hand. Magic.

Cresspahl hadn't been in jail twenty months yet and he wanted a trial. Wherever things led, he had to get beyond waiting for nothing but the next day.

Through the wet March of 1946 he'd been busy, which at least felt like movement. The camp on the western border of Soviet Mecklenburg had been meant as a holding camp, but a prisoner was allowed to volunteer for work without risk of punishment. The commandant didn't thank you if you went through a barracks from floor to ceiling until it was waterproof and draftproof as a house, so the other German prisoners wouldn't have anything to hold against Cresspahl either. But meanwhile he had his skill to set him apart from the future prospects that made the others crazy with rumors, arguments, bragging. So if he wanted to keep such a facility in good shape it wasn't to get thanks in return. When he carved himself a birchwood spoon, why not carve another for his bunkmate—though he would have preferred to teach that intellectual's two left hands how to do it themselves. If a thank-you wasn't enough, he might accept two pinches of tobacco, but he didn't let himself get talked into manufacture or trade. And since he divulged almost nothing beyond his name and, more or less, Jerichow, he thought he was simply being ignored in his bunkhouse, at best tolerated. Then, without warning, a sentry came to take him to the guardroom; he didn't get back until around midnight, and found that not a few people had waited up for him. This was a story he could tell. A wooden trunk was sitting in front of the commandant—Cresspahl had made several. This one had been confiscated direct from the woodshop, not yet bearing the initials of the person who'd ordered it. When challenged he confessed to having built this item of evidence. Questioned over its false bottom, he misunderstood even the second translation before finally admitting the possibility. Then came the order. It earned Cresspahl more sympathy than suspicion from his fellow prisoners—commiseration for forced labor. He spent almost a month over the birthday present for the commandant's granddaughter: a little chest eight inches high with three divided drawers, a rolltop, a wooden bolt, and, at your command sir, a secret compartment. This thorny assignment had, for once, let him think about something different, his own children: how he would someday build them an even more ingenious miniature dresser, and with real tools. His fee was two packets of Krüll, which he shared with anyone who asked—he knew all about how to act in the slammer by that point. But he needn't have bothered. The others had started acting like good neighbors; they were more worked up about the lower ranks of their guards ordering trunks too, for what could that mean if not that the Russians would be leaving soon, possibly as early as next week? Cresspahl, though, had to produce even more such containers for Germans, for their trips back to Röbel or Lauenburg, and so was protected from the masses' preposterous spiritual crises. He had been told: You, wait. That's how he managed.

He did not end up spending the winter in the barracks from which, despite the nearby Elde River, he'd hoped for some warmth at least in the morning hours. Starting in December 1946, he was kept beneath a solid house that he imagined was the arsenal in Schwerin. The basement was damp, but not from Pastor's Pond. His task was to write his life story again. He didn't produce much, for if running water froze in the cell overnight how were his fingers supposed to relearn how to manage a pencil? Also, the light from the yard, chopped into gray pieces by a grate in the ground overhead, made him go somewhat blind again. The first version of his second autobiography came out in basically tabular form, and so he was severely beaten; he counted himself lucky that the blows hardly ever broke his skin. He'd survived and starved too long on soup to trust his body to heal open wounds. He grasped that his invisible masters were interested in a complete delivery, not a quick one; and thus he was deprived of his childhood years. Born in 1888, son of the wheelwright Heinrich Cresspahl and his wife, Berta née Niemann, a day laborer's daughter, I was apprenticed to master carpenter Redebrecht in Malchow, Mecklenburg, in 1900, at Easter. They were all dead but there might still be some von Haases, whom Cresspahl remembered not only from when he was a five-year-old shepherd boy but from when he was a thirty-one-year-old member of the Waren Workers Council who'd dug up weapons on their family estate to be used in the agriculturalist Wolfgang Kapp's putsch. He knew all too well how that family treated sick estate laborers, even before his mother's death. He was very glad to have such people chased out of Mecklenburg to the other side of the Elbe, even if it went against the grain for him to denounce them personally. This produced such gaps in his chronological account that he got blows in the kidneys from a rifle butt when a year was graded as Poor in the interrogation room, in the neck if it came out Unsatisfactory. The young guys working for the MGB knew the approximate extent of treatment requested but not the daily reason for it, so in the underground corridors they seemed to be merely urging their charges on. They hardly ever seemed to care too passionately. No hatred was required to keep a prisoner awake, the truck engines making music outside in the yard during the interrogations took care of that, and for four nights straight a circular saw too. During the days he had to continue work on his writing assignment. Cresspahl earned himself a lonely week by taking the genealogical aspect of the question a little too seriously and detouring to his grandparents and the years after 1875. Solitary seemed fair. He was free to choose, after all. His new superiors, the expert from *Kontrrazvedka* and the auditor from the SMT, had handed him an analysis of his class position and his personal role in the wrong turns of world history, *i*'s dotted and *t*'s crossed, and it was his choice not to sign it. He didn't resist out of stubbornness, since he must have been wanting to go back home to his girls. It couldn't have been solely in service of the truth, since he was soon describing himself as a man who had been in this world for fifty-eight years and had never once made deals or spoken or cooperated with anyone. Possibly he was trying to come clean with the New Justice only to the extent that he could keep others out of it. Sometimes the men evaluating his learning process put an idea or two into his head, for instance an essay on the year 1922, and the name Hähn, privy councilor and arms dealer. Whenever the pupil failed a lesson he could almost perfectly picture the beating he'd be getting the next morning at daybreak, but even so he would sometimes escape from his life into blithe carefree daydreams of a different one, which could equally really have been his: not parting from Gesine Redebrecht in 1904, spending a while with her, with Mrs. Trowbridge starting in 1930, in Bristol, consistently avoiding Richmond, with a thirteen-year-old son Henry, or killed with them both by a bomb, being with Mina Goudelier starting in 1920, but not for long on Kostverlorenvaart behind the Great Market in Amsterdam, better on the Fella River, in Chiusaforte, where he could have not only learned fine inlay work but practiced it too, no not there, not where the Germans would occupy, so . . . Australia, if Goudelier's daughter would have gone that far with him, across other seas than Papenbrock's Lisbeth, who in this case would have survived November 1938, or else with all four women together, remembering other High Streets, lakeshores, Broadways, sunrises, picnics in the grass. He didn't take it personally that he was marginal to those lazily unspooling pictures, or hardly present at all. But when the Red Army gave him a pill it was nothing but aspirin. These didn't have to be dreams. Nor did his conscience bother him at being confined with food and lodging and a job he had a very poor understanding of while all around the prison people were helping each other get back to normal life through hard work (that was how he imagined it). Responsibility for his actions had been handed to the Ministerstvo Gosudarstvennoy Bezopasnosti, let them answer for his useless sitting around. With such abundant encouragement he had, by January 1947, written his way through his military service in Güstrow (which his idiot daughter never asked about), in February to his touchy feud with the SPD (and his idiot daughter thought she'd hold off on her questions), which added up to 260 pages of his life story but still only two pages typed up and signed, the first version. He persisted in considering himself his judges' partner, known by name and number, possessing the right to a trial and verdict, moving along a more or less agreed-on path, not only moving in time. In late February they canceled the agreement. He was ordered to report "with all his belongings" for transport.

"Belongings" were something he'd not had since his last move, and he joined the group in the barracks yard like someone just out for an evening stroll. The transport was on foot, in columns of unkempt men who'd been arrested just days before and carried out their guards' orders with downright Prussian ceremony. They took the doddering old man along out of curiosity, holding his arm as he groggily put one foot in front of the other, but they soon gave up on him, since all he could say when asked about his "case" was: I-I d-d-unno... He spoke haltingly, his sentences broke apart, there seemed to be something the matter with his throat too. – 'm fittyeight! he said, maybe because they'd called him Grandpa, but really more to himself, and they all chipped in to give the strange ragtag fellow a cigarette. It was his first tobacco in eleven weeks, it made him feel like his Australian dreams did, to the point where he later wasn't sure that their march hadn't actually started in Schwerin. Anyway his eyes weren't working too well either. Near Rabensteinfeld he realized which way they were moving, and when they reached various crossroads and the others cursed at their steadily eastward direction he thought the whole thing might be for his benefit. For the way through Crivitz should have reminded him of something, maybe a promise, he couldn't put his finger on it. At Mestlin there was something else he needed to think of, it nagged at him for the next six miles, then he remembered: the turnoff to Sternberg and Wismar and Jerichow, so now he'd missed it. Past Karow it was distressing not to see the rails that should have been off to the left of the road, it was like he was going the wrong way. He reluctantly believed it when he caught sight of Old Schwerin—something was missing at the train station, Krebs Lake confused him, but finally he saw the compass rose on the vane-less old windmill outside of town and stopped resisting: they were giving him one more look at Malchow. Only it was all high, high above him. Knowingly in disguise, as in a dream, he stepped back into the summer of 1904, with wavering songs from the lakeside boulevard wafting over the water of a Friday evening, he walked into the children's playground for the fair that lasted the whole next day, the Parchim dragoon band was playing, wearing their colorful fairy-tale uniforms, and three horsemen rode out through the town gate, and right in the middle of the leisurely crowd of the dead stood a young man with the master's daughter between Linden Alley and the big canvas tents, seen by all, discovered by no one, *Oh you're my darling but you've got no money, no clogs, no shoes,* in 1920 the workers seized the town of Waren and Baron Stephan le Fort of Boek shelled Town Hall with a cannon and the Strikers Council delegates couldn't get any farther with the people of Malchow, *those fellows're shootin at us now,* and a forester on a count's estate who'd refused to supply the estate owners with wagons for collecting wood and tried to bamboozle them was the only one to be driven out of his house. *Never hit man nor beast with a stick stripped of bark, whenever you do they're bound to die.* And that was Olden Malchow on the island, it was, the Gierathschen water between the island and the new town lined with lawns and landings and gables, Mill Hill—the one small bit of the mainland that hadn't let churches on—a storm a hundred fifty years ago'd helped—the subterranean folk needed somewhere for their Midsummers. A hole had been blasted in the embankment on the other side and sloppily filled in like the soil there couldn't bear it anymore, you could just about swim over to Wenches Hill, the old Wendish castle mound that a six-year-old had herded geese past, nowadays the subterranean folk were invisible when they walked out on Laschendorf farm in the daytime but a shepherd had once heard them cry *Give a hat, give a hat!* and he called for his hat and put it on and saw them standing in front of him, *Teeny little men with their three-corner hats, they jumped at him and scratched his eyes out and took his magic cap. The little folk in Wenches Hill made such lovely music, they say.*

Here lies Fünfeichen, the sanatorium! A long, brown, rectilinear building with its barracks and guardhouse, set in a spacious barren field abundantly equipped with muddy wooden walkways, barbed-wire passages, and squat watchtowers; behind its tar-paper roofs the mountains of Lindental and

Tollense Lake tower heavenwards—evergreen, massy, cleft with wooded ravines—and prominent signs on the fence inform the nature lover in Russian and German and English: OFF-LIMITS. ENTRY FORBIDDEN. VIOLATORS WILL BE SHOT!

Now as then the Red Army directs the establishment. Dressed in a belted tunic studded with medals and hanging far down over his baggy breeches, his head held high under the clay-colored cap, automatic rifle at the ready, the soldier herds the prisoner across the camp road; he is a man whom knowledge has hardened, holding his patients in his spell in his curt, reserved, preoccupied way, in amused amazement: all those individuals who, too weak to give and to follow laws unto themselves, put themselves into his hands, body and mind, that his severity may be a shield unto them.

It took till early summer for Cresspahl to come to; he was furiously intent on concealing this. In all seriousness he considered himself mushy, gamey, plucked out of the world and set to one side somewhere else.

For one thing, he couldn't find in his memory how he might have gotten from Malchow Abbey to Fünfeichen. He knew the Red Army from the first postwar autumn—they would have shot him on Wenches Hill if he'd slipped and fallen. He could hardly believe that the people in the transport—strangers—would have dragged him to Waren, Penzlin, Tollense Lake. He'd woken up on a lower bunk in Fünfeichen Camp without any idea how he'd gotten there, as if from nowhere, too weak to eat and too tired to open his eyes and weary of life. For another thing, he kept hearing talk of Neubrandenburg Camp in the tightly packed barracks. But this was Fünfeichen, two and a half miles from the Stargard Gate—as recently as 1944 the British had told him to take a look around this area, both at the Trollenhagen air base and at how the Germans were treating their prisoners of war at Fünfeichen. If he could believe his eyes he was in Fünfeichen's old south camp, barrack 9S or 10S, next to the barbed wire around the vegetable garden, facing Burg Stargard, and the fenced-in compound of rooms and workshops lay to the north just as it had in his old drawing. He couldn't be this wrong, could he? Why did everyone else think this was Neubrandenburg, and only he thought Fünfeichen? For a third thing, why, even now, could he not stop hoping for a trial, to get closure? Ending up here was his closure.

He tried to find the prisoners he'd come from Rabensteinfeld with. He barely knew any of their faces, and it's hard to find someone out of twelve thousand. The workforce was herded out of the barracks only when the camp command's Operations group and the German kapos working for them turned up to search the bunks. From this last piece of his past he found no one, for they'd all had more of their journey ahead of them, while he'd been parked here, disposed of for good. The kapos not only rummaged through the rags when they searched the bunks, they tipped over the bed-frames too; the prisoners argued for hours about confiscated or mistakenly switched property. Cresspahl just watched. When the soup was doled out he had to wait until someone shoved him their own bowl, contemptuously, like he was a sick dog, and by that time the tureen was often empty, and still he had to pay for the loan of the bowl by washing it. He would have had his own dish soon enough, except that you also had to pay for permission to work. What he had on his body no longer fell into the category of barterable goods. He volunteered at once when the German kapos needed replacements for latrine duty; he had to march in goose step for ten yards in front of well-nourished representatives of the Soviets, barking in snappy military fashion: I am an old Nazi pig and I want to carry shit! He didn't get the job though. He tried to look on the bright side—he'd been spared the stink—but soon realized that the other prisoners tended to move away from him, despite there not being much room to move, because he stank. He had lain too long in his own filth, unconscious or asleep or whatever it was. And now he was defenseless against fleas and lice. Hot water had a price, too, he could have paid it by informing on his bunkmates but he had no information. The kapos fetched him from the barracks at night and handed him over to the Soviets for leaving the barracks at night. He'd expected solitary but was only penned up closer to the others than he'd been in the barracks, except now in the dark, and with no food. Because a scarecrow's clothes were in better shape than his, a kapo reported him (for neglecting his appearance) to the Soviets, from whom he was instantly told to take five steps back. In the clothesroom the kapos had no witnesses and were free to torment him with beatings until he recited what they wanted: As an old Nazi piece of shit / I walk on a cripple's stave / My pants are full of shit / As I head for a shitty grave. The German personnel also had in mind that they were allowed to hand out clothes only from dead men. But he kept his old shirt and managed to wash the caked pus from the new one and after the third washing he could trade it for the bottom half of a fish can, rusty but with no holes. When the kapos went after a prisoner the others moved aside, uneasily, but it still looked cooperative, as if wanting to let the beaters move comfortably. Whatever he was supposed to learn from the whole process, Cresspahl probably got it wrong.

So many Mecklenburgers (though hardly any among the kapos), and it was so easy to set them against one another. Was that supposed to be the lesson? The kapos paid in bread, in half cigarettes, and very rarely with a job in the barbershop team: that was enough to break up any solidarity. Cresspahl saw one man (he refused to name him) that the others harassed just to pass the time, or because his scared, weepy carrying-on invited it. They won his confidence with wild stories from the eastern front and appeals to his comradeship, proved their friendship with gifts of soup and promises of a pipeful of tobacco, until finally he trusted them, made them promise not to tell, and told them about his background, being given leave to play the violin at Reich Governor Hildebrandt's state dinners and other occasions; before long the kapos were making him reenact his ceremonial postures and way of walking, the way you train an animal. Then he did cry, out of exhaustion or lost pride, but his pals didn't let him run off into the electrified outer fence, they gloomily kept an eye on him, hardly out of guilt or shame but because the Operations Detachment knew all about such deaths and took out their inconvenience on anyone involved in them. The men seemed relieved when the Soviets took their violinist away like a rabid beast; would they have been right if this had gotten them released? Not a single rumor involving release went around. Cresspahl listened in on one of the banned cultural discussion groups, this one about the Hague Convention with respect to War on Land and the illegal incarceration of civilians in a prisoner-of-war camp; he kept close to the speaker until the speaker's arrest, to avoid any suspicion of having denounced him; he refrained from commenting that Fünfeichen had been a Soviet "special camp" since 1945 under international law. One seventeen-year-old deserter, "also here by mistake," had confronted his elders, somewhat vehemently, over their shooting of hostages in the Soviet Union; they'd beaten him up for it that night and accidentally strangled him. An orderly who'd studied medicine for three years lectured on the soggy camp bread's actual caloric content vis-à-vis the calories in the camp administration's calculations, arriving at

the absolutely unintended conclusion that the Soviets must have adopted
SS concentration camp calorie charts; this was a student for whom no time
of day was too early or too late to clean out a prisoner's festering sore or
give him medical advice, they all listened to him talk, a single word would
have been enough to save him from the insulator prisons, and Cresspahl
too said nothing. What kind of virtues had he renounced? Or were these
new ones? In March new people were still being brought in who didn't
grasp the distance between civilian life and camp life; they blithely rattled
off their slogans from Socialist Unity Party election posters, with which
they'd opposed the lower allocation of paper to the bourgeois parties, and
before you could blink they were in lockup and they wouldn't be coming
back out. This process was referred to as "moving on," a kind of substitute
for dying. Cresspahl's thoughts kept running in circles around the news
that the Soviets couldn't get by without elections, and that paper was used
for such things. One new admit called it a war crime that the Soviets had
fired on the city of Neubrandenburg until it went up in flames, leaving the
whole area ringed by the old walls cleaned out except for Great Woolweavers'
Street, then he moved on; Cresspahl said nothing about the city's refusal
to surrender and tried to mentally sketch out the wiped-out town hall, a
cute little boxy building with a ridge turret perched up in the middle of
the roof, *built like itd been plucked out of a box of Christmas toys many long
years ago and set right down in the fore-city of Neubrandenburg's marketplace
for the magistrate and townspeople to play with a little.* Now admittedly
he'd grown stupid from exhaustion, from sitting in the stench and chatter
of the barracks day in and day out; he might be confused, seeing as his
thoughts so often slipped right past the others'; can he really have failed to
notice that he'd just lost heart? that he no longer did anything from the
heart? So how did he act when a new guy was brought to the barracks; only
yesterday he'd been sitting down to dinner at his own table in Penzlin and
now he was being shoved from bunk to bunk before finding a place on the
drafty floor—why did Cresspahl let him discover all by himself that he
was in prison, that he would never ever be able to get word to his family,
that this rotten dishwater was the very best that morning soup could be,
and that the path through the hospital led not to comfort but to a filthy
and miserable death? He knew what help the man needed; he hadn't been
given it himself. Was it indifference? What had he chosen to do?

He occasionally did something for friends. In August 1947 Heinz Mootsaak appeared in the barracks door, in pants and shirtsleeves as if brought in straight from the fields. He looked completely idiotic—after the silence between the barbed-wire fences and the wooden shacks he probably hadn't expected such a loud group in such close quarters; he was still the shy country boy who's polite when he enters a room full of other people. For him Cresspahl stood up and turned his back on him, not to betray mutual recognition, but so that they could meet later on by chance without arousing suspicion. Here he miscalculated, exaggerated. Heinz Mootsaak hadn't had the slightest idea who that decrepit bag of bones in tattered rags of mismatched uniforms might be, and by the next morning he'd already moved on to lockup.

In October—it was already pretty cold—Cresspahl was drawn into an escape scenario by two prisoners who may have taken his new concept of sociability the wrong way. They could hardly recruit him as a full partner; they were acting charitably. The old Cresspahl wouldn't have hesitated for a second, he'd have answered clear as day with the look on his face and said out loud just for the record: *Nonsense. Don't be idiots.* The one from 1947 did hesitate, to keep up good relations, and then answered helpfully with a Mecklenburg saying: *The nobility wont stand for that.* He evaded by asking for time to think it over and that was enough to catch him. Meanwhile it had gotten around the room that the glum old sourpuss had finally nibbled the bait, or else that a new trio was up to something. There was positively nothing to deliberate about in the plan. It would take months to pry three adjacent floorboards loose and reattach them so that no accidental footstep would make them pop up and yet so that they could be taken up within a few minutes during the night. They wanted to go under barracks 10S and 11S to the south edge of the camp, then right along the wire and past the middle watchtower, then under the whole length of 18S to the inner ring of barbed wire, under that to the auxiliary power unit, where they'd turn off the power and finally force their way out over the last fence, more or less exactly toward the Soviet staff barracks, behind which ran a road. One of them said he was an electrician. He tried to talk them out of it, out of neither pity nor concern, he just didn't want to be responsible for anything. He mentioned the Soviet guards' swivel-mounted searchlights, the quarter mile of crawling and tunneling in a single night, the open space for miles around. To be polite he at least praised the escape route for leading away from the kilometer-long eastern edge of the camp. He warned them of armed patrols in the Forst Rowa woods, the waterlogged fields of Nonnenhof, the Red Army's large off-limit areas north of Neustrelitz. One of the men pretended to be insulted, maybe he'd been the one who'd come up with the plan. They both thanked him, loud enough to be heard three bunks away, extra noticeable after all the whispering.

After the second twenty-four hours had passed Cresspahl thought he was out of danger—that's how long it took for him to be brought before the Soviet administration. At the staff barracks a signed and sworn statement was sitting on the desk: Prisoner C., Incitement to escape, Unscrupulous plot against Soviet People's property, Slanderous comparison between Red Army and feudal aristocratic caste. Supplemental attachments: sketches of the south camp and the escape route continuation via Nonnenhof and the Lieps Canal, reconstructed on the basis of the accused's suggestions. Cresspahl now enjoyed another opportunity to appreciate the Soviets more than the German kapos. The Soviets' Operations Detachment went unarmed down the camp road or into the barracks; they ordered no punishments worse than standing at attention for up to three hours, and if one of them did lash out it was clearly out of a desperation that had once been good-naturedness, which could now no longer put up with a prisoner's doing whatever it was he was now doing wrong. The worse punishment was the German camp officials accentuating their interrogations by keeping sausage and bread within the prisoner's reach, pouring coffee into cups before his eyes, ersatz coffee but hot, and with milk; the Soviets treated their interrogation rooms as offices. And it was true, they didn't beat him. For the Mecklenburg saying about the nobility he had to stand against the stove for an hour and a half, spine pushed back by it, hands firmly on imaginary pants seams. When, even after that, he could only explain the defamatory phrase in terms of the nobility's dominance in the 1896 Mecklenburg-Schwerin parliament and the remoteness of the Malchow railway station, the gentlemen presented him with a statement to sign. In it he was permitted to deny every accusation except for that first and last conversation, which had been seen by too many people, and he signed. By this point, around four in the morning, the officers were in a convivial mood, though not without contempt for this wreck of a human being. They thanked him for his love of the truth, regretted disturbing his night's rest, expressed the hope that he might fall back asleep soon. Then they handed him over to the German kapos.

The kapos held him in a detention cell in the north camp until noon the following day, taking turns in groups of four, using whips. Can someone refuse to speak simply because he's decided he doesn't want to speak? How can he know for sure that even shortly after losing consciousness he's kept silent? Did his lapse warrant them hurting him so badly right away that there was nothing he had to care about anymore but the pain? Can someone refuse to speak a word to others just because he doesn't understand them?

When the Soviets had had ample time to observe what Germans are capable of doing to one another, they ordered an end to the questioning. The last shift of kapos resented having to drag the copiously bleeding heap across the camp road themselves. The Soviets didn't let the regular prisoners help, but they did let them watch. They needed the kapos as sturdy hunting dogs, not gone soft or anything from being liked. Since the Russian guards supervised the whole transport, Cresspahl was laid almost gently on a bunk in the barbers' quarters in the north camp.

The wounds took until the following summer to heal; he could walk by early December. At which point he started all over again: food dish, hot water, foot wraps. He was immediately known among the north camp inmates as a crazy man, for when asked why he'd told the kapos nothing he actually had an answer, and it sounded credibly deranged:

– *Ididn likem*: he said. He hadn't liked them.

They tried again around Christmas and offered him a job in the burial squad,

> a chance
> to demonstrate
> a change of heart and
> atonement as well as
> the forgiveness
> of the community

with additional rations and a change of clothing. Since it was work, which involved physical movement, the prospect nagged at him. Why shouldn't he be able to do what other people could do? The bodies looked bloated, they no longer weighed much. Most often there were only a few to pick up each week, always two bearers per stretcher. It came down to the fact that he'd survive the day when they had to clear out the corpses from the storage cellar and lug them onto the truck; he'd have time to recover during the drive to the cemetery on the Fuchsberg. He didn't dread the task of undressing the bodies before dumping them into the mass graves, if anything he doubted he'd be able to dig the graves, at first. He didn't want to do it for the dead, nor to get a couple of extra potatoes in his soup, nor to survive—he wanted to have something to do. Some career military men who had appointed themselves the illegal German leadership of the camp around that time talked him out of accepting, making mild threats. They couldn't rely on him to remember the correct numbers, and for a while they firmly held on to him in the back row during roll call until the kapos gave up. The job went to a prisoner considered worthier of the extra rations and the drives outside the camp, and who wanted to be transferred to Sachsenhausen just because it was closer to Berlin. For the men in the burial squads were suspected of keeping count, and so were often replaced or sent off to other camps, that way the lists of the dead could only be put together out of approximate fragments. The number for Fünfeichen was 8,500, not always documented by names. And so Cresspahl lost a chance to escape before he even knew it, the kapos didn't get him out of the camp and still had to remove the two conspirators from the old bunkhouse; Cresspahl was compensated with a month's priority in getting a shave and owed thanks to nobody. Was this one of the things he was supposed to learn?

It had been a long time since he'd even thought about escape. He'd seen one though. The march to Fünfeichen had passed through the town of Goldberg, and as the column rounded a corner one of the prisoners stepped out of it onto the sidewalk, grabbed a thoroughly startled housewife by the elbow, and made her keep walking with him, loudly marveling at their reunion: – Elli, my goodness! he cried in excitement. The scene had apparently looked plausible enough for the Soviet guards; as they left town they replaced the runaway with a civilian who happened to be digging in his garden. For a while Cresspahl had held on to this example of Red Army principles of order, as something to tell Gesine; then the yarn had been told a few too many times in Fünfeichen and the gardener ended up getting shot for his unreasonable horrified reaction two miles past Goldberg, or else he was still in N22 today without any idea, sometimes the woman was named Herta and sometimes the man leaving the column had shouted: Hey, Aunt Frieda! Eventually Cresspahl himself doubted he'd ever seen it happen.

Flight, revolt, liberation—he was no longer susceptible to these things. The piece of land near Ratzeburg that the Soviets had traded to the British had grown in the Fünfeichen rumors to the whole strip west of a line from Dassow through Schönberg to Schaal Lake, and if American paratroopers weren't expected outside the Fünfeichen gates the next day then it would at least be the Red Cross from Sweden. Cresspahl recognized in others the feverish, frenzied effects of latrine gossip and feared them for himself, for he was in such a state often enough already, when his thoughts ran at such an unnerving distance from the talk around him. He had never read the warning sign on the camp fence from the front but he was perfectly certain that Western military commissions, even in Burg Stargard and Neubrandenburg, were being kept at a distance by multilingual prohibitions. He couldn't understand what the other prisoners expected from their former enemies. The camp workforce was shoveled in and out so regularly that informers were not immediately detected, however thickly larded with them the barracks were—any plot with more than one person involved was as good as blown. For himself he couldn't even envision an escape. Once he'd made it to the other shore of Tollense Lake he might be able to get to the fabled new border of Mecklenburg in nine days, but the Soviets would be waiting for him where he'd need to go to fetch the children, and as soon as his escape became known they'd arrest them. That meant he was less separated from them in Fünfeichen. And anyway escape from Fünfeichen was impossible.

Fünfeichen had become the world. Life outside the camp never entered it.

There were a few possible changes. These were: Deportation to the Mühlberg, Buchenwald, Sachsenhausen, or Bautzen concentration camps, all well known from new arrivals' reports. These were eternities like Fünfeichen—time did not pass there. You could also decide to die, voluntarily by starvation, voluntarily at the fence.

Fünfeichen offered any number of ontologies.

Still, Cresspahl would have preferred a trial and sentence.

June 5, 1968 Wednesday

– Where *were* you, Marie? Tell me where you were!

– It's a quarter to six p.m. and I'm here at home. Those are your rules.

– Where were you all day?

– What about you, Mrs. Cresspahl, you're not home a minute earlier than usual either.

– Should I have come home? Is that an accusation?

– You have a job, you're not allowed to leave work. Maybe if it's raining, or if there's a subway strike, but not for private matters.

– Marie. How did you hear?

– In the park.

– That's not your usual walk to school.

– Okay.

– We'd agreed—

– on West End Avenue. Like the police are lining the streets there! People have come up and talked to me there, again and again. I can take care of myself in Riverside Park too, on bright sunny mornings. I'm not a child anymore, Gesine!

– You're not understanding me.

– I'm *not* understanding you!

– When I got to Broadway they were sold out of *The New York Times*.

– I went to school through the park because on Wednesdays I have first-period gym. At the playground. In Riverside Park, on the corner of 107th Street and—

– Right.

– When I left for school it was like I was wearing an invisibility cloak. Eagle-Eye Robinson was up and about on the stairs with his back to me. The elevator door was open, Esmeralda's swanky purse was on the stool, totally unguarded, she was nowhere in sight. No neighbors, no bus drivers on the street. So the news would hit me without warning. There was a guy sitting on the bench by the memorial fountain for the firemen, all alone.

Young guy, nineteen. Not a college student, more like an off-duty shift worker. Baseball sweatshirt, long pants, thick white wool socks, not a tourist. Crew cut. He was leaning back on the bench, all comfortable, arms stretched out, not a care in the world. Radio next to him, steamer trunk, flustered voices. That's where I heard. Kennedy'd been killed.

– *Angeschossen,* not *erschossen,* Marie. *Erschossen* is more final than "shot."

– It's because I have to talk your damn German with you! *He was shot. He wasn't dead.*

– You don't have to use German if you don't want to.

– The guy was sitting there doing nothing, so relaxed, nothing to do, he was perfectly happy to let me listen without looking at me. Like everything had gone as planned. Like he was glad.

– What did you know at that point?

– The senator from New York had won the California primary. He was giving a victory speech at the Hotel Ambassador in Los Angeles. On the way to the press conference, in a kitchen corridor, he was shot in the head from behind. 1:17 California daylight saving time. When it was quarter past three here. I know, I know, you say *viertel fünf* in German, not *viertel vier*! He was lying on the ground, his wife kneeling by his side. The thing with the rosary. The last rites. Unconscious in the hospital. Then again, from the top: Robert Francis Kennedy, the senator from New York—

– You could tell in the subway that something had happened, but maybe not. Maybe the reason everyone was so gloomy, not looking at anyone, not saying anything, was because it was the hottest day of the year we've had so far. There wasn't necessarily anything worse going on than the usual tragedy that life sometimes is for some New Yorkers. Then, at Grand Central, I saw a TV in a window, something filling the screen, nothing from the loudspeakers. There was just one word on the screen the whole time, crooked, like it was written in dust with a finger: *Shame.*

– *Schande* in German, "a scandal"?

– Also that they felt shame.

– Yes.

– I tried calling the school as soon as I got to the bank.

– Gesine, would you have gone to school on a day like this?

– You'll get your note for Sister Magdalena.

– For tomorrow too.

– Do you want the rest of the week off?

– You're not a bad mother, Gesine.

– Am too. I was probably being ridiculous. I thought I had to talk to you.

– You were right, you did. I needed to talk to you. First I got super mad at the bank, for not allowing private phone calls, then at you because you follow their rules. Now I feel better. You tried.

– I tried calling home too.

– I was already in Times Square. There were so many people there, craning their necks, reading the line of news running around the building. Whenever anyone left he pushed his way out past the others, so depressed, so angry. One time I was almost knocked off my feet.

– You know, I saw so much politeness underneath Times Square that it must have thrown everything off schedule. A young black man, black leather jacket, Afro, wanted to let a fat white accountant go first. – After you, go ahead! he said to the befuddled white, who was expecting to be cursed at. – *After you, brother*: the black man said. In the subway! "Brother"!

– I didn't see any of that. In Central Park the middle class were out playing holiday. I heard: nice weather, Tonya's varicose veins she's so young!, summer clearance sale at Macy's, the intrigues on New York's baseball teams. It was the same on Broadway. Music playing in the supermarket like any other day. My cashier was griping about the customers without small change.

– I'd have been mad too.

– I was mad at you, Gesine! Because you told me that this was normal for America—John F. Kennedy, Martin Luther King—and now you were right again. Robert Francis Kennedy.

– The Ferwalters didn't know where you were either.

– I was walking around, alone in the city.

– Buying newspapers, one after the other.

– Not as classy as you, though. I also got New York's Picture Newspaper, *The Daily News*.

– Can I give you the money for them?

– I used my pocket money. Pocket money's for personal needs, right?

– I didn't stay in the bank at lunch, I went across the street. Two more times in the afternoon. I kept going downstairs, I was sure you were standing outside the building, waiting.

– I was!

– Mrs. Lazar just looks so strict, doesn't she. That doesn't work with children. She'd have brought you upstairs to me.

– I wasn't embarrassed! I was mad at you, because you'd expect me to do that too! I spent ten minutes admiring your beautiful lobby and then I left, so that you and your ideas wouldn't get me.

– Ideas about myself?

– Ideas about yourself! Who can possibly console me except Mother! And that I needed consoling at all! What if I wanted to be alone? As if you know me inside and out!

– I don't even know what you've decided on for dinner.

– Nothing! Not for me. There's a T-bone steak for you. And green beans.

– I'm not hungry.

– Gesine, you've been working, you need to eat. Tomorrow you need to go back to the bank. Eat. Or can you stay home tomorrow?

– I have to go to work.

In the end there wasn't much left standing of that knowledge inside and out. Where Mother wanted to make up, Marie wanted a deal. She showed signs of strain, the same as when she has to make herself speak nice about purchases, or doing the dishes; she would have been happy to go off into her room behind the curtained double doors. But she needed her mother for one more thing. She listened for the clicking of the elevator cable and was standing at the door at the first ring or the bell. And what were two furniture movers bringing this late at night into the Cresspahl apartment, which for seven years had been immunized against American television? What now overrode all educational, economic, and maternal considerations? The muscular men rolled a TV set over the threshold, and a mother was needed to sign the rental contract. Marie had the TV moved to her room and paid the $19.50 herself. Pocket money is for personal needs.

She must be embarrassed at having broken another agreement—she makes a point of turning the volume down whenever the ads interrupt the news. It'll be a long time before she believes me when I tell her that her love for a politician is starting to look from the outside a lot like how I fall in love.

"Marie H. Cresspahl, Class 6B
Teacher: Sister Magdalena
Subject: Science? History? Social Studies?

Preliminary Notes for Optional Essay
           ROBERT FRANCIS KENNEDY
Outline? Later as Table of Contents

Biography
1925 born November 20. Father a banker, shipping executive, speculator. 1 million for each child. Isolationist.
      Education: Catholic, in Rhode Island. Private prep school near Boston. Classmates' impression: K bad at small talk, bad at parties. Marines training program while at Harvard University. Served on a destroyer. Back to college without making contact with the enemy. Liked football but too small to play
1946 $1,000.00 from his father as a reward: No smoking, no drinking, not much going with girls
1948 B.A. from Harvard. Correspondent for The Boston Post in the Arab-Jewish War. Studies law in Virginia
1950 marries Ethel Skakel: a Great Lakes coal company, Manhattanville College of the Sacred Heart. Children: Kathleen Hartington, Joseph Patrick, Robert Francis, David Anthony, Mary Courtney, Michael L., Mary K., Christopher, Matthew, Douglas. Dog: Freckles
1951 Bachelor of Laws degree. Job in the Department of Justice. Internal Security division. $4,200.00 a year. Roots out homosexuals, then learns all about corruption in the Criminal division (under the Truman administration)
1952 Campaign manager for John F., wins him the job of senator. Then

in McCarthy's House Unamerican Activities Committee. And so what if Gesine was right about that. Joe McCarthy godfather of his oldest child

1955 Supreme Court attorney. Trip through the Soviet Union. If a Russian doctor saves his life, Communism can't be that bad

1957 Fights crime in the unions, using investigations and interrogations. Said he'd jump off the Capitol Building if he couldn't get Hoffa (Teamsters). Hoffa is acquitted. Kennedy doesn't jump. Refuses offered parachute.

Guest at Joe McCarthy's funeral

1960 Campaign manager for John F., wins him the presidency. "Jack works as hard as any mortal man can, Bobby goes a little further." Votes bought in West Virginia? Bobby is Attorney General and starting in

1961 Adviser to the president. Civil rights for Negroes. Attack on the Republic of Cuba

1962 Travels all over the world. Bali, Tokyo. Stood at Checkpoint Charlie in Berlin with just the tips of his toes on the white line, flowers in one hand and waving at the East German guards with the other

1963 John F. shot. Bobby head of the family. Fights with Lyndon Johnson. But gets Hoffa, eight years prison

1964 Resigns as Attorney General. Elected senator for New York. We'd been here three years. I was seven years old

1967 Calls for negotiations with the South Vietnamese Liberation Front. Role model for draft dodgers

1968 January 30: "I will not oppose Lyndon Johnson under any foreseeable circumstances."

March 17: "I am announcing today my candidacy for the presidency of the United States." Takes advantage of (Eugene) McCarthy's campaign

June 5: Wins the California primary, wounded by two bullets

June 6: Dies in Los Angeles, 4:44 AM Eastern Daylight Time.

Don't mention time of death. Looks too private.

Shorten the biography. Unfortunately this is the length Sister M. wants. Fill it out with other material.

Honorary doctorates from: Assumption College, 1957

Mount St. Mary's College, 1958

Tufts University, 1958
Fordham University, 1961
Nihon University, 1962
Manhattan College, 1962
Philippines, 1964
Marquette University, 1964
Berlin Free University, 1964

Books written: 2. <u>The Enemy Within</u>
              4. "How I Would End the War"
                 (DER SPIEGEL, April 8, 1968)
              1. ?
              3. ?

Justification for the importance of the topic:
    The news announcers sometimes say "President Kennedy" by mistake.
Possible future and all that
    Death in America (Gesine)
    Presence at a historical event via television. Historic
    Senator from New York

SIRHAN BISHARA SIRHAN

1944 born March 19 in the Armenian quarter of the Old City of Jerusalem,
     under the British Mandate. Father Greek Orthodox, waterworks
     supervisor
1948 Arab-Jewish War. Sirhan watches as Israeli soldiers kill relatives and
     family friends. The Sirhans move many times in the Arab Quarter.
     After the British withdrawal East Jerusalem comes under Jordanian
     rule, father working as a plumber for the new government
Education: Lutheran Evangelical school. "Did well in school," the best of
     the five Sirhan sons. Father wants to make sure that something will
     come of this one; beats him. Parents fight
1956 Suez War. Sirhan 12 years old
1957 U.N. and World Council of Churches pay for the family to come to
     the US under a refugee-admission program. They receive visas from

a limited quota; can immigrate on January 12. Come to New York City

1957–1964 (?). Sirhan at John Muir High School in Pasadena, did well enough to gain admission to Pasadena City College but dropped out
Mother had a steady job; Sirhan often unemployed. Liked to hoard his money
Doesn't smoke, doesn't drink. Can't stand being told what to do
Tends the garden, the neighbors like him, plays Chinese checkers with elderly neighbors, one of them a Jewish lady
Wanted to be a jockey but was only allowed to walk horses around after a run to cool them down

1965 Applies for work at a state racetrack. Has to have his fingerprints taken
After the Negro riots in Watts a man named Albert Herz in Alhambra fears for his life and buys a snub-nosed Iver Johnson eight-shot revolver for $31.95

1966 Works at Granja Vista del Rio ranch. Moves horses. Falls off one, injures chin, stomach problems. Doesn't think he receives enough compensation. Claims vision problems

1967 Israeli war against the Arabs. Loses his homeland
Since September 24 employed at a food store in Pasadena. $2.00 per hour. Gives tirades about the Israelis who have everything but still use violence to take Jordanian land. Meanwhile Mr. Herz has given his gun to his daughter, Mrs. Westlake. She became uneasy about having a gun in the house and gives it to an eighteen-year-old neighbor in Pasadena, who sells it in December to one of Sirhan's brothers

1968 In the store Sirhan boasts often that he is not an American citizen (which is required to legally buy a gun). On March 7, his employer makes a comment about Sirhan's work. End of that job
On June 4 walks into the Ambassador Hotel in Los Angeles.
On June 5 at 12:17 (3:17) a.m. shoots the whole magazine at Kennedy and his friends

Evidence against Mrs. Cresspahl: TV is appropriate. Useful for schoolwork even. Ads don't work
Now bring Kennedy and Sirhan together. Reasons why they met.

Death in America (Eagle-Eye Robinson, Gesine C., probably D. E. too).
Evidence or counterevidence?
Violence a national characteristic?
Conflict because immigrant nation, many countries of origin?
Violent eradication of the Indians
Darwinism transferred to pursuit of gain?
Nation enriched by
    War against the Indians
                Mexicans 1846–1848
                Spanish 1898
(Civil War 1861–1865)
National history as a Western movie with a guaranteed murder, usually by
    shooting
Murders in labor disputes: the Molly Maguires in the coal mining districts
    of Pennsylvania, 1854–1877
    Again 1937, during River Rouge plant strike, Dearborn, Mich.
The right of an American man to carry a gun. Toy. Ernest Hemingway.
Gun clubs. Gun manufacturers and gun dealers lobby. Annual gun deaths:
21,000. Per capita of population 1 gun in the cupboard.
Recent murders (1966): Richard Speck, 25, murdered eight student nurses
    in Chicago
    Charles Whitman, 25, shot at random down from the Texas University
    tower, killing 16, wounding 31
    Robert Benjamin Smith, eighteen, forced three women and two children
    to lie down on the floor in a cosmetics salon in Mesa, Arizona, like
    spokes in a wheel, shot them as planned, two survived
1967:
1968:
Attempted and successful assassinations since the Civil War (guns only):
    ABRAHAM LINCOLN, President, † April 15, 1865
    WILLIAM SEWARD, Secretary of State, wounded, 1865
    JAMES GARFIELD, President, † Sept. 19, 1881
    WILLIAM MCKINLEY, President, † Sept. 14, 1901
    THEODORE ROOSEVELT, ex-President, wounded during campaign,
        Oct. 14, 1902
    FRANKLIN D. ROOSEVELT, President-Elect, not hit, Feb. 15, 1933

1136 · *June 6, 1968* *Thursday*

ANTON CERMAK, Mayor of Chicago, † March 6, 1933 (instead of
  Roosevelt)
HUEY P. LONG, Senator for Louisiana, † Sept. 10, 1935
HARRY S. TRUMAN, President, not hit, Nov. 1, 1950
JOHN F. KENNEDY, President, † Nov. 22, 1963
MALCOLM X, Negro leader, † Feb. 21, 1965 (Broadway and 166th)
JAMES MEREDITH, Negro leader, wounded, June 6, 1966
GEORGE LINCOLN ROCKWELL, Nazi boss, † Aug. 25, 1967
MARTIN LUTHER KING, Negro leader, † Apr. 4, 1968
ROBERT F. KENNEDY, Senator for New York, † June 6, 1968, 4:44 ante
  meridiem, Eastern Daylight Time

Did Sirhan Bishara Sirhan have enough time here to learn the American
way of having a conversation? Eleven years, one hundred and forty four
days
Reason (from Sirhan's notebooks, found at 696 East Howard Street, Pasadena): For June 6, 1968, the first anniversary of the last Arab-Israeli
war, Robert F. Kennedy was due to give a speech, a plea for Jewish votes
in this country, a favor to the Israelis who had taken Sirhan Bishara
Sirhan's country away from him, or at least his part of it. Kennedy
needed to die before he could give that speech?
(But why are they letting that be broadcast on the news so that no one can
deny they've heard it? They won't be able to get an untainted jury anywhere
in Los Angeles. Again with no trial?)
Played Chinese checkers with an old Jewish lady
For this reason
From that day on
Then the first bullet entered Kennedy's right armpit, burrowed upward
through fat and muscle, and lodged just under his skin, two centimeters
from his spine, in one piece.
The other bullet hit an extension of his temporal bone just behind his right
ear. One centimeter farther right (viewed from the back of the head) and
the small bullet would have ricocheted off. As it was the empty tip of the
bullet hit the "spongy, honeycomb mastoid bone" and sent bone and metal
fragments into the cerebellum, the midbrain, the right hemisphere. The
brain, already damaged by lack of oxygen, was impaired in the following
functions:

Balance and movement control (cerebellum)

Vision (occipital lobe)

Eye reflexes, eye and body movements, nerve connections between ce-
    rebrum and cerebellum (midbrain)

Control of heartbeat, breathing, blood pressure, digestion and muscle
    reflexes, emotions (the brain stem, the "old brain")

So he wouldn't have wanted to live.

He took slightly more than twenty-five hours to die. He never regained
consciousness. After the three hour and forty minute operation the blood
was circulating properly in the brain, twelve hours later the circulation was
undetectable. He had to pump blood through his heart and breathe for
seven more hours. Then he was no longer able to give his speech.

Now I just have to write it all up.

The Air Force Boeing 707 with the coffin on board left Los Angeles International Airport at 1:28 (4:28) and is expected to reach Kennedy Airport
in New York in four and a half hours.

In Fremont, California, 2,400 workers left a General Motors assembly line
when a supervisor prohibited them from stopping work by saying Robert
F. Kennedy "got what he deserved." He allegedly explained his opinion by
saying: "All these Kennedys are ————————."

Outline ?

Contents

Sources: New York Times, Vol. CXVIII, No. 40,310 and 40,311

             Webster's International Dictionary of the English Language,
             1902

             Columbia Broadcasting System and National Broadcasting
             Company, news programs, panel discussions, medical dem-
             onstrations, etc., June 6, 1968, between 8 a.m. and 6 p.m.

             Telephone calls with friends

Addendum: Evening programs on the radio

WQXR (the New York Times station)

The announcer of the Seven O'Clock News had tears in his voice. The
commentators used words like "tragedy" and "saddening turn of events."
Mr. Apple recites in a rickety voice what he still remembers about R. F.
Kennedy.

Ads turned off.

General Telephone & Electronics brings you, in consideration of the trag-edy, a musical program without any interruption by commercial announce-ments. You are listening to music by Michael Haydn
WCBS

9:35 p.m.   The coffin is off the plane
               it's on the Triboro Bridge
               the funeral will be organized by an expert, Mr. McNamara
9:40 p.m.   eight to nine thousand people are standing at St. Patrick's
               Cathedral
               sirens in the air on the radio, everywhere
               the reporter describes where he's standing, the people along
               the street, whatever he sees. Calm voice, swinging in strong
               slow acoustic waves
               almost all the cars following it are government vehicles
               police whistling
               the close family is gathering for a private viewing. They've
               really left you shaken up
               they're arranging that themselves
the coffin is in its box, broadcast dead
only notes. Now I just need to write it."

                                                 June 7, 1968 Friday
On the south side of Ninety-Sixth Street, starting at West End Avenue, workmen are painting the curb, about a hundred feet of it to the number 19 bus stop. The men are using hand brushes fastened to broomsticks with two pieces of string. They are working away, unhurried, not without a certain pleasure in their expertise, they're about to take a break. Dave Brubeck, "Take Five." The yellow paint shines in the sun, fresh enough to eat. Life must go on. But we know one child who doesn't understand that.

I wonder if Marie knows that these TV sets have a way of imploding when someone watches them for ten straight hours with schoolbook in hand, as she did again today?

At the newsstand the papers were again stacked up higher than in normal times. Along the plywood fence around the burned-out building there are additional copies, it's hard to say how many. The line stretches south from the newsstand; the people coming from the north slow-wittedly follow their usual habit and just grab the topmost paper, holding out money in their other hand. This morning the crippled fingers are already busy with other people's money, though; the papers have been divided up into those available to anyone and those for preferred customers; now line up with everyone else, fifth on line.

– You, darling! the old man says severely, as if reprimanding. Today he wants to talk to you, doesn't he. – Don't you ever stand on line with me again! Are we friends or what?

The customers on line patiently, even approvingly, hear that the old man's on special terms with this lady and is willing to say so out loud. Today it seems the display of emotions is allowed, even entirely unaccustomed emotions.

In the subway fewer passengers than usual are waiting on the platform, though it's a work day. They get onto the train with almost no pushing and crowding, and who do we have here? a heavyset old Negro with a rheumatic bent back offering some random white woman his seat. – It's not easy for you either: he says. Are we still in New York?

Beneath Times Square the city is like itself again, so thick is the stew of people. On Lexington Avenue the people are walking shoulder to shoulder, as if all in a march. The sunlight here has shriveled up. Signs hangs on some of the shop doors saying they're closed, other stores announce that they will be closed tomorrow, and thus still manage to attract customers' attention the way they want. A young West Indian girl bats her eyelashes on a side street—she is wearing an elegant shirt, from Bloomingdale's at least, and showing off her thick eyebrows and thin legs, she has business to take care of too.

From the cafeteria entrance to Sam's counter is about sixty or seventy feet, and Sam calls to the kitchen as soon as he's glanced at the door: Large black TEA! so that he can hand over the brown paper bag two minutes later. Meanwhile he wants to know how things are going. – First with me! I want to, but I can't! he says, and he means the proper emotion he is incapable of producing. – Man, Gesine, this is going to be quite a day!

For the bank is working. That is, our allegedly adored vice president can't leave it at mere instructions, he has to explain the obvious in a memo:

Today is Friday, regular payday for most wage earners in the city, and all the checks need to go out before the weekend; For All Departments, de Rosny. If he wanted to he could have added: Incidentally, I also have the support of the Chamber of Commerce in this matter. The employees on the lower floors might be obediently counting bills, weighing bags of coins, checking accounts, or clicking conceptual money through the four arithmetical operations on calculators; on the sixteenth story we find the most blatant reading of newspapers. They are hardworking, these people who allow their employer two weeks' grace in which to pay them; they have long since turned to the center page, where the articles on Kennedy are continued from page 1. Mrs. Lazar, whose job is to defend the department with life and limb, barely looks up from whipping the pages backward and forward in an irritated, schoolmarmish manner. Here we have Henri Gelliston, who regards the banking business as the pinnacle and indeed the whole extent of earthly knowledge, absorbing the headline with a look of amazement: White House Plane Flies Body From Los Angeles. He's about to find out that the hearse there was blue and that Mrs. John F. Kennedy yielded precedence to no one, even in boarding the plane. As far as Wilbur N. Wendell is concerned, the financial business of all of South America might just as well suffocate under the spread-out pages of his *Times*—he is busy studying a photo of the cemetery personnel at Arlington measuring out the grave for tomorrow. Tony, Anthony, so intent on making us all forget that he was born in a poor Italian neighborhood of New York, our man with his rigidly perfected manners, is sprawled right across the desk to make sure that he doesn't crease the newspaper; like yesterday, the first page of a paper he normally wouldn't polish his shoes with—*The Daily News*, New York's Picture Newspaper—lies neatly folded in his weekly planner. It's as quiet as a reading room in the executive lounge; apart from one minor detail the sight could serve as an ad for *The New York Times*. De Rosny may know why he shouldn't make the rounds this morning: he'd be in for a shock at his subordinates' industriousness.

The employee by the name of Cresspahl betakes herself into her office none too swiftly either. She fritters away work hours next to our elegant Tony's desk. On the front page of the Picture Newspaper, on the left, the word "Final" is printed, which probably means Last Edition. On the right is the price, eight cents, so now you know. Below that, a weather report:

sunny and warm. You could put it that way. The letters in RFK DEAD are almost two inches tall. Why not five? Below that, in a thin black border, the dead man is looking the newspaper buyer trustingly in the eyes, somewhat concerned about the bad state of the world, his lips suspiciously loose, his face a little bloated. His hair is shaped into artificial dishevelment as ever, his left shoulder juts forward a little, dependably warm and attentive. His wife has been able to tug his tie closer to the top shirt button than he usually wore it. Cresspahl would be happy to buy this scruffy paper from Tony, she's not sure whether Marie has it, but she doesn't have the courage to suggest it. It would be for Marie, right? Who else would it be for.

All the papers now have to eat their words like old hats. *Ruthless*: it turns out he wasn't that. He may have fought more recklessly than wisely in his younger years, but the *Times* is willing to forgive him for that now, since he hadn't done so for a low or merely personal triumph. It still doesn't grant him a full regard for the legal process, it sees him as a warrior, and also as a big man who at his death was still growing. What is de Rosny to do now with his countless stories about Bugs Bunny, the crazy cartoon inventor who robbed his neighbors of health and property with, say, a motorized hammock—he will have to come up with a new victim, de Rosny that is. Want to bet it's Richard Milhous Nixon, who cries so nicely?

As if there were no homework in the newspaper. Not all the Czechoslovaks smiled and waved at the Soviet convoy rolling through the countryside, probably in greater than expected numbers, and with heavy equipment; the weight limit had to be raised specially from thirty to seventy tons, not a problem among dear friends. Such mutable bridges might have given the interior minister something to ponder, except he had his own secret police to worry about, which were acting like they were still answerable to Stalin. Write that down. Recently there've been up to thirty thousand cases in which internal security officers provided trumped-up charges for the prosecution of innocent citizens.

The person who, by three o'clock, can no longer stand such preparations for a trip to Europe is Employee Cresspahl. Marie doesn't answer the phone in the apartment. That may be a good sign. If she can't hear the phone she is far from the tube, the newscasters, doing homework at Pamela's, or in the park with Rebecca listening for the ice-cream man's bell instead. If you can't believe that, you'll think the child is at St. Patrick's Cathedral. But what's the point, after all the coffin is closed. She wouldn't care, she might still want to walk past it and brush the flag on the casket with her fingers. She shouldn't be standing there alone. Someone should be there to get her. Cresspahl decides to leave early, and can't tell anyone, even Mrs. Lazar has already left.

The line now ends on Lexington Avenue, at Forty-Seventh Street. It's so wide that walking next to it on the sidewalk is like walking on a balance beam. Too early to find Marie outside the angular plate-glass cookie of Chemical Bank—she must have joined the end of the line a long time ago. She's not in front of the Barclay Hotel, nor the Waldorf-Astoria. How yellow the General Electric building is: crazy Gothic with a crown full of holes that has a water pot in it. All the people standing still make you feel like you're walking faster—irrational but true. Business is merrily going on all around, hawking pins that say "In Memory of a Great American. Robert F. Kennedy. 1925–1968." Maybe buy one for Marie. Fifty cents each. Probably 100 percent profit. Here's another entrance to the IRT, Fifty-First Street, the next stop is Grand Central, from there it's twenty minutes to get home. The people are hardly dressed in mourning—this man could board a sailboat in those clothes, you'd expect to find that lady working in her backyard. Here we have a mailman who's gotten stuck in the procession once too often, and now even the phone booth is occupied. – I'm forty-five minutes behind schedule! he says to the people standing near him, who smile and nod back. That's how things go in New York when something's happened; anyway, he was only looking for sympathy, and found it. Where's this line going? Now it's winding around the Seagram Building block and turning south down Park Avenue. Seagram's is handing out plastic cups, though not with whiskey, water is good enough advertising. Nobody's visibly in tears—the conversations may not be happy but a certain good humor prevails. Here there are more commemorative buttons, now they're a whole dollar, maybe due to the fancier surroundings of the Embassy Club and the back of Chemical Bank. How much percent profit there? Here a garbage can is being stormed by two teachers intending to make paper hats for their whole class of boys. Such stately towers of business and at their feet the people are strewing plastic, paper, tin cans. Whenever someone collapses the line bulges out toward the curb; here two girls in too-tight pants are leaning against the pillars of Union Carbide, tired out. People faint not so

much from the muggy heat as from the car exhaust fumes. For other New
Yorkers are driving on Park Avenue, out to the country, or the beaches,
even if many have their automobile lights on as a gesture of mourning. Here
it takes an hour to move a single block, if you stay with the line. The police
have set up gray barricades to protect those waiting against line cutters.
There are a lot of children here, almost every third person looks underage;
but this must be about number five thousand, it'd be easy to miss Marie.
No one is talking about the reason they're all there, not even about Thursday's amendment to the gun laws. Previously, mail-order businesses were
free to send out pistols, revolvers, hand grenades, and mortars; now they
are limited to rifles and shotguns. Including the kind of rifle used for the
other Kennedy. Bankers Trust, the Colgate-Palmolive command center,
the headquarters of International Telephone & Telegraph. Looking back
from the corner, before the line turns west onto Fifty-First Street, you could
still see the Pan Am Building, where the Kennedy fortune is managed. At
Madison Avenue the police actually did form two rows, to let the line cross
the street. On this corner, one cold winter, Cresspahl too once walked up
and down, carrying a sign, outside the New York Archdiocese, the palace
of Cardinal Spellman, who so loved the war. Here the last stage begins,
and the soft-drink vendors are becoming aggressive. One vendor feels stared
at by an extremely ragged beggar in the line—he'll teach that beggar to
envy him, for a while he holds out the brightly colored cans so that they
invariably pass under the thirsty man's nose, until he turns away. Again
and again there is a Puerto Rican, a Negro, among the whites—about
every fifth person has dark skin. They were the ones who felt spoken to
when this millionaire spoke of them. What could they have believed he
would do? Among them most of the women are not carrying their shoes
in their hands, the men have only slightly loosened their ties. At the church
the police are in a holiday mood, moving nimbly between the elephantine
TV broadcast vans, chatting comfortably over their walkie-talkies, waving
up at the helicopters. The true lord of the scene is a cameraman, hanging
with his equipment high overhead in a seat shaped to his buttocks. This
close to the goal, people now begin to resist when someone tries to cut the
line, though not as viciously as on normal, unsacred days—with comments
referring to the dignity of the occasion, in a preachy tone where possible.
At the northwest church entrance, uniformed men lop off five or six heads

at a time from the front of the line, with wordless gestures. Inside there is something golden, brilliantly lit, to see. If Marie did go in she'd have wanted someone Catholic with her. She'd have wanted to do everything right: the genuflecting, the sign of the cross. She isn't here either, and for the next fifteen minutes, the length of time it can take to walk past the coffin, she doesn't come out the south entrance, and yet her mother has seen her many times and sees her again while walking away past the gray wall of Fiftieth Street and the weeping women in the hot western light.

Marie hasn't left the building. When the telephone rang she had just gone down to the basement to ask Jason for advice adjusting her TV antenna. She watched the whole route, starting at Lexington Avenue, up and down Park Avenue, all the way to the cathedral and past the coffin. She didn't need to go in person. She wasn't there, and yet she's even learned the basics about how to make a sign of the cross. She was there with the TV. Of course we couldn't find her today either.

June 8, 1968 Saturday

A day in front of the TV. But we won't spend it unsupervised. When Mrs. Cresspahl called D. E., Mrs. Erichson had to go get him from the car, he was just about to drive off, as Marie had called and asked him to, in fact. The child wants a referee too.

Bring her back to me, D. E.
To you?
Away from the Kennedys.
Didn't she get this obsessive joy in grief from you?
If it's from me get it out from her. Bring her out of it.
You're giving me free hand?
Get her back, D. E.

By eight thirty a.m. he's arranged his long bones in our apartment, on one of the Salvation Army chairs, with his back to the luminous park so he can't be suspected of paying insufficient attention. Next to him he's set out a tin with eight ounces of tobacco, three pipes, all kinds of implements, and now he requests a liter of tea—he's ready for a lengthy undertaking. He is dressed more for the weekend in the garden in New Jersey to which he invited us, down to his sneakers; with his expression of somewhat sleepy gravity he is giving a good imitation of a professor who's up to the task of one more long exam. The language is American English.

His preparations managed to put Marie off balance; his role forces her to be the organizer. She moves the TV set back and forth in front of him, apologizing for the distorted picture; he nods gravely. He may be an authorized professor of physics and chemistry but he doesn't know how to improve the technology of this kind of machine. – The tube is overworked: he determines, his objectivity an unanswerable reproach; Marie nods meekly. She can't prove he said it pointedly, but her pious feeling slips a little. Now she's sitting next to him and he can touch her consolingly on the neck, the arm, it's allowed. He strictly refrains, out of respect for her grief, and by reflecting her behavior he forces her to question it. Having expected nothing less from him than proper silence during the programs, she soon can't stand it anymore.

Around nine she sucks in air through her teeth, as if in sudden pain, for there on-screen a staticky distorted picture appears, sliced up into its own shadows, of the widow of the day in the moment of crossing herself. Her face shines out bright and clear in its jinxed surroundings. D. E. looks at Marie in surprise and perfunctorily explains: The raster, you know. She nods, innocent and teachable. The raster. I see.

Mrs. Cresspahl would have long since burst out, against her will but needing to score a point: This Robert Kennedy of yours, he had Martin Luther King's phone tapped! That's the kind of attorney general he was, just so you know! But now she's unable to make these further pedagogical mistakes, and is moreover amused by her sidelong glances at the pair sitting stiffly in front of the TV. She gets carried away by sudden mirth, she smiles, whether from gratitude or elation. She gets in return an indignant sidelong look from D. E., as if there's nothing to laugh about here, and obediently withdraws with the radio into the one room whose door can be firmly closed.

WQXR, the voice of *The New York Times*, broadcast on 96.3 MHz, is now going to show her educated readership how a Grand Old Lady of the World behaves upon the death of a murdered adversary. Cheerfully, respectfully, she describes a well-respected banking firm and recommends its services to the public. Worthy Auntie Times not only earns a little pin money by advertising for friends, she launches into the ether with plugs for her own in-depth features she'll be selling tomorrow. It's her station, after all, she refers to herself by name, she is it. She's not prepared to accord her fallen foe an iota of indulgence: she honors the dollar undeterred, no one's giving her anything for free.

In the other room, D. E. hasn't yet invited the child to visit a funeral parlor in New York where dead people are lying with their sharp noses pointed upward too, equally Catholic but with no prospect of a burial in the most chic cathedral on Fifth Avenue, but he is playing a game with Marie. Each player gets a point if they're the first to identify by title the dignitary being conducted through the checkpoint and into the cathedral before their eyes. They were tied on the secretary general of the UN, the head of the United Auto Workers union, the president of the United States, and the former head of the CIA; Marie scored wins on almost all the others, from poet Robert Lowell to Senator Eugene McCarthy—only with Lauren Bacall does D. E. say he got her first; Marie doesn't notice anything. Then they start guessing the colors in the procession since the TV set doesn't supply them: they sense the white of the seminary students, mistake the brown of the monks, the olive green of the army chaplains, the purple of the monsignori, and the violet of the bishops, but agree on the scarlet of the cardinals; by this point, Marie, simply by being forced to imagine a colored picture, has gained insight into the finer details of the staging. D. E. is able to compare one meaning of "service" to another, and she lets herself go along with him in estimating the costs.

She won't yet crack or laugh at jokes with him, but every now and then they give each other one of their old looks, sly and conspiratorial, like for instance when the surviving Kennedy brother's voice cracks near the end of his eulogy. She is still trying to honor his teary tone, but D. E. expresses some of her own suspicion with his remarks about the dead man's motto,

"Some men see things as they are and say: Why?
I dream things that never were and say: Why not?"
Once he's cited the source of the tearful quote (George Bernard Shaw), complete with a short history of Fabianism, he is able to add: Even when they borrow they take the best.

After that she looks a bit more suspiciously at the eight half-orphans carrying bread and wine in golden vessels up to the high altar; she is not moved to defend the water sprinkled on the coffin, meant to call down from Heaven God's purifying mercy, nor the swinging of thurible filled with incense, meant to carry the prayers of the faithful up to God. She's had to recite such things all too often in school, against her will. She gradually comes to see what's happening in the cathedral as a private ceremony, which is taking her Kennedy away from her, and during the playing of the slow movement from Mahler's Fifth by thirty members of the New York Philharmonic she can't yet put into words how the Kennedys look when they're borrowing, but she reveals the thought, with a painfully amused sidelong glance. The cheerfully galumphing "Battle Hymn of the Republic" unnerves her again; she can't defend herself against D. E.'s reminder that the tune was stolen from another song,

John Brown's Body Lies a-Mouldering in the Grave
about the abolitionist's attack at Harpers Ferry, West Virginia. The theft bothers her, as does the suggestion of a rotting body, plus there's the sense that this is educational material she will never hear from Sister Magdalena, and all the thinking she has to do about that dries the corners of her eyes. Before long she's arguing with D. E. over the placing of dead Catholics vis-à-vis the altar—feet toward the altar and head under the stars of the flag, she points out to him, so that eventually she cries out: But they're carrying him out of the cathedral head down!

At first the only joking she permits D. E. is at the expense of the other Mrs. Kennedy, the president's widow, who stood rigid and unmoving on the top step outside for almost four minutes, *you can all see me, right?,* never mind if the motorcade gets hopelessly delayed, she wants her share of the limelight, and finally Marie does say, half embarrassed, half annoyed: That's just what she'd like. She's practically inviting someone to shoot!

Her store of reverence took a serious hit with the news from London inserted into the program. The fact that a man suspected of the murder of Martin Luther King had been arrested at Heathrow Airport, that they finally caught him after such a long time but on this very morning, today of all days, a perfect link to the spectacle of the senator's burial—it's too pat, too calculated, it feels to her like a trick played by grown-ups who think kids are dumber than they really are. The precision work bothers her, and even if she doesn't quite doubt the truth of the report it still seems damaged somehow by its placement. – They're trying to distract us! she says angrily. She's been distracted.

She is also being unscrupulously unjust, heaping criticism on the president's widow for her desire for yet another bullet and further fame; the current president, Johnson, has long since finished his journey from the New York cathedral back to Washington; the train with her senator's coffin is still in Pennsylvania Station. The commentators on-screen are so at a loss that they allude to the train that carried the assassinated Abe Lincoln, tell stories from the history of the station, one mentions the renaming of Idlewild Airport.

– *Which I undertook solely to keep New York clean:* D. E. says incautiously, and immediately worried; she nods pensively, lips pursed. Her dead Kennedy cannot be separated from the staging of his last journey; his family represents him; this is how he would have wanted it. – No: Marie says. She would vote against renaming it Kennedy Station.

Her stubbornness persists for a while yet, the TV set stays on, but she's lost her agitation and excitement. The course of events has become predictable. She will see the old-fashioned observation platform of the last car many more times, and the coffin placed on six chairs there; the camera in the helicopter will show her both trains many more times; but she still has to face the American character of the drama. There are three trains—the first to intercept any explosives (one reporter quickly corrects his mistake, "dummy train," into the correct official term: "pilot train"); the third consisting of two diesel engines, for repairs and the consequences of any new assassination attempt. But it is none of the thousand famous friends of the Kennedys on the funeral train who are struck down, it is two onlookers in Elizabeth, New Jersey, hit and killed by an express train going the other direction on the opposite tracks. This interjection of the everyday disappoints Marie, but D. E. doesn't take advantage of the first sign of boredom, it's only at nearly two o'clock that he uses Annie's bath thermometer (prewarmed) plus some demented science to demonstrate that an implosion of the TV tube is imminent. It's Marie who presses the button, and as a favor to D. E. she takes him to the Mediterranean Swimming Club in the Hotel Marseilles. She keeps her eye on him as they leave the apartment. He says goodbye to Mrs. Cresspahl with a casual air, not a triumphant one.

It's hot on Broadway, as if the street is being roasted from below as well as above. A predictable crowd is dawdling busily along, with only the heat sweeping the east sidewalks sparklingly clear of people. With no fear of TV cameras, the Upper West Side goes about its business—women in curlers out shopping, young men in undershirts discussing the day in the shade of the awning outside the Strand Bar or carrying bags of laundry into the laundromats. Whatever the TV stations may have shown of the flags at half-mast on Fifth Avenue and the solemn crowds along the coffin's route, here it's a normal Saturday. Only a few stores cover their displays with black-framed photographs of the senator, or funeral ribbons, and hardly any are closed; Mrs. Cresspahl can get her four bottles of spring water (the tap water is disgustingly brown from deposits in the main pipes that have washed up from the changing water pressure, since children throughout the city have been turning the fire hydrants into street showers and the adults are sitting at home in front of their TVs for the third day in a row); she has no trouble finding the extras to go with the proper lunch D. E. has graced us with. And Marie eats up much of her sorrow with herring from Denmark on black bread from West Germany. She would have felt that it was indecent to be hungry, but she doesn't notice, because D. E. finishes not one second ahead of her. We'll hand the child over to you yet, D. E., you know how to be a legal guardian after all.

By around three the TV is repeating segments of the morning's broadcasts, since the train doesn't pass before the cameras often enough and the crowds on the platforms along the route to Washington can only produce the same waving, shouting, and swinging of signs yet again. Marie has the younger brother's eulogy practically memorized by now and knows in advance the place where his voice starts to break. Meanwhile the train has been driven at reduced speed for the onlookers so many times, and has been plagued by so many mechanical difficulties, that it's hours behind schedule, and one more of D. E.'s calculations works out: tired from swimming, Marie nods off, right in the middle of the discussion of whether the broken brake shoe on the last coach would be called a *tormoznoy bashmak* or *tormoznaya kolodka*. She is so fast asleep that she slides down until she's lying against the back of the sofa; she doesn't hear the hollow sound of the engine's bell on TV coming to an end, nor the closing door.

Riverside Park seems no emptier than usual, and maybe *The New York*

Times tomorrow will have counted for us to prove it. Mrs. Cresspahl isn't hoping to run into anyone on the steps, dried out in the heat—she's looking for secluded nooks and finds one just before the underpass to the Hudson River promenade, a staircase well sheltered by trees where she can put her head against Prof. Dr. Erichson's chest and cry uninterrupted, never mind propriety or pride. In such situations, some people administer regular strokes, down over the other person's shoulder blade, like you do for a disconsolate horse; this one here just holds tight, doesn't try to touch you more than you want, doesn't talk.

> *It's infection by mass hysteria.*
> *You're not infected, Gesine. You're not hysterical.*
> *Because I've been divided from my own child for three days.*
> *You'll get her back, Gesine.*
> *Because maybe she got her sentimentality from me.*
> *You think so? Don't you realize you're not sentimental. She's fallen into being a bit American.*
> *I am not raising that child right.*
> *Jakob wouldn't have minded. I wouldn't.*
> *You could say it now, D. E., if you want. But not out of pity.*
> *Just believe me when I say it.*
> *I believe you.*

By evening, faithful to the four-hour delay, TV has arrived in Washington too. The coffin's location is indicated by the flashbulbs the spectators are firing at it; the darkness is all-powerful. The family's stage manager has decided that the dead man should pass every Senate building in which he'd had offices. Welcoming cheers that die away shyly. Sharpshooters on the roofs, plainclothes police everywhere. The body has to spend four minutes saying goodbye to the softly lit figure of Abraham Lincoln—to the two of them next to each other on their two chairs, the TV picture is so distorted. And again: the Battle Hymn. President Johnson in the first car behind his felled opponent, with Secret Service scurrying all around him. The moon draws veils over the milling crowd, it cannot brighten the Potomac's dark waters. At the unloading, one of the dead man's sons insists on helping to carry the coffin and so has to hold it by the head end. The bearers move off

in the wrong direction at first, walking more or less toward the eternal
flame, and have to veer off at an angle over the rise. After the final service,
John Glenn folds the flag into snappy sharp corners and hands it to the
new head of the Kennedys. A state limousine has brought a cocker spaniel
from the dead man's home—it's Freckles, in person. *The* widow once again
feels the need to assert herself against the senator's: she makes a point of
laying small wreaths, and having her children lay wreaths, on her own
nearby grave sites. The other relatives kiss the new coffin, leaving it standing on the lawn. Again and again strangers kneel by the African mahogany,
brush their lips against it, pray. Marie sits on the bench with her legs drawn
up, holding her hand over her mouth, merely surprised at a ceremony that
her mother has described as taking place differently in Europe.

The radio says nothing about relatives not staying for the interment
here. Clearly one of her nephews has taken *The New York Times* aside at
some point during the day to point out the unseemliness of her behavior,
as well as the possible consequences for future business; now she reassures
her customers of her good taste with lugubrious classical music and announcers
reading the news in properly subdued voices. A station next to hers on the
dial ends its broadcast with an ad about the dangers of smoking.

The television department moves to views of the ocean, accompanied
by saccharine singing, and then to a photographic portrait, presented as
now the only thing left to us. The eleven o'clock news is sponsored by
Savarin Coffee. Their ad shows the expert surrounded by coffee plantation
workers anxiously awaiting his reaction to the drink. He approves, and
anthropological joy spreads across the Indians' faces. The expert then rides
off in his genuine South American railroad train. Also helping to pay for
the news is the roach spray Black Flag, *Kill & Clean*. If it were up to Marie,
we would not buy these products, for a while. Now music is being played
at the moment it's performed, continuously, interrupted by a photo of the
dead man that seems to be hung slightly crooked. He has his hand on his
chin, conversationally, and looks younger than he did three days ago.

At one a.m.: *THE GREAT GREAT SHOW*, tonight with a fable from
prewar Hungary: *The Baroness and the Butler*...Can't alienate the viewers.

D. E. has stuck it out the whole time on the chair next to Marie, having
roasted about two and a half ounces of tobacco in his pipe and cracked the
third bottle of red wine. It's not going to be him who gives up. Almost as

soon as Marie realizes they've switched over to normal programming, she asks for permission to turn off the set. She rolls it over to the apartment door, its cord wound around it, ready for the rental company to take it away.

– D. E.: she says. What do we have to do to get you to spend tomorrow with us?

– Drive with me right now across the Hudson and all the way to the New Jersey woods where my log cabin is.

– Okay: Marie says, looking at him affectionately, amused, in anticipation. She leans against his chair, arranges his gray hair this way and that. He has earned her thanks.

In D. E.'s car, before entering the tunnel to New Jersey, she turns to the back. It's dark enough there, her mother won't be able to see her face.

– *Thank you for letting me have this:* she says.

– Who, me? Mrs. Cresspahl is startled out of her doze, she almost thinks there's someone else sitting next to her.

– Yes. You. For letting me watch TV. That's what I'm thanking you for.

is the nation's official day of mourning, just as the City of New York decreed one yesterday. Marie wasn't interested in a trip to Arlington National Cemetery, to test the TV's representations against the fresh grave; what she wanted was an outing to Culver's Lake and Lake Owassa, to the Delaware River on the Pennsylvania border, and across Little Swartswood Lake to the country seat that D. E. calls his log cabin. They may be marching with flowers for RFK in Arlington; we saw people like ourselves out for a Sunday drive, people at the side of the road selling eggs and cherries from farms and forest paths, flaneurs strolling around the small towns, crowded coffee shops, children lining up at jingling ice-cream trucks, shores lined with people in colorful swimsuits. Marie watches us without the least disdain as we spend the whole early evening in D. E.'s shady yard, chatting idly, carefree in the green twilight; she appears more by chance than anything at the bay window of the kitchen, where she is advising Mrs. Erichson about preparing dinner, her occasional glances in our direction meant merely to reassure that she isn't going to bother us. She speaks German with D. E.'s mother, although with an American "Granny" slipping naturally over her lips. – Why are we making such a big dinner, Granny?

– How far have you gotten, Gesine?
– Yes, I need your advice. 1947. I can't get Cresspahl away from the Soviets.
– You should tell Marie more about them.
– She'll take it the wrong way, D. E.
– She gets today's Russians all wrong too.
– She's a stalwart anti-Communist. On that topic she believes what they tell her in school.
– A clueless anti-Communist, you mean. She's put a poem in her collection reprinted from the June 7 *Pravda*, by that guy, what's his name—
– Him. I know him.
– You know the one.
– I read all about him in *The New York Times*. In November of '66 he paid a visit to RFK...
– Gee, I just can't get enough of that name Kennedy.
– ...to the living RFK. It's a historical event. When they were voting on a civilian complaint review board for the New York police.
– *The vote of fear.*
– No sooner had Senator Kennedy cast his vote than who should ring the bell of his apartment on the fourteenth floor of the UN Plaza building? It's a visiting Soviet poet, he lolls around on a cream-colored sofa high above New York City and talks with this representative of American imperialism, and what do they put out as a communiqué? The poet: "I have faith only in politicians who understand the importance of poetry."
– The senator from New York: "I like poets who like politicians."
– And the poet, comforted, set off for home, reduced to a scarecrow but breast swelling with pride.
– Oh, I've just thought of the name. Eugene.
– Yevgeny Yevtushenko. Right.
– He's struck again. Maybe he meant it as an act of friendship for the dead man, not even Marie's quite sure.

– Tell me.

– "The price of revolver lubricant rises."

– You anti-Communist!

– That's what it says. And:

> Perhaps the only help is shame.
> History cannot be cleansed in a laundry.
> There are no such washing machines.
> Blood can never be washed away!

And:

> Lincoln basks in his marble chair,
> wounded.

But what does Abe like to do in the evening? Wasn't he at a play? Listen to the Yevtushenkos' Eugene:

> But without wiping the splashes of blood from your forehead
> You, Statue of Liberty, have raised up
> Your green, drowned woman's face,
> Appealing to the heavens against being trodden underfoot.

– Do you believe that?

– Marie even wonders if he believes it himself.

– I'm telling her things that don't fit her views, D. E. Things about the Twins, who ruled in Jerichow longer than any other Soviet commandants before or after them. They acted like gentleman: aristocratic. Refined. Superfine. They would have made perfect von Plessens. Estate owners from the nobility, and running Jerichow the way the von Plessens once had. Breakfast together, not before nine, each with his own server to wait on him, white linen, silver, punishment for the slightest spot of dirt. Departure for Town Hall at ten, to rule. They kept the mayor in a filing room where he was allowed to sign things; they were in his room, together even behind the desk, and the Germans had to keep a distance of three paces, the same as the hirelings from the nobility back in the day. Even tempered, never got mad, never drank, never went a single step in the town on foot. They weren't brothers—that was the one and only private fact about them the Jerichowers knew; they didn't even look alike—and rumor gnawed away at their nickname and could never figure it out. When they caught a subordinate fraternizing with Germans they'd have him hauled off like a mass murderer, and the beating would start only behind the fence. Terrible beatings. If a German came to them with a complaint, say Mina Ahlreep, and she didn't know the first name and patronymic of the Russian who'd shot the fake clock off her gable, the slanderer would find herself in the basement under Town Hall for the night, without trial, to give her time to remember the Soviet man's name, and no one would bother to explain this to her, and she'd be let out onto the street the next morning without a word. That was how disgusted the Twins were by Germans. Their arrival put an end to the all-night parties in Louise's front parlor, and while she did request compensation for her broken furniture and ruined parquet floor she didn't know Mr. Wassergahn's serial number. Pontiy had sometimes kept bonbons in his pocket for the *devushki*, these two didn't even say *idi syuda*, they shooed children away like chickens. They'd had the fence around the Kommandatura raised by two feet and even though they received no visitors in the villa they had a triumphal arch built in front of it, on which Loerbrocks the painter had to paint fresh slogans for Soviet holidays and anniversaries of great military victories. And if Loerbrocks isn't dead yet he can still crank out a portrait of Josif Vissarionovič Stalin from memory, although only in three colors and in size DIN A2 per German Industrial Standards, this being how he had to repaint him every Christmas. Stalin got his place at the top of the arch; the army and the army alone was the constant topic of the changing slogans below him, which meant that I knew the four case endings for *Krasnaya Armiya* better than for any other words. After work, still in unwrinkled uniforms and crisply ironed caps, the two Wendennych gentlemen would go riding out to the Rehberge Hill, now without adjutants. From ten to eleven we could hear their phonograph records: Tchaikovsky, Mussorgsky, Glinka, Brahms. These are not the Soviets Marie learns about in school, and she doesn't like it.

– Cresspahl wasn't kept in Fünfeichen forever.

– She pictures it like a cell in Sing Sing.

– If she had a more precise picture she wouldn't let you go to Prague.

– That reason has only existed for six months.

– Still, it's a reason.

– You, on the other hand, never once told a lie, even as a boy.

– But whenever I could since then. And liked doing it too.

– Marie should see the Russians of today.

– Who were eighteen in 1947.

– I am not going to help her school! Didn't I tell Marie how the Soviets got their hands on Cresspahl? That was bad enough. If I tell her the food they got in Fünfeichen, never mind anything else, she'll never trust Socialism for the rest of her life.

– You wouldn't be backing up Sister Magdalena, you'd be preparing Marie better.

– She's too young for that!

– She already knows all about the rapes in New York.

– That's what we get for letting you study physics and chemistry. You think truth has absolute value.

– Marie would know more about you too. She'd understand why you want to take one more trip to the other side. No, not that. But she might have some idea.

– I know what's in fashion in things aside from ladies' clothes, D. E. It's not chic to disparage the Soviets. But those aren't my reasons.

– So approximately when is Marie supposed to get this lesson?

– I don't know, at fifteen . . .

– In that case she'll hear about 1953 when she's an adult. We'll be allowed to tell her about your death when she's on her own deathbed.

– Fine. Cresspahl concedes. Erichson wins on points. Your solicitude for the little miss is just ridiculous!

– I owe her that much. She's about to get me a beer. The stories you know!

– You tell her about the camps. You'd somehow do it so that all she gets is justice, the rule of law, and humane treatment.

– Then you do it.

– School in 1947. Josif Vissarionovič was hanging on the walls of the seventh-grade rooms by then, much higher than the Austrian's pictures used to. Which made a faded rectangle very noticeable. But no one could expect the new leader to be short. His title had been expanded too: Wise Leader of the Peoples, Benevolent Father of the Nations, Generalissimo, Preserver of World Peace, Creator of Socialism, Guardian of Justice, "There Is Still Light in the Kremlin," Guarantor of a Truly Humane Future. Something's wrong with that last one, "Guarantor," we'd heard that word a bit too often.

– All correct.

– I have never once seen a portrait of him looking straight at the viewer, he's always squinting down to one side, as if someone there had stepped out of line, or sneezed. We were never allowed to talk about him that way at school—as having a physiognomy, as being human in any way. Someone ratted on Lise Wollenberg, who couldn't help laughing at the parting the *Vozhd'* had put in his plump mustache: the scare was punishment enough, plus she got an F in Russian and an F in conduct. She had reason to watch out. Schoolgirl Cresspahl also wanted the followers of this Leader of Peoples to give her her father back—that made two strikes against her. Was she just being scatterbrained? She dutifully learned the new history of technological inventions, a bit like how Marie learns what they teach her in religion: knowledge to regurgitate when needed. It hadn't been that feudalist jerk Karl Drais, Baron von Sauerbronn, who'd thought up the velocipede after seeing some Chinese drawings—it was a Russian serf, freed for biking from the Urals to Moscow, fifteen hundred miles. Russian feudal lords were more benevolent too, apparently. It wasn't Marconi who'd been the first to send wireless signals, we had a Russian to thank for that too. The demise of the Kunze-Knorr compressed-air brake at the hands of a Russian was taught in literary style: As the venerable Moscow scholar demonstrates braking tests to his German colleagues in a tunnel, and his system gently and firmly brings the train to a halt, one of the foreign bumblers lets out a groan: Awwf, Kunze-Knorr, eet iss feenished! The first car drove in Russia, the party didn't invent the airplane but a tailor from Minsk or Tula did, the pharmacy was Russian in origin, and the crane, and your caran d'ache, and the telephone, and every part of the railway, from *stantsiya* to *passazhirskiy* and *pochtoviy* cars. But if you learned all this you were allowed to take English classes with Mrs. Weidling, who wasn't arrested until the following fall.

– You forgot penicillin.

– An obedient little student like that writes an essay for school, "I look out my window...," and describes what she sees—the green Russian fence topped with barbed wire, the roof of the commandant's villa above it, and an American truck with a bulletproof grille over the headlights parked inside the open gate—and if she leans awkwardly far out the window she can see around the corner of the brickworks to the east, where the sun rises, as *krasniy* as the Red Army. She really liked that ending, Schoolgirl Cresspahl did; she was genuinely out to please and flatter. Mrs. Beese gave the essay back unmarked and kept her after school, and it had to be rewritten looking out the window at the schoolyard, where there was nothing at all to see. Mrs. Beese didn't tell Cresspahl the lesson she was meant to learn here, she had to find it out for herself, and two months later the girl handed in a plot summary of a Russian novel that mentioned in passing "the Russians' wild nature," "the wild nature of the Russians," thinking only about the part of the story where a Russian nobleman keeps a wild bear in a room and locks unsuspecting visitors in with it—she'd worked so hard on her summary and it got her sent to the principal. A Social Democrat, a teacher since 1925 and again since 1945, so furious at the oblivious child that he couldn't even explain her sin. He personally went to the school secretary and borrowed some nail scissors and cut out the four or six words and gave back her notebook. "This really won't do, child." Whether the slip of paper she should now stick over the hole should have corrected text or be virgin white—that decision exceeded his powers, it overwhelmed him, he flailed around like someone busy drowning and now you're asking him the time.

– That's not true.

– You see? And yet I'm supposed to tell Marie.

– Did that really happen?

– His name was Dr. Vollbrecht. The one who almost wasn't made principal. In his inaugural address he was supposed to welcome the Red Army as the bringer of true culture and humanity, and his wife had been raped at gunpoint by twenty-one Red soldiers. They kept him in the Gneez courthouse for three days, and he talked around town about a visit he'd made for family reasons, then eventually admitted he'd been arrested but only "by mistake." Then he gave the speech.

– No. You're pulling my leg. I'd do the same thing. The New Schools repudiating Pushkin? I don't believe it.

– You see. Marie would love to believe it. And she'd have another advantage over you.

– That it's true?

– That it really happened and I was there.

– *The shoe comes out the way the leather is.*

– Right, and *what can you do about it?*

– Erichson concedes. Cresspahl wins, and not just on points.

– Write to young Vollbrecht! Go ahead! He's a lawyer in Stade, the post office there can find him.

– Gesine. I wouldn't dare.

And so why the big dinner? D. E. stood up after the meat course, stuffed a napkin between his collar and neck the way all the best people do, and gave a speech for Marie. He'd originally been hoping to marry the Cresspahl family on this day too, but work had prevented him, and now he promised not to bring up the tiresome topic again until September. As a substitute might he offer an amateur theatrical production, rehearsed for two hours, with several parts, the cast of characters including a prince by the name of Dubrovsky, one bear (guaranteed untamed), . . .

– Does September work for us? Marie asked.

June 10, 1968 Monday

Marie was going back high above the Hudson, on George and Martha Washington's bridge; her mother was riding under the river, from Hoboken to Manhattan on the PATH train; Marie emerged from an unmistakable Bentley at the school entrance; Mrs. Cresspahl arrived under Times Square at almost precisely the usual minute, and already it was no longer her, she was cut off from her day of free time in the country, slotted into the way to work, already transformed, already an integral part of the day that's not hers, that's hired out. A drowning man is more reasonable—at least he struggles.

In the second of the three light boxes with which a cosmetics company frames the departures board in Grand Central Station, a photograph of the assassinated senator is still hanging, trimmed with black and purple ribbons. Clearly the arrangement had simply been forgotten.

De Rosny has hired someone to read *The New York Times* to him. And today again a confidential message is tucked in it for him. From London comes the portent that Soviet exercises on Czechoslovak soil were not meant to exert "a certain intimidation." Who would dream of such a thing. The military maneuvers had been scheduled for six months ago, i.e., an opportune January—they'd just been postponed. The Novosti press agency personally vouches that the leaders of Czechoslovakia have time and again confirmed their loyalty to the Warsaw Pact defense system. Another visitor is coming tomorrow, today—a high-level delegation for economic discussions—and they will definitely be discussing de Rosny, i.e., loans in hard currency. The usual calculations won't, of course, apply. For officials concede that the ČSSR sends to the Soviet Union manufactured goods that fall short of world market quality and are not favorable for convertible currencies, and doesn't look too deeply into why that is. In the other direction, the Soviet Union sends raw materials that are everything they should be. The equivalence between them is thus tantamount to a Soviet hard-currency credit for Czechoslovakia. This may not enlighten mathematicians or give much more than basic information for economists, but no one is trying to speak to such circles anyway.

Meanwhile, Employee Cresspahl doesn't touch a typewriter all morning, or anything else that might make noise in the office. The noise of the outside world is muffled, kept at a distance already. Without a word, almost assiduous from the silence, she is calculating numbers for a diagram based on the Czechoslovakian Five-Year Plan; behind her, lulled by the even breaths of the air conditioner, a visitor is lying on the sofa, asleep.

Amanda Williams, if she'd been at our school in Gneez, would have been given a nickname like Black Beauty. In high school. Or maybe Our Fine Filly, and not because of her curvy body but because a child like her moves quickly, stepping gracefully but nonetheless with a surge of power, whether coming out of a reverse-flip dive and plunging straight into the water or stepping on a teacher's foot; devoted without fail to her girlfriends, innocently out for her own advantage, surprised by some of her successes, in short far advanced in her training as woman and without much realization of the fact. A girl that the boys in the class are still proud of even if she's rejected them twice. And yet this whirlwind of a person can be found in a strangely tame state, crying and for the time being inconsolable over a lost ring, bungled homework, an avoided glance—still strong in her sobbing, defenseless against unhappy reality, like the shyest dolt in the rearmost row. This other Amanda crept, yes, slunk into Mrs. Cresspahl's office and before she could guess whether it was a sleepless night or alcohol the shirker's tears indicated another misfortune. Now nothing will come of our house on Long Island Sound, our man-free commune. Amanda needs forgiveness for this, as though it were the worst thing that could happen. She was one of the hundred and fifty million viewers who followed the massive coverage of the Kennedy ceremonies, and sounding just like *The New York Times* she calls herself emotionally exhausted but ready to make one more mistake. One that she again can't discuss with Naomi. She has reconciled with Mr. Williams, psychological counselor to New York's police; she is quite sure she's pregnant. She slept till noon, in the bank where she belonged but sheltered in an office that not even our vice president sets foot in without announcing himself first. She lay on the three-seat visitor's sofa for a very long time, her back trustingly to the wall, hands cupped and folded over her eyes, an overgrown child.

Strangers noticed nothing as they went down to lunch, even though she could check her makeup in no other mirror but Mrs. Cresspahl's eyes; she was talking in her usual galloping, easily overheard way too, and the other customers in Gustafsson's sandwich shop might well have taken the sharp rage in her voice for mimicry, for clever exaggeration:

– You don't watch TV, Gesine. You don't know this country. We used to have a TV show here, very popular, showing terrible accidents, you know. The mother of the sweet little boy who lost his arm in a garbage disposal sitting in front of the camera, the father of a hemophiliac son, the parents of a deformed child, and they'd all tell you everything, with photos, and the invited audience voted on the various diseases and travails, awarding third, second, first prize. The studio had a phone line where viewers across the country could donate money for the sufferers, or a wheelchair from up in the attic, or a brand-new garbage disposal, *do you even have a pig at home?!*

said Amanda; in Berlin she'd have been called a *flotter Dampfer*, a sassy girl; she has long since taken in the horrified and lustful looks of the men at Gustafsson's, through her skin, through her temples; she doesn't turn her bitter gleeful face away:

– Here's a series that would be a real hit, I'd call it *Fantastic Funerals*, copyright by me. An hour a week is probably enough. Your host: the ravishing Amanda Williams. I'd show the different rituals—the Catholic one, I have no idea how that goes, oh never mind I do since two days ago; the Jewish customs, Protestant, can't forget Voodoo, the white tears, the black tears. That'd be a real contribution to national education, don't you think? Knowledge and Sympathy—that's the slogan, to bring in the viewers. I'd interview the bereaved, show the bodies, have a group of judges for the flower arrangements. The funeral parlors, can't forget those. *It is a cold April morning, our melancholy coast guard cutter chugs through the biting wind out to Potter's Island, its cargo a heavy one, that no one wants to...* whaddaya think? What percent do you think the advertisers' sales will go up by? You could get everything into a show like that! Grass seed, weed killers, all kinds of makeup, insurance, US Steel, umbrellas of course... Whaddaya think? You know what that is, that's a million-dollar idea. Six months and I'll be rich! Do you think I'll still talk to the likes of you?

– You're thinking about money again. Just go play the lottery.

– You think I don't? I'll hold my press conference in the Hotel St. Moritz, out on the lawn. I'll tell the reporter from the *Daily News* "I'm not talking to you," so that the *Post* reports on it and the *Times* gives the whole thing a veneer of seriousness. What else am I supposed to think about if not money, Gee-sign?

We were together for half the trip home, to the destination boards in Grand Central. The bottles still shone on the frosted glass, not entirely unlike a penis. – A woman belongs in bed, the men in the ads! Amanda said.

She doesn't want to borrow money for an abortion. Not from Mrs. Cresspahl. No best friend could do more for a person than Mrs. Cresspahl.

If only she understood what she's done. The fact is, she was entirely elsewhere all day, since this morning.

June 11, 1968 Tuesday

– I won't give you a *Spiegel*: the old man at our newsstand says, hardly as friendly and forthcoming as last week, and someone coming home from work with dulled senses is especially taken in by his grumpiness. In fact he's protected his stacks of paper from the dripping rain with transparent sheets of plastic, they're items to display more than to sell. Maybe he feels like keeping everything for himself today. He scrapes a smile onto his stubble and smugly says: Your daughter's already gotten herself one!

Bringing something special home for Marie is harder to do. She'd rather get her toy cars from Herald Square than Upper Broadway, and anyway she's enjoyed her collection less and less as it's approached completion. She has two Bentleys. A men's outfitter on Lexington Avenue promises to print anything you want on T-shirts, and of course they had size 12Y in stock, I just couldn't think of the text, Marie doesn't feel the need to share her first name, PARTLY SUNNY TOMORROW is not something she'd want to promise the world too often, it would be a burdensome present. An extra pork chop, a kosher bundt cake, European chocolate—if she's in the mood for any of that she'll have it at home; she's in charge of the groceries. The lively Puerto Rican who's sometimes on Ninety-Seventh and West End Avenue hawking the tastiest hottest dogs and sauerest kraut in a one-mile radius is one last possibility—but today he's moved somewhere else, whether because of the policemen collecting their money or the nasty humidity in the air. So as I finish my walk to the apartment door all I'm bringing home is the wish that I were bringing something home, *and saying something stupid like*: Hey. Marie. The East German government is sending condolences to Ethel Kennedy too.

When Marie is startled, you can see it most easily in the eyes. She can't help the lurch of her pupils, she would have liked to keep her lids from snapping down, when she manages a mask of patience it's too late. At age four she still pursed her lips at unreasonable requests—protruding them resentfully at the ice-cream man speaking a foreign language, for instance— but this person will keep her face stiff at the oblivious adult, while thinking over and over that she has to accept it, especially from this one, has to behave herself with this adult who'll just never learn. Embarrassed for her mother she shifts her shoulders back and forth, she even stands up from an inner conflict between answering sharply and being considerate. She politely says: If you could at least stop repeating the name, Gesine.

– It was for your essay: her mother lies, submissive, and prepared well enough for the admonition that not every essay is meant for the eyes of the child's legal guardian. But Marie puts the news from Germany down on the table, with the cover folded back—it must show that Kennedy in front of colors of mourning—she sees that one of these evenings when we sit trapped, as if in a snowed-in post office with no horses, is soon underway, and we talk politely to each other, like strangers, and she says:

If it's no trouble.

If you're not too tired.

For at least a week, okay?

And:

Here's your weekly rations.

How are the East Germans consoling Martin Luther King's widow?

How was work?

And:

There was a *Versammlung* against the *Notstandsgesetze* in West Germany. Translate that for me?

What does this poet, Enzensberger, mean by "backrooms"?

What kind of workers does he want to go out onto the streets with, exactly?

What are these French conditions he wants?

And:

Dmitri Weiszand wants to know whether I'm going to Prague.

Can I learn Czech too?

I'm not arguing with you! Not at all.

June 12, 1968   Wednesday

Rain. Rain. Rain.

The Soviet Union is having trouble with its Socialist brothers and sisters in Czechoslovakia. Among them it had an erstwhile confidant, a major general, who last December attempted a military putsch against the scorners of Saint Novotný, though in vain. His employers may have forgiven him his lapse, and also that he then crossed the wrong border. They will hardly hate their former friend now that it turns out he's a big thief ($20,000 worth of clover and alfalfa seed). But the fact that he got his diplomatic passport from a Soviet general! That's serious. If it were only the *Times* from New York telling the tale that might be all right—let the world know. But for people in Prague to hear about it through a reprint in the newspaper *Lidova Demokracie*, that is just too much, and the ambassador in Moscow gets a sorrowful letter. It would really be a shame about those amicable international relations you've got there. If the appropriate authorities of the Czechoslovak Socialist Republic fail to take immediate action against their own news organs then look out! Alfalfa and clover seed, hmph. It may be true, but does that mean you have to put it in the papers?

– Your Soviets weren't so funny: Marie says. I'm supposed to tell her what they were like, she's been promised, and reconciliation depends on it. It's our Professor Erichson who's promised her—he feels that there's no such thing as an abstract truth, truth is always concrete. Why was Mrs. Cresspahl so relieved at every postponement? Why did she want to table the whole thing, at least until fall, preferably for a whole year?
– "My" Soviets.
– In *your* Soviet Mee-klen-burg. You were there with them, in the same place. You met each other. You know them.
– At age twelve. I turned thirteen in 1946.
– Gesine, tell me there's one child in Mecklenburg who doesn't know about my country.
– You can have a whole grade of schoolkids in Gneez.
– Couldn't I tell them how things are in New York, from Harlem to the Hudson?
– It would be just what you've seen. What you know. Just your truth.
– My truth.
– They'd never believe you, not from the word go.
– Gesine, I want to believe you.
– You think I have an ax to grind but you say you want to believe me. How is that going to work!
– I have an ax to grind too, Gesine. Oh yes. I do too.
– All right, I admit that things were bad for Cresspahl in Soviet prison. Sometimes. Worse than I want to tell you about.
– Starvation?
– Starvation too.
– Physical abuse?
– Injuries of all kinds.
– It happened to him because of a mistake, Gesine.
– It happened to him.
– The Soviets had won. They were soldiers, foreign ones. Why couldn't a clerical error have crept in somewhere? Maybe they'd misunderstood the foreign language, a lot sometimes.

– Some of the interpreters had learned their German from Nazi occupations and had to get to Russian through Polish.

– Gesine, am I being a bad granddaughter and daughter if I don't want to hear all the details about Cresspahl?

– It's not exactly a water-butt story.

– Okay, Gesine: He wasn't there for a while.

– He wasn't there. So he couldn't help me for a while, while I'd taken in all my earlier whiles with him. With his words, but more through the information that passed through moods, glances, shifts in facial expressions. I had Jakob's mother, but she was a stranger in Jerichow and couldn't bring home much more than the hospital and its neighborhood. With Jakob there was yet another way to share things, and just like he didn't bring children along on his business deals, he didn't tell us about them either. For the other families still in Jerichow I was the daughter of the mayor who'd been arrested—they were more likely to talk to Hanna. In Gneez there was truly no one who wanted me to count on them. What I can tell you now is nothing but what a thirteen-year-old happened to be there for, along with all the confusion that later knowledge imposes. Is that all right with you?

– What else haven't you told me about?

– Slata's disappearance.

– I'd almost forgotten about her! You were avoiding her on purpose!

– Slata opened the door to the first Soviets to walk into Papenbrock's foyer as if she wanted them to take her away from that house, that family. The Gneez military commander kept her as an assistant, not just a translator; he would have let her visit the Papenbrocks. She never got around to it. Louise had treated her like a maid for too long, Albert had merely watched without helping. So in Gneez hardly anyone knew that a Nazi "special unit" commander had hauled her off to Mecklenburg as a bride, with a child, to in-laws themselves linked to the air force and the Nazi Party by profitable business dealings. Instead they knew her as "the Angel of Gneez." She'd been in the country since fall 1942, it was impossible to lie to her in standard German, fancy German, or Plattdeutsch either, and there were a lot of people who credited her with their having made it out of a Soviet interrogation in one piece, their innocence more or less proven. Still, she was a stranger, there was no one who could count on special treatment except sick women, starving children, or a refugee who'd stolen potatoes not to sell them but because he needed them. She was nastily scrupulous in helping her boss, J. J. Jenudkidse, "Triple-J," keep tabs on the Gneez business world: the mighty Johannes Knoop had had to hand over his cart for transporting wood, never mind any "import-export." In these higher circles, her former future relatives were kept in reserve as a moral failing, a snare to be used down the line if needed, but not for now, in deference to their good Jerichow business partner, Albert. When they got mad they called her a slut and, can you believe it, a traitor. But the Angel of Gneez didn't live in the military housing on Barbara Street, protected from the Germans by an eight-foot fence; she left her son Fedya with Mrs. Witte during the day, in the requisitioned City of Hamburg Hotel, and slept there on the top floor, still furnished as Alma's private apartment, behind two doors not counting the hotel's main entrance. She spent some evenings downstairs in the former dining room with various officers from the Kommandatura and functionaries of the German Communists. There Slata understood almost no German, and especially not one young man's repeated attempts to strike up a conversation; he stood five paces away, kept his scornfully baffled eyes on her, with a deliberately gloomy expression, as if he weren't the future district councilman of Gneez. No. Not even Cresspahl's requests, with which he tried to circumvent K. A. Pontiy with even-higher-ups, passed through Slata's typewriter any faster than the rest, even though he'd talked with her under the Nazis about more than just the time of day, for example about Hilde Paepcke, who used to wear her hair in a scarf just like she did—clearly a woman he liked, too. In a twelve-year-old girl's eyes the district councilman was a stupid boy, but she wouldn't have minded turning out like Slata someday.

– I like how you look in photos from then, Gesine. *If I may say so myself.*

– But she was blond, Marie. That was considered pretty in those days. She was a grown-up; she was over my problems: what to do with your breasts, how a girl gets a baby. She was tall, almost willowy, but impressive. I loved to see how she held out her arm, or bent her knees to lean down. Such harmonious, flowing movements. She had a small, voluptuous mouth; I was mad at the language for saying my lips were "protruding." Slata nodded with her eyes when she listened to you. She would pass me on the street with a closed, withdrawn expression, preferring not to acknowledge me;

still, I felt invited to look back, be playful even. I would feel like we'd exchanged smiles after all, and said: Hi. Hey, how are you? You too.

– Such an important character. And you try to keep her from me.

– Then she disappeared. She was gone from my life. Once, when the midday train to Jerichow wasn't running again, I dropped in on Mrs. Witte, not knowing, just remembering when I'd had my lunches at the City of Hamburg, I wasn't thinking about Slata at all, and Slata was all Alma could talk about although she'd lost the power to form words. She just pointed around the room she'd given Slata as a bedroom, I followed the movements of her crippled finger, wanting to reassure her, and I set a nightstand back on its feet, swept up broken glass from the rug, hung some dresses back up, tidied up Fedya's torn-apart bed, and was just about to dash off and run to Jerichow on foot to warn Cresspahl but I had to go into Alma's kitchen and put on a kettle, get tea out of the can marked "Salt," all following her helpless breathing and panting.

– It happened to Slata because of a mistake, Gesine.

– It happened very suddenly. J. J. J. had driven up to the hotel like he did every morning, whistled cheerfully up to her window, but this time he'd brought four armed men with him and whipped up his anger by stomping up the stairs. That's how much he'd changed since the night before, but she hadn't.

– Did they beat her?

– Yes, because she resisted. Her child had a fever and needed to stay in bed.

– She was the wife of a Nazi, even if not legally. One who'd set villages in Ukraine on fire.

– Triple-J knew that when he hired her and trusted her. He'd forgiven her.

– She'd had a son with this Robert Papenbrock.

– He spoke Russian better, his name wasn't Fritz anymore, he answered to Fedya.

– Her name turned up in Cresspahl's files.

– Yes. But that's not why they picked her up.

– Gesine, you didn't want to tell me this because of that ax you have to grind. You think I'll misunderstand the Soviets again. But I'm understanding them.

– As long as no one gets beaten.

– Gesine. I don't like that kind of punishment. But I don't like when someone betrays his country. You're trying to tell me it's a good thing. First Cresspahl, then Slata.

– Tell it to Slata.

– I see. She came back. We can talk to her, try to explain. Someone explained it to her a long time ago.

– She didn't come back. And Fedya survived the trip to the Soviet Union, then died in the camp.

– Gesine, rewind the tape to Alma Witte. I wish I hadn't said all that. Let me think it over first. Next time warn me. Say: "Stop."

– Here Mrs. Witte had lost something: Fedya, who'd learned to call *her* Grandma, not Louise Papenbrock. A little three-year-old boy. She could carry him in her arms. *Where are you, where are you, my little chickee?* And she'd lost the mother with the child. A mother who could've easily lorded it over her landlady but she'd been quiet, a shade too independent but occasionally daughterly. This young thing had given her the respect she was entitled to. A Mrs. Witte liked that. And when the proprietress of the City of Hamburg Hotel praises Miss Podyeraitska's politeness for no apparent reason, it cuts a wide swath through public opinion, especially when she hints at the presence of other virtues too. The Angel of Gneez. In addition to that, Alma Witte had lost what the good townsfolk call pride. It takes more than hard work in a Mecklenburg country town to keep a hotel in second place behind the Archduke, with no close third. The district court judges had dined with her, the teachers and principals, army officers from good families. At night when she walked through the dining room the men would stand up to greet her. If someone from out of town wanted to be introduced to her, he'd better have one of the old well-established guests with him. One time, she'd told the Mecklenburg Reich governor's entourage to keep it down, and hadn't waited to see that her request was obeyed, and their corner had settled back down to the usual level. Commissioner Vick—from the police, not the Gestapo, because I'm an upstanding National Socialist!—had to watch his behavior or else she'd refuse to serve him. The Soviets had turned the building into an inn for functionaries of the new administration and visiting party officials, and yet she called Mr. Jenudkidse "chivalrous"; she'd joined them for dinner like an honorary chairman; merrymaking of the kind that went on at Louise Papenbrock's was unthinkable. Whether Mrs. Witte felt affable or respectful behavior was appropriate, the behavior always was appropriate. The thing is that her whole sense of propriety depended on her being accepted, recognized, responded to. Such mutual partnership had been wiped out by the raid on her apartment. She no longer trusted in the exchange of similar manners and mutually agreed-upon forms. The Alma Witte of earlier days would have turned up at Town Hall in her best Sunday clothes and requested that the commandant clear up the incident, diplomatically assessing whether to demand an apology or if she'd ultimately have to let the faux pas go. But they hadn't even waited for her to open the door, they'd crashed through it and broken all her rare frosted glass. They'd ignored her dignified protests and dragged guests out of her home, in defiance of all morality. They'd shoved her in the chest, and certainly not held out a hand to help her get up—a lady of sixty-five! Alma Witte submitted nothing in writing to the Kommandatura, neither a request for mercy for her young friend nor a petition for compensation for damages. She couldn't even feel satisfaction at J. J. Jenudkidse now spending his evenings off at the Archduke Hotel, now known as the Dom Ofitserov—it wasn't because he felt any embarrassment in front of her. Around town she was invited to comment on Slata's departure, and declined with sad dignity, as if refusing a course at the dinner table; again she was leaving an exaggerated wake of Soviet renown behind her, but actually she'd only wanted to avoid complaining. From a child she could demand that a shameful sight be forgotten. And I didn't need to be especially obedient to do that. To me she was a very old woman, why wouldn't she have fits or bouts of something. I hoped she felt better soon.

– You liked her too, Gesine.

– I've liked lots of people in my life.

– Couldn't it have been pity, Gesine?

– Pity for what. If she'd cried it would have been contagious and I would have too. But I couldn't be a pitying child.

– Am I jealous, Gesine? Of Slata? Of a proprietress of the City of Hamburg Hotel in Gneez? Is it possible?

– "Stop."

– No. No. I need to know.

– Mrs. Witte was never the same again, except outwardly. It wasn't the Red Army's manners that were her undoing—it was about her. Once, in spring 1946, I had to ask her if I could spend the night, the evening train to Jerichow had been canceled as well. She casually gave me permission, because one didn't set foot in Alma Witte's home as an imposition or to make some request, you had to follow the formalities of a social visit. Her salon had been repaired and she made me sit down in it for a proper conversation about the canceled train, sabotage?, requisition?, about the Gneez district administration office, about Cresspahl. She hadn't become nervous or afraid. And along with all that she was educating me in the finer points of middle-class polite conversation: replies in complete sentences, clear enunciation, euphemisms where appropriate and the whole truth when proper. She seemed undamaged to me. At about nine o'clock, unhurried, every inch a lady, she went downstairs with me into the former hotel reception desk, where she'd heard some noise that she planned to put a stop to. It was nothing but a lost Red Army soldier, two girls had caught his eye at the train station, a couple of junior teachers, guests of this establishment, chicks from out of town, they were supposed to just precede the young drunk to the Kommandatura, where he'd have gotten what was coming to him and a safe place to spend the night too. Now he'd stumbled into the Hamburg Hotel lobby and was waving his gun around in the half-open door to the reception area, admittedly too drunk to shoot, totally wasted in fact, but still drawn to the company of the young ladies who'd so mysteriously vanished into a wall here. That's when I saw Alma Witte's crooked index finger again. She pointed at the flailing figure in the lobby the same way she'd once indicated wrinkles in a table-cloth, spots on a knife, cigar stubs on the rug, whatever had to be straightened out, cleaned up, discreetly removed. But now there was no staff to leap to do her bidding; now she could not speak. This imperious person found herself surrounded by two educational experts, a woman who had almost qualified as a People's Court judge, Comrade Schenk emerging slowly from the dining hall—a man by the look of him—but not one of them understood what Mrs. Witte's trembling finger meant. It was a young female person who crept along the wall to the lobby, pushed the banging door shut, and turned the key in the lock, reaching up from her cautious kneel.

– He could have fired!

– He took his cue from the door. It was shut. The girls were gone. He just wanted some sleep.

– Why didn't any of you report him to the Kommandatura?

– Someone would've had to go out the back of the hotel, down a swaying ladder from Mrs. Bolte's apple yard, into the courtyard, over the wall, onto the street, and maybe right into the arms of another wandering lost soldier. Comrade Schenk forbade it, for the public good. At which Mrs. Witte forbade it again, pointing her finger at him outraged that he would give orders in her house. She wasn't vindictive. The drunk kid would've gotten a terrible beating at Town Hall and then another round after Triple-J had been woken up, because he would have reminded Slata's protector of where she'd lived. No, Alma Witte hadn't become nervous or afraid, and wasn't vindictive. She'd just lost her pride. The befuddled sleeper moved off before it was light out, and Mrs. Witte scrubbed the area between the inner and outer doors twice before anyone else in the hotel woke up. That's how she was now.

– And the person who locked the door, Gesine, was that you?

– I stood there, unable to tear my eyes away from that crippled, humiliated finger. I kept telling myself, over and over and over again: Don't laugh. Whatever you do, don't laugh. Why aren't you laughing, Marie?

– You know a lot more stories like that, don't you.

– A lot more.

– And you're sure I'll take them the wrong way.

– I'm afraid you might.

– Wait and see, Gesine. Wait and see.

The East German Communists plan to demand even more money from citizens of West Germany on their way to West Berlin. Now these citizens will have to pay not only for the tracks their tires leave on the roads but also for a visa, whether they're rich or poor, retirees or trucking companies; and a passport for foreign travel will be required too. There are three obvious reasons for the stratagem: They want to intimidate the people in the foreign city; they need hard currency to buy Western machinery and equipment; they are simply stressing their sovereignty and national dignity. They do not want to be misunderstood in such ignominious terms, and so they provide a reason of their own: it's about retaliating for the West German emergency laws, which don't apply to them.

Because give them a whole basketful of Easter eggs and they'll incorruptibly stick to the rules of international diplomacy. They do not get involved.

June 13, 1968 Thursday

The Czechoslovak Communists have put a new travel law before the National Assembly, all they have left to do is finalize the precise wording for the exceptions. The exceptions are citizens facing judicial proceedings, persons in active or upcoming military service, bearers of state or scientific secrets, and those who have damaged Czechoslovak interests on previous trips abroad. Everyone else is guaranteed the right to a passport valid for all countries and not requiring an exit visa, and they'll be able to go wherever they want for as long as they want and the homeland will welcome them back in friendship upon their return. Hopefully the Soviets won't be sad again when they read about this in a Prague paper, or in *Freedom*, out of Halle, East Germany.

The weather. It's supposed to be sunny, dry, and mild today, cool tonight.

– All right Gesine, can I set a trap for you? I was clumsy yesterday. Today I'll get you.

– Can I set a trap for you too, Marie?

– I know yours. You won't see mine.

– Mary Fenimore Cooper Cresspahl!

– And Henriette. Ready?

– The tape's running.

– Gesine, were the Soviets in your country more out of control than the British in India?

– They behaved like occupiers. The country was theirs, they wielded the power, and along with the glory they wanted to make sure they didn't get a raw deal.

– But the losers weren't all equally afraid of them. The ones who had something to lose. The middle class. What you call the bourgeoisie.

– If they were scared of the New Order it wasn't over their place in it. That had already been locked in.

– It was such a fat index finger, Alma Witte's. Chalk white, trembling. She was bourgeois.

– No. Take just the people in Jerichow, they weren't the Witte type. They genuinely wanted to surrender everything, starting with their sense of identity, if only they could keep their money, as a way to acquire possessions and more money. And the Soviets let them. The potatoes and wheat and milk went through their shops, just like before, and even the green Soviet fence went through their account books, they made money on others' labor same as ever. Even Papenbrock had been able to keep his granary, and his representative managed it for him, Waldemar Kägebein, who'd turned out to be right after all with his copy of Aereboe's *Handbook of Agriculture*. He charged a fee for receiving the grain, another for storing it, another for shipping it, and they weren't only written down in Papenbrock's books, they were deposited in the bank. If Louise could only charge forty-three reichpfennigs for bread, she just mixed in enough bran so that she could still make a profit. No one gives me anything for free either, she used to say, contentedly in a position to think: And no one's gotten much off me.

– They took her husband though.

– He was replaced by a trustee. Exactly as under the old laws.

– Wasn't she in danger too?

– If Albert came back and she hadn't taken good care his property, never mind if she'd let it get frittered away, then she'd really be in danger, that's what she thought. True, the Soviets might invite her on a little joyride who knows where: she thought she'd survive it, knowing she was innocent, the same way she expected Papenbrock home any day now, vindicated, pure as the driven snow. Besides, hadn't she been nice to the Red Army, hospitable even, when Mr. Wassergahn's crowd destroyed her living room parquet with their dancing? The only thing that could happen now was an accident of some kind, and for that eventuality she had Horst's widow in reserve, admittedly of inferior background, from the shoemakers' town, but still a daughter-in-law, predestined to take over managing the inheritance. Why would the chain be broken?

– Her friends in the nobility had run away from the Russians.

– That was a relief, as far as your middle class were concerned. The victors' punishment had fallen on others' heads, for now. How could your middle class keep up a friendship that had become impractical, which is to say bad for business? Pure friendship for morality's sake, without any value? There was no longer any point in imagining an alliance with the Plessens, the Upper Bülows; in fact, quite a few things came to Louise's mind that implied, if anything, a certain hostility: a greeting ignored or airily returned, failing to be invited to the von Zelck double wedding in 1942. Back then she would never have found fault, not even with a doubtful nod at the Lüsewitzes, at the fact that a member of the German landed aristocracy was keeping forced laborers locked in the farm stalls, foreign laborers but still—now she tucked her chin firmly into her collar and spoke of justice with pious severity. Another family, the von Haases, were staying in one of the Papenbrocks' attic rooms. They'd been deported from southern Mecklenburg, farther from their estate than the prescribed thirty kilometers. Louise nagged at them in the kitchen when they came to get water, and if their daughter Marga gave her the slightest bit of back talk Louise would shout after her: I bet your mother used to hit prisoners of war too! Which she had no evidence for at all, beyond her imagination. She wanted these people and the uncomfortable memories out of her house. She would have slammed the door in a fugitive von Bothmer's face.

– And denounced him.

– You don't trust me. You think I'm twisting the story around against her. Just to make her out to be bad.

– You hate her.

– There was nothing about her for a thirteen-year-old to hate, Marie. I avoided her because Cresspahl more or less told me to, and now Jakob wanted it too. Did I know why? Can you hate on command?

– That wasn't my trap, you know, Gesine.

– She would never have denounced him, it would have gotten around to the neighbors that she was being more accommodating to the Soviets than she needed to be. And besides, she still shared something else with the other Jerichow homeowners: they wanted their little entries in the nobility's good books. The situation might change again, after all.

– Back to what it had been? They'd lost!

– The Soviets were incomprehensible conquerors—they didn't introduce their own economic system in Mecklenburg. Not the big nationalized communal farms, their famous kolkhozes. They faithfully kept the agreement with their Allies, the Potsdam one, and took the land away from everyone who owned more than a hundred hectares, and of course from any Nazi leader. They did so earlier than promised, but did they do it in a Communist way? Socialist production is large scale, you'll learn that one of these days, but the Soviets handed out their stock of land in small parcels, many of them just five hectares, to farmworkers, small farmers, resettlers from the eastern territories, even old farmers got something, and the municipality of Jerichow, can you imagine? got fields to cultivate that had once been the nobility's, and a piece of the Countess Woods to boot. To approve so much property, in such quantities, both the concept and the reality, and provide the Mecklenburg world with it—that didn't look like they were planning to stay.

 – They must have done it with gritted teeth at least. Just to honor their treaty?

 – You don't believe they'd do such a thing, Marie.

 – Aha. So that was your trap. Right, Gesine?

 – That was not even the spring in the door of the trap. But they'd signed an agreement saying that the German people were not to be enslaved, and they stuck to it. They kept their version of Communism for themselves. Sometimes they acted in such a way that even the most ethical bourgeoisie couldn't help but approve. They communicated with the Germans through a newspaper of their own, and they could have called it *The Soviet Military Administration News*, *The Anti-Fascist Observer*, *The Free Red Front*, but they called it *The Daily Review—Tägliche Rundschau*, "The Frontline Newspaper for the German Population," and dropped the "Frontline" as early as June 1945. And that wasn't any random title, it had once been the name of a Christian paper with fiercely nationalistic leanings. The Soviets took that, too, from the booty they'd pocketed from the Nazis, all strictly legally. The middle-class concept of property counted for something with the Soviets.

 – Maybe they needed your bourgeoisie for a while, for economic reasons. But they didn't let them into the government. That would have been like promising to cut off their own arm.

 – Well, don't ask Sister Magdalena about the Potsdam Agreement.

 – You're kidding me.

– The Soviets couldn't make their position with regard to their share of the conquered people any clearer than they did with their leader's prophecy, painted on bedsheets and hung on town halls or painted in red Gothic on the front walls of school auditoriums:

Hitlers

Come and Go

But

The German People, the German State,

Remains

all center-aligned the way type designers and calligraphers like. When you have that before your eyes for hours on end you can't stop trying to translate it into Latin, with *et,* or even more elegantly, *atque,* it looked so classical. Wise as the Leader of Peoples working nights in the Kremlin, a perfect example of his style and yet the voice was off a little, it wasn't one of his feats of dialectics, just the ebb and flow of history: Hitler a recurring type notwithstanding the growing power of the international working class, eternity promised to a state identified only as German but that meant it included a strand of Mecklenburg too. It was nothing less than a lesson in irony, perfect for bourgeois minds.

– They didn't believe it, Gesine.

– If the Soviets were using perfectly good sheets for it? Cotton they otherwise could have slept on? Your middle class bowed their head and accepted it, they liked showing off how clever they were. How sly, how shrewd. As promised, the Soviets didn't just hand over the administration of their conquest to Germans, to opponents of Hitler's; as expected, they sent in relatives, German Communist Party émigrés trained in Soviet schools for this German state; predictably, they sent in people with them representing the class which, according to Soviet science, was the sole source of productivity and historical strength, and which, moreover, was overdue for an equalization of both income and power; to no one's surprise, the Communist Party arrived. Now it was their turn.

– Arm in arm with the bourgeois parties. Before K. A. Pontiy's very eyes.

– This commandant left them behind in Jerichow as a memento. After Cresspahl's arrest—

– "Stop."

– In fall 1945, Pontiy was no longer the Oriental potentate. His orders grew more detailed by the day, treating the former British Mecklenburg in accord with the same plans that applied to the rest of it. Sighing, he gave up his statistics. He would have liked to just issue orders. He ordered Mrs. Bergie Quade and Köpcke's wife to come to the villa for coffee, on the last Sunday in November, the Sunday for the Dead, and amazingly enough he served coffee. They could sit down, too, if only in the brown leather armchairs facing the corner of the commander's desk, but they tried to make up for this by sitting bolt upright, knees decorously together, expecting a discussion of their idiosyncratic bookkeeping. Instead it was suggested to them that they

    found
    a regional branch
    of a Party
    of German
    Liberalism
    (or: Liberality) and
    Democracy

while Bergie couldn't stop dreaming of filing a complaint over the removal of the old mayor; Mina was encased in an almost new dress, let out at the back with two gussets, acquired to be worn for the widowed Mr. Duvenspeck, she had just started feeling like a woman again; now they missed their cues, it didn't matter what else they said: *we're simple womanfolk*, you know, I'm just taking my husband's place, you know, I mean in the business, that's all, a political party's for special interests, *youve still got our men locked up*, you know, and what will the neighbors say! Commandant!

– Liberalism. Isn't that something to do with the gold standard?

– Not in that context. There it was the idea of stimulating the economy with the economic self-interest of the individual, unrestricted competition, a free market that the state protected but did not interfere with, international free trade, manage best by managing least, laissez-faire laissez-aller...

– Must've been a translator's mistake.

– Well, they were certainly willing. It was a gift, they weren't going to ask why they deserved it. Whatever they thought of this party's name, it did have a ring of the old days, of prewar times, pre-Nazi. They were clever about it, asking for time to think it over, pleading shyness, what with the public speaking. Bergie couldn't get it out of her head that Pontiy's adjunct

Wassergahn could be her son, she'd have no trouble pulling the wool over his eyes. Mrs. Köpcke licked her lips, she'd been chosen because she was a woman, and if the Soviets were offering tea and cakes for honest doings and dealings then she could cut herself as big a slice as any man. Each of them hoped to palm off the top spot onto the other, but that didn't yet get in the way of their friendship and trust. There was only one snag to be taken care of, and that was the neighbors' ignorant chatter about sucking up to the Soviets: they'd learned a thing or two from the reputation they themselves had created for Cresspahl. And here they both bethought themselves of K. A. Pontiy's shortest, curtest answer, which had sort of agreed to offset their political activities with the expedited return of their husbands from Soviet prison camps—wasn't that an honorable reason? It took some time to get it known among the good citizens of Jerichow. Duvenspeck, though in charge of the gasworks, was the most amenable to accepting it. Then, out of left field, Böhnhase emerged as the founder of the local LDPD (German Liberal Democratic Party)—Böhnhase the tobacconist, former DNVP (German National People's Party), sentenced to seven years in prison for the crime of bartering tobacco for bacon in 1942 and yet not recognized as a VoF (Victim of Fascism) but nonetheless ready and willing to serve as a pillar of anti-Fascist Liberalism, office hours whenever his shop was open, tobacco rationing no argument against the party, abolishing tobacco rationing an argument in its favor. Mrs. Köpcke had to admit, along with Bergie, that they'd underestimated the male appetite, and anyway Böhnhase had been too far away from the trough for too long. They both joined his party, now no longer the main offenders, just fellow travelers. They brought in others too: Plückhahn the pharmacist, Ahlreep the jeweler, Hattje from the general store, tinker tailor soldier sailor rich man poor man beggar man thief—the whole native population faced with a minimal state. A "night-watchman state," they called it. Translation from the German.

– Did Louise have to join a party too?

– She wanted to, Marie. It was voluntary. Allowed. Desirable. Louise, standing in for her husband, joined the Conservative party, which called itself a Union, and wanted to be Democratic like the liberals, but unlike them Christian. Christian Democratic Union, CDU. And that's how K. A. Pontiy achieved his public

expression
of my respect
for the cause
of the equal rights
of women

because even though Pastor Brüshaver didn't generally preach atonement for German war crimes, even in what he called "the social sphere," he did think party politics was irreconcilable with spiritual office, it was enough simply to call for an "honest self-reappraisal," and Pontiy was happy to have a woman in charge—

– Louise Papenbrock.
– Käthe Klupsch.
– She was the laughingstock of the whole town!
– Käthe Klupsch was incapable of laughing at herself, though. What she was best at was the forgiving tone in which she spoke of people who went over to the Communist Party or Farmers' Mutual Aid just to get a second residence permit or a claim to a plow or maybe a head of cattle from the stock of the land reform agency. Swenson, Otto Maass, Kägebein, whenever one of them asked another how things were going the other would say: Scared as shit, same as ever! It sounded much better in public when Käthe Klupsch announced: We have joined forces not for our personal advantage but for the cause.

– Well, whatever your trap was, Gesine, it blasted mine to pieces.
– Mine was just to show you that you're wrong sometimes with all your talk of merciless oppression by the Soviets.
– I was trying to prove I can learn a lesson. I can think the Russians are right, sometimes, at least when they punish a crowd like that. But now the old crowd's back on top.
– What do you call a double trap like that, Marie.
– You know perfectly well.
– Your English is better than mine.
– A *double cross*. Probably a *Vorspiegelung vermittels Tatsachen* in German, or something.

There once was a time when we believed Herbert H. Hayes—that time when he looked up the weather over Easter 1938 for us. Let's hope the New

York Weather Bureau never employs him anywhere but in the archives. They'd have to worry about him in the forecasting department. Today was neither sunny nor dry. It might have deserved "mild," if only for the persistent rain that wouldn't stop for hours.

June 14, 1968 Friday
The Czechoslovak government delegation is back from Moscow. Bringing gifts. The Soviet Union will increase its annual natural gas shipments to Czechoslovakia to three billion cubic meters (100 billion cubic feet). The Košice steelworks will receive two million tons of iron-ore pellets a year, though not until 1972. Do we think he's gotten the fear of God put into him, our confident Vice President de Rosny? No, the Soviets refused to provide a hard-currency loan, modest though the requested sum was, $350 million, a mere seven-eighths of their debts on the Western market. All the more quickly and happily will de Rosny provide more. We're not going to get out of our trip to Prague. Marie knows, too. She doesn't want to talk about it.

The *Times,* prim and proper Auntie Times, makes a decorous curtsy. She apologizes. She's made a mistake. In that Soviet poem on the death of the New York senator, it wasn't supposed to say that Abraham Lincoln basks in his marble chair. It should have said that the marble Lincoln "rasps." Marie could use this for her Kennedy folder. But she doesn't want to hear that name for a while.

– So, what are you not going to tell me about today?

Sometime before Christmas 1945, Erwin Plath came trotting through northwest Mecklenburg again—his home territory, and assigned to him by the Socialist Party in Hanover. You make an effort for a guest, and Plath got his meeting in Jerichow, twenty minutes standing in the brickworks drying shed, perfectly in view of the Soviet Kommandatura, so it wasn't only from the cold that he was shivering. It was a bitter enough pill to swallow that he had to admit a mistake before informing his audience of the new party line; they heckled him mercilessly, not even respecting his status as a messenger. Fourteen men and two women had come; he knew two as former card-carrying members, was willing to believe it about two more, for eight of them he could imagine neither a past nor a future in the Social Democrats, and in one case he thought he must be dreaming, hadn't he been kicked out of the party in 1938, following the full illegal procedure? What's more they refused to give their names, so we'll have to content ourselves with their initials, although we can assume that W. was Wulff, and B. was Bienmüller. P. was Plath and wrote out his name, Plath, and had come from headquarters—important delegate Erwin Plath. The others soon cured him of that. – In all my life: P. was still saying nineteen years later: I've never been through a party meeting like that!

W.   This meeting is now opened. Be it resolved: This is not a meeting. About the agenda, let it be unanimously agreed: There is no agenda. That takes care of the role of secretary. I ask that the election of the secretary be approved. Now get lost, you.

P.   The party regrets the erroneous directive of August of this year.

S.   Do we have a chairman? We don't have a chairman. Permission to speak can only be given by the chairman.

H.   You've gotten us into a fine mess, comrade. If the Soviets know any of our names now, it's your fault.

P.   Who's been found out?

L.   None of your fucking business.

P.   The party concedes that the attempt to acquire secret spheres of influence within the Communist Party has not succeeded. There are comrades who applied for admission into the Communist Party who have been asked to found their own local branch of the Social Democratic Party. It was wrong, I'm not ashamed to admit it, I'll say it again.

K.   Let's hear you say it again, mister. Like in school!

P.   There's no "mister." And who are you, anyway?

L.   None of your fucking business.

P.   We must apply all our strength to create a strong party organization as a counterweight.

W.   We're not in Krakow here. The Communist comrades in Krakow am See sent all their papers to the State Criminal Investigations Office in March '33. The Soviets probably found them there.

P.   That's beside the point.

L.   None of your fucking business.

S.   They don't know a thing about us. We didn't send any parcels to the Nazis and none to the Soviets either.

H.   But there's one man they know. And that's your stupidity, dumbass. It's your fault.

P.   Is it you, comrade?

H.   Me you can call "mister."

P.   Needless to say, the party will do everything in its power to cover for that comrade.

K.   Permit me to inquire: Do you have anything to cover him with?

S.   Because he can run away on his own. He doesn't need any chickenshit from the party for that. So that's one less of us.

P.   How many of you are then, anyway?

L.   I move that this is none of his fucking business.

W.   Since we have no meeting, no official agenda, and no procedure, there is no way to propose a motion. The motion is passed.

P.   The most important consideration, in case of unification with the Communist Party, is to create a strong counterweight within the Unity Party. If it comes to that.

S.   Feel free to come back when the party in the British zone unites with the CP.

P.   We must avoid any weakening of the party. But your case is different. You've still got to found a local branch!

H.   Register it, you mean. Inform on ourselves, that's what you mean.

P.   So you already have a local branch? And you're it?

L.   None of your fucking business.

H.   You'd like that, wouldn't you. Something to report.

P.   Children, children. I've worked my way north from Ludwigslust to Gneez. Local branches of the SPD hard at work everywhere. We hear about everything that goes on in the administrations, from the state level down to the districts!

S.   Then they can have a nice little chat with the Communist comrades about us being Socialist Fascists. What we meant by that coalition with the Nazis. What happened to the Social Democrats who emigrated to Russia.

K.   And will we have the pleasure, perchance, of hearing a word from headquarters to clear this up?

P.	Maybe you won't have to unify at all. All the more reason for you to be here as a branch!
A.	Anyway, it's only the Soviets who want a Unity Party. That doesn't matter.
P.	Children, children. You have no idea what's happening in the world.
B.	If you call us children one more time. Just one more time!
P.	But you have no idea! Oh, how the Communists lost ground in Austria on November 25! And how well the Social Democrats did! In the Soviet Zone in Austria! Four seats for them, seventy-six for us!
K.	Next you'll be comparing the Social Democrat wins in the local Hungarian elections with the defeat of the Communists.
P.	I almost forgot about that! Yes! That's how you'll do, too!
A.	Go ahead, help the Soviets.
P.	Only an independent SPD in the Western Zone of Germany will be in a position to support you.
B.	How on earth did Cresspahl ever come to it. A high opinion of you, I mean.
L.	None of his fucking business! None of his fucking business!
W.	The minutes have been read and approved. We will now proceed to the vote. For. Against. Abstain.
H.	Every time someone's cover gets blown we're going to hold it against you. In twenty minutes, next year, doesn't matter.
S.	You wanted something to report, didn't you. There it is.
W.	It is hereby resolved that there are no minutes. This meeting is adjourned. There was no meeting.

– So, what do you have today that you don't want to tell me about?

– A casualty. "Stop"?

– You're emptying your Jerichow out. Soon no one I know'll be left.

– Paul Warning wasn't in Jerichow. Because he'd helped out on Griem's land for a while he was allowed to call himself an agricultural worker and take part in drawing slips of paper out of a hat Gerd Schumann had obtained from the von Zelck manor especially for the occasion and was passing around. Warning drew four hectares of moderately good land, an hour from town by wagon, almost uncultivated. He couldn't live on that this fall with his wife and two young sons but next year he just might. But his work in the fields hadn't taught him much more than how to follow orders. When he'd gotten back from Dreibergen prison he'd been in charge of minding the town's cows, a job he'd been given for his wife's sake. He told no more stories of any kind anymore, leaning comfortably on his pitchfork handle as a cow lowed next to him, and no one discussed their stories with him anymore either. He had turned hardworking, eager, obedient, afraid of another trip to Dreibergen. After the war his wife became set on having a plot of land of their own, but he would've done better with someone to supervise him. The Narodnyi Komissariat Vnutrennikh Del picked him up on Christmas 1945, no one paid much attention. He was still under a cloud because of that business with *Our Lisbeth*, so neither his arrest nor his release aroused much comment around town.

– If he gets shot, you're all to blame.

– Peter Wulff took the blame. He was only trying to help get the browbeaten fellow back onto his feet when he brought him along to a meeting of former Social Democrats with Erwin Plath; he regretted it right away, because Warning thanked him so effusively for the show of confidence, for taking him back into the party, he actually spoke of happiness. That was no way to talk. It hadn't been meant like that. He'd only been trying to help.

– They'd needed him as a stopgap.

– Exactly. Still, Wulff would've enrolled him in the party again, no, welcomed him as a comrade, because he'd been unobtrusive at the meeting, levelheaded, and above all kept his mouth shut. Wulff wasn't the only one to feel that way after Warning refused to say a word about his interrogation by the Soviets, neither high nor to heaven—maybe the guy really had firmed up, at least in one spot. Wulff trusted Warning, all the more when Warning assured him, with a twisted smile and a painfully solemn handshake: *Nothingll happen to you lot.* On New Year's Day, Warning went and hanged himself.

– It was a crime to expect someone like that to keep silent.

– Warning hadn't told the Soviets a thing about the mood of the Jerichow Social Democrats. He'd withstood even his own family—his wife knew not a thing about the arrest except that it'd lasted four days. He didn't even tell her, or leave her a note saying, why he could no longer face life. All she had was the slip of paper in his breast pocket, a new summons to the Gneez Kommandatura "due to a formality."

– He hanged himself where the meeting had happened. So they'd believe him.

– Right. In the brickworks shed.

– But if he didn't snitch on anyone then someone must've snitched on him!

– Right. So he did leave a legacy after all. In his way.

June 15, 1968   Saturday, South Ferry day
Public Library day

Sometimes you need to look at it scientifically, as the man says. Before a fight starts the public is given details about the boxers, weight, earlier victories, etc. So,

In the Prague corner:

ČESTMIR CISAŘ, b. 1920. Known for his very short hair and candid way of speaking. Note: wears glasses. Graduated with a degree in philosophy from Charles University in Prague. No injuries from the Soviet purges! Served in 1956 as secretary of the Czech Communist Party regional committee, Plzeň; came back to Prague in 1957 as deputy editor of its newspaper, *Rudé Právo*; and in 1961 was put in charge of its monthly journal *Nová Mysl*, well known to sports fans as *New Thought*. Joined the secretariat of the CCP in May 1963, demoted that same September for an inclination toward cultural dialogue and listening to other points of view. In his new post as minister of education and culture, he began to reform the Czechoslovakian school system while remaining fundamentally true to the Soviet-designed Education Law of 1953, yet he loosened up the curriculum, reduced instruction in party matters, and did not station a watchdog to look over every teacher's shoulder. Too popular with both students and professors, he received from St. Novotný not the highest punishment but the post of ambassador to Romania, in other words, training in Romanian cultural policies. After Novotný stepped down, he was called to be the Secretariat of the Central Committee's man in charge of education, science, and culture, was mentioned as a possible new president of the country, and has recently been entrusted with delicate missions for the party chairman, e.g.: persuading the press to deal gently with the Soviet brothers. Stated occupation: journalist and philosopher.

In the Moscow corner:

FYODOR VASSILYEVIČ KONSTANTINOV, b. 1901. In leading positions in the Communist Party of the USSR since 1952. Author of the textbook *Historical Materialism.* Allowed to celebrate the second anniversary of the Stalin's death with an article, "J. V. Stalin and Questions of Communist Superstructure," in—but not on the front page of—*Pravda,* known to sports fans as *Truth.* Author of the sentence: "The forces of production continue to develop even under the conditions of Imperialism" (*Voprossy Filosofii,* No. 2 [1955]). Since December 1955 head of the Division of Agitation and Propaganda in the Central Committee of the Communist Party of the Soviet Union, results negative. Since 1962 director of the Institute for Philosophy in the Academy of Sciences of the Union of Soviet Socialist Republics. Stated occupation: Professor. Philosopher.

A-a-a-a-nd Cisař comes out swinging in the first round with a speech at a public meeting in Prague. The occasion is the 150th anniversary of the birth of Karl Marx, and in his speech Cisař casually describes Leninism as a monopolistic interpretation of Marx's views. That was on May 5.

Konstantinov is in fine form, quick in his wit, fast on his feet, and he counters as early as June 14, raining massive blows down on his opponent, which can be gleaned from *Truth* as follows:

Cisař's criticisms put him into the ranks of a Menshevik such as Yuliy Ossipovič Martov (Tsederbaum), 1873–1923, Russian socialist, cofounder of *Iskra* (*The Spark*). That's right, Tsederbaum.

It has become fashionable among contemporary revisionists to attempt to give a different, non-Leninist interpretation of Marxism, Marxist philosophy, Marxist political economy, and scientific Communism.

With the industrial and economic successes of the Soviet Union, Leninism has become the banner of the world's Communist movement.

Revisionist exponents of reform seek to discredit Leninism and demagogically preach a "rebirth" of Marxism without Leninism.

Communists have always considered, and still consider, Leninism as not a purely Russian, but rather an international Marxist doctrine. And this is the reason that Marxist parties of all countries have originated and developed on its basis.

Now turn your attention to the finish, as the man says, but don't lose sight of the timing!

Because where are the first secretary of the Czechoslovak Communist Party and the prime minister during this fight? They are off in Budapest negotiating a twenty-year friendship pact. What else are they saying? They are emphasizing the enormous importance of their alliance with the Soviet Union.

Referee to the phone!

Where, in contrast, one might well ask, are the delegates to the Czech National Assembly? They, with their president, Smrkovský, are off with the head of the Soviet Communist Party, Leonid I. Brezhnev, and even if every last one of them has the *Truth* with Mr. Konstantinov in his jacket pocket, the Soviet press agency is only allowed to report a "warm and friendly talk" and everyone's confidence that the visit "will help further strengthen the fraternal friendship and cooperation between our countries."

Is there any way Fyodor Vassilyevič Konstantinov's not going to lose? That his trainer won't throw in the towel? Or on points?

They need to look at it scientifically, too.

June 16, 1968 Sunday, Father's Day
The third Sunday in June, set aside in honor of fathers.
Der dritte Sonntag im Juni, vorgesehen zur Ehrung von Vätern.
Because someone's a father.

Equipped as usual by nature, they take credit for such an exception.
Proud of their procreation.
If there's any guilt involved, it wasn't theirs.

There have to be children.
So that a father can pass himself down, even just part of himself, into a future.

That they neither know nor need fear.
They just want to be in it.

That's how much fathers love themselves.
And their possessions shouldn't be left just lying around, so they make someone to keep an eye on them.
A name should remain, a rank, a right to power.
As always: inheritance.

The hope of being looked after in old age.
Fear of being alone.
Dying with someone there to see.

Such a child, a gage of marriage.
See the Civil Code.

Hunting around in the sacrificial victims to make sure that they are truly contained in them. Being like them.
They want to be the measure, whether filled or broken: the type is to be theirs.
Children should have it better than their fathers.
What fathers do for the better.

And if the children don't want to have anything?
Not the place of consciousness that knows its end to be the goal, not even themselves?

In Europe, fathers stagger along in the gutter, wearing paper hats, tooting horns, yelling, beer in their throats, to honor themselves.
Vatertag. Father's Day.
Boys go with them who haven't yet made a baby with a girl, but they will.
Father's honor.
Nature's wisdom.
Continuation of the human race.

Fathers know why.

The US wants to release some Czechoslovakian money. No, not the gold worth $20 million that belongs to them and that the US wants counted toward the compensation owed for property nationalized in 1948. This is only $5 million—annuity payments in the form of social security, railroad retirement, and veterans' benefits to which some ten thousand Czechoslovak residents are entitled by virtue of contributions they made while here, as long as their new government gave written assurances that the sums would actually reach their recipients, at a fair rate of exchange. – We are not thieves: the Czechoslovak Communists need to say.

Once again a Soviet poet has given voice to his feelings. This one's name is Voznesensky. He does it not for the sixty-six-year-old doctor shot and killed and robbed on Friday night in Brooklyn during a house call, no, he does it on the occasion of a less mundane death:

Wild swans. Wild swans. Wild swans.
Northward. Northward. Northward!
Kennedy... Kennedy...

and he laments the loneliness of the roots of the apple trees on Kennedy's balcony on the thirtieth floor, availing himself of poetic license, in the opinion of *The New York Times*, due to his failure to remember that Mrs. Kennedy lives on the fifteenth floor. The poet had also been struck by the dead senator's resemblance to Sergei Yesenin, a Soviet poet.

– You're right, it's been a week: Marie says: But do you mind not bringing up that name for a while more?

– Sowwy. I mean, Sorry.

– You wanted to try and see. That's fine. I would've done the same thing.

– You know, in the IRT the fans are mounted in pairs, and now they've taken out one of each pair. It makes everyone start sweating as if their whole body was cr—

– I know, Gesine, I'm being silly. It'll heal. Someday it won't matter at all.

– If only you'd have a good cry!

– You also hold it against me that I got over MLK's death in a couple of days. I didn't know as much about him, you know.

– How was it on the South Ferry on Saturday? First time on your own!

– Calm, gray water. I wanted to punish you. And I did.

– You did. No you didn't. You had to do it alone for the first time someday.

– Gesine, is it because I'm from Mecklenburg that I can't make up with someone just by trying?

– Let's wait a little more.

– Okay. So tell me something that's got nothing to do with me.

– Louise Papenbrock?

– Good. She's got nothing to do with me.

– With trap or without?

– Without.

– Your great-grandmother's new political importance made her uncomfortable. Sometimes the only thing she could use as a crutch was spite against her fractious son-in-law, Cresspahl, who'd warned other people besides her off all this government nonsense. Going against that didn't turn out quite right either, and it didn't help her sleep any easier. This was the first time in her life she'd joined a party, and she suspected tricks while thinking herself too good to ask questions. How happy she'd have been to follow Pastor Brüshaver in everything! When it was precisely he who was causing her more annoyance than anyone, enough to make her shudder in secret. She'd joined this Christian Democratic Union for her husband Papenbrock's sake, following the command she imagined he'd have given; she was only trying to keep him a place in it. But Papenbrock, it seemed to her at least vaguely, had kept business and politics strictly separate, even at the office, certainly at the dinner table, and now she'd brought politics into the home! Pontiy's unit had beaten an ignominious retreat, she was rid of Wassergahn's parties (she didn't see Second Lieutenant Vassarion as a political figure); secretly she was trying to get the large ground-floor parlor back into Papenbrock's property, and might well have earned a few square feet of it once she'd spent four days on her knees scrubbing it clean. To her it seemed that the room would be easy to conceal, as unsuitable for housing refugees in, she meant, and the current Kommandatura wasn't set on amusements involving dancing. Oh how tart she could look when she had to pretend to be kindhearted, pretend to be making a sacrifice willingly! Her smile slipped off her face quite often when she had to reopen the double doors for her friends from the Union so soon. These friends had known, even children had known, about this magnificent great hall, three-foot-high oak paneling with von Lassewitz fauns and nymphs above it, the plaster-relief hunting scenes, the deep bay of plate-glass doors at the back, the green light from the garden everywhere. (One child had wondered why the grown-ups used a room like this only for special occasions.) There would be few meetings of the Jerichow CDU for long stretches, and still Louise's ego would take a hit every time. Here was that Klupsch woman, the party chair, that old biddy; Louise begrudged her not the job but the place at the front, she would have liked to bang on the table herself. That Klupsch had more fat on her bones than those bones wanted to carry, still it reminded Louise of her own fullness of form amid all these shabby, emaciated figures around her. So few people realized that you could get fat from grief and sorrow, you could! Then this Klupsch was allowed to read the newspaper, the *New Era*, to the group—every now and then a copy made it all the way from Schwerin to Jerichow. This Klupsch could decide whose turn it was to talk. Kägebein, her own employee, might think of something he had to say about the temporary allocation of town land as garden allotments for refugees, without even asking her permission first. Then Mrs. Maass, to suit her husband, would say something about the injustices that had occurred in the expropriation of large landholdings, and Louise too had felt that some compensation was called for but now she could only nod. She'd only been trying to remind everyone she was there when she cosigned the telegram that the Jerichow local branch of the CDU sent to Colonel Tulpanov in late December 1945, informing him that he couldn't simply replace the chairman of their party on a whim, and now a certain Colonel Tulpanov, Soviet Military Administration, Berlin, had had his attention called to a certain Louise Papenbrock and the fact that she was causing trouble. She couldn't lean on Brüshaver for support; he just sat there, and in the front row too, like a visitor. He did speak up sometimes, of course, but only about German mistakes, about honest efforts at improvement. Louise was inclined to forgive him, he must have come up with these ideas in the Nazi camp, but why did she keep feeling like he meant her? Would he dare? It was exactly like when he would stand in the pulpit and preach about virtues like friendship that meant nothing unless they were turned into action. Did he mean . . . Louise's reserve in her dealings with the von Haases? He couldn't know about that. He had no right to tell her that. It often happened that she wanted to shout at every last one of the seventeen people present at the party meeting: What about me?! What am I getting out of this? Are you even paying me rent?

– Was there someone writing down everything Brüshaver said again?

– Not in church. Yes in Papenbrock's parlor.

– Then all they could do was talk.

– And they'd been given the room to talk in which the Communist Party hadn't been able to fill. That group, which met at Prasemann's Rifle Club, really did see it as a game of hide-and-seek with the Soviets. It was not only Duvenspeck (German Liberal Democratic Party) who let himself be heard expressing the opinion that in Liberalism the freedom of each individual was compatible with the freedom of every other individual, hence had to be restricted by it. After the Sunday in October when the CP collected a group of people to burn down the estate manors "which were a disgrace to the landscape," even though in truth that surely applied more to the farmworkers' cottages, the local historian, Stoffregen, just released from his labors dismantling the railways, gave a subtle lecture on the influence of Italian and English architectural styles on secular buildings in Mecklenburg, "which we were permitted to see for the last time this past Sunday." In the minutes there was only something about the urgency of the potato harvest.

– And then Stoffregen was arrested. Oh, Gesine…

– No. But that's how Stoffregen got himself known. People like Duvenspeck on the other hand, and Bergie Quade, even though they claimed that as housewife or civil servant they'd been purely apolitical, were needed for positions in the Anti-Fascist Women's Committee, or as municipal advisers, and maybe they felt more important when they could apply for a permit not merely as a private individual but by starting their letter: As a member and representative of the Christian Democratic Union…

– What exactly could they apply for?

– Whatever they wanted. They could petition for the removal of Friedrich Schenk as mayor, for the construction of a power line to Jerichow…

– But what did they get? What were the limits?

– I can tell you one of them. They had banded together as private groups—they were appointed, not elected to public office—but they had one mandate, assigned to them by everybody, and there was no getting out of it. They needed more living space. An urgent mandate, you might say. Imperative. There you are, Mina Köpcke, you've been running around after your workmen six days a week and Sunday morning is wasted on bills and taxes and now you're sitting on the sofa in the evening, Duvenspeck's there too, in his shirtsleeves, you wouldn't mind taking your blouse off too, at least undoing a few buttons, Duvenspeck's a little tipsy, now that doesnt hurt, jus' top off my glass there, fill it up, fill it, Eduard, cheers Edi . . . and here comes the refugees' oldest child walking into the room, right on schedule, wants to warm up the pillows for her brothers and sisters by the fire, a ten-year-old girl like that sees more than you think, the kids'll lose all respect for you just because they can't find anywhere to live, the Liberal Democratic Party hereby proposes to improve the lot of the resettlers and requests that the Soviet Kommandatura approves an allocation of living quarters from the occupation power's holdings at Jerichow-North airfield.

– So that was the limit.

– Right. They thought they'd pull a fast one Pontiy's successor—surely he could see the houses for the former civilian employees standing empty on the airfield, all those broken windows. They promised to have living quarters restored by the honest tradesmen of Jerichow. They provided proof that an airport like that is too big for just one company of guards. If not a single plane is flown in or out, then the strategic value must be—let's just say it, zilch. Now don't you agree, Mr. Commandant sir?

– Now who was this commandant?

– I didn't know him, I never once saw him. Around Jerichow he was known as "Placeholder," because he left after only three weeks. But I know what he answered, and I can imagine his despair at these screwy Germans, exasperation buzzing around in his brain like a swarm of bees—no clue about territorial tactics, right on the border with the British, they say this crowd almost beat us? It was a short answer, given with his very last scrap of patience, and I can hear his tone of voice too, imploring, beseeching, rising to outright fury on the last syllable. Guess.

– "The commandant regrets to inform you—"

– No.

– "The Red Army refuses to allow any interference in matters which—"

– Nope.

– "Get out!"

– No.
– "There's no such airport"?
– There! is! no! such! airport!

June 18, 1968 Tuesday

Brezhnev had tears in his eyes. In a two-hour meeting with the Czecho-slovak parliamentary delegation on Friday, things weren't going as Profes-sor Konstantinov wanted and as the Soviet news agency knew to be true. Admittedly, a representative of the People's Party said so, which is a party with a Roman Catholic orientation, but it is part of the Czechoslovak National Front, allied with the Communists; admittedly, he said it to that tiresome *Lidova Demokracie*, but anybody in Prague could buy a copy. Brezhnev denies that his country intends to intervene in Czechoslovakia's democracy. Many things that the now uncontrolled Czechoslovak press is spreading among its citizens are making him sad and hurting the Soviet Union's feelings, but there is no thought of intervention. Leonid Ilyich was prepared to justify himself before any international tribunal! He also concedes that errors have been made, though he doesn't say what they might have be. The general secretary of the Central Committee of the Communist Party of the Soviet Union, Leonid Ilyich, cried.

– They were always going to be bringing you Socialism, Gesine. They never denied that, right from the start.
– It was going to be Socialism. But not off-the-shelf Socialism. The Germans were going to make their own.
– What does "German" mean, Gesine?
– The German version of Socialism had to be something special. Sweepingly specific. In February 1946 the Communist Anton Ackermann wrote to the Germans: In particular cases the
  pronounced characteristics
  of the historical development
  of our people,
  our political and national idiosyncrasies,
  the special features

of our economy
and culture
will find full expression.

– What did he mean by these German idiosyncrasies? The robes the judges wear? How many doors the buses have? The color of their military uniforms? Blue for the navy?

– The German military was outlawed. Weapons, buildings, literature. Everything.

– Was it that you were supposed to do it in the German language, not in Russian?

– Yes. But imagine how people like Stoffregen the local historian started drawing up a list of German things! What was German about the state, about the people . . .

– Gesine, when're you going to show me just one person who liked it. Who was sitting in the driver's seat. Who did it because he wanted to. Who was enjoying himself. Someone like that. He knew what was going on and he liked it. You must know *one*!

– I do know one. Imagine that you're twenty-three years old . . .

– Sounds great, Gesine. Sounds great.

– . . . in the summer of 1946, you're the district councilman for Gneez, you've gone over to the Communists not for a bit of bread but across the eastern front, you've founded practically every third local branch in the area around Gneez, you're allowed to carry a gun, you talk to the Russians in their own language with a Moscow accent, you've got a room in the City of Hamburg Hotel, now with breakfast, but in winter Alma Witte has to heat it for you . . .

– His name's Gerd Schumann.

– That's what you're called these days, you've been given that name and by now you're even used to it, it's missing only a few deep crannies you can crawl all the way into, where you feel it to be really yours, where it couldn't be anyone else's. You shouldn't change it again, you should keep it for now, you've gone around to too many villages with it, people wouldn't know you; but who has the forms you need for another name, and the authority to stamp them and sign them? You do. You don't exercise this power too, there are enough other kinds that you wield.

– He's got everything he wants.

– You were one of the very first, the Soviets brought you into Initiative Group North, you were not with Comrade Sobottka in Stettin on May 6, you were still studying administration in Stargard, but you were there in Waren on the Müritz when the Sobottka Unit voted itself head of the party for Mecklenburg-Vorpommern, you're not on the wrong horse, you've proven your worth. No one's given you anything for free, you worked for it. And it's thanks to you that nobody's homeless in Mecklenburg now even though the population's doubled, 52 percent are resettlers from the East but they all have roofs over their heads, you've put them to work, they can feed the occupying power, feed the friends, they have food to eat themselves, and you receive bread for your labors too. Where 2,500 estate owners used to exploit the soil now you've helped settle nearly 65,000 new farmers, it was your party that repaired 26 large bridges rather than leaving them in ruins, the waterways are open again, except for the Bolter sluice, your accomplishments include 539 drivable trucks, 243 tractors, 437 automobiles, 281 motorcycles, laid rail, 11 omnibus lines running on schedule...your party got them all moving. You did that. That's what you have to worry about.

– And he can't have had any other worries, Gesine.

– Oh yes you can. You can have trouble with the party. The Red Army deploys you to Mecklenburg and a little knowledge of the local dialect would've come in handy. No idea what the people might be saying to one another, maybe right to your face. In a rural area you would've liked to know the acreage needed to feed a family, how much milk a cow actually gives, that people here still measure the land in rods. The same kind of thing had happened with the other comrades in Initiative Group North— they came from Silesia, Bavaria, the Ruhr, they were miners and clockmakers, some of them knew nothing but the inside of the party. One had waited it out in Sweden. Sweden! The party helped you, it sent you up and down the coast from one village to the next and soon the people were no longer laughing at you, you even proved to them that five hectares was enough to feed a family, not the fifteen actually set by the party back in 1932; hopefully the other comrades did as well as you did. You know the reasons: The German émigrés in the Soviet Union could only produce cadres of activists, and not even enough of those, certainly not agricultural or technical experts; take what you can get. Those the Nazis didn't kill off in their prisons and camps are broken, sick, exhausted people; have to make do with them too. You have to talk them out of the nonsense they've dreamed up away from the party. They come to you with their thuggish Socialism—total expropriation, large-scale agricultural production—you can't be a spoilsport, you have to let them find out for themselves that we can't entrust the administration of Socialist farms to the same estate managers who served the agrarian capitalists. One of them, who'd been in a camp since 1939, objects to you that after the brown straitjacket he has no desire to put on a red one—you explain the exceptional path of the German nation to that one. They demand from the party the immediate and complete seizure of power by the working class and you gently point out to him that Socialism can only be forged with the human material at hand, with farmers, the lower and middle classes, and of course with the working class in the lead; that's precisely why the Red Army has removed the large estate owners, the military leaders, the major banks, the leading industries. Sent them away. Others can't get it through their heads why Mecklenburg would demolish its proletarian centers in Rostock and Wismar; it falls to you and none but you to itemize that the workers at Heinkel and at Arado built warplanes, at Neptun they built warships and rocket parts, at Dornier seaplanes, and you pose the question of restitution in moral terms first, only then political ones. When they ask you to intervene in Soviet arrests, you just silently shake your head and suggest that when it comes to security the Russian friends trust none but themselves, and rightly so. Yet another person understands about the demolitions but not about the Razno-Export or Techno-Export stores where the Soviets are buying up gold, precious stones, porcelain, paintings, every last valuable possession down to the wedding rings, in exchange for cigarettes at precisely the black market rates; you ask that one: Who owns such things? He wouldn't happen to have any of that himself now would he? When they ask you about the years between 1935 and 1938 in the Soviet Union, or émigrés there who never came back, you're too young for a moment and then you ask about the harvest. You have your own burden to bear. You have no choice, you have to tolerate a Social Democratic mayor in Gneez who, you personally know for a fact, from a prisoner's statement, encouraged comrades to defect during the Nazi years, that is to say volunteer for the German Army; he survived

with his tobacco store and now they call him senator. And if that's not
enough you have to let the bourgeoisie into the administration for the time
being, as long as they weren't actual members of the Nazi Party, or if they'd
been locked up for refusing to give a Hitler salute once; actually what
matters more, more often than not, is that they know something about
business. The head of the Mecklenburg-Vorpommern State Bank is one
Dr. Wiebering, bourgeois anti-Fascist, all right, Forgbert's a Communist
and he's vice president and supposedly he'll pick up the banking business
but will he? As for you, you're a bit up in the air—every file comes across
your desk, you sign the permit, a duplicate of every order is filed, but now
this deputy of yours, Dr. Dr. Heinrich Grimm, what did he do after the
Nazis kicked him out of office as a district councilman? He says he behaved
properly. What does that mean? Who is this Elise Bock: almost all your
files pass through her hands and typewriter but who is she going around
with, why doesn't she want to join the party? Of course you'd trust her any
day over all these people who come running with their applications for
party membership, talking about their good will, offering up the exceptional
German path to Socialism as their justification, they don't have the faint-
est glimmer of an idea about the party, you need to find an empty building
somewhere or other in this district of Gneez where you can teach them,
sound them out, prepare them for the party, since you're not allowed to
refuse them membership. This language! *Kåååmen sei, so kåååmen sei nich;
kåååmen sei nich, so kåååmen sei; if they come then they dont come and if
they dont come they do come so its better when they dont come so they do come
than when they do come so they dont come* ... Once you've slowly finally
learned to understand the words then what are they talking about? At least
if it were a riddle, but no: it's a problem predicting the future, and what's
the answer? *Duven un Arwten.* You had to get that translated for you.
Tauben und Erbsen. Pigeons and peas. Hopes for the harvest. All right.
Not that you're homesick for Mannheim, the Allies have blown it to bits
anyway, but down there in Baden the people wouldn't look at you so funny
just because of how you talk. There's plenty for the Communist Party to
do in the Neckar region too. Now your proper place is wherever the party
sends you. But you could think of another place.
 – Don't make me a whiner, Gesine!

– You're twenty-three! You want everything to be perfect. The party must be pure. And all you've got is pure chaos. Hodgepodge. Odds and ends and none of it fits together.

– That I can understand. It's like in that Soviet film we just saw. Where the Red Army man loses his party book. To him that was worse than . . . than if you woke up tomorrow morning in a hotel room in Outer Mongolia and had lost your passport. I get him, I think. And if he can't handle Mecklenburgish right off then let him keep talking Russian. With his friends.

– That's what they were called. You were allowed to call them that.

– Dancing at the Dom Ofitserov! Not everyone gets to do that.

– As if you have time for that! You get to the office, for once you're going to clear your desk of the ten-day pile of leftover paperwork, and Triple-J phones you up. Mr. Schumann: he says. They'd almost gotten to first-name-basis brotherhood the night before last, hadn't they? Well, maybe he forgot. What else does he have to say? Wants to know whether you've been to the station. Have you been to the station, Mr. Schumann? That's it. End of conversation. You have someone drive you to the station, gun in your coat pocket, must be some kind of dustup going on there, what else could it be. What it is is a freight train full of resettlers, transfers, from Pommern, from Poland, and they're sick, and have lice, and now once again the city is faced with typhus. These few hundred people could infect forty thousand. Now you've got to waste three days—burying the dead, setting up a hospital in the Barracks of the Solidarity of Peoples, ordering the doctors onto night duty—while your Social Democratic mayor spends a few extra days on his official trip to Schwerin. Does Triple-J ever once show up, take a look around, intimidate the stretcher bearers a little? On the contrary, the station and the streets around it are declared off-limits to the Red Army. And what does Jenudkidse say on the fourth day? – Good boy: he says. You don't lose faith in him, you don't imagine yourself as his equal, but he could be nicer when he tells you certain things, not quite so patronizing. You get it, this unification with the Social Democratic morons can't be avoided. Tactical reasons are reasons. The whole People's Front thing has to happen. You give Triple-J reports on the problems with the bourgeois parties; you make it funny, with amusing details, you don't complain. You get the new farmers to trust their property, you remind them of the Count von Gröbern who told the Prussian parliament that he needed three oxen in his fields, two to pull the plow and one to drive it—finally the people believe that you're trying to bring them justice. In Wehrlich they invited you to the celebration after the drawing of lots. You danced. A woman put her arms around you, not out of gratitude, just because she felt so happy. You turned red, and the men helped you out of your embarrassment by slapping you on the shoulder, and for one afternoon you weren't an outsider. Then the SMA sends you men from its own Centralized Agricultural Planning Office— well-dressed well-fed gentlemen, one with a pince-nez—and at a public, authorized meeting they prove that Mecklenburg's climate and soil quality make it the best region in the country for the cultivation and propagation of seed potatoes, enough to feed half of Germany, it won't take more than, say, 1,500,000 acres of estate land staying in large, undivided plots. And there goes three weeks of agitprop. The people don't believe you anymore. They start asking each other if they're really working the land for themselves. This is the hot water the Red Army has gotten you into with its People's Front, 1936 model. All of a sudden you realize that they were just letting the bourgeoisie talk their talk, the land has been divided up and distributed and it'll stay that way. You apply yourself with a little patience and suss out the ultraclever variation being played out before your eyes and you forgive Triple-J for everything, almost everything.

– He was having his fun with the bourgeoisie.

– All you can do with the bourgeoisie is laugh at them. They're playing hide-and-seek with you and you're playing it with them. They think they're so smart when they can fill the post of building monitor with one of their own people, after the old one moves away or dies, and you just turn him, the second step is to warn him, the third is to reward him, and now the party knows everything it needs to know about what's going on in that building, or at least as much as they did before. When the elections for block monitor come up, the bourgeoisie get nowhere. Some people compare the new building monitors with the Nazi building wardens but you just don't get it, you weren't here then, those days are over; the question you maybe ask back is who they think should collect the fees for the ration cards? They think their meetings are secret; you're in stitches laughing at Stoffregen, this local historian who tallies up all the things about the new administration that are Mecklenburgish, i.e., conducive to Mecklenburg sovereignty and eventually unification with Denmark. In Rostock a Dr. Kaltenborn turns up trying to prevent the demolition of the Ernst Heinkel AG factory with the argument that the British don't consider Heinkel a war criminal; in Bützow, after a liquid-oxygen plant in the Peenemünde Center has been demolished and is being rebuilt, the owners come from the West and offer their services on the condition that you don't bother them with a second demolition later—after a while you can only shake your head at the ingenuity of these people who can't even figure out where they are. Let them think you've been Russified, that you're a helpless babe in the woods of German culture: one day you too notice how often the party slogans are inscribed centered on walls, and you put a stop to that nonsense, not mad, with a burst of laughter that takes you entirely by surprise, that expands your rib cage, they like that. Someday they'll like you too.

– The one thing he can't forgive Triple-J for. Slata?

– Yes, well, you are twenty-three . . .

– In that case I don't want to be that after all. She goes out with a German and he defects to the Soviets. Maybe at the same time.

– If Triple-J didn't mind, why should you?

– It's a dirty trick.

– Maybe Slata told a clean story. She hadn't run away with the British, she'd waited for her own people. What do I know?

– Exactly. What do you know.

– Now you need to take the insult with the injury. There's talk going around your own party that you'd have taken Slata if she'd have brought you Triple-J. You know what that's called: careerism. Their ideas of you don't match your idea of yourself. But you want them to.

– You have no way to know that.

– He had a photograph hanging in his room. It showed Triple-J, Jenudkidse's adjutant, his political adviser, and a random young woman standing behind the three of them, blond, sporty, the only one not smiling.

– Alma Witte. She shouldn't have showed you that.

– She did it to show me he was a brave young man. So that I wouldn't make any dumb comments when he walked past us. She too wanted to bring me up right. I was supposed to realize that even someone like that can have cares and sorrows like a normal person.

– That's why he stayed in the City of Hamburg Hotel.

– Almost directly under Slata's room.

– But he had power?

– Never before had a Gneez district councilman had so much power. It grew and grew every week, too, the more other people thought that he had all the power. He liked it.

June 19, 1968 Wednesday

This morning the blind beggar on Lexington Avenue (my days are darker than your nights) set up a yellow bucket of tasty-looking clear water for his dog. This evening the rim of the bowl is smeared and the water silted with dirt. Especially civilized passersby tossed their charity of coins into the water.

In the main hall of Grand Central Station, amid the monstrous blend of noise, footsteps, and tangles of voices, there is another, smaller sound, much better known, getting quite unreasonably louder in the ramps to the commuter trains. It comes from a man collecting the subway tokens from the turnstiles. The tokens rattle against the gray metal and the bucket scrapes against the floor when the man moves on. A wide squat bucket, the kind we had for horses to drink from.

At night, a storm stays over the river, not moving. Lightning flashes turn the park into silhouettes; sometimes, their bright white shaded, they light up only the opposite shore. Some, the very short, barely perceivable ones, etch sharp furrows into the brain.

As children, in haystacks, caught in a storm, we thought: Someone can see us. We are all seen.

PART FOUR

June 1968–August 1968

June 20, 1968 Thursday

WOKEN by a flat cracking sound in the park, like gunshots. People standing at the bus stop across the street, unafraid. Behind them, children playing war.

Our newsstand at Ninety-Sixth Street is covered. No papers today, due to a death. The old man could have at least written whether the death was his. The weeklies are covered, too, with a weathered plastic sheet. The customers come up as usual, stop a few paces from the grave-mound-like bundles, and peel off in an embarrassed arc. No one tries to steal anything. A customer still groggy with sleep expects the handwritten cardboard sign to say: Closed out of respect for...who?

In the tunnel under the subway platforms a boy in a yarmulke walks past a whiskey poster on which someone has added, in cursive, twice: Fuck The Jew Pigs. The boy holds his head as if he doesn't see it.

In Grand Central Station there was one *New York Times* left. Weather: partly sunny, partly cool. Kept: the photo of Adolf Heinz Beckerle, former German ambassador to Bulgaria, on trial for complicity in the 1943 deportation of eleven thousand Jews to the Treblinka death camp. Since he suffers from sciatica he is lying dressed in business clothes on a stretcher, between the blanket and pillow, and two Frankfurt policeman are carefully carrying him up the courthouse steps. Frankfurt am Main.

Sometimes the final stage of waking up happens only at the fountain outside the passage to the Graybar Building. Today two men are clinging to its sides, alternately bending down and raising their heads high like chickens, numbing their hangovers.

Today the beggar outside the bank has a red bucket for his dog.

Approximately thirty people can attest that Mrs. Cresspahl entered her office at 8:55 and did not leave until 4:05!

Four fifteen during this deferred lunch hour was the only appointment that Boccaletti the hair stylist could find all week for his customer Mrs. Cresspahl. The other regulars are sitting in the waiting room, including the two ladies who enjoy addressing each other with tender solicitude, each happily certain that the other is a lot worse off than she is herself. There were signs a long time ago, back when we were fleeing, in Marseilles, you remember. Mrs. Cresspahl would have liked to hear more of this spoken German but Signor Boccaletti summons her over in more of a hurry than usual. He's not trying to gain a few extra moments for the next customer, he's wanting to complain about how very very far away Bari is, where they do things differently. He flings two hands covered in lather into the air and only then can he cry: *Signora, uccidere per due dollari? Ma!*

(Giogrio Boccaletti, Madison Avenue, is requested to write to *The New York Times* advice column—discretion guaranteed—and say how much money *would* make it worth it.)

Delays on the West Side line's express track. The loudspeaker promises, in a growl that gets gruffer with each repetition: The local will be stopping at all express stations. It's impossible to imagine a human being behind that distorted voice, and anyway, local trains always stop at express stops! I didn't make it on till the third train, where there was not enough air to breathe.

For ten minutes I stood in front of a poster exhorting us to SUPPORT OUR SERVICEMEN. Below the words was an SOS in Morse code, and below that a photograph of a white soldier giving a blood transfusion to a black soldier. Support our servicemen. On the left, under a red cross: HELP US HELP. According to Amanda Williams's reliable information, this poster secretly means: The Americans are in dire peril in Vietnam.

Then two Negro women executed an almost simultaneous rotation of their bodies around their respective central axes, and moved their neighbors along with them, so I could stand facing away from the poster.

On Broadway another Negro, perhaps drunk, staggered into a deli and greeted the proprietor with a word I don't know. – And if you don't want to hear that then get lost! he shouts. He stumbles on between the glass cases and gives a revolutionary speech that no one understands a word of. The proprietor, in a slight crouch, hands on the counter by the cash register, watches the enemy from under his brows, not at all upset.

At home Marie has flowers. There were originally a dozen peonies, for six dollars, and – Then there was a Puerto Rican woman there with her little kid, nine years old, and the girl wanted some too and the mother kept saying: *But they don't last, child!* So I waited for the girl outside the door and gave her six of mine. Is that okay, Gesine? Hey, *talk to me!*

– I approve, Marie. But why were you getting flowers at all?

– It's Karsch's birthday today! Do they take out your memory too, at the bank? It's Karsch's birthday!

In the mail there's a letter from Europe, in which someone appeals to Mrs. Cresspahl's acquaintance with him and wants her to put that connection in writing, for a festschrift. A testimonial of friendship, made to order.

June 21, 1968 Friday

Military exercises on Czechoslovak soil involving the Soviet, Hungarian, East German, and Polish armies along with the Czechoslovaks officially began yesterday. According to Ivan I. Yakubovsky, marshal of the Soviet Union, only command staff and signal, transport, and auxiliary units would be involved. There was no indication of how long the exercises would last.

– Okay, Marie, what's needed to hold free and open elections?

– They had elections in Mecklenburg too? Well they could just use whatever was there, couldn't they.

– They could if they had to, Marie. So what would that be?

– First you need parties. You had those. Second, the people in the parties have to invite in people who aren't in the parties. They have to promise them something more or something different than the other parties. A party that's not in power has to have the same rights as the party that is in power. If the parties can't include all the people who aren't in parties, they have to persuade the rest with newspapers, fliers, posters. Third, when it's time to vote, they need arbiters or referees, who only care about the rules— people voting voluntarily, in secret, the votes being counted properly—and don't give a hoot about the parties. Then you need people who aren't sick of it all and actually want to vote. There are *some* people I know who don't even care anymore.

– But the borders had been closed since June 30, 1946. The Soviets had done that in their own interest, but still in the Control Council with the Western Allies. They'd also wanted everyone in Mecklenburg to stay in Mecklenburg and face the demands of the day there. The municipal elections were on the Mecklenburg calendar for September 15. Mina Köpcke, to her dying day, couldn't have said what she had in her hands except when it was Duvenspeck's soft neck; all the same, she too said: Why should we let anything slip out of them?

– I know who won. This is getting boring.

– It wasn't boring for the Socialist Unity Party's campaign manager in the Gneez district. It was dicey, downright unpleasant. In the weeks before the election he often had the creepy feeling that someone was standing behind him in the dark. He couldn't figure out who it was. It turned out splendidly for him and his friends; he would say: It's all nice and cozy! He wasn't stupid, he'd learned something from January's municipal elections in Hesse, when the Socialists had gotten eight times as many votes as his own party; the Gneez district was one of the first where the Social Democrats gave up on their party and joined him in the new one; eventually the Central Committee had no choice but to believe and obey the call for unification rising up from below. He'd talked himself blue in the face! He'd had to promise the Socialists so much: clean procedures for organizing the economy, which they were weirdly insistent on; not transposing every last thing Lenin said and wrote into the German situation; fundamentally honoring the particular German path of democracy, if only for as long as the capitalist class remained on the soil of democracy, and then, unfortunately, the path of revolution, which the Socialists seemed to see as opposed to democracy. Everything promised, signed, sealed, and transcribed. That suited him fine—he stuck to what the comrades from Kröpelin had done, having the resolution to unify the parties signed by the mayor and assistant mayor and the chief of police too. They started calling Kröpelin their *sister city*, in Platt. Oh yes, he'd learned. He'd run into Social Democrats who called unified meetings with him only when the local Soviet commandants ordered them to. Some of them didn't get it until they were ordered to resign early. There'd been a lot of evenings that were pleasant enough, even fun: he had signatures in his collection which plainly showed the exuberant zest of the vodka. These were the rogues he was sharing his party with now; it was for them that they'd abandoned the title "German People's Daily" in favor of Neues Deutschland, "New Germany"; more than half the members of the Unity Party were former Socialists; but it was also true that the votes people cast for them wouldn't be going to them alone. That reassured him. So why did he have that flickering feeling in his wrists whenever the municipal elections so much as flitted through his mind, not even settling into conscious awareness?

– He feared for his good name, this Gerd Schumann.

– You shouldn't say it like that, Marie. He didn't like hearing "Gerd," it had a falsely young ring to it, childish even. And just one syllable. When Triple-J said it there was almost nothing left. Slata had always called him "Comrade Gär-kha't" when he was there, though always as if he weren't. And she was truly speaking to him, he felt. As for "Schumann," what was memorable about that? It practically invited you to forget him. He felt detached from such a stillborn name himself. "Comrade District Councilman" was better—it at least reminded him of what he had to do. (How happy he'd have been to hear his nickname, "Redhead," if only he'd ever caught wind of it!)

– Maybe this Comrade District Councilman of yours was scared they wouldn't pick him!

– That would be enough to wake you up in the middle of the night, in sweat-soaked sheets? In August? In a building as cool, its walls as thick, as the City of Hamburg Hotel, in a room with a breeze from the west? Worries like that can ruin your sleep?

– Gesine, I was just saying. In case the voters saw Comrade District Councilman and his party as tools of the Soviets.

– Don't tell him that. You'd make his heavy eyes widen and darken with surges of blood; you'd have done much more than insult him a little. You'd have wounded him, truly ambushed him, his shoulders would crumple. You'd feel bad—a handsome young guy like that, reddish-gray stubble on his red face, innocent lips now bitterly pinched together. Almost desperately, practically paralyzed, he would ask you who, if not he and his party, was working in the national interest. No! For someone to see him, him of all people, as a stooge!

– All right then, sorry bout that. He's just friends with the Soviets.

– You can say that again. He's their ally. He knows that. He's grateful to them, and not in the bourgeois way either, where all that matters is material things. Though of course they help you that way too. When you need a car the commandant sends you one, complete with driver and as much gas as you need, vouchers too. Grimm doesn't get all that, Christian Democrat as he's unmasked himself as being—he doesn't even get time off for campaign trips, he needs to get the district administration in order first. If a bourgeois local branch in Old Demweis seems a little fishy, you can just say so and before you know it the SMA has revoked its registration. There were 2,404 municipalities in Mecklenburg and the Liberals wanted 152 local branches for them—they should be happy with 65! The Christian Democrats tried to register 707 local branches; they'll be lucky to get 237! Your party, though, gets an office everywhere, and your *New Germany* is for sale in every store, and the *Tägliche Rundschau* too, daily as promised; you think the Soviets should slog away with things like *Neue Zeit* or *Der Morgen*, which come out only twice a week anyway? At first your jaw drops when your party gets eight hundred tons of paper for marketing while the CDU and LDPD are allocated just nine tons between them—but then you see why. What do they have to say anyway. What do they know. The people have to be given the right information, you won't disappoint your friends; while the bourgeoisie are still wrangling with the local commandants for permits for their meetings or posters, you've already been sweeping through five villages. You don't need to submit your speeches for approval, and anyway you speak without a script. And if you're stuck in the deepest woods near the coast with engine trouble, who comes and gets you, in a jeep, with a spare car? The Red Army—they sacrifice time and manpower to get you to your next meeting, in Beidendorf, almost on time. And anyway, a Communist is the only man friends can know for sure is a natural-born foe of Fascism to the death; there was nothing to worry about there, that tremor, which passed through his brain as he fell asleep and sometimes half the night through, couldn't be coming from that.

– What else does he need to be grateful for, Gesine? It's like having Rockefeller help you in an election!

– What else is he grateful for? For being taught the right way to think! The Red Army doesn't just give him rent-free housing with Alma Witte, bring him food from the city's communal provisions, eventually give him a leather jacket and a pair of ankle boots, used but that's all right. No, his bodily comforts are not enough, and he would forgo those if he had to, as long as your friends go on making sure that your mouth doesn't get stuck, like the flounder's after he'd gulped down a dozen herring. The things they taught him! Let's take the word: *election.* In the beginning he used it to refer to something that actually exists. Everyone means the same thing by it, no one has more control over it than anyone else, it's a simple label for your current assignment from the party. Then J. J. Jenudkidse summons you to Town Hall, in the middle of a workday, and these are five minutes you will never forget. Triple-J, all fake unapproachability, is sitting behind an empty desk, in front of a three-foot-wide three-foot-high portrait of Goethe, next to Dr. Beese who is supplementing her income by giving German lessons in Town Hall. Both of them are giving you a silent, rogu-ish look, as if to say that you're in for a surprise. But no one purses his lips as impishly as Jenudkidse. He asks you one single question—just one word, a German one: *Wahlkampf.* "Election." And you've grasped once and for all your special ownership over the *Wahl* or choice, the different choices, the *Kampf* or struggle, the hostilities, and of course the enemies required for there to be such a thing; you wanted to explain it to Elise Bock but she just put the folder of signatures down in front of you again, perfectly calm, not interested in your excitement. You can hardly wait the few days until the meetings, until the moment when the respective mayor introduces you as the comrade from the district and at last you can start your speech! You don't come to the office for days, you can be reached only by phone and chance in the villages around Gneez, ten meetings a day are one too few as far as you're concerned and you show up to the eleventh like a boxer, and wherever you wake up you find a slip of paper next to the bed that you've scribbled full of the ideas that've come to you, that'll help you do even better! Then you think maybe you're feeling guilty.

– Keep talking, Gesine.

– The first harvest on free soil. The Junkers' ruthless exploitation, from the twenties right through to the liberation. Three hundred thousand more acres cultivated than in 1945. The Red Army halts the dismantling of the Neptun docks in Rostock, creates jobs by setting up an SAG. The Hanse-atic dockyard in Wismar is expanded around the Dornier factory, given harbor equipment from Szczecin (formerly known as Stettin). The Soviet Union is helping, as brothers, and not only today, it always has. The *Krassin,* the same Soviet icebreaker that saved the crew of the airship *Italia* in the summer of 1928 after it crashed and was trapped in the ice off Spitsbergen, also battled to rescue the icebound ships off Warnemünde in the winter of 1929, including the ferryboat to Denmark. But it wasn't about the Soviets, it wasn't about the dictatorship of the proletariat, it was about the New Beginning, the Reconstruction, in alliance with the anti-Fascist forces, including the bourgeois ones, insofar as they're honest. Neglect of the victors' anti-Fascist obligations on the part of the English and Americans, Nazis left in the government there, in the police, in the Schutzpolizei, in the Gneez gendarmerie. Swept out of power, the country cleaned up, parliamentary democracy, all democratic rights and freedoms to the people— under the protection of the Soviet Union.

– "SAG"?

– Sowjetische Aktiengesellschaft. Soviet joint-stock corporation.

– I wasn't asking for a definition, I was heckling.

– *When in Rome.* . . . Use the bourgeois economic forms at hand.

– Equal rights for women. Women get less tobacco rations on their cards than men!

– Alcohol too. Well, there it is. That's why Comrade District Councilman always carried a packet containing two cigarettes on him. He'd throw it in the general direction of the woman complaining, shouting: Take them! My last ones! And first things first: massive election turnout, victory for the Socialist Unity Party (for the name if nothing else), then we'll handle this. It looked cute, actually, him shrugging his shoulders in his leather jacket and giving a slightly pained smile—giving up his last two cigarettes!

– He wasn't a smoker himself.

– Of course not. Got his pairs of single cigarettes from the Red Army commissary.

– And then he lost the vote.

– Then he lost. In the September 15 municipal elections the LDPD and CDU received almost twenty-five percent of the votes cast. His party, along with the allied Farmers' Aid and Women's Committees, received a mere sixty-six out of a hundred. He was truly crestfallen, avoided Triple-J and everything. Only got through his first night by drinking. No matter how insistently he told himself that it had, after all, been a fight, the fact was he hadn't won it overwhelmingly. More than a quarter of the people in Mecklenburg didn't trust him. Plus he'd disappointed his friends. Now he thought he could put his finger on what he'd been feeling during the past few weeks: fear of failure, a premonition of defeat. Someone older would have felt relieved at least to know; at twenty-three, he was almost beyond help.

June 22, 1968 Saturday

In České Budějovice there's a bishop who'd been out of commission for sixteen years, i.e., expelled from his diocese and under house arrest. Last Sunday he was permitted to celebrate mass once again in his St. Nikolaus Cathedral, in the presence of three representatives of the secular authorities, who acted perfectly polite. The very next Tuesday, the police called him to tell him about a man who'd lost a large sum of money while counting it on a train at an open window. Might the custodians of law and order bring this unfortunate man over, to receive from the bishop the kind of consolation a police precinct couldn't give?

The Bishop from Budweis could only consider such a request, from the selfsame state that had deported him in March 1951 (then too using a detail of three men), as a most heartening symbol of his future in the ČSSR.

In the second autumn after the war, Cresspahl's daughter stopped giving Pastor Brüshaver the time of day. She didn't even try to pretend she hadn't noticed this man of the cloth. She saw him all right—who didn't? His thinness was not from the past year's hunger—the Nazi camp seemed to have restructured his whole body into a small-boned frugal model; the pants and coats of 1937 flapped about him, flapped from his careful, almost stiff movements too. Nor did Gesine give Brüshaver an ostentatious refusal to greet him—she showed that she recognized him, the way a person walks right by something familiar and of no further use. Just as Brüshaver had managed in the past without pride and severity, he tried for a while to nod at her—first, even though he was the elder! Then he'd just look at the child, without reproach, without seeming puzzled; so then the child could top it off by denying outright any acquaintance at all in this exchange of glances.

Jakob generally recognized soon enough when Cresspahl's daughter got such a bee in her bonnet; it's just he rarely managed to talk the bee back out. Jakob was dissatisfied with himself as head of the household.

The household had shrunk: he'd had only three people to report on the People's Census, plus Cresspahl, Heinrich, under the heading "Resident But Absent." The NKVD's Sunday labors in September had done their job, even more so the rumors trying to make all paths lead back to the mayor who'd been hauled off. By the end of September all the refugees moved out, even the teacher from Marienwerder, who'd rather live way out in the Wehrlich forester's lodge with two other families and look after her baby boy on her own than stay any longer among such dangerous enemies of the Soviets. The housing office didn't make up for these departures; even the new batch of Sudeten German resettlers were warned in time by the refugees already established in Jerichow to avoid the lonely house on Brickworks Road, right across from the Kommandatura—a place of countless house searches, a dead loss for future prospects. Living in isolation, like in a haunted house, were Gesine in her little room, Mrs. Abs in Cresspahl's big parlor, and Jakob on the other side of the hall. In the back part they used only the kitchen and, every now and then, put Mr. Krijgerstam or kindred business partners up in one of the pantries. It was a real household only in the evenings; at breakfast Mrs. Abs made lunch for the two others, then the door was locked until everyone came home from work and school, unsupervised. At that point there was sometimes a light on where Cresspahl used to do his writing: the child was doing her homework, Mrs. Abs was carding wool, and Jakob, on nights without overtime or business appointments, would furtively watch the others over the top of his Russian dictionary, head of the household, dissatisfied with himself.

His mother had handed him both the official status of head of household and the actual responsibility of running it even before Cresspahl's disappearance, as soon as he'd refused to participate in the land lottery. However much he'd disappointed her, the farm property had been intended to be his in any case. She didn't want to discuss it any further, not even attempts at explanation or apology. Her job cooking at the hospital left her just enough energy to make dinner and keep things moderately clean. It was he who'd decided that they should stay with this utterly parentless child, in a strange house, in a rural part of Mecklenburg without more than a few dozen square feet of garden—let him manage it. He was old enough. Let him be responsible. Anyway she was busy waiting for her husband. She described neither him nor Cresspahl as someone who would return as a judge to condemn Jakob's stewardship. And as for her, Jakob thought she was resigned, if not content. This strange child, Gesine Cresspahl, on the other hand was unfathomable to him. She had shaken hands with Brüshaver at Amalie Creutz's grave. Was it only because they'd been there to assist the mourners? She had obediently accompanied her father to the first church service this Brüshaver had held after the war—the fourth time total she had set foot in St. Peter's Church since her christening, same as Cresspahl. So why not since? She was only thirteen, after all; what could a child like that know about the pros and cons of the Protestant congregation?

He did see her making distinctions. If it was in fact contempt she was showing to various particular adults. If there was anything at all she was trying to show. So, for instance, she would sometimes come back on the same train as Dr. Kliefoth—they'd have shared a compartment and would walk together down Station Street to the corner of the market square; the old man and the child had no need to talk, they clearly belonged together. Were allies. From earlier times? Jakob had no way of knowing. This Kliefoth was a university-educated man, like Brüshaver, someone to show respect to—to him she practically curtseyed, while Brüshaver she left in the dust like an empty shopwindow. Then there was Louise Papenbrock, the girl's natural grandmother, and the girl would cross the street to avoid her. That might go back to habits from her father's time—impossible to know, as always. But she'd let Heinz Wollenberg stop her for a chat. Just because she took the train to school with his Lise? With Peter Wulff she would stop on her own; she would talk to him. Jakob could see this with his own eyes, and she'd tell him about it. Usually it was about Cresspahl. Then Jakob would keep his mouth shut and his eyes on the Cyrillic column in his book—he didn't think Cresspahl was coming back. (In his view, Cresspahl was dead.) If she needed comfort, she should go get it from the man whose job was to provide it. But to him she wouldn't give the time of day.

While well brought up children always greet their elders. Right, Jakob?
We certainly wanted you to learn such things.
Because you'd never been around people like Stoffregen.
There was something between you and the church, Gesine. After a year in Jerichow I knew that much.

Did you go to St. Peter's Church on Sundays, or out to Johnny's?

Gesine, we weren't from your denomination. I didn't feel like going to Gneez just because there was someone there from the Old Lutheran Church in Schwerin every three months.

Didn't I go to the Old Lutheran services in Gneez with your mother? I brought her there. I stayed there. I sang along with them!

Stoffregen was with the Nazis. He'd beaten children. Brüshaver spent seven years in the camps. Lost four children of his own. And instead of giving himself a rest he goes into politics.

Exactly.

And you won't say hello on the street.

He went into politics with the Soviets. The Soviets had my father. Brüshaver didn't get Cresspahl out of Soviet hands. He didn't even try.

That's how you divided people up? Into friends and enemies? Is that what children are like?

What were you like when you were thirteen, Jakob?

Lately the incomprehensible Cresspahl child had gotten involved in the black market. Johnny Schlegel had been able to unload another two sacks of wheat flour at Brickworks Road on the wagon's way back from the town scales—all aboveboard and in good faith, though Kägebein and the Papenbrock granary would probably have to chalk up a little extra loss to the Red Army. Or to himself. Or to no one at all. Whatever these two sacks might have turned into on the highways and byways of bookkeeping, in reality: Jakob thought: they'd been standing in the back pantry for some two days. Suddenly this Gesine forbade the conversion of the wheat. Because half belonged to Hanna? Her share of the profit could be forwarded. No. Because only Gesine was entitled to make decisions about her property? He'd be happy to discuss it with her. She didn't give a damn about his discussions, she didn't want to sell. He calculated for her that she had six thousand marks sitting in those two sacks, but money that would go bad. That was 160 hundredweight of coal. She could get a winter coat out of it—thread, lining, dependable tailoring—with a fortune left over. He knew someone who would part with a pair of winter boots in her size, used of course, for 560 marks, ten percent cheaper if paid for in wheat flour. This was an evening during the winter of 1946, when he was explaining to her the ways to commercially exploit her harvest earnings: the stove was already burning coal converted from butter (four pounds per hundredweight), the lamp burning the oil he'd laid in for the winter (one mandel-dozen eggs). He hardly seemed very enthusiastic in laying out these calculations for her because such transactions would cost him a lot of time, not to mention the distances, but he was happy to do his part toward paying a real rent in this house. He was even sure that he hadn't used a didactic tone, he certainly hoped not; all of a sudden the child leapt up—you try to understand it—snatched up her school notebooks as if someone was trying to rip them out of her hands, and ran off. Jakob was left with the slam of the door; a shake of the head from his mother, whose veiled derision was aimed at him, not the girl; and two shouts from Gesine that scared him. Not because they were unjust but simply because he couldn't make heads or tails of what she was shouting. Is this how children are?

Jakob didn't understand. The next morning the child apologized to him. Breathing heavily as she chewed. Asked if he'd really meant it. What, accepting her apology? Of course, it was nothing. No, his plan for the winter. Then this child stands facing the window and resists so stubbornly as he tries to pull her by her braids that eventually the older boy lets go and promises, in a dignified, distinctly reserved manner: Whatever you want, Gesine.

Vilami na vodje?
No. Not written with a fork in the water, as you put it.

This was on the Sunday before the state elections, so they had plenty of time to draw up the plan according to which the wheat would be converted into enough supplies to last until next spring. For a long time Jakob felt uneasy in these meetings because of Gesine's submissive acquiescence to everything. He felt like he was cheating her. She approved of whatever he wanted to lay in—shoe soles, new wool, fire starters; he'd have preferred an occasional protest. He was all the more taken aback by her one and only condition, which he had blindly promised to accept: not only the list of commodities was to be agreed on between them but every trade route, every business partner had to be discussed with her.

He thought she was curious—children are like that. He agreed, with misgivings. He tried to keep some things secret; this Gesine was liable to go to a partner and start asking questions. She was Cresspahl's daughter and she got answers, since they thought she already knew in any case. There was no way around it, he had to tell her Mr. Krijgerstam's business, and from then on this skillful veteran from the Baltic fleet rarely got from the firm of Abs & Cresspahl the bacon he needed to exchange for the oil painting in his Razno-Export, however set on it his sense of art appreciation might be. The connection with Knoop the bigwig ran dry for a while too—here Gesine had heard around town in Gneez more precise information than Jakob could come by in Jerichow: Knoop had been nabbed, he'd tried to go big a bit too fast. The NEP isn't so easy to tackle for everyone, Emil had to learn that the hard way. There was no doubt that she knew more about people in Jerichow. That's how Jakob ended up with Jöche, a friend until fall 1956; that's what brought him together with Peter Wulff, a bond as lasting and irrevocable as any on this earth.

Jakob had heard that the children in both Jerichow and Gneez schools carried on a trade in the ration stamps they were meant to hand in for their school meals. But this Gesine wanted to know about every shoemaker he approached, every lawyer who turned up, and this even after they were long since past the two hundred pounds of wheat flour. She learned too much. She ended up involved in business that was dangerous, and not only for children. This isn't how you teach children by example. This isn't how you head a household.

And why wouldn't she have it any other way—who could figure it out?

Maybe his mother was right and this Cresspahl child was in need of religious instruction. Gesine had a bee in her bonnet about that, he'd certainly realized that by now. But how should he try to talk the bee out of it?

June 23, 1968 Sunday

At midnight the American war in Southeast Asia became the longest in the history of the United States, if we assume that the Revolutionary War ended with the British surrender at Yorktown on Oct. 19, 1781. This war has lasted six years, six months, and now two days.

Yesterday five Vietnamese children arrived at LaGuardia Airport in a military aircraft on their way to hospitals here. The boys are named Nguyen Bien, ten, hit by a bullet that went through his back on Jan. 8; Doan Van Yen, twelve, wounded by rocket fire on March 4; Le Sam, eleven, third-degree burns by napalm on March 31; and Nguyen Lau, nine, paralyzed below the waist by a gunshot wound in the spine about nine months ago. *The New York Times* photographed the girl, eight-year-old Le Thi Thum, who came down the staircase in white pajamas, eager and smiling. The *Times* did not get any closer. In words she adds that the girl has a scar across her face and that her nose is there but lacks a bridge. A *Nasenbrücke*? *Nasensteg*?

– No. *Nasenbein.*

For Mrs. Cresspahl is traveling with her daughter through the towns and forests north of New York, on trains, on buses, in taxis, so they share the paper and one corrects the other's language. Every child has a right to an education. The town squares are quiet, looking forward to lunchtime; in one park, a policeman is motionless on his spot like a monument to himself, an equestrian statue with a radio to his ear; in the woods the creeks running down from the mountains are so clear that you'd think you could drink from them without risk of death. It's a day trip; it's a business trip. Every year around this time we have to find somewhere for the child to spend the summer: Marie has a right to a vacation. She inspects country manors, shantytowns, campsites in New Rochelle, Mamaroneck, Peekskill; what she cares about is how long the bus ride is to New York. For we've agreed to just four weeks in Prague and she might want to stay here and wait. She pesters the foreman of one construction site with serious negotiations: paying children are apparently supposed to transform the plot into a recreation area with their own hands, since the brochure promises "creative activities." The man is genuinely tormented—clearly it gives him a headache to confront matters like sculpture . . . cardiovascular activity . . . French courses in the rain. Two hundred dollars a month. Late in the afternoon, Marie finds a camp on Long Island Sound, half an hour from Riverside Drive, with a brisk lady at the counter holding out no creative prospects at all. She rattles off in military fashion what the place offers: Size of camp (in sq. ft.), two pools, completely supervised athletics, thirty-five years of day-camp experience, regular service to and from Manhattan, insurmountable chain-link fence cordoning off the camp from life-threatening natural water. And, due to the planes taking off or landing every two minutes from LaGuardia Airport across the Sound, a discount price of thirty-five dollars a week.

For six hours we've been meeting Americans who've been acting like friends, far above and beyond the requirements of business: the teacher whose art practice involves making mobiles, the custodian, the woman driving the taxi, even the hapless man asked to market a desolate construction site as a children's paradise thanks to the presence of a few forests on steep hills nearby. On one train, the conductor not only invited Marie into his cabin but let her hold the lever and push it forward and now she knows what's it's like to be all the way in the front when you drive into the tunnel under North River. In Yonkers we were allowed into a bar even though the male clientele had just started their afternoon drinking; the owner may have wanted to offer to one and all the Italian cuisine listed on his sign, and he brought out pizza, Italian-style. Marie decided in Yonkers. The soldierly conduct had won the day. That's where it'd be. Across from LaGuardia.

– You know, huh? You think you know me? Tell me, Gesine.
– Forty-five dollars for children.
– Fifteen dollars a week saved. That makes sixty.
– This committee is acting in the name of "responsibility," Marie?
– I'm not responsible and neither are you. Does the money bother you?
– No. It's just that you're doing it out of pity.
– I'm not necessarily the kind of child you were, Gesine.
– Pity isn't genuine, Marie.
– Pity's not bad. I soothe my conscience for four weeks. It's practical, is what it is, don't you think?

June 24, 1968 Monday
The results of the Mecklenburg state election of October 20, 1946, are known. The Socialist Unity Party won forty-five seats, the Conservatives thirty-one, the Liberals eleven; Farmers' Mutual Aid were able to send

three representatives to Schwerin, and the Cultural League for a Democratic Renewal of Germany received not enough votes for even one.

In this new election as well, the campaign manager for the Gneez district had made his rounds with an uneasy feeling, perhaps due to his defeat in September; moreover, the feeling was different. True, the honor of the assignment had once again fallen to him, though this time more than just towns and villages were at stake so his failure could be all the more dire. He drove such fears out of his mind, once he'd recognized that they were selfish. A similar sensation remained, though: the certainty that something was coming that might ruin everything. He could feel it in the back of his neck, like the premonition of a blow. He could ward off a sudden attack, he knew how to deal with insubordination—he'd made his name doing such things—but what should he do in case of a real disaster? All you could see by looking at him was fatigue; on the inside he felt limp and weak. It wasn't because of the many repeat performances each and every day—those were fine, they enacted the truth. So what was it then?

When he drove into Jerichow he thought he'd caught a glimpse of at least a little piece of it. It was the last day before the election and he'd never set foot in this windy backwater that called itself a town. Perhaps he felt some pricks of conscience for having avoided this Jerichow. Slata, the intended wife of a murderous Fascist arsonist, had lived here for three years in a capitalist businessman's house; he had no desire to see the house, and especially not these in-laws of hers. The father, Papenbrock was his name wasn't it, was probably long since lining his pockets again as a middleman, under the Red Army's nose, safe and sound under its New Economic Policy; what a pleasure it would be to deal with him once they'd turned a new page. He decided not to ask about this Papenbrock. Admittedly there was a private aspect to this resolution; maybe for now, or until the votes were counted, it was enough not to admit such weaknesses to anyone but himself.

He stood with his back to the window of Papenbrock's emptied office, incognito, since without his car, driver, and leather coat he thought himself unrecognizable enough. The woman who squeezed out the door next to him was Louise Papenbrock, who used to have a maid to send on such errands. Now she had to walk down Town Street in person to alert her comrades, and the Liberals too, out of Christian duty, for the SMA had again denied them a list of candidates. Even Alfred Bienmüller learned within an hour that a stranger had come to town and had a car with driver and leather coat parked behind the freight shed.

For now, the evening's speaker was strolling down Town Street like someone who wanted to buy himself a little treat in this new place, not that he had anything definite in mind. Nothing he was secretly worried about could ever happen to him here. Plus he didn't know the object of his fear, which made the sensation inherently unscientific. The mayor here was from his own party, though his two advisers were Christian Democrats, and as a result the town hadn't received the full allotments on its ration cards in the past few weeks, though it certainly had gotten almost half the printed matter. That would help. His friends had also availed themselves of an element of bourgeois democracy in which a French Conservative would give amnesty to political enemies or a German Social Democrat would send flowers to a war criminal's daughter, assuring themselves of correct votes—here the dialectic had merely brought about a reversal: no flowers, arrest instead of amnesty. Gerd Schumann had ceased to find such rhetoric from this Ottje Stoffregen fellow witty or amusing; Ottje Stoffregen was now, today, unbolting rails on the Gneez–Herrnburg line and using his delicate teacher's hands to carry them off for transport to the Soviet Union. They certainly hadn't skimped on using the printed matter they'd received, either—almost every shopwindow, every yard gate had a poster of sufficient size stuck to it.

As soon as he read the first one, he knew for certain that his worries had turned up and reported for duty in the right place. What a godforsaken dump, this Jerichow. If only he'd never set foot in it.

The notices summoned the public to appear at tonight's political rally and were signed by Alfred Bienmüller on behalf of the Unity Party. The text opened with a personal description: Gerd Schumann, member of the German Army, admitted to the National Committee for a Free Germany after his desertion to the Red Army, twenty-three years old, district councilman. There were countless posters, all saying the same thing. At the brickworks he turned back, for there was Town Street's name visible for the first time on a sign on the cemetery wall. It was clearly the main street and did not bear the name of Generalissimo Josef Vissarionovich Stalin. An old-fashioned sign, with trim lines around the Gothic script, written

white on blue, all so attractive and undamaged that it looked like it had
spent a few years wrapped in wool in a drawer.

The evening's speaker hurried back to the market square. Which was
called Market Square.

And he was in the right place, the location gave him an almost complete
view of the train station's facade ("Most everyone in Jerichow has to go to
the station at least once a day"). He could see his driver on the steps, slapping his arms for warmth, right under the bedsheets with a slogan painted
in black on it:

FOR IMMEDIATE MERGER WITH THE SOVIET UNION!
VOTE SOCIALIST UNITY PARTY (SED)

and not even centered.

He got into an argument with Bienmüller almost immediately. As a
district councilman, he was used to being invited into the parlor for a
little bite, a little drink. As a comrade, as campaign manager, he took it for
granted that people would agree with him. This Bienmüller didn't leave
his muddy workshop yard, held a truck crank in his left hand as though it
weighed nothing, even kept his felt hat on so his face was largely hidden,
and actually bent down to continue his work.

– That business at the station—that's provocation! It's worse than in
Gneez, where they sent postcards saying things like "Are you a intellectual?
Vote SED! For the Latin scholars: that's BUT!"

– Huh.

– And you claim to be a comrade!

– *Innt that watcha want, m'boy? Doncha wanna join the Sooviet Union?*

– I demand that we clear this up right now with the commandant!

– *We don have one. Got two.*

– You'll explain your posters there, my friend.

– *Cant go there withiss jeep. Occupation orders.*

– Listen, comrade, you're not going to be mayor here for long!

– *Spose not. I'mma third one already.*

The evening's speaker, in the middle of his march on the double to the
Kommandatura, was held up again, this time by the sign on Peter Wulff's
shop. He was vaguely familiar with that name. He'd had its file card pulled
from the lists of the old SPD in Gneez: member until the Socialists were
banned in 1933; courier services; illegal actions (voluntary); arrested during

Mussolini's visit to Mecklenburg (Bützow-Dreibergen); KZ Sachsenhausen 1939–1940; unfit for military service; not yet unified into the SED. Sloppy recordkeeping, probably. He was close to sixty, tall but bent as if he'd been a stevedore not a bartender, pale in the face, still blond. In the hallway shadows he looked merely massive, soft, but outdoors he unexpectedly proved forceful, much more aggressive than Bienmüller. In fact Peter Wulff had immediately taken a shovel off a hook and gone to dig in the garden ("*Our Petey's a good guy he juss forgets himself a little an lashes out sometimes*"). If you keep digging you don't have a free hand to start a fight with.

    – Hello, comrade.

    – *Red Front yer sposed ta say.*

    – Red Front, comrade.

    – *Notcher comrade.*

    – But you're a member of the Socialist Party, aren't you?

    – *Was.*

    – Your name's still in the card file. Now you just need to unify.

    – *Yeah Im thinkin it over.*

    – Yes, why don't we talk it over together?

    – *Nope. Juss bring me Cresspahl.*

    – What on earth is that?

    – *Our mayor.*

    – Don't you like Bienmüller then? Is he being removed?

    – *Cresspahls who we wanted. Now your guys have im. Bring im back. Go ask about it inna Kommandatura.*

    – I will just have to do that, Mr. Wulff.

    – *Or ask yer Slata, she knows bout it too!*

The evening's speaker might have been shaken by this reference to Slata. How could he realize that Wulff's singular possessive might have been just a grammatical plural in Platt—"Slata who's with you Russians"? The district councillor probably did announce himself a bit too forcefully at the Kommandatura, since he was a district councillor, and he was perchance not quite polite enough when the gentlemen didn't choose to receive him. In the end it would have been smarter, politically, to have his dispute on the administrative level, as the Wendennych comrades suggested, who had all sorts of second-rate complaints to deal with about supplying their district with adequate food, fuel, building materials. The district councilman, a friend of Triple-J's, may have taken the wrong tone in trying to show them the errors they had committed in their political work among the people of Jerichow. In any case, that in no way justified their taking away his gun. The moment stayed in his memory as a kind of pantomime: while he was distracted by Jerichow's favorite guessing game—which twin was in charge of politics and which in charge of military matters—an orderly had twirled him around on his axis, uncoiling from his body in one smooth, dreamlike motion his belt, his holster, his firearm. They handed him the army decree about German civilians' possession of weapons, in German, while he kept insisting that he spoke Russian perfectly, comprehension, speaking, even written Russian! They had him taken back out to Brickworks Road, with the firm promise: The request to punish him would be submitted to the SMA in Russian, not to worry, but only on Monday because of the election.

Later, he seemed to remember trying to take shelter in a house diagonally across from the Kommandatura—a strangely solitary building that made him feel like it stood at a great distance from this town. All he wanted was three hours of peace and quiet before the rally started. He couldn't face people again so soon. But he was refused, by a child, a girl, thirteen years old at most, who kept answering him in two sentences, now separately, now connected, sometimes in Low German or in standard German if he wanted: *Cant do it.*

– Why not?
– *The Russiansre right over there.*
– What's that got to do with it?
– Can't do it. The Russians are right over there.

He finally gave her up as crazy, feebleminded, a figment of his imagination. A man can imagine things like that in moments of severe emotional strain. Mirages, illusions like that, do exist.

As six o'clock drew near the market square was packed. He stood on the balcony of Town Hall with Mayor Bienmüller, flanked by the Wendennych Twins. The rally started half an hour later, because these commandants had insisted on a written list of his key points, signed and dated before witnesses. How are you supposed to give a speech like that! He began faintheartedly with the harvest, industrialization; it was still with far less than his usual verve, the swelling in his breast from within, that he mentioned the Bolshevik Leonid Borisovich Krasin, explosives expert and bank robber under the czars, representative of the new Soviet Russia in London and Paris, who had also managed, as commander of an icebreaker in 1929, to free a German rail ferry trapped by the ice off Warnemünde. Then he deployed the two weapons the party had put in his hands to ensure that the embarrassing results from September would not be repeated. The market square was quite quiet when he repeated the line from the election appeal of October 7: Our party stands for the protection of property rightfully acquired the workers' own labor.

Then came the ploy that experience had taught him was sure to draw cheers and applause, prepared beforehand with volume, pacing, and intonation marshaled properly: in words straight from Berlin, from the party's own mouth, manly opposition to the Soviet foreign minister and his recognition of the Oder-Neisse line: *Our* position, though, must be defined on the basis of *German* interests—Molotov is pursuing *Russian* policy!

– More than that: cried the evening's speaker: we need not say! *Our* party—pursues—*German* policy!

And at that point one of the Twins had to take his arm. He hadn't noticed that some people were crying down on the market square. Someone had fallen down too.

The rally was concluded by Alfred Bienmüller, as mayor and local chairman of the Socialist Unity Party. The guest speaker from district headquarters didn't understand everything he said, since he was still somewhat dazed; in addition, Bienmüller's variety of High German grammar left plenty of room for slipping into Plattdeutsch cadences.

– You all hadda good laugh at me: Bienmüller said. – We told you, didn we, that a kind and humane great power like the Sooviet Unron wouldn ruin a people just for territorial gain, righ'? Seems to me, seein' how even our Swede here didn...all right, Mr. Duvenspeck! You all laughed at us. Wouldn believe us. Now youve all heard it for yerselves, ya numskulls. And you know who youve heard it from! It wont just be good news for our refugees that theyll be allowed to go home again, lets givem a little good news ourselves. Since we havent given em much a that before. Shut yer trap, you! Now one more thing. Theres some rumors been goin round. We know whos been starting em too, and weve been payin the child support. Theyre not true. Theyre sayin that if a city gets too few SED votes the people therell get less on their ration cards, less coal, and less of everything that isnt there. As true as I'm standing here and reading that from this here piece of paper, that's how truly I'm going to rip this piece a paper to pieces right in front of you, that's how truly it isn't true! Thats not how we wanna win your votes! Look at us, look, an then vote! *Im not sayin this from the party, Im sayin it myself, as mayor. Now quiet! No one here* .... This meeting is adjourned.

And so the Gneez district councilman lost his election. In Mecklenburg as a whole, his party got 125,583 fewer votes than in the test run in September. He'd have liked to blame it on Bienmüller's closing speech but couldn't, on scientific grounds. Because, look, in Jerichow his party got a percentage of the vote equaled only in two, maybe three other Mecklenburg communities—more than seventy percent.

He never got his revolver back. That was definitely a loss, one his feelings could latch on to. Only it wasn't the real loss. What was it he'd really been afraid of?

Nowadays, when a leading member of the Czechoslovak Communist Party gets an anonymous letter in the mail, reviling him as a Jew and threatening that his days are numbered, what does his party's newspaper—*Rudé Právo*, "Red Law"—do? It prints the letter in its entirety, and he is allowed to respond to it just as openly. What is he allowed to respond? That anonymous letter writers like this only unmask themselves by adopting the tone of 1952. And what happened in 1952? That's when Rudolf Slánský was executed in the name of the people. We learned that in school.

June 25, 1968 Tuesday
The Czechoslovakian delegation to the national assembly explained to the Soviet Union, clearly and logically,

"that the conditions under which we began to build our socialist country after February, 1948, have changed and that the qualitative changes that have taken place in the economy as well as the socialist structure of our country called for rectification of mistakes, shortcomings, and deformations of the past and a modernization of the economy that has fallen shamefully behind.

But the new realities require a great deal more. They require a transition to a democratic, humanitarian and popular concept of socialism not only in the economy but also, and primarily, in public and political life, where socialism must provide new, wide-ranging concepts of rights and freedoms for the individual as well as society as a whole."

The Soviet comrades showed considerable tolerance for these explanations, perhaps placated by their choice of words. But it may also be true that one of these words got brought up too often. They listened with a certain lack of enthusiasm. Their leader—and no one denies this—had tears in his eyes.

The October 20, 1946, Mecklenburg parliamentary elections produced three results.

I.

On the night of October 21–22, the Red Army came out from behind its fence and paid some visits in Gneez. They parked large trucks so quietly at various locations around the city that the ensuing events that night went virtually unnoticed. Where the patrols entered a home they hauled off whole families. Accusations of harsh treatment are not appropriate, since the soldiers consistently helped the affected parties pack their bags and carry any item they wanted, from the kerosene lamp to the oak sideboard, down the stairs and loaded them carefully into the trucks. This took place repeatedly in some buildings, on other streets not at all. Toward morning, when the reports from eyewitnesses started overlapping and the relocators themselves were in passenger trains well on their way to the new eastern border, the conjecture was bruited about that this had been just another instance of the Soviet national character—impulsive, arbitrary. On the contrary. Comparing the eliminated addresses revealed that they all, although widely dispersed through the city, had two things in common: first, the departed residents had all had residence rights for at least five years—they were locals, by no means refugees (resettlers); second, the male heads of households had without exception been employed in the Arado factory by Gneez Bridge station. The Arado factory had been in a special category of war industries, because for one thing it had made rocket parts for the Peenemünde army testing site. As for the other thing, the prefabrication of parts for Ar 234 jet bombers, those behemoths with four BMW 003 engines—we'll keep that to ourselves. Any conclusion to the effect that the plant's dismantling and the rounding up of its labor force had logically followed from the rules of war must be rejected as rash. There was no way these actions could have been intended as an ethical favor to Great Britain, which had been harmed by the Peenemünde rockets, since the victorious powers had each reserved its own zone of occupation for dismantling and confiscating industries by way of reparations and—we must emphasize—the British had, during their provisional administration of West Mecklenburg, confiscated blueprints of the Arado Works for their own use, as war booty; the capitalist bandits hadn't even shied away from encouraging scientifically trained workers at that factory from coming with them when they were forced to exchange their Mecklenburg territory for the British Sector of Berlin. Moreover, nothing was dismantled near Gneez Bridge on the night of October 21–22, since, under the SMA's Order No. 3 of June 25, 1945, the machinery, assembly lines, cooling facilities, etc. of the Arado factory there had already been dismantled and removed to the Soviet Union on July 5, immediately after the Red Army entered Gneez. In this regard, we cannot warn strongly enough that re-hashed horror stories about piles of telephones in the courtyard of the Gneez post office being heaved onto army trucks with pitchforks, and other such tales, are to be avoided. The dismantling of Gneez-Arado took place under the supervision of a diplomaed (engineering science) high-school teacher attached to the Soviet rocket troops with the rank of colonel—that is to say, were carried out with the utmost care. Proof of which is the cataloging of the equipment: after each written entry, every machine was photographed three times: at rest; being operated by its trained worker; and finally from the rear, again attended by its operator, who was required to appear in the photograph visible from hair to toe. In this connection, one should also recall that the city's carpenters had turned their entire stock of lumber into custom-made crates, and been given orders to spend two whole days making wood chips, not as waste but as the product itself. The Arado factory in Gneez had had its power completely turned off in early August. Certain bourgeois elements bring up as a counterargument that the remaining workers didn't abandon the factory at that point and began manufacturing primitive tools from the leftover materials, supplying the population from September on with rakes, spades, stovepipes, pots, pans, metal combs, and rulers, or at least carrying out repairs on such objects. To which we must reply in the sharpest possible terms that in a great many cases the People's Police were unable to determine the origin of the material used (aluminum sheets for rabbit hutches!), and that the factory, situated in a country town as it was, carried out every imaginable kind of blacksmith work except for horses; that the man in charge of the factory, Dr. Bruchmüller of the CDU, who was elected in an illegal and arbitrary way, has not been cleared of the suspicion of having made off with whatever tools and tradable items were left in the Arado factory before the second dismantling in November of last year; that (here we come to the fourth and fifth points) ... the greater part of production went to fill private orders; and that the members of the former Arado factory at Gneez Bridge were sabotaging the circulating currency organized by the SMA with contracts stipulating payment in kind. The deportation of former factory employees can be considered just punishment on that account alone, permission for families to move with them as merciful. Since there can be no question that the above is true, not to mention any alleged contempt for the Fascist capitulation terms, the word *Osavakim* circulating among the population can only be rejected as enemy propaganda seeping over the border from the Western occupation zones. Those who allowed the interpretation of this Soviet word as an acronym for "Special Authority for Carrying Out Dismantlings" to get out should have their heads chopped off. (And anyone blabbing about how it's really something quite different—Osoaviakhim, "Obshchestvo Sodeystviya Oborone, Aviatsionnomu i Khimicheskomu stroitel'stvu SSSR,"

    for the Promotion
    of the Defense,
    Aviation,
    and Chemistry Industries
    in the USSR,

deserves to have more chopped off than his head.) Any and all further inquiries from the Free German Trade Union Council shall be met with the response that five-year labor contracts have been concluded with every displaced family and the Soviet trade unions will be looking after their interests henceforth. Copies of these contracts can be forwarded on request.

The narrow circle within which this discussion is taking place permits us to subject the tactical discernment of the Soviet Union and the Red Army to a well-meaning appraisal. If our friends had undertaken such a vitally necessary measure during the run-up to the parliamentary election, the results in the Soviet occupation zone would have been comparable to the vote counts in Berlin, where the SPD, under the protection of American and British bayonets, is still capable of opening its maw wide and receiving 63 seats out of 120 in total, whereas we could score only 26. By now the light must have dawned on even Comrade Schumann about why he's spent the last few weeks scared shitless. Yes, if only! The fact is, the Red Army did not invite these citizens from Gneez to the Soviet Union during the election campaign, or even one day before the vote. No, it was one day after the vote. Comrade District Councilman sure knows how to talk convincingly about a debt of gratitude to the Soviet Union, but when it's sitting right in front of his face he doesn't recognize it. In conclusion, since the call to vote placed the securing of peace and friendship with the Soviet Union above all else, it is a fact that the former employees of the factory at Gneez Bridge turned in their ballots and voted as they did.

II.

There was a kink in the October 1946 census. Osavakim affected people not only in the city and district of Gneez but also in other Mecklenburg businesses of armament-strategic significance, and still further in the other provinces of the Soviet zone—for instance, Carl Zeiss and the Jena glassworks, the Siebel airplane factory in Halle, Henschel in Stassfurt, the AEG factory in Oberspree, Askania Friedrichshagen in Berlin, etc. The census was to determine who was home on the night of October 29–30, as well as what job they claimed to have. Thus the undertaking failed to detect a type of migration undetectable by statistical means. In addition, the results implied that fewer specialists in heat-resistant glass or electrical measurement equipment (GEMA, Köpenick) resided in the Soviet occupation zone than in the zones of the Western Allies, for natural reasons. Here sciences other than sociology must be summoned to our aid. In the city and district of Gneez, Osavakim had disseminated among the peace-loving population the conviction that the Soviet Union now, at the conclusion of what was after all a whole year, considered the demilitarization of their

Germans complete and that their job census had proven that Soviet interest in military specialists was no empty delusion. Local rumor had it that anyone who volunteered for the Red Army as a mercenary in the war against Japan could count on like-new clothing, solid footgear, and regular meals. Here people's hopes for the future might be summed up with the question that itself indicated a dual result: *If I only knew where to sign up!*

III.

The Gneez district councilman spent one and a half days in a prison cell under Gneez City Hall. The cause was a quarrel initially about a gun that Triple-J's colleagues in Jerichow had taken from him. As it proceeded, Comrade Schumann unexpectedly, inexplicably even to himself, asked for Slata's address. (Just to write to her.) J. J. Jenudkidse was generally considered a placid commandant, uninclined to malicious or even impulsive behavior. He had the young man delivered to one such address. Sixteen years later, in spring 1962, he who had been that young man tried to explain to a woman that this had been the end of his education, his final renunciation of private desires, the complete submersion of his self into the party. This listener wouldn't have been a woman he was married to, but still, he would have mentioned neither Slata's name nor her whereabouts. He is married. This will have been an evening in the palace gardens in Schwerin, after a concert of serenades. He won't be going by the same name anymore. His last name would be the same as his father's, except for two letters, while for his first name he would be called exactly what his mother wanted. Two days after the parliamentary elections of 1946, seven days before the census, he would have been summoned to Schwerin. His name would have been waiting for him there. Personnel Department at the state administrative level, Security Department at the central ministry level. He never returned to Gneez. I never saw him again.

– But I, if I was coming along to Prague, I'd see him: Marie says. She'd see him. I'll recognize him.

All day long we've been waiting for the black rain that is finally hanging above the Hudson. At lunchtime the air was thick with humidity. Bone-dry people acquired a second skin of sweat as soon as they set foot outside an air-conditioned building. It was impossible to calculate in your head anymore: 89 degrees Fahrenheit minus 32 times five over nine makes something or other in Celsius. The upper edges of the buildings shimmered. After ten blocks, Lexington Avenue itself was blurry; whether the whole thing would have melted away after twenty blocks remained an open question. Now, at nine p.m., rain has come down from the north with two short lightning flashes in its midst, which stab into your eye, short-circuit something in your brain.

 – The New York rain, I'd miss that: Marie says. (Children bring the rain with them when they travel.)

June 26, 1968 Wednesday
The Czechoslovak National Assembly has unanimously voted to rehabilitate those who were unjustly persecuted, jailed, and tortured since the Communist takeover in 1948. The sentences may be voided or reduced if the legal rights of the defendants were violated. Survivors are to receive monetary compensation, maybe a new party book for the dead victim. There are also provisions for compensation for physical harm suffered during imprisonment, for court costs, and for material loss. The responsible judges, policemen, prosecutors, investigators, prison wardens, and Interior Ministry employees face the loss of their posts and/or possible further legal punishment, it all depends. The party functionaries, or so-called political leaders, who ordered the purges and persecutions are exempt from the new law. Nothing is going to happen to Antonín Novotný, who was there in the Central Committee of the ČCP since 1946. That's good news for authorities of other nationalities as well.

Every last representative of that National Assembly is the same as in Novotný's days.

Bad news for Karsch. In Palermo seventeen Sicilians and Italian Americans have been acquitted of having juggled with currencies and transported narcotics to the local Mafia or the American Mafia. Terrible news for Karsch. Now there's at least half a chapter in his book he'll have to plow over. The index is toast. No way he'll finish by the end of July. Oh well. We won't be like that about it.

Today Mrs. Cresspahl laughed about Mrs. Carpenter.

Mrs. Carpenter doesn't know that. She can't imagine anyone would, since she'd never do it herself. And there's no way she could prove it.

Mrs. Carpenter ("Call me Ginny") is a young person of thirty-one, five foot four, size 4, shoe size 7 1/4, all estimated in American measurements. In appearance a tall, attractive girl with broad shoulders, pear-size breasts, narrow hips, regular features to the point where each half of her face is a mirror image of the other, framed by harmoniously wavy hair that used to be straight but was always as white-blond as it is now. What's known on the Upper West Side as a Scandinavian type. She is rarely to be seen like this since she's always in motion. When she's driving she plays with the steering wheel, if only with her little finger; in any kind of conversation she moves a foot back and forth, stretches an arm, runs her fingers through her hair; when she walks, any onlooker is faced with a whirlwind of rapid attacks—jerking of neck, clutching of pearls, twisting of or rummaging through handbag, down to legs unheedingly hammering the pavement. On the tennis court this all seems connected to some kind of performance and so becomes enjoyable. Even when she's reading the paper she'll widen the whites around her narrow gray eyes to a surprising extent, as a display of attention, of presence of mind. When she isn't paying attention to her-self—when she's observing some child's nonsense, for instance, or when a first raindrop falls from a blue sky—the pretty monotony of her mask slips, revealing displeasure, what you might go so far as to call weariness of life; even that would seem only right, if not for the fact that her symmetrical features went crooked. Then the smile promptly returns. She thinks of herself as beautiful, desirable, ideal—others tell her so. Her calves might be judged flabby by a female observer; a European woman would be more likely to wrongly assume aftereffects from college hockey in Michigan. Anselm Kristlein spent half the length of a cocktail party unable to tear himself away from her long willowy neck, her deep alto voice, the earnest drollery she uses for verbal flirting; she is faithful to Mr. Carpenter in submissive fashion, almost as if incapable of doing otherwise. Once she brushes him with a smile, with girlish sympathy, with a delighted cry from across the room, it's hard for him to imagine she has any secrets.

Since the beginning, when she moved to Riverside Drive four years ago, she's insisted on us being more than just neighbors: friends. Marcia was in the same class as Marie then. Soon Marie was going over to the Carpenters' alone. She wanted to see for herself what exactly that is: a stepmother. Ginny put on a fake deep voice and accused herself of being an evil stepmother out of a fairy tale to anyone who would listen; the child listened in amazement, since this woman then quietly did whatever the child wanted anyway. (They could become partners in crime all the more easily since Mrs. Carpenter had no children of her own. Didn't want to have kids for now.) Marie went over, ostensibly to watch television; she also wanted to find out what it was like to live with a father. When Mr. Carpenter comes home from his chambers, that's when work really starts: here, beatified anew each evening, stands a young wife at the door, slightly red in the face from housewifely zeal; the furniture is waiting, comfortable, clean, more extravagant than he'd exactly wanted for a third marriage; fresh highballs at his preferred temperature are waiting by the window overlooking the Hudson. Now it's his turn. Stories from the office. How Elman was today. Whether Burns via Elman is going to foist the real estate case against the National Guard off on him. Carpenter, a colonel in the reserve, is now buried under household incidents and others that *The New York Times* has already told him about. The caresses all come off in a form it doesn't harm children to witness. He can escape as long as she hasn't planned a party, fifteen people, right before dinner, attention to be paid to acquaintances passing through town or intellectuals from Europe; but just then is when he's supposed to realize how lucky he is, for the liveliest voice is his wife's— a sound well aware of its loveliness. Indefatigably cheerful, she spins the guests around one another, speeding them up with delicate deliveries of excellent drinks, then transforms back into the ardent student she once was: philosophy major, sociology minor, cocooned in a private one-on-one conversation by the fireside, now immersed in an erudite discussion of an article in *International Affairs*, a magazine that in this living room lies out no better or worse than *Cosmopolitan, Newsweek,* or *Saturday Review.* The *Playboy* is not out. The household is run along strict yet generous lines—the guests reassure one another of that once they're back out on the sidewalk— but we'd never go there to borrow a pinch of salt. The Carpenters' maid, Isobel, from a village in the Alleghenies, looks a bit like the lady of the house after only two years, and not just because of her youth. A polished girl, she wants to stay not particularly for the half-orphan Marcia—she keeps Marcia rather at arm's length. Tessie, who used to help us, would never set foot in this apartment. Tessie is a subject of Her Royal Majesty the Queen of Great Britain; she likes living in the Bronx, she doesn't need to care what conclusions Mrs. Carpenter pronounces about the dark-skinned race as such.

Ginny Carpenter is without question a major power in our neighborhood, a pillar of our community. If it occurs to Governor Rockefeller that this Riverside Park is utterly useless and would suit him much better as an eight-lane highway for trucks only, Ginny will have ruined the spring of her phone dial within three days, by using it as you're supposed to for once in human history, and presto, here's is a rock-solid committee, fiercely named from the acronym for Save Our Riverside Park, and now Rocky is quaking in his wingtips. She serves as a member of almost every group concerned with the external beauty of our neighborhood, whether with respect to the large-tooth aspen on 119th Street or a trampled trash can on the river promenade. For a passably honest lawyer could hardly pay the expenses of such a wife on the East Side, a location befitting her social status, and so Mrs. Carpenter lives here among us, because of the housing and tree stock, the sunsets over the Hudson, and, not least, the incomparable mix of people here, whose sense of community she could hardly expect among the soulless apartment towers east of Fifth Avenue. – Never!: she says, stamping a little with her long foot. In fact, when she spots us walking on Riverside Drive, she backs up her Cabriolet ($6,780.00) especially for us and entertains us during the ride with the swanky sensitivities of a car like this, stopping without a trace of shame in front of our gray-painted front steps, where there's not even a carpet. – After all, we're neighbors!: she cries, beaming, a good-natured child, sincerely happy at all times.

She is certainly honest. It didn't take long before she noticed something. We don't live in a building you enter under a manned baldachin; we have just three rooms, with a view of the park from beneath the tops of the trees; no liveried doorman keeps watch over us. Our incomes are incommensurate, we can hardly repay invitations like hers in kind, so a pleasant neighborly relationship is preferable to a friendship in which one party feels bad. In circles too elevated for us, Mrs. Carpenter might express admiration for single working mothers supporting self and child year after year, like Mrs. Cresspahl for instance, she wishes she were a woman like that—if only she could get rid of the sneaking suspicion that this Mrs. Cresspahl is leading such a life for the sake of a half-baked feminist ideology, not because she wants to. She is willing to grant us our European origins—although her Europe consists of France, Spain, and Monaco; our neck of the Continent is more dubious even than Yugoslavia. No, she doesn't insist on being friends. Neighbors is just fine.

Today Mrs. Cresspahl is supposed to pick up her daughter from a birthday party at Pamela's. Marie insists on such formalities sometimes; she wants to show off her mother in her best clothes and a brooch at the neck, please. So it's change after work, out to Riverside Drive, elevator to the twelfth floor. And there was Ginny, through the half-open door to the Blumenroths' living room, doing four things nearly simultaneously.

She was savoring what she'd just strewn across the room: Utterly charming, no, dazzling; You look like a June day in the flesh; etc.

She was sitting on the edge of the sofa, eating cookies, hand cupped under her chin to protect her red silk from Lord & Taylor, her taut brow evincing a certain contemplation of how marvelously tolerant she was to be paying such an extensive visit to Jews (admittedly, rich ones); now, to whom could she say that, and from whom better keep it; finally, a gobbling curiosity: are these kosher cookies she's eating?

She was giving a lecture: In twenty years the blacks will have been driven out of Manhattan. We'll be living on a lily-white island surrounded by the black boroughs—the Bronx, Queens, Kings. Richmond County, no, that's not clear yet. It's very simple—economic factors. Our charming four-story brownstones, expensive sandstone on numbered streets, what could be their fate if not a return to being luxury houses for one family each?

She was fingering Marie's blouse, the concealed placket, the double-stitched seam along the button-down collar: it seemed un-American to her; suddenly she pulled the napkin from the child's neck, reached for the label, and spelled it out, aghast: from Geneva.

Mrs. Cresspahl doesn't recall how she waved her child out of there.

Mrs. Cresspahl will need to apologize to her surprised hostess for how she whisked past her. When the elevator doors slid shut before her, she started laughing. Twelve stories down she fell, laughing, seriously disconcerting Marie, and as soon as they got out to the sidewalk the child demanded an explanation, to keep her mother from laughing any more, in public like that. It's not so simple.

Listen, Comrade Writer. I've got something to say to you.

You laughed, Mrs. Cresspahl. Gesine. You did.

Maybe I did. But not just this once.

That may be true, Mrs. Cresspahl.

I gave you a year. That was our agreement. Describe the year.

And what came before the year.

No tricks!

How you got to this year.

And during this year we've agreed on, beginning August 20, 1967, I've seen Ginny Carpenter at Jones Beach, twice. Three times at the Philharmonic. For a meal in the city once. She loaned me her car—no, that didn't work out.

Renting a car cost less than owing her anything.

(I don't know about that.) She's a part of my daily life.

Not on Broadway: she has her meat delivered from Shustek's. Not in the subway: she's never ridden the subway in her life. When the Italian delegation invites you to the UN, you don't bring her along. You're afraid she'll say something embarrassing.

Gimme a break. It's like the thing last Thursday. When you want to show something about shopping you can't help making a drunk Negro assault me in the store and vent his sexual fantasies. I see Ginny Carpenter twice a week and you give her her moment in the spotlight exactly once in ten months: one striking, conspicuous moment.

An important moment.

I laugh every time I see her. Marie just has to mention her. It's not unfriendly laughter, there's no mockery in it at all, usually. It's just funny that someone like that exists. Almost never mocking. I'm glad she exists.

That America can be like that too.

Exactly. So write that down.

You want this to turn into a diary after all?

No. Never. I'm keeping up my end of the bargain. So write about her more often.

If I did, what was important about today's laugh might get lost.

There you go again with your quantity and quality! Add more of one if you want the other!

By accumulating more Mrs. Carpenter, all I'd get is Mrs. Carpenter. I

was trying to show that you're preparing for your departure. Reassuring
yourself that not everything you're leaving behind is essential. For instance,
Mrs. Carpenter. You want to make it easier for yourself to leave, at least to
leave this one person in New York.
    My departure? For three weeks in Prague?
    Business travel of this sort has a way of being extended, Mrs. Cresspahl.
    I'm afraid of losing New York but I just can't say it?
    Go ahead and say it, Mrs. Cresspahl.
    I create my own psychology, Comrade Writer. You need to take it as you
find it.
    So, you've never laughed like that about Ginny Carpenter.
    Agreed. You can write that. I've never laughed like that.

Mrs. Cresspahl had never laughed like that about Mrs. Carpenter. Like
that? Never.

In fall 1946, the Cresspahl child moved many of her things from Jerichow
to the county seat of the area, Gneez. She lived in Jerichow, she was on the
official lists in the registration and housing offices there, she got her ration
cards there (Group IV), it was there that she and her father had arranged
to meet again, in case he came back from the Soviet prison or wherever
else he might be from which return was conceivable. But she went to school
in Gneez, and the railway management often combined the afternoon train
to Jerichow with the evening one, and when there was no coal even for
that one she would stay until the next school day with Alma Witte, in the
room from which Slata had disappeared. She went back to Jerichow in the
dark, as if into the dark.
    Gneez was a big city. For a child born in Jerichow—who ever since then
thought of such enlarged one-street villages as the way the world was supposed to be, if not the only possible world—Gneez is a city that only makes
you think of bigger ones.
    Back then the train needed an hour to cover the Jerichow–Gneez branch

line—nineteen tariff kilometers, four regular stops and one flag stop, forty-one minutes according to the timetable. The train consisted of three third-class cars, the kind where compartments lining the corridor have a door on the left or the right alternately, plus two or three freight cars, delivering the potatoes, beets, and sacks of wheat collected in Jerichow to supply the needs of the city of Gneez. These cars drove back empty at night, as a rule, and as soon as the train got out of sight of the Soviet control officer in the engine routing center, the People's Police swung out of the empty boxcars and tumbled back along the long running boards to the passenger cars, where they might stay warm at least with card games. In the mornings, though, in rain or in frost, they would crouch along the edges of the box-cars next to their products of the country, 98k Karabiner rifles propped at an angle, implacable enemies of snipers, thieves, and black marketeers. If the district administration in Gneez had been able to meet its need for trucks by confiscations from the coast, this largely single-track rail line, too, would have been unscrewed and sent off to the Soviet Union, like all the second tracks in the Soviet occupation zone. As it was, the line was used, three times a day according to the timetable, and the Cresspahl child took it to her secondary school in Gneez, as the Educational Reform Law mandated.

The dairy train from the coast approaches Gneez along a wide bulging arc to the west, letting viewers build up a semicircular picture of the thin sharp spires of Lübeck, as in a peep box; at the Gneez Bridge station, then closed, the line heads south-southwest and the rising sun paints the windows; at Gneez station the Jerichow train rests on an almost precisely east-west line, and with only a little shunting it could be dispatched to Hamburg or Stettin, the two cities on the classic line, but now that they're both cut off by borders no train can get there from platform 4. Gneez had four platforms.

Outside the station was a plaza that took up more space than the whole market square in Jerichow, and it was surrounded by buildings like a market square too. To the right were the steel gates, more than six feet tall, to the freight loading area; next to them City Hall, in three red-brick stories, flying the Red Army flag; straight ahead the prince's mansion, converted into Knoop's storage and haulage firm, crossed hammers on the frosted-glass windows; to the left, alongside the track running onward to Bad

Kleinen, were bicycle sheds and the bay in the sidewalk that country buses used to pull into. In the middle of this incredible expanse they had laid out a genuine park, a square of grass now admittedly trampled black with bare trees here and there. The path running straight across the plaza, though, led to the showpiece of one's first impression: a four-story gray stucco building, its continuous columns and fluting rising clear up to the elegantly rounded hipped roof—a palace, the Archduke Hotel, built in 1912 and designed by an architect who'd believed in a future for Gneez as a major metropolis. Not only did the building jut into the rose garden with a restaurant and a three-story wing of rooms, it bulged out into the street in front half again as much, its ground floor enlarged into a café beneath graceful stucco garlands, a mighty portal to the reception halls, and another, more subdued one leading to the Renaissance Cinema. Only then, fifty-six yards down Railroad Street, did this colossus yield the frontage to midgets—bourgeois houses of few stories, painted white, with stores and bars at their feet. This was Railroad Street, which had been named after an Austrian for a few years and now bore the name of the place to which it led, from which it came. The name "Archduke" was still on the hotel's roof, attached to a wire frame in proud Roman letters, and just as the place had once scared off the less impressive traveling salesmen, nowadays it was kept for the better sort with a red-and-yellow tin sign on the bulging semicircular reception desk, illegible to most Germans, presumably to be translated as Officers' House but meaning only the officers who could read Cyrillic. This was Station Square in Gneez—what a rich country town had once resolved to create as a lasting monument, not ostentatiously, just humbly presenting what the city had to hand. The citizens of the new century had no desire to boast of more than that; their solidity was only to be made visible. This had been the site of political rallies since the 1914 war, and here was where the Red Army had established its civil government.

The square was guarded by a ring of streetlights, it didn't matter that they weren't on—maybe the panes of glass had been shattered by rocks or bullets—anyway, they stood so tall, making sweeping gestures, in stiff pairs, they were still candelabras, lacquered black. And between the pair, almost every one, a pole had been set up flying a red flag, or else a sheet was stretched, bearing words from the Red Army to the locals in their own language, German black-letter.

Anyone who found the Dom Ofitserov too threateningly grand might take a narrow path straight ahead, past Knoop's edifice of hereditary ownership, and might genuinely be shocked by the difference between the doorless side of the prince's mansion facing the station and the south facade with its generous balconies, statues in niches, and serenely sweeping outdoor staircase commanding the southern prospect. There had once been a park there, which had gradually been devoured by a neighborhood of new buildings that had burned down once every century since the fifteenth until the 1925 SPD planned to put up a middle-income public housing project there, with reduced-cost lots, credit assistance, and a salutary dislike of rushing things. As a result six units were finished only in 1934 and 1935, and as a result Gneez-Neustadt was depicted in photo books from then on as an example of Mecklenburg's flourishing under National Socialism. It was hardly what you'd call the city. It was a field of scattered red villas, each with its own fenced-in garden plot, organized in groups of six with frugal paved paths under the patronage of the Musicians Guild. Felix Mendelssohn-Bartholdy's name could not, it turned out, be restored on the customary enamel sign, but it could be recarved into two oak signs. This was "the new good part of town," assigned to employees of the administration and the parties, the imported brain trust, and now thickly settled with refugees, children's homes, and Soviet private quarters. Only after you'd wandered through this pattern of boxes, turning left and then left again, would you find yourself at the tail end of Station Street, at a modest square that had once held the widened city walls, the Lübeck Gate, the guardhouses Lisch the local historian had failed to mention, and a humorous image in bronze of the animal to which Gneez owed its nickname. Now all the square had to offer was the bridge over the city moat, a low-lying, nearly stagnant body of water as wide as a man is tall. Here was the start of Old Gneez.

On maps, Old Gneez resembles the attempts of early mathematicians to carve a piece of wood into a many-sided polygon approximating a circle. This crude disk, divided by thin veins, was split down the middle by Stalin Street, an artery for shopping, strolling, and through traffic big enough for two horse-drawn carriages to pass each other without moving aside. Almost everything east of this thoroughfare, down to the rose garden, was considered "the old good part of town," the collective address of people who could document ancestors there since Napoleonic times, or, when in doubt, refugees. To the west, the side streets might start off by putting isolated stuccoed buildings on display, but they betrayed their true nature with the crumbling half-timber at the sides and stood convicted by the cottages, small farms, and tradesmen's yards sloping away behind them. These were houses built not just for single families but for those who wanted a rental income too. Anyone walking through the Danish Quarter could tell by the doors. Factory-made, barely any woodwork or mottoes on the beams. Just workers. Happy with anywhere they could lay their heads. That's how it is, west side, can't be helped, right? Anyway, there were such crooked walls there that you hardly noticed the odd door handle. That's how several of those houses had avoided the looting. Gotten off easier in terms of being assigned refugees too. But even the Soviets hadn't been able to eradicate the border to the respectable part of town: Stalin Street.

Stalin Street, previously named from its orientation toward Schwerin, crept south toward the market square for a quarter mile and then vanished into the cobblestones, starting up again on the opposite corner but less grandly, and now as Schwerin Street once more. There was Bulls' Corner, Bleachers' Road, Coopers' Lane. There the child sometimes visited a building with a grand entrance and a cramped upper story of living quarters and servants' rooms. There she sometimes watched Böttcher at work. She liked that. It was across the street from the Chapel of the Holy Blood. Schwerin Street had once been a way to walk to school.

But the market square was unforgettable for a child from Jerichow. Its square footage might be comparable to the market square back home, but in Jerichow everything had been left at that; the square here was clearly the model for Gneez's modern ceremonial plaza by the station. Here the buildings often showed four rows of windows, one atop the other, each of its own dimension, in individually upward-scalloping facades, behind whose pinnacles was no mere empty air but an indisputable window to an attic room, which existed there too. They kept such a proud distance from one another; they left alleyways, *Tüschen*, between them, not from necessity but from self-respect. They had to have those. The roofs had their backs turned from the market square; like hair partings above faces, they were all supposed to be unique. There were pulleys built into the gables, on which every single gap had been upgraded to a half wheel with spokes; there were coats of arms painted there, from interlaced initials to a burning circling sun. (The south side of one building turned the long end of its roof to face the market with a mansard in masonry not to be found on any postcards from before 1932.) Here you had the Court and Council Apothecary. There you had buildings that spoke of history, and not only in their weather-beaten bricks: In this hall the citizens paid their contribution to Old Freddy's seven-year war (1756–63). In memory of the time of the French: arson and pillage under General von Vegesack. Friedrich IV, King of Denmark, spent the night here, December 19–20, 1712. The post office, formerly the palace of the counts of Harkensee, was on the market square, its Doric columns courteously retracted. On the west side a spacious building has raised its brows so high that the roof needs to keep to the horizontal for a while before bending downward in back. Its facade has double doors proportioned according to the golden ratio, with staircases to the second floor closing in on both sides. And yet it stands in a row with the other buildings, not insisting on a greater separation. This was the former City Hall. The double staircase had been meant to show respect for authority, for the man elected first among equals. The cellar below was to keep its view of the market square. But for twentieth-century views it was too modest. With all their grand ideas they still hadn't managed to wean themselves from linden trees, full and round of crown, all around the market square near the surrounding buildings; they had just kept on growing. The candelabras wouldn't grow. Station Square might suffice as a parlor for the modern era, but the market square was Gneez's good room, now as ever.

The city didn't end there—south of the market square was almost a third of it, known as the Ducal Quarter, designed by court architects somewhat more generously between the forceps formed by tree-lined avenues along the old fortress walls: police prison, district council office, district court, county court, palace theater, cathedral yard, high school converted into Soviet army hospital, and the esplanade, about a hundred yards long, between the city swimming pool and the Little Berlin housing development on Gneez Lake. At the corner of the cathedral yard there was Alma Witte's hotel, where the child from Jerichow sometimes spent the night.

The city of Gneez. First mentioned in the Ratzeburg tithe register in 1235. Approx. 25,500 inhabitants in 1944, just under 38,000 in 1946. District capital. Industries: Panzenhagen Sawmill, Möller & Co. Canning Plant (a branch of Arado). Apart from that, trades; no mercantile business to speak of except for one company. Surroundings: forest to all sides except the south; a ridge of hills to the east, 320 ft. high, forested under the gracious supervision of Duchess Anna Sophie of Mecklenburg. The last witch burning took place there in 1676, hence its second name, Smœkbarg (Smoke Hill). Along with Gneez Lake: Warnow Lake, Rexin. Train connections to Bad Kleinen, Herrnburg, Jerichow.

Ever since the Cresspahl child had been transferred to the Bridge School, she could have turned right straight from Station Square, walked down Warehouse Street, and crossed the bridge to the Bridge School in the suburb known as the Lübeck Quarter. If instead she wanted to learn more about the city of Gneez than she was assigned, perhaps that was due to the time she had to kill until the next train departed?

She had long since stopped being a stranger, someone who noticed the buildings first and the people second. She was still a commuter student, but she'd moved to Gneez with many of her things.

She would enter the houses. With the people there she'd talk business, and she had much more time to do so than Jakob. She asked Böttcher the price of a butter churn, compared his answer to what Arri Kern was hoping to spend, and Böttcher got the difference.

In "the new good part of town," the suburb around the station, she had a Russian officer's wife to visit. This was the supervisor of the district council office. Her German landlords tried to hound at least this one newcomer out of her house with grossly inadequate services—they gave Krosinskaya no bed linen, started rumors in the neighborhood that her kind could hardly be used to any. Krosinskaya didn't have a husband in the barracks on Barbara Street; hers was buried near Stettin. This meant she had to buy sheets and blankets. She bought liquor. Once, she took all her clothes off except her silk slip right in front of the Jerichow child, pushed up an invisible weight with both hands, and asked: wasn't she still beautiful? The child guessed her age to be about forty and gave her the adjective she wanted; she wasn't lying either. It's just that everything about Krosinskaya, from legs to breasts, was a little too large, too heavy. Krosinskaya always paid the exact amount. She laughed at her German hosts. They wouldn't give her any furniture, so what? So she lived in bed, spread out sheets of the army newspaper on the bare mattress and laid out her dinner every day on the *Krasnaya Armiya*: sausage and bread and onions, separately. She ate them with a knife. In other ways she was quite finicky.

Another Soviet family, employed at the station, were bringing up their little boy to hate Germans. He would kick over Granny Rehse's mop bucket and treat her like the lowest scullery maid every way he could. Granny Rehse would have enjoyed being affectionate with the seven-year-old; as it was, she didn't understand him. This was the Shachtev family, who didn't buy liquor, they bought LP records. It was supposed to be Beethoven's music and cheaper than you could get it at Krijgerstam's Razno-Export. They brought out some liquor after all, under protest; berated the German child as a Fascist brat; weren't above threatening her with denunciation once—all with the pointedly good manners that made any real familiarity impossible. Mrs. Shachtev had been a doctor before the war. Her darling child, Kolya, had had his own nanny back home.

The Jerichow child learned from Alma Witte, or from Wilhelm Böttcher, those little scraps of local history that newcomers so like to use to imagine they understand a strange place:

The cathedral burned down in the hot June of 1659. Every other building remained intact undamaged, so it was presumed to be a case of arson. (According to the calculations of the New York municipal weather bureau, June this year was unusually wet and cool.) The Church has been waiting for the city to donate money for a new spire since 1660. The city had to accept the Protestant faith at gunpoint; the cathedral received nothing but a new transept until 1880, with the city giving nothing for the tower. The city could wait. As long as the Church was annoyed, the citizens could accept that ships no longer used the blunt emergency roof of Gneez as a seamark but instead used St. Peter's Church, Jerichow.

The Lübeck Quarter's official name was Bridge Quarter, even though it was on the Lübeck side. Well, we can keep the big neighbor to the west, even its *name*, out of our city at least once, can't we! For another thing, there *had* been a bridge there, over the channel with which Johann Albrecht I of Mecklenburg, long before Wallenstein, had intended to link the Wismar Bay to the Elde and thence Asia Minor. Wallenstein had lent his name to the scheme; what remained was a putrid ditch between Arado Works I and Arado Works II.

Gneez Lake had once been named after a large farmer's village to the south, which was wiped out during the Thirty Years' War and then later in the seventeenth century came under the plow and turned into moors. Woternitz Lake was the old name. The higher Gneez rose in the world, the more urgently it wanted a city lake of its own—Gneez printed it on tourist brochures, screwed hands with a pointing finger onto the enamel signs already in the train station. True, the Reich's land surveying office hadn't budged. Gesine learned to listen to such stories without bringing up Jerichow's Town Street. The right thing to do when Gneez's "Town Lake" came up was to purse one's lips a little and give Willi Böttcher a sidelong glance. Then she almost seemed to belong.

She had to take care of things in Gneez. On September 1, 1946, when she started at the Bridge School, the signature *Abs* on the old report card had caught the eye of the homeroom teacher, Dr. Kramritz. He'd asked just out of curiosity, but her panic made her realize the truth: Mrs. Abs was not her stepmother, not her aunt, not anyone entitled to sign report cards. The Cresspahl child had no legal guardian at all.

In late October she heard about Control Council Directive 63. There were now to be "interzonal passports" for trips to the western zones. The border was open again. Whatever it was keeping Jakob at the Jerichow gasworks and Cresspahl's house was a mystery to her. He might go west any day now. Dream up a funeral to go to there, or a deal in nails, and the People's Police would give you the piece of paper you needed. Mrs. Abs wouldn't stay without him. But Cresspahl's child had to wait.

In Gneez you could see it. Brigitte Wegerecht had stopped coming to school from one day to the next, without an excuse for Dr. Kramritz or her friend. Then she sent word from Uelzen (British zone).

Rooms in Gneez would suddenly turn up empty overnight, or whole apartments. Leslie Danzmann scattered a glorious treasure of residential assignments over the refugees' heads. There were again families living all by themselves, behind their own door. When Dr. Grimm was due to take over the district council office as senior administrator, Krosinskaya energetically made certain suggestions and his family took a trip to Hamburg for a christening—no great surprise for so Protestant a family. He spent a long evening over wine in the Dom Ofitserov discussing the work Gerd Schumann had left behind after his departure; by the next morning he had swum across the lake near Ratzeburg. He knew what he was doing. Brigitte's mother, née von Oertzen, may have been complying with her husband's last wishes, or her brother's advice. Could Cresspahl's child have blamed Jakob's mother for doing likewise?

Jakob still went to visit Johnny Schlegel's often enough. He was in love with a girl there. Anne-Dörte was prettier, and smarter, than any younger girl could hope to be; she might be a countess and all that; but Gesine Cresspahl knew—she was thirteen, wasn't she?—that loves like theirs last a lifetime. There was no doubt about it. If Anne-Dörte was summoned to Schleswig-Holstein, Jakob would follow her there too. Then Cresspahl's child would be without the care to which she had a customary right and which the Abs family had temporarily given her.

Children who are alone in the world are sent to a children's home. There was no such place in Jerichow. The one that took in all the children from the area was in Gneez.

June 28, 1968 Friday

Yesterday, června 27th, in *Literární Listy*, the weekly journal of the Czechoslovak Writers' Union, published in Prague, authorized by the Ministry of Culture, price one crown twenty, was a letter to all the citizens of the country,

dělníkům,
zemědělcům,
úředníkům,
vědcům,
umělcům,
a všem,

signed by almost seventy workers, farmers, engineers, doctors, scientists, philosophers, athletes, and artists,

Dva tisíce slov, The Two Thousand Words:

"The first threat to our nation was from war. Then came other evil days and events that endangered the nation's moral integrity and character. Most of the nation welcomed the Socialist program with high hopes. But it fell into the hands of the wrong people. It would not have mattered so much that they lacked adequate experience in affairs of state, factual knowledge, or philosophical education, if only they had had enough common sense and decency to listen to the opinion of others and eventually agree to be gradually replaced by more capable people.

The Communist Party, after enjoying great popular confidence immediately after the war, bartered this confidence away for office piece by piece until it had all the offices and nothing else. We feel we must say this. It is known to both Communists and the others who are equally disappointed with the way things turned out. The leaders' mistaken policies transformed a political party and an alliance based on a great idea into an organization for exerting power, one that proved highly attractive to power-hungry individuals, to unscrupulous cowards, to people who had something to hide. Such people influenced the self-image and behavior of the party, whose internal arrangements made it absolutely impossible for people to attain leadership positions and adapt the party to modern conditions without performing scandalous acts. Many Communists tried to fight this decline, but they managed to prevent almost nothing of what was to come.

Conditions inside the Communist Party both epitomized and caused the corresponding conditions in the state. The party's association with the state deprived it of the asset of separation from executive power. No one was allowed to criticize political and economic decisions. Parliament forgot how to advise, the government forgot how to govern, and the leaders forgot how to lead. Elections lost their significance, and the law hardly mattered. We could no longer trust our representatives on any committee or, if we could, there was no point in asking them for anything because they were powerless. Worse still, we could scarcely trust one another anymore. Personal and collective honor collapsed. Honesty was a useless virtue, assessment by merit unheard of. Most people accordingly lost interest in public affairs, worrying only about themselves and about money, despite the fact that it was impossible to rely even on the value of money under this system. Personal relations were ruined; there was no more joy in work; in short, the nation entered a period that endangered its moral integrity and character.

We all bear responsibility for the present state of affairs. But the Communists among us bear more than others, and those who served or benefited from unchecked power bear the greatest responsibility of all. This power was that of an intractable group, spreading out from Prague into every district and community through the party apparatus, which alone decided who could or could not do what. The apparatus decided about the cooperative farms for the cooperative farmers, decided about the factories for the workers, and decided about the National Committees for the public. No organization, not even a Communist one, was truly under its members' control. The chief sin and betrayal of these rulers was casting their own whims as 'the will of the working class.' If we accepted this premise, we would have to blame the workers today for the decline of our economy, for crimes committed against the innocent, and for the censorship that hinders us from describing these things! The workers would also be to blame for the misconceived investments, the trade deficits, the housing shortage. Obviously no reasonable person can hold the working class responsible for these things. We all know, and especially every worker knows, that the working class had no say in deciding anything. Working-class functionaries were given their voting instructions by somebody else. Many workers imagined that they were in power, but it was a specially trained clique of party functionaries and state officials who actually ruled in their name. In effect these people had stepped into the shoes of the deposed ruling class and themselves became the new power.

Let us say in fairness that many of them long ago realized what a false game they were playing. Today we can recognize these individuals by the fact that they are trying to redress old wrongs, rectify mistakes, hand back decision-making power to rank-and-file party members and citizens, and set limits on the power, and size, of the administration. They share our opposition to the reactionary views held within the party. But a large number of officials have been resistant to any and all change. They still retain the instruments of power, especially outside of Prague, at the district and community levels, where they can wield them in secret and without fear of accountability.

Since the beginning of this year we have found ourselves in a process of regeneration and democratization.

It started inside the Communist Party—that much we must admit, even the non-Communists who no longer hoped for anything good to emerge from that quarter. It must also be added, of course, that the process could have started nowhere else, since for more than twenty years only the

Communists could conduct any sort of political activity; it was only the opposition inside the Communist Party that enjoyed the privilege of being heard by their antagonists. Now the efforts and initiative being shown by democratically minded Communists are only a partial repayment of the debt the entire party owes to the non-Communists hitherto refused an equal position. Accordingly, no thanks are due to the Communist Party. But perhaps we should give the party credit for making an honest eleventh-hour effort to save its own honor and the nation's.

What this process of regeneration has introduced into our lives is nothing particularly new. It includes many ideas and problems older than the errors of Socialism, and others which, having emerged from below the surface of visible events, should have found expression long ago but were instead repressed. Let us not nurse the illusion that these ideas are destined to prevail now because the power of truth is on their side. Rather, their victory will be decided purely by the weakness of the old system, obviously falling into exhaustion after twenty years of unchallenged rule. Apparently the basic defects of the system, already hidden in its ideological foundations, had to come to full fruition. So let us not overestimate the effects of the writers' and students' criticisms. The source of social change is economic. A true word makes its mark only when it is spoken under conditions that have been properly prepared—conditions that, in our context, unfortunately include the impoverishment of our whole society and the complete collapse of centralized government, which had enabled certain types of politicians to get rich quietly and at our expense. Truth does not prevail alone here—truth is merely what remains when everything else has been frittered away! So there is no occasion for a national victory celebration, merely a reason for hope.

In this moment of hope, albeit hope still threatened, we appeal to you. It took several months before many of us were able to trust that it was safe to speak up; many of us are still afraid to do so. But we have already spoken up enough, exposed ourselves enough, that now we have no choice but to continue and finish our efforts to humanize the regime. Otherwise the old forces will exact cruel revenge. We appeal above all to those who have waited on the sidelines thus far. Now is the time that will decide our future for years to come.

Now is the time for summer holidays, a time when we are inclined to let everything slip. But we must not forget that our dear adversaries will skip their summer break; they will rally everyone who is under any obligation to them, and take steps, even now, to secure themselves a quiet Christmas! Let us watch carefully how things develop; let us try to understand them and have our answers ready. Let us give up our impossible desire to have someone from on high provide the single possible explanation and the single correct conclusion. Everyone will have to draw their own conclusion, on their own responsibility. Common, agreed-upon conclusions can only be reached in discussions among all sides, and those presuppose freedom of speech—which may remain the only democratic achievement we have accomplished this year.

But in the days to come we must act on our own initiative and make our own decisions.

First and foremost, we must oppose the view, whenever it is voiced, that a democratic renewal can be achieved without the Communists, or even in opposition to them. This would be unjust, and foolish too. The Communists have a well-developed organization in place, and we must support its progressive wing. They have experienced officials, and, not least important, they still control the crucial levers of power. They have presented their Action Program to the public. This program should start to resolve the most glaring injustices, and no one else has a program worked out in such detail. We must demand that they present local Action Programs in every district, every community. Then we will suddenly face very simple decisions, to be decided the right way, as we have so long awaited. The Czechoslovak CP is preparing for its congress, where it will have to elect a new Central Committee. We demand that it be a better one. If the party says that it now plans to base its leadership position on the confidence of the public, not on force, let us believe them, but only to the extent that we can place our trust in who they are sending as delegates to the district and regional assemblies.

People have recently been worried that the progress of democratization might come to a halt. This feeling is partly a sign of fatigue after the thrilling events of the past few months, but partly it reflects the truth. The season of astonishing revelations, of removals from high office, and of heady speeches couched in language of unaccustomed daring—all this is over. But the struggle of opposing forces is merely taking place on another level, over the content and formulation of the laws, over the scope of practical measures. Besides, we must give the new people time to work: the new ministers, prosecutors, chairmen, and secretaries. They are entitled to time to prove themselves fit or unfit. Beyond this, we cannot expect much from the central political bodies, though they have, in spite of themselves, made a remarkably good showing so far.

The practical quality of our future democracy now depends on what happens to the factories and *in* the factories. Despite all our discussion, it is the ones who manage the businesses who have us in their power. Good managers must be sought out and promoted. True, we are all badly paid in comparison with people in the developed countries, some of us worse than others. We can ask for more money. But then it would just be printed, as much as we want, and devalued in the process. Let us rather ask the directors and the board chairmen to tell us what they want to produce and at what cost, to whom they want to sell it and at what price, the profit that will result, and how much of that profit will be reinvested in modernizing production, how much will be left over for distribution. Under seemingly boring headlines, our press is covering a hard battle being fought—the battle of democracy versus the feeding trough. The workers, as employers, can intervene in this battle by electing the right people to management and workers' councils. As employees, they can help themselves best by electing trade union delegates to represent their interests—honest and capable individuals irrespective of their party affiliation.

If we cannot expect much from the central political bodies at the present time, it is all the more crucial to accomplish more at the district and community levels. We demand the resignation of those who abused their power, damaged public property, and acted cruelly or dishonorably. Ways must be found to compel them to resign. To mention a few: public criticism, resolutions, demonstrations, demonstrative work brigades, collections for their retirement, strikes, and picketing their offices. But we must reject all illegal, dishonorable, or boorish methods, which they use against Alexander Dubček. We must reject so forcefully and completely the practice of writing vile anonymous letters that any such letters that are reported in the future will be known to have been written by the recipients themselves.

Let us revive the work of the National Front. Let us demand public sessions of the national committees. For questions that no one else will look into, we will set up our own citizens' committees and commissions.

There is nothing difficult about it: a few people come together, elect a chairman, keep proper minutes, publish them, and refuse to be intimidated. Let us convert the district and local newspapers, which have mostly degenerated to the level of official mouthpieces, into a platform for all the forward-looking elements in politics; let us demand that editorial boards include National Front representatives, or else let us start new papers. Let us form committees for the defense of free speech. At our meetings, let us have our own security forces. If we hear strange reports about someone, let us seek confirmation, then send a delegation to the proper authorities and publicize their findings, posting them on doors if necessary.

Let us support the police forces when they prosecute genuine wrongdoing, for it is not our goal to create anarchy or a state of general uncertainty. Let us avoid quarrels among neighbors and drunkenness on political occasions. But let us expose informers!

Summer travel throughout the republic will also make it more desirable to settle the constitutional relations between the Czech Republic and Slovakia. Let us consider federalization as one possibility for resolving the national question, but as only one of many important measures for democratizing the system. This particular measure will not in itself improve life in Slovakia. Having separate governments in the Czech lands and Slovakia doesn't solve anything. Rule by a state-and-party bureaucracy could still continue, and might even be strengthened in Slovakia by the claim that it had 'won more freedom.'

There has recently been great alarm over the possibility that foreign forces will intervene in our development. Faced with all the great powers, we can only defend our own point of view, behave decently, and not defy or challenge anyone. We must show our government that we will stand by it, with weapons if need be, as long as it does what we give it a mandate to do. And we can assure our allies that we will observe all our treaties of alliance, friendship, and trade. Exasperated reproaches and unfounded suspicions on our part can only make things harder for our government, not help it. In any case, the only way we can achieve relations on a basis of equality is to improve our domestic situation and carry the process of renewal far enough to someday elect statesmen with sufficient fortitude, prestige, and political acumen to negotiate and maintain such equality for us. But this is a problem that the governments of all small countries face.

This spring we have been given another great opportunity, as we were after the war. Once again we have the chance to seize control of our common cause, which bears the working title of SOCIALISM, and give it a form more appropriate to our reputation, once good, and the fairly high opinion we used to have of ourselves. This spring is over and will never return. By winter we will know where we stand.

So ends our call to the workers, farmers, officials, artists, scholars, scientists, engineers, and to everyone. It was written at the behest of scholars and scientists."

Employee Cresspahl got to work late today. First she played hooky and stopped by the Italian delegation of the UN—uninvited, without phoning first. Signora Sabatino couldn't quite believe that someone she knew only from the Rolodex for second-tier cocktails was standing here in person. But at the receptions she serves food and gives every guest an encouraging look, which says silently but clearly enough for everyone to feel they've heard it: Well? Another hors d'oeuvre? Just a little something? How about this one?

She had only one question. How could someone get ahold of a Prague paper from yesterday in New York today. The one, you know, that today's *Times....*

– *Ma!*: Mrs. Sabatino cried at once. – *Ma abbiamo quattro edizioni di questo manifesto!* La Práce, Zemědělské Noviny *e* Mladá Fronta! *Anche le Sue* Literární Listy! *Signora*, do take off your coat! Your hair's wet! You're the lady who sends letters for Signor Karresh, aren't you? I'll announce you to His Excellency Dr. Pompa, he is very busy at the moment, doing nothing whatsoever. Just two minutes, I'll go in and interrupt him with coffee. *Facciamo così, signora?*

But Mrs. Cresspahl left right away, through the rain, seven photocopied sheets under her coat. One has to at least pretend to be at work. And then she cheated the bank out of a whole workday; our Vice President de Rosny himself would have asked in vain what this Czech document has to do with a trip to Prague. Employee Cresspahl wouldn't just have reminded him that it was she and none other who was to take that trip in August to the land where the Socialists talk like this, on a mission from the bank. She'd likely have added how disruptive it is for bosses to interrupt one, or something like that. This was practically homework! Mrs. Cresspahl had her lunch brought up from Sam's! The radio, set to the Prague station, emitted foreign words, another country's music, it was hot to the touch when she took it home that evening. Today it looked like almost no work had been done in the office.

Komunistická strana, která měla po válce velikou důvěru lidí, postupně ji vyměňovala za úřady, až je dostala všechny a nic jiného už neměla. Musíme to tak říci....

No, even closer to the beginning: *Událostmi, které ohrozily jeho duševní zdraví a charakter.* Destroyed the integrity...? That's not the right word at all.

Today, too, our radio gives the good honest water levels of the Vltava, and it also offers the answers of some citizens.

Prime Minister Oldřich Černík denounces such letters before the National Assembly. He concludes by practically inciting deeds from which might arise things such as nervousness, unrest, and judicial uncertainty.

The presidium of the Central Committee of the Communist Party of Czechoslovakia believes its policy is under attack from this letter—the program of the National Front and the government itself in danger.

If you want to know what's possible for Socialism in our time, learn Czech, my friends!

June 29, 1968 Saturday, South Ferry day

The Rawehns, ff. Ladies' and Gentlemen's Apparel, had had a store on Gneez's market square since Napoleonic times. It had once been loosely affiliated with the famous Ravens of Wismar; in fall 1946 a coat for the winter should still turn out in a way that Rawehn deemed fashionable, all the more so if the customer was merely a tradesman's child from Jerichow, under the care of an old woman from even farther out, a refugee. Madame Rawehn, a short strapping woman not yet forty, in a city suit as tempting as it was unbreachable, acted by no means snooty toward this Mrs. Abs and her protégée, who promised to pay in wheat. Mustn't provoke rich customers. And it'd been a long time since she'd had such fine black worsted fabric in her hands, it had probably been lying in a drawer since 1938, a French drawer perhaps; she would have been happy to buy more than one and a half yards, double wide. Not to mention the tartan pattern lining. But how this Gesine Cresspahl looked at her! It made her check the mirror! Where she saw herself taking measurements—her whole body tight in its crouch, chestnut-brown hair done up in tight rolls, the hairdo known as the all clear: "Everybody up!" So it wasn't about how she looked. In the end it was just the defiance that girls at that age are so prone to show.

The girl was picturing a long coat, below the knee. Children wore short coats at Rawehn's. The girl wanted the buttons hidden. Brought eight large horn buttons with her, could you conceal those? The girl wanted a high collar, standing up around the neck; Peter Pan collars were in fashion for children, covering half the shoulders, with rounded corners. The girl would have preferred no belt in the back. – But that'll ruin the chic? Helene Rawehn cried. – Everyone will know this is our work, *whatll the people in Gneez think!*

She did not fail to realize that the thirteen-year-old was looking for support from her companion's face every now and then, the woman with such a hollow look about the eyes. She received glances meant to console and encourage, in which Helene noticed no sign of any knowledge of the art of tailoring. Plus the woman barely spoke. Madame Rawehn gave in about the belt in the back. She'd just fasten it with buttons at the side seams, removable at will. She could whipstitch the hem if the girl wanted to wear it Soviet-style. The coat would be big enough to grow into so she could wear it for two years. As for the visible buttons, the flared cut, and the collar, Helene refused to give an inch: she felt the art and the honor of the House of Rawehn (Raven) were at stake. In the end the child rarely balked during the fittings (on Sundays, after creeping diplomatically down the *Tüsche* and through the back door so as not to give the Soviet ladies in the waiting room with their English magazines too tempting a look at the fabric), and Madame Rawehn actually didn't cheat the child out of a single ounce of flour, even sewing the buttonholes by hand; she sincerely wished she could have put the finished piece in the display window to advertise her services, if these times had been like those of peace; she had worries of her own, about the husband missing near Kharkiv—Heini, that love-crazed skirt-chaser. Why shouldn't a child get to pout a little in times like these?

The child was unhappy with her coat. Not because it failed to serve its purpose. Slash pockets, once they tear, need crude seams; you can reattach patch pockets easily and it won't show. She didn't want a coat with a collar named after a little boy, and someone could grab her by it and the belt. She found herself in crowds so often these days, and the buttons seemed to come off by themselves; if they'd been concealed she would've kept them longer. She had planned the coat as one to do more than just live in: it had been meant as a durable shelter for the trip that the Russians might send her on, as they had her father. Now Gesine Cresspahl had a coat that was merely contemporary and elegant.

Ask Countess Seydlitz—she'll say she knows all about this subject too. She predicts that the child of a successful marriage will mature much earlier and more fully, acquiring a stronger sense of self or at least of the place from which it wants or desires, maybe also the place where it knows itself and can show that self to the world.

Marie Luise Kaschnitz, on the other hand, has seen how the perfect union of two parents can do damage to a child. They band together against the child, don't let her individuate, forestall her search for different possible avenues for loving, keep her trapped in inevitable self-denial; even at thirteen barely more than the child of her parents, almost entirely defined through them.

Both of these children can run back to their parents when the world refuses to understand them or hurts them—there is also the big-brother figure, *hes got nails on is shoes*—secure in their protection while still not lacking in self-understanding. The elders only set right what such children have not yet been able to learn to do for themselves; children learn from them how to remain undamaged even when things go wrong.

The mother had abandoned the child Gesine Cresspahl back in November 1938—at four and a half she'd already been betrayed. The father, indispensable and not only for that reason, but also as her ally in the English secret, had served as the mayor of Jerichow in a way that angered the Red Army, whether it was the business of the abortions or a certain insubordination, and now the Russians had him, unreachable, less in charge of the child every day, for he didn't see what she saw. There was a woman from the island of Wolin living in her house, whom she craved as a permanent mother, but she could hardly ask her: Take me as your very own child!

This woman helped—more than that, she accepted help, when a stove had been lit by the time she got home in the afternoon she was happy with this child who wasn't hers. Another thing I learned from her: Now you can have children of your own, Gesine.

There was Jakob Abs, Mrs. Abs's son, who treated her like a little sister. Whatever time he didn't spend working he spent thinking about his business affairs, and most of all about a girl who wasn't too young for him, a creature of unimaginable beauty, Anne-Dörte was her name. He left, not only to go see her but to get away from Jerichow. He studied his Russian from a book of zheleznodorozhnykh terminov; he was headed from the gasworks to an apprenticeship with the railway that would take him away, to Gneez, to Schwerin, and someday out of Mecklenburg altogether.

Those were who she had left.

So what is a child like this Gesine Cresspahl to do when she's about to turn fourteen on March 3, 1947, and doesn't have a single person in Jerichow or its surroundings she can count on? Will she become so blind with fear that she runs after anyone who happens to be around, from her father's friends to a teacher who for once doesn't ask where her father is? Or, another option, she could see herself as alone against the grown-ups—not in open hostility but without any chance of help from them? Can't she, too, regard herself as an "I" with desires, with prospects that just have to be kept hidden for the time being?

The child that I was, Gesine Cresspahl—half orphan, at odds with her surviving relatives in memory of her father, owner on paper of a farmhouse by the Jerichow cemetery, wrapped in a black coat—she must have decided one day to give the adults what they wanted while smuggling herself out of their reach and into a life where she'd be able to be what she would then want to be. If nobody told her, she'd just have to find out for herself. It's not about being brave.

Strangely enough, she thought of school as a way out. Her father had withdrawn her from the school in Jerichow and tucked her away in the Gneez academic middle school because the teacher in Jerichow, Stoffregen, liked to hit; also because she might accidentally betray him one day to the Sudeten German Gefeller, principal in Jerichow and regional speaker for the Nazis. The child concluded from the move that her father wanted her to pursue a higher education. That being the case, she had no choice but to take a deep breath and forward march all the way to where school ended at that fairy-tale place called Abitur, finals, graduation, and permission to make her own choice. No, she wasn't particularly brave. She was scared.

She started by lying. To enter seventh grade at the Bridge School in Gneez she'd had to turn in not only a sixth-grade transcript but also an autobiographical statement. This was a school administered by the Red Army, and her father was not on good terms with the Soviets. Or maybe vice versa. She couldn't know. But there was something else she'd learned. She put him in her statement, she described him as a master carpenter, self-employed, minimized his role in the construction of the Mariengabe Airfield, confining it to that of a construction worker, brought up the liberation by the Soviet Union, and implied that he was still living, working, and residing in Jerichow.

Anyone comparing the various autobiographical statements made by this Gesine Cresspahl over the years will be forced to conclude that there were several different people by this name. Or maybe one person who turned into a new one every year and didn't know who she was from one day to the next!

Zeal attracted attention—she decided on diligence. Just as she'd been able to supply Fontane's ballad "John Maynard" in her old school, whether as memorized recitation, answers in class, or essays, so too she delivered to her teachers in this new school the description they wanted of present-day life in Mecklenburg:

Structure of the Anti-Fascist/Democratic Constitution. I. Definition. The initial prefix, an attribute used only in compounds, expresses opposition. It is here directed against a form of government that in ancient Rome was symbolized by the bundled rods of the lictors, which oppressed the people through violence at the disposal of the few. We have no violence in Mecklenburg. Democracy, a combination of the Greek words for people and rule (*demos* + *kratein*), means the exercise of power by the people themselves. We can see in the Gneez district how the exploiters robbing the people were chased away by that same people or at least forced to find housing a minimum of thirty kilometers away from their property and forced to work. The people consists of the workers, the farmers, the petite bourgeoisie, and the middle bourgeoisie, in that order. (This was a dicey part for her, because her position in this ranking was rather unfortunate,

as a tradesman's child.) All this taken together characterizes a constitution.
II. Implementation. One example is the recent Educational Reform Law.

In Physics she wrote on demand: Aleksandr Stepanovič Popov, Russian physicist, born March 17, 1859, in Bogoslovsk, guberniya of Perm, died January 13, 1906, in what was then St. Petersburg, invented the telephone in 1895. (She believed it, too, taking no further interest in the origin of this story; up to age sixteen she could only think of telephones in the context of authorities and a few select bourgeois families, minions of the NEP.) Even in her final exams, in June 1952, this would still have been the right answer. One day, accidentally, certainly not looking for anything in particular, she opened the encyclopedia inherited from the Papenbrocks in 1950 to the page giving Alexander Graham Bell's life story. Even much later, she wished she didn't have to forget the year 1895 for that reason, and that she might find another reason to look forward to visiting Edinburgh.

In 1947 she was taking third-year Russian, still from Charlotte Pagels. The topic was the derivation of Mecklenburg words from the Slavic, a language group preceding Russian, well then. At the end Cresspahl raised her hand, with all the timidity this child had by then become known for, and asked permission to say something about Gneez. Maybe the name was derived from the Soviet word for "nest," *gnezdo*? An A in the roll book! (Such things hurt her standing with the other girls in the class, even Lise Wollenberg; she had to make up for it by bringing up her house's location right across from the Jerichow Kommandatura and stories about Lieutenant Wassergahn. Finally Lise came to her aid. – It's true: she said. – The Cresspahls were practically occupied territory!)

As long as you didn't take the slightest peek to either side of the lesson plan—you'd lose your balance and fall:

> *Bow your head and bend your knee,*
> *Silently think of the SED;*
> *Give us not just potatoes and cabbage,*
> *Also give what the First Secretary and also the Deputy of the Social-*
> *ist Unity Party of Germany get to eat and take home in their*
> *baggage!*

When a classroom full of girls is left alone just before lunch, freezing in their coats, fifty or fifty-five degrees in the room in the very best case, what crazy song-and-dance routines they put on, shrieking and hopping on the tables like madwomen!

Eat less sugar?
Wrong, wrong, wrong!
Eat more sugar!
Sugar makes you strong!

until Fifi Pagels came rushing in, entirely forgetting the price of sweeteners on the black market, remembering only her dream of well-behaved children circa 1912, wounded, crying: You wicked, wicked children!

In February 1947 Dr. Kramritz's class was studying the new Mecklenburg constitution, which the parliament resulting from the previous year's election had just adopted. All inhabitants of German nationality are citizens of the country. Civil servants are servants of the people and must at all times prove themselves worthy of the people's trust. II. Citizens' Basic Rights and Basic Obligations, Article 8: The freedom of the individual is inviolable.

Persons who have been deprived of their freedom.
Must be informed on the following day at the latest.
Which authorities have done so and for what reasons.
This curtailment of freedom was ordered.
They are to be given the opportunity without delay.
Of objecting to the curtailment of their freedom.

Herr Dr. phil. Kramritz rented two rooms in Knoop's building, the prince's mansion. When Knoop came back from his curtailment of freedom in March, that was the first his loyally worrying mother had heard of him since February 3. Knoop said nothing, even to trusted friends, about his place of detention or other events connected to his diminished freedom. What he liked to say in response, smugly, wearing a smirk no one could prove he wore, in broad High German, was: The charges were struck down. Just like Emil.

In March, Mrs. Weidling called on Student Gesine in English class even though she had long since reached the middle of the alphabet, going in fair and proper order. And for this lesson Mrs. Weidling had brought with her a young man in city civilian clothes, introducing him as a future New

Teacher whose training included sitting in on classes like this one. Dr. Weidling already had Soviet counterintelligence going after her husband pretty hard, you could scarcely blame her for not warning us. Who wanted something to be blamed for from those times. After a few grammatical questions to the *N, O,* and *P* parts of the class, the Cresspahl girl was called on and asked to recite a poem that had been distributed in parts for memorization. She always thought it was a mistake for the Soviets to allow English as a second foreign language; she was more than willing to spare Mrs. Weidling any disgrace; she started and kept going, with vile pronunciation and a childishly singsong rhythm but a perfectly automatic and acceptable sentence melody, the way she'd learned it from her father since 1943, whenever they were without earwitnesses, and which Mrs. Weidling's instruction had been unable to modify:

Recuerdo
by Edna St. Vincent Millay
born 1892

RECITED BY HEART

"We were very tired, we were very merry—
We had gone back and forth all night on the ferry.
. . . .
We hailed, 'Good morrow, mother!' to a shawl-covered head,
And bought a morning paper, which neither of us read;
And she wept, 'God bless you!' for the apples and pears,
And we gave her all our money but our subway fares."

Marie may not believe it, since we take that ferry to Manhattan and then use the subway to get to Riverside Drive. Marie is suspicious of stories where everything fits together—I've taught her that much. The truth is that in teacher conferences Mrs. Weidling had already been introduced to certain signs of the times: having us learn poems like "The Song of the Shirt," by Thomas Hood, 1799–1845, With fingers weary and worn, / With eyelids heavy and red, /A woman sat, in unwomanly rags, / Plying her needle and thread for her daily bread, the sociocritical indictment. It's just that she'd had acquired her academic rank at a university, not by marriage; she had traveled through numerous countries, thanks to the favors her husband did for the army; she may even have actually owned a copy of *A Few Figs from Thistles* (1922), and she really and truly did subject her visiting auditor from the land of the Soviets to a recitation of this ferry poem with the pernicious message that personal charity could take the place of systematic reform, if indeed it had any message at all—she did not permit herself, or her students, any sycophancy; as with Leslie Danzmann, it was important to her to think of herself as a lady. The Cresspahl child suffered a terrible defeat.

Whend you realize, Gesine?
Oh Cresspahl. You cant forgive me!
I forgive you. Tell me.
I didn see im at first. Then I realized he hadn talked the whole time. Just sat lookin mute. When I was done he said something to Weidling in English. Thats when I knew: Hes a Russian.
Wasnt too bad, Gesine.
It was for me. That was the first time I knew for sure you were still alive. But I'd betrayed us. You had to spend another year in Fünfeichen.
Please, Gesine. He was just sposed to check if I'd really spent years in Inglant.
And whether they could send you back to South London with a child who could pass for a native speaker.
That's right, Gesine. You might still have had the chance to learn Richmond English.
Would you have gone to England for the Russians?
I would've for you. That's what I wanted to ask you as soon as they let me go back to you.
We're getting to that soon. When we do, I'll say the wrong thing again.
Fer me, Gesine.

June 30, 1968 Sunday
Colonel Emil Zátopek, the man himself, who'd been held up to us as a model for the link between humanism and sports under the benevolent

Soviet aegis ever since his victory in the 5,000-meter at the International Allied Meet in Berlin's Olympic Stadium in early September 1946,

Emil Zátopek, who'd wanted to speak those two thousand words to all the people in his country, now doesn't understand why the party is angry at his hope that the guilty will finally be treated as guilty. – I see nothing counterrevolutionary in it: he says. He says: All those who signed the statement are concerned with the fast construction of democratic Socialism and human freedom. That's what he says.

And he's not alone—*Zemědělské Noviny*, the farmer's newspaper, says something similar, as does *Mladá Fronta*, the Communist youth paper for the whole ČSSRepublic. Now even the carpenter's son, winner of a gold and a silver at the 1948 Olympic Games in London, master of interval training, not only an icon for long-distance runners but a live model for the Soviets during a year spent living in Crimea, winner of three gold medals in the superfluous 1952 Olympics in Helsinki, for running

5,000 meters in	14:06.6
10,000 meters in	29:17.0
42,200 meters in	2:23:03.2;

holder of nineteen world records in total, head of Czechoslovakian military sports since 1958, chosen as athlete of the year in his country as recently as 1966, living in Prague, near the main train station, at U pujčavny (Pawnshop) 8, the Czech Locomotive, him too: Emil Zátopek.

The Abses managed to get me into Pastor Brüshaver's confirmation class for only two hours, then he kicked me out; I had to take dancing lessons two afternoons a week at the Sun Hotel in Gneez behind the district council office—but in the spring of 1947, because in the winter there had been neither heat nor daylight enough. I had no time for my homework, came back grumpy to Jerichow on the evening train, but my grumbling didn't sway Jakob or his mother: the child had to get what was proper for her. Dancing lessons.

They could see it in Jerichow, Jakob could see it at his training courses in Gneez: some things about bourgeois ways were to be preserved. They saw me as a middle-class child, never mind that my father had disappeared and one of my uncles was guilty of unspeakable crimes; it was almost like they had taken on the job of giving me a fancy education. In Jerichow as in the district capital, they saw high society unscathed, except for those who'd been caught with weapons in the Soviet Union, or in the Nazi Party's files, or with noble titles and title deeds too and overly profitable business deals with the old Reich. Or else in anonymous notes. The others were left to believe they would still be needed, and believe it they did. Whether trading in shoe heels or weighing out twenty-gram slivers of butter for the workers, they all felt certain that the system for feeding and provisioning the population would have been running even worse without them. No one in our class at school said so out loud, but almost from the beginning we'd thought of ourselves as divided into the natives and the refugees. The grown-ups extended the distinction to long-established citizenry versus newly arrived lowlifes; in part, no doubt, because the decorative wood carvings of the Sudeten Germans and East Prussians took a little money out of their own pockets. These newcomers had had to leave practically all their possessions behind; as for the articles of gold or paintings in oil that the right people in Jerichow owned, the plundering Soviets hadn't managed to find them all, not by a long shot, and in times of greater need these could be exchanged at the Red Army's Razno-Export for cigarettes, exchangeable in turn for butter or a sailor suit (Bleyle), worn just twice, that a refugee boy had managed to hold on to. This better sort had rarely lost sight of one another—even Gneez was small enough for that—and now they congregated again, in conservative political parties for instance, where they discussed the minimal or "night-watchman" state, or a future annexation by a Scandinavian country. The revolutionary Red Army had even left them Mecklenburg as an autonomous province; the irritating addition, "-Vorpommern," had been removed by the law of March 1, 1947, so now they had less to say and really you had to chalk that up as a win for Mecklenburg. The province of Mecklenburg. *Land Mecklenburg.* Article I, §1, paragraph 3 of the new Mecklenburg constitution defined the official state colors as: blue, yellow, red. These were also the traditional colors, but what business of anyone's is that.

These people showed what they thought of one another in other ways, too. Sure, Johannes Schmidt's heirs in Jerichow eventually let the SED use its loudspeakers free of charge for election campaigns; Wauwi Schröder, likewise in the musical and electronic field, but in Gneez, had two display windows and in one of them hung, through February 1947, a calligraphed sign in a gold frame:

> We consider it an honor,
> now and in the future,
> to put our loudspeakers at the disposal
> of the Red Army and the party allied to it
> in service of the anti-Fascist cause,
> free and without charge,

with the addendum:

> The microphone that was apparently forgotten about on September 19 we consider a token of our goodwill.

Plus two medium-sized azalea pots. After the next large rally, held in connection with the Moscow meeting of the Council of Foreign Ministers on April 24, Wauwi disconnected his microphone along with the remaining cables and also replaced the document in the display window with the latest dictum of the ranking functionary: The SED would continue, as ever, to oppose any change to the borders. These people would have been more than happy to let the refugees return to their territory beyond the Oder and Neisse—anything to have Mecklenburg to themselves again.

They found one another in the realm they considered their ancestral birthright: that of cultural functions. Proper table manners, nuanced forms of address, status-appropriate clothing—all self-explanatory. But how could one accuse a paint dealer of narrow-minded money-grubbing if he almost never missed a meeting of the Cultural League (for a Democratic Renewal of Germany), even the meetings devoted to interpreting a poem by Friedrich Hölderlin or some such? The old families of Gneez had collected Mecklenburgana, not just Lisch's five volumes or the *Yearbook* but glassware, silhouettes, chests, portraits of old-fashioned mayors, and views of the cathedral before the inexplicable incident from the summer of 1659. They had almost pulled together enough money at one point to give a commission to the sculptor Ernst Barlach—a bronze rendition of their embarrassing heraldic animal in as dignified a form as possible; nothing came of it after all, what with his disputes with the Güstrow and Berlin Nazis. Gneez was no Güstrow. They just put the Barlach books that the Nazis didn't like toward the back of their display cases; first of all, such poems had been the *dernier cri* around 1928, simply indispensable for one's self-respect; secondly, their eventual monetary value was perhaps only suffering a temporary setback. And Gneez had a writer of its own!—born as the son of a day laborer on the Old Demwies estate, true, but claimed by the good city of Gneez in Mecklenburg ever since being shipped on to the Cathedral School on a municipal scholarship in his eleventh year. He'd managed to publish a volume of poems and two novels before he had to flee the country because of the Nazis; even under the British occupation, the city council had requested to rename Wilhelm Gustloff Street after Joachim de Catt; to Triple-J, too, de Catt's emigration was credential enough. *Nu vot*, unusual legislation calls for unusual legislation. *Pochemu nyet? Mozhno. Imeyem vozmozhnost'*. Admittedly, "our poet" hadn't yet found his way back to his proud hometown, neither in person nor by letter. Were he to return from his transatlantic climes, Gneez would gladly forgive whatever had been a bit irksome in the likeness he'd captured of a Mecklenburg small town in 1931, Gneez was hardly petty; he should get his celebration, and for now Mr. Jenudkidse had already approved the second poetry recital in honor of J. de Catt. They found one another there too, not just in the lectures given by Mrs. Lindsetter, the wife of the chief justice of the district court, who publicly communicated her memories of the wartime-shortage recipes of 1916. The church was part of it—religion was clearly a component of proper decorum; the cathedral was more crowded during evening organ concerts than during religious services. Dean Marjahn's sermons were certainly edifying and innocuous; if he went on a titch too long on a major holiday, his ears were bound to be set ringing afterward by the tongue-lashings of conscientious ladies who'd been forced to take their goose out of the oven too late, apron tied over their Sunday dress, or found themselves behind on their carp. In the 1946 Hunger Winter too. Those ladies were still there. If Dr. Kliefoth had had his apartment cleaned out, that was just his bad luck. Anyway, in 1932 he'd gone and picked that backwater Jerichow to live in, not the upstanding city of Gneez, which could boast no fewer than two town chronicles over the centuries. Still, happy about it or not, one would probably have to take him back into the old fellowship—PhD, senior instructor, lieutenant colonel in the army, oddly respected by the Soviet authorities; he didn't come. *Ah never mind. Murrjahn was a stubborn dog but in the end he hadta give in.*

Cresspahl's child, though a commuter student from Jerichow and a bit of an awkward case given her father's arrest, was felt to belong—the elite families welcomed her with pleasure. The British, after all, not the Soviets had made this Cresspahl the mayor. What a chic black coat she wore. She took pride in her appearance; she didn't have refugees do her tailoring, she went to Helene Rawehn on the market square. And, just as propriety demanded at her age, she was taking dancing lessons.

They called their commandant "Mr. Jenudkidse," even to his face. They weren't going to be found lacking in proper manners. He liked it too, unfortunately. But they thought they could get him to commit to being polite as a result.

There were exceptions, characterized with the saying about the traces left on a person who's touched the devil. Leslie Danzmann, for instance: the Knoops, the Marjahns, the Lindsetters predicted a dim future for her when she too got involved with the new powers that be. Leslie Danzmann—old Mecklenburg family, English grandmother, navy lieutenant's widow, a lady. Turned up near Gneez right around the middle of the war, rented one of the most modern villas by the sea, lived absolutely comme il faut as the housekeeper of a gentleman who had something to do with the Reich Aviation Ministry in Berlin. No false moves. Classy. Then the people who still played tennis had attracted attention in Gneez; Leslie Danzmann, also, was made to work, drafted into the labor office. Force majeure. But did she have to go to the Russians and look for work in their administration? The fact that someone owns nothing but a lapsed pension and has never learned how to do any kind of respectable job—give piano lessons, be married to a doctor—what kind of excuse is that! Now she too had been arrested for a bit, part of the Cresspahl business, strange don't you think?, but did she take that as a warning? No, our fine Danzmann has gone and offered her services to the Soviets again. You tell children: Don't get too close to that. Now she's fallen right in—let go from the housing office, had to go to the fish cannery. Didn't she realize that Comrade Director of the Housing Office was inviting her to join the SED? Couldn't she think of any other answer besides: But what will the neighbors think of me, Mr. Yendretzky! She was pretty much right about that, in terms of the neighbors, but to go and blurt it out. As if you didn't teach children: Hold your tongue. Now she went to work early every day, on foot from the coast, on the dairy train to Gneez, standing at a stinking table all day cleaning flounder, boiling fish stew. No, she didn't complain. She's still one of us to that extent. How cannery women talk, a housewife with some experience

1272 · *June 30, 1968* Sunday

of the world can easily imagine it. You know their word for a woman's
private parts. A cultured woman won't put it into words. What happens
when a woman, a married woman, when she voluntarily lays down with a
man, they talk about that as ——. Well, working-class women, what do
you expect? What a hideous word too. Speaking of which, *when you think
about it its maybe not so far off really.* Such a word will never cross my lips,
Frau Schürenberg! Leslie Danzmann had it coming to her. If a girl gets
herself brought up all nice and proper and wants to live like that and have
everything come to her just the way she likes then she shouldn't go somewhere she can be kicked out of into a cannery! And did she show any
neighborly feeling, this Leslie Danzmann? She was right next to all that
fish, couldn't she ever bring some by? Just as a courtesy? Not once. If she
talked about her work at all it was to praise the proletarian women. So
good-natured, supposedly. Always helped her, she said. There was one,
Wieme Wohl from the Danish Quarter, known all around town, who'd
said more than once at the end of the day, before the bag inspection: Hey,
Danzmann, cmere, here's an eel. Tie it round your waist. If yer too squea-
mish I'll do it for you. 'S just for ten minutes, Danzmann! Don' be so
proud.... Danzmann had stayed firm. It wasn't pride, she said. – It's just
that it's not mine, girls! It doesn't belong to me! The women persuaded
her. In the end Leslie was willing to believe that fish, especially eel, never
made it to the stores, only to the private Red Army and party distributors;
she had no problem with that, she could see that. But then she'd insisted:
the eel wasn't hers. That's what happens to someone who lets herself drop
out of morality and respect for property!

Cresspahl's child didn't like going to dancing class. She did it because
Mrs. Abs told her to.

She spent those afternoons in Gneez with Lise Wollenberg. In dancing
class they were known to boys from elsewhere as the blond and brunette
from Jerichow. The dancing master was Franz Knaak, from a Hamburg
family whose members, with a single exception, had all been dancing masters since 1847. This one was fat and liked to speak French, emphasizing
the nasals; he was so proud of his mechanical gestures that he was able to
console himself for his ample corporeality with languid, brown-eyed glances.
First he taught them the old German dances—the Rhinelander, the Kegel—
all with references to the heritage of our fathers. Instead of something Soviet.

He let himself be talked into teaching the slow dance only after universal, almost deafening requests; he showed how the movements looked in such an oily, filthy way that we would be filled with disgust for them all the rest of our lives, at least that's what he hoped. He wore something resembling a frock coat, soapy at the neck, and held up the hem on each side with two fingers, demonstrating the single steps of the mazurka with a feeble spring in his step. What an unbelievable monkey: Gesine Cresspahl thought to herself. But she saw the absorbed smile on beautiful, merry, long-legged Lise's face as she followed Herr Knaak's leaps and hops; Lise knew so much about everything. – How'll you ever get a man if you don't learn to dance! she'd said, and all down the long end of the room the mothers were draped on worn plush chairs, Mrs. Wollenberg among them, dabbing their eyes. That wasn't how the Cresspahl girl saw it. She didn't want to get a man that way. She already knew one, and he went dancing with someone else.

She'd decided her coat should be black because she wanted to wear it in mourning for her father, *not* because he was probably dead but just in memory of him. That was only proper. She knew it. But it was something inappropriate to talk about.

On the evenings after dancing class she almost always ran into Leslie Danzmann on the train platform. She greeted her, stood far away from her as they waited for the train, and never got into the same compartment as her. Leslie Danzmann may have imagined another humiliation, this time due to the smell coming off her. But it wasn't that. Cresspahl's child rather liked the smell, if anything. She wanted to punish this Danzmann woman. She'd been let free, her father hadn't. She hadn't brought any news from him. She might even have betrayed him.

July 1, 1968 Monday

Sometimes I think: That's not her. What does that mean here, "she," "me"? It can be thought; but it is unthinkable. If she were alone, I would have to think: That's Gesine Cresspahl (Mrs.), a woman around thirty-five, not a lady, in the very best posture for elegant occasions—chin high, back straight and far from the back of her chair, gaze so mobile that it can shift from moment to moment between surveying the room and an indissoluble bond with only one object, only one person; from a distance I could tell it was her from her short hair in what the stylist intended as a feathered cut, but the overlapping close layers of a bird's wing now look too loose, too ragged over the forehead. Close up there is no mistaking her for anyone else, what with the cautious movements of her overly narrow lips, whether chewing or speaking; the shallow hollows below her cheekbones, skin sometimes stretched tight over them, straining to mimic the right behavior; the little wrinkles that have hardened in the corners of her eyes, the involuntarily narrowed pupils: the first thing I'd think is that she's scared, and hiding it, skillfully. She's on her guard, she's going to defend herself—but she wants to seem polite, friendly, ladylike. It would take a lover to observe specifically how she takes a deftly apportioned bite of fish from the end of her fork and dismantles it with barely visible chewing, so that her mouth is empty again at once, ready to smile or give an answer—we don't notice anything in particular. But, she is not alone.

She is just one of many people in a long, spacious dining room with very white vertical bands of cloth blocking the sun coming in through the floor-to-ceiling windows on two walls; she is sitting surrounded by men at one of the north tables and an empty, dirty sky is behind her, with the shy tops of skyscrapers, silhouetted like cutouts, reaching up into it— airplanes there would be less unexpected. She may know how to act in restaurants, be familiar with the comportment demanded by the damask tablecloth and silver place settings with a knife rest and three drinking glasses; her nod to the waiter over her shoulder is irreproachable as he bends down to let her examine the plate with the next course—she will have learned all these things. But this is the restaurant high in the East Tower of the bank, closed to the public, to ordinary people, even to employees. The head manager for office supplies is honored to be invited up into this circle of heaven, permitted to read the menu with its French formulations that he approves every day when it comes out of the in-house printshop. While Mrs. Cresspahl is not only lower in rank—that in itself would suffice to make the waiters slightly standoffish with her—she is also the only woman there today. Oh, women are brought here sometimes, it does happen. Only then they're part of the family, one of the bank's owners; they're wives, invited along when a vice president is promoted or shoved off into retirement and his nearly paid-off house on the better or worse side of Long Island Sound; ladies sometimes come on business from allied firms, after a contract has been signed, a scam's been pulled off; when the National Bank of the People's Republic of Poland dispatches for negotiations not a man but a Mrs. Paula Ford, a meal in these well-protected heights to honor her is indispensable. Less than a year ago Mrs. Cresspahl was still a secretary for foreign languages: she used to work down on the lower floors, in a big group office, with cassette players, and the voices speaking from them didn't belong to people she needed to be introduced to; she started even farther downstairs, at an adding machine in the Finance Department; what is she doing here? And she's not at just any table—she's at the one reserved for de Rosny, the true monarch of this bank, the Vice President of all Vice Presidents, deputy chairman of the board of directors. He receives state visits from the competition here, he conducts his seminars for the heads of the foreign departments, and at noon today he turned up with Mrs. Cresspahl. Maybe she's on a secret assignment for him, something statistical probably; still, she's one of the dispensable ones, owed two weeks' notice and then basta; yet everyone summoned to the table, with nod or call across the room, has had to say hello to this Mrs. Cresspahl following all due formalities, while some of them have run into her earlier in the day, with nothing more than a normal Hi. *Hi.* Now, though, what's called for is: *It's a pleasure.* . . . ; now she's sitting at de Rosny's right hand, as if hosting the gentlemen with their grave responsibilities along with him. But it's just a woman! De Rosny can do whatever he has planned, but this isn't what he should be doing. What does she want here!

She wishes she were somewhere else. She likes to go downstairs for lunch, out of the building. It may be hot downstairs, the forecast is 95 degrees, but she could have crossed Lexington and Madison Avenues to Fifth to buy blouses like the other "coworkers" with no time for department stores after work; she could sit in Gustafsson's fish shop on Second, leaning back, with Amanda Williams, with Mr. Shuldiner, with friends, in conversations where she doesn't have to watch out like a hawk the whole time. She'd be more than happy to give up the arctic chill that the appliances here fabricate for the bosses in exchange for the relaxed hour she's guaranteed by contract. She knows it won't be forever. She's one of the other class of people in the city, who can neither buy nor pay to operate such an air conditioner. Tonight, when she gets back to the Upper West Side, there won't be many of these expensive boxes overhead sticking out of the buildings; people will be sitting on the stoops, hoping for the protection provided by the naturally occurring shadows and nothing more, all they can do is push open the windows and hope for a breeze from the air rushing down the channels of the streets. Marie will keep the apartment door open to try to get a cross-breeze between the Hudson and the stairwell, to hell with burglars. The electricity can be turned off, the gas pressure lowered, the faucets left thirsty. The firefighters will once again have neglected to outfit their hydrants with spray caps, so children will have to use force before they can hop around in the spraying streams intended for use against fires. Anyone driving by of an evening, in a sealed and air-conditioned car, will see classic New York local color and not suspect a shortage of working showers on the poor streets. After the high-pressure system that's been moving so laboriously from the Gulf of Mexico over New York since yesterday, others will come to pay a visit, and someone like Mrs. Cresspahl will never officially own a doubly and triply guaranteed air conditioner— this single hour in the climate-controlled fortress of the bank may be hazardous to her ability to survive in New York. Since de Rosny wants her to, she is sitting in the cold with her back to the north while the breeze from the blades behind her caresses her back. Her shivers often turn into shudders.

She has a sense of what de Rosny's getting at by bringing her into this company of privilege-laden men; she knows that it isn't about her. If asked by his own ilk he'd say something about women's equal rights; no less a word than *emancipation* might cross his lips, with the cheerful earnestness that even his friends from the West Coast have a hard time reading mockery into. Then it would all be taken as one of his whims, and one tiny misstep would turn Mrs. Cresspahl into someone paying the price for it. As long as she sits up straight and yet puts one foot in front of the other in exactly the right place, he can accustom his subordinates, men though they are, to the presence of a woman at business lunches, and even to her competence to speak up, so that someday they'll discuss with her a matter of business where she'll be representing de Rosny—business in a country that they know very little about . . . but we won't discuss that now. De Rosny started with invitations to places like the Brussels and Quo Vadis, where his peers, friend or foe, were to help spread the rumor that he seemed to be consoling himself after all for the nasty situation with his wife, he's barely sixty after all, de Rosny, isn't he; here, in the boss's restaurant, the boys'll think what they're supposed to think if he wants them to. In any case, de Rosny has clearly forgotten how you're supposed to treat women—he doesn't need to give advance notice, it doesn't occur to him that she might need to prepare her schedule or wardrobe, when he calls he expects Mrs. Cresspahl to come as she is. So now she can no longer come to work in the older dress that's easy to clean, it's okay if she sweats in it; her small raise is eaten up almost every month by the shopping she has to do in stores that maybe the Kennedys' maids could afford but not a bank employee! She got lucky today, with her sleeveless ribbed-silk number from Bergdorf Goodman with a short jacket—formal enough, the color next to the white hopefully works with her hair color—only she'd tried to save on tailoring, it doesn't fit as well as it could, and up here she feels like she's freezing in it. The women who work as news announcers on TV get supplemental pay for their clothes, don't they? *Thats messed up.* Anyway, we hold our end up well enough in the art of conversation.

Today it plays out once again like a kind of test, because that's what de Rosny wants. He doesn't come across as manipulative, he seems fully at ease—the philosophizing boss. The younger men try to catch his eye and at the same time get their meat (grilled lamb cutlets with peas flown in from somewhere) off their plate—worshipful as puppy dogs they are, Wilbur N. Wendell, Henri Gelliston, Anthony Milo, despite the fact that they'd been dictating truly imperious letters to banks on other continents just an hour ago. They're invisible to de Rosny, who is busy recalling the years 1899 and 1900, as though saddened by the passing of time—the Open Door policy, the directives to expand American business abroad, the canonization of the faith that America must not keep its system, the best of all possible in business as well as politics, to itself but instead bestow it on other nations. Employee Cresspahl keeps her eyes on her plate: she has learned all about this in school, exactly the same facts, just with other words, along with the conceit that the thoughts of anyone ignorant of dialectical materialism were not to be taken seriously. De Rosny has brought his puppy dogs to the point where they want to prove themselves good students. Anthony, poor Anthony. He probably left Brooklyn too soon, left his recent-immigrant mother with her embarrassing peasant head scarf whom he now rides past every day on the commuter train from Long Island. He should have scouted out the lay of the land! Instead, falling for the new nationalism, our Tonio launches into the legends—the troops sailing to the Philippines from California, Dewey's victory in Manila Bay (1898), the sinking of the *Maine* earlier that year; blind with zeal he runs right into de Rosny's knife: Not even John Jacob Astor ever talked like that, young Mr. Milo. Think of our missionaries in China!

It all has something indirectly to do with Mrs. Cresspahl's secret assignment—this dispatching of American trade and traffic to the benighted nations; she can sense de Rosny's gaze passing over her out of the corner of her eye. No thank you. It's too soon for her to triumph over these better-paid men under de Rosny's thumb. Plus she's too angry at them. Does Mrs. Cresspahl own a house on Long Island? Does she have a stock portfolio? No, thanks anyway. Tomorrow Tonio will tell James Carmody: You were lucky you weren't there!

Now de Rosny decides to use ribbed silk as an example: international credit can't do it, of course, the poor natives can acquire the goods and services of the industrialized nations only when they get jobs, purchasing licenses, trade by means of which they can send the results of their own prosperity back to the USA, let's say. Now take the ribbed silk in this exquisite dress our Mrs. Cresspahl is wearing....

Thank you. That she does say, then she talks across the table with Mr. Kennicott II, about the Long Island Rail Road strike. Was it bad? Mr. Kennicott may be the head of the Personnel Department but this was a swish of the matador's red cape that got him, he's confused, he starts complaining about the heat in the stopped trains this morning. Mrs. Cresspahl won't let herself be herded into purely feminine topics. Let our purportedly universally admired vice president hold forth on barre ribs, Ottoman ribbing, ribs ondé—the lady isn't listening, her devoted attention is turned to Kennicott II and nothing seems to matter more to her than how it was on the Montauk line with eighteen out of twenty-four trains from Babylon not in service. She nods, she can imagine, who would doubt it.

Shortly before reaching the late-Egyptian evidence for ribbed fabrics, de Rosny gets bored; he generously yields the floor to Mr. Gelliston (Harvard Business School) and Mr. Wendell, letting them pronounce on how the Open Door policy grew and prosperity resulted under McKinley,

Roosevelt, and Wilson, from the Algeciras Conference to the Webb-Pomerance and Edge Acts, the requirements as act, as law, and of American business and the White Man's Burden. But we have a lady at the table who is not only charming and beautiful but fully educated in Marxism. What do you have to say, Mrs. Cresspahl?

– It is the indispensable duty of all the nations of the earth: she says, apparently gladly, and firmly confident in the preacherly voice by the fifth word, if anything falling too deep into the orotund hollow that the *d-y-u* leaves in her throat: to know that the LORD he is God, and to offer unto him sincere and devout thanksgiving and praise. But if there is any nation under heaven, which hath more peculiar and forcible reasons than others, for joining one heart and voice in offering up to him these grateful sacrifices, the United States of America are that nation.

Laughter. Applause. She does blush a little, why try to hide it. But it does come out cute, more feminine, diminishing her success somewhat. And again she's too angry, even more than when she read in one of Marie's textbooks Levi Frisbie's sermon dated five years after the French Revolution. Now there's a bet about this date, and she forgoes the prize, adding an extra year so that de Rosny hands it out to Henri Gelliston. The boss laughed so heartily that his eyes weren't free to do anything else; she catches his small, approving nod.

Now the conversation turns to dialectics, the railroad strike, the heat, constantly if cautiously circling around politics. The plane with 214 American soldiers on board that Soviet fighters forced to land on the Kuril Islands yesterday is not even mentioned: de Rosny frowns on the current president's policies, why force him into any awkward repetitions. (On March 16, de Rosny was not received at the White House.) The cost of summer camp, coffee, vacation plans. Mr. Kennicott II is given suggestions for restaurants in Amsterdam. Someone's already told him about one, what's the name again, something about a yellow bird. De Rosny advises against. Does Mr. Kennicott want to spend his time in Holland dining with Americans or stock market people? De Rosny knows another place, dark wood paneling, solid old-fashioned furniture, fatherly waiters, the floorboards tremble— some kind of schoolroom Latin name. . . . – Do you mean Dorrius?: Employee Cresspahl says cautiously, like a schoolgirl; she doesn't want to overdo it. (She's only seen Dorrius from the outside, it was too expensive for her; she knows more about it from D. E., whom of course all good things are there to serve.) De Rosny is now free to either ruin her offering or visibly praise her among and before his students.

– Dorrius! That's what it's called! de Rosny cries.

– It has three exits: Mrs. Cresspahl adds meekly.

Their duet is applauded, de Rosny bows for the both of them, and the amused chitchat about dialectics lasts all the way to the elevator. She can't get free of him there either. He still does not withdraw into his distinguished chambers; he chivalrously accompanies his team down to their office foyer. Where it turned out he was accompanying Mrs. Cresspahl, and it wasn't about chivalry, it was to have a word with her behind closed doors. She is suddenly so nervous that she stays standing in the middle of the room that's set up for her work.

De Rosny doesn't want to sit down either. He leans against the door, looks around at the charts on the wall, the documents on the metal bureau, seeking an opening.

Who is this de Rosny? What on earth is her connection with him? Was he one of the men who celebrated the fall of France on June 26, 1940, with a banquet at the Waldorf-Astoria? No, not him, but maybe his parents. She feels no threat from him with regard to anti-Fascist elements—Fascism's bad for business. Should she be suspicious of him for being anti-Fascist for the wrong reasons? What does he want, here in her room, behind closed doors?

She has before her a gentleman who has taken care of his body since youth. He won't die from that. It'll be an advanced old age indeed that gets him. He's kept his brain busy, but not forcing it or letting it drift into alcohol. This guy'll be sharp as a tack when death comes for him. Barely a wrinkle in his brow. A full head of thick hair, flecked with gray but not white like an old man's. Still, his eyes, usually cool and sharp, are dull today, hardly even still blue. He'll lose that look tonight, on the golf course on the Sound. She looks at him; she'd recognize him even in disguise; she can't let her look show what else she knows, which is that he's one of the people we were warned about in school. He is Money, hateful and malevolent. It has raised him; he serves it; if he does want to extend credit to the Czechoslovak Socialist Republic it's not to improve Socialism there. He understands the aspects of politics that can harm money. He finds it useful to send the Czechs and Slovaks someone who once lived in the vicinity. It doesn't need to be her, but it is her. Why isn't that disgusting?

– Mrs. Cresspahl. So here's the opening. And she clears her throat, and already he's brought to a stop. Which isn't what she wanted to do, she was trying to help him out of his embarrassment. – Sir?

– You're willing to do all these things for us. . . . You're going to Prague for us, taking your child out of school, from her home in New York . . . it might take three months, six months: he repeats, insists, but not with any regret in his voice. It's not sympathy he has in mind. Why isn't he looking her in the eye?

– Yes. Sir: Employee Cresspahl says.

– Would you do something else, too? Something . . . I can't tell you what it is, I've already said too much! You can say no. . . . : he has sped up; in anyone else she'd be sure he felt embarrassment, timidity, shame. He just gives a little smile. I saw Cresspahl's cat look like that, holding its paw above the mouse.

It's not the bank I'm doing this for.
I realize that.
You have no idea why I am doing it, Mr. de Rosny.
Maybe not. But as long as it's useful for us.
I don't need to say a word to you.
You can refuse the assignment. This is your last chance.
And then get my two weeks' notice.
You know the terms of your contract, Mrs. Cresspahl.
After two months I couldn't afford my apartment, after six I'd have to take Marie out of her school.
And if that's worth it?
You'll put me on a blacklist and I'd never get another job in any bank in New York State, Pennsylvania, New England.
You'd get compensation.
If I keep my mouth shut.
That's the way it is, young lady. *We could even make trouble with your visa.*
And of course you'd apologize.
Only in the moment. Now.

Say it, Mr. de Rosny. Just so I know.
Try to prove I was here in your office, Mrs. Cresspahl. Just try to prove it to anyone!

– I will not refuse to do anything that's necessary to carry out my assignment: Employee Cresspahl says, stiff and polite. She's annoyed with herself—she let down her guard for a single moment and now, in the empty space, there's trust. She's scared but not of the right thing.

– That's the kind of courage I admire: de Rosny says, turns, shoulders open the door, leaves it ajar, and is gone. He was never here.

In the remaining hours, Mrs. Cresspahl does her work as if every last bit of it had to be finished by five p.m. today. She can recalculate the LIBOR (London InterBank Offered Rate) again. She can convert it into Czech crowns a third time. She finishes with only two minutes to spare for the memo to the head of personnel: Dorrius Restaurant, Amsterdam, The Netherlands, has one exit on N. Z. Voorburgwal, two on Spuistraat (N. Z. = Nieuwezijds = New Side; there hasn't been an Old Side for about a hundred and fifty years): Sincerely Yours, G. C. When the evening heat assaults her on the street, she realizes she also feels a sharp edge of fear. That's what it's like when you're trying to forget something. Why is more and worse being expected of her than of all the people around her, who are cautiously approaching Grand Central Station and scared of nothing on this first of July 1968 but a sudden burst of sweat, the nun with the beggar's plate on her knees between the doors of the east entrance, the ragged old woman with her swollen legs asleep on the steps of the Graybar Building with a tattered paper bag held tight in her hand. It's not fear she feels, it's worse: it's like a farewell. Saying goodbye to New York.

July 2, 1968 Tuesday

The American military in Vietnam is battling the press, telling the flat-out lie that reporters' access to the news in wartime is as rapid and complete as reporters could possibly want. And the newspapers apparently believe it. Last week John Carroll from *The Baltimore Sun* went to Khesanh and saw with his own eyes how marines were breaking runways into separate steel plates and dynamiting their own bunkers. Since he assumed that enemy troops in advance positions could make similar observations, he sent the news home. The general from the Press Department confiscated Mr. Carroll's press pass for an indeterminate time; neither embassy nor military personnel will talk to him, and when he wants to get from one place to another no army vehicle will take him. The army says he is an estimated ninety percent right; apparently the remaining tenth of its opinion suffices for a ban. Maybe the retreat from Khesanh doesn't yet fit with what they're calling three months of ferocious defense

In Hesse, in the Federal Republic of Germany, Dr. Fritz Bauer has died. He was the chief prosecutor of the State of Hesse and one of the few people in office who from the beginning considered the Nazi crimes prosecutable under the law, and prosecuted them. He especially hunted down the murderers who tried to use clean hands as proof of their innocence, having washed away the stains, from Eichmann to a number of concentration camp doctors. Without him the Auschwitz trial from 1963 to 1965 would never have taken place. There are many sentences she thought of writing to Mr. Bauer, the child that I was—none were ever sent. Only sixty-four years old, and now he's dead.

The Gesine Cresspahl of the Soviet occupation zone had started a diary in spring 1947.

It wasn't technically a diary. (And this isn't either, for different reasons: here she's agreed to have a scribe—instead of her, with her permission—write an entry for every day but not of that day.) That one she wrote herself, but she left out whole weeks sometimes. It wasn't because she'd made a New Year's resolution. It was to keep things from being forgotten, that's true, but it was for someone else's sake, not hers. It hardly looked like a book or a notebook. Jakob's mother wouldn't have wanted to touch it; Jakob wouldn't have gotten past the first few lines; she had only a very vague sense of why she wanted to protect it. It lay between now these pages and now those pages of Büchner's *Economic Geography of Mecklenburg-Schwerin*, which is a dissertation fat enough for a dedication to the author's parents, thin enough to be a special issue; you could hardly fit more than a couple of slips of paper between its pages. There was no date on the slip of paper—it had to not look like a diary on second glance either. There were few complete sentences, in that adolescent handwriting, just words in rows, kind of like a badly arranged vocabulary list, many of them crossed out. One was still legible: "jagged." Now and then she forgot what she'd been trying to preserve. We find this word a second time. It bears the recurrent sense that Schoolgirl Cresspahl's face must look jagged when she's talking to grown-ups because that's how she feels on the inside. But what are we to do with an entry like "Ya kolokoychik" or "Packard? Buick?" It's gone. And there were not only Russian words in the list, crossed out or let stand, but also German words disguised in Cyrillic transcription. It has run away, no one will ever catch it. It wasn't much of a diary, and it was meant to be one for Cresspahl. If you write something down for a person then he's bound to come back. A dead person can't read, right?

"Ya kolokoychik" isn't crossed out, so it was nothing to be ashamed of at the time. But if *Ya,* "Yes" in German, *Ja,* could also be "I" in Russian, *Я,* as the Cyrillic letter here suggests, then it might also be a clever abbreviation. What did Jakob (Ja-kob, Я-kob) have to do with *kolokoychik,* a little bell? A sleigh bell, *Schlittenklingel,* maybe? Was that supposed to be a nickname for Anne-Dörte, who still hadn't taken him away (Schleswig-Holstein, *Schlittenklingel*)? No, let's hope not. She wouldn't have wanted to pick a fight, especially by name-calling, with a girl Jakob liked better than her. So was it the diarist herself? Was she the bell that was too small?

"Rips." An entry for black market dealings—ribbed fabric, *Rips*—or tears in that fabric, the English word *rips*? Not pain in her ribs (*Rippen*): her unavoidable daily dealings with Jakob hurt elsewhere. No, "Rips" was Bettina Riepschläger, the acting German instructor at the Bridge School in Gneez, not much older than the students in 7-B but entrusted, right after her own graduation and a two-month teacher-training course, with providing a classical humanistic education. A cheerful girl, never insisting upon professional dignity. We did whatever we wanted in her class; she did too. It often seemed like *she* was talking out of turn. The Cresspahl girl wanted to show her that she had no intention of taking advantage of a certain shared experience they'd had in the lobby of Alma Witte's hotel; what she liked best was just looking at her. Bettina had had her fine pale hair cut fashionably short and tousled; she would comb it with her fingers, coming away with strands of hair an inch or two long. Blond, experience had taught, was Jakob's color. As opposed to darker shades. Today she too will know that this fashion came from the movie based on a Hemingway novel, where the Spanish terrorists chopped off a girl's hair, but that Maria was supposed to be a brunette. Best not to mention to Jakob that cornflower-blue dress, hanging so perfectly, or those beautiful full-grown legs, that carefree bright voice able to switch from a tone of camaraderie to a firm one conveying rebuke yet nonetheless safety. It sometimes happened that Bettina acted her age, which was nineteen. She might say: "*Kinnings...*," and then we would be, for a little while, children. Lise Wollenberg cried once, she was so afraid that Bettina might take a walk in the yard with someone other than her; Lise was now trying to place her feet the way Miss Riepschläger did. She was from Ludwigslust. She didn't often speak in the roundabout phrases Dr. Kramritz used, the anti-Fascist democratic constitution or the leading role of the party of the working class just came up as though they were self-evident, because they were ready to hand. For this teacher we wrote essays like "My Best Friend." Cresspahl from Jerichow had slipped even more deeply into an unshakable need for secrecy so she didn't want to admit to any best friend, falling back on a dog. There was no dog, it was neither the one from the Kommandatura nor Käthe Klupsch's chow chow, she just made it up, body shape to behavior. She went so far as to claim that this Ajax would stay at the edge of the military pool, unafraid, no matter how much she splashed him as she swam by. For this and many other reasons: he was Schoolgirl Cresspahl's best friend. As a grade she received the question, in diplomatic red handwriting: "A bit sentimental, no?" She was very pleased. She now considered this Bettina one of the most reasonable and rational teachers she'd ever had in her life, and that was something about her she wanted to tell Cresspahl about. Rips.

"Škola." School. This was where our diarist had her concerns, worries even. For there were not many teachers like Bettina, who was "free" after school hours like we were. Teachers like Dr. Kramritz believed they were respected, even venerated, just because it was quiet during their classes; almost no one talked about him. Everyone knew that life in Gneez was very different from his exposition of the Mecklenburg state constitution. He had picked up his stiff knee in precisely the war he now described as the nation's guilt, not his own. But it didn't look right when he pressed his wire-rimmed glasses even more firmly down on the bridge of his nose—he seemed to be taking up arms. His punishments were all permissible under school rules; he enjoyed being obeyed. The refugee children were scared of him. Gesine Cresspahl found the trace of a scar on his nose revolting. Still, he was able to force the class to recite what he wanted them to. This was not the case with Miss Pohl, math and geography, one of the women called "Miss" throughout her whole career even though she was over fifty and not an inch of her body possessed delicate grace. Intensely red-brown hair in a crew cut, jet-black eyes, full cheeks, full chin. Always wearing her one green hunting suit, sometimes with matching hat. We called her breasts "the outwork"—in Mecklenburg the tenant farm at the edge of a manor estate, but she didn't know the term, being a refugee from Silesia. She was mad at the world over her share in the German losses—you could see it behind her even, sullen expression. She didn't care. Once a child had failed to understand an arithmetic problem after the second repetition, that child simply lacked a head for mathematics as far as this lady was concerned and was just given up on, even if she couldn't pass with that D+. (Gesine Cresspahl was seen as possessing a head for geography, due to an essay she'd written on the soil properties and economy of China; this mistake persisted into the following spring.) Mrs. Pohl, Miss Pohl may have practiced her profession like a chosen vocation at some time in the past; now it was just a job, the prerequisite of a residence permit and ration card—she would do everything the job required and no more. Student Cresspahl still believed in escape through learning, but with this kind of teaching, time seemed to trickle away and she often had the feeling that something was being missed. The part of this she wanted to tell Cresspahl about came from her memory of his having helped her once, in 1944, with school. In school. Against school.

"Antif." Now that was one of Jakob's tougher evenings. For Cresspahl's daughter didn't come running to him with trifles—certainly not every trifle, and definitely not running; she might be younger than countesses named Anne-Dörte but she'd long since stopped being a child. Jakob might think she was taking what she deserved from him as the man of the house; the fact was she didn't have anyone else to ask the questions she had learned in school as answers. She had a hard time with the word "anti-Fascism." Fascism was something Italian, after all. Jakob had been handed the same word as her, in his own retraining course; he looked deeply resigned now that he had to set it in motion again behind his broad hard brow. They often used to sit on the steps outside Cresspahl's door, with a view of the boarded-up headquarters, seeing little of the guard marching around or the picture of Stalin in the triumphal arch. Jakob, like Cresspahl, knew how to set his eyes to a faraway look. It struck her once again, unfailingly, that his temples looked so solid, his forehead curving so seamlessly into his skull. Why did he get his hair cut so short, so high on his head, when a few days later it would look like a pelt again. If you like a horse's coat, you.... She also couldn't stop thinking about the slight displacement of the wrinkles in the corners of his eyes—they looked so taut, so alive, like he was conscious of his every movement. She hadn't been listening very closely. Jakob was well into an explanation that the Nazis, with their "National Socialism," had stolen a word from the Socialists, maybe two, and that was why a word like "anti-" couldn't possibly turn up near "Socialism," but there was no reason not to say "anti-Nazism" if she thought people would understand her. – Okay.... No: the Cresspahl child said. It was shocking how suddenly a conversation could be over. She thought that was an ugly word. – A shitty word for a shitty situation: Jakob said. She didn't know where to go from there. She'd known the whole time that he was about to stand up, give a nice stretch above her, and say goodbye down from his great height—smiling, solicitous, like an adult to a child. – *Don' forget bedtime*: he said, his Platt already pretty Mecklenburgish, and before she knew it he was past the walnut trees and on the way to town. She took it badly, she wrote it down in her diary. "Antif."?

"One leg, bike." She'd seen a man who could manage a bike with one leg.

"A. in Gneez." She hadn't been able to let go of her—in dreams Alexandra came back to life, came back (and looked nothing like Hanna Ohlerich, who'd spent weeks sleeping next to her, in the same fever). Alexandra in a foreign country, wearing a head scarf so that two bright arcs stood out above her forehead, said in Ukrainian: Here, Gesine. Hold this little guy for a second. And then Gesine really had Fat Eberhardt Paepcke in her arm, he wasn't dead either, just asleep, and dreaming, like her. (In March a freight train had come through Gneez full of people from Pommern who'd been kicked out by the Poles. Gesine had caught half an hour of the train's stopover and run from car to car, plaguing the tired, dirty people on the straw with her questions about Paepckes from Podejuch. Just like in the dream, she knew that they'd died two years ago in April, and as in a dream she couldn't stop herself, running to the next sliding door, her brain a blur of shame and hope, almost crying, her speech slurry.)

"White bread." Three exclamation points. This was Dr. Schürenberg's stalwart resistance to the Communist occupation. Since officially there was no white bread, he would put it on prescriptions.

"R. P." A little line between the two letters had turned it into the formula for *Requiescat In Pace*. This didn't help lay the incident to rest very much, and it was something she'd actually done, not just something that had happened; the memory of it would come back so sharp and painful that she'd flinch, as if from a pinprick. Jakob's mother tried to talk her into letting that evening go; she would speak so softly, so comfortingly, until the child fell asleep, and the next morning there it still was, unforgotten. How can something that started as clear and cold and clean as the feel of a wet-honed knife turn into fear of guilt?

R. P. had shown up in Cresspahl's kitchen one evening. Gesine came home from the despised dancing class that was so indispensable for her education in finer matters, and by then she had progressed so far in higher etiquette that a sixteen-year-old cavalier was standing outside her door, the boy from the pharmacy, waiting to talk further with her about tango steps and the graduation ball. A stranger was sitting at the table in the kitchen. Since Cresspahl had disappeared there were so few strangers in the house, so rarely visitors; she desperately hoped this might be Cresspahl. That wish was ground to dust by a series of miniscule glimpses, faster than anything can turn into words in the mind. The man's shoulders, averted, were round not from age but from laziness. His whole body was too tall; even from behind she knew he would have a ruddy, healthy-looking face. Also, Cresspahl would surely have stood up at the sound of her footsteps, or turned around, said in Platt: *Look a that . . . .*

She was barefoot at this point—no one had heard her steps on the tiles. Sitting at the table with the stranger were Jakob and his mother, not acting familiar but polite enough, a little uncertain, as if for all their right to be there they still had to justify themselves. The man looked up when she stepped to the table, just casually, seeing nothing there but a child. – Hey there: he said, condescendingly, intrusive with his claim to being family, entirely at ease. – Get out: said Cresspahl's daughter, fourteen years old.

This was weeks ago and she was still trying to convince herself that it hadn't been hate. She'd just looked at him. She'd memorized his face: round skull, Mecklenburg type, a bit meaty. Big eyes, the blue that's supposed to mean honesty and that flickers so rapidly. Full, spoiled lips. So respectable, so well-fed. In a suit of re-dyed army fabric that fit as if custom-tailored. The rubber boots didn't go with the rest of the grandeur, but he probably planned to pick up leather shoes here. He still hadn't stood up. – Out! she screamed. – *You get outta here!*

She'd used the informal pronoun and felt bad about that once he'd left; she hadn't really had the right to speak so familiarly. Then it finally dawned on Jakob that this was her uncle, her mother's brother, Louise Papenbrock's favorite child that she didn't want in Cresspahl's house. Bah, he hadn't even gotten a beating. With a crooked grin and a shrug like someone found out, Robert Papenbrock had ducked out of the kitchen, afraid of a younger man who was simply stronger than him. He'd threatened to burn the house down. That was the one time their visitor had had a little stumble, Jakob saw to that, his face landing on the back door's sharp stone stoop. Then she hadn't even wanted to turn him in to the Kommandatura, plus she was too cowardly to; anyway, the cavalier from dancing class was still standing next to the house. The eldest of the Papenbrock line had moved off slowly, across the fields to the southwest, in a dignified saunter, until Jakob, at her urgent request, threw a rock after him. The high green grass was so like peacetime, the low sunlight so peaceful. The rock didn't hit the target, just the left kidney.

The Abses said yes to everything, until midnight. It took her that long to get her stories from the life of Robert Papenbrock straightened out—from deserting the country in the first World War, all the way across the Atlantic, to the fact that he'd been sitting at this very kitchen table. Her own vehemence tripped her up quite a bit: Cresspahl hadn't immediately said he'd throw him out, the elder bushes had still been there, but there was barbed wire in them, before that he'd sent Lisbeth to court, *that was my fathers wife she was,* speaker for the party, recruited Nazis in America, burned down whole villages, SS Sonderführer in Ukraine, kidnapped Slata and her arrest was his fault, beat Voss to death in Rande with steel bars, no, I need to ask Cresspahl about that! – Yes: Mrs. Abs said. – *Ida done the same thing*: Jakob said. – Yes.

That lasted one whole evening. The next day she woke up with an icy doubt impervious to anything she could think of.

She didn't need to stay afraid of this relative. He didn't set fire to the house. He was in too much of a hurry. That was how he ended up in a Red Army guard post by Dassow Lake and had to swim for several hours with a relatively severe flesh wound in one of his fat legs. In his letter from the other side of the zone border, from Lübeck, he called himself "crippled by gunshots" and testified to the genteel bourgeois breeding of the house of Papenbrock by solemnly adding: So I hereby disinherit you.

Maybe it was the right thing to do. But she'd kept this person from seeing his mother again. True, he hadn't tried to see his mother, he seemed to prefer entering Jerichow through a back door. True. She'd been in the right. There were arguments on the other side too. Whatever Cresspahl would decide about it, she needed to be the first to tell him about it. R. P. R.I.P.

But Cresspahl didn't send word, didn't come, was in "Siberia" or dead. His daughter was well prepared for the man who'd been in prison with him, for the woman to whom he'd shouted to send greetings to a house in Jerichow. It was for them that she always carried with her, in her coat as well as her dress pockets, a sheet of paper and an envelope. She would know when the moment came what the first, the most important thing was to tell him.

July 3, 1968 Wednesday

The Union of Soviet Socialist Republics has returned to the USA the plane that on Sunday it forced to land on the Kuril Islands, along with all the servicemen on board, the soldiers. The White House has somewhat apologized for the navigational error. The great and peace-loving Soviet Union gave the soldiers of imperialism red tins of Russian-made cigarettes as a present, too, before sending the death specialists onward to the Vietnamese. Not even three days later and the 214 killers are already on the front, fighting their allies, the bosom friends of every Soviet citizen.

A skilled and eager Communist would be capable of discussing the art of diplomacy here without missing a beat—how negotiations over reciprocal disarmament have been saved; children in my year who went to my school would have taken that as part of their job. I can't do it. I can force myself to, I can do it intellectually, but I can't in my dream! There I'm an honorary citizen of Sigh-da-mono.

Cydamonoe. The Marie of today refuses to believe it.

The other child, in April 1961 and through the summer, peering apprehensively out from under her bonnet at the city of New York, is who found it. That was a child whose hand in mine tightened into a vise grip when a rumbling line of metal boxes came thundering towards us underground, becoming a rolling prison, with dangerous sliding doors, and only gradually the subway, and hers. Marie was three and a half, four in July; she avoided the litter like everyone else on Broadway. She insisted on dressing for others in dresses, girls' suits; she thought pants, never mind jeans, were to wear in the apartment, and she accepted them, for Riverside Park at least, only when she started to see their advantages, financially. It might have been the New York weather too—the sweat-stifling heat and humidity that even our decorous Auntie Times calls "unspeakable" today, and she's right, and the suggestion of a curse only redounds to her credit!—that Marie was afraid of when she lay in bed at night and anxiously awaited what this incomprehensible city would send into her sleep. But fear is precisely what it now can't possibly have been, not in a Marie who plans to live in New York forever and always! In 1961, she lay in her room, the door ajar, unimaginably small, unbelievably chubby, staring at the "safe place" on the ceiling and talking to herself. Even if it wasn't about pushing away her fear, it was Cydamonoe.

She pronounced it the English way, with a sharp initial *S* sound and swaying, dark-brown vowels; anyone who heard her would take her for American. (Today she would say that someone taking her for an American proves the opposite.)

Anyway, four-year-old Marie knew hardly any graver danger, in dealing with peers, than that of revealing Cydamonoe. – You fly there? David Williams said, that immemorial autumn, truly thunderstruck. He was standing with her in a less crowded corner of the playground, hands behind his back, his face completely frozen with the thought that this foreign child was trying to pull his leg, lead him down the garden path, and everything else he didn't want her to do. A girl too. She nodded so shyly that he turned on a dime from a victim to an expert, superior because male. – Through the window . . . ? he followed up, still ready to devastate her with laughter. Marie trusted him not to snap her secret in two; a person has to say what's on her mind sometime; and anyway it was the truth: I can: she revealed.

David stared at her, eyes wide. He too had various special powers no one knew about but him. He nodded seriously, and said: Aha. Now that was something worth trusting a friend over. David Williams became a friend of the Cresspahls.

Not even Marie's mother learned anything more about Cydamonoe until a certain stormy night when Marie wanted to delay going behind her curtained door as long as she possibly could, and the only means she knew for doing so was telling a story. The words came out of her mouth all rounded with urgency—German, English, however it came out. She didn't look at me, ashamed of her betrayal as she was, and she would have fallen into stony silence mid-sentence if I'd let my face show the slightest doubt. She held her glass of juice in her plump little hands, wanting to drink, unable to stop talking.

Cydamonoe was a place you could get to only by air. The voyage there started the second it got dark in the child's head and she knew her whole body was asleep. The vehicle you flew there in was your head and your body, self-guided, no "Stewardessens" (blending German and English, *steward-esses* and *Stewardessen*). The flight lasted as long as it took to realize you were flying. The landing happened in the exact moment when the sun rose behind the earth in an eager leap, like a friendly dog, and it was day.

Cydamonoe was a colony for children—a Kinder-Garten in the intended meaning of the word, a child's garden. It was a time that compensated the child for the false day, from waking up until going to sleep.

As soon as Marie reached that place, surrounded by water, she breksted. In English she told me that "brekst" is what she did and in Cydamonoe language that's the word for "help yourself."

In Cydamonoe children help themselves, to breakfast or to houses. Anyone who needs a house just takes one that's empty. There was no reason to keep the one you have. And every house is equally nice.

In Cydamonoe the streets were grassy lanes and it was against the law to misuse them. But there were pedal carts, tricycles, and jump machines standing there ready, the same number as there were children. Not a single one less, not ever. The same as with the houses, the shared toys, the ice-cream cones: no child ever did without.

In Cydamonoe there were lots and lots of windmills. Presiding in the main mill were Kanga and her husband Kongo and their son Roo. Other than this Ministry of Agriculture there was almost no government or administration.

Unless you count the guards on the landing field. It's a position of honor, being the guard; every child serves sometimes, in rotation, unless they have a toothache.

The guards look at your passport and calculate whether the number of stamps qualifies the new arrival to be a citizen of the Republic of Cydamonoe.

Then they check the places of departure. It has to be one of these: Rastelkin, Rye, Korkoda, Shremble, Stiple, Roke, Kanover, Rochest, Kribble, Krabble, Idiotland, Ristel, Rastel, Kranedow, Scharry, Rinoty, Exremble, Rimble, Stevel, Stretcher, Sklov, Opay, Orow, Irokrashmonoe, Crestelmonoe, or Wrestelmonoe. There's no way to get to Cydamonoe from anywhere else.

There have to be thirteen vaccinations entered in your passport, along with a pill for every week. For Cydamonoe is the only country in the world that's worth living in.

As burdensome and unfriendly as this passport control is, all the children agree it must be. For Cydamonoe is a republic of children.

The grown-ups don't want to accept that. They're constantly sending spies in the craziest disguises. No, not dwarfs. Just normal grown-ups who think they know everything and that children never notice anything. And they're noticed right away, when they climb up out of the river in the morning and go to sleep sunbathing in the grass. The children immediately turn invisible. But they watch the intruder wander around the whole country, take hold of the rain machine the wrong way, bend the stamps in the post office out of shape. Many and many a time have the children debated whether or not to continue granting these unwanted visitors their hospitality since they only ever misuse it.

When the grown-ups come in a group, some children get so mad that they want to turn visible again. These grown-up groups inevitably adopt the same disguise and unfold their guns and shoot. Then they're done, but the children have had a bad night. Who wants to stand up in the dream meeting and admit: "In my sleep I too was at the Berlin Wall and I fired with the rest"?

They're so clumsy, the grown-ups, that they don't just damage things, they hurt themselves. One of them thought the toy factory was a bank and broke down the door and stole billions of billions of dollars and marks. ($4,000,000,000,000.00.) One smoked in public, threw aside their match, and put out their cigarette in the swimming pool. And all sorts of other things grown-ups can think up.

But then they're arrested, convicted, punishable, and they go to jail! In jail they get nothing but bread and butter and milk! The punishment consists of them having to find the hole to slip out through. No child will tell them where it is. Once they've found it, they're free. All they have to do is swim the three hours across the river surrounding the island.

Because of them, the children often have to misuse the many narrow passages and tunnels as escape routes. It takes so much to repair them, until they're good for playing in again!

Mr. CoffeeCan does that. Yes, there is one grown-up who lives in Cydamonoe. But it's the man in the moon. One morning there he was on the landing field, mute, fat and brown and round like the cans where the coffee lives, which you can see through the lid in his head. He didn't have to undergo the examination, he was given his passport and his shots and he promised to take his pills. He isn't always mute. He knows he needs to hang up a new fire bell every day. There are no fires in Cydamonoe but there are dangerous visitors sometimes.

Mr. CoffeeCan is a handyman. He takes care of everything. True, the children don't let him tackle the really tricky stuff, like the island's propeller. But he knows how to pump out the many swimming pools every day, and he's great at giving the birds haircuts. Stephen the policeboy even let him turn invisible once.

Day begins in Cydamonoe once the "entrance of the Stewardessens" fails to occur. Then comes playing, reading, swimming, feeding the animals in the countryside and the trees, and every afternoon at four thirty the class that every child hates: How to say goodbye. One of the games is called, and is:

Jumping up and down,
Kanga-Roo's around the town!

Because since Kanga has a job she gets time off, and since Roo needs to live with his grown-ups he does too. Kongo never has a day off. How could anyone invent even a game if someone showed up and it was just Kongo! Kongo's flour is usually multicolored, not white.

The children in Cydamonoe are alone, or with friends, however they prefer. Leaving a group because you're sad is not permitted, however. When a child has been alone enough and is done with that, they only need to think of being with the others and they are, quick as a wink, with a soft toot.

You can also summon children who aren't citizens of the Republic, just by thinking of them. If you've left, let's say, a Konstanze or a Manuela back in Europe, you can invite them for a visit. But they won't know they've been to Cydamonoe, and the next morning, when they wake up in Hannover or Düsseldorf, they'll have forgotten it.

And if for some reason something is missing in Cydamonoe, you go to the Wunsch und Wille building. Want and Will. It'll be there.

Marie doesn't know how the other children do it when it's nighttime. And you're not allowed to ask. As for her, she gets into bed with Tigger and his father a second before it gets dark, sleeps for a long time, and wakes up in the morning somewhere she doesn't recognize at all. She has to think for a long time. Then she realizes it's . . . New York City.

Back then she admitted it. And don't I still carry with me wherever I go a seven-year-old piece of paper on which the unevenly written letters authorize me explicitly and by name to visit Cydamonoe? – But only come if you don't know what else you can do! she begged me back then, when the thunderstorm was over and she was willing to try once more to go to bed. How short a four-year-old child is, lying there.

And now, for the Marie of 1968, none of this is supposed to be true, just because she's almost eleven. Just because New York is now hers—with every mile of its subway system, all its islands, all its weather, at all times— without a world of Cydamonoe to contrast it with! Because she can meet me at the Seventy-Second Street station for a stroll through Riverside Park, in a meticulously faded T-shirt and artificially aged jeans; because she can both keep an eye on the stairs up from the subway and suggest to the sturdy policemen next to them, with a sidelong look no one could prove against her, that he should think what she thinks: Are you really known as New York's Finest even though you've been caught taking bribes again and again? It used to be that she'd avoid such a massive fellow in uniform, because of his wooden billy club if nothing else; this one turns away from her as if she's wounded him. Is it possible she ever had such fat baby lips, with the words tumbling out so pudgily, as if covered in fuzzy skin? Her hair is almost as white-blond as it'll be in August. No stranger will realize that she's now caught sight of the person she's wanting to find; no one needs to know who she's waiting for. That's between us.

In any case, an honorary citizen of Cydamonoe has the right to occasionally speak in phrases such as "except for the fire bells of Cydamonoe," "according to the laws of C."—but only in code, never in front of witnesses, and no more than twice a year. Why today? Why today without the reprimand of a furrowed brow? Because today is the third of July, and the start of a long weekend, and we wish each other a good one, I her and she me.

July 4, 1968 Thursday

In the third summer after the war, Mecklenburg was safer than the city where we live now.

Yesterday a man in his forties, stocky, black-haired, white undershirt, black pants, dark socks, walked into the women's section of a public lavatory at Eighty-Fifth Street in Central Park and shot a twenty-four-year-old woman, the bullet passing downward out her throat and into her chest, killing her. He then climbed onto the roof and fired in all directions, calm, capricious. It was near the part of Fifth Avenue where people like Jack Kennedy's widow live, and more than a hundred policemen stormed into the peaceful area. One of them says he thinks he shot the killer ten times. Apparently the killer had lived in the Soviet Union, Bulgaria, and Yugoslavia, and come here with a Greek passport; there were pictures of Hitler, Göring, and Goebbels on the walls of his apartment. People on the upper floors of nearby buildings had a bird's-eye view. "The police were absolutely great," said Mrs. David Williams of 1035 Fifth Avenue. "It was as thrilling as anything you could see on television."

Around Jerichow there were mostly thefts, and dogs on chains enjoyed an unforeseen respect. Stealing food, up to ten pounds of flour, was considered a hunger tax; a bottle of liquor gone missing earned curses at the unknown perpetrator; news of neither tended to reach the police: why call in the upholders of the law to take a look around, you might just as well catch a rabbit by sprinkling salt on its tail. (Not much went missing at the

Cresspahls' place—behind the cemetery, so close to the Kommandatura.) It was seen as a sign of economic recovery when tools or machines were stolen, to work with. You could carve your house number into the shaft of the scythe, but what about the blade? And why would Duvenspeck give up his residence permit in Jerichow when Willi Köpcke came back from the Soviet camps—the director of the gasworks wasn't running away from just anywhere, and if Mina Köpcke was not to be seen on Town Street for quite some time, and then was seen tired and gentle as a lamb, it must have been some other misdeed that she was getting beaten up for.

The streets were practically safe, aside from the Soviet MPs and various marauders; a child could take a trip with no need to worry, especially if she was wearing an extra-big sweater and baggy pants that discreetly recalled a checked curtain, and was carrying her things in a net bag, so fellow travelers could see everything inside it, there was no need to grab it. Gesine Cresspahl got off the bus at the Kiel stop on Fischland and walked north on Fulge, quickly, away from the corrosive yellow stench of the wood generator; she'd trusted things three days earlier in Jerichow but not here. She shamelessly bypassed the mayor's office; a returning native didn't have to pay the visitor's fee, surely. Past the Baltic Hôtel, at the corner where Malchen Saatmann's place was, she turned right onto Norderende Road, as though intending to hire herself out to Niemann the farmer for the harvest, but she stopped in front of a very red cottage with a cane roof, surrounded by hedges and wild bushes and lush trees. This was her house here, and she didn't go inside. But it's why she'd come.

She'd forgotten that Alexander Paepcke had signed the property over to her father; it was hers only because she and Paepcke's children had come to feel at home here. The slip of paper on the post revealed that total strangers were living at this smallholding now—no one else in Althagen would need a nameplate. Only outsiders would be capable of neglecting to pull all the weeds from the stone embankment around the house. The southwest corner of the thatched roof was ragged—the rain would get in during the fall. Memory refused to supply anything.

She would probably have walked farther, on the firm sand between the thick hedges, to Kaufmanns Corner, to the Ahrenshoop Post Office bus stop—there was nothing else she was looking for on Fischland; it was only ancient habit that led her to the cottage where the Paepckes used to drop off the keys over the winter. She wasn't alone, she just felt that way; she greeted the people out for their early-evening stroll—greeted them first, without fail, not because she was younger but strictly according to the English custom, so that several of the men looked surprised. She gave them the slip. Finally she was standing in front of Ille, and each of them was terribly shocked by the other.

Ille had latched the top half of her door to the wall—a *Snackdœr*; suddenly she was standing so still that she was like a picture in a frame. She saw the child who'd always come with the Paepcke children, but they were dead, she knew that. Ille was easy to recognize—the same pensive face, the freckles even more pronounced, her brittle reddish hair like a man's. She was wearing, in the house, a white head scarf, the way people on Fischland do to mourn the dead; she had married her captain after all, at forty-two. The shock lasted the blink of an eye. Then Ille was the elder again, and said, barely reproachful, barely worried: *Gesine. You've run away.*

Gesine had run away from home, and Ille informed her that a note on the kitchen table in Jerichow wasn't enough for Jakob's mother. She had to go that very day *œwe den pahl*, over the fence and the border from Mecklenburg to Pommern, to the post office, with a letter saying she'd come here to visit relatives. Which was true, that more or less was what she'd had in mind. Ille also clarified that the child would be sleeping under the same roof as her, if she didn't mind. It was a bit strange to want to go to Farmer Niemann for work and bread, just because she'd once been friends with Inge Niemann. Ille herself had things for Gesine to do. It was understood and agreed from the beginning: Gesine was no longer one of the master's children. She was welcome here, and she would have to work for her bed and board.

The things for Gesine to do started the next morning in the garden: there were roots to pull, gooseberries and black currants to pick, beds of soil to break up. Carrying water to the kitchen three times a day; the potatoes she had to peel were counted in buckets, the milk canister she had to have Grete Nagel fill every evening held probably eight quarts. All that was missing was for Ille to let her near the stove. When it was precisely to give Gesine a proper respect for cooking that she'd taken her in. Gesine was allowed to make the cucumber salad, butter the bread. Carry the food to the rooms too.

For Ille had guests, paying visitors from the cities, as in earlier times. Except that a family of refugees was there too, though Ille sent them out into the fields with the farmers; they'd suddenly remembered the work that needed doing on a smallholding, and if these Biedenkopfs from Rostock wanted to stay with Ille over the winter, they'd have to pay in work, not rent. She took money from the temporary guests without a second thought, though. Gesine understood only when she found two piglets one morning in the shed behind the house, which she now had to feed and take care of as well; when a sewing machine was delivered and another time a laundry bucket with almost completely undamaged enamel. What Gesine had been planning to think about on Fischland hardly came into her head even once, she was so busy; she understood the folk wisdom and wanted to tell it to Jakob: her recourse to tangible assets now had a possible goal.

She had her opinion about the guests, too. They were not often friendly. They were people from the British and Soviet Sectors of Berlin; from Leipzig; from the state capital, Schwerin. One of them called himself a painter, though he hadn't been seen painting for two weeks. In the old days, something like that would have been reported to the municipal authorities. The others were a doctor and an East Prussian landscape writer who managed various internal affairs of the state of Mecklenburg from Schwerin and didn't want to say anything more specific about it. They got into lots of arguments and yet stayed together, on the path to the beach, in the water, as though there were something keeping them together above and beyond the room at Ille's. The artists defended themselves against something they called Production. That's what functionaries demanded of them. – Just let us process all this sorrow already! the painter groaned. – You'll see: his colleague in the realm of the Muses proclaimed, vaguely gloomy but trying hard to keep an honest countenance. Gesine saw the gentlemen one more time after that. It's true their bodies weren't exactly plump but their suits, hanging loosely around smaller masses as they might be, were made of enviable, well-looked-after fabric. Their faces were smooth, alert, lively. They didn't look careworn to her. She noticed how intently they dug into Ille's smoked roasts, how wastefully they tackled a chicken thigh with a single, encompassing bite. In her experience, people in mourning had a different way of eating. If the men were trying to process something here in the fresh air and sun and silence, why did they bring their wives along to fight with, why did they spend every evening in their cramped rooms where there was so little space between the beds? (Gesine didn't begrudge their children the vacation, that's how grown-up she felt; she was no longer speaking to the children of the Schweriners, ever since they'd tried to hire her to make their beds.) No, she was being unfair here. If the men were trying to attend to some sorrow, it was probably other people's.

The guests had understood right away the boundaries of where they were wanted and kept out of the garden, the stables, the kitchen, wherever there was work to do. Trapped in their rooms, they never heard any part of the conversation that the locals had on many evenings. Yes, Ille had visitors, like in Paepcke's day, whether they wanted a ladle of water to wash the beach sand out of their mouths or wanted to sit down for something serious, a chitchat or maybe a palaver or even a full-on story. Except that there weren't many men there, and not a few women kept their white head scarves on. No one greeted Gesine as Alexandra Paepcke's cousin—she gradually came to understand that here she was known and remembered because of her father. At the same time, no one asked her about Cresspahl either. They discussed what was happening around Fischland, so Gesine got to know Fischland as a place where things happened differently from the rest of Mecklenburg. Most of the houses had summer visitors like Ille's, pursuing endeavors of the mind. The Cultural League for a Democratic Renewal of Germany had more to say here than the number of votes they'd received in the Mecklenburg election would've led you to suppose. The government of the Soviet zone had set up a playground here for the intellectuals they considered well-behaved, or usable. Life in Hotel Bogeslav was like in the old days, except that people like Seipmüller the banker didn't turn up anymore. Actually, well, they did if they were from the British Sector, or even better, England. – Englishmen? Gesine asked by mistake. But she wasn't rebuked for her forward behavior, why should she be. That's right, Englishmen. The Kurhaus was called the Bogeslav now. They got special allotments "from the reserves," whatever and whosever those were. Fischland was doled out to the intellectuals of the Soviet zone like medicine—after two weeks they'd have to clear out for the next ones. There were some who'd been swimming here since June, though. One had gotten a building permit, in Ahrenshoop, thank God. As long as they don't start putting up their contrived buildings in Althagen. They went for horse-drawn carriage rides through the Darss. That's right, Gesine, during the harvest. Well, we get ours in whatever happens. Yeah, no one knows what happened to the hunting lodge of Reich Huntsmaster Hermann Göring, they don't let anyone near that place in Darss. Other than that, hardly a single complaint about the Red Army. Clearly they were trying a different tack with this corner of the world. Sure, they were armed when they went in search of Alfred Partikel when he went missing in Lower Darss Woods. Seriously, they wanted to save him. You know, Gesine, the painter. From Ahrenshoop, not in the Cultural League at least. What Gesine picked up about the business dealings of the locals sounded no less extraterritorial. It was like there was no tax office here, no Economic Commission for the Soviet zone, as if the police had no admittance. On Fischland, the category "self-sufficient" seemed to mean pretty much exactly what the word implied, not someone refused ration cards. Are you kidding, ration cards!? Now and then talk turned to the house with the sundial, so near the Shoreline Cliff. When would that crumble into the sea, do you think. With west-facing windows as tall as doors. Even if they board them up in the winter the wind gets into the room and dances with the sand. Something often said: You should do it, Ille. No harm in it. Just do it already, Ille.

After Gesine had fetched the milk, she was free to go wherever she wanted. Memory remained absent, all that came was the touch of a moment of the past that calls itself memory. What she wanted was entry into the whole of past time—the path through the faltering heart into the light of the sun of back then. One time they'd stood next to each other on the Shoreline Cliff and indisputably seen the outlines of Falster and Møn islands; Alexandra had turned slightly and her upper arm had jerked toward Gesine's shoulder, without touching it; the feeling of convergence lay in a capsule of her mind, as if buried, and did not come back to life. One time she walked through the lagoon pastures, up to her ankles in squelching water, wanting to secretly get a glimpse of Paepcke's cottage from the back, without the slightest hope left for anything but that touch of the past. She saw the overgrown hedgerow, the maypole, a corner of the Lagoon Room's window. The steel door with the chicken wire was secured with a padlock and chain. She heard a woman talking the way you talk to babies old enough to take in words. All of that brought lost time back only as a thought:

When we....; the words in her mind didn't come to life. Almost every evening, when fetching the milk, she came near the moment when Grete Nagel had offered her and Alexandra a glass of milk, but fresh from the udder, and the cow was turning her eyes to look at them. Now it was a little harder for her to drink milk. She didn't find anything more than that; and anyway it was probably just because Emma Senkpiel's milk in Jerichow was adulterated. In the evening, when the *Zeesenboots* sailed into the Althagen harbor, the cats splashed through the reeds and waited for their hosts, for their share of the day's catch of fish; cats, in the water! She still didn't hear Alexandra's voice. She tried to find expressive descriptions of Alexandra's voice in that moment; even the idea of it almost escaped her. Outside Farmer Niemann's three-story house there were three laundry lines and four people painting next to one another depicting the scene. It was like back then. It was solid and impenetrable, covering over the thought of Alexandra; all that remained was the knowledge that Alexandra was hidden under there, somewhere. In the evening the light from Malchen Saatmann's back room rested in the bushes. She could think: That evening when we still had to fetch bread from Malchen, Alexander was sitting loftily on the sofa, probably tipsy, and he said to his daughter: Well, child?— as if he didn't recognize her.... Gesine could think it. She could imagine it written down. It wasn't actually there. She was conscious that in this minute of standing still outside Mrs. Saatmann's friendly scattered homey light the wind stood still too, as if curbing its pace. She wondered if one day she would have forgotten this too, if it would someday be preserved only in words.

At last Ille did it. She asked Gesine for a "frightful" favor; it turned out to be merely accompanying her on an errand Gesine mustn't ask questions about. She had to keep silent the whole time. Ille's voice wavered. Gesine would've gladly promised her more if it would have made her feel better. The errand was a visit to an old woman in a cottage in Niehagen. Ille put a basket of eggs down in the vestibule, next to an assistant—the fee. Inside, by candlelight and windows draped against the sunlight, she had to put on the table before the conjurer a photograph of the captain and her wedding ring on a silk thread. The old woman avoided any fuss; her manner seemed to have been learned by watching a doctor. Her gaze was that of a businesswoman delivering something a customer has ordered for an agreed-upon price. An open, secretly covert look. She raised her elbows and crossed one hand over the other. The ring swayed on its thread from a previously invisible finger above the captain's face in the picture. It didn't sway, it hung perfectly still from the beginning. The ring didn't move for five full minutes. Where you count to three hundred in your mind. Then Ille started to cry. Back outside, the assistant, apparently the sister or partner in this enterprise, expressed her condolences absolutely as though to a widow—objectively, reasonably, as if such an outcome had been infallibly expected.

– You too? the assistant asked. Gesine had only promised to keep silent. Now that she'd finished accompanying Ille, she was free to run away.

Back home Ille didn't insist on talking about it. We didn't take offense at each other. We could talk to each other. Five days later or so I went back to Jerichow with my wages.

Fischland is the most beautiful place in the world. I say this as someone who grew up on a northern coast on the Baltic, somewhere else. If you've stood at the topmost point on Fischland, you know the color of the lagoon and the color of the sea, both of them different every day and from each other. The wind leaps up Shoreline Cliff and constantly sweeps across the land. The wind brings the smell of the sea everywhere. There I saw the sun set, many times, and I remember three times, the third one not too well. Now the dirty gold is about to drop into the Hudson.

That's when you knew that I'm not coming back, Gesine.
Yes, Alexandra.
That's when you were done once and for all with wanting to kill yourself.
Yes, Alexandra.
You were still thinking about it.
Yes, Alexandra.
But now you won't ever do it.
No, Alexandra, I won't.
I was just hiding, you know.
I know, Alexandra.

In 1947, during the summer, I was on Fischland. Never again.

July 5, 1968 Friday
Yesterday in Bonn, Fritz Gebhardt von Hahn, of the Department of Jewish
Affairs under the Nazi foreign ministry, appeared before the court again,
accused of complicity in the death of more than thirty thousand Bulgarian
and Greek Jews. The defense called a witness who had also formerly been
in a leadership role in the Nazi foreign ministry, wiretapping division.

He gave his first names; his last name, Kiesinger, was already known.
Profession: Chancellor of West Germany. Such silver-haired gentlemen
enjoy the West Germans' trust. The Social Democrats are in a governing
coalition with the likes of him.

When had he joined the Nazi Party? Right away, in 1933. "Not from
conviction, but not out of opportunism." What other possible reasons are
there? No one asked him that. He claims to have had nothing to do with
the party until 1940, other than paying his membership dues. At that point,
he was trustworthy enough to supervise the appraisal and interpretation
of foreign radio broadcasts. When the enemy stations mentioned the extermination of the Jews, Mr. Kiesinger simply took a skeptical position
and omitted the matter from the daily digest for his superiors, and as a
result the Nazis remained in the dark about what they were doing. (This
was how Mr. von Hahn could fail to find out what was happening to the
Jews he was sending on their way.) Similarly, Mr. Kiesinger's colleague von
Hahn had never heard the term "final solution" until the end of the war.
Only late, and gradually, very slowly, did the disappearance of those who
wore the yellow star, and stories from soldiers returning from the fronts,
make him think "that something or other wasn't right." That "something
very ugly was happening" with the Jews. Officially he knew nothing. Under oath. Leaves the courtroom without handcuffs.

In Soviet Germany, in Mecklenburg, on February 26, 1948, the Soviet
Military Administration ordered the end of denazification on and as of
April 10. It was said of the guilty that they were under arrest or that the
Western occupying powers were giving them shelter. The Americans were
in possession of a particularly capacious aegis: Dr. Kramritz taught the
fourteen- and fifteen-year-old children in class 8-A. Former National Socialists were now being expressly invited to join in the "democratic and
economic reconstruction," provided they "atone by honest work." Not
being in jail proved your innocence.

Atonement comes in various forms, of course—how could a child know them all?

The Arado Works in Gneez had now been expropriated in writing. Heinz Röhl had even legally forfeited his Renaissance Cinema, due to miscounted admission tickets when the Soviets released its booty of UFA films for the starving Germans, which was the profit motive, hence aggravating circumstances, not mitigating ones as he was probably used to getting under the republic. And yet there was a business king of Gneez, outside the law just like in the days of Freddy Numero Duo. Emil Knoop, we'd almost forgotten about him! As per the rules he was an ex-Nazi, and he'd come to town with quiet pomp and gentle circumstance and soon exceeded all comparison. I bring you tidings of great joy. He'd had a hard time to begin with, over the reputation from the old days he'd left in his wake. For his father, Johannes (Jonathan) Knoop, had always been considered a prominent businessman and upstanding citizen who could be forgiven such little tics as raising carp and rather gentrified hunting. He'd been doing business as Coal Merchant, Carriage Trade, Import and Export since 1925 (1851). When it came to getting in with the right people in Gneez, his boy Emil had often enough been a problem. Take 1932: it was far from clear to whom a businessman had the moral duty to pledge his allegiance. Johannes was leaning toward the German Nationalist Party. But his boy Emil ran off to Hitler Youth shooting practices with his father's whole gun cabinet. That was a dicey year. An expensive one, too, for now Johannes had to give money to both sides. And even if Emil's political savvy could be said to have been proven by 1935, the fact remained that he hadn't learned much more about his father's business than how to reach into the cash register; his teachers had apparently had to carry him across the high-school finish line. Then it was labor service that was supposed to reform him; he came back from it once he'd gotten a girl pregnant in Rostock. The things it took to make her see that her life as Mrs. Knoop in Gneez would be nothing but torment! He continued to learn from his father how to cut a fine figure in Gneez, with a sports car and silk scarf; this, along with alimony and other settlement money, was too much for the company so he had to enlist in antitank defense in Magdeburg so early that he became a reserve-officer candidate, then went off to the Polish war as a private first class and came back from the Soviet one as a first lieutenant. Not straight back to Gneez. In June 1945, at the Kiel harbor, the British released him into the civilian population since he could prove to their satisfaction that he'd never had anything to do with the NSDAP other than his party dues having been withheld from his officer's salary. During his practicum in the black market in Belgium, during his work in all the occupied countries in Europe (except Italy), it had certainly been better for Emil Knoop to be in the party. Whatever it might have been that kept him apart from his loving family for a little while yet, in a Hamburg office that apparently really looked like a counting house of yore, his sojourn there may have helped give his amateur understanding of business a bit of scientific backbone. In early 1947 he took over Gneez. Shows that people were coming from the West after all! He left the coal trade to his father. His qualifications for the transportation business were obvious, seeing as he'd brought with him a more or less brand-new American truck, the kind you could get enough spare parts for in Mecklenburg. He transported almost nothing within Mecklenburg. He spoke little about what he was doing; pretty much all you could get out of him was that he was assisting the SMA with liquidating various businesses. True, one day he'd said a bit loudly in Café Borwin: I've got to get everything for the Russians, *from tank to horse an saddle, don' know which way is up anymore!* Turns out he did, because one evening when he was arranging a deal in Jerichow's Lübeck Court Hotel a waiter came running up, pale as a sheet, and whispered: Mr. Knoop! Berlin's on the line, Karlshorst headquarters! – Right: Emil said, in his self-satisfied way: *They cant do a thing without me.* Turns out they could, sometimes, and then he'd spend a few days in the basement under the Gneez courthouse. He reformed that place in a matter of days, got hold of the keys of the other cells, had food delivered from town (from Mrs. Panzenhagen— liked her cooking more than his mother's), and acquired a record player with jazz discs from the thirties, which was apparently a bit of a burden for the guards and they let him go after six weeks (with feverish apologies). Johannes Knoop grew ever paler with fear until he was almost transparent. Gneez got a taste of Emil's views on filial devotion: by fall 1947 his parents were living in Hamburg, and not in the Pöseldorf neighborhood either, in fact quite far from Inner Alster Lake—out in the country, you might say. They seem to have written him rather few letters. True, Father ran Emil's old office, it's just Emil seemed to have forgotten it. To each his own business methods, whether inherited or acquired. Emil's new office was in Brussels. And why not, didn't the Soviet zone have a trade agreement with Belgium? Emil's office in the Soviet Sector of Berlin was called Export and Import, the one in the British zone was a room in a dentist's office and didn't seem to need any sign whatsoever. The fact that Emil was often away from Gneez made it that much easier for legends to spring up around him. A foreign truck, with a trailer, loading every last particle of wheat from Papenbrock's and the Red Army's granary and driving off toward Lübeck, the border crossing—that's not nothing. Soon Emil was respected, almost liked by the proper sort in Gneez. He could be living like Louis the Last in Belgium, could he not?, and yet here he was toiling away for Mecklenburg and the SMA. And did he go around bragging of his business success? No, he kept wearing the same hat every day, bit greasy by now. Did he not show Christian compassion, time after time? A Mrs. Bell was living in Gneez, in a room in her villa in the Berlin Quarter. Lucratively divorced in 1916, a rich woman who took care of problems over the phone. Now that her phone had been taken away, she couldn't handle the world. Emil went and sat her down at his own private phone. Needed a housekeeper anyway. Do you think Emil was the type to wear gold rings? No, if he had anything to be happy about (*"like a kid"*) it was more likely that, in addition to his white ("personal") *propusk* required for any long-distance transport orders from the Central Transport Authority, including border traffic, he'd been given another one, the red kind, authorizing travel through the whole Soviet zone, including border traffic! It was age-old wisdom, wasn't it: Just let the army haul a ne'er-do-well over the coals and he'll know what's what for the rest of his life. Y'can see it in his short haircut too. Tight, black, neat. And Emil never bought a round for everyone at the bar—only paid for the ones worthy of his love. It was nice to hear him tell stories, not about business but from his life: how he'd shot down two Viscounts near Cuxhaven in September '39 and made sure the crews were buried with military honors. How at the "Vistula estuary bridgehead" he'd discovered that they'd had a concentration camp by the name of Stutthof there, which was why he'd painted "Stutthof Remains German!" on his truck. You know, personal reminiscences. And now they finally knew what the weather'd been like on May 9, '45, when he'd skippered the crossing of the Baltic to Kiel: the sea was calm. Why begrudge a lucky stiff?—his interzonal pass was always in order, he could count on being exempted from local motor pools, the rationing board not only recommended him but attested to the legality of his fuel sources. No one envied him his driver, or his 275 pounds. He had such a calming effect. (Nobody wanted a closer look at his black boxy briefcase: too full of dangerous money.) When he did come a cropper—smuggling horses to Lower Saxony; getting beer kegs of "uranium" confiscated at the border—he would laugh himself silly telling stories about it later. A loyal soul, that's what he was. One time, he came back from the wider world of the steel trade to Gneez, where the potatoes on the state-owned farm weren't out of the ground yet. He promised fifty marks for every basket upended next to the trucks, and that night the trucks were filled to the brim and he threw a party for the workers too. He could use those potatoes. Took the small stuff too. And oh how he cried when Dr. Schürenberg told him about the diseases the schoolchildren were suffering from. Chinese beggar's disease, that's what they had, from eating pigweed? Emil couldn't bear to hear that, needed a triple brandy, quick now. What? suffering from scabies? under Emil's very eyes! Dr. Schürenberg didn't inform him that the word referred to ordinary itches; he painted a picture of the children's vitamin deficiencies. The children kept getting their ankles all banged up from their wooden sandals' sharp edges, never healed, led to inflammations of the lymph vessels, horrible pains in the groin. He'd seen Cresspahl's daughter (– *now thassanother good man!*: Emil roared, in tears) standing at the train station, legs so stiff she could hardly walk it hurt so much. – Cresspahl? said Triple-J, the town's military commander, J. J. Jenudkidse. For they were sitting in the Dom Ofitserov, guests of Triple-J. – I swear it!: Emil cried, sobbing. This was shortly before Christmas 1947. – An orange for every child: Dr. Schürenberg said. For he'd been to university and wanted to wipe out on the spot this unheard-of prestige that a common tradesman apparently enjoyed. – And a salted herring for every laborer!: Emil sobbed. Gneez held its breath for the next couple weeks. Emil could always back out by saying, truthfully enough, that he'd been ten linen closets of sheets to the wind at the time. But it happened, punctually too. The salted herring came. The oranges were handed out in schools and children's homes and hospitals. Triple-J provided the trucks, since this time Emil didn't happen to have any trucks "liquid" (such short notice!), while Emil saw to it that the things were pilfered in sufficient number from Hamburg harbor. Gneez had long since learned to believe in Emil.

That was his way of atoning.

And he was innocent, as proven by the fact that he wasn't in jail—a child could see that. A child saw him wreathed in one halo of glory after another. In March 1948, the Communists established the *National News* for him, dedicated to former members of the NSDAP or other patriotic thinkers, to help him feel at home in their Germany; three weeks later, when their People's Police confiscated all products of the press licensed in the West and shut down their distribution, they continued to allow people like Knoop a discreet subscription to the West Berlin *Daily Mirror* to counteract any hint of feeling not at home, mailed in a sealed envelope of course. When he did take a fall, nine years later, he had to say goodbye to a whole colony of boathouses, a pheasant-breeding facility, and the first canopy swing—called "Hollywood"—in all of Gneez and the district too, but for Cresspahl's daughter it came too late. She could grasp that the Communists had let him help them to rise above the level of commodity circulation, as long as they still had something to learn from him and the Soviet Union; she felt sorry enough for him when he was led off past white-faced government secretaries in his waiting room, but it was too late. She'd had to spend too long being ashamed of having reached into that sack of oranges.

July 6, 1968 Saturday, South Ferry day

is also the day when Auntie Times tells us what her special correspondent Bernard Weinraub wrote her from Saigon, South Vietnam, back under the date of June 27:

"AMERICAN IMPACT ON VIETNAM'S ECONOMY, POLITICS AND CULTURE IS PROFOUND

Ten years ago fewer than 1,000 American servicemen were stationed in Vietnam, and their presence was scarcely noticed.

Today, 530,000 American troops and 12,000 civilians are swarming through this tortured country, and their presence is affecting the very roots of South Vietnamese life.

... Lambrettas and cars. In 30,000 to 40,000 homes and in village squares throughout the country, South Vietnamese families watch in fascination 'The Addams Family,' and 'Perry Mason' on armed forces television. In college classrooms students read John Updike and J. D. Salinger. In coffee shops, young men who work for United States agencies and girls in mini-skirts sip Coca-Cola and complain that the Americans have taken over.

The American presence has also contributed to a tangle of more profound changes that remain, with a war on, contradictory and complex. Students, teachers, Government employes and businessmen insist, for example, that the influx of American soldiers, civilians and dollars is tearing the family apart and creating social havoc.

... 'An impossible situation has been created,' said an American-educated lawyer. 'The poor families come to Saigon from the countryside because of the war. The father has few skills, so he becomes a day laborer or drives a pedicab. Before he was respected by the children. He knew about the farm. He knew about the land. Now he knows nothing.

'The young boys wash cars for the Americans or shine shoes or sell papers or work as pickpockets,' the lawyer went on. 'They may earn 500 or 600 piasters [$5 or $6] a day. Their fathers earn 200 piasters a day. Here is a 10-year-old boy earning three times as much as his father. It is unheard of.'

Beyond the impact of Americans and American dollars, of course, there is the over-all, shattering impact of the war itself. Virtually every young farmer or peasant is forced to join the Government forces or the Vietcong; more than a million people have become refugees; the disruption of farms and villages has led an additional two million to flee to the cities...

... since thousands of families in rural areas are physically moved out of their farms by allied troops to create free-strike zones.

... 'The Vietnamese never wants to leave his village,' said a professor at Saigon University. 'They want to be born there and they want to die there.

'That is not easy for you Americans to understand, since you can move from village to village in your country,' he went on. 'But here it is very painful for a Vietnamese to leave his village, and when they are forced to move they hate you. It is as simple as that—they hate you.'

... Another [American] declared:

'It's easy to blame everything wrong here on the Americans—the Viet-namese love doing it. But, look, this society was damned rotten when we got here and what we're getting now is an exaggeration of the rottenness, the corruption, the national hangups.'

...Ironically the strongest American cultural influence has touched folk singing in the antiwar ballads of the most famous college singer in Vietnam, Trinh Cong Son.

The broadest social—and, by extension, cultural—impact of the Americans has fallen on the powerful middle class, who exclusively ran the Government's bureaucracy, taught in primary schools and colleges and served as lawyers, doctors and businessmen. This socially conscious class, to all indications, had little link to or sympathy for the peasants, or even the army.

American officials say privately that the disruption within this entrenched class is welcome. Middle-class Vietnamese are naturally bitter. Especially at their decline in status.

'A university professor may earn 18,000 piasters a month [$150], while a bar girl can earn 100,000 piasters [$850],' said 58-year-old Ho Huu Tuong, a lower-house representative who was a prominent intellectual in the nineteen forties. 'The intelligentsia are the disinherited, the lost, because of the American impact. We have lost our position.'

'Money has become the idol,' said Mr. Thien, the Information Minister. 'Money, money, money.'

The theme is echoed by poorer Vietnamese—the pedicab drivers, the small businessmen, the maids, the cooks—but for them the problem of status is irrelevant and the flow of American dollars is hardly unwelcome. 'How can I hate the Americans?' asked a grinning woman who sells black-market cigarettes at a stand on Tu Do, in the heart of Saigon. 'They have so much money in their pockets.'

...At the official level, only enormous American assistance—$600-million this fiscal year—keeps Vietnam afloat. The figure is exclusive of American military expenditures of more than $2-billion a month.

...Only 6 per cent of last year's budget was met by direct taxes on income and business profits in comparison with about 80 per cent in the United States.

This results in Government reliance on levies on foodstuffs, tobacco, alcohol, matches and other items that fall with heavy weight on the poor. And, through bribes and bureaucracy, the rich often pay no taxes at all.

... Since 1962, land distribution in South Vietnam has been at a virtual standstill and the bulk of the land remains in the hands of absentee landlords.

... There is a general feeling that Mr. Thieu, Mr. Ky or any other Vietnamese leader would have enormous political difficulties, even if they agreed to every possible reform that the Americans have urged.

For the heart of the Government or 'system' is an unwieldy, Kafkaesque bureaucracy that hampers progress at every turn. And in that area, the American impact has been minimal.

Paperwork, documents, stamps, bored officials, bribes are everywhere. Officials work four-hour days.

'It will take us at least a generation to change the system,' said one of the highest American officials at the United States mission. 'Maybe more than a generation.'

... A South Vietnamese publisher told an American recently: 'You are our guests in this country and Vietnamese have been very friendly to you. Do not outlive our hospitality.'

... 'Smugness of so many of them is appalling,' said a junior American official. 'If we were not at war it would be funny.'

But a student in La Pagode, a coffee shop on Tu Do, observed: 'Americans must fight for us so we can live in peace.'

Had the student volunteered to join the army? 'No, I must study, I am a student,' he replied."

© The New York Times

And who else does Auntie Times want us to get to know today? Lynn Tinkel.

On June 19, Lynn Tinkel, a twenty-two-year-old Bronx schoolteacher, was going somewhere with her friend James Lunenfeld, two years older than she, also a teacher, and was doing so on the INDependent's platform under Fifty-Ninth Street. The hour was late—two thirty in the morning—and she thought: Uhh: the thought came into her mind: I feel like taking a picture of my friend James.

But it is forbidden to take pictures in the New York subway! A wise Transit Authority rule forbids it, without written permission, signed and sealed. This was where Lynn had her idea, James his in turn, and that costs a cool $25 fine or ten days in jail!

Yesterday, Lynn stood before a man in robes, in the Criminal Court at 100 Center Street, presumably Chamber 5a (Traffic Court), and was acquitted. For her, it was the principle of the thing. If she felt like taking a picture of her friend on the subway platform.... The judge agreed and let her go in peace.

Now the Transit Authority thinks a closer look at this rule might be in order. For instance, it could explicitly tell photographers they can't use tripods, over which people have been known to trip; or that flashbulbs might blind a train driver or passengers ... that's what its closer look has yielded so far. Anyway, Lynn is free, and if the air temperature above Broadway was lower than 82 degrees Fahrenheit with a humidity index of 73 percent, would we go down into the subway and take photos of each other question mark?

There's something *The New York Times* has missed.

The sidewalks on Broadway are bordered with steel bandages that make the street corners steep and difficult to manage for people with baby carriages or even the kind of grocery carts that families use to carry home food for the entire week. Today, for the first time, our eye is caught and our soles are soothed by the gentle slopes that the city has sunk into the transition between street and sidewalk, a relief to taxpayers and recognition of its obligations; a down payment: as Marie says, still in a bad mood from the muggy air over the harbor, which made it hard for her to sweat.

Can this be? Something escaping the gaze of *The New York Times*—a change in the style of Broadway's furnishings on the corner of Ninety-Eighth, an aesthetic correction, and sociographical event? Alas, it is we who must make sure to mention it.

July 7, 1968   Sunday

Haven't we been steadfastly insisting that *The New York Times* was an auntie? Wasn't that our very own word?

We can prove it with her performance yesterday—her lecture on the profound impact of the US-American presence on the economy, politics, and culture of the part of Vietnam that this country intends to save from Communism. She's considered, double-checked, and articulated everything:

The South Vietnamese in range of armed forces television gobble up *The Addams Family* as eagerly as they do *Perry Mason*; the students read contemporary classics of New England and Pennsylvania literature; Coca-Cola's in the homes and the homes have been torn apart, as are families, by the unheard-of income structures and the forced separation from farm and house and village; the folk singers sing antiwar songs in American styles; the middle class is bitter at their loss of influence over politics and the ruling bureaucracy, bitter at the new status symbol, money (barmaids earn five times as much as university professors); direct taxes cover only six percent of the state budget; a once independent rice-producing country has to import rice; land reform is at a standstill; the pervasive influence of French and American bureaucracy has ruined the local variety: every consequence of the American war is at least mentioned, not even excluding the religious disputes. Only one blessing of Western civilization, while being another American import, does *The New York Times* pass over in silence: venereal diseases. What an auntie.

We could prove it with her manifestation today. Fully eight hundred lines on the brutality of the American police; severely, clinically, she bends over the sinners and asks what this might be about: because civilian citizens don't say otherwise? because citizens lay fingers on policemen too? because policemen like others' pain? because they're filled head to toe with contempt? because they're scared? stressed? because they're ashamed of their modest education? because the police academy fails to conduct psychiatric examinations? This is followed, to make the rebuke all the more stinging, by the blow that it was a New Jersey policeman who, without observing the legal requirements, bought the forty-year-old Smith & Wesson revolver that he then sold, equally illegally, to a second policeman, and only then did the firearm reach the hands of the man who shot and killed a young woman in the ladies' toilets in Central Park four days ago. She is going to make the policemen of this country behave if it's the last thing she does, this aunt.

A person of such stature should be able to take for granted that only appropriate opinions about her are current, namely these (disregarding of course the ill-bred definitions coming out of Moscow and its surroundings). But this noble simplicity and quiet grandeur is beyond her. Instead, risking aspersions on her self-confidence, she'd rather hedge her bets and disseminate on her own what one is to think of her. We have read, for instance, on an agèd enamel sign in Woodlawn Cemetery that: she is indispensable for intelligent conversation; in the subway, that: without her we cannot keep up with the times, and the tempting consolation that: you don't have to read it all, but it's such a pleasant feeling to know that it's all in there; we have read in bronze and marble that: she is the diary of the world; today, though, it's that: one of the nicest things about *The New York Times* is that you can get it delivered—this with a sketch that shows her in the act of delivery.

And so who do we see there?

An older person, not exactly maidenly, but chaste. An aunt.

A short person. What is it that pushes her head forward—is it gout, or so she can better peer over her pince-nez? Beady jet-black eyes, rectangular glasses. Lips curved up at both corners into a delicate semicircle; nothing remotely like frivolity or a vulgar grin. Controlled friendliness. Not a wrinkle anywhere on her face.

On her head a mountain of thick ringlets, falling over her ears. The evidence of hair curlers is clearly visible.

A chubby person, judging by the round shoulders draped in a black knit wool cape with a few stitches that have come apart, or going by the more and more bulging dress whose lower expanse forms a long narrow bell with the upper. (We'd imagined her as rather more lean.)

The clothes are dignified: a white dress with a geometric pattern and wide ornamental trim down the middle and at the ankle-length hem, although some isolated threads are hanging down loose there. (We were sure she'd be more smartly dressed.)

There she stands, her bulky body stiff and straight, her little feet turned neatly outward in their high-heeled ankle boots. Her limbs may seem gaunt with age, thin and brittle, but her left hand keeps a firm grip on a heavy roll of paper, although her right hand, with a splayed middle finger, rests on the carved handle of a cane, which she doesn't need for support since she's planted it at an angle in front of her, almost coquettishly, unlike what we'd expected. That's how she stands there.

That's how she looks, as shown to us by herself.

Hi, Auntie Times!

July 8, 1968 Monday

For more than a week, apparently, workers at thousands of Soviet factories and farms have been holding rallies, right in the middle of the harvest, and condemning, or so we hear, "anti-Socialist and anti-Soviet elements" in Czechoslovakia. The Prague paper *Young Front* declares itself bewildered. Precisely this, cries the *Truth* from Moscow right back at them, demonstrates that the *Mladá Fronta* journalists are among the "irresponsible." The chairman of the National Assembly of the ČSSR has also received letters from Moscow, Poland, and East Germany. Josef Smrkovský has kept their exact wording to himself; first he has to discuss it with the governing presidium of his Communist Party; still, he has acknowledged receipt by insisting that Czechoslovakia would not tolerate interference by other countries in her internal affairs. "Interference." That's all it is.

In May 1948 Cresspahl lay stark naked in a water trough in Johnny Schlegel's flower garden. Johnny was sitting on the bench next to the trough as idle as if the workday were over. It was early in the morning. The cats had sense enough to avoid the site of this spectacle; the stupid chickens kept their heads down and wondered why they were so often mispecking. Most of the time the chickens were the only ones keeping up a conversation. Every hour or so Johnny would knock on the sill of the open window behind him, and Inge Paap née Schlegel would come out with a bucket of hot water and put it down at the corner of the house, keeping her back to the two men, not once turning to look. Johnny, with his one arm, could not only carry the heavy bucket but handle it so well that the water poured over Cresspahl's body in a gentle rush, only a little spray reaching his head.

Since Johnny was no less flustered than his guest, he had a hard time keeping silent. He didn't care so much about the time—he'd assigned the work to be done on the farm, he wasn't needed there. He must be getting on in years for his mouth to be itching like that. And for now this Cresspahl knew only that his daughter was still living in Jerichow, with the Abses, in their own house. Couldn't he come up with any questions to ask after all those years with the Soviets? Johnny cast dignity to the winds and said, as if making some kind of calculation: Now that must have been a long trip Cresspahl'd just taken, all right.

That was probably a bit too close to sentimental for Cresspahl, and he put Johnny in his place by answering: *Yeah, bout the same as the one from Jerichow to the Damshagen pub.* This was a local story from the old days when people used to take trips only when a ship'd been wrecked on the beach. Fritz Mahler the cobbler and Fritz Reink the blacksmith were supposed to report to the soldiers but took a bye in Grems and annoyed the people there. Then they realized they'd been dummies and really should see the world a bit. Fritz goes right, to Damshagen, a mile from Jerichow; Fritzie keeps left until he, too, gets to Damshagen. They run into each other in the pub, and cry, Fritz! Fritz! Imagine meeting you here halfway round the world! In fact Schlegel's farm was near Damshagen too. Johnny admitted it.

But Cresspahl wasn't trying to snub him. Since both these world travelers had been from Klütz, he admitted in turn that on the long trek here from Wismar he'd been at the north end of Wohlenberg Cove and there, with the west wind blowing, had heard the bells of Klütz. How was it they'd kept their bells in Klütz?

– *They say what theyve always said*: Johnny confirmed, suddenly a bit uncomfortable, probably giving a sigh. Cresspahl at once took it personally. Because what the bells of Klütz say is:

> *It's true-ue, it's true-ue,*
> *the 'prentice boy is dead.*
> *He's lyin in the Piglet Pond,*
> *the 'prentice boy is dead.*
> *He never used to steal nor lie*
> *and never a cheat was he.*
> *Our Lord God, on high-igh,*
> *have mer-cy, mer-cy, mer-cy!*

and even if it's true that Cresspahl had been that apprentice boy for the past two and a half years, falsely accused, now lying at the bottom of a pond without any prospect for rehabilitation by any Lord God, he wouldn't stand for the slightest expression of pity, let's get that clear. That's why Cresspahl said, a little maliciously, that it sure did stink here in Johnny's yard.

Johnny promptly took a deep breath and let out a roar. For the boy Axel Ohr had been busy behind the barn for an hour already, trying to burn, with some old straw, a pair of men's underpants, a kind of undershirt, and a pair of felt boots along with a black rubber raincoat. So far he had managed only billows of smoke, no fire, and Johnny gave him a hell of an earful, effortlessly spanning the several hundred feet separating them. Now Axel Ohr had to carry the fire, such as it was, on his pitchfork around the corner to where the wind would scatter the smoke. Axel came slinking across the yard, shyly approached the corner of the house, and asked to be allowed to bury the things instead of burning them. The naked man as well as the clothed one just stared at him, in amazement, almost contempt, so that he turned back, shoulders slumped helplessly, and ashamed at having tried to quibble with an order from Johnny. Terrible dictator, Johnny was. Unpredictable too. Axel Ohr wasn't allowed to do any more serious work all day, for instance. Out came Inge with a fresh bucket.

Johnny's sigh had escaped him more because of the generally prevailing circumstances than anything; he felt a bit unjustly punished. So he just said: He didn't have any beer on the farm but he could manage a shot of liquor. That put Cresspahl in his place. His head had actually shrunk down into his shoulders at the memory of the sip he'd had to take earlier, as a proper greeting. – *Or maybe a cigar?* Johnny generously followed up, quite the master of the house making up for a bad odor with a good one. Cresspahl made an indecisive movement with his head, so Johnny left his nobly rolled tobacco on the outermost plank of the bench and stepped away for a moment, to see to things in the kitchen and bring Axel Ohr the kindling, which of course the boy wouldn't have thought of on his own. When he came back the cigar was sitting in more or less the same place, barely wet, but Cresspahl was even paler in the face than before, if that were possible. What was wrong with that man's stomach, he couldn't eat!

Then they poured out the broth and moved the tub, following the sun, which by that time had left the living-room windows. The chickens made a terrible fuss. Now there were three buckets of fresh water by the corner.

Johnny came over with the bench under his arm and mentioned in passing his obligations to Cresspahl. He spoke of Cresspahl's Gesine and her remarkable abilities as a farmworker, in the realm of wheat as well as that of potatoes. He still owed her two sacks of wheat but was planning to send her part of it in the form of smoked meat. What did Cresspahl, as legal guardian, say to that? Cresspahl asked what the date was. Because there'd been such a rush about signing the papers the previous morning in the Schwerin prison, plus he couldn't read the small print too well yet. Johnny left and came back with his schoolteacher glasses on his nose, holding Cresspahl's release papers in his hand, from which he read first the date and then all the rest. The naked man now wanted to take another stab at the cigar. Johnny Schlegel told him about the head of the Cresspahl household, Jakob. He was learning how to couple up freight cars at the Gneez station, but he didn't want to sell his sorrel horse. Maybe Cresspahl could have a word with him about that, man to man. Jakob was a man of the world in other ways, after all, with grown-up love affairs, including one on the farm with a certain Anne-Dörte until she decided she preferred her titled relatives in Schleswig-Holstein. Johnny was perfectly capable of going on to tell quite other tragic love stories that had taken place before his eyes—men are like that. But he had failed to notice—men are like that— Gesine's suffering during Jakob's visits, and Cresspahl would spend several years suspecting Jakob of a certain dislike, in private you might say, of the nobility. Now Johnny produced some lie about a canister of kerosene he was supposedly keeping for Gesine too. They had sworn one or one and a half false oaths before, on the other's behalf, these two; clearly one more wouldn't matter.

Axel Ohr took up position ten paces away and reported successful incineration. He'd washed himself too, to Johnny's lengthy surprise. Axel Ohr wanted to leave now. He was the boy on the farm, wasn't he. Though he had his doubts sometimes about whether what Johnny imposed on him in such a threatening tone were really punishments. This runaway city boy, sixteen years old, really should've realized that he'd been as good as adopted by the Schlegels and had, without really trying, learned practically everything Friedrich Aereboe had put in his book on general agricultural business management, even a bit more. Need to finesse the calculation of total deliverables, just ask Axel! Now he stood there waiting to hear his next repulsive assignment. He was to go meet the noon train at the Jerichow station. – With Jakob's sorrel...? he repeated, blushing, afraid he might have misheard. Thats right, on Jakobs horse. Johnny gave his ears a good thorough washing out while Axel waited for the catch. – M'boy! Johnny said, serious, looming. He could be so horribly High German sometimes. The catch was that Axel had to pick up a girl there, even if just a fifteen-year-old. She'd probably hold on to him on the horse. Axel didn't really know his way around girls too good, though he'd known one for years as Cresspahl's daughter. That's how Johnny was, always spoiling your fun. The boy resentfully went and saddled up.

Now Johnny gave Cresspahl a crash course in what he'd missed since the fall of 1945, from the creation of Soviet joint-stock companies in Germany to the regional elections to the Gneez principal who in May had been sent to jail for two years, for writing recommendation letters for schools in West Berlin: Piepenkopp showed firm character as a student, that kind of thing. Associating with the enemy of peace. Driving young men and women into the clutches of the enemy of world peace! Johnny'd had Richard Maass make him a book of blank pages, some good rapeseed oil it cost him too, and he wrote something in it almost every day. He read some to Cresspahl: about the Communist coup in Prague; the SED wished the Germans would do the same. People like you and me. Jan Masaryk, the Czechoslovak foreign minister, had jumped out the window of his own free will, they said. Cresspahl didn't happen to know anyone around here, or somewhere in Mecklenburg at least, who wanted to jump out a window so things here could go like there? Then Johnny explained what "spare peaks" were. That was the new name for surplus harvest yields after delivering the target quota, which you were free to sell to the Economic Commission at a higher price. Cresspahl was inclined to see this innovation as permission to conduct an agricultural business for profit again. Yes. Well. Theoretically, sure. But since Johnny'd had to say goodbye to patrons like Colonel Golubinin, the PSC had been paying quite a few visits to the farm. People's Supervisory Committee. They would hand around slips of paper about "monitoring production and commodity whereabouts" and then raise the target quota to what they saw fit. What did a post-office guy like Berthold Knever have to do with *Triticum vulgare*, much less *Triticum aestivum*? Now some farmers had to buy back wheat at spare-peak prices so they could sell it at quota prices. Naah—not Johnny. He was running the business with the other people on the farm commune-style, remember? It was precisely these progressive, *youd hafta say* advanced features of Johnny's business organization that were a thorn in the Gneez district attorney's side. *Men live longer than cows an learn somethin new every day.* Cresspahl showed that he'd learned something too by that point, whatever else he'd missed. – *Izzat book well hid?* he asked. Johnny nodded, proud, unconcerned. Five years later that book wasn't well enough hidden after all, and since he had the nerve to pretend it was a novel he didn't get out of jail till 1957. For now he was sitting on a bench next to a naked friend and gently refilling his tub with fresh water.

– *Heres yer big seal in the water!* Johnny Schlegel said as he led Cresspahl's daughter to the trough, which was now covered with two big wooden breakfast boards. This was totally wrong. Cresspahl didn't have a beard, his skull was long and high, and in Mecklenburg a seal was someone who gaily got away with risky pranks. Cresspahl sure hadn't gotten out of his intact. It did fit a little, because of the man's blank gaze from an indeterminate, unknowable distance. – *'E wont bite*: Johnny said, and the Cresspahl child desperately hoped that he wouldn't leave her alone with this person. First she only saw the ears, which looked so wrong next to his thin haggard face. They'd shaved him bald so his stubble looked dirty. The head between the edge of the trough and the start of the first board looked decapitated, especially since his arms were hidden. She didn't know where to look, she felt more ashamed than she'd ever felt, she was about to start crying. By that point Johnny had long since left his own garden.

– *Ive brought you summing*: the stranger said with her father's voice.

Johnny was staging quite the scene with Axel in the hall—it was about Axel having let the sorrel out into the pasture. So thoughtless. It dawned on Axel that he needed to get the sorrel again, and the rubber-tired cart, to take this Cresspahl to Jerichow. The valuable cart, which horses had so much fun with that it drove itself in front. He'd be driving like a young king. Well, a viceroy. Not on the way there. Any man with eyes in his head, if not a girl like Cresspahl's daughter, could see that she'd gotten her father back shattered, truly not a well man—you'd have to drive him at a walk. But Axel Ohr could already picture the rush of the return trip, whip planted picturesquely on his left thigh, road swirling with dust behind him between the choppy waters of the green wheat on the left, the sea on the right. Axel Ohr convinced himself to believe his luck, at least for that day.

You didnt cry, Cresspahl.
'Fonly I coulda cried, Gesine.

July 9, 1968 Tuesday

It's a normal American thing—for that reason alone Mrs. Cresspahl should have seen it coming. But she'd never imagined that de Rosny would expect this from her, even with apologies. The stockholders on the board must have pushed it through: this proceeding as medieval as it is futuristic. De Rosny *did* expect it from his Mrs. Cresspahl and informed her by mere interoffice memo, like she was a cog in a machine and the person renting the machine could request an adjustment, a depth control, whenever he wanted. Only in Westerns do civilized murderers announce what they're doing (you won't be going anywhere tomorrow), while it's the villains who shoot without warning, from ambush. Mrs. Cresspahl is sitting in a soft deep faux-leather chair with her back to an older technician. She can remember only his bluish smock; she forgot his face at once in her rage. She's in a room with no windows anywhere so she feels short of breath. The walls are painted in yellowing ivory as you'd expect in a hospital. A rubber loop is coiled high around her chest, a band interwoven with wires is stretched tight across her right upper arm, she has a metal plate affixed to each wrist. Heartbeat, breathing, blood pressure, skin moisture. It's the polygraph, the lie detector that no one believes in except the police, the military, and the business world. The empathetic voice behind her seems to be putting out bad breath. She has already been answering for a long time, heedlessly, tripped up by the question of whether or not she should lie. The walls are so thick that out of all the noise of New York she can only hear the humming of the fluorescent lights somewhere above her head.

ANSWER	Refuse? When my job depends on it?
QUESTION	Now the rules of this game are that you can only answer Yes or No from now on.
ANSWER	Yes.
QUESTION	Again, your birthday. March 3, 1933, was that right?
ANSWER	Yes.
QUESTION	In Jerichow, Mecklenburg, the Baltic.
ANSWER	Yes.
QUESTION	You said before what you were doing at six thirty last night.
ANSWER	Yes.
QUESTION	You said: "I was on the promenade by the Hudson. Since

the river was so calm, my daughter thought it must be ebb tide."

ANSWER   Yes.

QUESTION   "I looked at the time so I could check the tide table in *The New York Times.*"

ANSWER   Yes.

QUESTION   Did you do that?

ANSWER   No. Being invited into this nice room here made me forget.

QUESTION   Mrs. . . . Cress-pahl. You're getting agitated.

ANSWER   Sorry. No. Yes.

QUESTION   I have questions that I'm required to ask, along with others from the client. I'm not making them up. This is my job. You mean nothing to me as a person, so I have no interest in hurting your feelings, or in—

ANSWER   Yes.

QUESTION   It's also not true that I'm drawing any personal conclusions from your answers. The measuring instruments, oscillating in front of me or tracing out curves on the paper drum, take care of that.

ANSWER   Yes.

QUESTION   It's just a game, for us both.

ANSWER   Yes.

QUESTION   Your nationality is German.

ANSWER   Yes.

QUESTION   West German?

ANSWER   Yes.

QUESTION   East German nationality?

ANSWER   Yes.

QUESTION   West German nationality?

ANSWER   Yes.

QUESTION   Earlier you said, "I have about seven dollars in my wallet."

ANSWER   Yes.

QUESTION   "Maybe eight with the change."

ANSWER   Yes.

QUESTION   You're here because your bank wants to give you a sensitive, confidential assignment.

ANSWER	Yes.
QUESTION	You understand that your bank has to insure itself against risk.
ANSWER	Oh yes. Yes.
QUESTION	Do you feel loyalty to your bank?
ANSWER	No.
QUESTION	Do you mean the bank where you have an account?
ANSWER	Yes.
QUESTION	Do you mean the bank where you work?
ANSWER	Yes.
QUESTION	You came to the United States on April 29, 1961.
ANSWER	No.
QUESTION	On April 28, 1961.
ANSWER	Yes.
QUESTION	With a visa that let you work.
ANSWER	Yes.
QUESTION	Your name is Gesine L. Cresspahl.
ANSWER	Yes.
QUESTION	Do you go by only this name?
ANSWER	Yes.
QUESTION	Have you ever gone by a different name?
ANSWER	Yes.
QUESTION	Was that different name intended to evade an existing law?
ANSWER	Yes.
QUESTION	Multiple laws?
ANSWER	Yes.
QUESTION	Did you believe you were right to break those laws?
ANSWER	Yes.
QUESTION	You are not married.
ANSWER	No.
QUESTION	You have never been married.
ANSWER	No.
QUESTION	You reject the institution of marriage.
ANSWER	Yes.
QUESTION	Will you ever get married?
ANSWER	Yes.

QUESTION	You had a happy childhood.
ANSWER	Yes.
QUESTION	Not always happy.
ANSWER	Yes.
QUESTION	When you think about your biographical background, do you think it possible that you are psychologically damaged?
ANSWER	No.
QUESTION	Would you call yourself a stable person?
ANSWER	No.
QUESTION	An unstable person?
ANSWER	No.
QUESTION	You have never been married.
ANSWER	No.
QUESTION	Do you feel guilty toward anyone now alive?
ANSWER	No.
QUESTION	Toward anyone now dead?
ANSWER	Yes.
QUESTION	More than five people?
ANSWER	No.
QUESTION	Five.
ANSWER	No.
QUESTION	Three.
ANSWER	Yes.
QUESTION	You have promised not to talk to anyone about your assignment.
ANSWER	Yes.
QUESTION	Have you ever broken this promise?
ANSWER	Yes.
QUESTION	Would carrying out your confidential assignment pose any risk to you?
ANSWER	No.
QUESTION	Your daughter was born in New York.
ANSWER	No.
QUESTIONS	She was born in Düsseldorf.
ANSWER	Yes.
QUESTION	You have no loyalty to the bank you work for?

ANSWER   No.

QUESTION   Do you have an account at that bank?

ANSWER   Yes.

QUESTION   Do you have an account at another bank as well?

ANSWER   Yes.

QUESTION   You come from a Communist country.

ANSWER   No.

QUESTION   You come from a country that is now located on the other side of the Iron Curtain.

ANSWER   Yes.

QUESTION   In fleeing that country you have suffered losses.

ANSWER   . . . No.

QUESTION   You regret these losses.

ANSWER   No.

QUESTION   Would you betray the hospitality of the United States?

ANSWER   Yes.

QUESTION   Have you ever betrayed it?

ANSWER   No.

QUESTION   You have never been divorced?

ANSWER   No.

QUESTION   Are you suspicious of the practice of polygraphy?

ANSWER   Yes.

QUESTION   You consider the measurements from the so-called lie detector unreliable?

ANSWER   Yes.

QUESTION   Do you have the rest of the day off?

ANSWER   Yes.

QUESTION   All right, we're done.

ANSWER   No.

QUESTION   Would you prefer to take the sensors off yourself, or would you rather my colleague . . .

ANSWER   Yes. No.

QUESTION   You don't have any questions.

ANSWER   No.

QUESTION   Usually, other people, they have questions, you know.

ANSWER   Yes.

QUESTION They can hardly wait. But the results are still strictly confidential.

ANSWER Yes.

QUESTION In your case, I have permission to tell you your percentage of truthfulness. If you asked. A very cultured man, a real gentleman—French name, de Rosny...

ANSWER Yes.

QUESTION You are ninety percent truthful. That's confidential, of course.

ANSWER No.

QUESTION Yes. You're young, Mrs. Cresspahl, you still have lots of opportunities!

The man in the tunnel of the Ninety-Sixth Street subway station who always demands that the Jews get fucked has an opponent, who always crosses his graffiti out. Today the invitation has been forcefully restored.

And, please, who's writing "YOPA!" on the train cars, posters, electricity meters, and station pillars? What does it mean?

It's only quarter past eleven. The sun is making a cozy cave out of the garage on Ninety-Sixth Street. A policeman is there, questioning two employees, one white and one colored. They're sitting on a bench that's too narrow for two people, asses pressed uncomfortably together. The Negro doesn't look up. He lets the white answer. Only after being explicitly asked does he confirm the other man's statement, his eyes still on the floor: Yes, that's pretty much it, you could say that, mister, sir.

July 10, 1968 Wednesday

Now the Communist Parties of Bulgaria and Hungary have written to Prague too. (Romania is keeping out of it, apparently understanding the principle of noninterference in the exact same sense as the Soviet Union claims it applies with respect to its own affairs.) The letters are similar in content: all charge that the Czechoslovak Central Committee had not been sufficiently firm in dealing with the "revisionists" in its ranks, nor with the "counterrevolutionaries" outside the party, both of which groups were misusing the press, radio, and television to spread the truth about the past as well as the present. But Alexander Dubček, as well as Josef Smrkovský, do not wish to appear before a tribunal of their peers; they are more than happy to talk with individual partners. Meanwhile two Soviet regiments remain in the ČSSR, despite the maneuvers having ended on June 30. There weren't any repair facilities for their vehicles: they explain. They weren't given enough transport space on the railroads: they complain.

The blue workman's overalls Cresspahl borrowed from Johnny Schlegel were definitely clean—Inge had washed them. Cresspahl wore them for only a few hours a day. As if the half-day bath at Johnny's hadn't gotten him clean enough, he would often sit in a tub of water in the kitchen when we were out of the house.

– Well at least you've gotten him back from the Russians. Thank you: Marie says. – Congratulations, too, you deserve it. But this is you telling the story, it's not like you'll have the Red Army bring him back in a Mercedes with a motorcycle escort. Since he was innocent and all.

– He'd been sentenced.

– Release is a sentence.

– He wasn't sure of the exact words, and the numbers had only been read to him. But since there were three of them, it must have been paragraphs 6, 7, and 12 of §58.

– Under Soviet law?

– Soviet law. From 1927, partly.

– He was in England then, Gesine.

– And that's why the British had made him mayor of Jerichow; and maybe he'd betrayed something to the British about the Jerichow airfield before the Soviet commandant K. A. Pontiy arrived in all his glory. Up to three years deprivation of freedom per par. 6, Espionage.

– Paragraph 7?

– Sabotage against Business, Transportation, or Monetary Circulation, including to the benefit of earlier proprietors.

– If there was anyone in postwar Jerichow living like a . . . a movie star, Gesine, it was your man Pontiy.

– K. A. Pontiy hadn't changed his testimony. We tried to find him; by that point he was probably locked up in Krasnogorsk for the same paragraph.

– He really did interfere in Jerichow business.

– But Cresspahl did too. Hadn't he retroactively withdrawn, from the frozen accounts of the estate owners who'd fled, whatever he needed to borrow to pay municipal wages?

– And par. 12 punishes the fact of being locked up by the Soviets.

– No, par. 10 did that. Under par. 10 he faced imprisonment for having told them something about his life: Anti-Soviet Propaganda and Agitation. Under par. 12 he was charged with Failure to Denounce Counterrevolutionary Crimes. Six months minimum sentence.

– Robert Papenbrock.

– Or not reporting the visits from Emil Plath. The secret SPD. Or that he hadn't managed to pull together an official SPD in Jerichow himself, because Alfred Bienmüller thought it was ridiculous.

– But the Soviet commandant had forbidden the forming of political parties!

– Pontiy wasn't a witness in Schwerin. In Schwerin there was someone from the Soviet military police, with a machine gun strapped on him, and three judges in uniform. He could request others, by the way, if he thought these ones were biased.

– Well in that case he got out much too soon! According to just paragraph 6 and 12 he should have stayed in jail until October 1949.

– And if the punishment started on the day the sentence was pronounced it would have been till August 1952.

– You and he were lucky, Gesine.

– It was pure luck. Little Father Stalin abolished the death penalty, the "highest form of social defense," only in June 1947. As a rule, an SMT in Germany handed out twenty-five years in the labor camp. Releases from camps on Soviet-German soil started only in July '48. In August the Schwerin military tribunal sentenced a Rostock man named Gustav Cub and eight others to a total of 185 years in the labor camp for communication with a foreign news agency.

– Why was Cresspahl the exception, Gesine?

– That was his bad luck. It made people suspect him of having been given a little something for denouncing others.

– The people in Jerichow had known him since 1932! Since 1931!

– He hadn't been keeping tabs on the people in Jerichow. Today we think that the Soviets found out something about Cresspahl's news-gathering for the British in the war after all, and wanted to save him for possible use later.

– Since there was a par. 10, how could he ever tell you anything about Schwerin?

– He never did. It was probably eight years later, after I'd long since left Mecklenburg, that Jakob heard a word or two about it. He didn't have anyone else to talk to.

– Now he was scared. I'd have been too. Honest.

– He was sick, Marie. These water cures of his. . . . We had trouble keeping him from going to Town Hall to register that first night, with the official certification explaining his absence. The Cresspahl of the old days would've had the mayor come to him. The mayor now, for a change, was Berthold Knever—he'd risen higher than the postmaster Lichtwark ever did and become tentative and jittery under the burden of his new honor. Knever would've come as if following binding orders, with an uneasy conscience. If anything he was glad that Jakob had held the certificate up to him and asked for a ration card for Cresspahl without the necessary personal verification. Knever stood with his back to Jakob for quite a while, sighing; he was the first person in Jerichow to feel embarrassed at the return of his former superior. You know, when Jakob was telling a story he'd sometimes be overtaken by a laugh in his throat as if adding to his own amusement the pleasure he was giving his listener. It was easy to tell when Jakob was happy about something. Cresspahl was still worried he might have gone against regulations. As if rules were right simply because they'd been defined as what was right.

– Aftereffects of imprisonment.

– You are *not* allowed to read the books on the top shelf!

– I've read about that in *The New York Times*.

– It wasn't so bad that whenever I saw him, wherever he was in the house, he'd be sitting down. Meek and quiet, at Lisbeth's desk, at the kitchen table, on the milk stand. He still twitched when he walked and he hadn't minded letting Johnny and Inge see it, Axel Ohr was allowed to see how he'd gotten off the cart, but he didn't want me to see him like that.

– I would have been proud of him for that. As a daughter.

– His daughter was more nervous, until the limp went away. It was bad that he hadn't let Axel Ohr drive him down Town Street, Stalin Street, to let the citizens of Jerichow have a look—that we'd snuck in from the west on Cemetery Road and that for a while he stayed just a rumor. That he put Jakob off whenever he suggested in passing that they go into town. That sometimes as I sat doing my homework I could feel him looking at me as if he just couldn't get used to my profile softening along this line or that, around the eyes, that my hair was that smooth and straight and yet curled in a tiny wave above the braids. No one had ever stared at me like that.

– Someone has stared at me like that, Gesine. And I know who, too. But he wasn't being Mecklenburgish enough for you?

– I've learned it too now. This job of being a single parent.

– That's what I meant, Gesine. But you'd lost some respect for him?

– Not at all! I was embarrassed, nervous. Didn't talk to him without being asked. I was scared of having taken dancing lessons while he was in the camp, or maybe dead. Not to mention the reception I'd given Robert Papenbrock.

– What grade did he give you?

– Hanna Ohlerich had left very suddenly. Cresspahl didn't seem to care about that. I told him about it again, about what I'd said, I even resorted to lying. He nodded. I was breathing so hard that I had to turn away—he was staring so fixedly at me, in that new way of his. For Robert Papenbrock I had Jakob join me, as a witness, but in his telling Cresspahl's brother-in-law had left the house voluntarily after exchanging a few pleasantries about the weather. When Cresspahl learned the truth, he was almost glad. The dancing lessons: he thanked Mrs. Abs for those. He was on eggshells with Jakob; he seemed to feel he owed Jakob something it'd be hard to repay. As for my uptight behavior toward Brüshaver or Granny Papenbrock, he just abolished it. Brüshaver's mouth practically hung open when Cresspahl's daughter greeted him first, and deferentially. I was vindicated in my battle with Brüshaver over religion, and then I went to confirmation class on my own.

– So you passed.

– By the skin of my teeth. Cresspahl could talk to Jakob much more easily—Jakob was the more skillful doctor. I, on the other hand, brought up Alexander Paepcke's Aunt Françoise, the worthy old lady, who as a Mecklenburg MP had gotten the Althagen house released for her personal use; Cresspahl's daughter was afraid of what was to come, you see, and catching up on the past inevitably meant confronting losses. While Jakob, of course, had kept the pamphlet for the Mecklenburg parliament, first term, and updated it too: the MPs starting on page 64 had been neatly checked off if they still had a right to a seat, while others had had their biographies crossed out or their arrest by the NKVD indicated, their flight to West Berlin, to West Germany, their suicide. That's how Cresspahl learned a little something about the lay of the land he'd been released into.

– You were jealous of Jakob.

– I sat and listened, silently pleased. Anyone who talked like that wasn't planning to leave Jerichow for Schleswig-Holstein.

– But why did you stay! Cresspahl had friends in Hamburg, in England!

– He didn't have his Mecklenburg affairs in any kind of order yet. Of course he'd lost all his accumulated fixed or cash possessions while in service to the Soviets; for my sake he wanted to wait and see whether they'd honor my name in the land registry or confiscate the house too. He wasn't better; he would lock himself into the house for half a day whenever another wife came to visit this miraculous returnee to life from "Neubrandenburg" and asked for news of her son, her husband. Only one of his Hamburg friends had sent word, and that wasn't a friend, it was his old-time party comrade Eduard Tamms who needed a letter of absolution—they weren't done with denazification in Hamburg yet. He would never, ever work up the courage for England. That was where Mr. Smith had been killed in 1940 in a German air raid. No Arthur Salomon was alive there who might have put a word in for him; notification of his death had been sent out by the firm of Burse & Dunaway in 1946. And where else would he have wanted to go besides Richmond? The Richmond Town Hall had been damaged by German bombs. It's true that there was a hydraulic engineer in the British Sector of West Berlin to whom Cresspahl had once sold a dog with an excellent pedigree, and Gesine had run into him the previous summer on Village Road in Ahrenshoop, Cresspahl would be welcome to stay with him for a week. But he was too damaged for that.

– When was Cresspahl better?

– On the day when he managed to write a letter to Mr. Oskar Tannebaum, fur merchant, Stockholm, and thank him for a package. Written in one go. That was near the middle of June 1948.

– Now you all could leave.

– Now the Soviet Military Administration in Germany had shut down rail, car, and foot traffic between its zone and the Western ones.

July 11, 1968 Thursday

Alexander Dubček did call the two thousand Czechoslovak words disruptive, a reason for concern, and was far from subscribing to them; now the *Literaturnaya Gazeta* (place of pub.: Moscow) informs him what we should truly think of these words: If someone calls for public criticism, demonstrations, resolutions, strikes, and boycotts to bring down people who have misused power and caused public harm, this is, in direct language, a provocative, inflammatory program of action. It is counterrevolutionary. We can certainly hear the invitation to conceive of *literaturka* as revolutionary, especially in connection with the misuse of power.

At the end of the 1947–1948 school year the teachers at the Gneez Bridge School all agreed that they needed to keep an eye on Cresspahl, class 8-A-II. Only Miss Riepschläger, in the excusable carelessness of her youth, excluded herself from the others' cares. – Gesine has her father back, let her celebrate till she's blue in the face: Bettina said in her innocence. The older, more experienced pedagogues were perfectly willing to allow this for the first two days, a week at the outside, but it certainly was suspicious, wasn't it, if this transformation from a gloomy to an open, even confiding personality lasted longer than that. Frau Dr. Beese and Frau Dr. Weidling were constantly skirmishing over the psychological theories they had learned at different institutions at different times. Weidling resorted to dictation, which she gave with grammatical snippets, *titbits* (back-translation not out of vanity but for educational purposes). She was unaware that her voice, in the heat of the moment of elegant articulation, got rather bulgy, downright owlish in fact, so apart from five students the word *usually* took various fantastic forms, and those five all happened to be sitting around Cresspahl, although she hadn't been seen whispering. How could such a timid child suddenly put her graduation to high school at risk! Even worse: during the break Gabriel Manfras and Gesine went up to the board and openly (!) wrote what they'd heard—Gesine "usually," fine, and Gabriel "jugewelly," then he crossed her version out. The old Gesine would have pinched her lips, would have turned on her heel, stubborn and subdued. This one came running after Mrs. Weidling, pulling Manfras by the arm (!), and asked in a cheerful, friendly way for the correct spelling. *Now wouldja lookit that.* Dr. Beese asked if Cresspahl had gotten a demerit in the class book. No, there was no proof she had whispered the answer: Weidling replied, demoralized once more when she remembered how Schoolgirl Cresspahl had walked on with her, alone, and asking like an old friend if the Dr. got these titbits from British Broadcasting? She sometimes gave it a listen too. Was it conceivable—concluding a pact of silence with a child? Severity now as much as ever: Beese said dreamily.

Gesine simply felt like she'd woken up. All the dillydallying before a decision was gone, and whatever she did was right. She saw no reason why she shouldn't use a wooden briefcase as a satchel one day; she explained the rolling lid, the three compartments to anyone who asked (but not the secret compartment, or its place of manufacture, or its provenance from the personal effects room of a prison)—she was the daughter of a father who could make such a thing with his own hands, wasn't she? It was only right to share her confidence with Mrs. Weidling, if the teacher was going to reciprocate. (She regretted for rather a long time the sudden disappearance of the titbits from the lesson plan.) Even in Miss Pohl's class, her stalwart efforts and stubborn diligence had turned into willingness, thinking along as if enjoying it, delight at understanding; she kept her cool when Pohl slipped back into her earlier conception of pedagogical Eros and grumpily reproached her with comments like: Yes, Gesine, about time! or the one about two minutes before closing time; what she got for her pains was more likely to be a twinkle in Gesine's eye. Gesine not only had a B+ average in math now, almost all her grades qualified her for high school and she'd get permission because she now had a legally authorized head of household who could sign the application. (Jakob had gone to Jansen and started proceedings to be made legal guardian specifically because of Mrs. Abs's contested signature—now she could throw those papers right into the Gneez moat.) The future had arrived, and she'd been on time to meet it.

She was careful not to overdo it. She was one of the first in her class to show up at the office that Emil Knoop, in his inexhaustible patriotism, had cleared out and made available for the People's Referendum. When she got there Frau Dr. Beese was on duty, and since it was before the noon train it was just the two of them behind the windows that showed them one piece of Stalin Street after the next through crossed hammers on frosted glass. Gesine suddenly decided she could say something to Beese after all. Because constituting Germany as an "indivisible democratic republic" sounded fine to her, especially if there was going to be a "just peace" too, but she'd learned about elections a bit differently in school—not these ballot lists on open display and quizzing children aged fourteen and up about their preferences. She asked if this was another right way to do it. – I know your identity personally: Beese said grimly. She was missing lunch that day. Gesine mentioned being underage. – You just sign right there: Beese hissed, snide but somehow coaxing too, and the child realized that this might be important for her permission to attend high school. So she scrawled her name under German Unity, appeased her teacher with a curtsey, and skipped happily across the fluted tile floor of the enormous lobby onto Stalin's blistering hot white street.

Schoolgirl Cresspahl might have gotten her father back; did it entirely escape her what kind of father he now was? He certainly wasn't in much of a position to work, his earnings wouldn't even cover the school fees; but she acted as if she'd woken up, downright cheerful. The way things were seemed to be just fine with her.

Believe it or not, Cresspahl had been released with more obligations than just to register his new address. He was supposed to set up a wood-working facility with the machines that had been taken from him and manage it as a trustee. Even the telephone, previously seized as part of his business property, was reinstalled for him by technicians from Gneez in the interest of another business—the people's economy—and with the old number too: 209. Except the machines he'd driven into the drying shed of the brickyard in April 1945 weren't there anymore. From the carpenter's bench and disk sander down to the tiniest saws and clamps, they'd disappeared—and from right next to the Kommandatura, too, under the very noses of the Soviet military police, behind two-inch-thick doors and an untouched padlock. The room had been totally cleaned out. The noble Wendennych Twins stood there, nonplussed, with the itemized lists from the Schwerin SMT in hand, disgraced in front of this dispossessed German while a judgment from their very own army courts absolved him of this crime. Since they didn't believe in ghosts, for professional reasons, search teams from the Economic Commission started entering numerous workshops north of the Gneez-Bützow line in late May 1948, finding a dovetail jig in a carpenter's shop in Kröpelin, a crude-oil motor in the maritime boundary slaughterhouse in Wismar (now a people-owned ship-repair yard), and also some purchase agreements whose prehistories had a way of fading into obscurity just before reaching one Major Pontiy, one Lieut. Vassarion—business conducted at night, via handshake, sealed by insufficient written documentation. Cresspahl received furious letters from colleagues who at the time had paid in labor or goods for the equipment the Gneez prosecutor's office was now having hauled off to Jerichow. He seemed happy about the fact that the machines tracked down by mid-June weren't enough to reopen a business with, and he put up not the slightest resistance when the post office came to re-remove his telephone after half the brickworks burned down one humid Sunday morning. The honor of the Red Army blazed again in all its old glory; he'd been saved from having to manage anything. The Wendennych brothers had ordered the tardy fire brigade away from the more brightly burning main gate and into Cresspahl's yard so that it kept his daughter's house safe but was unable to save the future workshop. The prosecutor's office found enough molten metal in the rubble to satisfy them and declined to question Cresspahl after he'd had no choice but to refer them to the local commandants as the responsible parties. And what could he have said to their questions anyway? The commandants, nattily dressed and perfumed, came to see him with impeccable apologies and even accepted coffee, standing rigidly upright, after they had called his attention to the smoke in the air. The *People's Daily* reported the accident as an attack by unscrupulous elements opposed to world peace in the employ of the American imperialists; in Jerichow word went round about Cresspahl's experience with fires going back to November 1938; never again did the Twins pay a personal visit to Cresspahl, just as they consistently kept the Germans at a distance from their own residence and persons.

Gesine didn't mind. For one thing, she'd been in no danger from the fire since she'd been moved for the night from her room to Mrs. Abs's on the other side of the hall. For another thing, she wasn't seriously hoping for a return of the old days when Cresspahl would hoist a desk onto his shoulders, an oak top with two built-in stacks of drawers, and march that awkward monster straight through Jerichow to the exact spot in Dr. Kliefoth's study where what he'd ordered was supposed to be put. This Cresspahl was hardly up to supervising a workshop as a manager. She watched him in the yard earthing up potatoes—the ones that Jerichow's nimble fire brigade hadn't run over or trampled; he held the hoe stiffly, moved slowly, head hanging. There had been a time when he could make an interior door with nothing but an ax. He was here now. She didn't need everything all at once.

They were sitting one morning on the milk stand behind the house. Not only was there no school that day, she could sit next to Cresspahl for as long as she wanted to. Who cares if he didn't notice that the milk stand's uprights were rotting and needed shoring up. In the shade, wet with dew, the oldest cat was standing on stiff legs in the overgrown grass in front of them observing a blackbird chick that had fallen out of its nest, not fully fledged. The cat put down two legs in front of the others, not even bothering to sneak up. The screaming mother blackbird was in such a hurry that she dropped like a stone out of the tree, bouncing up already raising her head against the enemy, offering herself as a sacrifice, prepared to commit suicide. The cat gave her a sidelong look, gray and dispassionate, and stepped toward the chick, undeterred by the mother's shrieking. The cat would take care of the first one and then the second one. Gesine didn't know for sure if in earlier times she'd also have stood up and taken the dumbfounded cat away from its breakfast; now she came back with the predator under her arm, accepting the fact that the animal thought she'd lost her mind. She sat back down next to Cresspahl, keeping hold of the cat, which gradually realized it was being stroked but clung to its suspicion. What strange new customs were these? Then Gesine saw Cresspahl put down the stone he'd been about to throw at the cat himself.

Of all the arts these are the unprofitable ones, bringing in neither bread nor money. In the last week of June, Cresspahl's daughter saw how much trouble people could have with the money they'd set aside. Obediently, eagerly, she recited in school for Herr Dr. Kramritz certain things about the West German currency reform that he didn't believe and that she now felt uncomfortable saying: the surviving leaders of the Fascist war economy, aided and abetted by the leaders of the bourgeois parties and the Social

Democrats, were only interested in saving the rotting, crisis-ridden capitalist system—how stark a contrast with the currency reform in the Soviet zone. But she was exempt from the chaos raging among the people of Jerichow and Gneez starting on June 24, as was Cresspahl, and Mrs. Abs, and Jakob too. In their four savings accounts they had a grand total of two hundred and twenty-two marks after the devaluation; only Jakob and his mother had the seventy marks per head that could be exchanged for certificates with glued-on coupons at the post office. But many people owned greater sums, still worth a tenth of face value through June 27 and rather risky above five thousand marks, hinting at arms deals or black market business. Miss Pohl was observed storming up and down Stalin Street in Gneez past emptied shopwindows; by Saturday she had a genuine antique porcelain object from which punch might have been ladled were it intact, and an electric heater beyond repair (trading folks were occasionally moved to offer electrical appliances, given that the power had been cut off). Many felt sorry for Leslie Danzmann, who'd tried to pay back Mrs. Lindsetter, wife of the district court chief justice, the two hundred marks she'd borrowed a week before to buy a pound of butter—the worthy matriarch rejected her offer and refused to come down to even two thousand marks in paper money. Upon her humanity being appealed to, Mrs. Lindsetter avenged herself with the cryptic decision: Yes, well, then there's no help for it, I'll just see you in court, darling! Gabriel Manfras got a violin for Christmas from the Sons of Johannes Schmidt Musikhaus—guaranteed and unsellable for decades—though he didn't know it yet. Mina Köpcke, alarmingly inclined to the inner life and the exercise of religion ever since that nasty fight with her husband over a gasworks manager by the name of Duvenspeck, extended the range of her sentiments to the arts and acquired for a good three thousand marks two genuine painted pictures (oil), one an early-spring birch landscape with an overflowing stream in zigzag diagonals and the other a stag with its head in a position suggesting embarrassment. Pennies, five-pfennig pieces, and groschen were hard to come by, since they retained their face value for the time being; it was seriously said about old Mrs. Papenbrock that she'd rounded her bread prices *down*. The truth is that she baked less than the minimum daily quota during these days and Miss Senkpiel offered the rounding off—upward. Mrs. Papenbrock overcame her disdain of her son-in-law for once and went to Cresspahl for advice, because the balances in all of her accounts had been canceled the day before the proclamation of Order No. III of the SMA of Germany, and the sheepish gentlemen at the government bank hadn't cared to tell her why. Cresspahl assured her, though he didn't really believe it himself, that the Soviets confiscated assets only if the defendants were still alive, and spared her his opinion that she shouldn't even dream of Albert's release. Not that she failed to conveniently forget her offer to lend him the sum he needed to make up his per capita quota; with a gracefully raised double chin she turned around, almost exactly on the spot, and didn't shake his hand, content with the disappointment she'd predicted but for which she could never have found the right words. (This was the first time she'd been in the house since 1943.) Sunday had come and gone and money was still pursuing the Jerichowers with its useless offers; they were left to flop like fish on dry land. Everyone in the house felt bad for Jakob's mother, because the housing that Jakob had refused to consider after the war was now having its equity devalued only fivefold, which meant that the Abses would've had to make payments only until 1955, not 1966, for the property Mrs. Abs wanted merely so as not to have to welcome her husband back empty-handed. She knew she couldn't manage such a property—it was remembering Wilhelm Abs, his uncertain life on or under the earth of a Soviet camp, that she could bear only while sitting alone in her room, praying with unseeing eyes, unhelped by her tears. On Monday Cresspahl received two small packages in the mail containing paper money, payment for bills from 1943 and 1944, but he was not allowed to pay the thirty marks he had been short of his per capita quota after the deadline; Berthold Knever, now back behind the counter at the post office, found that the days passed a little more quickly during the currency reform, occasionally letting him think about something other than his troubles and exert a little authority over Cresspahl with a snippy tone, now no longer a dusky old parrot but one dusted with gray. Then Jakob turned up and gave him trouble aplenty; Jakob didn't shout at the mayor, he only had to look at him with his brooding, puzzled gaze and he got Cresspahl's certificates at once, with the coupons, without a receipt. Emil Knoop, unaware of any more pressing troubles, once again made sure he got the cut he felt he was entitled to, despite it taking a few private visits to the Soviet neighborhood in Gneez; his calculations, sweeping all before them, told him that the soldiers and noncoms must have spent almost all of their month's pay by this point, and the officers and employees of the Military Administration their biweekly salaries likewise, so, charitably, he planned to go in with them on their unrestricted exchange quotas for a mere 5, 4, or 3.5 percent fee. He came to regret his audition with the commandant brothers in Jerichow as a misstep, for when they threw him out onto the street he could expect only a denunciation, which meant a loss, of time if nothing else. Perspiring, a little on the overweight side by this point, he stood in the sun outside Cresspahl's house, again forgoing a visit to his "paternal role model." What did he have to be worried about? But nowhere and never in Jerichow or Gneez did those Western enemies of peace with their suitcases full of old currency turn up, and it was their evil machinations that supposedly justified the whole ass over teakettle in the first place. Cresspahl's daughter was spared all this. She didn't have to participate in the hubbub. They had nothing. They had nothing! In your mind, that can feel like a brisk, cheering wind.

Meanwhile, it wasn't only Mrs. Weidling and Mrs. Beese who were focused on the Western Sectors of Berlin, to which the SMAG was just then cutting off both rail and water connections—whose population they were no longer prepared to supply with potatoes or milk or electricity or medicine; there was a lot of talk about World War III and a little about the prospect that the Soviets might finally try to set up a trade with at least the British: West Berlin for the parts of Mecklenburg the British had gotten to first. The Cresspahl child was seen going to the Renaissance Cinema during these days, twice, for eight marks fifty each time, but hardly in that subdued and intimidated state so familiar—not to say consoling!—to a teacher's eye. She didn't even bite her lip anymore when she had no answer to a pedagogically well-founded question. She was granted promotion to high school, but what deplorable inconstancy of spirit this schoolgirl was remembered as having!

– And that, if you please, was the dividing of East and West Germany, Gesine! Marie says. It's not that she's homesick for one Germany. No, in the middle of West End Avenue, outside the entrance to the Mediterranean Swimming Club, what she cared about were the infamous Communists in Germany. – Now you couldn't get mad at the Soviets anymore! she says.

– It was the Western Allies who started it with currency conversion, you know.

– War was around the corner!

– In early July the Soviet authorities ordered the deployment of German troops under the new name KVP, the Barracked People's Police.

– Well, you had permission to go to high school.

– War was something I thought I could handle, Marie. I'd already been through one. No one had taken Mecklenburg away from me. I had gotten something else too.

– Did it last, Gesine? Did it last?

– Until September. When I came back from Johnny Schlegel's wheat.

– You see, Gesine?

– You mean, that it didn't last?

– Yes. Or are you trying to teach me the lesson that happiness lasts?

July 12, 1968 Friday

Freitag. Friday. Thirty-nine days to go. Not even six weeks.

Read the business section, Gesine! It's nine oh three—the workday has started. Consider the state of the pound sterling. Daydream about the Old Lady of Threadneedle Street, not *The New York Times*!

There's statistics too. The annual tally of major crimes has risen hereabouts, and those are only the reported ones. Car thefts are listed as plus 64.3 percent, robberies at plus 59.7 percent, murders were reported 20.3 percent more, rape sagged 6 percent. Yesterday a man in a black hat and dark glasses walked into the Woodbury branch of the Chemical Bank on Jericho Turnpike carrying a small vial of acid....

The Communist Party of the Soviet Union responds yet again, with the voice of its *Truth*, to the two thousand Czechoslovakian words. As though anyone'd asked them. They claim to have no quarrel with the true objectives of the new crowd in Prague; Novotný may have committed errors and may have shortcomings, but like this, with "subversive activities from right-wing and anti-socialist forces," it is not pleased. The new crowd are trying, in *Pravda*'s view, "to blacken" their sister Communist Party "and discredit" it. That's happened before, too, they say—twelve years ago, in

Hungary. Is it not the case that the party *has* squandered some of its credit? Is it true that the party has kept its hands clean since 1948, innocent and pure as the driven snow for all these years?

Whatever Employee Cresspahl does, August 20 will come. She may go to the Atlantic shore again, open the windows another thirty times, buy Marie her fall and winter things, go to bed with D. E. whenever she feels like it—she will use another two tapes "for when you're dead," Marie needs to get her crayfish soup, maybe one more dream will stay with her past the point of waking up; she will be thoroughly and completely caught in the illusion of being alive. The truth is that she's sliding on the slippery ice of time toward the appointment de Rosny has made for her with Obchodný Banka. If she's allowed to go by boat she'll leave New York on August 12, by plane it'll be August 19. She has to start on Wednesday in Prague. There'll be someone to meet her at the airport. *Pravda* mentions Hungary. That sounds like tanks, doesn't it. What if they go in by air?

It is almost silent in Cresspahl's office. The telephone has been asleep since work started. The sound of Henri Gelliston's adding machine occasionally sloshes through the door. From immeasurably far below comes the yowl of a truck, now gossamer-thin. Alarm system damaged. Pedestrians will be approaching the source of the noise with apprehension, leaving it behind with indifference. Up here someone is writing a private letter— and you're going to regret it.

Dear Professor, it says, I hope you don't mind my writing to you, a friend gave me your address, and since I don't trust New York psychoanalysis, because of the proverbial label of headshrinker if nothing else, and since I'm aware that any diagnosis at a distance is necessarily a misdiagnosis, so don't even bother, she would still really like to know if she should consider herself psychologically disturbed, since she is facing a change in her life circumstances for professional reasons, all-encompassing enough to prompt her to draw up a will and take precautions in case her psychological condition proves dangerous, life story attached, what a lot you're handing over to someone else!

The handwriting alone. You're making large unbroken round shapes with long sharp descenders—what someone once called "tulip writing." If you look closer, you'll see that the letters may be fluid in their middle sections but the loops often aren't entirely completed according to specifications: hence, "open." The upstrokes as well as downstrokes are impoverished (simplified), especially the latter are little more than vertical slashes. Still, if one does think in terms of tulips, these are short ones, standing upright. It's a pronounced handwriting (not spoken pronunciation of course: distinct, inked, marked). What will someone else see in it, though? And what will he make of the fact that you're using black ink?

"... as for absurd actions in my life I'm only aware of the usual ones, including my reaction to the death of the man who was the father of my daughter. Fundamentally I think of myself as normal. The exception: I hear voices.

... don't know when it started. I assume: in my thirty-second year but I don't remember a particular reason it would have started. I don't want to. But it takes me back (sometimes almost completely) into past situations and I talk to the people from back then as I did back then. It takes place in my head without my directing it. Dead people, too, talk to me as if they're in the present. For instance criticizing me about how I'm raising my daughter (b. 1957). The dead don't persecute me—we can usually reach some kind of common ground in these imagined conversations. But are they imagined? Are they illusions? I also talk to dead people I know only by sight, who spoke only enough words to the child me when they were alive as were needed to say hello or give me some candy. Now they draw me into situations I wasn't there for, which I in no way could have grasped with an eight-year-old's or fourteen-year-old's mind. In other words, I hear myself speaking not only from the subjectively real (past) position but also from the position of a thirty-five-year-old subject today. Occasionally, when I hear them, my situation from back then as a fourteen-year-old child changes into that of the interlocutor of today, which I could hardly have occupied then. Many of these imaginary conversations (which seem real to me) are generated from insignificant triggers: a tone of voice, a characteristic emphasis, a hoarseness, an English word with the same roots as the Mecklenburg one. These scraps are enough to create the presence in my consciousness of a person from the past, their speech, and thus circumstances from long before I was born, such as March 1920 on my grandfather's leased estate when my mother was a child. I can hear my mother and the other people in the room not merely as an eavesdropper but with the knowledge that it all was intended for me—everything that, by the end of the imagined (?) scene, proves to have been bequeathed by the people of the past to me, the me of today.

With living people, present or absent, this tendency (?) of my consciousness can also be misused, I mean as a special ability. For example, I can reconstitute my daughter's thoughts from muscular particulars, even if she's not saying anything, and then respond to them (in my mind), even during our worst fights, although I have no proof that the 'transmission' reaches her. As a result, the child is rarely safe from me—she's kept under almost total surveillance. My only excuse is that I do this involuntarily.

It's not only with the child—in everyday conversations, in the office, on the subway, with coworkers or strangers, a second strand runs alongside whatever is actually said, in which the unsaid becomes perceptible, I mean what the other person doesn't say or just thinks. The volume of this second, imagined strand sometimes pushes to the periphery of my attention what I'm actually hearing in the moment, but it never totally drowns it out. Again I feel suspicious of this word 'imagination' here, because even though I absolutely don't count on the authenticity of what I hear only in my mind, it does often enough turn out to be correct, to be something I knew. It's possible that I'm foisting this second acoustic strand onto the person speaking just to give my own opinion an advantage, to corroborate myself—this doesn't seem likely, since I sometimes 'hear' the most horrible things from people whose sympathy I'm always desperate for. I do concede that as a general rule such sympathy may always contain its own negation, but I cannot concretely apply this rule to friends or even acquaintances.

It doesn't cause problems. The second audio reel doesn't paralyze the first, especially not when talking to anyone where there might be professional consequences if I opened myself up to criticism. When I try to tell my daughter about her grandfathers in Mecklenburg and Pommern, it sometimes happens that the interruptions of the dead make me pause, but no longer than the triangle a thorn might rip in a dress. (Or else the child, especially considerate for her not-yet-eleven years, conceals her shock and fear at these moments, allowing herself no physical, gestural reaction.) Such automatic interpositions of conversation do bring about a slightly distracted state, but I can get out of that state at will, considerably faster if the child calls me (but not when a car horn honks outside the window or something like that)—but when she does it's instant, immediate.

Is this a mental illness? Should I adjust my professional obligations accordingly? Does the child need to be protected from me?"

"They talk to me." You snitched.
You! Where've you been?
Were you waiting?
Well, you dead are usually....
Pretty chatty?
Usually there.
We've been busy.
Tell me.
We have nothing to say.
You never once told me: Here we all are! *And now no one even wants to talk to me.*
What business of ours is the future?
What.... (This isn't for me, Marie asked it:) What... lasts?
We do.

Dear Anita *Red Pigtails,*

First off, hello. Since you asked, I am writing to you yet again about our dealings with the man we call D. E., who paid you a visit the day before yesterday as Mr. Erichson, fringed asters in hand, just as we'd told him to.

If this is a life together, then it's one involving a certain distance: he on the flatter land beyond the Hudson, we on Riverside in New York City; a life together at intervals, each visiting the other for a day and a half at a time. Visits make for plenty of goodbyes, though, and entertaining hellos. Still, he's cautious and avoids springing surprises on us; even after we've made plans he'll call from the airport to check that we still want to see him after ten whole days. We reply that we're looking forward to it, and to news too. Because when this guy goes on a trip, he comes back having found something.

You're thinking: presents. Those too; and we've liked almost everything D. E.'s brought back from his trips. For Marie there was the ingenious revolving sphere showing the temperature in Fahrenheit and Celsius, the air pressure in millibars and millimeters, and the relative humidity too— she's been keeping a record of her observations since June and doesn't need *The New York Times* for her weather. Only during the first year with him did we suspect him of trying to get into our good graces with filthy lucre; now we have, both of us, come to know and like his overly casual, worried look as he tries to assure himself that he's thought about us accurately enough during his absence. (Since after all one of us assesses the air in the American manner, the other one stuck in her European habits.) Presents.

We're more interested in the other things. The moment of pleasure when the car from the air force of this country, dressed in civvies, drops him off outside our short yellow stump of a building exactly when he said it would, within five minutes. (He champions a kind of axiom whereby a person can manufacture punctuality. This doubly amuses us: first, because he manages to do it; second, that we're allowed to make fun of him for it.) What we've been waiting for is the phase right after the hug and the handshake, which I initiate by inviting, practically begging him: Tell us, tell us! And Marie has already clapped her hands and spoken in Mecklenburg Platt and shouted: *You tell such good lies!*

News. Where he was. What he's seen, what's happened to him. For instance, the Irishman in London whom the city government has stuck in the ground, alongside a lever in an elevator in the Underground, singing in his eternal night of a *Johnny, I hardly knew ye*, too slow but believably mournful, with pauses in which he inserts warnings to his middle-class cargo to please stand clear of the sliding doors. In D. E.'s report he's right here with us, with his curly mustache and undersized bass voice—we can hear him and want to go see him. Or the furious old hag in Berlin who screeched at him to leave the country for the peaks of the Urals because he was crossing a totally empty street in her country at a red light, the way one does in America, and he did look a little like a student, with his long hair. (Are people really like that in West Berlin, Anita?) We also believe his insatiability for news from us, about school, about the city. Did we put one over on Sister Magdalena with our skills in the *imparfait* of *connaître*, so that against her will and nature she had to write in the book the letter that points upward? What's new with Mrs. Agnolo, what did Eileen O'Brady tell us, has James Shuldiner been hounding us again with his pronouncements on the narrow benches at Gustafsson's? And then too: the dress you were wearing, the vegetables Anita has growing on her balcony, do you still see us next to the pot in which a certain Anita is boiling up displeasure at American policies in Southeast Asia? From the top, back to front, stem to stern, no ulterior motives. As though each of us, in our various locations, had lived a bit for the other, stored it up, and brought it back, in the interest of reciprocal delight.

You'll say that that's how things are only between people who. . . .

Yes. (There's one exception. We do leave one thing out. Just as I wish he worked for somebody else, he'd be happy to see me not take on an assignment that's looming before me. [Version for the mail censors.] It's not much help to know that he's sworn an oath, or for that matter that my obligation too comes from without, rather than being a project of my own devising the way it's supposed to work in the fairy tale of an unalienated life. We have to settle this with each other by listening right up to the border where advice would turn into instruction. We manage. Is there any reason for me to say out loud that civilian flights from Europe arrive in the evening, not the morning? He knows that I know. He could recite exactly what I don't like about these trips and I'd have to agree on the spot and confirm it and sign it too.)

So, I admit to having reservations. But I can't think of one that makes me unwilling to trust him.

He was in London (aside from the other business) to go to Moorfields Eye Hospital and complain about the fringed veils that, to his eye, streetlights have lately been wearing. At our breakfast table he threw a napkin over his shoulder as a white coat and turned himself into a British specialist and aristocrat, lisping with senile glee and salaried compassion as he tells us: It is to be feared, Mr. Erichson, sir, that this condition is a sign of advancing age. . . .

I can hear you say: If someone goes and admits to a strike against him, a physical ailment no less, instead of sticking to his strong suits. . . .

That's the way it is, Anita. He's not afraid to trust us with anything. We all laughed.

Here we have someone who refuses to try to change us. True, he'd be glad to abolish in our case this country's rule that employees get only two weeks' vacation in a whole year and not a single day for housekeeping; D. E.

would offer me machines that clean the laundry and dry it and put it on the table crisply ironed. But since this household does get by with the communal device in the basement of number 243, and moreover wants to see in person the fish and fruit it's spending its money on, D. E. can have only one of us this Saturday. When the other of us then suggests that he take the measure once more, by ferry, of all the water between the island of Manhattan and that of the Staaten General, she can take his careful nod as deliberate assent, no mere favor.

You see, Anita: I let him have the child. (With one limitation: only once were they allowed to fly on the plane without me—a superstition of mine. Which he respects.) The child goes with him. If Marie is inviting him then maybe she wants a chance to discuss with a man what seems incomprehensible and irrational about her mother; and I don't mind, I think she should, I'm not afraid. Their latest shared routine is one where the first person says (confident, despondent, pleading): *God knows.* And the other (gloating, or reassuring, or giving information, or saying "next, please"): *But he won't tell.* Optional addendum (portentously): *"Will he??"*

With him, you'd be playing this game too after a while. (It was Marie who brought this funny business home with her, from her strict religious school.) Here's what he had to say about you: Yeah, she's someone I'd go steal a horse with.

Marie has been known to forget the condition that she call home every two hours from wherever she is in the Greater New York area. When she's with D. E. the ring of the phone comes tinkling in on the dot, cf. axiom above. (Whatever could you be thinking, Anita? That they don't have pay phones on the harbor ferries?)

In the basement Mr. Shaks (many thanks for your postage stamps!) insisted on helping with the old-fashioned washing machine, and on a conversation. We were well equipped for one of those, between the terrible humidity in the air and, especially, Mrs. Bouton. What, you've never heard of Thelma Bouton? Works at a jewelry store on Forty-Second Street, corner of Fifth Avenue. Man comes in yesterday morning with a shoe box, locks the door behind him. She asks what he wants. He shows her his bread knife. Armed beggary. She whacks him over the head with her broom. Man, did the guy beat it! The whole time I was nervous, fidgety. When I got back to the apartment I knew why. It's no weather to be wearing jackets with pockets, D. E. left the house in a shirt and pants, and there, abandoned on the table, were two pipes, a tobacco pouch, and the poking implement. I truly felt sorry for him.

Now, Anita, you're thinking: That's the way a person feels only about someone they. . . .

Yes. And when I crossed Broadway with my shopping cart (a "granny cart" they call it here), I missed him. For at the end of my rounds I stopped by Charlie's Good Eats to reward myself with an iced tea, and there I read what *The New York Times* had to say today about the difference between kosher caviar (from fish with scales) and caviar from lumpfish (merely spiny skin, not allowed). Third book of Moses, 11:9 and 10. Just to make sure I never forget what kind of city this is that we're trying to make our way in. As a further reminder, my gaze slips from the edge of the paper to the man sitting next to me, someone I know by sight. An old man, a looker-away-er, a stepper-aside-er, always holding his neck as if it's just been hit. One of the people they. . . . I thought: *A victim.* Unfortunately there is also the term: *to victimize.* His stare from the corner practically sliced off a piece of me, his attention drawn to my hand, to the *Times*, to my nose, what do I know; I promptly stood up from the stool and put on a show of suddenly not feeling well, for Charlie's hospitality's benefit. That was how things were, how desperately I wished I had someone with me walking down the steep street. Ninety-Sixth near us, you know, can look deserted on a hot early afternoon, with the only living thing left the TV set broadcasting the movements of tennis players from some basement.

At home I caught the first phone call. Marie had a win on points to report. The South Ferry, heading south, has Governors Island to port, and Marie was informing D. E. about the dirty rotten US Navy there.

ERICHSON (baffled): I thought it was just the Coast Guard stationed there.

CRESSPAHL (Socratically): And who does that gang report to?

ERICHSON (confident): The navy, and the president. But only in wartime.

CRESSPAHL (gently, not rubbing it in): Think about it. Vietnam. US Navy. Ships. Ship guns.

ERICHSON (embarrassed): This round goes to you, madam.

Second phone call: Marie has taken this gentleman—quite elderly, after all, almost forty; secretly afflicted with the time difference between Berlin and this Eastern Seaboard—she's taken this exhausted man along a pedestrian path away from the ferry terminal down Bay Street. Riverside Drive in the shade is 75 degrees Fahrenheit; there it must be almost ninety. The proposition is an honor, Marie rarely suggests it to me; will he know to appreciate it? Bay Street is a three-hour-long strip of dust with the brackish smell of the water between the piers and the warehouses wafting over it, lined with weather-beaten wooden structures—sheds, gas stations, decaying industry, and the little shacks promising beer in snaky blue or red neon. If you ask me, she's looking for an America that existed when my father was young. But it's true, when there's a wind there it comes in strong after a long sweep across the bay, and in the hazy distance there's a hint of the towers of the bridge over the Verrazano Narrows, a span of almost 4,300 feet, growing larger as you look.

Sir Doctor, in a walk with you / There's honor and instruction too: Marie sounds almost giddy in her latest location report. What happened was that D. E., near Stapleton, requested his companion make a short detour, just up Chestnut, and she granted him that privilege, since he'd invented some professional reasons for it. What they found there, though, on the corner of Tompkins Avenue, was the house in which Giuseppe Garibaldi waited from 1851 to 1853 for the chance to return to the Italian revolution, working for the time being as a candlemaker and famous only because of his housemate Antonio Meucci, who claimed to have invented the telephone before Alexander Graham Bell, a device like the one by means of which Marie casts a line of words across to the island of Manhattan. The only Garibaldi she'd known until then was the one poised in Washington Square in his *verdigris*...what's that in German? his green patina, with his saber firmly sheathed in its scabbard; Marie hasn't even been told that he draws and raises it every time a virgin walks past his feet; now you figure out how many times a day that'd be, Anita.

(In a city like this one, Anita, I've had to tell the ten-year-old child what else men want from women, as a precaution against one of them trying to force Marie to. She looked at me, glowering, disbelieving; held off asking questions until I was done, and then, with a kind of outrage, wanted me to confirm: You and D. E., you guys...you guys too? She didn't have the word for the deed; I'm planning to keep it from her for eight more years. Now how am I going to do that in New York City.) I got this far in my letter and

The earth had turned enough toward the sun that it received the false stains and colors and veils, beaming with poison, that show us each day the planet's end; at six thirty I received a dinner invitation. Can you guess what I asked in return when I accepted? That's right. What dress I should wear.

Now, Anita, you'll say: That's what you do for someone you want to....

You got it. I was to wear the "yellow-and-blue raw silk" one, and I was to go find them so deep in old Brooklyn that I needed to search the city map and the subway map too. Way down in the BMT zone, let me tell you. There I found the two of them with Chinese people, in what was more like a private lounge than a restaurant, and D. E. seemed to have known them quite a bit longer than a day or two. (Since I keep various secrets to myself, how can I deny him his?) And as always happens when he's the host, the proprietors fuss around with *"che bella signorina," "carina,"* all with exclamation marks, this time in Chinese of course, if you'd care to translate it for yourself. And I received a hand on my hand, and a hand on my cheek, because what was I wearing over my "yellow-and-blue raw silk" dress? A men's jacket from Dublin with a tie folded in the breast pocket. And what lost items did I have with me in my briefcase? I'm sure you've already guessed, my sympathetic friend of the house.

You're saying: When a man, I mean, if he sees that kind of thing....

And hears, Anita. Here's how it went:

– We chickened out. We took the bus from South Beach to Bay Ridge.

– Great weather for ironing.

– You'd rather be roaming around the desolate wasteland of Staten Island.

– Do you know what a fig tree on Staten Island shows? You're probably thinking: the time of year.

– On Ninety-Sixth and Broadway? At Charlie's? But he lives up in the Hundreds.

– Chopsticks for me. Are you gonna try to use chopsticks?

– Did the Germans ... take care of him?

– It was a German woman.
– People live there who remember Italian grandparents!
– He's just hanging on more than living. Used to be German.
– *God knows why.*
– *But he won't tell, will he?*
– His name's de Catt.
– Tell us, tell us!
– *You tell such good lies.*

All the while the proprietors were sitting at the next table doing the same as we were. Passing a bowl or a spoon to someone—they or we, it made no difference. We felt at home there. A ten-year-old boy was standing watch over us through the crack of the kitchen door, with military severity, making sure that we treated his parents with the proper respect. Marie wanted to talk to him, but alas he let his dignity keep him from noticing her existence. D. E. would've loved to stay with the Chinese late into the night (if only to get the boy to join us at the table), but we invoked Mrs. Erichson so that he'd recall, along with his filial obligations, the mail sitting in New Jersey waiting to eat up his time. We did it out of concern for him. And when we said goodbye, outside the three garages under our building on Riverside Drive, one of the mechanics, the middle one, Ron the blabbermouth, let slip to D. E. that he could drive his car anywhere now, not to worry, it'd make it to San Francisco and, hell, kill two birds with one stone, Tokyo—for it seems that a lady came by the garage that afternoon and reminded them specially of the needed servicing and checkup. That's right. This very lady right here with the gentleman, if he wasn't mistaken, yes that seemed to be the one.

But the one who laughed last was D. E., heading west in his swanky Bentley. A silent laugh alone in the night. Because he knows what time I get into bed and what's waiting for me under the sheets. It is Král's *Guidebook Through the Čechoslovak Republic*, 1928. So that I can find my around there now, if the mood ever strikes me, duly noted, Anita. I'd get by with the help of J. Král, associate professor of geography at Charles University, Prague, because D. E. arranged it for me.

Dear Anita. That's how things are with us. Less than more than different between what I wanted at fifteen before I knew better. I'm thirty-five though.

July 14, 1968 Sunday

Auntie Times provides an editorial for anyone who can't avoid taking a trip abroad. Remember the neediest!

"Flowery July.

May is violets and June is roses, but offhand we don't think of July as a floral month at all. But it is, and perhaps we tend to forget because there are so many roadside blossoms.

The mints come to blossom now, from inconspicuous bugle-weed to royal bee balm that is such a lure for hummingbirds and bumblebees. Jewel-weed opens its pouchy yellow flowers and the spotted species is a favorite nectary for hummingbirds momentarily sated with bergamot. Hawkweed flourishes in unkempt pastures, deep orange and pale yellow, and black-eyed Susans add vivid accents to every patch of daisies.

Tall spires of great mullein open little yellow blossoms a few at a time, deliberate in bloom as they are in growth. Butter-and-eggs, the little wild snapdragons, are deep orange and clear yellow, and their big cousins, the turtle-heads, open grotesque mouths, white and pink and cream-pale yellow. The deep blue of harebells and great lobelia fade to lavender in tiny spiked lobelia and Indian tobacco.

July is so full of blossoms that the days can't hold them all. Evening primroses have to wait for late afternoon to open their brilliant yellow flowers."

© The New York Times

In memory, July of 1948, that summer, is Schoolgirl Cresspahl's last vacation, even though she did go to work in Johnny Schlegel's fields, which were parceled into giant rooms by hedges of hazel and hornbeam, blackthorn and hawthorn, dog rose, elder, and brambleberry. As we plowed at 250 feet above sea level, the rows of thorn blossoms tumbled down to the Baltic like waterfalls, later joined by the unambiguous black of the elderberries, the red of the rosehips, the blue-black of blackthorn and brambleberry. It was a joyless vacation, for she was supposed to leave—leave Cresspahl and Jakob and Jerichow and Mecklenburg—but was supposed to like it. Could she live alone: that was what she was brooding on as she lay atop a cartload and looked down at the shining Lübeck Bay, over the hedgerows at the spires and chimneys of the city behind the haze of exhaust from Schlutup furnace works, at the boxy white dice-like buildings of Travemünde, at the contours of the Holstein coast to the north, the barber-poled lighthouse on the corner of Dahmeshöved, at the British zone, the West, the other side. She was anxious and happy to let Johnny distract her with his lecturing voice rising up from the depths—the *Lobelia inflata* in the pond in the yard also thrived on the Mississippi, was officinal, and its real name was Indian tobacco. He was trying to whet my appetite so that I'd say: Yes, send me away from you all.

Johnny was embarrassed around me too, as were almost all the adults on the farm. His cooperative now had a stud stallion and in late July a mare had been brought for mating, and Cresspahl's daughter had watched, unnoticed by Johnny, who would surely have diverted her attention away from the proceedings. That night, when he thought I was off at the children's home, I heard him raging like he wanted to rip the nose off Axel Ohr's face; but Axel had an alibi, at the children's home. "The child! How could you let the child!" But it didn't do me any harm at all. I did think it was too bad that people treated the two horses like such animals. Before the mare's hind legs staggered under the stallion's leap she turned her head to us for a moment, as if asking us if she could leave. And I'd have wanted to leave the two animals with each other, instead of immediately leading the distraught timid mare away. Now I was supposed to be forbidden to look. Even a year ago no one had cared when I reported that one of the black pied cattle was in heat. Now I was a child. But supposed to make a decision like an adult.

– But you're a big girl now: they said encouragingly. And I was! And I only laughed at Hanna's package from Neustadt, which included along with the tea and tobacco not a single piece of girl's clothing, though it did have a shirt that fit Jakob like it was tailored. Because I thought I knew how love worked better than her now, ever since I'd seen the engagement notice from Anne-Dörte in Holstein standing on the radio, done in style, on card stock, with a count's crown. My heart was pounding in my throat as I asked Inge Schlegel why the card hadn't been forwarded to Jakob. – She's gonna have to write to him by hand: she said, turning away, and that was good, because blood had surged into my face. So that was why Jakob didn't come even once that summer to the farm where Anne-Dörte had been. Thus love was a misfortune. The one you want isn't enough for you, the one who should come prefers to stay away, and anyone who's seen the course of it calls it cause for mourning. As for me, I was supposed to do without Jakob completely. And on top of that, I was prevented from telling anyone my secret.

It was because of the threat of war. Here too I wasn't a child, when they came to me with talk of the Soviet blockade against the Western Berlin sectors and the assurance that the divided Allies were in conflict elsewhere too about the final distribution of their war booty, just look at the Greek civil war, Gesine! There's the Bulgarian and Albanian attacks, the Truman Doctrine, *containment*—it's you who need to splain that to us, Gesine. And the Soviet Union doesn't have any atom bombs, get that through your head, Gesine. But she refused to see why she in particular should be taken out of it just because she could be. And there were so many times that she heard, in a grown-up tone of voice, unspoken: A child can hardly be expected to understand that; then she balked.

There were moments when I was convinced. One July morning we were standing on a hill behind the Countess Woods, Johnny with a watch in his hand, because it was going to happen at six o'clock sharp. The Red Army had posted notices asking the Jerichowers to open all their windows, including the ones facing south, and that applied to Rande too; Johnny's farm was behind a high furrow in the land, protected from the shock wave. We were about 250 feet above sea level and we could see Wohlenberg Cove, behind which the St. Mary's Church spire hinted how deeply Wismar Bay penetrated into the mainland; the spire at the end of Kirchsee on Poel Island was clearly visible; behind it the land rose up in arches of forested domes and hills into the pure brisk sunlight. All this I was supposed to give up. Since we'd lost sight of Jerichow, I thought, at a heartbeat after six, that it wasn't going to happen, then the first blast went off. The force of the succeeding explosions may have fooled me but I was sure that the earth had shaken and would knock us off our feet at the next blast. But everyone thought they'd felt the tremors. The first cloud of smoke appeared in the long silence—a cauliflower trailing a stem as it rose into the sky. As the whitish mushroom started upending its edges, the next one rose alongside it, and by the time the first had been gouged by the sea wind, there were four. It was in the middle of the harvest but that afternoon Johnny took me with him to what had once been Mariengabe Airfield. It was fenced off with a hundred-meter buffer, but even from a distance we could tell that the whole facility was gone, the buildings flattened, the runways chains of holes. It wouldn't be easy to rebuild that.

And it wasn't rebuilt—German forced laborers chopped it up by hand, the pieces were picked up and driven off, and Johnny showed me: the airfield had been located too close to the "future front line," the border between the Soviet and Western zones; it would have been in artillery range. And now that the British were starting to supply West Berlin by air, why would the Soviets leave them such a superb emergency landing place? Then it was me who was clever, and I countered with how popular the Soviets could have made themselves among the refugees if they'd given them the barracks as living space. He had an easy time disposing of that one: if they'd risked angering the Germans over it, just think how compelling their military reasons must have been! No, seriously, the Russian is seriously underestimated when it comes to tactics, even more so about strategy. I tried one more time with the Border Police Department that the Soviets had set up in June. For Johnny that was one more piece of evidence in his favor. "The Russian" was preparing for a war: he was arming his German allies. I should get out of here.

And things would be different than they were in "the villa." This was the vacation home that back in the Kaiser's time a Hamburg real-estate agent had had built on the cliff behind Schlegel's copse of trees—a shrunken miniature castle with too many windows and an actual tower. It had been allocated to the Protestant Homeland Mission as a children's home, which Cresspahl's daughter used to visit, for Axel Ohr's sake, so he could come too without it looking like he was in love with a certain Elisabeth from Güstrow, he, Axel Ohr! The children had a strict time of it there. What the churchly caregiver ladies demanded in terms of proper behavior at the table and at recess was enough to totally spoil anyone's appetite and the fun. Though anyone sick was treated with a certain tenderness. Almost every day these children ate soup made from pigweed, with noodles added, but it agreed with them, and by the end of those four weeks almost all had gained weight. Earlier Johnny had augmented their fare with groats and meat, as his business dealings and delivery targets allowed; the new lady in charge of the home had taken offense at a "blasphemous" remark of Johnny's, and Johnny had taken offense at that in turn. That's how Johnny was—if someone talked nonsense at him they were dead to him, whether or not children got hurt in the process. (Anyway, they'd be getting CARE packages, his conscience was clear.) Many of these children hadn't ever been to look at the sea, and on the last day of their stay they collected beach sand for the mothers who wanted to be able to scour again. And all this constant praying and the devotional hours! Johnny admitted it: There would probably be religion and religious practices to spare in England. But if I clenched my teeth, pulled myself together, was a big girl. . . .

I sometimes pictured myself in an English boarding school. It was in the countryside, far from any train station so I'd be caught in time if I tried to escape. The whole day divided up with no recourse; one hour of free time. I could only imagine the teachers as unforgiving ladies, so sparing with praise or recognition, in word or look, that I wouldn't get any. I would never be alone—in the dorms, in the giant dining halls, in my free time— and would always be alone. In England, too, food was rationed, but even if the Brits had closed Cresspahl's account at the Richmond Bank of Surrey they would still allow a *ration card* for his daughter. Enough for pocket money. Waiting for the post. School uniform. Permission to leave for the day. Hours and half hours punctuated by the tolling of the church bell: chiming the foreignness through the sleepless night. Practicing the "th" over and over in front of the mirror, tongue between the teeth! then forgetting the tongue between the teeth. The bustle of *cricket* on a blazing field of grass, and me in the middle as the German child, the Fascist child, she deserves it, never getting visitors, in her third year already.

– Were your reasons good enough for Cresspahl?

– He never let me get as far as my reasons. After a whole summer. He looked at me and nodded, and I was scared. Now I wished I had another day to think it over after all.

– It would've been better for you: Marie says, this fearless child who howls with homesickness on her first night of summer camp. Look at her, coolly lying on the grass in this hot humid garden; look how she hides her fear in a squint of her eyes.

– It would've been better for Cresspahl. So now I'd done him wrong, and I'd been a coward.

– I'm a coward too, Gesine. I don't like being without you either. Just because I think you care about me.

1398 · July 15, 1968 Monday

July 15, 1968 Monday

The Soviet Union, via *Pravda*, gives us the truth: how puzzled it is by the West's "morbid interest" in its war games in the North Atlantic. It complains about NATO reconnaissance planes in the exercise area and the presence of a British destroyer. Therefore, anyone who couldn't care less what Soviet warships are doing there with their Polish and East German pact mates must be healthy.

The Soviets have halted the withdrawal of their troops from Czechoslovakia. Since yesterday they've been meeting in Warsaw with their Polish, East German, Hungarian, and Bulgarian friends, about and without the ČSSR, and now that the official organ of the press has stated that "a decided rebuff to the forces of reaction and imperialist maneuvers" in that country "is of vital interest," de Rosny might as well give up. On the contrary, though, he sticks with Tito, according to whom no one in the Soviet Union could possibly be so "shortsighted" as to use force against the Czechs and Slovaks. De Rosny is a Titoist.

We were all required to be very mad at Tito. Immediately upon our official matriculation at Fritz Reuter High School this was presented to us as one of our main occupations, and that fall we often marched through Gneez to City Hall in a column of four hundred students, with banners on which we demanded Tito's overthrow, maybe adding a musical number about Spain's heaven that spreads its brightest stars above our trenches. There was no mention of the cold in that song, but now I get cold when I think of the word *Spain*. We had to stand in the cold for a long time until the market square was filled with columns of demonstrators (the ones from the Panzenhagen Sawmill were always late) and the three people on the City Hall balcony could begin their speeches. Whenever one was finished, we shouted our grievances against Tito in chorus, and I would have been glad to be as enthusiastic as Lise Wollenberg, who just that morning in Contemporary Studies had given me a wink while reciting Comrade Stalin's five criticisms of Tito, one of which (the false priority of agriculture) I'd had to whisper to her. Since she was my friend.

That's what she called me. When two girls have spent whole years of schooldays on the train for an hour, and walking to the station too, they'll eventually either ride in the same compartment on good terms or in separate ones on bad. The Cresspahl girl didn't have the courage for an open feud at that point. She and Wollenberg had been almost the only ones to find themselves reunited in the waiting room that ninth grade turned out to be, and Lise was many teachers' favorite—blond as she was, shyly girlish as she knew how to look at dangerous moments, jokily confidential when sucking up was called for. Cresspahl would have found it hard to say exactly what bothered her about Wollenberg. In the end, she secretly thought that this Yugoslav might know the economic situation in his own country more precisely than the wise Leader of Peoples in the far-off Kremlin, but still she called him the Marshal of Traitors on demand—we all lied, to please our elders. Lise exaggerated it, maybe, in the way she looked around her, a tolerant smile on her gentle lips, as though trying to tell us, tempt us: It won't hurt our grades... it's just a joke... we're just tricking Kramritz... it doesn't really matter....

The mistake was sealed when we picked a desk together in 9-A-II. That keeps you together even when you're pursuing other interests. She remained at my side while the boys in the upper grades checked out us girls in ninth grade for our suitability, taking our willingness for granted. Breaks between classes were like a marketplace. But one time it was just me, alone, who was asked to step aside with messieurs Sieboldt and Gollantz, eleventh grade, wearing long pants already. These gentlemen wanted to know what the people in Jerichow thought about blowing up the barracks and potential refugee housing. I had barely drawn breath, blushing with the honor I'd received, when Lise started gushing: Oh, the clouds from the explosions were like parachutes rising up from the ground, now she had a better sense of what atomic bombs must be like... word for word what *I* had told *her*. Sieboldt and Gollantz left at once. Lise answered my protest by saying they'd been asking her, and anyway, what difference did a word make? Gollantz did take me aside one more time, alone; he wanted to talk about the election of a class representative for the student government, headed by Sieboldt. Unfortunately I told Lise. She was only annoyed that the gentlemen hadn't approached her. She consoled herself in that grown-up way she sometimes had: Ah, well, they graduate two years before we do, where would that've left us. (Us.)

She probably realized how pretty it looked when she tossed her long blond curls next to another girl trying to keep her dark braids still, and so Wollenberg stuck with Cresspahl when she got invited to go for a walk or to the movies; she accepted for both of us. Up came Gabriel Manfras, stranded in 9-A-I; up came Pius Pagenkopf, Dieter Lockenvitz... and she'd already sworn that we were inseparable so I had to tag along like a chaperone. Sometimes I looked at her from the side when a bright scene was projected on-screen—hordes of horsemen thundering across the steppe to retrieve stupid Zukhra for noble Takhir—and she was cheering for the extras at the top of her lungs along with everyone else around us, the same as for the extras in *Kolberg* in April 1945, portraying the Final Germany Victory. She could get so carried away. She lived entirely in the present moment. At the performance of *Noah's Flood* by Ernst Barlach, I felt lots of people staring at us and at Lise's rapt intensity, so pensive, so poignant; during the intermission she could hardly control herself, she was giggling so hard over Mrs. Lindsetter, wife of the district court chief justice, who had fallen asleep and whose wheezing during the performance had not impressed Lise one bit.

With the boys she acted sarcastic and snippy to the point of total indecipherability. They had to talk seriously with the third party, me; even Manfras, who never talked much, suddenly had quite a lot to say about interior end moraines as exemplified by Gneez Lake. With almost every one of these boys I managed to beat a retreat under some plausible pretext. The next day Gabriel Manfras was even more introspective than usual. Pius Pagenkopf, tall, dark, and the oldest in the class, kept his head bent low over his notebooks for days after his time alone with Lise, so that he'd be sure to avoid catching sight of her. Lockenvitz, the shy, lanky, glasses-wearing top of the class, slumped to Cs in several subjects after declaring himself to Lise. And in early November, when new personal IDs were to be issued to everyone over fifteen, all three of these boys, separately, took me aside in secret and asked me to sneak a spare print when I went to Stellmann's with Lise. I told her. She laughed, deep in her throat, amused; she giggled getting herself ready for the occasion. A lot of sweet encouragement found its way into that passport photo. She gave me one, which I let Pius have. But one time Lockenvitz dropped something from his wallet— it was a passport photo of Lise Wollenberg, and before her very eyes he slipped it into his jacket at just the place where his heart lived and worked; she burst out laughing, flinging her head high like a colt. Manfras was said to have her standing on his dresser at home in 8 x 10 format, and not an enlargement of the passport photo either. One day, Pius Pagenkopf, walking by the first row, took Lise's ID picture out of his shirt pocket, tore it up, and threw the scraps onto her desk. She smiled quite happily and later asked him if he wanted another one. What was I supposed to say when she told me she acted that way because the boys were "so silly"? Neither Pagenkopf nor Lockenvitz was silly; no one would ever say Gabriel was.

We all wanted Pius as our class representative, and he would have been chosen if only Lise had kept her mouth shut about a kind of boy who was more serious, able to defend us in storm and tempest; Pius furrowed his dark eyebrows, like someone with a toothache, and crossed the name Pagenkopf off the list. Lise was by no means left speechless and started nagging Lockenvitz. He resisted for a while—he was a refugee and would have a hard time of it with the locals—but he put his name up for her sake and was elected on the third ballot. He would have to atone for that for a long time, because in December, when student self-government was banned, the members of the Free German Youth (FDJ) chose him as the head of our class group—he'd been our representative, after all. We'd get a day off and he'd have to go to meetings of the Central School Group Authority (ZSGL), where he found himself reunited with Sieboldt and Gollantz. We didn't unfold the notes he sent Lise during class, he was huffy enough already; he saw her laugh out loud as if overjoyed, but he got embarrassed, so we were mad at him. Once she sent a piece of paper to him—there was nothing written on it. Lockenvitz was being silly, he let his wistful gaze rest on me for a while (and he owned a passport picture of me. I'd given exactly one print away, to Lise). She arranged it so that a passage in our 1949 Class Day newspaper affirmed that Lockenvitz, friend to youth, loved em all, he didn't care, / loved all women, dark or fair.

"Us." She and I were supposed to put our names down together for the Society for the Study of Soviet Culture, which later become the German-Soviet Friendship Society. Dr. Kramritz had mentioned the benefits and advantages of "societal activities"; this was one of the less taxing ones. There was no doubt that Mr. Wollenberg had advised his daughter to join—he wanted to secure other flanks besides the one facing the LDPD; Cresspahl, who really could have used the extra protection, advised his not to. As a well-nigh British schoolchild, I was on the British side anyway and cursed them soundly when they crashed a Berlin Airlift plane near us and had to go to the Schönberg hospital. To make Lise, all by herself, step up to a desk with a stranger sitting behind it—I thought it couldn't happen to a better person. I'd gone with her as far as the door just to humor her.

But Jakob didn't think it was a good idea to let this Lise know about my aversion to Soviet culture, my profound dislike of it; he turned his head slowly back and forth. His categorical headshake. I grasped the damage I'd done only after he suggested: Keep on her good side.

For Jakob, I forced myself to thank Lise when she gave me a dress, now that she was getting more fashionable ones from the new government stores. Anyway, Jakob's mother was glad to see me dressed properly under my black coat; Cresspahl, like Jakob, looked me in the face or would notice the slightest scratch on my hand but worn collars were somehow invisible to them. That Lise was trying to spruce me up like a shabby backdrop really was too much, but I was spared an open breach because after the Christmas break Heinz Wollenberg at last decided it was beneath a businessman's dignity to send his daughter on the cold and dirty train twice a day; for people like Wollenberg the Gneez housing office could find a room for Lise at "a relative's." Besides, the ration cards had by that point been declared valid only at their place of issue; in Gneez there was often sugar or fire starters when there weren't any in Jerichow; Lise could bring some home on the weekends.

Now that we had different routes to school, I had to sit somewhere else in the classroom. When we saw each other only during the schoolday, I could march a few rows behind her and watch her from afar. There she was, swinging her legs in the air and zealously belting out the FDJ songs: "You HAVE a goal in si-ight / that GUIDES you through the world! . . . ."; there she was, hopping around merrily shouting the slogan against the Greek government, or the celebrations of Mao's victory in Suzhou, or the songs of hate toward that renegade Tito. We had grown apart.

She had a goal in sight; today she's a tax adviser in the Sauerland, West Germany. That dress from her, green organza with large polka dots, would have looked good on me on that Class Day, or for birthdays—but I only tried it on.

July 16, 1968 Tuesday

The worst part is that the bosses do it without warning. And then someone's standing exposed at the podium in the staff cafeteria, under the eyes of four hundred people, maybe in a suit that clashes with the yellow walls, but they have to keep quiet and act like they've completely risen to the dignity of the occasion. The ceremony is ridiculous but in the moment it does take your breath away—everyone acting reverent, following the lead of the CEO standing stiff as a board across from the person, trying to seem taller than he really is, and disgorging a speech of praise so tensely that the victim feels spat upon. This is one of the occasions de Rosny has set up especially for the titular head of the company so that he can feel like he's doing something. An unlucky victim may find herself on that day dressed to match the criss-crossed American flags on display behind the CEO; and some people have even made the mistake of wearing sandals.

Anyone whose number has come up would love to have slipped out for a haircut during lunch, but it takes you by surprise. It can happen on any workday of the year, so you half forget about it; this is why we have to submit our vacation requests six weeks in advance, though. Anyway, if you reflect on how ardent your work for this bank is, why would you be afraid of such a distinction. On top of that, participation in the event is considered voluntary, so some of the victims go just to show how devoted they are to the firm. All employees have to neatly initial a form to attest their attendance at the morning's events; anyone who dares can be free and out on the street by four. Employee Cresspahl has a sense of what's waiting for her outside—the cars are standing on Third Avenue with their hoods open because the engine coolant is boiling; how she'd love to get through the muggy heat of this afternoon in a less crowded train car, before rush hour. But no, she has a visitor.

– Give it up, de Rosny, sir: she says. It has turned into a game between her and her boss, ever since he's recently started making use of her and her office "for tea." He demonstrates the growth of the Czechoslovakian loan to her; today she's refuted him with the Warsaw communiqué announcing a severe letter to the leadership of the ČSSR from their comrades in the struggle. And where are these "aggressive imperialist forces" with their "subversive actions" going to go if not hell in a handbasket, assuming the central committee in Prague decides to show a little backbone before the thrones of brothers instead of bowing meekly? Now they're wanting to rewrite the terms of the Warsaw Pact to give every member country its turn as the supreme commander and put a stop to the political misuse of the alliance. That's got to be the end of the line, a bridge too far for the Soviets. De Rosny tilts his head at this and narrows his eyes in a way expressing doubt, as though he knew something more reliable than that, but in so doing he notices his wristwatch. – Should we go downstairs again? he says, urgent like a schoolboy suggesting they cut school. – Take another look at the big production?

He's allowed to call it that—he invented it. Employee Cresspahl is well and truly annoyed at the loss of a whole hour of time, but she doesn't want to give him any leverage by being impolite; she's already been led past all the possible escape routes (stairs, ladies' rooms) and is now sitting in the second row, in front of the podium, cut off from the aisle by de Rosny, who has one leg bent over the other at an angle as sharp as a stork's. Surrounded by his young men, Carmody and Gelliston, he can carry on a perfectly uninhibited conversation with his "young student." She feels the assembled gazes of the staff on her and remembers the other names people in the bank refer to her by; in sudden fury she decides that de Rosny's white double mane is a wig, or at least dyed bluish to match his eyes. De Rosny is pontificating. "We" are not aggressive, "we" are not subversive, "we" are going to teach "our" West German friends to hold their tongues so that "we" and "our" friends in England, in Denmark, won't get mad at a bungled deal. And what does Mrs. Cresspahl think about the Communists in Romania? They've come out against interference in Czechoslovak matters, haven't they, just like Tito? She's almost grateful when the dribble of music falls silent, making him do the same. The chairman is already standing on his platform and has cleared his throat several times. De Rosny feels compelled to whisper to his "young friend": Next time we'll use a curtain for this production!

The performance begins with an oration by the titular president. Mrs. Cresspahl has seen him so many times since the ceremony in which poor Gwendolyn Bates got a silver slap in the face for her excess zeal, and still she can't keep enough of R. W. T. Wutheridge in her mind for her to remember him, even as a still picture. "Rustic" they like to call him. But he must be one of those meek peasants, humble, awkward, following in his ancestors' footsteps, so fearful does he appear to her; his tailored suit looks too short on his little old body; seventy years have taken some of this blue-cheeked man's hair but have given him no dignity in return. The program: First he gives a speech to his own taste. Back then it was the team spirit and what America wants from us; this time it's the same thing, plus he wishes us well. Then the candidates are called up, they mount the carpet-covered wooden box and have to listen to a description of their services eye-to-eye with the Most Senior Spokesman. These speeches are written in de Rosny's office, though, which is why the openings always seethe with distinctions:

It is truly difficult to find the right words . . .

Let the presentation of this award set a precedent in every respect . . .

Not a single member of this firm, to my knowledge, has . . .

It must have been twenty-five years ago that . . .

One is unusually young; or she's already helped conquer Arizona, "her shield on her back, without laying it aside"; or his family has been working in the banking business for three generations. That's how Mr. Kennicott II is dispatched, another forgettable one. Now he performs an endless series of small bows, since "he will always be among the victors," in the personnel department of all places, while the laudatio's last sentence informs him that "he will be leaving us next year"; here de Rosny's sidelong look is meant to remind his "young assistant" of something, was it the white pumps in a desk drawer? is he trying to make amends? Now it's a young black woman's turn, whom we've often noticed in the elevator—her large eyes full of desperation and forgiveness, her motherly demeanor toward the pink-skinned men—now she is identified as Blandine Roy and praised for her accomplishments in the mail room; we recall the serious problems there've been, only in the interoffice mail, and so here they're honoring none other than a token black woman; we are all relieved along with her when she's allowed to climb back down from the stage and disappear into her seat. After her, Amanda Williams's name is called, giving her a nasty shock and prompting an angry look at Naomi sitting next to her. Because the aspirant is supposed to remain unsuspecting, and that means the bosses use an officemate or friend to tail the victim all day and make sure that they show up to the celebratory occasion. Now Amanda, before all our eyes, has to hear herself called lightning-sharp, but modest, and her candor makes the firm trust her commitment all the more. Suddenly Amanda looks awkward in her thin, washable dress, a yellow flower pattern that matches the walls; in her embarrassment she reaches her arm out to the CEO, so that he has to step over to shake her hand; but for the first time the whole auditorium claps, everyone is happy for her, and as Amanda returns to Naomi's side she is already giving her a forgiving smile, realizing what these five hundred dollars will be useful for, given her pregnancy. The next name announced is a new one, never before pronounced like that in this building, with a North German articulation: Mrs. Ge'sine Cress'pahl!

– Trick number 18!: Mrs. Cresspahl tells her daughter in the lobby of one of the fancy old movie theaters on Broadway, where they've taken refuge from the muggy blasts of heat on the street. They cared more about the air conditioning than either of the movies anyway, but Mrs. Cresspahl has a hard time thinking about anything but her public exhibition; she is almost unhappy with Marie's indifferent answers. Unfortunately, Marie is anything but outraged.

– What do you expect from de Rosny: she says.

– He pulled a fast one on me!

– To be dragged along somewhere by de Rosny his very own self is really like the English court. Dubbed a knight or something.

– And when I was standing up there he raised his miserable paper cup of his miserable tea to me like he was toasting!

– He was happy for you, Gesine.

– Until now people knew my name if they needed to know it, or if I told them. Now the whole staff knows it. And the speech is going to show up on everyone's desk on Friday, from the in-house print shop!

– Gesine, I don't like getting prizes in school either, but I need them. I'm standing all alone in the cathedral and wish I could run away.

– But you're trapped, by people and folding chairs, and the confinement makes you anxious.

– Right. Because folding chairs are handy for throwing.

– And for beating a person with.

– All you have to do is stand up straight for a while and keep your belly sucked in—

– Right.

– And breathe deeply and think about anything but your hair, which maybe isn't tied properly, and the next breath you take will make it come loose—

– I managed not to raise my hand to feel it!

– Then there's the president's medal and a check for more than eight hundred dollars.

– But everything they said about me was a lie!

– For you to hide behind.

– "Her studies at European and American universities." Two semesters in Saxony and a little economics at Columbia!

– De Rosny needs an educated assistant for his business, right?

– "Her origins in the Communist sphere have contributed decisively..."

– I was there for that, Gesine. They did.

– "to our ability to abandon our passive position in the Eastern European credit business."

– That was the official announcement. Now it's happening. We're on our way to Prague.

– And then I couldn't get away from the cold buffet afterward either, you know. Champagne and zakuski.

– You'd have expected an apology from me.

– Sowwy, Marie.

– Still, everyone could see that your suit's from Rome. It must have looked great on you there too.

– *Thank you very much.*

– Is that thing genuine silver?

– It is. We'll give it to the old lady out on Ninety-Seventh Street, begging. On the theater steps, I mean.

– D. E. should get that medal.

– He won't like the five-line symbol on it any more than I do.

– Still, you're engaged, Gesine.

– What do you mean I'm engaged?

– You've agreed to marry him. You need to give him something.

– You're right.

– Silver can be melted down.

– Yes.

– Then D. E. will get a silver ring from you.

– Yes.

July 17, 1968 Wednesday

Since Cresspahl's dumb Gesine balked at life in England, he had to take steps to help her get through one in the Mecklenburg of twenty years ago. As was right and proper, he asked his guild master for an interview. So quickly, so readily did Willi Böttcher agree to come to Jerichow for a visit that we could only think he was trying to keep the former prisoner out of his house, out of sight of the people of Gneez. He came on a Sunday, in a black suit, not sweating in the September heat, and sat down hesitantly, preferring to discuss the weather for a while. His good-natured devious face looked crumpled. When I came in with coffee and he humbly asked me to stay—a fifteen-year-old schoolgirl—I knew: he wants to confess something, and for that he needs someone Cresspahl won't use rough language in front of.

– Heinrich: he said heavily, and sighed. What was the good of pleading for nice weather now?

Cresspahl had asked him here to discuss his professional prospects as a tradesman, but if Willi had something on his mind then sure they could talk about that first.

Then it was Gesine Böttcher turned to, called on as witness; her visits to his workshop should let what he had such a hard time bringing out go without saying. But Gesine had watched him at work because she didn't have a father; all she saw was a lot of business. Revenue.

– Never mind revenue!: Böttcher suddenly cursed, as though it were bad luck and trouble too. It was back when—

he looked at me, I passed the look along to Cresspahl, and he gave Böttcher a nod, sparing him from having to say: when they'd nabbed Cresspahl—

that Böttcher's firm had had to keep its head above water with its share of the confiscated furniture that the Red Army kept stored there, as reparations, and then decided it would rather barter back to the locals (for material assets); that and the mechanical production of wood cubes for producing automobile gas had been their bread and butter. Their butter, to be precise. He couldn't exactly count on the reputation that stretched all the way into Brandenburg, which he'd earned with his bedroom sets and other standardized furniture—he stayed with mass production. Through early 1947 it was the watchtowers that the Soviets were ordering for their new prison camps; he'd delivered some all the way to the Polish border. *Ptichniki.* It was easy work, since the Soviets didn't need to see designs first—both parties had a pretty clear picture of what these towers should look like. Since it was good honest Mecklenburg work, it came at a price; every roof was done with beveled siding, for instance, solid enough to last a lifetime. They were worth 900 marks apiece but had to be billed at 2,400, the money had to be divided up so many ways. Of course the Soviets knew that Böttcher had to get his share of the profit and they got this price through the pricing authorities, the finance office, the Gneez commandant. Gesine had seen one.

His look was so pleading. For a moment, as if in a dream, I was sure I'd seen a watchtower in Böttcher's workshop, complete with guard and Kalashnikov. Then, as if waking from a nightmare, I remembered the tower I'd crawled under in the Countess Woods, and nothing could happen to me there because I was with Jakob. It was Cresspahl who'd had to live beneath such towers.

You wouldna built them things for the Russians, Cresspahl? Honest?
Not if they were keepin you locked up, Böttcher. Honest.

The two of them had a drink to this article of Böttcher's production—one schnapps. The bottle stayed standing between them, a monument to the part Böttcher had played in Cresspahl's imprisonment. But it was settled; he sat on a bit more of his chair than the edge, and eventually leaned back. It was true—to his chagrin, he was minting money. His workers were happy about the incoming orders; he let them have the scraps for home heating before they stole them, and continued to negotiate on their behalf for night-work bonus pay, ration cards for heavy labor too. Then came the picket fences for Heringsdorf and other penny-ante stuff; in 1947 he undertook the interiors for the Russian ships in the Wismar and Rostock dockyards. They are still bravely plying the seas, his cabins and berths—shoddy work's not in Willi's repertoire!—but he'd added a hundred-percent surcharge to cover wastage. (Thirty to fifty percent would have been reasonable.) Under these circumstances a complete child's bedroom for the director authorizing billings was handled with a handshake, not an invoice. Then, when the time came to enlarge the dockyard buildings to handle ship provisions, especially the "bazaars," he ran into temporary difficulties, not knowing his way around hustling food supplies as well as his various other areas of expertise. Then Emil Knoop returned to Gneez and helped him out in his hour of need.

What followed was the kind of aria to Emil Knoop's ability to draw profits out of thin air, one that Cresspahl's child could have joined in on. It did make her mad to recall the 1946–47 Hunger Winter when milk and honey were flowing on Böttcher's table. But what did it profit Böttcher, really, that he drove a Mercedes, that the Soviet guards at the free port of Stralsund raised the barrier because his sad frazzled face was ID enough, what good did all that high living with canned goods from Denmark do him? For one thing, he constantly had one foot in jail (– *Ive made my peace with that*: said Willi, gloomily, but still as if somehow looking forward to it). For another, the meetings with the Soviet gentlemen always ended up so terribly booze-soaked. In Stralsund a waiter felt for him and always served him water instead of Richtenberger kümmel (– *You c'n have the money fer it*: said Willi, dolefully—a dignified man with bitter religious disappointments in his past). He couldn't bribe all the waiters on the Mecklenburg coast, though, so it happened once that when stopping to take a leak between Rostock and Gneez he slipped and fell down a steep embankment and his Soviet business partners forgetfully drove off without him, in his Mercedes. All night on the wet ground. No. All of Gneez knew it as well as Cresspahl: Willi Böttcher didn't know how to drink. Not his forte. Lay in bed half a week afterward, every time. And then the wife! *The old lady! The ol' bat!*

All true. Böttcher's got his row to hoe: Cresspahl said, being friendly. His daughter was livid at Böttcher's geniality, but grown-ups were incomprehensible. Now we've told each other some stories, let's bury the hatchet. As if Cresspahl had told stories about Fünfeichen!

But for every line of Böttcher's business, Emil Knoop held an end of it in his hand; if Knoop balked, something went south. Willi had made some wall paneling for the Gneez Kommandatura. The invoice was approved by the pricing authorities, the finance office—Triple-J probably would've paid it by Whitsunday 1948 but there was a deputy sitting in his chair, behind him the 40" x 40" Goethe from the Gneez high school, refusing to pay at all. Willi went to the waiting room outside Emil Knoop's office

so early that he was second in line. Emil was about to leave on a trip to
Oostende; he had just enough time to give him a little information on his
way out the door: the deputy commandant had managed to get only a
sewing machine with a damaged base at a furniture distribution but was
interested in a young lady on Rosengarten Street and wanted to give her a
token of his affection. Willi Böttcher cast his mind back to medieval
techniques and made the deputy a new sewing machine base with all the
care an aspirant gives his journeyman's piece, complete with inlaid centimeter ruler and other intarsia. So then the deputy paid for the two hundred
square feet of wainscoting, had Böttcher sign for it, swept the money off
the table back into the cashbox, pointedly locked it, pulled a new receipt
out of his drawer, requested a second signature, and handed over the
money... By evening the negotiations had moved to Böttcher's shop, where
the deputy sat on the planer with him, only slightly drunk, rattling off
words of wisdom: You Germans, you think we're all dumb... (Oh, no, Mr.
Deputy! Please! How could you even *think*...?) We're better cheaters than
you, though.

Cresspahl looked long and hard at his guild master, whose word had
once been law in the craft and the bookkeeping of their trade all around
Gneez and who now had to make a double entry of every receipt if he didn't
want to be hauled off to jail by the tax investigators. He decided to try
another angle. He asked where Emil's power and glory had its limits.
– *Nowhere nohow!* Willi declared glumly. Although their conversation
once again managed to steer clear of the painful topic of Cresspahl's absence,
it still sounded for all the world as if he, Böttcher, were complaining to his
younger colleague. The latest about Emil Knoop was the saluting practice
he'd conducted with a Soviet guard outside the green fence around Barbara
Street in Gneez, in full view of German passersby, Soviet military personnel, even the commandant, J. J. Jenudkidse, who looked expertly on from
the comfort of his private villa's upper floor. Emil (Emile) corrected the
amenable Red Army man's hand position, pushed and shoved at the man's
feet, and was saluted by the Soviet ever more briskly, almost up to the old
Greater German standards—crowing vigorously, he rooted out aesthetic
errors: No! Like that! Look: Chock! Chockchock! Chock! until the
present-arms was solid and Emil, with a salute of his own, strode past the
guard to his meeting with Triple-J. Nothing happened without Knoop.

The people who said Knoop must have a twin may've been right. Because how could he be on trial in Hanover over a mislaid delivery of blue basalt and at the same time cutting a deal in Jerichow about demolishing the brickworks at the town's expense? Seriously. *You cant catch that guy.* He's off to Moscow, and not with a delegation, alone! As a guest of honor!

I think its time to catch im.
Hes got enough double receipts at the finance office, mine 're sheepdroppings fer him!
Willi—what if he had to help you?
Don' take it the wrong way, Cresspahl. Youve been away a long time.
He has a friend, doesn he?
Hes got lots a friends.
One friend: Klaus. Your boy Klaus.
Jå, Klaas. We think about im all the time. The old lady won' stop weepin and wailin. If hes still with the Russians, is he dead? Is he still alive there? If it wasn for him Id throw in the towel.
Then think of him!
Cresspahl, you're not . . .
Hes got a friend in Gneez whos in good with the Russians and now hes goin for a visit . . .
Emil! Emil Knoop!
If he cant get his friend out a Moscow—
Cresspahl I wont ever forget this. Come and see me, day or night, youll have whatever you want. Whatever you ask for, Hinrich!
If he cant pull it off then hes useless. Then hes through in Gneez.
Ive done nothing to deserve this from you. I wont ever forget it.
I'd rather you forgot it right now.
What?
You dont know nothin, you keep your trap shut, Willi.

This was the kind of operation Cresspahl was capable of by that time. His daughter took it as a sign of recovery, it was fine with her. He was casually picking a fight with the business tycoon of the district, and she was happy to do her part with comments about an Emil Knoop without the power or the glory to get his friend back from the Russians, until Mrs.

Lindsetter, the judge's wife, started talking and Dr. Schürenberg's wife and Mrs. Bell and all the rest of the ladies in their ladiness. The Knoop firm delivered a batch of Finnish timber to Cresspahl, from which he built a workshop behind his house—a large room on stilts at a right angle to Lisbeth's bedroom—and when the Schwerin State Museum inquired into whether he did restoration work it was Knoop who'd in all innocence written him a letter. Then the people from the antiques shop started coming by. Cresspahl had realized the fate of fine handicrafts in Mecklenburg but he thought he'd do well enough to live out his time there. It was his last retreat. From then on he only ever worked alone.

Emil Knoop never discovered who had dared to defy him; he'd written that letter in Schwerin out of sheer goodwill. He carried out the search for Klaus Böttcher in the sporting spirit we were used to from him. True, he did come back from Moscow alone. It was around Christmas when I saw a ragged young man on Station Street, dazed, staring at the people forming a line three persons wide, shivering in the cold, because the Renaissance Cinema was showing the Soviet war booty *Die Fledermaus*, with actors who'd been accessories to Fascism, as he had probably learned by then as well as we had. I didn't know how to explain this to him as I took him to his parents, and I had to see a man of almost thirty cry before I understood why Böttcher had been so desperate to have a good reputation with the Soviets, even when it hurt a fellow guildsman, and what had moved Cresspahl to such a forgiving stance, and I apologized to my father, deeply; as they say when they're ashamed: from the heart.

Still nothing but hints from "reliable sources," no indication of what the letter sent to Czechoslovakia from its allies actually said.

July 18, 1968 Thursday

The New York Times has read the letter to Czechoslovakia from the Warsaw comrades, and informs us that it included the following demands:

"Decisive action against right-wing or other anti-Socialist forces." Okay, that's fine. Agreed.

"Party control of the press, radio, and television." Because they'd made "groundless" charges that Soviet troops in the ČSSR represented a threat to the nation's sovereignty. Well, if they don't represent a threat, then agreed. But let them tell the people what they see.

"We do not appear before you as spokesmen of yesterday who would like to hamper you in rectifying your mistakes and shortcomings, including violations of Socialist legality." If that stays true, then agreed.

The New School taught us to rank one another according to our respective fathers. Just as Schoolgirl Cresspahl was a tradesman's daughter, Pius Pagenkopf was appended to a father with a leadership role in the Socialist Unity Party of Germany and high office in the Mecklenburg state government. Reactionary Middle Class and Progressive Intellectual—how could they share a desk from January 1949 all the way to graduation?

Pius . . . he'd once gotten stuck declining this Latin adjective; he must have preferred that as a nickname to a translation of his last name from Platt into High German (Horsehead). He was also the only Catholic in our grade. Pius . . . if only the mind would do our bidding! Of Jakob I have a sense of his closeness, his voice, his calm movements; of Pius I have only the memory of a photograph. We were nineteen and eighteen, standing before bare April reeds on the shore of Gneez Lake. A tall lean boy with a hard head, shoulders thrown back, annoyed at the camera, in a posture of resistance. He held a lit cigarette like a grown-up. And the snapshot tries to convince me that Pius's face was always so finished. All I know at the moment about the younger girl next to him, with the braids, is that her father wanted to forbid her from smoking, because she is concealing her burning tobacco product in a cupped hand. We look like a well-functioning married couple; we knew each other quite a bit better than our fathers cared to notice.

When ninth grade started, Pius was for me too almost nothing but Mr. Pagenkopf's son. Head of the Gneez finance office and a Socialist, he'd been removed in April 1933 and had to augment his 75 percent retirement pension in the freight department at the railroad station (preventive custody during Mussolini's visit to Mecklenburg). In 1945, the people of Gneez decided to see it as only fair when the British made him interpreter for their city commandant; they held it against him that he became mayor under the Soviets, and the Social Democrats in particular found him suspect for his speeches in favor of unification with the Communists, all the more so now that he was helping the Soviet administration in the district capital. Since 1945, the Pagenkopfs, on paper a family of three, again resided in a four-room apartment—cause for resentment in an over-crowded, occupied city; moreover, Pius's father showed his face in Gneez so rarely that even his son's girlfriend knew him only from pictures of speakers' podiums, or newspaper articles on the New Face of the Party or the Yugoslavian conspiracy. Of his nighttime Bohemianism in Schwerin, it was taken as fact that he had his pick of attractive women there, younger and wittier in conversation than Mrs. Pagenkopf, a farmer's daughter with an elementary-school education—he had to sneak her onto the "In." list, authorizing ration cards for the intelligentsia. With a father like this, Pius would obviously raise his hand at once in the FDJ constituent assembly; with a father like that behind him, he could simply wave aside his election to various FDJ offices as just another "societal activity"—Comrade Pagen-kopf took care of his son to that extent. It came as a surprise to no one when Pius, after the new TO government stores opened, was wearing a fresh sports shirt every three days, a hundred marks each, and leather shoes, two hundred and ten for a pair of those; he kept up bourgeois appearances, he did. The son of such a father could permit himself walks with the daughter of a tradesman (bourgeois), but paying visits to a Heinrich Cress-pahl's daughter was pushing it, and she was not a little shocked to see him at the door in December 1948, on Sunday, at coffee time. Then she thought she saw through his excuse.

They were under threat of a quiz in math class. If someone has a weak heart when it comes to math, surely he can go looking for a classmate—even if she lives in distant Jerichow. Now here he stands, a plausible smile of recognition in the corners of his mouth, nervousness in his eyes, because someone might get the idea that he'd been wandering around Jerichow Market Square just because, or else, say, trying to run into Lise Wollenberg, and not because he couldn't figure out where Brickworks Road was (straight, then right at St. Peter's Church). – *Dobri den'*, Gesine: he says cautiously, almost pleadingly. Turns out she can speak Russian too: – *Kak djela, gospodin*, she asks; she brings him into Cresspahl's room, *sadites'*; next comes *na razvod*, to work!, so that he'll finally believe she's believed him. Her feeling here was less compassionate, more urgent, the way seeing someone's wound demands a bandage. There was nervousness too, though, and with it the thought: Oh my distant homeland! which was sung in

Russian, *Shiroka strana moya rodnaya*, but meant in translation: Well this is a fine mess we're in, and it may get dicey.

But Pius did nothing halfway. When the geometry tutorial was over, the question was stuck in my throat and Pius answered it. We came to an understanding about our fathers—the younger man who served the Soviets and the older whom the Soviet had had in their clutches; both men had made it possible for us to do this, each in his own way. Cresspahl merely remarked that he hoped Pagenkopf Senior wasn't sticking anyone's head in the lion's mouth but his own. Now all that was missing were tiny scraps of paper and Mrs. Habelschwerdt's community spirit.

Ol' Habelschwerdt, nicknamed *Hobel* (the wood planer), had graduated high school in Breslau twenty-one years before and snagged a senior school-teacher to marry; unfortunately, with him missing "in the East" and her stuck with half-grown children, she'd gone to teacher training school surrounded by all sorts of young things. She taught us mathematics, chemistry, and physics. The boys in the class rated her as genuinely "acceptable" ("good enough for a new husband"); her legs were a solid A-minus given that she was forty; she'd acquired her nickname for her excessively harsh reprimands, overstraining her tiny voice. As a relative and now surviving dependant of a politically compromised person (NSDAP), she tried maybe a little too anxiously to guarantee at least one ("bourgeois") son's admission to the New School high school, plus she needed to hang on to her teacher's salary—she'd zealously memorized the words of the New Progressive Pedagogy and perhaps understood the meanings a bit less well. And so, a week before Christmas, she whacked the desk with her metal ruler (several times over, as if beating a bad dog) when a handful of paper confetti blew into the aisle from Pius's place; and thus she yelled at him, over all the thirty-nine student heads: You of all people should show some community spirit here!

In an English or American school, "You of all people..." would probably have become her nickname. Eva Matschinsky was admonished like this: You don't just lay your abundance down on the table like that, Eva Maria! You of all people... Habelschwerdt was taken aback by our laughter, having forgotten the youthful abundance of her own bosom; she had just been reminding Eva, and us, that as a barber's daughter (Reactionary Middle Class) she had to make up for her social origins with at least unimpeachable conduct. And Pius, of all people, should come across as entirely agreeable, given his father (Progressive Intelligentsia). But given Mr. Pagenkopf's position, she accepted with a sigh that Pius refused to give her—his teacher!—an apology. I alone knew: it was Zaychik who'd done it.

Pius shared a desk with him, Dagobert Haase (Platt for *Hase*, "rabbit," *zaychik* in Russian). They'd shared it since the start of 9-A-II, because they took the same route to school. Not a friend, a habit. High-spirited, pushy, clever, usable. But Zaychik just wouldn't stop passing notes. Playing Battleship right under Mrs. Habelschwerdt's nose, Pius cured him of that. But when a scrap of paper is passed from the right it's considered an affront against solidarity to shake one's head, and unfortunately this one was addressed to Pius himself (Eva's already wearing a . . . ; Eva has already . . .); Pius had ripped the message into tiny bits and left them on his opened book. The teacher neared, the book was slammed shut, the telltale cloud between the legs of the desk testified to Pius's lack of community spirit. Now it might be that such spirit abandoned Pius when it came to the community of teachers, but if such a sensibility was a virtue, a public virtue, then it was unjust to be told one lacked it because of someone else's offense. Worst of all, Haase Zaychik failed to avail himself of the honor code to which a member of the Free German Youth was bound—he didn't try to clear up the situation. The girl to whom he explained all of this, in a state of multilayered uneasiness, was also unattached.

And so began the first "work collective" in the Fritz Reuter High School in Gneez, two years before such things were officially introduced, and it was scandalous. First of all, classroom seats could be traded when the school year started, never in the middle except on a teacher's orders. Second, a boy or girl left over was to sit alone—if worst came to worst a boy and girl at the same desk might be allowed at the front of the room. But in any case . . . Cresspahl's daughter was almost sixteen and Pius was already seventeen! On top of that, the desk Pius had moved to with me was in the very back corner of the room, hard for a teacher to keep her eye on, and since Pius had offered me the chair next to the window, he also screened me from view down the aisle. The school might be "New"—if you didn't count the building, and the furniture, and most of the teachers—but this was an offense against propriety, letting young people of the opposite sex sit together at the same desk. Unheard of!

"Oh, Angelina, you've got to wait . . ." was sung in our direction before first period the first day after Christmas break; there was a lot of anticipatory giggling around us, because a visit from the principal was expected—Dr. Kliefoth, was held to have old-fashioned ideas, and in fact a corner of his eye did twitch when he caught sight of us, as if a fly had attacked him there. He tested the class his way. He started with Matschinsky, jumped to C when W was up, took some P's, then relaxed against the back of his chair, hands in his lap, initially with a stern sidelong glance from under his beetling brows. The stiff white tuft of hair on his skull was perfectly still, although the heat was by no means on full blast. Pagenkopf and Cresspahl had to translate, in alternating lines, the letter from E. A. Poe's "The Gold-Bug," which, unfortunately, opens "My Dear" and goes on containing phrases that would also be appropriate in a love letter. We had to deal with foggy light from the frosted-glass lamps, we were in no mood to giggle. Lise Wollenberg, whom the slight had made reckless, forced herself to burst out laughing and in return got a mark against her in the record book for disrupting the class (a delicate matter for someone from the bourgeoisie). He gave each of us an A. Kliefoth's position was murky: bourgeois, militarist, but on the other hand Progressive Intelligentsia as principal; after his tacit approval what could the Wood Planer do to us? Luckily for her, she saw the change in the seating plan actually recorded in the principal's handwriting; we saw her sit up with a start at that. Never again would she convict Pius of a lack of community spirit; the following year she even invited us for an afternoon coffee—together.

When the singing and jeering about our new desk started, Pius furrowed his eyebrows as if in pain and his lips grew taut the way they used to when he was standing under the horizontal bar, collecting himself for his leap. This was someone who'd stuck it out through every decision he'd had to make in his life. Since he stared straight ahead so haughtily, as if our intention alone guaranteed our success, I lost my trepidation and knew for certain that everything was going to work out fine. And since we'd apparently nodded at one another after Mrs. Habelschwerdt's sigh like two horses who'd been sharing a harness for a long time, we were considered a couple from that moment on.

Because of our fathers, it stayed a secret for quite some time that the Cresspahl girl went home from school with the Pagenkopf boy and did her homework with him, or that Pius gave up a half hour of sleep to meet Gesine at the milk train from Jerichow. We didn't shove our compact in anyone's face, even each other's. Cresspahl got through it because custom dictated that you had to go with someone; by this point she was afraid to look too closely into how things stood between her and Jakob. And now Pius always had someone he could walk right past Lise Wollenberg with, as if the thing with her passport photo had been settled when he tore it up.

July 19, 1968 Friday

– It's all gonna come down today. (Eagle-Eye Robinson)

– It's all gonna come down today, Gesine. And don't smoke so much! (Eileen O'Brady)

– Hope it all comes down today, my gardener made a bet with me. (de Rosny)

If only it all would come down today—the heat that's hanging over the city, making the mornings pale, the days hazy, the tops of buildings blurry at the edges, standing still in the sun unbearable because the heat from the sidewalk penetrates up through one's soles. Last night the dirt in the air left nothing but a small sweltering hole for the sun. After you've swum eight blocks through the hot liquid air, the artificial climate of the bank hits you like a blow to the heart. If only it all would come down today.

So what did Czechoslovak Communists' peers in East Germany, Hungary, Poland, and the Soviet Union have to tell them, and what did the presidium of the Central Committee of the Communist Party of the ČSSR reply?

They say: We've read it, and first off: greetings! But we *have* already addressed your concerns in our May plenary session.

Yet how could we instantly clear up all the conflicts that have accumulated over the twenty years preceding our January plenary session? If we start with healthy Socialist activities, it's inevitable that some of them will overshoot their marks, whether it be a little heap of anti-Socialist forces or the *fronde* of old dogmatic-sectarians. If we're trying to unify our new line, not even the party itself can remain untouched. Many of us are so accustomed to rule from above that the wishes from below always fall short. We wish to admit these facts, to our own party and to our people. You know that.

But you do have eyes in your head, so how can you possibly claim that our present situation is counterrevolutionary, that we want to give up Socialism, change our foreign policy, break our country loose from you. After everything you've done for us, during the war and in the years since, you mustn't doubt us. That's an insult to us.

We are friends in Socialism. And things can only improve with mutual respect, sovereignty, and international solidarity. We'll try harder. You can count on us.

You mention our relationship with the Federal Republic of Germany. Well, it is our immediate neighbor. And we *were* the last to take definite steps toward the partial regulation of mutual relations, particularly in the economic field. There were other Socialist countries that did so earlier and to a greater extent, without it causing any fears.

We thoroughly respect and protect the interests of the DDR, hand in hand with it. It is our Socialist ally. We do all in our power to strengthen its international position and authority. We said so in January and have done so in all the months since.

What we've promised to you, in agreements and treaties, we will respect. Our commitment to mutual cooperation, peace, and collective security is proved by our new friendship treaties with the Bulgarian and Hungarian People's Republics, and also the prepared treaty with the Rumanian Socialist Republic. (You know why we here bracket out China. And Poland.) No hard feelings!

The staff exercises of your forces on our territory are a concrete proof of our faithful fulfillment of our alliance commitments. We gave you a friendly welcome, we were where you needed us to be. The restlessness and doubts in the minds of our public occurred only after you repeatedly changed the time of your departure. Did we ever say to your face: Get going?

We know this: Give up our leading role and it's all over for Socialist society. For this reason alone we must understand each other on the question of what is required to lead. We depend on the voluntary support of the people. We are not implementing our leading role by ruling from above, but by acting rightly, progressively, socialistically.

Any indication of returning to the old methods of compelling obedience would evoke against us the resistance of the majority of party members, workers, cooperative farmers, and intelligentsia. That is just how we would imperil our political leading role, would threaten the Socialist advantages of the people, how our common front against imperialism would waver. That cannot be our hope.

We have our tactical plan. We've told you what it is.

First. We are going to give the specific people responsible for bringing the party into this unfortunate situation a good talking to. If that's justifiable.

Second. At the fourteenth extraordinary congress of the party we'll take a look at what we've done since January. We will lay down the party line, adopt an attitude to the federation of the Czechs and the Slovaks, approve the new party statute, and elect a new Central Committee with the full authority and confidence of the party and all of society.

Third. Then we'll tackle our internal political questions: the improvement of the socialist National Front, self-government, the actualization of the federal constitutional arrangement, the new elections, and the preparation of a new constitution.

Just now it's darn tough. We're winning, if also suffering drawbacks. But we have the situation in hand. The delegates elected to the congress are a guarantee that the future fate of the party will not be decided by extremist or unreasonable people.

We have clearly rejected the "2,000 Words." They were never dangerous words, but since you got so mad at them we want to tell you loudly and openly, so that all Czechs and Slovaks can hear us and understand: This must not be repeated, for that could anger our Soviet friends, from whom we require not ill will but patience. Nothing of this kind will happen again.

But believe us, it's been easier to do our job since we abolished censorship and restored freedom of expression and of the press. People are no longer whispering behind our backs but expressing themselves openly. For the first time, we know what they think of us.

If we now discuss a certain painful matter with you, but in everyone's hearing, and despite the fact that you have records of it in the files of your secret police already, this is actually an act of politeness and to be taken as information ex officio. The law about the rehabilitation of innocent people who in earlier years were persecuted illegally with the help of the law has been a success. Since it was passed, people are hardly ever even looking in this direction.

In September, immediately after the party congress, we will confirm the permanent existence of the parties of the National Front and pass a law clarifying the legal regulations for the formation and activities of various voluntary organizations, associations, clubs, and all that kind of thing. The enemies of Socialism will show themselves, and we will have the opportunity to effectively face them down.

Dear friends, are you trying to make us look bad in front of our own people? We can hardly return to the days when we could convince them that you weren't butting in when you were butting in. Help us save face. We cannot decide on our own policy anywhere but at our own congress.

So what are we asking you for, then? For time. For two months.

We are ready to talk with you. It was probably just a misunderstanding about the date of that meeting—it happens. But leave us in peace, just for a bit, it's touch and go here. Of course we've always been ready to talk. We will kiss your hand, we will embrace you cheek to cheek, if you'll leave us to act for just a little while yet, dear friends, just two months.

In the name of our common fight against imperialism, for peace, the security of nations, democracy, and Socialism.

Why don't you all say anything! You're still treating me like a child whose fun you don't want to spoil!
Maybe it will *be fun for that child.*
Yeah, maybe!
Gesine, you're forgetting: we have no power over the future.
But you always gave me advice when you were alive, for the future!
Then we could get you back, if we had to.
The fun is over.
Gesine, you don't want us to treat you like a child.

Today it all did come down—it's been four hours and still we're telling one another where we were when it caught us. D. E. claims he was standing on his mother's lawn after lunch, hose in hand, nose raised aquiver, and he put his equipment away because cool dry air from New York was moving past him overhead; he's more than a little proud of his nose, and we will remember him looking self-satisfied like this, exuberantly waving his wine glass around. Employee Cresspahl watched the beginning, neglecting her official duties: the light between the glass skin of the blocky office buildings had darkened and then turned exaggeratedly clear. All the edges sharpened to clarity. Then, at a quarter past four, came the first thunderclap. Marie is convinced she saw the very same bolt of lightning, in the wide cutting of Ninety-Sixth Street sloping down to end in the dark window of the river. She was outside the Good Eats when the first fat drops burst at her feet, and Charlie waved her in—a regular customer—but there was a man pressed against the Broadway side of the front window, lacking the change for a cup of coffee, who surrendered, shoulders slumped, to the rivulets flooding the sidewalk. Just then the rain was pouring torrentially down at the bank's palace, too, and from the thirteenth floor you could hear the cars tires whooshing on the wet asphalt. Just then D. E. had stopped at a streetlight in New Jersey, next to a pedestrian marching along as if in a parade, with a piece of cardboard over his half-bald head and letting the rain blacken his suit all it wanted. Just then Marie saw a Negro dancing across Broadway, a large cardboard box on his shoulders that he heaved up higher again every five steps, never bumping into anyone. Then the fire engine began to wail on Third Avenue. Racing mountain streams were pouring down D. E.'s windshield, but if he's said he'll be somewhere at six then there he will be, at 1800 hours, and we're grateful. On Lexington Avenue, in contrast, the commuters seemed to think it was more important to keep walking than to keep dry; clearly rain engenders less solidarity than snowstorms or heat waves—here in this country of ours. It was now twenty minutes since it had started coming down, and a men's clothing shop had its window sign ready: Umbrellas, On Sale. But Mrs. Cresspahl marched grandly on, under the roof of a folded *New York Times*. The beggar stationed on this side of Grand Central Station, who when on duty shocks people with his bared double leg prostheses, had taken a break and was now leaning against a wall inside the Graybar Building, his pant legs rolled down. When Marie stepped outside she learned a new kind of breathing, which D. E. can now explain to her as due to the plunge of at least ten points in the air humidity. In the subway it was still muggy, only half of the fans were running, the people stood grumpily pressed up against one another even though they had, after all, survived another week in New York. At quarter to seven the rain was so weak that it could only trickle, but still it had swept clear the clump of fog from New Jersey so we could again make out the opposite shore in its semidarkness. Then the thunder trampled back and forth over the Hudson, unable to let the river's water be. Now it's quiet, the asphalt mirror of Riverside Drive shows us the treetops in their close friendship with the sky. A squealing birdcall comes over from the park, like that of an injured young animal. A seagull? Yes, Marie saw it over the tops of our trees—a seagull sawing into the wind, the wind bearing down on our building.

July 20, 1968 Saturday, South Ferry day

At the table lavishly set for breakfast (American version, for D. E.), opposite the festively sunlit park, *The New York Times* came between us—we almost slipped into a fight. Twenty American-made machine guns have been dug up under a bridge between Cheb and Karlovy Vary. In five kit bags (or knapsacks) bearing the date 1968. Plus thirty pistols, with the appropriate ammunition. Near the West German border. And *Pravda*, Moscow, was able to publish the news yesterday morning, before the Czechoslovakian interior ministry could even announce the discovery. To a Professor Erichson, this means it's possible that such caches have been placed across the country, waiting to be found and to thus give the Soviet Union justification for any military invasion: Sudeten German uprisings. According to this expert, airborne troops are most likely. But there's a woman sitting at the table who's planning a trip to that part of the world in a month—she'd prefer to be presented with a slightly brighter picture. Then came Marie's glance, up from below, amazed at this new fashion of someone in our family criticizing a person for expressing their thoughts; both of them stared at me like I was simply overworked, I needed a break. They can have their outing, but during it they will have to listen to the Pagenkopf story: as a warning, as a promise, however they want to take it.

"Can Love Really Be a Sin?" This song, too—famously sung in a low, smoky voice by a Nazi actress and now put back to work, this time by Sovexport, to distract the Germans from their hunger—who do you think got this song sung at them in Gneez's Fritz Reuter High School starting in January 1949? It was sung and drummed and whistled at Cresspahl's daughter and Pius Pagenkopf. We were the Couple.

Lise Wollenberg believed it too. She'd taken as deskmate the niece of Mrs. Lindsetter, wife of the district court chief justice—a delicate blond who, despite her soft flesh, was nicknamed Peter because she'd always worn her hair cut short, since the early days of the Soviet occupation. It looked striking next to Lise's long curls. Wollenberg said about me: yes, well, with a father like that Cresspahl was well advised to suck up to the new regime.

But Mrs. Pagenkopf was not a fine lady with elegant clothes and hairdo and political slogans on her lips; to me she looked bent, stout, and worn-down, dressed as frugally as Jakob's mother. Her shoulders were hunched as though she had a lot of fear left over from the twelve swastika years and new worries too given her husband's "lifestyle" in Schwerin—which was, of course, how the good people of Gneez couldn't help but understand Mr. Pagenkopf's political activities. She was far too shy to let herself be drawn onto the stage at the Renaissance Cinema for the political address after a screening, much less when it was later moved up ahead of the films after people had started heading for the side doors en masse as soon as they saw the words "The End." She did read the front page of the Schwerin *People's Daily* and would have been perfectly able to spell out for her comrades what had happened to the SED since the first party conference in January 1949. (She actually helped us with our So-Sci essays.) The neighbors interpreted her taciturn manner as revenge for the times when the Pagenkopfs were people it was better not to talk to. She talked about me as "*your Gesin*," in a voice of fond reproach; she rarely talked to me. But since it was me her boy Robert had chosen, she soon found a rhyme: *Röbbertin his Gesin.* Anyway, if she had talked to me I'd have had to shout back. Since her near-deafness had remained incurable, she turned her right ear, not her eyes, to everyone but Pius—who knows if she ever once looked me in the face. It was as if Pius's mother lived in the kitchen; she was visible most of all in the ceaselessly washed windows, the polished floors, the scrupulously assembled sausage sandwiches that Pius carried in from the kitchen with the tea. Yes, there was tea. And butter on the bread, for the Pagenkopfs had three ration cards and would never be short of the fifty-five marks for a pound of margarine from the TO store. The sandwiches were generous.

After 1949 I was never hungry in the East again. To that extent, Lise was right—I was enjoying one of the pleasures connected to the ruling class.

I thought I should keep this Pius away from Jakob (I was after all being unfaithful to Jakob, whether or not he'd been with other girls). Several weeks went by and then I saw Pius talking to him: the tall, elegant boy in a polite pose in front of the stocky guy in his greasy railroad worker's outfit. Jakob's protecting hand was over me every step of the way.

Pius and I were a couple because we'd walk together from our shared desk onto the Street of German-Soviet Friendship to Pagenkopf's place, where we'd do our homework in the "salon." (The maid that Helene Pagenkopf had once been had filled the living room to bursting with flower stands, étagères, spindly little tables, and club chairs, leaving barely enough room to walk around a piano, the contribution from Pagenkopf Sr.) Since we left the house together too, we were a couple.

The teachers soon got used to it. When the beanpole gym teacher couldn't find me, he asked Student Pagenkopf to tell me the practice time. Naturally he'd be accompanying Student Cresspahl to the pool, with her swim things in the basket of his bike. He, like she, joined the SC Trout swimming club because his father had asked him to add more "societal activities" to his schedule. Since each member of a couple has to look out for the other, Pius discovered that children who excelled in a sport were rewarded by a transfer to a special school, where they received more training in their specialty than in practical subjects, and thus after their tournament victories would have to scramble professionally while never catching up to their peers. Cresspahl the front-crawl ace soon saw her times slump to almost normal. There was little that anyone could prove against her, since the other teachers reported steady performance from this student, and the gym beanpole banged his stopwatch as he accused Cresspahl of paying too much attention to Pagenkopf. Still, he did say I could stop coming to his practices, since he didn't like interfering with couples. He must have liked us, as a couple.

KLIEFOTH: What is all this fuss supposed to mean, Mrs. Habelschwerdt! It is precisely at their desk that the two of them are safe with respect to your...valuable concerns!

The world thinks it's cute when the two members of a couple are similar in certain ways, and I became a bit more like Pius by joining the FDJ, just like him. For his father had now seen fit to request a bit more societal activity from "my son's girlfriend" too. He required more than a bit, it turned out—my booklet sporting the yellow-on-blue rising sun soon proved insufficient and I had to get myself the tall narrow one with the black-and-red-and-gold flag waving in front of the Soviet flag, both diagonal flagpoles stuck into a circle. This latter booklet was for the Society for German-Soviet Friendship, and after Cresspahl read the Stalin telegram ("Hitlers come and go . . .") printed after my name he promptly raised my allowance by fifty pfennigs, "for the next ones." Small wonder that Pius was elected president of our FDJ class chapter at the start of tenth grade, and I his deputy; we held these offices to the end and they were noted in our transcripts.

We biked as a couple to the unofficial bathing spot on the south side of Gneez Lake and swam without the others across to the boathouses Willi Böttcher was in the process of building for the Progressive Intelligentsia; we came swimming back to the rest of the class together, and clearly we'd been talking to each other the whole time. When I happened to be there without him they sometimes still sang that question about whether love might be a sin, but Pius had cured me of my old bashfulness and they learned to ask about him through me. We were, after all, the ones who dried off with the same towel—the couple.

When two people have been a couple for a while, they go to the movies depending on the state of their wallets and the attractions of the film; when two people are far from being a couple, one of them has to pay for the other's ticket and spend ninety minutes laboriously exploring whether they might become one. If only one member of the couple is there, people keep a seat free for the other: next to Pius, "Keep that free for Gesine"; to you as you come in, "Here's your man!" In the FDJ meeting, on the field trip to the theater in Schwerin, on the potato fields during harvest service. When one of the couple is on card-checking duty, Gesine will take Pius's plate with her and bring him his school lunch. A couple has more time than other people; they can save the strolls, at least two afternoon hours, up Stalin Street and back down it, keeping a trembling lookout for the object of their longing: those in a couple already have it.

I should also tell you: Pius was no more Catholic than she was Protestant.

In spring 1950 we signed up together for maintenance duty with the German Railway, because this time old Pagenkopf had requested a more visible societal activity. For three weeks the couple poked around in the scruffy track beds of Gneez station, with shovel and pickax; in the photo you can see "my son's girlfriend" shoveling while Pius, amiably leaning on a handle, looks into Jakob's camera, a knit cap on the back of his head. The reward (the material incentive) was a free train ticket to any destination, but we were unable to take a trip together because Cresspahl needed my pass for a trip to "Berlin" (never referred to as "East"). So Pius went by himself to Dresden, detouring via Wittenberg on the way there for the sake of his father's reputation, returning via West Berlin for my sake, because when one person in a couple goes on a trip he brings back a souvenir for the other. Gesine Cresspahl, 10-A-II, now owns a ballpoint pen.

The last game was *pretty pathetic* but here we have Fritz Reuter High School versus Grevesmühlen, with Pius as center forward again. And look, two minutes before the starting whistle here comes Gesine. Over there, in that empty part of the bleachers, the one with the braids, straightening her long skirt around her legs. The one sitting up straight, so Pius can see her. Why should they wave to each other! he's already seen her. Look, she doesn't clap for him either. Well he already knows. They're a couple after all.

Yes, but can love be a sin?

In the winter the power cutoffs would interrupt us diagramming benzene rings or laying out the societal motivations of Lady Macbeth, and there would often be another hour before the evening train to Jerichow. Then it might happen that Pius would sit down at the piano and play me what he'd learned in eight years (he had diligently practiced Schumann's "Träumerei," and once, on a dusty, languorous summer afternoon, I heard him playing it from the street—he kept his dreams of Lise to himself). Other times it would be perfectly silent behind our dark windows. Early on, Zaychik and his girl Eva Matschinsky burst in on us with the excuse that they'd wanted to bring us candles. They saw Pius go back to the piano and Cresspahl calmly go on smoking—they must have thought we were uncommonly slick, and moreover they'd now lost their pretext for visiting. Pius had told me about his elder sister's death from typhus, I him about Alexandra Paepcke. We could certainly say: We knew things about each other.

One time—I was sixteen—the rail service to Jerichow was canceled and I spent the night at the Pagenkopfs', alone in a room. I didn't wait up for Pius.

Pius would have refused to tell me anything about the modified second line of the song about that girl Angelina who had to wait.

We were careful never to hold each other's hand.

In the summer of 1951, we were out biking and, at Cramon Lake, opposite the village of Drieberg, we stopped for a half-hour swim. While we were changing I was clumsy, he was clumsy, for the span of a breath our feet touched each other.

Just a fling wouldn't have been enough for me, Gesine.
Where no love grows, it's hard for sin to flourish.
Don't say her name, Gesine.
Don't ask me about Jakob.
But we didn't say a word to each other that time, did we!
No, Pius. We swam right across the lake.

Pagenkopf and Cresspahl spent vacation together. They biked to Schönberg, to Rehna. Pius lived at the Cresspahls' for two weeks! They went to the beach together every morning. It's six of one, half a dozen of the other, what they do when they're alone! That's our couple.

"MARIE H. CRESSPAHL   New York, N.Y., July 21, 1968

Dear Anita Red Hair,

It's still my birthday, but I want to write you my thank-you note today since you took the trouble to send me two full pages. Other than that I only got cards—one from Denmark, one from Switzerland, two from London, and the rest from the USA, mostly New York. Thirty-two in total.

I liked that your present can be worn in a blue leather envelope on a ribbon around my neck like a medallion and none of the clever nuns, not even Sister Magdalena, will suspect a watch. Because wearing a watch during class is 'verboten.' People say that here in German when a rule is totally unreasonable. Jewelry is also 'verbotten' (same), but they won't be able to see this under the blouse of the school uniform. Thank you and I'll remember you every time I wear it.

I hope the alarm built into this watch wasn't meant to teach me something. Because I always get up at the same time as Gesine, so that I can see her awake at least once a day. On Tuesday she went straight from the door to her bed and stayed lying there till the next morning. On the other hand, I'm always on time to school and have never once needed to take the 5 bus there. 'Don't take the bus, pay the fare like everyone else.'

To tell you the truth, I'm also writing to you because I have stationery with my name printed on it for the first time. It's a present from D. E. 'Because everyone older than ten needs some.' I turned eleven years old at seven thirty this morning.

I should tell you something about D. E., you probably know him as Erichson. Gesine's going to marry him. In the fall, when we're done with Prague. It's going to be *en petit comité*, with you as our best friend (and a mother-in-law too). As a result Gesine will become a citizen of the USA, and I'll be from a totally different country.

This was my first birthday without a party. I could have easily had ten people over. But it couldn't happen without Francine, the black girl who lived with us for a while until welfare came and got her. We've looked for her everywhere on the Upper West Side and even D. E. found not a trace. Francine would've been the first on my list to invite. Maybe she's dead. But D. E. would find a grave.

Anyway we need to learn how it goes as a trio, so this is the first birthday D. E. did for me. When I had to leave my room I put a blindfold on and went back to my room from memory too because I wanted to see the table only when they were both there. They were supposed to call me and most of all they needed to sing the song they sing in Mecklenburg to wake up the birthday girl or boy: 'I'm happy you were born.' D. E. sang it for me. Then I came in.

The table was set with the damask tablecloth that came to us from Gesine's mother. We normally use it only on New Year's Eve. How did they smuggle flowers into the apartment! But once you get to know D. E. you'll stop being surprised by miracles. Eleven candles, in all four colors, and the one for 1962 had a ring painted around it, 'because years are different from each other, of course.'

Before I'd cracked it myself. 1962 is when he met us. He likes to show you something to think about but then you've got to do the thinking yourself.

Your present was there. You know what, I just now saw the 'HMC' engraved on it. It's probably part of your job to think so carefully about other people, isn't it. Gesine gave me a model of the prewar English Daimler I've been missing for a long time. (Do you think it's dumb to collect things like that?) Jason, Shakespeare, and Eagle-Eye Robinson gave me a deluxe carton of chewing gum, which was very good of them but now they've given away my secret to Gesine. She thinks chewing gum is bad for your teeth. Mrs. Erichson gave me a two-yard-long shawl in the Mecklenburg colors (she's going to be my step-grandmother). From de Rosny, that's Gesine's highest-up boss, a savings account. (Seventy-five dollars.) From D. E. this printed stationery and a look as if butter wouldn't melt in his mouth. Don't trust anyone over forty.

But since he was watching like a hawk I acted like this was the end of it and innocently let them take me out for a walk in Riverside Park. Gesine was wearing the Copenhagen blouse, since he'd come over in a matching blue linen suit. (He still doesn't have a closet here.) So you see, they're arranging everything together.

At first I didn't suspect anything, since it was Sunday, and families often go for walks on Sundays. (Even though I was born on a Sunday.) They were discussing, like people on TV, whether or not there were evergreens in the park. 'You've got to keep your eyes open,' D. E. said, letting me think this was another piece of education in disguise. I did have to listen to how the little white beech on the slope below the retaining wall across from Ninety-Eighth Street was the kind of tree used for the wall of trees in the gardens of Versailles. But if you had kept your eyes open you saw a package next to the trunk, wrapped in colored paper, with ribbons, something even the most respectable person would steal it looked so tempting. Give up. We'll be fumbling around in the dark till the end of time if we try to figure out how he smuggled it there. I was walking behind him the whole way, he can't have thrown it. Give up. It was an ID bracelet, a silver chain with a tag saying my name and:

$$A_2$$
$$cde\ cD^uE.$$

For if I need blood from someone. After an accident. This is something a Czechoslovakian doctor can read.

Now you realize that D. E. must have broken into a doctor's office on Park Avenue. At least.

The third of the good things was an electronic calculator at the Memorial Fountain on 100th Street ('To the heroic dead of the Fire Department'). It was sitting there shining, way below the plaque to honor the horses that died 'in the line of duty' too. And you know Gesine, the educational ideas she has—she of all people says I can use it for homework, all four arithmetical operations plus percents. ('To get exponents you'd have to promise me something.') Only at home.

This Erichson was imitating Alexander Paepcke. That's an uncle of Gesine's (dead), he was an expert in things like this. D. E. doesn't want to be too much like a father. And that's why I agree to it.

Then came another thing, but it was the fourth and good things come in threes so it doesn't count. It was an apartment.

You're probably thinking: an apartment for the future married couple, Cresspahl & Erichson. That too. Up by Columbia University, where it looks so much like Paris, a fourteenth floor on Riverside Drive, five rooms, and they walked around in there like people in a bus station who have time to kill before they need to board. They called one of the rooms "the Berlin room." Obviously they'd secretly been here before. I don't know any more than that.

Because there's a door in the apartment and it had a sheet of paper like this one hanging on it, and behind it was mine. An apartment for me, with locks and a bolt, with its own bathroom, walk-in closet, air conditioner, phone, a hundred and thirty feet above Riverside Drive, with a view of the Hudson, the George Washington Bridge, the Palisades Amusement Park, the shore of New Jersey all day. The open space of park drew me in so much I felt like I was falling out the window. Down below, the thick bustle of the treetops along the roads, not as thin as the forest in West Germany when you fly into the Rhein/Main Air Base. Between the trees the number 5 bus came creeping up like a long strong animal. It had a very clean roof. I'll live a bit more alone in that apartment. Before we were two plus one. In the new apartment, he's one of the Two, I'm the One. New math. Group theory.

At night when he paces back and forth here talking, she runs along after him, just to make sure she doesn't miss any of his *statements*.

But she also lays into him. The Soviet Army has now signed the letter to the Czechs and Slovaks too. D. E. brings up airborne troops, she says he mustn't. It goes by fast, they often lose me: 'Not after Hungary!' Erichson: 'For most Americans the last war was in the Pacific...' Now you're supposed to think about Vietnam. But she's denying 'objectively comparable functions of power' and he's already ready and waiting with the concept of crowds.

It seems this apartment has another room with three windows facing the river. Now I hear them negotiating which one of them will get it—they both want the other one to take it. After their six years of practice it can't help but go well, can it?

Dear Anita, are you coming to see us in Prague or have you made yourself unwelcome in the ČSSR too with your travel agency? If they're rebuilding your Friedenau post office now, and you're losing your PO box, you'll have to shut up shop, won't you? You're hard to find in a PO box but in a four-room apartment with a phone the lights will give you away. (I'm sorry you lost your studio.)

There were relatives living in Friedenau until 1943, the Niebuhrs, also dead. We've just gotten a letter album from them, with photos, Gesine wanted to look through them alone. When she came back I thought she'd been crying. But does she let anything show?

My favorite dream about Friedenau is the market, because you can buy fish there and rhubarb and butter in bulk, not just sweaters and suits like sometimes at Fourteenth Street here. But how come the fishwife still asks after me?

When you come to New York I'll take you to Park Avenue, where it becomes a poor neighborhood (I'm only allowed to go to Harlem with a grown-up), and I'll show you La Marqueta with the Caribbean fruits, from habichuela blanca to aji dulce. The Puerto Ricans brought this market with them, and their neighborhood is called Spanish Harlem.

When you come for the wedding we'll only need to go swimming in the Hotel Marseilles. You can stay with me. Be my guest.

M.

P.S.
But my name will still be what you see on the top left corner of this sheet of paper and on the letters on the watch you gave me."

July 22, 1968 Monday

So what is it that threatens to end civilized life on earth? More than anything else, the bomb that produces heat through nuclear reactions: says one of the people who invented it, and he would now like to see the Soviet Union come to terms with this country, in this realm as in other hygienic regards. So industrious, scientists' regrets are.

Another expert, this one renowned in mathematics and philosophy, sounds antsy. The Soviet prime minister needs to assure Lord Bertrand Russell and the world that the Red Army renounces all use of military force in the ČSSR. Just so we know what's coming. Always these uncertainties about the future.

In fact the Soviets concluded their war games in Czechoslovakia three weeks ago and still they have their troops in the country. Their army newspaper reports from Moscow what they're doing there. They're looking for sacks of American weapons, and they've found another three.

From the late summer of 1948 on, the widower, the proud old bachelor Cresspahl was surrounded by three women. One you know; the second, a fifteen-year-old, you can guess; the third will surprise you. The first always wore an item of black clothing, a collar or scarf or something, mourning in advance, unfortunately; the second was often referred to behind her back as a hussy; and then there was the third, paying visits like back in the old days—Mrs. Brüshaver, the pastor's wife. Plucky of mouth, glasses stuck up on her head at an awkward angle, a careless part in her now-dull ash-blond hair, this is how she came over, careful not to seem to be looking around like a stranger. But her old path, between the Creutzes' greenhouses and the masters' villa, was now a Soviet restricted zone, off limits, so she had to come openly, down Brickworks Road from Town Street, a coat over her apron for decorum's sake, easy and relaxed from her first visit. But Cresspahl was pleased that she saw him busy in the kitchen with his daughter and Mrs. Abs, as if safe in a family, and dismissively asked her what they might do for her.

She started in as only a woman can, snatching something out of thin air; in her scattershot way she hit on how men were always bustling about and making a fuss and in general just you know. This was hard to contradict, and she tacked on, as it were reasonably, an invitation for Cresspahl to come by the pastorage and take a look at a window that was letting in rain, making puddles on Aggie's waxed floor. She thereby reminded us that we used to know her as Agatha, and reminded Cresspahl that his job used to be fine woodworking and carpentry in general. She had her opening. Now we had to mind our manners, and since in her pride Gesine Cresspahl forgot them, Mrs. Abs offered the guest a chair and a tin mug of coffee made of roasted rye. She immediately praised it. Because if a certain husband, hers in fact, hadn't taken her wifely advice then she'd now be drinking unhealthy imported coffee from a porcelain cup on a white tablecloth in Schwerin, as wife of the minister responsible for church matters in the state of Mecklenburg(-Vorpommern). In brief, Aggie was bustling and fussing and just-you-knowing as if the last time she'd dropped by was the day before yesterday and not ten years ago. Cresspahl kept his eyes on the stove into which he was putting more wood, maybe to warm the room a bit for her, and still he let himself be tempted into a question. – *Right?*: she said, the way only a woman who grew up somewhere between Grabow and Wismar can say it. The ministry post was something the Communists in the government had dreamed up as a reward for Brüshaver, whom they planned to introduce as a comrade from Sachsenhausen and Dachau. But they themselves *had written a "P" in front of that*, upset the apple cart, by mentioning their fellow soldier Brüshaver to their secret police K-5 a little too often, just because he kept bringing up, again and again, the matter of certain members of his congregation who'd disappeared and were staying wherever they were at the pleasure of the Soviet friends. (At this, someone in Cresspahl's kitchen felt her ears turn red with shame. She'd been refusing to greet the pastor on the street because she thought he'd betrayed her father.) And just as with the secular authorities, Brüshaver's stubbornness had made a hash of it with the religious ones, all because he'd had to refuse church rites to head senior detective Herbert Vick of the criminal police at his funeral. – Vick?: Cresspahl asked, dumbfounded, and not at the death. – Vick!: Aggie cried, quoting: "Because I am a faithful National Socialist!" Now the ten years between them were over and gone; now they were talking together again. The democratic civil administration of Mecklenburg had wanted to use Herbert Vick's arts, at least the criminological kind, for educational purposes too, at K-5 in the Neubrandenburg zone, and had hoped to repay his service with a Christian final benediction, as if the whole thing were just for show. Brüshaver, though, felt professionally obliged to consider, as a German and an anti-Fascist Christian, how this honored keeper of the peace had abstained from religious service and communion throughout his life; Jerichow as place of baptism scarcely mattered. So the Volkspolizei had had to find a pastor in Gneez to do the final honors, and Brüshaver was summoned to the state superintendency for a gentle warning. The Mecklenburg State Church was hoping to avoid a collision course; they'd told him so in writing, Brüshaver could frame it, just like his official certificate as "Fighter against Fascism" (category 4), if there were any frames to be had, and speaking of which, she'd dropped by today to discuss something about a window frame... Not a word about the Cresspahls, or the Abses, failing to attend her husband's sermons; not a word about Gesine's haughtiness. Thank you for that, *Fru Pastor Brüshaver.*

The next morning, Cresspahl cleaned one of his carpenter's rules, oiled the hinges, put it in his pocket, and really and truly walked partway into town, among other people, for the first time since October three years ago, since May of this one. Went out on a job.

It was a window ledge (*window breast*) on the upper floor of the pastorage. Aggie showed Cresspahl how she'd been bracing herself while polishing the window and the heel of her hand had gone right through what looked like perfectly intact enamel paint into the rotten wood, more than an inch, and she wasn't kidding. It turned out you could scrape off two thirds of the sill with your bare fingers. Aggie wanted an explanation, since the window had been repaired as recently as 1944. A master craftsman knows how to watch his words and refrain from appraising someone else's workmanship. In 1944 it had been Pastor Wallschläger—that shining light, annunciator of Nordic preeminence—reigning here. If someone had it in for him, all he needed to do was use the softest wood, black poplar it looked like, and make one or two channels in it with a spike or screwdriver, cover it all up with some paint, and leave Jerichow in good time. The rain, driven hence by the west and sea winds, will separate the ledge from the board (*window sill*) within a year, stealthily wash out the mortar, and before long leave nothing to keep frame and masonry together but the interior wallpaper. By that time it's too late to repair it—we're dealing with a total loss, which'll take more than ten pounds of tobacco on the black market to fix. – *I'll have to make a botch of it:* Cresspahl said soothingly, in English, since he had to get accustomed to his profession again gradually, and he didn't want to translate it, because it meant two things: to mess it up, to cobble it together. – Emergency first-aid for the winter: he promised, and Aggie was calmed, because he measured the window as if it might be saved. His keeping the sabotage from her is what I consider the second step in Cresspahl's return to life with people, instead of, as required, against them.

Now *you* try to find some cement in Jerichow or Gneez, just a paper cone full!, to slap over the masonry and bandage the rest of the ledge with, in exchange for the reformed currency of East Germany and some cheap words. You'd be more likely to run across a full sack of wheat. Then there's the problem of finding a hunk of beech or Cornish oak, 20" x 6" x 3", and let's not even mention the sodium silicate solution or synthetic resin to waterproof it with. If that's what you're looking for you've got to make your way around, offer at least conversation, and then when you come to inspect the wound in the wall with its makeshift covering you'll see Pastor Brüshaver standing in the garden, bent over the flowerbeds he's spading but still looking up as if he knew you. Conversation topics in that situation might include the days when the pastor had to make an appointment to talk to Mayor Cresspahl in Town Hall about a permit to hold an assembly (religious service). Or: that it's May again and here we have a new constitution, whose Article 44 sanctions religious instruction in secular schools, except maybe in Jerichow, where Brüshaver finds his charges waiting outside a looked door on School Street and the district commissioner conducts himself during the pleadings as though the Evangelical Church were a dispensable social group for an upright Communist and its Jerichow pastor more of a burdensome supplicant than a comrade in anti-Fascism. Potatoes need loose soil, Pastor. Hoe em before the sprouts show. When they get four inches high, hoe them again and pile them, pile em again when the plants are as big as your hand, *it'll do your waistline loads of good.* And then Brüshaver, with all his Greek and Latin, had to ask what this meant, and Cresspahl informed him: *Juss thins people say.*

Being neighbors. Teasing. Aggie Brüshaver now brought the ration cards over to the house, Street Representative for South Jerichow as she was ("since someone had to do it, and from me they'll get only the receipts, no character references"). When Cresspahl tried to refuse the vegetable fat and bacon Aggie had diverted for him from the Swedish Aid, he heard back that she was acting out of a sense of medical need, not charity, and a sixty-one-year-old patient needed to follow a state-registered nurse's orders. She'd noticed how my father held his head and before long I came upon her massaging his shoulder and neck muscles, and felt jealous, because he'd never asked his daughter to do that. – *Surely I'm closest to hand now*: Aggie said when he thanked her, and she gave him a pat to tell him to put his shirt back on. One time Jakob was with us for the weekend and she came in and fussed and bustled and lectured him as if reading him the riot act, or Leviticus. Jakob had gone to St. Peter's for Easter 1949, for the sermon on the resurrection, and she accused him of having sat there with his arms crossed till the end, even if in the back pew. – Like you were considering an offer!: she shouted, and after a while Jakob nodded, as if admitting it. And because I can still hear her, it gives me another chance to see him. Brüshaver had been getting along without teeth for three years now—they'd knocked them out of him in Sachsenhausen; finally Aggie talked him out of his suspicion of "German doctors" and he turned up with yellowish plastic structures in his mouth, chewing and chewing like someone when something tastes bad. – Say "*sixpence*": my father told him, and Brüshaver would attempt the English word, and they went on babbling away at each other in made-up words like two little boys. I once saw Jakob's mother looking at them, her lips stretched so tight it seemed they had to hurt—she was attempting a furtive smile. When Jakob's mother wanted to speak severely to Aggie, she called her "*young Fru!*" They had gotten to the point of confidences in the hospital. And if some forgave me out of Christian duty, others had to only, let's say, for reasons of residence—because I lived and belonged there.

For the Gesine Cresspahl of 1948 wanted only to tolerate her neighbors. First of all, she was now a student at the academic high school and had settled the matter of God for herself, in a way she considered entirely original; second, she could soothe her unbelief simply enough, by recalling the prayer that a Lutheran chaplain of the US Air Force had offered up for the crew of the plane about to drop the first atomic bomb on populated territory; she credited Protestant theology with enough tactical and strategic judgment to realize that a conventional destruction of the city of Hiroshima would have sufficed, given the state of war as of August 6, 1945, 9:15 p.m. (Washington time). Student Cresspahl was well aware of why the New State in its New Era tended to schedule its parades, conventions, and

work details to coincide with religious holidays; she felt she was superfluous in this duel, believed she was taking neither side by keeping silent about
how the cigar butt had ended up in the schoolroom, which was the justification and excuse for shutting out the church: the boy Ludwig Methfessel was severely reprimanded and told to obey his new teachers' every word.
Anything else would've meant being a tattletale. And anyway, what did
she care about the church!

The heathen girl, she cannot live in peace / If other heathens do not let
her be. Look at Jakob, carrying a rain-soaked cat into the house and holding the dripping bundle up by the nape of its neck before dropping it with
the report: Wet as Jonah! and only then does he notice Cresspahl's Gesine
sitting there and he lets his glance slip right off her, idly, as if she didn't
know about biblical whales anyway. Hear the proverbs Heinrich Cresspahl
comes out with that summer, English and Protestant at once: *Don't preach
to the converted! Don't mock the afflicted!* and Gesine has to translate them
for him into current German, as if she were too uncultured for Luther's.
Jakob's mother lets him tease her for her Old Lutheran peculiarities since
that at least gives her the rare chance to discuss religious matters, but this
fall she goes for the first time to Brüshaver's church, takes communion
from him. Finally, in October, the daughter of Johann Heinrich Cresspahl,
b. 1933, well known to the authorities already, appears in the pastor's house
of St. Peter's Church in Jerichow to request for a second time, in person,
permission to take confirmation class. Enjoying already the blessings of
her elders' permission and agreement. So eager to please, this child.

In the warmer season Pastor Brüshaver had gone for walks with his
charges, holding lessons in a clearing in the Countess Woods; there were
not enough of them to keep warm under the oversized dome of the church.
He tried to borrow a living room for this one hour a week on Saturday
afternoons, trying the Quades, trying the Maasses (strictly avoiding Cresspahl's house); the good citizens complained about all the dirt the fifteen-
year-old children would track onto their sacred floors. Right after the war,
Mrs. Methfessel had been pleased to refer to the "community of destiny"
in which Brüshaver and her husband had found themselves; now she was
no match for her bullheaded boy, Ludwig, practicing with his soccer ball
right outside the parlor just when the pastor was holding his classes. Mrs.
Albert Papenbrock had the biggest hall in Jerichow—and the firmest faith

in the Evangelical Church, to hear her tell it; she was afraid to stir up the displeasure of Albert's wardens by having hopefuls for church membership in the house. She wrung her hands with scruples and hesitations, she lamented in a slight whine: people were always expecting more from her than from anyone else. . . . Brüshaver reserved the back room of the Lübeck Court, now a rathskeller. The tenant, Lindemann, let it be known that gatherings had to be registered and authorized, just like club meetings. The Jerichow mayor's office prohibited the use of secular premises for religious propaganda. (This was the one after Bienmüller: Schettlicht, the bright-eyed agnostic from Saxony.) Brüshaver thought he could see Red Army policy behind this; he hesitated to test out his theory at the Jerichow Kommandatura; how could he have known that the Wendennych Twins would have bit Comrade Schettlicht's head off! Eventually Jakob lost patience and the German Railway shunted a workshop car onto Papenbrock's now governmental siding, with benches, as if set up for a meeting, and a stove, for which the gasworks donated a wheelbarrow full of coal; because wherever Jakob worked with people they were always willing to do him a favor, as he was for them, the way friends do. In this train car, under the light of barn lanterns, Cresspahl's daughter stuck it out till Christmastime.

She tried to play the humble child, eager to repent through hard work; she was also prepared to accept as only fair that she got little praise for rattling off the main elements of the sacrament of baptism. Baptism is not just plain water, obviously. But she had to force herself to sit still and she avoided looking at Brüshaver's face too much. It seemed to be stuck in a perpetual smile, but it was just strained muscles, torn tendons that pulled the corners of his mouth into a grimace, froze his crow's feet into the involuntary semblance of a grin. He also acted like the pinky of his right hand had always stuck out from his palm like that, the stiff hook at the end of a sweep of pain pulling his shoulder down. When he lifted his book with his index and ring finger before pushing his thumb onto it, as though by accident, his hand looked artificial, sinister. He didn't realize he groaned every time he used his lower arm—that's the kind of thing it hurts to look at. Religious instruction takes the form of a catechism; there was no refuge from Brüshaver's damaged voice, which sounded like there was something unpleasantly sandy in his throat, being turned around and around, every syllable another wound to the sensitive tissue there. Gesine obsessively told herself that these were what he'd brought back from six years in Oranienburg and near Weimar, to be counterbalanced against an official certificate that by now his comrades at the town hall, the Gneez district school commission, the district council authorities raised their hands in front of as though shooing something away. But she couldn't keep perfect control over herself, and it was certainly against her will when she heard herself say, through a drone in her ears as if she were talking underwater: she knew the part about the doctrine of ubiquity by heart and could recite it at will but couldn't bring herself to believe in it.

She said it and ran so blindly to the train car door that she almost toppled down the high step onto the platform and ran down wet cold Station Street into the dim abyss of Market Square, hid in the broken lightless telephone booth, racked by wheezing sobs, afraid of the twilight when everyone would see her.

Cresspahl remembered the winter of 1944 when she'd sought out that same booth to hide from school and the authorities; he came to rescue her before dinner even. He led her off like a child, one arm around her shoulder, and the route they took spared her the light on at home and the look from Jakob's mother, with her dark eyes, enlarged by her glasses; the journey took them into the marsh where only rabbits and foxes could hear that the bodily presence of Christ in the communion wafer seemed like cannibalism, and they didn't care. This was the last time he held her and walked her somewhere like a father; she retained one of his efforts to console her, the one that absolved her: *You gave him a chance.* You tried, Gesine.

The next afternoon she saw Mrs. Brüshaver come into the yard and disappear lightning-fast into the Frenchmen's room, which Jakob's mother, in her proper way, had cleared out for us to use as a dining room. In her hiding place, Gesine tried as fast as she could to think up various arguments against this emissary of the church—weapons in case she was discovered: Aggie had stopped instructing children in the Christian faith as early as 1937. Did she doubt what her husband proclaimed as articles of faith? She told Cresspahl to have himself hung upside down in front of an x-ray to get at the roots of the pains in his neck while she let her husband walk around with a case of Dupuytren's contracture, knots of tissue creating a thick cord in the palm of the hand, and a surgeon could take care of that; she was a nurse but turned her back on her husband's troubles with this government too, and went off to Jerichow's hospital leaving him to deal with all the paperwork of the parish too; are these the precepts for a Christian marriage, then, Aggie?

Aggie's response came through the closed door. She was in the hall with my father, thought no one else was listening, and asked him, despondently, as if asking for forgiveness for herself: What if the child's right, Cresspahl?

The sun hung in the western mist, already a quarter turned away from the earth; its low rays filled the room with a thick, blood-colored light. It was the first time I'd ever been in such a menacing red haze.

In March Cresspahl installed a new window ledge in the parsonage, handmade from a rail tie so soaked in carbolineum that dewdrops would sit on its surface without seeping in or running off. Meanwhile the Brüshavers had found a three-foot-wide section of crumbling wall, running alongside the chimney from the attic to the ground floor, bequeathed by enemies of the Mecklenburg State Church in 1944 with a few chisel blows to the copper flange. This was part of what Brüshaver had inherited. The pastor of Jerichow lived in a house that was falling apart.

The Sunday after Palm Sunday, 1949, there was a christening at the Brüshavers'. Aggie ("everything just grows like that with me") had had another child, a boy, Alex.

Those who challenge the omnipresence of Christ are neither worthy of confirmation nor equal to the duties of a godparent, it goes without saying, and Cresspahl's daughter wasn't jealous when she heard that, along with Jakob's mother, another child from confirmation class had been chosen to watch over Alexander Brüshaver's Christian conduct—a girl from former East Prussia who could not only recite the doctrine of ubiquity but believe it. Gantlik's daughter is who it was. Her name was Anita.

– Bit heavy on the church stuff, Marie?

– Did your pastor lose his hair too?

– Brüshaver without his biretta was a sight you did not want to see. The remains of a wound were still visible on his temple—a reddish indentation the size of a walnut.

– What was the Old Lutheran Church?

– Idiosyncrasies about justification, atonement, the trinity. If you ask me, a dispute about the right of association.

– Jakob's mother gave it up for you?

– Only children, who think they're the center of the world, believe things like that. No, she could only make it to the Old Lutherans in Gneez or Wismar once a month. She wanted to be able to go to church every Sunday.

– Were you being honest when you ran away and fell off the side step of the train car?

– Maybe I was being arrogant with my idea. Anyway it serves me to this day.

– Since you all had to lie everywhere, you took your own truth out on Brüshaver. Admit it.

– I admit it, Marie. And I wanted it to finally be over.

– You were much too young, Gesine. How's a child supposed to decide whether she believes or not. I'll get confirmed when I know for sure—maybe when I'm eighteen.

July 23, 1968 Tuesday

Enter Anita.

Not a "little Anna"—a big tall girl with strong shoulders like a boy, practically athletic from the work in the fields she'd had to do in the village of Wehrlich for nothing but food and a straw-sack pallet under a dripping thatched roof, because she was no local child, she was displaced, with almost no property to protect her, no mother, and a father who left her in servitude to the farmers and kept his pay from the Jerichow police for himself, apparently wishing ruin and death on his daughter. That's how things looked, and when the child came to town for religious services and confirmation classes, one and a half hours' walk and barefoot, she went right past her father with a calm, indifferent look, no anger. How could such a child—with no guardian, no support—escape from day labor to the state capital of Gneez, to an academic high school, to an apartment in the most desirable neighborhood, by the town moat, in a three-story building with running water coming out of the walls and light out of the ceiling?

When she first entered ninth grade the rumors had preceded her and gave her a nasty welcome: "the Russians" had helped her out. That was true insofar as the gentlemen commandants of Jerichow, the Wendennych

Twins, when they wanted to tour the country as conquerors from the Red
Land, took a detour through Wehrlich and had Anita, a fifteen-year-old
child, sit with them so she could translate what these Germans in Mecklenburg were trying to say. That was fair to the extent that the Comrades
Wendennych compensated her for her services as though she were one of
their own: with a purchase coupon for a bicycle, a Swedish import no less,
the crown jewel of the government store on Stalin Street in Gneez; the
citizens of Gneez called this the first bike in Mecklenburg that "the Russians" paid cash for; they called Anita "the Russians' sweetheart" while
they were at it. As a result, Anita could bike to Fritz Reuter High School
punctually on September 1, 1948—one and a half hours every morning,
one and a half hours back to Wehrlich, over unpaved country roads, into
the rain and the west wind of that cold wet fall. She only had to lock the
bike—it was safe from damage because even though dealings with "the
Russians" hardly constituted a recommendation, crossing "the Russians"
was a bad idea. A bicycle with white tires, TRELLEBORG stamped on the
tire rims. It's true that the Wendennych gentlemen also asked her how
she was doing and were scandalized at her habit of doing homework in the
former municipal library, now run by the Cultural League (for a D. R. of
G.), since she had no home and her slave driver of a host—he doesn't need
a name—might at any moment send her away from her books to go clean
out a pigsty; Jerichow's Kommandatura arranged with Gneez's to get her
a change-of-residence permit and have her assigned to Frau Dr. Weidling's
living room—out of turn, a favor. A dangerous one, only worsening her
reputation, even though Dr. Weidling had been hauled in by the *Kontrrazvedka* that November because of her carefree travels through German-
occupied country with a man in a black uniform, not because she meant
to leave Anita Gantlik a whole apartment to herself. But that's what people
said. And we were there the first time Anita was called on in class by Baroness von Mikolaitis, who was allowed, as an act of mercy, to sell her Baltic
origins to us in the form of Russian lessons; Anita humbly stood up, suggested
a curtsy, and gave the jittery older lady a longish answer. Its length was
about all we could understand of it, even after our three years of instruction
in Russian; it sounded a bit like: The Russian word for "train station,"
ma'am, *voskal*, is derived from the amusement park near London's Vauxhall
station, much like the park that Czar Alexander II Nikolayevich built in

his city of Pavlovsk, *rayon* Voronezh. Anyway the word *"voskal"* definitely came up. The baroness was not used to such fluent, unforced, natural speaking from us, and not up to following it either; in pure self-defense she found fault with the way Anita pronounced her *o*'s. Anita had made them sound dry, not elongated as in our Mecklenburgish. She thanked the baroness for her guidance, in Russian. The following week she raised her hand and told Mikolaitis that she'd pronounced her *o* for some *native speakers* (said in Russian, not English!) and they'd given it their seal of approval as standard Moscow pronunciation. If she sounded helpless, pleading, it wasn't an act—she was asking her instructor for a decision. The end of the story was that Mikolaitis invited Anita to take private lessons, hoping to learn a more natural Russian herself. A Solomonic move; in fact she was a coward; in general we found little worth emulating in adults. It was incontrovertible, though, that the loudspeaker above the blackboard would crackle three or four times a week and the voice of Elise Bock, school secretary now as before, would come through it: Gantlik to the principal's office. Anita said goodbye to her German or biology teacher with a slight sigh, curtsied per regulations, and packed up her notebooks as though saying goodbye forever. Two periods later, sometimes after three o'clock, she'd be back at her seat—having translated for Mr. Jenudkidse in City Hall; since Slata was gone. A modest girl. Walked into the school in her well-worn black suit as if joining a solemn rite. Spoke softly, eyes downcast. She probably thought that wearing her long dark-brown hair in braided loops around her head was the fashion in Gneez. A wide, squat forehead behind which there was a lot of worrying that fall. She was clumsy, too— borrowing notes for the classes she missed from none other than our top student, Dieter Lockenvitz. His hair stood up straight and white with distraction; under the pressure of his cogitations he failed to notice that this girl would have liked very much to sit down at his desk for a minute and have him point out various of his lines and formulas, especially for her, so that for once he'd notice her. When Lockenvitz would stand up at the board and try to force his way through to an algebraic victory—for in math his wheat bloomed half-choked with wheatgrass—her wide-open eyes would be fixed on him, visibly hoping for him, longing to help him; I trembled a little for her, she would've been a tasty morsel for Lise Wollenberg to gulp down. But only Pius and I saw the hopes and dreams going to waste. If she was ever happy that winter, it was when she'd forced her father to register her as a resident in Gneez and then skedaddle by return train—for the first time she was alone in a room, behind ice-cold glass, with a view of the fog and the freezing tops of the linden trees, in a foreign land, but on her own.

You know, Gesine, Gantlik wasn't my real name.

Was he your stepfather?

I wish, Gesine! Unitam! *If only he'd been a stranger with no rights over me.*

"Anita," is that a fake name too?

My mother saw a movie with a Spanish scene, heard a 1933 hit song. "Juanita." I forgive her.

But not your father.

Maybe when he's dead.

Our gentle Anita, thirsting for vengeance.

We were living on the Memel, where it's called the Neman, with a good Polish name that Gantlik's the stump of. The Germans came and offered us blue IDs—German People's Census Group One, for Persons of German Nationality with "Proven" Active Participation in the National Struggle— because of a grandfather from Westphalia. My bonehead father ups and joins the German Swastika Party because he likes seeing German tanks flatten Polish villages. Support for the Germans, and all of us along for the ride: mother, brothers and sisters. Gantlik.

Without a German passport the Germans could've easily conscripted him to work in Old Germany, Anita. Without his family. You all had ration cards, you were allowed to go to school.

A German school.

A school. You were allowed to go to the movies.

The City Mouse and the Country Mouse. *Or* Hitler Youth Quex.

And your mother could go to cafés with you, to restaurants, could shop in the stores.

And my father, as a citizen of the Reich under his German pseudonym, was compensated for the farm, was given a new one near Elbing. When the Red Army caught up to us in January 1945, we could show them in writing that we were Germans. My mother, my brothers and sisters, we buried them in an open field. My father, the German, he couldn't take care of an eleven-year-old child.

You pray, Anita. There's a request in there, about forgiving.

I do forgive. The three Russians who took me one after the other, all the Russians lock stock and barrel.

But never your father.

You mean Gantlik. Not till the day he dies. This was his war. He did it.

And then you were curious about the Russians. The kind of people who could take revenge on an eleven-year-old girl.

I was, Gesine. Still am today.

Do you know what we used to say when Triple-J summoned you out of the classroom? "Anita's off to give blood." Because it always had to be you. Because you came back so exhausted.

It was Pius who said that.

Pius was a good man.

I should say so. I didn't used to tell anyone about the Neman, the Memel, because I was scared you'd all call me Volksdeutsch *behind my back. Or "foreign war-booty girl."*

Student Gantlik rid herself of her father when she was able to trace, via the Red Cross, a sister of her mother's—a widow with two children, starving in the Ruhr District, to whom the words "Gneez" and "Mecklenburg" sounded like dinners with meat again. On paper this aunt became the head of Anita's household by the town moat, with Anita's pay the mainstay of the household budget; no sooner was the Western zone cut off from the Soviet one than she started whining about the sacrifice she was making for her niece, living in a region whose money bought less of everything, from butter to wristwatches, complacently forgetting that Anita had given her a roof over her head, that Anita's fees filled the common coffer, that it was Anita who was raising her aunt's two sons, around eleven years old. Her father still came up when we had to recite our genealogy to the school in order to be eligible for educational stipends (twenty-two to thirty-two marks). – My father's a worker: Anita said in as East Prussian an accent as she could manage—and wrote. Later the questionnaires became more nitpicky and general information was no longer allowed. – My father knocks rust off the Warnow shipyards in Rostock: Anita testified.

Did we profess to each other that friendship was our destiny? We most certainly did not. Anita borrowed neither paper nor pencil from the Cresspahl/Pagenkopf collective; she was also suspicious of such playacting of marriage among high-school students, or else maybe wanted to show respect for it by keeping her distance. In was Pius who, while walking past her desk, put down his extensive set of compass instruments for her, because all she had for geometry homework was a homemade protractor with no degree scale; once again Pius was trying to rub Lise Wollenberg's nose in something, plus it was hard for him to look on while someone was struggling. When Anita returned the things the next day, she thanked him with a giant sigh but ignored Student Cresspahl sitting next to him. While I was worried she would take any word from me as condescension, she was wanting not to impose. For she felt like an outsider, an undesirable, an intruder, a refugee. On a school trip, 9-A-II met a charcoal-maker building a pile and Kramritz the humanities scholar translated the sooty-skinned wanderer's Czechified comments into scientific fluency; Anita started explaining, in a voice squeaky with agitation, this work she herself had had to do as a child. Schoolgirl Cresspahl was eager to learn how you made charcoal for flatirons; Anita's voice grew softer, stammered, then ceased.

Anita, the outsider, found a patch of meadow with a path through the reeds on the south shore of Gneez Lake and thought she could be alone there; how startled she was when students from all four ninth-grade classes turned up in her habitual swimming spot, still off the beaten track in April. She covered up with her towel at once, embarrassed because she was well along in terms of developing a bust; long slim thighs and firm calves remained visible. – Nice legs: Pius said as we swam across the lake to the boathouses. – FEISTY legs: I corrected him; I'd learned that once and for all. When we got back we found her besieged by young men from tenth grade wanting to borrow her towel, complimenting her wavy, copious hair, offering her cigarettes—the usual male courtship rituals. In her confusion Anita said something dismissive in a shaky voice about how dumb people were who learned all about the structure of the human lung in school and then went and spoiled it by inhaling tobacco smoke. We—Pius and I—looked around for Lockenvitz, even though we knew he wasn't there, he was at a ZSGL session; the person who was, however, clearly visible on the edge of the group of swimmers with a cigarette between her fingers was the Cress girl, Cress on a Pole, *Röbbertin his Gesin*. What else can a person do in such a situation but proudly squint into the May sun and take a long slow draw of her cigarette—from Dresden, twelve pfennigs apiece you know, genuine imitation Lucky Strikes?

That was rude of me, Gesine; I didn't mean it.
And how could I tell you in front of all the boys there that Pius had once held your godchild at his breast—six-month-old Alex—and told me about the refreshing air that babies exhale?
Like fresh uncut silk crepe.
A breath I thought I might still have. If I wanted to keep Pius from hungering for it, I had to start smoking.
If I'd known I was causing you pain, Gesine!

That was one rapprochement; it wandered off into the reeds of Gneez Lake and was lost forever. What could Anita be expected to see but more contempt? At the same time we felt deeply sorry for each other. She for me because I'd troubled the pastor of Jerichow with a show of sincerity; the concerned and pitying sidelong look she gave me, which I could merely feel in the dim light of the confirmation car, I remember it to this day. I for her because she understood absolutely all the assignments in our science classes (math: A; chemistry: B+; biology: A) and yet the bottom line of all her equations was inevitably a God present in the molecule, the atom, the sparrows he makes fall to the ground by shooting them off the roof with nuclear weapons. Anita, authorized for Gneez, took it upon herself to travel every Sunday to St. Peter's Church in Jerichow, just because the dean in Gneez Cathedral supported the Mecklenburg pastor Schwartze (Ludwigslust) and denounced his very own bishop, Dibelius (West Berlin), as a warmonger and "instrument of American aggression," as "Atom Dibelius"; Dibelius had spoken of the administration of the Soviet occupation zone and its K-5 as a "government construct," and of the
    violence
    overstepping all lawful bounds,
    inner lack of authenticity, and
    hostility to the Gospel of Christ;
Brüshaver, on the other hand, wanted to try his luck again with Martin

Niemöller, now on the council of the Evangelical Church in Germany, signatory of the Stuttgart Declaration of Guilt, and author of the proposition that every occupying power should withdraw from the remains of Germany and keep the peace through the UN. That was why Anita was missing every Sunday when we raked the city parks in our blue shirts or dug up a third of the schoolyard for a Michurin garden; she went to see Brüshaver in her little black dress, probably dropped in on the Kommandatura to see the Wendennyches too because unlike us she was never was reprimanded for unauthorized absences. By then her name was Anita the Red, because swimming under the sun of the spring of 1949 had bleached her hair and let a reddish note shine through.

> *And I had a godchild in Jerichow, Gesine.*
> *And you took communion in Jerichow.*
> *Once every six months. Most times I wasn't worthy to.*
> *Because of evil thoughts? Tell me, Anita.*
> *Due to envious thoughts, Gesine.*

Anita could have stayed as a child of the house with the Brüshavers, but she was afraid of seeming to intrude, afraid above all of pity. Plus Aggie was just a nurse, whatever her degrees; Anita needed someone bound by a doctor's oath to keep her secret. If she'd trusted me I'd have come with Jakob's mother on the spot. That aunt from the British occupation zone let Anita do all the housework, naturally including the laundry, and they shared a bathroom but she didn't have the sense to ask a sixteen-year-old about her cycle. Everyone else Anita saw in the world were men. She went to the Gneez public health clinic, corner of Railroad Street and Town Moat, hoping the machine there might process her and let her come out the other side still anonymous. The bit about the machine was true enough. Behind those frosted-glass windows bordered with peacetime vines she learned about the gonorrhœa cervicitis that the Red Army had given her when she was eleven. She had almost *fayassn*, as they say in East Prussia—forgotten that act of revenge, thanks to constant efforts not to think about it.

Anita would later describe the quarantine barracks in Schwerin, to which she was whisked off with an infectious-disease certificate, as a camp. She was locked in with young and older ladies who'd acquired such internal complaints voluntarily, sometimes for money. Anita remembered the head doctor as a harsh, prudish woman—a bitch, "a Naziess" whom she could easily picture with a swastika on her smock. Anita was snarled at like she was guilty, or because a different guilt had come to light. The woman, with her medical expertise, accused Anita of dillydallying, but Anita had been detained in Poland when the children around Jerichow were being officially ordered to report for VD examinations (signed H. Cresspahl, Mayor), and the course of the infection was almost entirely lacking in visible symptoms, except for moderate discharge. The finding was that the infection had advanced to the cavum uteri, with endometritis specifica as the result to date. They congratulated Anita on having gotten away without pain; – Stop making such a fuss!

They used the formal, adult second-person with her because she'd been advanced into tenth grade; the radiation treatment and the sulfonamide drug that stained the urine red seemed risky to her. She escaped from the facility and made her way east, through forests and down footpaths, in the night. But there was one person who wanted her back—Triple-J in Gneez. Uniformed men in his service and pay were waiting from the Countess Woods to down in the "gray area" for just such a girl, creeping along by herself, unarmed, and claiming to be Russian. Alone in the jeep with a child who refused to give him information in his language or any other, he thought of a drinking buddy, Dr. Schürenberg, and gave him a bad scare by knocking on his door at midnight. Schürenberg at that time still had the right to place selected patients in the city hospital under his own care; it was he who finally notified the principal's office of the high school. And who was the third man with whom these two had sung and caroused in the Dom Ofitserov? None other than Emil Knoop, the man with the heart of gold ("by weight, Yuri, by weight!"), who brought the antibiotic, penicillin, back from Brussels and Bremershaven. Here one man was doing his job, and anyway he was sworn to help and to keep secrets in confidence; the second man was being diplomatic, since Comrade Jenudkidse could hear the wind of an East German state blowing across the fields of Stalin's foreign policy, and if the Soviet Military Administration was about to withdraw step by step from Gneez City Hall then a generous gesture would go over well. The third man, Emil, was not the sort to worry about laws and regulations describing such imports as a contamination of the anti-Fascist

German People's Movement with drugs of Anglo-American imperialism, not over a mere refugee girl (never mind that penicillin was being manufactured in the southern part of the Soviet Zone by a copycat people-owned pharma firm for the use of the higher echelons of the party and security force). You could learn a lot from Knoop—all of it illegal, unfortunately.

Anita spent the whole summer vacation of 1949 lying in bed, at first for just four days, because of the four injections she was getting, and then on orders of the referring physician, for malnutrition; we traveled by water, traveled to the Black Forest, passed beneath Anita's windows, and forgot her. The Twins of Jerichow, the Wendennych commandants, turned up at Anita's bedside in visiting hours to give her sweets and a volume of poetry by Aleksandr Blok. Triple-J appeared with his entourage, bringing red carnations, and decided to interpret the word "cystitis" on Anita's fever chart as tactfully as the Pagenkopf/Cresspahl students, who'd been sent—no, delegated—by their FDJ unit to call on Anita at the start of the school year. She looked disbelievingly at us, wide-eyed, not recognizing us right away—that's how permanently prepared she was to be alone, to stay alone.

Did praying help you, Anita?
It did help, moshno.
What did you think about?
I puzzled over the three boys in Red Army uniforms, one of whom was carrying gonococcus. Burning sensation when urinating, purulent discharge from the urethra—a man notices that, even during a war. So he knew what he was giving me.
And what did you read, Anita?
The kinds of things you read up on at sixteen when you've been told you have pyosalpinx, curable and infertility, permanent. That you'll never be able to have children. Mayakovsky. Nado
    vyrvat'
        radost'
            u gryadushchikh dney.
V etoy zhizni
        pomeret'
            ne trudno.

Anita stayed alone when she came to terms with the fact that if she went east she might reach the Havel River at best but never the Neman. She spent a school year staying by herself in the 10-A-II classroom while we had gym. If only she'd trusted Aggie Brüshaver. But she saw her as someone whom Christian marriage obliged to tell her husband, a man, everything.

"Anita the Red": that stayed with her. Because she still went and helped Colonel Jenudkidse with the German language, now in the Barbara Quarter, behind the green fence taller than a man's height. What were we supposed to think if not that she'd taken the Red Army's side? While the deputy president of the 10-A-II FDJ group had a terrible time unloading at least three copies of *Young World* journal among her fellow students, Anita used issues of the Red Army's *Krasnaya Zvezda* in Contemporary Studies class, even if it was from a subscription she shared with Triple-J. Her windy aunt now complained that Anita had recently started locking a certain room in the Weidling apartment behind her, both when she left and when she was there, merely because she was worried that the healthily boisterous lads, Gernot and Otfried, might damage her record player, and what was Anita listening to anyway, behind her locked door, allegedly without company? Tchaikovsky, every time. And the Red Army station, Radio Volga—the signal came in weakly from the Potsdam area. Insatiable was her curiosity about the Red Army of the Russian Workers and Farmers.

What she'd have to say to the latest news from the ČSSR would no doubt make sense to me. The Czechoslovak Communist Party leadership has rejected a meeting with their Soviet comrades and their followers in the latter's territory, accepted one in their own. As though it wasn't going to be a friendly match.

For the ČCP to make them rearrange their travel plans really is adding insult to injury. Why would they ever forgive that?

And they're wanting to send troops to the Bohemian border with West Germany.

Do you hear what you're saying? They want to send troops!

In Poland, three miles north of Czechoslovakia, they've driven up half a dozen army trucks with extra-high aerials, secured by two regiments of combat troops.

Gesine, if I were the Red Army I'd station myself in the Olza River valley

too. It's the easiest place, there are mountains all around. And what does an
army need when it's going somewhere?
  A communications center.
  You're learning, Gesine.

  "Red Anita," too—this out of ethnographic error and prejudice. For
while Anita continued to contribute more than her share to her aunt's
household budget (to keep her aunt in the household and herself with a
right to the apartment), she did keep a little something to herself for purposes that were . . . should we say private? Yes, if that means: secret. First
of all, she had to pay back Emil Knoop for the cost of her medication, at
a rate of six to eight East marks per every last one from the "West" (– only
death comes for free: Emil said in his jovial way, not noticing how she
started at the word). Finally, acting as a businessman, he gave her work to
do helping with his correspondence with the Soviet Armed Forces in
Germany, where Jenudkidse's help failed to reach. Her credit with Knoop
she left untouched, even when she had to fool her hunger with oats and
sugar roasted together with no fat. Then she would take Madame Helene
Rawehn, fine apparel, Gneez Market Square, utterly aback with fabrics of
pure wool and raw silk and terrify the young men of Fritz Reuter High
School with grown-up tailored suits, with tight skirts a hand's breadth
above the knee, with sweaters of a kind worn this year in France or Denmark and due in Mecklenburg sometime around 1955 if they were lucky.
Next to Anita, Habelschwerdt looked shabby and threadbare; but how do
you ban a student's appearance that's *comme il faut*, if a little too elegant?
It's to encourage and awaken Dieter Lockenvitz, we thought at first; except
he was precisely who she avoided. But she came to the class parties, accepted
invitations from twelfth graders and eleventh graders too; she didn't dance.
A gentleman who escorted this lady home would find himself heading
home with thanks but no handshake. Anita received requests for much
more than her towel; asked if she'd go for a walk at night around Gneez
Lake she asked the young men their intentions so openly that they had no
choice but to recognize as an imposition what they'd wanted to keep floating in the air above the promenade as a lovely dream. – What for? Anita
asked, unmoved, businesslike, and raising her head with a slight jerk, lips
pursed, clearly well aware of why and wherefore. She wore her blouses but-

toned all the way up, with a thin velvet ribbon in a double bow; "Bitter Rice" was sometimes shouted after her anyway, alluding to another Italian film notorious for very different reasons. The Anita from before had worn knee socks; cured Anita made use of stockings, nylon, seamless.

"*Red Pigtails.*" She'd had her hair cut while still in the hospital. A short, close-fitting plumage, crisscrossing her forehead in well-judged fashion, was all that remained of her braids. Fiete Semmelweis Jr. had left two tiny stray strands at the nape of her neck that stuck out startlingly red under the outer brown, shifting against and over each other every time Anita turned her head even a little.

July 24, 1968 Wednesday

On Sunday we watched an old man being taken from the bus stop bench across from our windows into a Knickerbocker ambulance—a bum in rags and a long beard, recognizable from the two shopping bags that contain his worldly possessions. He seemed to be about to cause trouble so two boys in blue made him get a move on. Since yesterday he's been back on the bench; he may live there. In return for giving back to society, needless to say, he entertains the waiting passengers: Eh, ma'am: he says: it was just that I ran into a syringe (points to his calf). So I had the police call me an ambulance.

His next sentence betrays the fact that he thinks he's in Alabama, and he wishes us a pleasant river voyage on the Manhattan and Bronx Transit Authority bus. They've shaved him a little, by force it looks like; he's a little cleaned up. He could use a shepherd and keeper besides the police department.

Anita, as a godmother.

Jakob's mother gave the baby Alexander Brüshaver a sterling silver food pusher; – *from Cresspahl an is daughter*: she said, for completeness sake. Anita would've given a lot for the matching spoon; she stood by the cradle empty-handed, clenched her teeth, looked furious. Brüshaver thanked them both for their prayers; Anita didn't yet venture to see any of her prayers as producing a result.

Easter 1950 was looming and with it a first birthday; Anita put a

Scandinavian bicycle up for sale, 600 km on the tires but well cared for, in good-as-new condition. Pius offered her eight hundred marks, cash in hand; the next day she asked him to a parley, in private, as if it were a matter of life and death. Lockenvitz had bid up the price: Pius told us, and we looked at each other in disbelief, from under furrowed brows. Lockenvitz may have an A in Latin and another in English, but he didn't have any money. Anita put down on the Brüshavers' table, as if it were nothing, a silver napkin ring with DEUT4:40 – A. B. engraved on it. Mayest thou prolong thy days upon the earth.

1951. Anita had turned into the kind of person who needed to learn to knit for this child. A two-meter-long scarf.

In 1952 was our Abitur; Anita made a wall hanging for Alex, without paying much attention, because while tying the knots she also had to memorize that force causes a change in a body's momentum m over time, following the equation $F = dm/dt$ (according to Isaac Newton). Until he was ten Alex fell asleep to a color rendition of IL FAUT *travailler* – TOUJOURS TRAVAILLER. The only formula she trusted, at that point.

In West Berlin Anita lived in a grimy building two blocks from Karl Marx Street in Neukölln, on a rear courtyard, with Mrs. Machate. Look at that, Anita has learned how to hug. The room was so cramped that there was just enough space between the bed and the wardrobe to prop up an ironing board for the guest to sleep on. First we confessed that each of us had done all right in the past four years. Once it occurred to me that the Brüshavers might have named their last child in memory of a former neighbor, I had to spend until morning telling Anita about Alexander Paepcke, in death a comfortingly good man. (Because Anita wanted to trade and sleep on the ironing board, and I refused, we woke up midmorning and lay in the one bed.)

On Anita's shelf in Mrs. Machate's kitchen I saw artificial honey and margarine; she gave me good butter and expensive smoked fish to take with me back to Alex. She rode the streetcar with me to Baumschulenweg, as if she still had papers for the East; friendship was one thing, intrusive questions another. One of her errands in the "democratic" sector must have been to get the messenger through the pocket search of democratic customs officers. So that Alex would get his needs met.

Anita was relentless with the child. Until he was eleven he got an orange from her every fourth day—never candy or chocolate. An electric tooth-brush when he was six.

In 1955 other children in Jerichow might have a schoolbag; Alex Brüshaver was equipped for his educational institution with a solid fountain pen. – Ballpoint pens have ruined all our handwriting: Anita said in her forth-right way.

In the fall, Anita began her letters to Alex *Your father Brüshaver is dead.* In the letters she had to avoid causing any trouble with the officials who opened and read and wrote reports to the authorities on them; even so, I wished they'd been kept.

Anita had worked out a basic diet for Alex's monthly packages, but she always thought of something she'd forgotten, something like band-aids. – Boys like to run around and they get scrapes!: she said, disgusted and angry at her prior forgetfulness.

And, inevitably with Anita, a children's illustrated Bible. Since what Alex was learning via the printed word were texts from the people-owned People's Knowledge Textbook Publishers:

Today the Young Pioneers are all on the meadow.

All are wearing the blue scarf.

"Be prepared!" some shout.

"Always prepared!" the others answer.

She owned a tasteful frame with a removable back for photographs of Alex. In 1956 she was definitely strapped for cash, with just enough to move near the university, but expensive enlargements of the Jerichow snapshots were a necessity. Once I noticed that there was no recent picture. Anita turned away. The photo showed Alex making the Young Pioneers greeting, with the famous triangle of scarf around the neck, hand to forehead, palm out, fingers clawed heavenward, promising his support to the oppressed of all the continents of the earth. How I had to beg to be allowed to see that one!

When Jakob had died and the funeral had happened, Anita the god-mother treated me harshly. She thought my presence at the cemetery would have helped me. Since she was talking over an open phone line from West Berlin to Düsseldorf, she spoke vaguely. As if a doctoral student in Slavic Studies knew ways to sneak into Mecklenburg.

– There are factions in the Red Army too: she said.

Anita connected to a Soviet military mission? Carrying messages? She didn't invite any questions.

In 1956 Anita already possessed a passport from the Republic of France, and it finally occurred to her: A boy needs a pocketknife with thirty-two attachments.

What a boy of eight could really use is a bicycle. So it was a good thing that the Gift Service GmbH, Genex, headquartered in Switzerland, was founded in 1957. Payment in Western currencies, deliveries in East German goods, but punctually, within the space of a month. Anita could even decide whether Alex should ride to the Baltic on a blue or silver painted frame, with or without a gearshift. (She avoided giving him unambiguously Western devices. Alex should grow up without the envy of other children, without warnings from schoolteachers.)

She suppressed any missionary impulses. She worked hard to forgive her classmate Cresspahl for leaving the Evangelical Church almost as soon as she'd found a paying job "in the West"; she even forgave her her argument that the Church has it so good uncontested under capitalism that it doesn't need a tax to help it out. Anita confidently expected that the child Marie would be given a Christian baptism; if she was upset and disappointed, it was for our sake.

In 1959 Alex Brüshaver was safely doing the right thing in school. He came in first in an essay contest and won a toy: a battery-operated tank, in olive battle color, that could roll on its treads and swing its cannon to face the class enemy at the same time. To strengthen Alex's will to defend the homeland. You'd think a child would love such items of mechanical art. Anita wasn't sure, and asked. He sent her a postcard with a picture of the East German custodian on one side, and on the other he'd dedicated the following to her:

What use is it to dream of peace?
Who defends the young state?
The doves themselves need armor,
That's why I am a soldier.

In his next mailing the thing itself arrived, in wrapping paper and olive-green ribbons. For years to come, Alex stood up every morning in school to hoist the flag and recite the slogans, the Song of Rebuilding included. "Youth, awake and rise up! Build up, build up, build up!"

In 1960, Mrs. Brüshaver was kicked out of the Jerichow pastorage but was given two rooms near the Rose Garden in Gneez. Anita took two weeks off to travel to Mecklenburg with paint, to help set up a widow's apartment, to spend fourteen days with Alex. (Whenever Anita considered a legal regulation unreasonable, she got around it without a second thought. Anarchism? Stubbornness? Mischief?)

Before we moved to New York there was a vacation Anita invited us to spend in West Berlin. For self-interested reasons, she insisted. She'd been going out with an émigré from the lands of Karelia for years, and now he wanted it in writing that they belonged to each other, and she wanted another woman to check him out first. Sometimes a godmother needs a godmother of her own. I had to swear to her twice before she entrusted me too with the explanation of why she would never in her life have a child besides Mrs. Brüshaver's in Mecklenburg. She'd told her boyfriend—he wants to be known as "the old man," nothing else—in their first year; she still wasn't sure if he was truly willing to forgo reproduction. The old man and I—he passed the test, we came back from a daylong walk through the Berlin woods near Schulzendorf, Anita was sitting with Marie in the Old Tavern garden in Dahlem. Marie was startled, the wind or she had knocked over a full glass. Anita was explaining the course of events to her. – *Le vent*: she said: *vous comprenez?* – *Le vent*: Marie said: *vous . . .*

The other matron of honor was Mrs. Brüshaver, – *because I'm closest to hand now*: the gallant lady felt. But the truly closest was Alex, twelve years old, in his confirmation suit and tie. So Anita had two children at her wedding. Protestant, of course, what else.

Anita watched the children, who were bored by the ceremonial meal, passing the time with pen-and-paper games. Anita wrestled down her prejudice and cried out: They're both good children!

For many years Marie thought of Berlin as a city flooded with breezes and sunlight, where you go to get married.

After the authorities in East Berlin built a wall through Berlin to keep their citizens from continuing to vote with their feet, Anita is said to have used a bar on Henriettaplatz as a travel agency that helped people cross the borders of the other Germany. She denies it. The bartender on Henriettaplatz had a different name, she says; that bartender was just twenty-four, had problems with her relatives . . . When Anita wants to she can easily look four years younger, even today. And she doesn't care much about names when they're printed on official paper, we know that.

Whoever it might have been, I took trips for Anita after I lost my job in New York. I tried out passports in transit from Prague to Warnemünde, from Trelleborg to Vienna. During these trips my name was often that of the people about to take these trips, and I pleaded an age that wasn't my real age too, just as Anita requested.

By 1962 the East Berlin philosophers had convinced themselves that cybernetics was a science and a tool, not an instrument of capitalist exploitation; Alex had long since been the owner of a beginner's computer-science handbook. Likewise books that state who actually invented the telephone. For reference.

At fourteen Alex was conceited. Couldn't pass a shop window in Gneez without checking his reflection. Making sure the dark lock was curled on the right corner of his brow. Anita was worried. – Who'd he get that from?: she asked (in letters to New York).

She sent him the American gold miners' pants with the studded pockets when he asked for them. Then, since she happened to know his size, she had a khaki-colored linen suit made for him. Anita won that round.

At sixteen Alex started smoking. After 1962 a citizen of the GDR could purchase Western tobacco products at domestic stores, the Intershops, assuming he or she could put West German marks or American dollars on the counter in such establishments. Anita sent her godchild no cash. Cf. Gneez Lake, "Lucky Strikes" from Bulgaria or was it Dresden?

In 1966 Alex was seventeen and signed his name "Alexander." He sent a photo from a trip to Poland, from which a round-headed Mecklenburger looked out at us from under curly tousled hair, with soft lips, but somber. His broad shoulders, wet from swimming, were like Anita's. Still, it bothered her that this photo might have been taken by a girl. – He's still just a child!: she cried.

The next year he was eighteen, of age under East German law, and for his birthday he was informed of two things. First, that as the son of a pastor he would not be permitted to study at the university (mathematics). Second, that he was invited to fulfill his military service requirement in the defense and protection of his Socialist fatherland. Anita had predicted the first; she was prepared for the second.

If Anita were the missionary type, she would have managed to convince him to work harder in Russian. She accepted his merely satisfactory grades in this language, if with a sigh. The hiking trips to Poland, he'd thought of those without her too. She may have been waiting for him to say he wanted to go to "where you got married" again; she didn't let herself try to talk him into it.

So how would Alex ever get the crazy idea into his head that Anita could take him by the hand and out of the country to wherever he wanted to go? He's a do-it-yourselfer, and he lets himself get caught in the Stettin harbor in the proven act of trying to leave a Socialist fatherland behind at his own discretion. Alex is sentenced to three years in a prison in Saxony. He's allowed to write to Gneez from there. Anita is left empty-handed.

And what does Anita write to tell us, as though she had no troubles of her own? She invites Marie to live in West Berlin for as long as I'm working in Czechoslovakia; she promises to keep a perfectly regular household—with no trips. Anita with no trips. She asks Marie to visit, so she can work on her own English.

As if she, too, has agreed to present me with the ČSSR as a country you don't take a child to. You send the child to a godmother.

July 25, 1968 Thursday

To dissuade Soviet troops from any thought of crossing the Czechoslovakian border to defend it, Prague television is showing the vigilant tanks, dogs, and barbed wire fences that they have there already. The West German government has decided to move the maneuvers they'd planned for Grafenwöhr and Hohenfels, near this border, to the area near Münsingen and to a mountain ridge known as the Heuberg, in the state of Baden-Württemberg, some 100 to 150 miles away. So that the Red Army can withdraw, to its homeland, eastward, with one less thing to worry about.

Dr. Julius Kliefoth was removed from his office as principal of Fritz Reuter High School before the end of the 1949–50 school year. His students had to get through the change without an official justification; were they supposed to think Kliefoth had shown "conduct unbecoming a teacher"?

Stubborn, that's what Kliefoth was. In 1947, summoned before the school board to accept a food parcel he'd been allotted so that at least the head of a civil service office would be properly provisioned amid the ravenous children, he refused any special treatment; apparently he was sufficiently taken aback to utter the word "corruption." A year later, in March 1949, the German Ministry of People's Education officially approached him and ordered, at the behest of the Soviet Military Administration, an increase in his salary and purchase coupons above and beyond his ration card, as well as preferential credit in case he wanted to build a house of his own. This was meant to keep people like him from going forth and building a log cabin in the Western occupation zones. Kliefoth would have loved a two-week visit to England. When reminded of his rank in the school administration, and how inappropriate it was to be subletting an apartment on Field Road in Jerichow, he declined to move into an apartment of his own on Cathedral Square in Gneez; he took the milk train to work, often didn't return home until evening, on the bare wood of the unheated compartments, and considered himself lucky when he'd managed to buy kerosene for his lamp. Now the Mecklenburg Ministry of People's Education lacked a lever with which they could remind him of favors received. *Kliefoth was a tough ol Murrjahn but in the end 'e had ta give in.*

The Mecklenburg Interior Ministry was disappointed with Kliefoth as well. He was ordered to report to Gneez City Hall on May 15 and 16, 1949, where they were holding the vote on the Third German People's Congress. It was a historic session in its exemplary eschewal of the word "election" or "choice," *Wahl*, boiling things down to a single alternative. The question was simply whether the eligible voter were for peace or against peace—whichever one you want, really. A Yes would install in power a Unity list of candidates from the existing parties, en masse, so that anyone's displeasure at, say, the Communists, over, say, their strangulation of West Berlin would also lessen the mandate of the Free German Youth; or a preference for the party of the Soviet Union, perhaps because it had let food and work materials back into that city for the past three days, would equally unintentionally advance the cause of the Cultural League (for the R. of a D. G.). Kliefoth was a civil servant; he failed, in his innocence, to realize that the authorities wanted to take advantage of the civil trust he enjoyed—things were surely aboveboard if *our Julius* was supervising them. Educated man and all, had ta respect him. Now he obeyed in all rigor, feeling bound by a formal, official assignment. On the first day, his polling place was run like a classroom. He looked at the voters like examination candidates, welcomed the uncomfortable ones with encouraging murmurs, obligingly spoke Platt. In *this* location Gneez voters, either presenting a valid ID or known to him personally, would step up to the urn on their own, the police having no other right than to escort non-local individuals out onto the street. Kliefoth leaned his head back to look at each person stepping up to his table, instead of merely raising his eyes—an effort growing slower and slower toward evening. If he looked stern it was because he hadn't been able to smoke—the dignity of the proceedings forbade it. He was the very picture of a civil servant carrying out an assignment the government had given him.

On the morning of the 16th, instructions arrived from Schwerin—a "Blitz Telegram: Rush To Desk," signed Warnke, Interior Minister. According to these instructions, Kliefoth was to declare ballots found unmarked in the urn as valid; the large preprinted YES was sufficient. If there was writing on a ballot, it would count as one of the desired votes, except where the text showed signs of a "democracy-hostile" disposition, whatever that was. By dint of these numerical chicaneries, Peace plus the Unity list found as much assent in Mecklenburg as 68.4 out of a hundred—888,395 people— but 410,838 people had managed their ballots in such a way that their NO was immune to metamorphosis. The presiding officer's signature was missing from the Gneez Electoral Commission report; Kliefoth had given himself a leave, for "philological reasons." For the historical files he had to revise this to a "sudden onset of medical weakness"; how could a belligerent and party-loyal minister like W. be expected to approve of a civil servant who took almost a whole Monday off on his own insubordinate say-so?

Fired because of his past: was Lise Wollenberg's opinion, stated with her well-known propensity to gloat. But when the Soviets, in their Decree No. 35, declared that "denazification" was complete in the Soviet Occupation Zone as of April 10, 1948, Kliefoth had not had to interpret his life story before the special court even once (unlike Heinz Wollenberg); Kliefoth had slipped away from Berlin's Hitler party as early as 1932, to the rural pastures of Jerichow, and since the start of the war he'd kept tucked away from it in the army. Of course the Red Army wanted in writing what had been ordered in the Demyansk Pocket under Hitler's supreme command

and his, Kliefoth's, responsibility as captain on the staff of the Second Army Corps, everything up to and including his final rank of lieutenant colonel, but the Soviet Military Administration must have deemed it satisfactory. For in 1945 they left him free with an honorable discharge, and in May 1948 they recommended him to their German Administration of the Interior as an instructor of tactics in the training academies of the newly formed German People's Police, the Volkspolizei, offering Kliefoth the temptation of two salaries, civil and military, and a doubled pension; he excused himself with a medical certificate that he was missing eight teeth, and everyone knew a soldier needed a full set of thirty-two to bring to the army's table. They'd offered him back pay from the army, too, retroactive to May 1945. Of course you'd be a bit mad at anyone refusing such munificence.

It was also said that he'd allowed his grip on the reins to get loose—we know who took the reins out of his hands. For that fall of 1949 was a season of meetings in the Fritz Reuter High School. Emerging from the Third People's Congress (which Kliefoth had indeed rubbed the wrong way) had come a German People's Council, and thence a People's Chamber, which on October 7 declared the territory of the Soviet Occupied Zone to be a German Democratic Republic and the inhabitants therein to be members of said state, with a constitution, a government, and for the time being the traditional eagle on black/red/gold stripes, all to be celebrated with solemn yet festive rites in the assembly hall, which lasted either two class periods or an entire morning. For each of these, Kliefoth asked one of "the younger gentlemen" to do him the favor of presenting to the assembled youth how these events between Mecklenburg and Saxony looked in the context of other circumstances in the world, how they advanced or hindered them, with particular attention to China; Kliefoth seemed to be asleep behind the red-draped table on the podium, his narrow skull with its tuft of white hair tilted forward, hand on chin; in fact he was calculating how much of the prescribed curriculum was being lost in the time these performances took up, and watching the afternoon, too, disappear in teacher conferences on curricular renovations, meetings he had to vouch for in person to the Mecklenburg Board of People's Education. When he eventually stood up to bring the ceremony to a close, his shoulders were bent, he seemed bowed down with the cares of his office, and the claws of the Picasso dove of peace painted behind him seemed to have him by the neck—he who had once been able to speak in a tone of confident authority, looking forward to his return to work. – In this spirit . . . : Kliefoth loyally said; true, he did sound exhausted.

Kliefoth had come a cropper over the new national anthem: proclaimed individuals such as Mrs. Lindsetter, solely to pride themselves on their musical understanding. For this additional requisite of a state—a song—had been integrated into the lesson plans of the Fritz Reuter High School for November. In 2/4 time, in a simple three-verse symmetry, it accompanied the rhymed resolve of a plural subject, a We, to rise once more from the ruins and turn to face the future, along with that of a singular subject, "you," to serve a "united German fatherland," "so that" (last couplet) the sun might shine across this land, "beautiful as ne'er before." Each grade rehearsed this pretentious good-natured piece under Joachim Buck (Julie Westphal was elsewhere, in Güstrow, studying for her job as a New Teacher). "Handsome Joachim," shining of tonsure, swirling of hair therearound, lips playing incantatorily, was adept in the preparation of state occasions, having been thanked for adorning official proclamations both in the Weimar Republic and under Reich Governor Hildebrandt (see *Mecklenburg Monthly Bulletin*, 1926–1938); he gave his respective all to the present authorities as well, hurled invisible weights in the palm of his hand from way down low up to the coffered ceiling of the school auditorium, conjured his singing underage throng with an elderly rowing motion of the arms that sometimes made him look like he was pushing a medicine ball, and nodded punctually from the neck when the last note had rung out—this was how he rehearsed the lower grades. He thought he owed the twelfth graders, facing their Abitur, a more substantial scientific underpinning, a "musical history of ideas" as it were, so he opened his instruction in the new state melody with a practice waltz from *The Theoretical-Practical Piano Tutor: A Systematic Course* by the musical pedagogue Karl Zuschneid (1854–1926), a 3/4 number that sounded like a model for the admittedly less jumpy anthem. Joachim turned his amply shining eyes upon his students, so that they might notice the blindly gliding fingers at the end of his long arm. With a variation of Zuschneid's rhythm he slipped into an impudent tune that, like the preceding, seemed related, by descent and by family resemblance, to the subject of the lesson, and proceeded to inform the class that this was a song from a 1936 film, *Water for Canitoga,* sung by Hans Albers and René Deltgen to a tune by Peter Kreuder (1905):

Good-bye, Johnny,	(Newly risen)
Good-bye, Johnny,	(from the ru-ins)
we were really great together.	(to the future turned we stand.)
But, ala-as,	(Let us serve your)
But, ala-as,	(good weal truly,)

now those days are gone forever (Germany our fatherland etc.); naive handsome Joachim, simply retaining and recognizing a melodic line he may have picked up during his studies, or at the Renaissance Cinema in Gneez thirteen years ago. Still, the criminal police, D Squad (successor to K-5), accused him as early as February of having imputed a borrowing, a plagiarism, a theft to the composers of the latest version of the anthem; still, his pretrial custody turned up correspondence neither with Peter Kreuder (Argentina) nor with Hanns Eisler (Berlin/GDR). Since handsome Joachim was willing to concede a passive knowledge of the constitution, from his reading of reports, he talked his way into Article 6, "Incitement to Boycott" and Related Offenses, and as a result Buck saw the light of day again in 1952, in Lüneberg, in the West, somewhat disappointed by the state of musical scholarship there, which dismissed the origins of the East German anthem as a bagatelle rather than anything newsworthy, still, surrounded once more by a community of followers thanks to his secular performances of "Oh Eternity, You Word of Thunder" or "The Heavens Declare"; a loss for Gneez, to hear Mrs. Lindsetter tell it. And Kliefoth? Principal Kliefoth received an official reprimand. Almost entirely lacking in musical culture himself, during the official faculty meeting he had simply smirked at the curious fact which the newly founded State Security Service, the Stasi, had unmasked as an attack against the establishment of democracy. – *What nonsense:* Kliefoth replied in his measured way, when the district school board accused him of not having denounced handsome Joachim on the spot, as he should have. The two gentlemen had been in former times, 1944, confederates—they had shared an academic semester; at that point the oaken chair was heavily shifted and out was cried: *Principiis obsta!* (Ovid). Kliefoth preferred Juvenal and cried out: *Maxima debetur puero reverentia!,* by which he meant not just twelfth grade but all the students he was responsible for. His adversary was dismissed even sooner than Kliefoth was, but not before ensuring a comment in Kliefoth's file.

The end of the professional line for Kliefoth came: it was furthermore said: with the academic subject of Iosif V. Stalin (b. 1879); others were sure: it was Christmas 1949.

1949 minus 1879 equals the biblical, magical age of seventy for the distant Generalissimo, and just as the people of the new nation, the East German republic, sent "the Soviet Union's Genius Helmsman," "the best friend to the German People" close to thirty freight cars of presents, along the rail lines that still remained (adding shamefaced apologies for the delay in supplying a planetarium for Stalin's own city), so too did the students of the Fritz Reuter High School, Gneez (Meckl.), make their offerings under the Loerbrocks portrait of the honoree (members of the festival committee: Sieboldt and Gollantz; responsible for the contribution of class 10-A-II: Lockenvitz). Julie Westphal—eye sockets clenched in rigid zeal, brow curtained with bangs of stone, bosom quivering in her jacket of mannish cut, this *Olsch* on the wrong side of fifty—had had her conducting skills freshened up in Güstrow by that point; under her baton, a female choir of ninth and tenth graders performed the birthday boy's favorite song, which, with its desperate longing for the grave of a lost love, Suliko, intoned by sixteen-year-old girls' voices, was apt to cast a pall over the proceedings; following Julie's choreography, the eleventh-grade students, dressed in regulation blue shirts and blouses, stepped solemnly forward and back, raising and swinging their flags; in Julie's mandated tempo and meter, the graduating seniors called in chorus what the younger audience responded to in chorus as a vow to the Architect of Socialism, the Lenin of Our Time, the Teacher of Vigilance in Confronting the Agents of the Enemies of the People, and whatever other personal descriptions Burly Sieboldt had gleaned from the daily press of Stalin's party in Germany. Cathedral Cantor J. Buck—handsome Joachim—on guest piano supplied the P. Tchaikovskian stylings, stiffly, vivifyingly armed with neither premonition nor warning. Final number: the new anthem. Principal Kliefoth was present as master of ceremonies, grayish green bowtie in his worn collar as usual, wearing the baggier of his everyday knickerbocker suits, his thin lips performing a dry chewing motion and the discomfort of a man abstaining from smoking out of respect for the occasion. Mission accomplished.

That was December 21. For the 24th, Kliefoth had authorized 10-A-II to give another festive performance. That was thanks to Anita. This foreign child, from "East Prussia," hadn't been satisfied with the information we'd given her about the man for whom the school was named—what she'd been told about his writings had been couched in the phrases and circumlocutions Mecklenburg children used to brush one another off. As a result of her shy inquiries, we rehearsed the description of the Christmas celebration in Chapter Seven of Fritz Reuter's Plattdeutsch monument *Ut mine Stromtid* (*Seed-Time and Harvest*, 3 vols., 1864) and performed it for our parents as a narrative with staged episodes. For what parents we had. Normally Anita would've had to pay for her suggestion by appearing on stage in person, but we were sufficiently embarrassed to cast Student Cresspahl, alas, in the role of Fru Pastor Behrendsen. In the words of the poet: *Everything about her was round,—arms and hands and fingers, head and cheeks and lips*; Cresspahl wound blankets around her hips and stooped and pretended to be forty and did her hair up in a bun—Anita was upset. Anita had invited the Brüshavers and thought Aggie would take offense at this embodiment of a pastor's wife scurrying *like quicksilver* round the Christmas tree and perpetually asserting that *surely she's closest to hand*. But Aggie laughed along with the rest of the audience, and clapped—*a good woman, she was*. Burly Sieboldt took a turn as Pastor Behrens, and Lise was *Lowise*, and *Rika with er loud voice* was played by Schäning Drittfeld who fainted on us right after the last *Julklapp* Christmas gift. There was no shortage of village youths—Fru Pastor had real pfeffernuesse and apples to hand out. We'd cut the part of melancholy Franz in favor of Jürn the coachman: Pius was Jürn, and the commentator, and had the last word with his *drive through the village, the songs coming from the poor little laborers' shacks, and up in the heavens God had lit up his great Christmas tree with a thousand shining lamps, and the world lay stretched out beneath like a Christmas table, which winter had spread with a cloth of whitest snow, that spring, summer, and autumn might cover it with Christmas gifts.*

That Dr. Kliefoth thanked the participants and wished them and the audience a merry "Christmas holiday" was the straw that broke the camel's back. Because he could have stopped us. He'd had on his desk for at least a week the directive permitting winter school celebrations only for the Generalissimo, or else for the Soli-boy, whoever that was. Kliefoth was likewise informed that the official designation of this break in the school's operations was henceforth "the winter holidays"; and that is what it has been called in Gneez and Mecklenburg to this day.

It meant "the Solidarity Child," Fru Cresspahl.
With a nightshirt, a lit tallow candle in hand, like the Darmol ad?
Or the Coal Thief caricature. But I must say, that part about the camel's back is an Anglicism, Fru Cresspahl.
All right: Which drop made the barrel run over? How did we lose you?
They could take their pick of reasons. Safety violation: no firefighter on the stage.
There was a bucket of water and a bucket of sand, Mr. Kliefoth—we'd thought of that.
But was there anyone wearing a helmet, axe in hand?
There was no medical team either.
Right! And whatever was wrong with Christiane Drittfeld? I remember her as a buxom lass, rosy-cheeked even. No, stout.
She was about to go away with her parents over New Year's, to the West. The need to keep silent, the secret goodbyes, were probably too much for her.
Moreover, you had the wrong author.
Fritz Reuter had given his name to the school! I say this in a dignified tone.
The wrong text.
Written in 1862, in Neubrandenburg, Nigen Bramborg!
In which books are also distributed to children, at the end.
"Writing books and slates and primers and . . ."
"And catechisms," *Fru Cresspahl! Utilization of a democratic-pedagogical venue for Christian purposes, that's what that was called. Propaganda, it was!*
"Quosque tandem!"
"Videant consules" *is what I said.*
But you weren't fired until the following April.
That was when the fat really hit the fire. There was sposed to be an essay writtn everywhere cross Mecklenburg, "What My Teacher Has Told Me About Stalin," and none came in from my school.
A kind of pedagogical public referendum.
Not in my school.

Plus it would've been better if you'd gotten a few less letters from your friends at English universities.

Or joined the National Democratic Party, where they'd gathered all the known Nazis in one place, and the riffraff from the army. That would've helped for a while.

So who's right, Lindsetter? Or bringing in Stalin? Or Christmas?

You figger it out. They could use my age too.

Dr. Kliefoth was a full year away from retirement age in 1950.

But you know who was called a Murrjahn, and was one too.

The last time Gesine Cresspahl saw her principal in the school was when he substituted for one of his "younger gentlemen" and taught a class in the map room. He had trouble handling the long poles wound with big heavy sheets. A thin line of spittle was on his lips after a Latin class with the seniors. He recognized her right away when it was her turn and she asked for the physical geography of South China, but he looked at her as if her eager greeting came as a surprise. Alert, cheerful eyes in steep-sloped sockets, tucked into thick wrinkles—an owlish look. And because Kliefoth disappeared in the middle of the school year, without an assembly to thank him and say goodbye, it was too late for a torchlight procession in his honor the first time he resigned, and later such a gesture was seen to be "inopportune," a translation for a simpler word. Because it would have meant a twelve-mile trip for his students, from Gneez to Jerichow, where Kliefoth was spending his premature retirement alone with Mr. Juvenal, Mr. Cicero, Mr. Seneca. And the stories going round about his ample pension also soothed a sixteen-year-old conscience. But Student Cresspahl was now on her guard in Jerichow, her own town! She avoided the path to the garden plots where Kliefoth was cultivating thirty rods of land with potatoes and tomatoes and onions and carrots the way he'd learned to as a child in Malchow am See. As if she wasn't so sure he would fill her hands with berries.

Friday July 26, 1968

When a Czech general suggests rotating the command of Warsaw Pact troops so that it's assigned to a state other than the Soviet one for a change,

Moscow snorts and accuses him of having divulged military secrets. In Prague the ruling presidium of the CP of the ČSSR gets cold feet, removes Lieut. Gen. Václav Prchlík from his high party post, and sends him back to the army. The Soviet air defense command announced "exercises," operation "Sky Shield," extending into regions near the border with Czechoslovakia, and now the Polish Communists, too, venture to criticize their Czech brothers for lacking the will to fight against the "forces of reaction" threatening them. The Associated Press adds a photo—a camouflaged Soviet truck on East German soil, a hundred yards from the border at Cínovec; a half-recognizable wheel looks about as tall as the two Red Army soldiers next to it.

A prosecutor in Frankfurt am Main has sought a life sentence for Fritz von Hahn, for the 11,343 Jews from Bulgarian-occupied Greek territories that he sent to Treblinka, for the 20,000 Jews from Salonika that he sent to the gas in Auschwitz. He'll get his sentence next month, maybe.

Employee Cresspahl plans to write a letter today. At five to nine she steps in front of Mrs. Lazar's fortresslike desk and tries to give her a smile; she may be here straight through to evening with this work she's assigned herself. She does it with the door open, without first taking out the colored ribbon and typing on white paper with a carbon underneath. She does it *with company equipment, on company time*—that's how reckless she is now. Because anyone who comes in, Henri Gelliston or another of the vice president's young men, will see a page of writing in a foreign language, not addressed to an allied firm, suggesting private business.

Salutation.

Missing. Could endanger the recipient. Because of the name, or the code name. He has renounced the usual adjective himself, although we'd much rather have begun with *Dear*...Unfortunately it would be something of a lie.

(Dear) (J. B.—cut); we can't do that. The salutation in German would say that we like and respect you, and also expect the same in return. And who is it who's prevented us from saying that? You have, by lying to us. The salutation sticks in our throat. The tongue in the throat, you remember. We speak to you with dissembled voice—no, not even to you, just in your direction. We give no address, neither Rövertannen in Güstrow, nor Christinenfeld in Klütz, nor Markkleeberg Ost in Leipzig (alter all the names!).

We don't want to make it any easier for them to look up your notorious registration card with the People's Police by giving a building number on any Street of Peace/of German-Soviet Friendship or even a Stalin one now renamed half after a mysterious Dr. Frankfurter and half after Marxandengels. Anonymouses of the world, unite!

We're saying *du* to you, the informal pronoun, to make it clear how we used to address each other; we're talking to you as if to an unknown cat, with shimmering fur or unkempt, it makes no difference, and needing our care or our contempt for letting herself go like that.

We're talking to you as a "we," to give you the excuse of the unfathomability of a group, and conversely so that you can presume for the time being, and write in your report, that one is speaking for others with whom he/she has taken your side, to ensure that you are trusted and the very mention of your name respected. Take your pick and you'll figure it out— also what you've destroyed.

In deference to your anxieties, you will find this in your mailbox but not brought and previously inspected/photocopied/registered/indexed by the German Post Office of your country, since we intend to pay only for conveyance and delivery, by no means for technology or personnel costs in Location 12. That is why you might receive this between bedsheets that a people-owned business, Lilywhite, or a Workers' Cooperative Union, Progress Laundry, returns to you. Or when opening a book you've requested to borrow. Or unexpectedly crinkling in your jacket pocket. Some way that it'll end up right in your hand, and yours alone.

So that it'll be well and truly concealed whether and that you have ever been an in-law/friend/sublettor with or of anyone named Gesine Cresspahl (cut this), a person still thinking of you from beyond your borders. So that you could be a nominal aunt of ours. A seminar leader, female; a teammate, male, whom we always had to greet with a balled fist or the cry of "Friendship!" Anyone from among that innumerable company of members of the Socialist community of humankind—we're quoting here. A man in a gray flannel suit (cut).

You should always be in a position to state for the record that this must have been addressed to someone else, you've never in your life been the author's Roman or countryman. Whether you're male or female, bearded or uncurtained—we say nothing. Nor about the business/laboratory/institute in the German Democratic Republic in which you so laudably ply your trade/science/ability/habits, albeit without glorious honor and recognition from your national government, but still so that certain of your patrons/sponsors/coworkers/pen pals deem it appropriate and worthwhile to honor the round number or some other number of your birthday with a collective reminiscence/tribute/festschrift.

It's no secret how these German-style festschrifts go: the jubilarian is supposedly never and reliably always asked whom he'd like to see included and who would be embarrassing, who an unattainable honor, who a scandal; in your case: whether you could make your peace with a publisher and place of publication abroad, where those honoring you can do so without harmful or awkward consequences for your honorable person. Far be it from us to reveal whether the editors here have found a publisher in Finland or France, Sweden or Switzerland; all we have to say about the place of publication is that it should be in a country on a large body of water between two oceans. Or three. Nicer typesetting, presumably. But printed in a British colony? Gibraltar? Hong Kong? *Our lips are sealed.* And let it be a private joke, among the like-minded, for your sake.

So we were deaf in one ear, while happily hearing perfectly well in the other, when the editors approached someone to open the string of pearls of expert dedications and obeisances with a biographical squib, which many years of contact and inclinations thereto made that someone capable of; and also at whose request: yours. *For your comfort and safety* I doublechecked, twice, in writing: yes, you asked them to ask me. It was clear in any case—who else could have given them my address, my apartment, down to the phone number, if not you. I (= we) had to take it as an assignment from you. Confirmed and attested in black on white. Here we had a place to begin, it seems.

We are, as you well know, subjected to five eight-hour days a week of work; I can tell you in confidence that it's more than that. Still, there's always the weekends. It's true, we could have foisted the job off onto a Comrade Writer we have handy, in fact totally in our hands; but since you suggested me, it had to stay with me, between us. My English, as you might well imagine—the stipulated language—unspools passably enough in professional matters, when it comes to *assets and liabilities* and credit lines resulting therefrom, but never in my life have I attempted belletristic prose with it. And that's what's needed to put down on paper a person's life, what can be known and presumed, what's been seen and heard. Don't you think? For other people to read as well, and recognize you there, for their amusement and instruction? I admit it, humiliating though it is: I needed two dictionaries on my desk. As though my English would disappear on the spot if I tried to use it to say how someone was (might have been) in school, how he looks biting into a Thuringian bratwurst (a cold boiled egg), how he gets through a storm at sea (a summons from the secret police / the East German Stasi), whether he can sleep easy or should take to his heels immediately. I started by moving around you like a tailor (male or female), trying to find out what's under the fabric and how my own might sit on your shoulders and limbs. I also tried to look at you like a young girl/boy with a crush on the special way you purse your lips, move the muscles around your eyes, place your legs. How you clear your throat, how you . . . I thought, as you know, about your parents. There was one thing about which I kept absolute and perfect silence. I praised what I liked, wove what bothered me into a stitchery of teasing. My thoughts hurt the whole time, I was working so hard; by the end I could sometimes feel your presence, as if you were now there. Fourteen and a half pages, two thousand characters each, and off to the main post office at eleven at night to send it off to the editor with the next airmail.

Then silence, and the date of the occasion came and went. Finally the explanation that you'd had my document smuggled over the border to you, in pants pockets, matchboxes, what do I know, so that you could read what I in particular had to say about you. What'n honor (but: "festschrift" and "jubilarian," qqv.). After another while, the information that you'd recognized yourself, actually both of us, in the piece and, while admitting to a certain diffidence, were happy to accept the portrait as on the whole accurate, knowing what I'd left out of it out of friendship.

Well all right then. 'Slong as you're happy. No problem. I waited for requests for changes. Again like a tailor.

But none came. Instead, the message that there's no possible way to publish our piece, because it's known that we're so-and-so.

You could've known that when you asked us, doncha think?

Obviously we'll withdraw the piece. True, we do have a contract (payment: zero); but we won't insist on it. Why should we stand in your way if you've got a hankering to become a factory manager/a Meritorious Doctor of the Republic/a coach of the national team/no-previous-criminal-record? with regard to your art/technique/physical ability to travel to the NonSocialistEconomicSphere, the West? On the contrary, we would like to see your knowledge or skills presented in Helsinki and Leningrad, Pasadena and Mexico City, by none other than yourself.

Without our needing to be there in person, of course.

You have stipulated a festschrift in the field of endocrinology/forestry/molecular biology/mathematics/art history/heating engineering—purged of the piece of life that you had in common with us.

Which makes us think that here, like there, you are transferring the needs of your government into your own person—exigencies of a kind that you simply impute to the GDR in an interpretation that is all too obsequious and far-fetched.

For if we do run into today's emissaries and guardians of your national government, they'll likely hold it against us that we left without asking the law, whose answer to such questions we knew in advance to be No and which punished even the asking with prison. And yet the machine guns remain unraised before us; the GDR says Good day and Have a nice trip; it provides room and board if we're willing to pay in our NonSocialist money, while keeping the non-NonSocialist money that should be ours locked up safe in its very own State Bank. Auf Wiedersehen, it says that too.

Possibly it's keeping in mind the useful services we might be able to render it after our farewell, namely mentioning it as a foreign (*ausländisch, outlandish*) state, as it is required to be for reasons of recognition (details under a three-letter abbreviation; direct mail to the editors). That would be one of our deeds worthy of gratitude.

You took up our time. Which is fine—I've liked a lot of people in my life. But you misused it, since you knew it would be in vain and for nothing; you *wasted* our time.

We understand the limitations you're operating under; but we're sure that you've brought a good part of them on yourself. Still, since you say so, all right: you can get only from us, via a private mailing address, a thousand little things of everyday life that your national custodian and his successors keep from you, from academic books to toilet paper. You're perfectly happy walking around in your country wearing a jacket made from fabric you've had us send you, a transistor radio at your ear that we sent you on your request. But it's impossible for you to admit to any contact with us professionally, publicly, or in official correspondence—even the proximity of our name would harm your career/cadre dossier/biography/reputation. We understand that. We in no way intend to keep you from perceiving your human rights.

Last night it was relayed to us, as indisputable sight and sound: you are walking around in your country with our memories of you, the eulogy you've swindled out of us so that you could hear it while you were still alive, the things we've preserved about you and considered valuable. We hear: you're reading it to friends, always in an intimate circle, as a plea for pity for your bad situation, in which you're unable, for reasons of state, to have such nice things about you printed.

Since last night we've been walking bent double, inwardly, we're so embarrassed. So ashamed.

We'd like to take back what we wrote for you, trusting you.

Elli Wagenführ. (Change the name. But how could Somebody Orother replace Elli Wagenführ?)

We told you about her, and that was not right. How she used to slip out of Peter Wulff's kitchen, plates in both hands, – Coming through!: she'd cry: *Hot and greasy!*, and the market-day clientele would declare that something hot would suit them nicely, even in the middle of the summer, and make remarks about her fat. Undid her apron strings. Looked forward to getting a slap. I'm sorry. I take it back. (Change the name. Pub in Jena.)

And the gorse. We walked past the gorse, the German broom, it was in full bloom; I couldn't help but express my pleasure in its blue and yellow. – Gorse? you asked: *Ginster*, like the guy who wrote the novel written by himself? You got our gorse; we contest your ownership of it.

And that we ever thought we had no need to take further precautions, and we could send you the collocation, a piece of the old homeland, a view of the Baltic: *blue as blue can be.* We're confiscating that back.

And that I expected my father to put up with you, when he had to say yes because he was trying to console me. If I was bringing him a stranger, I was vouching for that person too, was I not? So that he'd watch you as if you deserved his politeness, maybe offer you his hand, as a guest. How can I make that never have happened. I'm ashamed of it.

If I have to choose between betraying my friend and betraying my country,
I hope I shall have the guts to betray my country. —E. M. Forster
You all gotta look at it dialectically, doncha. Well, then, be glad.
And don't worry. We'll deny knowing you. We've never known you.
Will that help you out? No, you've had nothing to do with us. We
don't care two figs about you. Will this assurance help you/give you a
promotion/get you a lease on your apartment? Is your national variety of
self-understanding, your *identity*, relieved of any possible offense? We're
strangers. Always have been. How could we sign off in the end if we'd ever
been your acquaintances/coworkers/roommates. To other people, we say
Bye or *Take care* or *Mind where you're going*, sometimes by request *À Dieu*.
To you we say Enough and Never and Finis.

(Send a clean copy as a photocopy to be forwarded. Pretend to be covering a signature here.)

Today *The New York Times* wants us to feel sympathy for a housewife
(who herself prefers that her name not be mentioned). She comes into
Manhattan from Long Island to do some shopping. Suddenly, hey, she
decides why not meet her husband for lunch? Tries the phone booth on
the southwest corner of Sixty-Second and Madison. Her dime comes back
out—no dial tone. She marches twelve blocks north up Madison, trying
seven more public phones; the eighth doesn't even have a dial. She's three
dimes poorer now.

But the phone in the bank obeys for once. Sam sends a warm ham sandwich straight up from the basement at her request, with tea, brought by a
messenger, who as requested puts the paper bag down on the chair next to
the door without a word. He understood the dime she'd left there likewise.

Things are going reasonably well in international communication too.
Around when we're finishing our clean copy we get a call from the Stafford
Hotel, London, will we accept the charges? Of course. And there at the
other end of line, at an hour when the English should be asleep, is de Rosny,
a vice president, checking up in person.

– Working hard as always, my dear Mrs. Cresspahl? de Rosny pronounces.
He is imitating an Englishman. No, he announces to a colleague: Just look
how well trained my people are!

– But of course: Employee Cresspahl replies from New York, shamelessly.

– Desk still full then? de Rosny says, exaggerating the Etonian voice.

– Almost empty. Just finishing up now. Sir.
– Before the big trip, eh?

Which we'd have preferred to forget.

– Do I know this ... person? Marie wants to know back on Riverside Drive. If she were older than her proud eleven, you would have to call her look solicitous. Is her mother ultimately hurting herself? True, she's sitting there making the heraldic Mecklenburg ox-head—both fists on her temples. Isn't her mother plucking out something that offends her, and in the end it's a bit of her eye?
– I forget the year. You were eight and a half. We were visiting ... a Socialist country, planning to meet Anita, and instead we ran into this person and were glad that he was ... at least able to take trips in an ... easterly direction.
– This was the person you sang in public with, right?
– The wine was strong that night, Marie.
– "Marble Breaks and Iron Bends"?
– You were so ashamed of your mother.
– I was jealous. Just bursting into song whenever you're in the mood— that takes courage.
– *Which you did solely to keep New York clean.*
– "But our lo-ove will ne-ver end"?
– That's what he used to think, once, in 1955.
– So this is the person you—
– Careful now!
– also went places with before my time?
– We plead innocent, Your Honor.
– And why is Socialism bad in privately printed matter from the Non-Socialist Economic Sphere?
– Because its custodian has an unfortunate predilection for archives.
– Who delivers mail like this for you? Anita? Günter Niebuhr?
– I'm afraid we can't answer that, Your Honor.
– That's how you kick people out of your life?
– That's how I send them off, and wish them bon voyage.
– You want me to learn that.

– I want you to know. And since when does our apartment smell of roast cauliflower in the early evening, with the windows open? Were you cooking? The breadcrumbs are out, there's parmesan in the air.

– I ... It's a secret, Gesine. I'll tell you tomorrow.

– I'm much too tired to eat anyway. Is it all right with you if I go to bed now? If you let me sleep till ten tomorrow morning?

– Sleep as late you want, Gesine.

July 27, 1968 Saturday

Woken by the silence: it was roomy, it contained birdsong. All through the night sleep knew that the alarm clock was muzzled, and wake-up time it set for when the cars are deployed on Riverside Drive, the first children taken to the park. The dream showed a wood thrush, showcased a red-breasted thrush, went as far as to offer a tanager—all discarded. For all these are busy by this time of year remodeling their nests, raising their progeny. The one singing here was a wren, a *Zaunkönig*—king of the fence. A cheerful little monarch perched on the park's chain-link, beyond the hot still road, in the warmed shadows of the magnificent *hickories* ... the walnut trees, present in the dream as an oil print in Pagenkopf's hallway. I woke myself up.

Quarter to ten; greeted by a staging of breakfast: tea waiting on the hot plate, two places set, two eggs waiting under their little caps; only the napkins are still empty of rolls. *The New York Times* is there, and what's not there is Marie or even a note from her. The young lady is out for a mysterious morning walk.

Edward G. Ash Jr. of Willingboro, NJ, US Army, and David A. Person of Tonawanda, NY, US Navy firefighter, are reported as killed in Vietnam.

The British Communists are avoiding any hint of reproach of their great Soviet brothers, but they nonetheless stand there and find it just swell how the Czechoslovak party is tackling "the wrong of the past," insisting on Socialist democracy, and what do they serve for dessert? "Only the Czech people and their Communist party can decide how to deal with their internal problems." These number 32,562 people in Great Britain (not counting abstentions).

Antonio (Tony Ducks) Corallo, of the Mafia, got what was coming to him in the Federal Court on Foley Square. For attempted bribery of a Water Department official: three years in prison. But the maximum sentence would have been five years and a $10,000 fine. Now, assuming good behavior...

Yesterday a thirty-four-year-old man from Astoria (we almost lived there), Vladimir Vorlicek, walked into the gun department of Abercrombie & Fitch, bought shotgun shells for $5.50, surreptitiously loaded a shotgun—apparently such things are just lying around unsecured there—and shot himself in the head. He had arrived within the past year as a refugee, from Czechoslovakia. He would have made one more.

– Good morning, Marie! Look what we have here—such a beautiful child! Out visiting friends? What an elegant dress you have on, blue and white stripes, perfect with your blond braids, and silk ribbons on your bare shoulders too! Perfectly gellegant!

– Good morning, Gesine.

– Is something troubling you, young lady?

– Obviously.

– But today's not a day when anyone should feel troubled! It's the weekend, the sun is out, we could go right to the South Ferry, just say the word, Marie!

– It's that... Sometimes you like hard-boiled eggs for breakfast, Gesine. When they've been left to cool overnight.

– I do indeed! But I don't need any today.

– I wanted to make you some last night, but when they'd been on the stove for a while I started reading, then went off to my room with my nose in the book. There was a bang, and I thought of Eagle-Eye Robinson's old jalopy and its busted muffler. When I finally noticed the smell, the saucepan on the gas was black and warped and the eggs had exploded all over. Up to the ceiling.

– You sure did a good job cleaning up.

– *Danke.*

– German's the language of the day, then?

– Okay.

– In that case you need to call it a *Stielkasserolle*, a handle-pot, even if the people here somehow imagine it's a pan. Oh, sorry! Sowwy.

– Here you go. The closest . . . handle-pot I could find on Broadway. Aluminum too. With my own money.

– The old one was old, we should've thrown it out a long time ago. Amortized for four years. Tell me, classmate, are you in the mood for a quick lesson on amortization law? The keeper of the household budget deliberates, approves, and authorizes the expenditure.

– Make it halfsies.

– Half and half! Done! So now smile! I'm the one to blame, with my sense of smell! Roast cauliflower!

– I fear, Madame, that this, Mrs. Cresspahl, is a sign of advancing age.

– Is today a South Ferry day, Marie?

– I'd rather have *brunch*. The tape recorder is saddled up, toast's on its way, and a lemon for the tea.

– Supposing, *posito*, we had a guest with us from the ignorant *Wildernis*—from, let's say, Düsseldorf: how would we translate that for him?

– *Breakfast and lunch in einem.* A big . . . midday breakfast. *Gabelfrühstück!* Breakfast with a fork!

– Instead of fish with a spoon and scrambled eggs with tongs.

– What do you charge for an hour of German lessons?

– An hour of "Contemporary Studies," you mean. I'll take one *insalata di pomodori e cipolle. Puoi condirla?*

– *Coming right up! Coming right up!*

– Contemporary Studies: that was a New Subject, insofar as the Nazis would've called it "Ideological *Weltanschauung* Inculcation," and also insofar as there would be a new instructor at the Fritz Reuter High School teaching it to class 10-A-II in 1949–50. Her name was Selbich—not much older than twenty, we'd heard, and the principal pro tem. Teaching this kind of subject would be seen as quite useful probation if she was out to get her promotion made permanent.

– Selbich . . . Selbich . . .

– Principal replacing Dr. Kliefoth.

– Oh boy. His successor was an outsider, and young, and female. That's not easy.

– And that is precisely why the seventeen-year-olds decided to give her the benefit of the doubt: it must have been the dignity of her office that kept the new principal from shutting the classroom door behind her herself, and give the nod for the task to the lowest in the room, Mrs. Lindsetter's niece, Monika ("Peter"). We were perfectly ready to make allowances for her teetering along as if her feet hurt (– Not like any woman alive: Pius whispered), standing up stiff and straight as a commanding officer reviewing soldiers on parade, and surely she couldn't keep her grown-out blond hair from hanging down so stringily unless she brushed it for half an hour every morning. The students of 10-A-II rise to their feet and stare at the new Contemporary Studies teacher's shirt. For she was wearing, with a brown skirt, the blue FDJ shirt, complete with epaulettes and an emblem on the sleeve. At this point Kliefoth would have made a hand gesture to release us, sure of having the whole class's attention; this person inspected us at length before saying: Sit down! And since when do I like quince jam?

– Since D. E. sent us some from Lenzburg, Switzerland, Gesine.

– All right, I'll let that go. Less edified (than I by this jam) was 10-A-II by this instructor's first question. She asked in a sharp voice: why were we all, without exception, in civilian garb rather than sporting the proud blue shirt of the Free German Youth? Pius looked at me as if wanting some kind of cue or advice. I gave my head a little twitch, meaning: Go for it! By this point our quick precise silent communication system ran practically perfectly, eluding the pedagogue's eye or at least not being provable. I knew Pius would needle her, and now that I'd recognized her I was hoping she'd join in our game. Pius raised his hand, received a stiff nod, stood up, and said in exaggerated Mecklenburgish: The blue shirt, our garment o' honor it is, ma'am. It's only on festive occasions we'd wear that. Lise Wollenberg made a similar false move, which she too would've known better than to try if she hadn't recognized this Mrs. Selbich. She blurted, unasked, without standing up to speak, familiarly, quoting from the dress regulations: *Plus a course a girl don' often have a black dress to wear every day now* (her eyes clearly on Madame Principal's brown-clad hips). But Bettina had changed more than her name—she'd lost her sense of humor, and spoke differently, in a hard voice, as if wanting to threaten us, as if we were dirt—

– Bettina Riepschläger?! It was her?

– Bettina Riepschläger, married name Selbich, divorced name Selbich too. She demanded "Silence!" in a voice as imperious as it was clumsy, and also demanded to know who the 10-A-II FDJ class president was. That was

Pius again, and while she made every effort to intimidate us by announcing that shameful conditions had been permitted to spread unchecked in our class, our whole basic attitude was in need of serious reassessment—

– Were you "a bunch of pigs"?

– she was derailed by Pius's lengthy explanation of the enormous sums of money we'd paid at the district office for a mere one shirt each, which we certainly wore for rallies, street marches, and year-end meetings, but which was too good even for potato harvest work details,

Our blue shirts black with the sweat of toil . . .

and as for the girls in our class, every last one had had complaints about the ungainly footwear that went with the uniform. – I reserve the right to return to this matter again: this new Bettina announced, as if about to hand out punishments. The old Bettina would've made it back safe to shore with a smile, telling us we must think of every moment as a festive occasion. It all could've still turned out fine.

– The things a teacher training course can do to a person!

– And a failed marriage too. And having applied to be a party member. And who knows what else.

– Had she . . .

– She'd thrown in the towel. Upset the apple cart. And this was the first time Pius shook his head when I told him something: that in middle school she'd been friendly, fun, someone you could trust, someone you studied hard for just to make her happy. Pius made a face as if now he had to start all over again if he wanted to get me; his brow was furrowed with concern, even.

– But I bet Lise Wollenberg showed up to Selbich's Contemporary Studies class the next day in a blue FDJ shirt.

– Black skirt, too. Civilian shoes though. It didn't take long before it was all tripping off Lise's tongue: that the employers in capitalist West Germany are atremble at the sight of the freedoms that the workers have won in the German Democratic Republic and will someday bring with them to the West.

– Kliefoth had had to make predictions like that too.

– A Julius Kliefoth says whatever he feels like saying. He'd translated cognitive therapy into his own terms and decided that teachers should put at children's disposal whatever the contemporary moment actually contains. If Austria gets a peace treaty all for itself, or Indonesia independence, he would in the first case assign an essay on economic geography, in the second expect us to know at least the country's population. When the Bulgarian politician Traicho Kostov admitted to planning to assassinate Dimitrov and join his country to Yugoslavia, then denied both charges, and then was executed anyway in December 1949, Kliefoth passed that information on to us as news. He held press conferences with us; we were allowed to be like reporters and ask him: Is it true that ... ? (that England has diplomatically recognized China? We could have set him up so many times; the thought of his astonished reaction, those drawn smacking lips, was enough to dissuade us. We had an agreement with him.) From the newspaper principle he transitioned to the newspapers he'd actually been allowed to subscribe to before the war—three months each one, from various French *départements* and English *counties* in turn. How beneficial this practice was for fluency in a foreign language, he said; how it nourished one's awareness of contemporary events. (Sitting in front of him were children getting a vague sense of what he had learned to do without, children who already knew that possessing a West German paper meant censure in school, while showing it to anyone else meant jail.) When Zaychik insisted on wanting to learn a foreign word for *Düsenjäger*, Dr. Kliefoth wrote to his academic friends in St. Andrews or Birmingham; he defined *jet* to us as best he could in technical terms as the *Düse*, and we learned that a *fighter* was a battle plane, a weapon at the ready. We could hear in his voice the staff officer well acquainted with airplanes from the eastern front when he added: Frightful thing, that.

 – Did Bettina believe the things she wanted to hear back from you in Contemporary Studies?

 – I hope so, for her sake. How terrible for her if she didn't! If that was part of her burden, she must have seen in our silence the mocking sympathy we felt for Dieter Lockenvitz when he stood up by the map stand in the front corner and had to report tidings of joy with respect to the imminent demise of the West German economic system, as a result of more than two million unemployed. He writhed, shuffled his feet, tried to hold tight to the map stand, and Bettina critiqued: The concept is correct in itself but you're getting stuck in it; you're twisting it around like you're trying to look at a ball from all sides!

– Look at that. She's trying to make the sale.

– This was one last remaining bit of the earlier Bettina, wanting to win over a boy not much younger than she was: Come on, we're not so different, you and me, we can come to some kind of agreement . . . It's just that Bettina had developed some blind spots. She had no sense that her students might possibly be agonizing over the news from January 1 that ration cards had been abolished in the territory allegedly facing such imminent economic demise. No eyes to see that he was avoiding the gaze of the pair of students in the southeast corner of the classroom, because only recently he'd debated with them whether the much-lauded collective labor contract of May 1950, with its mandated acceptance of centralized planning, wasn't actually a total abnegation of worker's rights, and whether a woman gutting fish in the people-owned business FishCan really was in a position to comprehend her individual share in the ownership of the factory or at least of her labor. Bettina should have realized that Student Lockenvitz's recitation was stumbling over his own thoughts.

– And the fact that you all were lying like an American president—minor detail, right?

– Since when is school an institution we trust with anything more than the prescribed curriculum? I'm sure that when it comes to your Sister Magdalena, too, you know in advance who's going to win any argument.

– I just wish you'd won *once*.

– I did. By the length of a bathing suit.

– Tell me! *You tell such good lies!*

– "Now comes the time of victories": the nation's custodian had said in April, but coal sometimes failed to turn up for the evening train to Jerichow, where my swimsuit for the Baltic was. If I woke up in the morning at the Pagenkopfs', I would head out with my bathing suit for Gneez Lake and swim a few hundred meters there, usually with Pius, who would've preferred to sleep longer but who forced himself to be the good chaperone. When we didn't have time to detour to Helene Pagenkopf's laundry line on the way back, we'd take the wet things to school. It was May, the windows were open, they'd be dry by fourth period on the sill in the sun. Keeping my face turned to the teacher, I would sometimes stick my hand out the window and feel the fabric, which smelled of fresh water.

– And Selbich had it in for you.

– Maybe, since the sight of me reminded her of a time and a situation when things were going better for her. When she caught me with my forearm on the window ledge, she yelled at me and said all sorts of infuriated things about people who fondle swimsuits; she got tangled for a minute in the fact that when a person is changing into a bathing suit he or she is naked for a moment... and this while someone is standing here telling you about the personality of Comrade Stalin, the wise leader and guarantor of the world peace bloc!

– Telling "you" with a plural? Who were "you" besides you?

– She meant Pius and me. Even though the Gneez swimming area had separate changing rooms available and mandatory. Pius was already halfway out of his chair.

– What a sight! Big strapping boy decks helpless New Teacher!

– He'd have been sorry, that's for sure. I held his jacket tight with my right hand and moved my lips as if telling him something. If he understood it, it was the word "Kliefoth." For in 1939 Kliefoth had resigned from his teaching post because he'd pulled an eighth grader back from thin ice but the boy was in uniform and started proceedings: You, sir, have insulted the honor of the Führer's coat. Bettina, too, was wearing her heraldic blue that day, and assaulting it might have cost Pius his graduation. Instead of him, Schoolgirl Cresspahl rose, leaving Pius with all his thwarted manhood behind, and walked up to Bettina Selbich, perfectly calm, without any permission to do so. Selbich started to panic and shouted: Sit down! and eventually, in the informal form: Stop, Gesine!

– It was like she suddenly recognized you again.

– If being in tenth grade has any advantages, one is that pupils are to be addressed with adult, formal pronouns—but I could let that go. The other one is that teachers aren't allowed to grab or touch you.

– Oh to be in tenth grade!

– I stopped right in front of her, one girl facing another, and looked at her as obligingly as I knew how—like this, look—

– That's your nicest one, Gesine.

– and pursed my lips a little and showed her the tiniest bit of the tip of my tongue.

– No one else saw it.

– It was nothing she could ever prove. She alone had understood what I was telling her there, one woman to another; she was shaking in her blue shirt as I turned and walked out the door. She was shrieking, this Bettina was.

– A tenth grader could let that go.

– And could march, wrapped in all her dignity, straight to the principal's office where she asks Elise Bock for a piece of paper and an envelope, accepting Elise's invitation for a cup of coffee. Rumor later turned that into: FDJ-member Cresspahl wrote to the FDJ ZSGL

– What on earth is that?

– to the Free German Youth's Central School-Group Authority and filed a complaint against FDJ-member Bettina Selbich, Principal (pro tem). The truth is that I hid in the map room, so now Bettina also had to worry that I'd run out onto the street; punctually at the start of the next class I was standing behind my desk. Pius smiled the way Jakob sometimes did: relieved, just a hint in the corners of his eyes, up from under his brows.

– He was grateful.

– No, but he forgave me for having ruined his chivalry. We were scared. The principal's office had a cabinet full of radio equipment and a microphone, she could issue an order through the loudspeaker in our classroom that I come to her office. That would not have been good.

– But not a peep.

– On the other hand, the rumor I mentioned started going around, peeping with all its might. It said Mrs. Selbich had slapped Cresspahl's daughter in the face so hard that the girl had to see a dentist. It insisted that after Student Cresspahl left the room, class 10-A-II started acting up—she had friends and allies, of course—so that Mrs. Selbich felt the need to put her chair on the front desk and climb this tower with the aid of a second chair to keep the class under surveillance from above, putting on quite a show of the Riepschläger calves and thighs in the process. (Unfortunately for Bettina, rumor wasn't exaggerating in this case; Pius swore that had actually happened.) The alleged complaint miraculously turned into charges of mistreating a student, filed at the city's DA office: it was said that Mrs. Selbich had tried to strip Cresspahl's daughter; Pius and I refused to comment. But in town I was often and ardently greeted, the way I imagine beautiful princesses passing through town used to be in the old days; news of the spunky schoolgirl defying the throne of the principal had already reached Jerichow, too. I went to get our milk at Emma Senkpiel's and she took my can to the back room and brought it back heavier than usual. Twelve people watched me weigh the free extra weight in my hand, all looking like gleeful co-conspirators. So it cost a few marks extra. Back home Jakob's mother found a dozen eggs in the milk; during the ten-day ration periods in May, we redeemed our egg coupons for margarine.

– You're lying, Gesine. Those are my eggs that exploded!

– And thank you very much, otherwise I would've forgotten about Senkpiel's.

– Now for the complaint.

– Burly Sieboldt caught up to us the next day at the swimming place off the beaten track; he used to just come up to me publicly in the schoolyard. He had an air of secrecy, of something circumspect. Talked to everyone there until he had me alone and could take me aside. As Chapter Secretary of the FDJ ZSGL, he had nothing but praise for my having Elise Bock's sheet of paper in my breast pocket, blank, and the envelope, unaddressed; – *now thatsa matter for my mothers own son*: he said, every inch the functionary in charge, clearly having premeditated what he wanted to do, and not telling me. He acted like an unexpected task had suddenly appeared in the middle of his neatly organized schedule, an impossible but rewarding mission. He was known as Burly because he had something bull-like about him—*Bullen* not *pigs*, remember; anyone who didn't know him and unexpectedly found themselves in Sieboldt's paddock would feel menaced, but I was *Cresspahl sin Gesin* to him. He liked keeping it vague, and he knew his reputation.

– Gesine, is this going to be another water-butt story?

– Don't worry. All that happened was that Granny Rehse, whom Bettina Selbich in her new magnificence had hired as a cleaning lady, gave notice; now Bettina had to clean her own apartment on Cathedral Court. The landlord gave notice, too; Bettina won that suit but the general tone on the stairs in the building was quite different now. A garbage can might be left somewhere in the dark hall, for instance, and Bettina might take a little spill.

– You're all so mean.

– I agree. And Jakob, two hours away at the Güstrow Locomotive Engineers School, had by then been friends with Jöche for a long time; Jöche liked being Jakob's lieutenant. Bettina ran into a patch of bad luck traveling by train. The conductors always checked her ticket much more suspiciously than the other passengers', who then tended to move away from her. The railroad police would walk through the whole train not paying attention to anyone, and then pounce on Bettina, check her ID— only hers, openly suspicious. How could they know by sight someone who'd moved there from far-off Ludwigslust! Bettina got careless; she misplaced her ticket somewhere between Schwerin and Gneez. Questioning at the Gneez main station, a report filed. How did the passenger present herself? Distracted. Sufficient grounds to consider her capable of the offense (subreption of conveyance services)? Premeditation is suspected.

– The main station…

– Yes indeed. Connection to Jerichow.

– She had no way of knowing that a railroad employee was a registered resident with the Cresspahls in Jerichow!

– That thread of Ariadne was unwound for her by someone else. Someone who had something bulky about him.

– Oh my distant homeland!

– The Chapter Secretary at Fritz Reuter High School had certain questions from the FDJ head office that he needed to discuss with the principal, also an FDJ-member. Overburdened as he was by his duties in office, as well as preparing for his finals, he could only manage appointments in the late evening hours. He was observed in Cathedral Court during the night several times.

– Oh my distant homeland!

– We had an ally on the faculty too: the beanpole gym teacher. He never failed to wave us over when he saw his former star swimming with Pius (we were The Couple). And so we heard that someone had suggested at the grading conference that Colleague Selbich give Student Cresspahl a higher grade than her usual "Good" in Conduct this year. She apparently sat there stiff as a board. But in fact this student had not been caught in the slightest breach of school rules all year. She finished tenth grade with a grade in Conduct of: Very Good.

– And once bitten, twice shy?

– Mrs. Selbich ignored the back right-hand desk in 10-A-II whenever she could. She had to spend three weeks, too, on a page in the class book which she'd had to replace by hand, having written something reckless on the original page before coming to her senses and tearing it up in front of the class.

– I'd have felt sorry for her by now.

– Me too. She even started combing her hair in class, unconsciously I'm sure—the Riepschlägers hadn't raised their Bettina like that. Two years earlier she'd have never allowed that, neither from us nor from herself. She usually noticed the wide-toothed comb in her hand only after she'd passed it through her hair—not especially helping her hair either, by the way.

– You and your bathing suit and Comrade Stalin.

– Now hanging—the suit, not the comrade—with Loerbrocks the painter. He'd been made our janitor. And there it was for all to see at the edge of the schoolyard. The Cresspahl Monument. Bettina probably wished it was back on the window ledge outside 10-A-II.

– Make it up to her!

– We were obedient. She expounded the decline of capitalism in general (miners' strike in the USA) and particular (a month of every West German's salary goes to pay for the military occupation); we repeated this back on demand and refrained from asking how much per capita the East German worker paid for the Soviet occupation. The rise, in contrast, of Socialism: the pact between Stalin and Mao, a $330 million development credit. If anyone wanted to hear why such sums were calculated in dollars, that desire was duly suppressed. While Bettina combed her hair. Zaychik interpreted the liberation of India as the fall of the British Empire; the sound of the British airplanes helping to break the blockade of Berlin still rang in our ears. Gabriel Manfras spoke at length about the Soviet gift of work standards, numbers of work units, time norms—flush with quiet enthusiasm, it seemed. Bettina Selbich praised the vigilance of the Socialist battalions, the trial of ten priests in Czechoslovakia for treason and espionage in April 1950, sentences up to life in prison; Anita recalled the troubles that had befallen Pastor Brüshaver on account of Herbert Vick's bequest, obeyed Bettina, and regurgitated what Bettina wanted; Bettina kept combing, head to one side, with tugging motions. Triumph of the World Peace Movement! The British have had to stop their bombing of Helgoland. We sat before her in the hot June light, the scent of the linden blossoms wafting in; rather inattentive, since the only thing we could learn in this class was a way of behaving. Bettina confirmed the younger Seneca yet again: *Non vitae, sed scholae discimus.* We learn not for life, but for school. One student, at least, was definitely daydreaming about a time when trips to the vicinity of Helgoland would be permitted once more. In any case, this New Teacher had ruined any chance she had to ask about our obedience, our patience. Like we would tell her anything. We were exaggeratedly polite and deferential in her classes, you could hear a pin drop—half a pin drop; her class put us to sleep. That was the first time I hoped I would never become a teacher anywhere they were trained and transformed from Bettina Riepschlägers to B. Selbichs. After three such classes at most I would have crawled out of the classroom in tears, without argument or discussion. She kept at it, though. Now you say what you wish for, Marie.

– I wish you could sleep as late as you want and need to, every night. *Yours, truly.*

July 28, 1968 Sunday, South Ferry day, even though it's the second-to-last day to edit Karsch's book. Are we really cocky enough to smuggle the proofs into the office disguised as work? Written words are getting the upper hand here. J. B. since June; for almost a year, the days that the other friend of our youth, Comrade Writer, has wanted to write up. We'll be so happy when there's an end to all this un- published writing.

The New York Times brings us my dream from yesterday morning.

And says that the East German Communists are again spreading what they call the fact that "life may appear quiet and normal in the streets of Prague these days," but it's a facade—apparently they know all about fa- cades—and behind this one is "a creeping counterrevolution." "The coun- terrevolutionary tactics employed in Czechoslovakia are more refined than they were in Hungary." And the blows against the rectification of this country, how refined will they be?

Down with Bettina! that's what Marie wants. But the teacher and acting principal only stumbled in the summer of 1950, though repeatedly; she might have fallen.

We tried. As 10-A-II's teacher, Bettina let Pius register our candidates for the trip to the FDJ's Whitsunday rally in Berlin but insisted on examining them herself, primarily with respect to the added condition that they keep their distance from the Western sectors of the city. She accepted Pius of course—he was our class president, after all, and son of the meritorious Comrade Pagenkopf in the district capital, where via the Department of Popular Education he could spit in the soup of an unprotected New Teacher whenever he wanted. The deputy class president, Cresspahl, claimed homework as her reason for not wanting to go, would you believe it. She didn't bring up her father's warning. In early May they were still saying "Free German Youth to Storm Berlin!" and Heinrich Cresspahl considered the lessons that Gesine had brought home from her New School. According to which the West had thoughtlessly picked up right where the Weimar Republic had gone off the rails; he remembered policemen in shakos attacking demonstrators with billy clubs, or shooting, and didn't want to have his child "storming" Berlin or anywhere else, nor did he want his daughter returned to him all beaten up. He practically begged her, promising her a solo trip to "Berlin" over the summer to make up for it. Gesine reserved the right to refuse that trip too; she always willingly submitted to her father's concerns; so eager to please, this child. (And because it was still a comfort to Cresspahl when someone listened to him, paid attention to him.) She didn't tell him the real reason, of course: It might happen that Jakob remembered his filial duty on Whitsunday and paid a visit to Cresspahl's house. Gesine thought to await this eventuality in a deck chair by the milk rack behind the house, pretending, for Jakob, to be reading for school.

So Student Cresspahl was absent. Gabriel Manfras declared, in a guarded way: Everywhere we go we must show how sincerely we stand for peace; Bettina believed him (as did we). Lise wanted to take the opportunity to go shopping in West Berlin and made no bones about it, neither to us nor to Gabriel, who was disconcerted to hear her parrot what he'd just said, cheerfully, not quite exactly. Anita was smart; she talked her way out of the trip with interpreting duties for Triple-J and Emil Knoop. In fact, she wanted to make some money at Emil's adding machine. Student Matschinsky had every right to feel tricked. She'd wanted to go so that she could be with Zaychik over the holiday too (Dagobert Haase was dreaming of going to see the West Berlin car show but pretended he was curious about the new construction in the "democratic" sector); now Eva awkwardly hemmed and hawed. Dieter Lockenvitz took the same line as Zaychik, if rather more finely drawn: he spoke of the limited autonomy of the superstructure, i.e., new Berlin architecture as an expression of national form. Since he did so with a straight face, and citations, moreover, from the works of J. V. Stalin on Marxist linguistics, what could Selbich do to him? (He'd never been to Berlin: we thought.) Eva got her permission, maybe because Selbich felt a need to ingratiate herself with 10-A-II. Where the earlier Bettina would have smiled and heightened Eva's anticipation, today's Bettina said dismissively, contemptuously: Ah well. You don't have the consciousness.

(Such pronouncements—unconscious students in 10-A-II!—were by that point the topic of avid questions on the part of those who had no pedagogical dealings with Selbich. Even Julie Westphal, who after all was no spring chicken, always liked hearing the story retold of how her younger colleague and superior had presided over the class from her vertically extended desk.)

Pius took the trip with more than the required accessories (blue shirt, toilet kit, fighting spirit). (He was traveling as the Pagenkopf/Cresspahl collective's representative.) And so Gesine had paid a visit to Horst Stellmann's on Stalin Street in Jerichow, asking him for an "instant" camera. – Eyes to the wood: Stellmann said, in the old soldier's phrase, slightly pulling down the skin under his left eye with his finger; – Eyes peeled: Gesine responded, always willing to go along with the games a grown-up wanted to play. Stellmann dug up a Leica from his rearmost drawer, truly moved by the thought of how accommodating he was willing to be with Cresspahl's daughter. But she wanted something less conspicuous, something that could pass the new luggage inspection at Nauen or Oranienburg without raising any suspicion of black-market dealings with West Berlin. Horst eventually brought out a humbler bellows camera, three hundred marks deposit instead of two thousand, which you could raise to the eye and then tuck away in nothing flat. How startled he was to catch a glimpse

of Cresspahl's daughter on Town Road in Jerichow on Whitsunday, nowhere near any surveillance activities in Berlin.

Pius came back on the Tuesday after Whitsunday, reporting train delays
that suggested a certain indifference on the part of railwaymen when it
came to transporting young human freight in the interests of peace. Accommodations in a business school in Berlin-Heinersdorf, on straw; fistfights
with students from Saxony over nighttime thefts; a five-hour shuffling march
to the platform holding the country's custodian and the head of the FDJ.
Honecker was his name, not yet thirty-eight at that point, and he weighed
the takeover of West Berlin against the bloodied heads of his Young
Comrades. As compensation, he offered up something bizarre about potato
bugs. Berlin residents annoyed at the blue-shirted visitors getting free rides
on city transportation. Zaychik and Eva had made it to the expo at the
radio tower. Dieter Lockenvitz set out for the Congress of Young Fighters
for Peace, at Landsberg Avenue station on the ring road, with opening
remarks by the poet Stephan Hermlin; he later said he'd gotten lost, and
remained missing, untraceable. Pius knew what Gesine was waiting for but
droned on and on; by then the two of us liked to tease each other, like a
married couple. Finally she swallowed her pride and asked: Did you get her?

Pius had her, in his box. The youthful, still confident principal, in charge
of the delegation from Fritz Reuter High School, Gneez—how could he
lose sight of her! She made it easy by falling into a helpless panic at the shy
earnestness with which Burly Sieboldt, in Berlin too, tugged at her blue
blouse, as though he wanted to reveal his admiration to both her and an
audience. She was dazed, letting Pius follow her as if under a cloak of invisibility, until he eventually surprised her on Palace Street, Berlin-Steglitz,
American Sector, West Berlin. Outside a shoe store—she was still just a
young thing, Bettina was. When she saw Pius, camera raised, it must have
dawned on her with a stab of anguish that she could not accuse a single
student from Gneez of a peace-betraying excursion to West Berlin as long
as one of them possessed a photograph showing the principal and FDJ-
member succumbing to the temptations of capitalism on the level of commodity circulation. Which is why she tried to take his camera away. But
Pius had strong hands, from gymnastics on the high bar; he also asked her,
familiarly, if she wanted it to unload it for West marks. Wouldn' advise
that, Comrade. Since the West mark is about to collapse and all. (So that

she could see at least some of what she extolled in her lessons as an economic law of nature had stuck with him.)

Better safe than sorry. To be safe, Pius sent word apologizing to the head of the Gneez youth delegation (sunstroke; and through Axel Ohr, so that Bettinikin would suspect Student Cresspahl might be involved); he went home on a different rail line from the one on which the railwaymen were shunting the school transport back to Gneez. Horst Stellmann was simply delighted by the secrecy with which he was asked to develop the film; grown-ups are like that—letting themselves get distracted by the Western shop sign and not noticing the person under it. And that was where the Pagenkopf/Cresspahl work collective let it stand in the campaign against Bettina Selbich; but she couldn't know that. She defied our blank looks with a pride through which we could see a quaking terror. (Her gray eyebrows were a little mismatched; how I'd once enjoyed looking at them.) Were we unfair to her? Maybe. Until the end of the first week after Whitsunday—*may*be, Marie.

Marie is eager to hear if Bettina managed to keep it together instead of hightailing it out of Gneez. Moving somewhere she wouldn't have to deal every day with students who had her in their power and pocket. Out of shame, if nothing else. There's no way to solve this riddle, Marie, here in the murky aggrieved haze of Staten Island, with a view of the Verrazano Bridge's west pier. Selbich hardly seemed up to defiance and the strength required for a move. Unless she'd decided, under that unevenly cut blond hair of hers, that the photographic evidence might just as well catch up to her in Zwickau, at the other end of the country. Would we have been so cruel? We might, if we had to be.

End-of-year grades in Contemporary Studies: for Pagenkopf, B; for Cresspahl likewise, "Good."

– The look she gave me in Steglitz: Pius told me, about that scene on the corner of Palace and Muthesius Streets between the policewoman, caught in the act, and the thief, magnanimous: it was like what she wanted most of all was to bite me! Tssss! Like a snake. (Sometimes Pius acted younger than me.)

It was just the two of us, tucked under the shoreline cliff west of Rande, muffled by the roar of the Baltic. True, one of us expanded on the description until we got to venom, snake-poison—but just between us. It must have been through osmosis that Bettina S. soon got a new nickname, first in our class, then throughout the school, and that this is how she is still remembered: "blond poison," the German phrase for a blond bombshell. Selbich, The Blond Poison. TBP. After summer vacation in 1950, Julie Westphal told her about this sobriquet she'd acquired, pretending to do it out of pity. Luckily, the phrase's author slipped through her fingers; our Blond Poison must have thought to the end that it was a malicious invention, not by accident.

Whatever nicknames might say about a person's behavior, Pius was safe thanks to his family and his apparently telling Bettina what she wanted to hear in a tone that was even more devout than was strictly required. Gesine had no nickname. Marie had one only in nursery school, in 1961–62 ("our lil' kraut"). And it is this young lady, the most steadfast of the children in the Cresspahl line though in no way the bravest, who asks a favor once we're past the Verrazano Bridge. The trip to Czechoslovakia looms. Could we maybe test the waters in the restaurant on the East Side, where the people speak and act Czech?

– Perfect! That's why you're wearing a dress instead of pants! That's just what I have a checkbook in my bag for! Let's go to your detested Svatého Václava!

– On Riverside Drive I still thought we wouldn't. Now I think I need it.

It turns out Jakob reconsidered the visit he owed his mother (in Cresspahl's house). He sent a photographic version of himself, taken privately, in postcard format. It showed a long swimming pier with a lifeguard's station and Island Lake in Güstrow with boats in the water. Jakob sent his regards from a training course that had been unexpectedly extended. When he did lie, it was only to spare others' feelings. A training course has breaks. In breaks you can take a girl out on a boat ride. And that was why Gesine Cresspahl had stuck out the Whitsunday sun in Jerichow, in her dress for special occasions, from the West—all she got for it was sunburned knees.

July 29, 1968 Monday, Dirty Monday

To be fair, if you look at it objectively, we do leave our apartment in the lurch when one of us goes to the corner of West End Avenue where the summer camp's orange bus is waiting and the other one lets the subway whisk her from the Upper West Side to Midtown and the desolation of work; we leave our twenty-seven hundred cubic feet of inhabitable space floating in the wasteland of Manhattan's architecture, unprotected, miles away, and that in a city where a dignified bum tries to steal Marie's grocery cart while she's watching through a window. Where, sitting on a bench by the river with Mrs. Ferwalter, we keep a wary hand on our brown paper package that contains nothing but laundry, at some cost to our intelligibility in the conversation. Where philanthropists passing through town count their cash outside in broad daylight, within reach of greedy observers, and a Mrs. Cresspahl grabs the wallet of this trusting man of the world, this Anselm Kristlein, and holds it tight at her side and only then apologizes for overfamiliar behavior. The fact is, we deserve punishment.

And we've expected it. The statistical average of two murders a day in the five boroughs of New York suggests a daily quantity of additional crimes as well. Ever since our Mrs. Seydlitz, trusting the sharp eyes of the doorman who watches over the elevator doors in her building, nonetheless found herself facing a seventeen-year-old boy's knife—his fear more dangerous than his weapon—we were disappointed, we shuddered slightly, at the fact that this course of probable everyday events had continued to pass us by. Now, after seven years here, it was our turn. Time to put behind us what the city administration's criminal science bureau has specified, just for us, as the degree to which hitherto unrealized events are possible. So that we'll be safe till the next iteration of what we're owed.

We enjoyed the bliss of the commonplace until Marie came home today to find a door with a dangling lock, which made her stop and listen and retreat downstairs; until Mrs. Cresspahl poked the lamely hanging piece of woodwork with a (gloved) finger and immediately noticed two crooked cracks in one of her storm windows. Marie has come to the point where she can laugh at the slow-motion gesture with which her mother raised both hands to her hair, and actually the hairdo was in almost as perfect shape as it had been when she'd left Mr. Boccaletti's beauty salon. The apartment was trashed.

We know what to do, we kept our fingerprints to ourselves for the time being and went down to the basement to use shamefaced Jason's phone. But does the NYPD know what to do?

New York Police Department: How do you know they came through the window?

Citizen Cresspahl: Because the window's broken.

NYPD: You have children?

C.C.: One.

NYPD: Well then.

C.C.: Are you planning to send someone over, or would you rather we just chitchat for a while?

NYPD: When did you move in?

C.C.: May 1961.

NYPD: And when are you moving out?

C.C.: Is there any chance that the law enforcement branch of government might want to see the scene of the crime in person?

NYPD: You can fix the window yourself.

C.C.: Then I guess I'll turn around and ask a private agency.

NYPD: Hey! Listen you, now calm down.

By the time a boy in blue from New York's Finest appeared, stranded in the doorframe, we could work out for ourselves what had happened before we arrived. The time was missing—the alarm clock stolen. But in some minute or another after 8:25 a.m., someone entered an empty lobby on Riverside Drive. At 243 Riverside Drive, to be exact, where there's always supposed to be someone watching out for our money, either Eagle-Eye Robinson or Esmeralda. A glance to the left of the elevator, at the open door to the stairwell, which according to fire regulations is to be kept closed at all times. How often we've daydreamed of taking a razor and cutting the thread tying the door to the heating pipe! Someone in a hurry, someone who doesn't belong here, settles for the next floor—apartment 204. Since the elevator is in motion right next to it, he has to manage with a few stabbing strikes around the clever stupid lock, with a mighty blow that rips out the chain anchored to the frame (by four two-inch screws). He sees from the keyhole that the people here can lock the door from the outside; if anything moves inside then they're home. Silence. In he goes. Puts the brass cylinder back where it was, more or less, so as not to be noticeable. What does he see?

Salvation Army furniture on hardwood floors (no rug), casually laid out, as if no one here ever had to turn their back on each other. Luxury?

Yes, two windows facing the western light of Riverside Drive, the woodsy park, the distant glittering of the river. Waste of effort. Better to scram.

But no, maybe he's thirsty, and there's a friendly refrigerator just waiting for him, to the left of the door. If someone gets mad because what he wants isn't there for him—a cold beer—he'll pull out one shelf after another, everything bangs gently onto the tiles, mixing the tomato paste, mustard, milk, and liverwurst. From that point on he leaves traces, our visitor.

Along the back wall of the middle room there's a structure of wood and glass—perfectly natural that the green curtain might scare a person. There's a key in the lock, but how could anyone know that, a few blows here and there does the job too. Books. More books. Still, people keep money in books, between the pages, he's heard that. The empty books anger him and he swipes them off the shelves by the row, including those that are too old for such treatment. *Outline of the History of Mecklenburg*, by Paschen Heinrich Hane, second preacher in Gadebusch, printed 1804, unlisted in ADB, NDB, Brunet, Kraesse, Cat. Schles.-Holst. State Bibl.—the fragile leather spine on that one breaks; likewise *Everyman's History of Mecklenburg, in Letters*, Printed in Neubrandenburg by C. G. Korb, Printer to the Grand Duke, 1791, motto: Moribus et hospitalitate nulla gens honestior aut benignior potuit inveniri. Yeah, right! Stomp.

The secretary that the Dane left us glances over with its many drawers, all with locks, better we just break it open, the glassed hutch too. Ha, some loot! A folder with *Taxes* written on it. Still, taxes have to do with money. Overwhelmed with the presence of mere information, he'll fling that across the room into the slimy sauce of edibles and broken glass.

To the right he sees curtained glass doors, they give way under a light kick revealing a room with a fleece carpet, a child's painting *al fresco* on the white wall, a table with a typewriter. All right then! We'll take that.

The tenant has sent her child down to the lobby, under the super's protection, to wait for the NYPD. The tenant herself is waiting in, as close as possible to the middle of, the room. Before her calm eyes the front door opens, rustling in the breeze, a finger reaches in. She says to the hand: *Marie, je t'en prie!* but the body part belongs to a different person, a man, who shows his confused, half-polite face and stutters. Must've made a stupid mistake, sorry, he'll just try the stairway door next to this one. All while taking slow backward steps from the woman. She watches him knock next door, until a second man, invisible behind the wall, comes up in the stairway and tells his friend, as if they were alone: Good idea to take care of the super. Both stumble off, abashed but relaxed before the unarmed female, only starting to run when they get to the super's floor, and they burst out the last door onto Ninety-Sixth Street into a cop car, which traps them in the corner of the sidewalk with the bridge underpass, because Citizen Cresspahl is shouting something excitedly, in Italian: *Al ladro! Al ladro! Fermateli!*

Then Marie has finally followed her out and for the first time ever she sees handcuffs being used for real. (All things considered, it feels like something performed for her, a fairy tale—all going off without a hitch.)

Admittedly, these two men don't have anything on them, and the policemen were only trying to do a (clearly hysterical) lady a favor, but after they'd traipsed around all the addresses the gentlemen supplied and found no place of residence anywhere, after one had tried to slip away from them into a subway station packed with rush-hour traffic, the team of patrolmen, one after the other, called up Citizen Cresspahl asking for forgiveness and thanking her—her assistance had given them some points in the precinct bosses' tally; the suspects were junkies, too. – You did the right thing, ma'am! Calling us right away, that takes care of it.

Meanwhile the man with the powder had come and he was dusting the shards of window on the floor with his little brush; with Marie watching him so closely as he worked, he'd rather have taken the whole window with him. His partner had found marks from the crowbar on the bottom frame, and, on the hooks attached to the outside wall that the window washers use for their belt, a belt for window washers, and, on the sidewalk below the window, a bucket with wash rags inside that had fallen over.

Do we insist on filing a complaint, which would only make more work for the NYPD? We ask for a police report.

Missing: One portable typewriter with European keyboard. One shortwave radio, on which we listen to the water levels in the ČSSR every night. A tape recorder, including the tape from Saturday (gone: one Blond Poison), in fact all the cassettes that would have been gathered and sent to a bank vault in Düsseldorf the day after tomorrow. One document folder with private correspondence and nothing but some loose change, not even a foreign passport. Such a hurry he was in, no? (Except that our visitor found

the time to fill the toilet bowl almost to the rim with his indigestibilia.)
And? One leather bag from Switzerland, big, with stamped initials. For
carrying stuff away with, first, before repacking, y'see? Your initials, if you
don't mind, on the double.

Once we can touch the telephone again, the young lady from the phone
company tries to make a fuss about our disavowal of any long-distance calls
that might have been placed from this number since this morning, whether
to Eugene, Oregon, or Yokohama, Japan. What's that, you want official
confirmation? Please remain on the line. *Ne quittez pas!* Here's a representative of the Twenty-Third Precinct.

It was still light out, we'd cleaned up the broken things and shard-filled
sludge, laid out the mistreated books on spread nets like wounded birds;
in came Jason, looking somber. He had pulled himself together, out of the
shame of this having happened to us under his watch, above his very head!
for he'd been in the building all day. With him came Eagle-Eye Robinson,
bashfully feeling the crispy furrows of his hair with his fingertips—he
should have been keeping watch. Together they measured the shattered
door and spent till midnight putting in a similar one, admittedly numbered
1201 but freshly cloaked in steel, with an undamaged lock and a chain latch
attached to the wall with rivets. Since such installations make noise (i.e.,
so that tenants next door might remain unaware that we're treated like
favorite children), they invited us downstairs to the super's office, to watch
TV, some ice tea for the younger of the ladies.

We both decided we'd rather take a walk. Passed from the shady Hudson, through the catacomb tunnel under the Henry Hudson Expressway,
to the Eighties on Riverside Drive and back. Maybe we were looking for
Marjorie. (If, Mrs. Cresspahl, the city of New York has ever done you harm
or made you suffer...) It was too late at night. She was nowhere to be seen.

July 30, 1968 Tuesday
The Soviet Politburo, largely unlocatable since Saturday, emerged yesterday
morning, nine men strong, in fifteen green sleeping cars that a red, yellow
and green diesel engine pulled across the damp wheat fields in Czechoslovak territory from Chop, a Soviet border town, into Cierna, led by the

party chief, Leonid I. Brezhnev, who was greeted at the brick station by Alexander Dubček and fifteen of his advisers. Kisses? Embraces? None. A three-and-a-half-hour meeting, then each delegation ate on their own in their own train.

No communiqué unless we fish one out of *Pravda*, which informs the hosts, scout's honor, that: the Soviet Union supplies their country with virtually all its petroleum, four-fifths of its iron-ore imports (border crossing point: Chop/Cierna), 63 percent of its synthetic rubber, and 42 percent of its nonferrous metals. Soviet prices are also more advantageous to Czechoslovakia than ones in the Western markets, where favoritism and discriminatory trade practices are rife.

Unless we bend our ear to the NY *Times*. This energetic lady, with her hypnotic compulsion to research every angle, opines: a Soviet invasion of Czechoslovakia would be a disaster for the French Communists. But she also concludes, on the evidence that the Soviet government has banned its own journalists from traveling to Czechoslovakia, that its own propaganda is a fabrication. But what if the Soviets only wanted to protect their reporters—a valuable cadre—from a future where people visiting Prague might have one or another hair on their head harmed?

On the first day of school after the Whitsunday trip, those who returned were given their welcome, along with those who'd stayed home to pen a love poem to Comrade Stalin, or to TBP, or to a girl he'd noticed sunbathing as he peeped through the gaps in a gooseberry hedge. At first many failed to notice the welcome. Gneez, like Jerichow, was covered with posters—why would they notice the DIN A5 sheets plastered on the glass in the main entrance of the Fritz Reuter High School and in rows at eye level around the walls of the building? They showed members of the Free German Youth, in formation, the color blue all too recognizable as well as the question to the FDJ'ers: What are you marching for? The desired answer came so automatically that Pius hadn't bothered to keep reading and had forgotten all about the handbills by the start of second period; Gesine too. Equations with two unknown variables, with three, can challenge the free German youthful brain, distracting it.

Then, right into the middle of the math problems being rehearsed under Mrs. Gollnow, burst Bettina's voice from the loudspeaker—hoarse, despondent, desperate, brittlely harsh. All students are to remain in their classrooms, ignoring any bells. Teachers currently in the room are in charge.

It was evening, a late-May twilight, before the last students were let out onto the street. The criminal police (D Squad) started their questioning with the seniors, so six hours passed before 10-A-II's turn. At first Mrs. Gollnow conducted class as usual, finishing the day's planned lesson; then she offered extra one-on-one tutoring to anyone who wanted it; eventually she started telling what she called "tales" from her life. What it was like at Leipzig University; her correspondence with the writer Joachim de Catt, who went by the pseudonym Hinterhand. The windows were wide open; there was plenty of air; around noon the 10-A-II classroom started to feel like a prison. A merry one, for a little while. For Dr. Gollnow—who to universal gratitude decoded her first initial for us: Erdmuthe—would rather let us see her as an ingenious person than do without out of pride any longer: she was a smoker, and admitted it. Referendum: permission to smoke in the confines of a room meant for educational purposes. Inventory: all available tobacco products. Communist distribution: to each according to his need, not his merit. Still, by around two o'clock the filterless Turf cigarettes

Thousands Under Russian Flags.
Thousands,
I tell you.

as well as the hit-or-miss imitation Americans were gone, and secret terror was creeping up to our throats, since Gollnow had banned all speculation about the quarantine. Something must be going on out there that affected the whole student body. Was Gneez in flames?

At around three o'clock, a doggedly uncommunicative Loerbrocks, guarded by a civilian unconnected to the school, handed out rolls from the cafeteria: dry bread with no water or soup; before long it hurt to swallow it. The silent guessing, the confused (sometimes scornful) questioning looks, the helpless shrugs; it soon got hard to keep up one's confidence. Anyone who needed to go to the bathroom could give two knocks on the classroom door; they would be let out, but accompanied by a male or female officer, who refused to say anything. In 10-A-II they started calling students by seating position, not alphabetically (did the school office have a copy of

the seating chart?). So Gantlik came before Cresspahl, Wollenberg before
Pagenkopf, and no one came back. Cresspahl was the last person waiting
with Gollnow, who had run out of anecdotes and whispered something
about Good luck!, as if this student might be in particular need of it. A
burning, hungry look had come into Dr. E. Gollnow's eyes.

Gesine did have good luck. In the hall she saw the single raincoat abandoned among the countless empty hooks and she slipped it on as if it were
hers. She felt paper in a pocket; while waiting outside the principal's office
she was even able to read some of what was written there in block letters.
Elise Bock's job was guard and watchman; she gave the student a soothing
look and had already snatched the scrap away when the incoming call rang
the bell of her phone. Shadows of trees behind Elise's back.

That was neatly done, Anita. Thank you, thank you, thank you.
*The cops first covered 10-A-II as a whole, with TBP smack bang in the
middle of it. But you're the target.*
I went numb racking my brain trying to figure out why.
*They wanted to know if you were mad at the state. Over the shitty deal the
founders thereof gave your father. Fünfeichen and all that.*
Always direct and to the point, our Anita.
*Since I was in a hurry. Also if you'd skipped the Germany Rally so you
could secretly go to West Berlin—*
Where I don't know anyone except a German shepherd.
*—and collect handbills showing free German young people marching
under and behind barbed wire.*
So that's what I get for serving in the FDJ.
*They don't give a rat's ass about that; if anything it's a strike against you,
Gesine.*
Which is why you hid behind block letters.
*Keep guessing, but later. Right now they're after your head. They want to
know if you've got someone with the railroads.*

A student stepped into the principal's office, the interrogation room,
with head lowered, braids feeling heavy; she barely lifted her head to look
at FDJ Comrade Selbich, who was staring at her from behind her desk,

fists clenched, and who jerked her head toward where the visitors were. A set of upholstered chairs, confiscated from the Bruchmüllers; on one a Mecklenburg man with the badge of the Unity Party on his lapel, almost too tired to take the trouble to be crafty; next to him a young man Bettina's age, who would have plunged Lise Wollenberg into a fit of jealousy if he picked another lady instead of her—a gentleman. Fabric of elegant cut on his chest, knees showing off the creases of his freshly ironed pants. A stern, mocking look which said: Don't worry, we'll get you too. The student said: My name is Gesine Cresspahl, 10-A-II, born on . . .

– *There are serious matters, ver-r-ry serious matters* that we have to discuss with you . . . : this upright citizen began, in a mix of Platt and High German—the nice uncle who doesn't like punishing anyone, unless it be deserved, or needed. An upraised palm stopped him in his tracks, like a well-trained animal: – . . . to discuss with *you:* he said again, using the formal pronoun: *We wancha to see right off that we're treatin you with all due respect. Tenth grade, all that horseshit.* Now, you probably know where Hans-and-Sophie-Scholl Street is in Schweri-en?

If that's all you want to know, Mr. . . . (no name given to fill the pause). From the main train station in Schwerin you take a right onto Wismar Street, in other words south toward Stalin Street, continue to St. Mary Square, now called Lenin Square, where the Dom Ofitserov is, and, to the east, the arcade to the palace, known and loved across the country. Past that, Kaiser Wilhelm Street, nowadays the Street of National Unity, branches off to the right, still heading south, and leads to Count Schack Street, going right and left. That's the shortest way, I think. Count Schack Street, every young Mecklenburger knows that address—that's where you go dancing, at the Tivoli! There are only twelve numbered buildings on that street; the municipal health insurance building used to be there, part of Mecklenburg State Insurance, and Pastor Niklot Beste lived at 5C, he was a member of the High Consistory after the war, state bishop of the Evangelical-Lutheran Mecklenburg State Church after 1947. Count Schack Street is part of the original Schwerin suburbs. Adolf Friedrich von Schack, born in 1815 in Brüsewitz just outside Schwerin, member of the Munich School of poets starting in 1855, made a count by the Kaiser in 1876, died in Rome (Italy), 1894. His epic poem *Lothar* . . .

How happy, I! Oh childhood bliss,
The golden days of life's sweet dawn!
A light we in our blindness miss,
Last glimpse of infinity shimm'ring on,
It shines upon thee yet!

Those who cherish this opus know all about his street, whatever name it now bears. From the left, eastern half, you can look down toward Castle Lake. In New Mecklenburg, this part was renamed for the Scholl siblings.

– Shut UP, Gesine! Shut up already! She's making fun of you, Comrade, this brat, this . . . bitch!: Bettina Selbich shrieked, raising and shaking her fist so that her blue shirt seemed to flutter all over. The local interrogator's partner was up in a bound, sending a whiff of fruit over to the accused, who sat there looking as meek and contrite as could be. This stranger busied himself about his comrade. Your nerves, my dear lady. It's been a long hard day, a blow to our World Peace Movement, please calm down, perhaps out in the waiting room if you'd rather . . .

Thenceforth it proceeded as if tea were laid out on the low table with the crocheted doily, as if the lady being held there were constantly being offered cakes, a glass of sherry if she wanted. So, the student knew about the Scholl siblings? Yes, they were students during the time of the Nazis, Hans and Sophie, executed in February 1943 at ages twenty-three and twenty-two in Berlin-Plötzensee for having distributed leaflets at Munich University. – Excellent!: came the grade from the Sovietnik, glancing at his German trainee as though encouraging him to learn these dates too, though not with much confidence he would. – And we: he said, with a touch of delight, with clear amusement: We are from the M.f.S. on Hans-and-Sophie-Scholl Street in Schwerin. We are looking into the leaflets that arrived last night at the Gneez station and were handed over to a total of four distributors, one of whom patched up your high school. Perhaps it was you, Miss Cresspahl? Would you like that?

What followed was a back-and-forth of verbal blows, today I'd say: a squash game; but one with my skin at stake. (– Skin is always on the out-side: a friend likes to say.) The only thing that made it easier was the fact that the tempo stayed the same, furious as it was, racing past the Mecklenburg minion as Achilles did the tortoise, thus numerous times, because an infinite series does converge on a finite sum, both in mathematics and out; a microphone from (the people-owned business) RadioTech had been placed, as a precaution, on the extended leaf of the cabinet:

And may I ask what M.f.S. stands for? *Ministerium für Staatssicherheit*, the State Security Service. Thank you very much. Don't mention it, happy to help. Was the founding of the M.f.S. somehow skipped in Contemporary Studies? It was, as far as I can recall. The historic date of the law of February 8, 1950? Maybe because of the excitement over the Peace Rally trip to Berlin. Name of instructor responsible for the omission? The Bl— Bettina Selbich. Incidentally, we already know everything, FDJ Comrade Cresspahl, all we need is confirmation from you. / So, she claims as an alibi that she arrived in Gneez on the milk train, after the school had already been wrapped in paper inimical to the state? Since the freewheel on her bicycle is broken and you can't get a replacement for money or coupons. There's a little device to separate a driven wave from a driving one, trademark Torpedo, ready and waiting for Miss Cresspahl, you can get it at any bike shop in West Berlin. Denial of having made any shopping trips to West Berlin. But FDJ-member Pagenkopf seems to have no problem paying visits to that den of iniquity. Pagenkopf is well aware what he owes to his father's position in the leadership of the Mecklenburg State Unity Party. And to himself? The FDJ class president does have a proper consciousness, yes. / Occasional overnight stays with the Pagenkopfs in Gneez due to arguments with her father? Not at all, he knows and agrees to it. Political agreement too? My father tries to understand the nature of contemporary events. With Miss Cresspahl instructing him? My father is not a talkative man, and also too weakened for extended conversations. Grandmother in the LDPD? Not an illegal party. Grandfather in custody with our Soviet friends? The proceedings are up in the air. A brother-in-law of Cresspahl's in the West, working for a ministry? Not on speaking terms with the family. Cresspahl himself imprisoned, most recently in Fünfeichen? My father describes it as a verification; trust is good, control is better, as LENIN says. Excellent, and now here is a quotation from STALIN! "Never in world history has there been a party as powerful as our Communist Party—and there never will be." Your grade in Contemporary Studies, Miss Cresspahl? B. Well, we'll have to discuss that with our colleague Mrs. Selbich. / Please, what was your first thought when you saw these handbills! Visual advertising defeats its purpose if it irritates the viewer. You are criticizing the use of visual advertising, such as why smooth paper is available for it but only wood-fiber stock for school notebooks? Or that there is more fabric available for propaganda banners than consumer textiles? Oh, no, nothing like that; just that the fliers were keeping the light out of the front staircase. Why do you say "fliers" rather than "posters"? Because of the size of the paper. And now your second thought, if I may ask. The form of address. "Young friend!" No, it said "FDJ'er." Like biker, gameplayer. To Mecklenburg ears it could sound somewhat childish, or maybe South German. The Red Biker bike messengers in Munich? No—modes of locomotion or athletics should be kept separate from the discriminating name of a youth organization which ... Worth considering, I might pass that along to my superior. All right, quick now, Comrade J. V. Stalin's birthday? December 21, 1879, New Style, in Gori, near Tiflis, Georgia. Why "in Rome (Italy)"? Because there's a Rome near Parchim, Mecklenburg, about four hundred souls, Mr. Inspector. / The advancing darkness invites us to respect proper form concerning two gentlemen and a lady alone in an interrogation. (– Hee-hee: bleated the Mecklenburg colleague.) Might we have a light turned on? At your service. Thank you. Look friendly, now, we are bringing in another witness. The principal? No need, she can mind the phone. My first interrogation—how different the dream is from the reality! Hello again, Mrs. Elise Bock; you, Selbich, get us some coffee, quick now. / Student Gantlik. Member of FDJ class chapter; employee of the local Red Army commandant. Student Lockenvitz says he got lost in Berlin. A new, strange city. Student Lockenvitz's social origins? Something about farming in Prussian Pommern. This young friend's attitude towards the government's decision to hand his homeland over to the Poles? To the People's Poland: is how Lockenvitz puts it. Jakob Abs, officially registered as living with Cresspahl, Brickworks Road, Jerichow, as a courier of leaflets from West Berlin? Of posters to paste up. Travels by rail on a free pass. After graduating with honors from the Locomotive Engineers School in Güstrow he registered for a course in Elements of Materialist Dialectics. The third tenet of this doctrine? The transformation of quantitative changes into qualitative changes. Railwayman Abs's private life? Handball. His plans for the future? He's a grown man, why would he discuss things like that with a seventeen-year-old girl! / Student Cresspahl comes to class in a white blouse. Blue shirt only for festive occasions. Turns up at school in a petticoat, dragging in the fashions of a declining empire. Completely incorrect: a petticoat is a woman's underskirt. I hereby regret falsely accusing this FDJ friend of coming to class in an underskirt. In fact it was, out of vanity, a full, lightly starched skirt, made following illustrations in the democratic press. Student Gantlik has been found guilty of Protestant leanings. Well she is extremely interested in Max Planck; the physics here is way above Student Cresspahl's head. Planck, the one stamped on the back of a West German two-mark coin? I've never in my life had a piece of Western currency in my hand; never seen it; no hide, no hair. Any liking on the part of Colleague Selbich for senior-year student Sieboldt? Only hearsay; it does look like she's in love. Is it mutual? The principal was too young to have any influence on Abitur final grades. The principal seems to have it out for a certain someone. If only I knew why. Hypothetically, just between you and me? For myself. Psychology, is that it? and now, quickly, to your third thought upon seeing these criminal postings on the wall of the school, showing young friends in the FDJ behind barbed wire. Barbed wire? I never saw that.

Here Student Cresspahl paused, for the first and only time. She was saying something true, for once, but she felt uncertain. What arises, what happens, when consciousness suddenly formulates a perception it had shrugged off nine hours earlier? An afterimage? On the anonymous scrap of paper in the coat pocket, "barbed wire" had been just a pair of words; now the twisted lines with their braided-in barbs were a mental image, and underlying them was the tone of voice from the evening's broadcast of the BBC: *barbed wire*, in English. How, from the miserable feeling of tedium last night at yet another wave of posters, could the resolve arise to testify to barbed wire, as strong as if it had been taken in the morning?

– After intensive self-examination: Student Cresspahl began to confess, but then stopped.

She remembered Kurt Müller. "Kutschi," chairman of the Communist Youth League in Germany in 1931. Sentenced in 1934 to six years in prison for "Preparation for Treason," then moved to Sachsenhausen concentration camp. After the elimination of Hitler's battalions, state chairman of the Communist Party, Lower Saxony; deputy chair of the national party, 1948; member of the West German Parliament, 1949. Under the protection of parliamentary immunity, paid an official visit to the German Sovietnik

Republic, and was reported as "missing" on March 22, 1950. Two months later, the M.f.S. had confessed and admitted that same date as the date of Kutschi Müller's arrest. He was sitting behind bars and wires on this very evening; if the members of the FDJ were marching for anything, it was, in fact, for this reinforced wire.

She remembered a boy in 10-A-I arrested over a pop song. Tipsy at a class party, he had altered the dreamy image in the first line of a sentimental number: "When, by Capri, the red sun sinks into the sea." Instead of "sun" he'd sung "fleet"—to be flip, and probably feeling sure that his position as president of his FDJ class chapter was bulletproof protection. Paulie Möllendorf it was, and his fast talk in front of the court had probably hurt him more than helped. Four years in prison.

She remembered Axel Ohr. Axel, though eighteen, wanted to go to the Germany Rally of Free Youth too, his luggage seeming a bundle of newspapers; he had almost seven pounds of electrolytic copper inside it, which he was planning to sell in the forbidden half of Berlin, to buy baling twine for Johnny Schlegel's agricultural commune. Johnny got off unscathed because Axel had dreamed up this contribution to the work in the silent chambers of his own mind; Axel was threatened with the maximum punishment, five years in prison. True, there was a law against exporting nonferrous metals, but that didn't help bring in the harvest. Axel was in pretrial detention in the basement, a dungeon surrounded by wire with barbs. When the New Free Youth went marching in their blue shirts, it was also for that.

Young Friend Cresspahl repeated, after lengthy consideration: she had noticed no barbed wire. Asked what the FDJ were marching for, she gave the desired answer. She was admonished to inspect any visual advertising in future with greater attentiveness (she'd claimed morning sleepiness), in the interests of dialectically utilizing the perniciousness she herself had invoked. And keep your ears open too, got it? – *Vas slushayu*, yes sir: Student Cresspahl said, which went over well with the interrogator although it was also something of a bitter pill since he was equally proud of his nationality and of his skill in concealing it. With a sudden laugh like that of someone annoyed at himself, he answered with sudden unexpected rudeness: *Da svidanya*. Until next time. That's a promise.

Outside the gate of the educational institution almost every student

Cresspahl had ever exchanged a word with or shared a smile with stood waiting. About seventy of them were there to make sure this child would be returning to their midst. People shouted "Hurrah!" the way brave young princesses used to be cheered in the old days. There was singing.

Lise Wollenberg had gone home.

And Student Gantlik, just visible on the bridge over the city moat, made off in a hurry as soon as she'd seen enough. She continued to consider it unwise for the time being to reveal even the scrap of a connection, a bond, between herself and Student Cresspahl. Yes you do talk like that, Anita.

We almost unanimously felt that Bettina must have thrown herself at the investigators from Schwerin while bullying and threatening the students under her as though we were dangerous vermin, lepers, contagious, keep your distance! (and again, though, like she wanted to bite us). Maybe we stepped aside a bit too eagerly when she came marching up with the two gentlemen in their leather coats. She was drooping now; we heard her lamenting, as she said goodbye: And it had to happen in my school, of all places, Mr. Inspector!

She now turned violently on us, ordering us to get water and scrub brushes from the janitor's and get the rest of the handbills off the school walls. (The school's front door—two large slabs of oak, prewar manufacture, from 1910—had been taken off its hinges and hauled off by the Gneez police.) And so the young dandy from Hans-and-Sophie-Scholl Street, Schwerin, was once more forced out of his black cherry–colored car, polished to a mirrorlike sheen (from the people-owned firm Eisenacher Motor Works, EMW, not a Bavarian BMW), to reprimand Comrade Selbich and keep the crowd of suspected culprits from further studying even the remaining small print as they scratched away at it.

And he singled out Student Cresspahl again for a parting word. He planted himself in front of the young lady in a comradely pose, in his made-to-measure easy-to-clean suit, and informed her: his name was Lehmann. (I would recognize him to this day, from a harelip too hastily repaired. But let him languish in boredom in Leningrad or Prague; why should I bother him.) – A name to remember: he added, revealing himself as one of the ruling powers of this New Mecklenburg.

Now after this did Bettinikin still manage to make the leap from principal pro tem to principal?

Anyone worried about that will of course set out on the long summer vacation of 1950 with a heavy heart, unsettled, practically troubled, with little prickles like a swarm of ants all over their brain as they fall asleep.

– Three times you could have nailed her during the interrogation: Marie says; she's complaining.

– First of all, Bettina did get her knuckles rapped. Plus we had promised each other: only in an emergency.

– If that wasn't an emergency then tell me what is!

– *Coming right up!*

July 31, 1968 Wednesday

The New York Times wants to show us a helicopter from which four crates are dangling, with supplies for Marine outposts near the Demilitarized Zone in Vietnam. A photo that looks like propaganda; no news value whatsoever.

In Kosice, the gentlemen from the Kremlin and those from the Hradshin are keeping the topic under discussion at the Junction Club in Cierna to themselves. The ones from Moscow are reported to have stomped out at 10:30 last night, looking rather angry, and boarded their green train. In order to have something, anything to report, Auntie *Times* describes the Czechoslovakian train cars as, unlike their Soviet counterparts, painted blue.

Pravda, the press organ of Soviet Truth, reprints the East German understanding of quiet, normal life on the streets of Prague these days, along with their conjectures about what's going on behind the facades. As evidence. It also puts out, in photographic facsimile, a letter from ninety-eight workers at Auto-Praha asking the Soviet troops to linger in the country.

And a New York City councilman has spent a week living in East Harlem, posing as a writer; now he says he knows about life there. He saw no rats, but said he didn't think rats could stand that building on 119th Street between Park and Lexington.

Personnel changes during the first half of the 1950–51 school year in Gneez, Mecklenburg:

First, to open the new term, a stiff-legged man (blue shirt) climbed the podium to the lectern facing the assembled students and introduced himself as the new principal, with all the powers and privileges pertaining thereto, and with the enameled badge (SED) showing clasped hands (KPD, SPD) on his lapel: Dr. Eduard Kramritz. He pressed his wire-framed (now gold-plated-wire-framed) glasses into the sores on his nose and announced: Some of you already know me. Applause. The rest will get to know me— soon. Applause.

Of course Bettina Selbich was innocent in the matter of the posted query to the members of the FDJ about why they were marching. But at an institute of secondary learning conducted with all due vigilance such questions never come up in the first place, do you follow that, Comrade? In addition, the district school board had received two letters, from the typewriter of the councilman, since replaced, and from the hand of Dr. Julius Kliefoth, both evincing knowledge of Latin, remarking on the moral maturity required in anyone called upon to thoughtfully supervise the course of education in young student souls (by this they meant us; Kramritz being made principal must have come as an embarrassing surprise to them). The Unity Party, meanwhile, showed a certain generosity in not rejecting Bettina altogether; it extended her waiting period as a candidate for membership by a full year.

Changes in the teaching staff: Dr. Gollnow is retiring, two years past the mandatory date. In her place we have Eberhard Martens—soldierly bearing, blond crew-cut, "the Evil Eye." Student-teacher in German, fulfilling his internship with the members of what is now class 11-A-II: Mathias Weserich, MA in language and literature, Leipzig University: another limper, somewhat more flexible at the knees, whose greeting took the form of a bow from the neck, his mouth pulled open to almost a rectangle full of unnaturally white teeth. Colleague Selbich's new assignment: instructor in German, and also Contemporary Studies. Applause.

Student Gantlik (alone) and Students Pagenkopf and Cresspahl (together) had paid a visit to Erdmuthe Gollnow at the start of the summer. Tight bun, friendly gaze down into cups of apple blossom tea, grandfather clock, dresser with knick-knacks, sofa with curved wooden arms. Anita had been stymied by the niceties of visiting; it was from Anita's two schoolmates that Mrs. Gollnow later heard that Anita too had meant to ask her to seize the day when the keys to the principal's office were dangled in her presence. The old lady sighed, and sighed again, and thanked them for the trust they placed in her, and said she was too weak. (In terms of health she was in better shape than Alma Witte.) – Ah, yes!: she croaked in a bouncy voice: Ah to be sixty again!

As the assembled faculty stepped humbly over to the right side of the podium, the Central School-Group Authority of the Free German Youth (FDJ ZSGL!) clambered up and took their places behind the red-draped tables, a wall of cloth. (That, Marie, was to keep any undignified leg movements from diminishing the devotion of the Young Friends on the auditorium floor.) Beneath the talons of Picasso's bristling dove, Sieboldt and Gollantz surrendered their offices, thereby entering the Rostock University groups. The secretary and treasurer resigned, pleading overwork in view of their coming Abitur. Elected as new secretary to organize the school group, by a vote of 288 to 23: Dieter Lockenvitz, 11-A-II. As president, with 220 votes and numerous abstentions: Gabriel Manfras, 11-A-II. Young Friend Manfras, step forward!

We'd never have thought that Gabriel had it in him to give a speech! Yet what a ringing voice this taciturn child suddenly launched from his throat. Maybe he was making up for the silence he kept from first period to last, from class visits to the theater to end-of-year parties; our old idea that he was shy was now instantly forgotten. The meeting now proceeds to the election of the presidium. Nominations please. Dr. Kramritz, as friend and partner of the FDJ school group. Acclamation. The beanpole gym teacher, because he rakes us over the coals politically too. Good-humored laughter. The members of the ZSGL, of course. I propose as first member of the honorary presidium Comrade Josef Vissarionovich Stalin, a shining example to us all for his mighty labors for peace; his daily efforts for the improvement of the proletarian capital; the opening of the Great Northern Seaway; the draining of the swamps of Colchis; not least as thanks and reward for his completion of that work of genius on Marxism and questions of linguistics. Frenzied applause, breaking off suddenly. The president of the People's Republic of Poland, Bolesław Bierut, in honor of the peaceful encounter of our two peoples at the Oder and Neisse Rivers. Comrade Mao, liberator of the People's Republic of China and partner of Comrade Stalin. The writer Thomas Mann, in memory of his late brother Heinrich, recipient of the Goethe-bicentennial National Prize, who displayed in his journey to Weimar the realism that shines forth from every buttonhole of his writings! The author of the work *The Socialist Sixth of the World*, a theologian ostracized in his own land, Hewlett Johnson, the "Red Dean" of Canterbury! The cheering, standing audience is requested to go easy on the bleachers. Now Young Friend Manfras has the floor, to present an appraisal of the prospects for world peace, and also in Gneez.

Gabriel looked strangely at us, gripped the front of the lectern with his right hand, propped the knuckles of his left against the bottom edge in back, looked down at his manuscript, and was ready to give a speech. (The boy standing there had been given advance warning that he would be nominated and elected; he had a lecture all prepared.) Young Comrade Manfras began, appropriately, with the date: September First, the Day of Peace, we too pledge that. The criminal invasion by North American troops and their South Korean mercenaries into the northern republic, whose leader we all. Well might the West Germans groaning under the yoke of capitalism fear the coming war—they are buying droves of sailboats to flee in, hoarding gas, standing in long lines outside the South American consulates; we, on the other hand, enjoy safety and security under the newly elected general secretary of the newly founded central committee of the Unity Party, W. Ulbricht, and the disgraceful use of the nickname *Sachwalter*, "Custodian," for Walter U. can only reflect pitifully on anyone with a German dictionary at his. The Party's vigilance, as demonstrated in the unmasking of leading comrades Kreikemeyer and company, co-conspirators of the American agent provocateur Noel H. Field and his disgusting three-way marriage; this vigilance we too shall. The imminent collapse of the British Empire at the side of the USA can only. The hateful interview of the West German chancellor with the organ of high capitalism, *The New York Times*, showing only his contempt for humanity; his proposal for the quick reestablishment of a German military force will inevitably lead to. We adjourn this meeting with the song: "We are the Young Van-Guard / of the Pro-le-ta-ri-at!"

In Gabriel Manfras's whirlwind world tour, he had woven in the obscure German word *Diversion* more than once, and at first those among us who knew some Latin thought: What an old-fashioned fellow. But when he added into the mix the people with the paste brushes who had been so interested in the goal the FDJ was marching for, and called them American diversants, the grammatical connection was at last broken for his listeners; only after the song could we find out from Anita that there is indeed a Soviet word, *diversiya*, meaning in no way a distracting maneuver but rather an attack. From the side? No, a frontal assault, or all around actually: Anita said, embarrassed. If only she'd finally realized that we'd long been impressed with her work for Triple-J, as jobs go!

As for Gabriel Manfras, we now had a pretty good idea how he'd spent his summer.

Dr. Kramritz, too, had undergone a course designed to hone him to a fine political edge, during which he had kind of misplaced his family. Lost sight of his wife. And so propositioned his colleague Bettina Selbich, who by then was sporting a tight-fitting blouse, non-blue, and a charmingly humble manner. In case of divorce, so he'd know where to turn for refuge. Rumors wanted to supply a slap in the face at this point; an eyewitness, Klaus Böttcher, had seen a couple in tears on the wooded path winding its way around the Smœkbarg. But now Bettina's landlord won his eviction case; she could find a single room only in the Danish Quarter; she was commended by her party group for moving closer to the working class; she was scared of Wieme Wohl. And who should move into the full apartment on Cathedral Court, three rooms with kitchen basement bathroom and a view across the parish meadows down to the rows of poplars on the shore of Gneez Lake, but the reconciled Kramritz family. "Protecting the cadre of specialists," it's called. If you want to protect your cadre, choose wisely.

The news of Thomas Mann's signature on the Stockholm Appeal—calling for a ban on nuclear weapons irrespective of whose—had consoled us about our own. A year later we were ashamed.

This "document" was not new to me... as part of a photomontage purporting to show me in the act of signing the Stockholm Appeal in Paris in the spring of 1950. I am shown on this occasion wearing a suit that I did wear in summer 1949, but did not bring to Europe in 1950. The black tie I had tragic cause to wear in mourning in May 1949 is visible in the photograph too. How this came to pass is something I am neither able to discover nor interested in. What I do know, and what

I have said, truthfully, is that I did not sign my name to the Stockholm Appeal. © Katja Mann

Kreikemeyer and company, that meant German Communists in French exile, imprisoned, Kreikemeyer helped to escape in 1942 by Field, the American Unitarian, then leader of the illegal German Communist Party in Marseilles. Seven years later, Willi Kreikemeyer was installed as the head of the German Reich Railway, Jakob's topmost boss. In May 1949 he'd gone out on a limb for his party when the West Berlin railwaymen went on strike for payment of their wages in the currency of the city where they worked and bought their bread. On May 5, Willi K. promised them payment in West marks, then retracted his commitment. One dead in clashes with the police, and several wounded, were added to the weight he bore on his shoulders for the party. On May 28 he promised up to 60 percent payment in West marks, and: refraining from any reprisals. In late June, to keep his party from losing face, he broke his word again and fired 380 railway workers without notice or transfer to locations in the East German Republic whose very currency they'd scoffed at. Willi Kreikemeyer, member of a party and adherent of its constitution that claimed to respect professions of religious faith, promised the Jehovah's Witnesses twelve special trains to take them to a congress in Berlin, that was July 1949, he took their money and then canceled the trains—all for his party. Now that party has been accusing him, since late August, of having passed addresses to the American OSS. Jakob went around dejected in the summer of 1949; a loyal member of the FDJ will of course recite such things on the evenings of his training course; if I'd interrupted, he would have asked me: And what kind of school do you go to, Gesine?

Once the Carola Neher club was done with her, I commissioned from D. E. Willi Kreikemeyer's life story; all three scholars with all their expertise in registers and sources and cross-references could find no lifespan for him extending past August 1950.

As for the West German chancellor, Bettina Selbich clued us in to the illuminating similarity between his name and that of the President of Columbia University, commander since 1950 of the armed forces of the North Atlantic Treaty Organization. Eisenhower, Adenower. Contemporary Studies.

As for the North American president, we were supposed to ridicule Harry S. Truman because he fraudulently used his middle initial to claim American dignity when in fact the S stood for itself, not a whole name; there was also Truman's former job selling neckties and suchlike menswear, which we were to invoke as proof of his inferiority. Contemporary Studies.

The first time the East German Republic observed Activist Day was October 13, 1950, and Elise Bock was awarded the title "Activist of Merit" and a tidy sum of money. One last greeting from Triple-J, who was now free to return home. The administration of Gneez had been turned over to the Unity Party; his successor was a military commander who moved out of the city into the woods around the Smœkbarg.

On August 15, the government of the East German Republic (a person, too) requested some kind of convoluted operation involving ballots having to do with the People's Chamber and the state, district, and municipal administration. It counted 99 percent yes votes, and another 0.7 percent on top of that.

The Waldheim trials started in the summer of 1950 and on November 4 it was time to start the executions. Cresspahl wore no crape for the man he might have remembered as his father-in-law. The Cresspahl child still felt sympathy for Albert Papenbrock, because there had been a time when she hadn't been allowed to take candy from anyone; he sat sadly under the sun umbrellas at the outdoor tables of the Lübeck Court in Jerichow, forced to consume a whole large ice cream by himself. Gesine Cresspahl wasn't brave enough to show up to Mrs. Selbich's class with mourning crape on her sleeve; by that point Selbich was quick to apply to Principal Kramritz for demerits. Thomas Mann's family suppressed his letter to the custodian in the collection of letters published for the time being; in fact he did write the *Sachwalter* in July.

Some ten trials took place within an hour. No defense attorneys were allowed, no witnesses for the defense allowed to testify. In handcuffs, though almost none were accused of real crimes, the accused—the men and women found guilty before the trial—were brought before the court, which, by the book, pronounced prison terms of fifteen, eighteen, twenty-five years, even for life. [...] Mr. President! Perhaps you are unaware of the horror, the revulsion, often fake but often deeply felt, that these trials with their death sentences—and they are all death sentences—have called forth on this side of the globe; how conducive they are to ill will and how destructive of goodwill. An act of mercy, as sweeping and summary as the mass sentencing in Waldheim has all too clearly been, would be such a blessed gesture, serving the cause of reconciliation and hope for détente—an act of peace. / Use your power . . . ! © Katja Mann

But the custodian needed his power to set up judiciary performances of the sort his wise leader and teacher Stalin had showed him in Bulgaria, Hungary, Czechoslovakia. Why should he restore the honor of a few useful dead when only fifty-one thousand among the living in his country found the courage to mark their ballots with a No—only as many people as lived in Gneez, plus Jerichow.

Klaus Böttcher was sitting in his dad's kitchen, cooling his feet in soapy water. In comes his wife, Britte, and she says: Hey, there're three men here, *all in black suits, they want something from you.* Klaus is out the window, dangles from the sill high above the shop yard, drops down, and takes off, barefoot, over the fence, the moat, the city walls, and keeps going, in the direction of West Berlin. In Krakow am See he has to go to ground at a carpenter colleague's, his bare feet are bleeding so badly. Britte can read her husband's mind and gets a call put through to Krakow. – Y'can come back, Klaus, they're all from the college, they wanted to go in together orderin a boathouse from you, dummy!: said fond Britte. When asked about the consciousness of guilt his behavior suggested, Klaus would always repeat, embarrassed anew each time: *Hows the hare supposed to prove hes not a fox?*

In December 1950, Jakob's mother applied for an interzonal travel permit. This was the piece of paper that would officially authorize a trip from Jerichow to Bochum, West Germany. If she'd been correctly informed, there was a remnant of Wilhelm Abs's family living there. The Abses would write to one another at very most in the event of a death, or a birth, two weeks late; she was old, of course, and wanted to get as close as she could to the news she feared. Jakob made time to go back and forth among the various offices and authorities; Cresspahl's daughter lacked the kinship necessary to help. So it took until January before Mrs. Abs had collected:

a police registration certificate,

police certification of a clean criminal record,

a handwritten autobiographical statement (fourth draft),

proof of the political or economic reason for the trip (here Cresspahl and Jakob invented an inheritance for her in the Ruhr
district, and Dr. Werner Jansen, attorney by trade in Gneez,
conjured up on his typewriter when his staff was out of the
office a district court's affidavit of delivery with a West German
dateline),

a statement from the Unity Party endorsing the trip (which Mrs.
Brüshaver got through via the CDU office for V.o.F. [Victims
of Fascism] in Schwerin),

a statement from the Gneez tax office confirming the absence of
any outstanding tax liabilities;

and then all she had to do is get everything translated into Russian. Lotte
Pagels took twenty-eight marks for that, with all its Krijgerstamian mistakes. Anita, you would've done it as a favor, admit it! But since Anita was
avoiding eye contact with Student Cresspahl, how could the name Abs
mean anything to her? And how useful she could have been as an interpreter
with the Sovietnik in Gneez City Hall whose job it was to "advise" the city
administration in the sovereign German republic. It probably wasn't too
much to expect for Gesine to make an effort and approach Anita with the
request; Gesine was against the trip, Mrs. Abs seemed to be preparing for
it very carefully, sometimes people take a trip and don't come back; she
used shyness as another excuse. If the application came back denied it
would be her fault.

Aggie, into December, was busy doing what a govt. exam.'d lic.'d reg.'d
nurse considers her job. She hid behind Dr. Schürenberg, district medical
examiner; Dr. Schürenberg summoned Cresspahl, examined him plausibly
enough, and wrote out a certificate attesting him unfit to work.

In 1950, for the first time since 1937, New Year's Eve was celebrated in
the Cresspahl house. There was no carp, but Jakob brought crayfish. It's
true that crayfish are best in the months without a letter *r*: in the opinion
of Hedwig Dorn, in *The Housewife's Helper*, an opinion shared by Frieda
Ihlefeld; still, one doesn't have to take it so literally, if one doesn't want to,

even Ihlefeld seems to regard it as a kind of folklore. For the first time we in Cresspahl's house were something like a family. Gesine watched from afar as Jakob's mother scrubbed the live creatures with a birch brush in cold water, then brought them to their death in boiling; while the church-goers in the family were out at services, Gesine stood by the pot, eyes on the clock and the paper with the recipe, and she ladled off the floating fat, added wood to the fire, let it cool, scooped out the red roe butter; distracted, though, because Jakob at the window spent a half hour showing her how a young man of twenty-two shaves for a nighttime celebration. Maybe the New Year's carp was missing—the fun was there. Cresspahl wrote the final lines in his last account books. Four people confessed their resolutions for the coming year; four times Jakob poured Richtenberger aquavit into Gesine's glass.

Jesu, let me gladly end it, / This my freshly entered year. / Thy strong hands' upholding lend it, / Ward off peril and its fear. / Lastly, in Thy mantle furled, / I shall gladly quit this world.

Oh now dont be leavin us just yet, Fru Abs.

Ive had it. These engines, these wornout tracks, let the devil ride em. Godet Niejår, *Gesine!*

Happy New Year everyone.

You're asking—

For what's different here in New York in the state of New York. You know that this is one of the places to which West Berlin newspaper publishers send tiny porcelain bells to families one of whose members has been killed trying to kill members of other families on the other side of the world in Vietnam. For one difference.

Well, take yellow. Here yellow is in different places. I mean the whole color family—genuine yellow or as near to yellow as ocher or canaries or anything else in the zone between red and green, not only *any of the colors normally seen when the portion of the physical spectrum of wavelengths 571.5 to 578.5 millimicrons specif. 574.5 millimicrons is employed as a stimulus*: as Webster says, but, you know, yellow. Here yellow is in different places.

Not only in eggs, Mongols, jaundice, sponges, butterflies, marsh-marigolds. I've never seen as much yellow as here.

Here someone jealous, envious, cowardly, melancholy, treacherous, a deserter, or someone like Brutus (because he was not an honorable man) may be called yellow. Yellow people here are contemptible; the tabloids here are the yellow press, like the yellow *Bildzeitung* in Germany; there are yellow oaks and yellow perch.

Underbidders are yellow dogs, who sign yellow-dog contracts, which means they agree not to join any union but a yellow one.

Someone yellowing here is throwing his weight around.

The language here believes that certain natives in the southwestern part of the country have yellow bellies, yellow like sulfur.

You see yellow lines on one-way avenues, with yellow writing reserving a car's width for certain vehicles only.

Two yellow lines divide the two-way avenues.

One yellow line divides the two-lane side streets.

Yellow in broadly applied lines marks off the pedestrian areas in inter-sections.

Yellow are the casings of the traffic lights unable to speak words, ca-pable only of round disks of color.

On yellow rectangles the authorities warn drivers of curves or children ahead and recommend certain speeds.

Yellow signs surround men at road construction work, and they say: Danger.

The barricades, planks on four angled legs that police place around buildings gutted by fire or use to keep the curious away from festive first-nights or parades, are yellow, sometimes with a touch of orange but the yellow remains unvanquished.

The edges of long-distance railroad platforms are painted yellow.

Yellow has a national quality—think of the only yellow platform edge in all of West Berlin: at the US Army station in Lichterfelde.

The platform edges in the subways are yellow; the railings are painted yellow; the platforms under the passenger's feet say Stand Clear, in yellow.

In subway stations the first step of a staircase and the step before a landing and the vertical edge of the last step are smeared yellow, sometimes the whole landing too.

The curbs in front of fire hydrants and bus stops are yellow: No Parking. Yellow is the color of the entranceways to garages, yellow the curbstones.

Post office steps are marked with yellow dots.

Gold, admittedly, but still yellow because not quite as red as gold, are the numbers and names and logos painted on the glass doors of buildings and stores and bars.

Official suggestions, too, such as: You are advised against coming any closer, or: Don't even think about smoking on public transportation, or: Please note that this car's name is 7493.

In the revolving doors of official buildings you find little arrows on yellow stickers. More and more the old street signs are being replaced with yellow ones.

Gravely the heads of famous ladies look down at you from the upper edge of an edifice that announces in yellow and gold: I am the Metropolitan Museum; I'm free of charge; I am very rarely closed.

Yellow wherever you look.

Yellow are the light fixtures in the windows of Western Union.

Western Union is a telegram service. What President Johnson keeps saying is: Great Society.

Yellow: Johnson commented two years ago about the dress of a wife of a Philippine visitor of state: yellow's my favorite color too. Actually: she confided later: My favorite color is pink.

Yellow are the raincoats of the workmen crawling under the street and looking for holes in the gas pipes.

The air here is yellow when it's suffocating.

Yellow circulars are carried around here, I pass you a note on yellow scratch paper, and many ballpoint pens, disguised as pencils, are yellow. Sometimes even orange juice.

Becoming tarnished in accord with nature is surely what the brass on the outside doors of genteel hotels, apartment buildings, banks would prefer to do; their baseboards, doorknobs, peepholes, handles, the surfaces of their noble locks are scrubbed yellow; their hydrants, mostly twinned, are shined yellow. The massive shingles of the exorbitant doctors are polished yellow, to a line of sheer gold, only the rational mind still considers it brass.

And golden triangles on the glass doors of fancy buildings are there to keep you from bumping into them.

Yellow are the envelopes known as manila. Yellow Pages are what they here call what you know as a business telephone directory.

The butter is suspiciously yellow.

Whereas it might get serious here, much like on the other side of the world, the signs indicating shelters against radioactive fallout are yellow. Prophetically placed therein are the three triangles above the little circle in which, in yellow, the number of persons who can here be saved is supposed to be stated but regularly isn't, as if it were something unknown.

Yellow are the Broadway Maintenance trucks that wash and sweep the streets, that carry away trash and/or cars that need to be towed. Yellow are the cars of many taxi fleets. Yellow are the symbols, products, packaging, and delivery vans of numerous enterprises and institutes.

But why? That they do not know.

Yellow is a color that attracts attention: they say. But why it does so, no one knows.

Maybe because a nephew of the country's first president owned an ocher factory?

Yellow is yellow: the answer runs.

And those who tell you that are authorities. It's true and I admit it: the authority says: Even if it was my favorite daughter who called me yellow I'd give her a good smack. But I feel that we, and by we I mean our whole nation: We can thank our lucky stars that we can at least kill these peasants in Viet Nam or whatever it's called there for reasons other than that their skin is yellow. The only people who can understand our reasons are those who belong, and who know: What Yellow Means. End of quote.

You have to admit, finally, that nobody in New York or any other city in this country is killed because of his yellow skin. In the first place, there are darker shades in the mix. Second, this is a free country. You need to see things in a yellower light!

—for it.

August 2, 1968 Friday

The *Times* would have so loved to report that the Soviet and Czechoslovakian delegations sat down and broke bread together. But she, too, was
merely given the communiqué mentioning something about an atmosphere
of complete frankness, sincerity, and mutual understanding. They're planning to meet again tomorrow in Bratislava, but this time with the leaders
from Poland, East Germany, Hungary, and Bulgaria. Will they throw a
wrench into whatever the Soviet Union may have signed at the Cierna
railroad junction?

And how was the weather in July? *The New York Times* has worked it
out and tells us: Unseasonably hot. We must've had a miserable time of
things around July 16. A Tuesday. We could've done without a half of it.
Don't wish your life away.

Anyone who remembers German class in grade 11-A-II in Gneez in
1950–51 will of necessity cry: Schach! Schach!

The teacher was Mr. Weserich, a student teacher from Thuringia, and
the Cresspahl/Pagenkopf collective had already gotten to know him slightly
toward the end of the previous summer. They'd seen him on a bench outside the dressing rooms at Gneez Lake—it was early, he thought he was
alone, and he was adjusting the screws on an aluminum structure at his
left knee, which was where his leg ended. His mouth formed another square;
he looked like he was in pain. We were horror-struck.

But it was he who opened by apologizing. – Well that's that: he calmly
said once he'd pushed himself up into a standing position. – For Führer
and Reich; I believed it too: he added, leaving the rest to us, trusting fully
to our diplomatic skills. As a result he already had a reputation when demoted Principal Selbich introduced him to us, in her sour way. – We will
be reading *Schach von Wuthenow* by Theodor Fontane: he said, announcing his intentions as clear as daylight. How we would have quaked in our
shoes if we'd understood what he meant.

We had German four days a week. Weserich told us about the century
of Fontane's life, starting on May 5, 1789, with Count Mirabeau, deputy
of the Third Estate; he was perfectly open in laying out his traps but we
failed to see them. He told us about Fontane's childhood years, his time
in England and France; read to us from letters to his family, *car tel est notre*

plaisir, as the king and Fontane's father used to say. Neat, clear High German, drawn from his mind while his gaze was elsewhere. On September 11 he had the effrontery to ask us our first impressions after reading the work by Th. Fontane mentioned at the start of the semester. Out of the blue, one week to the next, with shining eyes full of anticipation!

Anita raised her hand—she was willing to sacrifice herself. He ignored her hand but smiled at her, and her alone. The rest of us, numbering about thirty, were permitted to remonstrate that there was only one single copy of this work in the Culture League library; that only novels like *Effi Briest* were on our shelves at home; we tried to talk him out of his plan. The upshot was that he complimented us, praised our resourcefulness, and promised to repeat his question on September 18. – We'll be seeing one another quite a lot this year: he promised.

To keep him favorably disposed to us, we each contributed a thirtieth of what Elise Bock charged to type out a hundred and thirty printed pages; Pius procured the mimeograph stencils on a visit to the FDJ district office. (– Thou shalt not muzzle the ox when he treadeth out the corn: he admitted, but only in his collective work group.) Before the pages could be run off, though, Anita had to swing from City Hall a certification of harmlessness and authorization to reproduce a text. On the 18th, there we were with our bundles of rough spotty paper, and Zaychik the rabbit was already looking forward to what he was about to say.

– *Issan old story*: Zaychik said: You bed 'em, you wed 'em!

The visitor thanked him for this instruction in Mecklenburg folk wisdom. And he was right—what had spoken from Zaychik's mouth was the spirit of the Gneez townsman-farmers (and the banished nobility); he didn't even realize the speculation he was inviting about his parents' marriage, or about his own dealings with Eva Matschinsky. She shrank in her seat, blushing.

Dagobert Haase stood there, naive and slightly chubby in body, grumbling and defiant in manner like someone who follows instructions but doesn't have to. And he said: It's about a hunnerd an fifty years ago. A cavalry captain has a girlfriend that maybe he wants to marry. Suddenly he falls for her daughter, twenty years younger, but because people're crackin jokes about the pockmarks in her face he wants to duck the consequences. The king orders him to marry, and he does, but he shoots himself after lunch. He leaves his name and the child to her.

Zaychik obligingly turned half around to let us see in his face what he thought: Ain't that always the way?

Mr. Weserich thanked him for the plot summary. Might Haase be prepared to answer an additional question?

Zaychik let his head fall forward—the silent sufferer. Upon request, he named the main character (same as the title), the daughter (someone named Victoire), the mother's maiden name ... (not sure about that).

The address of the von Carayon family? this German teacher asked the room, past Zaychik, explicitly to spare him, and when Student Cresspahl could only give Berlin, we were permitted to return to the opening of the story and begin again:

"In Frau von Carayon's salon on Behrenstrasse in Berlin, a few friends had gathered on the customary evening..."

We were then informed that people of rank at that time ... but it wouldn't be worth the trouble, presumably, to ask what the year might be?

– 1806: Anita suggested, and then had to say why. – Because the characters are talking about the Battle of the Three Emperors at Austerlitz as something that just happened, and that was in December 1805, on the 2nd.

... at that time chose their addresses with great care. Where they lived expressed their self-regard and was held up to others. Therefore—alas!—he had no choice but to inform us that Behrenstrasse runs parallel to and one block south of Unter den Linden; the von Carayons were blessed with a house on the corner of Charlotten Street, a short walk from the Opera, the Lustgarten, the Palace. Behr Street is named after the heraldic bear of Berlin—this opinion is widespread, but the truth is that the street honors the engineer Johann Heinrich Behr, to whom Berlin owes French Street and, as of 1701, Jerusalem Street and Leipzig Street as well. Well known to every tried and true Berliner and now to every member of class 11-A-II, from personal experience, at least since September 11, if from a different source. Moreover, were we to consider that the author of this tale surely eschewed any mere coincidence, why would he mention an architect from the turn of the seventeenth to eighteenth century in the very first line? Perhaps to infuse the past era of the story with a hint of an even older past? Make sense? And are any of us now inclined to turn to the subtitle? "A Story from the Time of the Gensdarmes Regiment"? In response to the resulting determined, stony silence, a young student-teacher spent the rest of the class expatiating on the origins of the name of this regiment of cuirassiers, bearing swords instead of lances in the cavalry of Charles IV of France. A nod to the author's French background, perhaps? *Gens d'armes, au Moyen Age, soldats, cavaliers du roi?* Since our session, full of fascinating moments for which he was in our debt, was now drawing to a close, he ventured to request that by Wednesday we at least try to *read* the first two pages.

Class 11-A-II needed almost three weeks for the first six pages of the novella, and no matter how much you stared at Mr. Weserich for wasting all this time he refused to lose any sleep over it. We started to look forward to his outbursts of cheerful despair, when the perfectly clear words "in England and the union states" actually failed to call forth in our minds a picture of the United States of America, or to ensure that we learned more about the origins of the von Bülow gentleman, Adam Heinrich Dietrich v. B., than that he'd been arrested for his writing. Could it truly be the case that there was only one single encyclopedia in the whole city of Gneez, loaned out to someone else for the next several years?

No one could accuse Weserich of pettiness. We were inclined to work with him; we were equipped to handle the Latin quotations, thanks to Kliefoth, and now and then even translated one ourselves (*hic haeret*). After a while Weserich realized that, though a knowledge of Latin might be helpful in the learning of French, it could by no means replace instruction in the latter. This surprised him; he didn't want to admit it; was this reason to challenge the intellectual fathers of the Educational Reform Law who had replaced French with Russian? Thenceforth he had us present to him utterances in Fontane's second language for translation into German—always at least three at a time, please, on that he must insist. – How the time is running away from us! he'd cry, and this was late October, and we were on chapter two. So we looked things up in the dictionary, things such as *embonpoint, nonchalance*, the realm in which a gourmet excelled and the one in which a gourmand; we asked old people if they'd ever seen that kind of sinumbra lamp (an oil lamp on a pedestal, casting very little shadow). When Mathias Weserich was happy with our knowledge, to the point of putting on a show of surprise and disbelief, it was meant to be fun for us and so we did him that favor.

Two weeks of class on the riddle: Why did Fontane give titles to his chapters here, unlike in *Under the Pear Tree* only three years earlier, or *Count Petöfy* one year after *Schach*? What is a title. It is placed at the top (but why are paintings signed at the bottom or the side?); it indicates what is to follow. It's a courtesy to the reader, who at the end of a chapter is invited to take a breath and then know in advance where the voyage is going—to Sala Tarone, to Tempelhof, or Wuthenow. Yes, and is it supposed to whet our appetite? Such writers do exist, but we are dealing with Fontane here. A title is a milestone along the path: Wanderer, after twelve miles you will be in Jerichow. A sign at the edge of town—when a stranger reads "Gneez" it doesn't tell him very much at first, but once he's entered that city he knows where he is. A title as a warning. As an ornament, accompanying the old-time fashions of Berlin in 1806. Perhaps. The question remains: What is a title?

We had something of a mishap regarding the Sala Tarone Italian Wine and Fine Food Store on Charlottenstrasse. The gentlemen have to squeeze their way through rows of barrels and the cellarman enjoins caution: – There are all kinds of tacks and nails here: he says. *Pinnen und Nägel.* There was a boy in our class named Nagel. We could have acted like adults; the next day, his name was Pinne Nagel, Tacknail. He took it well. Underneath, he was glad that he now had something of his own, a nickname. From then on he'd say, about tricky math problems or cramped quarters: There are all kinds of tacks and nails here. He survived eleventh grade, Pinne Nagel. Today he's a jaw surgeon in Flensburg.

But what precisely is a *Pinne*, our Mr. Weserich begged someone to inform him. He understood the difference between a *Pinne* and a *Nagel* only after we'd connected the dots of the Little Erna story for him, with piety and tact: Lil' Erna's Grandpa's lyin' in his coffin and her mom wants to make him look just like he used to when he was alive but she can't get the beret to stay on his bald head, she fumbles and fumbles and then finally Mr. Piety-and-Tact comes by and she tells him the problem and he says Give me a minute I'll take care of it and when she comes back it's right there on Grandpa's head just perfect and she says How'd you do that? and he says Carpet tacks! It was the same with the Plattdeutsch during Schach's visit home: Weserich truly acted like it was all Greek to him. We translated why the old goat was always butting Momma Kreepsch where she hurt—in writing, since he asked us to. One time he came to us with reproaches: We'd kept a word from him. Right at the beginning, as early as the fourth chapter. We were crushed and promised to make it up to him. It was about Aunt Marguerite, "who spoke with a pruned mouth the Berlin dialect of her day, which almost exclusively used the dative case"— this without quotation marks around the offending term. We'd acted like everyone knew what this meant! That was the word, then, and he asked us to show him what it meant, and he stood in front of one schoolgirl after another (we'd convinced him that only girls pruned) and watched her protruding mobile lips, then thanked her. We responded in kind, gathering up our skirts at our side, which were below the knee in those days. *We curtsied.*

We were already in Wuthenow, page 122 of our transcript, chapter 14; we'd had enough of Schach (the person, after he'd spoiled the boat ride on the lake for us with his lachrymose shirking, not the book), when Weserich invited us to expound (with no notes!) on how we'd made this Schach's acquaintance. A forty-five-minute debriefing, right to the bell. It turned out that the weeks and weeks frittered away at the start of the year had paid off: we found the last line of the first paragraph where he is mentioned as absent, and nameless. The gentlemen there—von Bülow, his publisher Sander, von Alvensleben—are conversing with their hostesses, the Carayon ladies. Von Bülow is looking to start an argument. He quotes his man Mirabeau's comment about Frederick the Great's celebrated state as a fruit that's already rotten before it's ripe. In the sermon, he gives himself airs, as if by chance, with the maxim: *nomen et omen.* Not the *est* we learned in school, but *et*—name *and* destiny, bringing them into closer and more pregnant proximity and significance. After von Bülow's emphatic pronouncement that "Europe could have stood a bit more of the harem and seraglio business without any serious harm," whose name is announced midsentence? Cavalry Captain von Schach, the Shah between two women; his adversary is there already and will have the last word to the end. Fontane and the science of names. Fontane and the art of introducing a character.

A list of characters: Josephine, Victoire, Schach, Aunt Marguerite, the king, his much-bemoaned queen, Prince Louis, General Köckritz, the Tempelhof innkeeper...

A list of places, settings: The Carayons' salon, the tavern with the tacks and nails, the carriage ride, the (invented) church in Tempelhof, the villa

on the Spree at Moabit across from the western *lisière* of the Tiergarten
(our consultation of reference works should by now have led us to a place
where we might find the reason for this word choice), the parade in Tempelhof, the bedside scene, Wuthenow am See, Paretz Palace and its park,
death on Wilhelmstrasse. Make sense? A vote, in writing, anonymous, of
favorite locations. The lake came in first—we were again mostly from
Mecklenburg by this point; the students from the Memel (the Neman) or
Silesia had to accept it. Pius showed me that he'd voted for Paretz. Student
Cresspahl's favorite image was of the swans that came swimming up from
Charlottenburg Park in a long line.

Another ugly incident: Schach is going on and on about the prince, his
gracious lord, whom he loves *de tout mon cœur*: he tells Victoire. But, he
says, with all his adventures in love and war the prince is "a light that burns
with a robber." Again we'd tried to slip a word past our German teacher!
He was left standing there completely unaware of what a "robber" on a
light might be in this Northern Germany of ours! We agree that we have
earned our punishment and request an ample measure of it, as schoolchildren used to be made to say. A robber is a light with a wick that gives off
a very sooty smoke—that "steals" the candle wax away. When candles were
still made of wax...

Anita saved herself the trouble of the curtsy we'd all adopted as a way
to tease Mathias Weserich. She had the chance; she outsmarted herself. It
was common practice in our class to turn to the back left corner of the
room whenever it was Dieter Lockenvitz's turn to speak; Anita, too, liked
watching him talk. If the talk was rebellious, her eyebrows rose in concern.
There were certain details of a story from the time of the Gensdarmes
Regiment that displeased Student Lockenvitz. In the fourth chapter and
the Tempelhof churchyard, hazel and dog rose bushes grew so lushly that
they formed a thick hedge, "notwithstanding the leaves weren't out yet."
A student would get a red mark for that "notwithstanding." In the chapter
called "Le choix du Schach," it said, "After arrangements like these one
parted"—was this a misprint? or something wrong with the grammar?
What annoyed (i.e., *ärger*'ed, and by now we could think *aigrir*'ed too)
this student most was Fontane's habit of giving words of direct discourse
in both the subjunctive and quotation marks; Weserich interjected questions to keep the boy's spirits up, although he regularly conceded the points

anyway. But students were now officially required to form collective work pairs, one stronger student and one weaker, and Anita, who could have put herself in a position to observe this Lockenvitz for hours, and from close up, too, instead chose a girl, Peter (Monika), who was weak in chemistry and math.

When Weserich interrupted his aimless drifting among us to stop and stand by Lise Wollenberg's desk, we would see the phrase come to life: she was "hanging on his lips." She was, and she wouldn't have taken it particularly amiss if he'd solemnly ushered her out of the classroom and offered her his hand and his heart. But Weserich must have had some experience with girls like this who throw back their head when they laugh, whinnying like a colt; it was only in the seventh month of our collaboration on a man from the Regiment Gensdarmes that he gave her a speech, for her alone.

– My dear Miss Wollenberg! he said.

– You are looking at my mouth, as though something were missing there. You mention the color of my teeth at a volume that cannot but reach me. I now have the honor of confiding to you that no hair grows around my mouth because the skin there is transplanted. My teeth have an unnatural appearance because they were made in a factory. Do you have any other questions? Would you care to tell me where, in this story about a cavalry captain, von Schach—you remember him—where you suppose the person telling it is?

– Nooo: Lise said, straining for insolence. We felt sorry for her, the big blond child caught in the act of trying to be frivolous with a grown-up ("and with true horror maketh sport"). But we didn't hold Weserich's counterattack against him, after all the embarrassment Lise had caused his colleague H.-G. Knick.

Something different for a change. Who is the narrator? How does he conduct himself in performing this activity? Was he present at all the events that have taken place? Would those involved have wanted that, or allowed it? When are they outside the range of his observations? when they're writing letters. Once the letters are written, the narrator tells us what they say. What does he refrain from telling us? Why do we learn of the stolen hour of love only from the use, twice, of the informal second-person pronoun *du*? Good taste, or tact, or a well-developed ability to cope with life? Lockenvitz, let me give you a striking term for your collection, one which will bear you aloft on its wings to your final exams and beyond: the authorial narrative situation.

He knew where the ice was thin, our Mr. Weserich, and kept off it. Von Bülow, staff captain but also political essayist, admits, in the quoted subjunctive that so vexed Student Lockenvitz, to an abhorrence of pubs in which he felt "police spies and waiters were strangling him." There were pubs like that in Gneez; birthday parties had long since ceased to be thrown outside the house. Here Mathias Weserich could play innocent—he was from Thuringia. In his first appearance with Schach, von Bülow mentions the indissoluble marriage between church and state; Weserich could casually remind us to always stay in the temporal frame of the story. When Victoire writes her friend Lisette a letter that mentions "your new Masurian homeland," he knew that he had before him a child who had lost his own home in that part of the world; the discussion turned on the claims Victoire felt entitled to make from life, as revealed by this letter; how could the teacher suspect that Anita, too, felt herself to be a person "restricted to no more than her lawful share of happiness." He probably didn't even notice the silence that greeted his mention of a "Möllendorf" infantry regiment.

If we take the variety and energy of the relationships between the characters to be the mainspring of the narrative, then what happens if we place Aunt Marguerite at the center?

As the New School curriculum expected of Mr. Weserich, he paid due attention to the social critical element. Two classes worth of discussion of the concept of honor, the attitude towards it; dishonorable actions. Make sense? A passing ideological government inspector could sit in on our class without anything to worry about, or any need to question us in Weserich's absence—no harm would come to his career as a result. Fontane had supplied the novella with salt on which the Regiment Gensdarmes organized a summer sleigh ride on Unter den Linden; when asked what the lords intended to do with the soiled but expensive condiment afterwards, the nobility, in full consciousness of their omnipotence, replied: As long as it doesn't rain. It'll still be good enough *pour les domestiques.*

– *Et pour la canaille*: someone says; for the people, known as the mob. Weserich impressed upon us that the idea had come from the youngest cornet; we thought we knew everything we needed to know about seventeen-year-olds.

Time passed. The Israelites went out into the land. Marlene Timm, inevitably nicknamed "Tiny Tim" despite her average height, received official permission to go visit relatives (aunts) in Denmark—this was much marveled at, she was merely a guest among us; Axel Ohr was taken care of, five years' hard labor; Jakob hadn't been given the chance to drive more than a couple of engines, it's true, and was transferred to signal stations between Gneez and Ludwigslust for disciplinary reasons, meanwhile earning credits at the Transportation Technical College in Dresden, which might as well have accepted him as a full-time student; in March, Jakob's mother was refused permission to travel to West Germany; Heinrich Cresspahl, Brickworks Road, Jerichow, had his pension reduced when he'd faithfully reported his income from repairing chests and *sideboards*; his daughter actually did go to West Berlin to get him whittling knives, the kind with retractable blades; Oskar Tannebaum sent a *"petticoat"* from Paddington, which according to Cresspahl was a railroad station in London; in November of 1950, in the city hall of Richmond, Cresspahl's intended home town, the second version of Picasso's dove of peace was on view; the Americans got a punch on the nose in Korea; the seasons took their course; and still we were reading *Schach*. Schach!

We had discovered that he remained invisible throughout the hundred and thirty pages; intentionally, we were willing to assume for Fontane's benefit. Almost everyone called him "handsome"; therefore vain: opines Josephine de Carayon. Von Bülow mocks him as His Majesty, Captain von Schach. Victoire sees "something of the solemnity of a church councilman about him." He is occasionally knowable through his actions: when he poses as the conscience of his regiment and then denies it; when he gives a needlessly nasty report about Victoire at the prince's; when he cravenly hides from his mamma on the stairs and from his duty in Wuthenow; in short, behaves in such a way that Josephine de Carayon is moved to weigh her own family against his made-up Obotrite nobility. All of us thought his chickening out was obvious and inexplicable; Anita had the last word. She stuttered at first, stumbled over a word; we took it to be nervousness, common enough among seventeen-year-olds. – Getting her pr-pr-pregnant: Anita said: she could accept that. What were we to think it was but an ordinary linguistic mishap? Anita could pursue a train of thought while speaking as resolutely as if she were alone. – But to not even try (and to need to be ordered by his king, and by his queen) to be a good person!

It had slipped out of her involuntarily, unwillingly; she braced herself for our laughter over this old-fashioned term. We were embarrassed for her; we were proud of her. Who knows, if it had been Eva Matschinsky we might have laughed; because it was Anita we all stared straight ahead, I even saw some nods of agreement; and no one outside of that class ever heard Anita say what her conception of a person's honor was.

– The Gensdarmes Regiment was also abolished two years later in the army reforms: Zaychik said, to break the silence. He had learned to eat crow, our Dagobert with his *ol' story.*

A full hour's deliberation on the *beauté du diable, coquette, triviale, celeste,* and fifth and finally the *beauté, qui inspire seul du vrai sentiment.* (The only girl embarrassed by this: Lise.) On who Berlin's Alexanderplatz was named after, and what a member of the nobility can do with a pockmarked girl once his prince and gracious lord has transfigured her for him so that he can see a *beauté du diable* in her.

And does von Bülow's pronouncement at the end reflect the author's judgment? He's just a blockhead. (Would the class please be so kind as to enlighten its teacher about "blockheads"?) Because of his logic-chopping. We've had this already: the omniscient narrator. Here it was Lise Wollenberg who found an argument for why we had to consider von Bülow as separate from his creator: because of the finest white clothes, "something at which Bülow in no way excelled."

We are nearing the end. We know because Weserich, with a ceremonial air, takes us back to the beginning: the title. We were categorically prohibited from consulting Fontane's letters (– Declarations of intent say nothing about the work itself); he quoted one to us, the letter from November 5, 1882, which explores various possible titles for the novella: "*1806; Outside Jena; Et dissipate sunt; Numbered, Weighed, and Given Away; Before the End (Fall, Downfall)*." What could class 11-A-II in April of 1951 adduce to Mr. Weserich as reasons for the final choice of title?

– Because a person's name is always the most honest declaration: Lockenvitz (he got that from Th. Mann).

– Because the others almost all imply a judgment, forestalling the reader's own. Fontane wants his readers to decide for themselves!: Weserich now taught us, and now we were to start in on the delight and pleasure of reading a novella by Th. Fontane about the year 1806 again, afresh.

But we ruined it for ourselves. It was Lockenvitz who blew it. We were responsible too. Lockenvitz, now a member of the Pagenkopf/Cresspahl collective, asked us in passing if we thought Mr. Weserich himself would pass a test. It's true, we gave him permission; we predicted only that this student would complain about Fontane again—the first sentence, for instance, the hiccup that the present participle there could give rise to.

What Lockenvitz presented, though, right after the Easter lambs, was a journal from the half-capital, in a colorful jacket band—called *Form*, or maybe *Sinn*, in any case East German national culture's emissary to the rest of the world. In it (vol. 2, pp. 44–93), the reigning expert on Socialist literary theory wrote, about Fontane's *Schach von Wuthenow*, that the novella was a "lucky accident." The critique of Prussian culture it contained was "unintentional," was "unconscious," Georg Lukács wrote.

Lockenvitz had requested permission to read this out loud toward the end of class time, to spare Mr. Weserich any possible embarrassment in front of the students. Weserich listened, his mouth forming a rectangle, as though listening to a terrible pain. He thanked his student, asked to borrow the valuable printed journal, and stalked out of the room on his one leg. (Whenever the stump of the other *aigrir*'ed him he'd always recited the start of the poem about the knee that wanders lonely through the world / It's just a knee, no more.)

He was out for a week. Student teachers do sometimes need to travel on professional business, just like other teachers: thought 11-A-II. The one who came back, though, loathed us.

Schach was canceled. For the rest of May and June he rushed through Fontane's novel *Frau Jenny Treibel*; we had two weeks left over at the end of the school year. He still listened to what we said when we interrupted his speaking with our own; he nodded, as if at something he'd expected. He refused to allow any of what he called "jokes." The stove was out, the egg was broken, the dish was eaten.

Lockenvitz was ashamed, sheepish, crushed. Whether or not he'd actually hoped for a duel between a high-school class in Mecklenburg and a grand dialectician, it had all gone wrong. He tried, he asked for permission to add something about Count Mirabeau, after whom Victoire de Carayon

called herself Mirabelle: evidence had been found after this French revolutionary's death that payments had been made to him from the French
royal exchequer; the removal of the besmirched ashes from the Panthéon
surely must have been known in 1806? – Your Herwegh's like that too:
Weserich said drily and dismissively. (Herwegh receives somewhat merciless treatment at Treibel's hospitable table.) – Acts all grand at the head of
the 1849 worker's rebellion in Baden, but when things went wrong he fled
across the French border, disguised as a day laborer!

The informal pronoun—*your* Herwegh—didn't gratify Lockenvitz, it
choked him. This child of conflict and dissent, we saw him gulp. He lowered his eyes. He sat down without a word.

Lockenvitz wrote a twenty-page essay about *Schach von Wuthenow*,
without asking for help and without being asked to write it at all, and
mailed it to Weserich the German instructor during the summer; only
years later could he again feel proud of having discovered that Fontane
never grants Schach a first name—a custom of the nobility, to be sure, but
also a comment on the person. Our Weserich resumed his studies at the
University of Leipzig; he didn't have time to correspond with a schoolboy
in Mecklenburg. Mathias Weserich's dissertation on *Schach von Wuthenow*
was printed in Göttingen, across the border.

We knew he was using us the way a biologist uses guinea pigs, and we
weren't mad. We'd also raced against him swimming, 100 meters, by
stopwatch, not cheating him by swimming slower on purpose. It was clear
from his shirts that he didn't have a woman to look after them. And maybe
grown-ups were like that: after they've been shot in the mouth once, they
take steps to avoid a second bullet. He'd owned one single suit (gray summer fabric) that he wore every day with a handkerchief in the breast pocket
and a tie—as if he owed us respectable attire. And he had taught us how
to read.

August 3, 1968 Saturday

The New York Times still has not been able to prove that Leonid Brezhnev
and Alexander Dubček had lunch together, but thanks to the time difference across the Atlantic she can at least tell us this much: This morning

the two men embraced at the Bratislava train station. The way Auntie hears it, Brezhnev's feeling friendly, having received written appeals from the leaders of three Communist parties: the Yugoslavian, the Italian, and the French.

But the way the East German leaders are threatening the Czechs and Slovaks with lip-smacking references to the Soviet Union's overwhelming military might—we have to look away.

Helicopters are again allowed to fly to the city's airports from the tower above Grand Central Station. A Douglas Commercial, type 8 has crashed near Milan—fifteen dead. We're flying soon too.

Charlie in his Good Eats Diner, after two hours of frying and cooking, certainly doesn't look like he's been playing genteel leisure sports. Would they let you into a club with such messy, unevenly cut blond (yellow) hair? His customers wear their shirts untucked, loud lumberjack plaid, a bit stained too. This morning the men were razzing one another about their golf handicaps, though, and not as a joke.

This is something about America we'll miss: Marie ordered a patty on a bun with onion, and what does Charlie shout back toward the hot grill? – *Burger takes slice! Do it special for my special lady, now!* and Marie looks down, blushing, as she should. And proud, because she belongs.

A special message in the entrance down into the subway:

$$\sqrt{\text{RADICAL}}$$
is a state of mind.

And, as if no one would ever burgle an apartment whose inhabitants were two hours by car out of town, we spent today, from morning to early afternoon, at Jones Beach, thanks to the Blumenroths since this state park is accessible only to people with cars. Mr. Blumenroth, burned red under his thin frizzy hair, may have given the Cresspahl household a new catch-phrase: *There's a reason for everything!*

He expressed this harebrained wisdom after deciding that his supervision of Pamela's games on and under her inflatable raft was sufficient. After she'd drifted some seventy feet out to sea, Mrs. Cresspahl went with him to the rescue. (Once, in the Baltic, she swam for three hours chasing a ball, out of stubbornness. The ball put wave after wave between itself and

her before drifting off toward Denmark.) Pamela took a long time to come
to terms with the confiscation of her plaything as a grown-up measure; her
father spent a long time looking stupefied with reasonableness, he'd endured
such a fright. Only after a while did he start up again with the sidelong
glances meant to remind us of our meetings at the Hotel Marseilles bar;
Mrs. Blumenroth had her hands full with the job of overlooking her husband's goings-on. To keep him from saying it, she said it herself: That's a
bust you can be proud of, Mrs. Cresspahl.

– Thanks very much: she replied, in the American way of accepting,
not denying, a compliment, which this time she found tiresome for a change.

What do we know about Mrs. Blumenroth?

Born in 1929. "I'm from the Carpathians." Yes, the Germans came and
got her. She wasn't allowed to take anything with her. Except her clothes.

Arrival in New York: 1947. Marriage: 1948. Fear of having been made
infertile. Pamela: 1957.

A harsh Hungarian accent in her tinny voice. She knows that her voice
was softer and gentler as a child, hence her preference for whispering.

She admits to one flaw: an inability to lie, unless she consciously intends
to, which hasn't yet happened.

Her black hair is maybe dyed. Cut very short, in heart-shaped curls; one
sharp point drapes her brow. A face with few wrinkles, its expression more
fearful than approachable. When she wants to laugh, what comes out is
invariably: Ha!

"*I'm fussy, nervous.*" A younger parent would be more patient with
children.

One time, she almost laughed. Her husband had put together a new
bed and now the guest was to test it, sit on it. Mrs. Cresspahl's verdict:
Quality merchandise. Mrs. Blumenroth: Ha! Ha!

Unusually tidy home. Everything always put away promptly.

What she found hard to take after the war was how a woman from a
good background, with a sense of what's proper, could slip so easily into a
false, uncertain position.

Stubbornly working hard to keep a well-groomed appearance; always
afraid that the roof is going to fall in.

"At my age, my back can't help hurting."

She would take in a German child as a foster daughter.

And now Pamela, a possible companion for Marie's later life.

She stands with her chest flung out, her head thrown back atop its short neck. Opens her mouth wide—everything is pulled back and down, as if her head had grown straight out of her rib cage. Her whole face laughs. Marie beams when she sees her friend.

Marie carries out plans, pursues things; gets excited. Pamela behaves like a second child. A "girl" in the European sense.

She'll turn into a practical, nice woman. Not especially intelligent, but unshakably proper. We want to see it all. We want to go to Pamela's wedding.

On the beach there were a lot of head shapes and physiognomies like those of people in Germany, as one often sees on the streets of New York—doppelgangers, especially of the poet Günter Eich, sit in great number on the benches and at shop counters and bars. You never run across an Ingeborg Bachmann. But there are also people whom you're glad to find are false alarms—certain stately blonds, for instance. Memory awaits an illuminating flash of similarity with Mathias Weserich, with Wm. Brewster (in his younger years).

In the afternoon, at the playground in Riverside Park, various members of the public are relaxing; someone who recognizes Mr. Anselm Kristlein there will have been fooled for a while before realizing it's him. Maybe because she knows he's in town. In secret, incognito—but if that's how he wants it, he shouldn't have called Ginny Carpenter. She called him back that night, at his hotel on Central Park South; Kristlein always avails himself of the most expensive option, since cheap purchases have cost him dearly before. Ginny told the story giggling with delight at his cautious questions over the phone: – Yes...? Always wary over the phone. One knows so many ladies in this city, one might turn around and want something from him. Better not to name any names for the time being. The *tête-à-tête*, the *souper à deux* with the wife of reserve officer Carpenter—the usual for Anselm. Ginny's words. He's had himself examined at the Mayo Clinic: he says. Golden words. He's come to New York to collect donations for antiwar events in Europe; this nimble gentleman invites Ginny to come advise him while shopping on Fifth and Madison Avenues. He inquires circuitously, casually into any recent pregnancies that might have emerged in Ginny's circle; when she tells him one, he flicks the fingers of one hand as if burned. Mrs. Carpenter has promised him a check from her husband's hand—he doesn't have an American bank account to deposit it into. What is someone like Anselm Kristlein looking for on Manhattan's West Side, in this neighborhood whose shabbiness Ginny so complains of? He couldn't be looking for her?

Anselm Kristlein in our park was recognizable from the insistent looks he was casting over the top of the real estate section of the London *Times* at a young woman sitting two benches away and keeping an eye on a three-year-old girl's path from the sandboxes to the fountains; he could barely tear his gaze away from her bright red blouse of rough material, the reddish hair sitting on her neck, wound up in a knot with apparent casualness and consummate skill, from her dry but unwrinkled brow, lightly freckled, from her lips, from her monstrously blue sunglasses that shielded this face from him. So that's what he likes? Then he better do something.

What with trying so hard to disguise his looks to the side with glances at his paper, he's let the child he's here with run away. Maybe it's Drea. We saw him dash around almost desperately in search of this child, from one playground structure to the next, back and forth, and he was already halfway up the stairs to Riverside Drive when he succeeded in getting what he would have denied he was looking for: a wave from the woman.

She raised her hand and swung her outstretched arm until he saw her and she could point to his child at a corner of the fence, drinking from the water fountain; she had already walked over and said something to the child and returned to her place before he was standing at the fountain.

Holding his child's hand, he walked over to the woman and explained: *She did not understand you. She does not speak English.* The woman nodded. Her own child was sitting under her arm; she moved her arm gently. She made sure she had something to occupy herself with. In her other hand she held her magazine, waiting; both she and her child looked patiently at the man and his child.

We've seen him suaver than that. He stood with the soles of his feet stuck fast to the concrete ground. He'd started a conversation and wanted to extend it. – *Thank you:* he said, instead of asking to borrow the magazine. The woman said Hmm, twice, with such finality that he finally let his child drag him away.

Later I saw him on his bench staring helplessly at the woman as she went past him to the ice cream man, who had just parked his cart on the park path; I passed right into his line of sight but he had eyes only for the woman's firm petite ass.

Later he was with his child at the swings, two places away from the woman with hers, and sometimes he missed a push busy as he was storing up for the weeks to come the memory of how she let the box with her child hit her raised hands and then with a firm little push, only slightly visible in her beautiful bare feet, sent it back up into the air.

He was still there when everyone left for dinner; when I sat down by the window at around nine, I could still see, through a gap in the leaves, the young gentleman standing in his stylish wool shirt, looking up, with jutting chin; and if he'd recognized me a few hours earlier—

(but Mrs. Cresspahl wears her sunglasses in front of her eyes, or in her dress pocket, never pushed up on her head. The oils in her hair can leave traces on the lenses, which would then look like dirt to anyone standing behind you)

—I'd have been able to, maybe even would have wanted to, tell him he'd be waiting in vain till next Saturday, and so, in his desperate need to take the sunglasses off this woman too, just once, would he dare to tell her what happened to come to his mind?

Mrs. Cresspahl was tempted to go out to the street, make herself known, invite Mr. Kristlein up for a nighttime glass of something, one for the road. But she realized in time that he was waiting for someone else, wanting to get to someone else. He'll definitely make the attempt; we can leave him to it.

And to flick his fingers like that, in such a year.

August 4, 1968 Sunday, South Ferry day

– Gesine! You were up past midnight listening to the record of the variations for that student Goldberg. The quodlibet twice!

– Sowwy. There was a party in the apartment upstairs. I wanted my own noise.

– Got you! You thought I was picking a fight! The music gave me sweet dreams.

– Marie, I want to make a bet with you: We're not going to have any fights with each other until October. Starting in October.

– I bet I'll win!

The joint communiqué out of Bratislava from the Soviet Union and its charges: twist and turn it however you want, all it says is what they've been saying all along, from the victories scored by Socialism to the West German thirst for revenge. It closes with a mild affirmation of national self-determination from all signatories, without mentioning Czechoslovakia. The Soviets promise to withdraw their last sixteen thousand soldiers. Censorship is still abolished. Freedom of assembly and association remains in place. One single concession: the leadership in Prague has asked newspaper editors to refrain from printing articles with opinions that might sadden their allies. Articles with facts seem to be allowed.

On the second to last day of October, part of the trial of Sieboldt and Gollantz was held in the auditorium of the Fritz Reuter High School in Gneez. Principal Kramritz had been instructed to put a sheet of paper on Elise Bock's desk; those who wished to testify had to print their names and sign it. They all received postage-paid postcards, machine-numbered, with letterhead but no text: their invitations. But if they turned up outside the auditorium on Monday afternoon with nothing but their FDJ membership booklet, the two uniformed women at the check-in table promptly turned them away. The women wanted to see each student's "PID," the new personal ID—maybe because they were suspicious of the administrative approach apparently in style in the youth chapter headquarters (mimeographing stencils and paper gone missing!). Also, police-issued documents are harder to forge and easier to trace. Then anyone who showed up in a lumberjack instead of a blue shirt was turned away by Bettina Selbich: for "insufficient consciousness." That meant, in the end, that there weren't many students in the assembly hall; it was largely minders from out of town.

– A shirt in October?

– Student Cresspahl had bought a blue one two sizes too big for her so she could wear a sweater underneath. Pius pretended not to notice. Lockenvitz froze.

– I wish I knew what you think about him!

– Work it out for yourself.

– A *"lumberjack"*?

– See? You don't know Canadian!

– Do too. A woodcutter. *Every man jack.*

– In the fall of 1950 it came into fashion to wear jackets of lightly ribbed crepe, with wide collars, a zipper you'd leave open, and inside and outside zippered pockets. The way the woodcutters supposedly dressed in Canada.

– That's called a *lumber jacket*!

– We didn't know Canadian either.

– Like the Indian headbands here?

– What those jackets meant was: the wearer comes from people with Western money; he likes Canada.

– But Pius had one.

– *Elementary, my dear Watson.*

– Like blue jeans these days in Budapest? And East Germany?

– What do I care! Where people obey a custodian who's jeered at and whistled at outside City Hall in Bratislava!

– Gesine, you said: not till after October.

In memory the auditorium is an oak-dark room, lined with paneling six feet high, filled with benches as sturdy as in a church, topped with a coffered wooden ceiling. At the moment it was a great hall for displaying the colors of flags, in which the FDJ didn't come off too well—there were twice as many of the Unity Party's reds, sometimes with the clasped hands, sometimes not, as well as the black, red, and gold of the national flag adorned with the symbols of the peasants (ring of grain opening upward) and the workers (hammer). (Contemporary Studies with Selbich: We are proud to leave the eagle, that circling vulture of bankruptcy, to the reactionary forces in West Germany!) On the front wall, above the red-draped table for the judges, was Picasso's dove of peace, second version. The décor made it clear that this was an official gathering, not that of a club or some other group. Manfras and Lockenvitz, the highest-ranking functionaries, were sitting on the 11-A-II bench most compliantly for the occasion. Silence, as in a funeral hall, viewing the coffin. Once the blue of the People's Police completely surrounded the school building, the armored transport vehicle from Rostock drove up to the gates. An armed company escorted the accused up the six turns in the stairs to the auditorium. We heard the clicks from the open doorway and we knew: their handcuffs were just then being taken off. Sieboldt and Gollantz presented straight, almost rigid backs and a deliberately relaxed gait as they were led to the podium and took their seats between four constables. Two boys, nineteen and twenty years old, dressed in their dead fathers' Sunday suits. Imperturbable faces avoiding the least sign of greeting, even one they could've managed unnoticed with the corners of their mouths or their eyelashes. But they were looking, very carefully too, to see who'd come to bid them goodbye. Then the presiding judge realized his mistake and ordered them to look to the side. This judge was a chatty man, helpless, fussy as an aunt: How *could* you, but that's *terr*ible, this depravity at such a young age—that's how he talked. The prosecutor was likewise hampered by a bourgeois upbringing; he had a penchant for nasty insinuations which he offered as delicate irony. About the defense attorney, not one word—except that he too was wearing the state party's button on his lapel. They'd brought along their own lackey, who called them the Honorable Court for our benefit. It was cold in the auditorium. From the high windows came the pale glowing light that exists only in October.

— Now Burly Sieboldt will be able to tell you all what was on those fliers!

— Student Cresspahl had come to see Gollantz and him one more time. The way you go to see someone you're never going to see again.

— To pay your last respects?

— When you're seventeen you can feel that way. But we did know the verdict in advance. Little Father Stalin had reintroduced the death penalty on January 13—the highest measure of social protection—but for these two it'd only be twenty-five years. The usual.

— For a few fliers.

— And Pius had proven to me once and for all that we were friends. Because of his father, the Pagenkopfs were thought to agree with the custodian's government, and they of all people got something slipped through their mail slot. One time in June, Pius waited for me to ask him for the table of logarithms, and what I found between the pages might have been left there by accident. So when he handed the picture with the barbed wire and printed words over to Section D, fulfilling his obligations as a vigilant friend of peace, he'd be able to swear with a clean conscience that he hadn't shown it to anyone. When I finished reading it, a look hung in the air between us of the kind you experience maybe three times in your life, at most, if you're lucky.

– You dried off with the same towel! You slept under the same roof! But you only trusted each other once you could get him sent to prison?

– From that moment on I had another brother.

Ex-Students Sieboldt and Gollantz were accused of private and conspiratorial visits to West Berlin. The East Office of the West German SPD was located there, the Investigating Committee of Free Jurists was housed there, the Task Force Against Inhumanity was operating there. East German courts had proven that these groups had blown up a bridge, had set fire to a barn. Jakob, on the other hand, had told stories—and I believed him—of a railcar found in Rostock with forged freight papers, diverted from Saxony, the butter in it now not going to the people of Leipzig, assuming it was still edible at all. But Sieboldt and Gollantz had no interest in taking out other people's anti-Communism on *their* friends and neighbors and relatives, for instance by disrupting the distribution of food any more than the East German authorities had managed to do by themselves just fine; they'd gone to West Berlin with an idea of their own. So much the worse: concluded the court. They'd accepted from one of these groups, which were all registered with the West Berlin district courts, a picture of young people marching in a column behind reinforced wires, but had done so on the condition that their own text be added to it. So much the worse: concluded the court. The defendants were merely forced to admit the shameful infamy of these printed remarks, while at least two students had them more or less memorized: That the slogans about Peace and the Struggle for Peace were just euphemisms for the securing of what the Soviets had acquired in Central and Eastern Europe; since the Soviet Union, too, now possessed (by theft) the atomic bomb, it had started preparing an offensive, by manpower reinforcements and additional arming of the Volkspolizei, by propaganda among the members of the FDJ to join this

army-in-disguise, by appointing one of its leading officers to the Volkspolizei's central administration; what are you marching for, members of the
FDJ? That was what Students Sieboldt and Gollantz had worked out.
Aggravating circumstance: Verbal disparagement of the World Peace Movement. Namely by claiming that Picasso's dove of peace had appeared in
French newspapers armed with a hammer and sickle. The English apparently described it as *"the dove that goes bang,"* now would you mind translating for us this outrageous insult to the striving for world peace? *Die
Taube kommt mitm Knall* but a little less casual. My stars, where ever did
you hear such a thing?

– Gesine, you daredevil!
– I was a little scared when it came up. But Burly Sieboldt said, unhurried: Oh, it's in the air; and he directed his gaze to the air over Student
Cresspahl's head, but toward where the balcony around the assembly hall,
blocked off for the day, was filled with armed men.
– What if he'd suspected you! Just the idea that you had betrayed him
and he'd have brought you down with him!
– Things were carefully set up to deal with such matters in that German
democratic country. If Cresspahl's daughter tells her classmate Sieboldt
what she's heard on BBC radio, he is required to report her. If Sieboldt
seems happy to hear something worth knowing from his classmate's mouth,
she is required to report him. But Sieboldt's family would have disowned
him forever if he'd denounced someone. That's what denunciation meant.
Cresspahl would've never spoken to or looked at his daughter again if she'd
been praised for the arrest of a neighbor's child.
– To hear you tell it, it's all pretty easy. But someone denounced them.
– Everyone knew that Gollantz was practically engaged to a girl from
his senior class, one Lisette von Probandt. They were "the Couple" in their
year; the children in ninth grade just watched them ... the same way the
former ninth graders had watched Pius and me. Now if you put a girl
under arrest and give her the third degree ...
– So Sieboldt had something to blame Gollantz for.
– Meanwhile the Honorable Court tried to get Gollantz to admit that
Sieboldt had led him astray. Gollantz stood his ground so that he'd be
given exactly as many years as his friend.

– That darn Statue of Liberty, do you see how her arm is drooping? They're going to close it off to visitors any day now, it's not safe.

– *Elementary, my dear Mary.*

The accused were repeatedly told to express greater contrition. For they seemed quite content when they were shouted at, threatened, and cursed, as if they'd have been disappointed more than anything if they weren't. As if they were expecting it. And the children in their blue shirts sitting before them could tell what the accused considered reason enough to be happy, reason enough to feel the meager serenity that stiffened their backs in the face of twenty-five years of forced labor for sabotage:

> attempted continuation
> of reactionary student self-governance,
> a vestige
> of the pseudodemocratic inheritance
> of the Weimar Republic,
> by means of
> obtaining under false pretenses
> high
> and highest
> ranks
> of the Central School-Group Authority
> of the Free German Youth;

for espionage:

> scouting out
> the vulnerable flank
> of the Peace Movement
> of the Republic;

for terrorism: since they truly had undertaken to spread a view in Gneez and its high school different from the view that the ministry of the interior (which they insisted on calling the ministry of war) expected;

for illegal association (Sieboldt with Gollantz). Then Mr. Kramritz stood up and thundered about the "Abiturs obtained under false pretenses"— in fact they had gained acceptance to the university by working hard in the subjects being tested. Then one Bettina Selbich took the floor, stammering, recalling nighttime visits from FDJ officeholder Sieboldt; if her victim had chosen to speak, he would surely have said: The cavalier takes his pleasure and holds his tongue. He spared her, and if it was hard for him, it was after all how he wanted to think of himself later. Manfras, too, spoke up, with a "position statement" of the kind that the new tradition of democratic justice called for; his indignation, his voice trembling with rage, were perfectly understandable to the defendants, and to us too. For it was just when the FDJ school group had been about to mail off its protest against the murderous incursion of US troops into the peaceful land of Korea that they'd set him up. Disgraced him. Wounded his political conscience.

– Now of the circa eight million people earning their living in the vicinity of this ferry the *John F. Kennedy,* surely one or two of them remember that it was the other way around?

– We knew it too. Because when we were ordered to a schoolwide assembly at noon on June 26, Bettina's efforts at the lectern were aimed at making everything the imperialists' fault. That was one piece of edification. To demand we approve lies by acclamation, vote yes to untruths, was a mockery and a game to any child who knew how to use a radio. And who had been chosen, outside the auditorium door, to suggest the wording? Who came back with a mosaic flawlessly assembled from the costume jewelry of newspaper language? Sieboldt and Gollantz. And whom did they thank for his resolute editorial assistance, whose skill with words did they extol for the succession of FDJ leadership in the Gneez high school? Gabriel Manfras. They'd chosen him to ascend the Town Hall balcony that afternoon and read in passionate tones to the people marching on the square below a text that seemed unobjectionable to him; now it turned out he'd been manipulated into cooperating with a falsehood, rewarded for his political work with the taint of doubting the cause of peace. He had a right to be mad about that; the defendants could respect that.

– In conclusion.

– Sieboldt and Gollantz thanked the court for its efforts, again denied any consciousness of wrongdoing, each for himself, and voiced one final qualm: Maybe it would have been more appropriate under the circumstances if they'd been allowed to witness the afternoon's proceedings wearing the garb of honor of the Free German Youth?

– No! I could never do that.

– Maybe you could, Marie. Some people do when whatever they have is behind them and they're looking at twenty-five years in the slammer. Never to take a ferry across New York Harbor. Losing your girl. Never once to wake up except from the clang of a blow on an iron bar. To know that your only baggage will be your memories from age nineteen and twenty.

– If I were Lisette von Probandt and had a memory, I'd hate life.

– The twenty-five years turned into just five, at which point a West German chancellor visited the Soviet Union. Sieboldt and Gollantz were handed over with the rest of the prisoners of war; they studied law together in Bonn and Heidelberg and were accepted into the Foreign Ministry in 1962. Soon there'll be an embassy where we can go visit them.

– So the Soviets educated two civil servants for the West Germans.

– That's called cadre development! And Lisette had her seven years of waiting. She married Gollantz, and Sieboldt is their child's godfather.

– I could never forgive someone that way.

– You could, Marie. You will. You'll learn.

(Sunday, too, is South Ferry day when Marie says it is.)

August 5, 1968 Monday

On ČSSR television, Alexander Dubček announced: The conference in Bratislava had given the country new scope for its liberalization, it "fulfilled our expectations" (not: all of our). He was apparently trying to hide his party's satisfaction.

Yesterday in Florida, as was only proper for a Sunday, a man with a girl about two years old hired a Cessna 182, to sightsee over the area: he said. Then he pulled out a revolver; the plane had to fly to Cuba.

Yesterday a Convair 580 collided with a small private plane over southeastern Wisconsin and proceeded to land with the crushed wreck of the smaller plane, and its three dead bodies, embedded in it.

We're flying soon too.

Student Lockenvitz.

(Because you want me to, Marie. Only what I *know*.)

In the spring of 1950 we invited him to join the work collective of Young Friends Pagenkopf and Cresspahl.

For selfish reasons. We wanted to learn from this tall, lanky, starved boy how he could think in Latin. – Eundem Germaniae sinum proximi Oceano Cimbri tenent, parva nunc citivas, sed gloria ingens: he said casually when the subject of the Obotrite nobility came up.

Social background, father's profession: Farmer. On a 1949 questionnaire: Agronomist. In 1950: Director of Municipal Gardens, Parks, and Cemetery Plantings in (*don't worry, I won't say the city's name. Besides, you always pronounced it the Polish way. Anita was the only one who could understand it, if even she did*) of one of the larger communities in what is today the People's Poland. Bourgeois.

Political background, parents' party membership before 1945: None. Before 1933: German National People's Party. Imperialist. His father had kept his distance from the Nazis—Lockenvitz insisted on that. So how did he explain that he spent fifth grade in a NaPolIn? He said his father was given a choice in 1944: being drafted into the army or professing his faith in the Hitler state some other way. Heavy financial burden, the fees for a National-Political Educational Institution. But these places were unlike the Hitler Youth Ordensburgs in their lesser emphasis on physical ability. Take his glasses. The metal frame sent rusty trickles down his nose in hot weather.

And then why did the Soviets take his father away, if he was in neither the army nor the party? In February 1947 he was "last seen lying dead on his bunk." (A witness statement; his mother was hoping for a pension. The pension was denied, provisionally in 1947, definitively in 1949, cf. husband's previous social position. Application for educational stipends for Student Lockenvitz: Approved.) On the questionnaire in Contemporary Studies, Lockenvitz said: My father had an argument with the owner of our house; he was falsely denounced. Once he could trust us, he confided, asking us to tell no one else: That was when the Soviet Kommandatura was in our house.

Arrival in Gneez: Age eleven. They'd decided to try to defend that city in the East, so his father had sent the family with the relocating German Army in the direction of the western front; the city is now rubble. Mother's occupation since 1945: Garden worker. Son's class: Proletarian? No: Wage workers.

First apartment in Gneez: Across from the cemetery, with Mr. Budniak, the gravedigger, in a single room. Since 1949: Two rooms near the dairy. Starting in March 1951: An apartment converted from barracks in the Barbara Quarter, once the Soviets had left (and demolished a third of the barracks). In the plaster on the top of the barracks' facade were the outlines of the German eagle and the circle he'd been sitting on, the circle for the swastika.

An only child. Peasant relatives in father's birthplace, Dassow am See, where he spent his holidays, paid in kind for his help in the harvest. 1948 to 1949: twenty hours a week working in a bicycle repair shop on Street of German-Soviet Friendship; he needed the money for books. (The city library closed at five thirty, but you can read until midnight.) Starting in 1950: express messenger for the district of Gneez, German Postal Service, which was why Anita had forced him to take that Swedish bicycle; (without him realizing, absentminded as he was, that at the price she gave him it was practically a gift). He was paid twenty cents per tariff kilometer; bonus if it was raining: fifteen cents. Whether or not it had been raining was decided by Berthold Knever. One time a woman in Old Demwies had been waiting so anxiously for her letter with the red sticker and the address crossed out in red—her pass for the West—that she gave him an egg. But he spent a lot of the afternoons in the sorting room just waiting for an express delivery to make; and doing his homework.

A sensitive child. With a name like that! Nickname (bestowed by Lise Wollenberg): Dietikin. And Lockenvitz, when your hair is actually in *Locken*—blond unruly waves—with a *Vitz* or *Fitz*, a tangled patch, at the back! He lowered his head and pressed his lips together, as if deciding to take action; but cf. here GOETHE:

> For a person's name is not like a coat, which merely hangs about him and may, perchance, be safely twitched and pulled; it is a perfectly fitting garment, which has grown over and over him like his very skin, and at which one cannot rake and scrape without wounding the man himself. (*Dichtung und Wahrheit*, Pt. 2, Book Ten)

Such a child, if he had his way, would have such books in his house ready to consult at all times.

An afflicted child. During all the many moves, a framed photograph of his father, an enlarged driver's license picture with the staples clearly visible, was more important to him than all the furniture put together. Mrs.

Lockenvitz, however, was just thirty-five when her husband "was seen" for the last time; all she took from him was the mission to get the boy to the gates of a university. (His father had a degree in agronomy.) That was why, after Carnival in 1949, there was a photo in the window of Mallenbrandt Pharmacy with a story to tell about the festivities: a young woman with her breasts squeezed together by her bodice. A child who feels ashamed. A sixteen-year-old beaten by his mother because after a man had spent the night he'd taken his father's picture off the wall and hidden it; because he made his mother feel ashamed. At one point, when electrical devices were in short supply, Lockenvitz had mounted over his window a bell from a sleigh left behind in the east, with a cord of sack string coated in pitch hanging down, he was so eager for visitors; now he unscrewed the bell, ignored knocks on the door.

A young man who knows how to enter a room that contains a lady, how to manage his knife and fork now that Mrs. Pagenkopf sometimes brings a third plate in from the kitchen for him. Who insists on the good manners of thanking her for every snack, with a servant's bow from the neck; who declines to accept another sandwich—just to be polite—he would stay hungry for a long time. Until we could convince him that there were none of the "eavesdroppers who never hear anything good" at our house. It took a long time.

Because it hurt him to tell a lie. When his school demanded it, so much the worse for the school, as far as he was concerned; he did his best to let the teacher in charge know how he felt too. Bettina Selbich watched him nervously as he recited the seven commandments of the Stockholm Appeal:

I vow to
stop railroad trains,
unload no military cargo,
withhold fuel from such vehicles,
disarm mercenaries,
refuse to all my children or spouse to serve with the country's
    armed forces,
withhold food supplies from my government,
refuse to work at a telephone switchboard or for a transportation
    system—
to prevent a new war.

Bettina felt she should say something about his speech. He'd set all kinds of traps for her before; she tried once again and asked him where he'd gotten that text. Anita said, to no one in particular, in a respectful voice: It was in *Pravda*, first week of July.

(We thought she was trying to protect you. Or was it that she used to slip sheets of paper with transcriptions from her Russian reading into your notebook?)

With us he took a cautious approach. But then Zaychik and Eva came over—memorizing nitrites and nitrates had gotten boring—and shot a questioning glance at Pius's POB RTT radiogramophone, and when Pius as the host gave his nod, they shut the windows but turned the knob straight to Radio in the American Sector. RIAS broadcast a hit parade on Fridays—Zaychik was delighted to hear Billy Buhlan singing:
Yoop-de-doo—
You can't slam your head through a wall!
Yoop-de-doo—
This should have reassured Lockenvitz. For Bettina had informed us in Contemporary Studies that listening to Western stations was forbidden, explaining: Musicians who use their offerings for opportunistic reasons to adorn Mr. Adenower's road to war will forever be void of the humanism that might let them interpret the immortal symphonies of Mozart and Beethoven!
Lockenvitz waited until it was just the three of us; remarked: This text from West Berlin does call forth a sociological analysis, does it not? The other side must need to pacify the population, lure them away from making any demands. Lockenvitz was talking to the two of them the same way he'd heard them talk in school. Pius looked at me, brow furrowed; I shrugged as if baffled. We were all acting like diplomats! Pius tried again. So, what kind of music did Lockenvitz like?
Lockenvitz did rather like "boogie-woogie."
This was American jazz from the early years, recently promoted, by government decree, from the music of imperialist-decadent exploiter to progressive insofar as it had developed from the work songs of an age of openly practiced slavery. This boy went in for conversations by the book.

Then the East German government brought about what it had promised to its youth at the Germany Rally. On June 23, it communicated the following warning to its allied governments: American terror planes had dropped large quantities of potato-bugs over the territory in its control, in an effort to harm Socialist agriculture. In late September, the students of 11-A-II started pacing off the furrows of the potato fields around Gneez, heads bowed, seeking out *Doryphora decemlineata*. Now *If yer wearin butter on yer head you shouldn go out in the sun*—they were all embarrassed at a state power expecting them to believe this nonsense about agroterrorism and prove their belief by joyous action in the field. You would need a whole book of its own, Comrade Writer, to describe those afternoons, lasting so infinitely long, the earth turning east toward the sun so infinitely slowly.

And Lockenvitz showed his true colors to us, at least as the son of an agronomist; thunderstruck by the memory, he cried: Ha! Those crafty imperialists! The potato bug hibernates two handspans deep in the soil and appears as soon as the temperature exceeds fifty degrees. Early May, in other words. Now when is the Germany Rally to take place? End of May. So the bugs arrive on schedule, the females dutifully lay their eggs in batches of twenty to eighty, about eight hundred per bug in total, the larvae hatch after seven days, and they need another fifty days after pupation until they're ready. In July! Not on June 23. Not by Whitsunday. *Boys n girls!* If we have potato bugs here in Mecklenburg, they must be descended from the ones that were first sighted in southwest Germany in 1937! They're thriving here because the land-reform policies cut down all the hedgerows, and in those hedges there were nests, and in those nests there were birds that exterminated this pest! And because pheasant breeding went out with the nobility's estates!

– We: he'd said to the two of us. We'd done it.

Now he'd do it to entertain us, too, for instance when he pontificated to Bettina S., carefully exaggerating, losing himself as if unwittingly in the labyrinths of thoughts: These six-legged emissaries of American invasion. But our land is armed and ready. We have the pheasant, do we not. Small game that lives in bushy terrain, also in cabbage patches. Eats caterpillars and worms and beetles, pests in general! A bird that's easy to hunt since it's not a good flier. But what people hunt is the greater foe—the fox. Hence the pheasant's proliferation. Historical research can trace the economic

1516 · *August 5, 1968 Monday*

brutality of the American aggressors back to the *Lend-Lease Act* of 1941. Under the pretense of aiding the heroically struggling Soviet Union with food and weapons, they smuggled in 117 different kinds of insect species and weed seeds!

Baffled Bettina was about to go put another A next to his name in the book, but just to be safe she asked a follow-up question. These facts from the war years were entirely new to her, and since she intended to bring them up at an agitprop meeting in the state capital . . . might she ask Student Lockenvitz where he had come upon them?

– Of course: he said: In the *Literaturnaya Gazeta*.

(And wouldn't you know it, Bettina went and asked the school's Russian teacher if this was an émigré journal.)

The student body of the Fritz Reuter High School, four hundred people, found a total of seventeen stray potato bugs; nine of them were ladybugs. Lockenvitz wanted to do what a friend should, and asked us: Did we also know that there was a watch list posted on the distribution shelves of the German Post Office, and that pretty much every day a couple of letters would go spend the night with the Stasi (the State Security Police)?

Now *this* Lockenvitz was someone we could ask about his meeting with Hermlin, the poet, on Landsberg Avenue. Lockenvitz had squirmed his way around a lie: On a streetcar for Grünau he'd gone astray and ended up in Schmöckwitz, was invited into a house there for discussions about art in Mecklenburg, about Barlach the sculptor; tea, red wine. Lockenvitz borrowed a pair of shoes from Pius; his own had been waiting to be repaired for four weeks. He told us his thoughts without holding anything back: Our Socialist accomplishments all presuppose someone they've been taken from, someone who's now standing in the corner and sulking. What's been holding up our American shoe-resoling plants?

This Lockenvitz of ours was who we picked when 11-A-II suddenly had to delegate someone for an FDJ training course in Dobbertin, near Goldberg. At first, when we saw Manfras vote against absenting himself from home and curriculum, when Lise Wollenberg used her vote to avenge herself for being neglected and punish Lockenvitz in general for having ancestors from somewhere else, we kept our hands down. Then Pius, with the powers vested in him as head of the school-group authority, asked: What did the candidate himself think about taking such a trip. – Any organizational secretary for the ZSGL must constantly strive to extend his or her understanding of theory: he answered, like someone agreeing to sacrifice himself for us. Second round of voting: Unanimous—as was in fashion.

In November 1950, he left; in January, we had him back. It went badly. Start to finish: a flop, a mis-hit.

Literally. The start: In November the Ministry of State Security picked up Mrs. Lockenvitz's brother in the Wismar shipyards; charges of sabotage and espionage. Mrs. Lockenvitz tried to hit her son who was off to practice getting into the mental universe of such a ministry. He grabbed her wrists and said, as if conducting a medical evaluation, that she seemed to be hysterical; distracted by curiosity, she asked him what the symptoms of this illness were and didn't like his answers. Now he was off in another town and mustn't even think of going back to Gneez and the apartment in the Barbara Quarter.

He never told us exactly how it ended in Dobbertin. It must have been something like an instructor wanting to hear more about the third principle of dialectics—that could easily lead to a bad grade and a "Badge for Superior Knowledge" in bronze instead of gold.

For his first question to Bettikin had been: If quantity necessarily changes its nature as it increases and is transformed into a qualitative difference, how does that work when you're comparing Turgenev's brain to an elephant's?

(LOCKENVITZ, from before his course in Dobbertin: Children should be spared this. In 1946, when I went to answer the doorbell in Budniak's house, there were two people standing there asking about Mrs. Scharrel. Mrs. Scharrel lived on the second floor and was a black-marketeer, professionally. Mrs. Scharrel: Just tell 'em I'm on my way to Wissmar! That was hard for me, but you do what grown-ups tell you, right? The first time, you forget—if you're lucky. In 1948 the catechist asked us: Who had never told a lie in their life. I raised my hand, because no one else wanted to. And presto! I'd traded up from one lie to two. Now the process is running fine, from a technical point of view. But children should be spared.

The child Lockenvitz, in 1949, after having worked his way through the

Old Testament for a second time, requested an audience with the cathedral preacher of Gneez and gave him a well-organized explanation for why he would henceforth not be coming to the meetings of the congregational youth group. We bring this up to remove any doubt about the fifteen-year-old we're dealing with here.)

He was stubborn. Introverted. Teasing Bettinikin had lost its appeal. His grades slipped in Latin. He lost weight—in memory he is sitting lost in obsessive reflections behind his cheap glasses, wearing a blue shirt that hangs on him in folds. Then came January 12, 1951, when an eighteen-year-old high-school student was sentenced to death in Dresden for "Incitement to Boycott" and for the attempted murder (with a pocketknife) of a People's Policeman; in Gneez, the regular police went into the Renaissance Cinema, not even in disguise, to find out once and for all who was murmuring or laughing whenever the custodian appeared in image and sound, speaking his southern German dialect. Sachwalter Walter considered the sentence appropriate, both before and after it was reduced to fifteen years in prison. This provoked Pagenkopf's female partner in the work collective to thoughtlessly comment: If it's really true that this statesman is such a thorn in the Americans' side, why haven't they bumped him off yet? It's been three years!

Luckily for all of us, she did this outdoors, one evening on the Gneez ice rink. So Lockenvitz could do a few figure eights alone for a few minutes, then curve back into our circle and show us how he'd now learned to think. The ice was gray in the evening darkness, you had to keep your eyes fixed on the track. Sometimes there was the sound of a blade grating; the night surrounding us and Lockenvitz's hard, even, almost adult voice kept getting bigger and bigger:

– It used to be that when the commanding prince fell in open battle, this damaged the troops' morale. Today it would only lead to needing to close ranks. The result is always uncertain; the successor may be even more aggressive. You have to guess what strategy he has in mind, whereas before, you knew what you were dealing with. Any individual is surely expendable, even if they hold power; unless he has charisma, and the abilities that go with it, which is rarely the case. Not counting our dear friends in Moscow, needless to say. Conclusion: The machine is running and it will keep on running. Second: Even now, war is not a *free-for-all* with no rules, where every side is allowed to do whatever it can. People in the highest circles invoke such rules or norms precisely because they are occasionally (secretly) broken. One such tacit norm rules out murdering the opposing leader, other than in open battle. If such excellent rules were rashly, consciously violated, then trust in the validity of all the agreements that limit behavior would wither. The consequence might be a counterstrike with nerve gas against the capital of the offending state. Conclusion: Fear of negative effects rebounding on the perpetrator of a major violation of norms. And that's why everything stays the way it is.

– Grammarian: he'd said a year earlier when the current 11-A-IIs had been asked to state their choice of profession. – What do you want to be now, Youth Friend Lockenvitz? A historian?

– A Latin teacher: Lockenvitz said grimly.

That was the January when, in Western Germany, the Allied High Commission met with the chancellor, his assistant, and two generals at the Hotel Petersberg to discuss whether Germans should once again be rearmed.

That was the January when the East German Volkspolizei sent recruiters into high schools, wearing blue shirts under their uniform jackets, to talk to the boys of 11-A-II, one Youth Friend to another. They promised training in devices that rolled, swam, and flew. Lockenvitz made an appointment with Dr. Schürenberg, specified to the minute; in the hall of the villa on what they called Quack Lane in Gneez, he performed twelve knee-bends, repeating the exercise in front of the doctor's desk; he was given a piece of paper certifying "vegetative dystonia."

To make the school administration believe it too, he applied for exemption from gym class. From then on he would leave the schoolhouse when the Phys. Ed. beanpole hounded us onto the pommel horse or spun us around the high bar; he'd go for walks by himself. At handball or soccer games he would crouch behind the goal, elbows propped on his knees, chin on his folded hands, watching, coming back down to earth when a girl asked him what the score was.

At the start of the 1951–52 school year, nominated for a second term as organization secretary, he declined the candidacy, giving as his reason:

Academic demands. (Still, there wasn't that much he had to do: convene us for marches, campaigns against bandit potato-bugs, and assemblies; report once a month to the central council of the FDJ, on preprinted questionnaires, that we had done this or that in the cause of peace, and that so-and-so many members of the school's chapter had subscribed, for money, to the organization's newspaper, *Young World*.) He was a solid A student in Latin, English, German, and Contemporary Studies, with Bs in the other classes, except for a C in chemistry, which really rankled.

For Christmas of 1951 he found a bag hanging on his mother's door, filled with pfeffernuesse, walnuts, a pad of ink-proof linen-stock paper, and a pair of knitted gloves not made by a machine. It was a freshly washed gym bag, with a drawstring, the kind girls used. Lockenvitz came to see and thank Gesine Cresspahl.

She was dissatisfied with herself, for not having had the idea first; she assured him she was innocent.

(If only you knew that it was from Annette Dühr, 10-A-II. She was so good-looking, so pretty with her hazel eyes, dark-brown braids, a face that invited trust. Later she became a stewardess for the East German Lufthansa; she was allowed to go through training with Pan American, and when she got back her picture was on the cover of Berliner Neuen Illustrierten. *She liked you, she wanted you to like her. You could have found her so easily—all you needed to do was walk back and forth across the schoolyard with her gym bag visible in your hand. Annette reached out to you, in secret but still; she had every right to think you were conceited for having other things on your mind besides girls. But it would have been better for you if you'd wanted to find her.)*

Lockenvitz would now come join our work collective at the appointed times and leave as soon as the math or chemistry homework was done. Pius asked me, once and only once, to pose the question of how Lockenvitz imagined these tasks fitting with a woman's talents; I refused, I was scared of Lockenvitz's mother and had no desire to hear her say he was in unrequited love with anyone. Lockenvitz probably meant it as an apology for his guarded manner, as a gift, when he brought us a note explaining what was keeping him aloof from us:

People insert between events and the free apprehension of those events a number of concepts and aims, then demand that what happens conform to them.

We urged him to fob this off on Selbich as evidence of the nature of the field of contemporary studies under an imperialist regime, especially since she would never in her life figure out who'd written it (G. W. F. Hegel, 1802). He shook the locks from his brow with an exasperated laugh—as though he were done playing games with Bettinikin.

Pius and I kept our mouths strictly shut when we saw him one November afternoon coming out of the building where Bettina S. had been rewarded for her loyal endurance with an apartment.

We were mad at Zaychik for half a year. He wanted to start a correspondence with some socialistically inclined English girls, along with a schoolmate. Lockenvitz did him the favor, even wrote something to Wolverhampton for the sake of peace and the mail censors. Then he found out that Zaychik had included in the envelope, by way of introduction, a photograph of Pius instead, because he thought Pius was more attractive to a young girl's eye (in fact the girls of 11-A-II considered Pius merely "striking," while Lockenvitz was "our handsome young man"). Hopefully it did him some good to hear that we took his side in such a momentous thing.

Lockenvitz was the first person in our school to wear plastic-framed glasses, which he could prove he had bought on Stalin Street. (Opticians were a protected species all across Mecklenburg, safe from in-depth tax audits; they allowed themselves practically metropolitan window displays— almost never was an optician brought before the court in Mecklenburg.)

He owned no Canadian-style jacket.

During vacations we each went our own fine way—Pius, Cresspahl's daughter, and Lockenvitz too.

He had been careless about one factor in his calculations, if indeed they were calculations. Vegetative dystonia doesn't exactly go with long-distance bicycle riding.

He rode like a healthy person, twenty-five miles an hour was nothing. He could've been in Jerichow in half an hour! But he took his two-wheeled trips in the other direction on weekends. We could only hope that no one would notice.

Matthew 16:26. Yeah. Shit.

My dear Marie, this is everything I *think* I know about Dieter Lockenvitz.

August 6, 1968   Tuesday

If we want to get through today in one go, we'll need numbers.

I.

A New Yorker who has their apartment broken into can wait till they're blue and yellow in the face for the insurance payment to come, but if they've paid their premiums into a plan that de Rosny has dreamed up, they can send in a list of missing items on Tuesday, certified by the Twenty-Third Precinct, and get a cashier's check in the mail precisely one week later—good money, legal tender from Manhattan to Leningrad.

Just as de Rosny's bank wants its cut from the insurance underwriters for the people he calls "my colleagues," so too an in-house travel agency should make its profit from the money that these colleagues can afford to put into vacations. And anyone who enters this room on the eighteenth floor without the financial institution's five-line symbol above her heart, without a nametag, in a white linen suit like a passerby off the street, will have it pointed out to her that this business is not open to the public.

– I am aware of that: Mrs. Cresspahl replies, content. Here for once she is not known as "our" German, "our" Dane. The girl behind the counter with a beehive of blond hair keeps her lips tightly pressed; her morning is not going well. We wish we could show her the cartoon from the latest *New Yorker* that we kept for D. E.'s amusement: Under a sign that says SERVICE WITH A SMILE stands a butcher in an apron, handing a customer the bag with her purchases; he looks a little baffled, questioning, serious. The lady shoots her nose into the air with irritation; her mouth is creased with indignation. The caption below says what she's asking: *Well?* (Where's that smile?)

Here things go very differently from the usual sales transactions—we're asked questions, short and snippy: Bank ID? Social security number? Department? Supervisor's extension?

Employee vs. Employee. We're going to whip this girl into shape though.

There are mornings when we too find it hard to force that grimace of fake friendliness onto our face, but it's from the explicit demands of people like her that we learned to. We'll show her the lay of the land, particularly the path that leads to the telephone of the ostensibly admired Mr. de Rosny, without speaking his name. And here you have it, a once-in-a-lifetime opportunity, step right up, free of charge: the chance to see an employee's face ring the changes from shamefaced to scared to meek to submissive, and finally to heartfelt. – *I am ever so sorry, ma'am! My apologies—!*

Now we both felt a little ashamed and settled down into a perfectly normal discussion of how you can cancel a reservation for two to Frankfurt/Main on the evening of August 19, plus a car rental, the convertible in which we'd planned to drive to the border crossing at Waidhaus in the Upper Palatinate Mountains, hello there Czechs and soldiers! The date and time can stay the same but we now want to fly on Scandinavian Airlines, Pan American is fine too if you can arrive in København in the morning. That's how our friend Anita wants it; you probably don't know her. There must be a hotel on the beach somewhere near Kastrup Airport, where people can check in early in the morning and stay until, say, early afternoon. To catch up on our sleep, you ask? Yes, that's just what we were thinking; now we understand each other, don't we. If the hotel dining room is usually crowded we would also like a reservation for a table for four. Even though we are only two travelers? That's right, thank you for being so thoughtful. The thing is: we don't want to share the table. Then a reservation for a flight to Ruzyně at around four p.m. Really, even an American travel agency should know the names of the airports in Communist countries! Ruzyně, in Prague. Prag. Praha. We'd have to stop in Schönefeld, outside of Berlin? Passing through East Berlin doesn't especially bother us. And now what about that car rental, have we forgotten? The circumstances have changed, we don't think we'll be able to manage that. Impossible, but thanks anyway, *as the actress said to the bishop.* What's that, you want to send a telegram to a Communist country so that at eight p.m. on the 20th there'll be a car waiting for us from the people *who try harder*? The same way you're trying? You know what, we are going to send you a postcard. Do we have our visa? We do. International driver's license? Yup. The bill goes to the bank? It does. Linen too hot to wear when it's 75° out? You'd be amazed how cool it keeps you. Try Bloomingdales. No, thank *you!*

II.

A good hour before the Fifth Avenue department stores are overrun with people on their lunch breaks, Mrs. Cresspahl is to be found as a customer in a luggage department. It was supposed to have been Abercrombie & Fitch but someone from Czechoslovakia shot himself there on Friday the week before last. We would have recognized the door as the elevator went past. About this store, we'd say: It's maybe 3 percent cheaper here.

Is it the linen suit, the crocodile leather handbag, the footwear from Switzerland? Can you tell from her hairdo that a Signor Boccaletti has taken this customer into his care? Whatever the reason, the manager approaches to serve this client in person. So much for the commission for the younger salesladies. Good morning, she wishes us; gorgeous weather, she calls the shining dirt outside the windows; what can she do for us, she asks.

Hello too. We'd like two large suitcases, here's the size. They should look as shabby as possible, please.

What? You want low-quality merchandise in a store like this?

Like they're made from a worn-out carpet. But solid, and each with two wraparound straps, and locks that even at first sight can clearly be opened with bare hands.

I think I'm beginning to see what you mean.

These might be all right. But only if this distinguished establishment also carries two aluminum shells that can fit perfectly into them.

I see I see!

That's what we want. We've seen how a gentleman by the name of Professor Erichson prepares for his travels, and we liked it. We're adopting this D. E.'s practices, you might say.

When the customer requests delivery to Riverside Drive, a less respectable address, the full-figured woman betrays a certain hesitation at the sight of the checkbook we've opened. Decision time, my good woman. We look her right in the eye; she's facing the choice between more than two hundred dollars in revenue and not trusting us. The bank that the check is drawn on is two blocks away. If the lady decides she wants to call that bank, we'll have to allow it. She has the right to request our employer's address; the right to ask Mrs. Lazar if we're creditworthy; we could be mired knee-deep in suspicion of fraud. At this precise moment in our negotiations, she decides to smile. Is it dramaturgically justified? It clearly is, because now she tells us: I can see it in your face, you'd rather break a leg than cheat an old woman! Believe me, I can judge people . . .

And since it's true, we would, we give her a good look when she comes marching into the store's restaurant—every inch the supervisor who can set her own lunch breaks, but then turning into a kind and friendly woman, somewhat harried, telling us about her insomnia, no pills help. Her name is Mrs. Collins, she lives in Astoria, Queens. What a coincidence! There was something else she wanted to say: it was a week ago today that a man came into the store, in one of those South American hats, he bought suitcases like you, Mrs. Cresspahl. You understand, forty years helping people choose suitcases, you wouldn't believe what . . . I certainly do believe it. Six hundred dollars, paid in cash. And the next day he came back, asked for me especially, said he liked the service he'd been given . . . Not as much as I did, Mrs. Collins! And introduced himself as the impresario of a ballet troupe—such people do exist! Of course they do. He wanted a present for every ballerina, a reward, a bonus, I don't know; came to $2,000 altogether. That's a sale you like to make! You're perfectly happy to accept a credit card! We don't carry more than three tens around on the streets of New York either, Mrs. Collins. And the next day it bounced. A stolen card. A two-thousand-dollar loss! We don't like to have to go to the management either. There, you see, Mrs. Cresspahl? I just wanted to tell you that after we gave each other that look before, will you forgive me?

III.

The New York Times has taken a look into people's wallets in New York and northeastern New Jersey. A factory worker in that area, assuming an average hourly wage of $3.02, has to slave away for one hour and forty-four minutes for a rib steak in a restaurant.

The Bratislava conference has swept into the mists all the daily fare that's been coming from the Moscow press—the suspected counterrevolution, anti-Communist plots, etc. What does *Pravda* suggest? That none but the imperialist "enemies of Socialism" are to blame for the fact that such a debate has arisen at all.

At LaGuardia Airport they've opened a STOL runway—Short Take-Off and Landing. Want to bet D. E.'s going to take us for a look at the thing next Saturday?

IV.

When Mrs. Collins came running back into the restaurant, she had a message. Would we be so kind as to call New York, such-and-such number? Thanks, Mrs. Collins.

But actually Employee Cresspahl was angry. She hadn't told anyone at the bank where she was going to buy luggage this Tuesday morning; for a moment she had the intolerable idea that someone was following her. *That she might be under surveillance!*

There's a remedy for that. What are all the things the Czech word *hrozný* means? Terrible, horrible, frightful, appalling, dreadful, gruesome, harrowing. And what personal name does *hrozný* remind you of? *Hrozná doba*, time of terror. *Hrozná bída*, unspeakable misery. *Hrozná zima*, terrible cold. *Hrozná počasí*, frightful weather.

By the time she gets to *to jsou plané hrozby*, "they're only warning shots," she can think calmly again and arrive at the idea that someone might have gone into her office and looked at the desk calendar. It's written right there: the time, the name of the store. And what is this time, in which she is out and about? It is within the span of time she has rented to the bank. And what was she doing in said time? Buying luggage for a trip that the bank is sending her on, a trip she'll moreover be compensated for. That's what Anita would say. You see how docile a person gets once they've become an employee, Anita.

V.

The address was "good," a nice place in the Thirties on Park Avenue, a lawyer's office. We first met Mr. Josephberg at one of Countess Albert Seydlitz's parties—a man you can go off into a corner and speak German with, about Kurt Tucholsky, one of his former clients in Germany; about Tilla Durieux, who alas kept marrying men other than Mr. Josephberg. "For the actor posterity weaves no wreaths": these husbands were clearly the exceptions. Then D. E. heard me mention his name and gave us another connection to him: this man, ennobled by emigration at the very beginning, February 1933, is D. E.'s lawyer. And now he's ours. Anyone D. E. trusts, we trust.

– *Is it ready?*: Mrs. Cresspahl asks from a phone booth in the Grand Central post office, should she come right away? – *Mr. Josephberg urgently requests your presence*: his secretary confirms, formally, as if she's forgotten all my appearances with Marie in her waiting room. Or is it supposed to be sarcastic? Because of course you need to be there in person to sign something? It's a quick hop on the subway running under Lexington Avenue. And it's a happy occasion. After Anita told me about an American school in the south part of West Berlin, we've added an addendum to the Cresspahl will.

Anyone taking a trip should leave behind a last will and testament. I hereby bequeath everything I own to my daughter Marie Cresspahl, born July 21, 1957, in Düsseldorf, the daughter of railway inspector Jakob Wilhelm Joachim Abs. The life insurance policy number is. Marie is requested to keep until her twenty-fifth birthday all the Mecklenburg books with a date of printing before 1952. The child is to be brought up by Mrs. Efraim Blumenroth.

That was right, and it was wrong. Mrs. Blumenroth lives on Riverside Drive, so Marie could keep her school, her homeland; children will survive with the Blumenroths, even if they lack a mother of Jewish descent. How could I dream that Anita would be prepared to do without trips, for Marie! So now we've worked it out this way: A lady in Berlin-Friedenau, tried and found true for twenty years, will be responsible for bringing up the child; the child's legal guardian, however, will be D. E., who is required to go to Berlin in person four times a year and check whether everything is being arranged properly for the child. That's what I was going to sign, and I was glad it was ready.

VI.
– How are you feeling today, Mrs. Cresspahl?
  – Fine, thanks, Mr. Josephberg.
  – Heart? Circulation?
  – I had no idea you were taking up medicine, Doctor! Yes, I'm all right. Maybe a little tired from work.
  – Please forgive me for not being able to talk to you today the same way I've so enjoyed in our earlier conversations.
  – Let's get it over with, Doctor. Is someone suing me?
  – It's worse than that, Mrs. Cresspahl. Please forgive an old man for making a personal remark, based on what he feels he knows about your life.

– All right.

– This is going to be the worst thing you'll have heard since your father passed away.

– All right!

– The last will and testament of Dr. Dietrich Erichson states that you are to be the first person notified in the event of his death.

– He's dead.

– He died in a plane crash near Helsinki-Vantaa Airport, Finland. On Saturday. At eight a.m.

– What kind of plane was it.

– A Cessna.

– He's licensed to fly a Cessna!

– Both Finnish and American police have identified him beyond a doubt.

– People are incinerated in plane crashes.

– Indeed. The doctors estimate that Mr. Erichson may have lived for five minutes after the impact. Without regaining consciousness of his situation.

– Consciousness of being smashed to bits and on fire!

– Yes. Forgive me, Mrs. Cresspahl.

– This is the kind of thing that *The New York Times* would report.

– The government that employed the deceased voiced a wish to have the news suppressed.

– How do they identify someone who's been incinerated?

– From the teeth.

– Why couldn't it be a bullet in the chest? An injection? A stabbing!

– Clearly the deceased had been instructed to leave a copy of his dental records where it would be readily available.

– Why am I hearing about this only today.

– Because the American board of inquiry had to fly from Washington to Helsinki.

– That's ten hours!

– Because the gentlemen in question preferred to release the news of his death only today.

– A photograph!

– There are no photographs of the site of the accident.

– There are official photographs, taken by the board of inquiry.

– If you make a formal request, I can contact the authorities responsible and ...

– Now I believe it.

– Mr. Erichson left everything to you, Mrs. Cresspahl. His mother has the right to live in the house until she passes away. Aside from the real estate and monetary assets, there are various copyrights—

– No.

– If you'd prefer it, I can inform Mrs. Erichson.

– No.

– My deepest sympathies, Mrs. Cresspahl. Please be assured that anything you need in the coming weeks—

– Could you ask Mrs. Gottlieb to walk me to my office? Without telling her what ... what you've just told me?

VII.

The office—the only place in New York where you can be alone, behind a locked door. When someone dies, whatever you do or were doing turns into a reproach; playing in the water and flirting at Jones Beach. In a storm Jakob's mother used to set a lit candle on the table and pray. We were in such a hurry when we were hunting through Minneapolis that we assumed the edge of the wall frayed by the broad noonday light, the surface of light beyond it, was the famous river and we didn't look closer. And that was fine, because we were definitely going to take a trip to Finland together next year. He wanted to fly over the Alps with us; we had a date in Rome. According to Protestant belief, God can see what's written on airplanes. The aggressive honking of horns on the streets of Manhattan—how could we ever have felt homesick for sounds that just come from rudeness. Also, the planes rising along a diagonal offend an eye accustomed to order, to the perpendicular. A child is sitting comfortably on the floor, leaning a shoulder against the wall, raising and lowering something while making two connected sounds, almost like a melody. A rhythm in which a tired body unwillingly feels itself as nothing but a firing of nerves in the brain, with a feeling of complete despair, keening helplessly with those two sounds each pulling the other behind it. A heavy pendulum, blocked in its swing just before it snaps, the pauses lengthening ever so indiscernibly slightly.

In my day it took eight hours to fly to New York. Sometimes, when I arrived in Hamburg from Copenhagen on summer afternoons, the blocked
light in the passport room felt like home. When I like something, *D. E.'s
glad.* Guh-ZEE-neh! people say, with a pleading tone in the second syllable,
like they're trying to trap me with the name; D. E. does it differently, I like
hearing him. *Big Maries dead, lil Maries a-waitin for D. E.* He said
"My daughter"; once. – *Gimme another, Mr. Pharmacist, he said. An she
did.* And the white ball, like a cherry bomb, dangerously heading straight
for a closed eye, cheating the gaze, making the brain echo, but sometimes
nice, like birds flying, white midsize birds, maybe seagulls. There are
people who don't mind flying only because the situation includes the possibility of an unexpected crash, yes look out and that's it your life's over,
and so the moment, like arguably every other moment, contains a demand
that you organize and settle your personal affairs once and for all, including your death. Those who adopt such an attitude cite philosophical reasons.
D. E. was flying to Athens, way down below a tiny little patch of prepared
ground amid a boundless body of water, – Will we hit the target? I can see
what they mean about helicopters; we'd want to at least hear our own crash.
Comes back from a trip and suddenly knows, on top of everything else,
about the Gothic origins of the churches of Prague buried under the Jesuit
Baroque. He was definitely there. Took a look around as a favor to me. "Jan
Hus and the Symbolic Function of the Chalice for the Utraquists." Imagining: being on a flight over JFK and never leaving the airport; the child
that I was. *I expect to die very soon; would you permit me to make arrangements that would keep you cared for? At least on behalf of the child?* Lying
down, seeing the white sky lagging behind, swept by the dry branches of
the treetops. You're bad at suffering, D. E.! You turn everything into cause
and responsibility and pay what you owe accordingly, then forget people.
– Why should I suffer, Gesine? A bus has a long breath. Airplanes grind
the air, don't they? Today I'm the cat waiting for the host who'll disappear
someday—scabby, tunneled through with pus, limping, blind in one eye.
DOES THE AIR OVER MANHATTAN MAKE YOU UNHAPPY? IT MAKES
US TWICE AS UNHAPPY. A year ago the old dial tone in the telephone
gave up the ghost—since April 1967 there's been a bell-like, purring, plump
tone after the 9. The variations for Goldberg on Saturday night, they were
already D. E.'s dirge.

VIII.
– Please free the line, Mrs. Cresspahl. We have an international person-to-person call for you.

– This is a test. This is a test.

– Anita! You're calling me at the bank, you know.

– There's something we need to talk about. It'd be too risky with Marie around.

– Indicative, Anita. It *is* too risky.

– Helsinki airport, indicative?

– So I'm told.

– Was it yours?

– If I can believe it, it was mine.

– Do you want me to go to Helsinki?

– There are no remains.

– But there is a death.

– Anita, he had a piece of paper on him whenever he traveled that said in the four major world languages: To be cremated at the place or location of death with no music speeches flowers or any religious or other service *whatsoever*. You know, so he wouldn't put me to any unnecessary trouble when he died.

– Tell me what I can do.

– Come to Prague in two weeks. My vacation.

– *Ty znayesh'*.

– Tell me what to do.

– Does Marie know?

– When I tell her it'll destroy her.

– Let me think about it until tomorrow morning. Can you hold out till then?

IX.
– Well, Mrs. Erickssen!

– Evening, Wes.

– How's Mr. Erickssen?

– He's fine. Away, I'm afraid. But fine.

– What can I do for you, Mrs. Erickssen?

– A drink.

– Most certainly. But what kind of drink, that is the question.

– Something to pick me up, Wes.

– Mrs. Erickssen, with all due respect: could it be that you need something different to pick you up?

– Anything.

– I'll get you a taxi, Mrs. Erickssen.

X.

Waiting at Riverside Drive, of course, is airmail from Finland. A map of
Meklenburg Ducatus, Auctore Ioanne Blaeuw excudit, excusably a bit
naive in its geography, with Muritz Lacus blithely combined with Calpin
Lacus, but Fleesen Lake still awaits discovery; a friendly yellow griffon
appears on the coat of arms instead of the Mecklenburg *oxhead*. Still, there's
no doubt about the Mare Balticum: two jaunty galleons sail the sea and
right by the brightly colored gold-rimmed windrose above the Bay of
Wismar you can read what in truth it really should be called: Oost Zee.
Above to the right you can picture Finland.

If you put on your makeup until Marie gets home and then sit looking
out the window the whole time—maybe you can get through it.

We're in time, just barely. On WRVR, 106.7 on your radio dial, "Just
Jazz" is starting. D. E. asked us to tape it for him. How could we forget.

It's done. We've deceived Marie.

The child sleeps through the night while at two a.m. her mother goes
shopping on Broadway; there was everything—hashish, heroin, hits, but
no sleeping pills. This too has been known to happen: instead of helping
make breakfast, the mother stays hidden behind closed doors, Marie saying goodbye in a cheerful voice: *Walk, don't run! A fall is no fun!*

Eagle-Eye Robinson steps out of the elevator with a letter in his hand—
airmail, special delivery, stamps from Suomi. The text begins: Dear Ilona!
Then the "Ilona" was crossed out and replaced with: Gesine. Oh, your
jokes, D. E.

At the bank, the room for the young gods Wendell, Milo, and Gelliston has been cleared out, down to the floorboards. In Cresspahl's office, the furniture has been stacked into a tower and covered with a tarp. The telephone, complete with its connection box, has disappeared.

– We sent you a telegram: the girls in de Rosny's lobby claim. – Here's the carbon!

Dear Mrs. Cresspahl due to damaged cables your section of the sixteenth floor is closed stop we will inform you as soon as you can return to work stop this will not count against your vacation time stop *have a good time*

Employee Cresspahl requests an appointment with Mr. de Rosny. On the spot. At once!

It's her own fault. She should've realized that the telephone exchange keeps a list of all international calls. Has to keep a list. Someone heard Anita and me, a second person translated it, a third person put us in their files, a fourth person explained us to three more people at a meeting. *Hrozebný, hrozivý, hrozící!* Threatening, menacing, impending! *Hrozím se toho,* it terrifies me! *Hrozba trestem,* threat of punishment!

De Rosny sends word that he is very busy at the moment. During her stubborn two-hour wait, Employee Cresspahl realizes that, all the same, her lapse of discretion has resulted in a thoughtful gesture. De Rosny has invested in this employee. It truly would be a little loss for him if she broke down. A machine is overloaded so he turns it off for a while. *Dům hrozí sesutím,* and we hope it does! The house is threatening to collapse!

Before lunchtime, de Rosny coughs up an appointment: Monday, August 19, at nine a.m.

Hrozný?, python! *Hrozitánský,* monster!

– My best regards to the vice president: Employee Cresspahl says. She can see that he's gone to a lot of trouble. At least six movers hauling desks at the crack of dawn. If it's a game, she'll play along. She won't set foot in this building before August 19! *Hrozná doba.*

We need to apologize to Wes. Wes sells alcoholic drinks. Drunks disgust him. Mrs. Cresspahl may have looked that way yesterday.

– Wes, I just want to say, about—
– *My dear Mrs. Erickssen!* Don't mention it! All bartenders hand out medicine; you needed a taxi, you needed to go to bed, I could see that with the naked eye!

– Send me the bill, doctor.

– I'll send it to the professor, Erickssen. *A sweet man.* The kind of husband a woman can only dream of.

– Goodbye, Wes. *Thank you kindly.*

– Allow me the honor, Mrs. Erickssen.

– In the middle of the day? Unaccompanied by a man?

– Today I am the man accompanying you, Mrs. Erickssen.

D. E. spent parts of his life here—parts he liked. We were together here. This is the best place to reread the letter from Finland.

Even on rereading it's news of a trip. Finnish neutrality. The Port of Helsinki. What professional business brought D. E. there?

Eventually "Ilona" sticks out—not a woman, an abbreviation, a hint at a code. With just a pencil from Wes and the back of an Irish betting slip it's tricky business. A machine would crack it in five minutes but Mrs. Cresspahl spends two hours deciphering D. E.'s ILoNa.

D. E. has been to Prague many times. (But never with a passport that had my name in it, Gesine.) So the best thing for us to do at passport control in Ruzyně Airport is act like we have all the time in the world, since the young men behind the bulletproof glass are going to read our documents the way other people read poetry. D. E. recommends that we keep a car while we're there—it's a hassle to take the 22 to the Czernin Palace, the Foreign Ministry, especially when the streetcar bangs into the loose rails in the city center or is driven downhill in Mediterranean style.

– Does he always write such tricky letters?: Wes says, refilling his friend Erickssen's wife's glass after half an hour. And does she want to take Erickssen's ticket for Ireland now? It's ready for him.

Once at the Czernin Palace, D. E. recommends a wine bar called u Loretu, with outdoor tables. Diagonally across from a café where an uncle will inquire, in a doctorly manner, into the condition of our shoes, at which point he will adjust Marie's sandals and repair at most a torn strap. He will offer us wine as if we were in Italy.

The best thing to do, then, would be to find an apartment on Paris Street in Prague. After the opening of the ČSSR to capitalist tourism in 1963, our money will make us welcome. We should be careful of young men who come talk to us without looking at us—they just want our foreign currency.

So we might be an irresistible object of interest to craftsmen, but as for turning up any paint, Gesine, a faucet, a windowpane—God help you. You'll probably take frequent trips to Frankfurt, on a commuter flight that rarely runs. If you need onions, for instance. But if we know you, you'll have friends in a village somewhere within a month, Gesine. And all the better to eat you with in Frankfurt, Gesine. *À dieu, yours, truly—*

– Give my regards to Professor Erickssen!: Wes requests when I get up to leave, and he walks alongside Mrs. Cresspahl behind his forty-foot-long bar until she gets to the door, feeling the awed looks of the remaining gentlemen on her back. A guest of honor, that lady. Food and drinks on the house. Wife of an aerospace engineer or something.

Mrs. Cresspahl goes for a walk, all the way to the Upper West Side. On Forty-Second Street she passes a shop selling *Der Spiegel*, but she'd rather stay true to the old man on Ninety-Sixth Street. – I've kept it aside for you for a long time, sister!: he says. "That just as when you were alive / the clocks still run, the bells still ring…"

Waiting at Riverside Drive is de Rosny's telegram, signed by Kennicott II; starting at seven o'clock, Radio WKCR will be bringing us "Jazz and the Avant-Garde," with pieces by Eaton, Monk, Tristano, and Taylor, we'll tape them for D. E. There are some illnesses where music is life-threatening.

– Mrs. Cresspahl, Berlin is on the line.
– Gesine! Say something! Let me hear your voice!
– Your school friend Cresspahl speaking.
– Say the date, the day of the week!
– Anita, why are you crying.
– Say something!
– Wednesday. August 7th.
– It's really you.
– Unfortunately.
– I've been calling all day, every hour, and the exchange keeps saying: This line has been disconnected.
– Construction in the bank.
– I was shaking in my shoes!
– I'm not like my mother, Anita. As long as I have a child I need to take care of, I'll try to live. I don't have a husband I can leave the child to either.

– Promise.

– Yes. I promise. Now your advice please.

– Are you still going to Prague, with Marie?

– If it's up to me.

– It'll destroy her, like you said. At first I was in favor. But there's no coffin for her to look at.

– And she'll hold it against me for ten years that I waited a single day to tell her.

– Try. In Prague, after the 20th, I'll help you. Do you give me permission to go to Helsinki?

– If I knew why. Nothing's there.

– That's what I want to see for myself.

– But only tell me about it when I ask you. Not until Prague.

– *Ty znayesh'*, Gesine. What else are you doing today?

– What's a double widow who couldn't go to either funeral supposed to do? I'm listening to music.

– That's poison, Gesine!

The person scratching at the door is our Eagle-Eye Robinson, with two large, expensively wrapped packages and the business card, the warm greetings, the home address of Mrs. Collins, Astoria, Queens. Yesterday morning I was still alive. And there's Marie behind Mr. Robinson—enthusiastically looking forward to unwrapping the suitcases. Now the lying starts.

– Why are you wearing sunglasses *indoors*, Gesine? *"Indoors"*...

– *"Im Hause."* There're workmen in the bank. I banged my eye.

– Did you go to Dr. Rydz?

– No, another doctor. I'm supposed to rest my eyes like this for three days.

– Does it hurt?

– Yes. He gave me pills too.

– I was wondering... But are you tired?

– Go ahead and ask. I'm just slow.

– Is today going to be a normal evening?

– Should we do something different?

– I'll cook, even though it's your turn. It just dawned on me that something else must have been going on during that August of 1951 when Cresspahl wanted you out of the way in Wendisch Burg.

– In July the Stasi searched Cresspahl's house. The pretext was that he'd started making a lot of money from his work, more than his pension. The truth was that this state couldn't get it into its head that it could wrong a person a second time, and a third time, and this Cresspahl would still try to follow the law. But your something else had started earlier.

– Is it anything to do with Jakob?

– With Jakob too. Because it's reciprocal: the same way I've liked a lot of people, one or two have liked me.

– I know one person, who's flying on Scandinavian—

– On Finnair.

– and looking forward to seeing you.

– And to seeing you. You're even prettier than I am.

– Gesine! The Papenbrock hair!

– Widow Papenbrock was feeling crabby about the Cresspahls. When the state power, after Albert's death, confiscated the mansion in town, the warehouse too, the *ol lady* waited for us to invite her to move in. Cresspahl wouldn't risk his little finger for that. And it would have meant the Church taking over the house. She left for Lüneberg, where there was still some of Albert's real estate. We took her to the Hamburg line since we were hoping this would be our last goodbye. She didn't wish me especially well, but she still said, despite herself: At least you got our hair.

– And your lovely breasts, nice and high.

– Marie! What a thing to notice! Anyway, my breasts were just hypothetical among the young men of 1950. None had seen them bare.

– They wanted to.

– About that I was unaccommodating. Which damaged my reputation, because whenever someone dreamed up an affair with me and it didn't happen, he just made one up and spread the story around anyway.

– It's like weeds.

– They never stop growing. One of these boys was a literary type; he slipped a piece of paper with a quote on it into my bag, something like: "Not that Gesine had turned into a highly sensitive woman of delicate feeling all at once. She remained the way she was. Self-confident and timid, voracious and cowardly, longing for all 'the higher and finer things in life' that were starting to be shown in the cinematograph theaters." It took me forever to figure that one out! It was a Gesine in a novel.

– I'm sorry to hear that.

– Go look at our cookbooks—there's one from 1901, published by Appleton and Company in New York, *European and American Cuisine*, and written by the proprietress and president of Brooklyn Cooking College, now what was her name?

– Gesine Lemcke. I don't like that.

– You have the same name as other children too.

– I wish no one but you had your name.

– The reason I was given it was that once upon a time Cresspahl wanted to run away, across land and sea, with Gesine Redebrecht from Malchow. You got yours from Jakob's mother.

– One part of it's true. You were self-confident. Are.

– That's easy when Jakob's watching over you like a little sister.

– No kisses after dance class?

– I was waiting when it came to that too.

– Are you trying to teach me some kind of lesson here?

– You want me to tell you stories. I also had admirers who were satisfied when I vaguely knew they existed. One was my classmate for almost four years. In 1951 he wrote on the blackboard: "'Effi Briest,' a very pretty name I feel because it has so many 'e's and 'i's—those are the two fine, delicate vowels." Theodor Fontane.

– You knew who that was.

– And since I withheld what he wanted from him too, I think I'll at least not tell you his name. Actually I should start being vague with names in general from now on. When Cresspahl hustl—arranged some Danish business for Knoop, Gesine was invited aboard a boat, a yacht in Wismar harbor, for the toast. We don't want to cause trouble for the guy over his unpatriotic dealings with Communist Germany; but I'm grateful to him for a cruise to Denmark.

– Past the East German coast guard.

– They didn't have a wall floating in the water yet, in 1950. A Danish sailor can do anything, and will even smuggle a girl on board. As long as Cresspahl knew about it, and as long as everything stayed proper between the young lady and the older gentleman (around thirty), no kisses on the cheek, I was happy to learn navigation.

– Gesine, you were on vacation in Denmark when you were seventeen! That's why you showed me Bornholm!

– It wasn't a good idea to talk about it, though. What a Mecklenburg sailor can do, and does, is talk in his cups—the devil take him. So here was another story involving me, it was pure dumb luck that the police didn't get wind of it.

– There was the boy who lived upstairs from the Jerichow pharmacy.

– No name for him either. But I had a hard time getting him to realize that if he has a crush on someone who sees herself as long since taken, that's his business. They sometimes act like they have a right to you, boys do.

– Self-confident.

– Sometimes a bit too much. I liked to go dancing, because it meant I got to move—

– And because people like to do what they're good at.

– not because of the hands on my back. When two boys locked horns over me, I let them settle it between themselves—pretended not to notice. I wasn't anyone's property! But now here's another story about Cresspahl's daughter. Sometimes people mix up their own desires with other people's, you know. The truth is: I never led anyone on. I could never stand those anguished looks.

– There were the overnight stays at the Pagenkopfs'.

– And Lockenvitz sometimes came to Jerichow, when he could still show friendship, and stayed until morning. There were nights I was under the same roof as three men.

– Pagenkopf, Lockenvitz, Cresspahl...

– And Jakob. You're right, he's in a different category. But it was Jakob who tried to defend my good name in Jerichow on Town—on Stalin Street. All I know is that he came home bloodied; the next morning I was put on a train to far-off southeast Mecklenburg, to visit the Niebuhrs. How shocked Klaus was to see me handle the H-Jolle dinghy like a man! Luckily for me, he'd already gotten together with the girl from the teacher-Babendererdes, Ingrid. The other Ingrid, you're thinking of Ingrid Bøtersen. Four weeks with them on Wendisch Burg's Upper Lake and Town Lake before Cresspahl sent word. I found out right away what everyone in Cresspahl's house was trying to keep from me: Jakob had spent eighteen days in the basement under the Gneez district court for assault and battery.

– I had a boy who got into fights for me too once.

– Do you like how it feels?

– When someone insults me I'd rather take care of it myself.

– See? And now Jakob had something that would stay on his criminal record for several years.

– Did he do that a lot, get into fights?

– Don't worry, Marie. We both learned our lesson that time. I stopped going dancing except at school events. I would have to say that my conduct with men, since 1951, has been practically unimpeachable.

– Is that "pruning," what you're doing now?

– That is pruning. Someone once offered me a private lounge car! A West German Railways one!

– What, like Hitler had? You're lying, Gesine!

– Hitler didn't come from money. He just stole from the state. No, believe it: a real live millionaire brought me up to the mountaintop, showed me the treasures of the world, and said: All this is yours. The mountain was Platform Three at the Düsseldorf train station and the AllThisIsYours was a thing in which Hitler might have taken his fits for a spin. A kind of converted sleeping car.

– You and a millionaire!

– If you're a prosperous citizen of the USA on good terms with your government, there's nothing to keep you from stopping by the woods around Mönchengladbach and checking out how your army is working to defend Western Europe.

– And instead your eye is caught by a secretary with the Papenbrock hair, sitting prim and proper at her desk, knows her way around a typewriter too, has a gellegant Jersey wool sweater on, so you offer her—with her superiors' permission, of course—a modest railcar that you're forced to ride through West Germany since the rails are in such bad shape in the US.

– Envy is an unbecoming quality in a bank, Marie. That's a message from de Rosny *himself.*

– I'd've liked to see it.

– What's to see? A cramped four-room apartment, cabinets like on a sailboat, train phone, telex.

– Paintings on the wall. Framed. And seven guest rooms.

– One guest room—mostly occupied by the valet, who also does the cooking when the boss hosts a dinner. Other than that: a double bed. After six months gallivanting around that would've been the price.

– Would he have married you?

– I could've counted on a severance package after two years. He's still riding the rails from Munich to Hamburg every day, or maybe Hamburg to Munich. On special occasions they'll pull him through the Ruhr instead of the usual into Frankfurt and back out of Frankfurt. From Wunstorf they can couple him to the express to Regensburg. He forgave me, by the way.

– Can I ask about Taormina?

– I liked traveling with him; you could really talk to him at the table. He also seemed to grasp that I do what I decide to do, not what my hormones or glands tell me to. He made way too much of an overnight trip to Taormina, in separate rooms.

– And then came the man you'd been waiting for the whole time.

– Then came Jakob.

– You were . . . twenty-three.

– And a half. Now since you're talking about handsomely placed breasts, I should probably warn you that it's considered a bit ridiculous nowadays for a woman to wait so long. I'm sure you don't want people laughing at your mother.

– Please, dear lady, I ask you. Everything we tell each other is in strictest confidence! And would you be so kind as to make yourself at home, though I am retiring to bed. You can play the variations for Goldberg as late as you want, and the quodlibet twice.

I've never read a newspaper at midnight before. In East Germany, the press and the TV have suddenly stopped hurling their trash at the Czechoslovakians. They do suppress that the custodian was booed in Bratislava, even told *Damoi!* go home! The official report is: "Passers-by waved and called out friendly greetings again and again."

Last night a radar system for the flight paths around New York failed.

Planes circled in the air above JFK for more than a hundred minutes, unable to land.

We're flying soon too. And actually we've read the paper after midnight plenty of times! On Eastern European time. After we've come home.

— *What kind of a caller are you? Can't you dial the number for the time first?*

— Sorry, Gesine. It's just me. Anita.

— Okay.

— I was off by an hour with the time difference. Are you—

— I'm okay, as they say here; in German it'd be different. At the moment, the worst thing is that D. E. knew about Jakob. Knew that Jakob was the only man I wanted to live with, to have near me. Men do like to be the one and only, and if possible the first.

— Maybe he wasn't stupid. Maybe he was what your friend Anita calls a good person.

— He was. But that he knew—

— He was very happy he got to spend six years with you. Put that on the balance sheet too.

— Anita, I need you to keep telling me things like that. For a while yet.

— *Ty znayesh'.*

August 8, 1968 Thursday

Delivering a death announcement.

The buses threatened on D. E.'s stretch of road to New Jersey are now running: the whole lower deck is higher than the driver's seat; no smoking. The windows are tinted so dark blue that the landscape is barely visible. And so, memories. — *Oh, you can't buy memories!*: Esther once said. *And you can't get rid of them either.*

The bus comes out of the tunnel south of Hoboken. That's where, years ago, D. E. took the child and me to an apple-juice shop at the marina where the men were eating mussels from stoneware bowls and tossing the shells into the sawdust on the floor. Marie was studying him seriously, her friend and host. Back then she was still a child who might take a candy from a lady stranger on a bus but would then, after she ate it, hand back the wrapper—*to keep our city clean.* She was so delighted when he demonstrated the flick of the wrist she could use to send her shells whacking into the wood paneling. – Chock!: D. E. said. I guess he did have fun with us.

South Newark. He invited us to Newark with a topography: On Sunday mornings Newark consists of a church respectable citizens emerge from with calm expressions on their faces. Also worth mentioning is a statue behind the station, immortalizing in white and treacly fashion the first and to date only American citizen to have been sainted: Frances Xavier Cabrini. The main street is called Broad Street, located four hundred steps away, comporting itself like the local idea of *downtown!* (sing that word)— the setting for a parade caricaturing Polish peasant costumes. It's called the PATH, as you probably know. Van Cortlandt Straat, then left. *Yours, truly, D. E.*

We went there to meet D. E. in rattling icy weather, under the Hudson, to a scabby landscape piled high with never-decomposing garbage at the edge of a putrescent river. D. E. had his Polish parade to show us in Newark, with its dark-skinned participants marching like clockwork; then a cellar in which you could eat pea soup with pieces of ham à la Mecklenburg. Herr Professor Dr. Erichson was so happy when we ordered seconds! He was amused to see that a mother knows the precise moment when a frozen child's nose will start to run once she's inside and warm; Marie trustingly stuck out her face right into the napkin being held at the ready. D. E. enjoyed being with us, there's that too.

It's a surly Mrs. Erichson who opens one wing of the double door to D. E.'s stately farmhouse. Her expression is stiff, smooth white hair is stiffly sticking out from under her black riding cap. Jacket, pants, boots, and bow at the collar of her blouse are black. She's already had one visit today, from a pair of gentlemen in sports jackets who pulled something out of their pockets on a chain and quickly tucked it away again, as if they'd actually showed it to her. They wanted to take a look at D. E.'s study, maybe rummage around a bit too; she showed them the door. Now she's in a bad mood, and a little anxious. In a foreign country you need to show deference to people sent by the authorities, don't you think, Gesine?

She's relieved to hear that she'd acted within her rights. Reluctantly, because she was just about to go out riding, she brings the second visiting party of the day across the hall, opens the kitchen door, marvels at but allows the visitor to lead her into the living room instead and seat her safely in an armchair so that she won't fall at the moment of the news that her only son, the focus and pride of her old life, has allegedly and by hearsay met his death in northeast Europe, in a plane he's known how to fly for four years. She sits there as if waiting for an execution. Then comes the blow, and the slump of the head and the sagging of the body to make it look smaller. Then, all in Platt:

    – Dyou believe it, Gesine?
    – Im supposed to. I have to.
    – Burned up n buried n now theres nothin?
    – Thats how he wanted it.
    – Now you can jus stick me in tha ground too.
    – Youre gonna live a long time yet. You were off to go ridin somewhere n put the fear a God into that horse. You need to take care a his business.
    – But I got a letter from im, written on Sunday!
    – Postmarked.
    – Written, see?
    – I see it. But its your sons lawyer, sayin—
    – Dyou have an inheritance certificate with you, Gesine?
    – Lets not have any a that.
    – You won' kick an ol woman outta her house.
    – You can stay here forever.
    – Are you pregnant, Gesine?
    – Nope.
    – Dyou wish you were?
    – How could I bring up another child without im.
    – Littl Marie. Hows she holdin up?
    – Ive been afraid to—
    – Can you come stay with me?
    – We need to go to Prague.
    – But he just died.
    – He wouldve wanted it that way: first you do what you need to do.
    – Jå. Thats how he is. An once youre done with Prague?
    – Marie has to go to school. You should come stay in New York.

– Thats so far away from im. What, youre leavin?

– The taxis waiting outside. I have to catch the bus. Maries waitin at home. You can come with.

– No. Im gonna go for a ride.

In Spring 1951, Robert Pius Pagenkopf enlisted with the Armed People's Police at the Aero-Club in Cottbus. He was the only one of the three hundred and seventy high-school students at that time to do so; a lot of students were leaving school after eleventh grade then, since many parents felt that that was the equivalent of diplomas from the old days when there'd been a one-year military service requirement. These young people decided to go to the West, most not realizing that compulsory military service was awaiting them there with open arms. Pius went for the other side. Since we'd only been acting like a married couple, he made the decision by himself.

I wantd to be alone, Gesine.

Pius, if I was bothering you—

Stop it, Gesine. You were the girl for me.

Pius, Id—

Its fine. It's just that, later, I always compared other girls to you. That wasn't good for me. Marriage is hard, Gesine.

Y'left me sittin alone at our desk.

You would have gone your own way after graduation, without me. I could tell we'd be separated, I wanted to break it off myself.

To be alone.

All this peace struggle shit, Gesine. They were right you know, Sieboldt and Gollantz.

Like there's no political reeducation in the army!

There it's service, Gesine. In the army my superior has to be able to believe what I tell him, and no member of the force can doubt that I believe it. There're no more winks, stiff smiles conveying and commending your lies in one. There I can think whatever I want and no one has to hear it.

That means you'd never have another friend, Pius.

I thought I still had you, Gesine. We'd managed to create that.

And what did you plan to do if there was a war?

Then I'd be where they pushed the button. In the end, what I did with the plane would be up to me—I'm in command, I decide.

Pius's first enlistment was for three whole years; a cold glory hung in the air around our desk with plenty of room left over for Student Cresspahl as she sat through the last year of school in 12-A-II, alone, in a much smaller room on the fourth floor—one of fifteen students, alone at her desk, with a window view of the cathedral and the courtyard. We tried to talk Pius into staying through the Abitur. Even his father, the functionary of merit in the party administration in Schwerin, was scared, notwithstanding the significant boost to his reputation this new "societal activity" on his son's part would give him. You can lose a son that way. Helene Pagenkopf stuck to weeping for weeks; when Pius took the woman in his arms and stroked her shoulders, you could see how big he'd grown. Six feet tall, plus another couple inches. When we said things about the advantages of a terminal certification of knowledge in the sciences and humanities, he smiled at us for still believing in such things. As if the science of equine dental anatomy, say, would be of any use in later life. Whatever physics he'd need in the coming years, the air force would take care of teaching him. Student Lockenvitz was jealous of Young Friend Pagenkopf for the tactical savvy of his plan, not so much for the course of action itself, which was not an option for him anyway, given his eyesight. And yet he too would talk to Pius, encouraging him to consider the value of a Latin proficiency certificate, recognized by universities around the world; then Pius looked stern, keeping his dark eyebrows rigid, apparently feeling pestered.

Pius's decision was such a rare jewel in the crown of the New School's educational aims that he could easily have slacked off for the rest of the year and still received final grades that matched his standing in January. But being lax and being Pius were two very different things. Pius stuck to the syllabus and thereby kept Student Cresspahl in the habit of schoolwork—the form that learning is meant to take in one's youth. The thing is, he knew what his future held, which gave him a perspective far wider than that of school. In a ninth-grade class in 1951, the FDJ had a competition for selling their newspaper, *Young World*; it was won by a resourceful fellow who deposited his whole bundle with Abel the fishmonger on Street of National Unity, which cost him some money but saved him from having to pester passersby. It was the talk of the day at school. Pius just shrugged. Made you feel like a kid next to him. In 11-A-I there was a boy named Eckart Pingel who avowed in Contemporary Studies: In the Soviet Union they also have the biggest pigs! That was going to take him down a notch in class; Bettina Selbich put in a request for disciplinary proceedings. The thing is, Ol' Pingel wasn't just any father, he was the foreman at the Panzenhagen sawmill—proletariat nobility. Word started going around the working men of Gneez that Pingel's Eckart was getting thrown out of school just for telling the truth. That was why he was allowed to talk his way out of trouble at the teacher's conference, invoking recent Soviet advances in breeding the common domestic pig. Bettina threw the excuse right back at his head; he could recite from the textbook his class had unearthed for him (his school class). Now it's true, Eckart Pingel avoided mentioning his scientific findings too often, but everyone knew it about him and he wore it as a badge of honor that he'd hit on it first. Pius laughed too, but just by snorting some air through his nose; it came across as rather disparaging. His belonging among us, as one of us, fell from him layer by layer like an onion; he looked at us as if from a great distance. He was almost grown-up. There were evenings he spent in the Danish Quarter—without telling his mother, but without making a secret of it either. Afterwards his body would smell different, and to his silent, eyebrow-raising surprise, his friend Cresspahl started expanding her morning toilette routine to include perfume. Pius also went to bars frequented by the railwaymen of Gneez, including the Linden Pub, where the women conductors sometimes danced on the tables. For the assembly to conclude the 1950–51 school year, Gabriel Manfras proposed that the FDJ school group "delegate" Youth Comrade Pagenkopf from its ranks for service in the Armed Police; Pius looked at him so hard and so long that Manfras, who in no way had the guts for such service, finally turned red in the face for once. Pius was "bidden farewell" by the students and faculty.

He went to Cottbus for military basic training, was accepted as a fighter pilot, promoted to PFC and then corporal; he signed one letter as a "cornet." Mrs. Selbich remained part of the life of 12-A-II, as homeroom teacher, and suggested to Student Cresspahl that she read to the class from his letters, so as to share the edification of Pagenkopf's patriotic example. Cresspahl was tempted. For the letters discussed how mail censorship was handled "in our outfit": the recruit had to hand in his private letters in the guardroom, unsealed. That makes a person careful about what he puts down. Another thing the recruit has to learn: that the Comrade NCOs read the contents of incoming letters aloud to one another with gusto and commentary—not so good when they're written by a woman who's not his mother. When it is his mother, that can turn out badly too, for instance if she writes that she's worried about her "child," who has now been un-masked as a momma's boy. – To hear the old-timers tell it, it's worse here than in the army: Pius told us in writing; he sent his news via civilian mail, contrary to regulations. Gesine would've loved to make all this public in class, as a model case of Stalinist vigilance. But she had the feeling Bet-tinikin would snatch the letter out of her hand the moment she brought it to school; it contained, among other things, forms of address like the Russian word for "little sister" (Pius was a year and a half older than her). She denied that they were corresponding.

Gesine had an awkward time with her own letters to Cottbus. First, she had to avoid calling him what she was used to calling him, because she didn't want to hang a nickname around his neck, especially with the extra weight that'd be added in the barracks—but for her he was "Pius"; he was "Robert" and "Rœbbing" for his mother. Second, how could she tell him in a letter that would be read by others that three "bourgeois" people from Gneez had been sent to take a course in Socialist orientation; of course they all distrusted one another; but as soon as they walked into their room in Schwerin the first one covered the keyhole, the second one blocked the window with his back, and they both gave the third one advice as he scoured the room for the microphones; they came back to Gneez after four weeks in total harmony, sworn friends, and were appointed revenue officer, dairy manager, and head of personnel at Panzenhagen. A whole new network of relationships (though well known in its essentials) was forming throughout the city—it sometimes no longer mattered that X had known Y for some twenty-odd years: now how could she write that without blowing his political credentials for forever and a day? That's why she was relieved when he asked again what'll happen to Abel the fishmonger in England: He'll turn into *Able*, so he'll change his shop sign to "Ebel," so then people will call him *Eeble*, and then he'll, and so forth. Glad, too. For she took this to mean that he was being taught English again, and in case of emergency might be able to transfer into civil aviation. The whole Pingel family had left in a westerly direction after Eckart's "early graduation," clearly not happy with the school—that was another item not suitable for correspondence. What she liked best was when Pius came to visit and went for walks with her around Gneez Lake and had brought her a present. Because Cresspahl was once again feeling up to exertions of paternal force and had privately threatened the tobacconists from Jerichow to Gneez if they ever sold his daughter something she might smoke. So Pius turned up with cigarettes from China, brand name Temple of Great Joy (men in Pius's squadron could volunteer for duty in that People's Republic). There's a photo from this visit—our only photograph.

In 1953, Gesine Cresspahl took up residence in the state of Hesse, West Germany, and was worried that she might have lost Pius, too, in the move. She had every reason to think that Pius had learned to disapprove of such freedom of movement; and surely he wasn't allowed to correspond with residents of enemy countries. But the old friendship was rust-free! Pius now sent his letters home to "My dears." Gesine was included among his dears, otherwise Helene Pagenkopf would much rather have kept writings from her son's hand than dutifully forwarded them to *Röbbertin sin Gesin*. In 1954 Pius extended his term of duty and became a professional officer, a lieutenant by Christmas, and Gesine complained to her Robertino (having finally brought herself around to that form of address) about how hard it was to get by with her English in an American-occupied province. By then Pius had his Himalayan cattle firmly under control—the Yak-18 for training, the Yak-11 for doing—and was allowed to come back from the Soviet Union; stationed in Drewitz: squad leader (acting). Gesine sent the elderly Mrs. Pagenkopf a tiny electric shaver that a young man might use; Pius was now flying MiG-15's—in formation, but one time on his own, which was why he was transferred to be in charge of parachutist training in 1955. Gesine thought this was a demotion and that Pius had been grounded, or *gegroundet*, as it was called in the hybrid language spoken where she was working now. That can happen to a person for health reasons or as punishment. So she was happy to hear that he was uninjured; he had taken his fighter on a joyride under the autobahn bridge that crosses Zern Lake west of Potsdam. Eventually his regiment forgave him: First Lieutenant, Merseburg.

In January of 1956, the custodian of East Germany admitted that he

was training young people to fly for reasons other than their own enjoyment of the pastime; those "clubs" of the Armed People's Police were now
part of a National People's Army, NPA. As if a People weren't National
already. Six months later the air force of the Red Army, now known as the
"Soviet" Army, started asking around among its underlings in the GDR:
any pilots available? They should be ones whose flying ability had stood
out to a marked extent. Comrade Pagenkopf, for this predicate had now
been granted him, had his file card pulled from the registration offices of
Gneez and elsewhere; his personal data was now entered into "the most
desirable passport in the world": the one with the emblem of the Soviet
Union. Gesine didn't send out many notices of the birth of a healthy baby
girl in July 1957; Pius gave the child a doll inside a doll inside a doll, with
instructions for use: In this country they call the smallest, innermost one,
which can't be opened, the soul. Major Pagenkopf started another round
of basic training: on MiG-21A, 21B, and 21C's, to prepare to tackle the
MiG-21D, an all-weather interceptor (known to NATO as: "Fishbed").
Gesine was undergoing a rigorous training course too, at a bank in Düsseldorf; Pius was busy with an Su-7 ("Fitter"), a heavy fighter-bomber
suitable for nuclear assignments. In photographs he is always standing
alone now, a young man in a tailored suit meant to look British; his look
is haughty, distant; to a junior lieutenant he is a model, to an East German
officer a person commanding respect. Because the air force of the GDR is
under the air defense of the Soviet Union; the former was given no "Fish-
beds." Pius as bearer of state secrets; he gave out as his view that the Cau-
casus resembled Grunewald less than Göring had contended—an air
marshal from the old days; Gesine could now understand that this meant
he too was being taught the history of the war, and must by now be up to
the Battle of Stalingrad. Gesine was dispatched to the USA to study advanced tricks in the replication of borrowed money; Pius, undaunted, asked
"My dears" about Marie's latest adventures in American English. When
supersonic jet fighters boomed over West Berlin to scare the population,
they were piloted by people other than Pius—he was a test pilot, a valuable
commodity, a protected cadre. Medical exams every month; rest cures in
the sanatoriums reserved for cabinet ministers and up. And unreachable.
Anita, with all her skill in traveling, spent a long time looking for him in
the Soviet Union and never once saw him alive. He now could pronounce

his *o*'s like a Muscovite. Gesine was out on her ear from her first job in Brooklyn; Pius was testing whether any modifications were needed to the Su-9 ("Fishpot"), a fighter plane with a top speed of Mach 2, not given to the NPA. Maybe that's why he didn't visit his homeland. After he'd come home, rumor had it that in 1962 he'd shown up at his mother's place one night at midnight. After President Kennedy was assassinated, Pius wrote a letter meant to console a Gesine in New York City. For form's sake, dismissively, he mentioned to "my dears" a short marriage to a Masha (a Marie). He was alone, and always would be. Did he find himself in his work? His last job was on a Tu-28, a long-range ultrasonic fighter; he commanded a machine that was a hundred feet long, wingspan sixty-five feet. Colonel Pagenkopf. Want to bet that the Russians said the *k* in his name more like a *g*? And since he had earned the affection of the Soviets for his services improving their airborne weaponry, in December 1964 they sent a welded casket back to Gneez, Mecklenburg, instead of burying him onsite. It would have taken industrial-grade machinery to open it. Almost thirty-three years old, Pius lived to be.

(We would like to thank Herr Professor Dr. Erichson for the technical descriptions above. He procured this information on trips over the course of more than two years, in discussions with confidants in both the US and West German air forces [among whom we are especially requested not to single out one Mr. B.], all at times when he would have no doubt preferred to relax and drink a glass of, let's say, tea. Thank you, D. E.)

For information about Pius's funeral ceremonies we would like to thank our school friend Anita Gantlik. With her collection of documents, she, a Protestant, traveled to Gneez, to the Catholic service that his Socialist parents had agreed on. According to her, then, the delivery of the matter to be transformed was announced by two tolls of a bell. There was mention of our brother (formerly: our servant) Robert Pagenkopf. He was given the "viaticum" he had long done without. For them, too, there was a "This is My body, this My blood." Pius's mother stepped forward to take Holy Communion; the elder Pagenkopf stood stiff as a post, conscious of his guilt. Then it was said: We are beginning the Catholic rite of burial. We knew that already. First sight of the coffin in the chapel. Lots of kneeling. Joyful anticipation of Pius's union with God. "Angels will usher him into Paradise." Parting at the grave, with incense.

No military presence. The coffin without a flag of the Red Army or the NPA. A brass plate on the coffin with his full name. His address for eternity.

Among the mourners I noticed. The wreath ribbons read. This Gesine from New York could surely have come up with something more appropriate than *Ræbbing sin Gesin*. Oh, it can be a dative in Platt? "To Robbie from Gesine," not "Robbie's Gesine"? *You dont say.* An elaborate Mecklenburg lunch, conversation with the priest.

Delivering two death announcements.

As for our work, we're right there in *The New York Times*, page 1, column 3: Czechoslovakia wants $400 million to $500 million in hard-currency loans to buy industrial equipment. De Rosny: At your service!

A sad and upset child is waiting on Riverside Drive, wanting to commiserate: A telegram came, and unfortunately I opened it. It's from D. E. in Finland. He's had an accident. Forgets to put his address, the scatterbrain! Now we can't write back! Signed: Eritzen.

Now that is Anita's handwriting. Make sure you give it its due, Comrade Writer!

Handwriting of Student Gantlik comma Anita: No deformations; excellent; especially in telegrams.

– And is your eye feeling better, Gesine?

August 9, 1968 Friday

We'd learned it once and for all—the way to get to LaGuardia Airport is to take the West Side line to Times Square, the Flushing line to Forty-Second Street at Third Avenue, the airport shuttle to Long Island. Amid all the rubble of abandoned factories, the private houses built too small, the actual garbage, the cemeteries living on after their death—in the middle of all this an airport shows what's possible, with a glass semicircular two-story building of enormous halls for the processing of waiting, with generous coffeehouses and stores (containing nothing but products of a folklore gone to seed), with marble and other genuine stone, with clean floors and no muzak and a Mayor Fiorello LaGuardia incompletely hewn from a block of granite, as an artwork that has its place here. From the upper level you can look out at the air traffic; it's quite elegant how the countless planes use the space around the two ramps, quickly, in orderly fashion, rolling up to the gates and deigning to receive a little help at departure from the small bullish (yellow) tractors, until they can safely unleash their strength. The airfield's location on the water makes it easier to see in all this merely a well-established, reasonable sport when the beasts start racing—slow, controlled—until they lift their nose, retract the nose wheel, gracefully rise up into and over the dirt while augmenting it with their viscid exhaust. We stand there for a few minutes and then another plane aims at the runway from the north, seems to spread its wings, sits politely, gingerly down; it will come taxiing right up like a polite taxi. That's the one meant for us.

And who are the Cresspahls this morning? Merely travel companions, or an escort, a guard detail, for Annie and her children, the capitulating remnants of the Killainen family?

When Annie called us last night, she categorically refused to come over to the Cresspahl apartment. We had to go find her (because you're my friend, Gesine) in a hotel at Lincoln Center, where included in the cost of the night's room is the youth of the building, its proximity to the workshops of art, the wall-to-wall carpeting, hygienically sealed toilets, interchangeable furniture, leather intimacy your hand sticks to. Annie wanted to show us that she's brought money with her—a kind of independence. From a friend. We were going to go to a restaurant, two adults with four children in total, until Marie offered to supervise as F. F. Junior, Francis R., and Annina S. Fleury tried the room service. Thanks, Marie.

Annie née Killainen insisted on the restaurant, a velvety cave hollowed out of East Midtown, lit by blood-colored candles (how striking that one woman there looks, the one with the sunglasses), tended by supercilious waiters whose snooty French you could rip off their faces with a single complete sentence in that language. Annie orders, Annie lays her purse on the edge of the table—she's paying; what she has in mind is putting on a show of security.

It turned out to be not so easy for her to play the carefree lady with three kids in a Finnish small town, who'd run away from her American husband, the Romance Language specialist F. F. Fleury, over an argument about Vietnam. Especially since the specialist in question did, as promised, get himself sent to southeast Asia by a Boston newspaper and has since confessed and reported the error of his ways, to Annie too, in patient, shamefaced articles; in fact, the paper fired him over his coverage of the body bags that an American helicopter team brings along as a precaution on its missions against the enemy that the emissaries of Western culture refer to as "goons"—his coverage of the filling and transport of these bloodtight bags. Pleading letters. But if Annie needs someone at her side for her return to her husband, that seems like a warning sign: Cresspahl wants to suggest. And in so doing she would eat once more the bitter bread of responsibility, she would offer herself up as the scapegoat for future rifts in the Fleury marriage; she refrains. F. F. Fleury, he's really humbled now, bowing and scraping with remorse, scraping hard?

Annie nods, a bit ashamed of herself, forces herself to be honest and admits: *En jaksa enää.*

She can't do it anymore—life without a husband is too much for her. So what else can we do? We call the Mohawks and reserve six seats in a very small plane that hangs low from its wings—it calls itself a Vista Jet even though it has visible propellers (maybe it has hidden turbines) and it rises stubbornly into the air at always the same steep angle. Annie's two elder children stick to their defiance, their exaggerated obedience; Francis R. Knock-knees Fleury is three now and looks down at the unfamiliar landscape completely confused—a hilly country of thick woods in which highways, gas stations, and bulk-purchase stores have heedlessly cleared openings. Admittedly there was also something Norwegian about it, with the white and red painted slate, scattered hamlets or isolated jewelry boxes located high on hilltops with barely visible roads leading to them. We'll be flying somewhere soon too. Anyone sitting under the wings can see a leg being extended until all the joints are straight enough for it to stand. The airport doesn't seem built for bigger planes—it consists of just one narrow wooden barrack. The lone aircraft marshaller walks up to the taxiing Mohawk until it obeys him and comes to a stop. Then he puts down the brake chocks, takes off his earmuffs, and fetches the cart for the luggage that the passengers are allowed to retrieve under the open sky, as if theft were very rarely a concern in Vermont. The Cresspahls turn away from Mrs. Fleury right away; they want to confirm their reservations for the next flight to New York/LaGuardia; they feel they don't need to witness the scene where Annie sinks sobbing onto the chest of her lawfully wedded husband—a limp overgrown child with her tailored suit askew. The Cresspahls, too, must have their hands shaken, he insists on that; in silence, as if someone's died.

Then a drive down Main Street, past the stores with their adamantly understated airs. The bakery calls itself Bakery and poshly disdains to advertise Super-8 bread or suchlike big-city substitutes for the real thing; the other rural stores show similar restraint. Then a walk. The proximity, the presence of the university causes the glass doors of the shops to bear requests such as: No bare feet. The clothes look respectable; buyers can as a rule leave the souvenirs alone without disgrace; the windows seem washed daily. The hotel on the corner is wrapped in a porch on which new swing chairs in traditional style are resting all alone with their boredom. Annie's future world. The house, built by a *gentleman farmer* around 1840, out of stone, and with an oxblood-colored barn added, at first sight sheltered by old maples and bushes but at second hearing revealed to be closely surrounded by neighbors in prefab houses and the streets they drive wildly down. The inside badly cleaned, violently straightened up—Annie's future life. The hotel sent lunch; the guest is offered a slice of toast by the chastened, dejected couple. Here Mrs. Cresspahl said, without believing it, the line from Martje Flohr's toast that one says in such situations, ever after etc. How happy Mrs. Cresspahl is, how relieved Marie, late that afternoon when they get back to the airport and the dispatcher looks at them like familiar faces! He'd already tinkled the brass cowbell once, which here announced a takeoff.

The New York Times is handed out. Marie busies herself with Svetlana Stalina Alliluyevna and her latest howling. She wants to tell the world: she's planning to buy a car, the best there is in America! she has thrown her Soviet passport, the most desirable in the world, into the fire!

But they really have pondered and planned it, the East Germans. In mid-July they ordered a partial mobilization of the 650,000 men in the National People's Army reserve for an invasion of Czechoslovakia. Three weeks ago it almost happened.

This was an excursion. And how can we take one to Mecklenburg? Anita does it for us.

She went there on Ascension Day / in the very merry month of May, and from her train window she observed with concern the stones clearly visible amid the low growth, how they'd grown since 1964, some of them now larger than children's heads, *hardheads*. She thought back to the times when the day laborers would have been out with buckets collecting them, the farmers behind them even madder. The estate owners used to take care, since fields without stones saved machines from damage. Apparently there was no slot for clearing the end moraine in the work units of the AyPeeSees. Agricultural Production Cooperatives, that is.

When an Anita wants to partake in the Gneez station restaurant, then it may well say right there on the door that it's closed but a waitress will see that the waiting room, with its loud group of construction workers over their beer and schnapps, is no place for such a lady; she'll open up early. Neat and tidy fresh tablecloths. Flowered wallpaper, chairs upholstered in plastic, bamboo stands holding leafy plants, next to current newspapers on awkward racks; delicate tulip-shaped lights (electr.) on the walls. Then an Anita will wrinkle her nose, as if something smelled sour. The waitress will notice and immediately apologize for the just ten grams of butter for the bread roll—if the customer orders another roll she's allowed to set out ten more grams. Today: this young citizen of Gneez says: used to be a holiday, now theyve taken that away.

We don't permit ourselves any provocations.

Service to Jerichow is canceled due to work on the line: it says in the ticket window, which only opens twenty minutes before the train is due to depart. Behind it sits a public official—about sixty, punctilious uniform, white shirt and tie; on the phone. Passenger at the wrong window: better teach her a lesson. After ten minutes he honors her silent waiting and tells her the departure times for the railway replacement bus. Anita takes a taxi to Jerichow. It's an exception, she feels, that nowadays all you have to do to catch a cab is walk out of the Gneez mail train station, and in forty minutes one appears.

The driver's a disappointment, a Mecklenburger, a yakker. So, the lady's visiting relatives I suppose? But Anita saw a horse waiting indulgently for his farmer who was standing on the corner, *chatting away*; that's just how people are. There are actually people out picking where the road crosses the rails; maybe they're maintaining the line to Jerichow. The new construction in Gneez: factories in exposed concrete, barracks as temporary storage for fuel, fertilizer, farm machines. The industrialization of the north. Communal Administrative Association (Casket Warehouse—Woodworkers).

Windmills with no sails, wooded sections, a thirty-foot rise and the first glimpse of the gray line under the sky: the sea. This used to be Anita's route to school; she speaks of "your" Mecklenburg. She had to spend five years there.

Because of the stones, she asked. They must break the harvest equipment, no? – Auh: the man said: we jus' set the combine t' two feet!

He was eager to hear her address in Jerichow so that he'd have something to report. Then Anita—he'd already noticed something foreign in her accent—held out a box with some *papyrossi* sticking out, filterless, the way only the Russians smoke them daily. Now there was silence. – To the train station: Anita said.

At that very place she was met by a weather-beaten plywood sign on the monument to the fallen: Learn, Ye Who Have Been Warned. To the Victims of the Imperialist Wars.

Jerichow's Town, Ad.-Hitler-, Stalin-, Street of Peace.

Buildings in various conditions. Some of the mostly one-story buildings have been cleaned recently, with wider windows added, some new doors. Others, if they bear the mark "CHA"—Communal Housing Administration, the sign of ownership by the state—may have bare stone showing, uncovered and gnawed by decades of sea wind, and outside window frames scoured gray by the rain. Dangerous-looking bulges in the timber framing. The finest paintwork on the interiors, though; flowerpots; irreproachable, tightly drawn curtains made of Dederon, the miracle synthetic fabric of the East.

Blessed are those who withdraw / From the world without hate … (Goethe)

An antenna on almost every roof, for receiving TV signals, pointing in a westerly direction.

What felt weird to Anita: the scarcity of visual advertising. About eight flags along Town Street. Empty mounts on almost every front door.

The Karstadt department store was Magnet. (Because it attracts, Gesine— "Karstadt: Quality Attracts.") A table saw could be sold only to someone with an Essential Non-Private Purchaser ID. Electronics reserved for repair work. Schuko plugs and sockets only upon presenting a Specialist Worker Letter. Refrigerators were free.

A private business was selling radishes, turnips, apples. Potatoes. They were out of tomatoes. Outside butcher Klein's shop window there was a line of people equipped as though planning to stay there until closing time.

There are no picture postcards of Jerichow.

How startled Anita was to be greeted on the street, by an old woman in a headscarf and nylon coat! From that point on she said to anyone who looked five years older than her: *H'lo.*

There is no building on Jerichow's Town Street with the inscription: Do what's right and fear no man! nor a building with a carved, green-painted hedgehog on both wings of its double door! unless maybe it was next to the collection point for used glass. That was where there was one knocked out of the row and down into the cellar, an extracted tooth.

Peacefully alongside each other: boxes with announcements under glass, this one public, that one private:

It's up to you, your word and your deed. The Military Police Cabinet is open from to. Youths and maidens, live and act like the revolutionaries of today! Fanfare Corps rehearsals starting now.

German Shepherd Breeders Club invites you. Rabbit Breeders Club, Pigeon Breeders Club. A trophy is being awarded for the first time—who will be the proud winner? We'll find out in August! The shooting competition will be held on.

The display case outside the evangelical parsonage contains an illustration of the naked man that the Soviet Union donated on November 4, 1959, as a gift and monument for United Nations Plaza in New York. A work by Yevgeny Vuchetich; pendant piece at the Tretyakov Gallery, Moscow. The male nude has bent a sword so far that it looks like a plowshare at the other end; hammer held out in his right hand. WE SHALL BEAT OUR SWORDS INTO PLOWSHARES (Isaiah 2:4). Nation shall not lift up sword against nation, neither shall they learn war any more!

The roof of St. Peter's Church is half dismantled, the other half already covered in new bricks, biting red but that'll fade in the sea wind. The construction scaffolding, the ladders look long unused, unclimbed; the piles of rubble at their feet have dwindled. As happens every couple of centuries.

At the cemetery office, they shake the hands of even out-of-town visitors. It's called Department of Landscape Gardening, Funerary Facilities Branch. Although the graves of the house of Cresspahl would be hard to miss. They've smudged the letters of your father's gravestone by removing the rust. The planting looks as if the state had to pay the municipality for the selection: lily of the valley. Your mother's cross is falling apart: the cast iron is flaking, you can stick two fingers right through it. Jakob's slab is standing upright like a price tag; the 1964 rosebush is growing nicely. Your place is still empty, Gesine.

The house on Brickworks Road—your house—has been divided. The smaller half belongs to the People's Solidarity Veterans Club, closed unfortunately. The other half may turn into a kindergarten later. So far there's only a future kindergarten: Off-Limits to Children Not Attending This Kindergarten; Parents Are Responsible for Their Children. Much later. It's so dilapidated tradesmen would need weeks to fix it. The roof covered in Eternit. That doesn't bother any storks.

On the Bäk, Anita talked over the fence with older people, complimented the hyacinths. Yah, the roots on em are from the West! In some front yards are car tires, painted white and filled with earth, as flower bowls—a new Mecklenburg folk custom? Teams of horses pulling panel wagons; sullen boys on dirty tractors.

On the Bäk, a group of children, eight years old, in civilian shirts, shouting in chorus: We demand that the Volkspolizei be permitted to search this house! The inhabitant of that house standing there with a laugh on her face, agreeing. Kids, righ'? Most of the children are wearing genuine blue jeans and have Bowie knives too.

An RFT column (large loudspeaker) outside Emma Senkpiel's store; silent for now. In Emma's store Anita was given, against regulations, a glass of milk. Gesine, there's no one in Jerichow who'd recognize you.

The phone booth on Market Square has been repaired. You can tell because the pavement around it went missing during the repairs. Now the door opens onto the street instead of the sidewalk. When the Gneez Taxi Cooperative then refuses to send a car to Jerichow in good faith, as an indefensible burden on the People's national economy, a person can really feel stranded in Jerichow, abandoned on Öland Island. The railway replacement bus was scheduled for much later, five o'clock; the conductors certainly don't take the timetable too literally (helpful warning from a policeman in a green uniform).

Anita crossed the street to the former Wollenberg store; speaking insolent Mecklenburgish, she procured herself a bicycle. She had to walk it on the main street, due to the cobblestones and the scandal it would have been to ride it in her short skirt. Then she rode the twelve miles south in an easy hour, attacked again and again by a plane painted red/white/red, which was supposed to be scattering fertilizer this afternoon. The pilot may have been enjoying Anita's bobbing skirt.

What Anita felt was lacking, in a northern region like this: a sign with a basket of eggs painted on it, and a hand with a pointing finger: "1000 ft." People with portable tables on the streets, offering "Eel, fresh from the smoker"; raspberries, strawberries, picked by old women in gardens close by.

In the woods west of Gneez, on the Lübeck–Rostock road (ferry connection to Denmark), she came across the Happy Transit Hotel. Formerly an excursion destination, now a solid two-story building standing there aglow in its white scratch coat of plaster, reflecting in its golden-tinged windows the woods and Anita on her bicycle; in the back, a row of bungalows made of prefab components, every little cabin equipped with a TV antenna.

The man behind the reception desk thought she must have gotten lost; he nodded imperiously over to the placard across from the photographic depiction of the nation's custodian: Payment accepted here in foreign currency: marks, pounds, dollars, French francs. That was fine with Anita— her question was: Why did the Unity Party insist on parity between the German currencies?

With West German people in transit sitting all around her, Anita ate grilled eel off fine china with silver cutlery, drank a Chablis from a crystal glass. Let the girl who's learned everything the college of hotel management for the obtaining of foreign currencies had to teach her explain the procedures: Now that you've finally finished your meal, it's time for me to clear away your bread basket! that's how I learned it! In the middle of northwest Mecklenburg, Anita was waited on for dollars.

There is no Joachim de Catt Street in Gneez.

As for the name "Street of National Unity," you can still make out traces of Unity. Other than that it's named for the first President of the German Democratic Republic and it still leads to Schwerin.

Also in Gneez, no lines outside the drinking establishments (in the City of Gneez Hotel, a line outside the former manager's office, where Western detergent and chocolate and liqueurs are swept off the counter in exchange for Western currency, double-quick). But, Gesine: your Mecklenburg now does its drinking early in the day. The restaurant in the main train station was still closed, the waiting room packed with beer drinkers. Isolated conversations: Ten thousand tiles put on, half of em loose; only a blockhead'd talk about that. – But therere folks who'll talk bout it.

There they accepted the country's legal tender from Anita again; piqued. There it had been a long time since any customer had asked for a tea with lemon, though it was on offer, according to the menu. (You could see the calculation. The complaints book was lying out on the counter.) Then the tea came too. Everyone looked at the stranger accusingly. A beer's what you have at around five o'clock, that's a given!

The banknotes showed Humboldt on the fives, Goethe on the twenties, Karl Heinrich Marx on the hundreds.

On the rails, in front of the two streaky windows, a heavy diesel train of Soviet make was wearing down the foundation. There was still the word "Deutsche" on the mark coins, but it had already disappeared from the pfennigs.

All of Anita's attempts to get rid of the bicycle ended in awkward failure. None of the men had so many hundreds of marks on him while out for a beer. They watched with confused forebodings as Anita clambered up with the conveyance into a first-class compartment on the express to Neustrelitz. For fifty-five miles the conductor argued with her over the obvious fact that storing such means of transportation in the luggage net of an express train is not allowed, verbotten! When she transferred to Berlin, she left the bike behind, locked to a public bike rack. In the forests west of Neustrelitz the Red Army is sleeping and drilling like peas in a pod; there, before long, they'll be drawing lots for the prize of a men's bike of East German manufacture. In case there are factions in the Soviet Army, and Anita sends them letters with bike lock keys in them.

That was on Ascension Day. The military restricted zone, the gently rolling countryside, it shone in the distance. (—ANITA.)

August 10, 1968 Saturday

Yesterday a derelict known only as Red climbed to the top of the mast of the old lightship at Fulton Street. He wanted to talk to Mayor Lindsay. *The New York Times* shows us, in three photos, how he fell to his death; she tells us the kind of film she used, the shutter speed. Instructions for us?

A British passenger plane crashed yesterday in Bavaria. Forty-eight people on board, all dead. We're flying soon too.

In Hitler's schools we were warned against the stunted shadow of the man in the plutocrat's hat: "The Enemy Is Listening." In the New School we learned to warn one another: An FDJ Friend Is Listening.

At first we were suspicious of the loudspeakers in every classroom, since they seemed to simply replace the hand-carried notes that had done fine communicating school announcements until 1950. Maybe the devices contained equipment that transmitted sounds in the other direction. That might work to monitor a teacher; we didn't think it'd be able to pick out one student's voice from the thirty in a conversation during break. You'd need a person for that.

In the hour of the study of contemporary events, we'd been taught about the criminality inherent in Hitler's language, for example in the word *Untermensch*, "subhuman." During the break after that class, Zaychik, amused at the memory, carelessly remarked: *If Ive ever in my life seen a one a those it was Fiete Hildebrandt.* He meant former farm night watchman— "after-hours agricultural surveillance monitor"—Friedrich Hildebrandt, appointed by Adolf Hitler as gauleiter and Reich governor over the good state of Mecklenburg; Pius approvingly mentioned that Hildebrandt had been shot in 1945, in an open field near Wismar; Cresspahl denied it: he'd been sentenced to death in 1947 by an American military court and executed in 1948 in Landsberg am Lech, Bavaria. She'd heard that from her father, who kept an ear out for the postwar life paths of peacocks of that sort. As recently as five years ago, the mere name Hildebrandt had been a daily threat to him—Wallschläger, that shining beacon of the church, had included this special commissioner for the defense of the Reich in his prayers in church in 1945. At the June 1950 teacher's conference, it came up that 10-A-II showed a regrettable interest in information that the state media rightly withheld from the East German people as being unhealthy; showed, in fact, a treasonous concern for the fate of criminals. We looked around at our classmates; who among them was listening in on us and passing our casual chitchat along to the authorities?

Which of them had brought himself to deliver Teacher Habelschwerdt to the knife (disciplinary transfer), by furtively quoting her stupid comment about community spirit? True, something called "community spirit" had been one stated pedagogical goal in Hitler's schools, but anyone who'd spent years needing to recite this surely might misspeak the words once. Was Mrs. Habelschwerdt now squandering her gifts for the natural sciences as an arithmetic teacher at Niklot Elementary School because of one of us, someone we went swimming with, maybe even shook hands with sometimes?

Gabriel Manfras was the last person we thought of. First of all, how could we believe that the First Chairman of the FDJ school group would waste time and effort filing reports? Then, we felt protective toward him, which made it hard to see him properly. Gabriel Manfras was afflicted with a mother who used to thunder at him, even five years after the war: *Our Führer will return and he will judge you!* Gabriel Manfras was haunted with the memory of the crowd lining the road among whom he, too, quivering with enthusiasm, had waved and shouted "Heil!" when Hitler's man in Mecklenburg had staged a rally including a drive through Gneez. Of course he'd want to get distance from that; and so we accepted the repellent seriousness with which he now professed another brand of Socialism. We smiled only a little when he told us about his triumphs as a "People's Correspondent," when an article in *The Schwerin People's Daily* was signed "gms"—a report on a skating or skiing competition, say, where the US team had won, a fact that "gms" neglected to mention though he did say that the Soviet Union had finished in an honorable second place.

Student Cresspahl could still recall the elementary-school days in Jerichow when she'd wanted this quiet, darkly brooding boy with the razor-sharp center-part to finally notice her. Once, as a joke, for her own amusement, she told a story about Soviet Darwinism without paying attention to whether Gabriel Manfras was in hearing range: Michurin, the Soviet man of science, is giving a lecture about insects. He shows his listeners a flea standing on his right hand, orders the flea to jump to his left, and the flea does it, repeatedly. Then the professor pulls the flea's legs off and orders it over and over to jump; the insect refuses to comply. Here, the professor announced, we have scientific proof that amputating a flea's legs causes deafness... Gesine Cresspahl laughed—delighted by the twisted logic, enjoying having others laugh with her. She should have paid closer attention to the labored, contemptuous smile that Manfras was forcing onto his face.

Student Lockenvitz was no doubt making a subtle grammatical point and nothing more when he applied his linguistic stethoscope to the chest of the word *Volkspolizei*, trying to diagnose a possessive or accusative genitive. The German People's Police—who was the possessor, who the direct object? Policing by the people or of the people? It was pure semantics for him when he translated *res publica* as "affair of the people" and detected the tautology in the term "People's Republic." Even the question of why this label was granted to China and Poland but not, for the time being, to a "People's Republic of Germany"—even that would be used against him, later. Thanks to Manfras.

A book was going around school on hidden paths: *I Chose Freedom*, the work of a defector from the Soviet Purchasing Commission in Washington, DC. It told of compulsory spying on colleagues, institutional falsifications in industrial manufacturing, brutality during state police interrogations, concentration camps and forced-labor colonies in the Soviet Union. This Victor Kravchenko had had to sue a French Communist newspaper for slander, after it had called him a lying agitator in the pay of the Americans; a Paris court found that his evidence was true and convincing. When Burly Sieboldt loaned the book in confidence to Cresspahl's daughter, he simply trusted she'd know who she could pass it along to; Lockenvitz found it badly written, or at least badly translated into German, at which point Pius decided not to read it, he just wanted it summarized. Up came Gabriel Manfras with a trusting look, and he nudged the conversation to the topic of the enemy's arguments, that it was necessary to know them before, and were they not to be found in a book by the name of? Gesine denied any knowledge of such a book—among other reasons, because it might do painful damage to Gabriel's idea of the Soviet Union, where the heart of man beats so free in *shirokaya natura*. She thought the book's contents could bring about a fight with Gabriel, in which his feelings would be hurt; she wanted to spare the boy.

On the market square of Gneez, the new one, a loudspeaker on a pillar droned on and on all the livelong day, from morning, when the sleepy workers emerged from their trains, till night, when they'd earned their rest. The plaintive cry rang out: We don't want to die for the dollar! – That's fine: Pius said, brooding: but why is all the business at the Leipzig Fair conducted on a dollar basis? Manfras rushed that question to Instructor Selbich. But Pius was almost a soldier, rallying to the defense of the republic, he was not an easy target. So she pretended that "someone" in 11-A-II had asked her that question, and expounded to the class the temporarily unavoidable exigencies of the world market—not having an easy time of it, and pressed by Student Lockenvitz's invocations of Socialist autarky. As far as the Pagenkopf & Co. collective was concerned, he'd been caught red-handed—the spy, the informer, Manfras unmasked as someone ready to do whatever dirty work the Unity Party wanted. From now on we could protect ourselves, but how could we warn the others? Writing something in block letters on the board would have gotten us a house visit from men in uniform or, worse, not in uniform. We made do with surreptitious nudges in the ribs or casually clearing our throat when someone among us started candidly holding forth about a foreign general and marshal with troops stationed in Mecklenburg. A covert nod in Manfras's direction as he sat there, head lowered, pretending to do his math—we avoided even that.

Hünemörder came back to Jerichow and Gneez from the Lüneburg Region in the West, true to his vow never to return until Friedrich Jansen and Friedrich Hildebrandt and all their trash had been smoked out of Mecklenburg. He'd brought with him a few pounds of nails and tacks, thinking to open a hardware store in Gneez; with his solid business sense he had it all figured out, he just needed a saleslady. He couldn't believe it when he heard that Leslie Danzmann was available. Danzmann, the fine lady? That's right. After losing her job at the housing office she'd done so again at the people-owned business FishCan; repeatedly accused of embezzlement and unlawful appropriation of eels etc. and prevented from giving evidence in her own defense, she had finally, in her pride, given notice. She'd applied to the Schwerin CDU, helped once again by her past reputation; was allowed to help out reporting on legal matters in *The New Union*; was saved for a while from the fright it gave her to be offered under-the-table merchandise as a preferred customer—from the butcher, at the dairy—goods that hardly came up in the sales patter but made themselves known in the final total price. Her column, "Courtroom Glimpses," made her name known for a while in almost all the cities and towns of Mecklenburg, but then what was written in the files about her past life caught up with her again. Leslie Danzmann was available, any hourly wage would be fine. Grateful, she dispatched with friendly homespun phrases the lines of buyers pushing up against Hünemörder's mostly empty shop window. After two hours of commercial activity the People's Police was informed, showed up in pairs, and led Leslie off, her wrist cuffed to Hünemörder's. No one knew what Hünemörder got for his attempt to sabotage the people's economy via individual distribution of quota-regulated commercial goods, because that was handed down in the capital; Emil Knoop, through whom this supply line should probably have run, had just set sail for Belgium (by this point Knoop had barges crossing the border for him). Leslie Danzmann was held in the basement under the Gneez district court for a few days, not knowing what she was charged with, kept busy cleaning the cells and passageways. She says she was released the moment she'd finished straightening up the detention areas. This was the latest piece of social instruction Danzmann had received, but what improvement in her social consciousness would it bring her?: the Cresspahl girl asked, in a circle of friends, noticing too late Manfras's encouraging face as he walked up to them.

Bettinikin was furious. The brooch on her blue shirt quivered. (– Where the brooch sits is out in front: this saying, too, had been brought to her notice.) But she had to let it go with a vague threat against those whose sympathy for persons of the Reactionary Middle Class . . . Student Cresspahl gave a deliberate smile. She, like Bettina, knew about a certain photograph showing the teacher wistfully confronting the middle class.

The potato-bug uprising brought matters to a head. Class 12-A-II had been ordered out to the fields for the purpose of learning to distinguish between Coccinellidae or *Rodolia cardinalis* and *Leptinotarsa decemlineata*. Three students were missing. Whether they'd planned it or were just being absentminded, Students Gantlik and Cresspahl decided they'd rather take a stroll around the Smœkbarg, maybe because they could be sure that the rest of the class was out of town. Zaychik said he'd had to load coal into his auntie's cellar. All three were summoned in writing to justify their actions before the teacher's conference. There, Instructor Selbich confronted Student Haase with the fact that, after storing the briquettes—an act defensible in the interests of the people's economy—he had found the leisure to patronize the Renaissance Cinema. Instead of leaping onto his bicycle and hurrying to join the potato-bug inspectors! While we waited in the classroom for our *consilium abeundi*, Zaychik told us who'd screwed him over: outside the movie house he'd run into Manfras, excused for political service. (A photograph exists of this bench of public penance: Zaychik stands with his coat collar looped around the hook of the map stand, neck skewed sideways, arms slack, as if being painfully hanged.) A contrite and repentant Anita was saved by her contract with the Soviets. A contrite and repentant Cresspahl had a guardian angel circling overhead who had taken a picture of Bettina in West Berlin. Zaychik was credited with the fact that at least the work of filmic art he'd chosen to view was *The Council of the Gods* (East Germany, 1950, not shown in West Germany), thus informing himself about the imperialist conspiracy linking IG Farben, Adolf Hitler, and Standard Oil, so he got off with a severely worded reprimand, thanking the faculty for their lenience.

Anita took it upon herself to notify the party in question. Student Gantlik did not ordinarily go up to Student Manfras's desk during a break as if she had something important to tell him; the class fell silent and everyone saw the furious twitching of the two reddish spikes of hair at her neck, heard her voice ringing with passionate intensity: Anyone who takes the things we tell each other in private, family matters, personal business, and hauls it to the principal's office, brings it up before the Party, is... he's...

What was the worst condemnation Anita could come up with? He was...a bad person.

Gabriel kept his face blank, his head still, tried to look as if he was listening closely, even nodded once or twice like someone willing to endure even this for the higher political cause.

Since then, we've had reason to think of him when anyone mentions *Les Lettres Françaises*, or slander in matters whose truth has been established. This in turn brings before our eyes his appearance at the rally at the end of the 1951–52 school year, where, standing behind the presidium's red table, he contemplatively sang along in chorus the words that had been handed down to us since July 1950 as both statement of fact and confession of faith:

> The Party, the Party, is always in the right!
> Comrades, Comrades, it is always with you...
> The Party's given us everything—
> The sun, the wind, it gives for free.
> Born from the Party is life itself.
> What we are, we are through Thee!

We are definitely familiar with what a court in East Germany has determined about people like you: the term "informer," the court found, is not an insult but a job description. Since after all a building monitor's duties include supplying the political leadership with information about the population.

You'd better believe we remember you. It was you who turned our class 10-A-II into a place of intimidation. It is thanks to you that school, from eleventh grade on, was one long fearfest. Hope you're happy.

For the Party *has* given you almost everything—the sun, the wind, and never a headwind either. It started by accepting you as a candidate in 1951. It continued by promising you a slot at Humboldt University in Berlin a year in advance. It showed its trust in Young Friend, later Comrade, Manfras by permitting him to complement his Marxist studies with visits to, stays at the *British Centre* in West Berlin. It imposed one restriction, which we find fair enough: Since his father was a smallholder, not a farmworker, he is deficient in proletariat aristocracy and thus still excluded from the meetings near the Werder Market, Berlin, every Tuesday, in which decisions are made about East German policies, foreign and domestic. And thus Comrade Manfras tries all the more zealously to expound these decisions to others; Anita sees him on TV sometimes, for a few seconds. For this he is rewarded in abundance—for free, like the song says. He can walk into the State Bank and help himself to whatever he needs from the foreign currency drawers, for unrestricted trips to the lands of his enemy. His English is apparently international now, with a British tinge. A villa on Müggelsee, a car, cadre protection, shopping privileges in West Berlin—it's all there. His one dream, though, is to be accepted into the diplomatic service. But there's a built-in barrier, practically insuperable if you notice it only in your thirty-sixth year. In his articles reporting on the high society of his country (consisting of the likes of him), the telephones always ring "madly," even though each of these devices can be counted on only to do what its electrical current makes it do. He has issues with participles and will hardly earn an honorary doctorate for descriptions of people like: "The coffee-making, rose-breeding minister's wife..." But maybe we're wrong and he'll end up an embassy counselor someday. Hopefully somewhere other than Prague.

– Two questions: Marie says.
– Motion granted, your honor.
– At one point you gave Pius the rank of general.
– It's been three and a half years since he... But when I think about him as if he'd stayed alive, he'd be a general by now, major general at least.
– On the other paw, you think you have this Bettina Selbich under control.
– You're saying she could slip out of our grasp at the drop of a hat?
– You're in a catch-22. You guys took her picture doing some forbidden window-shopping in West Berlin—
– But?
– The guy with his eye to the viewfinder was there too—if it ever came to producing the evidence.
– Lucky you've only told me this now!

Back home on Riverside Drive the daily telegram from Helsinki is waiting. Today it says: Patient temporarily unable to drive. Signed: Eritzen.

August 11, 1968 Sunday

In Vietnam yesterday, near Tabat, over the Ashau valley, a US fighter bomber of type F-100 Super Sabre went into a dive and fired rockets and guns at American troops. Eight dead, fifty wounded.

Over West Virginia, a twin-engine Piedmont Airlines plane tried to make an instrument approach to Charleston's airport, 982 feet above sea level. Crashed and burned just short of the runway. Out of the thirty-seven people aboard, all but five lost their lives. We're flying soon too.

Before we do, Marie wants a children's party, as long as it's not called a goodbye party. It's just cause they're my best friends: Pamela, Edmondo, Michelle and Paul, Steven, Annie, Kathy, Ivan, . . . and Rebecca Ferwalter, which is why we've made plans to meet Rebecca's mother on a bench in the park to negotiate kosher items on the menu.

She watches us approach, clearly not wanting to be there, her bare, too-fat arms buttressing her on either side; she is trying to look pleased. Mrs. Ferwalter is back from the part of the Catskills she calls "Fleishman." Rebecca found a boy there named Milton Deutsch, called Moishele (Moses). Moses Deutsch loves Rebecca very much and hits her; Rebecca cries it out with her mother then goes back over to Milton as soon as she catches sight of him from afar. Mrs. Ferwalter says, vows in fury: Never again will she pick a place Milton Deutsch might be!

Park-bench conversation.

Will the Nazi Party come to power in Germany?

Most people in Germany don't want that.

What's their platform?

Changing the borders, to start with.

Do the Americans have the right to get involved?

If the government in Washington wants to do it, it'll do it.

My dear Mrs. Cresspahl, please leave it to me. I'll bring Passover cookies, they're colorful, thick frosting, children like them at parties, they taste like marzipan. The last time we baked them at home was in '44. Our village was part of Hungary then. Transports had been coming through since 1941, and people were being rounded up in the country. In May 1944 they took everybody. I had a Catholic passport, religion Catholic. The Germans took one look at me and arrested me. The Hungarians and the Germans, they were made for each other. They were all soldiers. Sorry, what are Swabians?

People living in a southern German province called Swabia, we thought.

Were the Swabians more for Hitler than the rest?

The rest were too.

These were Danube Swabians.

(Transylvanian Saxons?

No. Those were anti, you know.)

We were taken to Auschwitz. I was there eight months. Most were sent straight to the **crematorium**. A lot of the **wardens** are still running around, you'd be amazed to see where. The same way you and me are sitting here talking right now I once talked to Mengele.

I was **selected** for the **depot** to do **distribution**. In the kitchen two girls carried baskets behind me. I divided up the margarine and dropped it in the pots. The girls immediately fished the margarine out and tossed it into buckets of water to harden it. There was a good woman there, my **boss**, her name was **Frau** Stiebitz. She looked the other way.

Can we put that aside?

– Do it but watch out.

Mrs. Ferwalter now explains what a block is, with parallel vertical hand movements marking straight lines: The buildings there were like this. There were girls in one block, thirteen years old. After hours she would bring buckets of soup there. One time she was stopped on the way by a Jewish **Kapo**: You're stealing, you pig.

– And you pay for yours?

The Jewish **Kapo** threatened to report her and the next morning, after standing for hours, she was in fact called forward and accused of resisting a **Kapo** and theft. **Frau** Gräser, the head of the women's camp, said: You're going to be shot. Call a **guard** over.

Frau Gräser had fallen for a girl, and made this girl her right hand. Frances was her name. Frances said: But everybody does it. If you really like me, do me a favor, let her live. She's good in the kitchen you know.

The sentence was commuted to one hour's kneeling on sharp gravel while holding two stones in raised hands. It took many weeks before her knees were back in their normal shape.

Frau Stiebitz didn't say a word during all this. You have to understand. That's how it was in 1944: the Germans were *fed up* (this in English).

When we got there, there was nothing. Then they planted some trees, like for a park. The ones who were still alive had turned into *Tiere* by then (*animals*, not *beasts*).

When we got to Auschwitz we were **deloused** ("you know, some kind of disinfection") and had our heads shaved. The hair grew back, of course, and **Frau** Stiebitz liked to say: Oh how pretty. It was, too. Yes, the **selection** was like a beauty contest. **Frau** Gräser, too, she said once: You could be a beauty queen.

As part of my **punishment** they shaved a road through my hair that had grown back. I went and had the rest cut off too. Twenty-one years old I was.

We worked in two shifts. The day shift was all right. It was bad in the night shift. There were seven crematoriums going in our corner. At the end of the night shift the sky was as red as fire. I heard people screaming: *"Help, help!"* (this in English).

You'll understand, Mrs. Cresspahl. You're a **woman**.

From Auschwitz we were taken west to an ammo factory, maybe in Germany. I saw a sign: Geh-len-au. It was a small camp, to hold the French.

We saw the English parachutists jumping. We were herded to the station and locked into boxcars. The people who lived in that town were looting the stores. Just half an hour more and the English would've been there, but the train pulled out. We were taken to Mauthausen. I was **liberated** in Mauthausen.

In 1945 **Frau** Stiebitz went into hiding in Austria. The prisoners got clothes for her and an American pass (she drew a very long rectangle in the air with two fingers) so she could get back to Germany.

The first couple days after the **liberation** (May 9) we lived on a farm. Good food, real milk, red apples from last year (this in a housewifely tone). But we were scared, there were SS hiding on the farm next door. They could come right out and start all over again. One **warden** in Mauthausen had fifteen-year-old girls brought in to him every night.

The Jewish **Kapo** who'd caught her with the potatoes, she saw her after the war in an office building in Tel Aviv, Israel. I'm going to turn her in. Then a friend advises her: Why do you want to tackle all that? running around to the court, testimony, signatures. I let it go.

In Israel then, everything was rationed and people were leaving the city to go foraging in the country. This very **Kapo** comes into a kitchen through the back door and shouts something. The farmer sitting in the front room, she'd been a prisoner in Auschwitz, recognizes the voice and screams. Everyone runs out onto the street, catches the **Kapo** as she's running away. She got a year in jail.

Another girl was brought to court in Israel from my home village, she was terrible to everyone except me. She'd been made **Kapo** in Auschwitz. Back then you'd be let go if as many witnesses testified for you as against you. I went up and spoke for her. She's an old friend, she's a bad person.

But God punished her. She married a man who didn't treat her right; she's divorced.

The really bad thing was: that the Germans forced the Jews to kill each other. Shove relatives into the fire still alive.

(Rebecca has tripped and fallen while running:) *"My child, I have waited for you so long, eighteen years!"*

(Rebecca gets a sandwich roll to make her feel better; there's fish an inch thick between the bread halves:) You see! (Since Rebecca is constantly being stuffed with food she's a little fat, despite her petite frame.) If only my child would eat like yours!

We left the ČSR legally, with passports. We could take all our **belongings** with us. 1948. It took eight or ten days to get to Tel Aviv.

My brother got black-market sugar on the black market; it was rationed. Six months in jail: The sentence was due to start the next Monday. He had no desire to wait till then and went to Bratislava, over the border to Vienna. The police showed up on Monday. And so with the help of the Almighty we're now in New York.

So it's agreed, yes, the cookies for the children's party I will bring, Mrs. Cresspahl?

August 12, 1968 Monday

The New York Times wants to prepare its readers in advance for an anniversary: seven years ago tomorrow, the custodian of East Germany cut off his part of Berlin from the Western Allies' sectors with a wall, to prevent his citizens from leaving and those of West Berlin from visiting. Exceptions were permitted: if there is a death in the family; if the legal retirement age has been reached. "When I had my birthday I felt happy": a woman from the **democratic** Berlin writes to her daughter in the other one: "getting older. Now it is only five years until I can embrace you." The wall is manned with two East German brigades and three training regiments, totaling about 14,000 soldiers.

On October 7, 1951, the East German national holiday, some select households in Gneez, Mecklenburg, as well as two in Jerichow, received identical anonymous letters for the first time. The envelopes and sheets of DIN A5 paper were blotchy, pulpy, bulgy, easily torn, like the paper the government agencies used for their communications; the text was always written on the same typewriter, with the *e*'s and *n*'s unfailingly misaligned. Someone who, like Cresspahl's daughter, copied these missives out by hand before turning them over to the German People's Police as testimony to her Stalinist watchfulness received piece by piece a preliminary list of the workings of justice in Mecklenburg since 1945.

(The sender presupposed that his readers were familiar with the fact that Z might stand for *Zuchthaus*, "jail." He counted on their hunch that the series of letters SMT stood for "Soviet Military Tribunal," LDT for the "Long-Distance Tribunal" passing judgment from Moscow. He also relied on the supposition that a literate individual in Mecklenburg could easily picture from ZAL a *ZwangsArbeitsLager*, a "forced-labor camp," and understand by "verh." not *verheiratet*, "married," but *verhaftet*, "arrested." Clearly he was in a hurry, or else rarely had access to the ramshackle typewriter in question:)

1945

Prof. Tartarin-Tarnheyden, JD, from Rostock, b. 1882, verh. Nov. 20 1945; sentenced by SMT to 10 yrs. ZAL.

Prof. Dr. Ernst Lübcke, b. 1890, scientist, detained by Soviet officers on Sept. 8 1946; taken to the Soviet Union, disappeared.

Fred Leddin, b. 1925, chemistry student, verh. Sept. 27 1947; sentenced by SMT to 25 years ZAL.

Hans-Joachim Simon, science student, verh. on September 27, 1947; disappeared.

Herbert Schönborn, b. 1927, stud. jur., verh. Mar. 2 1948; sentenced by MVD (*Ministerstvo Vnutrennikh Del'*, the Soviet Ministry of Internal Affairs) special court to 25 years ZAL.

Erich-Otto Paepke, b. 1927, med. stud., verh. Mar. 8 1948; sentenced by SMT Schwerin to 25 yrs. ZAL.

Gerd-Manfred Ahrenholz, b. 1926, chemistry student, verh. Jun. 23 1948; sentenced by SMT to 25 yrs. ZAL.

Hans Lücht, b. 1926, med. stud., verh. Aug. 15 1947; sentenced by SMT Schwerin on Apr. 30 1948 to 25 yrs. ZAL.

Joachim Reincke, b. 1927, med. stud., verh. 1948; sentenced by SMT Schwerin to 25 yrs. ZAL.

Hermann Jansen, b. 1910, Catholic student minister for Rostock, verh. 1948; sentenced by SMT Schwerin to 25 yrs. ZAL.

Wolfgang Hildebrandt, b. 1924, stud. jur., verh. Apr. 3 1949; sentenced by SMT Schwerin to 25 yrs. ZAL.

Rudolf Haaker, b. 1921, stud. jur., verh. in Apr. 1949; sentenced by LDT to 25 yrs. ZAL.

Gerhard Schultz, b. 1921, stud. jur., verh. May 6 1949; sentenced by MVD special court to ten years ZAL.

Hildegard Näther, b. 1923, ed. stud., verh. Oct. 8 1948; sentenced by SMT Schwerin on June 9 1949 to 25 yrs. ZAL.

Jürgen Rubach, b. 1920, ed. stud., verh. Feb. 8 1949; sentenced by SMT Schwerin on June 9 1949 to 25 yrs. ZAL.

Ulrich Haase, b. 1928, lib. arts stud., verh. Sept. 22 1949; sentenced by SMT Schwerin to 25 yrs. ZAL.

Alexandra Wiese, b. 1923, applicant to University of Rostock, verh. Oct. 18 1949; sentenced by SMT Schwerin in April 1950 to 25 years ZAL.

Ingrid Broecker, b. 1925, Art History stud., verh. Oct. 31 1949; sentenced by SMT Schwerin to 15 yrs. ZAL.

On Dec. 17, 1949, an SMT in Schwerin sentenced eight defendants, including two women, to up to twenty-five years ZAL.

Jürgen Broecker, b. 1927, applicant to University of Rostock, verh. Oct. 21 1949; sentenced by SMT Schwerin on Jan. 27 1950 to 25 yrs. ZAL.

On Feb. 17 1950, a Schwerin SMT sentenced one Helmut Hiller and eight others for alleged communications with the SPD's East Office to a total of three hundred and seventy five years ZAL.

On Apr. 16, 1950, a Schwerin SMT sentenced high-school students
Wolfgang Strauß
Eduard Lindhammer
Dieter Schopen
Winfried Wagner
Senf
Klein

Olaf Strauß
Sahlow
Haase
Ohland
Erika Blutschun
Karl-August Schantien
to a total of 300 yrs. ZAL.

The president of the Mecklenburg state youth council of the Liberal Democratic Party, Hans-Jürgen Jennerjahn, was sentenced in the same trial.

Horst-Karl Pinnow, b. 1919, med. stud., verh. Apr. 2 1949; sentenced by Soviet LDT in May 1950 to 25 years ZAL.

Susanne Dethloff, b. 1929, applicant to U of Rostock, verh. May 4 1949; sentenced by Soviet LDT in May 1950 to 10 years ZAL.

Günter Mittag, b. 1930, med. stud., verh. early June 1950; sentenced by SMT, term unknown.

On Jun. 18, 1950, Hermann Priester, teacher, from Rostock, was sentenced to ten years Z; in the Torgau penal institution, Volkspolizei Constable Gustav Werner, known as "Iron Gustav," beat him so badly that he suffered a broken thigh bone. When he was unable to stand up, the VP constable screamed he was a faker and stomped on him, breaking his pelvic bone. Hermann Priester died of aftereffects in late June.

Gerhard Koch, b. 1924, med. stud., verh. July 13 1950; disappeared.

On Jul. 15, 1950, the district court in Güstrow in the Hotel Zachow ibidem sentenced nine leading employees of the credit union cooperative to a total of eighty-four years Z. Among them Arthur Hermes, b. 1875. Hans Hoffmann, JD, because he had tried to transfer the assets of the farmers' self-help association from Mecklenburg to Göttingen. (Two tanker ships, five tank railcars.) "Unfortunately, he succeeded." Prof. Hans Lehmitz, b. 1903, natural sci., member of the Unity Party: fifteen yrs. Z.

On Jul. 18, 1950, the district court in Greifswald sentenced additional members of the cooperative to Z.

Friedrich-Franz Wiese, b. 1929, chemistry student, member of the LPD university committee, verh. Oct. 18 1949; sentenced by SMT Schwerin on Jul. 20 1950 to twenty-five years ZAL, by SMT Berlin-Lichtenberg on Nov. 23 1950 to death.

Arno Esch, b. 1928, stud. jur., LPD Mecklenburg executive committee member, verh. by Soviet security officers in the night of Oct. 18–19 1949 upon leaving the Rostock branch office. Opponent of the death penalty. "I have more in common with a liberal Chinese than with a German Communist." "In that case I have established that we do not have the freedom to make decisions here. Please enter that into the record." Sentenced to death on Jul. 20 1950 by SMT Schwerin per §58 Par. 2 of the RSFR (= Russian Soviet Federative Socialist Republic) penal code: Preparation to Commit Armed Rebellion. Mocked during pretrial custody for his pacifist position. The death penalty was reinstated after his arrest, only when he'd long been in prison. Executed in the Soviet Union on June 24 1951.

Elsbeth Wraske, b. 1925, English stud., verh. Apr. 11 1950; sentenced by SMT Schwerin on July 28 1950 to twenty yrs. ZAL.

On Aug. 8 1950, SMT Schwerin sentenced Paul Schwarz and Gerhard Schneider, both members of Jehovah's Witnesses and therefore both previously in Hitler's concentration camps; sentenced on Aug. 1950 to 25 yrs. ZAL each for "Anti-Soviet Activities."

Siegfried Winter, b. 1927, ed. stud. and most famous handball player in Rostock, verh. Aug. 16 1949; sentenced by SMT Schwerin on Aug. 27 1950 to 25 yrs. ZAL.

Karl-Heinz Lindenberg, b. 1924, med. stud., verh. Sept. 16 1950; sentenced by Greifswald district court on Oct. 21 1951 to fifteen years ZAL.

On Sept. 28, 1950, the Schwerin district court sentenced high-school student Enno Henk and seven others, charged with distributing pamphlets, to up to fifteen years Z.

Alfred Loup, b. 1923, ed. stud., verh. July 3 1950; sentenced by SMT Schwerin on Oct. 31 1950 to 25 yrs. ZAL.

Gerhard Popp, b. 1924, med. stud and chairman of the U of Rostock CDU chapter, verh. Jul. 12 1950; sentenced by SMT Schwerin on Oct. 31 1950 to 25 yrs. ZAL.

Roland Bude, b. 1926, Slavic stud., FDJ school group leader, Rostock, verh. Jul. 13 1950; sentenced by SMT Schwerin on Oct. 31 1950 to two successive 25 yrs. ZAL.

Lothar Prenk, b. 1924, ed. stud., verh. March 24 1950; sentenced by SMT Schwerin on Dec. 9 1950 to 25 yrs. ZAL.

Hans-Joachim Klett, b. 1923, med. stud., verh. March 23 1950; sentenced by SMT Schwerin on Dec. 12 1950 to 25 yrs. ZAL.

On Dec. 18, 1950, a Schwerin SMT sentenced fourteen former Volkspolizei officers to death for "anti-Soviet agitation and forming illegal groups."

On Apr. 27, 1950, the Schwerin district court sentenced a defendant named Horst Paschen to life in prison for "agitation for boycott in conjunction with the murder of a coast guard."

Joachim Liedke, b. 1930, stud. jur., verh. in June 1951; sentenced to five years Z.

Gerhard Schönbeck, b. 1927, philosophy student, verh. Sept. 6, 1950; sentenced by Güstrow district court on Aug. 22, 1951, to eight years Z.

Franz Ball, b. 1927, classics student, verh. Jan. 18, 1951; sentenced by Greifswald district court on Aug. 22, 1951 to ten years Z.

Hartwig Bernitt, b. 1927, biology student, verh. June 29, 1951; sentenced by SMT Schwerin on Dec. 5 1951 to 25 yrs. Z.

Karl-Alfred Gedowski, ed. stud., b. 1927, verh. June 26, 1951; sentenced by SMT Schwerin on Dec. 6 1951 to death.

In the same trial:

Brunhilde Albrecht, b. 1928, ed. stud., verh. June 29, 1951; fifteen years ZAL.

Otto Mehl, b. 1929, student of agriculture, verh. June 29, 1951; 25 yrs. ZAL.

Gerald Joram, b. 1930, med. stud., verh. June 29, 1951; 25 yrs. ZAL.

Alfred Gerlach, b. 1929, med. stud., verh. June 29, 1951; death.

Above the entrance to the Soviet Military Tribunal (SMT) courtroom in Schwerin were posted the words: JUDGMENT SHALL RETURN UNTO RIGHTEOUSNESS. On the dais was a court of three officers. Present in the room, besides the accused: an interpreter, guards, and larger-than-life-sized portraits of Stalin & Mao. Accusations: Contact with Berlin Free University; production and circulation of leaflets; possession and circulation of antidemocratic literature. Verdicts justified under §58 of the Russian Soviet Federative Socialist Republic's penal code, Paragraph 6: Espionage; Paragraph 10: Anti-Soviet Propaganda; Paragraph 11: Formation of Illegal Groups; Paragraph 12: Failure to Report Counterrevolutionary Criminal Activity. Karl-Alfred Gedowski (qv.), in his closing statement: To decide in favor of one ideological worldview, one must also know the other.

Gerhard Dunker, b. 1929, physics student, verh. Dec. 24, 1951; disappeared . . .

The author of these thoughtful missives may have been circumspect, mailing the letters with different postmarks from Stralsund, Rostock, Schwerin, Malchin, Neubrandenburg; he gave himself away with his selection. He was apparently indifferent to the fact that Peter Wulff had been accused of having, in the years 1946 to 1948, cheated the state (which didn't exist before 1949) out of a total of 8,643 marks of income tax, business tax, and sales tax, and whereas he was found in May 1950 to have long refused to pay the 8,500-mark fine as per a settlement arrangement with the Gneez tax office, he was sentenced in July as per §396 of the tax code to a seven-thousand mark fine and three months in jail—Wulff belonged in his annals. Nor did the author seem to care about economic policies, e.g., that farmer Utpathel, in Old Demwies, went to jail for two years over failing to deliver his quotas of meat, milk, wool, and oilseeds; this despite pleading his age of seventy-three years, the poor quality of the seeds supplied by the state, the loss of his entire herd to the Red Army in 1945, and the cattle plague of 1947; the local court in Gneez conceded these "objective difficulties" with the caveat that, as a progressive farmer, he should have mortgaged his business and procured cattle on credit to fulfill his obligations to the state and the people; for Destructive Activity Against Large-Sized Farm (104 acres), confiscation of property; for Economic Criminality per Ec.Pen.Reg. §1 Par. 1 Subpar. 1, two (2) years in prison. Z. Now Georg Utpathel's farm sat uncultivated, abandoned to cannibalization by the neighbors—apparently a bagatelle for someone more interested in legal proceedings against high-school students, someone who deemed only purely political, ideological penalties worth communicating; that's how they'll catch him, and his copyists too: Jakob said, and he took Cresspahl's daughter's notes away, supposedly to discuss them with his friend Peter Zahn. Her pages were thus kept safe with an unknown third party in the railroad union headquarters in Gneez, who would send Cresspahl's daughter her property after Jakob's death, in an envelope with a Dutch postmark.

In the meantime, the nameless court reporter (who never used a mailbox in Gneez) kept his involuntary subscribers up to date on the treatment of hotel and tavern owners on the Mecklenburg Baltic coast taking place under the codename Operation Rosa—just for variety. Maybe he was trying to avoid monotony, and that was why he also slipped into the string of personal stories this comment from the Soviet News Agency, TASS, about the death penalty: It bears a profoundly humanistic character, in that...Then he returned to his focus on high schoolers, telling us about Burly Sieboldt's transfer from Neubrandenburg penitentiary to an unknown location, and his preoccupation with university students in Mecklenburg, as if he was planning to apply for admission: in Rostock, the State Security Service, the Stasi, had pocketed the "People's House" across from the university, for instance, and built cells in the basement and on two floors, and the interrogators threatened to apply Hitler's infamous *Sippenhaft*— punishing the prisoner's whole family—and indulged in beating suspects when the mood struck. For instance. Or, again, he'd direct his attention to the future that Mecklenburg's university students faced, explaining to his recipients the origin of the name of "Bützow-Dreibergen" prison—from the three hills (*Drei Bergen*) on the southwest corner of Bützow Lake, whose shores the facility was meant to be built on; he told us about the first head of the facility after 1945: the journeyman locksmith Harry Frank from Bützow, who passed himself off as a privy councilor until he had to hang himself in a cell in June 1949; told us about the goon squads named after Volkspolizei Lieutenant Oskar Böttcher that rampaged through the overcrowded prison. This information reached us in an objective, dispassionate tone; only once did the compiler give way to anger, ending one report with an appeal: Mecklenburgers! All we're known for now are the turnips our political prisoners get as feed—"Mecklenburg pineapples." Is that what we want?

After the Christmas—the winter—break, the following students were arrested in Gneez and around Jerichow: Gantlik, Dühr, Cresspahl; evading capture: Alfred Uplegger, then in 10-A-II. The men in their leather coats arrived at his farm just when he was busy chopping wood with a long-handled ax. *Hows the hare supposed to prove hes not a fox*: he deliberated, and hit back. With assault and battery against the state, he had suddenly committed a real crime, he could see that on his own; he took to his heels for West Berlin. One student had been in jail since the start of vacation: Lockenvitz.

On January 3, 1952, Jakob paid a call to the Volkspolizei district headquarters in Gneez to ask the whereabouts of Cresspahl's daughter; he could afford to speak calmly since he was noted in their files as a violent man. Since even a man in a blue uniform doesn't especially like meeting such a character when he's angry, for instance on a dark night on a lonely path between garden plots, the people at headquarters gave him a reasonable response: they would've clued him in a long time ago if they knew anything; *you know your Johnny, Jakob!* Jakob took a leave from work and settled in for a long wait in the lobby of the villa in the Composer's Quarter where the local State Security sorted out short-term deliveries in the basements until they were ready to be transferred to Hans-and-Sophie-Scholl Street, Schwerin. Two of our gentlemen promptly opened the door for him, meticulously went over his documents with him—union ID, Free German Youth ID, police ID, Society for German-Soviet Friendship ID, social security ID, German Reich Railway ID—and then he could begin. Rueful and sympathetic of mien, they advised him to go by Volkspolizei district HQ, the agency responsible for Missing Person cases; in this building, the name Cresspahl was unknown even by hearsay. – That's what we keep telling you, Mr. Abs!

The door to the waiting room was ajar, and Cresspahl's daughter could hear Jakob clearly until he left, disgruntled, a citizen who'd come to look into something and found his own personal credentials examined instead. Student Cresspahl was standing on the hardwood floor for her second day, three hours at a time, strictly ordered not to move. The interrogators wished the suspect to keep her gaze fixed straight ahead on a nail driven into the wall four inches above average eye level, on which, in a gilded frame, hung a colorized photograph of Marshal Stalin. Unprompted speaking was frowned upon in this building; speaking when requested to do so by the gentlemen was recommended in the strongest possible terms. The whole time Jakob was standing in the lobby, it was hard for Prisoner Cresspahl to breathe, due to the gloved paw being held over her mouth. When the front door closed behind Jakob with a sighing, satisfied smack, it started again: Raise your head! Arms out! Palms level! Writing exercises were scheduled for the end of each three-hour shift: repeating her life story, followed by discussions of any variations from the version written the day before. Jakob's appearance had given the interrogation personnel a new weapon. How to respond to the question of whether high-school student Cresspahl was involved in a sexual relationship with this railwayman? This was followed by more stationary gymnastics, a good fit with the suspect's annoyance at this idiot Gesine Cresspahl, who, on a dim Wednesday

morning in January, had boarded the milk train to Gneez and sat down
in a compartment by herself, making it possible for her to be loaded with
hardly any fuss into the back seat of an EMW at Wehrlich station. And
now for a short appraisal
  of the criminal activities
  of the enemies
  of Socialism;
we've even convicted the second-in-command of Czechoslovakia, you know,
that Rudolf Slánský; now, if you don't mind, Young Friend Cresspahl!
Raise your head! Arms out!

She got herself just one slap in the face, toward the end of the ten-day
inquiry—she'd fainted. On the night of January 12, when she came back
to Cresspahl's house, she got a hug from Jakob as if he knew what he was
doing, as if he'd made a habit of that with her.

That was a Saturday. The next day, at lunchtime, Anita came from church
to see us—another first. We both started talking at the same time: Hey,
I've got something to tell you! (Just between you and me.)

Guard duty in the villa that had once been Dr. Grimm's had been so
carefully arranged that neither of them had had any idea that the other
was housed on the other side of the wall, being fed bowls of Mecklenburg
pineapple, sleeping under filthy blankets and the smell of many different
sweats. They agreed about who they were afraid they owed this stay and
treatment to—the interrogations had primarily poked around the origins,
statements, and proclivities of "our handsome young man," Lockenvitz.
We were offended, our sense of manly toughness disappointed. We appreciated that he might want to buy time on the backs and palms of three
unwitting girls; still, disappointing. Until Jakob played Solomon for us
and said: Heaven protect him from such complaining women! Did we
think we'd ever get a husband at this rate? Just think about what they'd
have to do to someone before he'd let a girl get hurt!

Anita liked it at my father's house. There was Cresspahl, who squared
his shoulders for her when he said hello and looked her in the eyes as he
thanked her for coming over. *There was an ol woman* who said grace before
the meal. There was a young man who pulled out a chair for her, served
her food, waited on her with talk and stories, and you could get a straight
answer out of him too.

We recognized our third co-conspirator in a gym class where we were combined with 11-A-II. Annette Dühr was walking stiffly—she'd probably had to stand with straightened knees longer. She'd been seen leaving something at Lockenvitz's apartment door; they hadn't believed her as much as they did us. The glass face of her watch had been broken. She had blue welts on her back, from the beatings. She was missing a tooth. She avoided our eyes, pleadingly; she didn't want to be part of a group like this.

One girl felt left out: Lise had been hidden in Maass the bookbinder's attic as soon as two 12-A-II students went missing. Mrs. Maass would have taken her out to the Countess Woods in the night, to a waiting car, the moment the Stasi seemed to be coming for her, and driven her to safety in West Berlin; all *for the cat, for the birds*, for nothing. Like she had nothing to offer, this useless Lise Wollenberg.

By that time nobody would say a word to or take a slice of bread from Gabriel. His own school class pressuring him, the Dühr family imploring him to get the Central School-Group Authority to intervene to help the missing girl, he had declared: such requests were signs of a regrettable lack of confidence in the Socialist state. – Our security forces know what they're doing—no more than what's necessary. You don't ask questions. You help them!

Maybe Manfras was insulted by the indifference the girls had shown him since the summer of 1951; we would strike a yearning pose and sing right to his face, until he inevitably blushed, the current hit: Don't look at me that waaaaay / you know I can never saaaay / (no to you).

Someone else came from Cottbus, with medicine: Pius, ordered to Gneez to give a statement. He brought Temples of Golden Joy and a rebuke: we had never actually seen a denunciation against us in Lockenvitz's hand, or with his signature. The investigators had proceeded on the assumption that the perpetrator must have roped in accomplices. And who would willingly type up what a young man asked them to? Girls, that's who. – And you of all people, Gesine! He took special care to protect you!

(I deserved that. After Easter vacation of 1951, henceforth to be referred to as spring vacation, Dieter Lockenvitz left the Pagenkopf & Co. work collective. Just stopped coming, with no explanation. Asked in class whether there'd been a fight, he said he was in love with Gesine Cresspahl, he couldn't stand the hours spent watching the favors enjoyed by his rival,

Pius. Since then Pius and I had tapped our fingers to our foreheads in public, calling him crazy, but we let him have his way. He'd worked it out so that no one could attest to any dealings between Student Cresspahl and him—or a single one of his mistakes—in more than eight months.)

Lockenvitz's trial was held on the morning of May 15, 1952, in the district court; though the transcript was to state that it was a public trial, no public was present in the courtroom. Students Gantlik and Cresspahl had made provisions by committing the criminal act of successful bribery of court employee Nomenscio Sednondico; this N. S. alerted class 12-A-II via Elise Bock so punctually that a riotous assembly of young citizens in proud blue shirts had gathered in the courthouse even before the start of the proceedings; shouts were heard: Friendship prevails, friendship prevails! and: We are the defendant's school class! Among the importunate throng was Colleague B. Selbich, who'd had to leave school with her subjects to smother their open rebellion as much as possible; the fact is, we owed it to her officious cowardice that we were able to see him one last time—former high-school student Lockenvitz.

The Stasi had visibly done to him what his newssheets accused them of. They could have hidden some of it behind a pair of glasses replacing the ones they'd broken, if they hadn't been so cheap. As it was, he was brought in with his face bare, seemingly blind, stumbling; he slumped in the dock, hanging onto the chair as if even this was beyond his strength. He held his head in a listening pose; he avoided looking at us. Since his upper front teeth were elsewhere, he had trouble articulating certain syllables.

Witness statement from MANFRAS: The defendant's work in the ZGSL was, in practical terms, sabotage.

(Whatever work there was to do in the Free German Youth organization, Lockenvitz had done it; Gabriel's role was to give the annual addresses, his overview appraisals of the state of the world. Now he accused himself of lacking the vigilance that Great Comrade Stalin always . . .)

Witness statement from WESTPHAL: Dieter Lockenvitz assisted in the Culture League's library starting in 1948, organizing, cataloging, and placing orders for the collection; he is familiar with the premises. How could I suspect him of leaving a window open so he could climb in at night and use the typewriter?

Witness statement from LOCKENVITZ (MRS.): My son is a secretive child. He can't have gotten that from me or his father.

Witness statement from SELBICH: Missing. (Afternoon walks in the Rose Garden, Gneez.)

The prosecutor, during his training for the People's Court, must have skipped his German classes. Wild grammatical flailing. Somersaulting voice while mispronouncing the foreign words.

The defendant's attempt to obtain a diploma underhandedly. (His Abitur would have been the kind you see once a decade [except for chemistry]. He was meant for an era when people were rewarded according to their abilities.)

The defendant's monstrous ambition (am-BITZ-ee-own) to make public the judgments of the court kept under seal by the criminal chambers of the sovereign republic in the interests of the state! Collection of Subversive Information.

Terrorism. (Since he'd also sent his correspondence to the district court judges in New Mecklenburg, to affect and intimidate them if possible.)

Motion to have the defendant's mother in the courtroom arrested, for suspected complicity. (Gerda Lockenvitz, b. 1909, garden worker; sentenced to 2 yrs. Z. for Neglect of Child-Rearing Obligations and Active Collaboration.)

The implement used in committing the crime—one (1) bicycle, Swedish (foreign!) manufacture—is hereby confiscated for the use of the state.

(No comment whatsoever was made about how a child not even originally from the country could have gained access to secret files and records of closed trials. The detailed information in the reports about June 18 and July 20, 1950, and December 6, 1951, were just asking for a cross-examination. Yet the court acted as if no one not sitting on the bench knew a thing about the details of Lockenvitz's one-sided correspondence; perhaps this meant that he was still trying to protect his sources.)

Question: Do you admit that you are an enemy of the first workers' and peasants' state to exist on German soil?

Answer: I admit to an unambiguous German and Anglo-Saxon genitive. I admit to proclaiming the law in the public square in Germany.

Fifteen years in prison. And since the Soviets had decided not to take an interest in this lone-wolf criminal, he was spared a trip on the Blue Express to Moscow—a coupled-on prison car disguised as a vehicle of the German mail service. He also forfeited the privilege of learning to mine coal in Vorkuta or cut trees in Taischet. He also missed the Soviet amnesty of 1954, which annulled the verdicts of military tribunals. Since he'd been convicted by a German court, he served two-thirds of his sentence.

In September, the interrupted correspondence resumed:

Gerhard Dunker, b. 1929, physics student, verh. Dec. 24, 1951; sentenced by Güstrow district court on June 17 1952 to eight years Z . . .

In the beginning, 12-A-II knew where Lockenvitz had been taken: to Bützow. Two students in that class were allowed to choose a job for him, since he'd also told them which companies placed orders for convict labor:

People-Owned Business Rostock Shipping Combine,

P.O.B. Güstrow Garment Works,

P.O.B. Cadastral Unit, Schwerin,

P.O.B. (Combine) WiBa Wittenberg Basketwork Manufacture,

P.O.B. High-Voltage Installations, Rostock,

Wiehr & Schacht, Bützow;

they had some idea of his daily menu and were able to calculate from his reports an hourly wage of ninety-four cents, which left him at the end of the month, after the deductions for tax and social security and imprisonment costs, with fifteen marks, just enough for two pounds of butter and four jars of jam; they knew the maximum allowable contents of the packages they were sometimes permitted to send him as a reward for good conduct:

500 grams of fat,

250 g cheese,

250 g bacon,

500 g sausage,

500 g sugar,

and, up to the maximum total package weight of 3 kg: fruit,

onions, and store-bought cookies in their original packaging;

Anita could bring herself to send such a package only once, and it was returned; the sender was required to be living in Lockenvitz's jurisdiction and be related to him.

Thanks to his spywork, we were able to picture him with a one-inch crew cut, in hand-me-down Volkspolizei overalls, saluting the constable by doffing his cap and averting his gaze to six feet in front of and three feet behind this dignitary as he strode past, assuming a military posture, marching in formation, sleeping (never alone) next to a shit bucket. We left him alone.

Were we expecting his final statement to include an apology for our ten-day detention and questioning, or what? If Pius was to be believed, Lockenvitz probably thought no one had been arrested but him. Jakob said: *Thass somethin you gotta learn: bein stuck in the slammer.*

Starting in the summer of 1952, after those responsible for administering East German justice had disciplined Lockenvitz, they began to have their doubts about whether the secret arrest and incommunicado imprisonment of fellow citizens were sufficiently daunting to those remaining on the outside thus far. Maybe it was this high-school student's publicity campaign that helped inspire the criminal courts to start publishing their verdicts in the provincial newspapers. Let people read the deterrents in black and white.

Or was it simply disturbing to watch an eighteen-year-old boy sacrifice his future—from which he had every right to expect admission to university and, with luck, a profession of his choice—for the truth, whatever kind of truth, a proven fact or not? Remembering Lockenvitz sets our thoughts aflutter slightly. Birds starting up in the dark.

We got word from Gneez that his mother had returned there as soon as she'd served her two years. She tried to wait in Gneez for her son; however, the cathedral preacher whom Anita had gone all the way to Jerichow to avoid took the trouble to thunder down from the pulpit against her, using words that the Bible offers for the casting out of the undeserving. They say she's waiting in Bavaria somewhere.

Starting in 1962 we could have made inquiries about Lockenvitz. But his schoolmate Cresspahl decided she'd rather wait and see whether Anita would take back or tone down her threat from 1952: If I ever run into him in the subway and he offers me a seat, I'll stay standing!

The fact is, we sold Lockenvitz down the river. To give Anita the last word: We are guilty before him.

August 13, 1968 Tuesday

The New York Times on her front page shows us how an East German delegation in Karlovy Vary is greeted by a Czechoslovakian one: without Russian-style embraces and kisses. The onlookers cheered for Alexander Dubček; they bestowed a silence on Comrade Ulbricht, and later the two crews ate at separate tables. In her three-column history of the East German custodian's life, the World's Chronicler mentions a 1957 exchange of words between "Walter Ernst Karl" Ulbricht and one Comrade Gerhard Ziller. The former's subordinate: While we were in concentration camps, you were making speeches in Russia; you have always been safe. The latter's superior: I will never forget what you've said here; we'll discuss the matter later. Subordinate: (goes home and shoots himself). We wrote a tall question mark in the margin next to this story, since we want to ask someone for information to assuage our doubts—until memory, once again present, reports for duty at the place where said person now finds himself.

(Yesterday's telegram from Helsinki: UNABLE TO WRITE – ERITZION.)

Employee Cresspahl has now promised her daughter that she can do whatever she wants through next Tuesday; Marie has hesitantly renounced the military swimming drills in her summer camp. Yesterday they went to Chicago; because the flight takes more than an hour. (Because unfamiliar men keep calling the Cresspahl telephone in New York acting familiar, with urgent questions to ask about a certain Missing Person; also because one has neglected to report that person's possible demise.) Marie liked that the passengers on this airborne commuter line simply take a number and pay the stewardess on board, who is equipped with a money pouch at her belly like a train conductor. In Chicago we took the rattling trains on the Loop downtown. We looked for the hotel where we stayed in 1962, like a princess and infanta; torn down. In Marina City's round towers on the Chicago River, we toured a model apartment as if we were planning to move in; there was a gentleman in the elevator in an Italian jacket, winking confidentially. Marie thought that's how it goes when a lady gets a proposition; he was definitely from a different society. And, so that the telephone behind the locked door of the Cresspahl apartment can spend the day ringing into the empty air, today is perfect for an excursion out to Rockaway Peninsula in the Atlantic, taking more than an hour to get to by subway—the only stretch where you have to pay a second token.

Here we have a child about to take a trip in seven days that she is not looking forward to—the country is too foreign; she wishes she could talk it over with someone but he is unreachable at the moment on the Gulf of Bothnia in the Baltic. So it's time to give her something, a foretaste, long saved up to be used in case of emergency. Does Marie know that Jakob, in the fall of 1955, wrote a letter from Olmütz, Olomouc, where he was learning the operational techniques of dispatching at the *hl. n.*, located at railway kilometer 253 from Prague?

In Brooklyn the train to the beaches of Rockaway is crowded already. All of the Negroes among the passengers are going farther than Forty-Fourth Street; the white-sand beach, to Sixtieth Street, is indeed covered with none but the pink-skinned, lying in pairs on their blankets. The men are holding their hands still on the girls' backs; it looks quite unimaginative. On the subway, a young black man has nudged his napping girlfriend in the ribs, tipping her head onto his shoulder; while she puts on a show of comfortably snuggling up to him, he gives himself compensation for his goodness by feeling her upper thigh.

– Jakob used to work where we're going? Will we go see it?

We'll go see it, in ten days, if that's okay with her. We'll look for a family, Feliks and Tonya, with two daughters who'll have left home by now—they'll know who we are when we say Jakob's name. Jakob lived *en famille* there; he told the story of how the days began: in the morning there was only a big blue-black window in watercolor, with a pot-bellied lamp in front, on a peaceful white tablecloth, trying to put a plump dent in the darkness outside. At that table, with the guest from Mecklenburg, was the gentleman of the house, still drowsy but acquainted with the work of the day and certain to master it. For now he waits with concealed amusement to see which of his daughters will be first. On this morning of Jakob's letter, it was the younger, just seven years old, who fetched plates and silverware for five from the cupboards and set the table, all with a tense, worried look about her, perhaps meant to express: Yes, what would you do without me! Then the mother sits down with her tea and coffee pots, four people are already eating when the elder daughter comes to the table, sluggishly half-asleep but in a rush, handed a piece of bread while she's standing, eating while she walks, everyone's sympathetic awareness that she has a quiz in school today guarding her back, and not just any quiz: Russian. By now the wind was going at the darkness of the sky with a grater, making long pale slashes start to appear. These people liked to talk. About the farmer expostulating to his cackling chicken: Now they wouldn't getcha for those eighteen heller a yours! (that was the price of an egg, approximately: eighteen heller, eighteen cents). Or: Lookit how that redbreast's puffing up his feathers on the wall, it must be zero degrees outside. Hope the jay comes. Nest robbers have it hard too; a whole swarm of blackbirds just flew at him. Blackbirds? That's right, "black-birds." By now the left, northeast half of the sky is almost entirely cleared, the right half dissolved into streaks, so they *were* clouds; now the light comes leaping in. North wind. Wear your hat today, it'll be cold. Then they all said Bye, or Adieu, and everyone's day began at last; Jakob went to the train station.

– Jakob couldn't speak Czech!

If Jakob wanted to get along with the people from the Czech railroad he would have to spare them his Mecklenburg Russian. What Jakob quoted in his letter: *Protože nádraží je velmi daleko.* (Because the station's far away.)

Ne, jejich manželky jsou Češky. (No, careful! Their wives are Czech.)
Ještě dělám chyby. (I still make mistakes.)

– The things you can do, Gesine.

But there was a boy standing at the window for Jakob every morning, four years old, waiting for his friend:

– I see you.
– *So do I.*
– *Well, see you later.*
– *Will do.*

And he knew his way around station talk, among Czechs:

– I can beat you, doesn't matter you're tall!
– Go ahead.
– Cause I'm short, I can run fast.

Feliks: black goatee above a perpetually white shirt collar; bald circle surrounded by hair. Tonya: A kind look from behind awkward glasses, despite her worries; hair in a bun.

What surprised them both: that such a young man, just twenty-seven, was so good at living alone! She ironed his shirts.

North Moravia district, Marie. On the Morava. I'm sure you'll be getting to that in school *fore long:* the Punctation of Olmütz. Around seventy thousand people. An archbishopric. A St. Wenceslaus Cathedral. The biggest pipe organ in Moravia in the St. Maurice Church. Church of the Virgin Mary Visitation on Holy Hill! The Olomouc language island!

– That sounds like lots of lonely walks.

Feliks the railroad man took his colleague Jakob along when he went out for a beer. The family took him to Prague, three hours by express train, and led him from the corner of Kaprova and Maislova ulice to Dušni ulice, Mikulášska, Celetná ulice, to the Old Town Hall, the Fishmarket, the Kinský Palace, the Karolinum, the Assicurazioni Generali building, the Workers' Accident Insurance Institute building, to Bílkova ulice, to Dlouhá třída: so that he could take pictures there, as a good friend in West Germany had asked him to. Since she was unable to visit Czechoslovakia herself at the moment. Since then she'd had a standing invitation. That night they went back to Olomouc and found a wrecked apartment.

– Some people must've taken a trip there from Riverside Drive, New York, and broken in!

They'd forgotten about the cat and not left the basement window or back door open for her to slip out of. The cat, however, knew as one of her work obligations that she must relieve herself only outdoors; she felt a pressure in her body, and in her distress she jumped from china cabinet to sewing machine, from the egg basket into the molasses barrel. How sheepish she was when they came back, her human employees. How cruel she thought it was for them to punish her with a laugh and a warm bath. She had problems enough with the son, the affectionate blond boy, useless for hunting birds and mice, too lazy. To be unmasked like that, before the younger generation!

Not at all like dogs: Jakob wrote. With them, scratching is more of a symbolic act. But cats want to bury what sticks unpleasantly in their noses. You need to fence off a flower garden from a cat—and try finding wire here!

– And so Gesine sent some chicken wire from West Germany.

To thank them for the information, she did. By that time Tonya and Feliks trusted the colleague from Mecklenburg, despite his having been raised to follow Luther and being therefore destined for Hell; they told Archbishop Josef Beran about him. On June 7, 1948, Prime Minister

Gottwald signed the new constitution because the president for life, Eduard Beneš, had refused, and he asked the archbishop to accompany him in a thanksgiving service. A year later, though, the archbishop of Prague was prevented from preaching, in August he was robbed of his rights and his ability to leave the house, and in March 1951 he was banned from Prague. As for the titular bishop of Olomouc, on December 2, 1950, he was put away for twenty-five years. In Communism there are governments where you never know.

And to make sure that our colleague Jakob returned to his homeland knowing all about Olomouc, the railway workers entrusted him with the story that the city was most recently famous for. This was the perfume-box plot, and no one was supposed to know about it. The bombs came to Prague in wooden boxes marked "Perfume," one meant for the leader of President Beneš's National Socialist Party, Peter Zenkl, one for the Minister of Justice, Prokop Drtina, and one for Foreign Minister Jan Masaryk. The general secretary of the Communists announced in a public meeting that Peter Zenkl's people themselves had sent them. Now there was a carpenter near Olomouc, named Jan Kopka, concerned by the party's manhunt since he'd made the boxes himself and knew their intended use too. He went to confess, was accused of lying by the chief of the party police, and had to sign a statement saying so. There were still democrats in the Ministry of Justice and they rearrested Kopka, searched his carpentry shop, and found machine guns, hand grenades, ammunition. Kopka, as a Communist, wanted to share and share alike and named a fellow comrade, a railwayman named Opluštil; a much bigger arsenal was found at his home, which he must have gotten from the Olomouc Party Secretariat, and when Opluštil seemed reluctant to hide the guns, he was warned: you could be crushed between two cars, or fall off a train, without anybody ever knowing how it happened. The person telling him this, Communist Deputy J. Juri-Sosnar, had made the perfume-box bombs himself and was caught because they had the same serial number as explosives from the Olomouc depot, and now who'd been the one to tell *him* to do it? One Alexej Čepička. Klement Gottwald's son-in-law. So the case never came to trial, and you'll already have heard about the situation with the archbishop, Jakob. And now who jumped out of a third-story window the following February? Former Minister of Justice Drtina. And for what did he spend the next five years and three months in prison when he didn't die? For false accusations of attempted assassination. That's what we're known for here in Olomouc, Jakob.

Jakob, in Cresspahl's English household, had gotten used to tea, and there it was ready and waiting on the warmer at Tonya and Feliks's (all that was missing was the juice of a fresh lemon; and the tea lights). A young man abroad, you have to take care of him, don't you, and Tonya took an extra trip to Brno where there had been lemons the day before yesterday. Feliks built some tea lights.

Tonya was embarrassed about her figure; Feliks didn't mind it.

A love affair under her supervision, she didn't begrudge him that, despite the pain. But being lied to (betrayed), that went against her self-respect. A person's got to keep her self-respect.

Jakob learned from Feliks that in the Middle Ages sneezing was thought to be a sign of the plague, hence the good wishes. What do your Italians say about that, Gesine.

Each of them thought, about the other: if they do it, it's for the best.

– So you knew back then what he wanted to discuss with you, Gesine?

Now Marie wants to know why she's never seen a letter from Jakob in Moravia. Because it's safe in Düsseldorf. Will Gesine Cresspahl swear to her daughter that this letter exists? She will, she does, hand on heart. (And even if it was lying under oath, I'd do it again.)

But the child is looking out at a beach in America. Next to beachgoers at leisure, there is work being done—a backhoe with its snout full is creeping on treads toward the point of a jetty, shaking its load into the net of a crane that's making its own space to stand that much longer. Along the broad boardwalk, "colored" workmen are tearing the foundations of rotted bungalows out of the ground with crowbars, piling the slabs up neatly. May makes everything anew, as they say—the permanent season of speculation.

Behind the boardwalk, crooked weather-beaten collapsing wooden shacks that one can rent as temporary apartments or summer houses, even if the owners' phone numbers are bleached away, peeled off. One of the handwritten blurbs: *All the bungalow people can kiss my dick.* In the shimmering sky, airplanes towing advertisements. YOU LOOK SUNBURNED. COOL IT OFF WITH ... Stands selling meat products that may as well be factory-made. Tin cans of twenty-seven different drinkable liquids. Marie trusts the ice cream she can buy here; not the kind you get abroad.

Coming back on the wooden beach path, she gets a splinter in her foot by the second step, but keeps stoically still as she's learned to do in camp, savoring her multicolor ice cream while her mother tears open her skin with the point of a scissors. But the splinter breaks apart into several pieces. A plump, quickly spherical drop of blood appears under the scissors. Again we have a limping child.

When the beach narrows, the housing projects approach the water, the ones where the people live who want to be called Negroes—people with formal manners, looking friendly. Four seventeen-year-olds are trying to carry a fifth into the water, because a school of sharks was sighted off the coast last Saturday. In the abandoned shop windows are the advertising insignia of the "whites." A grandfather with three children and their fishing rods to play with; he's left his own at home. A region capable of lush vegetation, going to ruin under the industrial garbage. A single-story wasteland all around (as a writer once said). Amid the hurrahing of a crowded subway platform, one of the women is reading a book: *The Loneliness of the Individual in Modern American Society*, it says on the cover, in German. Marie saw it, she laughs. Sighing, brave, she says: Still, if we could only stay.

Two men entered Union Dime Savings Bank at Park Avenue and Fiftieth Street at about 9:05 a.m. yesterday, dressed neither especially well nor especially badly ("about what a police lieutenant would wear," in the police's estimation); one was armed with a pistol, the other with a machete or meat cleaver. When they were back out on the street with $4,400, bank employees behind them shouted "Thief! Thief!" and no taxi would take the fare, during the morning rush hour and everything, and they spent the rest of the morning at the Seventeenth Precinct station. (One had just been released from Sing Sing in June, where he'd been serving time for additional episodes practicing the art of bank robbery.)

The custodian of East Germany left Karlovy Vary so incensed at the refusal of his Czechoslovak colleagues to muzzle the press that he had his own press refuse to say where he'd been for twenty-seven hours.

Citizens of Czechoslovakia have given forty pounds of gold and the equivalent of nearly $20 million to a fund to strengthen their Communist Party; the party, though, would rather they shortened their frequent breaks for coffee or beer; cut waste; worked harder. One worker, in a letter to *Prace*, the labor newspaper, asks why. When young workers have to wait for ten years to get an apartment, and still have to pay 40,000 crowns ($2,500). We need new machinery in our factories! And something like the feeling that work pays!

Permission to leave high school—a diploma, a certificate of readiness, the Abitur: Student Cresspahl acquired it several times.

Once from her teachers, in the form each saw fit to give it.

From her Latin teacher, a hunchbacked, timorous old man who over-looked with a show of absentmindedness the fact that his favorite disciple in grammar, the famulus Lockenvitz, had left the class apparently never to return, while Miss Gantlik and Miss Cresspahl had been absent for ten days without the required excuse notes from their parents. He gave himself away by not calling on them until February, when they'd presumably caught up on what they'd missed. He flinched a little if anyone mentioned, in regard to his Marcus Tullius Cicero, that this orator against state corruption might have dipped into the till to satisfy his own need for ready cash, or, worse, if anyone brought up the fact that it was Christian missions to Western Europe that had been responsible for the spread of Latin; he'd already gotten burned once, and badly, by history: disciplinary transfer out of Schwerin. He would have had a heart attack and fluttered away on the spot if a class delegation, appealing to his well-proven moral sense, had requested instruction on how to react to the unfortunate custom of one student memorizing and reporting what the other students casually said during tours of gasworks and breweries. All he longed for was to reach retirement, leisure time in which he could compose his deeply personal monograph on the Schelf Church in Schwerin. Anyone who stood their ground with him on the ablative absolute received an A as a final grade: in gratitude for considerate treatment.

In English, Hans-Gerhard Knick gave the graduating Cresspahl girl an

A. He had learned this language with the help of LPs and believed he could speak it after he'd gone to the World Festival of School and College Students in Berlin in 1951, while still in short pants, and a group of socialistically inclined British girls had responded indulgently to his efforts at playing the translator. When Cresspahl, having carefully read T. Dreiser's *Sister Carrie*, slipped into conversation the word *conductor* instead of *guard* for a *Schaffner*, Knick at first tried to correct her, then quickly gave up on her. She also enjoyed a certain amount of protection given that she was planning to go to university and study a subject he himself could have used a review in; and another certain amount from something Lockenvitz had bequeathed to her in the FDJ: he'd known Mrs. Knick in their lost homeland, as a well-to-do bourgeois, not a daughter of the Workers and Peasants as befit the wife of a language instructor who hoped to be accepted as a candidate for the Unity Party.

There was a B in Russian on G. Cresspahl's final transcript, mainly because of her taking part in a plot to help a young teacher named von Bülow learn the language well enough to teach it. This von Bülow was already scared, due to her noble ancestry; the psychological tips she'd been offered in her training courses had thoroughly confounded her, since they had so little to do with the actual behavior of 12-A-II students in Mecklenburg. Instruction in Russian was therefore administered by Anita. Which was a sacrifice. For there on the lesson plan was Stalin's essay "On Dialectical and Historical Materialism," teeming with "Furthermore... Therefore... Therefore perhaps... Thus ends... Thus transforms... Thus must... Furthermore...," followed by the same author's discussion of "Marxism and Questions of Linguistics." *Vas slushayu.* None of us could have bought a pair of nail scissors in Kiev or Minsk with any of that. This Eva von Bülow left for Hamburg at the end of the 1951–52 school year and is still there, an interpreter in the West German/Soviet steel and shipbuilding business.

In Music a B from Julie Westphal. Because the Cresspahl girl had been happy to remain among the second altos—gaining some extra free time when the first-string school choir had to rehearse for their summer tour of the Baltic resorts, followed by time for unsupervised vacations. Also because Candidate Manfras had informed this Westphal that the Cresspahl girl once described one of her, Westphal's, teacherly opinions as "nonsense":

this being in reference to Julie's verdict that the song "The Moon Has Arisen" should vanish from the musical repertory of a democracy due to the plea therein that our sick neighbor too should sleep peacefully: solicitude that undermined the ideological vigilance of the class-conscious member of society, since the neighbor might well be an enemy of the people in disguise, whom it would be criminal to let sleep in peace. Third, because, while the Cresspahl girl had listened to and recited back Mrs. Westphal's lectures about the cosmopolitan reactionary nationalists and enemies of the Soviet Union such as Paderewski, Toscanini, Stravinsky, and other composers and musicians, she had then asked her teacher for a demonstration of these scandalous traits in the works of the condemned musicians—just a few bars on the piano, Mrs. Westphal, to give us an idea.

In chemistry and biology, an A from a little old man, weak and womanish (an "Auntie") like the Latin teacher but fat, almost spherical. It was from him that we were given, in tenth grade, the block of instruction meant to explain to children the sexual needs and abilities of the human being; that was when this drooler, a lady-killer in his own mind, had thrown a sop to his thwarted libido by reciting to the boys, with a wink, forefinger quivering erect near his eye, the line from Goethe—"The thought alone will lift Him"—followed by the poem:

When you're aware
Of Him hanging there,
So loose,
So big
In your trouser leg...
You've a dirty mind!
And I like your kind
("Heinrich Heine")

(Now where would a girl in 10-A-II know that from, where would she have heard it? Guess! Your best answer would be: osmosis.) He was still bustling around in front of us, getting all excited about examples of "e-vo-lution" in nature; in 1952 he offered his students the myth that bananas caused infantile paralysis, the same canard he'd offered the children of 1937, another period in which you couldn't buy bananas. The students in chemistry and biology had their doubts that this teacher, given that he'd been trained at Heidelberg University, actually did revere Stalin's favorite son the Soviet biologist Trofim Denisovich Lysenko; still we dutifully recited to him that whether plants passed on acquired characteristics depended entirely on environmental conditions. The fact that they did this was the sum total of our knowledge in this field, which was why Anita, on a tour of a seed-growing and hybridization farm, went up to the man in charge with a question about Michurin and his pupil Lysenko. This man was a chaired professor, holder of multiple doctorates both earned and honorary, winner of the National Prize, who had decided it was more important to stay in his field of experimental study than to worry about the temporary circumstance of the New State appropriating his results. Anita speaks to such a man in a modest, respectful tone that he can't help but notice. Maybe he had a backlog of anger stored up from a meeting in Rostock or a session of the academy, but furious, stern as a privy councilor, he laid it out for her and her alone that somatic detours might cause a fixing of genetic properties perhaps once in 106 million years—otherwise the theory of the evolutionary progression of life would collapse. You won't find any Lysenkoist cultivation here, young lady! We were standing nearby, saw her downcast eyes and flushed face. At moments like that we missed them—Pagenkopf, Lockenvitz; they would have taken measures, each in their own way, to keep a girl in their class from being hurt. Fortunately, Comrade Professor himself realized in time that it was Anita's school that should be ashamed of itself, not Anita; he put his arm around her shoulder and took her on a little stroll, to tell her a thing or two about productivity appraisal and seed-grain certification, as well as the fact that in a small country agriculture can't afford to take chances with arbitrary measures in genetics. We stood around our school biology expert in a group, ignored his embarrassed babbling, and hoped that Anita would be brought back to us consoled. – Hail Moscow and Lysenko! Student Gantlik said (when no Youth Comrade Manfras was nearby either): that afternoon she renounced a career she'd been aspiring to.

Both Gantlik and Cresspahl got A's in math and physics, from Eberhard Martens, nicknamed "the Evil Eye" because he had kept from his days as an NCO a searching, hypnotic gaze ever on the lookout for criminal activity. The kind of teacher who sticks to his syllabus long after it should have dawned on him that only three of his students had grasped the concept of value assignment rules (not functions, because "the essential content of the concept of a function is the fact of assigning a certain value, by virtue of which certain objects may be defined as belonging to others, not the dependence of the magnitude assigned"). He was bashful with us, trying to solve the riddle of our stiff courtesy. We had heard him tell smugly confiding stories, in a broad Mecklenburg accent: *I hardly ever sweat, the marches in Russia got me out a that habit; the others were always drinkin; theres just one sitcha-ation when I sweat*...We'd also heard him tell Special Instructor H.-G. Knick, man-to-man, about a certain noteworthy encounter on the streets of Warsaw in 1942: *Someone comes up to me, bats her eyelashes till I notice that her breasts are outta phase with her walk, so I put the make on her. Turns out the little monster'd crosslaced rubber bands from her garters to her bra, would ya believe it*...Technically racial desecration, I spose. "The Evil Eye" tried to leave East Germany in 1954 but baggage check at the border found what looked like private photos of Heinrich Himmler and the SS general who'd ordered the Warsaw Ghetto leveled and the survivors sent to their deaths—two years in jail. We kept up our obedience to this teacher through graduation.

We could have relaxed a bit more around our German and Contemporary Studies instructor, but as a rule we preferred not to. Because in 1952's ninth grade there was a girl named Kress, half of Cresspahl, and when asked who Comrade Stalin was she offered the guess that he was President of the Soviet Union. – Sit down! F!: our little Bettina screeched, and in the same breath: Your whole family's under suspicion as far as I'm concerned! Since Bettinikin had never seen this Kress before and knew nothing about her family either, a different girl in 12-A-II knew just which student she really had it in for.

Serious of mien, we recited in German class stanzas from "The Cultivation of Millet," a poem that the contemporary writer Bertolt Brecht had published the previous year:

20
Joseph Stalin spoke of millet.
To Michurin's pupils he spoke of dung
          and dry wind.
And the Soviet people's great Harvest Leader
Called the millet an unmanageable child.

21
But she, the moody daughter of the steppes,
Was not the accused as they interrogated her.
In Lysenko's greenhouse in faraway Moscow
She testified to what helps her, what disturbs her.

Her thoughts possibly dwelling on a different house, also far away, where
a student named Lockenvitz was being interrogated about what was bothering him, Anita interpreted for Mrs. Selbich the poetic goals of these lines,
namely, providing a scientific foundation for the Marxist concept of social
development—mankind's being shaped not only by his social milieu but
also by the inheritance of virtues acquired therefrom (and she included
the difference between this environmental theory and those of Marx's
contemporaries, while strictly avoiding the term *sociology*, at the time still
outlawed as an expression of imperialist pseudoscience).

Moreover, "The Cultivation of Millet" had been adorned with a musical setting, which could be sung with a lengthening of the final "a" in each
line:

1
Tchaganak Berziyev, the nomaaaad,
Son of the free desert in the land of Kazakhstaaaan...

and how was Bettinikin to take this if not as a somewhat childish excess
of enthusiasm within the framework of the curriculum?

In Frau Selbich's class we studied another work by the same author,
"The Herrnburg Report," a poetic recollection of how the West German
police at the border crossing of Herrnburg had treated West Germans
returning from the All-German Rally of 1950. The Schleswig-Holstein
interior ministry had ordered these young people to submit their personal
information and place of employment for registration, and that they be
given medical exams because they had slept on straw; they fought back
with fists and stones, bivouacked in the open for a night and a half, then
eventually gave in and held out their IDs to be stamped "Processed" or
"Valid." For Brecht the poet, this turned into their having "planted" the
flag of the Free German Youth on the roof of the Lübeck main train sta-

tion, and having been victorious; he also passed the following verdict on two party chairmen in the Federal Republic:

> Schumacher, Shoemaker, your shoe doesn't fit,
> There's no way Germany can walk in it.
> Adenauer, Adenauer, show us your hand,
> For thirty silver pieces you have sold out our land.

This news item in musical form was sung at the Third World Youth Festival of the FDJ in Berlin, and the socialistically inclined English girls there, surrounding our H.-G. Knick in his knee pants, might well have thought that what he translated for them was *awful*:

> Germans taking Germans into custody,
> Just 'cause they've gone from Germany to Germany...
> Roadblocks and fencing,
> Why even try?
> Look at us dancing
> Merrily on by.

We were crazy enough to suggest a performance of this choral work at Fritz Reuter High School in Gneez (Herrnburg being just a stone's throw away, after all), thereby delighting Bettina S. (at her pedagogical success). Julie Westphal put a stop to that; she had an inkling of our puzzlement at a poet who could be outraged at West German police measures by virtue of being largely immune to East German ones. But the school had achieved its true pedagogical purpose. By only presenting Brecht's hackwork to us, which had earned him the National Prize (a hundred thousand marks), the school kept us away from his *One Hundred Poems*, which came onto the market that same year, 1951—we had every reason to think they were equally maggoty.

Anyone willing to part with a used copy of Bertolt Brecht's *One Hundred Poems*, in any condition, preferably with dust jacket, is hereby requested to name their price to Mrs. Gesine Cresspahl, Address:..., c/o Státní Banka Československá, Prague 1.

Bettina worked hard denouncing cosmopolitan enemies of the people.

What she knew about Rainer Maria Rilke was that he was a lyric poet alien to the people; Stefan George she called a stylite. But what to say about Jean-Paul Sartre? The Cresspahl girl submitted that this individual had published a book named *L'Être et le néant*, aka *Being and Nothingness*, in Paris in 1943, under the Nazi-German occupation—enough for an A. Oh, how we missed Lockenvitz!

He'd still been with us on our class trip to see Ernst Barlach's works; he'd worn a suit to Güstrow, while Cresspahl wore her Sunday best because her father had suggested that this was proper when visiting a dead man. The Mecklenburgers, always under the leadership of Fiete Hildebrandt, had so plagued and tormented Barlach that he'd died in 1938, in Rostock, but he'd wanted to be buried in Ratzeburg, in the West. Here, before the hovering Angel in the Güstrow Cathedral, before *The Doubter*, the young woman from the terrible year of 1937, we listened to Bettina's interpretive mush and then went back a second time to contemplate the sculptures in silence. (Lise Wollenberg managed to pin the nickname "Fettered Witch" on her former friend Cresspahl, due to an alleged resemblance *en face* to the statue in question; these days Lise was occasionally stared at, by boys, as if she were out of her mind.) It was with a set of reproductions of the "Frieze of the Listeners" that Gesine Cresspahl moved to Hesse, to the Rhineland, to Berlin, and to Riverside Drive in New York City.

That trip had been in September 1951; in December, an exhibition of Barlach's works opened in the German Academy of Arts in Berlin, NW 7; the following January, an instructor in German and Contemporary Studies used the SED's newspaper, *Neues Deutschland* (*New Germany*), to teach us

What are the circumstances in which we construct the genitive as "des neuen Deutschland"?

Why do we here say "an issue of des Neuen Deutschlands"?

what Bettinikin had misinformed us about four months earlier. The SED had dispatched its official art expert to the Academy—one Girnus, well-versed in the practices of Formalism so inimical to the people—and Girnus was willing to concede that the Nazis had treated Barlach as someone inimical to their sort. But Barlach had been defending a lost position;

Barlach had been, in essence, a retrograde artist. Taking no inspiration from the 1906 Russian Revolution. Wrapping a world of "the barefoot" in a halo of sanctity. What, in contrast, had Stalin said about this world of barefoot pilgrims in his opus *Anarchism or Socialism*? He had responded to it by saying: The truth is, rather, that . . . Barlach's orientation toward a decaying social stratum had barred his access to the great progressive current of the German people, per Girnus. Insulated him from it. That was the whole secret of the growing isolation he had chosen for himself.

We dutifully wrote an essay for German class about said whole secret, scrupulously distinguishing between what a certain N. Orlov had written in the newspaper of the occupying power, the *Tägliche Rundschau*

> Daily Review*! Latest issue!*
> *Faily review, no one'll miss you!*

and certain ideas of the sculptor Ernst Barlach (now promoted to the status of Formalist) about the connection between the three-dimensional world of ideas and "more solid ideas of the material involved: stone, metal, wood, firm matter." We lied like troopers; we were working toward our final exams.

Ever since their visit to Barlach's lakeside house on Inselsee in Güstrow, the students Gantlik and Cresspahl had shared an agreement, a secret. Both of them had turned away from the art-critical tour-guiding on offer from their instructor, Selbich, and found themselves on the ridge of Heather Hill, at the top of a slope well known to the children of Güstrow as a sledding place but which also opened onto a sweeping view of the island in Inselsee and the gently rising land beyond the water, dotted with backdrops of trees and roofs, radiant since the sun had just managed to scatter some dark rainclouds—may this sight be before me in the hour of my

> *We don't give a damn if you think it's a bit much, Comrade Writer! You write that down! We can still cancel this whole book of yours—today if we want to. The plans we've made for our death shouldn't be beyond you.*

dying. We told each other our private thoughts about people's essential need for the landscape they grew up in, learned about life in. We told each other how much we liked each other. For the rest of the school year we were still considered two people, strangers to each other, but in fact we were joined in friendship.

Anita almost cost herself a diploma. She was a member of the Free German Youth and so she was expected to come out in favor of the resolution of the Fourth FDJ Parliament of May 29, 1952, stating that serving in the Barracked Volkspolizei was an honorable duty for all members. She, Anita, who had sworn only two years earlier that she would refuse any job, even just in a telegraph office, that was involved in any war effort, was now picked to march like the Leipzig FDJ girls with their rifles slung across their backs, the boys carrying theirs shouldered. A future was being prepared for Anita in which she too could acquire the FDJ sharpshooting badge, twenty-one rings in three shots for First Class. Anita sat in the class chapter meeting with her head lowered, neck tendons red and taut, stubbornly silent. Who knows if she was still even listening when Gabriel Manfras spoke up in a threatening way about a balance between academic achievement and the political consciousness required as an accessory to any assault on the citadel of scholarship.

Student Cresspahl, presiding over the meeting, suddenly said, sounding very upset: I could slap myself! Here we are discussing the Stockholm Appeal and military service and not even noticing that Anita is sick. You're not feeling well, are you, Anita? Go straight home. A vote on student Gantlik's indisposition. For. Against. Abstentions: None.

And so School Group Fritz Reuter, Gneez, could telegraph a unanimous endorsement of militarization to the FDJ central office in Berlin—unanimous approvals were in fashion. And Anita moved to West Berlin as soon as she had the piece of paper with her academic achievements in hand.

Suitcases were prohibited on trains to East Berlin stations—this was meant to hinder citizens from fleeing the country. Anita deposited a suitcase at a station south of Teltow.

She pinned the following onto her clothes for the trip: her Large Sports Badge, her Small Sports Badge, her Insignia of the Society for German-Soviet Friendship, her FDJ Insignia, her badge "For Correct Knowledge" (silver), and a membership badge for the German Socialist Unity Party that she'd been deft enough to pilfer from a Contemporary Studies teacher; she suffered under the cool, disparaging looks of the other passengers, especially since she also forced herself to shout "Friendship!" as a greeting to anyone in uniform. On her second day in West Berlin she left the Auto Hotel where a certain Mr. Cresspahl had put in a good word for her and took the train back across the national border to fetch her luggage, medals and insignia on her breast. The luggage wasn't there. She put up a fight, as befit someone wearing all those party insignia ("The party seminar starts tomorrow, and here I am without a towel!"), and succeeded in getting her suitcase sent to East Station, against regulations ("You'll be hearing from me whether it actually gets there, I promise you!"); she tried to transfer to a westbound tram. On the stairs leading to the platform for trains to Spandau, she saw a table across the way with Red Army soldiers. She dashed in comradely fashion over to the Russians. They were happy for the diversion and flirted with their German ally; considerate, watchful, they interrupted their conversation by crying: Run, Comrade, your train's coming. Across the border her hardware attracted attention; she brought her left hand toward her shoulder several times, scratched a little through her overcoat, slipped one medal after another into the palm of her hand, and let go of it in her coat pocket.

Had there been any other funny business during the Abitur exams? Of course. There's one legend about English texts hidden in a rotten bench in the assembly hall—but here we should, in all fairness, fall silent, since most of those involved (implicated) are still alive, and living where they acquired their certifications.

My first Abitur had been my last encounter with Lockenvitz, on May 15, 1952.

My second was dated June 25, and was accompanied by the general remarks:

G. C. has been a conscientious, reliable student, who did her work thoroughly and independently. Her initiative has been a model for her classmates.

Societal activities:

G. C. has been a member of FDJ since 9/10/1949. She has performed good organizational work and consistently striven, successfully, to gain greater understanding in questions of ideological worldview.

Certificate #: Zc 208-25 3 52 5961-D/V/4/59-FZ 501.

There it was again: that banned word *worldview*. Mrs. Habelschwerdt had to pay for that misspeaking. New School, old words—you try to figure that one out, if you have to, or want to.

My third Abitur took place in Jerichow.

In the final days of June, Cresspahl's daughter was biking home from a swim in the Baltic on the Rande country road at the strange time of about five o'clock, just when the retired senior secondary-school instructors in English and Latin stop working in the garden plots behind New Cemetery and head home to brew their tea, a habit acquired during their years at the universities of London and Birmingham. There he was, an old man in a torn shirt walking with rake and hoe over his shoulder, and his former student Cresspahl said hello as shyly as she felt. He replied just as he had two years ago, and pretended to be appalled when the child seemed about to dismount and accompany him part of the way. He wouldn't hear of it; he begged the young lady to forgive his unseemly attire.

To be quite sure she would no longer have to see it, he sent her up ahead into town with precise instructions about the croissants and crumb cakes and "Americans" she should buy in the former Papenbrock bakery. By the time she arrived at his two-room apartment on Jerichow's market square, Kliefoth had shaved and put on a black suit; he was standing at the door like the young lady's most obedient servant. It was the guest herself who then had to eat all the pastries, every last crumb, while making a confession that covered two years of school. He sat upright at the table, his gaze steady. He was quite at ease, you could see it from the way he held his cigar away in the air, benevolently observing her. The student herself was uncertain of a good outcome.

– *Iam scies, patrem tuum mercedes perdidisses*: Kliefoth eventually said, challengingly.

"You will soon know that your father has gotten nothing for his tuition money." What they've taught you in that school, Miss Cresspahl, is poor equipment indeed for a life of study and learning.

Cresspahl's daughter spent only half the summer vacation of 1952 by the sea; every weekday, she had to go to Kliefoth's apartment with a bag of pastries right after lunch and receive instruction by means of a book which included this maxim: *It may be fairly said that English is among the easiest languages to speak badly, but the most difficult to use well* (Prof. C. L. WRENN, Oxford University: *The English Language*, 1949, p. 49).

And when she left for university she was given, as a present, Gustav Kirchner's *The Ten Main Verbs of the English Language: In British and American Forms* (Halle/Saale: 1952), a reliable tool with which she would eventually move to the other side of the world.

For as long as she still came back home to Mecklenburg, the student Cresspahl continued to visit this teacher. And every time, she had to eat pastries in his presence, because that was one of his notions about young ladies.

He gets an update from us by letter every year, and as many as seven more, if we feel like it.

Student Cresspahl once asked him, in passing, what life was like for a ten-year-old child in 1898 in Malchow am See, Mecklenburg; he sent her thirty pages in a handwriting like embroidery:

"I myself might have been the ten-year-old country lad of '98, but we city boys kept our distance from these *post numerando* coeval 'country Moritzes' (local corruption of 'local militias'). In M. the average pediatrician would chuckle in amusement because the teacher always went around in '*Mähl-spich*' (shirtfront and high stiff collar) while the townsmen and tradesmen put on theirs, '*Kreditspitzen*,' only for important walks through town—heard in passing and relayed without comment: '*Didja hear, Heinrich? Fritz A. gotanother assfull this morning.*' Now how did our ten-year-old get from the countryside to the city? Via bicycle, then still called velocipede, Plattd. *Vilitzipeh*, I know of only one case and only in dry weather. Out of all the estate boys only a coachman's son and the district governor's walked with me, the latter having already covered the three miles from his estate on foot. Residents of lakeside municipalities (Petersdorf, Göhren, Nossentin) came to the city (on Sundays) mainly by rowboat. To be cont'd. 9/20/63. Kl."

All because I was curious how my father might have grown up. But what does Kliefoth have to complain about—he can devote a whole week to Robert Burns's poems when he wants, and sometimes even discovers one he'd forgotten.

We send him, via Anita, the cigars and tobacco that are his due according to his need and his merit (the same way Brecht wanted to supply a fresh rose every day, in East Germany, for the poet Oscar Wilde); as a result, his letters invariably begin: Admonishing finger raised at the spoiling of a useless old man ...

He signs his letters with a teacher's siglum, as though grading a paper.

He starts them with the words: Dear honored lady and friend Miss Cresspahl.

If only we deserved them.

My third Abitur: that one counts.

August 15, 1968 Thursday

At JFK N PODGORNI, a ticket agent, or at any rate someone required to wear a nametag to that effect on his uniformed chest, so he must be used to outlandish incidents, and maybe he's been working for this same airline for six years: anyway, this morning he looks doubtfully at two ladies named Cresspahl wishing to travel to California with no luggage apart from whatever they have in their coat pockets, possibly including a firearm; if it were up to him he'd have frisked them both. Life's dealt you lemons, Mr. Podgorni; good day, sir.

What makes us want to go to San Francisco for the day? We want to fly in over the bay with the Golden Gate. Marie should see the giant wheel that pulls the cables hauling cable cars up over the city's hills. The boxy Spanish-style houses on the hills, shining white in the earth's vegetation burnt brown. Maybe at the main post office we'll run into the same beggar who thanked us for a quarter there six years ago by informing us: *You're a real lady, that's for sure.* We'll need a window seat at Fisherman's Wharf. And why are we allowed to do this? Because Marie expects a return flight to New York City at nine p.m. or thereabouts. Because we want to reacclimate ourselves to long-distance flights. And why do we want to do this? Because there are strangers' voices arriving over the phone lines in New York, Italian as well as American, asking about one Professor Erichson. Because a telegram from Helsinki could arrive there at any moment, informing us that someone is unable to speak. Would the two ladies with the name starting with C. please be the first to board the aircraft? We would like to welcome the C. sisters on board our 707 for this morning's flight to San Francisco.

– To get used to goodbyes: the younger of the traveling C.'s guesses after the climb during which she surveyed her earthly belongings, namely the island of Manhattan and the two-story orange ships in the harbor. – I'm never going to leave my home for good!

– Easy for you to say, with so many institutions of higher learning there, and the likes of Columbia right around the corner.

– Gesine, do you think I should go to college?

– If you want to learn how to see all the sides and corners of things, and how they fit together with other things, or even just how to look at a thought and arrange all its interconnections simultaneously in your head. If you want to train your mind until it takes over everything you think and remember and want to forget. If you want to become more sensitive to pain. If you plan to work with your head.

– And if all you'd ever learned in life was how to milk cows or boil potatoes for pigs?

– Then lying would be just as bad, and guilt, and responsibility toward other people. But your memory would be less sharp—life would be easier, I think. Like Benn says, "To be stupid and have a job / that's . . ."—sounds good to me. There's no one else in the world I'd admit it to, Marie.

– If you'd stayed in Jerichow you would've gotten married in St. Peter's, three marks for the wedding decorations, four marks for choir and organ music, without the painful singing.

– The grain of truth in that is that I'd like to be buried there. If you can get the town to open up the old cemetery one more time. It doesn't need to be my own grave; Jakob's is fine with me.

– Because the earth never passes away.

– Right. Because I'm superstitious. Official statement from the earth of today, thirty thousand feet over Chicago.

– You'll have to give that to Dr. Josephberg in writing. Because if we crash, we'll die together.

– I hope so.

– D. E. will take care of it for us.

– D. E. can cook, D. E. can bake / and the day after tomorrow / the child he'll take. *And there will be / an end of me.*

– *Of him*, Gesine. Rumpelstiltskin.

– Saying goodbye in 1952 was like the first time, in 1944. Cresspahl took his daughter to the front door, leaned against the frame, said his last words to her. *Make sure ya wear yer scarf.* As if I was only going to Gustav

Adolf Middle School in Gneez, not Martin Luther University in Halle, on the Saale River. *Just tha he was smokin like a littl man bakes.*

– But my grandfather was tall!

– *The littl man*—in Mecklenburg, that meant the poor man. He heats his stove with brushwood, which "smokes like a chimney." The richer people used beech logs, which give off a fine, even smoke.

– Ah, when someone's about to lose something.

– He chain-smokes.

– Now tell me your dowry.

– My dowry was a rented room in Halle, on the moat, five minutes walk to the Saale—Jakob had arranged that for me. They sure do get around, those railwaymen. A wooden chest with a compass-rose carved on the lid was delivered there: Herr Heinrich Cresspahl, Master Carpenter (ret.), Jerichow had equipped his daughter for a life on the Saale with a winter suit, two new summer dresses (Rawehn, Fine Apparel, Gneez Market). Dr. Julius Kliefoth had contributed: FEHR, *English Literature of the Nineteenth and Twentieth Centuries: With an Introduction to English Early-Romanticism*; KELLER and FEHR, *English Literature from the Renaissance to the Enlightenment*; WÜLKER, *A History of English Literature from the Earliest Times to the Present*; the *Columbia Encyclopedia* of 1950; a MURET-SANDERS bilingual dictionary from 1933. From Jakob's mother: a bible, with an inscription on the flyleaf: 1947, acquired for a hare; God Bless G. C. away from home. There was also a bank account at the postal check office, Halle/Saale.

– That's pretty bold, having your scholarship money delivered by the state.

– No scholarship money for me—I was from the Reactionary Middle Class.

– But your father paid taxes! And you'd served the state's youth group with flying colors!

– For Cresspahl, the state was someone he didn't have a contract with, but it had power over his labor. He didn't want any help with his daughter's tuition or expenses from them. Sent her 150 marks a month, thirty less than children with proletariat pedigrees could pick up from the dean of student affairs, 8–9 University Place.

– That would've made me mad.

– I was fine, Marie. I could buy butter.

– Mad at the government, I mean.

– Please step back from the platform edge! At a moment's notice I could lose the offerings from the Department of English Language and Literature (6), fall semester, September 22 through December 19, 1952:

History of American English;

Modern English Syntax, with seminar;

English Conversation Practice;

Hist. of Eng. Lit. under Industrial and Monopoly Capitalism, with seminar;

Hist. of Am. Lit. under Imperialism;

and to get all that, Lib. Arts Stud. Cresspahl showed up bright-eyed and bushy-tailed to the mandatory classes in Russian, pedagogy, and political economy; wrote up neat and tidy in social sciences that Trotsky, in his vanity, had once offered to die for the Revolution as long as three million party members watched him do it. When the Communist Party of France gave the university a banner showing Picasso's dove of peace (third version), this student voiced no objection, she clapped along with everyone else at the ceremony—and even if she'd been enrolled in biology, she wouldn't have said that doves are nasty creatures that destroy one another's nests and that any house they choose as a nesting site is soon sorry.

– Such a quiet child. That must've stood out.

– The Cresspahl child had learned from her friends Pagenkopf and Lockenvitz. If she had to walk a tightrope, she'd make sure there was a net underneath. When asked for one of the most important sentences in American literature, she obediently recited what J. Lincoln Steffens (1866 to 1936) had said about his visits to the Soviet Union:

I have been over into the future, and it works;

and if you also knew and could produce on request that the English called a *Kommode* a *chest of drawers*, not a *commode*, you were in good shape. She'd learned her other insurance policy from Pius: societal activities. At Martin Luther University it was enough at first to sign up for a swim class in lifesaving. She swam fifty meters underwater in heavy clothes and with a weighted backpack, turning to come up for air; how could anyone spying on her guess that this was to make up for the disgusting shower on Moat Street that she could use only once a week? A student like her, who needs to squeeze in an additional fifteen hours a week just for English, has no time to hold office with the young German free. And if she's offered one, then she's seven steps ahead now that she has an upper-level swimming certificate to show them—she spends two hours a week going to a club that the interior ministry founded in August 1952 to teach young people telegraphy and marksmanship.

– No, you're lying, Gesine!

– Pius Pagenkopf's decision-making power as commander of an armed aircraft was now to be his friend's, too, with the help of a small-caliber rifle. She thought she'd deliberate at her leisure over who she would finally aim the gun at and pull the trigger.

– You don't even have a gun license, Gesine!

– Since when do I need a piece of paper to shoot?

– You battle-ready amphibian, you!

– Envy, *my dear Mary*, is not an attractive quality—even for a bank. *Although bankers have human feelings, too.*

– I give up. I believe you.

– You're welcome. Service with a smile.

– Now something about Saxony.

– I'll tell you about three or four people in Halle. The first two considered themselves a couple and charged twenty-five marks for a furnished room in the second-best neighborhood. The woman worked for the manager of a People-Owned Business and had strayed just a titch out of her marriage into getting to know her boss better. His mood was how her day went. One time she came home and proudly reported having straightened Comrade Director's tie in the nick of time before a meeting. That wasn't how I'd pictured things in a People-Owned Business; by now I have a feeling I know what an East German executive secretary had to do to get ahead in those days. The man who was merely her lawfully wedded husband felt forgotten, neglected; he developed a habit of knocking on the door of his female sublettor, at night when possible, to discuss wives who don't understand, wives who go off to meetings and conferences past midnight. Student Cresspahl left the slopes of the Reilsberg before the second month was up and moved to a place near St. Gertrude's Cemetery in Halle. The sign on the head of streetcar No. 1 gave its destination as "Happy Future" (a street name); the house by the stop was impoverished, with one bathroom for four parties on a landing between the floors. The people living there were suspicious of the newcomer, partly because she was awkward with the local variety of German, partly because her clothes looked as if she could afford more than they could with their ration cards or coupons. The landlady made an effort—she needed the twenty marks. She washed the window, swept out the mansard that Anita recognized from a single description as "Schiller's death chamber." On January mornings the water in the lavoir was frozen. That was when I vowed to myself that if I ever had a child—

– *Thank you ever so kindly.*

– . . . that child would grow up in a room of his or her own, not sublet, with hot running water and a shower.

– I'm so happy to have you as a mother. I'll miss you so.

– *A tua disposizione, Fanta Giro.* Now should we order some champagne from this miserable airline?

– Live a little, they always say. I want my steak well done. *If you please.*

– The fourth person in Halle was of the Gabriel Manfras variety.

– Snooping out attitudes and opinions.

– My file had been transferred from the district headquarters in Gneez by then, and just as Faust wanted to learn what held the world together in its innermost core, so too did the university's party chapter want to learn Student Cresspahl's. Any lingering effects, perchance, from her father's stay in Fünfeichen concentration camp? or the failed house search last summer? The boy pretended to be a suitor, followed me around, acted surprised to happen upon his classmate at eleven at night on Peißnitz Island between the "natural" Saale and the "shipping" Saale, and oops, he'd given himself away by waiting on the Bridge of Friendship. He soon gave himself away for real, letting slip things about Gneez and Jerichow that an ordinary person living outside of Mecklenburg would hardly know. His victim acted innocent, though, and with plausible pauses and hesitations told him the stories that were no doubt already in her file and that he'd been briefed on. He was a fan of the dialectical principle that any fact, even the abolition of the name Nightingale Island, must be seen in the light of *cui bono*

– We've had that! I know that one: "for whose benefit?"!

– so that "your fact" has now been transformed, or extinguished. He also wanted to make out. He'd probably managed to sweet-talk his way into a girl's bed once. The way men go on about my breasts—praising them as if I had anything to do with it! As if I could take them off and put them on!

– Not to mention the prettiest legs on the whole number 5 bus north of Seventy-Second Street.

– *Grazie tanto*, you American. I like it better when people look me in the face; that wasn't easy for our little stool pigeon. He thought he was on his way to a complimentary fling; I kept him around to go places with me like a big dog, and it cost him, or rather the ministry's "reptile fund," quite a chunk of money. I wouldn't go with him to the dance hall on Thälmann Square—the Tusculum, free admission, free feeling-up—but he could make things up to me with an invitation to the Golden Rose on Rannisch Street or old Café Zorn on Leipzig Street, now renamed after Klement Gottwald for geographic reasons. He might have thought he was in the home stretch when I watched his slim wrists gracefully twisting and turning as he spoke, which he clearly was well aware of as one of his good points. He tried to get his future lover drunk and trip her up with a more incriminating fact than that she'd also have liked to study Romance Languages; by the time she admitted, with reservations, that she considered a double major to be a "bourgeois remnant," Grün's Wine Cellar at the city hall had gotten the price of two bottles of Beaujolais out of him and the girl was still sober. She'd graduated from Cresspahl's school, which taught that a slug of Richtenberg aquavit was medicine; she'd celebrated New Year's Eve with Jakob at the Linden Pub in Gneez, where the unit of measure was a double shot of vodka—and she wasn't going to tell a young agent in Saxony that she'd smacked the cap off a Red Army soldier's head that same night, supposedly by mistake, but intentionally, as a sign of discontent with his outfit's post in the Countess Woods, *izvinite, pozhaluysta!* When my second semester started, I was especially precious to this young man, having come back from mysterious Mecklenburg still on the fence about when to become his—then I ended our little game of spying via propositioning.

– Too bad. I was kind of enjoying that. Still, he doesn't deserve a name.

– Let him go to . . . Really Existing Socialism! And he got there with an invitation to Frau von Carayon's salon on Behren Street, aka Ludwig Wucherer Street in Halle, where older students behind splendid late-nineteenth-century facades discussed aspects of Diamat—Dialectical Materialism —that left them unfulfilled. Maybe Jean-Paul Sartre's investigation into nothingness and being, *Das Sein und das Nichts*, Hamburg, 1952. Undergraduate Cresspahl knew these men from sharing study tables at the university library; they said hello when they saw her, with a certain scornful acknowledgment, and now she was out to get them. For the snooper's sake, she started objecting to the rule that a female guest was welcome in these gatherings only when a male one vouched for her loyalty and discretion; now he had another reason to admire her, as a pioneering fighter for women's emancipation. Now she got scared and called in reinforcements.

– I know that one! In Platt, from you: *My big brother, he's got nails on is shoes.*

– Jakob showed up in the city of Halle on the Saale in a German Reich Railway Sunday uniform, a star or two on his epaulettes, and patiently took *his lil sister* around from one student hangout to the next until she found her handler and pointed him out. While I put on an untroubled smile, Jakob went over to him and played a few bars; on Sunday morning, when we strolled to Pottel & Broskowsky on Orphanage Ring, a middle-class restaurant and wine bar with neat clean tablecloths and silver cutlery, the snitch stared right past us—his expense account wouldn't cover that. It was probably dawning on him that his victim wasn't as defenseless as he thought; this dish was spicier than he'd be able to finish. He no longer aspired to scale my upper arms in darkened projection rooms. The smile was stiff on his face. Lib. Arts Stud. Cresspahl could act like she'd forgotten him.

– What I wouldn't give to know what Jakob told him!

– I'm afraid I was curious too, unfortunately...

– It's not curiosity, it's just that I always want to know everything.

– Marie, your father always felt that a man does what he knows he needs to do and makes sure he gets it done, but he didn't feel the need to tell a young woman about it.

– Even if she's grown up with him, twice, like a sister.

– What do you think he said?

– "I have a criminal record, sir. Grievous bodily harm."

– Such big guns for a two-bit kid? When I asked Jakob what he'd said, he remembered what it was and smiled—but he was smiling at me too, with a slight note of warning, as if wanting to keep me from unbecoming behavior. With Jakob I was always the younger one. He decided to celebrate with a morning at Pottel & Broskowsky, Cresspahl's Gesine all to himself

—she should conduct a privatissimum on one Professor Ertzenberger and how amusing he found the pronunciation of a certain first-semester student from Mecklenburg. Professor Ertzenberger had left for a university in western Germany after January 12, when Great Comrade Stalin discovered, brought to light, and crushed a conspiracy of Jewish doctors in his very own city of Moscow. After colleagues in the halls of a university in Halle stopped speaking to him.

– I'd leave a country like that too. What I wouldn't give to know why Jakob stayed!

– You and me both. Maybe it was because he'd promised to work for the German Reich Railway—someone had to do it.

– But you were already thinking about leaving the East.

– That's what you think because you know what happened later. There were so many things that started the process, I remember only the first one: I told Jakob and he nodded, even though we were sitting under a roof with no holes, tended by gentlemen in long white aprons under their tailcoats, duck on our plates and wine in a bucket of ice. He asked me to think it over for three months.

– Think what over? Whether to leave Halle on the Saale?

– That part was easy—by the time I left I'd known that for six months. I knew which spires and towers were people's favorites there; that they think a little square called Reileck is the best in the world; I'd learned to understand their language. But I avoided walks that went by Robert Franz Ring (they like Rings there instead of Streets), because the Saxony-Anhalt Ministerium für Staatssicherheit was located there. Penitentiary Halle I —the "Red Ox"—was at 20 Church Gate. I now knew that right around the corner from Grün's Wine Cellar was Halle II prison; unfortunately I had places I needed to go on Short Stein Street between the polyclinic and the main post office. How would you feel slinking to the Paulus Quarter to stick an unsigned note under the door of an apartment on Ludwig Wucherer Street that says that someone wants to have confidential discussions of existentialism and can smile and smile and be a snitch!

– So they didn't need you there, and you left. We're over Omaha, Nebraska.

– Also, since May 1952 there was reason to think that the custodian, Sachwalter Walter, might close the borders. That was when the Stasi took over guarding the border. They drew a patrol strip ten meters wide along the demarcation line, plus a third-of-a-mile no-mans'-land, *plus* a three-mile restricted zone, from which they resettled anyone they knew to be unreliable: merchants, innkeepers, craftsmen, major farmers. You know, the ones the government had attacked with taxes and fines, making itself unpopular. The trap was shut right then.

– Volunteer soldiers like that must realize they'll have to move in on their neighbors?

– A kid who's grown up in the countryside, seeing backbreaking work all around him, usually for other people, with no hope of getting anything for himself—the recruiters for the Armed Police just promise him a decent uniform, better food than the farmhands get, light duty, and financial support for a whole long life and he's more than happy to sign up. An apprentice in the city, tired of endless grinding and scraping, maybe tired of work altogether, signs up for a fixed term because then he too gets a ration card with more coupons and a housing permit. (Conscience doesn't stand a chance against material incentives —ANITA.) Anyway, an experienced head of state will know to deploy his Thuringian recruits in Saxony, the Saxon ones in Mecklenburg. By the way, no more state of Mecklenburg.

– What? You're kidding me, Gesine.

– There was a Law for the Further Democratization of the Structure and Function of Government Institutions in the States of the GDR—July 23, 1952. You were only allowed to say "Mecklenburg" in a linguistic or anthropological sense. Otherwise it was now three regions: Rostock, Schwerin, and New Brandenburg; the state parliament and state government were transferred there. They picked up a piece of West Prignitz in the south, and Uckermark in the east. But since the law abolishing the states referred to the states, the regional legislatures kept electing representatives to the state senates until 1958, who had to keep showing up and declaring that they had no objections to the law of summer 1952.

– Are you sad about the end of the Blue, Yellow, and Red?

– I miss the blue, because Rostock's golden griffin looked so good against it. I miss the red and gold, for Schwerin. The red of the tongue in the black buffalo head for the Wendish lands. Another piece of one's origins wiped out.

– And you left Mecklenburg because the workers and peasants later rose up against the government of the workers and peasants.

   – These stirring words, Marie!

   – That's what they teach us in school.

   – American schools tell you that as the first and most important thing to know about Socialism so that you'll ignore the Negro uprisings from Watts to Newark!

   – Gesine, you said not till October.

   – Sowwy. The Gesine Cresspahl of back then didn't know a single worker well.

   – Excuse me, there was *one*.

   – Two, actually; because of one mistake. In May 1953, Lib. Arts Stud. Cresspahl was actually short of money, and had forgotten to get a free train ticket from Jakob, and wanted to discuss something with Anita. To save some money she took the train just to Schkeuditz and then stood on the autobahn cloverleaf between Leipzig and Halle, book bag under her left arm, right arm raised and waving. That lasted one and a half hours. Most of the drivers in the West German cars flicked their brights, which meant "Sorry!" because picking up passengers in the transit zone could get them in trouble with the People's Police. Round flashes of lightning, brighter than the morning sun. The people who eventually did stop for a demoralized undergraduate were two beefy guys moving furniture from Saxon Vogtland for some POB; they were pleased with the company and kept their guest quiet by repeatedly trading stories featuring ladies waiting at night by the side of the road prepared to remunerate their free ride in various positions on the bench behind the driver, at which point he almost steered the unwieldy truck into a ditch from sheer anticipation. On Frankfurter Allee in Berlin, which had been rebuilt in honor of Great Comrade Stalin, they turned on the girl they had, until she forked over twenty marks, more than the train would've cost. Good-natured threats of being prepared to get rough.

   – How sleazy.

   – Only fair, if you ask me: a lesson on the community of interests between workers in the transportation industries and students between Halle and Leipzig. It's true that that was the very year when a compass, representing "technical intelligentsia," was added to the hammer and ring of grain on the East German national emblem; that wouldn't have stopped the two

Vogtland guys from being just as ready to kidnap and extort money out of an engineering student. Anyway, we were—

– "We"?

– Anita and her Mecklenburg friend were constantly amazed at what the workers in East Germany put up with: changes to the collective labor contract in January 1953, namely the addition of "Socialist content," which meant raising the work norms, which to wage earners meant a slow decline in the amount of food they could buy for their money. The custodian wanted to take back the higher wages he'd decreed the previous summer; excess purchasing power gave him a hard time, since he'd opposed things like the primacy of consumer-goods industries on "scientific" grounds and now had too few shoes and pots to put on the market; because the party is not a human being, the party is always right.

– You knew Eckart Pingel's father in Gneez.

– Ol' Pingel would have greeted Undergraduate Cresspahl with a quick wink, meaning the cheerful, amused question: So, Gesine, you here too? He'd have taken his cap off before shaking hands and starting a conversation. If I'd asked him about the engineering work quotas courtesy of the Soviet Union, he'd have sidestepped the question as overly intrusive. Because around then, when Eckart Pingel had practically run away from school ("because he told the truth"), his father saw anyone allowed to go to college in the New State as one of its minions—an ally of the authorities.

– You knew farmers.

– Not many. After the war, the nobility's estates near Jerichow were given away to settlers (except for the von Plessens', to the south, and a much smaller one, formerly the Kleineschultes', on the Baltic; the Red Army kept those two to handle their own supply of meat, flour, butter). (And a third one, the Upper Bülows', taken over in one piece as a people-owned farm under contract with the Wismar city hospitals.) Not many of the people who'd taken over five- to ten-acre plots of land in 1946 were farmworkers from the old days—who understood the business and knew better than to try to make it with less than twenty-five. There was one single village with only peasant farmers, since the fourteenth century. Traffic sprang up there in the black-market days, so the Cresspahl house got some potatoes for the cellar: but it was Jakob who took care of that until 1950, by which time Cresspahl had

relearned how to go for walks around the countryside. The Cresspahl child
had been going to school in the city of Gneez since 1944, and recently even
farther afield. She didn't know any farmers. She'd taken a detour on her
bike at Dr. Kliefoth's request, once, through Pötenitz and Old Demwies;
she reported back on empty farms abandoned by their settlers when the
custodian, after only six years, tried to take his gift back by converting the
farms into Agricultural Production Cooperatives. (*Now we know!*) She'd
heard unwatered, unmilked cows bellowing in pain; she was cured of the
superstition that no Mecklenburg farmer would ever leave a head of cattle
without food and supervision for a single night. Didn't know any farmers.

– Georg Utpathel.

– He ended up in the usual way, but at least he'd been in jail a long time;
he could make himself feel better, tell himself he'd lost his farm to the law.
Wait, I knew one farmer!

– Johnny Schlegel.

– He was one of the exceptions. An educated man, with opinions about
how they'd run agricultural communes in the Weimar era. According to
one of these opinions, a proletarian working the fields, even if granted
(bribed with) a cottage and garden plot and grain allowance, would never
consider his labor his own—it only went to maintain and increase the
landowner's or leaseholder's property. Under the scourge of Hitler's and
Darré's agricultural laws, Schlegel had to work his three hundred acres in
the old feudal way; now that they'd lost their war, at home and abroad,
he'd handed out his inheritance in ninths to refugees from the lost eastern
territories, as long as they were farmers or willing to learn to be. For each
of these gifts, nominally loans, he'd entered an invented amount of money
in his farm's books and at the land registry; he operated an agricultural
commune on his own terms under the protection of his friends in the Red
Army. Even in 1951, an inspector from a people-owned land purchasing
and incorporation business wouldn't scare him off the road. Then came
the East German government's scientific recognition that a Socialist agriculture meant large-scale farms; then came their shock that in 1952 some
people on the Baltic near Jerichow had long since been working in a cooperative advanced far past Socialist Type III, in which only the collective
use of the land, draft animals, vehicles, and tools was supposed to have
been socialistically introduced. At Johnny's farm, household tasks were

done in common by all the members too—the food cooked in one kitchen, meals eaten at one table. The fictitious sums of money had now turned into the kind with which Mrs. von Alvensleben could be bought out for her share when her children asked her to join them abroad to fulfill a grandmother's duties; that money came right back when Mrs. Sünderhauf brought her brother over from the West, where he'd had to work underground, mining in the Ruhr. Assessed as farmers with midsized holdings, the members of Johnny's project were required to deliver quotas several times higher than what was due from the settlers and small landholders: eight double centners of wheat per hectare instead of two, seventy-five of potatoes instead of twenty-five, fifty-nine of meat instead of thirty-eight; and still, as late as the end of 1952, they were in good enough shape that Johnny could reply to a worried visitor: like this!

– Gesine! How can you bend your elbow and make a fist in an American airplane?!

– This is an international flight. *Io sono di Ierico.*

– You gave the old man across the aisle such a start! He knows what that gesture means.

– *Vi forstår desværre ikke amerikansk, kære frøken.*

– And now you'll say something like: Envy is an unpleasant trait even in a Socialist administration? *Socialist rulers have human feelings, too?*

– How can you even think such a thing! No, they longed to learn what held Johnny's world together/in its innermost core; the quota experts carried out an in-depth investigation. The 1952 harvest had been so-so, the Schlegel collective had fallen behind on milk; the collection officers magnanimously and per regulations gave him permission to deliver pork instead, and if that meant he was short of his pork quota, he could deliver *that* in beef instead.

– That means he'd get even less milk in his buckets!

– No, he was allowed to keep his pledged cow in his own stall—he just had to pay for it.

– For his own cow?

– At quadruple the price. If he'd actually handed it over for his quota, only the 1941 fixed price would have been credited to him.

– I'd make mistakes in my books, too, with all these twists and turns.

– Johnny's books were perfectly exact and complete. Alas for him. Now the tax inspectors could decode from regular "withdrawals" that Johnny, in fall 1947, had gotten from the von Maltzahns a wedge of land that had been bothering him for fifteen years—a few acres—and he had paid the money for it into their foreign account in Schleswig-Holstein via West Berlin. Private foreign-currency transactions.

– Arrest?

– In February 1953.

– Ah-hah! said the judge. Very bad.

– Excellent: thought the judge. And Otto Sünderhauf had exchanged the money for his share in Frankfurt, where he only had to put down twenty-three Western marks to get one hundred Eastern ones. The criminal exchange rate of the imperialists.

– Supply and demand.

– And thus the defendants were found guilty of being profoundly arrested in capitalist ways of thinking.

– That makes two!

– That made four. After Sünderhauf, Mrs. Bliemeister and Mrs. Lakenmacher were brought in for questioning. It turns out Johnny's collective followed a different plan than the one they'd handed into the authorities in duplicate, triplicate, and more. In that plan, provision was made for the death of young animals.

– Gesine!

– You think it's only babies who die prematurely? A calf can catch cold and die of pneumonia too.

– That's what doctors are for.

– Out of the five veterinarians in Gneez, three had "made their way West" by that point, Dr. Hauschildt in the lead as always. When Johnny factored into his calculations his own knowledge of veterinary medicine and what expert assistance would have cost, a certain amount of lost headcount was to be expected. And the state—the same state the veterinarians were fleeing—turned this into accusing Johnny of slander. Economic criminality. Incitement to Boycott. And when Johnny, in his closing statement, wanted to know why the court was tearing asunder what the *Krasnaya Armiya* had sewn together for him: that was breaking the Law for the Protection of Peace.

– *They threw the book at him.*

– Fifteen years in prison. For the other defendants: eight to twelve. Confiscation of property. By April, Johnny's cooperative had been cleaned out. The members had hightailed it to the refugee camps in West Berlin, with all their children. Inge Schlegel stayed a while longer; she wanted to try to save the house at least, and someone had to take care of Axel Ohr, send him his packages in prison. Now it was clear where Johnny had miscalculated: she needed him there. If a woman alone is trying to keep a large farm in working order, it's going to have sagging doors and holes in the roof after a month. She'd been left with a single horse: *Jakob sin Voss*, the sorrel. Once the horse had been shot, she left. That's a story . . . like the one about little children falling into a rain barrel.

– Well, I have to learn to be brave. Tell me.

– Don't ask, Marie.

– I'm eleven years old already!

– You'll be sorry.

– It's on me.

– Jakob's sorrel was listed in the books as one midsize workhorse. That requires, per year:

    10 double centners of hay,

    16 d.c. straw,

    20 d.c. turnips,

    18 d.c. grain feed,

    and 30 d.c. green fodder,

some of which it can forage from the fields on its own. Now if you figure that a centner of oats cost twenty-five marks in 1953 . . .

– then a horse like that will break Undergraduate Cresspahl's budget.

– The spring semester of 1953 ended on May 9; by that Monday I was visiting Inge Schlegel. She held me by the shoulder when *Jakob sin Voss* was led past us; I followed him into the large fodder-preparation kitchen. The man holding the lead turned around with a goofy grin on his face, like he was inviting me to come watch a show, a surprise. The horse walked cheerfully along, with friendly nods at the guy's encouraging patter. A few ribs were showing; he was totally healthy. His looks said: you did let me go hungry for a while, you humans, but now you're taking care of me again, I'm glad we're back on good terms. When the bolt gun was placed on his forehead, he trustingly closed his eyes; this was a new one from the humans.

After his death, knocked onto his side, his legs jerked violently, every which way, and kept beating against the echoing floorboards. It looked like painful agony; from a scientific point of view it was just residual functioning of the nervous system. The sweet-tempered animal *Jakob sin Voss* had suddenly turned into a disgusting piece of meat wrapped in blond fur; still recognizably him, from the open eyes.

– Gesine! You didn't wait outside the door?

– How could I know that the stranger was a butcher from Gneez! I saw his two assistants with the knife too late.

– The next time I brag about how old I am, Gesine, just put a stop to it then and there. Give me a slap in the face if you have to.

– We are now over Salt Lake City, Utah.

– You'd had enough.

– I still had to watch Elise Bock's bedroom furniture being auctioned off in Gneez—it was People's Property once Elise moved to West Berlin. People crowding and pushing in a narrow, dirty yard outside the open shutters of Elise's windows; a man in a threadbare suit inside, with the Unity Party emblem on his lapel, holding up photographs for the gathered crowd: a chair, the lamps. The bidders, Alfred Fretwust in the lead, hooted their humorous comments like a bunch of kids, or drunks. That was when my leaving started.

– Were you legally adult?

– Under East German law. Cresspahl and Jakob's mother stayed up a whole night with me, listening. I was scaring an old woman. Cresspahl hoped the child would reconsider. He said something about recuperating and feeling better. "A vacation at Anita's."

– And Jakob?

– Jakob gave Undergraduate Cresspahl a free ticket to Halle University, not via Stendal but for the route Gneez–Güstrow–Pritzwalk–Berlin. But the child at border control, without complete papers, under suspicion, liable to end up behind bars! He prevented that. And he'd realized that in June the mornings are bright, the sunlight dances in the woods, the lakes near Krakow and Plau glitter—that was to be her farewell sight. Only when the conductor gave her back her ticket with its brown horizontal stripe and the Reich Railway stamp, like a coworker, did she realize: Jakob had given her a round-trip ticket.

– *Welcome to San Francisco, Gesine!*

And what are the Chinese doing in SF?
Some of them are standing around glumly in a shooting gallery where you aim a BB gun at moving targets. They see a European tourist and her American child exchange words in a foreign language. The lady walks up, takes a rifle, and in ten shots has won an alarm clock, the grand prize. They clap, unenvious, these spectators. That's what the Chinese are doing in S.F.

August 16, 1968   Friday
Trying to find today's *New York Times* in New Orleans is like *chercher une aiguille dans une botte de foin*; a copy turns up like something exotic in a bodega on Canal Street offering mostly products of the foreign press, and is sold with a ten-cent surcharge—air freight. The only news for us: yesterday there was a fire in New York. At shortly past noon a midsized fire stripped bare the Rockaway Parkway elevated subway platform: exactly where we spent Tuesday with Jakob's letter from Olomouc, ČSSR. Marie asked for the page with the photo of the site, despite the resulting increase in the weight of our luggage, in preparation for a discussion of coincidence with D. E.; – for when we're back home.

Marie can't get enough of the Chinese of San Francisco—their sympathetic way of watching the yellow- and black- and pink-skinned people dealing with one another on the sidewalks and in the cable cars, making room for people according to fragility and age, in solidarity. Maybe also because they remind Marie of a Sunday walk in New York in July with D. E., where a dark-skinned fellow citizen was lying on a wall along Riverside Park with his eyes closed, a wall with a fifty-foot drop; asleep and trusting the sun. – That's all we've managed in our city!: concludes a shamed and disappointed child.

What with her delight in the boats of Fisherman's Wharf it's easy to miss a bus, even a taxi, to the San Francisco Airport; she approved our suggestion that we make the trip triangular. When a young lady in the company of an older one marches past a liveried hotel porter with no luggage except a ticking package, the house is honored to put them up for the night: *if* we act like we do this every day, like D. E.!: the child cries, looking forward to seeing him again.

Marie brings up Professor Erichson, who has departed this life in a northeastern part of Europe, once again when she praises her mother for rebooking a plane reservation: the way he's taught us to do it!: she declares. She carefully observes New Orleans for him, hoping he's never been there and she'll be able to tell him that you get out of that airport only in a six-seater limousine whose driver takes his last two passengers, unasked, to a family-run hotel between Canal Street and the Mississippi and drops them off at a narrow staircase with the shout: *Folks*, I'm bringin you some'un! And again a reception clerk was amazed when we actually copied a passport number into the register!

As long as we're irrevocably booked for a return flight to New York tomorrow morning, she's willing to accept a city on the Mississippi. The river does seem yellow to her, dirty; its harbor ferry is a poor substitute for the one in her city. The balconies in the Vieux Carré, the wrought-iron ornamental grilles outside the inner courtyards with magnolia trees inside, long shiny leaves and pinkish white flowers—she looks upon all of that as a quotation from the Europe looming on Tuesday and not a moment too late; she doesn't complain but she does mention the heavy hot humidity, the cool musty odor, – like a cemetery: she now finds it, making Mrs. Cresspahl shudder in anticipation of a discussion of coincidence, since now it will be expanded to include the topic of premonitions. What earned the city points for Marie was a big turn-of-the-century hospital, from which emerged dignified dark-complexioned fellow Americans, looking concerned. The newspapers printed on yellow and lavender paper—she likes that just for the variety. The unused areas in the restaurants are dirty, in her view; only the front halves of the grills are shiny, unlike in New York, where the whole surfaces are polished. Some streets near Canal Street are so poor and rundown that Mrs. Cresspahl, too, wonders how a person gets here— surely not by plane. In a luncheonette, Marie liked the cat longingly eyeing her double-decker sandwich.

On June 9, 1953, the custodian of the East German Republic made a few suggestions to his citizen Gesine Cresspahl, with respect to her possible return into his clutches.

His party, he said, intended to disclaim one of its virtues of the nonhuman type: infallibility. It had, in fact, committed errors. One consequence of which was that numerous persons had left the Republic. This applies to you, Miss Cresspahl!

Since the party had gone so far as to reset the scales to zero with Peter Wulff, as promised—"to zero grams!" as it liked to say in its zeal—it planned to go so far as to allow him to reopen the grocery store adjacent to his pub. It intended to supply him with goods to sell, even. And no need to worry, for now, about the taxes and social security deductions not paid since 1951. An end to repressive measures, Mr. Wulff!

Now as for the others near and dear to you in the Republic, Miss Cresspahl. Ever striving to stay true to our principles, we have converted a cooperative farm on the Baltic near Jerichow to "Devastated" status, so that no receiver would want to touch it with a ten-foot pole, and if Mrs. Sünderhauf, Mr. Leutnant, Mrs. Schurig, Mrs. Winse and all the children—*The Englishmin*, Epi, Jesus, Hen and Chickee, and the others under eighteen—cared to return to Johnny's agricultural endeavor they would get their property back along with aid in the form of credit and inventory. How do you like that, Gesine Cresspahl.

We plan in earnest to send your Georg Utpathel home from custody along with all the other people sentenced to just three years under the Law for the Protection of the People's Property. We would prefer to keep the ones we've convicted of graver crimes, such as Johnny Schlegel, notorious atheist and enemy of the nobility. But maybe not Otto Sünderhauf, let's talk.

The last time you paid a visit to Wendisch Burg you were mad at us for having harassed a girl by the name of E. Rehfelde over her Protestant faith and adherence to the Church; we'd persisted until Klaus Niebuhr and his girlfriend Ingrid Babendererde renounced their graduations too and left the country, obviously thinking that this would preserve their equality under the constitution. Well, Rehfelde is to be readmitted. If Students Niebuhr and Babendererde decide to return to Wendisch Burg, they too will be permitted to make up their final exams. What do you say to that?

And as for you, Lib. Arts Stud. Cresspahl. We made an exception in your case when we let you go to university, but in future this will be our general policy for talented young people from the middle classes. Once we no longer consider that a handicap, Miss Cresspahl, you might even get a scholarship.

Regarding your father, too, would you mind taking into account the following couple of concessions. The additional food cost we imposed in April will be abolished as of June 15—that's this Monday. We will also inform Jerichow City Hall that Mr. Heinrich Cresspahl, Brickworks Road, is again entitled to coupons for rationed articles, effective immediately.

So now tell us what you think, young lady. Just come back—we'll act as if you've just been on vacation. If we have already confiscated any of your belongings, we'll give them back. Or make restitution. Ration cards, German ID—it'll all be yours. Please come, Miss Cresspahl, and bring your friend Anita too!

These were some of the suggestions that the East German custodian's Socialist Unity Party made to Cresspahl's daughter in the event of her return.

You spent the summer months of 1953 in the Grunewald neighborhood of West Berlin, Miss Cresspahl?

As you already know, apparently.

In a mansion in Grunewald?

In a house in ruins from the second floor up.

Would you care to tell us the name of the street?

Forgot it.

The name of your host?

I don't recall.

The circumstances behind your connection to this household?

You know already. A dog named Rex. Or King. Or Voshd, whatever you want to call him.

What can a dog born in 1933 have to do with anything twenty years later?

I saw him again before he died. A stubborn patriarch of a German shepherd, gray-black all over. When he went outside he didn't seem blind. A hundred and twenty-six in human years.

And that was why you were in Berlin no later than 1951 to obtain carpentry tools by the criminal conversion of Western currency?

I was seeing a family friend.

Friends because you shared the presence of a dog in your family photos? Or because of business relations in 1944, 1947, 1949, and 1951?

No comment.
Someone gives you a room and breakfast and a house key and pocket money
all because of fond memories of Cresspahl?
Strange but true.
We're supposed to believe that, coming from you?
Take it or leave it.

Anita worked for department stores and ad agencies over the holidays, addressing envelopes, one half West pfennig each, until she found people who would offer her one mark per page for translations from Russian. (Let us refrain from discussing those bastards; we will say: they wanted the work done for the Department of Cultural Cooperation at the French Army headquarters, West Berlin. That'll have to do.) We had a standing arrangement to meet at Nikolassee streetcar station for Wannsee Beach whenever Anita had time. We had to keep our eyes peeled "for the less expensive pastimes"; we were too poor for movies or plays. Again and again, whether we were swimming the Havel from north to south or I was spending the night at Anita's room in Neukölln on Mrs. Machate's ironing board, she would be surprised to hear the latest argument her friend Cresspahl had dreamed up to give her a reasonable path back to Jerichow or Martin Luther University. One time it was that she'd remembered the news that in April all the Jewish doctors Stalin had accused of a plot against the Soviet Union had been released and fully rehabilitated, professionally and civically. Mightn't one draw a line from that straight to an eventual rule of law in the East German republic?

– Tell that to the two who died under torture, Kogan and Etlinger!: Anita said. – Tell it to the Jewish writers who that bloodthirsty killer had shot just last summer!: Anita said.

Stalin had died on March 6: Cresspahl offered.

And how did you feel when the East German newsreels in Halle showed the funerals from Moscow and the East German ceremonies with their lowered flags and inconsolable music?

Cresspahl admitted that the sight had caused in her, too, a creeping nausea.

So the passing of Stalin, which fills all progressive humankind with deepest sorrow, is an especially heavy loss for the German nation? The

Socialist Unity Party will remain forever true to Stalin's victorious teachings? Forever?

That was what they'd promised: Anita's friend admitted.

And now Anita could have said: See? But she didn't give advice; she was helpful, she reviewed the vacillating Cresspahl child's papers and checked them for anything missing, anything invalid. – Technically you'd be safe on a trip to Halle anytime until September 10: she concluded, exhaling deeply—it was practically a sigh. Anita and the freedom of a Christian.

Lib. Arts Stud. Cresspahl spent June 16 on the Havel; on the 17th, as she was going to check with her own eyes the radio reports of an uprising in the Eastern sector of the city, the streetcar she was on, line 88, was stopped at Lützow Street, where it normally crosses Potsdamer Street and runs to Kreuzberg along the border to the Eastern sector—by West Berlin police who were trying in vain to move the curious off to the south, one by one. (She wasn't cocky enough to attempt a streetcar ride into East Berlin itself; the station patrols could easily pack her off to Halle on the Saale sooner than she wanted to go.) And so she experienced the uprising only as news, in words and pictures, and as hearsay from students who made it from Halle into the refugee camps in West Berlin:

Two or three hundred women stood outside Penitentiary II on Stein Street, shouting: Let our husbands out! A column of striking workers from the Buna and Leuna plants who were marching up saw this and stormed the gate, taking the prisoners out of their cells, many of them women and in bad physical shape. The workers cleared out the court building. A female warden waved her pistol around, was beaten up. The Unity Party's headquarters on Willi Lohmann Street, the district headquarters at Stein Gate, the headquarters on the market square: stormed. Volkspolizei were waiting at the gates of the Red Ox, by the Church Gate—guns drawn, safeties off. The crowd pushes open a side door; is fired on from the roof; disperses. Here there were apparently people wounded. The main post office remained in police hands until morning. At around six p.m., about thirty thousand people are gathered on Hallmarkt. The speakers' demands: General strike against the government; loyalty to the Red Army. Discipline. Punishment for hoarding, looting, killing. Dissolving the government. Free elections. Reunification with West Germany. Around seven p.m., Russian tanks come rolling from Obermarkt; cautiously. Joining the pieces of paper that had already come sailing out the windows of the stormed government buildings were copies of a flier signed by the garrison commander and military commandant of the city of Halle (Saale), declaring a state of emergency, banning demonstrations and gatherings, imposing a curfew for the hours between nine p.m. and four a.m., and threatening armed force against any resistance.

There is a photograph of the striking workers, men and women, marching into Halle. It shows about ninety people in all—the women in summer dresses, the men mostly dressed as if for work, in gray or dark overalls or pants and shirts. They are in uneven rows, arms swinging, a few people waving at one another (unaware of the camera). Two people have brought luggage. There are eleven bicycles visible in the picture; why would these people have brought such expensive articles with them if they were planning to cause violence or expecting to suffer it?

On June 21, the Central Committee of the East German Unity Party gave Citizen Cresspahl one additional suggestion, for the event of her return: The uprising in its republic must be understood as merely events that happened. As the work of the American and (West-)German warmongers who, disappointed at the gains of the peace movement in Korea and Italy, wanted to throw the torch of war across the bridgehead of West Berlin ... discovered by means of bandits with weapons and secret radio transmitters being dropped from foreign aircraft ... trucks full of weapons on the Leipzig-Berlin autobahn ...

She got a letter from Gneez saying that workers at the Panzenhagen sawmill had opened the cellars under the district court, shouting: We want our exploiters back! She presumed, in all modesty, to know the workers better, even by sight, than the East German custodian, and know their complaints: the revoked discounts for train tickets, the family fights caused by reduced minimum pension rates, spa treatments now counted against annual vacations, workplaces polluted by informers, the sense of *travailler pour le Roi de Russe* as exemplified by the Unity Party's insistence on a 10 percent increase in work norms the very day before—on the morning of June 16. She would have gone back anyway, if everyone from Gneez to Halle were now allowed to say: We've seen who's in charge in this country—the Soviets. When she did decide to leave, it was hardly because the Americans were the occupiers in charge of that other Germany; it was because she was afraid of being called on in a seminar at the university by the Saale and expected to recite that on a certain date, X, it was not the workers who...

Memory offers—insists—that she arrived at the Berlin-Marienfelde refugee camp. The writer today may not be sure that it was already in operation in July 1953; the mind asserts that it was under construction starting on March 4. In any case, whether in Marienfelde, on Kuno Fischer Street, or on Karolinger Square, she there for the first time met a young man from Wendisch Burg—a skinny boy, bullheaded, with blond hair then, absently trying to strike up an acquaintance on the basis of his connection with the fisherman-Babendererdes and the teacher-Babendererdes as well as the Wendisch Burg Niebuhrs. On a stroll around Dahlem, near the West Berlin university, he observed the local students disdainfully and called them "all these beautiful young people"; she at first thought him conceited about being an upperclassman (physics). She described her amazement that Klaus Niebuhr would give up his school, his residence in Mecklenburg, all for the idea that he should renounce his citizenship to avenge an insult against a girl named Rehfelde. This Erichson (dipl. phys.) liked that; he immediately accused Miss Cresspahl of similar conduct. – For five years you accepted the gap between your thoughts and the things your schools demanded of you; now that the gap has grown just a little bigger than you'd like, you're through. Ever heard of the third principle of dialectics, the transformation of quantity into quality? You can apply it somatically too: he said in response to her excuse that she wasn't feeling well. Hardly a courtship. He let himself be flown out of Berlin before she'd even reached Preliminary Examination I in the refugee emergency admittance process.

The official questioning grew more and more repulsive from one office ("station") to the next. The medical examiner determined she was twenty years old and nothing he had to worry about. Station Two was responsible for determining responsibility. After the referral, the police, and the registration came Station Seven: preliminary examination by the Task Force Against Inhumanity. This group didn't take a liking to Undergraduate Cresspahl, nor did the next—the Investigating Committee of Free Jurists—since she blamed them for their part in the verdict against Sieboldt and Gollantz and moreover made fun of their initiatives, like the one according to which people in the "Soviet Zone" were to proclaim their resistance by boycotting movie theaters on a given Wednesday, and as a result, obviously, everyone rushed to the Renaissance Cinema in Gneez to shore up their political reputation. Here she was given reprimands, bad grades, as she realized once she got to Station 7c, Police Commissioner's Office, Section V (Political Section)—they looked at her like a bad, recalcitrant schoolgirl. For 7d, British Counterintelligence, she'd gotten Anita to brief her about the prison camp in Glowe on the island of Rügen, where around four thousand forced laborers, in exchange for bread and margarine and potato soup, slogged away at a circuit rail line around four runways for bombers and jet fighters, at a naval base for submarines and light surface craft; this was one of the rumors going around Mecklenburg. (Unfortunately for the Soviet strategy. Cresspahl was still mad about the "Red Corners" on public squares, known as Stalin's icon altars; she and Anita agreed that the Soviets had brought in their tanks on the 17th so carefully because they were only carrying reserve troops and equipment for the brutal strike should it be necessary.) Alas, the rumor was known to the British gentleman with the woolly mustache as well; he waved his pipe with regret. The recording secretary, with nine rings too many on her fingers for a woman only twenty-five years old, gazed with preemptive schadenfreude, not fellow feeling, at this girl from Mecklenburg trying to buy support for her refugee ID with such cheap coinage. The next question was about the students at the Fritz Reuter High School in Gneez who'd volunteered for service in the Armed People's Police.

The interrogatee twisted her statement away from that topic to Martin Luther University in Halle, where students in all departments could use small-rifle and radio-unit training by the banks of the Saale as a way to keep their noses clean; she then said she wasn't feeling well; she was sternly admonished to return to resume the examination.

Outside, in an offputtingly undamaged neighborhood of villas and empty sidewalks with only a maid every now and then waking a dog, she was alone with her concern that she had not much helped Prisoner Lockenvitz, and might have harmed NCO Pagenkopf. If this was the price of an official exit to West Germany, she'd rather slip through the bushes when no one was looking.

Anita found it, that path through the bushes. Did her friend Gesine know the lawyer on Lietzenburg Street who'd paid off debts in installments on behalf of Johnny Schlegel?

That was how Gesine Cresspahl came into a permit to move to the state of West Berlin; out of turn, too. She was allowed to register as a permanent resident of the Grunewald district of the city at a regular police precinct, not with Section V. Such a person with such a file has the right to a West Berlin personal ID. With a loan of a hundred and twenty West marks (the ticket alone cost over eighty), she flew in the second-to-last week in July as a private person to Frankfurt/Main, in a Douglas Clipper type 3, at night.

A person can imagine they recognize, under the wings of a DC-10 in transit from New Orleans to New York, while still over the Atlantic, the offshore island, the whitish shelf of land where Mrs. Cresspahl tried to vacation a year before. Marie, looking ahead, not down, sees the island of the Staaten General, Manhattan, Long Island.

– *Welcome home, Gesine!*

August 17, 1968 Saturday, South Ferry day

Waiting with Eagle-Eye Robinson at Riverside Drive is a single telegram. From Helsinki, of course, with the signature mangled: CANNOT CURRENTLY BE MOVED – ERISINION.

For breakfast, a telegram from Helsinki: NO NEED TO VISIT – ERISINN.

With the regular mail, an official-looking letter postmarked from Germany: from the Psychoanalytical Research Institute, Frankfurt am Main. Not counting the time in transit, the answer took less than a month. A professor taking the trouble to write three and a half pages to a bank employee named Cresspahl, on his private stationery! in his free time!

And he's never even had the pleasure of making our personal acquaintance. (As he says in all sincerity after reading our letter.) He refuses to attempt a long-distance diagnosis, due to insufficient information and too narrow a basis for judgment—nor had she wanted one. But he is willing to say: If I hear the voices of the dead, of people not present, and they answer me, it may be due to the predisposition of the person having this type of experience. Please take from my inferences only what's useful to you. There must be a firm bond between such a person and her past; there's no way she can have put it behind her. She's on the right track when she assumes that we're dealing with aftereffects of wounds, of losses; she is wrong when she thinks that it's about Jakob, or Cresspahl; in fact it started with her mother, who was "de-ranged" out of her place in this world. We're talking about you, Lisbeth née Papenbrock! Alienation, yes; delusion, no. It's just that you haven't dealt with this first rejection by the mother and put behind you (the second rejection, the third rejection). There's no risk of your passing it on hereditarily. There's just one thing that isn't right, Mrs. Cresspahl: your sometimes knowing your child Marie's answer before she says it. That can be a self-serving move, trying to protect the child and, in her, yourself—but for the child such symbiosis will soon turn dangerous, restricting her independence. You yourself described it in your letter as an illegal activity ("kept under surveillance"), and that gave you away, Mrs. Cresspahl.

"You need to have the courage—the considerable courage—to reject defense mechanisms, even though doing so cannot help but feel like negligence, given your life experiences. You would save some time if you chose to avail yourself of a, I know the word is on the tip of your tongue: a "*headshrinker.*" This metaphor really hurts you more than it hurts my American colleagues; it keeps you from making use of a medical service that could help you reach a more appropriate sense of inner security. Why not try it, it's harmless—you can break it off whenever you want. Kind regards, A. M."

What he clearly omitted: any concerns about an inability to work. Based on how I come across in a letter, I am equipped with what I need for a job abroad, in Prague.

"Dear Professor, I am somewhat ashamed to admit that I don't know how to express my..." Serves you right, Gesine Cresspahl. You asked him to do something difficult, now rack your brains over a thank-you letter. It'll take you three weeks to write it!

Over breakfast, the news from Bonn in *The New York Times*: the West Germans have thought long and hard about the treaty that they inherited, dated Sept. 29, 1938, when Chamberlain, Daladier, and Mussolini gave Hitler the Sudetenland. Hitherto this treaty had been regarded as "no longer valid." Now the people of the ČSSR might get their way and a signature under the wording: "null from the outset."

After Marshal Tito, it's now the president of Rumania paying a visit to Prague. Nicolae Ceauşescu describes how you do it: a small Communist country can totally accept credits in convertible currency as long as it remains in a military alliance such as the Warsaw Pact. If a delegate from a New York bank turns up in the capital of a small Communist country the day after the day after tomorrow, what's the problem.

– So now Undergraduate Cresspahl at a West German university: Marie requests as soon as she's done supervising the casting-off of the ferry.
– Lib. Arts Stud. G. C. at a University of... what did they call universities in West Germany?
– One was named after Johann Wolfgang von Goethe, was located in Frankfurt, and was willing to accept this rising second-year student from Halle on the Saale into the English Department. (And do you know why? Because I'd been enrolled at a university. Anita's Abitur meant nothing in West Berlin—she'd had to retake all her exams.) When I saw the tuition and fees I forgot about that.
– Your father had Western money! A few thousand pounds at the Surrey Bank of Richmond, with interest accrued since 1938!
– I'd left Cresspahl's country, left him, against his will. Just think how much more unreasonable I'll be when you leave me! He also probably thought his assets there had been confiscated as enemy property.
– Your father was trying to punish you.
– That would have meant he was trying to get his daughter back. No, she should have it her own way and live accordingly. As for academia, she'd seen through her illusions.
– Too bad, if you ask me.
– "Dr. Gesine Cresspahl"! Can you imagine?
– "Professor Cresspahl" sounds pretty good.
– Sure, "Prof. Marie Cresspahl"! You become one.
– We'll see, Gesine, won't we.
– And what kind of job can you get with a degree in English?
– Teacher.
– I'd lost all desire for that career at the Socialist high school in Gneez. Standing in front of a class knowing that you're hiding something, that the students think you're lying—no thanks.

– In a free country you could teach what you wanted.

– In grammar, poetic meter, form—sure. But I couldn't analyze the content with the kind of dialectics that made sense to me in 1953! Anyway, all I really wanted was the language.

– So because of your father...

– If I wanted to get that unraveled by a *headshrinker*... a psychoanalyst headhunter, Marie, then we wouldn't be able to take any more trips to New York via Frisco and Louisiana. A translation school was enough for me, and if it happened to be located in a river valley on the left bank of the Rhine, then in the morning mist it would look like Flanders after the battle. There you needed the abilities of Hitler's chief translator at your fingertips no less than you did the proverbs of Solomon. There the students would graduate and leave the nature conservancy park of academic jobs and pensions for life in the wild as working translators. Lots of chip-laden shoulders there. Narrow-gauge academics. Someone pointed out one of them to me who'd been in a translator's squad for Hitler's army, a former actor in Leningrad; no hands. Another one, when in his cups, used to brag about his many seductions; he was why I avoided Russian. Italian, French— yes. At least we learned how to speak; chockchock!: as Emil Knoop would say. Besides, Dr. Kliefoth and two semesters in Halle had hardly been able to fix everything from H.-G. Knick's classes. *Knickei*—a real Grade B egg. He'd sent us off with the information: The use of the passive is very common in English. That was that. Lots of *remedial teaching*.

– Simultaneous translation?

– That's a cinch, I can do that in my sleep. No, consecutive interpreting, at a conference, that's the pinnacle, the real art—translating a forty-five-minute lecture and saying it as if you'd written it yourself. Here is one of my many professional dreams that never came true: being elected a member of the AIIC, the Association Internationale des Interprètes de Conférences. They only accept you after two hundred days of conference work and if five colleagues vouch for you. For that I would've had to pay for ten semesters on the Rhine, at Schifferstadt, instead of my six minus two for previous experience.

– How did you pay for it, Gesine? You show up there with five marks in your pocket. A dollar and twenty-five cents.

– Probably more like seventy-five cents. Student Cresspahl would've been fine working in the institution's kitchen; but that would have made the rounds among the fifteen hundred students; it wasn't done. So here's your version of the American hardworking-dishwasher story: Student Cresspahl standing behind the counter in a cloakroom in Mannheim at night saying Thank you for every dime someone left on her plate. Visitors from the school included Rhine maidens, heiresses from the great houses of Düsseldorf or South America, who even in their third year still thought it was funny to come out with Germanisms like *"yes, yes"* or *"I have it not necessary"* instead of "I don't need it." They complained to the management: indecorum. At a nightclub the glasses should be washed in public. Next came the night shift in a factory making toys and garden gnomes. And if a lecturer needed something typed or translated, just ask Cresspahl; she charges a bundle but what she turns out is ready to turn in. After that, she was in demand in the northern neighborhood of Frankfurt where the streets are named after writers—from Franz Kafka past Franz Werfel and Stefan Zweig to Platen—and the families of the American occupiers lived. They went out at night and left their children in the care of one Miss Cresspahl, paying her German money; she wanted to learn nursery rhymes and fairy tales from the children, and how you say, in American, "On your mark, get set, go!" In her last semester, when she felt sure of a diploma, it seemed justified to pay her for holding conversation classes.

– You were starving again, Gesine!

– It was my own fault; I needed a typewriter. I went hungry the scientific way, with yogurt and brown bread every two hours; with practice you can do it.

– And two cigarettes a day.

– No more smoking till after 1955.

– And you were homesick for Jerichow, for Gneez.

– I'd seen the 1953 May Day parade in Gneez. Armed People's Police marching past the stage on New Market, swinging their brown-uniformed limbs, wearing expensive boots (and holding tight to their rifle straps, to keep from falling); the comrade from the district office screamed, as if he had a knife to his throat: Today we still say Gee-Dee-Ääh, but next May we will be able to say Uuu-Gee-Dee-Ääh! A belated decoding of Goethe's remark that was on display at purely academic occasions on the front wall of the auditorium:

I HAVE NO FEAR THAT GERMANY WILL NOT SOMEDAY
BECOME ONE; OUR GOOD ROADS AND FUTURE RAILROADS
WILL DO THEIR PART, BUT ABOVE ALL LET IT BE ONE IN
OUR HEARTS…,

center-aligned. This was a declaration of civil war. I was supposed to want
that? Only armed force would bring about a Unified German Democratic
Republic. Student Lockenvitz had already commented on this, quoting
what he'd found in Voltaire about the Holy Roman Empire.

– That it's neither an empire nor Roman nor holy. I've done my homework.

– Homesick! You don't get it at all. At Gneez main station, one Alfred
Fretwust, prison warden under the Greater German Reich, had gotten
lifetime rights to the bicycle stand. So what if he'd turned a pair of soldier's
boots into credit in a Hamburg bank account, even during the war. So
what if he'd been in Bützow a couple times. In the time of the New Economic Policy he'd accepted payments for motorcycles in the Industrial
Products Government Store on Great Comrade Stalin Street—motorcycles
that were never, ever delivered. Now here he was again. When it was still
going well, he rented allotment garden sheds on Grosser Werder—to be
alone, to meet female friends. Never drank more than a shot of liquor an
hour during the day. At home every last plate licked clean as if by a cat;
family life in the kitchen; a stupefying naked Venus over the marital bed.
Insistently played the good middle-class citizen, which others were willing
to believe since he had enough money coming in. An informer. Only when
a drunk drunkenly called him a crook did it come to blows. Now here he
was again. Had to watch over the bike stand at the station. Thirty cents
per bike per day at most. And since he needed his sleep, of course, the wife
with all her pride actually did the work. Alfred Fretwust, prison warden,
free and clear, denazified at first go-round, unpunished—I'm supposed to
feel homesick for him?

– And yet you did go back, to see Jerichow.

– I did go north for a visit once, to the Holstein coast in the West, at
Whitsun, and in the slowly creeping line of day-trippers from the city I
could see the gray sea under an overcast sky, above the shining yellow of
the rapeseed in bloom and the rain-deepened green of the meadows, with
a remarkably straight line of land at the very end; in the evening, in the

harbor, the northernmost stretch of the Mecklenburg coast, blue with white patches, a hand's breadth, and next to it the sea turning inward at *Great Point* and *Lesser Point*, and behind that bay, more or less, was Jerichow. Past the coastal hedge at the edge of the land you could look over the bay, with the west side to the right and across from it, unconnected, the east side under the inky, wind-chased cloudy sky, irregular, with peaks like jutting bluffs, coves like harbors, needle-fine spires like steeples, cracks like lurking guard boats. When I close my eyes I can remember it perfectly. That same that different roaring.

– *When the oak blooms 'fore the ash, / summer rains come hard and fast. Y'know that, Gesine. But when the ash the oak precedes, / summer's warm and dry indeed, like in 1952. This afternoon I saw my big oak trees, they'll be green soon. The ash is standing there deaf and dumb! On May 1, we used to, now y'know I'm older than you Gesine, we used to take off our clogs an socks, there weren't no shoes 'cept on Sundays. We'd go cuttin thistles outta the rye barefoot. Nowadays I'd rather wear gloves. Back then the winter started in October and lasted till February, it did, and snow too! We walked to school on top of the hedgerows and when someone slipped off into the soft snow we were twice as far above him as we were tall. Now winter lasts a lot longer. On First a May the rye should be high enough to hide a crow! Nowadays you can see a mouse runnin through it! No. And we only have one hay harvest. Before, the first one was in early June, the second in early August, you call that the aftermath, we call it the rowen. Who still feeds with hay nowadays. I gotta say, the seasons've all shifted. 'Tsall the atomic bomb's fault. There's no summer anymore. Didja ever think! . . . Yer not sayin anythin, Gesine.*

– *Why do we see so clearly in Mecklenburg?*

– *'Ts cause a the humidity in the air. But the people over there, I mean your father, they got our afternoon's weather this morning.*

The Cresspahl cousin stayed only one night. Being so close when there was nothing I could do—it hurt.

– Nostalgia is a painful virtue, Gesine. *Daughters have human feelings too.*

– *Right.* I too was expendable. When the Maritime and Merchant City of Wismar wants to celebrate its seven-hundred-and-twenty-fifth birthday in 1954, it can do so just fine without a visitor from Je—, from the Rhineland near the Main. The commemorative publication reaches her because her father sends one: a thick volume on glossy paper with a lot of corrected history, and notices from the government stores praising the New Courses, and the saying, which they call Mecklenburg folk wisdom, that when an old person is left in the lurch by the housing office his grandchildren will always take him in.

– In 1954 you turned ... you became an adult, Gesine.

– Twenty-one years old. And Johnny Schlegel's attorney in West Berlin, acting on behalf of Dr. Werner Jansen, attorney at law, Gneez/Meckl., in accord with the last will and testament of Dr. Avenarius Kollmorgen, sent me a sealed package.

– And woe is you if you don't tell me what was in it!

– I'd be happy to.

– You better.

– It was two gold rings. "Upon reaching your majority, my dear Miss Cresspahl, the undersigned is permitted to lay at your feet." "Since, owing to the intervention of untoward circumstances, I myself." "For any marital connection, so long as it be one you have chosen, I offer my devout." There was a way of speaking that went to the grave with Kollmorgen.

– Wedding rings! From the grave!

– They're ... for you. Yours.

– Like I'm ever going to get married, Gesine!

– That's what we said about me too. Don't forget.

– So, no plans to return to Jerichow or Halle on the Saale.

– The radio took care of that. "The Soviet Union has invented penicillin." One time an announcer said a song title with a sigh: "'*An* American in Paris'—oh, if only!" So taken with his own agitprop brilliance that he didn't realize the obvious comeback: how desirable it would be to have only *a* single Soviet in the East German republic, on vacation in Ahlbeck by the Baltic. It's as if they hoped to win over the airwaves! As if they thought they could divide the sky.

– Which party did you support in Western Germany, Gesine? You could vote now.

– In 1954 the Social Democrats, at a party congress in Berlin!, declared their willingness "to participate under certain conditions in joint efforts to safeguard peace and defend freedom, including by means of military action."

– Now if I know you, that threw cold water on the Socialists as far as you were concerned.

– Look at that, you do know me. The president of the country was a member of the Free Democratic Party who in 1933 had helped prop up Hitler with the Enabling Act that finished off the Weimar Republic. Now he was telling his citizens about *Vergangenheitsbewältigung*—that they had to overcome or work through the past—and since this wasn't an act of labor or a material object—

– *To accomplish. To master.*

– the only verbs left were "to prevail over," "to subjugate." All while he avoided any public "working through" where his own personal past was concerned. The chancellor, meanwhile, was a Christian Democrat—what kind of expression is that!—and he had a little dog which was allowed to yap "Quite right!" in the Bundestag whenever the chancellor spoke of a "reestablishment of German unity in freedom," for example on the day of the June 17 uprising. Then, with his other hand, he drew his republic into the economic nexus of the European Coal and Steel Community and locked it into a military organization named after the North Atlantic. There was a national song about him, which premiered on May 16, 1950, in Munich.

– If only I wasn't so shy, Gesine.

– So what you're saying is that you're embarrassed for your mother on a half-empty ferry where you don't know a single tourist.

– Okay. If it's a sing-along I'll take the second part.

– *On your mark. Get set. GO!* "Oh my Papa / was a most amazing clown / Oh my papa / was a gray-ayt ahtist! / Oh my papa / was so splendid to look at . . ."

– Defamatory to the state! Punishable by law.

– It definitely was in East Germany. In the West, anyone who sang it with tears of devotion wouldn't know who they were praying for.

– Gesine. This was supposed to be your home country!

– Student Cresspahl tried to make it so, starting when she moved to Düsseldorf and had a job and was living in a furnished room near the Flingern North post office, with a widow who was the treasurer of her local Communist group and crabby about a tenant who'd left her party comrades in East Germany behind; no visits from men allowed. The disinherited child wasn't looking for any men anyway—she divided her evenings between the central pool on Green Street and the state library on Grabbe Square, where people were considerate toward a patron who wanted to see newspapers from the past, year by year, one after the other. Catching up on the time she'd missed since 1929. Reading, reading; like after an insidious disease. She thought of Düsseldorf as the end of her travels; tried to get used to the smooth, joined facades of the row houses. Kept change at the ready on November 10, for the children carrying lanterns for St. Martin; wished she weren't in town the next day, when the carnival started. Avoided the cartwheelers. Read up valiantly on Jan Wellem and Karl Immermann; started a collection, with the guidebook *Welcome to Your New Home*, with *Düsseldorf at the Turn of the Century*. Walked to Kaiserswerth; found a hint of Jerichow—a shed for unharnessing painted oxblood-red in a dilapidated garden behind an inn. In a pub, when she saw a master craftsman's certificate with a swastika in the official seal, she furtively stuck a postage stamp over it, but then again the stamp still showed the head of the man who'd betrayed his state and was now head of state in this country here.

D'you see that guy telling off the waiter? Runs a photo shop now. If we'd won the war he'd'a been sitting pretty. Brought down sixty-four tanks, he did. One time he got ten with fourteen shells, broke open a whole flank. Knight's Cross, they gave 'im some land in Bohemia too. He just let 'em get closer and closer, using the ones he'd already taken down as cover. His turret gunner panicked—said it wasn't courage, he was just nuts. Nice guy, not conceited at all. You're so quiet, Miss Cresspahl, is something wrong?

I can't get a bite down with this kind of talk, even if I were hungry. Thanks for inviting me out. I have to go now.

Düsseldorf was a home once the name Cresspahl had a separate phone and a door to her own apartment she could lock. The allied British and American militaries, on whose behalf an employee in the woods outside Mönchengladbach was negotiating with local German officials over the assessment of and compensation for damages from maneuvers, wanted her safely housed and easily reachable. A simple converted attic—one big room with a small bedroom and kitchen, all the windows looking out at the sky. Düsseldorf-Bilk, that was my neighborhood, in pincers of rail noise from the streetcar lines and the tracks to Krefeld and Cologne. Near Old St. Mary's; every day a view of the memorial plaque to "THE BILK OBSERVATORY, DESTROYED ON THE NIGHT OF JUNE 11 TO 12, 1943"; center-aligned. In a building with brows over the windows and two balconies—truly like raised eyebrows. There were little parks, refreshment stands, you could stroll to the South Cemetery; a few blocks north was the city pool on Konkordia Street. Anything that was missing in the apartment when Jakob came to visit Düsseldorf he plastered on, screwed in, glued up, varnished over. For Jakob I splurged on a yellow silk blouse with a loosely hanging collar and long ribbons, even though I knew it was wasted on him—he looks me in the face.

– But before that you visited him in Jerichow!

– Who told you?... There's someone who's told stories about me, that I was on an official trip to Berlin and I broke the law on the East German stretch of the line and got off the train and snuck through the woods toward Jerichow. Well, since it's you, I'll admit it. It didn't work out well. I got myself into a situation that Jakob had been trying to protect me from. One Mr. Rohlfs, who wanted to talk to me about Jakob; he already had me in his files, from Gneez to Berlin-Grunewald to Mönchengladbach. I can't believe how completely we all trusted Jakob!

– How did my father like Düsseldorf, the West?

– He couldn't care less. He wanted to know if I was getting my eight hours of sleep every night; he walked me to my bus to work every day; he asked when was the last time I'd been to a dentist. He brought me a shawl from Mecklenburg! When I got home to Bilk, by Old St. Mary's, Jakob had roasted me sausages à la Jerichow—a man who can cook with blood and flour, raisins, marjoram, thyme, and apple slices, just so his Gesine can eat a meal like she remembers from back home! After he'd familiarized himself with the fine-food shops on Count Adolf Street in Düsseldorf there was no sign of envy. Okay, so the ten kinds of bread day in and day out, he wished that they had those in his country too, or rather the country he'd come for a visit from. When we walked past a construction site and saw bricks being unloaded as gently as porcelain, wrapped in thick paper, tied six times over, he sighed. And yes, he grumbled about the railway in the Western republic running express trains with just one engineer. Or because the trains would start suddenly, smoothly, without warning. He was just visiting, there to see Cresspahl's daughter. There were some things he thought were funny. The jolly ol' lady who'd gotten fat sitting behind the cinema's ticket counter taking one last walk up and down the aisle before the feature presentation, with an atomizer, numbing the guests with bursts of scent. Humphrey Bogart in *The Desperate Hours* on a day like any other. The words people said to the tune of the North German Radio call sign: "Is the rá-dyo páid fór?" How two kids fought: A Persian lambskin coat's just sheep; You're a sheep, my mother has one. He was bothered, though he didn't show it except by a shudder in the shoulders, when he saw in an ad a character actor expelled from the East, turning a phone conversation into a chance to use and recommend an electric shaver, for filthy lucre. When Jakob recognized something in me that he knew from before, a smile would crinkle the corners of his eyes—like when I paid the bill without asking him at the Park Hotel on Cornelius Square in Düsseldorf, just as I had at Pottel & Broskowsky on Orphanage Ring in Halle; he was in my city, he was my guest.

– He could have stayed.

– The things we discussed for the following year, and the years to come through 1983—arrangements in the invisible, plans for a future—now they're all just stories like the ones where small children fall into a rain barrel; it hangs by the thread of a minute whether someone will come and save them.

– You know the drill, Gesine. Say it.

– He goes back east, across the Elbe; in the morning mist he crosses a railyard he's been in charge of for two years and a shunting train gets him; he dies under the knife. Cresspahl arranged the funeral. Only told Mrs. Abs and his daughter after Jakob was in the ground. That was good for one of the women, bad for the other. The first one missed her chance to kill herself—she wanted to tidy everything up first, put her house in order. That's how life arranges things so people will live. Later, by the time someone came along to prevent me from killing myself, I'd almost forgotten about it.

– Who can stop you from doing anything, Gesine!

– It was a very strong person. When I stuck my finger into her palm, she made a fist; she could dangle three feet in the air, holding on tight. A contented person, constantly sleeping, waking up with soft guttural sounds. Four weeks later, she looked at me like she trusted me. By the third month she knew my voice; returned the smile of a Communist widow in Flingern North. In October 1957, she listened to me, signaling agreement with her voice. On St. Martin's Day she turned her head toward where my voice was coming from. By Christmas she was looking in the same direction with both eyes. In the new year she starts to talk, going in for the usual: yeah, yeah, my, my; she looks sweetly, but distantly, at her grandmother. In February she laughed when a bottle fell over, even though it was hers. She's proud of her toys; she knows they're hers. In April she crawled under my apron when Cresspahl came into the room. In May she tried to stand on her own. In June she knew the way to the South Cemetery, to the Hofgarten; she threw toys out of bed to make her mother get them back. In July she could crawl up steps, stand up for a moment or two, knew her name.

– It almost sounds like you liked me.

– When it came to you, the difference between good and bad had been wiped out—that's why in North German mothers call their children: my heartbeat. *They're so dumb, these mothers, they've got their kid on their hip an they're shouting Where are you my little chickadee, where are you?!* We lived in a symbiosis, if you'd care to go look up that word; it's something we'll soon be putting a stop to. You got sick if I was even a little upset.

– You know the drill, Gesine. Say it only if you want to.

– In September, when we walked past our house with the raised eyebrows, the instruments were sharpened, the patient prepped. A trailer was on the curb, a yellow sign on the front fence. The next day wreckers knocked out the house's teeth; they carefully carried the doors and windows off to the side, the reusable material. Then they sawed through the house's bones, broke its spine, cut it apart from its neighbor—the neighbor played deaf. A red-and-white poster appears on all the doors next to the victim. At eleven a.m. the house suffers a blast wound and collapses into a heap, a pile so small you could hardly believe it. Beams are still sticking out, the remains of balcony railings. The dust tastes like an air war. Two Caterpillar power shovels pull up to clear the rubble, two conveyor belts. The cast-iron fence stays intact almost to the very end, until a single smash of the shovel breaks it and sweeps it away. A young tree gets tangled up in all this; a blow to the roots and it's gone. The bared walls of the adjacent buildings look so un-protected, with their three sealed door openings, that they seem to be shivering in the sun. Up in the shimmering air, that's where I lived with Jakob.

– And so what did I get sick with?

– A fever. Almost 106°, the medicine couldn't fight it. You were uncon-scious for two days. When you woke up, there was Cresspahl again at your bedside, watching his heir.

– You were in line ahead of me though.

– Jakob's child—she had priority. For a Marie, daughter of Jakob, Cresspahl even broke the law. According to East German law, people were to be arrested and sentenced if, in their letters abroad, Location 12 found any complaints about the wisdom of the custodian—imagine what the law threatened for private transactions in foreign currencies! But instead of notifying the Gneez tax office or the East German post office about his account at the Surrey Bank of Richmond, Cresspahl went to see a lawyer on Lietzenburg Street in West Berlin, Inge Schlegel was another client, and he drafted for him a letter in English. A postcard came to Jerichow with Easter wishes from Anita; version for the censor; translation: a bank is relieved to report from Richmond, England, *bankers have human feelings too, believe you me!*, that one *Mr. Cresspahl* will admit to all those pounds sterling that have been saved up and accruing compound interest since 1939, unfrozen three years ago and now at the disposal of former enemy aliens. Cresspahl, almost sixty-nine years old, boarded a plane for the first time in his life to bring a bank statement to Düsseldorf. That was half of it. From Düsseldorf, Cresspahl traveled to that office in the forest outside Mönchengladbach and made himself known by means of that *half penny*, minted 1940, on the front was a jaunty galleon and on the back was GEORGIVS VI and as many letters of DEI GRATIA OMNIUM REX ET FIDEI DEFENSOR as the coin had room for. Faith and loyalty were given their reward; Cresspahl received his thirty shillings. That was the other half. Cresspahl, citizen of East Germany, in a will drawn up in Düsseldorf, packed two big piles of pounds sterling into a box made of rods of the law that neither you nor I can break into; if needed a legal guardian with tes-tamentary authority could.

– So who is my legal guardian, besides you?

– Just me for now I'm afraid.

– I want it to be your Erichson.

– He ... he has enough problems at the moment; would Anita be all right?

– Maybe, after I've talked it over with D. E.; maybe. Was I hostile to my grandfather?

– At first his black overcoat from 1932 scared you; but then you liked the velvet lapels. Before long you thought it was funny to copy us; you'd sit down across from us, cross your legs, fold your hands, and look resigned, head hanging like you were sad. Cresspahl was upset that how he looked had saddened a child; he held out his hand to you, a big hard carpenter's claw, and you punched it with your cat-paw fist. You went to sleep without fear when he told you stories about once upon a time when the devil was still a young lad who had to go fetch kümmel for his grandmother.

– And my own grandmother? Who I'm named after?

– Mrs. Abs was now afraid of a Jerichow where someone like Mr. Rohlfs with a Stasi badge might take her aside and start asking questions about one Gesine Cresspahl—she stayed in Hanover. We invited her to come live in Düsseldorf; she only came for visits. So by day you were brought up in a kindergarten, not by a grandmother. She would look at you, Jakob's child, and the tears would come to her eyes. She was worried her grief might be bad for you. Wanted to live alone and die alone. She was buried behind the palace in Hanover.

– Why don't I remember?

– Because it was kept from you.

– Why did Cresspahl go back to Jerichow? He could have stayed with us.

– *When it comes to dying we're all masters and apprentices.* He wanted to take care of that alone. Just not be a burden to anyone, even his own daughter. He kept his promise: he took Joche and Muschi Altmann into the two rooms that had been managed by the German Reich Railway for Jakob. There was no danger

Fer me to be sittin here dead and none to see me

ol' people can see farthest ahead.

– Am I going to be a rich woman when I turn twenty-one?

– It'll be enough for five years of college.

– Still, Gesine. You could've used it when you needed it.

– It would have been three times more than I needed. Anyway, he did give me something from it: for the child. A child who'd been thrown back into sublet rooms because commerce in the West German city centers was smashing to bits anything the bombs had left standing; how could a grandfather stand to see that! He furnished a garden apartment on Lohaus Dike—for the child. Paid the rent for a year, so that her mother could start another course of study, this time for banking—for the child.

– He should've given you a car.

– I paid for that myself, once you'd learned to talk; I was happier about it that way. From a big dealer who advertised his chariots with the sign of a hand (secondhand). You had to have a car. Hard for you to understand today.

– We took trips to Denmark.

– You spoke Italian as a small child, and French.

– But never went to England. For your father.

– I would tell you what stopped me, if I knew.

– The trips to London with D. E. cured you?

– *Thanks, Doc.*

– Now there's something I have to say to you. Something serious. Düsseldorf had become your city, like Berlin for Anita.

– And like the Niebuhrs feel about Stuttgart.

– When you want a treat, you go eat in the Düsseldorf Central Station restaurant. When a bridge is dedicated in Düsseldorf and named after a president of the federal republic, you grumble about the old man and go see it. It's your bridge. Heinrich Heine's praise of Düsseldorf—you couldn't agree more. You're ashamed for this city when it disavows that same Heine. And suddenly you're up and off to America with a defenseless child under your arm! Gesine!

– It wasn't Gesine, it was Employee Cresspahl. When a bank "on friendly terms with us" offered her two years of advanced training in Brooklyn, New York, she had to act thrilled and grateful. Deference pays—maybe she wouldn't be fired quite so soon. For propriety's sake she demurred just a little; secretly she was relieved.

– You've let me believe to this day that New York was my decision!

– It was your plan, at least the general outline. Crédit Lyonnais or some firm in Milan would've been all the same to me. I wanted to get out of that country for a while. In 1959, in Cologne—just around the corner—a synagogue had been defaced with swastikas and slogans: GERMANS WANT JEWS OUT. Dora Semig had put in an application concerning her husband and they ordered him to report to the Hamburg municipal court by September 2, 1960; if he failed to do so he would be declared dead. That was one thing.

– That would've been enough for me.

– The other thing was the career of a certain West German politician. This is going to be boring, Marie.

– Well, just so I can never say you haven't told me, on board a South Ferry in fact, in New York Harbor, afternoon, direction Manhattan.

– All right, grin and bear it. As a young man he was in the Nazi student organization. When he was twenty-two he applied to their Motor Corps, fulfilling the prerequisite: politically reliable and prepared to burrow ever deeper into the National Socialist mindset. In the war he was an "Officer for Militaristically Inspired Leadership" at an antiaircraft school in Bavaria; prerequisite: National Socialist activism. After the war he said he was in the resistance; he was in charge of the denazification proceedings in Schongau, where he was the district commissioner. At a public gathering in 1949, he shouted: "Anyone still willing to take gun in hand, let his hand wither!" Starting in 1957 he denied he ever said that. By then he was the West German Minister of Defense. In April 1957, when eighteen scientists from Göttingen University warned against equipping the German Army with nuclear weapons, he called one of them an "ivory-tower professor"; he himself is a high-school graduate. In the capital's press club he described the Professor of Physics and Nobel Prize Winner Otto Hahn as "an old fool who can't hold back tears and can't sleep at night when he thinks about Hiroshima." In June 1957, fifteen recruits drowned in the Iller at a training exercise that they hadn't been properly prepared for; the minister responsible, rather than resigning, celebrated his wedding the next day, ordering up a platoon of MPs—practically wartime-strength, with steel helmets and white leather gear—as an escort. Didn't go to the ceremony for the victims. That same year, he came out with this pronouncement: he was not a conscientious objector, but nevertheless was no coward. The following year, he provided the West German republic with a national hero: On April 29, 1958, a traffic cop named Siegfried Hahlbohm was on duty at an intersection outside the federal chancellery in Bonn when the minister's vehicle of state crossed it, ignoring the policeman's hand signal and forcing a streetcar to brake abruptly. Hahlbohm reported the minister's driver (who already had five previous offenses) for four traffic violations and two criminal infractions: Causing a Traffic Hazard. The minister vows to remove this officer from the intersection; when his efforts become public, he calls it "a betrayal of state secrets." In October 1959 there was a meeting of "organized bearers of the Knight's Cross" in Regensburg; the minister sends along three army officers with salutes and music and his regards. In 1961 he smeared a political opponent, who'd had to emigrate during the war, by saying: "But there is one question we can surely ask of you: What did *you* do during the twelve years on the outside? The same way people ask us: What did you do during the twelve years on the inside?" I read that when I was already in New York, relieved to be out of Mr. Minister's reach. The next year, he provides his officers with a "full dress suit" featuring an ornamental lanyard, known in Hitler's time as a "monkey swing"; he prescribes for the other ranks a belt with a buckle that says: Unity and Law and Freedom. After that, he tried to destroy—with denunciations, with lies—a West German news magazine whose editors had conscientiously investigated his financial dealings and official conduct. He knowingly lies to the West German Bundestag: "This was not revenge on my part. I had nothing to do with the whole affair. In the truest sense of the word: not one thing!" After that, he had to step down from the government for a bit; in 1966 a West German government again found him good enough to be a Minister of Finance. He can't get a hunting license without shenanigans and dirty tricks. He wants to be chancellor of West Germany with his finger on the nuclear button; what they say about him in the Bundestag is that: Anyone who talks like the Federal Minister of Defense would shoot, too.

   – That's just rude, Gesine.

   – If I were ever tempted to feel homesick for West German politics, I'd just hang up a picture of him.

   – He doesn't get a name?

   – He deserves the name he's made for himself.

– And so now we're in March 1961, on our way to NYC. New, York, City!

– Since Employee Cresspahl showed herself to be duly compliant, she got four weeks' vacation first. We spent it in Berlin with Anita.

– Where you have to watch what you say! If you try to buy a superlong sausage, they'll ask you if you're feeding a big family. I was so proud of my mother when she shot back: Nope, I'm founding a hermitage! Berlin, city of airplanes.

– Airplanes above the rattling skylight. Fitting into the gaps left by ruins, skimming roofs, adding to the church tower, skyscraper, rain. In parks, stadiums, gardens, on streets and balconies, everywhere there were planes looking down, veering off, sending in others. Invisibly high but far-seeing, the jet fighters of the Red Army, the Beautiful Army, the *Krasnaya Armiya* squeezed through the sound barrier and threw off that punching, booming, breath-stopping blast of sound. When we took off for Paris, we saw Anita down on her abandoned balcony, waving.

– And now, all aboard the *France*, for New York!

– Still, I know a certain child who for a long time could draw how the furniture was arranged by the garden windows in Düsseldorf. Who was almost in tears when she thought back to a birthday party where everyone sang in chorus: Now you are three! Now you are three!

– But I turned four in New York. We've finally gotten to what I remember. *Welcome home!*

August 18, 1968 Sunday

Cresspahl's daughter was living in New York when Cresspahl died in the fall of 1962. America is too far away for me to imagine. *Sevenny-four years's long enough.*

He tried to fall asleep on his back. He wanted to be found close enough to morning; he wanted to spare them any trouble with a stiff corpse that hadn't lain down in bed the way it would lie in the coffin. They used to break bones in such cases, before. But he turned to the side, even if only his head, as he went to sleep. In the morning, as the night thinned out in his

brain, his head turned his nose straight up. He already felt himself being
carried out, tipped over slightly in the narrow door to the room, then finally
out in the cool winter sunlight striped by the bare hedgerows. The jolting
on the pavement sent gentle waves of blood surging up behind his brow as
he heard Prüss the medical officer say: In cases like this it's hard to say how
long you have to live.

This morning the sleeping daughter once again saw herself stand up,
swing hand over hand out the window and onto Riverside Drive, down
the green-patinaed pier of the bridge to the street below. Following doctor's
orders she was wearing only a coat over her nightgown. Pulled the car door
shut behind her, quiet as a thief; let the wheels roll eastward to the entrance
to the passageway under Broadway that in waking hours the subway crosses.
By now she was escorted by black-lacquered carriages—trapped. The trip
went as if on rails; all she had to do was press the dead man's switch. When
she arrived under the cemeteries she found a circular, concrete-lined cave
hollowed out for her and divided by hospital doors. Behind the first of
these doors was the clothes closet; she was supposed to change here for the
operation. The doors reappeared along the inner arc of the hallway; these
were labeled Heart, Lungs, Kidneys, Blood. At the last door she was handed
a small package: the remains of the autopsy.

Let's start the day over.

At five a.m., the radio station WNBC plays popular works by Mozart
and Haydn. At six, WNYC follows with Brahms's *Requiem* and Schubert.

A weekend day. No work. Marie wants to throw a children's party, to
say goodbye.

The New York Times, number 40,385.

News from Bogotá, Jerusalem, Iraq, Cairo, La Paz, Peking, Biafra,
London. Who would question its comprehensiveness? Yesterday morning,
gunshots were fired at a Long Island Rail Road commuter train; one young
man dead, another wounded.

Pravda has hinted at what it wants readers in Moscow to accept as the truth: If workers in Prague have beseeched the Soviet troops to stay longer in their country, that is because they are being subjected to "moral terror." On every Prague street corner there are agitators and gathering demonstrators, all "subversive activities by anti-Socialist forces." Just to clarify things, yes?

About the chancellor of West Germany, that mild-mannered usherette the *Times* today sees fit to report that: he went boating on Starnberg Lake and saved a dachshund from drowning.

In South Vietnam, northern forces and their guerrilla allies attacked in nineteen places. American forces, under machine-gun fire, allegedly lost only ten men, ascribing five hundred casualties to the other side. These round numbers.

Tonight at six, radio station WNRV brings us "Just Jazz" with Ed Beach. We'd wanted to record it, but we've already missed it.

When we were on our way to the U.S. of A., it'd been just five years in April since a staff sergeant of the marines (one beer and three shots of booze in his belly) had led a party of inexperienced recruits into the tidal wetlands of South Carolina where six were drowned. MPs stood guard over the flag-draped coffins as if the men had died for their country.

That's why Marie, just last year, thought we had a duty to buy every single record by Pete Seeger: because he'd sung about the incident: "But the big fool said to push on!"

When we got here America had fewer than a thousand advisers in South Vietnam. The new president, J. F. Kennedy, increased their number to three thousand in 1961, ten thousand in 1962. Always these round numbers. In 1964 the commanding officers of the destroyers *Maddox* and *Turner Joy* claimed to have come under fire from the coast of North Vietnam while in the Gulf of Tonkin; they could report no damage; in August the new president, Lyndon B. Johnson, was given free hand by Congress. The Marines landed in 1965, without a declaration of war but bringing the number of Americans in Vietnam to a hundred and forty-eight thousand. Local guerrillas killed eight Americans on February 7, 1965; the bombing of North Vietnam began and, starting in April 1966, was carried out by eight-engine B-52 bombers. The Soviets didn't move. 1967 saw the start of the chemical defoliation of Vietnam's forests. All the better to bomb you with. One air force general whom the Americans number among their allies calls Adolf Hitler his political role model. After the Communists' Tet Offensive in March 1968, an American president acknowledged his mistakes; LBJ announced he would not run for reelection. His successor might be Nixon, a Tricky Dickie, nix on him; he announced as his 1968 slogan that instead of negotiating for an American defeat we should be negotiating "how we can push even harder for a victory." The awareness of being implicated, not far from guilt, that weighed on our shoulders through the dirty Algerian War of the French, 1954 to 1962, is back—it's just a different war this time.

What was the first piece of foreign policy the USA offered its guests the Cresspahls? They'd only been here two weeks when troops, with President Kennedy's approval, attacked Cuba's Bay of Pigs.

That summer, the party that is always right walled in the city of Berlin and put up a fence around its citizens. The initial fear: had there been deaths. – None on the first day: Anita said into the phone: maybe in the next few years.

In December, Employee Cresspahl, dragged at high-speed under Manhattan and the East River for two half-hours a day, lost her job in Brooklyn. She had happened to be walking by the branch's information counter and tried to be nice and help an elderly customer—a woman who was trying to look American and who spoke with a German accent. Saxony. East.

German bonds issued in dollars? We do have those.

Could it be something from Saxony?

We have municipal bonds from Dresden and Leipzig, from 1925 and 1926, each paying 7 percent, maturing in 1945 and 1947.

I got a tip that you can get those for a song.

You have been informed correctly, ma'am. That's because they're excluded from the 1952 London Agreement on German External Debts. It's by no means certain when they might be guaranteed.

So you'd advise me against it, Miss . . . Crespel?

Whoever gave you that tip is not exactly your friend, ma'am.

The reproof from management: Miss Cresspahl, we pay you to *sell* securities! Here's your notice. If you're so good at giving investment advice, go open your own broker's office, don't screw us out of a commission!

Starting in January, the unemployed Miss Cresspahl, with a four-year-old child as an adviser, blew through her savings traveling from the Atlantic Coast to the brown beaches of Oregon and had no one to discuss her troubles with but the talking road:

Stay on the Sidewalk
Prepare to Stop
Slow Traffic: Keep Right
Be Patient: Passing Lane Just Ahead
Center Lane for Left Turns Only
No Passing
No Parking
CORVALLIS, pop. 38,400
Please Drive Carefully (We Need Everybody)
This Lane for Passing Only
Railroad Crossing
R x R
NO XING
Falling Rocks
Trucks Entering
Right Lane Must Exit
Soft Shoulder
Thank You
Thank You

and she often felt like the pigtailed girl on the sign who's leading a smaller child by the hand across an implied road with zebra stripes. Children, children!

Then Anita turned up with her illegal propositions. Anita paid the expenses. Gesine was a tourist with an American passport, in Prague, asking the way to Wilson station, long since renamed Střed. A tourist with French papers trying to exchange Czech crowns at Berlin-East station.

Now that our widely revered Vice President de Rosny has entrusted his subordinate Cresspahl with the transfer of a few million into the Czechoslovakian national budget, he's admitted to her why he gave her a job despite her prior record: because she admitted her offense. Or because of the nature of it.

A job in data entry. Nobody heard one word more from this "coworker" than was necessary to be polite. Employed and under observation since 1962. Found suitable in 1967.

In 1962 one Prof. Dr. Dr. D. Erichson found us and proposed marriage after he'd gotten to know Marie; was given, for the time being, the name D. E. because Marie liked the tiny hiccup between the American D and E sounds. Dee-ee. Later she realized she'd meant: Dear Erichson.

In 1963 I was still from somewhere else. Capable of a laugh when I saw an office building, steel and glass and concrete, and its name was inscribed on it in lavish aluminum and that name was U.S. Plywood Building. And if my translation of a gold phrase on a green delivery van was correct, it said: Theatrical Moves—Our Specialty. My throat still tickling with laughter, I stepped into an elevator with thirteen men and saw them all doff their hats. Such things happen in the beginning—or what I thought of as the beginning.

I felt secure: I'd been to the Social Security Administration. Down on Broadway, between restaurants and stores, a startlingly businesslike entrance with two brass door handles. On the second floor a room as large as a baseball diamond, with no partitions. Closest to the elevators, little groups of chairs to wait on. Then a desk, ceaselessly asking via posted notice: May I help you? On a pillar, the photograph of the president, framed in black as if he were dead; matted under the photo in the same frame, the signature that the Soviet prime minister respects. Along the wall, writing surfaces as narrow as the ones in German post offices. The file card wanted to know the name the applicant "goes by," as well as the one acquired at birth. I hereby declare under oath that I have never applied for a *social security number* before. Necessity is the mother of deception.

When the old-fashioned printed card came from Jerichow, Meckl., in the fall of 1962, I lingered in the bar of the Hotel Marseilles. The ladies there were all in tweed and adorned with the accessories recommended on the women's pages of the news magazines, but they were waiting for the husbands who paid for that lifestyle, while I was waiting for Marie and paying for myself. The men were smiling. One, with his glasses pushed up on his nasal cartilage, busy with the paper, with the stock market pages, like it was a Book of the Times—this absentminded professor asked about George.

– They nabbed him in Brooklyn.

– But he lives in the Bronx.

– For knowing all sorts of inside information about the "weather." What'll it be?

– The same. Nah, probably not. Something similar.

– What I gave you?

– You're the better doctor.

– Here's your Ballantine's. Came here all the way from New Jersey.

That was like a permission to watch other people living, even if it seemed impossible to go on with one's own life. Then a parched-looking beanpole stepped up to the bar with frantic gestures and needed to know:

– Where can I get some water!?

– If you can't find it anywhere else, then right here. Sir.

– Gimme a glass of water.

– Free of charge: Mr. McIntyre said, indicating with a private pursing of the lips that there are some rude dirty dogs too old to learn new tricks. McIntyre, shaking the last drops from a bottle into a customer's glass like a sacrifice, a gift, a holy offering. McIntyre, whom they'd recently unexpectedly sent to an island, dressed in easily visible clothes, so that he couldn't tell stories from behind the shelter of a bar for a while—things that only the FBI claims the right to know.

In 1963, D. E. for the first time ventured to suggest: that I try to enjoy life. I went along. And I found it hard to break the habit of Mr. McIntyre's company. These were conversations that were worth it: McIntyre took on a teacher's responsibilities, always with an apology, and told me how English words were pronounced in America, that here a "public holiday" meant a legal one and a "proposition" was just a suggestion, not, as in England, a suggestion and a deal and a case and a consideration and an alternative and a plan and a sentence and a declaration. All this among taciturn men who'd likewise found the day's events unsatisfactory and who expressed their wishes so monosyllabically that Mr. McIntyre assumed an air of mock defensiveness. One of them, annoyed by the ice cube in his glass, dropped it into McIntyre's hand like a tip; he said: Just what I've always wanted. And I told myself that I was enjoying life, because in ten minutes the kindergarten bus was due to arrive and the bellboy would announce Marie's name and she'd walk into the bar, looking at us with a serious and friendly look like Jakob, but speaking a natural American English that by this point a certain someone would ask Marie to produce for her. Then we would walk hand in hand down the sloping street to Riverside Park, and I thought that just being alive was enough.

In 1964 the business of being homesick for New York while still in New York started. The sounds alone: they insisted that I admit it, I felt alive. Even though the big red fire engines were heading into danger, after all, rushing by as if already too late amid the throng of cars down below them idling in place; even though the firemen's helmets and coats, black and striped with yellow, were still stained from the old days when misfortune had been unpreventable and fires were like the plague; even though the mighty wail of the siren, lurching back and forth every second, and the animalistic roar of the horn resounded with the old fear; even though the expert at the back of all that efficient technology steered the overlong vehicle out of its spot so casually that it seemed like he'd accept an accident with a sportsmanly shrug.

In July 1964 a policeman, more than six feet tall and over 220 pounds, shot and killed a skinny black kid who, with some others, had been harassing a pink-skinned fellow American by throwing bottles and trashcan lids. The people of Harlem fought for four days and three nights, with cocktails à la Molotov, bricks, looting, and arson, against New York's boys in blue with their riot gear, billy clubs, guns, and tear gas. For weeks afterward, a German woman carried her passport around the city with her to prove she was a foreigner.

In 1965, in March, the American military started dropping incendiary bombs over Vietnam. Napalm.

In a bank in New York City, a foreign-language secretary's office was supplied with a removable plastic nameplate outside the door on the left, and it said: MRS. CRESSPAHL.

On November 9 at 5:28 p.m., when the lights went out in the northeastern United States, the residents of New York City were concerned. One woman from abroad, who had tried to worm her way into a new homeland's favor by studying its history, brought up August 1959, when electric power had gone out for thirteen hours in the area between the Hudson and East Rivers from 74th to 110th Street—this was part of the history of the Upper West Side, her neighborhood. She recalled June 1961: on the hottest day of the year the subways had stopped, elevators left hanging. Everyone has their own special story about the blackout of 1965: since Mrs. Cresspahl had managed to take the bank's emergency staircase down to the street and make her way from midtown to Riverside Drive on foot but was still expected to contribute a story, she described the conductor of the Wolverine Express diesel train in Grand Central Terminal who'd talked her into buying a sleeper ticket to Detroit for the night. She nods when someone explains the blackout as a computer failure in a key position in the network controlling the Niagara power plant; she emits grunts of skeptical assent when someone persists in suspecting a military exercise preparing for the coming civil war. She doesn't need to know everything; it's enough for her to have realized that night that she was alive. She returned to the candlelit windows overlooking the park, to Marie's silhouette, as to a home.

It was getting harder to say goodbye, even if those goodbyes led to vacations in Denmark, in Italy. One evening in 1966, in the Copter Club on the roof of the skyscraper that Pan Am has planted on Grand Central's shoulders, I was stunned by the quantity of haze through which a whirring-winged craft was to carry us to the airfield now called JFK. The lake in Central Park was a paler rag pickling in pallid brine. Two office slabs stood sentry, presumptuously clear and black and white, before the towerscape of buildings draped in fog. Park Avenue was visible up to Ninety-Sixth Street, you could see where the streetlights bordering the center strip stop, where the trains of the New Haven and Grand Central lines come up out of the tunnels. Trains would be safe on such a foggy day. The south brow of the Newsweek Building insistently proclaims in red: 77°; 7:27 p.m. By this time the helicopters were taking off every fifteen minutes, their flight numbers corresponding to the departure times. The rolling boil of the copter blades came out of nothing and after a while vanished back into nothing. Marie asked to look at our tickets, checking for the reservation back to the place we were about to leave.

In 1966 a man named James Shuldiner, thirty-one, tax adviser, first tried to strike up a conversation with a lady from Germany—in a smoky little restaurant, at a red-and-white checked tablecloth, in a cramped little pocket behind the passage between the drink bar and the food counter. *Everybody here lives on the verge of crime. And one crime leads to the next.* Once: he lectured: a society fosters hostile energy instead of transforming it (*police brutality, glorification of transgressions, violence against small nations*), murders like the ones in Chicago every day are only to be expected. (The next murder of the year was about to take place in Austin.) – On the other hand, these killings are setting a record it'll be hard to break! For a long time his Mrs. Cresspahl tried to keep secret from him that since 1961 she, too, had considered herself a student of New York City. Mr. Shuldiner felt she'd given him advice when he married a Jewish girl disgusted by the work nurses had to do in Switzerland. Now she's cooped up with her unclean skin in a sparkling clean apartment on Broadway with a grand piano and a guitar. Marie, to be polite, accepted a graham cracker from the skinny and arrogant Mrs. Shuldiner, who then snidely asked her if she was starved at home. James looked abashed, felt shame, regret. He gave us sidelong glances meant to solicit shared responsibility; we pretended we didn't see them.

Everyone in New York has their taxi-driver story; Mrs. Cresspahl has two on tap. The first driver, after admitting to her his Jewish descent, which she'd already gleaned from the ID card showing his face and license number, then told her he'd contracted a form of impotence from sexual intercourse with a German girl. Can't get erect, you understand what I'm saying, lady. Would you be willing to give me the only treatment on earth that might help?

The second was taking her to St. Luke's Hospital with Marie—a child who had something wrong with her knee, a 104° fever, terrible pain in the joint; in her distress she begged for help in German. As the mother carried her child up the hospital steps, trying in vain to cradle the hanging head in her elbow since the girl's braids were so close to trailing on the dirty sidewalk, the driver shouted after her: I hope your kid dies, you German pig!

In 1967, same as every year, a foreigner has to present her visa at the government office at the bottom of Broadway where they register resident aliens; every year the men there ask her what moves her to stay in NYC when she could also be living and making money *in that wonderful country, Germany.* They look incredulous, baffled, when the applicant informs them that if she had the choice between New York City, Düsseldorf, and Frankfurt, she would pick New York, but she wouldn't know what to decide between Düsseldorf and København. The compliment she was trying to pay the officers' homeland remained undetected. Since then she has taken to vaguely bringing up the exchange rate between "deutschmarks" and dollars; this gives her an air of prosperity and speeds up the process of renewing her permit. The expressions they'd have on their faces if she invoked a certain poet as her sworn witness, and sand-gray, the color of New York lions!

In 1968 we decided not to follow the law according to which we're supposed to take things slow and wait for events to take their course, await the gradual progress of history before dark-skinned people can live in friendship with pink-skinned neighbors: we plucked a girl named Francine out of a melee of stabbings, an ambulance, police. This little person with wide-set eyes sometimes appears in fuzzy morning dreams, tilting her head and weaving her stiff stubborn braids, and she says, both mocking and longing: "Yes ma'am, Yes ma'am"; when she leaves, she places a white kerchief fringed with lace over her dark gaze and dark head—the color of mourning. She may have died; she is lost.

In 1968, at the start of our eighth year here, I heard two dark-skinned men talking about me at the Ninety-Seventh Street bus stop. I wasn't trying to eavesdrop. When I eventually did start trying, and failing, to tell if it was English or Spanish they were speaking, I realized how far I was from the dream that I would ever understand this foreign language.

In 1968 came what for now is the last message from D. E., who liked the way we lived. That agreement about a birthday apartment for Marie on upper Riverside Drive will stay unsigned. D. E. had word sent that he's gone, an airplane has carried him off, to his death.

The air-freight ticket agents give us some backtalk. Two big suitcases, another one like a wardrobe, for Prague—a Communist country, whaddaya think yer doing, lady? The lists, the permits? – We're not diplomatic personnel, sir. The bill is going to a midtown bank. Do you see that green piece of printed paper under my hand? the hand I'd be happy to pick up if you want? So the shipment will be waiting for me at Ruzyně Airport tomorrow evening, yes? – Absolutely. Since it's for a lady like yourself. Have a good trip!

– You wouldn't be giving up your apartment, Mrs. Cresspahl?

– What crazy ideas you have, Mr. Robinson (Eagle-Eye).

– It's just, a boyfriend who takes his girlfriend… Someone saw you looking at apartments in Morningside Heights.

– Just visiting someone, Mr. Robinson. You can hear from the telephone ringing that we're planning to stay on Riverside Drive.

– My apologies, Mrs. Cresspahl. And you can be sure: no one else is going to break into this apartment!

– We'll see you a little later this year.

– Understood. Yes indeed, Mrs. Cresspahl.

– This is the operator.

– We haven't placed a call.

– You have recently called abroad several times, Berlin . . .

– Helsinki once.

– We're afraid there's a steep bill on its way.

– It'll get paid. That's no reason to disconnect our line.

– We were wondering if maybe it would be easier for you if you paid in installments, Mrs. Cresspahl?

– With customer service like yours, we'll definitely be staying with you.

– Our pleasure, Mrs. Cresspahl.

We arrive by subway under Times Square at the wrong time. Thick columns of people surge toward us out of the shuttles from Grand Central, diverted onto the three different staircases by the traffic police. – *All the way down. All the way down.* The authorities are acting paternalistic today. As soon as they see us, they clear the middle lane. – *Make room for the lady! Make room for the child!*

In Grand Central Terminal the streams of people flow through one another, formed of such well-aligned and coordinated movements that everyone is out of everyone else's way two steps in advance and gets where they're going faster than if they'd been trying to hurry. Three escalators run down from the Pan American extension—motionless terraces of people detach themselves with a jolt as they make the transition onto the walking surface, as if on ice. Straight lines swerve deliberately off toward the next destination—left and right to the commuter trains, a soft left to Lexington Avenue and the Lexington Avenue subways, a soft right to Madison Avenue and the hotels, straight ahead to Forty-Second and the tiny information rotunda. People flow in from Lexington Avenue through the double doors on countless thousands of feet, swim off beneath the low four-leaved domes, are replenished from the exits of the Graybar Building, rush dense and uncrowded at us beneath the barrel vault with the starry sky in gold, seemingly incised there. Under this high canopy we go in the wrong direction.

Waiting around the corner are the airport buses, elephantine bumble-bees. The tinted windows pull a curtain of shadow before the city. The ride will pass between the cemeteries, to a terrain where bushes and lawns are trying to turn an industrial zone into a park. We will wait till the very end; wait for the loudspeaker announcement that calls us back to New York. Until they say that this is the last and final call for passengers to board the airplane. *Passagererne bedes begive sig til udgang. Begeben Sie sich zum Ausgang. Please proceed to the gate now.*

August 20, 1968 Tuesday. Last and final.
In a beach hotel on the Danish coast, across from Sweden. In a dining room for families: wicker furniture, linen tablecloths. In the garden, behind the bushes leading to the promenade. On the beach. From noon until four.

An eleven-year-old child, her voice soft with exhaustion, weary. A lady, around thirty-five, coming downstairs behind Marie, in happy anticipation because she'd been called to reception. Anita had promised Prague; Anita is more than capable of already being here to welcome us in Klampenborg.

The porter, the driver, the waitress; hotel staff.

– Thank you for waking us up on time. *De har vist mig en stor teneste.*

– *Ingen årsag!* There's a gentleman wishing to see you as soon you're ready.

The gentleman is out on the patio—shrunken but standing straight by force of will, dressed in formal black and white, with snow-white hair—arms raised, he delights in the welcome. A raven, trying to hide how moved he is.

– No! No! (This is what older people from Mecklenburg do.)

– Herr Kliefoth. Marie, say hello to my instructor in English and proper manners.

– *I'm very pleased to meet you, Dr. Kliefoth. My mother has told me stories about you.*

– I think it would be a good idea to avoid German. This country was occupied by the Germans once.

– *D'accord, mine leewe Fru Cresspahl.* I am here illegally as it is. Your friend Anita, she puts an eighty-two-year-old man on the train to Lübeck, sends an ID to Lübeck that will let him travel on to Copenhagen, and the Jerichow police *never know a thing.* But the name in the passport is Kliefoth, it's my picture—I could keep it, just like this.

Seen from the front Kliefoth's head is narrow; in profile, forgotten depths are visible once again. At the table he rests his head in his hands, making his glasses slip up a little higher, their top rim over his eyebrows. Now the dark pupils are exactly in the center.

– That you took all this trouble, Fru Cresspahl. A stopover in Copenhagen for the sake of a useless old man.

– We have Anita to thank for that. She didn't like the idea of our changing planes in Frankfurt. We do whatever Anita tells us to do.

– She booked me a room here for ten days. If it's all right with me!

– *Shes a good person, that Anita; we think so too.*

– Please. A lot of the time all that's missing are the onions. The same goes for what used to be called tropical fruit. It's only when one runs across an advertisement for a fish-smoking plant in a magazine from 1928, mentioning thousands of tons of smoked eel—*you start to wonder. Theres no smoked eel in Jerichow or Gneez.* No, the reason I'm looking forward to our meal is for company's sake; it'll *give us a chance to talk.*

– *Hvad ønsker herskabet?*

– Pickled herring. Mackerel in tomato sauce. Smoked eel with scrambled eggs—go ahead and laugh! And which wine ... *hvilken vin vil De anbefale os til det?*

– It's six thirty in the morning for us, Herr Kliefoth. In our school we're ranked by numbers. I'm number four in my class. What was my mother like in school?

– It is due more than anything to my being the oldest of the survivors. I have to go to the cemetery when I want to talk to anyone.

His eyes close with exhaustion. Reaching under the temples of his glasses he massages his own with the thumb and index finger of the same hand. The skin around his eyes is gray, heavily wrinkled, unmoving. Sitting there like a dead man—until he wakes himself up with those clambering fingers.

– What was said at my father's grave, Herr Kliefoth?

– Hokum. So I threw a wrench in it. *I wrote a P in front a it.* Now what would have happened if you hadn't liked the wine?

– I would have sent it back. I learned that from a person who ...

– Now what makes you think of that, of all things! Jakob came to see me five times during the year after you left when he could no longer keep an eye on you. Came to read your letters, wanted to know what was going on at interpreters' school. Your father was a dependable, caring man, my dear young Miss Cresspahl.

– Herr Kliefoth, I'm only eleven. Please, call me Marie.

– Your mother, Marie, was about five foot four in May 1953. She wore her grayish black hair in a bob. Broad shoulders, narrow hips. When she was in Jerichow she liked to wear pants that would allow her bare legs to tan. Dark eyebrows, wary glances, thin lips—careful preparation for her adult face.

– What's it called in Jerichow when there's no wind like this?

– "Fine ladies' sailing weather," Fru Cresspahl. Present company excepted, of course.

A voice of jagged hoarseness, booming bass when relaxed.

– Herr Kliefoth, I dream about it sometimes. I'm on a Polish ship. It stops over in Liverpool then docks here in Copenhagen. Arrival in Rostock on the Old Channel, views through the Doberan Woods, Wismar or Gneez station. Or, if I'm not allowed Jerichow, Wendisch Burg. At worst Neustrelitz, Waren, Malchin, where no one knows us, where I can make enough money for an apartment with a view of a lake, a little dock for a boat, winter mornings on the ice, shadows of reeds, a fire in the stove ... but Rohlfs is dead or never made it to major with his unconventional ways. We're only allowed to travel through Mecklenburg in transit; if we stop at a hotel it's under supervision; there's no way to choose where we want to stay.

– If only a person like myself might be a rich man someday, Fru Cresspahl. *I say this truly!*

The old man's pants are pulled up to his nipples. His threadbare clothing has been shortened every so often. We thought of cigars, of tobacco— we forgot about fabric for a suit.

– I've bequeathed my furniture to a museum in Rostock. If you were related to me, Fru Cresspahl, you could have gotten the table and the wardrobe—they are presents from your father, after all. I have an agreement with my landlord. In the event of my death he will keep the remaining furniture, but he has to arrange for my removal.

Kliefoth kneads his hands, thinking. The pain narrows his pupils.

– I cut myself once and put my foot in Jakob's hand while standing on the other foot. He looked at it, then let the foot slide down in the same rhythm as my hand on his shoulder; the movement passed through my whole body with no pain. I think that happens to someone only once in their life.

– *Må jeg bede om Deres pas? De er nok med Deres underskrift, resten ordner jeg.*

– *De er meget elskværdig.* You're very kind. *Hvor meget bliver det ialt? Det er til Dem.*

– My wife had a problem with her . . .

– I've had to tell Marie the essentials, Mr. Kliefoth.

– with her nursery. A woman like that has children flocking around her apron, in the kitchen, in the garden. Fundamentally there is only one thing we know about life: that whatever is subject to the law of becoming must perish according to that same law. I certainly shall, don't worry about that. My Latin has become wobbly; my memory is barely adequate these days. I can only be grateful to destiny for treating me so mercifully. And I thank you, my dear Fru Cresspahl. You've helped it.

– Herr Kliefoth, may you live as long you want to.

– Your father granted me the honor of his friendship. One of his opinions went like this: History is a rough draft.

– As for how we've been doing, we've written it down, up to starting our job in Prague—1,652 pages. We'd like to give them to you, if you don't mind. All that's left to add is the two-hour flight south. What could happen to us on a Československé aerolinie plane, ČSA, operating internationally under the letters O and K? We have a confirmed reservation, OK? We'll call you tonight from Prague.

– *Will you take good care of my friend, who is your mother and Mrs. Cresspahl?*

– I will, Herr Kliefoth, I promise. My mother and I, we're good friends.

As we walked by the sea we ended up in the water. Clattering gravel around our ankles. We held one another's hands: a child, a man on his way to the place where the dead are, and she, the child that I was.

[January 29, 1968, New York, NY–
April 17, 1983, Sheerness, Kent]

Translator's Acknowledgments

MY ENORMOUS thanks to Astrid Köhler and Robert Gillett, Patrick Wright, and Holger Helbig for giving so generously of their time and expertise in reviewing much of this translation; to the organizations listed on the copyright page; and to the many editors and copy editors at NYRB Classics. All remaining errors and stubborn decisions are, of course, my own. I would also like to acknowledge the earlier, partial translation by Leila Vennewitz (Parts 1–3) and Walter Arndt (Part 4) of a heavily abridged version of the original, published as *Anniversaries: From the Life of Gesine Cresspahl* in 1975 (Part 1 and half of Part 2) and 1987 (the rest of Part 2 through Part 4). I referred to it often and borrowed some of their many inspired solutions to difficult passages.